# The Adventures of Audie Dale Smith

A novel by

## Clay Hutto

**PUBLISHED BY HARBINGER PRESS**

Revised abridged edition

# The Adventures
# of Audie Dale Smith

# April 3, 1978

He dreamed about *her*. He knew he would before finally falling asleep last night. Now in the morning of his twenty-first year, Audie Dale Smith lay in bed feeling like he'd slept only for a few minutes. But when he looked at the clock radio that she'd given him for Christmas, he leapt out of bed. He'd overslept. Dale had already missed his first class.

As he dressed, he tried to remember the strange dream. He'd dreamed she had become fat. Dale rubbed his eyes. His fingers pressed on the side of his head, near his temple. Near that old football scar she'd once touched. His head ached. He shook it. He almost felt as if he had a hangover.

Dale left his bedroom and walked into the bathroom and after urinating he washed his face and stared at himself in the mirror. He looked as somber as he felt. His dark eyes brooded even in the reflection. He rubbed his chin and felt the short stubble. He hadn't shaved in two days, but he didn't feel like scraping his light beard this morning. As he dried his face with the towel, he thought of that dream again. She wasn't fat. She was pregnant. He tried to catch the elusive images before they vaporized from his memory. Yes, he'd dreamed she stood in a gleaming white building – maybe the First Church – and as happens in dreams it changed in a surreal way from a church to a castle or a fortress or some other kind of large and impenetrable building. She looked serene standing there, dressed in a white gown, her belly gravid, her light brown hair still too short and wavy.

Dale put the towel on the rack and rubbed his eyes again. Dreams were strange. He always dreamed in color, and almost everything in that dream was white. Except for her eyes. They were their normally bright blue color.

He shook his head. She wasn't pregnant in real life. He knew that. She was still a virgin – at least technically.

He forgot about the dream and decided not to fret about what happened last night. He thought there was still a small chance for them to get back together. He'd write her another letter. It had worked the last time. Just thinking that they weren't really over, made him feel better.

Dale walked into the living room and saw his sister, June, sitting cross-legged on the couch, still dressed in her nightie. She held a pink pillow against her middle while watching television. He wondered why she wasn't at her high school. She had two more months left in her senior year.

"Why are you home?" he asked.

"Why are *you*?" she replied in an even more sarcastic voice than usual. Eighteen and she already suffered from world-weariness. Or was it something else this morning?

"I overslept." He yawned and stretched and then walked farther into the living room until he saw his mother sitting at the kitchen table drinking coffee and smoking a cigarette. "Why didn't somebody wake me?"

Jesse took a puff from her cigarette and blew the smoke out of her nostrils. "You usually git up on your own."

That he did. He vaguely remembered the clock radio blaring before he punched it off. That was two hours ago. Now everything seemed strange to him, as if he were still in his dream. He closed his eyes and remembered what happened last night. They'd argued, she'd left, and he let her go, then he changed his mind and ran after her. But instead of showing her he was there, he left. That was what made him feel so strange now. He wasn't used to their being apart.

He opened his eyes and stared at June. She sat on the couch in that odd position, as if practicing yoga, except she held a pink pillow against her middle. He knew boys thought her pretty. Like Dale, her face had a pleasantly congruous mixture of Jesse's and Blackie's features, except June had a fair complexion, reddish brown hair and hazel eyes and Dale had a dark complexion, like his father, and dark brown hair and eyes. June's figure – of which she showed a little too much at that moment – could best be described as voluptuous. He looked at her bare legs and thought she should put on some real clothes. She knew he didn't like it when she walked around the house in her nightie. Dale liked looking at full-figured women, but not his sister. In fact, he worried her figure would attract the wrong kind of guy.

He noticed June watching some inane soap opera. The melodramatic dialogue disturbed him. However, the actresses looked good, but in an artificial, manufactured way, like they weren't really women but highly polished and refined life-sized dolls.

"Why aren't you in school?" he asked June again.

She frowned at him and hugged the pillow tighter against her abdomen. "Because I don't feel good."

"You mean you're sick?"

June rolled her eyes. "Not exactly. I just don't *feel* good."

Dale looked at his sister more attentively and noticed again her hugging her pillow. He got it.

"Oh," he said, trying not to frown.

"Yeah, *oh*."

He turned away and walked into the kitchen. He opened the refrigerator and looked for orange juice. There wasn't any. Instead, he grabbed a carton of milk and drank from it.

"Look at you," Jesse scolded. "You're a man grown now, and you drink out of the carton like a kid."

He guzzled the last drops of milk from the half gallon carton, then with his left hand he squeezed in the sides until it collapsed. He liked doing that. He felt strong. He wiped his mouth with the back of his other hand and burped loudly.

"Excuse you!" cried June from the other room.

Dale didn't know she had such good hearing. He'd drunk the milk too fast. He tossed the empty carton into the trash can next to the door that led to the garage.

"Need more milk."

"Well, you gonna have to buy it yourself," Jesse said, now working on her second cigarette.

Dale walked over and studied his mother's face. Jesse had once been pretty. He remembered the story she'd told him about a man working for a photo magazine who had taken her picture on her twenty-first birthday with one of those big, old-fashioned cameras. That was just before she met Blackie. Dale had seen that portrait of her. He remembered her prominent cheekbones, the green eyes, the long black hair, the lipstick-red lips. He thought she looked a little like Maureen O'Hara, although not as beautiful, but with a similar bold Irish face. He'd been surprised by his mother's attractiveness. But now, he saw a chubby, middle-aged woman who looked older than her forty-three years. Her face sagged, wrinkles branched out from the corners of her eyes and mouth, and her black hair, although dyed, looked flat and lusterless. Her green eyes, expressionless and subdued, were preferable to that glow she sometimes had: an eerie brightness that foretold trouble.

Jesse noticed Dale looking at her. She wished him a happy birthday. Dale said thanks, a little surprised she'd remembered, although he guessed a mother had less reason to forget her child's birthday than anyone else.

"Now you're twenty-one," she said. "A man grown."

Dale said yep. He waited. He thought she might tell him he should pay rent. However, he knew Blackie's child support covered him until he graduated from college.

"I forgot to make you a cake."

Darn, Dale thought. He had looked forward to one of her Jiffy cakes. He didn't tease her, though. Instead, he told her he could always get a cake at the bakery. Nor did he expect a present from Jesse. If she continued to stay sane, that would be the best present of all.

Dale walked over to the wall that separated the dining room from the living room and leaned against it. June still watched *The Young and the Restless*. He shook his head. He couldn't understand how she could watch such junk.

She caught him staring disapprovingly at the television. She frowned. "Whattaya you lookin' at?"

Dale didn't understand why she felt so hostile to him this morning. Even *that* didn't usually make her this crabby.

"Say, Junie, aren't you going to wish me a happy birthday?" he asked in a teasing voice. She glared at him. "Don't call me that."

Dale grinned. She'd recently told them all to call her June instead of June May. Now she didn't want to be called Junie. He thought she was mighty particular.

"Say, what is wrong with you besides you're not feeling well? You've been glaring at me all morning."

June hugged the pillow tighter. "You've made things difficult for me. I was thinking about going to GNC, and now I can't."

Dale didn't know she planned on going to Galilee Nazarene College. He didn't even know she planned on going to any college. She wasn't a very good student, after all.

"How have I ruined it for you?" He knew he'd sort of ruined it for himself. But he only had four weeks left of classes.

"Because of what you did!"

Dale wondered how she'd heard. Well, the high school was only a few blocks away from the college. She went to First Church. Maybe she'd heard Sunday morning. Was the newspaper really causing that much of a ruckus?

"I'll tell you what, June. Just tell people that I'm not your brother. There are lots of Smiths. Just pretend to be another one."

"I *wish*," she said with surprising conviction.

Dale shrugged. Now June blamed him, too. Well, he'd expected some controversy, but not this much. He guessed he really was in trouble.

"Maybe people will forget about all this by next fall. Then you can go to GNC and people won't blame you for being my sister."

June shook her head. "I doubt it. I'll just have to go to another college."

Dale had enough. She was overreacting. Everybody was overreacting. He went over to the desk that Blackie had built for himself six years ago when he started college on the GI bill. Dale now used it. He fished out his car keys from a small wooden bowl, grabbed his wallet, and headed for the door.

"You goin' to see your daddy today?" Jesse asked.

"Yeah. I'm supposed to stop by later this afternoon."

Jesse blew out some smoke. "Tell him I heard about his whore."

Dale stared at his mother. He didn't know she knew about Cleoma. He glanced over at June. She pretended to be engrossed in the soap. Well, maybe she was engrossed. But he knew she'd told Jesse.

"Yeah, I'll pass along that information. I gotta go. I'll see y'all later."

As Dale left his home and walked to his car, he glanced back to the house he'd lived in since the fourth grade. The modest ranch-style white brick house stood in a fairly large yard. It contained three bedrooms, one and a half baths, a garage, and all the modern appliances it had when his father had bought it twelve years ago. Except for a panel of fake black rocks decorating the front of the house, a rustic touch, the house looked like all the others on the block. He had never paid much attention to it. But now, knowing he'd soon be leaving home for good, he thought how mundane it looked.

He climbed in his car, a '67 Chevy Impala, started it up, and drove to the college. As he drove, he looked out the window at the simple homes he passed and examined them with the same melancholy appraisal he'd used with his home. He'd either walked, biked, or driven this route hundreds of times from grade school to high school to now college. In a reflective state of mind, he thought how little he knew about his hometown and the people who lived their private lives inside those inexpensive homes.

Dale parked in the most remote lot, as he had done for the last two years. As he walked to the student union, he noticed a few students he vaguely knew staring at him. Last Friday, when the student newspaper came out, he'd not thought much about the stares and whispers. But today he had an idea of just how much trouble he was in. He dreaded encountering the critical gazes he knew he'd attract. He wasn't as shy as he used to be, but he still didn't like people gawking at him.

As he walked, he remembered why he liked the GNC campus. It was a small, neat campus with nearly 2,000 students, never raucous or tense like the large state universities he'd visited. Dale appreciated GNC's friendly and relaxed ambiance. People had usually left him alone even when he wrote a controversial editorial, feature story, or movie or record review. But now, after the April Fool's parody issue, he knew people were mad at him. It seemed like everyone on campus resented him, except for Teri and Professor Cooper and maybe a few others.

Dale, as editor of the student newspaper, *Smoke Signals*, had penned increasingly iconoclastic editorials during the last few months. But none of those pieces had generated the outrage he'd already encountered from the parodies he'd written for the April Fool's issue. Part of the problem was that people were already worked up over a continuing religious controversy. He guessed a satiric supplement had arrived at the wrong time. Still, he couldn't believe he was in any serious trouble. Then he thought of how Amanda and Chris had behaved to him last night. If they were that upset with him, then other people would be, too.

In the past, his writing had provoked scolding letters to the editor. A couple of his professors had looked critically at him during class; one of the student leaders and a former friend, Robert Henshaw, made oblique remarks that seemed to question Dale's judgment. But now, after the publication of the parodies, it looked like he'd crossed the line.

When Dale opened the door to the student union, he didn't see anyone in the lobby. He turned right and walked down the hall leading to the back of the building where the offices of the student government and the student publications were located. He unlocked the door, pushed it open, and breathed in the musty odor. Even with the windows up, the room smelled of paper, ink, wax, ragged old furniture, dust, and assorted food odors from meals snuck into the office. He savored the smell.

But his satisfaction dissolved when he saw a pile of letters to the editor scattered on the floor. Dale closed and locked the door. He picked up the letters. Some were scrawled by hand; some typed. Three letters were sealed in faculty envelopes. He knew they were all complaints and he wasn't in the mood to read them. He walked over to his desk and tossed them in the growing letter pile. Dale wondered if he'd set some kind of dubious record for eliciting the most negative letters to the editor in the history of *Smoke Signals*.

The phone rang and Dale, although knowing he shouldn't, picked it up. An elderly man's voice asked to speak to the editor. "Speaking," Dale said. The man then delivered a harangue for three minutes, calling him a disgrace to the Nazarene community. The old man said, yes, my friend, there was a hell, and Dale was headed straight for it. He said Dale had done irreparable damage to the reputation and good name of Galilee Nazarene College. He said –

Dale hung up. He didn't mean to be rude but his head ached. He'd heard enough. The old codger didn't want to hear his side of things; he just wanted to rant.

He decided not to wait around for another harassing phone call, or even worse, the appearance of an irate student, faculty, or staff member. He didn't have the patience today to listen to close-minded, humorless, religious zealots tell him off. Dale smiled a little at his thoughts; was there such a thing as an open-minded, droll, religious zealot? If so, he'd like to meet one.

He locked up the newspaper office, then strode quickly down the hall. He wanted to make it to the darkroom before classes got out and people swarmed campus.

He turned the corner fast and sharp and almost knocked down Sylvester Fish. Fish said, "excuse you!"

Dale said "sorry," although he didn't really feel the near collision was his fault. Fish had a tendency to lurk.

"Oh, hello, Smith," said Sylvester Fish, who always called Dale by his last name.

"Hello, Fish," replied Dale.

He stared at Sylvester: unsuccessful student journalist; English/religion major, campus busybody, and Dale's nemesis.

"How was your weekend?" Fish asked in an uncharacteristic pleasant voice.

Dale wondered why Fish was acting so civil. Maybe because he knew he had a horrible weekend. He'd spent Saturday night with Rusty, his best friend since childhood, but even Rusty's manic energy hadn't removed Dale from his funk. Now, as he stared at Sylvester Fish, he knew why he'd never trusted him. Fish didn't seem to have any eyes. He did, of course; but they were small, gray, and slit-like, obscured by his large, thick-lens tinted spectacles. Fish had a pallid complexion, incongruously jet black hair worn short and neat, a sharp nose, and a long thin mouth that extended like a scar over his jowly, nearly chinless lower face. Although average in height, five foot ten or so, he seemed shorter because of his strange posture: his shoulders hunched and his body sagged as if he were carrying some invisible heavy burden. Dale thought him a decidedly unappealing character but couldn't quite work up any animosity towards him.

But it was apparent Fish didn't like Dale. Or maybe didn't approve. He thought him a bad influence on campus life. Too much of a free thinker. Yet Fish never openly voiced his disapproval. For Fish was subtle – or so he thought.

"Coming or going?" asked Fish.

"Going."

"Have you been receiving a lot of response about Friday's paper?"

Dale knew Fish knew he had. Fish had probably spied underneath the door and seen the pile of letters to the editor.

"You could say that."

Fish smiled his usual toothless smile, really more a slight upturn of the corners of his mouth.

"Some people on campus, of course, aren't as broad-minded as I," Fish said, leaning closer to Dale than he preferred, so far forward, in fact, that he feared Fish might fall right into him.

"Yes, I've always noticed that about you, Fish," said Dale, "your broad-mindedness."

Fish's semi-smile returned for a moment, then his mouth grew straight and grim. "Have you checked your mail yet?"

Dale detected a slightly sinister tone. "No, why?"

"You might want to."

Dale studied the impassive face of Fish. He remembered that Sylvester worked part-time in the campus mail center. All the better for him to gather bits of information. So Fish knew he'd received a letter. Dale could guess from where and who.

"Thanks, Fish. I'll check the mail on my way out."

"Certainly. Just thought you'd like to know. It appeared to be an important letter. From the administration."

Dale nodded, growing annoyed with Fish's blank face and insinuating voice. He tried to look into his nemesis's eyes but they were as hidden as ever.

He moved away, but Fish sidled over to partially block his path. "By the way, have you talked to Amanda recently?"

Dale stiffened. He knew Fish had always been interested in Amanda.

"Not recently," he said tersely, not wanting to mention that he had argued with her last night.

"Sorry to hear," replied Fish, now taking a couple steps back.

"Yeah, right."

He suddenly felt angry and didn't want to say anything more, otherwise his wrath might overtake him and he'd say or do something to Fish that he'd regret.

Dale strode past Sylvester, imagining Fish's disapproving gaze as he left him in the gloomy hallway. Fish ordinarily didn't bother him, but today his insinuations had gotten under his skin. Especially when he mentioned Amanda.

Dale, lost in thought, didn't notice any other students checking their mailboxes. He deftly turned the combination key, snapped open the box, and reached in and found the letter. It felt important: high quality paper and an embossed seal. It looked important: a rigid, immaculate white envelope with imprinted scarlet words in the left corner: OFFICE OF THE DEAN. He tore open the envelope, pulled out the letter, and read the terse message that he was requested to attend a meeting with members of the publications board to determine whether he, Audie Dale Smith, should be removed from his position of editor of the student newspaper. The inquiry would be held this Friday at four o'clock in the afternoon. If he could not attend the meeting at that time, he was instructed to call the Dean's office. Otherwise, he was expected to be there to discuss his involvement in the student newspaper controversy.

Dale had been sort of expecting such a message, but the hollow feeling he felt in his belly nevertheless surprised him. He really was in serious trouble. Maybe he'd be kicked out of the college and not allowed to graduate. If that happened, he didn't know what he'd do.

After he finished reading the letter, he became aware of being watched. He glanced up and saw a couple of students, two plain-faced girls he once had a class with, staring at him and whispering to each other. Dale realized they were whispering about him. His face flushed, as from embarrassment, but the feeling felt more intense like the old feelings of shame he'd felt when he was younger. It bothered him that people he didn't know well knew about his problems.

Dale turned away and strode out of the student union, still aware of eyes following him and voices whispering.

He walked swiftly to the science building and dashed down the stairway to the photo darkroom. He opened the outer door and saw with relief that no one was present. He decided to spend a few hours working in the silence and gloom of the darkroom. He knew the yearbook was behind schedule. He thought he'd help out and develop some rolls of film and make some prints. He worked for two hours in silence and solitude, and the work helped take his mind off his troubles.

He stopped at one o'clock. He decided not to go to his afternoon Shakespeare class. Instead, he opted to get some lunch off campus, then head over to Blackie's.

Dale waited until classes were in session, then he left the darkroom and walked to his car and drove to Braum's, his favorite ice cream parlor and restaurant. He ordered his usual lunch there: a plain hamburger, fries, and an extra-thick chocolate shake made with real ice cream. Then he drove to the City to see his father.

He drove out of Galilee, down Highway 66 that led to Oklahoma City. He motored past the turnoff to Lake Overholser, drove through several miles of rural, undeveloped land, then entered into the thicket of buildings and cars and people that made up the state's largest city.

Dale turned into the parking lot of The French Quarter, where his father lived. The apartment building's only distinctive feature was its New Orleans motif; otherwise it looked, smelled, and depressingly felt like most other generic apartment complexes.

He parked his car next to his father's patrol car. Then he got out and walked to Building Three, passed the mailboxes where he saw his father's full name printed on it: Forrest Blackburn Smith.

Dale jogged up the stairs to the second level and knocked on his father's door. The door cracked open. He wondered if the door had been left ajar. He knocked again. Then he heard Blackie growl, "get the hell in here," and Dale walked in.

Blackie stood in his khaki ranger uniform, fastening his Sam Browne belt with its holster and .38 revolver. Dale immediately noticed his father's grim expression.

"Why the hell didn't you come in?" Blackie asked.

Nearly fully dressed, he only lacked his polished, black boots. Dale thought his father looked a little funny standing in full uniform, gun belt strapped around his waist, but wearing only white socks on his feet.

"I don't know," Dale said.

Actually, he did know. He thought maybe Cleoma was in Blackie's apartment. Dale had caught her sneaking in before. Since she managed The French Quarter, he guessed she had a right, but he still didn't like her snooping.

"I got to leave soon," Blackie said. "We got another suicide."

Blackie sat down in his easy chair and pulled on his boots. He looked at Dale with a truculent expression as if his son had done something to infuriate him. For a moment, Dale wondered if Blackie had heard about the newspaper parody. But he wouldn't be angry about that. If anything, Blackie would think his satire hadn't been iconoclastic enough.

"What's wrong?" Dale asked.

"The bitch's pregnant," Blackie said, bitterly.

Dale at first had no idea who or what he was referring to. For a second, he wondered if Blackie was referring to a real bitch; maybe he'd bought a dog. But as soon as the thought crossed his mind, he knew that was absurd. Blackie didn't like pets. He'd never allowed them to have one.

"Goddamn her, the bitch is pregnant."

Dale knew for certain the bitch wasn't a dog. Blackie's tone sounded too resentful, too personally affronted.

Then he guessed. "You mean –"

"That's right. That bitch Cleoma." His father's dark eyes flashed with anger.

Cleoma: Blackie's girlfriend. Or, as Jesse put it, Blackie's whore. Of course, Cleoma really wasn't a whore, not technically, but Dale didn't like her either. His father got to know Cleoma soon after he moved into The French Quarter three years ago. Knowing who was pregnant helped clear Dale's mind a little, but he still couldn't quite comprehend why Blackie was telling him about Cleoma's infidelity.

"That's too bad," he said, not knowing what else to say. "I mean, it must be a shock to know she's been seeing someone else and –"

Dale stopped when he saw Blackie glaring at him.

"Someone else? I wish."

"You mean …"

"Damn right. It's mine. At least that's what she says."

Dale couldn't quite believe his father had fathered another kid. He shook his head as he stared at Blackie, who now stood silently fuming. He wondered how a man his age could do such a thing. After all, at forty-three, he looked his age: a bit of a paunch on an otherwise sturdy frame; average height (two inches taller than Dale), and a dusky complexion, which

11

ordinarily would have obscured a few wrinkles and sags on his lumpy face if Blackie didn't drink and smoke so much. Only Blackie's thick dark hair gave him a touch of youth. If his face wasn't so bumpy, a result of fights and accidents, he might have been good-looking. But his twice broken nose, scars over his right eyebrow and under his lip, a crooked jaw, and a couple of chipped teeth gave his face a patched-up look, as if the various busted parts of his face hadn't quite been reassembled properly.

"I-I don't know what to say," Dale finally stammered.

"You and me both. Goddamn *woman*." His father said the word woman with as much ferocity as he had bitch.

"What are you going to do?"

Blackie shrugged. "Beats the hell out of me."

Dale didn't know what to suggest. He'd never been in such a situation. Well, back in high school, Wendy, his girlfriend, had told him she was "late." Initially, he'd thought she meant late for their date. She'd just blurted out those words when she slipped inside his car. When she elaborated, he'd felt his stomach collapse even though he knew the odds of her being pregnant were small. After all, they'd only really done it once.

"I guess I'll have to marry her," Blackie said.

"Marry?"

Dale felt aghast. The idea of his father marrying Cleoma repulsed him. Even though he'd not been around her that much – from choice – he knew Blackie was making a big mistake.

"Yeah, Cleoma wants to get married. And she wants to keep the baby. Of course she would. That's how she gets me to marry her."

It sounded to Dale that Blackie didn't like Cleoma much either. "You don't have to, though, do you?"

Blackie shook his head. He already looked beaten. "I don't know. She can cause trouble." His father peered at his son in an annoyed way, as if he'd already said too much. "Well, I didn't mean to lay all this on you."

"That's okay."

"No, it isn't. It's my problem. Anyway, I have a present for you."

Dale felt a little surprised. Blackie hadn't given him a birthday present since the time he'd turned eighteen.

His father went over to one of the few pieces of furniture in his apartment, a coffee table, on which the television stood. He picked up an unwrapped, squarish black case and gave it to Dale.

Dale opened it. A wristwatch. A Timex. It had one of those expanding wristbands that he didn't like.

"Thanks," he said.

"Yeah, well, it ain't much but I haven't had much time to shop."

"Yeah, I know."

Blackie told Dale to walk with him to the parking lot. He had to get back to the station. Otherwise, the incompetents he had working under him would probably screw up.

"Just another snafu," Blackie said, as they left his apartment and walked downstairs. "You know what that stands for, don't you?"

"I think so. Situation normal, all fouled up."

Blackie snorted. He told him the real phrase, using the obscenity. Dale felt a bit shocked. His father had always cussed, but he'd never heard him use that taboo word before. He guessed Blackie thought he was ready to hear it now that Dale had turned twenty-one.

"Anything going on with you?" Blackie said, in a way that told Dale he didn't have the time or inclination to really listen.

Dale decided not to tell him he might be in serious trouble at college. Instead, he told Blackie that he might take a trip to Europe after he graduated – if he graduated.

"Europe?"

Blackie didn't sound too impressed. Dale didn't think Blackie had ever been stationed in Europe while in the navy. Maybe that's why he didn't seem too interested.

"You got the money for that?" his father asked.

Dale said it didn't cost that much. If he stayed in youth hostels, used a Eurorail pass for travel, and just carried a knapsack, he could see a lot of European countries on the cheap.

Blackie grunted.

They arrived at their cars in the parking lot.

"Well, I better get going," said Dale. "You have to go to work."

"Yeah. I'm late already."

Dale started to get in his car when Blackie said, "goddamnest thing, isn't it? Thought I was finished being a father and now I'll have another kid."

Dale nodded, got in the car, and started it up. As he drove out of the parking lot, he looked into his rearview mirror at his father getting into his patrol car and thought about Blackie's last comment: *finished being a father*. Did his dad really think that? Dale thought anyone who really wanted to be a father would never think they were finished being one.

Dale drove through the outskirts of the City and followed Highway 66 back to Galilee. He felt a little depressed and decided not to go home right away. When he came to his turn, he passed it and drove on. Looking out the windshield, he focused beyond the light traffic at the scenery before him. The earth, flat as a tabletop, shined green with spring renewal. The verdant color wouldn't last long. In a couple of months the heat and dryness would burnish the earth a dusty brown. He looked at the sky and noticed the bright blue color and the white fluffy clouds scudding across the horizon. If the air wasn't so muggy, it would be a perfect day.

But even the near perfect day didn't lift his spirits. He drove past the old, abandoned children's hospital where his mother had spent four years of her life. About a mile west of Galilee he turned south and headed for the only elevation in these parts, a hill he called Reinhardt's Summit. It wasn't much, just a bulge in the rolling, flat land with some trees ringing it. But Dale liked going there and looking out at the sky looming over the prostrate earth.

A road didn't run to it or even wind around it, so he parked his car on the side of the road and hiked a few hundred yards. He used to visit the hill often; his visits had been less frequent of late because of how busy he was. But now he needed to walk up the hill again.

He passed through a clutch of cottonwood trees that stood like sentries. Then he walked up the hill, moving quickly, his eyes focused on the top of the mound. The climb wasn't difficult; it didn't wind him at all, but because of the heat and humidity he was sweating when he reached the summit. His wiped the sweat off his forehead with the back of his hand, then turned around and faced east.

Perhaps the hill stood fifty feet high, but the height seemed greater because the rest of the land lay so flat. Dale saw his hometown before him from the new perspective of height. Galilee looked like a neat, gray oval on the land. He noticed how small it appeared against the earth and sky. About ten miles farther east, he saw the outskirts of the City. Buildings, stores, church steeples, and the faint outline of the few skyscrapers that congregated in the center of the small metropolis. Turning back to his hometown, he noticed that Galilee wasn't much – just a small town, dwarfed by the City to its east, and overwhelmed by the green land and the vast blue sky. It sat in the expanse of earth like a quarter on a pool table. He thought about his problems back in his hometown. Did it really matter what the people in that town and in that little college thought of him?

In the past, he came to this insignificant hill, this bump on the earth, and gazed out at the land, sky, and the town. In moments of doubt and loneliness, he came here; it was his form of prayer; a meditation between his soul and the greater natural world around him. He knew if the Nazarene elders or his friends knew of his attitude, they might accuse him of pantheism or even paganism. But he came here to think, reflect, ponder, in short to put things in perspective. Wasn't that one purpose of prayer?

Dale thought about some of the people he knew who were down in Galilee right now: Amanda, Chris, Rusty, Wendy, Mary Jane, Teri, Coop, Jenny, Henshaw, Hawkins, and many of his friends and teachers from high school that he'd pretty much already lost touch with. He thought about his mother, sister, and grandparents. He considered all of them, saw them in his mind's eye living their lives down in Galilee, going about their daily duties as they always did. He worried about his mother's sanity; worried about his father's predicament; and worried, too, about his own situation at college. Most of all, he worried about *her*. As he thought about these concerns, he also thought about a mystery: his existence. Of all the places to be born, of all the times, he had been born here. It seemed strange to him that he'd grown up in this small, religious town, a town even more conservative socially, politically, and religiously than the rest of the conservative state and region. Soon, he would leave this place and venture out into the greater world. But for another month, he'd have to live in this unusual place and somehow make it through the upcoming tribulation.

Dale's eyes left behind the shiny disk of Galilee and scanned west, taking in the big, open sky that towered above the temporarily fertile earth. Then, before he saw it, he smelled it. He smelled the electricity, the water vapor, and the first draughts of cooler air. His eyes moved farther westward and he saw it. He'd been wrong about this being an almost perfect day. A sea of dark clouds gathered on the northwest horizon: large, roiling, blackish clouds. A storm was coming. And it would be a bad one.

# Book 1: *Witnessing*

### Chapter 1: *Trumbo offers to be Dale's guide; fight with Rusty*

Dale sat with his mother and sister in the Kingdom Hall on a Sunday afternoon in late July. Like the others, they sat on padded aluminum folding chairs, the kind made to be easily stacked. In front of the room stood an older man asking the brothers and sisters questions from *The Watch Tower* magazine.

Dale thought the "meetings," as the Jehovah's Witnesses called their gatherings, were more like school than church. He'd figured out that was the point. Jehovah's Witnesses disliked hierarchy and rituals. Dale, something of an egalitarian at age fourteen, rather approved of this simple approach. Unfortunately, he wished the meetings weren't so boring.

He sneaked a look at his mother and sister. June May appeared more bored than Dale. She slumped in her seat and when she began to slip farther down than thought permissible, Jesse elbowed her to make her sit up straight.

Other than keeping an eye on June May, Jesse seemed engrossed in the instruction. She wore one of her few dresses, a modest navy blue one that even Dale could tell looked a decade out of date. Her ordinarily naked face showed a few touches of makeup. She sat silently in her padded seat, listening intently to the elder as he asked a question drawn from *The Watch Tower*. Then her eyes dropped to the open pamphlet and anxiously searched the text. Once, she tentatively raised her hand before the elder called on another sister. Jesse pursed her lips in frustration.

Jesse had told Dale that this Sunday she would answer at least one question. The past two Sunday meetings Jesse had listened just as intently as today, but she'd never got the nerve to raise her hand like a dutiful student and answer the rather easy questions.

Jesse had encouraged Dale to answer a question too. But he felt even shyer than Jesse. He pretended his real reluctance was his disdain for how easy the questions were. "The answers are right there on the page," he had said. "Why is it such a big deal to answer?"

Now, after attending two Tuesday nights, two Friday nights, and three Sunday afternoons, plus having Greta coach her every week, Jesse felt ready. Dale thought his mother took answering the easy questions far too seriously; it was as if her spiritual salvation depended on answering a simple question from a grade-school-level pamphlet.

Over the past three weeks, Dale had learned a lot about the Jehovah's Witnesses. He'd learned they practiced the one true religion, that God's real name was Jehovah, and that other "Christian" churches were simply part of Christendom. He'd also learned some things he found strange: Jehovah's Witnesses didn't celebrate holidays or birthdays; they didn't salute the flag or pledge loyalty to any nation; and they didn't accept blood transfusions. He still didn't understand fully why the Witnesses were against these things. He'd heard Greta and others explain. They'd quoted Bible verses to buttress their arguments. He didn't like those rules, but the idea that Christ's Second Coming was imminent enticed him. He'd learned they were living in the "End Times." At any moment, He might return and History would end. The spectacular nature of the idea appealed to Dale's overactive imagination.

Even stranger to Dale than the Jehovah's Witnesses ideas were the people. The brothers and sisters were generally unattractive people who wore unstylish clothes. Their passive demeanor – except for a certain gleam in their eyes when they quietly spoke about Jehovah – puzzled him as well.

However, since the Witnesses he'd met had also seemed genuinely gentle and modest, he wondered if his distaste for them was mostly unjustified. After all, why should people place so much emphasis on appearance? Dale didn't care about expensive clothes or stylish haircuts. He thought the kids he knew at school fussed too much about such superficialities. And he didn't think people should make judgments about people's personalities based on casual contact the way they did in junior high. So the idea that a true Christian would appear odd to those in "the world" began to make some sense to him.

He watched as Jesse raised her hand, this time with confidence. To his surprise, the elder called on her. Dale sank in his seat. He felt almost as embarrassed as if he were the one being called on. He couldn't look; he waited. Then he heard her voice, quavering a little, rather quiet, but clear and loud enough that her brothers and sisters could hear her give the correct answer. Correct answer! Dale looked at his mother and saw her smiling a rare smile while her hands holding open *The Watch Tower* trembled.

He began to understand. These people were outcasts; they were not part of "the world." The fact that most of them didn't easily fit into society for a variety of reasons – lack of education, low income, poor health, general unattractiveness – had been turned into a reason for their special status. After all, hadn't the disciples been outcasts too?

These people thought they were today's disciples. Disciples of Jehovah. Dale, however, still wasn't sure.

After the meeting, several Witnesses came up to Jesse and congratulated her on her answer. Dale thought at first that maybe they were joking; after all, what was the big deal? The answers were right in front of them. But they *were* sincere in their compliments. Doing Jehovah's work, no matter how small, is always a big deal.

One of the people complimenting Dale's mother was another woman almost as small as Jesse. Her name, Mrs. DuBois. She'd introduced herself at the first meeting. A petite woman, just a shade over five feet, she was one of the people who seemed "normal" to Dale. She dressed like a modern woman, although more modestly, but with a certain quiet taste. She even wore a little jewelry, an unobtrusive broach or a small necklace of imitation pearls.

Mrs. DuBois's daughter, Juliette, stood next to her mother. She smiled and said something nice to Jesse as well, then glanced in Dale's direction. He'd been introduced to her at that first meeting three weeks ago, and Dale, intensely shy around any girl his age, had stammered a hello.

Dale now looked at Juliette with some interest. Small like her mother, she wore her brown hair short which emphasized her delicate neck. Her face, although not pretty, had a pleasant look to it: large grayish eyes, a short nose, and a small but not thin-lipped mouth. In a way, she reminded Dale of June May's old dolls. Maybe the one that wet or the one that talked when you pulled a cord.

Dale found Juliette attractive, but at his age he found almost any girl attractive. Juliette also possessed that eerie poise that girls seemed so easily to acquire as they reach adolescence. Dale, on the other hand, had no poise. He felt like he was cracking apart almost every minute from all the strange sensations and emotions colliding inside his body and he feared everyone could see.

Mrs. DuBois and Juliette quietly left and were replaced by Greta. After offering Jesse her congratulations, she turned to Dale.

"I saw you looking at Juliette," she said.

Dale blushed. He had no control over the blood rushing to his face. He said nothing although he tried.

"You know, Witnesses marry young."

Talk about jumping to conclusions, thought Dale. Greta was like the cow jumping over the moon. Still he stood mute.

"But not that young," said a deep voice from behind them. They turned and saw brother Trumbo, a tall, lean, sandy-haired man of forty that Dale also included as one of the normal ones.

Mr. Trumbo rested his large right hand on Dale's shoulder. "Don't worry, Dale," he said, impressing Dale that he remembered his name. "We don't allow our young brothers to marry until they reach, oh, at least fifteen years of age."

For a moment, Dale believed him and a vision of his wedding to the more-mature-than-her-age Juliette flashed in his mind. Then Mr. Trumbo smiled his big, manly smile and Dale realized he'd been joking. He grinned more out of relief than amusement.

"Oh, brother Trumbo," Greta said, giggling.

Dale had never heard sister Greta giggle; in fact, he'd thought her incapable of such a frivolous sound. But Trumbo made her feel girlish; he made most of the women in the Kingdom Hall act girlish because he was a handsome, charming man who paid them due attention.

"Are we ready?" Trumbo asked, looking first to Jesse, then Dale.

He'd arranged for Dale to come over to his home after the Sunday meeting. Ostensibly, it was intended for Dale to spend time with his two sons and join them and some neighborhood friends in a game of basketball. But Dale suspected the visit was to provide evidence that Witnesses could have fun just like worldly people – in fact, more fun because they knew how short their time was.

Jesse nodded, made bashful by the impressive figure of Trumbo.

"Don't worry about Dale," he told Jesse. "I'll bring him back later this afternoon."

"Oh, she won't be worrying," said Greta. "We girls are going out ourselves."

Greta put a hand lightly on June May's shoulder to confirm her inclusion.

"Excellent," said Trumbo. "And where are you ladies going?"

"Shopping," said June May indifferently.

Dale guessed it wasn't the activity that bored her, since like most girls she was wild for clothes, but rather whom she was going with.

"Thought we'd shop for new outfits," said Greta. "The circuit assembly's coming up."

Dale already knew the circuit assembly was like a convention for Jehovah's Witnesses. He looked at his mother and felt surprised to see something of an eager look on her face, as if she genuinely felt motivated to shop for an appropriate dress. He guessed she really wanted to fit in.

"Well, don't you ladies get too carried away," teased Trumbo. "I know how shopping can go to your heads."

Greta giggled again. "Oh, brother Trumbo."

Trumbo smiled. "I'll have Dale back for dinner," he said to Jesse and then they parted.

As he walked away with Trumbo, Dale glanced back. His mother and sister stood dwarfed by Greta.

Dale walked with Trumbo out to his car, a brand new Oldsmobile Cutlass. He stared at the car. Its shiny black exterior gleamed from the caresses of hand washing.

"You like the car?" Trumbo asked.

Dale nodded. He hadn't expected a brother to have such a cool car. And the Cutlass was a sporty make, too, the kind he especially liked.

They got in and Trumbo started it and they both listened to the throaty hum of the motor. Then with effortless skill, Trumbo guided the car out of the small parking lot and zoomed down the road, showing he didn't mind using a little speed to get around.

"Barbara and the boys already left in her car," he said, referring to his wife and sons.

Dale nodded, noting that Trumbo had two cars. Another unusual characteristic, he thought. Some witnesses didn't own even one car.

They drove down the road for a couple of miles, then Trumbo turned and drove through several neighborhoods, each block presenting increasingly larger and more expensive homes. As he drove they talked about baseball. He asked Dale which team was his favorite. Dale said the Astros. Several former Oklahoma City 89ers were now with the Astros. He'd seen Cesar Cedeno, J. R. Richard, and John Mayberry play when he went to a couple of games with Rusty and his family. He asked Trumbo his favorite team.

"The Cubs," he replied.

"Why the Cubs?"

Dale looked at Trumbo's right hand that casually steered the car. It had large knuckles with small sprouts of sandy hair on it.

Trumbo said he grew up in a Chicago suburb – on the northside, he added, a detail that apparently meant something to Trumbo but not much to Dale.

"One of these days the Cubbies will win the World Series." Trumbo glanced at Dale with a meaningful look on his big face. "Just like one day Christ will return to earth. And it could happen at any minute."

Dale knew the Cubs wouldn't win the World Series at least until October – if then. They weren't very good anymore. But he didn't say so. He didn't say smart alecky things; he just thought them. Instead he nodded at Trumbo and examined the man's face. Everything about it was big: large, cool blue eyes, a Roman nose, a wide mouth, and most prominent of all, a strong jaw and chin. All the features fit in a way that made him handsome in a rugged way. The only kind of handsome that Dale acknowledged.

They arrived at Trumbo's house. He pulled into the wide driveway as Dale looked at the attractive, two-story house. While Trumbo occupied himself in the back of the car, Dale got out and looked at the open interior of the garage. He saw all sorts of things stuffed in racks and hung on hooks on the wall: bats, gloves, baseball jerseys, two football helmets, water skis, boxing gloves, golf clubs, all kinds of tools, a power saw, hammers and wrenches and screwdrivers and machines he didn't remember the names of. Other stuff as well: lawn chairs, sprinklers, hoses, a barbecue grill, sacks of potting soil, flower pots, two lawn mowers, one the regular kind, another the kind you rode; rakes, shovels, a weed-wacker; and most interesting of all, a motorcycle. And not a little one, but a large, gleaming black beast of a machine. There was so much stuff that Dale didn't have time to identify it all. He had never seen so much stuff.

They got out and Trumbo took him inside and showed him some of the house. Dale marveled at how spacious and clean it was. It smelled good, too, like the outdoors after a brief shower. The large family room (as Trumbo called it) featured a big leather couch, cushioned chairs, long polished tables, a white shag rug and even a fireplace. Another room had a stereo with dozens of albums, a color TV, and more supple, expensive-looking furniture. And in the study, a sturdy desk sat in the center of the room and big bookcases stuffed with all kinds of books stood against three of the walls. The books were not just Witness's books, but novels and books about history, science, geography, sports, and politics. Dale, who liked to read himself, recognized some of the titles, in particular the novels by Dickens and Twain.

In the splendid kitchen, with its gleaming appliances and small black and white television, Dale met Trumbo's wife, Barbara, or Babs as Trumbo called her. He'd seen her before, of course, at the Kingdom Hall. She had blond hair and bright green eyes and a pretty face. In contrast to Trumbo, everything about her seemed compact: her figure, the features of her face, even her movements as when she turned back to the counter to make snacks.

Then they went out to the backyard. Dale heard the harsh voices of the boys before he saw them. Their voices sounded like crow caws as they cut through the air. He thought it odd that on such a hot day they would play basketball. He recognized Trumbo's two sons, Joe, the eldest, and Michael, the youngest. He'd met them briefly at the Kingdom Hall and hadn't been that interested. Joe, already seventeen, treated Dale with the casual contempt of an upperclassman. Michael, on the other hand, at age eleven, Dale's sister's age, was too young for a real friend. Michael hadn't even entered puberty yet and he looked like a little kid – even though he was already as tall as Dale. Both of them were blond like their mother, but Joe had his father's rangy build.

Trumbo interrupted their game and quickly introduced Dale. The two other boys looked to be fifteen or sixteen; both gangly and pimply and the taller one, Fred, had braces. They glanced indifferently at Dale, probably thinking his short stature meant he was as young as Michael and thus of little value. Trumbo excused himself, leaving Dale behind. The four boys resumed play – not inviting Dale since it was awkward to play with five – and he stood to the side watching.

It wasn't a real basketball court, not even the playground kind, but it wasn't bad. A large slab of concrete covered the back corner of the yard. A regulation free throw lane had been painted on the concrete. On the back end a pole stood ten feet high, with a backboard and goal attached. Dale could tell it was a good basketball board and goal; when the boys bounced the ball off the rim it didn't clang and the pole didn't sway. Whoever created the "court" did a swell job. Once again, Dale felt impressed and envious.

Trumbo returned with a pair of sneakers and tossed them to Dale.

"I should have told you to bring a change of clothes. But I think these shoes will fit."

Dale sat down in the lush grass on the side of the court and changed into them. The shoes, Converse All-Stars, still relatively white and unsoiled, didn't quite fit. They were a little too big. He glanced over at Michael, who awkwardly waved his arms in an effort to guard his taller brother. Dale frowned; it annoyed him his feet were smaller than Michael's.

Now properly shod, Dale joined the game. He still felt awkward in his dress clothes, black slacks and white dress shirt. He took off his clip-on tie, unbuttoned his collar, and rolled up his sleeves. The other boys were dressed in casual clothes, but Trumbo still wore his slacks and white dress shirt, too, a fact that impressed Dale who knew he did it for his benefit.

Then Trumbo performed another generous act: he picked Dale for his team. Actually, he just told everyone that he, Dale, and Michael would take on the three big boys. Joe, Fred, and the other kid whose name Dale never got, yelped derisively at the challenge. "Two kids and an old man," said Fred, his braces looking ferocious in his toothy mouth. "You guys won't stand a chance."

Trumbo laughed and promptly whistled through his teeth, signaling the start of the game. Then he took the ball from Joe and hit a perfect jump shot.

"Two zip," he said.

Basketball was not Dale's preferred game. Since it seemed to favor tall kids, he disliked it. Almost a foot shorter than the three boys on the other team, he did what he could, which was to dribble, which he was okay at, and pass the ball to Trumbo. Trumbo played dazzlingly. He hit almost every shot he took. He sank jump shots from the top of the key; he dribbled under the basket and hit a reverse layup. Adept with either hand, much stronger, and demonstrating a keen shooting eye, he clearly dominated the game. Dale and Michael mostly kept out of his way and fed him the ball. Fred and the other kid weren't much more useful than Dale, so the game quickly came down to a battle between father and the eldest son. Joe, as good an outside shot as Trumbo, didn't have his father's strength yet and the game turned on Trumbo getting under the basket and outmuscling him. The winning basket (they played to twenty-one) happened when Trumbo drove to the basket and sank a lay-up while knocking Joe down in the process.

"Game," Trumbo said, only now showing his age with his somewhat labored breathing. He reached down to help Joe up, but his son refused his hand and scrambled to his feet.

"You all right?" Trumbo asked.

"Fine," Joe said, stalking away.

"You can call a foul."

Joe didn't answer. The rest of the boys stood awkwardly, not sure what to do or say.

"Okay, let's snack," Trumbo said, letting the basketball drop with a plop onto the court.

Dale exchanged his Converse All-Stars for his dress shoes. Then he joined the others at the picnic table where Babs had left snacks: little ham and cheese sandwiches, potato chips, apple juice, and chocolate chip cookies. He piled the food on a paper plate and first took a bite of the cookie. Unsurprisingly, it was delicious. Homemade.

"How'd you like the game?" asked Trumbo. The others were gathered at the other end of the table.

"Okay," said Dale.

"I bet baseball is more your game," Trumbo said encouragingly.

"I like football, too."

"Well, you can come over in the fall and play football with us. Touch, not tackle."

"Okay," Dale said, tentatively biting into a sandwich.   Ordinarily, he didn't eat anything with cheese on it but he didn't want to be an impolite guest. The sandwich, cut like a triangle, tasted good, although it took him another bite to get used to the chewy cheese.

"Dale," asked Trumbo, "do you know what I do for a living?"

Dale nodded. He thought someone, maybe Greta, had told him. "Don't you keep track of planes on some machine?"

"An air traffic controller," said Trumbo. "I'm an administrator now, but that's what I used to do. And that was an important job. People's lives were at stake."

Dale nodded again. He had a vague idea of the job. Maybe he'd seen someone doing such work in a movie.

"You make a mistake and people die," Trumbo said.

That interested Dale. "Did you ever make a mistake?"

Trumbo grinned. "No, but there were a couple of close calls. The point is, Dale, I was like a shepherd for all those planes and all those people in the planes. I looked out for them. I guided them to safety."

Dale thoughtfully chewed on a cookie.

"I just want you to know that I'll be your air traffic controller if you ever need any guidance."

Dale swallowed. He knew Trumbo was making an important point, but he didn't think he was going to be on a plane anytime soon. Jesse didn't like to fly.

"Okay," he said.

"Good," said Trumbo.

He looked for a moment like he might say more but instead just grinned. His wife opened the patio door and told him Mrs. DuBois was here. Trumbo got up and went in. Dale saw him shake hands with the diminutive Mrs. DuBois and then Juliette came into view behind the glass patio door.

Officially, Dale still classified himself as a girl hater. He and his best friend Rusty had declared themselves to be that back in grade school. Even then they didn't really hate girls. It was just a way to protect themselves from their distracting presence. Since moving on to junior high, however, Rusty seemed to have forgotten his pledge. He talked to girls, flirted with them, was rumored to have even kissed one although he never confessed that to Dale. For his part, Dale had remained true, if not in thought then at least in deed. Better to pretend he hated girls rather than admit they unnerved him.

One of the enemy approached. Dale tried not to notice.

"Hello," said Juliette softly.

He glanced up and matched her quiet hello. He nervously noticed that the other boys had left. Now he was alone with her.

"Want some food?" he offered.

Juliette shook her head no. Dale played with the cheese in the middle of the sandwich until he noticed how silly it looked, then stopped. He glanced at Juliette again and observed her passive doll face looking at him in a way that puzzled him.

"You're sweaty," she said.

They'd all gotten sweaty playing basketball, even those, like Dale, who didn't do much but stay out of the way. None of the guys cared, of course. But leave it to a girl to notice.

"Yeah," he said, "it's hot."

"Yes, I like the warm weather, don't you?"

"It's okay," said Dale, who tended to be noncommittal about weather.

After a pause, he grew a little bolder, looked at Juliette for a full second, and noticed to his satisfaction that he was a couple of inches taller.

"How long have you been going to Kingdom Hall?" he asked.

"All my life."

Dale noticed she hardly moved her mouth when she spoke. When he asked another question, he looked more closely at her mouth.

"Do you like going?"

"I suppose," she said, her lips moving more perceptively this time. "I mean, that's not the point."

"I guess not," Dale said, although liking something ordinarily was rather important to him. He wanted to ask her if she had a dad because he'd never seen a Mr. DuBois. But he didn't. That might be a sad story and he didn't want to make Juliette burst out bawling.

"Are you going to be in the ninth grade?" she asked.

"Yeah."

"Me too."

She mentioned the high school in the City she'd be attending; he'd never heard of it.

They lapsed into another period of silence and before Dale could think of something not completely goofy to say he saw her mother appear at the open patio door.

"I've got to go."

Dale nodded and Juliette turned and walked to her mother. He noticed she wore hose like adult women do. He also noticed again her slender neck, especially the naked nape. He felt a little stirring of lust but not much. Juliette was a little too doll-like to incite much passion.

Mrs. DuBois noticed him and waved good-bye but Juliette didn't. She simply stared with her big gray eyes until she moved out of view.

The boys came outside again but without Trumbo, and instead of playing as teams they played a game of "H-O-R-S-E." Dale didn't win, but he didn't come in last. (Michael did, who pouted when put out of the game.) He knew he'd be a better shot if he hadn't almost cut off his two smaller fingers on his right hand. He'd done that at age five playing with a gardening knife. The two fingers had been saved, but they didn't function quite right.

After the game of H-O-R-S-E the boys went back to the picnic table to scrounge for leftover food, then it was time for Dale to go home. He said bye to the two brothers and the two neighborhood boys and joined Trumbo in his car. The garage door had been closed so he couldn't look more closely at all the stuff piled in there. He felt especially curious about the motorcycle.

"Is that Joe's motorcycle?" he asked.

"No, it's mine," Trumbo said. "It's getting old. I'll get a new one soon."

As if reading Dale's mind, Trumbo glanced over and smiled. "It's too dangerous for the boys to ride."

"But you ride it."

"I have experience. I know how to handle it."

Dale wondered how Joe would ever get experience if he weren't allowed to ride it, but he didn't say anything. Trumbo certainly wasn't strange in the way the other Witness men were. Most of them seemed either tall and skinny or short and fat. They all seemed too meek and mild for Dale's taste. Maybe that was the right way to be if you were a Christian, but to him it still seemed a little sissified. Trumbo certainly wasn't a sissy. Dale felt himself starting to admire Trumbo, but he didn't want to feel that way. Such feelings seemed like a betrayal to Blackie.

Trumbo once again drove his car with skill and speed. When he could, he passed cars and anticipated lights and in a few minutes they were racing down Highway 66 that connected the City to Galilee.

Trumbo pointed to a sign that led to the Wiley Post airfield. "How'd you like to fly in a plane sometime?"

"I don't know."

"I mean a small plane, not a passenger jet. A twin engine Cessna, for example."

"Maybe."

"I have a pilot's license," Trumbo said. He grinned at Dale. "I'll take you up in a Cessna sometime. I've already taken my boys. Babs won't go, though." He glanced at Dale slyly. "Well, you know women."

Dale grinned back. Actually, no, he didn't. But Trumbo obviously did. Another reason to admire him. Actually, Dale couldn't believe he was a Witness. He drove fast cars and motorcycles, played sports, and he even flew planes. And he had an important job. In fact, Trumbo seemed awfully worldly for a Witness.

"I thought Witnesses were supposed to be preparing for The End?"

Trumbo nodded solemnly at that question, his eyes locked on the road as if he were anticipating The End even as he drove. "Yes," he said, "we are. And I am. But that doesn't mean you shouldn't live life to the fullest. In fact, I think that means you should live it with even more gusto than non-believers."

Dale didn't understand. "I thought Witnesses should have just ordinary jobs. So they have more time for going door-to-door and stuff like that."

"Well, many do," Trumbo admitted.

"But not you."

"Well, we recognize that some Witnesses have to have important jobs. Jobs that help people – even non-believers. Doctors and nurses for instance."

"Air traffic controllers?" asked Dale, although he remembered Trumbo was now an administrator.

Trumbo nodded. "Well, yes, some might think that's an important job." He paused for a moment, scanned the road, then increased the speed of his Cutlass to pass a slower car. "Let me put it this way," he said, his voice a little lower, more confidential. "Even Witnesses don't agree on everything."

Trumbo glanced over at Dale and grinned just enough to make him wonder if he were joking. Before Dale could respond, the exit appeared and Trumbo turned off and had to negotiate the traffic. They both grew silent and in a few minutes Trumbo stopped the car outside Dale's house.

"Here you go," he said.

"Thanks for the ride," Dale said. "And, oh, thanks for letting me come over this afternoon."

"You bet."

As he exited the car and started to shut the door, Trumbo spoke. "Say Dale. We'll talk more. I bet you have a lot of questions you'd like to ask me."

"Yeah, I guess."

"In the meantime read the Witness book for teens. You have that book, don't you?"

"Yeah, I think so."

"Good. You read that and then we'll talk some more."

"Okay."

Dale shut the car door and waved bye as he walked to his house. Trumbo's car sped off and Dale heard the wheels squeal when the Cutlass turned the corner too fast.

He heard his mother playing on the old piano when he walked in. She played one of the Witness songs: "Myriads and Myriads of Brothers." She'd already learned it from just hearing it a few times at the meetings. She stopped when he stepped into the room.

"Did you have fun?"

Dale thought about the question. "Yeah," he finally decided.


Dale sat on the floor, his back braced against the wall. Rusty reclined on his bed with a pillow propped behind his head as he flipped through *Mad* magazine.

"*Mad* ain't that great anymore," Rusty finally decided.

He tossed the magazine to Dale. He hadn't seen that edition before, but he took Rusty's word for it. For the past few years both had been goofy over *Mad* magazine. Before that they devoured comics: *Superman, Batman, Flash, Weird Tales, Captain America*, and still occasionally sneaked a peek at *Archie*, although both boys had publicly declared it sissified even though privately they lusted after Veronica and Betty. At their age even cartoon girls inspired carnal thoughts.

"How was your vacation?" Dale asked.

"Okay," Rusty said.

He didn't elaborate. He hadn't said much about the "vacation." Dale knew he and his family drove all the way to Maryland to see his new dad's parents and brother and sister. Then the boys stayed a whole two weeks with his step-grandparents while his mother and stepfather honeymooned at Niagara Falls and took a trip through Canada and New England.

Usually Rusty talked a mile a minute and when he wasn't talking he was doing something. He was always, as his uncle Jim put it, "on the go, in the know, puttin' on a show." Dale, Rusty and Rusty's two brothers had just finished a lopsided game of Wiffle ball in the backyard. Since it had been decreed that Dale and Rusty always had to be on the same team, they had creamed Rusty's younger brothers, 15 to 3. The game had only lasted four innings when Sandy and Gavin quit, utterly vanquished and demoralized.

"How did you like Maryland?" asked Dale.

"I didn't," Rusty said. He stared at the ceiling.

"Why not?"

"The O'Malleys were always telling us to be quiet."

"You mean your grandparents?"

"Step-grandparents. Whatever that means." Dale waited to hear more. After a pause, Rusty continued. "I mean they wanted us to stay with them; I mean they made a really big deal about it because I didn't want to stay with them. I mean none of us wanted to stay with them. We didn't even know them. And then they kept on complaining. Definitely uncool."

"Were they mean to you guys?"

"Nope. Just uptight all the time."

Dale nodded. He rather envied Rusty's facility with slang.

"What were they like? Your, I mean, the O'Malleys?"

"Old."

Rusty, who'd picked up a baseball, tossed it in the air and caught it with his other hand, the ball making a pleasant smack when it landed in the palm of his hand. "Even older than Granny."

Rusty was referring to his mother's mother whom they had been living with, well, as long as Dale had known Rusty, which was all the way back to first grade.

Now Rusty, his mother, and his brothers were living in a brand new house with a brand new father. Dale had seen the stepfather a few times before he married Rusty's mother. He had no opinion of him. Neither good nor bad because he'd never had any close contact with him. He looked like an okay guy. Average height, average build, average looks, average clothes, average everything. Dale once mentioned that to Rusty and Rusty nodded, "yeah, Mr. Average," and the name, in private, stuck.

Dale looked around Rusty's new room. Larger than the room he'd shared with his two brothers in their granny's house, all kinds of stuff filled it. Books, magazines, sports equipment, records, posters of Lance Rentzel, Muhammad Ali, and Neil Young tacked on the wall, college pennants also tacked on the wall, and clothes scattered all over the room. Most of the stuff Dale had seen displayed in Rusty's old room. But besides the new furniture, including an impressive desk with a typewriter on it, one particular item interested him. Another poster, one he'd never seen, of Raquel Welch and she wore only an animal skin bikini. That poster definitely qualified as contraband for a girl hater's room.

"Where did you get that?" Dale finally asked. He'd been sneaking peeks at it for ten minutes.

Rusty glanced dismissively at it then tossed the baseball almost to the ceiling and caught it with equal nonchalance. "Like it?"

"I guess so."

"You guess so?" Rusty raised his upper body while his legs remained extended. He looked like he was doing a sit-up. He gave Dale a challenging look. "What's wrong with it?"

"Your mom lets you keep it up?"

"Sure."

Dale doubted his mom would. It was far too worldly. He wondered if he should mention the whole concept of worldliness and hear what Rusty thought. But he didn't. He knew he couldn't properly explain the concept. He wasn't even sure he agreed with it. And he was sure Rusty would ridicule the idea although Rusty occasionally went to church.

Dale looked at the poster again and recognized it as a still photo from the caveman movie *One Million Years B.C.* that Raquel Welch starred in a few years ago. He'd seen it when his mother took him, Rusty, and June May to the drive-in. He remembered feeling an odd sensation when he saw Raquel and the other women in their animal-skin bikinis. Not lust exactly; more like a momentary jolt of surprise and curiosity. He'd been just a kid then.

"Another thing," Rusty abruptly said, "they made us go to church. *Catholic* church."

"The O'Malley's?"

"Yeah."

"What was it like? I mean, the church?"

"Different. I mean it had a priest and a lot more stuff in it."

"That's because it's part of Christendom."

Rusty looked at him. "Huh?"

Dale shrugged. "Nothing."

Rusty threw his legs over the side of the bed and sat up. "I'm hungry. Want something to eat?"

Dale didn't have Rusty's enormous appetite but he said yes. The two boys left the room. He followed Rusty down the hall, past the living room, to the kitchen. On the way he saw Rusty's mom and stepdad sitting together on the couch in the living room watching TV. Sandy and Gavin were stretched out on the floor only a few feet away from the tube along with the family dog, a beagle named Roscoe.

Dale regarded Rusty's mom like any other mom. She seemed preoccupied with adult concerns but mostly seemed like a nice lady. For a mother, she was pretty with striking dark blue eyes and black hair, the same features as Gavin, the middle brother. Rusty and Sandy, whose real names were Garth and Garrett, had blue eyes too, but lighter in color, and reddish blond hair. Dale guessed they must have looked like their father. He'd never seen their real father, not even a photograph of him. All he knew was he lived in Georgia and Rusty's mother had divorced him when the boys were really little.

The kitchen looked just as new and nice as the rest of the house. It even smelled new. A faint odor of paint and new furniture and even sawdust permeated the air. Rusty opened the shiny fridge and scanned the inside.

"Peanut butter and jam?" he asked.

"Sure," replied Dale.

Rusty slopped both the peanut butter and the grape jam on his bread whereas Dale spread just the peanut butter more precisely on his. Then, each holding a cold glass of milk, they went outside to the backyard and sat down cross-legged on the grass. They ate ravenously and silently.

When they finished eating they wiped their mouth with the tail ends of their T-shirts. Rusty stretched out and patted his belly.

"Nothing hits the spot like PB & J," he said, then he burped.

They both laughed and Dale, now also stretched out, looked at the darkening summer sky. He listened to the lazy buzz of insects. The air smelled good: fresh and summery. He felt content.

"Summer and the living is easy," he said.

"What's that?"

"Words from some song I remember."

Dale remembered it was one of the songs his mother used to sing to him. She'd play the guitar and sing a lot of different songs when he was little.

"What song?"

"I think it's called 'Summertime.'"

"Makes sense."

They drew silent for a while, listening again to the natural world turning from day to night.

"Boy, you were gone a long time," said Dale.

"Yep," said Rusty. "Say, you never said what you did last month."

Dale considered telling Rusty about the Kingdom Hall and the Jehovah's Witnesses and even Juliette and Trumbo, but something warned him not to. He wasn't sure how he felt about going to the Kingdom Hall. He wanted to believe the Witnesses. If for no other reason, he wanted to make his mother happy. He thought maybe the Kingdom Hall helped her. But he didn't like some of their rules, especially not saluting the flag and not fighting in wars.

"Nothing much. Just messed around."

"Yeah, that's what we mostly did, too."

Another pause in conversation. The sky grew dark. Stars blazed brightly. Dale identified the Little Dipper and the Big Dipper. He and Rusty had memorized some of the constellations last summer.

"So, are you going to be Catholic now?" Dale asked. He didn't know why he asked the question. It just popped into his mind.

"Whattaya mean?"

"Your stepdad must be Catholic. His folks are."

"Yeah, I guess he is."

"So are you?"

"Why?" Rusty rose on his elbows and peered at Dale through the semi-darkness. "Why you asking?"

"Just wondering." He knew he should stop talking but he didn't. "I mean, if your stepdad's Catholic he's not supposed to marry a divorced woman."

"So?"

Dale lifted his upper body with his elbows. "Well, that's adultery, isn't it?"

Rusty jumped to his feet. "You calling my mother something?"

"Nope."

"Heck if you ain't," Rusty said. Dale couldn't see him so well in the dark but his voice sounded unusually angry. "Take it back."

"Take what back?"

"You know."

"Okay. I take it back."

"Say it."

"Say what?"

"My mother's not a …" Rusty either couldn't think of the word or didn't want to say it.

"Okay," Dale said, "your mother's not .. whatever."

Dale's vague confession seemed to calm Rusty. He started to sit down again when he said, "Besides, if I were you I wouldn't talk."

Dale, although shy, had a temper and on a few occasions Rusty had seen him explode. Now Dale jumped up and shoved his chest at Rusty. A head shorter, his chest only came to Rusty's belly. "Whattaya mean?" he growled.

"What did you mean?" Rusty countered.

Something in Rusty's tone infuriated Dale. He grabbed him around the waist and wrestled him to the ground. Rusty quickly recovered and grabbed Dale around his neck. The two squirmed in the grass, rolled over once, twice, three times, tried to free one hand to hit the other, got their legs tangled with the other's and basically grappled pointlessly for several minutes. Dale, although shorter, was as strong as Rusty and in their present antagonistic embrace, neither could do much harm to the other.

Finally, exhausted, they broke free.

Dale rolled away, then got to his feet. He heard Rusty, between breaths, muttering curse words, which meant he still felt angry. Dale's fury, as it usually did, died almost as abruptly as it had been born. He tried to say something, but he felt winded too, and didn't know what to say.

Rusty strode past him without a word, opened the back door, went inside and a few seconds later Dale saw the light of his bedroom flash on. Then he heard the song "In-A-Gadda-Da-Vida" blasting from the stereo in Rusty's room. The racket only lasted a few seconds before the volume lowered to a deep rumble.

Dale took in a few deep breaths and walked toward the end of the backyard. He felt a burning sensation and reached up to his forehead. He'd been scratched. He also felt a little sore in the belly where Rusty had sort of kneed him. Otherwise, he wasn't hurt.

Dale noticed the pup tent near the fence. He and Rusty were supposed to spend the night there. They were too old to have "sleep overs" in a bedroom; that was for kids. But camping together was appropriate for their age.

He wondered if he should go home. He hadn't had a fight with Rusty in a long time. Not since they became best friends. Both knew there were certain areas not to venture into. Rusty, who wasn't particularly sensitive, and Dale, who was overly so, knew the safe ground to occupy about certain topics. They'd tease each other and argue about all kinds of important questions such as which baseball team was better, the Braves or the Astros; or who was a better cowboy, Dale's favorite, John Wayne or Rusty's choice of Clint Eastwood; or what was the better kind of music, the new stuff which Rusty liked or the "old" stuff like the Beach Boys that Dale preferred. But all that was kids' stuff. They had never argued about anything personal or really embarrassing. They respected each other's privacy.

Dale knew why he'd pursued the topic of Rusty's mother's remarriage. According to the Witnesses, it was a sin to commit adultery. People who remarried for any reason other than adultery of a spouse were also committing adultery. And Catholics, who weren't supposed to divorce, sometimes did and called it something else. But that was because Catholics were part of Christendom, a false religion. Rome, in fact, was the whore of Babylon.

Dale stopped walking and looked up at the inky sky. Maybe God or Jehovah would speak to him. Tell him if all that stuff was true. All he knew was that Rusty was his best friend. His best friend ever. And he didn't like fighting with him.

The two of them were buddies of the first rank. In a lot of ways, they were opposites: Rusty, tall, lanky, with blue eyes and reddish blond hair and freckles, and a malleable face that he used to great comic effect; Dale, short, wiry, with dark brown hair, brown eyes, a dusky complexion, and a serious face that tried never to show too much emotion. They thought of themselves as brothers. Better, because Rusty never treated his two real brothers as well as he treated Dale.

In grade school, they were famous for their partnership. When assigned different homerooms in fourth grade, they devised a trick to sit together for lunch. If Rusty's class went to lunch first, he'd step on his shoe lace untying it, then stop, kneel down and take as long as he needed to tie it until Dale's class arrived. Then he'd get up, with a surprised look on his face as if to say "boy, those shoelaces are darn hard to tie," and he'd join Dale in line. When Dale's class went first, he did the same. But Dale didn't perform his role with the same aplomb as Rusty. He looked sheepish as he rose from his task and sneaked into line whereas Rusty always included a flourish, sometimes giving a little salute to the suspicious audience, other times not merely stepping on his shoe lace but stepping on the heel so the entire shoe came off.

For all of grade school, they were inseparable. Always sitting with each other at lunch, always playing on the same teams during recess, staying overnight from time to time. They shared books, baseball cards, toys, and food.

But what made them great friends even more than their shared experiences and interests was their idealistic regard for friendship itself. They had a romantic view of boyhood friendships forged from juvenile books and movies. Inspired by some forgotten film, they had once pricked their respective thumbs, squeezed out drops and mixed their blood in a solemn ceremony of blood brothers. The act, performed with all the dedication of youth, was as serious as any adult oath or vow. They believed in their friendship. They believed with the passionate conviction of children.

The previous summers had been full of activity. After delivering their paper routes, they returned home for some additional sleep, then usually got together later in the day to play sandlot baseball or race their bikes or go to the town swimming pool or see a movie matinee. They'd ride their bikes to their favorite ice cream place, Braum's, and see who could eat the most. They'd tied at seven dips. Sometimes Dale would simply hang round Rusty's granny's house, pretending to be one of the brothers too. They played Wiffle ball in the backyard, played board games, watched TV, and listened to records on Rusty's hi-fi. And they always had plenty of fun food to eat like hot dogs, hamburgers, chips, and soda pop.

Dale grew nostalgic contemplating those times. He walked back toward the red brick house, the same kind as his but newer, and considered walking home. Seven blocks; it wouldn't take long.

The door opened and Rusty emerged. Dale had been so lost in thought that he hadn't noticed the lack of music coming from Rusty's room.

"Still here?"

Those words probably would have provoked Dale, but the memories of their boyhood exploits had mellowed him.

"Look," he said, "I lost my temper."

"I'll say."

"So … I'm sorry."

"That's okay." Then Rusty added, "I'm sorry, too."

They could have said more. Dale knew Rusty was bothered by his mother's remarriage. He obviously didn't like his stepdad that much, and certainly didn't like his new step-grandparents. But now Dale was leery of asking any questions remotely personal. They never had talked about personal matters. They just lived in the moment, often forgetting reality in favor of fantasy and play-acting and day dreaming. Now, no longer children, they could have enlarged their friendship by talking about more serious matters. But Dale stood silent, although he reached out his hand.

Rusty shook his hand and Dale felt better. They were going back to the old rules when personal problems weren't discussed or even commented on.

"You wanna go in and watch some TV?" asked Rusty.

"Okay. What's on?"

"A John Wayne movie."

Rusty clapped Dale on the back as they walked into the new smelling house.

## Chapter 2: *Football practice and meeting the new kid, Clifford*

Dale, like his friends, looked forward to ninth grade. It was their time to be top dogs of the junior high school. Galilee had only one junior high and one high school and both were housed in the same building. The younger kids' lockers and classrooms were on the south side closer to the principal's office, the teacher's lounge, the cafeteria, the music and band room, and the gymnasium. The high school kids were in the north part of the building. Junior high kids never strayed into the high school area for fear of being snatched by an older boy and manhandled – well, at least shoved, teased, and "scalped" – which consisted of an older boy rubbing his knuckles over the top of the younger kid's head.

Before school, however, came football practice. Two-a-days were held the last two weeks of August and the junior high team practiced on the infield of the track. The junior high locker room was located just off the side of the elementary school playground. Just large enough to stuff thirty boys into it, the building had been painted green for some unknown reason (the school colors were "crimson and cream"). Dale and his friends, after suiting up, would walk over to the playground and lie down on the lower end of the teeter-totters.

Six of them were positioned thus in late August, near the end of two-a-days, before the afternoon practice. The day's high had been 98 degrees, the first day in two weeks that the temperature had been below 100.

The boys, however, were acclimated to the heat. Fully suited up in their white practice uniforms, they looked like bulky mummies as they lay rigid on the lower half of the teeter-totters. Dale reclined on the far end, Rusty to his left, and the other four boys to Rusty's left.

"Seen any of the new girls?" asked K. C. Cash, from the far left end.

K. C., short for Keenan Clark, had awed all the boys by showing up for practice driving a motorcycle, and sporting long sideburns. Coach Carpenter even let him keep the sideburns.

"Nothing special," said Butch Bigelow, best friend of K. C. and middle linebacker for the team. Like K. C., he'd also grown his sideburns long and drove to practice on a cycle.

"What do you think, Sonny?" asked K. C.

Sonny Schoendienst, even though he was the quarterback for the team, didn't say much. He usually had to be asked a question before he spoke. But he had been the first one to get a motorcycle and that confirmed his coolness. Besides, all the girls regarded him as the cutest boy.

"Yeah, nothing special," he said in a bored way as if the question wasn't even worth considering.

"That one girl looks really good," said Wally Wainwright, the slowest player on the team except for the really fat linemen. Since he wasn't big enough to play the line, not fast enough to play end, and not skilled enough to play the backfield, his position on the team was somewhat of a mystery.

"Which one?" asked K. C., who had earned himself the reputation of being something of a Casanova last year. The team's fullback and leader, he'd dated three different girls. Most boys hadn't been on even one date.

"You must mean Amanda," said Rusty, surprising Dale that he was in the know.

"Yeah," said Wally. "Amanda Meeks. Saw her with my sister the other night. Not bad."

"Yeah, not bad," said Bigelow, with feigned indifference. "But she's stuck up."

"Well, she talked to me," said Wally.

"That's because she knew you're Wendy's brother," said Rusty teasingly.

Dale began to suspect that all of them, except him, had attended some social function. He wondered why Rusty hadn't informed him.

"No, really. She's nice," insisted Wally.

"Yeah," said Bigelow, "but she's a goody-goody."

Dale noticed that Butch had the lowest opinion of her, which probably meant he was the most interested.

"How do you know?" asked Wally.

"I know," said Bigelow, whose real first name was Bentley. "She goes to my church."

Bigelow's opinion seemed to settle the debate for the time and the boys moved on to evaluating the other females of the ninth grade. Almost everyone agreed that Roxanne Robideaux was the prettiest with her strawberry blond hair, sly blue eyes, full lips and curvaceous figure. Almost everyone agreed Mary Jane Morgan (since they didn't count the new girl Amanda yet) ranked second in beauty, with long dark hair, big brown eyes, a wide mouth, and a long, model-like figure. And most everyone agreed that Wendy, Wally's twin sister, was the friendliest. In deference to Wally, they didn't elaborate too much on Wendy's physical attributes, but she was a pretty girl, with yellow blond hair, bright green eyes, and a big smile. Butch didn't care for her freckles and Sonny thought her hips were too big, but almost everyone agreed she was the nicest.

"Who cares about nice," said Bigelow.

"I like nice," said Rusty.

But Dale knew Rusty had once told him that Wendy annoyed him, she was a busybody: always organizing things either at school or for get-togethers after.

"Like what you want, Grimes," said Bigelow, who, like everyone else this year called guys by their last names to sound more grown-up. "What I want to know is who will put out."

Some of the guys laughed in a harsh, not entirely convincing way. There followed an excited discussion about different possibilities with different girls, with the most potentially receptive girl who was not a skank being Sadie Smith.

No relation to Dale, but he'd sat in the desk behind hers almost every year since second grade. Butch, K. C., Rusty, and even Wally began speculating on the possibilities of Sadie.

Dale admitted to himself that she was sort of pretty but he sensed something a little sad about her. He'd gotten a good look at her all those years sitting behind her and he'd

28

watched her mature into an attractive girl, with her long, white-blond hair, fairly cute face, and an alluring figure. But she often seemed a little "blue" as his mother termed it; her clothes didn't have the same new and fashionable look to them as the popular girls' and he guessed that bothered her.

Dale heard K. C. say that a sophomore had gotten to second base with her. Butch said he heard a junior had gotten to third base. Then Rusty said he'd gotten all the way home, but it was so obviously untrue and said with such mocking conviction that they all laughed, even Dale and the only other boy not to have participated in the bull session: Chris DeVille, the team's back-up split end and safety. He'd moved to Galilee just last year.

Before Rusty could elaborate on his joke, the boys heard the coach's whistle and they trudged over to the practice field. While walking over, Dale increased his pace and caught up with Chris DeVille. Guys like Butch would dismiss him as another "goody goody"; he made pretty good grades, didn't goof off in class, respected the teachers, even the incompetent ones, and believed in good sportsmanship on and off the field. Therefore, he remained thoroughly dull to the coolest guys.

"You didn't say anything back there," said Chris.

"You didn't either," said Dale.

"Not my kind of topic, I guess," said Chris, who had blond hair, blue eyes and a friendly face dominated by a large, wedge-like nose that seemed even larger compared to his comparatively small eyes and lips.

Dale nodded and wondered if Chris was as ignorant of sex as he was. Not only in practice – most if not all the junior high boys were in that category in such a religious and socially conservative town as Galilee – but also in theory. Dale remembered as a seventh grader eavesdropping on a conversation a group of ninth graders were having. Their talk grew increasingly graphic, their boasts increasingly fantastic, and Dale got an education on sex that he'd never had before. In fact, he'd been so woefully ignorant up until that point that he'd thought men made women pregnant by kissing them. A man sent his seed through a kiss into the woman and it swam down to her belly and in a few months a baby would be born. Dale couldn't remember how he acquired that fairy tale. Probably Jesse told him that when he asked as a little kid. Jesse never liked talking about sex and his father hadn't been around much to enlighten him either.

The older boys' descriptions had been so vivid and crude that Dale remained in a daze all during practice. His mind struggled to comprehend it all. The man's part made sense; after all, he had that part and although it hadn't yet reached any sexual capability, he could imagine how it could. But the woman's part especially puzzled him. The older boys' descriptions were almost horrifying, disturbing him even more than the scary things he'd seen in a horror movie; worse, because a horror movie is only make believe and part of the fun is pretending you're scared. But this sex stuff sounded really scary because it was real. Dale wondered how people could actually do it. Especially women. It sounded painful and embarrassing. And judging from the older boys' raucous boasts, they sounded like they enjoyed inflicting the pain.

Then last year in health class the boys received their first instruction in sexual reproduction. Dale had dreaded that segment of the class in part because the high school football coach, Ray Aldo, a gruff ex-Marine who'd killed Japs in World War II, taught the class. He scared all the kids by just walking into the classroom and glaring at them. Fortunately for Dale's peace of mind, that part of class, a whole week's worth, was taught by his junior high assistant football coach, Reeve Carpenter. Dale liked Coach Carpenter, a giant of a man, with a head disproportionately small in relation to his huge body. However, Coach Carpenter had a classically handsome face. He reminded Dale of Superman, especially since he had the same kind of dark hair with a short curl in front. His six foot seven height alone commanded respect. But Coach Carpenter also seemed to have a genuine interest in the boys and rarely raised his voice.

Coach Carpenter gave the class the basics of sexual reproduction, describing it all in a matter-of-fact way without any stammering or embarrassment. When one of the boys snickered, Coach paused and stared in his direction, which quickly silenced him. Hearing sexual congress described in a rational, medical kind of way made it sound less scary and shameful to Dale. But it still sounded sort of weird.

That was last year. In the meantime, Dale had seen a few girly magazines and seen a few suggestive scenes in movies, although Jesse always told him to put his hands over his eyes when an actress began to disrobe (Dale would peek through his fingers, anyway). He reckoned he'd seen dozens of naked women – in photographs or brief glimpses in movies – and his initial revulsion for sex had been replaced by increasing curiosity and a sense of adventure. But he still felt absurdly ignorant; most of the other guys talked as if they knew everything about it. Even Rusty had gotten a little boastful. The only other guy not to engage in the bull sessions was Chris DeVille. Dale didn't know whether that was due to his rectitude or his ignorance.

But Dale didn't get a chance to interrogate Chris before the start of practice. As soon as they walked on the field, Coach Carpenter kept them busy with drills, scrimmages, and sprints. After all twenty-seven boys were panting from exhaustion, walking with their hands on their heads to help deep breathing, uniforms stained with sweat and dirt and grass, Coach called them together for a practice-ending pep talk. In two weeks the season would begin.

Coach Carpenter wasn't much for pep talks. He had such a deep voice that some of the players had trouble making out some of his words. His voice resounded as if coming out of a deep well. But he mostly got his point across. Just the fact that a huge man stood before them and spoke confidently about the upcoming season gave them hope.

Last season the Galilee Junior High team hadn't won a game. Its record, 0-8. Which wasn't as abysmal as one might think considering Galilee played many of their games against city schools twice their size. Nevertheless, going winless discouraged the team and Coach Carpenter, whose primary job was coaching high school basketball and teaching physical education, had been asked to take over this season. He'd been asked by the athletic director to instill in the junior high boys the necessary confidence to start winning. Now Coach Carpenter, his voice echoing in the hot late afternoon air, told the boys that a positive attitude was half of winning.

Dale wasn't worried about that so much. He worried about playing teams with opposing players who weighed 160, 180, even 200 pounds. Thankfully, the growth spurt he'd been waiting for seemed to have started that summer and by the time two-a-days started he measured five foot three and weighed 120 pounds. Still shorter and lighter than most of the players on the team, he was fast, strong for his size, and Coach liked his hard working attitude. He'd won starting positions in the backfield on both offense and defense.

Coach Carpenter finished his pep talk and led the team in three cheers of "Go, Junior Gophers!" Then the boys jogged back to the dressing room and undressed and showered. That is, the older boys did. As an unwritten rule, only post-pubescent boys who played showered; typically no seventh graders and only the few eighth graders who played showered. Of Dale's classmates, only K. C., Sonny, and Butch showered last year.

Dale remembered those dreadful days of football as a seventh grader. The ninth graders tormented the plebes (one of the less derogatory names they used), berating them, shoving them out of the way, making them fetch like dogs ("Hey, plebe bring me some tape like a nice doggie"). For abuse, the freshmen would take off their chinstraps and whack the top of the seventh graders' helmets. The impact of the chinstraps metal snaps on their helmets produced a shrill noise that would make the plebes' ears ring. Even more abusive because it was so humiliating was "jock-masking." A freshman would take his sweaty jock and wrap it around a plebe's face making him wear it like a mask. And the most abusive act of all was "flushing" a plebe. The freshmen would grab a particularly pathetic plebe, drag him to the toilet, dunk his head in the bowl, and flush. If they really felt cruel, they'd pee in it before flushing.

Just last spring in the senior high locker room, Terry Harte, a freshman, had been flushed. Harte, talented enough as a freshman to run on the high school track team, incurred the jealousy of the upperclassmen. They ganged up on him and dragged him to the toilet. Harte struggled so much that he cracked his head against the toilet tank and knocked himself out. The four upperclassmen who'd perpetrated the prank had been severely punished. They were suspended from school for a week, given a negative citation on their official transcript, and upon their return to school were made to run an extra mile of laps after track practice for a week.

Dale had witnessed all the above abominations except a flushing and had been a victim of some of the milder bullying. He'd been spared the worse torments not because he was so small (he only weighted 100 pounds as a seventh grader) but because he pretended not to be afraid. He actually felt petrified most of the time but learned quickly that showing fear provoked attack more than a defiant attitude, both in the locker room and on the practice field. The plebes who were abused were almost always the ones that shied away from contact in drills or cowered in the locker room. In a way, the hazing was meant to toughen up the younger kids and weed out the weaklings. But it had been taken to extremes the last few years and the previous head coach, a rather bookish young man named Mr. Wickfield who taught social studies, evoked no fear and thus lacked authority to discourage the attacks.

So, the school administration promoted Coach Carpenter, all 230 pounds of him, to head football coach and directed him to instill discipline and, perhaps, turn the team into a winning one.

Dale welcomed the change. He'd been disgusted with the treatment of the plebes when he was one and later when he wasn't. At the start of the season, he, Rusty, and Chris vowed never to mistreat any of the younger kids.

So with a new season starting, and with a new coach and a new attitude, Dale felt a sense of optimism as he and Rusty left the locker room. They talked about the upcoming games, again against bigger schools, but they felt the possibility of success for the first time. Rusty's granny's house stood only a few blocks down the street from the track field. He stopped off there while Dale decided to go on to his house.

After a few blocks of swift walking, Dale saw one of his teammates about half a block away. He recognized him as one of the new kids. After a few minutes he caught up with him because the guy, also a freshman, walked so slowly.

"Hey," said Dale.

The kid stopped and turned around. "Hey."

Dale couldn't remember his name. He looked at the guy, who stood five foot nine or so, with a sturdy build, a long face, a bulbous nose, curly brown hair, and most noticeable of all, old-fashioned glasses, the kind with thick black frames.

"I'm Clifford," the kid finally said.

"Yeah, right. And I'm –"

"I remember your name," Clifford said, almost as if he felt offended that Dale doubted his memory.

Dale nodded and noticed that Clifford looked sweaty, more sweaty than he would have been from just walking in the fading heat. Trickles of sweat rolled down each side of his face and his sport shirt looked rather damp, as if it had been used as a towel. Dale concluded that Clifford hadn't showered. Obviously, it wasn't because of the unwritten rule of pre-pubescence. So Dale wondered why.

Instead of asking that, however, he asked what school he went to last year.

"Lyons," Clifford said.

Lyons was Galilee's archrival – only because Galilee sometimes beat them. It was a school about the same size as Galilee, located about thirty miles south of the City. When Galilee visited last year, the town looked sort of ragged and worn-out. Dale remembered hearing that a meat processing plant located in Lyons had closed a few years ago.

"Oh, yeah. The Lyons Lions."

"Yeah, well, we beat you guys last year," Clifford said defensively. Everybody made fun of the school's name.

"I know. By an extra point."

Dale thought about that game. Last game of the season. Last chance to avert a winless record. Junior Gophers scored late in the game and decided to go for the two-point conversion because they wanted to win and because they had a lousy place kicker. Instead of giving the ball to their best player, Terry Harte, the bookish coach, Wickfield, thought he'd outsmart the Lyons' coach with a fake to Harte and a bootleg by the quarterback, Sonny Schoendienst. The play didn't fake anybody out; the Lions tackled Sonny in the backfield. Game over. Season over. And the shame of not only being winless but losing to the crummy Lyons Lions.

"Well, you're on our team now," said Dale.

"Yeah," said Clifford, but he didn't sound too happy about it.

They began walking. They talked about the team, the upcoming season, and school starting next week. Dale asked Clifford if he'd met anybody else besides his football teammates.

"Nope."

Dale hoped that Clifford, the new guy, had met the new girl and would tell him about her. Dale hadn't wanted to ask the other guys questions about her because he felt shy about girls, even around his buddies.

They walked and Dale went along with Clifford's route although it took him out of his way for a few blocks. They'd crossed into the poorer part of town, across the proverbial train tracks, and followed a narrow street until it turned into a gravel road. Clifford slowed down a little and turned to Dale.

"You live around here?"

Dale nodded. "Well, farther up that way," he said, pointing north. Clifford's brown eyes narrowed behind his Clark Kent eyeglasses.

"Ain't you going out of your way?"

"Not really."

Of course he was, but Dale found Clifford interesting for some reason. It wasn't only his new-kid status; there was something a little odd about him, a little off. His clothes looked old-fashioned, like something out of the early '60s. Chinos, striped sports shirt, scuffed brown shoes, white socks. But there was also another incongruous quality that Dale couldn't quite define.

They walked down the gravel road listening to the crunching underneath their shoes. When they came to an alley, Clifford suddenly stopped. He looked uncomfortable, standing rigid, his hands almost in fists, not looking at Dale.

"Well," Clifford said, "I gotta go."

"Okay." Then Dale realized Clifford wanted him to go on. Dale started walking. "So long."

"Yeah, so long." Clifford turned and walked down the alley.

Dale slowed, then stopped, then crept back to where he'd left Clifford. He looked down the alley just in time to see Clifford turn into a yard of mostly dirt and then into a small, ramshackle house that looked more like a shack with its low, almost sunken roof and thin-looking walls.

Dale felt that unpleasant feeling surge through him: part pity, part revulsion that almost made him sick to his stomach. He'd felt such a feeling before, most recently when he'd gone out with his mother to witness. Sometimes he felt that burning sense of shame when he heard something embarrassing about his mother's sister, Wanda. How she got another divorce or was back on welfare or, more recently, how her youngest daughter, Bobbie Sue, had been sent to the girls reformatory. But none of his poorer relations lived in a shack.

Dale shook his head in pity and turned away and walked home.


**Chapter 3: *Dale starts school, gets sick, and sees her***

With his new status as a freshman, Dale had planned to wait for school to begin by joining the most popular students in the courtyard outside the main entrance. He hadn't done this much his first two years of junior high. He felt too shy to join the throng of kids that socialized and goofed off before the bell rang. Instead, he usually waited at the smaller west entrance with the outcasts and misfits.

So the first day of classes his freshman year, when he should have strode triumphantly to the junior high section of the courtyard, he stood at the obscure west entrance with Vern Jurgens and ten other antisocial types.

Dale actually liked Vern. They'd been friends since second grade. Vern, a stout, round-faced boy, went to a Mennonite church as did his two older sisters. None of them were allowed to show any skin save their face and hands. Because of that, Vern couldn't play organized sports or even attend gym classes. That removed him from Rusty's and Dale's circle and prevented him from being an even better friend. But Dale talked with him at school and sometimes visited Vern so he could go ride his horse, Smoky.

Dale knew from sight Vern's two older sisters. Both were in high school at Galilee and both looked the same. They always wore long dresses that dropped down to their ankles. The full, heavy skirts concealed their legs and hips. When they sat down, the dress hems moved up just enough so one could see they wore old-fashioned woolen hose. Both girls eschewed makeup on their homely faces. Both had long, straight brown hair that they never cut. The eldest girl's hair went down past her backside so she had to toss it to one side so she wouldn't sit on it. The younger one had the same kind of hair that only went down to her waist. They reminded Dale of Vern's horse. When they walked, hugging their books to their heavily clothed bosoms, their hair swayed like Smoky's long tail.

Dale and Vern exchanged their customary greeting:

"Hey."

"Hey yourself," said Vern.

Being such a religious kid, Vern took delight in occasional rudeness, especially to his friends.

They talked about nothing special: their upcoming classes and Smoky. Since Vern lived on the northern edge of town, Dale didn't see him as much as he'd have liked. Vern lived too far for Dale to walk or bike so he had to get Jesse to drive him over. And she didn't like driving him there and then turning around two hours later to pick him up.

Standing at the west entrance, Dale felt glad he at least had Vern to talk to. He glanced around and noticed that the other ten kids stood to themselves like solitary statues – seven boys, including the class brain, Isaac Gould, also a Mennonite, and three girls. The ten were either too shy, underdeveloped, or deliberately antisocial to join the other students or even talk to one another. Dale would have pitied them if he weren't afraid he might be doomed to their fate too if he didn't outgrow his adolescent bashfulness.

In spite of his shyness, however, Dale really wasn't an outcast or misfit. He performed well enough in important areas of school life to avoid that designation. Most importantly for a boy, he was athletic. He'd always been the fastest boy in his class, winning all the recess races or the sprints they ran in gym class. He was one of the best baseball players in little league, and even in football, despite his small size, he was considered one of the better players. Only in basketball were his shortcomings evident.

In the other important areas, Dale acquitted himself well, too. Although he hated to admit it, he probably was a good-looking kid. His female relatives had always fussed over him, and told him how handsome he was. Dale knew kinfolk were biased, but since he had to look at himself in the mirror at least long enough to wash his face or brush his teeth, he knew he wasn't bad looking. He had a crooked tooth, though, and so didn't like smiling. He thought that was just as well. He mistrusted boys who smiled too much. He preferred to cultivate an unsmiling persona; it created an aura of mystery and toughness that he craved.

Being short was a problem. In fact, that was the primary reason why he felt shy and uncomfortable in social situations. Most of the girls were still taller than he was and therefore he didn't like being around them.

The other important area was personality. Dale, although quiet, was suspected of having a good personality. Suspected because he didn't reveal it very often, but in rare moments he could say something funny or make an insight that would impress the average adolescent. Just as important though, he was best friends with Rusty, the most popular boy in his class. That brought Dale some reflected popularity.

Grades weren't considered an especially important measurement of popularity, although most of the popular kids did get good grades, especially the girls. For boys, doing too well at school showed sissy tendencies so even the bright boys, like Rusty, Dale, Vern, and Wally demonstrated a nonchalance, if not disdain, for making good grades. The only boy who didn't was Isaac, who was reputed to have an almost genius I.Q.

For the girls, the most important characteristic after beauty was "niceness." Encouraged by the culture of the town, the church, and the school, the most popular girls in Galilee were not only pretty, they were nice: friendly, considerate, polite, and proper. Although niceness was beginning to be disdained by the wider culture, in Galilee it remained important.

The school bell rang and Dale walked inside with Vern and the others. The ninth grade row of lockers was located on the east end of the building so Dale and Vern maneuvered through the jabbering students going in the other direction. He found Rusty waiting for him at their locker.

Every year in junior high, Rusty and Dale shared a locker. It was a requirement of being best friends. The third guy varied year to year. In seventh grade it had been Quentin Osteen; he had been more of a friend from grade school. In eighth grade, it was Vern. But not being an athlete eliminated him for freshman year. In fact, Rusty and Dale were like a binary star system that once a year pulled in a straying planet. Since they had such a strong and united bond, the third person usually became a buffer or a sidekick and only lasted one school year before leaving the solar system and floating off to a more hospitable environment.

This year the third guy was Wally Wainwright. Wally met the athletic requirement, sort of: he played but wasn't very good. He was bright but didn't earn especially good grades. But his personality was a problem. He fluctuated from being ingratiating with the more popular boys to being contemptuous of the hoi polloi. Part of the problem was that he was the twin brother of Wendy, the most popular girl in their class. It was pretty clear to everyone that Wally envied his sister's social standing. She was considered the leader of the girls and was also genuinely nice and pleasant to all.

"Hey, man," said Rusty when he saw Dale. "Where've you been?"

"Little late getting here."

Often he was late, but even when he wasn't he gave that excuse for why he wasn't seen in the courtyard.

"I don't mean that," said Rusty. He noticed Vern, who passed by on the way to his locker. "Hey, Vern, man."

"Hey, yourself," said Vern.

Rusty slapped Vern on the back as he passed, then turned to Dale. "I mean Saturday night. I thought you were coming over to Wally's."

"Well, I was. My dad just got back, you know."

"Yeah, your dad. Say –"

But before Rusty could say more, Wally arrived.

"Hey, Wallace," Rusty greeted.

"Hey, *Grimey*," Wally rejoined, just letting Rusty know he could play the name game too.

Rusty chose to ignore the insult; Rusty was good at ignoring things he didn't like. "I was just telling Smith here about your shindig Saturday."

Wally looked at Dale with an offended air. "Yeah, Smith, why didn't you show?"

Before Dale could even attempt an answer, Rusty butted in. "Should have been there, sport. Without you, it turned out uneven. Five girls and only four boys."

"Oh yeah?" Dale said, curious. "Who was there?"

"Wendy and Wally, of course," Rusty glanced at Wally who frowned as usual over the order of he and his sister; after all, he had once complained, he was older than Wendy by five minutes. "And Roxanne, Mary Jane, Gretchen –" Dale noticed Rusty listing only the girls.

"And besides Rusty," interjected Wally, "K. C. and Butch."

"That's only four," said Dale.

"Yeah, four boys," said Wally.

"I mean girls."

"Ah, Smith noticed," said Rusty.

Dale frowned. Now he was officially no longer a girl-hater. Well, they were now freshman and he'd been the only holdout since beginning junior high.

"Well, you're right," Rusty continued. "Amanda was there."

"Amanda," said Dale, who realized he liked the way the name sounded.

"Yeah, the new girl," said Wally.

"Yeah, and she ain't half bad," said Rusty.

Dale wanted to hear more about this new girl but the second bell rang. The boys grabbed their science books and headed to class.

"Science first thing in the morning," said Rusty, "who's idea was that?"

The first class passed slowly, as it did on the first day of a new school year. When it ended, Dale joined Rusty as they walked to their locker. Dale gave the usual terse greeting to the guys he hadn't seen yet because they didn't play football. But he couldn't work up the nerve to speak to any of the girls. They didn't seem to mind. They greeted him by his first name, his school name. They said, "hello, Audie," in their lilting voices as they passed him in the hallways. Dale nodded, trying not to blush. He scanned the hallways, looking for an unfamiliar face. He hadn't seen the new girl yet.

In algebra, Dale sat in the back with Rusty, Wally, and Vern and realized he felt worse than he did earlier that morning. He'd woken up with a sore throat and a headache. He thought the ill feeling would pass. He didn't want to miss the first day of class. He rarely missed class. Last year, he'd not missed one day.

"Hey, man," Rusty said in a low voice, leaning over, "what's wrong with you?"

Dale shook his head. He noticed he had a hard time swallowing. "I feel sort of crummy."

"Yeah, I can see that. And you got some weird lump on your neck, too."

Dale touched the side of his throat with his fingers. It felt swollen. It felt sore when he touched it. Then he realized he had another lump on the other side of his throat.

"You better go to the clinic and get that checked out," said Wally, who often dispensed medical advice. Since he got sick or hurt so often, he thought he was an expert.

Dale nodded but he didn't want to. He especially didn't want to raise his hand and call attention to himself. Rusty grinned, knowing of his pal's shyness, and raised his hand instead. The teacher, a young woman with a plain face and large glasses, walked over. Almost immediately, she instructed Dale to go to the clinic.

For three and a half days, Dale lay in bed with the mumps. He'd never missed so much school. He also missed football practice, and as he sat in bed and read he worried that he might lose his starting position. Blackie had taken him to a clinic at Tinker Air Force base in the City. As a retired career man, Blackie and his family got free medical care. Since Oklahoma no longer had a navy airfield, they were allowed to use the air force base.

While recuperating, Dale remembered the last time he had felt so sick. He'd been five when he caught the German measles. Blackie had been stationed in Antarctica for the first time, so it was up to Jesse to take him to the doctor. But she didn't do it. Jesse, after her own harrowing experience in the Galilee children's hospital, had an aversion to doctors and hospitals. She didn't even take the kids to the dentist. So Dale had remained sick in his bed, delirious from his illness, and had only vague memories of that time. He remembered not being able to taste food and feeling hot, weak, and thirsty. Compared to that, the mumps weren't so bad. He even got to eat his fill of ice cream.

By Thursday evening, Dale felt almost normal. He got up and left his room and joined his parents and June May in the living room. As soon as he entered the room, he felt the tension. Blackie and Jesse weren't arguing, but they weren't talking to one another. Blackie, still enjoying his "retirement," rose late, lazed around the house, then usually went fishing in the afternoon. When he came home, he cleaned the fish, then settled down in his E-Z Boy and drank beer and watched television until dinner. Jesse, not used to having Blackie around, often left the house to see her parents or her sister. The source of the tension, other than the unusual situation of having Blackie permanently home, was the Jehovah's Witnesses. Now that Wanda had spilled the beans, Jesse wanted Blackie to come along to the Kingdom Hall.

Jesse suggested that to Blackie while the four were having dinner Thursday evening. She wanted Blackie to come Friday; that meeting seemed more like regular church with the elders giving short "talks."

Blackie paused between bites of steak. "Those people have church on Friday night?"

"Not church," said Jesse. "They have meetings."

"Same thing," he said, sticking the speared steak into his mouth. He then lopped off a large hunk of potato and ate it, jacket and all. Dale thought it odd his dad ate the jacket of a baked potato. The rest of them excavated the potato from the jacket.

Blackie caught Dale staring at him as he chewed. "Whattaya you looking at?"

Dale shrugged. Blackie saw him looking at the half-eaten potato. "Forgot I eat my taters like this, eh?" he said sarcastically.

Dale nodded.

"That's where the vitamins and minerals are," he said, poking the brown, wrinkled potato skin with his fork; Jesse had baked the potatoes a little too long. "If you'd joined the navy at sixteen like me, you'd have learned to eat anything you could get your hands on."

"What about tomorrow night?" Jesse asked.

"Are you kiddin'? You think I want to spend my Friday night going to some *Kingdom Hall* with Bible thumpers?"

Dale had heard that term, Bible thumpers, before but it was one of those phrases that puzzled him. He'd never seen any brother or sister thump a Bible.

"I s'ppose you'd rather sit home and play poker and get drunk?" Jesse said.

"Hell, we could go out and get drunk." Blackie glanced at Dale and June May a little sheepishly. He tried not to cuss around them, but easily forgot when angry or drunk.

Jesse put down her knife and fork. "I'm tryin' to be a witness for Jehovah," she said emphatically.

Dale could tell Blackie was tempted to utter some witticism in response, one of the things that infuriated Jesse, especially when he used words she didn't understand. But Blackie restrained himself.

"All right. But I still ain't going on Friday night."

Jesse resumed eating, somewhat mollified. She'd heard what Dale heard: not going on Friday night. That left open the possibility of going on Sunday or Tuesday.

Friday at school the routine changed. An all-school assembly was scheduled. Sixth-hour classes were cancelled and all the students were to meet in the auditorium to hear a local country and western band, the female lead singer being a graduate of Galilee. Then immediately following, a pep assembly would commence honoring the high school football team members and cheering them on in preparation for their opening football game at home against Wheaton.

Since the assembly would need the use of the spotlight, the members of the audio-visual club were called into action. Rusty and Dale were the new freshman members of the club, a distinction that puzzled Dale. He hadn't even known they had been selected. Since all but one of the other members were on the high school football team, Rusty and Dale were pressed into service. When fifth hour ended, they raced to the auditorium and clambered up the stairs to a booth that housed the spotlight and projection machines and other AV equipment. A senior boy waited for them, a glare in his eyes.

"You're late," he said.

"Hey, we rushed here," said Rusty who didn't seem impressed to be in the presence of a senior.

"Yeah, well, I've been waiting five minutes." The senior wore round spectacles and sported shaggy dirty blond hair.

"So?"

Rusty looked around, touching a cable, poking at a lens, examining a 16mm film projector. Dale moved around more cautiously. He'd never seen such equipment before. He looked at the spotlight, a black cylinder on a stand, and reached to touch the back when the senior pushed it away.

"What are we going to do for ya?" Rusty asked.

"Nothing. You don't do nothing. Don't touch anything unless I say so. Just watch."

"Just watch, eh?" Rusty leaned against the wall, the thumb of each hand hooked into the front pockets of his bell-bottomed striped pants. "I thought you learned by doing."

The senior boy sneered, then turned and started fiddling with the spotlight. First he plugged it in, then he cleaned the glass lens, then he lined it up at the window looking down at the auditorium floor. Below they could hear students milling in: shuffling feet, the rumble of voices, an occasional shout and whistle. The first assembly of the year and the kids were a little rowdy and high spirited.

The senior slapped his forehead. "Rats, I forgot the filters." He gave Rusty and Dale a disagreeable look as if they were responsible. "Look, I'll be back in a minute." He started to leave, then stopped. "And don't do anything!"

Rusty, still reclining against the wall arrogantly, nodded. Dale nodded too, and the senior disappeared.

Rusty went over to the spotlight. "Interesting," he said, taking hold of the handle. Dale went over and examined it as well.

"How did we get picked for this job?" he asked.

"Mr. Baines picked us," Rusty said.

Mr. Baines was the elderly social studies teacher that advised the audio visual club. Except that it wasn't exactly a club. Baines selected students. He usually picked a couple of boys each from grades nine through twelve. They were responsible for the sound and lighting for plays and assemblies and operated projectors when the teachers showed films in class.

"Why?"

"'Cause we show promise. Who cares why? We get out of class. We show films. Sounds fun."

Dale and Rusty had Mr. Baines for social studies last year. The old man, with his big shock of white hair, looked like a venerable senator himself. He liked leaning back in his chair and telling stories about politicians and the deals they made. Dale remembered him explaining political deal-making with the phrase, "you wash my back and I'll wash yours" a lot. Every time he said it, Dale pictured a big slob politician standing in a bathtub washing another big slob politician's back. His mental image only went from the waist up.

Rusty flipped on the switch of the spotlight. Instantly a beam of light thrust itself into the shadowy auditorium. A couple of kids noticed and waved. "Hey," he said, "this is neat."

Dale put his head out of the window and looked at the light dancing across the auditorium when Rusty began moving the spotlight up and down and left and right.

"Look," said Dale, "there's our class in the back."

Rusty turned the spotlight to the left. "No," said Dale, "right." Rusty easily corrected the direction. The spotlight smoothly cast itself over the back two rows.

"I'm getting pretty good at this," Rusty said with his usual self-admiration.

The large, illuminated circle settled on a section of the back row where several girls sat. Dale watched as one by one they turned to see where this intrusive light came from. They seemed a little startled by the appearance of the light. Dale watched with amusement as first Wendy, then Roxanne, then Mary Jane turned around, squinting into the light, before shielding their eyes. Then Dale saw a girl he'd never seen before. She too had turned her face. Because her large blue eyes didn't look directly into the light, she didn't squint or shield them. Instead she held her head high, her heart-shaped face tilted up, a small smile on her full lips.

Dale had never seen anyone so beautiful.

Suddenly, the light disappeared and the girls, including the beautiful one, turned away. Dale pulled his head back in just in time to see the senior grab the spotlight from Rusty.

"Just testing," said Rusty.

"Just for that," said the senior, "you two can go."

Rusty shrugged and he and Dale descended the stairs to the auditorium. When they entered, they saw the country and western band, The Mavericks, standing on stage, preparing to play. The group consisted of four guys and one girl, the vocalist. Dale and Rusty didn't try to find seats with their class. Instead, they sat down on a couple of stools standing against the auditorium's back wall. Dale looked to his right at the back row of seats where the girls sat. As the music began, he saw her.

He would always remember the song, "If Not for You." He would always remember how she looked. From his angle, he saw her in profile. Her features seemed perfect. Her hair, light brown, hung in a thick wave past her shoulders. Even without her face being bathed in silver light, he still thought she looked angelic.

Dale didn't have to ask Rusty who she was. He knew. She was Amanda Meeks.

**Chapter 4:** *Clifford creamed; Blackie gives Dale a civics lesson*

Rusty became the next freshman boy to get a motorcycle. He showed it to Dale after school. It stood parked with three other motorcycles, K. C.'s, Butch's, and Sonny's. Rusty walked over to it and caressed the gas tank and black fake leather seat.

"She's a beaut, isn't she," he said.

Dale examined the silver and green machine: a Honda 90. Sonny, who had been the first to get one, had a Yamaha 90. But Butch and K. C. drove Kawasacki 125s. Still, Dale was impressed.

"Yeah," he said casually, not wanting to show too much admiration, "it's swell."

"More than swell," Rusty corrected. He jumped on and kick-started it. He revved the engine by twisting the throttle. He leaned down and cocked one ear closer to the engine's sweet rumblings. "Hear that baby sing?" he said.

Dale nodded.

"Get on back. I'll give you a ride over to the locker room."

Dale hopped on the back of the seat but didn't grab hold of Rusty's waist like some girl. Instead his hands grabbed the underside of the seat and he almost fell off when Rusty jerked the cycle forward.

They sped out of the school's parking lot, turned down Kerr Street, and drove two blocks to the junior high football locker room.

Rusty parked the cycle and locked the front wheel. He stood admiring his demon machine when Dale asked how he got it.

"A gift from Mr. Average," he said, still gazing at the cycle like a fat man gazes at a sizzling steak. Then, knowing he sounded ungrateful, corrected himself. "Martin."

"Your stepfather gave you that?" Dale said, thinking maybe he should reconsider Mr. Average.

"Yeah." Rusty finally tore himself away from the beautiful machine. "Think he's trying to bribe me?"

Dale shrugged and before he could say more the team's other three motorcyclists roared onto the makeshift parking lot. K. C. Cash, Butch Bigelow, and Sonny Schoendienst dismounted their cycles, locked them, and then K. C., Butch, and Rusty immediately engaged in a boasting contest about whose cycle was the toughest, the fastest, or just plain ol' better. Dale walked with Sonny to the locker room. Both of Sonny's parents taught at the high school, which normally would have made him an object of teasing. But Sonny had an aura of coolness that discouraged teasing. He seemed supremely indifferent to everything, even insults and quarterback sacks. As they walked to the locker room, Dale noticed that Sonny walked gingerly, still sore from the game.

After they put their pads on they marched back to the playground. The six of them, Rusty, Dale, K. C., Butch, Sonny, and Billy Joe Barton, the team's best player, reclined on the teeter-totters and waited until practice officially began. The talkative ones, Rusty, K. C. and Butch, launched into their usual banter, while the quieter ones, Sonny, Dale and Billy Joe listened and occasionally uttered a sentence, a word, or a grunt.

Thus engaged, the six almost didn't notice Clifford Oates, who had started the team's first four games as an undersized tackle and was still considered by his teammates as a new kid.

Rusty saw him first. He stood up and watched as Clifford walked swiftly toward the locker room. Then the rest of them stood up and looked. Clifford walked with a comic intensity; in fact, he did almost everything with a fierceness that seemed disproportionate to the task. His face wore a grimace throughout the day. Such an expression was understandable in algebra or in class in general, but to look like he was marching into battle every minute of the day seemed ridiculous, especially to Rusty who had an opposite attitude. So, leave it to Rusty to discover a catchphrase that perfectly summed up the absurdity of Clifford's demeanor.

"Where's Cliff-ferd?" he shouted.

Clifford turned in their direction and did not smile. He glared at them and continued his march toward the locker room.

The six roared with laughter, even Dale. He couldn't help it. Rusty had a genius for mimicry and facial expression. And Rusty was simply repeating, although with comic exaggeration, the pitiful inquiry made by Clifford's little cousin after their last game, which they lost, of course. Sitting in the bus waiting to return to the locker room after yet another defeat, the players were somberly quiet. It wasn't fun having to endure a nineteen-game losing streak. So quiet was the bus that they could hear their own breathing. Nineteen in a row? That might be a state record. (It wasn't. The Bowlegs Boll Weevils lost twenty-eight consecutive games.) Then the players heard a tentative rapping on the school bus door. It stopped. They heard light footsteps walking beside the bus. Rusty, sitting next to a window, looked down and saw a little kid, probably just nine or ten, rather raggedly dressed, looking up at the school bus as if trying to scan the faces of the players of the team even though they were concealed in shadows. The kid stopped and looked up in a bewildered manner and wailed, "Where's Cliff-ferd?"

Everyone on the team turned and looked at Clifford. He remained frozen in his seat, a scowl on his reddening face, his Clark Kent glasses hiding his eyes. He looked completely absurd sitting rigid in his seat as the little kid's plaintive query echoed in the bus.

Suddenly, the team broke into laughter. Perhaps it was just a chance to break the tension of losing yet another game; perhaps it was because the little kid's voice sounded so out of place, coming almost from nowhere and sounding so countrified and ignorant that it evoked laughter and not pity.

Then Rusty stood up and perfectly imitating the little kid's bewildered, rustic voice said, "Where's Cliff-ferd?" and everyone on the team except Clifford roared with laughter: loud, raucous laughter that seemed to be mocking fate itself.

Clifford stiffly stood up and marched out of the bus. Dale craned his neck and tried to get a look of him and the little kid past Rusty's laughing face. Clifford and the little kid seemed engaged in a serious conversation, the boy looking worried and almost crying while Clifford nodded and spoke a few sharp sentences before climbing back on the bus.

Of course, another wag, one without Rusty's exquisite timing, repeated the comic phrase and inspired another round of laughter, although this time not as spontaneous or filled with relief. Before another kid called where's Clifford and further debased the joke, Coach Carpenter boarded the bus and the players grew silent again. Coach, so tall he had to stoop inside the bus, looked at his players less in disgust and more in pity, and said nothing.

Now, three days later on the playground, the six of them still laughed at the reference. Rusty, who had the innate comic sense not to milk a joke, sat down on the teeter-totter as Clifford disappeared into the locker room. The laughter faded, and they resumed their joshing and boasting for a few minutes before the coaches whistled the start of practice.

They reluctantly rose, the mighty six, and lumbered over to practice. All of them had a sense of foreboding. Of the four previous losses, two had been close. But this last loss had been embarrassing. Not only the score, 36-0, but also the way they'd lost. Shutout! The offense couldn't even function. True, the Sequoyah boys were much larger and overpowered the smaller offensive line of the Junior Gophers, but as the game wore on Coach Carpenter and Coach Wickfield, now the assistant, thought they had given up. They not only lost, they got whipped! The fact that coach had said nothing after the game worried the boys. The less said after a humiliating defeat, the worse they expected the next practice to be.

After calisthenics, Coach Carpenter called the team together. His face looked uncharacteristically severe. He towered over the players and looked down at them. He said we were embarrassed last game. To lose is one thing, but to quit is another. He especially singled out the line for giving up. So, he said, it was time to return to the fundamentals of blocking and tackling.

Out of the corner of his eye, Dale saw Clifford sprinting toward them. Something looked odd. He looked more closely and as he did so did the rest of the team, including Coach Carpenter. Then Dale identified the incongruous element. Clifford wore cleats that didn't match. Not only was the right cleat a different style, without two white stripes on the side, it looked at least three sizes too large.

Dale looked at Rusty, hoping he wouldn't do the "where's Cliff-ferd?" He didn't. He knew it wasn't the right time. However, Butch Bigelow said scornfully under his breath, "way to go, Mouthpiece."

Rusty started the nickname after Dale told him that Clifford kept his mouthpiece in all the time. Most guys spit theirs out at the end of a play, letting the piece of plastic with their teeth imprints dangle from a strap attached to their facemask. Not Clifford. He clenched down on the mouthpiece not only between plays but while standing on the sidelines and even before practice had started. Dale had to admit that was odd; he hated that piece of plastic stuck on his teeth and spit it out as soon as he could. But then, Clifford had such a curious intensity to him that Dale imagined he always clenched his teeth.

Clifford joined the group and Dale noticed, true to form, he had his mouthpiece stuck in his mouth and his helmet buckled. Dale looked at Coach. Clifford's tardiness couldn't have come at a worse time. Coach Carpenter, normally judicious, became offended. Clifford had arrived late at an important practice, in the middle of his talk, and was one of the lineman who'd performed so poorly last game.

"Surry, Cuch," Dale thought Clifford said.

"Take out your mouthpiece," said Coach.

Clifford opened his mouth and let his mouthpiece drop out. "I couldn't find my right cleat," he said, eyeing his teammates suspiciously.

"All right, boys," Coach Carpenter said. "Form a circle around Oates."

They did, forming something that resembled a circle around the puzzled Clifford. Coach then took a football and tossed it to Clifford.

"I think you need a taste of what Schoendienst got Thursday night."

Dale glanced over to Sonny, who stood without his usual swagger. In fact, he looked sore just standing there.

"A volunteer," said Coach.

None of them knew exactly what they were volunteering for. They stood looking at each other.

"Where's one of our leaders? One of the linebackers?" said Coach. Bigelow took a couple of steps out.

"When I say so, hit him."

Bigelow looked from Coach to Clifford.

"Hit Oates as if he were the opposing team's quarterback." Coach Carpenter turned to Clifford. "Oates, hold the ball over your head."

Clifford stood motionless, considering his fate. Then he slowly raised the football above his head.

Coach turned to Bigelow. "Hit him hard. Now!"

Bigelow rushed Clifford, lowered his helmet and hit him square in the belly. They both fell into a heap and Bigelow got to his feet and then hit Clifford again, diving into him like he was a tackling dummy.

Dale winced at the first contact, then watched in disbelief as Bigelow pummeled Clifford again, one, two, three times. Coach Carpenter strode over and grabbed Bigelow by the back of his shoulder pads and yanked him off the supine Clifford.

"That's enough!" Coach said.

Bigelow broke free of Coach Carpenter's grasp and Dale thought he might attack Clifford again, but instead he stalked away, panting hard through his mouthpiece. Lying on the ground, Clifford tried to rise, but instead curled up in a heap. He made odd chuffing sounds like a wounded animal.

Coach Carpenter reached down with his large hands and tried to straighten him out. "You just got the breath knocked out of you. Relax and try not to breathe in right away."

Clifford finally found some breath. He opened his mouth and breathed in and then started crying. He cried for just a few moments, but it was enough to make Dale and the rest of the team ashamed of him. Dale knew he'd do the same, but he still felt embarrassed about Clifford showing weakness and since that made him feel ashamed of himself, he then resented Clifford all the more.

Coach helped Clifford to his feet. He'd stopped crying but still made odd noises, sort of gagging as if he was trying to hold in his emotion but couldn't quite do it.

"Walk around and shake it off," said Coach.

That's what coaches always told players who were hurt to do: shake it off. Clifford did. He stumbled away from the circle of teammates and walked in a dazed circle, his larger cleat making his walk look awkward.

Rusty elbowed Dale and then nodded his head toward the ground. Clifford's mouthpiece lay in the dirt. Bigelow had knocked Clifford's mouthpiece off his face mask.

"Some hit, huh?" said Rusty.

Coach then ordered the rest of the team to engage in tackling drills. He blew his whistle loudly and when the first two boys didn't hit hard enough, he yelled, "show me some guts," and blew the whistle again and the next two boys, Billy Joe Barton and K. C. Cash, collided with impressive force.

"Good hit!" shouted Coach Carpenter.

When Dale's turn came, he felt glad he wasn't facing one of his friends. His opponent was a lanky eighth grader named Martin Dewberry. Dale didn't like him much, so he rammed into him with all his might and sent the poor kid tumbling backward. Dewberry, to his credit, immediately jumped to his feet and said, "good hit."

Then Clifford rejoined the team and got in line. When it was his turn to tackle, Coach stopped the drill. He looked at Clifford's opponent, which was Rusty, and motioned him aside. Rusty quickly stepped aside and Dale didn't blame him. For all his bravado, Rusty didn't relish contact like the bigger guys. That's why he played split end.

Coach pointed to Bigelow. Butch took the ball from Rusty and stared at Clifford. All the boys stared at Clifford. His face looked stony and resolute. Then Coach blew his whistle and the two boys ran toward each other. Clifford lowered his shoulder and rammed into Bigelow just below his shoulder pads and the two collapsed in the dirt, the blow resounding loudly in the air. Both slowly got their feet. Then Bigelow said, "good hit," and Clifford nodded and all the boys felt better since Clifford had redeemed himself.

Coach then had the boys scrimmage. They hit each other with admirable ferocity. After scrimmaging, they ran wind sprints. Dale raced ahead of the rest, followed by Rusty and Billy Joe Barton. They ran five sprints of forty yards each. Afterwards, the boys were exhausted, panting hard through their mouths, walking with hands held on top of their helmets like prisoners of war. Two lineman, Leroy Lemmon and Sam Mears, walked over to the sidelines and vomited. Coach looked pleased.

They huddled up for the post-practice evaluation. Coach looked at them, sweaty and weary, and simply said, "good practice."

The boys felt the ordeal was worth it. They ambled off the field toward the locker room. Dale walked with Rusty and Chris DeVille, who had showed surprising tenacity.

The boys were in good spirits in the locker room. They joked and talked but didn't engage in any horseplay because of their weariness and because they didn't want to provoke their tough coach.

Dale hitched a ride on Rusty's cycle to Rusty's granny's house. Rusty was meeting his mother and stepdad there, so Dale said so long and started walking home. He walked swiftly, feeling rejuvenated after the shower. He walked two blocks when he saw Clifford Oates ahead of him. Dale slowed down. At the street corner, Clifford turned right and Dale lingered until he passed out of sight. He felt a pang of sympathy for Clifford but not enough to join him. Instead, he cut through an alley just to make sure Clifford wouldn't see him and walked swiftly to his own troubled home.

Blackie sat in his E-Z Boy chair, watching the news. In his right hand he held a can of Coors. He'd just got home from the police academy and hadn't yet changed out of his slacks and white dress shirt.

Dale came into the room. He felt surprised to see his father home. "Hi," he said.

Blackie grunted. Dale sat down on the couch. He glanced at the television: A serious man read a story about Vietnam protestors.

"Damn hippies," growled Blackie. He looked truculently at his son. "Don't you ever become a hippie."

Dale had no intention of becoming one. "Don't worry."

"I don't worry about anything," said Blackie. "I'm a fatalist."

He finished the beer and went into the kitchen and got another one. He popped the top of the can and settled back in his chair.

Dale wasn't sure what a fatalist was but it sounded interesting. "What's that?"

Blackie took a swig of Coors. "Beer. Want some?"

Dale shook his head.

"Oh, I forgot," Blackie said somewhat sarcastically, "you don't drink beer."

Dale decided not to defend his abstemious ways. Blackie sometimes forgot he was only fourteen.

"No, I mean what's a fatalist?"

"Oh," Blackie grunted. "It's someone who doesn't give a damn."

Blackie certainly seemed to qualify, thought Dale. Although he suspected that it was partly an act.

"I suppose your mother and sister have run off to the Kingdom Hall," Blackie said.

Dale nodded.

"Why didn't you join them?"

Dale shrugged. Actually, he wanted his mother to get used to him not going on Fridays because next year he would be playing football games then. Jesse didn't like the idea. Is football more important than Jehovah, she had scolded.

"How's school going?" Dale asked, thinking it was sort of funny he was asking his dad that question.

"School?" Blackie replied critically. "You mean the academy?"

Dale nodded.

"Fine and dandy."

Dale waited for elaboration, but none came. Dale hadn't seen much of his father the last few weeks since Blackie had started attending the police academy. He still worked most nights bartending.

"So, are you really going to be a cop?"

"No, I'm going to be a ranger," replied Blackie, finishing his second beer.

"You mean like in the movies? A Texas ranger?" The idea interested Dale. He wondered if Blackie would ride a horse.

Blackie let the question hang while he fetched himself another beer. He returned and looked suspiciously at Dale.

"By fifteen I'd already taken a few drinks." He sat down. "And done a few other things, too."

"I'm still fourteen."

Blackie regarded him with a mock tolerant expression. "Oh, that's makes a *big* difference," he admitted.

Dale knew when he was being condescended to. He frowned and sank back in the sofa and glanced at the TV. More bad news. Dale didn't have much interest in the news or politics or protesting. Witnesses weren't supposed to care about worldly things.

"I'm going to be a lakes and parks ranger," said Blackie, making an attempt to mollify Dale.

"You mean the guys that make sure you got a fishing license?"

Dale had seen them when his parents took him fishing. That didn't sound nearly as interesting as a real ranger, a Texas ranger.

"That's one of their duties."

"Why do you have to go to the police academy for that?"

"Because rangers are officers of the law. Just like cops, except in the parks and on the lakes."

Dale still wasn't too impressed.

"There's a lot of crime in the parks and on the lakes," Blackie said, then took a long drink of his beer, annoyed with his son.

"You mean like people not wearing their life vests?"

"No," said Blackie sharply, "like drug trafficking and prostitution and even homicides."

Now Dale was impressed but a little incredulous. "I've never heard of that."

"That stuff goes on in the City parks mostly. Especially around nigger town."

Dale frowned. He knew you weren't supposed to use that word.

"My, my," said Blackie. "Aren't we delicate." Then he leaned forward in his seat. "You got a lot to learn about the world, boy."

Dale didn't doubt that. Then, almost as on cue, a news story flashed on the screen about the Black Panthers. Blackie stared at the television.

"See what I mean. The niggers are revolting. Going to kill whitey."

"Black people should be treated like everyone else."

"Where do you get such ideas?"

Dale guessed he got them from going to church and the Kingdom Hall and hearing ministers and elders say that all people were the spiritual children of God. Blacks weren't any different than whites. Dale believed that. He didn't have any personal experience to give him ideas of racial equality. There weren't any blacks in his school or in Galilee. He'd heard some whispering that maybe Leroy Lemmon was part black. He played tackle on the junior high team. The biggest guy on the team, over 200 pounds. His skin looked dusky. He had very curly hair. Dale liked him. Leroy laughed easily and seemed a little shy and didn't smash guys in practice even though he could.

"Listen, I grew up with niggers," said Blackie. He glanced at Dale. "Sorry. *Negroes.* That's what they were called back then."

"Didn't you like some?"

He thought he'd like Bob Gibson or Gale Sayers if he met them. They were two of his favorite sports stars. But Dale didn't care much for black music. Rusty had an album by Sly and the Family Stone. Dale thought the music sounded too loud.

Blackie considered the question. "I had a colored friend when I was little. But it changes when you grow up, especially in Alabama."

Blackie got up for more beer. This time he returned with two cans.

"The world is a hellhole," Blackie announced.

Dale looked at his father, wondering what prompted that bleak assessment.

Blackie took a long drink of beer. "I joined up at sixteen. A year later, my ass was in Korea. Life on board a destroyer during a time of war isn't for the *delicate*." He gave Dale a surly glance.

Dale thought about saying it's better than the infantry. He'd seen war movies. The guys on the ships seemed to have it better than the guys on the ground. But he said nothing. He knew better than to interrupt Blackie during his reminiscences. His father only talked about his life while drinking.

"There weren't many niggers in the Navy. They don't cotton to water." He smiled and took another swig of beer. "But we had this one guy. Had a Mick name, for God's sake. McKenzie or McNally or something. Anyway, he wasn't a steward like most coloreds. Instead, he was a boatswain's mate. You know what that is, son?"

Dale shook his head.

"No, I s'ppose you wouldn't. Anyway, he was senior to me. I was just a maggot. That's what they called sailors who didn't have any stripes, yet. Damn, he lorded it over me. Knew I was from the South. Gave me shit all the time."

Blackie paused, took another drink, then looked straight at Dale.

"We had a fire below decks. During maneuvers so we couldn't get enough men down to stop it fast enough. The fire blasted through a whole compartment before we stopped it. Killed a dozen men. I went down with a clean-up crew. Saw McKenzie. Burned to a crisp. Burned blacker than he was before. Had to scoop up what remained of him with a shovel. Goddamn. The stench. Nothing stinks like burned human flesh."

Dale felt his stomach turn over. He had a vivid imagination and he could see in his mind the charred corpses.

Blackie suddenly changed the subject. "So, what are you going to do tonight?"

Nothing sounded very fun after Blackie's story.

"I dunno. Mess around, I guess."

Blackie nodded. "Mess around," he repeated.

Then Blackie rose from his chair and walked toward his bedroom. Dale got up and looked down the hall. Blackie closed the door on his way in. Dale knew what he was doing. That's where he did his serious drinking, the kind with whiskey.

### Chapter 5: *Galilee wins first game; Dale and Rusty visit Sundance Prep*

In the huddle, Dale felt the tension. He looked at his teammates' faces. They all looked weary and anxious. They knew this was their last chance. They had played better after the tough practice where Clifford had been creamed, but they still had lost two more games by close margins. Now, this last game against the detested Lyons Lions was their final hope to avert a second winless season.

Galilee and Lyons were tied, 6-6. They were in the fourth quarter. Only two minutes left in the game. Lyons had the ball on the Junior Gophers' 27-yard line. Third and three. They expected a run. Bigelow called the play.

"5-3 stunt right," he said. Then he added, "Remember. These guys aren't Lions; they're pussies!"

No one laughed. Instead they broke huddle with a roar.

Dale watched the Lyons' split end jog to the scrimmage line. He sensed something. Maybe it was all the time he and Rusty had played sandlot football. But Dale had a feeling that the Lyons' receiver was going to get a pass. He could tell by the way he stood, a little nervous, glancing at his quarterback.

The Lyons' quarterback called the signals. The center snapped the ball. Dale looked at the end running toward him and just as he thought, the end cut his route short and veered to his left. Dale, anticipating the move, raced forward at the correct angle. He cut in front of the Lyons' player just as the ball arrived. He opened his arms and let the ball settle against his belly just below his pads. Then he wrapped his hands around the ball and ran.

Dale saw nothing but an open field ahead of him. He marveled at how green the field looked. He raced past the white chalk lines. He heard his excited breathing echoing inside his helmet. From out of the corner of his eye, he saw several Lyons players chasing him. But Dale knew they couldn't catch him.

Only after he crossed the goal line did he hear more than his own heavy breathing. He heard cheers from his sidelines and from the few spectators in the stands. His heart thumped in his chest. He felt out of breath. He flipped the ball to the referee. Then he turned and felt his teammates pounding him about his shoulder pads and helmet.

Galilee missed the extra point when K. C.'s kick flopped like a flailing turkey, so Galilee led only by six. Lyons could still win the game.

Dale, still a little winded more from the excitement than his run, lined up for the kick off. The tension he'd felt before the interception now returned. He prayed, "Oh, Jehovah, let us win," even though he knew praying for selfish reasons was wrong.

K. C. kicked an erratic ball that bounced crazily between two Lyons players. One of them kicked the ball, and the advancing Junior Gophers collided with the Junior Lions and then a mad scramble ensued. Dale saw the ball squirt out of the scrum and he ran toward it, but before he got there Clifford pounced on the ball.

Dale and his teammates swarmed Clifford and pounded him with congratulations. After the recovery, Galilee ran out the clock out with two quarterback sneaks. The horn sounded; the game was over, and Galilee had won its first game of the season.

But what a sweet win. After shaking hands with the Lyons' players, Dale and his teammates ran off the field, jubilant. They roared incoherent boasts as they ran toward the team bus to take them back to the locker room.

Following Rusty to the rear of the bus, Dale saw Clifford already sitting in his seat. The lenses of his glasses were fogged and he sat rigid in his seat, his face unsmiling.

"That was a heads-up play," Dale said.

Clifford glanced at him and nodded but didn't say anything. Dale joined Rusty in the seat farthest in the back. Rusty was ebullient. He'd scored the team's first touchdown, catching a seventeen-yard pass from Sonny.

He clapped Dale on the shoulder. "Hey, man, we both scored." Then Rusty added salaciously, "if only we could score in another way."

Dale doubted that possibility. He didn't even have a girlfriend and wouldn't know what to do with her if he did. Rusty was rumored to be seeing Roxanne Robideaux. But seeing was a long way from scoring and Dale smiled as Rusty got in a friendly shoving match with Billy Joe Barton. Billy Joe, tall with lean muscles, grinned. His long, light brown hair hung so straight and smooth around his head that it looked like a helmet. He had a big, horsy face with a long nose, prominent nostrils, and large lips. When Sonny, Billy Joe's best friend, strolled to the back of the bus, even the lackadaisical Sonny slapped Billy Joe on the back. Dale was reminded how much better winning is than losing.

Then he looked a few rows ahead and saw Clifford sitting rigidly in his seat, not joining the celebration. Guys around him were standing, talking, boasting, recounting their heroics, real or imagined. But Clifford sat apart, silent and alone. Dale wondered if Clifford regretted recovering that fumble.

In school the next day, the halls of the junior high side were abuzz with the news of the victory. Since it was the school's first win in two years, even kids who ordinarily didn't care about the football team congratulated the players as they strode down the halls between classes.

Even Vern Jurgens, who rarely mentioned school sports to Dale, leaned over in class and said, "so you guys finally won one."

Dale grinned and Vern tried to keep his unimpressed look on his face. Dale understood why Vern downplayed the win and everything else athletic. He envied the boys who played sports. Dale knew from playing sandlot football with him that Vern was a good athlete. He would have made a dandy fullback. But his religion forbade him to play.

That bothered Dale. Why shouldn't a guy play football? Even if the end of the world was near, what was wrong with sports? Dale didn't know if Vern's religion believed in the imminent coming of Christ, but if not, then why the strict behavior? The question puzzled him so that he forgot to pay attention in English class and couldn't answer a question when called on.

Dale tended to daydream in class. In his next class, algebra, a subject he disliked, he sat in the back with Rusty and didn't listen to the teacher, Miss Mueller. Instead he remembered his touchdown, the first he'd scored this season, and wondered if *she* had been impressed. She wasn't a cheerleader; she was pretty enough and Dale thought she certainly could have been one if she wanted. But he decided she was too ladylike to jump around and yell and shake pom-pons. Not that Dale disliked cheerleaders. Lustful urges seemed especially urgent when he watched them at pep rallies. Four of the five cheerleaders were ninth graders: Wendy, Mary Jane, Roxanne, and Carmen Castro. All were cute. But to Dale, none compared to Amanda.

Since Amanda wasn't in any of his classes, Dale had to content himself with catching glimpses of her walking through the hall, always accompanied by two or three other girls. Even if Dale could muster the courage to approach her, he'd be dumbfounded by the presence of so many females. So instead, he admired her from afar.

The high school football team had a late afternoon game with Sundance Prep, a private school in the City, so sixth-hour classes were canceled for the pep rally. After the rally, students could board school buses for the trip to the game. Since basketball practice didn't start for another two weeks, Dale and Rusty had a free afternoon. They decided to go to the game.

Four buses made the trip. They drove east into the City then turned north on another highway. Dale looked out the window as the bus entered into a wealthier part of the city. The houses were even bigger and nicer than Trumbo's home.

The buses slowed down at the entrance to Sundance Prep. The school had a security gate, rolling green fields, and impressive red brick buildings. The Galilee bus passed the security gate, drove up a wide, winding drive and came to a stop outside the athletic complex. Rusty elbowed Dale in the ribs.

"Man, look at this place. You know, I heard Lance Rentzel went to school here."

Rentzel was a former Dallas Cowboys flanker and had been Rusty's favorite player even though Rusty said Lance had recently been arrested for indecent exposure and marrying Joey Heatherton. The Cowboys were the boys' favorite pro football team. That faint connection between the Cowboys and Sundance Prep awed both of them.

Dale and Rusty joined the other Galilee fans as they walked to the visitor's side of the sparkling football stadium. Once again, the boys were astonished by the quality of the stadium and the carefully tended football field.

"Man," said Rusty, taking a seat, "it looks like a pro field."

Dale nodded. It looked like the football fields on television. The stadium even had a large, modern electric scoreboard.

He looked down at the Galilee sideline. He didn't really know any of the players. Most ninth graders were afraid to go into the high school half of the school. Rusty, however, knew a couple of the guys on the team. One of them lived close to his grandmother and drove a really big cycle, a 450. The guy's name was Piersall and both Rusty and Dale had seen him pop a wheelie across the entire four lanes of 39th Expressway. The boys had been duly impressed.

Dale watched as Coach Aldo stalked the sidelines. A big, burly ex-Marine with a bullet-shaped head, short, spiky gray hair, and a brawny face, all the junior high kids lived in terror of him. Last year, Dale had to take shop in eighth grade with Coach Aldo. The coach was hardly there, however. He began class, glared at the boys and told them to keep busy and out of trouble, then left for most of the period. But Coach Aldo was unpredictable. Once he came back in the middle of class, caught Bobby Brown goofing off with a sander and grabbed the kid by his collar, picking him up off the ground, and slapped his face. After he released the bawling Bobby Brown, Coach Aldo said he'd better never see anyone else abuse any of the tools again or they'd get even worse. No one goofed off after that.

Dale remembered the tattoos on Coach Aldo's bulging forearms. They reminded him of

Blackie's. Coach always rolled up his shirtsleeves for shop class. But now Dale noticed Coach Aldo wore a suit as he paced on the sidelines.

The game started and Dale and Rusty watched as Sundance Prep dismantled Galilee. Not only did Sundance Prep overpower the high school team, but they also scored on elaborate pass plays like sending five receivers out at a time, plays that other high schools never ran. They also scored on trick plays: halfback option passes, double reverses, and flea flickers. At halftime, they led, 45-0.

Dale heard an old man sitting in front of them say that Coach Aldo was over the hill.

"He runs the same offense he did twenty years ago," said the man, who looked old enough to have invented that offense. He wore a red sweater with his white shirt and tie, so Dale figured he must be from Galilee. The old man turned in disgust to the scoreboard and Dale noticed his amazingly wrinkled face. Like a big, red raisin with eyes.

"Still runs the T," muttered the old man. Then he recounted to a middle-aged man sitting next to him how Galilee used to have good teams. For a decade they were one of the best small schools in the state. "But Aldo's old and stuck in his ways," the old man concluded.

Dale thought it strange that such an old guy would be so unsentimental.

"The last good team we had was when Comingdeer played," his younger companion said, who, with his ruddy complexion and similar features looked like he might be the old man's son.

Dale remembered Comingdeer. Robin Comingdeer, a full-blood Kiowa. He made All-State as a halfback. That was four years ago, which seemed like a long time to Dale. But he still remembered Comingdeer. He ran with a beautiful abandonment. He'd race down the field like a swift pony, cutting across the grain, finding open ground, and when the opposing team finally caught up and surrounded him, he'd hurl himself at his opponents, knocking them backward for another five yards.

"Remember Comingdeer?" Dale asked Rusty.

"The Indian guy?"

"Yeah. Remember when we went to a high school game back in fifth grade?"

"Yeah, they let us out early. It was a playoff game."

Dale nodded. The last playoff game Galilee had been in. Since then the high school had suffered three losing seasons in a row. And now they were getting smeared by Sundance Prep.

Dale and Rusty walked to the refreshment stand and bought Cokes and Snickers. They walked to the Sundance side of the stadium, the section that was built into a hill. Then they walked back, taking in the splendid stadium and the magnificent field, thinking how great it would be to play in such a place.

They passed the concession stands and restrooms and turned a corner to walk back to their side when Dale suddenly saw *her*. She and Mary Jane were right in front of them. Dale and Rusty jerked to a stop to prevent colliding into them.

"Hi," said Mary Jane.

"Hi," said Amanda.

Dale stared at her. He'd never been this close to her before. He looked right into her eyes and saw how bright blue they were; he thought they sparkled like jewels – which kind he didn't know because he didn't know anything about jewels. But they were pretty. Her whole face looked pretty. More than that. Regal. Yet kind. A face of a princess who's never haughty, only nice.

"Hey, girls," said Rusty.

Dale stood mute. Amanda smiled at him. A beautiful smile of perfectly straight, white teeth. And dimples in her cheeks. Then her smile faded and Dale noticed how lovely her lips were: a smaller upper lip and a full lower lip. He also noticed a pronounced indention between her nose and mouth, a vertical groove – that spot that he didn't know the name of, but found interesting.

Dale realized he must be staring but he couldn't help it. He'd been too surprised to be shy.

Amanda looked at Mary Jane. Her face seemed more concerned than annoyed. Her expression seemed to say, "is he always like this?"

Rusty elbowed Dale out of his trance. "Say hi to the girls, Smith," he said, his eyes never leaving their faces.

Finally Dale managed to croak, "hi."

The three of them started chatting while Dale, now self-conscious again, only snuck glances at Amanda. She wasn't too tall; maybe two inches taller than he was. That gave him hope. While they talked, he didn't listen to their words; rather, he heard Amanda's voice like he'd hear music. A lovely melody that didn't need lyrics at all.

Mary Jane congratulated Rusty on scoring a touchdown. Rusty swelled in response and feigned an "aw shucks" attitude. Then Amanda turned her blue eyes to Dale.

"You ran so fast when you scored your touchdown, Audie."

Dale nodded.

"The winning touchdown," she added with a smile.

"Yeah," said Rusty, "you wouldn't think such a little guy could run so fast."

Dale wanted to punch him. Best friend or not, he should not bring up his shortcomings in the presence of girls.

Then the girls excused themselves and Rusty and Dale watched them walk away. Dale noticed with approval that Amanda's dress came down to her knees whereas Mary Jane's hovered four inches higher, the current fashion, he supposed.

"Hey, that Mary Jane's something," said Rusty, still admiring her. Dale thought she was pretty but skinny.

"Skinny? Naw, just …" Rusty searched for the word.

"Bony?" said Dale.

Rusty turned and playfully shoved him. "I like 'em thin, man." Then a more thoughtful expression fell over his freckled face. "What did Amanda mean, the *winning* touchdown? Mine counted just as much as yours." After a thoughtful pause, Rusty glanced down at his pal. "You should have said more."

Dale felt the elation of being in her presence shrivel up inside him. Yeah, he'd blown it. He probably looked like a dope.

"I acted like a Maynard."

Rusty agreed. "A real Maynard."

The term referred to the awkwardest, goofiest kid that had ever humiliated himself in Galilee junior high history. A kid that only attended Galilee for one year in seventh grade. He was so goofy, Rusty had once said, that he didn't even know how goofy he was. A complete fool, dope, and doofus. His name was Maynard. They couldn't even remember his first name. Something Maynard. Everyone called him Maynard. And since he was the ultimate jerk, soon his name came to symbolize that pathetic state of existence.

Instead going back to the stands and watch the second half slaughter, Rusty and Dale joined a few other boys in a game of touch football above the home stands of the stadium. They used a jumbo Coke cup for a football and stuffed hotdog wrappers and napkins inside for weight. It worked pretty well. They played touch football and ran up and down the top of the hill with all the Sundance Prep people below them. At one point, they made such a racket that a bald man sitting in the stands yelled at them to stop "horsing around." A few minutes later, after Rusty and Dale had vanquished their opponents, Rusty sailed the Coke football down five rows and it conked the guy on the head. The boys ducked and waddled out of sight while hearing the guy sputtering, "Who threw that? Who threw that?"

Dale had hoped to see Amanda again, but she apparently left the game early. He and Rusty walked back over to the visitors' side of the stadium as the final buzzer sounded. Even the buzzer sounded better than any Dale had heard. Clear and emphatic. The two boys looked down at the field, watched as the high school players disconsolately shook hands with the Sundance guys, then slumped off the field. Dale felt sorry for them. Then he looked at the fancy schmanzy scoreboard. The results glowed in red bulb light: Sundance Prep, 72; Galilee, 0.

Rusty shook his head. "And you want to go out for the team next year?"

## Chapter 6: *Dale's basketball debacle*

Dale sat on the bench watching his teammates lose. The Junior Gophers basketball season hadn't been as dreadful as their football season. As the season dragged to an end, the team record stood at 5-10. With a loss assured in this final game, it looked like they would finish with more than twice as many losses as wins.

Throughout the season, Dale had been an observer. He hadn't even played a minute in any game. Part of the reason was that all of Galilee's games had been close. They seemed to either win by two or lose by three. If some of the games had been blowouts then he'd been put in for a mop-up role. But Dale didn't mind. He knew he wasn't very good and the idea of going out on the court and making a fool of himself wasn't appealing. He preferred sitting on the bench and watching his teammates scrap against taller opponents with occasional peeks at the cheerleaders. He even didn't mind practice. He liked the stuffy gym during the winter. Even though Oklahoma winters were usually mild, occasionally a cold front would barrel down from the Rockies and smash the state with ice and sleet. When that happened a few weeks ago, Dale especially liked being in the warm, steamy gym when outside it felt cold and icy.

He liked the camaraderie, too. There wasn't as much pressure or tension in basketball practice as compared to football. Part of that was because Dale didn't have to worry about playing. So, he got to goof around with the two other guys who didn't play much, Wally Wainwright and Matt Jones.

So as long as he didn't have to play, Dale rather liked basketball. But he began to worry about this game. The Junior Gophers had played Wheaton close the first half, trailing by only four. The taller Wheaton team dominated the second half and built a ten point lead. Dale knew if the margin worsened it was only a matter of time before Coach Wickfield sent in the reserves and since the team only had ten players present Dale knew he'd be one of them.

He dreaded that moment. Not only did he lack skill, he also disliked the intimacy of a gym. The court only stood a few feet from the bleachers. People could see you as plain as day. In football, a guy had pads and a helmet to help disguise him. In baseball, after striking out he could slink back to the dugout. But in basketball, there was no place to hide.

The starting five of Rusty, Chris, Billy Joe, Sonny, and Sam Mears, the eighth grader, were valiantly struggling against Wheaton. Dale didn't know why Galilee kept playing the Reapers. Wheaton was a growing agricultural center ninety miles north and now more than twice the size of Galilee. It wasn't even in class A anymore. Dale guessed that Coach Aldo, who as athletic director negotiated the schedules, still regarded Wheaton as the small town it used to be twenty years ago when he became coach.

Dale watched Rusty as he hit a twenty-foot jump shot. Rusty was the best player on the team. For most of their boyhood, he and Rusty had played mostly football and baseball. In junior high they both went out for basketball and Rusty immediately showed talent. His uncle Jim bought him a basketball backboard and goal and even made sure it stood regulation height over the garage door. Rusty started practicing and he, his brothers, Dale, and other friends included basketball in their seasonal sports activities. The practice paid off. Basketball looked like Rusty's best sport.

Last week at Oilville, Rusty scored 25 points. Just getting into double figures in junior high was impressive, but 25 was outstanding. Galilee won, too, 49-41.

This game, though, was a different story. Wheaton put their best player on Rusty and he had a hard time getting open. When he did, the Wheaton guy, who stood two inches taller, kept getting in his face forcing poor shots. Rusty had scored only nine points so far, five of those on free throws. He also had four fouls. Soon as Dale thought of that, Rusty picked up his fifth, an offensive charge.

Rusty's agile face twisted itself into a grimace. "Charging?" he shouted. "That guy fouled me!"

The ref disagreed and opened his hands for the ball. Rusty heaved it down the court in disgust and the ref whistled him for a technical foul.

"You're out of the game!" shouted the ref. He didn't look much older than Coach Wickfield, who could pass for a high school senior.

"Fine," Rusty yelled back. "I already fouled out anyway."

He stormed over to the bench. Coach Wickfield stared at him, his eyes hard underneath his stylish glasses.

"Oates," said Coach. "Get in there for Grimes."

Clifford, who played the game more like football than basketball, sometimes even knocking guys over with his fouls, jumped off the bench, peeled off his warm up jacket and raced to the floor.

"Way to go, Mouthpiece," said Rusty.

Clifford didn't dignify the phrase with even a look. Ten seconds after play resumed, he knocked a Wheaton player to the floor while trying to block a lay up.

Dale looked at Rusty who rolled his eyes.

Wheaton built up a twelve point lead with five minutes left. Coach Wickfield subbed K. C. for Billy Joe and Butch Bigelow for Sonny. A minute later, and another five points added to the deficit, Coach put in Matt Jones, the other eighth grader, who also had played very little. That left Dale.

Two minutes left and twenty-one points behind, Coach called time-out. "Okay, Smith. Go in."

Dale considered asking Coach to let him stay on the bench. Maybe he could fake a bellyache. But when he saw Coach's owlish eyes peering at him, he knew he had to go. He peeled off his warm-up top and joined the four other subs on the court. He didn't like standing on the court in his basketball uniform. He felt like he was playing in his underwear. He glanced at the stands. Since they were playing at Wheaton, only a few adults had made the trip; hardly any students, and only a handful of pep club members, and thankfully not including *her*. The cheerleaders, however, were present, and that alone made Dale feel bashful and clumsy as he stood on the court.

The whistle blew, and Dale stumbled down the court, feeling trapped in a nightmare where no matter how hard you try to run, your feet feel stuck in cement.

Ordinarily, one player, even one as crummy as Dale, couldn't inflict too much damage in two minutes. Although naturally athletic, in basketball he felt so nervous and self-conscious that he could hardly stop shaking and control himself enough to make routine plays. As the game slowly wound down, he surprised even himself by his ineptitude:

First mistake: he dribbled the ball off his foot.

Second mistake: on an in-bounds pass, he threw the ball to a Wheaton player.

Third mistake: he accidentally tripped his opponent while trying to make a steal and that caused the Wheaton kid to skin his knees pretty badly. The referee called a technical because he couldn't believe the foul wasn't intentional.

Fourth mistake: he missed the entire basket and backboard when he tossed up a twenty-foot shot, his first of the season.

Fifth mistake: not anticipating a pass off a screen, he turned his face just as the ball arrived, resulting in the ball bouncing off his nose and rolling to the other end of the court.

In a little over a minute, Dale had made five errors resulting in eight points for Wheaton.

For the next fifty seconds, Dale played error-free ball. That was because his teammates kept the ball away from him and went from man to man to a zone. Then, in the waning seconds, after Wally Wainwright missed a shot, the ball bounced off two colliding players and rolled down the court. Dale rushed to the ball, and dove just before a Wheaton player did. Dale grabbed the ball, controlled it, and felt the Wheaton guy fall on top of him. The whistle shrieked; a called foul. Dale got to shoot a one-and-one free throw.

The players walked down to the other end of the court. Dale stood at the free throw line and gazed at the basket. It sure looked tall and far away. He knew he'd be a better shot if he didn't have two bad fingers on his right hand. His three good digits could control a baseball or a football; but a basketball was too large. Often it slipped slightly out of his hand.

The ref tossed the ball to him. He took aim. He felt his knees wobbling. He felt short of breath. He imagined thousands of eyes staring at him (there were only 77 people in the entire gym, counting the concession workers and janitor). Even though he'd only played two minutes, he felt drenched in sweat. One drop fell from his brow and stung his eye. He ignored the pain. He ignored the skeptical crowd. He took aim, tried to relax, raised his arms and flicked his wrist and watched the ball not even hit the front of the rim.

Through the shrill whistle, Dale thought he heard laughter.

The ref had called a lane violation on Wheaton. He motioned the boys to line up again and tossed the ball to Dale. This time, he aimed at the back of the rim, and decided to shoot a little to the left because his shots tended to veer right. He went through the same motion as before, but made those adjustments, and to his amazement the ball swished through the net.

He'd scored!

He missed the second shot and when he turned to run down to the other end of the court he saw his teammates rise and give him a mock standing ovation. Dale blushed and almost tripped over his own feet as the buzzer sounded. His humiliation had ended.

He walked into the visitors locker room and sat down on a bench next to Rusty. He expected his pal to say something, maybe even congratulate him on scoring even if it was a second-chance free throw.

But Rusty said nothing. He still felt angry about fouling out, and chagrined about not scoring at least ten points which he'd done in every game thus far. He had no interest in congratulating Dale over a puny point.

In fact, Dale had begun to wonder if Rusty thought of him as his best friend anymore. Rusty spent more and more time with Sonny and Billy Joe. Both started. Dale wondered if Rusty felt embarrassed to be best friends with a sub. After all, he was the best player on the team.

The boys didn't shower or change clothes. Coach Wickfield wanted to get an early start. The bus had to drive two hours back to Galilee over icy roads. The players could change and shower in the Galilee gym.

In the bus, Dale sat in the same seat with Rusty but they didn't talk much. Instead, Rusty complained about the bad officiating to K. C. and Bigelow sitting in the seat in front of them. Then the three boys talked about their cycles and, invariably, they got around to the girls. They evaluated the freshman cheerleaders, Wendy, Mary Jane, Roxanne, and Carmen. K. C. and Bigelow said Roxanne had the best legs and Rusty said Mary Jane. No one asked Dale, although he had an excellent view to judge. On the bench he could easily glance over and see them do their routines. He especially liked the way they swirled around and their white pleated skirts rose above their hips and their crimson tights flashed into view for a moment. That image and the resulting surge of blood made him realize he was just as lustful as his friends. Dale thought there was no comparison. Roxanne not only had the best legs, she had the best figure, and a beautiful face. In fact, she looked so ravishing most of the boys were in awe of her and few dared approach her. But of the few, three of them were present and engaged in a deep conversation at that moment.

Then Dale heard *her* name mentioned. Dale stopped breathing for a second. He listened more closely. He heard Bigelow say her name again. The Butch said something characteristically crude: how Amanda wouldn't be so stuck up after he stuck something up her.

Dale stared at Bigelow. He'd never liked him much, but now he almost hated him.

Bigelow noticed. "What's your problem, Smith?"

"You shouldn't talk that way about girls."

"Oh, yeah? Who should I talk that way about? Guys, maybe?"

"You're supposed to treat girls with respect," Dale said, saying something that he remembered his mother telling him when he was little and had punched a bossy neighborhood girl in the belly and made her cry. They were only five.

"Get him," sneered Bigelow. "Score a stinking point and you think you can give all kinds of advice."

Before Dale could respond, Rusty told Bigelow to shut up. K. C., who when not unduly influenced by Bigelow could be a nice guy, agreed.

"Maybe Smith is right," he said. "After all, girls dig that stuff."

That prompted a discussion of what girls liked and how to use that information to the boys' advantage. Pausing in the middle of the conversation, Rusty glanced over to Dale. He grinned and Dale grinned back.


## Chapter 7: *Birthday surprise; cycle accident; birds and the bees*

A day in early April, two weeks after baseball and track season had started, Rusty gave Dale a ride home on his motorcycle. Rusty dropped him off and Dale, seeing the '67 Chevy parked in the driveway, wondered if something was wrong. He didn't think his dad was supposed to be home.

He told Rusty so long and watched him pop a small wheelie on his way down the street. Dale turned and started to walk inside his house when he saw his father at the door.

"Is something wrong?" Dale asked, thinking of Jesse.

"No," said Blackie. "Why?"

"Well, you're home."

"I worked six days last week."

Dale nodded. He'd forgotten. Blackie's work schedule varied; day shifts, evening shifts, night shifts. And he still worked bartending on most weekends.

Dale started to walk inside when Blackie stopped him. "Wait. Why don't you check the garage?"

"You mean something's wrong with the garage door?"

"No, check inside."

Dale studied his father. His dusky face looked completely neutral, like it did when he played poker.

"Okay."

He went over to the garage door and lifted it up. He listened to the rumble of the door as it rolled open and stared in surprise at a motorcycle parked in the middle of the floor.

"Like it?" Blackie said from behind him.

"Yeah. Is it yours?"

"No, it's yours."

"Mine?"

"Yeah. For your birthday."

Dale had almost forgotten his birthday. He hadn't expected any presents, especially one this expensive.

"How much did it cost?"

"Doesn't matter."

That's a first, thought Dale. He went over to the bike, kneeled down and scrutinized it. He liked the metallic blue color. It was a Honda, which was good. Then he saw the engine power. Only a 70 cc. All the other guys had at least a 90 cc.

"I know Rusty has one," said Blackie. "I guess a lot of the boys do. So, I thought you should have one too."

"Thanks, Dad," said Dale, still a little disappointed.

"You don't sound excited."

"I am. It's a cool bike."

"You know, at your age I was milking cows twice a day, not racing around on a goddamn motorcycle."

Dale stood up. "Yeah, I know."

"You ought to show some gratitude, you spoiled hippie."

Dale hadn't cut his hair for a couple of months. It covered his ears and hung almost to his eyebrows in front.

"I'm not a hippie. And I am grateful. I said thank you."

"You know what I once got for my birthday?"

How would he know? Blackie had never told him. "No, what?"

"A kick in the teeth."

"Come on."

"That's right. One of my older brothers kicked me in the teeth."

Dale looked skeptically at his father. "Which older brother?" Dale thought he had three.

"Why the hell do you care?"

"Just wondering which one would do such a thing."

"That bastard Thornton."

It always surprised Dale how much Blackie disliked his older brothers. The few times he mentioned them, he often called them bastards. Dale knew his father also had an older sister. He'd never called her names, but he rarely mentioned her.

"He didn't kick any teeth out, did he?"

"No, I have teeth like a mule. Just busted my mouth. Bled all over."

Dale realized that Blackie had never spoken at such length about growing up before. He almost smiled.

"Your mother didn't want me to get you anything."

"Yeah, I know."

"Something about Jehovah's rules. They don't celebrate Christmas and they don't celebrate birthdays."

"That's right."

"Why the hell not birthdays?"

Dale didn't quite understand that either. "Something to do with Jehovah's creatures shouldn't think of themselves as special. Or something like that."

"Well, they're right about that. Human beings aren't special."

Dale didn't like such talk. "I think we are."

"Not according to your Jehovah's Witnesses."

"Well, that doesn't mean we have to think people are scum."

"What do you know about people?"

"Not much," admitted Dale.

"That's right. So let me tell you, people will stab you in the back. People will take your last dime. People will shit all over you."

Dale frowned. "I wish you wouldn't talk like that."

Blackie shook his head in disapproval. "You're too sensitive, boy."

"Should I be like you? A cold-hearted bastard?"

"That's more like it. Talk back to your old man. Call him a bastard."

"I didn't mean it."

Blackie folded his arms across his chest. "I should have been around more to knock some sense into you."

"Well, you weren't."

"No, I was serving my country. Stuck at sea half the time. Living like a coolie."

"Dad, that was your choice."

"Was it?"

"I mean staying in the navy. You could have not re-upped all those times."

Blackie considered his son. "Well, at least you're smart. Too sensitive, though. The world doesn't open its arms wide for the sensitive, especially men."

Dale didn't say anything.

"You need to be hard and tough. Or you'll get knocked on your duff." Blackie paused. "And this religion horseshit. You don't really believe it, not a smart kid like you."

"It's not about being smart."

"No? Then what?"

"I don't know exactly. It's how you feel inside."

"*Feelings*?"

"More than feelings." Dale shrugged. "I don't know really, but I'd like to find out."

"Why this Jehovah crap? Why not go to the Baptist church? Or even the fancy Nazarene church?"

"Because Mom started going. Maybe it helps her."

"But tell me, son. You don't really believe all that Jehovah – " Blackie substituted a less harsh word for the benefit of his son – "stuff, do you?"

Dale thought about the question. "I don't think so."

"Good," Blackie said. "I don't want any son of mine to not salute the flag or be a C.O. or go out *witnessing*. You can be a Baptist like I was and believe in something natural, like eternal hellfire, if you want."

"Okay," said Dale.

"Okay," said Blackie.

After a pause, Blackie asked Dale if he wanted to ride his motorcycle.

"Sure. I just need to go in for a minute. I'll be right back."

Dale walked over to the door that led to the kitchen and stepped in. He saw Jesse sitting at the kitchen table looking intently into a cup of coffee like she was seeing the future unfold before her.

"Hi, Mom."

Jesse looked at him. She looked a little haggard and depressed. "You don't believe in Jehovah no more?"

Dale wondered if she had overheard them in the garage or if she just guessed by his reluctance to go to the meetings. "Sure I do."

"You know The End may happen any time."

"Yeah, maybe."

"If you don't believe, Dale, you won't be saved."

Dale tried not to show his impatience. What a day, he thought. He tried changing the topic. "Did you see the cycle Dad bought me?"

"Witnesses don't celebrate birthdays."

"We're not celebrating exactly," Dale said, thinking boy ain't that the truth.

"Jehovah's creatures have no right to celebrate their births. It's Jehovah who gives us life. And only He can take it away."

Before Dale could think of an appropriate response to that observation, June May appeared. She walked into the kitchen with a vexed expression on her cute baby-fat face. Dale would have never thought he'd welcome her arrival.

"Ain't fair!" she cried. "Ain't fair Dale gets a cycle. We ain't even suppose to get presents at all, and he gets a motorcycle."

"I didn't ask for one."

"A motorcycle costs a lot more than a dress or a record player or a *Barbie*," she protested, listing in reverse order her most recent presents. Her last birthday occurred just a few months after Jesse became a Witness, but Jesse relented and bought her a dress.

"June May," said Jesse wearily, "why don't you just hush."

"What about me? Why don't I get something that good?" June May stomped her foot. "I want a motorcycle too!"

"Girls don't ride motorcycles," said Dale.

"Some do. I've seen them."

"Oh, where?"

June May thought for a while. "In movies."

Dale realized she meant that movie they had seen a couple of summers ago. *Hells Angels on Wheels* or something like that. Jesse, needless to say, didn't like it.

"Those girls were playing biker chicks. They're not real."

"They are too real," said June May. "A movie is real. It has real people in it."

"Well, the girls were just riding on back."

"One girl wasn't. She rode her own cycle. And another girl rode on back with her."

Dale remembered that odd couple. "Well, you're too young to have a motorcycle," he said, thinking it best not to refer to the two biker chicks on one cycle; he remembered Jesse, in particular, not liking that.

Before June May could continue her protest, Blackie opened the door and poked his head in. He saw the three of them standing in the kitchen and glanced for a second longer than usual at Jesse. "I thought you were coming, Audie Dale."

"I am."

"I want to see the cycle," June May cried. She raced past Blackie. "Daddy give me a ride, please!"

Blackie turned to look at her. "June May, don't touch that bike." He looked back at Dale. "Come on, now."

Dale nodded and Blackie closed the door. Dale heard him scolding June May for jumping on the cycle and almost knocking it over. Dale looked at Jesse. She stared into her coffee cup.

"Mom, are you feeling okay?"

Jesse smiled a small, unconvincing smile. "Sure, just a lil' tired. Go ahead. Go ride your motorcycle."

Dale waited for a moment, watching to see if she did anything strange when he heard Blackie bellow from the garage that he sure as hell better come out there, and he reluctantly left his mother still staring into the cup of coffee.

The rest of the guys weren't impressed with Dale's Honda 70, but he decided not to care. He enjoyed riding it to school, parking it with the other guys' bikes, and he didn't have to rely on Rusty to give him rides any more. A week after Dale got his motorcycle, Wally Wainwright got one too, also a Honda 70. Now Dale didn't feel so self-conscious about his little cycle.

A Saturday in mid-April and Rusty, Wally, and Dale were riding their cycles over to K. C.'s house. Dale and Rusty hadn't worn their helmets. On such a warm, pleasant spring day, Dale liked feeling the warm breeze ruffle his hair. Jesse would have pitched a fit if she'd known. She didn't like him riding a motorcycle to begin with, but she always insisted he wear his helmet. Dale usually did, although he didn't like it. Part of the fun of riding a cycle was feeling free, and nothing felt freer than zooming down the street, hearing the engine hum and feeling the wind in his face.

They drove four blocks when they came to an intersection. The three boys' cycles were side by side at the stop sign. Dale, on the far left, could easily see traffic coming from his left, but Rusty and Wally blocked his view on the right. Sitting on his cycle, he felt impatient, as he often did of late, as if he wanted to speed everything up so he could plunge into his future. He heard Rusty rev his engine; Wally did the same. Then Rusty slipped the clutch just enough to make his cycle jump. Wally did the same. And Dale, thinking the other lane was free of traffic, released his clutch and zoomed forward. As soon as he passed Rusty and Wally he saw a car hurtling toward him. The old Ford's brakes squealed. Dale saw the startled face of the young man inside the car. He acted instinctively; there wasn't time to turn away from the car, or speed up to evade it, so Dale jumped off his cycle. He landed on his feet and watched as the Ford hit his bike, knocking it over and shattering the left turn signal. The young man, who looked college age, jumped out of the car and stared at Dale. They both walked over to the cycle.

The young man apologized; he hadn't seen him. Dale picked up the cycle and inspected it. It looked mostly undamaged. Just a small dent in the exhaust grill and the smashed turn signal. He got on and jump kicked it. The engine started immediately and sounded as good as before.

The young man talked but Dale didn't listen closely. He was thinking how close he came to getting hurt. If he hadn't jumped off the cycle the car would have plowed into him. He also wondered why the cycle hadn't been damaged more. Maybe not having him on it made it less resistant to the impact. As Dale considered these possibilities, the young man handed him ten dollars for repairs. Since no one had been hurt there was no reason to report the accident, he said. Dale took the money and said okay. Then the young man got back in his car and sped away.

When Dale turned to look at Rusty and Wally he noticed both were looking at him with odd expressions.

"Man, you were lucky," said Rusty.

"How'd you know to jump off?" asked Wally.

Dale shrugged. "I just reacted."

He doubted he'd been badly hurt if he hadn't jumped. The car braked almost in time. But, he thought, you never know.

Rusty asked if he could still ride his cycle. Dale tested it. It rode fine. The wheels weren't out of balance or anything. So the three boys rode away and made it safely to K. C.'s house and related the incident to him, with Wally, given to embellishment, making it sound more life-threatening than it was. But as Dale listened, he realized that it could have been different. What if the young man had been driving faster? What if he hadn't braked in time? What if Dale hadn't jumped off the cycle before impact? What if he'd been seriously injured or even killed? What if. All those possibilities. Why certain things happen and certain things don't. How all that affects us in ways we can't fully understand. And for the rest of the afternoon, the "what if" question popped into Dale's mind from time to time and he saw different paths his life could take, and he tried to imagine how different it all would be on another path than the one he was on.

Dale disliked glee club but since he wasn't in band he had to take it. Glee club alternated days with gym class so both classes only had boys in it. In some ways, Dale liked not having girls around. He felt less self-conscious and goofed off more, especially in glee club where he and Rusty would often sing the wrong lyrics to the songs. They'd substitute words that sounded similar to the real words. Their favorite incorrect words were slime for time, glove for love, and, daringly, thighs for eyes. (The funniest altered lyrics they'd ever mockingly warbled were: "When I look into your thighs, I know it's slime for glove.")

They never used really bad words because Dale and Rusty were comparatively "nice" boys unlike the small number of juvenile delinquents who made farting noises with their hands underneath their armpits, smoked cigarettes in the alley during lunch hour, and pretended to be hoods.

The song Rusty and Dale liked making fun of the most was "Raindrops Keep Falling on My Head," which they changed to "Raindrops Keep Falling on My Fred." The change made no sense, which was exactly why both boys liked it so much.

The teacher of the class, Mr. Werhmeier, pale and thin and almost completely bald even though his face didn't look very old, was called "Worm" by the boys. It wasn't so much his last name that inspired the moniker, but more Mr. Werhmeier's appearance. His long, thin body would gently undulate as he conducted the glee club. His face, pink, smooth, and hairless, seemed almost featureless with his small eyes, small nose, and slit of a mouth. And his head, devoid of hair except for a few wisps of ginger-colored follicles around the sides, added to his overall vermicular appearance. Dale thought of the comparison. He mentioned it to Rusty as a private joke, but Rusty, amused by the comparison, began freely using it and other boys picked it up. Rusty felt even more delighted when he learned of Mr. Werhmeier's first name, Herman. From then on, their teacher was Herm the Worm. Dale, even though he often felt sorry for the man, still couldn't resist laughing at his expense and also calling him that ridiculous nickname.

When Herm the Worm heard the wrong lyrics, he'd stop the song and stare in the direction of Rusty and Dale. They put on their most innocent-looking faces. Rusty looked especially convincing. He'd knit his brows in concern and glance to his right and left as if to help ferret out the malefactors.

"All right boys," Mr. Werhmeier would chastise, "let's do it right. It's a lovely song. No need to change the lyrics."

Usually, Rusty and Dale would then sing the correct lyrics but one day they kept singing the wrong words and other boys heard the wrong words and they started singing them too. By the second verse, half the boys were singing "raindrops keep falling on my Fred, but I won't worry because I am just dead," and Herm the Worm waved his hands and glared at them.

"This is not funny," he said, which made them start giggling. "I mean it," he said. "It's not funny to burlesque a song like this."

The boys started laughing out loud. And Dale, while laughing, thought the word burlesque sounded interesting. Rusty did, too.

"It's not funny to burlesque a song," Dale mockingly whispered to his buddy.

And for the next few weeks they warned their chums not to burlesque the algebra, not to burlesque the Maynard, even not to burlesque the macaroni and cheese when they ate in the school cafeteria.

In the spring, the boys glee club and the girls glee club practiced together for a week in preparation for a chorus competition at the state university in Stillwater. It was supposedly a big deal, this competition, but Dale and Rusty only cared about getting out of class for the day and riding in the school bus all the way to the Oklahoma State campus.

The glee club members boarded the bus early in the morning and, as was the custom, rode in sex segregated groups. Two hours later, the bus pulled into a parking lot on campus and the kids walked to the music building and nervously awaited their turn. The glee club members were dressed in school colors, crimson and cream, with the girls wearing attractive dresses with a red skirt and a white bodice and the boys wearing garish red slacks and white shirts with red stripes. With all the deep red they were wearing, Rusty said they looked like survivors from a horror movie.

As the choir members waited, they grew nervous. Even the most mischievous of the boys, like Rusty and Dale, felt the burden of musical achievement and school pride descend upon their shoulders. What if they goofed up? What if the sang the wrong note or wrong word

(Rusty and Dale were especially concerned about that). But when their turn came, they mounted the stairs and tried not to look at the audience members, mostly fellow singers from other schools, and concentrated on singing their three songs.

Mr. Werhmeier had selected three contemporary pop songs, "We've Only Just Begun," "Cherish," and one up tempo tune, "Joy to the World." Rusty had suggested to the teacher that he include "In the Year 2525," a song strangely overlooked in their repertoire, but Herm the Worm had ignored him.

The glee club sang the first two songs well enough and even Dale actually sang instead of mouthing the words as he usually did. Then they started the last song, "Cherish," a song Dale actually liked although he would never have admitted it. It was, after all, a love song. He heard the voices of his classmates singing, and he felt a strange feeling. The song seemed to express what he had been feeling ever since seeing *her*. Like all songs, it was more than the lyrics. The melody, rhythm, harmony, and lyrics combined into an emotional force that entered his ears and exploded into his brain and then went even deeper into his mind where there was no name.

As he sang, Dale looked down three rows and to his left where *she* stood. She looked as radiant as ever. It was more than her pretty face; it was her whole being. Dale watched her mouth move, watched her lovely lips grow round, then long, then gently close together. Dale forgot his self-consciousness that he usually felt when singing. Instead he sang each word as if he were singing it to her, but imagined he sang in a perfect voice that did justice to the sentiment. By the song's end, he felt tears in his eyes. He ruthlessly blocked out further emotion before any tears fell.

The audience applauded with more enthusiasm than the usual polite clapping. Maybe they actually did a good job, thought Dale. He looked down at Amanda who smiled and bowed her head in modest appreciation. Then Dale quickly looked away before anyone caught him looking at her. He glanced at Rusty and raised his eyebrow to signal he wasn't really impressed with the whole deal and Rusty smirked in response.

They dismounted the stairs, left the stage, and gathered around Mr. Werhmeier who commended them for their performance. "Indeed," he said, looking at the boys in particular, "I was pleasantly surprised."

Dale smiled a little. Poor guy probably expected them to croak off-tune or sing the wrong words. Then the teacher said they all had an hour to explore the campus before meeting at the bus at three o'clock.

Rusty, Dale, and Chris DeVille walked around until they found a campus directory. They located the football stadium and walked over there, but the gates were locked so they couldn't go in and actually walk the field or climb the stadium stairs like they wanted to. They walked back to the student union to get a snack. They tried to act nonchalant around the college kids, who looked more like adults than even the high school guys. Dale, throughout their wanderings, kept his eyes open for her. He wanted to see her again, even if from afar.

When the three of them left the student union they walked up to a small hill that overlooked the commons. Most of the college kids were in class, but a few strolled the long walkways that crisscrossed the verdant expanse of field. As they stood and looked across the commons, they imagined when they'd be old enough to go to college and how far off in time that seemed.

Then Dale saw her. She walked with three others, her best friend, Mary Jane, and unbelievably, two boys, K. C. Cash and Butch Bigelow. Dale stared as they walked down one of the walkways that angled toward the student union.

"See that?" Rusty said.

"Yeah," said Chris.

Dale could not speak. He continued to stare at the four of them as they strolled almost parallel to him, no more than twenty yards away. Dale felt his heart jump when he saw

Amanda smile. Bigelow walked next to her, on her left, while Mary Jane was to her right. What had Bigelow said to produce that smile? What could Bigelow ever say that would evoke that reaction?

"Boy," said Rusty. "Those guys have some nerve."

They watched the four of them until they walked into the student union. Then the three boys ambled back toward the fine arts center, sipping their Cokes and trying not to be impressed with K. C. and Butch. Impressed was not quite the right word for Dale's reaction. More like disturbed. He couldn't quite believe that Amanda had consented to walk with Bigelow. Then it occurred to him that maybe she hadn't consented. Dale knew how Bigelow sometimes foisted himself on people. Maybe he just showed up and she was too polite to tell him to scram. But then, why did she smile?

The boys walked back to the parking lot and boarded the bus. A few kids were already sitting in the front seats. The most popular boys always commanded the rear seats and Rusty headed back there. Chris hesitated, then he joined Rusty and Dale.

The rest of the glee club returned in threes and fours and ten minutes later Mr. Werhmeier boarded the bus along with the pianist Mrs. Baker. The driver started the bus and Dale, who'd been lost in thought as his classmates boarded, looked forward and noticed something radical. Some boys and girls were sitting together.

Maybe it was the call of spring. Maybe it was simply time for the boys and girls to mix in a more adult way. But it surprised Dale even as he smelled the sweet breeze of springtime floating through the open window and felt the warm rays of the sun.

Rusty noticed too. Without looking at Dale, he said, "man, I'm getting in on that."

He strolled up the aisle and motioned two boys sitting behind two girls to move over. They squashed themselves together toward the window and Rusty found enough space to sit and angle his body so he faced across the aisle closer to where Mary Jane and K. C. were sitting. One seat farther up, Dale, to his deep disappointment, saw Amanda sitting with Bigelow.

"Things are changing," said Chris.

"Yeah," said Dale. And he didn't like it.

Then, taking a different route out of Stillwater than when entering it, the bus rolled to a stop at a traffic signal in the downtown area. Dale, slumped in the back seat, trying to ignore the now four mixed couples ahead of him, didn't see the sign. Instead, sitting six seats ahead, Rusty first saw it.

"Look," he said, pointing out the window. Most of the kids turned where his finger pointed. "Audie's!"

Dale jerked his head up and looked too. On the corner stood a building with a sign hanging over it that said in neon *Audie's Bar and Grill*. Dale couldn't believe it. He didn't like his first name. Blackie had named him after the most decorated hero in World War II, Audie Murphy. Dale admired his heroism, but he knew Audie Murphy from his mostly mediocre westerns he'd seen on TV. But what really bothered him about the name was that he didn't like being compared to another guy, especially a famous guy, although most kids had no idea who Audie Murphy was. Some of his teachers did, though. Another reason why the name bugged him was that Audie Murphy was sort of a little guy. That made his bravery more impressive, Dale guessed, but it also seemed to confirm that Dale was fated to be a little guy, too.

He heard the kids laugh. Then their heads turned toward him and he saw their eyes staring at him. He blushed.

"Hey, Audie," shouted K. C., "do you know the guy that owns that place?"

Then Bigelow: "Hey, Audie, is he a relative?"

More laughter. Dale felt like telling Bigelow that relatives usually share last names not first, but he said nothing. He bowed his head, acutely embarrassed and a little ashamed that someone with his first name would own a bar. He couldn't bear to look up and see if

Amanda laughed with the rest of them.

The light turned green, the bus moved forward, and Dale was spared more torment.

"Don't let it bother you, Audie," Chris said.

"It doesn't," Dale lied. He slumped in his seat as the bus drove out of Stillwater.

As the bus rolled down the highway on its way back to Galilee, Chris tried to make conversation. A nice, self-effacing guy, his classmates often overlooked him. Dale liked him and appreciated his effort to cheer him up. He just wasn't in the mood to talk. Instead, he stared out the window at the green stalks of wheat pushing themselves out of the dark, reddish brown earth.

When Dale looked forward, it seemed that eight boys were playing a game of musical chairs. They sat with certain girls for a few miles, then moved and sat with other girls. They were like bees buzzing from one spring flower to the next. Dale noticed with surprise that even Clifford was one of them. And the girls didn't seem to rebuff him or any of the other bees as they vainly sought to pollinate them.

The only flower Dale cared about was Amanda. His disappointment, so profound when Bigelow sat next to her, eased as he saw a succession of boys sit next to her for a few minutes, only to move on. Amanda wasn't rude; she just didn't encourage them. Her proper behavior reassured Dale somewhat. He had begun to doubt her exalted status when he first saw her with the odious Bigelow. Now, he realized that it was part of a ritual, a casual interaction demanded by nature herself. Dale considered joining the bolder boys. He, too, could sit next to her. He could smell her mild perfume and glance more directly at her soft, smooth skin. He could even "accidentally" brush against her downy arm or, more thrilling, accidentally touch her leg with his. Instead, Dale sat in the back seat of the bus and watched her from afar. She still remained his secret.

**Chapter 8:** *A bad break at the baseball game*

Dale ran into the dugout with his teammates after the top half of the fifth. He'd misplayed a grounder. Instead of immediately reacting and going after the ball, he'd hesitated, thinking the play was the shortstop's. The grounder skipped through the infield on his side of second base. The mistake, although not technically an error, had allowed a run. Now Galilee trailed Agra by two runs.

Charlie Comingdeer, the starting pitcher, caught up with Dale. He brushed against him as they walked toward the bench.

"You shoulda had that, freshman," he said menacingly.

"I know."

He glanced at Comingdeer. Charlie's dark eyes glared at him. Comingdeer was only a sophomore himself. He had moved to Galilee last fall, but already he thought of himself as boss. Maybe he was naturally that way. Or maybe he had an extra reason: he was the younger cousin of the great Robin Comingdeer.

Dale sat on the bench next to Rusty, the only other freshman on the high school team. Since there wasn't a junior high baseball team, both had decided to go out for the high school team. Amazingly, both had made it. Dale understood that Coach Carpenter had a lot to do with it. He liked both Rusty and Dale. Rusty, a pitcher, didn't play much. Dale, however, started most of the time at second base.

"What's his problem?" asked Rusty.

"We're losing."

"Yeah, I guess pitchers don't like it when their infielders don't make plays."

Dale saw Rusty grinning, but he didn't feel like playing along. He'd made an error in the second inning. He thought he had the grounder, but the ball suddenly jumped up and skimmed off his glove. A run scored on his error and Galilee, which had only won three games that spring, was losing to a team it had beaten once already.

"Just a jest," said Rusty.

Dale forced a grin. "Yeah, I know."

He knew Rusty liked to needle him because Dale played more than he did. That was just because Rusty was a freshman pitcher. Dale looked down the bench at Comingdeer. He wasn't especially tall, but he had a barrel chest and unusually long arms. His black hair hung down to his shoulders Indian style – appropriate since he was, like his famous cousin, a full blood Kiowa. Dale wanted to do well when he pitched. He wanted to like him if for no other reason than his relation to Robin Comingdeer. But Charlie acted too aggressively and often criticized Dale. When not pitching, Comingdeer played shortstop and would stare at him from his position like he thought a freshman had no business being on the field.

Dale knew the two main reasons he played at all were because Galilee had a lousy team and because Coach Carpenter liked him. But today, Coach Carpenter wasn't managing the team. He was attending a basketball clinic in Tulsa. Instead, Coach Aldo, who coached high school track in the spring, was managing the team today. Dale saw him standing at the other end of the bench looking at the line-up card taped to the dugout wall. He took off his cap and Dale noticed the nearly bald bullet-shaped head and his rugged face and the muscular, hairy forearms. Just a month ago, he'd told Dale he should run track rather than play baseball. Dale said he'd like to do both but his first love was baseball. He'd surprised himself by sort of disagreeing with the fearsome coach.

"Hey, man," said Rusty, elbowing Dale, "you're on deck."

Dale jumped up, grabbed one of the smaller bats, and swiftly walked to the on deck circle. He practiced his swings while watching the Agra pitcher strike out Tim Middleton.

Dale walked up to the plate and crouched in his stance. He watched a ball go by, swung and missed the second pitch, fouled off the third, then leaned over the plate as the fourth pitch dived into the catcher's outstretched glove.

"Strike three!" called the ump.

"Come on," said Dale, who normally didn't protest calls. "That was outside."

"You heard the call. You're out."

Dale shook his head and slumped back to the dugout. As he passed the other guys on bench, he heard Comingdeer sneer, "that's a freshman for you." No one else said anything.

Dale flopped next to Rusty.

"Man, that pitch *was* outside," Rusty said, offering encouragement.

"Sure was."

"Wish I'd get calls like that."

Rusty had only pitched in two of the team's ten games, both times mopping up. He'd given up seven hits and three runs in four innings.

Dale hadn't done much better. With that strikeout, he calculated his batting average to .233, seven hits in 30 at bats. At least he was above .200. He feared if he'd went below that mark he'd be benched for good, crummy team or not. Actually, when three of the track guys, including Terry Harte, didn't have a meet they joined the baseball team and then they weren't so bad. That's why today's game felt so frustrating. Those three were present and still they were losing.

Dale thought about the season so far. Three wins and seven losses. He had only seven hits, all singles, but he'd stolen five bases and hadn't been caught once. He also had the honor of breaking up a no-hitter. It happened last week against Quanah Parker, an Indian school about forty miles northwest of Galilee. Comingdeer had pitched a great game, allowing only one run, but the Quanah Parker pitcher had done even better, no hits, no runs, no walks – a perfect game – in six innings. Dale came up to bat in the top of the seventh with two outs and no one on base. Coach Carpenter had told him before going to the plate to squat down as low as he could and take the first three pitches. Dale did. Two balls, then a strike.

Dale stepped out of the box and looked at Coach. A take sign. Back in the box he didn't swing at a pitch that looked pretty good. To his surprise, the ump called it a ball. Now, 3-1, Dale glanced at Coach Carpenter again. Another take call. Dale took his squatty stance and waited.

The pitch looked perfect. Right over the plate, maybe a little low, but Dale liked low pitches, so he couldn't stop himself. He swung. At first he thought he'd missed. His swing seemed to have hit only air. But then he saw the ball, looking amazingly white on the dirt, trickle down the third base line, hugging the base path of the run-down infield. Dale, surprised, hesitated for only a moment. Then he put his head down and ran with all his might toward first base.

With each stride he took, he kept expecting to see the first baseman reach out with his glove and snag the ball. He heard his hard breathing, felt his joints jolted by the pounding of his legs on the solid earth, and heard excited shouts and yells from all around him. Then he lunged forward, his foot tripping over the bag, and a second later heard the ball plopping into the first baseman's mitt. "Safe!" called the ump. Dale toppled to the ground, jumped up immediately, and dashed back to the base. The first baseman, soon joined by Quanah Parker's coach, yelled at the umpire, protesting the call, but the ump remained adamant. Safe. End of the perfect game.

Galilee's next batter struck out and the they lost, 1-0. But Dale had gotten his team's only hit. Although, it wasn't much more than an accidental bunt, it counted. So far, that had been his best play of the season.

Now, a month later, Galilee's next batter popped up for the third out. Dale shrugged at Rusty and took his place in the field. Comingdeer threw the pitch and the batter took a fierce swing only to pop the ball into shallow center. It was a windy day, not unusual for an Oklahoma spring afternoon, and the Galilee centerfielder, a senior named Dick Reinhardt, first backtracked five yards, fooled by the big swing. Then Reinhardt realized the ball had been popped up and raced forward. Too late. The ball landed with a soft thud in shallow center and hardly rolled at all.

Dale, who'd been covering second, trotted back to his spot. He waited for the pitch when something caught the corner of his eye. He glanced to his right and saw a '67 Chevy driving down the road behind the baseball field. It was his dad. He must have taken off early to see the game.

Blackie had been to one other game before this. While taking infield practice before the game, Dale had seen Blackie sitting in the back row of the stands by himself. Dale hadn't been pleased to see his father. It was more than the usual adolescent embarrassment kids have for their parents. In fact, he felt rather ashamed of his father. He worried that he might show up with his breath stinking of alcohol or people might overhear him cursing. Both fears were unjustified. Blackie had reduced his drinking since he'd become a ranger. He only drank beer on his days off and Dale hadn't seen him drunk for months. And, although Blackie was quite capable of shocking some of the delicate sensibilities of some Galilee baseball fans with his rough language, he sat on the back row of the bleachers and didn't say anything.

Nevertheless, it bothered Dale now to see Blackie park the car and get out. He knew he should be pleased that his father cared enough to show up. But Blackie wasn't like the other parents that Dale saw with Galilee kids. He had tattoos, smoked, drank and swore, and didn't go to the First Nazarene Church. He reminded Dale of how removed he and his family were from the popular people, the "high class" of the town.

Comingdeer struck out the batter and Dale forgot his father and focused his attention on the next hitter. Another left-hander. Dale shifted a couple yards deeper in the infield and waited. Two pitches later, the hitter hit another pop fly to center. Dale raced back toward second, then slowed down and watched as the ball again fell safely in shallow center, five yards away from Reinhardt's outstretched glove.

Reinhardt retrieved the ball and tossed it to Dale covering second where the Agra lead-off man stood, having advanced only one base. Dale threw the ball to Comingdeer who snapped at it with his glove. Then Comingdeer glared into centerfield. Dale knew what he was thinking. He'd made good pitches to those two batters, only for them to get on base because of misjudged fly balls. Comingdeer felt angry and Dale didn't blame him.

The next batter struck out. Then, with two out, men on first and second, a righty came to the plate. Dale got into his infield stance and waited. This was an important batter. If Comingdeer got him out they had a chance to win in the next inning, since they were only down by a run.

Comingdeer quickly got ahead of the batter. Strike one. Then a ball. Then another strike. Then a curve missed for a ball. Two and two. Then Comingdeer threw his fastball and the hitter swung but only made partial contact. Dale watched the ball sail high into the hazy blue sky toward shallow center.

This time Dale didn't hesitate. He sprinted past second, his eyes intently focused on the ball as it lazily looped through the air. He felt his legs churning underneath him as he stretched out his glove. He didn't hear anything but his own breathing. He didn't see anyone. He only saw the ball as it fluttered down toward him, just beyond his glove. Dale extended his arm as far as he could when he ran into something solid and fast moving. His shoulder slammed into that hard thing, then he felt something kick him in his lower right leg. Dale fell forward, tumbling through the air, before landing on his back. The collision reminded him of being tackled in football: a sudden, violent sensation that he couldn't quite comprehend until it was over.

And as he would in a football game, as soon as Dale hit the ground he jumped up. When he did, he felt his right leg buckle and give way. It felt like he'd stepped forward only to discover he didn't have a right leg. He fell face down in the springy outfield grass and felt an indescribable pain shoot through him.

Stunned, Dale looked ahead and saw the ball slowly rolling into the outfield. Then he noticed Reinhardt crumpled on the ground to his right. Dale tried to move but an intense pain roared through his body, starting from his lower right leg and instantaneously burning a path to his brain.

He clawed at the earth. He dug his fingers deep into the foamy dirt and gritted his teeth, hardly believing how viciously the pain wracked his body.

He heard someone yell for the coach. He saw cleated feet running toward him. He couldn't raise his head high enough to see whose they were. Instead, he writhed in agony on the field.

"Look at his leg," Terry Harte said. "Man, it looks bad."

Dale knew it was bad; he could feel the pain burning into every inch of him.

"Yeah," said Middleton. "It looks like a fish tail."

Dale didn't know what they were talking about. A fish tail? How could a leg look like that? He raised his head again to see the fish tail leg. But the pain seared inside his body with even more intensity when he moved. So he tried to stay as still as possible and dug his fingers deeper into the dirt.

He heard Rusty's voice, telling him to hang in there, buddy. You're gonna be okay, he said, but his voice didn't sound convincing. It was slightly too high pitched. Unlike teachers and others, Dale could always tell when Rusty was lying.

"See, that's what happens when freshmen play," said Comingdeer.

"Shut up, Charlie," said Harte. "Can't you see he's hurt bad."

Dale saw Coach Aldo's cleats before him. Coach Aldo told the players to get out of the way. Then Dale heard the old man say something about setting the leg. He taught health. He was a coach. He'd set bones before. He'd even set a fellow marine's busted leg. Dale grew fearful. The idea of Coach Aldo grabbing his leg and forcing the bones back in place was too awful to contemplate. Dale tried to tell Coach Aldo to leave him alone, but instead he groaned.

He listened to them discussing the difficulties of setting bones, especially one broken this badly. Middleton asked Reinhardt if he was okay. Reinhardt said yeah, he just felt sore in the chest. Coach Aldo told him to go to the dugout and wait for him there. Then he returned to speculating on how to go about setting such a bad break.

Dale felt the pain burn through him and he couldn't believe how much it hurt. He didn't cry, though. He couldn't do that in front of his teammates. Instead he gritted his teeth so hard they began to ache and continued to dig his fingers into the earth like as if he were trying to dig by hand to China.

Then Dale heard his father's voice. He'd forgotten about Blackie. His father's voice sounded surprisingly calm. But then Blackie had been in wars too, just like Coach Aldo. Blackie said he'd found a phone and called an ambulance. Then he kneeled down closer to Dale and told him to hang on, the ambulance would be here soon.

Coach Aldo suggested they do something now about the break. Blackie said they'd wait for the ambulance and take him to the hospital. Dale heard Coach Aldo grumble that you shouldn't wait too long to set a bone.

Dale thought it was taking forever for the ambulance to arrive. He tried not to listen to what they were saying above him. Instead, he prayed for a while, still to Jehovah, but asked for strength and nothing silly like a miraculous healing. Then he concentrated on memories and images that were potent enough that they might take his mind off the stunning pain. He thought about scoring the touchdown in the last football game of the season; he thought about Amanda complimenting him, how her full pink lips curled into a smile. He thought of getting the hit that broke up the perfect game. He thought about the naked nape of Juliette's neck. He thought about eating seven dips of Braum's ice cream. He thought about Amanda again, the dimples in her cheeks and that interesting groove above her lip. He thought about the picture of a nude woman in *Playboy* that he'd especially liked. Then he asked forgiveness from Jehovah for thinking unclean thoughts, but dad gum it, his leg hurt like heck and only feelings as intense as the pain helped a little to take his mind off his agony.

The ambulance finally arrived. Some men opened a gate in the outfield fence and it approached from across the outfield grass and stopped a few feet from the prone Dale. He saw the white shoes of the ambulance attendants. They stood with the black cleats of Coach Aldo and Blackie's thick brown shoes. Dale almost laughed. It struck him as absurd that all he could see were feet and grass and dirt. Like a worm. Like Herm the Worm. Like a snake. Like the wily serpent in the garden of Eden.

Dale heard them talking. Their voices sounded extraordinarily casual. Why not? It was a delightful spring day, although a little windy. Just because there was a kid sprawled on his belly with a fish tail broken leg that shouldn't interfere with the pleasant spring day. Then Dale heard Blackie tell them to take him to the hospital at Tinker Air Force base.

"That's thirty miles away," one of the attendants said.

"He has to go there," said Blackie.

"It'll take a lot more time," said the other attendant.

"That's where he has to go."

Dale didn't understand why Blackie didn't tell them to take him to Galilee General Hospital. Maybe his leg looked even worse than it felt and Blackie thought he needed to go to a bigger hospital. Whatever the reason, Dale didn't like it. He wanted the pain to cease now.

Dale braced himself when they loaded him on the stretcher. The attendants, Coach Aldo, and Blackie kneeled down and told him to relax. Then they gently picked him up and in one smooth but astoundingly painful movement, they settled him on the collapsed gurney. Dale thought he might burst out bawling then, but he held it in and only uttered a few groans. Then they picked up the gurney, which jostled him enough to provoke another jolt of pain but not nearly as acute as before, and loaded him into the back of the ambulance. That hurt too, being slid into the gurney slot, and Dale groaned again. The ambulance doors slammed shut behind him, the side doors opened and shut, and finally the ambulance started and they drove off the field.

The siren howled as soon as the ambulance hit the road, and Dale felt himself jostling around in the back. When the ambulance turned onto the highway leading to the City, Dale grabbed hold of the sides of the contraption he was on to keep from sliding off. Wasn't he supposed to be strapped in? He glanced forward and saw the two attendants through the rear window. They both looked unsuitably young, like college kids. One had long, blond hair and a mustache, and the other had shorter black hair and long sideburns. They chatted with each other as the ambulance raced down the highway, the siren's scream obliterating their voices. Dale waited for them to look back his way, but they never did. Their casual attitude seemed to say, no big deal, hauling this injured kid to the hospital thirty miles away. We've seen a lot worse.

Bad thoughts flooded Dale's mind. He tried to replace them with good thoughts: the pleasant memories that he'd thought of before. He tried, but the pain wouldn't let him. He remembered Blackie telling him about the sailor who'd gotten his legs cut off by a snapped aviation landing cable. Blackie had seen it while serving on the Franklin Delano Roosevelt, an aircraft carrier, off the coast of Vietnam. One of the jets snapped the steel cable during landing. The cable whipped through the air and cut through the crewman's legs like a hot knife through butter. Those were Blackie's exact words. *A hot knife through butter*. And Dale, who was ten at the time, thought about how odd it would be to be standing one moment and falling legless the next. Now Dale sort of knew. He remembered asking Blackie if the crewman had died. "Of course," Blackie said. "He bled to death in a couple of minutes."

Dale then thought about his mom. He remembered her defeated face as she sat in the car while Blackie took her to the sanitarium. He remembered feeling vaguely guilty, as if he'd done something to her. Maybe if he'd been a better Witness she wouldn't have gone crazy again. Maybe if he'd refused to salute the flag at school and witnessed to other kids and went door to door in Galilee, she wouldn't have gotten sick again.

It didn't matter now, Dale told himself. It was over. And then he thought this too would soon be over. All he had to do was endure it a little longer. This too would pass. Didn't the Bible say those exact words? So Dale repeated those words in his mind, this too shall pass. This too shall pass.

The ambulance had to stop at the security gate, and then it raced down the street to the hospital emergency room. Dale groaned again when lifted out of the ambulance and wheeled into the hospital. He felt dizzy and he hardly noticed the nurses and doctors and gleaming machinery and the clean floor and spotless white walls. The astringent smell enveloped him like a cloud and permeated into his nostrils. He didn't mind the smell. It reminded him of getting well, like the time he'd almost cut off his fingers and had to stay in the hospital at the Corpus Christi Naval Air Base.

One of the nurses spoke softly to him as they wheeled him to an examination room. He couldn't quite hear what she said, but he liked her soothing voice. They busted open the doors to the room and lifted him off the gurney onto a long, cold examination table. This time they turned him over so he was face up and he squinted his eyes at the bright light above him. He should smile, he thought, like *she* did when he saw *her* face bathed in the silver light. So Dale smiled. And the nurse, the same one with the soft voice, noticed. "What are you smiling at, young man?" she asked, puzzled, and Dale saw her face and it disappointed him to see that she wasn't young the way he imagined her.

Suddenly, they all left him. He heard the doors shush as they swung shut and he looked around by moving only his head. They'd left him alone. He didn't understand it. He dropped his head back against the cold, hard surface and stared at the bright light. His leg throbbed and he didn't think he could take the pain any longer. He closed his eyes and felt utterly alone. He felt abandoned by everyone, even God. For the first time, he cried. Not for long, and only a few tears. At that moment, the loneliness was worse than the pain.

They rushed back in, the doctor and the nurses, and he saw the doctor down by his leg looking at it intently. The doctor was dressed in his surgical gown, cap, and mask, and Dale thought he looked just like a doctor in a movie. He felt the doctor gently touch his leg, more a tap than a touch, and a guttural moan rose out Dale's chest and escaped through his mouth.

"We're going to have to operate," the doctor said.

He moved closer. Dale noticed he had kind-looking brown eyes with thick eyebrows. The doctor explained that he'd broke his leg too severely for him to set it in the normal fashion. He'd know more when he saw the X-rays, but it looked like a compound fracture of the tibia and the fibula.

Dale nodded, actually knowing what the doctor meant because last year in health class he'd memorized almost all the bones of the body. He couldn't quite remember all the bones of the hand and foot; this and that phalanges, and so on, but right now it didn't matter.

They took him for X-rays, then wheeled him into the operating room and moved him to the operating table and Dale groaned again, wondering how many more times they were going to move him like a sack of potatoes.

Someone cut off his baseball pants and someone else cut off his jersey. Another someone, gowned, capped, and masked like all the rest, placed a rubber mask over his mouth and nose and asked him to count backwards from a hundred. Dale thought that was a silly request. Count backwards? But he was good at numbers so he started: 100, 99, 98. He felt a little woozy, but he got to 89, which was the number Rusty wore in football. But before he could think of 88, a deep, welcoming darkness came up from nowhere and embraced him completely.

Dale woke up in darkness. At first, he felt like he was floating in completely black space, like being stuck in the deepest, darkest cave on earth. His mind cleared a little, and he realized he was lying in a bed. Something felt heavy on his right leg and he forced his eyes to focus down there. He saw in the midst of all the darkness, a white blotch of some kind. He stared at it until it formed a shape he could recognize. He identified it as a large white cast covering almost all his right leg. His leg was suspended and he felt tubes stuck in his left arm, tape clinging to his skin. He yanked his arm once and before he could do it again, a nurse, not the old one he'd noticed before, but a middle-aged one, appeared and told him not to do that. Keep still, she said, don't remove those tubes. Dale felt her warm hand on his arm and he relaxed. The next thing he knew he tumbled down into the cave again and it felt good.

Dale awoke famished. He winced at the bright light overhead and noticed that grown men filled all the beds in the room. Then he remembered he was at the Tinker Air Field hospital. All these men were air force personnel. Some of them might be pilots, but then he realized probably not. He was no doubt with the enlisted men.

A nurse arrived at his bed and asked him if he was hungry. You bet, he said. She also asked if he needed to relieve himself. He bashfully said yes, and she left and came back with a bedpan. Dale looked at her and noticed to his relief that she wasn't very young or very pretty. In fact, she had a plain face. He took the bedpan and peed like he'd never peed before, almost filling the metallic basin. A few minutes later, he got breakfast. Cereal, eggs, bacon, toast, orange juice. He ravenously ate everything but the eggs. He didn't like eggs. Especially the kind with the runny yolk.

Later in the day, his surgeon visited and said the operation had gone well. Dale asked the doctor what those two odd objects were sticking out of the cast. They looked like small spears covered in plaster of Paris. One was a few inches below the knee, the other three inches farther down. The doctor said they were pins to hold the bone together while it healed. Dale moved his leg just a little. They didn't seem to hurt him, although the idea of having big pins stuck in his bone didn't sound good.

None of the other patients spoke to him. The beds were too far apart to really carry on a conversation, although Dale did hear some young men talking loudly to the guys closest to them. The television was mounted on a platform at a sharp angle from Dale's bed so he could only see a wedge of the picture. He didn't care much. He'd never watched television anyway except sports and an occasional show like *Star Trek* or *Get Smart!* Even though he couldn't see it well, he could hear it, and after awhile the constant blather of the television began to annoy him. He asked the nurse for something to read and she brought him boring stuff like *Field and Stream* and *General Mechanics* and *Time* so Dale had to content himself with *Time*, although he didn't care much about news and politics. He couldn't understand why they didn't have *Sports Illustrated*.

Blackie showed up later in the afternoon and gave him more information about his leg. Dale asked him how long he'd be in the hospital and Blackie said the doctor wanted him to remain throughout the weekend. Then, if everything went well, they'd release him and he'd have to stay at home for another week before going back to school.

Dale asked Blackie if he'd seen Jesse yet.

"Saw her yesterday."

"How's she doing?"

"She's still out of it."

Dale then asked about June May. Blackie said she stayed with their grandparents after she got out of school and until Blackie got home from work.

Dale didn't know what else to say. He suddenly felt tired and depressed. Blackie said get some rest. He'd visit again tomorrow.

"Bring something to read. A *Sports Illustrated*."

Blackie said he would and then left. The rest of the afternoon, Dale slept. Then he ate dinner and listened to the network premiere of *West Side Story*, occasionally getting a peek of Natalie Wood when she danced close enough to the right side of the screen.

Dale decided boredom was the worst thing about being hospitalized. None of his friends visited him, but he didn't expect them too. They'd have to drive all the way to Tinker and get special permission to come on the base. The Reinhardt family sent a ceramic baseball cleat filled with a bunch of flowers. Dale liked the cleat but didn't care about the flowers. He wondered if Dick Reinhardt was okay. He guessed he was. He'd been up and walking soon after the collision. Reinhardt, even though he was a senior, wasn't very big. He probably weighed 150 pounds, which was twenty-five pounds heavier than Dale. Dale tried remembering exactly what happened, but he mostly just remembered colliding with him and flipping head over heels, then getting up and feeling his leg collapse.

Reinhardt had a younger sister in Dale's class, Gretchen. She was pretty with dark red hair, a sharp-featured face, and narrow blue eyes. She reminded Dale of a fox. She stood a little on the short side and had an attractive figure. Dale never talked to her. She was very mature for her years and some of the boys thought her haughty. Her father owned a trucking company and just last year the Reinhardts moved into a large, expensive house close to Lake Overholser. But Gretchen and Dick still went to Galilee high school.

Then Dale remembered that the junior high pep club's picnic was next weekend. The girls were allowed to ask boys to the picnic. It wasn't exactly like a date, but it was a social event that excited everyone, especially the girls, and Dale realized he wouldn't get to go even if some girl asked him. He told himself he didn't care. But he had daydreamed for weeks that Amanda would invite him.

Blackie on his next visit brought the *Sports Illustrated* and a couple of comic books although Dale didn't read comics anymore; that was kids' stuff. He also brought some candy, which Dale still enjoyed, and they had their usual terse conversation. Later, when Dale had to do the *other* bodily function, he refused the bedpan and made the nurse bring him crutches so he could go to the actual bathroom that was fortunately on his side of the room. The nurse scolded him, but peeing was embarrassing enough and he sure as heck wasn't going to do the other in her presence, even if she were middle aged and plain.

When the doctor came by for his daily visit, Dale asked him how long he'd have the cast on. Dr. Praetorius said five months, maybe less if he healed quickly. Dale hoped he was a fast healer because football practice would start in four months. Then the doctor asked him if he remembered what happened. He told him and Dr. Praetorius nodded. You probably cracked the bone during the collision, he said. Then when you got up you did the worse damage, separating both bones and almost breaking the skin. Not breaking the skin was good; it reduced the chances for infection. Then Dr. Praetorius went into more medical detail than Dale cared about. All he knew if he'd just laid on the ground like most guys would have, he'd have been a lot better off. It was football training, Dale thought. They were trained to get up as soon as they hit the ground.

The weekend finally ended and Dale felt much better and his leg seemed to be mending well, so they released him from the hospital. His father had brought him some old jeans and had split the lower part of the right leg for him. Dale put on his own clothes and hobbled out of the room. He paused, turned and looked at all the airmen that hadn't said a word to him and thought if had Rusty's gall he'd say "see ya later guys" in a loud, mock-friendly voice. Instead, he just nodded a good-bye.

Back in the car on their way home, Blackie told Dale some good news. He'd gotten a promotion. It came with a raise and use of a patrol car.

"That's good," said Dale.

"Yeah, maybe our luck is turning."

Dale sure hoped so.

## Chapter 9: *Dale gets his letters and makes a big decision*

Dale crutched his way to the auditorium for the end-of-school-year awards assembly. He'd gotten pretty good at walking with his crutches. When he wanted he could swing his legs and pump his arms, producing impressive speed. However, now he hobbled more carefully, maneuvering through the crowd of students as they rushed to the auditorium. If he wasn't careful, some kid might trip him and he would have hated falling down in front of everyone.

"Hey, gimp," said Rusty, catching up with Dale.

"Hey."

"After the assembly, some of us are going to Pizza Hut. You wanna come?"

Dale frowned. Rusty didn't seem to understand the imposition wearing a cast to mid-thigh. "How'd I get there?"

Rusty considered the question. "Yeah, man, you're right. Can't ride on the back of my cycle with that leg of yours."

Dale nodded his head and tried to keep a peeved expression off his face.

Rusty looked critically at Dale's injured leg. Dale had used magic markers to turn the cast into a multicolored, psychedelic mural with cartoons, designs, and favorite expressions covering every inch of the plaster. He hadn't known that casts were supposed to be autographed by his friends. A few people had signed his cast anyway, the ink lost in the swirl of colors and weird drawings.

"That cast is a drag," Rusty said. "When you getting it off?"

Dale said another three months.

Rusty whistled. "Man, that's a long time."

Dale waited for Rusty to say something else as astute as his last comment but instead Rusty shouted to someone walking down the hall. Dale glanced up and saw Sadie Smith waving. For a moment, he thought she was waving at him, but quickly realized she was waving at Rusty.

"See ya inside," Rusty said.

Then he quickly walked past him in the direction of Sadie. Rusty caught up with her and Dale watched as the two of them walked together down the hall. Sadie's long, white-blond hair reminded Dale of the mane of a Palomino. He'd always liked those horses the best, with their tawny coats and snowy manes and tails.

Fortunately for Dale, the entrance to the auditorium didn't have any steps. He crutched his way inside then maneuvered to the back row of seats and saw Wally sitting on the end.

"Move down," Dale said.

Wally grinned at him, then turned to his left and started talking to Sonny.

Dale waved the rubber end of one crutch at Wally. "Hey, man, I said move down a seat. I gotta sit on the end because of my leg."

Dale knew no one liked to relinquish the end seat, but Wally, glancing at the crutch in front of his face, then at Dale's determined expression, acquiesced. He told Sonny to scoot down, and Sonny told Billy Joe and Billy Joe told Roxanne and she told Wendy who told Gretchen who told Sadie who told Rusty who told K. C. who told Mary Jane who told *her* who told Carmen who told Carrie and she moved to the open seat. Students were supposed to sit in assigned seats, but kids didn't anymore. Dale sat down, keeping his right leg extended almost into the aisle. For protection, he extended one crutch alongside his leg like a boundary so no dopey kid would accidentally stumble against his broken leg. It amazed Dale how few people paid attention to his broken leg.

He noticed Vern sitting in the seat in front of him. Vern turned around and glanced at Dale's extended leg.

"Does it itch yet?" he asked.

Dale remembered a year ago Vern had broken his arm when he fell off his horse.

"Yeah," Dale replied. He used a dismantled coat hanger to reach into the cast and scratch his knee. That's as far as he could poke it inside his cast.

Vern grinned and shrugged in the vague way boys offered sympathy, then turned around as the assembly started. Dale didn't listen to much of the ceremonies. One reason was that he hadn't done as well as he usually did in his studies. He never did his homework, which lowered his grades, in part because for a while he sort of believed the End was coming anytime. If the End was imminent as Trumbo and other Witnesses said, then why do homework? Why take school seriously at all? So Dale ended up making two As, three Bs and a C in algebra. He'd never made C before so the grade bothered him. He hated algebra. The teacher couldn't control the class. Once, Rusty, Bigelow, and K. C. grabbed the class brain, Isaac Gould, and shoved him out through the window, dumping him in the bushes. After Isaac climbed back in, the teacher, Miss Mueller, didn't do anything. She didn't even tell the principal, which Dale wasn't sure was a point in her favor or not.

Dale noticed Isaac Gould sitting next to Vern. Gould, like Vern, was a Mennonite and always wore long-sleeved shirts completely buttoned. Unlike Vern, who sometimes rolled his sleeves up a couple of folds on hot days and never buttoned the top collar button of his shirt, Gould never folded his sleeves or left a button unbuttoned. Worse, he wore bow ties and white socks with his thick, black dress shoes. He never wore blue jeans or the striped bell-bottomed pants that had been in fashion the past year. Instead, he wore the kind of clothes that Dale imagined country bumpkins wore decades ago.

Aside from his old-fashioned clothes and buttoned-up style, Gould was an odd-looking kid. He was tall, skinny, and had a strange haircut. He cut his blond hair short on the sides and in back, but a thick thatch of wheat-colored hair sprouted on top. Tiny reddish-brown freckles and black, thick-framed spectacles dominated his face. The freckles looked like buckshot spread against his pallid, plain face. His glasses had even thicker frames and lenses than Clifford's.

But Gould was the smartest kid in Dale's class, maybe the whole school. He always made A grades. He was also a musical whiz, playing the violin so well he'd made the state youth orchestra this year as a freshman. Of course, no one liked him.

Gould's unpopularity, however, didn't faze Isaac at all. He seemed, in fact, oblivious to the resentment and ridicule he inspired. He dominated class discussions, answering every question if the teacher allowed him. He'd answer grammar questions, literature questions, history questions, and especially math and science questions. He would even correct the teacher when the need arose. He was a know-it-all and utterly indifferent to groans, moans, catcalls, and insults from his classmates. The only things he didn't know anything about were popular culture and sports. When Dale had asked him how many home runs Babe Ruth hit or what movie won the Academy Award that year, Gould had simply said, "irrelevant."

That response had provided Rusty and Dale with a new word to abuse for about a week. When Dale asked Rusty his opinion of quadrilateral equations, he'd say "irrelevant." When Rusty asked Dale about the function of the spleen, he'd say "irrelevant."

In some ways though, Dale secretly admired Gould. He respected his intelligence, but what equally impressed him was how indifferent he was to the opinion of his classmates.

Dale wished he could acquire such aloofness. He pretended to be aloof. He tried to maintain a stoic bearing, especially as he hobbled through the halls with his broken leg. But inside, it bothered him that no one seemed to care. He didn't expect much sympathy from his male pals; it was part of their code not to openly express sympathy or pity. But Dale thought they were taking it too far. After all, he'd injured himself playing baseball, for the school, in a heroic attempt at catching a pop fly to win the game. But no one seemed to remember.

The girls were more expressive. Most of them had told him how sorry they were about his injury and Dale had accepted their solicitations with admirable stoicism. But none of them had cried or even looked misty eyed. They hadn't fulfilled his romantic expectations. Many times Dale had sat in class daydreaming about performing some heroic deed, usually athletic in nature. He'd envision himself scoring the game-winning touchdown, diving over four monstrous defenders and getting crunched. He'd see his poor, crumpled body stretched over the goal line as thousands of Galilee fans cheered and praised his name. On the sidelines, Amanda, transformed into a cheerleader, wept from fear that her love might have perished in his heroic effort. Then his apparently lifeless body stirred. Dale slowly climbed to his feet, his body wracked with pain over the vicious blows, as the stadium grew silent. When he finally rose to his full six-foot height (it was a daydream after all), the crowd broke into a joyous celebration over the victory and Dale's immortal performance. Then Amanda, so fetching in her pleated cheerleader skirt, ran to him and Dale nobly accepted her embrace.

Reality, Dale had learned, was far different. True, he hadn't done anything heroic. He'd just overreacted to a Texas leaguer and then crashed into a bigger player. But Dale hadn't wailed and wept like some guys, and rather than be commended for his toughness, no one said anything to him. He realized that the game he'd been injured in was just another game that people hardly paid attention to, and it didn't help that Galilee had lost, 5-4. No legends would be constructed featuring Dale. No hosannas. No cheers. No beautiful women shedding tears over his wounds. Nothing but ordinary greetings, some teasing, and dumb questions ("Did it hurt?").

Strangest of all was the realization that when you're not part of something, you're quickly forgotten. Dale had missed six days of school. He'd missed the pep club picnic.

But no one, not even Rusty or Chris or K. C., had filled him in on what happened during the time he was absent. It was as if those six days had vanished from his official record. Dale felt curious about whom Amanda had invited to the picnic, but he didn't dare ask anyone directly. If he did, then they'd understand he liked her, or even had a crush on her, (when it was much more), and that knowledge would profane the intense feelings he had for her. Also, he feared everyone would think it comic that a boy as undistinguished as he would have designs on a girl as perfect as she.

So he didn't ask. No one told him. He didn't know and never would. That was another lesson he'd learned. Out of sight, out of mind – a phrase he'd heard before but never fully appreciated until he returned to school. Dale folded his arms across his chest, oblivious to everything except the feeling that perhaps he was growing cynical. And at so young an age!

Dale felt Wally elbowing him. He turned to say knock it off when Wally said, "Coach is calling your name."

Dale looked at Wally without comprehension. Wally nodded to the auditorium stage. "The baseball team's getting their letters. Coach Carpenter just called your name."

Dale looked up and saw twelve guys standing on stage with Coach Carpenter. Dale hadn't been paying attention as usual. After the academic awards, the coaches handed out the athletic letters. Dale struggled to his feet, grabbed his crutches, and started to hobble down the center aisle to the stage. But the idea of everyone watching him unnerved him and he decided to go down one of the side aisles where fewer people could see. He turned and crutched himself past the back of the east section of seats, turned north and proceeded toward the stage, then paused and swung his broken leg up one stair at a time until he disappeared into the wings of the stage. A few seconds later he appeared on stage to laughs and mock cheers from the audience. He noticed his teammates, all high school guys, staring at him like he was the nerdy ninth grader they all knew him to be (Comingdeer's expression showed pure contempt), and then he saw Coach Carpenter's face. The giant of a man had a slightly amused look on his face as he handed Dale his letter.

"Congratulations, Audie," he said. Then in a lower voice, "sorry I wasn't at the game."

Dale took the award, nodded at Coach Carpenter, and joined his teammates in line. Coach's few extra words made Dale feel better and he forgot the laughter still bubbling from the seats below. Coach Carpenter concluded his remarks, and the players began to exit the stage, but Coach told Dale to remain. Dale stood alone on stage for a few seconds, feeling completely self-conscious as if a giant spotlight were showing his pathetic person to the whole school. Then Coach announced the names of the junior high football lettermen and Dale felt better when Rusty, Sonny, K. C., Butch, Billy Joe, Clifford, Leroy, Chris, Quentin, and five eighth graders joined him. Rusty, who stood next to Dale, whispered, "why the heck did you go up the wrong stairs?"

Dale shrugged and Rusty shook his head in amusement. What could Dale say? He felt embarrassed walking with crutches? He didn't want everyone to see him hobble up the stairs? He felt afraid he might misstep and fall? That was one of the differences between Rusty and himself. Nothing seemed to embarrass Rusty. He liked being known. He enjoyed telling jokes and horsing around and making a spectacle of himself. And why not? Rusty was good at it.

The junior high football lettermen were applauded and those who were going to get basketball letters were told to stay while the others exited the stage. Dale took the same roundabout route to his seat. When he finally got there, Vern grinned at him.

"Better hope you don't get any other awards," he said.

Dale grinned back. He knew he wouldn't because the basketball letters were the last awards. Dale then looked at Gould and saw he held five awards, for best student in algebra, science, English, history, and music. He'd won every freshman academic award except one, physical education, which, like Vern, he was forbidden to take.

With the end of the awards assembly, school was officially out. Yearbooks had been handed out the day before and now most of the kids passed theirs around to have them signed. Dale didn't have his with him. Carrying it and walking with his crutches was too awkward so he'd left it at home. Most of the people he wanted to sign it had signed it yesterday, including Amanda. Dale admired her signature, loopy in its feminine script but with a distinctive flow that suggested she had some artistic talent. She'd just signed her name. No comments like some of the kids added; but it was enough that she'd signed it. Not all kids signed everyone's yearbook.

Dale didn't feel like hanging around. He still felt removed from his classmates in spite of getting his two letters. So, as unobtrusively as he could, he hobbled out of the auditorium and went over to the grade school to meet his sister and wait for their grandpa to pick them up. The grade school got out of school thirty minutes later than the high school, so Dale waited in the playground. He sat in one of the swings and swayed back and forth a little, careful not to drag the heel of his broken leg. He retrieved a paperback book from the back pocket of his jeans and began reading it. Entitled *The Comeback Kid*, it was a story about a baseball player who had been beaned by a pitch and now felt afraid to stand in the batter's box. That hadn't happened to Dale, but he sympathized with the hero's predicament. Of course, the Comeback Kid eventually overcomes his fear, wins the big game with his heroic play, and charms the heart of the prettiest girl in town. Half an hour later, Dale closed the book without satisfaction. Such stories didn't seem to have the appeal they used to have.

Dale saw June May exiting the grade school building with her friend Sheba Smith. The two girls walked over to him. Dale pretended not to notice them until they stood before him.

"I thought Sheba could come along," June May said.

Dale glanced at Sheba. He thought she looked quite a bit like Sadie with a fairly plain face until she smiled and then her dimples made her cute. She had the same Palomino-colored hair as her older sister but her eyes were blue-green and didn't look as sad. She smiled shyly at Dale. He realized that to her he must look sort of impressive, the way Dale thought older kids looked when he was her age.

"Does it hurt?" she asked, pointing to his cast.

"No."

"You have horns in your leg."

"They're steel pins to help the bone stay connected."

Sheba made a squeamish face like most girls did when they heard that. Dale almost smiled.

Grandpa Walsh's car pulled up next to the playground. He drove a baby blue '63 Ford Falcon that Dale sort of liked. The car had a small engine, though, and to Dale it sounded no more powerful than a lawn mower. The three of them went over and got in the car. Grandpa gave them a hearty howdy-do and then the Falcon puttered down the road.

June May asked Grandpa to drop her off at Sheba's. Grandpa nodded and asked Dale how he felt. Dale said fine. Then Grandpa told for the third time the story of his older brother, Orville, who'd been kicked in the shin by a mule, breaking his right leg. "Not as bad as yourn," Grandpa admitted. Dale nodded. Seemed like everyone in his family broke their right leg. He didn't say that out loud because Sheba sat in the back seat with June May. He smiled at himself. He felt shy even around a seventh-grade girl.

A minute later, Grandpa dropped the girls off. Dale told June May to come home by five to help with supper. Blackie actually cooked supper when home, that was mostly TV dinners or canned stuff he brought home in bulk from the commissary at Tinker. They'd been eating a lot of fried Spam of late and Dale was getting rather sick of it. Sometimes he and June May went over to his grandparents and had supper there. Dale loved his Grandma's cooking, but he felt she resented them a little. Not for making supper for them; she enjoyed cooking, but because maybe she blamed them in a small way for Jesse's illness. She'd never said so, and Dale thought maybe he was imagining it. But he felt she acted a little distant with them.

As Grandpa drove to Dale's house, he said he and Grandma had been out to visit Jesse. He said she was doin' better. She almost seemed herself again.

"That's good," said Dale.

Jesse had been hospitalized for six weeks now and Blackie had said the insurance was just about used up.

"Yep, she's goin' be comin' home soon, Audie Dale, don't you wurry."

"I'm not," Dale said, and that was the truth. He'd decided not to worry about anything anymore if he could help it.

They approached the house when they both saw a man standing next to a large black Harley-Davidson motorcycle parked in the driveway. Grandpa slowed the car and stopped it next to the street curb.

"Who's that feller?"

"Just Trumbo."

"Trumbo? You know that feller?"

"Yeah." Dale wasn't sure if he should tell Grandpa that Trumbo was a Witness. "He's a friend of Dad's," he said, telling himself he wasn't telling a lie exactly, just stretching the truth. Okay, stretching it a whole lot.

"It's all right," added Dale. "I know him. Dad will be here in a little while."

"If'n you say so."

Dale got out of the car, thanked his grandpa, and watched him drive away. Dale hobbled over to Trumbo, who stood next to his impressive machine, grinning in his manly way.

"Thought I'd surprise you," Trumbo said in his deep, hearty voice. "Say, was that your grandfather?"

Dale said yeah. He looked more closely at the Harley. It sparkled in the sunlight. Like all of Trumbo's vehicles, it looked freshly washed and polished.

"I'd give you a ride, but I see you can't straddle a bike with your cast on."

"Guess not." Dale couldn't even straddle his Honda 70, which was a lot smaller than this cycle.

"Well, some other time." Trumbo looked more closely at Dale. "Sorry about your family's tribulations."

Dale almost grinned at that word. Other people would say bad luck, but Witnesses didn't believe in luck. Everything was a consequence of Jehovah's will. Good or bad. Bad things were tribulations. That was one of the ideas that puzzled Dale. If everything was a result of Jehovah's will then why bad things at all? Why Satan?

Dale asked Trumbo.

"Jehovah doesn't make us do what's right. So Satan can tempt Man. We don't have to succumb though."

Did Satan make Jesse go crazy? Did Satan make Dale break his leg? If so, that seemed to suggest that Satan was the equal of God.

"No, not at all," said Trumbo. "Satan was a rebellious angel. He doesn't have the power of Jehovah."

"But God lets Satan tempt and deceive."

"Yes, but only to test us. To strengthen us. We grow stronger through adversity."

Dale considered that point. It made sense. That was how it was in sports. But Dale wanted to know why some people have so much tribulation and others don't.

"Only Jehovah knows that," admitted Trumbo. "You know, a lot of Witnesses were put in Nazi concentration camps because they wouldn't renounce Jehovah. Most of them suffered horribly and died."

"Like the Jews," said Dale.

"Yes, but of course, Witnesses died as members of the true religion."

Dale didn't say anything. He wondered why Jews didn't count as much as Witnesses. He knew Jesus was a Jew. He learned last semester that millions of Jews had been exterminated in the concentration camps. Actually, the teacher hadn't spent much time on that in class. Dale had read about the holocaust later in a book about World War II for teenagers.

"I thought I'd come by and see how you're doing. We haven't seen you for over a month at the meetings."

"Yeah, I know."

"Didn't sister Greta call and ask you and June May to come with her?"

Dale said yes.

"I know a lot has happened these past few weeks," Trumbo said somberly. "But you'd find spiritual nourishment at the Kingdom Hall. We could help you and your sister persevere through these tribulations."

Dale nodded his head.

"I would be glad to stop by Sunday to give you and June May a ride to the Kingdom Hall. Joe and Michael would be happy to see you again. You boys haven't seen each other for a long while. After the meeting, I'd take you and the boys for an airplane ride, like I told you once."

Dale didn't say anything. He felt Trumbo's cool, blue eyes studying his face; his gaze felt like it peered into Dale's very soul.

"What do you say, Dale? Would you like that?"

Dale looked up and met Trumbo's gaze. "I don't think so."

Trumbo's eyes, so blue and intense, narrowed. "Why not?"

"I don't want to go to the Kingdom Hall anymore."

Trumbo said nothing. Dale couldn't match Trumbo's gaze, so he looked away. He looked at the cycle and resisted the temptation to run his hand over the smooth chrome.

"Dale, is your father making you do this?"

He stared angrily at Trumbo. "No, it's my decision."

That was true. Blackie hadn't said anything lately about the Jehovah's Witnesses. He hadn't blamed them for Jesse's illness. He hadn't forbade Dale or June May from going.

"Why, Dale?" Trumbo asked. His voice sounded both gentle and subtle.

"I don't want to anymore."

"That's not a very good reason, is it?"

Dale paused before speaking. "I don't believe in that stuff anymore."

Now Trumbo's voice had an edge to it. "What *stuff?*"

"Well, stuff like not saluting the flag. Not receiving blood transfusions. Not celebrating Christmas or birthdays. Not playing sports."

"We're not against playing sports."

"The high school games are played on Friday. You have meetings on Fridays."

Trumbo grinned. "That's true. But it doesn't look like you'll be playing any football with that leg."

Dale frowned. "The cast is coming off in a couple of months."

"Your leg won't be healed in time."

"Maybe it will. Maybe Jehovah will miraculously heal it."

Trumbo shook his head. "You shouldn't mock the powers of Jehovah."

"Okay, I didn't mean it. But I'm still not going to the Kingdom Hall anymore. I'm not going to be a Witness." He shrugged. Trumbo was sure making it hard for him.

"All right, Dale, but remember that Christ could return at any moment. By the time you change your mind, it might be too late."

"I won't change my mind."

"Very well," Trumbo said, his voice no longer hearty. Instead, it sounded grave and full of sorrow that Dale had forsaken Jehovah and would never attain an earthly paradise.

Trumbo swung a leg over the Harley and steadied it with his big hands. He pressed the ignition button. The motor answered immediately with a deep, throaty rumble. Trumbo looked at Dale one final time, shook his head, and gently let out the clutch, easing the big black machine forward and across the lawn and out the neighbor's drive. Dale watched as Trumbo sped down the street, his fairly long, sandy hair fluttering in the wind.

# BOOK 2: *The Year of Zero*

### Chapter 1: *Dale gets his cast off and encounters APH*

The man with the circular saw poised the instrument at Dale's mid thigh and winked. Dale braced himself. Then the man lowered the blade into the cast and Dale watched as the whirring saw spit out small puffs of dusty plaster.

The saw moved down Dale's leg, gradually splitting open the cast. He'd forgotten how loud the little saw buzzed. He gritted his teeth as the man curved the saw around the ankle and down the foot. Finished, he turned off the saw and with his two large hands began carefully splitting the cast. Dale wanted to help, but he had to sit and watch as the man opened the cast by cracking the old plaster of Paris apart like he was splitting a husk.

Dale lifted his leg out of the ruptured cast. His right leg looked liked a long, hairy pole. The skin looked strange, shiny and smooth, almost like it was made of plastic. Two dime-sized discolorations, where the pins had plunged into the bone, shone on his skin. They looked like small gunshot wounds, Dale thought, although he'd never seen any gunshot wounds. The knee and ankle were swollen. The area of his leg where he'd broken it, between the ankle and knee, had a knobby elevation as if a small, hard hill had formed on the smooth plain of his leg.

Dale flexed his leg and noticed with dismay how much muscle had atrophied. His calf muscle looked half the size it was before the accident. Even his thigh muscle looked smaller.

Dr. Praetorius entered the room. He examined the leg with admirable professional detachment, like a craftsman analyzing a mended piece of pottery.

"Not bad," he murmured, his thick but sensitive fingers feeling the bone. "How does it feel?"

"Fine," said Dale. He winced when he bent his knee.

"Your joints will be a little sore," said the doctor.

Dale nodded. He watched as the man who had cut off his cast tossed it into a trash bin. Dale could smell the stinky cast from where he sat. Dead skin and hair coated the inside of the cast.

"Let's see how you walk," said Dr. Praetorius.

Dale carefully got to his feet. He gingerly applied pressure to his right leg. He then put his full weight on his feet for the first time in four months. He took a step. Aside from his ankle and knee feeling sore, the leg seemed fine, although he had difficulty keeping it straight. He took another step, hobbling a little. Dale walked outside the room and into the hallway. He saw Blackie standing in front of Dr. Praetorius's office. He came over and watched along with the doctor as Dale walked down the hall and back. With each step, his leg felt sturdier and his walk grew mechanically smoother. Still, he couldn't help feeling this wasn't the leg he used to know. It was like he'd gotten a new, worse leg and he wished he had his old one back.

In Dr. Praetorius's office, Dale sat down as the doctor explained a few additional details to him and Blackie. He remembered the first time they'd changed his cast, eight weeks after breaking the leg. The same man had sawed off his cast. When the cast broke open, Dale's leg recoiled up toward his body as if it didn't want to be exposed. It throbbed and ached and looked thinner and strangely hairy. The leg reminded him of mossy branches he'd find lying in a creek bed while hunting for crawdads. When Dale sat on the bench waiting to get the leg X-rayed, he tried to keep the injured leg straight but it kept curling up and quivering. He felt nauseous and even though Dr. Praetorius said the leg was mending very well, he felt like the leg didn't really belong on his body. It looked like an alien and disgusting thing.

"Did you hear that, Dale?" Blackie asked him.

"What?" Dale replied, embarrassed that he'd been caught not listening to the doctor.

"You have to takc it casy with your leg."

"For how long?"

Dr. Praetorius stroked his chin. Except for his large, brown eyes and bushy eyebrows, the rest of the doctor's face looked rather ordinary. Dale thought he looked more impressive with his surgical mask on.

"Limited activity for at least a week. Then gradual activity after that."

"Can I run?"

"Not the first week. After that, take it easy. Test your leg. Your muscles will need time to build back up. Your joints are rusty; they'll need time to get back in smooth functioning condition. Your leg will tell you how to proceed if you listen to it carefully."

Dale grinned, imagining his leg growing a mouth and actually talking to him.

"What about Dale playing football this fall?" asked Blackie.

"That's probably not a good idea."

"Not at all?" asked Dale. Two-a-days started in two weeks, the season two weeks later.

"Well," reconsidered Dr. Praetorius, "it's possible. It depends on how well your leg functions. The bone has healed. But for some time it will be vulnerable. Especially to violent blows," the doctor paused, "as experienced in football."

Dale wondered if the doctor had played football. He looked sturdy enough. He wasn't tall but he had broad shoulders and a muscular body. If the doctor had played then he'd know how much Dale wanted to play. He slumped back in his seat, feeling glum.

"We'll see how the leg progresses," Dr. Praetorius added in a more cheerful voice. "You healed faster than I anticipated, so maybe the leg will respond more quickly than usual. We'll know after the next examination in two weeks."

Blackie and Dale thanked the doctor, shook his hand, and left his office. Dale tried to walk as normally as possible, but he knew he looked funny with the right leg of his jeans split to the thigh and his unbalanced gait.

While walking to the car, Dale asked Blackie if he'd ever broken a bone.

"Not any big bones," Blackie said.

Dale thought some guys have all the luck. Then Blackie told him twice he'd gotten pretty banged up in car accidents. The first time was after getting married to Jesse. They were driving back to Galilee from Oklahoma City. A truck hit them from behind and the collision broke Jesse's good leg and threw Blackie clean through the front windshield. Lucky he hadn't been killed. The broken glass gashed him across the top of the head. Blackie stopped walking and lowered his head and showed Dale a ragged scar traversing the top of his skull. No hair grew on the scar so it looked like an erratic creek cutting through the jungle of dark hair. Dale was impressed.

The second accident happened two years ago in Washington D.C. Blackie said his car skidded on a wet street and rolled down a hill before hitting a tree sideways. He escaped with just a few scrapes, bruises, and a busted nose and jaw.

"I didn't know about that," Dale said.

"I wrote your mother about it. At least, I thought I did."

They got to the car and Blackie drove off Tinker Air Base into the city traffic and then turned on Highway 66 to Galilee. They didn't talk much. Dale thought how boring the summer had been. He'd read a lot, listened to his records, and even watched television. June May liked television and Dale would make fun of her programs and mock the commercials until she screamed for him to leave her alone. Then he'd go outside and sit in the grass and bounce a rubber ball off the garage's brick wall. He got pretty good at it. His record was tossing the ball 144 times without making a bad throw or missing the rebound.

He'd also made up the Imaginary Baseball League. Consisting of ten teams, Dale created players and imagined them playing games as he tossed the ball against the brick wall. He'd gotten so carried away with the IBL that he'd started keeping statistics. Calculating the batting averages and pitchers' ERA gave the fantasy games a tactile reality. He'd spent hours playing imaginary games and then compiling imaginary statistics, which, on paper, became reality. His favorite team, the Freedom Flyers, consisted of players with presidential names: Billy Truman, a fleet black second baseman; Ed Eisenhower, a clutch-hitting third baseman; Doc Monroe, ace of the pitching staff; and his favorite, Legs Lincoln, a rangy, power-hitting first baseman.

Jesse got out of Coyne Campbell in June – just before the insurance terms changed and Blackie had to pay more out of pocket. Dale heard his father talking about that on the telephone and wondered if they'd discharged Jesse too soon. When he first saw her, she didn't seem quite well. Her eyes looked dull, she didn't talk much, and most of the time she sat on the couch and watched television with June May or by herself. But as the days passed and she took her medicine, she got better. She started cooking meals again and cleaning the house some, and doing other simple household duties. She still seemed a little depressed. Dale kept waiting for her to talk about Jehovah but she hadn't so far. He wondered what the doctors at the sanitarium did to her to make her forget about Him.

Dale hadn't seen many of his friends that summer because of the broken leg. He couldn't visit Vern and ride his horse, and he couldn't go with Rusty to swim or play sandlot baseball. He couldn't deliver newspapers and he couldn't mow lawns for pocket money. Worse of all, he couldn't ride his motorcycle. Dale suspected he'd missed out on a lot of fun. Even though he was still almost morbidly shy, he resented not being able to participate in some of the group activities that Rusty told him about.

When Jesse came back home and Dale thought his home reasonably normal, he invited Rusty over a few times. But Rusty, always on the go, grew restless doing sedentary things like playing board games like Monopoly and Strat-O-Matic and listening to records, so he didn't come over too much. He and Dale had learned to play chess, but both were so competitive playing games that involved any ego that the chess threatened their friendship. If Dale won, Rusty got angry; if Rusty won, Dale did. So they wisely avoided chess and played games that emphasized luck over skill.

Blackie turned the Chevy onto their street, and Dale saw his Grandpa's Ford Falcon parked on the curb. Dale followed Blackie into the house and showed everybody he could walk again. Grandpa and Grandma talked about all the broken bones their kids suffered, and Dale glanced over at Jesse who seemed strangely detached about the whole proceeding. June May said Dale's leg looked funny.

"And it smells, too," she said, holding her nose.

"Yeah, but not as bad as you," Dale said.

"Shut up," June May replied.

"Even my withered, wounded leg that hasn't been washed for four months and is covered in dead skin and hair smells better than you," Dale proclaimed. His sister often inspired Dale to almost poetic heights when insulting her.

"Shut up!" June May cried.

"Nothing can compare to your stench, Junie. Nothing can compare to the fetid odor you ooze when you walk into the room." He'd just learned the word fetid. He had been waiting to use it.

"Momma! Daddy! Make Dale shut up."

"Dale, don't aggravate your sister," Jesse said, but with no energy in her voice.

"That's enough, Dale," Blackie said. "Your sister doesn't smell and you know it."

Actually, Dale knew June May did smell. But she didn't really stink. She smelled of all the girly stuff she smeared all over herself. He thought she overdid it. She even wore cheap perfume around the house during summer vacation.

Grandpa and Grandma had to leave and Blackie walked them to their car. June May went to her room. Dale looked at Jesse and asked how she felt.

"Fine," she said. "Bet you're glad to get that cast off."

"Yeah." Dale looked at his mother. She looked tired. Her eyes didn't shine. She was normal.

Blackie came back in and got ready for work. He changed into his uniform and said he'd see them that evening and left. Jesse went to her room for a nap. Dale decided he'd take a shower, a real shower for the first time in four months. In the shower he turned on the water really hot and blasted his mended leg, feeling the hot water dislodge all the dead skin and clotted hair. The extra hair on his hurt leg puzzled him. He'd meant to ask Dr. Praetorius why his leg got so hairy but he'd forgotten.

After the shower, he dressed in his old clothes and walked to the garage and took his motorcycle out. He rolled it down the block about halfway so starting it wouldn't bother Jesse. When he kick-started it he listened with satisfaction to the engine's hum. He'd missed riding his cycle. He knew he had to be careful still, so he only drove the cycle around the block a couple of times, then put it back in the garage.

Later that day, Rusty and K. C. stopped by. Dale rolled up his jeans and showed them the leg. They were sitting on their cycles. K. C. got off his and kneeled for a closer look. Rusty didn't. He remained seated on his cycle with a frown on his face.

"What's that bump?" asked K. C.

"It's a calcium deposit," said Dale. "Helps protect the bone."

"Isn't a bone that's been broken once harder to break a second time?" asked K. C.

Dale nodded. "Yeah, I think so." He looked over at Rusty, who didn't look very interested in the conversation.

K. C. stood up and smiled. He had a wide mouth with lots of big, straight teeth in it. He'd grown a mustache, a real mustache, and Dale thought all he needed was a pair of round spectacles to look like a younger version of Teddy Roosevelt. K. C. even had the stout build and loud voice. Dale waited for him to say, "bully!"

"That leg is sure gross, Smith," he said instead.

"Yeah, I know."

"Will it be strong enough to play football?"

"I don't know yet. The doctor said maybe."

"I'm not going out for football," Rusty interjected.

K. C. and Dale looked at him. "Why not?" asked K. C.

"The team will be lousy."

"Maybe not," said K. C. "We got a new coach."

Dale hadn't heard about that. "We did? What happened to Aldo?"

K. C. shrugged. "Either he got fired or quit or retired. Hear different stories from different people."

Dale felt mixed feelings at the news. On one hand, he felt a little afraid of Coach Aldo and thought he was old fashioned, so he was sort of glad he left. On the other hand, he also respected him because he'd been a marine in World War II. Thinking of him standing on the sidelines at Sundance Prep watching his team get slaughtered 72-0 made Dale feel sorry for him.

"I think I'll concentrate on basketball anyway," said Rusty.

Dale wondered why Rusty hadn't told him that before. Dale wasn't sure if he wanted to go out for the high school team if Rusty wasn't going to.

"Hey, Smith, man," said K. C., "you want to come over to Wally's tonight?"

"I dunno. What's happening?"

K. C. glanced at Rusty and smiled slyly. "You'll find out."

Dale looked at Rusty. He just grinned.

"Come on, what is it?"

"Just be over there at six or so," said Rusty. "We'll have some chow, play Wiffle ball, and … well, you'll find out."

Both Rusty and K. C. smiled in an enigmatic way. K. C. mounted his cycle and the two of them said see ya tonight, and they raced down the street and turned out of view.

Dale, watching from the driveway, wondered why they got all secretive on him. What bothered him more was Rusty saying he wouldn't play football. He should have guessed. Last spring while they were standing around the broad jump pit on the track field, Comingdeer and Terry Harte ambled over and asked them if they were going out for football next year. Rusty and Dale both shrugged. Dale would have said yes, but he didn't like the way they asked the question. It was like they thought the idea was ridiculous. He thought Rusty had put on an indifferent act for the same reason.

"I knew you guys were a couple of pussies," Comingdeer had said with his usual sneer.

"Ah, who needs them anyway," Terry Harte had said, but with a smile. Harte, probably the school's best athlete even as a sophomore, wasn't a bad guy. He stood about six feet, with a lean, muscular build and thick blond hair. What Dale noticed most of all were his narrow, greenish-gold eyes. They reminded Dale of the eyes of a lion or some other big, ferocious feline. Even when he smiled his big, toothy smile, Harte had those predatory eyes.

But now Dale realized that Rusty hadn't been putting on an act. Maybe he really had decided that football wasn't his sport. Rusty in junior high had been a little contact-shy; in high school the hitting would be even more intense. Dale thought maybe football wasn't his sport either. He only weighed 130 pounds now, and Comingdeer and Harte both probably weighed 180. Dale wasn't sure if he could take the beating guys like Comingdeer and Harte could inflict.

Well, Dale decided, if he did chicken out at least he could blame it on his leg.

That evening at six, Dale got on his motorcycle and drove over to Wally's house. K. C. and Rusty were already there. They played a game of Wiffle ball; Rusty and Dale teamed up as required by law and won. Then they ate hot dogs, chips, and guzzled root beer. Then more Wiffle ball. Then more food; this time Wally's mother added a plate of brownies and a half-gallon carton of milk. The four boys didn't use glasses to drink the milk; they took turns chugging it from the carton until it was all gone.

After gorging themselves, the four boys reclined in the grass of the backyard and felt contented for a few minutes until Rusty stood up and said, "ready?"

Wally sneaked a look around his yard, although Dale didn't know why. It was *his* backyard. The only other creature besides them was Wally's cocker spaniel, Waldo, who whined from his pen. Waldo had wanted to play Wiffle ball, too.

"Okay, let's go," Wally said in a rather mysterious voice.

Dale followed them into the house, or rather a new, small addition of the house that Wally's dad had specially built for Wally a year ago. Connected to the main house by only a short walkway, the addition wasn't much larger than an ordinary-sized bedroom but it had the allure of being physically disconnected from the house and thus psychologically independent of parental authority. Dale had never been in Wally's new room. As soon as he entered he realized he was in the realm of the teenage boy. Large posters of Jerry West, the band members of Bread, the girl from *Laugh-In* (the one that wore a bikini with graffiti painted on her exposed flesh), and oddest of all, Albert Einstein sticking out his tongue, were tacked on the walls. On one table stood a lava lamp with a doughy substance churning inside that Dale found rather repulsive. An actual stereo, with detachable speakers and separate components, stood against one wall. Dozens of albums and scores of 45s were stacked next to it. Against another wall, a small black-and-white television. Scattered on the chair and on the unmade bed were all kinds of clothes: jeans, bell-bottom trousers, sweaters, T-shirts, and dress shirts. Wally tossed the clothes off the chair and bed into a heap in a corner.

"Have a seat, fellas," he said, as he looked up at the ceiling.

Dale sat in the now uncluttered chair and watched as Wally grabbed a stool and climbed on it. He reached up and pulled on a rope that dangled from an attic door. Wally pulled open the door and reached inside. He brought out a box. Wally tried to step down while balancing the box, but his foot slipped and he dropped the box, spilling its contents.

"Hey, man, watch out," said Rusty, who'd been behind watching Wally.

Dozens of magazines flopped on the carpeted floor. Dale looked at them. To his astonishment they were *Playboy* and a magazine named *Penthouse* that Dale had never heard of.

"Gotta be careful," scolded K. C. "Don't want to damage the goods."

Dale scrambled over to the clutter of magazines, all of them featuring naked women on their covers – so many that he didn't know which one to look at first.

The other boys joined him and they kneeled before the pile of magazines. Dale couldn't believe how many there were. Ten, twenty, maybe thirty magazines. And all of them dirty.

"Where did you get all of them?" Dale asked. He felt a thump of exhilaration like he did before running a race.

"Some lady let us have them," said Wally.

"What?"

"We were cleaning up her yard and clearing out a bunch of stuff from her garage," said K. C. "She had a lot of things in boxes and we carried them to the curb to be thrown out with the trash. One of the boxes had these in it."

"But not on top," said Wally.

"No, not on top," said K. C. "Beneath a bunch of boring stuff like textbooks and old notebooks."

"Why would a lady have *Playboy* magazines?" asked Dale.

"She didn't," said K. C. "They belonged to her son."

"Yeah, he died a couple of months ago," said Wally. "I knew him, sorta."

Dale looked at Wally.

"I mean, I saw him around some. He went to college. Central State, I think."

"How'd he die?"

"Car crash. On Highway 74."

"Will you guys quit being so *morbid* and look at what we got here," said Rusty. He picked up an issue of *Playboy* and flipped through it. "Man, this is great."

Dale thought so, too. In fact, it was almost like finding treasure. He scanned the covers of the thirty magazines and tried to decide which one to pick first. He selected one called *Penthouse* and opened it to a picture of a completely nude woman on her hands and knees with her backside directed right at the camera. Her head was turned back to the photographer and she had a wicked smile on her face. Or at least Dale thought so, once he took his gaze away from her exposed posterior that showed every private part of her.

Dale felt as if someone had clunked him on the head with a huge mallet, like in cartoons when the cat is conked on the head by the mouse and then the cat sees birdies twittering and tweeting as they fly around his swelling noggin.

Dale took a deep breath. He'd never seen such a picture before. He didn't even know such pictures existed.

"Man, look at this," said Rusty.

Dale looked up, doubting Rusty's magazine could top his. Rusty showed the centerfold from *Playboy*. The naked woman wore the same kind of demure smile that all the girls in *Playboy* seemed to have. She posed from the side so only her breasts and buttocks were visible as she frolicked on the beach. That was the quality that Dale thought sort of odd about *Playboy*. The nude women always seemed to be posing with an utterly normal expression on their face or with inviting smiles as they did something mundane like dusting the house or gardening or preparing to play volleyball. It was as if they were naked almost by accident. The photographs in this *Penthouse* magazine weren't anything like that. Dale flipped through a few more pages. These women didn't seem wholesome or girl-next-doorish. They looked like they enjoyed being naughty and they were presenting their bodies in stunningly explicit ways that continued to shock and awe him.

Rusty let out a whoop as he glanced at Dale's magazine. "What the heck!" he shouted.

"Keep it quiet," scolded Wally. "My mom can't find out."

Rusty reached over and grabbed one end of the magazine. This photograph showed a nude woman sitting in a chair with her legs spread open. She smiled wantonly.

"Man," Rusty said, almost in a pant, "this is even better than APH!"

"Yeah," Dale said. APH: short for After Pubic Hair. That historical epoch had only recently begun. Dale remembered just a few years ago when all the pictures he saw were BPH – Before Pubic Hair.

"What are you guys talking about?" asked K. C. Rusty took the *Penthouse* from Dale and showed it to K. C. "What the hell?" he said, so stunned he actually used a swear word.

"How did this guy get so many of these magazines," asked Dale.

"I guess he collected them," said Wally.

Dale checked the date on some of them. "Yeah, some of these are old. Last year."

"Hmm, I wonder if there are any BPHs in there," said Rusty.

So the boys diligently checked the historical record. They couldn't find one issue of *Playboy* or *Penthouse* that didn't have at least a peek of pubic hair. Dale hadn't been quite as impressed by the appearance of pubic fluff as Rusty had been two years ago, although he did think it a welcome advancement. But when he started going to the Kingdom Hall he stopped "reading" *Playboy*. He couldn't buy them, of course. You had to be eighteen to do that, and no store in Galilee sold them anyway. But every now and then an enterprising boy such as K. C. or Bigelow would get his hands on one. Older brothers were a useful resource. So, Dale got to see his fair share of nude women artfully displayed in these magazines and always felt the same odd combination of feelings: lust and sheepishness.

And frustration, too. After awhile, looking at beautiful naked women resulted in great frustration unless you relieved yourself of that tension. Dale did that too, and never felt any remorse even though one of the Witness books said it was wrong. He didn't understand how it could be wrong if it sometimes happened anyway when he slept. He'd once asked Trumbo about what his pals called "jacking off." Trumbo, as he did with such important questions, thoughtfully considered it before pronouncing such activity, which he called onanism, not a serious sin just a minor one. Onan was a character in the Old Testament who'd sinned by "spilling his seed." Trumbo said onanism was mostly a problem of wasting one's time and resources. Dale remembered that was the word he'd used, *resources*. Dale had nodded then, but he didn't think he was wasting any of his resources. Anyway, he seemed to have a big supply.

Dale had found the name Onan so interesting that he'd used it for a player in the IBL: Onan Seeds, a switch-hitting catcher. He played on the Hebrew Patriarchs, a team with all the players named after Old Testament characters. Dale's favorite players: Nimrod Hunter, a power-hitting centerfielder with a cannon for an arm; and David King, a hard throwing right-hander with outstanding control. Sort of like a righty Sandy Koufax.

The boys grew quiet as they examined each photograph with an almost scientific thoroughness. Dale couldn't believe these girls looked so beautiful and yet were so willing to be revealingly photographed. Especially the ones in *Penthouse*. They showed, well, they showed everything. The more Dale looked, the more he wondered if this was a good thing. His mother had told him he should treat women with respect. Dale wondered if the women in these magazines had been treated with respect. They certainly looked like they were enjoying themselves. And yet something didn't seem right.

Rusty and K. C. said they had to go. Dale stretched and felt sort of funny the way he did when he overate. Maybe he was over-lusting.

Wally asked them if they wanted to camp out. K. C. and Rusty said they couldn't. Then Wally asked Dale if he'd stay over.

"I'll have to call and ask."

He wasn't sure at first if he wanted to, but Wally had asked him with such a plaintive voice that he would have felt bad saying no. Besides, he wanted to do something different on the day he got his cast off.

Rusty and K. C. said see ya later and left. Wally, who looked liked he'd grown two inches since school let out for the summer, said they'd better put the magazines back in their safe hiding place. Dale agreed and helped Wally gather them and stick them in the box. Then Wally balanced precariously on the stool and stuffed the box back inside the attic closet. Dale used Wally's phone and called home and Jesse gave permission for him to stay over. He handed the phone back to Wally and wondered how Wally got all his stuff. Wally's dad worked as a trucker for Reinhardt trucking firm. Dale supposed he didn't make a lot of money because he didn't think truckers did. But Mr. Wainwright seemed to be on the road a lot, so maybe he made more money that Dale supposed. At least, Wally and Wendy seemed to have nice clothes and all the other necessary teenage amenities.

Wally played records by Creedence Clearwater Revival and Cream on his impressive stereo. Wally explained in too much detail about the subtleties of his stereo system and Dale was reminded of Wally's tendency to brag or talk at too much length about things that only concerned him.

"How's your leg?" Wally asked rather abruptly.

"Fine," said Dale.

Then Wally started talking about his knee. He often claimed he had a bad knee. In football last year he had a bad knee. In basketball he had a bad knee. In track he had a bad knee. Sometimes it was his right knee, other times his left knee. Dale thought Wally was exaggerating but maybe not. Wally was the slowest non-fat kid he'd ever seen. Once, when they played on the same little league team, Wally hit a line drive down the right field foul line that tumbled in fair territory and rolled all the way to the fence. For any normal kid, that would have resulted in a home run. Dale remembered standing in the dugout and yelling at Wally to run. Wally looked like he was moving in slow motion as he lumbered around the bases. To Dale, it was like one of those nightmares where you try to run as fast as you can but no matter how hard you try you can't seem to move but an inch at a time. Except this was like watching someone else's nightmare. Finally, Wally lurched to third, then hesitated, ran a few feet down toward home, and then retreated as the ball came to the plate. A sure home run for almost anyone but Wally had only made it to third.

"Did you hear about the new football coach?" asked Wally.

"Yeah. Are you going out?"

"No," Wally said. "My knee."

Dale nodded. Then Wally said he'd met the new kid in their class, a big guy called Rich Erickson.

"Is he going out for football?"

"No, he said he's going to concentrate on basketball."

That was what Rusty had said Dale remembered.

"There's also a new teacher."

"Oh, yeah?"

"Yeah. Everybody calls him Rabbi."

"Rabbi?" Dale wasn't exactly sure what that was. Something Jewish, he thought. "Is he a Jew?"

"No. He graduated from the Nazarene college. He helps teach youth Sunday school. He's not a Jew."

Dale wouldn't think so. He didn't think there were any Jewish kids in Galilee. At least, he'd never met one. The only thing he knew about Jews was that they had been God's chosen people in the Old Testament, then in the New Testament they turned against Jesus. That meant they were going to burn in hell. Dale didn't think that was fair. Some of his favorite Biblical characters were from the Old Testament.

"Why is he called Rabbi?" asked Dale.

"I dunno," said Wally. "When I saw him he looked like a big fat baby."

"When did you see him?"

"He hangs around the softball field when the high school guys from church play. He takes some of them for Cokes afterwards. He's taken Rusty."

"Oh, yeah?" Funny Rusty hadn't mentioned that. "Why does he look like a big fat baby?"

"He's sort fat like a baby. You know, kind of shapeless. And he wears glasses."

Most babies that Dale had seen didn't wear glasses. But he knew what Wally meant.

Before anything more could be said, they heard a soft knock on Wally's door. Wally checked to see no illicit magazines had been forgotten and yelled, "What is it?"

The door opened and Wendy appeared. Dale thought she looked sort of dressed up for a late summer night. She wore a yellow skirt and fancy-looking red blouse.

"What do you want?" Wally asked.

Wendy frowned at her brother, then smiled at Dale. "Hello, Audie."

Dale said hi.

"I just saw your light and wanted to say good night," Wendy said.

"So, good night," said Wally.

Dale thought Wally was being a little harsh with his sister, who couldn't help that pathetic state. Wendy and Wally were twins and they looked a lot alike, except that Wendy was pretty and Wally wasn't handsome. They had more or less the same features: green eyes, freckled snub noses, and large mouths with big teeth. Wendy's hair was a golden yellow; Wally's dirty blond. Wendy's features seemed to fit together better, plus she always had a big, bright smile. Wally often seemed glum and resentful.

Dale noticed additional differences. Wally looked like he was going to be fairly tall; Wendy didn't. In fact, as Dale discreetly examined her, she didn't look any taller than she did last school year. However, her figure looked more buxom than Dale remembered. And her hair, which had been worn fairly short and curled at the bottom, was now longer, completely straight, and parted in the middle.

Dale noticed Wendy looking at him. Her expression looked rather serious for a moment then it changed to her usual cheerful look.

"I heard you got your cast off today," she said, smiling brightly like it was her leg that had been freed.

"Yeah." Dale hoped she wouldn't ask to look at his leg like K. C. had. He'd feel funny rolling up his pant leg to show her.

But she didn't ask.

"Where've you been?" asked Wally. "On a *date*?"

"Not exactly," she said, smiling almost bashfully.

"With who?" Wally demanded.

Dale thought it rather odd that Wally wanted to know so much about his sister's personal life.

Wendy glanced at Dale. "With Terry Harte," she said demurely.

Dale detected a coquettish attitude with Wendy, which he was beginning to pick up from other girls as well. He looked at her face. She wore a self-satisfied smile and kept twisting what looked like a yellow scarf in her hands. She seemed nervously excited and kept glancing at Dale. He couldn't figure out what was wrong with her.

"Big deal. Where'd you go?"

"Oh, nowhere special," she said in a sort of sing-songy voice.

"Did he kiss you?"

Wendy nearly blushed. That is, a crimson glow crept into her full cheeks but didn't spread all over her pale face like Dale had seen on a few occasions in school. Like the time Wally said her bra strap was showing in front of a crowd of kids.

"Did he feel you up?"

"Wallace!" cried Wendy. "Don't talk dirty!"

"*Wendy*," Wally replied, saying her name with mocking exaggeration because she didn't have a more formal name.

Dale felt surprised by Wally's language, too. He felt himself blush, but he had a darker complexion than Wendy so it wouldn't show nearly as much.

"Well, I'm leaving if you're going to start talking like that," Wendy said.

"So leave," Wally sneered.

"And for your information," Wendy said, sort of wriggling in the doorway out of nervousness, "Terry did neither. He's a gentleman, unlike you."

"Some gentleman. You ought to hear how he talks in the locker room."

"Wallace!" Wendy cried, then paused and collected herself. She looked at Dale in a sort of funny way again. "Good night, Audie."

"Yeah, good night," said Dale, acquiring Wally's cool indifference.

Then Wendy slammed Wally's door shut and they heard her go into the main part of the house.

"I think she likes you, man," Wally said to Dale.

"What?" Dale asked incredulously.

The idea that Wendy, one of the most popular girls in his class, would have any interest in him seemed preposterous. After all, she just went on a date with Terry Harte. Then Dale remembered a time in grade school when he and Wally were sitting on swings and Wendy came over. She and Wally engaged in childish banter, and Dale recalled how she kept looking in his direction with an odd smile on her face. He wondered then if she might like him, but he was a confirmed girl hater and he put the idea out of his mind.

He looked at Wally and saw him grinning, no doubt amused by Dale's shocked expression.

"Just kidding," Wally said.


**Chapter 2: *Dale meets Mr. Benedict; the Pizza Hut adventure***

Dale stood for the school song with 500 of his fellow classmates. The music blared from the auditorium stage, a little off-key, but it stirred Dale nonetheless. He watched intently as the cheerleaders pranced on stage, waving their pom-pons and swaying their bodies. Then the new coach, Marlon Dorfman, led thirty-five football players up to the stage.

From his seat, Dale studied Coach Dorfman. He looked to be around six feet, big shoulders, thick legs, and a face that reminded Dale of an ancient Roman general such as Julius Caesar: broad forehead, aquiline nose, thin but well-defined lips, sturdy chin and jaw. He was balding on top with short, wavy black hair on the sides and graying, rather longish sideburns. When he spoke, Coach Dorfman had a deep, rumbling voice that furthered the idea of a Roman patrician. Dale began to admire the new coach. He seemed almost noble in bearing, especially in this splendid setting of vibrant music and vivid color.

Dale nudged Rusty and asked what he thought of the new football coach.

"I heard he's a jerk," Rusty said out of the corner of his mouth. Like Dale, he clapped along with the school song, although not very enthusiastically.

Dale had heard rumors, too, mostly how tough and demanding Coach Dorfman was. But Dale didn't think that was bad. After all, Galilee had suffered through four straight losing seasons. Last year they won only one game. You needed a take-charge guy to turn around a floundering program.

Coach Dorfman introduced the teams and Dale wished he could be standing with the players. He felt frustrated and angry that he hadn't been able to start football yet. He'd asked Dr. Praetorius about playing during his last visit and the doctor had said not yet. It would still be too risky. But he said Dale's muscles and joints were looking good. In two weeks, if his leg continued to improve, then he'd give permission for Dale to play football.

Two weeks! He'd already missed two-a-days. Tonight, Galilee opened the season at Wheaton and he wouldn't be on the team. He'd miss the next game, too, the home opener against Sequoyah. Dale felt his whole body tighten in frustration. He never thought he'd miss football so much. He never thought he'd feel so cut off and isolated. He felt like a man stranded on a desert island who from a distance can see a lot of people having fun on shore.

The spectacle of the all-school pep rally began to intoxicate Dale. Everything about it stimulated his senses and roused deep, almost primal feelings in him. He stared at the one cheerleader in particular, Laurie Page. She was a senior, so he had no hope of even speaking to her, but if it weren't for Amanda, she would be the girl he dreamed of every night. She was short, no taller than five foot three, with a curvaceous figure, long auburn hair, and a cute face, highlighted by her large blue eyes and rosy lips. She smiled, and Dale noticed she no longer wore braces. Now he upgraded her from cute to beautiful. He gazed at her every move, only momentarily shifting his eyes to the row of football players standing on stage wearing their crimson football jerseys. Dale realized he coveted one of those jerseys more than anything else in the world.

After the assembly, Dale and Rusty walked out of the auditorium, through the lobby into the gym. Dale's head was still full of the sights and sounds of the pep rally and he didn't even see Mr. Benedict standing right in front of him as he and Rusty entered. He bumped into the new teacher, eliciting an oomph sound from Mr. Benedict.

"Sorry," Dale said, puzzled how a boy his size could cause Mr. Benedict to make an oomph.

"Be careful, Audie," Mr. Benedict said. "You might injure someone."

"How could anyone injure you, Mr. Benedict, with all that blubber protecting you?" Rusty said, laughing.

Mr. Benedict raised an eyebrow and peered critically at Rusty. "Blubber? Some who have known my wrath will attest that my bulk is pure muscle."

"Oh, yeah, right," said Rusty, faking a punch at Mr. Benedict's sizable belly that protruded over his wide white belt.

Mr. Benedict immediately reacted with another "oomph" and jerked his chubby body backward so violently that he almost stumbled and fell.

Rusty and Dale laughed. Mr. Benedict's pudgy face frowned and he reached a rather large hand out and grasped Rusty's wrist. He gave it a twist.

"Hey, man," Rusty said, breaking free of Mr. Benedict's grasp, "that hurts. Well, it would hurt if you were a man and not a woman."

"Very amusing," said Mr. Benedict.

Dale, who had been observing the rather strange horseplay between student and teacher, decided that Wally was partly right. Mr. Benedict had a body that looked like an overgrown, pudgy toddler. His arms and legs looked short for his torso. He had a prominent belly but comparatively slender limbs. He had baby-like jowls and cheeks but with the shadow of stubble on them. He had a big mouth and his nose was long and thick. Heavy, black eyebrows hung over large, stylish spectacles that seemed to magnify his brown, rather froggy looking eyes. He wore his black hair in the shaggy style of a college student.

Dale guessed the reason why Mr. Benedict was called "Rabbi" was because his nose, eyes, and eyebrows looked vaguely Jewish, at least in a movie kind of way, which is the only way Dale knew about Jews. In fact, Dale thought Mr. Benedict looked a little like the guy that starred in *Fiddler on the Roof* as the fiddler, except Mr. Benedict didn't have a beard.

"Hey, is everything set for tonight?" Rusty asked.

"I presume so," said Mr. Benedict.

Dale couldn't decide if he liked the rather formal way Mr. Benedict talked or not. He sounded sort of pompous, but Dale learned some new words listening to him.

"You *presume*," Rusty mocked. "Are we going or not?"

"Of course," Mr. Benedict said, almost apologetically.

"Smith's going to come, too," Rusty said, giving Dale a glance.

Mr. Benedict turned and looked at Dale rather closely. "Certainly. Audie is invited as well."

"Invited where?" Dale asked.

"The Rabbi has graciously invited us to attend the game with him," said Rusty, mimicking Mr. Benedict's rather florid speech.

"I've asked you not to call me that at school," said Mr. Benedict, glancing around to see if anyone overheard.

"You mean tonight's football game?"

"Right-tee-O," said Rusty. "The Rab—sorry, Mr. Benedict's going to drive to the game tonight and he's invited a few of us along."

"Who?" said Dale.

"Me, you," said Rusty, first pointing to himself, then Dale, "and Rich," he pointed down to a tall blond kid shooting a basketball that Dale had in a couple of classes, "and Kevin." He pointed to another kid, not as tall, with light brown hair who guarded the shooter. Dale recognized Kevin Stephenson. He was a junior and didn't play football. He was a pretty good basketball player, though. Not very physical but with a deft shooting touch.

Dale hadn't planned on seeing the game. He knew his dad wouldn't drive all the way to Wheaton to see a game without Dale in it. "Okay," he said, joining in on the fun, "I'll presume to go."

"Ex-cellent," Rusty replied. "Mr. Benedict has a pretty cool car. A 1957 Edsel."

"What a prevaricator," said Mr. Benedict.

"Okay, it's really some foreign job. Not bad though."

"A *Saab*," said Mr. Benedict and for a moment Dale thought he was making another odd noise like the oomph before he guessed that was the name of Mr. Benedict's car.

"I guess it's big enough for the five of us," Rusty said, before he abruptly shut his mouth and stared at Mr. Benedict. "Well, that is if Mr. Benedict can stuff his blubber into only the front seat and not ooze out like the Blob or something."

When Dale saw Mr. Benedict's reddening, offended face, he joined Rusty in laughing. Mr. Benedict reached his big mitt toward Rusty again, but he was too quick for him this time.

"No, you don't son of Blob," said Rusty, dancing out of the way. "Say, Dale, when was that Blob movie made?"

"I guess around 1950."

"Weren't you born, er, oozed out around then, Mr. Benedict?" Rusty feigned to his right, then skipped to his left, again avoiding the grasp of Mr. Benedict. "So, you are indeed the Son of the Blob!"

The boys laughed again and Mr. Benedict scowled at them, his froggy eyes blinking from behind his glasses. The lenses were large but the frames were gracefully thin, which Dale thought didn't seem right for a pudgy guy.

"This is no longer amusing, Rusty," hissed Mr. Benedict.

"Oh, sorry," Rusty said, with a deadpan tone and expression. Then, in his mocking voice: "I certainly don't want you to start *blubbering*!"

"Hah, Hah," said Mr. Benedict. "But the joke's on you. I've decided not to chauffeur you to the Wheaton game after all."

Rusty opened his arms in supplication. "Okay, okay," he said. "Can't you take a joke?"

"To a certain point, yes," said Mr. Benedict. "But you have a malicious tendency to push it too far."

Rusty nodded. "Yep. I've been told that before."

Dale grinned. He sort of had. Clifford hadn't said it so eloquently, but he'd said about the same thing after being mercilessly teased by Rusty.

"Anyway, I must leave and prepare for our journey," said Mr. Benedict. He turned and nodded at Dale. "See you this evening."

Dale nodded back and watched as Mr. Benedict chugged out of the gym.

"Why is he driving us all that way?" asked Dale.

He didn't know Mr. Benedict very well. He was Rusty and Dale's history teacher this year and they'd had five classes so far. He seemed to be a pretty good teacher. At least he knew some historical stuff.

"Who cares why," said Rusty. "You want to go, don't you?"

"Yeah, I guess."

"You guess. It'll be fun."

Dale nodded, wishing he could be part of the team rather than just be a spectator watching from the stands.

New coach, new season, old result. The Wheaton Reapers, 28; Galilee Gophers, 7.

Riding back to Galilee after the football game, Dale, sitting in the back with Rusty and Rich Erickson, felt depressed. He knew if he'd been on the team nothing different would have happened. Just the same, he felt like he'd let down the team and his school.

"Some game," said Rusty.

"Yeah, they stunk," said Erickson.

"They didn't get beat as badly as last year," said Kevin Stephenson from in front.

The three of them began discussing the poor play of the football team. Dale glanced over at Rich Erickson sitting on the other side of Rusty. He stood maybe an inch over six feet, and had a long, thick body. He didn't look especially muscular. His shoulders slumped and he looked thick around the waist, but he certainly appeared big enough to play football. Kevin and Rusty, on the other hand were kind of skinny still and Dale couldn't imagine them helping the team much. But Erickson could. And now he sat in the backseat of Mr. Benedict's car ridiculing the football team.

"Why does Galilee even have a football team," Erickson said. "It just gets beat all the time. My last school was about the size of Galilee and we didn't have a football team. But the basketball team was really good. Won the district tournament last year."

If there was one thing Dale didn't like about new guys it was when they started making unfavorable comparisons about their old school to Galilee. He stared at Erickson. He had long, blond hair, longer than Rusty's even, and his eyes didn't match in color. His right eye was golden brown while his left eye was green. The mismatched eyes sort of bothered Dale. But the girls seemed to like it. He'd heard some of them refer to Erickson as "cute." Dale didn't know about that; he thought Erickson had a sort of smirky smile that showed a crooked bicuspid. And even though Dale also had a crooked bicuspid, he was beginning to dislike Erickson.

"If you know so much about football," said Dale, "why didn't you go out for the team?"

Erickson looked at Dale. "You talking to me?"

"Yeah. You're the one criticizing the football team."

"I play basketball. It's a better sport."

"It's a sport for –" Dale paused, remembering that the three of them played basketball – "guys who don't like getting hit."

Rusty frowned at him. "Who says?"

"What about you, Smith?" asked Erickson in his smirky way. "Why didn't you go out?"

"I can't yet. Because of my leg."

Dale heard Rusty chortle. "Now, you're sounding like Wainwright, except it's your leg instead of his knee."

Dale almost wanted to punch Rusty. He, of all people, should know the truth. He'd been on the baseball diamond when Dale broke his leg. He saw how bad it had been.

"Oh, yeah, I can hardly run but I'm making excuses."

"I didn't say that. It's just that we all get injured. I hurt my ankle pretty badly last year in basketball and played through it. No one felt sorry for me."

"Yeah, basketball's hard on the ankles," said Erickson.

Dale resented Rusty insinuating that he wanted people to feel sorry for him, because it was true. He started to say spraining an ankle is a lot different than a compound fracture of both the tibia and fibula, but he didn't. After all, he was outnumbered 3-1 in the argument. Still, Dale felt especially bothered that Rusty seemed to be siding with Erickson.

"Why don't you young men talk about something else," suggested Mr. Benedict. "Something affirmative in nature."

"Yeah," said Kevin. "We need to develop a positive attitude. Basketball season is not far away."

Dale didn't like that they were writing off the football season already. Galilee had only played one game so far. They could turn it around. Dale thought they had the nucleus for a good team. There weren't many good senior players, but the juniors had Harte and Comingdeer. Hart had scored Galilee's only touchdown against Wheaton, a dazzling sixty-three yard run in the third quarter. And Dale thought in another year several of the sophomores like Billy Joe Barton, Leroy Lemmon, Sonny Schoendienst, and Butch Bigelow would be pretty good.

"Say, Smith," asked Erickson, "you play basketball?"

Dale hesitated. He knew Erickson would make fun of his short stature if he said yes.

"No, I just ride the bench," he said, trying to use the same deadpan voice Rusty was so good at.

Rusty and Kevin laughed but Erickson provided only a smart-alecky smile. Before he could make an unflattering comment, Mr. Benedict pointed to a Pizza Hut. They were in the northern suburbs of the City.

"How would you young men like some pizza?" he said. "My treat."

They all cheered the offer and Mr. Benedict pulled into the parking lot. They got out and Rusty playfully shoved Dale just to let him know they were still best buddies, and they went inside and sat down at a large, circular booth. Mr. Benedict ordered one large pepperoni, then raised two thick fingers.

"Make that one large pepperoni and one large with everything." He turned to the boys. "Is that satisfactory?"

The boys nodded and Rusty said, "oh, yeah, that's satisfactory," and then they discussed the usual topics: sports (except football), girls, more sports, music, the latest movie they'd seen, and the new school club Mr. Benedict was sponsoring, FCA, Fellowship of Christian Athletes.

"There are chapters all around the country," Mr. Benedict said. "Members attend regional and national conferences. Our regional conference will be in Dallas in November. We could travel down and stay in a hotel. See the sights. Take in a Cowboys game. Eat at a fine restaurant."

Rusty glanced at Dale and raised his eyebrows, as if to say ain't this cool or what? The idea of seeing a Cowboys game appealed to Dale. He wasn't that interested in the rest.

The pizzas arrived, cutting short the conversation. The boys grabbed a slice each and gobbled it down. Then another slice. Then they each guzzled a large root beer and Mr. Benedict offered refills. Dale, who only ate the pepperoni because he didn't like all the stuff on the Supreme, had thought that Mr. Benedict had overestimated their capacity for food. They'd already eaten hot dogs at the Wheaton game for dinner. But it turned out that Dale had underestimated the gargantuan appetites of his friends. Mr. Benedict, he noticed, had kept up with all of them, including Rusty and Erickson, who had four slices each.

Finally, they were finished. They slumped in the booth, sated with pizza and root beer. Dale noticed all the boys' bellies looked almost as rotund as Mr. Benedict's.

The check arrived and Mr. Benedict graciously accepted it from the waitress and reached into his back pocket for his wallet. His chubby face, which a moment before had beamed good will and magnanimity, suddenly collapsed in despair.

"My wallet," Mr. Benedict gasped. "It's missing."

The boys looked at each other with concern. Mr. Benedict stood up, his belly jostling underneath his lavender dress shirt, and checked his other pockets.

"How could this be?" he asked, his froggy eyes opening wide in disbelief.

"Did you leave it in the car?" asked Kevin.

"I don't think so. That is, I don't recall."

"Better check," said Rusty.

Mr. Benedict walked out the restaurant. Dale watched him chug to the car. Dale thought he had an odd walk; he pumped his arms fast, but the rest of his body moved slowly.

The waitress, a middle-aged woman with a long, homely face, large, camel-like lips, and orange hair walked over to their booth.

Rusty looked at her with a raised eyebrow. "I think he's trying to run off without paying," he told her. Rusty turned to Dale and gave him a quick wink.

The woman stared at Rusty, her small, watery blue eyes widening, her camel mouth falling open in surprise. Rusty solemnly nodded. The woman turned and swiftly walked away.

Mr. Benedict burst through the door, his face ruddy with worry. "I did not locate it."

"Locate what?" Rusty asked.

"My wallet!"

"That's bad," said Dale.

"Very bad," said Rusty.

"Did you look in the glove compartment?" asked Kevin.

"Yes," said Mr. Benedict, wiping his sweating forehead with a handkerchief. "I searched everywhere."

"Under the car?" asked Rusty with sweet innocence.

"Under the car?" repeated Mr. Benedict, not quite grasping the meaning of the question. "Why, for goodness sake, *under* the car?"

Rusty shrugged. "I don't know. You said you searched everywhere."

"I didn't mean literally," spluttered Mr. Benedict.

"Oh, but that's what you said," replied Rusty as if making a valid debating point.

"Did you check in the seat?" asked Kevin.

"Yes."

"Did you check in the glove compartment?" asked Erickson, with a smirk. Dale thought he was catching on.

"Yes."

"Well, those are the two most likely places to put a wallet," said Kevin, who hadn't caught on.

"Except under the car," said Rusty.

"Will you please stop referring to under the car," pleaded Mr. Benedict. "It makes no sense."

Rusty made a mock-offended face. "Just trying to help."

He stood up and dug into his pocket. He fished out three quarters, two nickels, and four pennies. He offered them to Mr. Benedict.

"Oh, thanks, that will help a great deal," said Mr. Benedict, with a rare display of sarcasm.

Dale dug into his pockets and turned up one quarter, two dimes, and four pennies. Kevin held a crumpled dollar bill in his palm. Erickson offered nothing. He shrugged. "I spent all my dough at the game."

Mr. Benedict ran a hand through his thick, black hair. He took off his glasses and rubbed his eyes.

"How about a credit card?" suggested Rusty.

"They're in my wallet!" said Mr. Benedict loudly, finally losing his patience with stupid suggestions.

"Well, I guess we're cooked," said Rusty.

"Maybe I could call my father," said Kevin. "I guess he could drive all the way over –"

A short man with a fuzzy mustache and expressive eyes appeared. He wore a thick white tie with his red shirt. He looked suspiciously at Mr. Benedict.

"Hello," he said rather grimly. "My name is Mr. Perriwinkle. I'm the manager. Is there a problem?"

Mr. Benedict smiled nervously. "I think perhaps I lost my wallet."

Mr. Perriwinkle glanced at the boys and did not smile. He cleared his throat. "Were you trying to leave without paying a few minutes ago?"

"Of course not."

"One of these young men told the waitress that was exactly what you were trying to do."

"Nonsense!" cried Mr. Benedict. "She must have heard incorrectly."

The waitress stood behind Mr. Perriwinkle, but since she was a head taller her face hovered above the manager's face as if together they formed a two-headed totem pole. Her mouth dropped open.

"I heard right, mister," she said. "That boy right there said you were tryin' to go without payin'." She pointed to Rusty, who feigned a look of complete innocence.

"I think you misheard," Rusty said in a dignified, slightly offended voice.

"Heck if ah did."

"It doesn't matter," said Mr. Benedict. "I was not attempting to leave without paying. After all, I returned."

"Maybe your car wouldn't start," said the waitress.

"Nonsense," said Mr. Benedict. "I returned on my own accord. I want to pay my debt."

"That's happened before. People wantin' to skip out but their cars won't start."

The waitress said this with such conviction that Dale concluded it must have happened recently.

Mr. Perriwinkle took the bill from the table. He glanced at it, then looked at Mr. Benedict. "You owe twenty-one dollars and thirty-five cents, not including the tip."

Rusty cleared his throat and gave the waitress a critical look. The other three boys laughed. She blushed and said, "well, kiss my grits," then turned and marched away.

"I'm sure we can work something out," said Mr. Benedict, smiling nervously.

"Such as?" asked Mr. Perriwinkle.

"If I give you my word that I will return first thing tomorrow with the money, would you let us go?"

"How do I know you live around here?" the manager said, his eyes narrowing.

"Well, what else do you propose?"

Mr. Perriwinkle considered the question but before he could answer, Rusty, knowing it was time to conclude the prank, stood up and said he would pay the bill.

"What? With your eighty-nine cents?" Mr. Benedict cried.

"No," Rusty replied. "With this."

He produced Mr. Benedict's wallet and flipped it open, revealing three credit cards in the interior pockets and the edges of several bills in the mouth. The boys laughed.

"Where … how …did you get that?" Mr. Benedict stammered.

Rusty flipped the wallet to him. "In the driver's seat. It must have fallen out when you shoved your bulk out."

"Rusty …" Mr. Benedict hissed.

"This is not funny," said Mr. Perriwinkle, his mouth grim underneath the fuzzy mustache. "Please pay your bill and *leave*."

Before Mr. Benedict could apologize, the manager returned to the cash register and the boys scurried out of the booth and headed for the car.

Three minutes later, Mr. Benedict got in the car and glared into the rearview mirror at Rusty.

"Did you give her a tip?" Rusty asked.

"Who?"

"Our lovely waitress."

"Yes."

"How much?"

"What do you mean, how much?" shouted Mr. Benedict.

"Five or ten percent?"

"I don't remember," their teacher said wearily. "I just put enough down to make it even."

"Okay, if you want to be remembered as a tightwad."

Mr. Benedict sighed. "Let's just resume our journey. We're almost home."

The boys agreed. Mr. Benedict started the car. Suddenly, Rusty said, "wait a minute," and told Erickson to let him out.

"What now? Where are you going?" cried Mr. Benedict.

Erickson opened the door to let Rusty out. Then Rusty, who had been standing outside the window, disappeared. Mr. Benedict and the three other boys looked around, trying to locate him. Rusty reappeared. He rapped on the window and Erickson let him in.

"Just checking underneath the car," said Rusty.

The boys laughed.

Mr. Benedict said very amusing and put the car in gear and drove out of the parking lot.

## Chapter 3: *Going out for football and seeing "her"*

On a sunny day in October, Dale stood on the sidelines watching the varsity scrimmage. The defense, composed partly of second-stringers, was outplaying the first team offense. Coach Dorfman blew his whistle and berated the offense for the second time.

"Hold your blocks," he said to the lineman. "How the hell can we run a play if the line doesn't hold its blocks?"

Dale glanced at Chris DeVille, who shrugged. It was a bad sign when Coach Dorfman started cussing. He might keep the team in practice a half hour longer; he might make them run an extra lap; he might even make them run sprints until one of the players vomited. Or Dorfman might grab a player by the facemask and whip his head around while shouting in his face.

Dale had experienced Dorfman's fury during his first day of practice three weeks ago. It happened on a Tuesday, because Dale had only gotten permission to play from Dr. Praetorius the day before. It was the third week of the regular season and Galilee had lost its first two games: on the road at Wheaton and their home opener against Sequoyah. Dorfman was already in a bad mood before practice began; by the time tackling drills started he fumed at the team's lack of spirit during calisthenics. When tackling drills started, Dale, eager to show his enthusiasm, got in the ball-carrying line first. Coach blew the whistle and Dale raced toward the running lane marked by two reclining blocking dummies. The tackler, K. C. Cash, rushed toward him. Dale knew K. C. had an aggressive way of tackling and often dived at a runner's legs, so as he approached K. C. in the running lane, Dale faked to his left and cut to his right and zipped past the lunging K. C. He turned and saw K. C. sprawled on the grass and smiled to himself, expecting to hear Coach commend him on his shifty move. Instead, Dorfman ran over to Dale, stuck his face right in front of Dale's facemask, and yelled, "what the hell was that? This is a tackling drill! You're supposed to make contact with the tackler, not make some fancy move!"

"Sorry, coach, " Dale had said, "I forgot. It's my first day."

Coach shoved Dale back toward the line of players. "I don't care if it's your first day. You've played football before. The purpose of tackling drills is to practice tackling! Now, get over there and watch."

Dale had trotted back to the end of the line. As he passed Comingdeer, he heard him sneer, "good job, sophomore."

Earlier on that same day, Dale hadn't made a good first impression either. He'd gone down into the high school locker room before practice and felt excited to be in such a hallowed place. He even savored the rank smell of stale sweat, fresh paint, and other generally unpleasant odors that permeated the long brick room. He found Coach Dorfman sitting in his office, wearing only his coaching shorts, socks, and cleats. Dale stared at the coach's hairy torso. Thick, black hair ran from his belly to his chest and even curled over his shoulders. Dale thought he looked like a big black bear.

"What do you want, son?" Dorfman had asked him.

Dale said he wanted to go out for the team.

"At the start of the third week?"

Dale told him that he'd just got medical clearance to play. He started to tell about breaking his leg last spring in baseball with all the gory details when Dorfman impatiently nodded and cut him off.

"Yeah, you're the kid who busted his leg running into centerfield rather than staying at your position."

Dale thought it wasn't quite like that, but he didn't say anything.

"Well, I guess that shows you have spirit at least." Dorfman scrutinized Dale. "How much do you weigh?"

Dale said a little over 130.

That information did not impress the coach. "You really want to play, eh?"

Dale said he really did.

"All right. Tell Cookie to get your equipment." Coach Dorfman paused. "You got to provide your own jock. You have one handy, don't you?"

Dale said he was taking gym this semester so he had a jock and other stuff in his P. E. locker.

"Okay, go get it. And try not to be late."

93

That encounter was three weeks ago. Since then, Dale had practiced but not been in a game for even one play. Galilee hadn't won any of those games, their record now 0-5. But homecoming was Friday, against the Agra Armadillos, and Dale thought they could beat the Armadillos.

Standing on the sidelines, Dale couldn't help but resent how he'd been treated. After every practice, his knee had fluid on it. His ankle swelled. He had to wear a special pad on his lower leg to protect the bone. Dale practiced hard and didn't complain and endured the insults from Comingdeer and other upperclassmen and yet no one seemed to care. None of the coaches showed appreciation that he'd come out for football with a right leg that still wasn't in shape. He loped more than ran because his right leg didn't have the strength of the left and so it couldn't quite keep up. He was the smallest player on the field and yet he didn't back down during tackling drills even though he often got knocked off his feet. Even though he knew he had to prove himself on the field and he knew football coaches and players were particularly contemptuous of self-pity, he felt he deserved some appreciation, if only a slap on the back or a that-a-boy.

The shrill sound of Coach's whistle broke Dale's reverie and he saw one of the cornerbacks squirming on the ground. Dorfman went over and motioned for the trainer to come over. Dale recognized the injured player as Kimbo Jones, a senior who started at cornerback. He held his knee and rolled on the ground, moaning.

Dale watched as a couple of players not scrimmaging helped Jones off the field and to the bench where he'd be examined. Then, to his surprise, Dale heard Dorfman call his name.

"Smith. Get in for Jones."

Dale grinned when he heard that, mostly because of the names. He jogged over to the defensive huddle and listened to Butch Bigelow call the defensive formation. They broke huddle and waited for the offense. Dale took his place at right cornerback and looked at the receiver, a senior named Jerry Dewberry. The quarterback, a tall senior with scarecrow scrawniness named Hank Henderson, barked the count, then took the snap and faded back to pass. Dale reacted well and followed Dewberry on a short sideline pattern. Then he heard the whistle and looked back to see Henderson lying on the ground, sacked for the fourth time.

"Dammit!" yelled Dorfman.

He rushed into the disarray of players tangled together. He looked for one lineman in particular, spotted him, and grabbed him by the facemask.

"Oates," he shouted, "what the hell are you doing?" Dorfman yanked Clifford's facemask back and forth, making Clifford's head swing. "That's the second time you've let your man get to the quarterback. Last game you failed three times. What is it going to take for you to learn to pass block?"

Dale remembered that Clifford had always been better at run blocking than pass blocking. Pass blocking required the blocker to react more than act. Clifford's intensity made him better at acting than reacting.

"I guess it's going to take something extreme for you to learn," Dorfman barked. He let go of Clifford's facemask. Dorfman turned and looked at players standing around him. "Harte, sprint ten yards down field."

Harte, who'd been playing halfback, ran ten yards away from the coach. Dorfman then took the football from Henderson and motioned Clifford to take a couple of steps to his right side until he was directly in Harte's line of attack.

"When I toss the ball to Oates," Dorfman shouted to Harte, "I want you to start running and hit him as hard as you can. Give Oates a taste of his own medicine."

Dale glanced at the sophomores. Surely they remembered what happened last year in junior high. Dale looked at Sonny, Billy Joe, Leroy, K. C., and even Butch, but none of them appeared to be concerned. Then Dale looked over at Chris standing on the sidelines and he saw him shaking his head in disbelief.

Dale could hardly believe it himself. Different coach, different season, different team, and yet Clifford was the sacrificial goat again. Dale looked at Clifford. His white practice uniform was covered in grass stains and soaked with sweat. He stood nearly motionless, his body rigid, but his hands trembled just a little as they hung down at his sides.

Dorfman tossed the football to Clifford. He tossed it high so Clifford had to reach for it. Harte sprinted down the field. Just as Clifford wrapped his hands around the football, Harte exploded into him. Clifford grunted as Harte knocked him backwards. The football squirted into the air and both players tumbled to the ground. Harte, instead of ramming Clifford again as Bigelow had done, simply climbed off and walked away.

Clifford lay on the ground groaning. He groaned for a few more seconds, then stopped. He turned on his side, got to his knees, and finally stood unsteadily on his feet.

"Okay," said Coach, "huddle up for another play."

The offense ran a simple off-tackle play on the opposite side of the line from Clifford to give him a little more time to recuperate. Then another run to that side. Then a halfback counter to Clifford's side.

The next play Dale guessed would be a pass. When the offense broke huddle, he looked at the five foot eleven Jerry Dewberry, who tried to keep his face as neutral as possible, but Dale saw an eager look in his eyes.

At the snap, Dewberry ran the same sideline pattern that he'd run before, then turned his route and raced up the sideline. Dale guessed he'd do that. He raced step by step with Jerry and saw the ball floating toward them. Just as Dewberry stretched his arms out, Dale forced a burst of speed that propelled him past Jerry. Then Dale leapt into the air and grabbed the ball. He gripped it tightly as he fell, fending off Dewberry's grasping hands.

Dale tumbled on the turf and quickly rolled to his feet. He looked downfield to the other players and heard Coach praising Clifford.

"That a boy, Oates. Good block."

Dale trotted back with the ball and tossed it to Henderson. He glanced at Dorfman. "Good play, Smith. That-a-way to go after the ball."

Dale smiled to himself. All it took was an interception to get some recognition.

Coach Dorfman seemed pleased with the team's effort. He made them only run five forty-yard sprints to close practice.

After practice, Dale walked with Chris to the bus when Comingdeer passed by. "Hey, sophomore, don't let one play go to your head," he said. "You still ducked two-a-days."

Dale knew it wouldn't matter explaining why he couldn't have come out for two-a-days. Comingdeer wasn't the only guy to resent him for missing pre-season. Even if the other guys knew he had a valid excuse, they still didn't like someone skipping the toughest time of the season. But only Comingdeer and Bigelow, the two most aggressive guys, kept reminding Dale about it.

Dale and Chris took their seats near the front of the bus with the other sophomores.

"Ignore the jerk," said Chris, referring to Comingdeer. Charlie razzed Chris, too. He razzed all the sophomores. But Comingdeer especially liked taunting Dale.

"Okay," said Dale. "I'll try."

"You made a good play out there. I think the coaches were impressed."

"Thanks."

He grinned at Chris. They were becoming pretty good friends. Dale didn't think Chris was shy like he was; he talked to people and was friendly. But he was self-effacing. Dale thought maybe he lacked confidence. Chris's parents were strict. They were Nazarenes, like many people who lived in Galilee. His father worked in the Nazarene college administration. Dale didn't remember his exact position. His mother was a homemaker. Chris had an older sister and a younger brother. Like Chris, they had blond hair, blue eyes, and large, straight noses. No bumps, lumps, or curves. Just big, straight, and long. Chris said he had a "Gallic" nose because he was French.

If Dale were going to confide in anyone about his secrets, it would have been Chris. Even though Dale felt he could trust Chris, so far he hadn't revealed anything really personal. Nothing about his father or mother. Nothing about attending the Kingdom Hall last year. And especially nothing about *her*.

Chris sometimes talked about his family. They seemed like really good people, but strict. Chris wasn't even allowed to see movies, except for Disney films. Officially, Nazarenes weren't supposed to go to movies; but more and more of them did. And his parents were even more adamant about the other Nazarene prohibitions against drinking, smoking, swearing, dancing, and premarital sex. When Chris told Dale about these things, he understood why the high school didn't have dances or proms. Galilee High School was a public school, but with the college and First Church only blocks away, the school had a strong Nazarene influence. Many of the teachers had gone to the Nazarene college; even more went to the First Church. So, in an unofficial way, the high school was like a Nazarene school.

Dale began to realize how influential the Nazarene code was in the school. Even though there were non-Nazarenes attending Galilee, and even non-religious kids, most of the popular and admired kids were Nazarene. The usual characteristics of popularity, such as athletic ability, good looks, and personality, were important; it was just that an additional ingredient, character, especially of a Nazarene kind, was important, too.

That day on the bus ride back to the locker room, Chris told Dale about some of the other influential Nazarene families, including the Meeks. He told how deeply involved the Meeks were with the Nazarene church. Amanda's mother taught education classes at the college and her father served as an elder in the church. The Meeks had lived several years in northwest Oklahoma City and Amanda, her older sister, and younger brother had attended the big, public Cimarron City school.

Dale and Chris often had interesting conversations while riding on the bus. The rides usually lasted ten minutes and that provided them with enough time for Chris to explain some of the subtleties of Nazarene culture. Chris had asked Dale if he'd like to come with him to the First Church sometime and Dale had said maybe. He didn't tell his friend that he was still recovering from his Witness experience.

After showering and dressing, Dale, as he usually did, gave Chris a ride home on his motorcycle. Chris lived on the southern side of town, the nicer part because there were more trees and a few hills to break up the flat land. Chris hopped on back of Dale's motorcycle and they sped down Kerr Street, across 39th Expressway, then rode six blocks until they got to the far end of Chris's street. Dale couldn't drop him off at his house, because Chris's mother would strongly disapprove of her son getting a ride on a motorcycle.

Chris jumped off the cycle. "See ya."

"Yeah, tomorrow."

Dale watched as Chris walked down his street. Then he zipped down the road and instead of turning north, as he usually did, he turned south. Feeling a little adventurous, he decided to explore the fancier part of town with the big houses not far from Lake Overholser. He drove farther south, felt the road rise a little in elevation, and entered a neighborhood with expensive houses, immaculate lawns, and tall trees. It was a bright, Indian summer day. The sun glowed in the clear, fresh blue sky. Even the trees in this part of town were better. Their leaves were turning color and instead of the usual murky brownish-yellow, these trees' leaves were bright gold, burnt orange, and even vibrant scarlet. As he proceeded down a tree-lined lane, leaves brilliant with color, he saw *her* getting out of a large dark sedan and walking toward a white two-story house.

Dale slowed his cycle and crept close enough to watch her but not close enough to attract attention. Amanda wore the same blue peasant dress that he'd seen her wearing that school day. She also wore a pink choker, a velvet piece of cloth that encircled her delicate neck. All the pretty girls were wearing chokers that fall.

Following Amanda was her mother. She looked the same size as her daughter, both about five foot five with trim, shapely figures. From a distance, they looked almost like sisters, except that Mrs. Meeks dressed in a dark skirt and jacket and she wore her honey blond hair short and elegantly styled. She looked exactly how he thought a lady professor would look like.

Dale's heart thumped in his chest. He felt a little sick to his stomach, partly out of excitement but also because he felt anxiety at seeing how far beneath he was to her. As he observed how lovely Amanda looked, and how perfect her home looked, with its gleaming white façade, sparkling green lawn, and the tall trees that surrounded the property, it was sickening evidence that he had little chance of ever attaining her.

Amanda and her mother disappeared into the house. Dale blinked and wondered if they had been a mirage before his fevered eyes. He turned his cycle around and drove back to where he belonged.

**Chapter 4:** *Blackie gives a civics lesson; Clifford confides in Dale*

"Nixon's a sonofabitch," said Blackie. "Why are you wasting your time going to see him?"

"My history class is going," said Dale.

Mr. Benedict had arranged for his history and government classes to attend a Nixon re-election rally in downtown Oklahoma City.

"Some reason."

"You like McGovern better?"

Dale didn't follow politics. He didn't know much about either candidate except that Nixon was a Republican and McGovern was a Democrat. Dale knew Grandpa Walsh was a Democrat. So maybe he was, too.

Blackie grunted. "He's worse. If I have to make a choice between a crook and a fool, I'll take the crook."

Dale wasn't sure what his father meant. Personally, he thought if the choice was between crooks and fools maybe you should find someone else. He said so to Blackie.

"Find someone else? Good idea. Who?"

Dale shrugged. He didn't know.

Blackie took a drink of beer. He reclined in his easy chair, still in his ranger uniform, although minus the tie and with the top buttons of his shirt undone. In a few minutes, he'd change into civvies and drive to the City to attend his college night class. The GI bill paid for his classes at the Oklahoma State extension center in downtown Oklahoma City. With Blackie working during the day and taking classes at night, Dale hardly saw his father. Not a historically uncommon situation.

"Our last chance was MacArthur," said Blackie.

Dale guessed he was referring to General MacArthur, the old guy who always wore sunglasses and smoked a pipe.

"But he chose not to run," Blackie added, grinning darkly as if those words had special meaning.

Dale didn't understand. Talking politics with his father, which he rarely did, mystified him.

"We need a strong leader," continued Blackie. "Someone who won't back down to the Russkies." Blackie drained his Coors and looked thoughtfully at the empty can. Dale knew he was deciding whether to have another, a violation of his weekday rule. Blackie then leaned back in his chair, resigned to his quota. "We had our chance. We should have blasted the Russians to hell at the end of World War II. Then we wouldn't have had to fight in Korea and Vietnam."

Dale said he thought the Russians were our allies then.

"Of convenience only. FDR was too accommodating. Hell, he was almost a commie himself."

Dale knew Grandpa admired Franklin Roosevelt. He often said FDR helped the workingman. But Blackie, who'd always been a workingman, didn't like him. Politics was sure puzzling thought Dale.

Jesse walked into the room from the kitchen. She'd just finished washing the supper dishes. Dale looked at her as she sat down on the couch and lit a cigarette. She'd stopped smoking when she became a Witness because she would have been disfellowshipped if she'd continued. Then, at Coyne Campbell, she became a smoking fiend. Dale remembered Blackie bringing her a carton of Pall Malls to the sanitarium every visit.

Dale knew Jesse wouldn't be able to illuminate any of Blackie's political observations. She was more in the dark about politics than Dale. He doubted if she even knew who McGovern was.

"Ain't you goin' to your *class*?" Jesse asked between puffs of her cigarette.

"Yes," said Blackie, "I am."

"Drivin' all the way to Oklahoma City just to go to some class. Seems a might strange to me."

Blackie gave her an annoyed glance. "It's for career advancement."

"Yeah, I bet," said Jesse out of the corner of her mouth. The rest of her mouth sucked on her cigarette.

Dale waved the drifting smoke away. He hated it. Back when she drove him and June May to school, he'd get out of the car smelling the smoke on his clothes. His fourth-grade teacher had once took him aside and told him about the dangers of underage smoking. She said he should at least wait until he turned eighteen.

Dale handed Blackie the permission slip for him to attend the Nixon re-election rally. Blackie signed it with a flourish and gave it back.

"Sometimes I wonder what else you do over in Oklahoma City besides goin' to class," Jesse said, this time her mouth unencumbered because she'd taken the cigarette out. She flicked a nub of ashes into the ashtray and blew smoke out of her nostrils.

"You know what I do," said Blackie, getting out of his chair. "I go to class. Criminal justice on Monday and Wednesday. Sociology on Tuesday and Thursday." He walked down to hall to the bedroom to change.

"Funny thing for a ranger to have to take a course on *criminals*," she said, her voice sharp with sarcasm. "You'd think he'd know all 'bout that since it's his job."

Dale looked at Jesse wondering if she was jealous of Blackie taking college courses. She hadn't even finished fifth grade.

"What are you looking at, mister?" she asked Dale, the cigarette back in her mouth. Its fiery end glowed more fiercely when she inhaled.

"Nothing."

He thought he liked her better when she was a Witness. He got up and said he was going to his room. Jesse nodded, still puffing on her cigarette and told him to turn on the TV on his way. He did, then walked past his sister's bedroom and heard music from behind her closed door. June May had retreated into her room as soon as supper concluded. Dale put his ear to the door. The Partridge Family. He hated them almost as much as the Osmonds. Shirley Jones, however, was very appealing. She reminded him a little of Amanda, except that Shirley had short hair. Shirley, not the skinny Susan Dey, was the only reason he sometimes watched the stupid TV show.

Dale started to go into his room when Blackie came out of his. Blackie asked about the football game tomorrow.

"Yeah, it's homecoming," said Dale.

"Are you guys going to finally win a game?"

"We have a good chance."

Blackie grunted and started to walk away.

"Hey, Dad."

Blackie stopped.

"I'm going to start on defense tomorrow. At cornerback."

Blackie looked surprised. "That's good, Audie Dale. I guess you've had to work hard for that. Especially because of your leg."

Dale felt a glow spread inside him. It wasn't exactly a compliment, but it was as close as Blackie got.

"I'll come watch tomorrow."

Dale felt the glow extinguish itself. He wasn't sure he wanted Blackie present. Dale feared he might drink in the stands even though it was against the rules.

Blackie grinned sardonically. "I'll be watching from the car," he said, almost as if he read Dale's mind. "Your mother wants to stay in the car."

Dale felt embarrassed and nodded his response and Blackie said he'd see him later. Dale went inside his room and closed the door. He went over to his stereo and put "Good Vibrations" on. He sat down in the old chair by the bed and listened. Then he heard his parents arguing from the living room. He couldn't make out the words exactly; he just heard their harsh voices for a minute before the front door slammed shut. Dale went over to the stereo and turned the volume up near the end of the song where the Theremin soars above the melody. Tomorrow would be an interesting day.


"Who's that man with the president?" asked Sadie Smith.

Dale turned and looked past Rusty to Sadie. Rusty had led Dale and Chris to the open seats near the middle of the auditorium when he saw Sadie sitting there. Dale wondered why Rusty couldn't make up his mind which girl he preferred.

"Oh, that's Ed McMahon," said Rusty, turning to Dale and giving him a wink.

"The man on TV?" said Sadie, her brown eyes widening.

"Yeah, you know. Johnny Carson's sidekick."

Dale looked more closely at Vice President Agnew. He sat in a chair on stage while President Nixon spoke. Dale wasn't really listening to what the President said. He looked very serious though, as did the Vice President. Dale thought he did look a little like Ed McMahon. Blackie watched *The Tonight Show* and last summer Dale sometimes joined his dad. Blackie enjoyed the show. He often grinned at Johnny Carson's jokes about politics. Dale preferred the skits where Carson would impersonate a used car salesman or a swami.

"So, why is Ed McMahon here with the president?" asked Sadie, finally seeing the oddity of having a talk show second banana on the same stage with the President of the United States.

"Rumor has it that Ed might become secretary of defense," Rusty said in a hushed, conspiratorial tone of voice.

"What?" Sadie turned to Rusty with a bewildered look on her face. When she saw Rusty grinning, she knew she'd been had. She playfully slapped Rusty on the arm. "Oh, you."

Dale thought when Sadie smiled she looked cute. She had pronounced dimples in her cheeks that he liked. But her brown eyes didn't go with her white hair. She also didn't seem very bright.

Rusty didn't mind that. He'd once said, "why do I care if a girl has a brain? I'm more interested in the other areas of her body." Dale had been rather shocked when he heard that. Rusty had sounded like Bigelow. Besides, Dale knew such talk was just idle boasting. None of the sophomores had a car yet, and according to K. C. it was awfully hard making out on a motorcycle seat.

Dale looked farther down the aisle and saw Mary Jane Morgan and Amanda sitting together. To Amanda's right sat the aforementioned K. C. and Bigelow. Dale wondered if they had sat next to the girls by design or chance. Even though he'd been trying not to think or dream or fantasize about Amanda anymore, he couldn't help but wonder about the significance of the seating arrangement. Dale had Amanda in only one class, Mrs. Page's English class. She sat in the front with Mary Jane and Roxanne. Dale sat in the back with Rusty and Erickson. His perspective wasn't very advantageous for seeing Amanda. He had to stand up and pretend he needed to sharpen his pencil in order to get a good look at her. Sometimes he'd sharpen his pencil three times a class. Mrs. Page, who was one of the few perceptive teachers, once asked Dale why he needed to sharpen his pencil when they were reading an assignment in class, a short story by Poe. Dale had to think of an answer quick. "So I can take notes," he said. Mrs. Page had nodded skeptically but accepted the improbable answer. She knew not to delve into the curious behavior of sophomore boys if it didn't disrupt the class.

From then on, when they came into English Rusty would ask Dale if he planned on taking notes. Dale didn't know if Rusty guessed his true motive or just thought he was acting goofy.

The president leaned closer to the podium and spoke more loudly and deeply. Something about the silent majority. Dale wondered if he meant people like him who were shy and didn't say much. Except how could they be the majority? Most kids Dale knew were always blabbering, especially the girls. Seemed like they were always whispering to one another, giggling, and talking all kinds of foolishness as his grandpa might say. Dale scrutinized the president. He seemed very serious. He made a fist and shook it. Dale thought he had a funny nose. Sort of like Bob Hope. And his eyebrows were thick and dark like Mr. Benedict's.

Sadie laughed out loud and Dale turned and saw her trying to repress her laugh, her shoulders shaking as she giggled. Mr. Benedict, who sat in the row in front of theirs on the end, turned and glared at them. His black bushy eyebrows furrowed in disapproval just like the president's did when he mentioned the Democrats.

The speech finally ended. The audience stood on its feet and clapped, and music blared from somewhere on stage, and the president and vice president came to the front of the stage and waved at the crowd. It reminded Dale of a pep assembly, except there weren't any cheerleaders.

The cheering went on for a few more minutes, then the president and vice president disappeared into the wings of the stage and Dale's class got up and marched out the auditorium back to the school busses.

Rusty was still busy teasing Sadie so Dale and Chris sat together. Dale looked out the window just in time to see Amanda boarding the other school bus along with Mary Jane and Roxanne. No sign of K. C. or Bigelow, which pleased Dale.

"What did you think of the president's speech?" asked Chris.

Dale shrugged. "It was okay."

"My dad says it's a choice between the devil and the deep blue sea."

"You mean the election?"

"Yeah."

"Which one is the devil?"

Chris shrugged. "He didn't say."

Dale thought about those words. He didn't quite understand their meaning. He guessed it meant neither choice was desirable, but what exactly was wrong with the deep blue sea? Maybe he should ask Blackie. He'd been a sailor for twenty years.

"Yeah," Dale said, "my dad said almost the same thing."

Finally, Galilee won a football game. They'd beaten the Agra Armadillos, 28-12. Terry Harte scored four touchdowns, two on long runs, one on a short run, and one a thrilling eighty-nine-yard punt return. Dale started on defense, but he hadn't played very well. Agra scored one touchdown on a fifteen-yard pass to their tall split end that was a foot taller than Dale. He asked the other cornerback, Glen Dennison, to cover him, but Dennison, although five-eleven, didn't want to. "He's your man," he said.

On the touchdown play, the lanky Agra split end put a hand on Dale's shoulder that prevented him from jumping for the ball. It probably wouldn't have mattered anyway because the ball had been thrown high and Dale wouldn't have reached it. The Agra guy caught it with one outstretched hand, the other hand engaged in the illegal contact. Dale complained to the referee but he didn't call offensive interference. At the time, in the third quarter, the score narrowed Galilee's lead to 21-12. In the huddle, Comingdeer looked like he wanted to punch Dale. But Agra failed on the two-point conversion when Dale decided to knock the receiver off his feet before he came off the line of scrimmage. That was illegal too, but the ref didn't see it. Dale wasn't sure if the Armadillo quarterback would have thrown to the tall split end, but a pass play had been called. Harte and Comingdeer teamed up to sack the quarterback.

On the next defensive series, Coach Dorfman took Dale out. Jerry Dewberry who replaced him didn't do any better. Agra marched down the field, mostly with short passes to the tall guy. Then, on a blitz, Harte tackled the quarterback for a big loss and Agra had to punt. Harte returned the punt for a touchdown to clinch the victory.

After the game, the players raced to the concession stand to get their free cup of Coke and for the first time that year Dale heard all the fans telling them how good they had played. The old guy with the raisin-face that Dale had learned was Old Man Reinhardt, slapped him on the shoulder in congratulations. It wasn't just Dale. He slapped every player he saw on the shoulder. He thought it was sort of odd that so many old folks cared about a high school football game.

Dale boarded the bus and sat with Chris. Sweat soaked Dale's uniform. It'd been a warm, sultry night for October. He looked out the bus window and saw the immense golden harvest moon. In spite of his mediocre play, he felt happy about his team finally winning a game.

Chris said he'd played a good game.

"Not really."

He'd made a couple of tackles and before Agra started throwing passes in the second half he'd done pretty well. But it wasn't fair guarding a player a foot taller. Dale stood only five foot four. When he thought he'd never be as tall as Blackie, it depressed him. Dale had asked Dr. Praetorius if breaking his leg would cost him some height. The doctor considered the question knowing the answer was important to Dale. He said, not much. The break might have slowed his growth for a short time. Maybe it would cost him half an inch to an inch.

A whole inch! If only he hadn't broken his leg chasing that dang pop-up. By now, he might be five foot five and since he was still growing he might creep close to Blackie's rather unimpressive height of five foot ten.

"Hey," Chris said, seeing Dale's melancholy expression. "What's wrong? We won, after all."

Dale tried to grin. "Yeah, that's right." He thought about Chris not getting to play much. He played only on the special teams. Dale realized he didn't have any right to sulk. "You played good."

Chris shrugged. "I got knocked down every time I ran down field on the kickoff."

"Yeah, but you took out a blocker."

"You mean he took me out."

Dale smiled his typical no-teeth smile. He looked up when Clifford sat down in the opposite seat. Sweat streamed off his face, plopping down on his already-soaked jersey. His glasses were steamed over. They looked like goggles.

"Good game, Clifford," said Dale.

"Yeah, good game," echoed Chris.

Clifford turned to them but didn't say anything. His mouth remained a grim line underneath his bulbous nose and opaque glasses. He shoved over when his fellow lineman, Leroy Lemmon, lumbered onto the bus and collapsed his 230 pounds into the seat. No other sophomore wanted to sit next to Leroy because he took up so much room and sweated so profusely. But Clifford had no choice. It only seemed fair, Dale thought. Clifford, although he was fifty pounds lighter, sweated like a hog, too.

The players celebrated as the bus took them back to the high school locker room. Guys were telling jokes, laughing loudly, making ridiculous boasts, crowing about the plays real and imaginary they'd made. Coach Dorfman let them go wild. First win of the season, breaking a losing streak of twelve games.

Dale glanced at Coach Dorfman as he sat in the front seat with the assistant coach, John Blocker. Dorfman turned back at that moment and saw him. Coach's hazel-colored eyes coolly observed Dale as he said, "Should have got you a stepladder, eh, Smith?"

Dale nodded, not immediately understanding the implication of Coach's words. Dorfman's thin lips pressed themselves in a partial smile, then he turned back to the assistant coach to resume their conversation. Dale, now fully aware of his meaning, blushed. What about the play when he took that tall guy's legs out from under him, he thought. The bigger they are, the harder they fall. But the words seemed hollow even as he thought them.

The players filed out of the bus and into the locker room, eagerly anticipating homecoming festivities. The school hosted a party in the cafeteria with food and soft drinks and a local band playing music acceptable to Galilee standards. Most of the upperclassmen with girlfriends made only token appearances at the party before heading off to restaurants or a movie in the City or to other less reputable locales, such as Lake Overholser, or as some of the guys called it, "Lake Holdhercloser."

After changing and showering, Dale joined Chris outside the gym. Chris asked Dale if he was going to the homecoming party. Dale knew all the popular sophomore girls would be there. But he didn't feel like it. He still felt disgruntled for being taken out of the game and from Dorfman's joke.

"I don't think so. Are you going?"

Chris shook his head. "My dad said I had to get home early tonight."

Dale thought that rather odd. It was a Friday night after all. He waited for an explanation but Chris didn't elaborate.

"Need a ride?" Dale asked.

"No. My parents are here."

He nodded toward the parking lot. Dale saw Chris's father's car, a fairly new Ford. Inside he saw the silhouettes of Chris's parents.

Chris said "see you," and Dale said the same, and then he got on his motorcycle, kick-started it, and drove toward his home.

After driving north five blocks, Dale caught sight of Clifford walking on the sidewalk. He slowed his cycle down and put the engine in neutral to reduce the noise. Clifford stopped and looked at Dale, his expression neither friendly nor unfriendly.

"Want a ride?" Dale asked.

Clifford shrugged but climbed on back, and Dale took off and drove two more blocks before turning right and driving seven more blocks east. Dale remembered where Clifford lived but he stopped about half a block before the alleyway.

Clifford got off and said thanks.

"Why aren't you going to the homecoming party?" Dale asked.

"Why aren't you?"

"Didn't feel like it."

"Me neither."

The lenses of Clifford's glasses were completely clear and Dale could see his brown eyes even in the dark because the moonlight shone so brightly. His eyes had that curious intensity to them, as if he had X-ray vision and could see, if he stared hard enough, through brick walls and steel doors.

"I'm surprised you're not going to the homecoming party. Your buddy Rusty will be there."

"Yeah." Dale noticed Clifford's eyes had narrowed even more than before. "You don't like Rusty much, do you?"

"No."

"Why not? Everybody likes Rusty."

"Not everybody."

Obviously Clifford didn't, but Dale wondered whom else. Sometimes, Dale noticed some of the guys who thought they were junior hoods didn't like him. Those few guys who hung out in the alley behind the parking lot and smoked cigarettes. The bad kids. But that was an insignificant minority.

"I know he sometimes teases you. But he's really a good guy."

"I hate him," said Clifford.

Dale almost laughed. Clifford said it so seriously that Dale thought he was joking at first. Rusty, in fact, sometimes made a joke with that same kind solemn voice, his deadpan voice. But Clifford wasn't joking.

"That doesn't make any sense."

"Rusty started it all. The nicknames. The teasing. The effort to make me ridiculous in the eyes of everyone. That's why I get picked on all the time. Even in football."

"Rusty doesn't even play football now."

"But he began it all," said Clifford, now with more passion. "His joking, his taunting, made it all possible. That's why coaches always pick me to punish. He started the ..." Clifford paused, trying to think of the right word. "He started the infection," he finally said.

Dale didn't know what to say. An infection? As if Rusty were a mad scientist that made some virus that infected everyone in school so they'd ridicule Clifford?

"I'm as smart as Rusty. I'm probably better at a lot of things. But Rusty gets to define me as a fool when he's really the fool."

Dale thought what Clifford said made some sense. Not the part about Rusty being a fool. In fact, he sort of envied his friend. He was tall, funny, smart, and athletic and the girls thought he was cute. But Dale agreed with Clifford that the popular kids always seemed to determine what was cool or what wasn't. Sometimes Dale thought they were held in a high regard they didn't entirely deserve. But he didn't think it was some kind of plot or deliberate scheme like Clifford seemed to think. It was just sort of the way it was.

"Just because I live with my uncle and aunt and they're ..." Clifford paused. "I'll tell you, Audie, because I know you won't tell anyone."

Dale wondered how Clifford knew that.

"I had to leave Lyons because my family got in some trouble. My father that is. I don't want to go into specifics. But I came here to Galilee to live with my uncle and aunt. Well, my uncle is sort of slow. I mean, he's retarded. But he's not my real uncle. I mean, not related by blood. Anyway, they're poor. They don't have any money to buy me cool clothes or a motorcycle or anything like that. I have to work during summers and weekends to buy my own clothes and to save for lunch money during the school year. I haven't told anyone this because they'd only tease me more. But I think you have already guessed."

Dale had never heard Clifford say more than a sentence before. Now, he'd spilled his guts. He was right that Dale had guessed there was something wrong at his uncle's house. That wasn't hard to do once he saw the house. He also remembered seeing Clifford last summer mowing lawns. He heard from one of the guys that he worked weekends at Whataburger, a hamburger chain. Dale realized that Clifford had it a lot worse than he did. He'd try and remember that when he started feeling sorry for himself.

"Sorry to hear that," Dale said. He didn't want to say anything too gushy because that was something teenage boys shouldn't do.

"That's okay. I just wanted you to know so you wouldn't think I was a total Maynard."

Dale almost smiled. Rusty must have called Clifford that during one teasing session.

"And I want you to know that I don't hold the fact that you're Rusty's best friend against you. You're different than Rusty."

Dale nodded again. Yes, he certainly was. And most of the differences were undesirable.

"Well, I got to go," said Clifford.

"Sure," said Dale.

He watched Clifford turn away and walk ten yards, then turn left into the alley. Dale tried to imagine what Clifford's room looked like. It probably wasn't any bigger than Dale's closet. Maybe his uncle's house didn't even have heat. Or running water. Was that possible in Galilee?

Dale started the cycle and drove down the gravel road, listening to the crunch of the pebbles underneath the tires. The moon seemed even larger than it did a hour ago. Dale gazed at it and promised he wouldn't join in on teasing Clifford anymore.

**Chapter 5:** *Dale doesn't letter; the boys see a zero in Dallas*

The gym smelled like an old, wet sock and Dale loved it.

He and Chris stood in front of the bleachers. Outside it was a chilly, windy November day. Inside, the gym felt warm and cozy. The pungent smell welcomed him. Football season was over. Galilee had won three of its last five games to finish the season 3-7. The highlight of the season was when they beat Lyons, 35-14. Dale even got to play offense. He carried the ball four times for twenty-one yards. But he didn't score. After the Lyons game, he noticed that Clifford ignored the celebration even more than he usually did. Dale sort of understood. Clifford's heart remained with his old team.

Winning only three games might not sound like a successful season, but considering the football team had won only three games in two years before the Dorfman era, Dale believed the team was headed in the right direction.

Those football players who were going to play basketball had a week off before practice began. Dale wasn't sure if he would play basketball. He wasn't very good at it, but Rusty and Chris were going to play. Galilee didn't have a wrestling team, which would have been a good sport for him, so it was basketball or nothing. He didn't welcome the idea of not having any sport to play after school. He didn't relish the idea of going home. Like Blackie, he didn't like spending any more time than he had to in the increasingly tense household.

Dale and Chris walked down into the locker room and gathered their football equipment and checked them with Cookie, the guy who served as bus driver and equipment manager. He was a lean, grizzled old guy who always looked like he needed a shave. As far as Dale knew, Cookie didn't like cookies or any kind of sweet. In fact, Dale had once seen the top of a bottle of whiskey sticking out of Cookie's jacket pocket. He knew it was whiskey because it looked like the kind of bottle Blackie kept in his bedroom dresser top drawer along with his revolver.

The boys checked in their helmets, pads, pants, and jerseys to the uncommunicative Cookie. Dale had never heard him speak more than a few words at a time. Usually he grunted or made other disagreeable noises indicating his disdain for youth. He kept a toothpick between his thin lips and silently sucked on it. Once, he'd taken it out of his mouth and Dale noticed that the end of the toothpick had been chewed to a flat and pulpy nub.

Equipment checked in, Dale and Chris walked up the stairs back into the gym. A couple of workers were busy polishing the gym floor so they couldn't shoot any baskets. Down at the other end, Dale saw a group of guys sitting on the bleachers. They were sophomore and junior football players who weren't going out for basketball. Dale took note of Clifford, K. C., Bigelow, Leroy Lemmon, and several juniors. The most prominent guy was the obese, redheaded lineman, Doug MacDonald, who everyone called Fat Mac. He weighed even more than Leroy, probably 240 pounds, but for all his weight he wasn't especially strong and often got pushed around by linemen 30 or 40 pounds lighter.

Behind him, Dale heard the rush of wind as the front gym doors opened. He turned in time to see Coach Dorfman striding toward them.

Coach glanced at them and nodded his head slightly to acknowledge their presence but comparatively low status. He strode past them, then suddenly stopped. He turned and looked at Dale.

"Why aren't you with the other boys?"

He meant the guys sitting down at the other end. Dale didn't know why he should be with them.

"What do you mean, Coach?"

"Didn't you hear we're starting an off-season weight and conditioning program?"

Dale thought he'd heard something about that, but he really hadn't paid much attention.

"A memo is on the bulletin board in the locker room. Surely, you heard some of your friends talking about it?"

"Yeah, I guess."

"You're going to be a part of it, aren't you?"

Dale shrugged.

Coach Dorfman glanced at Chris as if to say why this is Smith kid such trouble. First, he comes out late for football. Now he isn't with the other weight and conditioning guys. Why don't you talk some sense into him?

"We're having a meeting in –" Coach checked his wristwatch – "five minutes."

Still, Dale didn't say anything. Dorfman's commanding attitude caused his usual reticence to be even more pronounced. He knew Dorfman probably took that as a sign of his contrariness, but he just felt tongue-tied around the coach.

"Smith, are you going to be part of the weight and conditioning program? You need to stay in shape before track starts."

Finally, Dale managed to say, "I was thinking about going out for basketball."

Dorfman looked at him with mild amusement on his big, brawny face. "Now, why would you go out for basketball? It's not your kind of sport, is it?"

"Well…" Dale tried to think of a reason. Coach was right. It wasn't his kind of sport. But Dorfman's tone annoyed him. He seemed to assume that a short guy like Dale had no business being on a basketball court. "Well, I like it."

That wasn't exactly true. He liked the cozy confines of the gym when it was cold and blustery outside. He liked the atmosphere during the games, the people in the stands, the cheerleaders in front of the bleachers, the frenetic activity, the shriek of the ref's whistles, the cheering, the crowd's rumbling. He liked all of that as long as he sat on the bench. And he liked being around his buddies. Dale glanced down at the weight and conditioning guys and saw only K. C., Clifford, and Leroy that he felt friendly with. It did not seem like an inviting group.

"Look, Smith," said Dorfman, "it would be better for you to join the weight and conditioning group. It's the best way to bridge the time between football and track."

"I'd rather play basketball, Coach."

Dorfman looked like he was gritting his teeth. His big jaw jutted out even more than it usually did and his lips flattened. His hazel eyes narrowed on Dale.

105

"I was thinking about lettering you for football, Smith. Now, I don't know. You don't seem to be a team player."

Dale had expected to letter. The rule was that a player had to play in half plus one of all quarters.

"I thought I had enough quarters," he said.

"I think you have nineteen," said Dorfman.

"Twenty."

"Okay. But you need twenty-one."

"But I missed two games because of my leg. Isn't that like an injury?"

"The team played ten games, Smith."

Dale felt himself getting angry. Now his jaw jutted out like the coach's. "I started the last five games."

"That's only five games," Dorfman said. "Look, you show me you're a team player and I might overlook the fact that you missed two-a-days and the first two games."

"But I couldn't come out then. I wanted to. The doctor wouldn't let me."

"Like I said, show me you're a team player. Then I might give you the extra quarter." Dorfman started to walk down to the weight and conditioning guys. "Coming?"

Dale stood motionless except that he felt his hands clenching in frustration. Coach was being unfair, he thought. He'd worked hard in football. He'd risked further injury. So what if he hadn't played that well. He'd tried. He thought the coaches would have appreciated the effort.

He shook his head no.

Dorfman gave him a contemptuous look and strode down the gym to the gang of guys waiting for him. Dale glared at them. He didn't want to be around them. Some of those guys were jerks, especially Bigelow. But the biggest jerk of all was Dorfman.

"Boy, that's not fair, Audie," said Chris.

Dale shook his head. "Let's go."

They walked out of the warmth of the gym into the cold teeth of the wind. Dale pulled his windbreaker closer around him. He wanted a letter really bad. He wanted a letter jacket. Now he'd have to wear his silly windbreaker instead.

They walked over to the parking lot, bowing their heads against the battering of the wind.

"Boy, that's *dang* not fair," said Chris, causing Dale to smile bitterly because even in the face of this injustice Chris couldn't swear.

"No, it's not," said Dale.

But then he remembered what Blackie often told him: who said life is fair?


Mr. Benedict negotiated the Dallas traffic as clumsily as he negotiated himself. He lurched the car to the left lane, which was precisely the wrong thing to do, then slowed his Saab down trying to get back to the center lane. Mr. Benedict and the boys heard car horns bellowing behind them.

"You have to get to the right lane," said Kevin, as he sat in the passenger seat reading a Dallas metro map. "The exit's coming up soon."

"Good move, Rabbi," said Rusty. He turned around and waved at the car honking its horn.

"This traffic is unbearable," said Mr. Benedict.

Dale, from his seat in the back, could see Mr. Benedict's sweaty neck. His collar looked damp. Dale turned to Chris, who shook his head at their teacher's incompetence.

"There!" Rusty said. "There's an opening."

Mr. Benedict attempted to turn into the center lane, but a car sped up and closed the gap. Mr. Benedict abruptly turned the car back to the left, prompting another blast of a car horn.

"Too late," said Rusty, with a laugh.

Dale glanced over to Rusty, who sat on the other end of the back seat. Rusty seemed to be enjoying their predicament.

Mr. Benedict made another tentative attempt to cross into the center lane, but once again another car cut him off. Rusty told him to force his way in, but their teacher told him that was too dangerous. He continued to drive in the left lane, speeding up, then slowing, trying desperately to find an opening.

"Flip your turn signal on," Rusty said.

"I have already done that," said Mr. Benedict.

His voice took on comic shrillness that made Rusty laugh. Rusty rolled down his window.

"What are you doing?" asked Mr. Benedict. "Roll it up. You're allowing cold air in. We'll all catch our death!"

Rusty leaned out the window, not just his head but also almost half of his body. Mr. Benedict cried for him to stop. "Get back in here!

Chris grabbed Rusty by the legs to anchor him. Rusty waved at the nearest car in the center lane. He motioned the driver to slow down and let them in. Dale looked out the back window. A car in the center lane slowed down, and Mr. Benedict slipped into the lane.

"Uh oh," said Kevin, turning his head toward his window. "That was our exit."

"Beans!" cried Mr. Benedict, using one of his stronger euphemisms.

Rusty, still hanging out the window, waved off the car in the far right lane. It, too, slowed and Mr. Benedict finally made it to the right lane. Rusty popped back in.

"You can flip off your turn signal now, Rabbi."

Mr. Benedict stared into the rearview mirror. "I'd like to flip off something else."

The boys laughed. "Hey, Rabbi made a joke," said Rusty. He leaned forward and pointed. "Take that exit. We can drive back on a side street."

Mr. Benedict did as instructed and ten minutes and two wrong turns later they were at the Happy Trails Motor Inn. As they got out of the car, Rusty spread his arms wide in mock appreciation.

"Swell digs. The FCA sure knows how to go first class."

Minutes later they were in their rooms. The four boys shared one room with two queen-sized beds. Mr. Benedict also had a room with two queen-sized beds and Rusty teased him that he'd have to connect the two beds side to side in order to accommodate his blubber.

The boys wanted lunch. Mr. Benedict, in no mood to rejoin the horrendous Dallas traffic, didn't want to go out. The boys decided to order delivery pizza. Mr. Benedict retired to his room to apply a warm washcloth to his aching head. The pizza arrived. The boys devoured it. Then they explored the motel, running through the hallways and shouting, incurring the wrath of an old man who called them "hooligans."

"Say, Dale," asked Rusty, "what's a hooligan?"

"It's what old guys say instead of Maynard."

They ran to the courtyard and peered at the empty pool. "Hey, they drained it already," said Dale.

"It's November, you know," said Kevin.

"We didn't bring our swimsuits anyway," said Chris.

"Beans!" shouted Rusty.

He jumped onto the concrete floor of the pool. The other three boys followed. A few dead leaves, some twigs, part of an old newspaper, and several hamburger wrappers lay near the drain. Rusty kicked at them.

"We have to go the FCA convention this afternoon, anyway," said Kevin, who as a junior demonstrated his usual farsightedness.

"Boring," said Rusty.

"That's why we came down here," said Chris.

"That's not why I came down here. I came down for the chow. The Rabbi promised to feed us a spread at Marco's."

Marco's was a fancy Dallas restaurant that Rusty had once eaten at with his family. It specialized in steaks and seafood. Rusty told Dale he'd eaten fourteen jumbo shrimp last time and that was three years ago. Now he could eat a lot more.

"Gee, that's awfully nice of Mr. Benedict," said Chris.

"Mr. Benedict is a nice man," said Kevin.

"Mr. Benedict is a S.O.B.," said Rusty. He paused as the boys looked with surprise at him. "S.O.B. Son of Blob."

The boys laughed.

"Do you know Mr. Benedict's first name?" asked Dale.

Rusty smiled. "Laughton." Then he spelled it so they wouldn't confuse it with the town in southwestern Oklahoma.

The boys tried to think of some way to make fun of the name. But it wasn't a funny name.

With that bit of unfunny information, the boys climbed out of the pool and headed back to their room. They put on ties and coats for the conference. Mr. Benedict didn't have to get back on the highway, so he drove without incident to the convention center. As they passed through Dealy Plaza, Mr. Benedict pointed out his side window.

"This is where President Kennedy was assassinated," he said solemnly.

Dale remembered that day. He'd been in first grade in Bishop, Texas. His dad had been stationed at nearby Kingsville Naval Air Station. Early in the afternoon, Dale noticed some of the adults were upset. His teacher, a young woman he thought pretty, cried. Later, at home, Dale asked Blackie why the president had been killed. Blackie said the president "knew too much." Blackie didn't explain, so Dale thought it must be dangerous to know too much. For a while, he tried not to learn too much in school, but he couldn't help himself.

"He was a great man," said Mr. Benedict.

Dale didn't say Blackie had a different opinion. In fact, once while drinking he'd said that Kennedy deserved what he got.

They arrived at the convention center and listened for three hours to athletes talking about how their faith made them better people and better athletes. Tomorrow, the boys would have to attend a non-denominational church service before going to the Cowboys game. Dale thought it was a fair trade. After the afternoon gathering, Mr. Benedict valiantly fought traffic as he drove to Marco's for dinner. Dale, who'd never been to many restaurants because Jesse didn't like going, was impressed. Marco's had big, comfortable booths with leather seats and wood-paneled walls. He thought it was too dark though. The boys had appetizers first, then feasted on chicken, ribs, and shrimp. Rusty won the shrimp-eating contest, gulping down twenty-one jumbo shrimp. He arranged the crustacean carcasses in a circle on the edge of his plate. Dale thought they looked like an exoskeleton necklace.

Pleasantly stuffed, the boys climbed in the car and Mr. Benedict drove back to the motel. In their room, the boys watched television. Rusty turned the dial and Dale, seeing the beginning of an old movie he remembered, told him to stop.

"This is a funny movie," he said.

"What is it?" asked Chris.

Dale wondered if Chris could watch movies on television. So far, Chris hadn't turned away.

"It's called *A Funny Thing Happened on the Way to the Forum*."

He saw it as a kid at the drive-in with his mother and sister. His mother didn't like it much but Dale thought it was funny, even though he didn't understand some of the grown-up mushy stuff.

The movie started with the comic title song. Rusty turned to Dale, his agile face showing approval. Then Zero Mostel appeared, his rotund body squeezed in a ridiculous orange tunic.

"Look, it's Mr. Benedict," observed Dale.

The boys laughed.

They laughed throughout the movie, amused by the antics of Mr. Benedict's look-a-like. Dale didn't think Mr. Benedict looked exactly like Zero Mostel. For one thing, the actor appeared much older and had a more agile face. And Zero Mostel didn't wear glasses. But otherwise, he and Mr. Benedict had a similar fat face, big nose, froggy eyes, and large mouth. And funniest of all, they both had the same flabby, blimpy body.

During one of the comical moments in the movie, with the boys convulsed in laughter, Mr. Benedict opened the door. As he stood in the doorway, Rusty turned and pointed, "hey, it's Zero!"

Rusty rolled off the bed in laughter. Dale followed. Chris and Kevin, less given to uncontrollable bouts of mirth, guffawed but didn't fall on the floor.

"Zero? What are you referring to? And what's so amusing, may I ask?"

Rusty rose to his feet and pointed at the television. "It's you. Or he's you. You're both Zeroes."

Mr. Benedict walked over to the television and peered at the screen. Zero Mostel made grotesque motions, distorting the features of his fat face and contorting his corpulent body to "converse" with the buxom Silent Woman. The boys found this scene hilarious, especially with a flesh-and-blood replica standing in their room.

Mr. Benedict studied the television and when he recognized his similarity to the star, he stiffened and gave them a reproving look.

"Very amusing."

"Hey, Zero, mind closing the door?" Rusty said.

"I'm leaving," said Mr. Benedict. "After the film I'll return to inform all of you about tomorrow's schedule.

"Sure thing, Zero," Rusty said.

"Okay, Zero," said Dale.

"You bet, Zero," said Chris.

Only Kevin didn't respond in kind. But he laughed.

Mr. Benedict turned and exited the room, shutting the door just a little too loudly.

Rusty turned to Dale and said he was right. This was a funny movie.


**Chapter 6:** *Dale learns about the deviousness of girls*

Dale sat in the scorer's box adding statistics. It was halftime of the Galilee varsity basketball game against Oilville. The Gophers led 28-21, and if they won this game they'd have a 7-9 record going into the last two weeks of the season. One of the reasons he decided to play basketball was because he liked Coach Carpenter. Dale thought he was a pretty good junior high football coach but he was even a better basketball coach. He'd taken a team with no player taller than six foot two and made it competitive.

Dale didn't suit up for the varsity. Instead he kept statistics along with Chris. Sitting in the scorer's box, they got an excellent view of the court. The only sophomores that suited up with the varsity were Rusty, Erickson, and Billy Joe. So far, they'd played a couple of minutes in the few lop-sided games Galilee had played.

Dale, waiting for Chris to get back with their Cokes, busily added the half-time totals. Bent over the stat book, he sensed someone hovering over him. He looked up and saw Wendy and Carmen Castro smiling at him.

"Hello, Audie," they both said at the same time.

Dale said hi.

They both were smiling their big girly smiles, showing all their teeth, their eyes bright and merry. They had that look he'd learned to recognize in girls: they had a secret and they were bursting to share it.

"Audie," said Wendy, trying not to smile so broadly, "has anyone asked you to the Gopherette banquet?"

The Gopherette banquet was the high school version of the junior high pep club's spring picnic, except that it took place around Valentine's day and the couples attended a fancy banquet. The girls had to ask the boys to it.

Dale shook his head. He was growing suspicious.

Wendy, still beaming, took a couple of steps to one side and gave Carmen an encouraging look. Carmen sidled over to be directly in front of Dale. No longer smiling broadly, she looked a little shy. Her dark eyes behind her cat's eye glasses didn't quite look directly at him.

"Would you like to go with me to the banquet?" she asked.

Dale hadn't expected to be asked by anyone. He noticed Carmen had a little mole not far from her lower lip. He rather liked that. He thought girls called such a mole a beauty mark.

"Sure. I guess."

Wendy moved closer to Carmen. "We thought the four of us could go to the banquet together."

Dale was confused. "The four?"

"I asked K. C.," said Wendy, who lowered her eyes, and Dale noticed she had some bluish gunk smeared on her eyelids. She raised her eyes and looked at him, her smile fading just a little. "He's going to drive us."

As with a motorcycle, K. C. had been the first boy to get a car. It was an old car but a cool one. A '65 Mustang convertible, cherry red, and in excellent condition or as K. C. had proclaimed himself, *mint*.

The girls explained the arrangement and giggled together. Then they said bye and Dale watched as they walked down toward the concession stand. Carmen was small and cute, with black hair worn in a sort of old-fashioned curly hairdo instead of straight and long like most of the girls. She'd been a cheerleader in ninth grade and would probably try out for the varsity squad next year. He thought she was nice, but quiet like he was. They probably hadn't exchanged more than a few sentences since grade school. He knew her family was Cuban. Her father worked as a mechanic at the Reinhardt trucking plaza. Her brother, Roberto, a year older, played guard on the football team. Dale liked him. He had good sense of humor and didn't razz the sophomores like most upperclassmen.

Watching Carmen walk away, Dale guessed she was probably a little over five feet tall. He wondered if the girls encouraged her to ask him because they matched up well. He knew that was how girls thought: arranging pairings like they were the matchmakers of high school society.

Chris returned with the two cups of Coke. He gave one to Dale and sat down.

"What did Wendy and Carmen want?"

Dale felt embarrassed. He didn't want to say. But Chris pressed him so he told. Dale asked Chris which girl had asked him.

"Peggy," he said.

Peggy Mullins. Some of the guys called her "Piggy" because she was chubby and had a turned-up nose. But she had blond hair and a sort of cute face. She talked a lot. Teachers often had to reprimand her for talking in class. She wasn't one of the popular girls, but she hung around with some of them and perhaps that's why she talked and gossiped so much. Dale didn't really like her, but he didn't tell Chris that.

"How are you going?" Dale asked. Chris had turned sixteen in December but he didn't have a car.

"I guess my father will have to drive us," Chris said, sounding like he regretted the whole deal already.

Chris then changed the subject. "Rusty told me you got a C in driver's ed."

Dale saw Chris trying to repress a smile.

"Yeah."

They all had gotten their grades over Christmas break. Rusty saw Dale's report card one day when he was in Dale's room. Of all the classes to get a C in, Rusty thought that was one of the funniest.

"How'd you manage to do that?"

Drivers' education was one of the easiest classes. Chris had taken driver's ed in the summer and got the usual A.

Dale tried to explain. First, he missed his night driving time and the teacher, Mr. Nash, wouldn't let him make it up. Dale had been in the first group and had simply forgot after football practice. But Mr. Nash had been adamant. No make-up. Dale got a zero. Knowing even a B was now mathematically impossible, he started goofing off in class. He'd deliberately cause wrecks and run over pedestrians when he drove the car simulation machine. He'd expected to get a F. But Nash gave him a C.

"He should have allowed you to make up the night driving," said Chris.

"Yeah. And later in the semester he let a girl make up her night driving time."

"That's unfair!"

Dale smiled. He liked Chris's sense of justice. "Yeah. Well, I think Nash doesn't like football players. Sonny and Billy Joe got B's."

The C in drivers ed still rankled Dale. Other than that, he'd done pretty well last semester. Three As and two Bs. He got A's in English, American history, and gym. B's in typing and biology. Like Rusty, he hardly ever studied. Most of the material was covered in class anyway and what wasn't Dale didn't worry about. In fact, instead of studying school subjects, he spent time reading books not covered in class. He'd read one book recently, The Psychology of the Adolescent that he'd checked out in the library. Some of the information that stuck in his mind was that most friendships were based on propinquity. That meant people tend to be friends with people that they share experiences with. Such a pragmatic definition bothered Dale, who'd always had a romantic view of friendship. But the more he thought about it, the idea made sense. He'd noticed that he and Rusty had drifted apart a little during football season. Dale and Chris, on the other hand, became good friends because of football. It wasn't only proximity, of course; friends tended to have a natural attraction to one another and share common interests and attitudes. But Dale reluctantly admitted that it was hard to stay good friends with someone who wasn't around.

The other memorable bit of information he found in the book had to do with girls. The book described puberty and he, of course, had firsthand knowledge about the male experience so he was interested in the female experience. Some of that stuff had been covered in biology, but this book described the process in more detail and discussed psychological factors as well. The information didn't make girls less mysterious to him. But he did think about them in a different way. He tried to imagine being a girl, for instance, and began to appreciate their complexity.

One the more interesting questions the book raised was the source of sexual attraction. Men, as Dale knew, tended to focus on how women look. They were especially attracted to women with small waists and large bosom and hips. Younger women tend to have a higher degree of fat on the hips, buttocks, thighs, and breasts and also had smaller waists and slenderer limbs than older women. All that made visual sense to Dale, of course, but the book said there didn't seem to be any biological advantage to this. That is, women with more curvaceous figures weren't necessarily more fertile. Men, however, on some instinctive level seemed to think they were. The authors concluded that nature was deceiving men. Dale thought back to the *Penthouse* he'd seen at Wally's last summer. So, had he been deceived?

The book referred to the fleshy parts of the girl's body as "fat pads." The term amused Dale and he told Rusty and Chris about it. He even told his sister about girls having fat pads but June May wasn't amused. "Are you calling me fat?" she'd asked in an offended tone.

Dale tried to explain that it was just a term a psychology book used about – and then he dropped it. He didn't want to tell his own sister about the specific areas of the female body that had fat pads on display.

The second half of the game was about to start, and Dale and Chris got ready. As they assembled their papers, they saw Roxanne Robideaux walking past the scorer's table. She wore her pep club outfit, and the tight red sweater and tight short white skirt clung alluringly to her curves. When she walked by her whole voluptuous body seemed to shimmy and shake. Dale looked at Chris who was still following her with his eyes.

"Nice fat pads," Dale said.

Chris, speechless, could only nod in agreement.


The backseat of K. C.'s Mustang was narrow. Dale sat close enough to Carmen that he could smell her perfume and feel the warmth of her body. They weren't touching though, and he tried to keep his legs not spread too far apart so his knee wouldn't knock into hers. Dale and Carmen hadn't said much to each other since he escorted her to the car. Both of them would glance at the other and start to say something, only to stop. It seemed as if their natural shyness only increased in each other's presence.

Wendy, on the other hand, couldn't stop blabbering. Sometimes she'd turn around in her bucket seat and talk directly to Dale and Carmen. At that moment, she was telling them about her little brother, Riley, only five years old, who had told her about his girlfriend in kindergarten.

"It was so cute," Wendy said. "He wanted to give her a crackerjack ring as an engagement present."

That didn't sound cute to Dale. A boy that age should hate girls, or at least pretend to. But instead of informing Wendy of this, he merely nodded.

"I thought Riley was six," said K. C.

He leaned back in the seat and steered with one hand. After six months of driving he already felt nonchalant about it.

"No, five," said Wendy. "Don't you remember? He was born when we were in fifth grade. Well, I remember. I would, of course. It's not every day your mother tells you she's pregnant."

Dale nodded. He shyly glanced at Carmen. She sat perfectly still and ladylike. When the hem of her green gown crept above mid-calf, she tugged it down an inch.

Wendy then proceeded to talk about her older brother, Denny. She said he'd started a new job as a contractor and was going to marry his high school sweetheart in June.

"You mean Shari?" asked Carmen.

"Yes, Shari," said Wendy.

Carmen said she remembered her. Wasn't she all-school queen? Wendy said yes, and Denny was all-school king. High school sweethearts and Galilee High royalty.

Dale remembered Denny Wainwright. He'd played quarterback on the team that went to the state playoffs. The same team with Robin Comingdeer. Denny was sort of a little guy, too. He must have weighed only 150 pounds. But he was tough. Those guys played only five years ago, but to Dale it was like a golden era. His memory had burnished that year into a nostalgic glow.

K. C. was thinking the same thing Dale was. "Wasn't your brother the quarterback –"

"On the team that went to the state playoffs," Wendy finished for him. "That's right!" She laughed. "It's funny how many people remember that."

"That's because it was the last good team Galilee had," said K. C.

"Oh, I bet you guys will have a good team next year," Wendy said with genuine enthusiasm. "Won't you, Audie?"

"Yeah, I think so," he said, and for a moment he caught Wendy looking at him with a strange attentiveness – like she was measuring the size of his nose.

"Oh, definitely," she said with her usual cheeriness.

She turned around. K. C. glanced into the rearview mirror at Dale. His expression looked as puzzled as Dale felt. Something odd seemed to be going on, but Dale wasn't sure what it was.

The banquet was held at Maxine's in northwest Oklahoma City. Dale had never heard of the place. But Wendy said it specialized in French cuisine. The only French food Dale had ever eaten was French fries and he supposed they really weren't French at all.

Two couples were seated together at round tables that displayed elegant white tablecloths and silver candleholders. A floral arrangement decorated each table. Dale and Carmen sat at a table with K. C. and Wendy. She continued to chatter. Dale and Carmen ate their dinner mostly in silence, exchanging shy smiles from time to time. Wendy talked about her classes, about her friends, and about the cheerleading tryouts that were coming up in the spring. She talked about her family. K. C., usually garrulous himself, smiled as Wendy continued her monologue. He still had long sideburns but he'd had to shave his mustache off for football. His shaggy reddish brown hair hung down to his eyebrows. When he smiled, Dale noticed the perfect rows of large, square teeth.

Dale glanced around the banquet hall. He saw Rusty sitting with Sadie at a nearby table. Rusty noticed him and winked. Bigelow and Mary Jane also sat at the table. Dale could hardly believe Mary Jane had asked Bigelow. But you never knew about girls. The four of them had arrived together, with Bigelow driving. His car wasn't as cool as K. C.'s. It was just an old Ford.

At the next table, he saw Sonny Schoendienst with Roxanne Robideaux and Billy Joe Barton with Gretchen Reinhardt. At another table, Wally sat with his date, Carrie Bacon. She was cute, with medium-length brown hair and glasses. Erickson and Merry Singleton were the second couple. In contrast to her name, Merry had a rather dull and stolid personality. She had long brown hair and big brown eyes, but not an especially pretty face because of a big nose. She reminded Dale a little of a cow. However, she did have the biggest breasts of any of the sophomore girls.

Dale looked for Amanda. He scanned the tables but couldn't find her in the sophomore section. He did locate Chris and Peggy. They were sitting with Leroy Lemmon and a girl named Louise Henderson. Louise, a brunette, was the tallest girl in Dale's class, almost six-foot tall and she had the longest hair of any girl in school except for Vern's sisters. Neither Chris nor Leroy looked especially happy. Dale shook his head in sympathy. These kinds of functions were designed to please the girls: new dresses, flowers, and the fancy food. Dale would have preferred to go on a picnic like the junior high kids did.

At the front of the banquet hall, a trio played soft instrumental music. The president of the pep club, a senior girl named Mildred Davis, who Dale didn't think very pretty, acted as hostess. She welcomed the guests, talked about things that Dale didn't care about, then let them alone to eat their fancy French dinners. He didn't know what the heck the main course was. It looked like some kind of little whole chicken. Wendy said it was a squab. Dale had never heard of it, but he ate it anyway and it tasted okay.

After dinner, Hank Henderson, older brother of Louise, was crowned Gopherette beau. Dale liked Henderson. He and Rusty called him Hindu because he had a birthmark shaped like a dot near the center of his forehead.

After the crowning, Hindu kissed Mildred and everyone clapped and the string trio played more music. Then a raffle of modest gifts took place. Dale had one winning ticket. After the banquet was over, he went up to the front and claimed his prize, a valentine's box of chocolates. While there, he saw Amanda. She stood next to a tall, handsome boy that Dale had never seen before. Amanda smiled as she talked to a pretty junior girl, Amy Mears, and her date, Kevin Stephenson. K. C. came up to Dale and asked what he'd won. Dale showed him the box of chocolates and then asked K. C. whom *that* guy was. He didn't refer to him as Amanda's date because it would suggest he was jealous. K. C. glanced over.

113

"That's Bobby Henshaw. He goes to Cimarron City."

Cimarron City was the largest high school in the City. It was located in the Northwest suburbs of Oklahoma City, so it wasn't that far from Galilee. Dale knew the Nazarene kids that went to Cimarron City also attended the First Church in Galilee. Dale supposed Henshaw was one of them.

"You know him?" Dale asked.

"Yeah. He goes to First Church."

Dale nodded and didn't ask any more questions. He didn't want K. C. to get suspicious of why he was interested in Henshaw. The two boys went back to their table and escorted the girls back to K. C.'s car. On the drive back, Dale managed to ask Carmen how she liked the banquet. She said she enjoyed it. Wendy talked about the music, the decorations, and the dresses the other girls wore, and often turned around in her seat and asked Dale what he thought of her observations. Usually he just shrugged; he didn't have much of an opinion about decorations or dresses.

K. C. drove to Carmen's house first. It was a modest white clapboard house only about five blocks away from Wendy's. Dale walked Carmen to the door. He stood five feet away as she opened her door. Carmen said she enjoyed going with him to the banquet. He nodded. She seemed to be waiting for something. Dale glanced back at K. C. and Wendy to see if they were watching. They were. He didn't want to kiss Carmen in front of them. Actually, he didn't know how to go about kissing a girl at all. Instead, he nodded at her again and said good night and all but ran off her porch.

Back in the car, Dale sank in his seat and wondered if he should have tried kissing Carmen. He wasn't sure what you did first. It looked easy in the movies. But on her porch he felt like nothing worked right. His arms felt heavy; his feet felt stuck in place; the idea of moving toward her and putting his hands on her and actually putting his mouth against hers seemed like such an advanced act that he'd need months of training before he could attempt it.

K. C. and Wendy made small talk as he drove to Wendy's home. Dale caught Wendy looking at him in the rearview mirror. At least, he thought he did. Her eyes flickered away as soon as his met her reflected gaze in the mirror. He almost blushed. He was certain she was spying on him because he'd acted so oddly with Carmen.

K. C. put the car in park as he took Wendy to her front door. Dale peeked out of the window. Maybe he could learn something from K. C. After all, he was reputed to be quite the ladies' man. But to Dale's surprise, Wendy smiled, thanked him, and quickly disappeared into her home. K. C. stood abjectly on her porch for a few seconds, then turned and moped his way back to the car.

Dale got in front as K. C. drove back to his house where Dale had parked his cycle. They didn't say anything for a few blocks. Then K. C. shook his head and said he didn't get it.

"Get what?" asked Dale.

"Wendy."

"What about her?"

"I don't get why she asked me to that stupid banquet if she doesn't like me."

Dale considered the question. Of course, he couldn't figure girls out at all, so there wasn't much reason to ask him.

"She must like you."

"Then why didn't she talk to me?"

"She did. She did a lot of talking."

"She did a lot of talking, but not to *me*," said K. C. Driving with one hand again, he rubbed his chin in thought. "Maybe it was a setup."

Dale thought that sounded interesting. "A setup? Like a trap?"

"Yeah," said K. C., liking that word better. "A trap."

"Why was she trying to trap you?"

"Not me, my friend. You."

Dale didn't understand. "Whattaya mean?"

"Why did Wendy want the four of us to go together? Why was she talking to you so much? Why was she looking at you so much, making sure you noticed *her*?"

"Beats me," said Dale.

"Because if the four of us went together, in a sense you'd be going with her."

"Then why didn't Wendy ask me instead of you?"

"That's the trick," said K. C. "She doesn't want to be so direct. If she asked you herself, you'd know how she felt. She wants you to like her before she likes you. Get it?"

Dale was starting to. But he thought it all sounded unnecessarily complicated. And worse, were girls so devious?

Before Dale could object to K. C.'s theory, they arrived at the Cash residence, an attractive brick house. As they got out of the car, K. C. noticed something and reached into the back seat. He retrieved the box of chocolates and gave it to Dale.

"You know, you were supposed to give this to Carmen."

Dale took the box. Suddenly, it made sense to him. He wondered if Carmen thought him a complete Maynard.

"Man," K. C. said, with a big smile. "You've got a lot to learn about girls."

Didn't Dale know it.

**Chapter 7: *An exchange with Comingdeer; talking to Earl at Bible study***

Dale stood at the back line of the court and readied himself. Coach Carpenter blew the whistle. Dale lunged forward, sprinting to the free throw line, then quickly pivoted and raced back to the back line. Another pivot and on to the half-court line, then back again. Finally to the other end of the court and back. As he crossed the back line, he saw in his peripheral vision that he was a few feet ahead of two upperclassmen Terry Harte and Glen Dennison.

Dale leaned against the brick wall and gasped for air. He wasn't much of a basketball player, but he ran shuttles faster than anybody.

He put his hands on top of his head and paced. He breathed deeply through his nose and felt sweat coursing down his face, soaking his jersey. The warm gym smelled musty and old and he liked that smell as it mingled with the odor of his and his teammates' sweat.

Basketball season was nearly at an end. The team finished the regular season at 9-11, three games better than last year. The varsity still had to play in the district tournament and there was a small chance that they might win it. They'd split with Agra and Lyons during the regular season, but they'd lost two close games to Oilville. If the varsity played well, they might win the district tournament for the first time in six years.

The junior varsity's season was over and they'd done almost as well, finishing 7-9. Rusty had led all scorers, averaging almost seventeen points a game. Erickson and Billy Joe also averaged in double figures and Sonny led in assists. Dale played in most of the games as a substitute and even scored in seven games. He still felt awkward on the court but most of the JV games were sparsely attended so he felt less self-conscious. He'd gained some composure with experience, but best of all basketball practice had helped strengthen his right leg. He still ran a little unbalanced; his stronger left leg made it difficult for his right leg to precisely keep pace. But his knee and ankle no longer swelled up. Dale thought he'd made the right decision to play basketball rather than join Dorfman's weight and conditioning class.

Coach Carpenter summoned the team together and gave a short pep talk in preparation for the district tournament tomorrow. Then he dismissed the team and they walked down to the lockers. On the way, Comingdeer brushed against Dale and gave him a scornful look. Dale matched Comingdeer's stare.

"You know," Dale said, "you better get used to having me around. I'm going out for baseball again."

Comingdeer wasn't used to sophomores mouthing off. His dark eyes stared at Dale for a few seconds, then he said, "make sure you stay out of my way."

Dale watched him descend the stairs into the locker room and turned to Rusty and Chris, who had been watching.

"I don't think he likes me," Dale said with mock concern.

"That's too bad," said Rusty. "You two would make such an attractive couple."

Chris and Rusty laughed and the three of them walked down the short stairway to the high school locker room. Inside, Dale heard Mr. Benedict's voice from the coach's office. He followed Rusty as he headed there. They found Mr. Benedict sitting in Coach Carpenter's chair, his belly more pronounced with his slumping posture.

"Better not let Coach catch you in his chair," said Rusty.

Mr. Benedict immediately pulled himself out of the chair, but so quickly that he knew he looked ridiculous. Before he was completely on his feet, he slowed himself and almost fell back in the chair. Dale and Rusty chuckled at his awkwardness.

"I'll have you know that Coach doesn't mind," Mr. Benedict said.

"Then why'd you jump up so fast?" Rusty asked.

Mr. Benedict chose to ignore the question. "Where is Coach Carpenter? I have important information to convey."

"I bet you do," said Rusty.

"Indeed I do," Mr. Benedict said.

He acted as something of an unofficial factotum for Coach Carpenter. Mr. Benedict wasn't remotely qualified to be an assistant coach but he was willing to perform useful non-athletic tasks to assist the coach.

Rusty walked over to the grill wall that separated the coach's office from the rest of the locker room. The grill had small diamond-shaped holes in it. Rusty put a couple fingers through the grill and turned to Mr. Benedict.

"I don't think I'm coming over tonight."

Mr. Benedict looked displeased. "And why is that?"

Rusty and Dale heard Coach Carpenter's deep voice echoing in the stairway. They started to leave the office.

"Just joking," said Rusty. "I'll be there. After all, I need all the spiritual guidance I can get."

Dale and Rusty walked back into the locker room. They saw Chris standing at his locker. Dale asked him if he was going over to Mr. Benedict's for the weekly Bible study. It was something that Mr. Benedict had started during basketball season. Rusty, Dale, Stephenson, Middleton, and a few other guys went over to his apartment on Thursday nights for the Bible study, but they ended up listening to Mr. Benedict's records and eating his food more than studying.

"No," said Chris. "I got to study for a geometry exam."

Unlike Dale and Rusty, Chris studied. He made okay grades but not better than Dale and Rusty.

Dale glanced over at Erickson, who sat on the bench before his locker in his practice uniform waiting for the upperclassmen to get out of the shower. Rusty sat down next to him and told Rich that he'd talk to "Zero" – that was what he was calling Mr. Benedict now – about Rich being allowed to come to the Bible study again. Mr. Benedict had kicked Erickson out of his apartment at the very first meeting.

Dale thought Erickson didn't like Mr. Benedict. Erickson hadn't joined FCA and he looked bored in history class. He also had his driver's license and didn't need Mr. Benedict's chauffeur services.

Erickson said he had better things to do than go to Benedict's and Rusty shrugged. Then Rusty, Dale, Chris, and Erickson undressed and went into the shower. Sonny, Billy Joe and Wally were already there. Shower etiquette was about the same in high school as junior high. Upperclassmen showered first. All the guys had learned how to shower quickly and efficiently and keep their field of vision above the waist. Dale didn't know if this behavior was learned or instinctive. But he, like the other boys, had employed it from the first. It was as if they never really focused on each other, although sometimes by accident he did notice something personal about the other guys. For example, last year with an unintentional glance, he'd noticed that Billy Joe wasn't circumcised. Back in ninth grade, Dale didn't know he was "uncircumcised;" he'd just thought poor Billy Joe was deformed.

As Dale rinsed the soap off, he wondered if girls practiced the same kind of decorum in their locker room. The girls' lockers were on the other side of the gym and were strictly off-limits. He remembered Sonny and Bigelow back in junior high kneeling down and peering into the heating vents on the outside of the building, thinking they might get a peek. They saw nothing but a brick wall, but guys would occasionally try just the same, hoping no doubt that someday the walls of Jericho would come tumbling down.

Dale and Rusty quickly dressed and walked outside into the mild evening air. Chris said so long. He was getting a ride home with his older sister, who stayed late on Thursdays for some club activity. Erickson and Wally took off, too. Dale and Rusty got on their cycles and drove to their homes. Dale turned off first and waved as Rusty motored seven more blocks north.

Dale parked his cycle in the driveway, noticing that his dad's car wasn't there. Blackie was taking four classes a week in the spring semester, so he just had time to change before driving to the City. The only time Dale saw his dad was during the weekend, but even then Blackie kept busy studying during the day and drinking at night. Dale thought it sort of odd that his father studied more than he did.

Dale had supper with his mother and sister and while they ate, June May talked about all the exciting things happening in seventh grade. He hardly listened; June May seemed to have adjusted to junior high a lot easier than he had. She didn't have his almost morbid shyness for one thing. She had lots of friends, socialized, and didn't have to worry about getting "racked" like Dale had when he was in seventh grade. Getting racked was a sadistic game some of the boys played. They would pass a victim and slap at his groin with the back of their hand. If they hit him just right, the kid would crumple because they had "racked his balls." This vicious game went on for weeks until the infamous "Something Maynard" tried to rack Billy Joe Barton and Billy Joe beat him to a pulp.

Dale decided not to relate this bit of history to his sister and mother, but he remembered it without any fondness. He'd been racked a couple of times and the memory still made him wince.

Even though Jesse wasn't much of a cook, Dale ravenously ate everything on his plate – pork chops, fried potatoes, carrots, and two pieces of white bread – along with half of June May's dinner. As a little kid, June May usually had second helpings, but since succeeding to the seventh grade she had cut that out, now concerned about her figure. Dale liked to say, "what figure?" when she used that as an excuse not to finish the food on her plate, but in fact she was developing a shape along the Roxanne Robideaux line.

After spending an hour in his room reading one of his non-school books, a book about sleep and dreams, Dale emerged into the living room and told Jesse he was going over to Rusty's. Dale hadn't told Jesse about the Bible study at Mr. Benedict's. He didn't want to mention the Bible to Jesse for a while. So far, she'd shown no sign of wanting to return to the Jehovah's Witnesses and he didn't want to remind her of anything religious. Dale also hadn't mentioned Mr. Benedict. He didn't know what Jesse would think about a grown man spending so much time with fifteen and sixteen-year-old boys. Dale sometimes wondered about that, too. But Mr. Benedict served a purpose as both an object of ridicule and as a source of food and transportation.

Dale found Jesse sitting on the couch smoking a cigarette. If some sculptor had wanted to capture the essence of Jesse in stone, he would have picked that pose: her short legs not quiet touching the carpeted floor, her right hand holding a lighted cigarette, her mouth distorted as she blew a plume of smoke.

"I'm leaving, Mom," he said, checking the TV to see what she was watching. It looked like the syndicated rerun of *Perry Mason*.

"All right," she said, her eyes focused on the television screen.

Dale noticed cigarette butts and ashes filled the ashtray on the coffee table.

"You're smoking too much," he told her.

Jesse nodded, then took a long draught on her present cigarette.

"I'll be back around ten," he said as he walked out of the room. He heard Jesse say, "be careful" as he shut the door.

Dale rode his motorcycle south, past the high school, the college, and downtown, and then turned east and rode another five blocks. Mr. Benedict lived in the Wildewood Apartments and Dale thought he had a pretty nice place. His apartment stood on the third floor and it had a terrace and a clear view. One could see the lights of Oklahoma City from the terrace.

Dale knocked on the door and Mr. Benedict opened it and said, "welcome, sir," as he always did with a passable British accent. Dale didn't know if he was pretending to be a butler or a lord, but either way it was an odd thing to do deep in the heart of Oklahoma.

Dale breezed in and saw Rusty and Kevin Stephenson, holding hot dogs, sitting on the floor next to the stereo, while going through albums. Their numbers were dwindling. Chris had attended a couple of meetings. but his parents didn't like him going out on school nights except to a real church. K. C. sometimes came. Wally had been over a few times. Erickson had come only that one time. Usually Kevin's friend, Tim Middleton, came with him. But since Dale was a little late, he guessed Middleton wasn't coming either.

Just the four of them seemed a little too cozy, but Dale joined Rusty and Kevin. Mr. Benedict had dozens of albums, some of them from the '60s that Dale especially liked: The Association, the Mamas and the Papas, the Four Seasons, and the Beatles. Rusty preferred the contemporary albums like Credence, Sly and the Family Stone, Nilsson, and Neil Young. Rusty especially liked imitating Neil Young. He had a similar look, so when he played "Heart of Gold" he'd creakily stand up like an old cowpoke and howl in the same kind of whiny voice as Neil Young. Everyone laughed, especially Mr. Benedict.

"Hey, look at this," Rusty said.

While munching on a hot dog, he held up the Frank Zappa and the Mothers of Invention album, *Uncle Meat*, which Erickson had brought over several weeks ago. After hearing a spoken obscenity, Mr. Benedict had forbidden the record to be played. Erickson kept playing it anyway and then Mr. Benedict snatched it off the turntable. They'd argued and Mr. Benedict kicked out Erickson. In his angry departure, Erickson had forgotten to take the taboo album with him.

"Let's play it," Rusty said with a sly smile.

Dale nodded, but Kevin, who unfortunately displayed signs of maturity on occasion, shook his head no. Rusty ignored him, and put it on the turntable as Mr. Benedict asked them what they wanted to drink.

The boys called out their orders and Rusty waited, his hand poised with the stylus above the revolving record. Just as Mr. Benedict came out of the kitchenette with the soft drinks on the tray, Rusty dropped the needle. A pop, a hiss, and then "Electric Aunt Jemima" boomed into the room. Mr. Benedict jerked at the loud music, and when he recognized the song, he jerked some more. He sloshed Coke and root beer from the glasses, and two of the half-empty cans toppled to the floor.

"Beans!" he cried.

He looked in horror at the soda oozing out of the spilled cans onto his pinkish shag rug. He quickly slid the tray onto the table and reached for a towel to mop up the mess. As he kneeled, dabbing at the carpet, he shouted:

"Turn that off, Rusty! I told you never to play that vile record in this apartment."

Rusty laughed. He turned the volume up.

Mr. Benedict stood and walked over to the turntable. For a moment, Dale thought Mr. Benedict, his chubby face red with vexation, might smash the record. He held a fist above it. Then he relaxed the fist and reached his hand down and tried to pick up the stylus. Unfortunately, he executed the attempt with his customary clumsiness and the needle squawked loudly as it scratched the record before being lifted off.

"Hey, careful there, Mr. Zero," Rusty said.

Rusty had stopped calling Mr. Benedict "Rabbi." Now he preferred to use the moniker "Mr. Zero," or just plain "Zero," or, for variety, "Son of Blob."

"Did you bring this criminal record?" Mr. Benedict said, holding up the *Uncle Meat* album.

"No," Rusty said. "It was already here." He stood and went over to the table for his glass of root beer. He took a sip, then turned dramatically and pointed at Mr. Benedict. "Indeed, sir, it is *you* who have committed the crime!"

"What are you talking about?" replied Mr. Benedict, clearly offended by the word "crime."

"I mean that it was you who stole the record from the innocent Erickson," Rusty continued with the exaggerated air of a television show prosecutor. "No doubt to play it in the privacy of your abode and to engage in all sorts of deviant practices."

Mr. Benedict grew visibly disturbed. He pushed out his fat lips, his froggy eyes behind spectacles bulged out, and his corpulent body stiffened so much that his belly shook.

"Stop this!" he cried. "Stop this asinine charade!"

Dale, enjoying the spectacle, glanced at Kevin. He didn't seem to be enjoying it as much.

"Tell me, Mr. Zero," continued Rusty in the same theatrical manner, "how many times a day do you listen to this deviant record?"

"Stop saying that," said Mr. Benedict.

"Ten, fifteen, twenty times? Do you even forsake nourishment and repose in order to memorize this depraved recording?"

"Stop it, Rusty. I mean it," said Mr. Benedict. His voice wavered between a command and a whine.

Rusty, who easily grew bored, suddenly stopped. He resumed his normal demeanor and picked up his glass of root beer.

"Oh, quit blubbering," he said, taking a drink. "Can't you take a joke?"

"May I remind you that this is supposed to be a Bible study group, not a …" Mr. Benedict searched for the word.

"A comedy group?" interjected Dale.

Mr. Benedict frowned. "That's enough. Now, fellows, business before pleasure. Let's commence with the Bible study."

Dale and Kevin got up, grabbed their drinks, and sat on the couch while Rusty sat at the dining table and Mr. Benedict sat in a chair next to the table. He picked up his Bible and noticed that none of the three boys had theirs.

"What now?" he asked. "Did all three of you forget?"

All three nodded.

"Very well. Then I'll read a short passage and then we can all discuss it. You'll have to listen carefully since you can't follow along."

Mr. Benedict read I Corinthians 13. Dale knew the verses, and half listened as he thought about Mr. Benedict trying to get him to attend the youth Sunday School service he led.

Dale didn't have anything against going to church. In spite of his rejection of the Jehovah's Witnesses ways, he still believed in God and didn't object to church. He just didn't think he wanted to go the First Church. It was so big and so many people went there that he knew he'd feel self-conscious. Amanda and her family went there, and although he was tempted to go just to see her, he knew he'd feel ashamed that his family wasn't with him.

Then when Mr. Benedict read the fourth verse, Dale listened more closely: "Love suffereth long, and is kind; love envieth not; love vaunteth not itself up, is not puffed up," and Dale thought of Amanda. He decided he'd do all those things for her. He would bear all things, believe all things, hope and endure all things.

Mr. Benedict finished the passage and asked what they thought. Kevin said that it meant if we didn't love one another, all our other deeds would mean nothing.

"Very good," said Mr. Benedict. "So we should always love one another, shouldn't we?"

"Yes," Kevin said.

Rusty, who had just finished drinking his root beer, burped.

Mr. Benedict glared at him.

"What about forgiveness?" Rusty said, smiling. "Isn't that part of love?"

Mr. Benedict grew milder. "Yes, it is."

"But what kind of love?" asked Dale.

Mr. Benedict frowned at him. "What do you mean, Audie?"

Dale couldn't remember the names for the different kinds of love. He'd read somewhere that there were Greek words that described different kinds of love. As he thought about it, he remembered one of the words, *eros*. That meant romantic love. There were also words for love for God and love for friends.

"I mean there's different kinds of love. Is Paul talking about love for God or love for people? Or does he mean, you know, mushy love?"

"Well, Audie," Mr. Benedict mused, "I would think he means all kinds of love."

Dale didn't think so. Like so much of the Bible, he thought there was more to it than what was taught in Sunday school or the meetings at the Kingdom Hall. He started to say so, when Rusty suddenly hurled his lanky body over the couch and fell on top of him. The two of them grappled for a few seconds while Mr. Benedict told them to behave. Finally, Rusty disengaged himself and toppled to the floor. He laughed while Mr. Benedict continued berating him. Then Rusty's smile faded. He squinted his eyes and made a face and rolled over on his belly and moaned.

"I don't feel so good," he said lowly.

Mr. Benedict, alarmed, toddled over to him and knelt down. "What's wrong?" he asked. 'Tell me, what's wrong?"

"I feel sick," Rusty groaned. "I think I'm going to throw up."

Rusty stumbled to his feet, his face contorted, his hands flailing for the now standing Mr. Benedict. He threw his hands over the shoulders of the shocked Mr. Benedict and started making awful hacking sounds.

"Uck, uck, uck," Rusty barked, then moaned, "I'm going to puke, Mr. Benedict. Help me, help me!"

Mr. Benedict tried in vain to free himself from the slumping Rusty. His chubby hands grabbed hold of Rusty's arms and tried to pry them away.

"No, Rusty, not here. Go to the bathroom!"

"Uck, uck," Rusty responded, then moaned, "I can't make it, Mr. Zero. I'm gonna barf right on your shirt."

Kevin jumped up and tried to assist Mr. Benedict in removing Rusty. But Dale remained seated, grinning, waiting for the payoff.

Rusty made a loud "blaaaugh" sound and Mr. Benedict howled in horror, his pudgy face pale as if he were the one sick, and threw his arms back in a vain attempt to escape.

Nothing came out of Rusty's mouth except a loud, raucous laugh. Rusty broke free and pointed a finger at Mr. Benedict.

"You ought to see your face," he managed to speak between guffaws.

Mr. Benedict looked down at his still immaculate white shirt. Then he turned his pale and terrified face to Rusty, who now stood bent over at the waist howling with laughter. Dale laughed too; Mr. Benedict's face looked goofier than any face created by the real Zero. Even Kevin laughed, although he shook his head in disapproval.

"This is not funny," said Mr. Benedict. He tried to regain his dignified bearing. "This is not at all amusing, Rusty."

Rusty's laughter abruptly stopped and his mouth grew slack. He grabbed his belly and moaned.

"What? An encore performance!" cried Mr. Benedict. "Really, Rusty, don't you think you're overdoing it?"

Rusty shook his head. Dale thought he really did look in distress.

"I'm not joking this time," Rusty croaked. "I feel crummy. Really crummy." Rusty's body jerked in a pre-heave. He covered his mouth with a hand. "I'm going to earp for real this time."

Rusty dashed out of the room and moments later they heard him vomiting in the bathroom. One loud "blaaaugh," then a quieter one. Dale looked at Kevin, who frowned at the unpleasant sound. Mr. Benedict had a sickly look on his chubby face as if he might throw up himself.

They heard a flush, then Rusty walked into the living room, looking almost normal except he was pale and subdued. He flopped down on the couch and wiped his forehead.

"Man, I really talked to Earl then."

Talking to Earl was a phrase Rusty, Dale, and a few friends used to describe vomiting. Dale wasn't exactly sure of its derivation. He thought some kid had thrown up on another kid named Earl back in grade school, hence "talking to Earl." Dale thought he remembered the sick kid turning to Earl as if to speak and then "blaaaugh!" That was possible, thought Dale. He'd thrown up once in first grade. One minute feeling fine, the next hurling sick onto his desk.

Dale noticed that Mr. Benedict seemed close to talking to Earl himself. He stood unsteadily on his portly legs, his face pale and sweating. Rusty noticed, too.

"Boy, I really tossed my cookies. I really blew chunks. I really vomited my guts –"

Suddenly, Mr. Benedict started a pre-heave and his blanched face contorted itself into an awful sick mask. He lumbered out of the room and next they heard an unearthly high-pitched wail followed by the sound of splattering vomit.

"Beans!" They heard Mr. Benedict cry. "I missed the bowl!"

The three of them, even the still recuperating Rusty, howled with laughter.

Rusty rolled over on the couch, laughing until tears came to his eyes. He looked at Dale, who was in a similar state of hilarity.

"Man," Rusty said, "don't you just love Bible study?"


## Chapter 8: *Parallel parking, dangling hands, and mopping up*

A few days after Dale's sixteenth birthday, Blackie took off work and drove him to the Licensing Bureau to get his driver's license. He easily passed the written test. He'd expected he'd do just as well on the driving part, but when he tried to parallel park he misjudged the distance to the curb and bumped into it. Dale grew angry. He wanted to do perfectly. He hit the steering wheel with his fist and the examiner, a middle-aged policeman named Booker said, "that's enough."

"What?" Dale asked.

Booker told him to return to the parking lot. Dale started to protest, but the cop's determined look silenced him. After he parked, he asked Booker if he'd passed.

"Of course not. You have to learn to control your temper if you want to be behind the wheel, young man."

The cop left and a few minutes later, Blackie arrived. He told Dale to move over. He got in and started the car.

"The officer told me what happened," Blackie said grimly.

"He didn't let me even try again."

"That's because you lost your temper. What's wrong with you?"

Dale didn't exactly know. He'd always had a bad temper about things he cared about. When he was little, he and his dad were watching the Dallas Cowboys lose to the Green Bay Packers over at Grandpa Walsh's house. That was the second time Dale remembered Jesse getting sick. Blackie had taken emergency leave. Dale and his father watched as the Packers won the NFL championship in the last seconds when Bart Starr snuck in from the six-inch line on a field frozen solid by sub-zero temperatures. Dale threw a fit. He remembered rolling around the floor, banging it with his fists, and even bawling. He couldn't help it. He wanted the Cowboys to win so badly. They'd lost the title game the year before to the Packers in the closing seconds in Dallas. The '67 loss had been too much to bear.

Another time, while playing little league baseball, Dale struck out during his first time at bat. He'd been counting on having a perfect game, but the strikeout ruined that plan. The next two times he came to bat after that he deliberately struck out just to punish himself. In a game later that year, he got so mad when he struck out that he threw his bat and helmet. The umpire kicked him out of the game.

During the last few years, he'd become better at controlling his temper. But when he failed at something he cared about he still became irate.

He sulked all the way home. He'd missed morning classes to take his driver's test and now he'd have to return to school without a license.

Blackie pulled into the driveway and before he turned off the engine, Dale bolted from the car and slammed the door shut. Before he knew it, Blackie was in his face yelling at him.

"You better watch yourself, Audie Dale," his father warned.

"Who's going to make me?" Dale snapped back.

Blackie grabbed him by his shirt collar. Dale grabbed his father's hands and tried to throw them off, but Blackie tightened his grip and shook him.

"Don't smart mouth me, boy, or I'll kick your ass."

"Let go," Dale said, but he'd lost his bravado. He was still a little afraid of his father. Blackie had never hit him with his fists, but he'd slapped him with the back of his hand once when Dale was around ten.

Blackie released his collar and stared at him. Dale avoided his dark, angry eyes. He stood motionless in the driveway, trying not to cry. When he felt like that, he thought of something physical and hard. Dale thought of his favorite car, an Oldsmobile Cutlass, and driving it as fast as it would go. That annoying emotion faded.

"All right," Blackie said, his voice no longer threatening. "I got to go to work."

Dale nodded. He raised his eyes and saw Blackie looking at him strangely. His face seemed to show faint signs of pain, as if he had a bad toothache but didn't want to admit it.

Blackie turned and walked into the house. Instead of following his father, Dale opened the garage and took out his cycle. He kick-started it and peeled out of the driveway, leaving a skid mark.

As he drove, Dale calmed down. He drove north to the edge of town, to a pasture where Vern kept his horse stabled. He parked on the side of a gully and looked for Smoky. He saw him, a gray gelding, running with a couple of other horses. Dale looked at the sky. Dark clouds were massing at the northern horizon. He smelled the approaching rain. The clouds didn't look too threatening; no towering thunderheads.

Dale remembered how angry he felt when Blackie grabbed him by the collar. For a moment, he thought he might punch his father. He wondered what would have happened if he had. He guessed Blackie really would have kicked his ass.

He smiled and drove home before the rain came.

The next day at school, Rusty asked Dale why he hadn't been in class yesterday. Dale lied and said he'd been sick. He doubted that Rusty believed him, but before Rusty could pursue the matter he stopped short.

"Look," Rusty said, pointing down the hall. Dale looked and saw Mr. Benedict standing outside his class talking to Mrs. Page.

"So?" Dale replied.

"Look at Benny's hand." They had taken to calling Mr. Benedict "Benny."

Dale noticed that Mr. Benedict's right hand, covered in a bandage, hung at an odd angle.

"He must have hurt it," said Dale.

"Yeah, but he's still holding it weird."

Actually, Dale had always thought Mr. Benedict held his hands weirdly. Unlike most guys, he didn't let them hang loosely at his sides. Instead he clasped them together or put them on his waist. Dale also thought that Mr. Benedict had an odd way of moving in general. It wasn't awkwardness; in fact, just the opposite. He seemed to move, in spite of his bulk, with a kind of finesse. It was only when he tried acting like a tough guy that he grew awkward.

"Well, Benny *is* weird," said Dale, and that made Rusty laugh and the two of them continued on to Mr. Benedict's history class.

Things hadn't been going well in Mr. Benedict's American history class of late. Perhaps Dale and Rusty had been unduly influenced by Erickson's contemptuous attitude, or perhaps they could no longer keep the teasing and taunting strictly outside class as the once had, but whatever the reason the class had grown tense the last few weeks. Dale recognized the uncomfortable feeling of tension. He felt it often at home. The friction between Blackie and Jesse slowly increased until it provoked a fight. Dale felt the same kind of tension building in Mr. Benedict's class.

Dale was annoyed with Mr. Benedict for a valid reason. A few weeks ago, the class wrote a paper in response to watching the movie *Fail Safe*. Mr. Benedict wanted the kids to pretend they were the President like Henry Fonda. What would they have done if a B-52 bomber got through Russian air defense and dropped a nuke on Moscow?

Dale wrote that he would have done what the Walter Matthau character recommended: blown Russia to hell. Dale knew Blackie would have approved, but he had his own reasons. Mostly, he did it to be contrary. He knew what the "right" answer was: do what Henry Fonda did and regretfully but nobly obliterate New York City. But the more Dale thought about the decision, the more he questioned it. So, from a contrarian impulse to bug Benny, he'd progressed to wondering if the conventional response really made sense. How could a president actually kill millions of his own people, even if they were being sacrificed for world peace? Maybe Dale would have been less skeptical if the president's friend hadn't been asked to pilot the plane with the bomb in it and drop it on New York City, knowing the pilot's wife and kids were there. Even the president's wife was in New York City, so she'd be vaporized, too. The movie's preachiness annoyed Dale. And he didn't like being expected to regurgitate the same kind of sanctimoniousness for a class paper.

Mr. Benedict, predictably, wasn't amused with Dale's paper. He accused him of not being serious and gave him a D. Apparently, everyone else in class, even Rusty and Erickson, had written that Henry Fonda did the noble thing.

Now, sitting in class, Dale was still peeved at his poor grade. Mr. Benedict had said he could write his paper over for a better grade, but he resented being pressured into accepting the status quo.

Class started and Mr. Benedict launched into the history of the cold war. Dale glanced over at Erickson and saw him slumped in his seat, his expression showing utter boredom. Then Dale looked at Rusty who sat attentively listening to Mr. Benedict. In fact, Dale thought Rusty looked like he was regarding Mr. Benedict with awe – a most unusual expression. Rusty held his mouth slightly agape. He narrowed his eyes in concentration. He nodded his head solemnly with each sentence Mr. Benedict uttered. And then Dale looked from Rusty's face to his desk, where he saw his right elbow propped on the desk and his hand dangling at the wrist.

Dale smiled and rested his elbow in the same manner, the hand hanging loose at the wrist. Then Erickson delightedly did the same. Dale imagined the three of them sitting all in a row in the back with their limp-wristed right hands.

Mr. Benedict noticed and he didn't like it. As he lectured, he tried not to stare at the three of them. Finally, Mr. Benedict could stand it no longer. He stopped speaking and glared, prompting several students in the front rows to turn and look back at them. Mr. Benedict was about to reprimand them, but he'd already caused too much interest to be directed their way. He didn't want the whole class to see the three rebellious students mocking him. Mr. Benedict pursed his lips, contained himself, and continued his lecture. When class was over, he confronted the three of them as they left the room.

"I want you to stop doing that," he hissed at Rusty.

"Doing what?"

"You know perfectly well what."

"I have no idea what you are referring to," Rusty replied, using his pompous Mr. Benedict voice.

"Yes, you do." Mr. Benedict paused, waiting for one of them to acknowledge their rude behavior. But all three feigned complete innocence. "The *hands*," he whispered angrily.

"The hands?" Rusty replied, saying the word innocently but rather loudly. Mr. Benedict glanced nervously around as if Rusty had uttered a naughty word.

"Yes, stop doing that."

"Doing what?"

"You know perfectly well what. Quit holding your hands like that."

"Like what?"

"Dangling them!" Mr. Benedict said the words so loudly and angrily that kids walking by stared at him.

"Man, what are you talking about?" Rusty replied, turning his hands up in wonderment. "Hey, we got to split, Benny."

"And quit calling me Benny," hissed Mr. Benedict.

"First hands and now Benny," said Rusty. "Well, we got to go now, *Mister* Benedict. We got a baseball game this afternoon."

As they walked out of class, Dale heard Mr. Benedict say, "I'm warning you, boys ..."

Dale joined Rusty and Erickson in laughter as they left Mr. Benedict fuming at his classroom door. But Dale wondered if they were going too far. They'd made Mr. Benedict angry in class before, but he always got over it by the time they next saw him. However, something in his agitated voice suggested he might not get over it this time.

The game against Quanah Parker High did not go well and Dale wondered if Mr. Benedict had hexed them. For the first time this season, they were losing by a big margin, 7-3, and with no one out and two men on base in the top of the seventh inning, Coach Blocker decided it was time to take Rusty, today's pitcher, out.

Dale stood at his second base position. He started at second unless Comingdeer pitched, and then he moved to shortstop. So far this year, he'd been doing all right. He was hitting .282 and had stolen nine bases in ten games. Galilee's record of 4-6 was still a losing one, but they had played a lot better than last year. In their last game, Galilee had beaten Lyons, 4-3 in dramatic fashion. With two out in the seventh, Dale led off with a single. He then stole second and Rusty drove him in with a line drive to right field. Dale had slid headfirst into home, just like Pete Rose and touched home plate just before the catcher slapped him with the tag. It was Galilee's best win of the season and all the guys mobbed Dale and Rusty.

Their new coach, Blocker, had helped make the team better than last year's. As fond as Dale was of Coach Carpenter, he had never coached baseball before. Coach Blocker on the other hand, had played baseball in high school and had more expertise.

In the fall, Blocker served as the high school assistant football coach and Dale liked him better than Dorfman. Blocker was short, only an inch taller than Dale, but built like a bulldog with a broad, sturdy chest and shoulders and short, powerful legs. Dale saw him in football practice knock down Tim Middleton, who was five inches taller and twenty pounds heavier with a tackling dummy.

Blocker called time and walked to the mound. He signaled for the infielders to gather around. Dale joined Comingdeer, the shortstop; Danny Robideaux, Roxanne's younger cousin, and the only freshman starter who played first and pitched; Tim Middleton, the junior third baseman; and Erickson, who caught. Blocker told Rusty it just wasn't his day and took the ball from him. Rusty felt angry with himself for pitching so poorly. Dale recognized that self-disgust and patted his pal on the back. Then Coach Blocker asked if anyone, besides the team's two other pitchers, Robideaux and Comingdeer, wanted to pitch. He needed someone to "mop up."

Dale waited for someone to volunteer, and when no one did, he said he'd pitch. Rusty looked critically at Dale. Dale knew what he was thinking: he'd never pitched before, and Rusty thought pitching was part of his domain. But heck, thought Dale, if no one else was willing, he'd give it a shot.

Coach Blocker gave Dale the ball. Then he rearranged the positions. He moved Rusty to left field and brought Chris in to play second. Dale took the mound and after five warm-up tosses, he faced his first batter. Erickson didn't give him a sign; there was no need. Dale didn't know how to throw curves or sliders; he just threw a slow fastball and an even slower change-up.

Dale had pitched before, if throwing a rubber ball against his house's garage brick wall counted. So he pretended he was in his backyard, wound up, and flung the ball toward the plate. The ball bounced a foot in front of home plate. The wild pitch advanced the runners to second and third. His next pitch also dived into the dirt, but Erickson saved it. On the third pitch, the Quanah Parker batter belted the ball. Dale turned and watched the ball sail over the chain-link fence. Rusty didn't even move from his deep left field spot. He turned his head up, watched the ball fly over, then tossed his glove up in the air in disgust.

Two of the runs were charged to Rusty, so Dale sort of understood his pal's displeasure. The ump tossed a new ball to Dale and he proceeded to throw another wild pitch. Then a pitch high for a ball. Then another pitch in the dirt. This time Erickson, instead of hustling after the ball, strolled to the backstop and threw the ball back to Dale so hard that it stung his hand under the glove when he caught it.

Eight batters and four runs later, Dale finally got out of the inning.

Walking back to the dugout, none of his teammates said a word to him. Galilee scored two runs in the bottom of the seventh but lost the game, 14-5. On the bus, sitting next to Chris, Dale calculated his earned run average. It wasn't hard. One inning, five earned runs. ERA: 45.00.

"Well," he mused aloud, "at least my ERA is under fifty."

Chris chuckled and slapped him on the right shoulder. Dale winced and said, "watch it, man. That's my pitching arm," which was a better joke. The mood lightened and Rusty, sitting with Erickson in the seat behind Dale, laughed and forgave him with a little shove.

Dale looked out the window as the bus left the baseball field, heading back to the high school. Winning was more fun, but even in a losing effort playing baseball was still enjoyable. Dale liked everything about it. The smell of the grass, the feel of the dirt, how the blue sky loomed over the field, even the wind in his face. He liked the way the white ball with its red stitching sailed in the air. Liked the crack of the bat. Liked how the uniform felt against him. Liked sitting in the dugout with his teammates and hearing them say the same phrases they'd used since little league: *way to get a piece of it, hum it baby, good eye, shake it off.* It wasn't frenetic and violent like football. It wasn't repetitious and claustrophobic like basketball. It had poetry and finesse and a bucolic beauty to it. To Dale, it seemed like the perfect game.

**Chapter 9:** *A peculiar punishment; Dale asks a girl to the all-sports banquet*

For five days, Dale, Rusty, and Erickson tormented Mr. Benedict with their limp wrists. Sometimes, rather than directly dangle their hands, they'd employ subtle variations such as pretending to mop their brows with the back of their limp hand, or they'd hang their hands over the front of their desks as if their arms were too weary to hold them up. Each day, Mr. Benedict grew angrier. He glared at them during class and on their way out he'd follow them into the hall hissing they should stop or he'd retaliate. He even cancelled the Thursday night Bible study. Then, on the following Monday, he barred them from entering his class.

Dale and Rusty were about to enter when Mr. Benedict blocked the doorway with his bulk. Mr. Benedict stared at them, his face resolute and aggrieved.

"Hey, Benny," said Rusty. "What gives?"

"You two are not coming in here," Mr. Benedict said.

"Okay," said Rusty. "Fine with us."

He turned to leave. Mr. Benedict grabbed his arm.

"Where do you think you are going?"

"Leaving. You said we weren't coming into your stinking class."

"But I didn't say you could leave."

"Then what are we supposed to do? Just stand around in the hall for the entire hour?" asked Dale.

"You are to report to Mr. Blocker's room," Mr. Benedict said. He pointed down the hall. "Now, go."

Dale and Rusty shrugged and ambled down the hall to Coach Blocker's room. They knew Coach didn't have a class this period. When they got to his room, they saw Erickson already sitting at a desk in the front row. He was the sole student. He wasn't happy.

Dale and Rusty walked into the room and saw their coach standing in front of his desk with an encyclopedia opened up. They waited.

"Hello, boys," said Coach Blocker.

"Hi, Coach," the boys said.

"Take a seat," Blocker said, then added, "any seat" as a little joke.

Dale and Rusty took desks next to Erickson. They looked at him and he shrugged.

"I heard you three have had your differences with Mr. Benedict," said Blocker. The boys said nothing. "So we – Mr. Benedict and I – decided to make an arrangement."

Coach Blocker then proceeded to tell the boys that they were to write down all the information he read to them. Write it down word for word. If, at the end of class each day, they had kept up they would be allowed to practice and play in the baseball games. If they were one word short, they'd be benched.

Rusty looked at Dale as if to say, is this guy serious? He was. Coach Blocker told them to get ready. Dale and Rusty scrambled to find their notebooks and pens. Then Coach picked up the encyclopedia, the Americana, and began reciting information on Afghanistan. Rusty looked up, an uncertain smile on his face. Falling behind, he quickly began writing all the facts pertaining to Afghanistan. Ten minutes later, Coach started on Albania. And so it continued, Blocker reading word for word the encyclopedia's description of world nations.

Fifty minutes later the bell rang. Rusty, Dale, and Erickson got up, showed their notebooks before exiting the classroom. Coach Blocker said, "Good work, boys."

On their way to the locker room, Erickson asked if Blocker was insane.

"What if he gives me writer's cramp?" asked Rusty. "How will I pitch then?"

Dale shook his head. It was a peculiar punishment. For the rest of the semester he expected Mr. Benedict or Coach Blocker or the school authorities would relent and let them back in the history class. But they didn't. By semester's end, the boys had made it to Madagascar.

Dale pulled off his sweats and hammered his blocks into the hard grass track. He crouched down, put his feet into the footrests, then got up and made an adjustment. Back in the blocks, he put the thumb and knuckles of each hand on the chalked starting line, and counted down to himself. When he heard the imaginary gunshot, he bolted forward.

He practiced his start three more times before the umpire appeared for Dale's heat of the 100-yard dash. The umpire told the boys to get ready. "On your mark," he said. Dale crouched down in his blocks and waited. "Get set." Dale raised his hips and coiled his body like a spring. Then he heard the clipped shot of the starter's gun and he sprang ahead, digging his right spiked shoe into the short, dry grass and shot forward.

He pumped his arms, stared straight ahead, and thrust first one leg then the other in a short, powerful stride. In just a little over ten seconds, he lowered his head and thrust his chest at the finish tape. He slowed down, disappointed that two runners had finished ahead of him. He knew sophomores weren't supposed to win, but he'd hoped on his home track he'd qualify for at least the 100-yard dash.

He walked off the track and Coach Dorfman checked his stopwatch. "Ten-four," Dorfman said. "Not bad."

Dale took his sweats from Chris, who'd brought them from the starting line. They walked back to the spot in the infield where the other Galilee guys were. Rusty, reclining on one of the old gym mats, shielded his eyes from the sun.

"How'd you do?" he asked.

"Don't think I'll qualify."

Dale and Chris sat down on the mat beside Rusty. Dale thought if he couldn't qualify in the 100, his best event, then he had less of a chance in the 220. But the 440-relay team had qualified for the finals, so he'd be running with Terry Harte and the two seniors, Jerry Dewberry and Kimbo Jones. He might get a medal yet.

Dale hadn't planned on going out for track. He'd been mad at Dorfman for not lettering him in football and had decided to punish him by playing only baseball. But when Dorfman said the track team could use him, Dale relented. After all, he knew he was fast and all he needed was a little encouragement to go out for track.

He made sure Dorfman knew baseball came first. Dale would play in the baseball game rather than run at the track meet if there were any scheduling conflicts. But Dorfman, who as athletic director made the schedules, had dropped a few baseball games to prevent any conflicts.

The worst part of track was getting in shape. Even after all the running Dale had done in basketball, he was unprepared for the regimen used in track. Dorfman even made sprinters run longer races to build endurance. The first run was a cross-country race. The coaches bused the players to the northern edge of town and made them run the five miles back to the school. Even though the run was difficult and monotonous, Dale sort of liked running with the guys as they traversed the countryside back to town. The grass was turning green, leaves on the trees were budding, the sky had that early spring turbulence, and Dale, hearing his breathing and feeling his heart pump as he ran, felt part of the whole natural world reviving itself after winter.

The next ordeal involved running quarters on the track. The track team, except for the big guys who only did field events, had to run several 440s. Fifteen boys lined up at the starting line. They jostled for position. Some of the sophomores had been pushed to the far side, but Dale slipped in between two seniors, Glen Dennison and Jerry Dewberry, closer to the inner lanes. Coach Dorfman said get set. Dale felt a strange excitement like electricity shooting through his body. He felt as if this race had universal significance. It was his first as a high schooler. He felt afraid he might be left behind or fail in such a way that he'd be ostracized and shamed. He heard Coach Dorfman yell "go!" and he sprinted ahead, squeezing past the two seniors for a second, before they hurled past him, almost knocking him down.

That had been two months ago. Now the season was almost over. After the Galilee Invitational, the team would go to the Wheaton Invitational, one of the largest track meets in the region, then finish the season at the district track meet in Agra.

Rusty and Chris got up for their next event, the 110 high hurdles. Dale and K. C. walked with them over to the starting area. Rusty and Chris peeled off their sweats and warmed-up. Dale and K. C. gathered their sweats and walked together to the finish line. K. C. asked Dale whom he was taking to the all-sports banquet.

"Gee, I don't know. Who you taking?"

Often the boys asked the same girls who had asked them to the Gopherette. The highlight of the all sports banquet was the dispensing of awards for best players in football, basketball, and "all-around" athlete. The winners got trophies. It was sort of a big deal for the athletes.

"Gretchen," K. C. said.

"Really?" He didn't know K. C. was interested in her.

"You know, you ought to ask Wendy."

Dale shrugged. "I don't know."

"You gotta ask somebody, so why not her? She likes you, you know."

Dale suspected that was true. Ever since the pep club banquet, he'd caught her gazing over in his direction as they stood before their lockers at school. He felt embarrassed when Rusty or K. C. teased him about Wendy's interest. Dale couldn't understand why Wendy liked him. They were so different. And he still pined for Amanda. He'd tried not to think about her as much, but he still found himself daydreaming about her in class and sneaking glances at her as she walked down the hall. He'd thought about asking Amanda to the all-sports banquet but was afraid she'd say no. Dale thought Amanda was too high above him for her to seriously consider going with him. It would be like a princess accepting the attentions of a peasant.

"So whattaya say?" asked K. C. "Are you gonna ask her?"

The all-sports banquet was the next weekend. You were supposed to ask a girl at least a week in advance.

"Maybe," said Dale.

"Go ahead and do it, Audie. Everybody thinks you should."

Everybody? It amazed Dale how people gossiped. Now he wasn't so sure he wanted to. He felt that contrariness rise inside him.

"Maybe," he said again.

K. C. shook his head over Dale's stubbornness. They arrived at the finish line in time to see Rusty finish third in his heat. His time was pretty good but probably wouldn't qualify.

The three then watched as Chris finished fourth in his heat, knocking over two hurdles. Dale thought Chris ought to consider a different event.

The four walked back to their camp and flopped down on the mats. Dale thought this was the most boring part of track – the waiting. He had to wait between his events; if he didn't qualify, he had to wait until the finals were finished. When they were on the road, they had to ride in the bus all the way back to Galilee. Dale spent maybe a minute running and hours waiting around.

K. C. asked Rusty whom he was taking to the all-sports banquet.

"Sadie," Rusty said. "Sweet Sadie, slinky Sadie, sexy Sadie."

Dale smiled at the word "slinky." Sadie was sort of slinky; when she walked, she moved her hips more provocatively than the other girls.

"Slutty Sadie," said Bigelow.

Rusty glared at Bigelow. "Who says?"

"I say," said Bigelow.

Dale stared at Butch's porcine face. He wore his hair short and recently had gotten a haircut, so now the bristly hair on his round head resembled even more the prickly hair of a boar.

"And are you speaking from personal experience?" demanded Rusty.

Bigelow offered his usual insincere smile. "Not exactly."

"Not exactly," mocked Rusty. "Then keep your mouth shut."

"Why don't you make me, Grimes."

Dale sized them up. Bigelow, linebacker and discus man, six feet and solidly built. Rusty, three inches shorter, with an adolescent scrawniness. No contest. Bigelow would easily win any fight.

"Ahhh, I don't want to," Rusty said, dismissing Butch with a wave of his hand.

"Just as I thought," said Bigelow.

"Who are you taking Bigelow?" asked Dale, trying to help Rusty save face. He waited. He hoped it wasn't Amanda.

"Amy Mears," Butch said.

Dale was surprised. She was a junior and pretty with her really long, red hair. Usually, sophomore boys didn't date older girls. But Butch was mature – at least physically.

The confrontation over, the boys drifted back to their separate territories in the camp. Dale joined Rusty and Chris. He sat down on the mat and watched as Sonny over at the pole vault faulted at fourteen feet. Dale had heard he was taking Roxanne. He wondered if they were going steady, something sophomores rarely did.

"Who you taking?" Dale asked Chris.

Chris looked a little embarrassed. "Carmen. Hope you don't mind," he quickly added.

"No, I don't mind. She's a nice girl."

"Yeah, she is."

Dale watched Sonny as he sprinted down the pole vault track. Sonny stuck the pole in the slot and leaned back, using the pole to lift his lanky body into the air. He nearly cleared the bar when his elbow knocked it off. Third miss. Disqualified.

Dale wondered if there wasn't some kind of conspiracy at foot. It looked like everything was falling into place for him to take Wendy to the all-sports banquet. He still wasn't sure he would.

"I heard you're taking Wendy to the banquet," said June May as she, Jesse, and Dale sat at the dinner table.

"Where'd you hear that?" demanded Dale.

"Through the grapevine."

"What does *that* mean?"

"You know, kids talking."

"Gossip," said Dale. "Why are seventh graders talking about high school kids?"

"We talk about all kinds of things," June May said, sounding very mature. "After all, we're in the same school building."

Dale dropped his fork on his plate and got up from the table. "I'm finished."

"Dale," Jesse said, "where you goin'?"

"To my room."

"Wendy's a cheerleader," said June May to Jesse. "Like I am."

"Is that so?" Jesse said.

Dale tried to ignore his sister, but he remembered overhearing some girls talking about the cheerleader tryouts. Two sophomores made next year's high school squad, Wendy and Mary Jane. Carmen, Gretchen, and Roxanne were the only other sophomores to try out. *She* didn't try. Dale wondered why. She was certainly pretty enough. She also had a good figure. Maybe she thought cheerleading too undignified.

"I'll be the only eighth grade cheerleader next year," June May said. Dale thought her voice sounded awfully conceited.

"That's nice, honey" said Jesse.

Dale walked down the hall into his parents' bedroom and got the phone. It had an extra-long line so he and June May could take it into their rooms.

Inside his room with the door closed, Dale picked up the receiver and paused. Yesterday, he'd done the same thing. He'd felt more nervous than he did before running a race. His heart had thumped in his chest and his mouth had felt as dry as sandpaper. He'd dialed her number and listened to the ringing, but when a woman's voice answered, presumably Mrs. Meeks, Dale had panicked and hung up. The next day at baseball practice he overheard Tim Middleton telling Kevin Stephenson that he had asked Amanda to the banquet.

Dale now dialed Wendy's phone number. He felt strangely calm, almost indifferent, even though he'd never asked a girl on a date before. To his surprise, Wendy answered. Her voice, bright and slightly husky, came through the line with amazing clarity.

"Hello," she said.

"Hello, Wendy. This is D -" he paused, remembering to use his school name, "Audie."

"Oh, *hello*, Audie," Wendy said, her voice as warm and welcoming as melted butter on popcorn.

Dale, not one to beat around the bush, asked her to the banquet. She accepted. He said fine. He'd pick her up Friday at six. She said that would be *wonderful*. Then she said good-bye in that same gooey voice and he said good-bye and hung up the receiver. He wondered if he'd done the right thing.

The all-sports banquet hadn't been as boring as the pep club one. For one thing, the food wasn't as fancy. Just basic he-man stuff: steak, potatoes, green beans, salad, roll, and apple pie alamode. And no fancy restaurant in the City. Instead it was held in Galilee's best restaurant, The Wagon Master. And no romantic trappings. No valentines, no smoochy music, no bows and frills. Just basic, down-to-earth, unpretentious surroundings. After dinner the awards for best athlete for each sport were given. Then the guest speaker, one of Dorfman's former players and now a young head coach for a high school team in the Texas panhandle, spoke. He kept his speech short, told a few jokes, and then the evening was over.

Dale and Wendy sat with Rusty and Sadie, who had rode with them. Rusty didn't drive yet. He would turn sixteen in two more months and was already thinking about the car he planned to get. Dale, who got his driver's license on his second try and parallel parked perfectly, drove them in the '67 Chevy. Blackie had bought a new car the month before, an Oldsmobile, but not one of the cool ones like the Cutlass. Instead, it was an Olds 88 and had a yellowy green color that Dale disliked. Blackie didn't think the color made much difference. The car's price had been reduced a few hundred bucks and Dale knew that was why Blackie bought it, ugly color and all. Jesse disliked it too, because it was too large for her.  She had to sit on a bigger pillow to see over the dash.

During the speech part of the banquet, Rusty nudged Dale and nodded in the direction of Mr. Benedict and his date, a woman Dale had never seen before. The happy couple was sitting four tables away.

"That chick sure is a dog," whispered Rusty.

"Who is she?" Dale whispered back, thinking that Rusty's evaluation was unkind but accurate; she did look a little like a golden retriever with her flowing blond hair, long, plain face, and big nose.

"I think her name's Bea."

"Bea?"

"Yeah, like in buzz buzz."

Dale looked more closely at Mr. Benedict and Bea. He'd never seen Mr. Benedict with a grown woman before, except for female teachers. They both sat rather stiffly. They didn't seem especially romantic.

"Is she his girlfriend?" Dale asked.

"No. Benny doesn't have a for-real girlfriend."

"How do you know?"

"Ever seen one around him until now? Ever see any photos of one in his apartment? Ever hear him talk about one?" Rusty turned and glanced over at Mr. Benedict. "Tell the truth, I don't think he's ever had a girlfriend in his zero life."

After the banquet, before leaving, Dale and Wendy said hello to their friends: Chris and Carmen; Billy Joe and Mary Jane; Sonny and Roxanne; Wally and Peggy; K. C. and Gretchen; Leroy and Carrie; Erickson and Merry; Clifford and Louise. Dale slyly looked for Amanda and saw her with Tim Middleton. Dale tolerated Tim, even though many of the sophomores didn't. He was the sort of guy who considered himself a leader but didn't have enough talent to back it up. He was a little bossy, especially to the sophomores, but not obnoxious like Comingdeer. Middleton was about average height, average build, not fast or slow, not handsome or ugly, sort of a younger version of Rusty's Mr. Average stepfather.

It could have been worse. Amanda could have gone out with Terry Harte or another impressive upperclassman. Or she could have gone out with one of Dale's friends. Or worst of all, she could have gone out with Bigelow. But Dale didn't feel too jealous of Middleton.

Dale drove Rusty and Sadie back to her house. Rusty had driven his cycle over there. He dropped them off. On the way to her house, Wendy talked about the different couples, focusing on the girls' dresses and what kind of corsages they had. Dale thought about the cars he'd seen in the parking lot. He now drove the '67 Chevy with Jesse driving the Olds, even though she disliked it. The Chevy wasn't a bad car. It needed a paint job. The hot Oklahoma sun had already faded the blue color. Otherwise, it was an okay, basic car. Nothing fancy; no bucket seats or mag wheels or souped-up engine. Not even an air conditioner, which annoyed Dale. But Blackie had grown up without air conditioning in stifling Alabama and he thought spending money for one in a car was a waste of money.

They arrived at Wendy's house. The light of the living room cast a weak reflection on the porch. The April evening was warm and clear. When Dale got out to open the door for Wendy, he looked briefly at the night sky with its crescent moon and glittering stars. The spring night made him feel a little romantic, so when he escorted Wendy to her porch he felt he should kiss her good night. Obviously, she thought so too. She stood on her porch, looking nervously at him, her green eyes wide and alert, not making any effort to scoot inside the door as she'd done with K. C.

Dale hesitated. He'd never really kissed a girl before. His cousin Tammy had kissed him once, but that was her silly idea of a game. Dale had been ten at the time. Dale had seen people kiss in the movies. It used to yuck him out. Later, when he stopped being a girl-hater, he'd watch the smooching and wonder how a guy did it. Where did the nose go? Did the guy turn his head slightly or let the girl turn hers? Where did he put his hands? Now, he found himself forced to put into practice something he'd only thought about in theory.

"It was a nice banquet, Audie," Wendy said, obviously trying to motivate him. "Thank you so much for asking me." She smiled encouragingly.

Dale stammered, "you're welcome."

He shuffled his feet, looked down at them as if they were misbehaving, and then glanced back at Wendy. He abruptly leaned toward her. He meant to slightly angle his face but he forgot and his nose bumped into hers.

"Ouch," she said.

"Sorry."

"That's okay."

He tried again, this time maneuvering his nose out of the way like a pro and his lips touched hers for a moment, then quickly withdrew. Like feeling a tiny electric shock, he drew back almost instinctively. Still, her lips felt very soft and that feeling pleasantly surprised him.

"Good night," Dale said as he bounded off the porch.

"Good night," Wendy called.

He heard her open the front door as he swiftly walked to his car. He turned back and saw Wendy quietly closing the door. He looked at the silhouette of her head from behind the curtained door window. Then she moved out of sight. Dale got in his car, started it, and drove away.

As he drove, he shook his head. What could a girl like Wendy see in a Maynard like him?

**Chapter 10: *Dale gets a tip from Clifford; going to a swimming party***

With the end of school, Mr. Benedict forgave them. Rusty and Dale never officially apologized, but they stopped dangling their hands and that seemed to satisfy their teacher.

With more free time, at least until they got summer jobs, Rusty and Dale spent a lot of time over at Mr. Benedict's apartment. The complex had a pool and they'd go over and swim sometimes twice a day. Mr. Benedict kept his refrigerator well stocked and they raided it with impunity. The teasing eased somewhat; Rusty preferred an audience when he tormented Mr. Benedict and Dale didn't really count. So, the boys settled into a languorous early summer ritual of swimming, snacking, seeing an occasional movie, and listening to records at Benny's.

The routine changed when Rusty turned sixteen and got his car, a comical '65 green Rambler. Now he needed money to pay back his stepfather. Rusty had thought about working his usual summer job, delivering papers, but it didn't pay enough. He needed serious moolah. So when Erickson's father, a carpenter, informed Rusty that a roofer friend of his had an opening, he took the job.

After a week, Rusty told Dale that his boss had another opening. Dale showed up early in the morning and the boss, a broad-shouldered, clean-cut man of thirty, showed him the basics and Dale went right to work. The only problem was that he had never roofed in his life and didn't possess any natural skill. Two hours later, the boss noticed that Dale had laid down a quarter of the shingles crooked. He pointed to the disarray and said they'd all have to come off. Dale hung his head. He didn't have a very good sense of geometry. He always had difficulty making his wood working projects square in shop. At the end of the day, the boss and Dale agreed that roofing wasn't his cup of tea.

Dale needed another job. He thought about mowing lawns, but a lot of boys did that and there was too much competition for yard work. He wasn't sure what else to try. Then one day in June, he ran into Clifford.

Dale saw Clifford walking down the street on his way home and he stopped his Chevy and gave him a ride. Dale hadn't seen Clifford since school let out. Clifford climbed in and nodded. Dale nodded back and noticed that Clifford was wearing a white and orange striped shirt with Whataburger stitched over the pocket. Whataburger was a Southwest hamburger chain. Dale had eaten there a few times but he preferred the local joint, Sooner Shack, or for a great shake, Braum's.

"How do you like working there?" asked Dale, pointing to Clifford's shirt.

"It was okay. Today's my last day."

"Did you forget to give back the shirt?"

"It's mine," said Clifford, not amused. "They make us buy them," he added less severely.

"Why is today your last?"

"I quit." Clifford turned and gave Dale a meaningful look. "I'm leaving town."

Dale wondered if Clifford was running away or maybe joining the navy like Blackie did at his age. He tried imagining Clifford as a swabbie. He could.

"Where you going?"

"Back to Lyons."

Dale glanced over and saw Clifford almost smiling.

"That's good. I mean, sounds like things are better with your family." Then he quietly added, to indicate it was still a secret, "and your father."

"Yeah," said Clifford.

Dale turned and drove to the gravel road and the alley. About a block away, Clifford said here was fine. Dale stopped the car. Clifford didn't move. Dale began to feel awkward sitting in the car with him.

"They're looking for a replacement," Clifford said.

"Who?" Dale had forgotten about Whataburger.

Clifford pointed to his shirt.

"Oh, yeah."

"If you go in, ask for Mac. He's the manager."

Dale nodded. Clifford started to get out of the car, then stopped. He turned to Dale and stuck out his hand.

Dale, although a little surprised, quickly shook Clifford's hand. Unsurprisingly, Clifford had a strong, tight grip.

"Thanks," Clifford said.

He said the word with more feeling than usual when given a ride. Dale nodded and noticed that Clifford's eyes didn't have that fierce stare. He didn't know what he'd done to deserve this uncharacteristic farewell. Had Clifford really been that lonely?

Clifford got out, shut the door, and started walking. Dale suddenly remembered something. He leaned his head out the window. "Hey, Cliff, we'll be playing you guys this fall."

Clifford, without turning around, said, "yeah, and we'll kick your butts."

Dale took Clifford's advice and asked for "Mac" at the Whataburger. A huge, corpulent man with frizzy red hair and a pale potato face came out of the office. He stared at Dale.

"Yeah," the big man said.

"Clifford said there was an opening here."

"Clifford?" asked Mac. He thought for a moment. "Oh, yeah, Oates."

Dale waited.

"So, you want to apply?"

Dale said yes and Mac asked a skinny girl to bring an application. The girl did and Dale filled it out while Mac retreated to the office. Finished, Dale walked over to the office and peered inside. Mac said come in. Dale did and handed him the clipboard with the completed application. Mac perused the application, then leaned his bulk back into the chair and looked at Dale.

"Says here your last job was as a roofer."

Dale nodded.

Mac glanced again at the application to make sure. "For one day."

Since he didn't say it as a question, Dale didn't know if he should answer. He waited.

"Well, you're hired if you want the job."

Dale said okay and started to go. He stopped. "What's your, uh, full name?" he asked the gargantuan redhead.

"MacDonald," he replied.

Dale smiled. "That's sort of funny. You know, hamburgers."

"*Mac*Donald," the man said. "Not *Mc*Donald."

Dale nodded although he didn't see much difference. Mac told him he could start the afternoon shift tomorrow and to come in at eleven. Before leaving, Dale paused, realizing that Mac must be Fat Mac's older brother. They looked the same except Mac was even more humongous. Dale considered telling him he knew his younger brother but decided not to presume on his connections. He noticed Mac eyeing him with his small blue eyes, so Dale nodded and left.

Back home Dale told Blackie he had a job. He had neglected to tell him of his one-day adventure in roofing.

"About time," Blackie said.

Blackie believed in developing the work habit when young. Dale had a different philosophy. He didn't see the value in working at a dull, boring job simply for money. But he supposed it was time to start.

Dale arrived at Whataburger the next morning and listened to the skinny girl as she explained the routine. The distinctive feature about Whataburger was they made the hamburgers fresh. Customers watched as the cook grilled the meat and toasted the buns. Then, with alacrity, the condiment specialist assembled the fixings on the burger. Then fries and drinks were added and the freshly prepared meal was presented to the pleased customer. So, quickness was essential.

Dale said he had no problem with that. He'd always been quick at everything: quick on his feet, quick at reading, quick at doing math, quick at going to sleep. A regular Speedy Gonzalez. He half-smiled. The skinny girl didn't. He noticed she had bronze skin and long black hair.

She said in a sour-kind of way that the other essential attribute for the Whataburger employee was a smiling, happy disposition. Dale realized he'd have to work on that part. He didn't smile easily; at least not broadly. But he'd try to be enthusiastic.

His four-hour shift passed slowly. First days always seem slow, of course. He got a lunch break at one o'clock and got to sample the freshly cooked, speedily assembled Whataburger himself. He liked it better than he remembered.

Dale drove back home after work and felt like a success. His second real job and he'd lasted more than one day. He didn't know if he'd continue to pursue customer service jobs in the future, but for now he wasn't displeased.

The week went by faster than expected. Dale got the hang of the job quickly, and regarded himself as the fastest condiment specialist of all the employees. (They hadn't let him cook any hamburgers yet.)

Dale and Rusty still visited Mr. Benedict's apartment, but not as much now that they were workingmen. In the evening they'd go over for a swim where they'd find college-age guys lounging along with girls on the patio chairs and recliners. Rusty would belly flop or cannonball into the pool and splash them. One of the guys threatened to beat him up. In response, Rusty squirted water out of his mouth.

Dale avoided Wendy. He didn't even go over to see Wally in case he ran into her. He wasn't sure how he felt about her. She was nice and pretty, but Dale didn't have the same strong feelings for her that he had for Amanda. He thought dating Wendy would be unfair to her. He was also unsure about dating. It sounded sort of grown-up and tedious. He still preferred goofing off.

So did Rusty, but Dale guessed that wouldn't last. Dale caught him more than once ogling the girls lounging at the pool. One of them, not the prettiest, but cute just the same, wore a skimpy bikini. She never got in the pool though. She just reclined on a lounge chair and had her boyfriend smear lotion on her suntanned skin. Once, while he and Rusty were swimming, they saw her lie on her belly and unhook her top. Dale knew how Rusty's devious mind worked. Rusty was trying to think of a way to scare her so she'd jump up topless. Dale shook his head and grabbed Rusty's arm.

"She'll scream," he warned. "And her boyfriend will beat us up. Or worse, she'll call the cops."

Rusty laughed but decided not to throw any soggy grass at her.

He did, however, go on an official date with Sadie. Rusty told Dale about it the next day at Mr. Benedict's. He related the affair with a studied casualness. They went to see the movie version of *Tom Sawyer*. Dale didn't ask for any details of the date, even though he was curious.


Wendy and Mary Jane organized a swimming party in late June and Dale decided to go. He'd grown two inches since last summer and now stood a towering five foot five and one quarter. That meant he was taller or about as tall as most of the girls in his class and he began to feel a little more confident around them. At least, he didn't feel like a squashed worm. So he and Rusty drove out to Twilight Beach in the northwest part of the City. Twilight Beach wasn't really a beach. It was a big hole in the earth with a muddy bottom. But people who went there could pretend they were at a real beach. It had sand.

Dale and Rusty spotted their classmates on the north end of the beach. They strolled over to them and tried not to stare at the girls as they swam and dived. Wendy, Mary Jane, Gretchen, Carmen, and Roxanne were present. To Dale's utter disappointment and great relief, Amanda wasn't.

Dale had only learned to swim a couple of summers ago. He'd almost drowned three times, once at Twilight Beach with Rusty and his brothers and another time at Turner Falls, a lake and resort area seventy miles south of the City, with his cousin Tammy. Both times he'd stepped into a deep depression and gulped a lot of water before finally finding his footing and getting back to lower water. The first time occurred when Blackie had once tried to teach him to swim when Dale was five. He did it the old-fashioned way by tossing him into the water while fishing off the Texas gulf coast. It didn't work. Dale simply sank into the warm water and Blackie had to jump in and save him. Blackie never tried again, and it wasn't until Dale turned thirteen that he learned by himself to do more than dog paddle.

Dale and Rusty joined K. C. and Wally in the water. For the moment, they preferred to observe the girls at a distance. None of the girls wore revealing swimsuits, although Mary Jane wore a two-piece. Still, they were a sight to behold. Dale liked the way their wet hair stuck to their naked backs. He liked the way their smooth skin glistened under the sun. He marveled at how water streaked against their sleek, padded bodies – characteristics that reminded him of seals.

Sometimes when Dale looked at them too long he couldn't come out of the water. He knew his swim trunks would show his arousal, so he stayed put until "Gilbert" subsided. That's the word Dale and Rusty used for their penises. The origin of the word was misty, but Dale thought it referred to a kid back in grade school named Gilbert who'd caught his pecker in the zipper of his pants. He'd zipped up too fast, a hazard common to all young boys not yet dexterous enough to zip and go. Anyway, the word seemed appropriate at the time and Dale thought it sounded more sonorous than the typically rude words for penis.

More than once, Rusty joined him in the deep end, treading water. They tried not to ogle the girls so their tumescence would lessen.

"Having problems with Gilbert?" Dale asked the first time Rusty arrived. Rusty nodded, not taking his eyes off Mary Jane. "Just imagine how long we'd have to stay out here if the girls had worn bikinis."

Rusty nodded, imagining it vividly.

Wally and K. C. were the only other boys at the swimming party. Chris, Sonny, Billy Joe, and Butch had been invited too, but they didn't show. Dale knew why Chris didn't come. He worked full-time in the summer at his uncle's lumberyard. In exchange for that labor, Chris got to play sports during the school year.

Four boys to five girls was an advantageous ratio thought Dale because the boys couldn't easily pair off with the girls. Dale, after saying hello to the smiling Wendy, tried to avoid her without appearing rude. The boys had initially stayed amongst themselves but as the afternoon wore on, K. C. and Wally began swimming and diving with the girls. Rusty and Dale, now unaroused enough to join, swam over and Rusty immediately dunked Mary Jane. She screamed, went under, and then bobbed up, squeezing water off her smiling face. Mary Jane wore the skimpiest suit: a two-piece that wasn't a bikini but by Nazarene standards was quite daring. Dale still thought she was too skinny; he could see her hipbones jutting out of the top of her suit bottom. Mary Jane had a pretty face even though her nose had a little bump on the bridge. As Dale studied it, he decided the nose bump gave her face a distinctive touch.

When Mary Jane floated on her back, Dale noticed her exposed navel and he felt a lustful urge. Out of deference to Rusty, however, he put the thought out of his mind.

K. C. dunked Roxanne. Even in her one-piece she made Dale dizzy. He decided her distinctive facial feature was her eyes. Not just the deep blue color, but also the heavy-lidded quality to them. He remembered a time at the drive-in watching a movie that starred an actress with such sly eyes. Wanda had called them "bedroom eyes." Dale hadn't understood the meaning of the term then, but now sneaking looks at Roxanne, he understood.

Wally dunked Gretchen. The water streamed off her sharp nose and pointed chin. Those features and her narrow, light blue eyes reminded Dale again of a fox. Dale had heard one of the older boys at the pool at Mr. Benedict's describe a girl by that word. "She's really a fox," he'd said. When Dale looked at the girl in question, he noticed she had long, black hair and he felt confused.

With the all the dunking going on, Dale knew he had to get on the act to confirm his maleness. He swam over and dunked Carmen.

Caught by surprise, she emerged from the water spluttering. "Why are you being so mean?" she cried.

"It's just a dunk," Dale said, remembering how even her shoulders felt sleek and soft as he pushed her down.

"Not that. I meant why are you being so mean to Wendy?"

"Huh? I'm not being mean."

"You're not paying her any attention."

"Sure I am."

"No, you're not," Carmen said, splashing Dale with water and swimming away.

Dale looked over and saw Wendy by herself treading water. She looked pensive as if she were having difficulty understanding the chemical properties of H2O. Dale felt a pang of guilt but before he could swim over to her, K. C. thrashed his way to Wendy and dunked her. She squealed in her throaty, almost hoarse girlish voice that Dale both found appealing and a little annoying. When she came back up, she was smiling like her usual self, her blond hair heavy with water, making its color darker like that of wheat.

136

The girls escaped the boys and went to the diving board. The boys watched them dive a couple of times, admiring their shape more than their form. Then the boys joined them, determined to show them how to really dive.

Dale stood in line with Roxanne, Mary Jane, and Wendy in front of him. He watched them climb the steps to the diving board. Before they dived, each girl reached behind her and pulled her swimsuit back down over the bulge of flesh that had popped out. Dale regarded the act as poetic.

Rusty dived like a madman. He jumped arms and legs akimbo. Wally dived like he was falling out of a tree. Dale dived legs first. He was afraid he might lose his trunks if he dived headfirst. Only K. C. dived with precision and élan. He'd been a lifeguard for three summers at the Nazarene church camp he attended. Dale had to grudgingly admit that, except for K. C., the girls did it better.

When the five girls took a break and laid supine on the sand, Dale looked at them from the shallow water. Their heads pointed in his direction. Each girl had a distinctive color of hair: Wendy's yellow blond, Roxanne's strawberry blond, Gretchen's red, Mary Jane's brown, and Carmen's black. Dale imagined Amanda's light brown added to the mix.

The day wore on and still Dale hadn't really talked to Wendy. He saw her putting on a stoical façade. He felt guilty, but he kept telling himself it was for the best.

Wendy and Carmen were the first to leave. Dale saw them gathering their stuff when Wendy dropped her coin purse. Dale jumped out of the water and trotted over and picked it up. He tapped her on the shoulder. Wendy turned and the expression on her face startled him. She looked like she was about to cry. But when she saw him offering her the coin purse, her eyes brightened and she smiled.

"Thank you, Audie," she said, almost shyly.

Dale said you're welcome and she looked at him a little longer than was necessary, her smile slowly fading, and then she turned and joined Carmen. Dale watched them walk toward the showers, noting how nice their cheerleader legs looked and how their bottoms fetchingly cantered underneath their swimsuits.

After they disappeared from view, Dale felt a melancholy mood pass over him, like a cloud obscuring the sun. Then it passed, and he raced over to the springboard and jumped headfirst into the water.

### Chapter 11: *An incident at work; a revelation at Lake Thunderbird*

Dale, while working, worried that some of his friends might come into Whataburger during his shift. He felt silly wearing the orange and white striped shirt and the absurd paper cap. And the idea of being seen by someone he knew, especially a girl, filled him with trepidation.

The chances were not great, however. He only worked twenty hours a week and the Whataburger was on the eastern end of Galilee, just off Highway 66 that led to the City. Most of the people who stopped were hungry commuters.

Then one day in mid-summer, it happened. He saw Amanda and a skinny, blond girl that Dale supposed was a church friend, getting out of a car in the parking lot. As he watched them walk toward the entrance, he felt as if he were cooking on the grill instead of the 95 percent pure beef patties. He glanced down the line of customers and saw five hungry people gazing at their sizzling hamburgers. In a few moments the hamburgers would be arriving at his condiment station, topless and ready for dressing. Dale glanced at Amanda and her friend, both smiling and talking as they reached the entrance. He had to think of something. He could not allow her to see him working this ridiculous job.

Amanda opened the front glass door, still absorbed in her conversation. Dale suddenly buckled over. He moaned, but not very convincingly, and scurried out of the service area. He heard Mac at the grill call him. Fortunately, Dale had used his middle name and Mac bellowed "Dale" instead of "Audie," keeping his identity unknown to Amanda.

Dale ignored the bellow and considered what to do next. He saw the skinny girl, Maria, walking toward him. He ducked into the bathroom and turned on the faucet. Maria banged on the door.

"Mac said to get out here now," she said but in the same kind of perfunctory way she did her job.

Dale faked puking sounds, then tried to talk to Earl for real. Nothing came out. But the banging stopped.

He sat in the bathroom for ten minutes. Thinking the coast was clear, he unlocked the door and sneaked out. Standing in the doorway to the grill area, blocking it almost completely, was Mac.

"You're fired," he said.

Dale had always appreciated his laconic manner and never more than now. He didn't argue. He didn't really like working in food service. He did his menial functions efficiently but that was never enough. He'd been criticized for not smiling. He didn't aim to please. Curious criticism, since it came from the dour giant himself.

Dale shrugged and threw his paper hat in the trash. He clocked out and, not taking any chances, removed his orange and white striped shirt, folded it, and stuffed it under his undershirt. Then he crept out of the back door and stealthily slithered into his Chevy. He waited another five minutes, then started the car and drove through the parking lot. She was gone. And with a turn onto the highway, so was he.

Out of a job, Dale wasn't sure what to do next. He supposed he'd get a paper route. Maybe deliver *The Oklahoman*. It paid better than the local paper. But before he could pursue that avenue for employment, Rusty called and invited him on an overnight visit at a cabin at Lake Thunderbird. Mr. Benedict would take them.

"Benny has a cabin?" Dale asked.

Rusty said it belong to a friend of Mr. Benedict's. He was just borrowing it. Dale said he wasn't sure.

"C'mon," said Rusty. "It'll be fun."

Going over to Mr. Benedict's to swim and eat his food was one thing. Being in his company a whole day and night sounded less appealing to Dale. He asked who else was going. Rusty said Kevin was coming, too.

"Okay," Dale said, "I'll presume to go."

Dale drove to Mr. Benedict's apartment the next morning at six. When he arrived, he saw only Rusty and Mr. Benedict. He asked where Kevin was.

"Sick," said Rusty.

"Sick?" repeated Dale.

"Ill," said Mr. Benedict. "Unfortunately ill. He called late last night to inform me. The summer flu, he believed."

Great, Dale thought. It was better to have at least three guys to gang up on Mr. Benedict. Just two of them along with their teacher changed the dynamics; sometimes Dale felt left out.

They got in the car and zipped out of town, riding Highway 66 to the City. On the way, Rusty teased Mr. Benedict about the eight tracks he had in his glove compartment. The Carpenters? Bread? Where's the good stuff he wanted to know.

Dale didn't say much. He felt sleepy. He wasn't used to getting up so early. He stared out the window from his seat in the back. They were moving through the western suburbs of the City. The urban area seemed to be continually spreading itself farther and farther out. Dale remembered his grandpa telling him that Oklahoma City used to be twenty miles away from Galilee. Now it didn't seem more than a few miles.

Dale closed his eyes and when he opened them again he saw semi-green fields and clutches of small trees. He must have fallen asleep. He heard Rusty telling Mr. Benedict about the swimming party. He talked about each of the girls with fickle enthusiasm. Dale thought Rusty was like a honeybee buzzing from one sweet flower to the next. Dale, on the other hand, buzzed for only one flower.

Ten minutes later, Mr. Benedict turned off Interstate 35 and drove on a paved two-lane street before turning again onto a dirt road. They drove for half a mile until they came to an A-frame cabin. Dale was impressed. It looked like a nice place, not a run-down, rickety old shack like he'd expected. Even better, the cabin stood only forty yards away from the lake.

They carried their stuff into the cabin. Dale liked the way it smelled: Woodsy and fresh. The interior was appropriately rustic with a bare wooden floor and unfinished walls. It had a small half-kitchen, a bathroom, one regular-sized bedroom on the ground floor, and a smaller one in the loft. Dale noticed there was no TV. He thought that was okay. After all, they were roughing it.

Rusty and Dale changed into their swim trunks and raced down to the lake. Not yet noon, the day was already hot. Dale looked at the sky and knew the few hazy clouds would be burned away by afternoon. Late July and the temperatures were already creeping past one hundred.

Dale looked at the lake and noticed farther out a number of treetops sticking out of the still water. The trees were devoid of bark and looked starkly naked in contrast to the dark water. Some of the white tops were broken and jagged. The boys swam and horsed around for an hour, then went back to the cabin for lunch.

They took off their sneakers before walking into the cabin so they wouldn't track any sandy mud in, but their feet were still wet and Dale noticed their moist footprints on the wood floor. Mr. Benedict did, too.

"You're still wet!" he cried. "Didn't you dry off outside?"

"Yeah," Rusty said. "We're dry enough."

"You certainly are not." Mr. Benedict waddled over to Rusty and drew a fat finger down his leg of his trunks. He held the moist finger dramatically in front of them. "You're still wet. You're dripping water all over the cabin floor."

"No, we're not," said Rusty. "And so what, anyway? It's a cabin, not a palace."

"We have to keep this cabin in pristine condition," Mr. Benedict said. "It must be immaculate when we leave."

"Then why the heck are we here, if we can't have any fun?"

"You may have fun, just tidy fun."

Rusty rolled his eyes. "Tidy fun? Sounds like a new detergent."

He and Dale chuckled.

"Let's eat," Rusty said.

They started to walk into the kitchen. Mr. Benedict blocked their way.

"Not until you change," he said.

"If we change now, we'll just have to change back later," said Dale.

"I insist."

"Man, Benny, what is your problem?" Rusty asked. "You're overreacting. It's just a little water. It'll dry, man."

"Go and change or you will not receive any food."

"Oh, yeah?"

"You heard what I said. Now –"

Before Mr. Benedict could complete his sentence, Rusty slipped past him and went into the kitchen and began stuffing food into his mouth. He crammed in lunchmeat and bread, then poured mustard straight from the jar into his full mouth. While he chewed he danced a little jig of defiance.

"Rusty," hissed Mr. Benedict as he moved menacingly toward the kitchen. "I'm warning you."

Rusty grabbed a tomato. He tossed it in his hand like a baseball, feeling its texture and weight.

Mr. Benedict halted in his tracks. "Put that down, Rusty. Unhand that tomato."

Rusty, still chewing, shook his head. He suddenly reared back and threw the tomato hard against the living room wall. It hit with a splat and the split pulp slid down the ragged wood wall, leaving a slimy red trail.

"Rusty!" shrieked Mr. Benedict.

"Strike one!" called Dale.

Rusty grabbed another tomato. He held his arm loose, letting his wrist go limp before snapping it into position.

"Don't you dare," warned Mr. Benedict.

With a flick of his wrist, Rusty threw the tomato at Mr. Benedict. It hit him square in his belly, slightly staining his white polo shirt, before bouncing off mostly intact to the floor.

"Oomph," grunted Mr. Benedict.

Rusty grabbed a stalk of celery and flung it at the still-shocked Mr. Benedict. It bounced off his head and hit Dale on the leg.

"Hey, watch it," said Dale.

"Apologies," said Rusty in his pompous Mr. Benedict voice.

"Rusty, stop this immediately!" shouted Mr. Benedict. "Please stop throwing vegetables!"

"Isn't a tomato really a fruit?" asked Dale. He'd learned that in his eighth-grade health class.

Momentarily distracted by the question, Mr. Benedict paused long enough to get conked on the head by a clump of cauliflower.

"Stop it!" Mr. Benedict squealed. "Stop throwing those fruits and vegetables!"

Dale nodded approvingly. Mr. Benedict was even a better student than a teacher. Rusty meanwhile armed himself with a carrot. He wielded it like a knife, holding it at the thicker end and with a grim look on his face he slowly advanced toward his teacher.

"Stop, Rusty," Mr. Benedict pleaded. "Please, stop."

Mr. Benedict backed up his bulk. A maniacal gleam appeared in Rusty's eyes as he slowly advanced.

"It's too late, Benny," Dale said solemnly. "You've driven him mad."

With that diagnosis, Rusty leapt at Mr. Benedict, thrusting the carrot repeatedly against his protruding belly. Mr. Benedict reacted as if being impaled with an actual knife. He threw his arms back and wailed. When, on the third stab, the carrot's narrow end broke off, Rusty ceased his assault and stumbled back to the kitchen, laughing.

Dale laughed, too, and Mr. Benedict, one pudgy hand grasping his belly as if holding in his guts, glared at them.

"Look at this mess you made," he scolded.

"Well, clean it up," said Rusty.

"Do you mean that I should clean it up?"

"Yeah. You started it."

"Started what?"

"Bugging us."

"Oh. And the fact that I *bugged* you is reason enough to engage in a wild, felonious assault on my person as well as despoiling this lovely cabin –"

"I wouldn't say it's lovely," said Dale. "Nice, maybe."

"—and now I should be the one to clean it?"

Rusty took a bite of the broken carrot. "Yeah."

"Oh, you are too much, Rusty Grimes. And to think that I invited you and your accomplice to this splendid cabin. To think –"

"Shut up and let's eat."

Mr. Benedict stopped his ranting. His froggy eyes blinked behind his glasses.

"We'll *all* clean up the cabin after we eat lunch," Rusty said.

Mr. Benedict tried to resume his dignity. He tugged his slightly soiled polo shirt completely over his big belly.

"That would be satisfactory," he said.

"Okay, then," said Rusty. "Is there someplace around we can order a pizza?"

After lunch, a pizza not included, the boys went for a swim while Mr. Benedict cleaned up. After swimming, they played an improvised game of baseball using a fallen tree branch and a dead fish's severed head. After five hits, the fish head disintegrated, putting a premature end to the game.

They walked around the shoreline and speculated on where the other cabins were located. They wondered who was staying in them. Perhaps a beautiful girl and her invalid mother? Maybe a homicidal maniac roamed the woods surrounding the mysterious lake. Rusty and Dale would have to save the girl and her mother. They imagined a ruthless battle with the homicidal maniac. First Dale would heroically grapple with him only to be knocked unconscious (Dale thought it should be Rusty), then Rusty would engage the battle and just as he was being overpowered by the maniac who, after all, has the strength of three men because of his lunacy, Dale revives, and together they subdue the subhuman. That left only the question of who gets the girl.

"How good-looking is her invalid mother?" asked Rusty.

They walked back to the cabin and saw Mr. Benedict sitting in a chair on the back porch watching their return. He hadn't joined them for a swim, which was a relief to the boys. They didn't want to see Mr. Benedict's pale, hairy, blimpy body in anything but the most proper of clothes. However, as they approached, they saw he had changed into Bermuda shorts. That was bearable, they supposed.

They had barbecue for dinner. Mr. Benedict cooked the chicken and pork on the grill outside. The barbecue was pretty good, except Dale thought it too spicy. He drank an extra bottle of root beer and still his mouth felt hot.

After dinner, they went inside the cabin and played Monopoly. Rusty and Dale ganged up on Mr. Benedict and finished him off quickly, then spent an hour trying to defeat each other. After the momentum seesawed back and forth, the boys called it a draw. Rusty and Dale often preferred ties because neither one had to lose.

They tried a couple of other board games but they were boring. The cabin didn't have a record player so they listened to the radio. The station the radio was tuned to played a lot of mushy romantic stuff, the Carpenters, Bread, Roberta Flack, stuff like that. Rusty turned the dial.

"Who owns this cabin anyway?" asked Dale.

"You noticed the young lady I escorted to the all-sports banquet?" asked Mr. Benedict. Dale nodded. How could he have not?

"Her father, Mr. Webb, owns the cabin."

"Oh yeah?" Rusty said, busy changing the dial. "Does he listen to slop like this?"

"I presume not," said Mr. Benedict. "Probably Beatrice prefers that type of music."

"Beatrice?" both boys said.

"Yes, that's her name."

"Is she your girlfriend?" Dale asked.

"Well, not exactly," replied Mr. Benedict.

"Why not, Benny?" asked Rusty. "Are you too good for her?"

Mr. Benedict stiffened. "Of course not. I'll have you –" but before he could continue, Rusty found the right station and shouted, "Hey, it's Doctor Demento!"

Rusty had told Dale about this radio program before but Dale's stereo at home couldn't pick it up. The host, Dr. Demento, played really weird songs and sometimes Rusty would sing a snippet at school. Playing right now was "Tiptoe through the Tulips." Dale and Rusty weren't too impressed; it was weird but not funny weird.

The next song, "Gitarzan," they liked better. Rusty jumped up and started grooving to the song.

"Hey, I'm the monkey," he said, imitating the monkey part of the song. Rusty crouched, letting his arms hang long and loose, then elongated his agile face into a monkey-like look as his voice produced convincing simian sounds. Dale laughed and took the part of Gitarzan. He puffed out his chest and gave a pathetic imitation of a Tarzan yell, but it made Rusty laugh. Then Rusty pointed to Mr. Benedict and said, "Now, you're Jane." But Mr. Benedict refused to assume the role. He sat in his chair and crossed his hairy arms. That made the boys laugh all the more because they imagined him as the unwilling Jane, flabby body and hairy arms included.

The next song was even better: "Sarah Cynthia Silvia Stout Would Not Take the Garbage Out." Rusty held his arms up signaling quiet. He nodded. He remembered this one. They listened. It delighted them, Rusty once again, Dale for the first time. And why not? Lots of alliterative description of disgusting food. The boys tried not to laugh, because it would drown out the poetry. But when they heard "blobs of gooey bubble gum," they looked at Mr. Benedict and erupted in laughter. They still teased him as being the Son of Blob.

"Turn that off!" Mr. Benedict shouted. "Turn the dial!"

Rusty held a hand up, signaling silence.

"I said turn it off!"

"It's almost over," Rusty said.

Mr. Benedict could not tolerate another syllable. He rose from his seat and quickly – but not too quickly since he was so slow – walked over to the radio. He got there just in time to cut off the closing sentence, which didn't matter because it wasn't funny.

"What's the big deal?" asked Rusty. "Can't you take a few chunks and blobs?"

"Quit saying that," Mr. Benedict said.

"Which word?" asked Dale. "Chunks or blobs?"

"Both!"

Dale started chanting chunk in a passable baritone: "Chunk, chunk, chunk." Rusty followed in a higher voice with "blob, blob, blob."

"You're making me ill," cried Mr. Benedict.

Dale, knowing Mr. Benedict claimed to have a sensitive stomach, imagined the Sylvia Stout song might have disagreed with him so he stopped chunking. Rusty, however, added three more blobs before he concluded in an awful falsetto.

"Thank you," Mr. Benedict said.

Dale thought he looked pale. Maybe he was about to talk to Earl. But no, Mr. Benedict returned to his seat and mopped his fat face with a lavender-colored handkerchief.

"Let's engage in a less raucous activity," he suggested.

That sounded boring to the boys.

"Like what?" asked Rusty.

"We could talk," said Mr. Benedict.

"About Beatrice?" asked Dale.

Mr. Benedict pursed his lips. "No, not that. Something else."

Dale's mouth was dry. He said he was getting another root beer. Did anyone else want one? No takers. He walked over to the fridge and pulled out a cold one. He returned to the couch and flopped down.

"We could tell a story," he said, glancing at Rusty.

"Yeah, Benny. We heard this story while we were out swimming."

"What do you mean heard? Heard from whom?"

"Well, the cops came by," Rusty said.

"I didn't hear a car."

"Well, they weren't actually cops," said Dale. "They were rangers, lake rangers. They came by on a boat."

"Oh, certainly, lake rangers came by on a boat," repeated Mr. Benedict but Dale could tell he was beginning to wonder.

"That's right," Rusty said. "They came around while we were swimming. At first, we thought they were going to chase us off or something. You know, for swimming without a license."

"A license is not required to swim here."

"We know that but we didn't know if they knew that," Dale said.

"Yeah, anyway, the cops, I mean, rangers said we had better be on the lookout." Rusty gave Dale a quick, sly glance.

Dale saw that Mr. Benedict didn't want to be lured into this conversation but he couldn't help himself.

"Very well," Mr. Benedict said, showing some annoyance. "On the lookout for what?"

"Whom would be a better word," said Rusty.

"Whom? What do you *mean*?" Mr. Benedict asked with asperity.

Dale and Rusty looked at each other. Then Rusty solemnly intoned, "there's a maniac on the loose."

"Hah! I don't believe it."

"It's true," Dale said with as much sincerity as he could muster. "They said a maniac broke out of the hospital for the criminally insane."

"And they think he's in the woods somewhere," added Rusty.

"Probably close by," said Dale. "The rangers asked us if we kept any guns in the cabin."

"Do we, Mr. Benedict?" Rusty asked with a convincing mixture of innocence and fear.

"Very amusing," Mr. Benedict said. "Very amusing, indeed."

"Look, Dale," Rusty said, pointing to the skeptical Mr. Benedict, "he doesn't believe us."

"Maybe he'll believe us in the morning when he wakes up drenched in blood." Dale realized he hadn't quite made sense, but he liked the imagery.

"Yeah, maybe missing a head," added Rusty, not helping the logic any.

"That's enough, boys," said Mr. Benedict.

He rose from his chair and walked over to the window and peeked out. Night had fallen and there weren't any streetlights like in town. Even with the illumination of the moonlight, they could barely see the road because it was so dark.

"It sure is dark out there," Rusty said, as he followed Mr. Benedict to the window.

Dale joined them. "Look," he said dramatically. "A full moon."

Rusty gasped. "Oh, no, Benny."

"What? What is it?"

"The maniac always attacks on a full moon."

"No wonder the lake rangers looked so concerned," said Dale.

Dale noticed Mr. Benedict peering into the darkness as he nervously bit his lip. Was he really believing their story?

"Dale," asked Rusty. "What do the locals call this maniac?"

He had to think a little about that. He didn't think the two of them got that far. "The Mad Sickle Man."

"The mad cycle man?" Rusty gave Dale a quick perplexed glance.

"Not cycle. *Sickle*," Dale said, almost hissing. "Remember? The maniac kills his victims with a sickle." Rusty still showed some confusion. "You know, the thing old-time farmers used to cut wheat."

"Oh yeah," Rusty said, recovering nicely. "That's what he uses to cut the heads off his victims."

"Right," Dale confirmed. "He slices them off in one, clean stroke."

"Well, at least the victims don't suffer much."

"Depends," Dale said. "Sometimes he tortures them before chopping their heads off. Sometimes the Mad Sickle Man first cuts off a finger, then a hand, then an arm, then –"

"That's enough, boys!" Mr. Benedict cried. "You know I don't believe you!"

"Dale," Rusty said in a hushed voice. "Did you see that?"

"See what?"

"That … that reflection."

"You mean like a reflection off a sharp farm tool of some kind?"

"Exactly."

"No … wait! Yes, I think I see it. Out there! Look, Mr. Benedict."

Dale pointed out the window beyond the dirt road, back into the inky woods. Mr. Benedict leaned forward. As he did, Dale, out of the corner of his eye, noticed Rusty sneaking behind the two of them.

"Aarrgh!" Rusty yelled, as he jumped on the back of their teacher. Mr. Benedict screamed – actually screamed – and stumbled into the wall with Rusty screeching in his ear.

"Stop it! Stop it!" Mr. Benedict cried. He tried to pry the wiry Rusty from off his back. "Unhand me!"

Rusty let go and retreated to the living room laughing hysterically. Dale laughed loudly too, remembering Mr. Benedict's high-pitched wail. How could a man that fat produce such a thin sound?

Mr. Benedict steadied himself and reached into his pocket to retrieve a handkerchief. He mopped his sweaty brow and let out a long, relieved breath.

"I knew you were fabricating," Mr. Benedict said, now fully recovered. "I knew it. You can't fool me."

"We can't?" Rusty said, suddenly serious again.

"Who says we were fabricating?" Dale intoned with an equally somber voice.

Mr. Benedict looked at them with uncertainty. His froggy eyes behind his glasses blinked with fear.

"I want the truth! You *were* making up the whole thing. No lake rangers, no maniac on the loose, no sickles! Tell me now!"

Dale looked at Rusty and saw that he was tired of playing the game.

"Of course we were making it all up," said Rusty, almost in disgust. "You're worse than a girl."

"We made it up while swimming today," said Dale.

Mr. Benedict forced a smile. "The vivid if not sanguinary imagination of you two lads," he said. He faked a chuckle. "I must admit that you almost convinced me at one point."

"When? The decapitation part?" asked Rusty.

Mr. Benedict's smile faded. "That's enough of that. Amusing story. Rather like a Grand Guignol."

Dale asked what that meant and Mr. Benedict briefly explained. Something to do with gory French drama. Being a teacher helped further calm him. He walked over to the kitchen. He said it was getting late and before bed, he preferred a cup of warm milk. He began preparing it. He asked Dale and Rusty if they would like some.

"Are you kidding?" Rusty said.

Dale said no to the milk and got another root beer. Rusty said, "isn't that your fourth?" Usually it was Rusty who drank the most.

"Fifth," Dale corrected.

The boys allowed Mr. Benedict to talk about nothing while he drank his glass of warm milk. Dale wondered why he didn't add Hershey's syrup or Ovaltine, the stuff Rusty and his brothers used. Rusty, not drinking, yawned.

The boys only half listened as Mr. Benedict talked about his two older sisters and his mother back in Iowa. He remembered how they used to drink hot milk before bedtime. He talked about how nice they were to him, always fussing and making sure he was well cared for. He enjoyed their attentions. It helped make up for the taunting he received from the boys at school for being chubby and clumsy.

Dale didn't hear anything about a father. He asked about that.

"Oh, my father died of a heart attack when I was young. He was rather overweight and worked too hard. He was a lawyer. He died at age thirty-nine." Mr. Benedict stared down at his almost empty glass of milk.

"That's too bad," said Dale.

"Yes," Mr. Benedict agreed. "I was eight."

Serious talk bored Rusty. "Let's turn on the radio."

"It's too late for that." Mr. Benedict got up to carry his glass to the sink. "It's after midnight." He returned and looked at the boys. "Aren't you two exhausted? You've been up since before six in the morning and you've played all day. I know I'm very fatigued."

Dale suddenly did feel tired. He looked at Rusty. His eyes were half closed.

"All right," Mr. Benedict said. "To bed we go. I'll take the couch. Which of you boys would like to sleep in the loft?"

Dale said he would. Rusty headed off to the bathroom. When he came out, he said "good night" in a sleepy voice, then paused. "Hey, we had fun today."

Dale nodded and Rusty went into his room.

In the bathroom, Dale brushed his teeth and washed his face but didn't feel the urge to pee. He'd had three root bears since his last visit, but he just shrugged and climbed the short stairs to the loft. The bed there was more like a mat, but he didn't mind. He felt like he could sleep on anything. He heard Mr. Benedict in the bathroom gargling but before Dale could chuckle he fell asleep.

He woke up in the middle of the night needing to pee. Dale knew he shouldn't have drunk the last two root beers because he hated getting up in the middle of the night to use the bathroom. Still groggy, he padded down the stairs, aided by a dim hall light. He passed Rusty's room when, from the corner of his eye, he saw something or someone standing before Rusty's bed. For a moment, he thought maybe there really was a Mad Sickle Man on the loose, but he shook that thought out of his mind and peered into the room from the doorway.

It was Mr. Benedict. He was gazing down at the sleeping Rusty and even in the semi-dark Dale could tell his teacher had a pained expression on his face. Mr. Benedict suddenly sensed another presence and gave Dale a startled look. Dale didn't say anything; he was thinking more of the imperative need to relieve himself. He used the bathroom and when he opened the door he saw Mr. Benedict waiting for him.

"What's up?" asked Dale.

Mr. Benedict motioned Dale to follow him into the main room. Dale, now more awake, began to think Mr. Benedict was acting very strangely. What was he doing in Rusty's room? Why was he gazing so intently at Rusty while he slept?

"I want you to know, Audie, that nothing happened," Mr. Benedict said.

"Nothing happened?"

"I just looked."

Dale thought this was weirder than some of his dreams. He suddenly felt uneasy. He felt like he did when his mother got sick. She'd wander the house in the middle of the night. Her ranting voice would wake him.

"Nothing happened," Mr. Benedict said. "Nothing ever does."

Dale said okay.

"Just pretend you didn't see any of it."

Dale said sure.

"Just go back to bed and forget all of it."

Dale nodded. He turned and went back to the loft. Lying on the mat, he wondered if he should go back down and check on Rusty. He decided he didn't have to. He was pretty sure Mr. Benedict wouldn't go into Rusty's bedroom any more, but if he did and tried anything, Rusty would wake up and punch him.

Dale had a hard time going back to sleep. But finally he did, hoping everything would be like before on the ride back to Galilee, but knowing it wouldn't.

# BOOK 3: *Wendy*

### Chapter 1: *Sadie's secret; bull-in-the-ring*

"Did you hear about Sadie?" Wendy asked Dale.

He shook his head no. He sat on the hood of his Chevy in the high school parking lot.

"She had to go stay at her *grandmother's*," Wendy said.

Dale waited for more. Wendy fidgeted as she did when nervous. She looked like she expected more of a reaction from him. He shrugged. "So?"

"She's going to be gone until next semester."

"Well, that's too bad."

He didn't know why Wendy seemed so concerned. Sadie had never been one of her good friends. He did wonder, however, how Rusty would react. He'd dated Sadie some that summer, although of late Rusty seemed more interested in Mary Jane and Roxanne and the other pretty high school girls.

"Sadie left for her grandmother's just *last week*," continued Wendy, speaking in an exaggeratedly clear way as if she were explaining a problem to a child.

"Yeah, so what?" He thought one of Wendy's least desirable characteristics was her excessive concern with other people's business.

"She'll be gone for *six* months."

"Well, I guess we'll all miss her until she gets back," said Dale, looking at the courtyard to see if Chris was ready.

"Oh, Audie," Wendy said, smiling broadly, "you're so naïve. That's one of your more endearing qualities."

Dale felt like he'd been insulted. He was about tell off Wendy, even if that hurt her feelings, when Chris and Carmen approached.

"Hey, what's your schedule?" asked Dale.

Chris said English, world history, calculus, Spanish, chemistry, and chorus.

"So we have two classes together," Dale said.

Chris asked Carmen and Wendy their class schedules. They told him and then asked what the boys were doing next. Chris said he and Dale were waiting for Rusty. Wendy said she had cheerleading practice. Carmen said she was going along with Wendy.

"Bye, Audie," Wendy said, smiling.

Dale noticed Wendy had *that* look in her eyes. A look his Grandpa called "calf love." He didn't want to encourage her.

"Bye," he said without enthusiasm.

The girls left and Chris joined Dale on the hood of the car even though there were patches of rust.

"Wendy and Carmen are really nice," Chris said, looking in their retreating direction.

Dale glanced over, then looked back to the courtyard. "What's your point?"

"Hey, what's eating you?"

"Nothing."

Actually, Dale was getting tired of this expectation that he should date Wendy. Not only did Wendy think that but everyone else did, too. Yeah, he thought, she was nice. Cute and smart and really, really nice.

A tall, skinny kid named Andrew Smith walked by. He had curly red hair, snow-white skin, freckles, and extremely pale blue eyes. Sometimes Dale couldn't even see the irises of his eyes from a distance. Some of the kids speculated that he might be an albino. But Dale had seen a real albino at the Wheaton track meet last spring and Andrew was no albino. For one thing, albinos had pink eyes. Andrew Smith was just a really pale kid.

"Hi, guys," he said as he passed by.

They said hey back.

"Now the only Smiths left in our class are you and Andy," said Chris.

So Chris had heard about Sadie, too.

"Wendy said she'd be coming back for spring semester," Dale said, suddenly wishing he hadn't said that. He sounded like the rest of the kids, especially the girls, who talked about people all the time.

"Well, until that time it's only you two."

There were several other Smiths in other classes. Dale wished he had a less common last name. People who didn't know him sometimes confused him with Andy. It didn't exactly insult Dale, even though Andy was pretty dumb. He and Andy were almost complete opposites. In fact, they would be if Andy were a girl.

"It's sort of funny," said Chris, "that you two guys have the same name and yet are so different."

"Maybe people should start calling me htims." Dale pronounced it "huh-tims." Of course, he didn't know how to really pronounce the word. He'd just made it up.

"What do you mean?"

"Because it's the opposite of Smith."

Chris shrugged. He still didn't get it.

Dale grinned. One thing about Rusty, he would have gotten that reference.

And wouldn't you know it, think of the devil's name and he appears. Dale and Chris got off the car and walked over to the courtyard. Rusty and Rich Erickson were talking to Roxanne and Gretchen. The two girls were sitting on a white bench wearing summer dresses. They looked lovely.

When the girls saw Dale and Chris, they said hi. Dale still felt nervous around Roxanne. When she said hi she smiled perfectly. Her lips had a natural reddish-pink color that really didn't need lipstick. Dale thought maybe her upper lip was a little too big. He preferred a smaller upper to contrast with a full lower. But her lips were nevertheless beautiful. Her eyes, with that sly, almost sleepy look, appealed to the boys. Maybe they were "bedroom eyes." Maybe they gave the boys false hope because Roxanne, as far as Dale knew, was chaste like most of the Galilee girls.

Dale noticed that Roxanne's blue eyes had a darker hue to them, especially in contrast to Gretchen's rather light blue. He remembered reading that Elizabeth Taylor was reputed to have "violet" eyes. He decided Roxanne's eyes looked like that color.

If anything, Roxanne looked almost too gorgeous. Dale thought some of the girls disliked her for that. Some said she was vain. But he didn't see her combing her strawberry blond hair, which she wore long with bangs, all the time; she didn't fuss with her face either like some girls. Some of the guys thought she was stuck-up. But she always said hi to him. Her only obvious drawback as far as Dale could determine was that she wasn't very smart. She didn't seem interested in any class and he'd never heard her say anything perceptive. He acknowledged that Roxanne was the most beautiful girl in high school, but he thought she lacked something besides smarts. She lacked … Dale couldn't think of the word. Something indescribable. Whatever it was she lacked, he thought Amanda had it. That's why he couldn't forget about Amanda.

The others had been talking and Dale hadn't really been listening. He heard Chris kiddingly say, "he's lost in deep thoughts as usual," and Dale snapped out of it and saw them smiling at him. Well, not Erickson or Rusty. Erickson in particular had a sardonic frown on his face.

"Is our philosopher ready?" asked Rusty, he didn't say it in a mean way. He just didn't have any interest in intellectual speculation or reflection in general. Whenever Dale talked about something "philosophical," Rusty got bored. He lived for the moment; he didn't like thinking about what things meant.

Dale said yeah and the boys said bye to Roxanne and Gretchen and walked into the high school and got their locker assignments. Rusty had decided to locker with Dale and Chris. Dale had thought maybe he wouldn't, breaking one of their rituals. Rusty had wanted Erickson to be the third guy, but Dale wanted Chris. To settle the impasse, they threw for it. Dale threw down a rock and beat Rusty's scissors. Rusty got mad and Dale thought he might locker with Erickson anyway. But in the end, he honored their deal.

Dale asked Erickson whom he was lockering with and he said Sonny and Billy Joe. Erickson then said "see ya later" and split. Rusty, Dale, and Chris checked out their locker, now in the junior class section, and then walked to the gym.

Rusty asked Dale his schedule. He said English, world history, business machines, bookkeeping, art, and gym. Chris asked why he was taking business machines and bookkeeping. Dale shrugged. He didn't really know. That was what the school academic counselor, Mr. Simon Smedley, recommended.

Dale remembered sitting in the counselor's office last spring as Mr. Smedley searched his files for Dale's records. Mr. Smedley wore a rumpled gray suit, a yellow bow tie and rather small, square-shaped glasses. Dale noticed a button missing on his blue shirt and when the counselor stepped from behind his desk, he saw that his socks didn't match; one was brown, the other blue. Mr. Smedley kept muttering, "A. Smith, A. Smith," and Dale shook his head and thought Mr. Smedley reminded him of the old teachers, the ones hanging on for retirement, except that Mr. Smedley wasn't that old. Maybe forty. Finally, Mr. Smedley found the records and flipped through them while Dale looked around his small, junky office. The counselor said according to Dale's aptitude scores he should consider a career in business. He said he didn't really need to take geometry or chemistry or a foreign language. Dale shrugged. He took algebra as a freshman and hated it. The only foreign language offered by the high school was Spanish and Rusty, who took Spanish I, said they spent most of their time repeating one Spanish phrase after another. Dale didn't like speaking in class; he felt self-conscious of the way he spoke. He knew he wouldn't be able to pronounce the Spanish words properly so he didn't really want to take the course. But it puzzled him that Mr. Smedley thought he should take business courses. Dale didn't have any interest in business. He'd rather take more courses in English or history. Or philosophy if his high school offered it, which it didn't. Mr. Smedley said one English class and one history class was sufficient for a student of Dale's background. So, business machines and bookkeeping it was.

When they got to the gym, Chris said hiss father wanted him to do some work around their house before football practice. He told Dale and Rusty he'd see them later.

Dale and Rusty shot some baskets until Cookie came up from the bowels of the locker room and told them to scram. Rusty bounced the ball toward him and it hit Cookie in the shins prompting a growl from the old man. Dale had heard one of seniors last year saying that Cookie was a former coach who'd fallen on hard times and Dorfman had given him his job. As they walked out of the gym, Dale scrutinized Cookie and thought it was possible he'd been a coach. He hated kids enough.

Dale walked with Rusty to his car. He thought Rusty seemed unusually quiet. He wondered if he was thinking about Sadie.

"Did you hear about Sadie?"

Rusty leaned back against his Rambler and looked at the bright blue sky. "Yeah, I heard."

"So, is that what's bugging you?"

"What? Sadie? No. I wasn't seeing her anymore."

Dale waited. There was something else.

"Did you know Mr. Benedict resigned?" Rusty asked, looking at Dale in an almost suspicious way as if he'd heard something about it and hadn't told him.

"No."

Dale should have been surprised, but he wasn't. He didn't feel that little punch that accompanied a real surprise.

"Sort of strange," Rusty said. "Mrs. Page said he abruptly resigned two weeks ago. The school had to scramble to find a replacement."

"Yeah, that is strange. You'd think he'd give the school more time."

Rusty looked down at the ground. He seemed lost in thought. "He didn't say anything to you, did he?"

"Mr. Benedict? No, he didn't say anything to me."

Dale thought about the time at the cabin, although he knew Rusty wasn't referring to that. He remembered how strange it had been riding back to Galilee with Mr. Benedict. Rusty had been his usual irrepressible self. When he teased Mr. Benedict, their teacher had hardly responded. He sat passively, almost glumly, in the driver's seat and stared at the road as he drove. Even when Rusty called him Mr. Zero or Son of Blob, he didn't react much. When Rusty asked, "what's wrong with you, man?" Mr. Benedict said that he was tired. Eventually, Rusty gave up and listened to Mr. Benedict's tapes. Rusty didn't like that music much, the mellow and romantic music of the early '70s, but he was so discouraged he didn't make fun of it.

Dale hadn't been in the mood to talk either. He pretended to sleep during part of the trip. When Rusty grew frustrated with the lack of talking, joking, and general stimulation, he turned back to Dale and asked, "hey, am I missing something here?"

Dale caught Mr. Benedict looking at him in the rearview mirror. His eyes had a strange look in them. Not fear, exactly, more like they were pleading. Dale told Rusty he wasn't missing anything. They were just tired. Rusty stared, but said nothing. He knew something was wrong, but he didn't want to make a big deal out of it.

"Did you have a fight with Mr. Zero back at the cabin?" asked Rusty.

Dale said no, he didn't.

"That's what I thought because we were always together and I don't remember any real fight or anything. I mean, we pretty much tormented the slob, but we always did that."

"Why do you ask?"

"Because everything changed after that trip."

"Like what?"

"For one, you stopped going over to Benny's apartment."

"I told you I had to get ready for football."

"Yeah, right." Rusty studied the sky. Dale could tell he didn't like thinking about such mysterious matters. "And Mr. Benedict changed, too."

Dale asked in what way.

"He stopped being so pompous. He didn't *respond*. He wasn't any fun anymore. So, I stopped going. The only other guy ever there was Kevin, and he's too well behaved.

Erickson wouldn't come over. You know how he dislikes Benny."

Dale remembered overhearing Erickson talking to Sonny last year and saying "yeah, he's queer" and Dale hadn't thought much about it at the time. Just Erickson disparaging someone he didn't like. But Dale now thought he was talking about Mr. Benedict. He wondered if he should tell Rusty about that night in the cabin. He hadn't told anyone about it. He couldn't tell his parents. Jesse probably wouldn't understand and Blackie would understand too well. Dale had thought about telling someone at school or even the Nazarene church but what would he say? That Mr. Benedict liked watching Rusty sleep? That sounded ridiculous. The more Dale thought about that the weirder it seemed to him. No, not weird exactly. Strange and sad.

Dale debated whether to tell Rusty what he'd seen. He didn't know if that would do any good. If he had told him the next morning after it had happened, Rusty might have done something. Rusty wasn't especially aggressive; he didn't like fighting. But he might have punched Mr. Benedict if Dale had told him. A violent response didn't seem right. Maybe if Mr. Benedict had actually tried something; maybe if Dale had seen him slobbering or moaning or doing something disgusting, he would have told Rusty. Heck, he would have slugged him himself. But Mr. Benedict seemed pathetic and unthreatening as he stood over Rusty's bed and watched him sleep. Dale didn't understand it. It puzzled him in the same way his mother's illness puzzled him. He wondered what was really going on inside both of them.

"So, you're not going to say anything?" Rusty was referring to Mr. Benedict's sudden departure.

"I'm as surprised as you."

"But he didn't say *anything*. About leaving, I mean."

"Yeah, that's odd. But odd things happen in life."

Rusty grinned. "Spoken like a true philosopher."

Dale shrugged. Maybe he'd tell Rusty the truth sometime.

"And the darndest thing about it," Rusty said with a shake of his head, "is that I sort of miss Mr. Zero."


Dale followed Chris onto the bus. He liked how his cleats clattered on the bus floor. When they wore steel cleats, the guys, especially the lineman, really made a racket.

Dale sat with Chris in the middle seats of the bus. The seniors sat in the back, the sophomores in front. Two-a-days were almost over. They hadn't been as hard as Dale expected. Last year the guys acted like two-a-days were hell on earth. But now that they were almost over he thought that while they were exhausting at first, once he got in shape the practices began to get a little tedious.

Coach Dorfman had taken the team to Red Rock Canyon State Park, located about thirty miles west of Galilee, for the first day of two-a-days. After the morning practice, without pads because the first week they didn't wear pads, the team had a picnic lunch together. Coach warned them not to eat too much but some of the guys, in particular the two big linemen Leroy Lemmon and Doug MacDonald, ignored him. Then in the afternoon practice after the usual drills and scrimmage, Coach made the whole team run up the dirt road that led to the red rocks. The guys who heeded Coach's advice didn't have too much trouble. They felt exhausted when they made it to the top but nothing else. But Lemmon and MacDonald and a couple of other guys made it only halfway before they got sick. Dale, at the top, could hear them barfing below. It was almost funny listening to their retching sounds echo in the canyon. Fat Mac then got so overheated he collapsed. Blocker put him in his air-conditioned car and drove to a clinic. Turned out he was just dehydrated and he only missed one day of practice.

Practice got tougher when they put on pads, but Dale, now weighing 147 pounds and standing five foot and five and one half inches, didn't feel completely overmatched as he had last season. And since the backs and ends had contact drills with each other and not with the linemen, he didn't dread tackling drills. Terry Harte and Charlie Comingdeer were the most powerful backs. Both weighed 180 pounds, but they always drew one another in the tackling drills. It was like watching two stags crash into each other when those two collided.

"The last day of two-a-days," said Chris, with a relieved smile.

Chris didn't weigh much more than Dale; maybe ten pounds more. Since he played end, he and Dale sometimes drew each other in the contact drills. Dale always got the better of it because he was four inches shorter and could get leverage. Once he'd hit Chris under his shoulder pads and knocked the air out of his pal. He felt sorry for Chris as he watched him writhe on the ground, making hiccupping sounds until he caught his breath. From then on he tried not to draw him. If he saw Chris coming up during his turn, Dale would slip behind Sonny or K. C. One time he couldn't change places and Dale didn't hit Chris at full speed and Coach Blocker yelled at him.

"Maybe Coach will go easy on us today," said Chris.

Dale shrugged. He appreciated that Chris had never taken personally the smashes he'd received from him.

K. C. and Butch Bigelow sat in the seat in front of them. They were talking low and occasionally snorting, at least that's how Dale characterized Bigelow's nasal laugh. Bigelow increasingly reminded him of a pig; well, more like a wild boar because he was a predator. Dale disliked the way Bigelow liked hitting guys, especially smaller guys. Butch enjoyed hurting them.

"I heard someone knocked her up," K. C. said lowly. Then Bigelow said, "well, it wasn't me, man," and he snorted again. Dale knew immediately whom they were talking about. Now he understood the meaning behind Wendy's comments about Sadie going to her grandmother's.

Dale felt shocked, the way he felt back in seventh grade when a freshman, Glen Dennison, talked cruelly about Dale's cousin, Tammy Walsh, not knowing she was Dale's cousin. Dale sort of liked Dennison. He wasn't as mean to the seventh graders as most freshmen. Dennison had laughed in a scornful way as he told Jerry Dewberry that Tammy was a slut. Dale remembered feeling his face burning with shame. Even though Tammy was two years older than he was, he spent a lot of time playing with her when he was in grade school, especially during the summers. He liked her even if she was a girl. Dale had wanted to punch Dewberry, but he also felt somehow tainted by his association with Tammy. Then two years ago, Tammy dropped out of tenth grade. She had a baby and she didn't go back to high school. Dale felt both sorry and angry with her. She seemed to be an example of how some of his mother's family seemed to live down to the hillbilly or even white trash level.

Dale must have been staring at Bigelow without realizing it because he heard Butch say, "what are you lookin' at, Smith?"

Dale thought about saying "oink, oink" but he didn't have Rusty's impulsive ways so he said, "nothing."

"Good. Keep looking that way," replied Bigelow. That didn't quite make sense to Dale, but he didn't expect Butch to express himself logically.

"Did you hear that?" whispered Chris. Dale nodded. "Do they mean that Sadie is ..." Chris couldn't bring himself to say it. Dale understood. It was a big word.

"Yeah, I guess."

"*Boy.*"

Dale wondered if Rusty knew. He didn't seem to have any idea as to why Sadie had left school. Of course, Rusty tended to practice an out-of-sight out-of-mind form of friendship. Dale wondered if Rusty could be the father. What a strange idea. He didn't think so. As far as he knew, Rusty had never even done the deed, let alone done it so successfully. Dale looked at Bigelow again. Still engaged in a sneaky conversation with K. C., Bigelow

151

was a different matter. Butch puzzled Dale. He was a Nazarene boy but he wasn't nice or considerate or openly religious at all. Dale guessed Bigelow was just one of those guys who goes to church because he's required to. His parents were heavily involved in church activities. Still, it was hard to believe that Bigelow would get a girl in trouble and be so callous. Dale stared intentionally at Bigelow this time.

Bigelow felt the stare and turned his head just enough to glare back at Dale. Neither boy said anything. But they both knew what the other was thinking.

Coach Dorfman boarded the bus ending the stare-off. Dorfman told Cookie to get the bus moving. Dale thought Coach gave them an almost mysterious look as the bus lurched forward.

The last day of two-a-days started as expected. They did their calisthenics and drills, including Dale's favorite, the three-man roll. In that drill, three men get in a row on their hands and knees; then, on the whistle, the middle guy rolls to his right, the guy on the right leaps over him, then the guy on the far left heaves himself over that guy and so on until coach blows the whistle to stop. It was sort of like the players were juggling themselves. Dale liked the drill, but that was because he was quick and agile.

Then the offense ran plays while the defense practiced strategy. Then they scrimmaged, the first team offense against the mostly second team defense since the best players played both offense and defense. Dale scrimmaged with the offense at halfback. Even though he suspected that Dorfman didn't like him, he'd won a starting spot on both offense and defense.

After scrimmage Dale expected the usual end to practice: sprints. He liked them, too. He outran everyone, including Terry Harte, although he usually just beat Harte by a nose. His right leg felt almost normal. He hadn't done anything special that summer. No lifting weights or special conditioning. He'd just swum and played sandlot baseball. But he'd done that a lot and the exercise had strengthen his joints and muscles of his right leg until it was almost as strong as his left leg.

Coach Dorfman blew his whistle and waved the players over to him. Dale trotted over wondering why they weren't running sprints. He waited for Coach to start his post-practice evaluation, but instead Dorfman said: bull-in-the-ring.

Some of the players cheered. Coach said, "Two groups. Sophomores go with Coach Blocker. Upperclassmen stay with me."

The ten sophomores followed Blocker down field. The remaining twenty-two players formed a circle. Dale looked at Chris, who shrugged his shoulders as to say "how could I forget," then the two of them got in place. Dale remembered the guys talking about bull-in-the-ring last year, but he didn't really know what it was. They'd just refer to it, usually to let him know how "lucky" he was to have missed it. Of course, they said lucky as if they meant "chicken."

The players now standing in a circle, Coach pointed to Terry Harte and told him to start the count. Harte said one then the next guy, K. C., said two and so forth until it got to Dale who said twenty-one and then the count ended with Charlie Comingdeer. Coach nodded at Comingdeer. He left the circle and stood in the middle of the ring. Dale realized he was the bull.

Coach called one. Harte shot out and collided with Comingdeer. Their collision sounded like a clap of thunder.

"Good hit!" Dorfman said.

Then he called twelve. Billy Joe Barton smashed into Comingdeer. Coach called his next calls more quickly in succession. First, Middleton dashed out and hit Comingdeer. Before Charlie could quite regain his balance, Dorfman shouted eleven and Robbie Castro bolted out and hit Comingdeer, making him lose his balance. Then Coach said five and MacDonald, all 240 pounds of him, lumbered toward Comingdeer, but MacDonald was so slow that Charlie recovered and slammed into the much bigger player.

152

"Good hit!" shouted Dorfman. "Way to attack the big guy!"

After three more calls, Comingdeer was clearly exhausted. But he hadn't been knocked off his feet. "Good job," Coach said, as Comingdeer joined the circle. Harte took his place and handled the hits with admirable perseverance. Strong and quick, no one could knock Harte off his feet, not even Lemmon who got a better start than MacDonald. Dale waited for his number to be called. He felt tense and almost sick to his stomach the way he did before a race. But Dorfman hadn't called twenty-one yet and so Dale remained in his stance anticipating his number because if a guy didn't respond immediately Coach would yell at them for not quickly reacting.

Bigelow was third in the ring. Dale, who'd been less eager with Comingdeer and Harte, now hoped his number would be called. He got ready. He dug his cleats into the grass and made fists of his hands. After three numbers, he heard twenty-one! and he bolted just as Coach finished saying the number. Dale raced at Bigelow, lowered his shoulders, and hit a glancing blow off Butch's shoulder pads. Bigelow grunted, but easily stayed on his feet. Dale rebounded off him and almost lost his balance. Forty pounds made a bigger difference than what he'd anticipated.

Bigelow, to Dale's disappointment, did almost as well as Harte and Comingdeer. Then Coach made MacDonald the bull. The big redhead did pretty well at first. No one knocked him down. But he grew tired. After five hits, Dorfman sped up the process and before MacDonald could break free from one collision another player arrived and soon a human traffic jam developed and MacDonald fell to one knee before three players knocked him down. He lay sprawled on the turf panting and tried rising to his feet only to collapse.

"Okay, okay. Help him up, men," Dorfman said with disgust. "Looks like we ought to call this elephant in the ring."

Harte and K. C. helped MacDonald, wheezing and stumbling, to the sidelines. Coach paused. He looked over the players. Dale felt his heart thumping in his chest, more out of a sense of foreboding than exertion.

"Okay, Smith, you're the bull."

There was only one Smith on the football team so Dale couldn't pretend Coach meant another Smith. He took his spot in the middle of the ring. He bent his knees and lowered his shoulders in anticipation. He saw the eyes of his teammates glittering from inside their helmets. He could hear them breathing, short puffs of breath like they were trying to blow up a balloon.

"I don't think you got a taste of this last year," said Dorfman, smiling. He paused. "One!"

Harte hit him like a battering ram. Dale stayed low, but Harte got enough weight under him that Dale felt himself fly off his feet but not high enough to make him fall.

"Four!"

Lemmon came barreling at him, a moving mountain. Dale knew he couldn't let Leroy get a head of steam so he ran forward and crashed into him before Lemmon took three steps. Dale heard himself grunt involuntarily from the impact. For all of Lemmon's blubber, he was nevertheless surprisingly solid. Dale felt like he'd smashed into a truck. Lemmon had absorbed most of the blow, but it didn't stagger him at all. He used his heavy arms to shove Dale back five yards.

"Twenty!"

Chris hit Dale with unexpected force. Dale almost fell then, but he regained his balance. Then Coach called number nineteen and Sonny hit him. Sonny, who weighed only 160 pounds and played quarterback, didn't deliver much of a blow. But Dale felt surprisingly tired. He'd only taken four hits and already he gasped for breath and felt his stomach heaving and his limbs burning.

Coach called seven and Middleton rushed forward. Dale wanted to give Middleton a good hit. He still resented him for taking Amanda to the all-sports banquet. But in his eagerness, Dale missed most of Middleton and had to dig his cleats in the ground to stop. He heard

Coach yell thirteen. Before Dale could completely turn around to face the charging sound behind him, he felt a blow overwhelm him and knock him off his feet. From the ground, he saw Bigelow standing over him, smiling.

Dale jumped on his feet and tried to ignore the urge to collapse and end the torture. He felt dizzy and weak. He didn't seem able to crouch anymore. Coach shouted twelve and Billy Joe hit him hard and Dale felt himself flying backward in the air before crashing into the dirt. He felt like never getting up.

"Had enough?" Dorfman said.

He said it with such disrespect that Dale grew angry. His anger helped pull him to his feet.

"Good," Coach said. "Twenty-two!"

Dale dreaded hearing that number even more than Harte's number one. Panting, nauseated, drenched with sweat, he could barely hold his head up. He felt like bawling and giving up. It wasn't the pain or exhaustion that threatened to unman him as much as it was the feeling that everyone was against him. He felt alone. It was as if all his teammates were generating a force of will against him; the force generated energy that pummeled him with more power than the actual collisions. But he resisted the urge to give up and cry. He steadied himself as best he could and watched as Comingdeer charged him. Comingdeer then rammed him with astonishing force. While flying backward through the air, Dale felt as if he were falling into a dark pit. He almost wanted to laugh at how hard he'd been hit, but before he could he was swallowed by the darkness.

He opened his eyes a few seconds later, feeling Harte and K. C. tugging him to his feet. Dorfman peered into his eyes. Coach didn't seem to be in focus, and at first Dale couldn't hear him although he saw Coach's mouth moving. Then Dale's head cleared and he heard Dorfman say, "You all right, Smith?"

He nodded. Coach slapped him on top of his helmet, which didn't really help Dale's condition, and said, "good job." Then he blew his whistle, the shrill sound echoing in Dale's head. Coach waved for the sophomores to join them. Dale stumbled against Chris.

"You okay, Audie?"

He nodded.

"Man, you looked funny flying around like that," said K. C.

Dale nodded.

He tried to listen to Dorfman as he evaluated the teams' practice, but Dale's mind drifted back to the last time he'd been hit so hard. It was in eighth grade. He was approaching the ball carrier and almost had him when the runner cut left and Dale turned around in full stride and got hit square in the chest by a bigger kid. Dale must have been knocked five yards down the field. He had a cold and a stuffy nose and he'd been hit so hard that all the snot exploded out his nose. Dale had no idea where the mucus landed. He hoped on the guy who cleaned his clock. The blow and hitting the ground hard knocked him out for a few seconds. When he came to, he was sprawled on his back with completely clear sinuses.

Dale tuned in Dorfman to hear him say he expected *this* team to be winners. No excuses this year. He said they'd scrimmage tomorrow against Sundance Prep. Some of the guys muttered curse words under their breaths. Dale wondered if Coach knew Galilee's recent history against Sundance Prep. Dorfman said he knew it was a bigger school but he wanted the Gophers to face a tough scrimmage opponent to make Galilee stronger for the regular season. Dorfman said they'd had done well during two-a-days. Then Harte led the team in chanting Go-phers! Go-phers! and practice was over.

Dale slowly walked to the bus with Chris. Now that he had recovered enough to speak, he told Chris, "Yeah, that was an *easy* practice."

Chris laughed and slapped him on the shoulder pads. Dale joined the team on the bus. He felt like a real member this year. Even with an aching body, that felt good.

**Chapter 2: *Clean livin', Bigelow's threat, getting hurt at the scrimmage***

Grandpa spat a stream of tobacco juice into the empty Folger's can. He noticed Dale looking at him.

"You don't chew, do ye?" he said.

"Nope."

"You don't smoke neither?"

Dale shook his head no.

"Too young to drink, I reckon."

Dale nodded. He remembered Grandpa taking a snort, as he called it, when Dewey visited once. His uncle passed a bottle in a brown paper bag to Grandpa and he looked to make sure Grandma was still in the kitchen before taking a swig. Grandma found out anyway and cussed him.

"Well, that's good, Audie Dale," Grandpa said as he rubbed his grizzled face. Then he took his chaw of tobacco out of his front shirt pocket and gnawed a hunk out of it. "That's mighty good," he added, chewing vigorously. "A young feller ought to practice clean livin'."

Dale knew why he practiced clean livin', as Grandpa called it. Part of it was living in Galilee. Most of his classmates didn't smoke or drink either. Of course, a lot of them were Nazarene kids and the Nazarenes were pretty strict. But the other reason was that Dale had never liked his parents smoking and drinking and cussing. Even as a little boy that kind of behavior bothered him. He guessed he rebelled like most kids do, but in his case he rebelled to clean livin'.

Grandma, Jesse, and June May came out of the kitchen and sat down. June May, upset about something, flung herself down on the couch next to Dale.

"What's your problem, little lady?" Grandpa asked.

June May frowned. "Oh, it's *mother*."

Jesse shook her head. "She's been going on about it for days."

"Goin' on about what?" Grandpa asked.

"A boy asked her out on a date and I told her no."

"He's a *sophomore*," said June May. She turned to Dale. "In high school."

Dale rolled his eyes at his sister's redundancy. "What's his name?"

"Marty Dewberry," she said, as if Dale should be impressed.

He knew the kid, all right. Younger brother of Jerry Dewberry. He didn't play high school football and he reminded Dale of a sheep dog with his long, shaggy, dirty blond hair that hung all around his head except for a window for his goofy face.

"He's a jerk," said Dale.

"He is not!"

"It don't matter nohow," said Jesse. "You ain't goin' out with him or any boy. You're too young."

"I married when I was near sixteen," said Grandma.

"Well, Mama, June May's only thirteen."

"Yep, that's a might young. To get married."

"See, Momma. Grandma thinks it's okay if I go on a date," said June May.

"Didn't say that, June May," Grandma corrected. "I said a might young for gettin' hitched."

June May tossed herself back against the couch and pouted. Dale shook his head in disgust at his silly sister. "You can't date at thirteen."

"Just cause you don't date even at *sixteen* doesn't mean that I can't."

"Yes it does, June May," said Jesse.

"Oh, *mother*," June May said. "Don't you know that girls develop faster nowadays?"

"What'd she say?" Grandpa asked.

He spat in his Folger's can again. This time, in deference to the women, he'd picked the can up and held it close to his face so he wouldn't have to spit so far.

"Somethin' about developin'," said Grandma.

"Developin'?" repeated Grandpa. "What in tarnation does that mean?"

"It means maturing," said June May, almost smugly.

Dale had to admit that June May was maturing outwardly but she still was a silly child inside.

"Don't care how developed you are," Jesse said, "you ain't going on no date at thirteen."

"*Mother*!"

The phone rang and put an end to the debate for the time being. Grandma rose heavily from her chair and picked up the phone. She said hello loudly. She listened for a while, then talked some, and Grandpa asked who was calling.

"It's Pearl," Grandma said.

Pearl was Dewey's wife. Dewey was the second oldest Walsh son and the father of Tammy and two older boys, Otis and Billy Dee. Dale considered his uncle Dewey as the most taciturn man he'd ever encountered, even more uncommunicative than Cookie. Dale guessed Dewey had never said more than ten words in his presence. Most of the time he just grunted. He'd worked construction all his adult life and was now a foreman. Dale remembered how sinewy his arms looked, toughened up by years of hard work. Dale had been afraid of his uncle as a little boy, even though Dewey had never done anything mean to him.

Grandma hung up the phone. She bustled over to her chair and collapsed into it.

"Whale, what'd she want?" Grandpa asked. He had a rather low opinion of Pearl. He'd once called her a blabbermouth.

Grandma shook her head. "Billy Dee's back in prison."

"Awl be," said Grandpa. "Weren't he just let out?"

"Yes'm. Three months ago. But he got arrested for selling that dope. He's goin' back in for a long time this time."

Grandpa began talking about how the younger generation was going to hell in a hand basket. In his day, the Walsh family was poor but honest. Everyone worked hard and was law abiding. No shame was ever brought to the family. Grandpa didn't understand what was happening to his grandkids. Some were on welfare. Some of the girls were having babies out of wedlock. Some of the boys were going to prison. Now, Billy Dee had done even worse by selling that evil dope, which was a damn sight worse than alcohol. At least whiskey only got you drunk whereas dope made you crazy. Grandpa looked at Dale. He asked if any of his friends took dope.

"No. Least I don't think so."

He'd heard a few rumors. Some of the bad kids who smoked cigarettes were reputed to have smoked marijuana, too. Dale had heard some speculation that maybe a few of his classmates had tried grass. None of his close friends. But maybe Sonny, Billy Joe, and Leroy had tried it. Dale didn't believe it. They played football.

"You ain't ever goin' try that dope, are you Audie Dale?"

Dale shook his head. "No, sir, I ain't."

Grandpa nodded and spat in the direction of the Folger's can. He missed by a hair. "You keep at your clean livin' ways," he said.

Dale sat next to Vern Jurgens in their business machines class. He couldn't help but wonder what Vern was doing here. He was one of the smartest boys in their class. But then Dale remembered that Vern wasn't going to college. His religion didn't think that was important. Boys were supposed to get practical jobs after they graduated from high school.

Vern would probably be a carpenter. Dale remembered all the impressive stuff he'd made in eighth-grade shop. A gun rack, a cabinet, even a baseball bat on the lathe.

"Why are you taking this class?" asked Vern.

Dale wondered that himself. So far, the class had been as tedious as it sounded. He was pretty good at it though. He'd easily mastered the ten-key machine. But he'd always been dexterous and quick with his fingers. Just to keep the class work interesting, he'd started doing all the calculations without the machine, just by hand, the way he did when adding stats for the IBL.

Dale's next class, bookkeeping, was even more boring. Worse, Dorfman taught it. Dale was one of five boys in the class. The other fifteen students were girls. So, that was interesting. All the popular junior girls were in the class, including Amanda. She sat up front with Mary Jane, Roxanne, Gretchen, and Wendy. Dale sat in the back with Sonny and Billy Joe – who were not college material.

So far, the class had been easy. Much of the time, Dorfman entertained the girls. They asked him questions about the football team and the businesses he'd managed before going into teaching. Dale, to his amazement, had learned that Dorfman once managed a Whataburger in Agra. On second thought, that didn't surprise Dale. Dorfman would make an excellent Whataburgerian.

Rusty was in four of Dale's classes: history, English, gym, and art. They didn't have much opportunity to goof off in history or English. Coach Blocker taught history and he often spent most of class reading from the history book and having students write down what he read. The first time that happened, Rusty said, "déjà vu," and he, Dale, and Erickson chuckled.

In English, Mrs. Page was a dynamic teacher and she didn't take any guff. If Rusty or Erickson or some other smart aleck started goofing off, she'd glare at them until the guy straightened up. Dale thought it was kind of funny that Mrs. Page exerted such authority in the classroom, because she was a small woman. But she had such a magisterial presence that even consummate cutups like Rusty and Erickson didn't provoke her.

Dale respected Mrs. Page. In sophomore English, she read *The Merchant of Venice* to the class and did it so well that she inspired Dale to read *Hamlet* on his own. Besides sophomore and junior English, she also taught speech and drama. She supervised the high school plays, including the all-school play, the "big production" that was staged every spring. Dale had heard that Mrs. Page was the cousin of the popular '50s singer from Oklahoma, Patti Page. At first, he'd doubted the rumor. After all, Mrs. Page's name was her married name. But when Wendy told him that Mrs. Page's maiden name was Vivian Fowler and Patti Page's real name was Clara Ann Fowler, Dale changed his mind. Whether or not Mrs. Page and the famous singer were related, Dale could believe Mrs. Page had show-biz folks in her family. Still attractive in her mid-forties, she had an impressive "stage" presence in the classroom. Dale could easily imagine her as a professional actress. But instead of going on stage, she taught high school, was one of the women leaders in the First Church, and had raised three children, all girls. Two of the daughters, Portia and Laurie, had been voted all-school queen. The second daughter, Emily, had been popular as well. Since Dale liked Mrs. Page, he refused to goof off even when tempted by Rusty.

The art class was a different story. A new teacher, Miss Roach, who immediately had a difficult time keeping control of the class, taught it. Rusty and Dale sat at one end of the room, Butch Bigelow and K. C. sat at the other end. Simply put, Miss Roach was outflanked. Dale tried not to goof off too much; he actually was interested in learning how to draw better. He'd always been a pretty good cartoonist. He'd draw a succession of cartoons in the margins of his paperback books so when he flipped the pages they moved like an animated cartoon. But he wanted to learn to draw "for real" and thought the art class would help.

Sitting in class the day after bull-in-the-ring, Dale wondered why Bigelow was taking the class. He doubted that Bigelow had even one artistic bone in his hulking body. He suspected that Butch, along with several other students, took an art class with a new, young teacher thinking it would be easy.

On the way out of class, Bigelow "accidentally" bumped into Dale.

"Sorry," Bigelow said sarcastically. "Didn't mean to knock you down. *Again.*"

Dale stared into his porcine face. "Only because you hit me in the back."

He'd exaggerated. Bigelow had hit him more on the side than the back, but Dale knew Butch would have had no compunction smashing him in the back if he had the chance.

"Yeah, right," said Bigelow.

"Hey, Bigelow," Rusty said. "I hear old MacDonald calling you."

Bigelow started to say something ruder than usual, when K. C. intervened.

"Cool it, guys," he said. "We're all friends here."

Bigelow glared at Rusty. Dale wondered whom Butch now hated more, him or Rusty.

"I'll see you, *friend*, at practice," he said to Dale.

Dale shook his head. Just like Bigelow to forget they had a scrimmage today. His threat didn't matter anyway. They both started on defense and Bigelow practiced with the line during contact drills. So he wouldn't have a chance to smash him.

Bigelow and K. C. turned and walked away. Dale and Rusty stood to the side, allowing the rest of the kids to leave the classroom. As they filed out, some of the girls looked at them. The only girl that Dale and Rusty knew well was Carmen. She was a pretty good artist already. She drew horses really well. Carmen paused and gave them a suspicious glance, like she had just seen a wanted poster with their faces on it. Then she scurried down the hall to catch up with Peggy.

"I think I know what they're thinking," said Dale, glancing at Rusty.

"Oh, yeah? And what would that be, mind reader?"

"You know. About Sadie."

Rusty shook his head in disgust. He leaned closer to Dale as they walked down the hall. "It wasn't me," he said lowly. "I only got to first base with her." He took a few more steps. "Well, make that second base."

"Third base?" asked Dale, although he wasn't exactly sure of the definition. He knew baseball, he didn't know girls.

Rusty shrugged. "I'll tell you this, I never made it all the way home."

He looked somberly at Dale. Dale believed him.

The seniors were motivated against Sundance Prep. Some of them like Harte and Comingdeer had played in the massacre two years ago. Even though a scrimmage was a lot different than a regular season game, the seniors, and the whole team, had a lot to prove that Friday.

Galilee held its own. Sundance scored three times on six possessions, whereas Gailee scored twice on five possessions. But what impressed Coach Dorfman the most was how hard his team hit. They were smaller than the Sundance team, but they were "taking it to them," as he remarked during a time out.

Dale started at cornerback on defense and right halfback on offense. He'd done pretty well. He'd made two tackles and covered his man effectively on defense. On offense, he'd only carried the ball three times for relatively short yardage. But Harte, the left halfback, broke two long runs for scores and on both runs Dale threw good blocks.

During the break, Dale felt a surge of confidence in himself and his team. They were doing better than he expected against Sundance Prep. Last week in their first scrimmage against Agra and Quanah Parker, Galilee clearly had the better team. Dale was beginning to think this year would be different. Maybe they'd finish the season with a winning record for the first time in five years.

Near the end of the scrimmage, the two teams brought in their second units. Dorfman left

Dale in on offense, moving him to left halfback. Dale wanted to stay in. He hadn't run the ball as much as he'd liked. But he did worry a little about the second team linemen. They were mostly sophomores, and Sundance Prep's defensive linemen outweighed each guy by at least twenty pounds.

Chris trotted into the huddle with the play from Dorfman. He told Sonny, the quarterback. Then Sonny said, I formation, slot left, 22 trap. That meant Dale would move to the slot position just outside the tackle. Sonny would fake the ball to the tailback to the right, drawing the nose guard and middle linebacker in. Then Dale, pausing for two counts, would race down behind the line and take a hand off and cut up into the line on the right side of the center. If the nose guard and linebacker fell for the trap, it meant a big gain.

Dale liked the play. However, if the two defensive players didn't fall for the trap, then the runner usually got smashed for a loss.

The offense lined up and on the second hut, Sonny took the ball from center and did the fake as Dale sprinted behind the line. The play went according to plan. He snatched the ball, cut straight up, raced through a big hole, and juked the safety and almost broke the run for a touchdown. A gain of twenty-three yards.

Dale trotted back to the huddle, a little winded. Billy Joe brought in the play. 22 trap again. Dale knew Coach Dorfman had a penchant of calling the same play again if it had resulted in a big gain the first time. Coach believed in running a play until the defense stopped it. Dale didn't agree with such strategy. He thought it better to run a variety of plays to keep the defense on its heels. He especially didn't think Dorfman's strategy made sense with a deceptive play like a trap.

They broke huddle and Dale lined up at slot again. Maybe the Sundance defense thought their formation was a trick. Whatever the reason, the play worked again, but not for as many yards. This time the safety was ready and tackled Dale after eight yards.

Chris brought in the next play. 22 trap. Dale glanced over to the sidelines at Dorfman. Same play, three times in a row? And a trap at that? He thought it was a crazy call. They broke huddle and Dale took his slot position. On hike, he raced behind the line toward Sonny as he had the two previous plays. But this time, the nose guard and middle linebacker weren't suckered. They hit Dale just as he took the ball from Sonny. Dale ducked and the two bigger players could only grab him around his shoulder pads. They tugged on him. He kept moving his feet. The three of them did a little dance before he felt a crushing blow in his back followed by searing pain.

Another Sundance player crashed into them. Then another. Dale, stuck in the middle, couldn't fall to the ground. The tacklers held him in place while the crowd of players grew larger but hardly moved after it absorbed the next tackler.

The ref blew the whistle, signaling the end of the play due to lack of forward momentum. The tacklers released Dale and he tried tossing the ball to the ref. But when he moved, an intense pain exploded near his shoulder blade and shot down his side all the way to his thigh. The pain hurt so much that he could hardly breath. When he didn't move, the pain stopped. But if he turned his back just slightly, the pain returned in all its fury.

Dale took small steps away from the huddle. He tried to signal the coaches. He held up his hand but the excruciating sensation forced it down. Dorfman and Blocker came over. They asked what was wrong. Even speaking prompted the burning in his back. He mumbled something about injuring his back and Blocker helped him to the sidelines.

Dale took off his jersey and shoulder pads and Blocker lifted up his undershirt and examined the space below his shoulder blade. He said he didn't see anything serious. Maybe a bruise. Some reddening. Dale told him it hurt so much it made him nauseous and dizzy. Blocker said it was probably just the heat. He told him to sit out the rest of the series.

However, he didn't know if he could sit down. He moved gingerly toward the bench. He figured out if he didn't move the left side of his back, the pain didn't appear. So he walked by taking a regular step with his right leg and just scooting the left leg. It worked. He made it to the bench and carefully sat down. Chris joined him when Galilee went on defense. He asked what was wrong. Dale shook his head. He didn't know. Just an agonizing pain in his back when he moved a certain way.

The scrimmage ended. Galilee had done pretty well. Coach Dorfman was pleased. Galilee would have lost a real game against Sundance Prep, but the score wouldn't have been anything close to 72-0. The Galilee seniors felt a special kind of vindication. They bitterly remembered the massacre at Sundance.

The players walked to the bus. Dale hobbled along with them, but he moved so slowly that he soon fell behind. As he carefully climbed the steps to the bus, wincing at the pain, he noticed some of the seniors, especially Comingdeer, staring at him. He knew what they were thinking. No blood, no broken bones, then no real injury. But surely they didn't think he was faking it. They'd seen him endure a beating in bull-in-the-ring just yesterday. Why would he fake an injury now?

Dale carefully sat down next to Chris. He tried to listen as Dorfman critiqued their performance. When Coach finished, Harte led them in cheers. Cookie started the bus and drove it back to the high school. In the locker room, Dorfman came over and asked Dale how he felt. He said his back hurt pretty bad. Where, Dorfman asked. Dale told him. Then Coach asked him if he could pee, and Dale said he thought so. They went over to the toilet and Dale peed and Coach said there wasn't any blood so his kidneys were okay. Coach told him to rub some Bengay on it and then use a heating pad that night and it should get better.

But it didn't get better. The next morning, Dale could still barely move. Blackie came in his bedroom and found him lying on the floor flat on his back. Blackie said he'd take him to the hospital at Tinker on Monday. Dale spent the entire weekend on his back on the floor. He even slept on the floor. As he laid there, he grew angry with Dorfman for running the same play three times. The defense had been ready for it the third time. Ready and mad. Then Dale wondered if he was destined to have bad luck. First a broken leg, now this, whatever this was. At least with a broken leg people can see you are hurt. But this ailment was invisible. People, especially coaches, didn't respect what they couldn't see.

Dale decided it was time to care less about sports and more about something else. He knew he had no chance of playing any sport past high school. He was too small to play football even in high school. He was comical in basketball. He was good at baseball but he'd never received any real instruction on how to play the game better. Even if a little guy could make it in baseball, like Freddie Patek, the five foot four shortstop for the Kansas City Royals, Dale already knew a guy had to get the training and instruction to have any chance past high school, even if he did have talent. As for track, he was fast, but he already knew that the fastest guys were black. At the Wheaton Invitational last year, one of the state's largest meets, the black guys from Ralph Ellison High School won all the sprints in class A.

So Dale knew that his sporting days were numbered. He decided to do his best while in high school but not to take it too seriously anymore. He knew part of the reason why he loved sports so much, aside from the competition and camaraderie, was because athletics offered an escape from the tension and ugliness of home. But it was time to stop having romantic fantasies about sports. It was time to care about something else. Dale reached for the book next to him. He opened *Great Expectations* and began reading. Just for the fun of it.

### Chapter 3: *Wendy praises Dale; the power of the olive*

Dale woke up and didn't feel the pain. He carefully rolled over and still no burning. He stood up. Except for a little soreness below his shoulder blade, he felt normal. It had taken two weeks but he'd finally healed.

He quickly got ready for school and walked into the kitchen for breakfast. Instead of Jesse, he saw Blackie sitting at the table reading the sports page.

"Where's Mom?"

Without taking his eyes off the paper, Blackie said she'd taken June May to school.

"So early?"

"She had cheerleading practice before school."

Dale reached into the cupboard for a box of cereal. Blackie noticed him extending his left arm, something he hadn't been able to do for two weeks.

"What's this?" Blackie asked, dropping the paper onto the table. "You finally okay?"

Dale poured the Rice Crispies into a bowl. "Yeah. I woke up feeling fine." He reached into the refrigerator for a carton of milk.

"About time," said Blackie.

Dale filled the bowl with milk and listened to the Rice Crispies pop. He thought the worse thing about being hurt is that it separates you from healthy people. Blackie, like Dorfman, thought he should have willed the injury away. He tried. Every night for two weeks he urged his body to heal itself. But, as the doctor at Tinker said, a pinched nerve takes time to heal. Jesse and Blackie took turns rubbing wintergreen oil into his back and Dale slept on a heating pad. He went to school like usual, tried not to move his back, which was impossible of course, and came back home and laid on the floor with the heating pad and read. He finished *Great Expectations* in seven days; *A Tale of Two Cities* in three days. Now he was reading *David Copperfield*.

"Have you ever had a pinched nerve?" Dale asked.

Blackie took a sip of coffee. "Have you ever been in a line-crossing ceremony?"

"What's that?"

"First time a sailor crosses the equator, he crosses the line. They make you strip to your skivvies, then you run the gauntlet. They beat you with tubes and paddles and hoses." Blackie took another drink of coffee. "I was sore for a week. Had welts all over my back. Bruised head to toe. But I lived."

Dale found talking to his father frustrating. For every bad experience he had, Blackie had a worse one.

"Well, it takes time for a pinched nerve to heal," Dale said.

"So it does."

"I was in a lot of pain."

"So you were. What do you want me to do about it?"

Dale shrugged. "Nothing. I guess it doesn't matter now anyway."

Blackie stood up. He was dressed in slacks and shirt. No uniform. "You're beginning to find out that most things don't matter."

Dale was in no mood to debate him this early in the morning. He didn't believe that though. "You're not going to work today?"

"I'm going in late."

"I guess being sergeant has its advantages."

"That's right. And one of these days I'll explain it all to you."

"Explain what?"

"Getting ahead."

"Why don't you explain it to me now?"

Blackie looked at him as if trying to guess how much he weighed. "You're not ready yet."

"Ready for what?"

"Ready to find out how things really work."

Dale shook his head. "I don't know what you mean."

"My point exactly." Blackie got up from the table. "But when you begin to understand, then I'll tell you."

Blackie walked out of the kitchen and Dale put his bowl in the sink. He didn't know if his father knew what he was talking about or not. Was the fact that Blackie hardly talked to him, and when he did he spoke in such a cynical way, supposed to be part of a plan? Or was it just an act? Dale thought the latter.

Dale grabbed his car keys and headed out the door. He looked at the sky. It looked cleaner and bluer than yesterday. He looked at the scattering of trees on his block. Even their turning leaves, mostly dull gold, looked brighter. Just feeling healthy again and not being stunned by pain made the world seem a lot better. And he wasn't going to let Blackie spoil that feeling.

Dale noticed Wendy looking at him. Throughout the school day her face alternated from hope to joy to despair depending on how he responded. If he saw her looking his way and he responded with a nod, or anything affirmative, she beamed. If he ignored her, her face crumpled into a frown. If he looked annoyed, her frowning face turned into a mask of sorrow and Dale feared she might start bawling.

In the classes they shared, Wendy, who always sat in the front, would turn around from time to time to check on Dale, as if making sure he hadn't fled the room. Her behavior often annoyed him because it was so obvious. The whole school knew Wendy had a crush on him and he was being mean to her. Even Coach Dorfman had implied that Dale was being insensitive to Wendy. Dale didn't think he was being mean. He just didn't know how to respond to such devotion. It baffled him. The only thing he could compare it to was how he felt for Amanda. But in his case, he kept his feelings secret. He never telegraphed his ardor. If anything, he pretended he didn't even know Amanda existed. Inside of course, he felt like he was falling apart when she walked by. Sometimes he couldn't even breathe freely. He avoided direct contact with Amanda as much possible, which wasn't difficult because, as usual, they only had two classes together, English and bookkeeping. He snuck glances at her from afar. He became a consummate actor. He casually looked in her general direction, his gaze falling on something completely uninteresting, and he pretended to study it while he actually studied her. He noted every change of her expression, heard every modulation in her voice, and memorized the different clothes she wore, the slight changes to her hair, and the subtle changes of her moods. Dale was more than an actor, he was a spy.

There was one important difference. Dale thought he was socially inferior to Amanda. He thought being obvious with his affections would make him look ridiculous. Wendy, however, had greater social status than Dale. Maybe that allowed her to be open with her feelings. It also put pressure on him that he resented. If he decided to date Wendy it would be his decision. And no one, or no thing, not even peer pressure, would change his mind.

On Friday in late September, Dale saw Wendy gazing at him in a more lovesick manner than usual. She stood at her locker, wearing her cheerleading uniform, pretending to talk with her locker mates, Carmen and Roxanne. But every other sentence, she peered in his direction, her green eyes as attentive as a doting dog's for its master. Dale pretended he didn't see her mooning face, but he felt guilty when he saw her grow fretful so he nodded at her and watched her face radiate a sunny smile.

A moment later, he looked up and saw Wendy standing before him, that same smile still lighting up her freckled face. He knew she was violating a rule of hers. She never approached him directly. She never said more than hi to him. It was important for her to retain her feminine advantage of responding to the male's overt move.

"I'm glad your back is better," she said.

Dale nodded. "Me too."

"Are you going to play tonight?"

"I guess. At least some."

"I imagine you went through a lot these past weeks."

"Yeah, I was getting pretty tired of – " Dale paused. He didn't want to say pain; that wouldn't sound manly or stoical enough. "Tired of the bother."

"Oh, certainly."

An awkward pause. Dale wanted to leave, but he could tell that Wendy was bursting to say something else.

"Audie, I just wanted to say how proud I am of you," she said, her eyes searching his face. "I know how much pain you must have been in. My older brother hurt his back once playing football and I remember how hard it was for him. He could hardly walk, just like you. But he didn't complain. Neither did you. I just wanted to tell you I thought you acted, well, with incredible courage."

Before Dale could say anything, Wendy walked away hugging her books to her bosom. Her gait quickened until she caught up with Carmen and the two of them disappeared into a crowd of retreating students.

Dale felt himself glowing. He reached up with one hand and felt the heat emanating from his face. He glanced around, hoping no one had overheard. But the halls were almost empty of kids.

He slammed his locker shut and walked down the hall recalling Wendy's words. It surprised him how her words warmed his heart. He felt a delightful surge of pride. Courage. What a wonderful word. A word he had longed to hear applied to himself since he was a little boy.

He ran into Chris and Quentin Osteen. Chris looked at Dale with surprise.

"Hey, what happened to you?"

"Huh?" Dale responded.

"You look funny."

"I do?"

"Yeah, like you're getting sick or something."

"No, I feel fine."

Chris studied Dale for a moment. "Well, okay. Hey, we're going to be late for the pep rally."

The three boys walked to the gym and joined the rest of the team on the third row of the bleachers. The pep band struck up the school song and Dale watched as the cheerleaders pranced on the gym floor. Instead of watching Valerie Long, a pretty blond senior girl who'd earlier that day had been crowned all-school queen, his eyes flickered over to Wendy. She jumped and waved her pom-pons and opened her mouth in a big smile as she cheered. Dale envied her emotional frankness. She wasn't phony about anything. Unlike him, she wasn't afraid to let everyone know how she felt and what she wanted. He felt his feelings for Wendy beginning to change.

Dale glanced over to Quentin. He'd heard that he liked Wendy. Quentin was a tall, lean, blond-headed guy who got braces over the summer to fix his buckteeth. Dale had always liked him. They had been pretty good friends in junior high, but now, since he went to First Church, he was more Chris's friend. Quentin had always seemed impressively mature for his years. He never goofed off in class, and in spite of his bad teeth, he never taunted or picked on other kids as a diversion from his own shortcomings.

The pep rally ended and Dale watched Wendy leave with Mary Jane. Before she disappeared out the door, Wendy glanced back at him. He gave her a little smile and her eyes brightened.

Coach Dorfman told the team to remain seated on the bleachers. He waited until all the kids left the gym, then he introduced a man wearing a dark suit. Dorfman said the man's name was Dr. D'Amato. Dale, whose mind was elsewhere, jerked his head to attention when he heard the name.

"Hey," he whispered to Chris, "did Coach say Dr. Demento?"

Chris looked at Dale as if he were crazy. "No. Who's that?"

Dale shrugged and turned his attention back to Dorfman and the doctor. Coach said Dr.

D'Amato was a psychologist and he was here to help the team acquire a winning attitude. Winning was as much mental as it was physical, Dorfman said, and he thought after years of losing what this team needed most of all was confidence. Dr. D'Amato specialized in helping his patients learn how to be confident, how to succeed, how to win.

Dale scrutinized Dr. D'Amato. He didn't look especially athletic. He looked about average in height and build. His face reminded Dale of a hawk with his small and alert eyes, beaky nose, and thin lips. He had unusually long gray hair, too, swept back off his forehead in a way that reminded Dale of one of those classical music conductors he'd seen on the public television channel.

Dorfman finished his introduction and motioned for Dr. D'Amato to work his magic. The doctor gazed with supreme confidence at the team. He nodded once, then twice, and smiled slightly. Then he spoke with an impressively resonant voice. Dale found the voice compelling. He listened more closely. Dr. D'Amato said the power of positive thinking was essential to success. In order to succeed, a person had to eliminate all negative thoughts and focus on positive thoughts. For an athlete that meant visualizing a positive performance. He should imagine himself performing his particular assignment flawlessly. See yourself succeed. See it in complete detail. If you're making a block, see yourself executing the block with perfect technique. The same applied to any other assignment: tackling, throwing, catching, running.

So far, Dale thought all that made sense. But the doctor seemed to think such an attitude was part of some kind of mysterious process that only he could reveal to the team. Dale began to feel a seed of skepticism grow inside him.

Dr. D'Amato said sometimes a player needed a totem to help him get in touch with his positive energy. He said they were probably familiar with totem poles that Northwest Indian tribes used to make. The Indians attributed great power to these totems. It was as if the carved images amplified their own sense of power. Well, the same principle worked on a smaller scale. Teams did that with mascots, school fight songs, other such familiar symbols. But individuals could create their own totems. Dr. D'Amato said the totem could be almost anything. Even a mundane object. All the person needed to do was attribute a special power to this ordinary object. This object would then help amplify the positive energy within that athlete. Now, Dr. D'Amato wanted them to use this as a totem for tonight's football game.

Dr. D'Amato paused. Then Dorfman handed him a jar of pitted olives. Dale hadn't even noticed the jar of olives that had been perched on the front bleacher. The doctor unscrewed the top of the jar. He reached inside and removed one olive, holding it between his thumb and index finger. He showed it to the team. He said, this olive is your totem. When you feel a need for positive energy, simply eat an olive. The doctor popped the olive in his mouth. He chewed, then swallowed. That's all you have to do, he said. These olives will amplify your positive energy. Before the game, when you imagine yourselves performing your duties perfectly, when you want to instill positive energy in your mind and body, symbolize it with the olive. In the course of the game, when you feel your confidence waning, when you feel your energy ebbing, eat an olive. Your positive energy will be restored. You will succeed. You will win.

Dale looked around to see if anyone else thought the doctor crazy. All his teammates near him, even Chris, stared at Dr. D'Amato with rapt attention. He looked farther down his row and saw Matt Jones, a sophomore, with a doubtful expression on his face. Jones, who had taken over Dale's halfback position for the first two games, was an interesting guy. He was half Japanese. His father, then a marine officer, had met his mother while stationed in Japan. Matt, whose proper name was Matsui, had an older sister, Koko, who had been named all-school queen three years ago. Dale thought she was quite pretty in an exotic way. His older brother, Kimbo, had graduated from Galilee last year. Dale had sort of wanted to dislike Matt. After all, he was competing with him for the halfback spot. But he'd liked him before this year, and now, seeing that skeptical look on his face, Dale liked him even more.

Coach Dorfman thanked the doctor and the players, except Dale and Matt, applauded. Then Dorfman summarized the doctor's ideas as if preparing a class for an upcoming quiz. Essentially, think of olives as giving you power, confidence, positive energy. During tonight's game, when you feel tired or doubtful, pop one in your mouth and those negative thoughts will disappear.

"Are we gonna win tonight?" Dorfman said loudly.

The player shouted yes, but not with the intensity Coach desired.

"Stand up! Are we gonna win?"

The players jumped to their feet. "Yes!"

Better. More enthusiasm.

"Can't hear you. Are we gonna win?"

The players yelled with such fervor that Dale thought they'd all gone loco. They were like one loud, blind force of positive energy.

Coach said he'd see them at five sharp.

The players clambered from the bleachers. Dale understood the need for motivation. The team had lost its first two games. Wheaton, in the traditional opener, beat them 21-7. Then Sequoyah, another bigger school, won 14-7. Terry Harte, who earlier that day had been voted all-school king, had scored both game's touchdowns on long runs.

Dale hadn't suited up for either game. He watched from the press box along with Wally, who filmed the games. The team had played well. They were just outmanned by bigger opponents. But maybe Coach was right. Maybe Galilee had gotten used to losing. Maybe all they needed was more confidence to turn close losses into victories. But olives?

Dale walked out the gym with Chris and Quentin. He could tell that both of them had bought Dr. D'Amato's theory. Dale didn't even bother to make fun of Dr. D'Amato's ideas. Who knows, maybe he really was Dr. Demento.

In the small stadium locker room, Dale stood with his teammates and heard the band playing the fight song. Coach finished his pep talk, stared at them like a mad scientist, then told them to go out there and WIN! The players, led by Harte and Comingdeer, rushed through the doorway, ran through the end zone, raced past the two rows of cheerleaders and pep club members, and burst through a large paper hoop. Dale, somewhere in the middle with the other juniors, followed the leaders over to their bench. When the players fanned out to the sidelines, he saw, to his amazement, twenty jars of pitted olives standing on a long, wooden table along with salt tablets, water jugs, and paper cups.

Dale walked over to the jars. Already some of the linemen were popping them into their mouths. Surely, they didn't need positive reinforcement yet. The game hadn't even started. Maybe they were just hungry.

Leroy Lemmon chewed on an olive. He picked another out of the jar with his thick fingers. He offered it to Dale.

"No, thanks," Dale said.

He didn't like olives and even if he did he wouldn't have eaten one. He thought the ritual silly superstition.

Lemmon gulped the olive down. He beat his chest like a gorilla. Dale thought, maybe the olives had totemic power after all.

The game started and Galilee's opponents, the Humble Horned Toads, dressed in gray and green uniforms, started off well. Humble, a school in the less populated western part of the state, scored first on an end around. Dale, playing cornerback, saw it coming when the receiver he was covering reversed his field and took a handoff from the halfback. All the Galilee players, no doubt full of positive energy, had over-pursued the halfback. Dale got caught up in the confused throng of his teammates. The Humble end had clear sailing to the end zone, a run covering fifty-two yards.

After the missed extra-point kick, Dale returned to the sideline. He noticed several players eating olives. Even the guys not playing were munching on them. It must have worked. On Galilee's first possession, Sonny hit Billy Joe for a forty-two yard scoring pass. Harte kicked the extra point and the rout was on.

Harte scored on a long run next. In the second quarter, Comingdeer recovered a fumble and three plays later scored on a two-yard dive. At halftime, with Galilee leading 21-6, the players smelled victory – and olives. After fortifying themselves with more of the fruit, the Gophers scored twice more in the third quarter, Harte on a thirty-five-yard run and Matt Jones on a seven-yard run. Dale, who was supposed to only play defense until he got in better shape, got on the offensive act in the fourth quarter. On an option play, he cut off Harte's powerful block and ran twenty-one yards for an oliveless touchdown.

Final score: Galilee 42, Humble 6.

The players and fans were jubilant. The players rode the bus back to the high school roaring the school fight song.

Chris, who had alternated at split end, attributed the win to the power of the olive. He and Dale were standing outside the locker room after showering and changing into street clothes, their backs pressed against the brick wall. Just then Matt came out of the locker room along with another sophomore who started at defensive end, Sam Mears.

"Hey, Matt," said Dale. "Did you partake of the olive?"

Matt smiled and shook his head.

"See, Chris. Matt didn't eat one and neither did I and we both scored touchdowns."

Chris said he still thought the olives helped.

"What helped was playing Humble, a school our size," said Dale.

Chris, Matt, and Sam all agreed about that. Matt and Sam said so long and left. Dale asked Chris what he planned to do. He said some of the gang was going to Pizza Hut to celebrate. Dale, who still tended to shun social gatherings, asked who made up this gang.

"Wally, K. C., Rusty, Roxanne, Mary Jane, Gretchen, Carmen, and Wendy," said Chris. "Oh, yeah. And me."

Dale raised an eyebrow. Chris was going out? Then he saw Mary Jane and Wendy, in their cheerleading uniforms, waiting to get into Roxanne's car. Wendy paused and looked over at them, smiling invitingly.

"Okay," Dale said. "I'll go."

## Chapter 4: *Mouthpiece; homecoming; and rounding second base*

While walking down the hall on his way to English, Dale noticed Mrs. Heath signaling him. He walked over and she asked if she could speak to him for a moment. Dale said sure. He'd never had a class with Mrs. Heath. She taught psychology and sociology and home economics. He'd heard she was a good teacher.

Mrs. Heath said she was finishing her master's thesis and she needed a teenage boy to be a case study. She wondered if he could help her.

Dale wasn't sure what she meant. Case study?

She said all he'd have to do was take a couple of tests for her. Maybe he could take them this coming Saturday afternoon. The tests would only take two hours at the most. She knew giving up part of a Saturday was asking a lot, but she would bake a cake for the occasion if he consented. Thea, she added, would be there.

Dale thought it over. Most Saturdays he watched college football before getting restless and going out and tossing the football around himself. Sometimes he joined Rusty and his brothers for a game of touch football. He didn't mind taking tests. In fact, he sort of liked taking them as long as they weren't about boring stuff like algebra. He definitely liked cake. He knew Mrs. Heath was an excellent cook. She sometimes contributed cookies, brownies, and cupcakes to bake sales, and hers were always the best. As for Thea, Dale didn't find that fact especially tempting. Thea was a sophomore, and he talked to her from time to time. She was a petite brunette with interesting blue eyes. They weren't that large or brilliant but Dale liked how the blue color contrasted with her dark, curly hair. Thea was sort of on the plain side otherwise. In fact, as Dale looked at Mrs. Heath, who was also a petite brunette, he noticed that the mother was quite a bit prettier than the daughter.

"Okay," he said. "I'll do it."

Mrs. Heath thanked him and told him to arrive tomorrow around two at her home. She said after she got the results, he could come over again and she'd explain what it all meant. She gave him a late slip, thanked him again, and Dale ambled off to his English class wondering why Mrs. Heath had picked him.

In the auditorium after the all-school pep rally for homecoming, Dale watched the students leaving. Wendy, with the other cheerleaders dressed in their crimson uniforms, strolled out. He liked the way the red contrasted with her blond hair. She saw him and waved and Dale nodded, still embarrassed at such public displays. Then the pep club girls, also dressed in red uniforms, followed. He noticed Amanda among them. She was talking to Roxanne and Dale, feeling that familiar romantic ache, thought back to two years ago when he first saw her here in the auditorium. How long ago that seemed.

Dale stood with the other football players, all of them wearing their crimson football jerseys, a tradition on game day. They were waiting for Coach. Dorfman wanted to talk briefly about the homecoming festivities at halftime. He was late, and the guys milled around at the front of the auditorium. Dale felt a nudge in his shoulder and turned and saw Rusty and Erickson.

"What's up?" asked Dale.

"Hey, man," Rusty said, "I heard something interesting. Actually two interesting bits of info."

Dale waited.

"Did you know that Clifford is on the Lyons football team?"

Dale nodded. He noticed Erickson grinning behind Rusty. Dale didn't understand why the two of them were smiling so slyly.

"Well, we're gonna have a surprise ready for him at the game tonight," said Rusty.

"Like what?"

"You'll find out," said Erickson, his bicolor eyes gleaming with a mischievous intensity.

Dale started to tell them to leave Clifford alone, although he didn't know what they could do. Wally, standing by the stage, called Erickson over. Erickson gave Dale a departing grin and joined Wally. Then Rusty leaned closer to Dale.

"Interesting info number two: guess where Mr. Benedict, a.k.a. Rabbi, son of Blob, Mr. Zero, and Benny, ended up?"

Dale had no idea. He hadn't even thought of him these past few months. He shrugged.

"In *California*," Rusty said in a voice that suggested there was something nefarious about that.

"So?"

Rusty grew thoughtful. "Yeah, so." He shrugged. "I thought maybe that meant something to you."

California mostly meant the Beach Boys to Dale. And the things that the Beach Boys sang about: surfing, hot rods, girls on the beach. None of those things seemed to go with Mr. Benedict.

"Imagine Mr. Benedict on a surfboard," Dale said.

"Better yet," said Rusty, "imagine Mr. Benedict *as* the surfboard."

They laughed.

"He's teaching school out there," said Rusty. "I got a postcard from him."

"Where in California?"

Dale had always been interested in geography. Back in grade school he used to draw maps of the United States freehand when he finished his class assignments. His fourth-grade teacher praised the accuracy of his maps and said he ought to become a cartographer. Dale thought she meant a guy who took pictures of cars and he had no interest in that.

"Around San Diego. He said he's rooming with a friend who's teaching at the Nazarene college in Point Loma. Benny said he was teaching high school as a substitute right now." Rusty paused. "Strange to think he's way out there."

"Yeah, it's strange."

Rusty snapped out of his momentary reverie. "Well, got to go. Got to get the surprise ready."

"Hey, what's going on?"

Rusty grinned and winked at him. "No comprehendo, amigo," he said in the Spanish-accented voice he'd lately assumed. "You'll see at the game la noches."

Dale sat next to Chris on the bus as it headed to the football stadium at Galilee Park. The players on the bus were silent, trying, no doubt, to visualize success. The team had stopped consuming olives after winning their third game in a row, but Dorfman still emphasized visualizing success. So far, it had worked. Galilee had won five straight games. If they beat Lyons tonight in their homecoming game, the Gophers would be guaranteed a winning record for the first time since 1967.

The football team was the talk of the town. Attendance was almost twice what it had been last year. During the game when Dale glanced at the crowd sitting in the stands, he felt astonished seeing so many people watching them play. It seemed like half the town was coming to their games. Blackie and Jesse came, too, but they stayed in their car. Blackie parked the Olds outside the chain-link fence behind the south end zone and watched from there. In the Quanah Parker game, after Dale scored a touchdown on a twenty-eight-yard run, he saw his dad and mom sitting in the car as he trotted around the goalpost. Seeing them was strange since his parents didn't do anything else together anymore.

Even the Oklahoma City paper had trumpeted Galilee football success. It ran a big story on the sports section front page, with photographs of Terry Harte, Charlie Comingdeer and Coach Marlon Dorfman. The headline said, *Dorfman Makes a Winner of Galilee*, and featured a photo of Dorfman staring into space like a battlefield general, his eyes narrowed, his jaw jutting, his balding head shiny. Dale had read the story and it told how Galilee had suffered through five losing years but Dorfman, in his second year as head coach, had made the team winners. The story mentioned the names of Harte and Comingdeer the most. And for good reason. Harte led the team in rushing and scoring and played "monster," sort of a roving linebacker on defense. Comingdeer played fullback in the wishbone and middle linebacker on defense and was known for his vicious tackles. The paper also mentioned a few other players: MacDonald and Lemmon, who anchored the line; Sonny Schoendienst, the junior quarterback; Billy Joe Barton, who led the team in receptions and also played safety; and Butch Bigelow, who along with Harte and Comingdeer gave Galilee the three toughest linebackers in their district.

Dale didn't see his name mentioned in the story even though he alternated at halfback with Matt Jones and started at cornerback on defense. But he knew he wasn't one of the stars on the team. He just did his part, which against Lyons would be more than usual. Matt had twisted his ankle in practice and would miss the game. That meant Dale would play offense the entire game. He was looking forward to it because he'd get to carry the ball more than his usual four or five carries.

The bus rolled toward the park and Dale looked out the window and saw the stadium lights ablaze. He heard the band playing and the crowd cheering even though the bus had yet to turn onto the stadium road. Dale felt an excitement rise inside him. He turned to Chris. He saw the same emotion in his buddy's eyes. All the players felt it. They felt connected to some positive energy that stretched like an electrical cord from somewhere in infinity to each player on the bus and on to each fan in the stands. Dale thought of a poem he'd read recently in English class: *The Body Electric*. Yes, this was his body electric, here at this moment, in this place, with his teammates before his hometown.

The team took the field and went through their warm-up drills. Dale looked down the field at the Lyons team. He sort of felt sorry for them because of their lousy uniforms. Just brown jerseys and white pants without even a stripe on the side. Their helmets were white, too, with one brown stripe down the middle. Why would a school want brown and white for its colors? Dale guessed someone had thought brown an appropriate color for Lions. But he thought brown was such a mundane color for a football uniform that it bothered him.

Galilee's uniforms, until this year, had been crummy and plain, too. But their new uniforms were pretty cool. Instead of their old, plain white helmets, they now had crimson helmets with two white stripes and a decal of an menacing gopher on the side, baring its teeth like it was going to gnaw right through the opponent's face. Dale didn't think rodents were very scary in general, but the drawing of the gopher looked plenty mean. The rest of the new uniforms were neat, too. They had two sets of uniforms: red pants and jerseys with stripes or white pants and jerseys with stripes. Dale liked the stripes. Little touches like that made a uniform look special. Tonight, a special night, they wore both their crimson jerseys and pants.

After warm-up, they trotted back to the locker room for the pre-game skull session and Dorfman's pep talk. The team was so pumped up, Dorfman didn't have to say much. He said two things. First, he wanted them to knock Oates's jock off. The players cheered. Second, he simply said, win number six. The players exploded. They chanted Go-phers! Go-phers! Go-phers! Then they raced past the pep club and cheerleaders and smashed through the paper hoop on their way to their sideline. That's when Dale saw the posters.

Rusty, Erickson, and Wally were standing in the front row of the visitors' side of the stands. Rusty held a large horseshoe-shaped poster. Erickson and Wally held posters, too, both rectangle in shape with writing on them that Dale couldn't quite make out. It wasn't until he trotted onto the field for the kickoff and took his spot on the far left of the field, close to the visitors' stands, that he saw exactly what the posters were.

The horseshoe poster wasn't a horseshoe after all, but a depiction of a giant mouthpiece. Someone, Dale guessed Rusty because he could draw some, had made marks like teeth imprints on the mouthpiece outline. They had mounted the poster on a stick and now Rusty waved it in the air. The other posters had thick block letters written on them that said "Mouthpiece Oates" and "Where's Cliff-ferd?"

The three of them saw Dale looking. They waved the posters and started chanting, "Mouthpiece!" "Where's Cliff-ferd?" Dale appreciated the absurdity. He smiled in spite of himself. He wondered if Clifford had seen the posters yet.

After the kickoff, Lyons lined up on offense and Dale quickly found Clifford. He played left guard and Dale recognized his stiff walk as he approached the line of scrimmage. Galilee's defense easily stopped Lyons on its first possession and the Lions punted.

When Galilee broke its offensive huddle, Dale saw Clifford playing right linebacker. On the fifth play of the drive, Dale carried the ball for the first time. He took the pitch from Sonny, avoided one tackler, cut back toward the middle, and three guys hit him. Two of the tacklers quickly got up, but the third remained on top of him. Dale looked past the face mask and saw Clifford staring at him. "Tell your friends that they're real funny," except it sounded more like "Trg yug frenz thug thr relg funnig" because Clifford still had his mouthpiece in. Clifford shoved him as he got off. Dale let his mouthpiece fall out and dangle by the strap. Then he laughed. He laughed so hard that the referee came over and asked if he were okay. Dale tried to stop laughing, nodded at the ref, and rejoined his teammates in the huddle. Comingdeer glared at him. "What's so funny, junior?" Dale almost started laughing again.

Galilee scored three plays later when Harte ran forty-three yards for a touchdown, highlighted by his knocking a Lions player, Clifford, on his back. That was the beginning of the end for Lyons and Clifford.

Galilee led 21-0 at half. Dale joined the rest of the team on the sideline and watched the ceremony crowning the football queen, a senior named Amy Mears, the older sister of Sam. Like her brother, she had bright red hair. It hung all the way down her back in a shimmering wave. Dale thought the senior girls weren't as pretty as the junior girls. Roxanne was the only junior to be in the homecoming court. Harte had been dating her recently. There was a lot of competition to date Roxanne. Some of the junior boys thought it was unfair they had to compete with the seniors.

In the second half, Galilee scored three more times in the third quarter and for the first time that year the second team played most of the fourth quarter. Dale stayed in and carried the ball nine times in the fourth quarter and ran for a forty-nine yard touchdown. Dale faked out Clifford on the run, juking to his right and watching Clifford stumble to his knees when he cut left and raced down the sidelines.

Lyons finally scored late in the fourth against the second team defense to avoid a shutout. Final score: Galilee 48, Lyons 6. It was Galilee's biggest win in years.

When the game ended, Dale tried finding Clifford to wish him luck, but Clifford, along with a few other Lyons players, didn't hang around to shake hands. Instead, they ran into the visitors' locker room.

Back on the bus, the boys went through their usual post-game boasting and cheering and laughing. Six wins in a row. Dale would have never believed it. Lyons was also their first win against a district opponent. The next two games, their last two regular season games, would be against Agra and Oilville, also district foes. If Galilee won both, they'd be going to the state playoffs for the first time in five years.

Dale felt happy, but when he thought about Clifford he felt a little sorry for him. He knew it must be tough to come back to his old school and get beat. Seeing those posters must have made it worse. But Dale couldn't help but see the absurd humor, too.

"Did Clifford say anything to you?" Dale asked Chris.

Chris shook his head. "He was too busy panting," he said, not trying to be funny.

Dale took Wendy to the homecoming party held in the high school cafeteria. The staff had decorated the large room in the crimson and cream school colors. The theme of the party was *American Graffiti*, so a lot of older photographs, mementos, and paraphernalia from the early '60s were displayed. Dale and Wendy had seen the movie five weeks before on a double date with Chris and Carmen. Dale had liked it. He liked all that old stuff, the music, the cars, and the general atmosphere of the time. While watching the movie, he thought how the town of Galilee still had an *American Graffiti* kind of feel about it. In a lot of ways, the town and school seemed to be more in 1963 than 1973. But he sensed that was beginning to change.

At the movie, Dale had held Wendy's hand for the first time. He felt her excitement radiating from her hot, moist hand. He'd kissed her again that night, this time for more than a second, and when he drove home that night he realized that they were going steady, even though he had never said anything specific.

Ever since then, Wendy waited for Dale after the football game on Fridays and they'd go to Pizza Hut or West Oaks or one of the other places the kids gathered together. On Saturdays, he usually took her to a movie. After seeing *American Graffiti*, they saw *Papillion* and Wendy hadn't liked it much. Dale thought it was sort of long, but he found it interesting. He guessed one of the reasons Wendy didn't like the movie as much was because there was a scene with topless native women. Dale had felt Wendy's hand tense when that scene came on, but he'd played it cool and didn't say anything like "ooh la la" like Rusty would have done.

At the homecoming party, Dale and Wendy saw Chris and Carmen standing in line for refreshments. At the other end of the cafeteria, an oldies band from the City played a vaguely recognizable version of "Chantilly Lace." Although dancing wasn't officially banned – Nazarenes didn't condone dancing – none of the high school functions included it. The cafeteria didn't have room for a dance floor anyway. Dale saw some kids standing close to the band and swaying to the music just the same.

"Are you going to the movie tomorrow?" asked Chris.

The high school was showing a special screening of *Brian's Song* for homecoming weekend.

"Sure," Dale said, then he looked at Wendy as if checking and it briefly annoyed him that he had started doing that. He turned back to Chris. "I guess you have to go to a movie named after yourself." Dale knew Chris's middle name was Brian.

"If I'm Brian Piccolo, then you're Gale Sayers," Chris teased.

"Boy, I wish," Dale said. Sayers had been his favorite pro halfback.

"You don't have to wish. You already run like one of them."

Dale knew who it was before turning around. Butch Bigelow.

"What do you mean, like one of *them*?" Dale said, turning and seeing Bigelow's broad, white face.

"You know what I mean," he said. "All that fancy dodging and shifting. You wouldn't do that against me. I wouldn't fall for it."

"You don't have to worry about that," said Chris. "We're on the same team, after all."

Dale looked past Bigelow and saw K. C. and Gretchen behind him, and a step farther back, Amanda. He churned inside like he did whenever she was near. He was too nervous to defend his style of running.

"You never run at guys. You don't try knocking them down," said Bigelow. Like most big guys, Bigelow thought football was all about knocking guys down.

"That's because Audie is smart," said Wendy. "He knows how to out think them."

Dale wished she wouldn't get involved.

"Out think them? Run away from them," sneered Bigelow.

"Well, he ran away for a hundred yards tonight," said K. C., as usual trying to reign in his aggressive friend.

"That's right," Wendy said. "What about that?"

She tightened her hold on Dale's arm. Dale felt himself growing angry. If the girls weren't present, he thought he might throw a punch or at least tackle Bigelow.

Dale looked over at Amanda and saw her biting her lower lip. He didn't know if she did this because she felt worried about the argument or if she was bored. He loved her voluptuous lower lip.

"C'mon, Butch," said K. C., tugging at Bigelow's shoulder. "Let's go listen to the band."

"Sure, sure," said Bigelow, suddenly smiling like they were concluding a friendly conversation.

He turned and the four of them walked away. Dale watched, trying to see who Amanda walked the closest to. She didn't cooperate. She walked next to Gretchen. Dale desperately didn't want her to be with Bigelow.

Wendy and Carmen and Chris were talking, but Dale didn't listen. He watched Amanda as she stood at the other end of the cafeteria. Dale still couldn't tell who she was with. Maybe neither. Maybe the four of them were just informally together.

"Say, Audie, did you hear?" asked Chris.

"What?"

"I said Butch is just jealous."

Wendy and Carmen agreed. Chris said that Butch wanted to play offense, too, but he wasn't fast enough to play halfback. Dale, still looking at the four of them at the other end, thought that might be part of the reason. He noticed that K. C. and Butch, both of whom had seemed so big and mature in ninth grade, hadn't grown much since then. K. C. hadn't grown any at all. He wasn't much taller than Dale now. Butch had grown a couple of inches but it looked like his growing days were over, too. Dale didn't fully understand the source of Bigelow's antagonism; Butch just didn't like him. He didn't like Rusty, either.

Dale and Wendy and Chris and Carmen got their refreshments, punch and cookies, and sat down on the ugly plastic cafeteria chairs. Dale listened to the three of them chat. The usual stuff. School and people. Idle gossip, he thought.

After a while, Wendy put her hand on his and squeezed. Dale looked at her. She seemed to be glowing. "Want to go?" she asked.

Dale said okay and he and Wendy said good-bye to Chris and Carmen and walked out of the cafeteria to the parking lot. Dale wondered why he hadn't seen Rusty. He asked Wendy if she'd seen him.

"He and Wally are going with Peggy and Merry to see a late showing of the *Exorcist*," she said.

"The *Exorcist*?" It was a new movie about the devil that everyone wanted to see. People were standing in long lines that curved around the block to buy tickets. "That's sort of weird."

"No," Wendy said. "That's good." She smiled.

Dale didn't pursue the point. They got in his car and he drove her home. When they got there, the house was dark but the porch light was on. Dale escorted Wendy to her door and started to kiss her good night when she asked if he wanted to come in.

He hesitated. He'd been in her home before, but not alone with her.

"It's not that late," she said.

Dale guessed it was only ten-thirty. They hadn't stayed too long at the homecoming party.

"What about your parents?"

"Mom's asleep. She goes to bed early. So does Riley. And Daddy's on the road."

Wendy's father seemed to always be on the road, hauling stuff all over the country.

"Well …"

"C'mon. We can watch TV. I'll make some popcorn. We'll turn down the lights and pretend we're at the movies."

Dale nodded and he followed her into the dark house. Wendy turned on a lamp. He noticed how lived-in the Wainwright house seemed. Old, comfy furniture, worn rugs on the floor, scenic pictures of the outdoors, a photograph of Mr. Wainwright standing beside his rig. Dale breathed in the odor of the house. It wasn't a bad smell. It smelled like fried food, detergent, cigarettes (her father smoked), flowers, and other kinds of earthy smells that he couldn't identify.

Wendy led Dale into a smaller room off the living room. She turned on a portable black and white television and asked him what he wanted to drink. He said an "uncola," making a joke about the TV commercial, but Wendy didn't get the reference so he said a 7-Up.

Wendy left the room and Dale looked at the television and noticed an old Elvis movie playing. He'd probably seen it before at the drive-in. After a few minutes of watching, he identified it: *Tickle Me*. It was the one where Elvis works at a dude ranch when he's not singing and carrying on with the chicks.

Wendy brought Dale his glass of 7-Up and for herself a glass of Tab and put them on the table. She turned off the lamp and the only light in the room came from the bluish glow of the television set.

They drank their soda pop and watched some of the movie. Dale remembered how silly it seemed to him when he was eight. Now, he thought it completely preposterous.

Wendy snuggled up against him. She said he played really well tonight. Dale shrugged.

172

He had played well. He had almost as many yards rushing as Terry Harte, although most of them came in the fourth quarter when the Lyons players were tired and demoralized.

Wendy snuggled even closer. Dale knew she wanted him to put his arm around her so he did. Then he felt her hot, moist breath near his face and he turned and found her lips.

Wendy's kiss was surprisingly passionate. Dale felt his usual awkwardness come over him. He responded in all the ways he thought he should, but he felt curiously divided as if his mind had departed from his body and now floated somewhere above them.

His body, however, reacted appropriately. He began touching her and Wendy murmured her approval and he continued his exploration, not entirely sure what he was doing but letting nature take over.

Dale put one hand on Wendy's thigh and another hand under her cheerleader's blouse. He couldn't decide which route to pursue first. Her thigh felt really nice. Soft and supple and especially warm as his hand advanced under her pleated skirt. The other hand liked what it touched too. He moved it farther under her blouse and encountered her brassiere. Unlike most of the other cheerleaders, Wendy had large breasts, and Dale was surprised how large and substantial the bra felt. She moaned. He pushed his hand under the bra and felt the incredibly soft mound of flesh and his fingers touched her erect nipple. Meanwhile, his other hand curved around her hip and felt the slick fabric of her tights. His fingers pushed under and clutched at the soft, cool flesh of her lower buttock.

He wondered if he had gotten to second base yet. The baseball metaphor confused him a little. Did the bases symbolize the different areas of a girl's body or did they symbolize different acts? It all sounded so simple, like an orderly procession from base to base. But none of this seemed simple to him.

Dale continued this course of activity for a while; he didn't really know how long. In the background, he heard the Elvis movie conclude, with the King singing the closing song. He was more or less in the same areas and they were still kissing, but now Wendy's mouth was open and their tongues were engaged in sort of a duel. His initial excitement had faded into a state of frustrated arousal. His body wanted to go farther and faster but his mind wasn't sure how to proceed.

Then when Wendy changed positions and uncrossed her thighs, he removed his hand from her bottom and positioned it in her lap, gradually moving his fingers under her skirt in front. His fingers crept forward, encountered the front of the tights, and stopped. Everything there seemed too tight and bunched up to find a path underneath the cloth. He hesitated. She reached down and pushed his hand against the center of her tights. He started awkwardly stroking that area and Wendy moaned more fervently. He rubbed harder. After more moans, she suddenly gasped, and hugged him so tightly that he felt as if he were being squeezed by a boa constrictor. With a shudder, she gasped then gently moved his hand away from down there. She sighed and her body grew slack and he removed his other hand from under her bra and blouse. Then she kissed him in a kindly way, not with the previous passion, and got up and asked him if he wanted something more to drink. He said just water. She brought him a glass, took a drink of it herself, then he gulped down the water.

Dale, realizing the night was over, unsteadily stood up. Gilbert didn't seem to get the message. His penis thrust against the interior of his jeans with such determination that he began to feel nauseous. He walked awkwardly to the door. Wendy, smiling sleepily, offered her mouth and Dale kissed her and said good night. Wendy said good night and call me tomorrow. Promise?

He promised. He heard her softly shut the door behind him as he hobbled to his car. He got inside, started it up, and drove away from her house. As he did, he saw Wally, in a Volkswagen Beetle, pass him. The Chevy's headlights briefly illuminated the interior of the Bug and Dale saw Wally gazing at him with a surprised look, as if he'd never seen Dale before in his life.

As Dale drove home, the pressure in his pants subsided and he thought how odd it all had been. He'd kissed and fondled Wendy some before, but it had never gotten that far. He wasn't sure what to make of it. He liked the feeling in spite of the lingering frustration. But mentally he felt odd. For one thing, he felt like he had just encountered a new and complex machine but someone had neglected to give him the operating instructions. It was like trying to assemble a bike without the manual. Dale guessed he did pretty well not really knowing what he was doing. He remembered how soft and warm and sleek Wendy felt. He remembered the taste of her mouth and the warmth of her breath. He felt like trying again. Then he remembered he'd probably get another chance tomorrow night.

## Chapter 5: *Unusual test scores; Time; a close call*

Dale scooped the last bite of chocolate cake into his mouth, savored the sweet flavor, then swallowed. He gulped down the last of the milk.

"Would you like another piece, Audie?" Mrs. Heath asked.

"No ma'am, thank you," Dale said, although he was tempted. The piece he just ate was almost twice as large as Thea's. It was the best cake he'd ever tasted besides his grandma's. Maybe better.

"How did you like it?" Mrs. Heath asked.

"It was great," Dale said.

Mrs. Heath laughed at his enthusiasm. "Why, thank you for the compliment. Although I think you exaggerate."

"No, ma'am. I mean it."

Dale thought of Jesse's cakes. She didn't make homemade cake or homemade anything. She baked Jiffy cakes, the kind of mix that didn't even require an egg. But on Dale's and June May's birthdays she used Duncan Hines with an egg and also bought canned frosting from the store. Dale liked them just the same, but now after having tasted Mrs. Heath's cake, he didn't think a cake made from a mix would ever suffice.

"You're a polite young man, Audie," Mrs. Heath said. "I've always noticed that about you."

"I try to be," Dale said, which was the truth. He *tried* to be polite even to teachers and coaches he didn't like. Dale glanced across the room to Thea. She sat in a chair reading *Little Women*. He'd seen a few other girls reading that book. It didn't interest him.

"As I promised you a couple of weeks ago, I have your test results. Now, the first test you took was the California Personality Assessment, CAP. Quite a few psychologists use it to determine a young person's personality. Would you like to see your test results?"

Dale said sure.

Mrs. Heath provided the two-page test results. The first page gave the numerical scores in the seven different categories. The second page charted Dale's scores against his age group's norms. She explained the significance of each score and each category. Most of what Dale heard didn't surprise him. He tended to be introspective, introverted, and independent.

Dale nodded. "Yeah, I guess I'm an 'I' kind of person."

Mrs. Heath laughed softly. "There is also an interesting, somewhat unusual aspect to your personality."

He waited.

"Well, you scored high on both typically masculine and feminine traits," said Mrs. Heath. Dale thought he saw her right eyebrow rise a little. "That is, you scored high on qualities generally thought to be masculine: aggressiveness, independence, and initiative. But you also scored high on qualities generally thought to be feminine: sensitivity, intuition, and empathy."

Dale glanced over to Thea. He thought he saw her looking at him from over the top of her book.

"Does that mean there's something wrong with me?" he asked lowly. He felt embarrassed to have high feminine scores.

Mrs. Heath smiled. "No, not at all. It just means your score is somewhat unusual. Most boys your age score fairly high to high in typically masculine categories and girls your age score fairly high to high in feminine categories. Most don't score high at all in the opposite sex's categories."

Dale nodded, but he still didn't like the sound of it. He wondered if Mrs. Heath was saying in a sneaky way that he was a bit of a sissy. Blackie sometimes told him he was too sensitive. Now, this test was confirming that damning assessment.

Mrs. Heath noticed his troubled expression. "Your scores are unusual, that's all. Frankly, I find them most interesting."

Dale noticed when Mrs. Heath smiled her blue eyes seemed to twinkle. He tried to remember what happened to Mr. Heath. He thought he'd heard that he'd died a few years before Mrs. Heath came to Galilee to teach. Dale thought Mr. Heath had died of some sad disease but he couldn't remember which one. He wondered if Mr. Heath had both high masculine and feminine scores.

He leaned closer to Mrs. Heath and quietly asked how Thea scored. Mrs. Heath said in a whisper that she'd scored high on the feminine and low on the masculine. Dale thought as much. Thea seemed very feminine in a quiet, unobtrusive sort of way.

"I was curious," said Dale in the same low voice, "why you wanted me to take this test."

"I needed a boy your age for the case study. But I thought you might enjoy taking it. You see, I once saw you carrying a certain book. *The Psychology of the Adolescent*. That's not an everyday sight seeing a high school boy carrying such a book for his own edification."

Dale smiled his typically no-teeth smile. He liked that word edification. He'd have to remember it. He assumed that Mrs. Heath was familiar with the term "fat pads." But he wasn't sure how to work it into the conversation.

Mrs. Heath asked him if he planned on taking the psychology/sociology course next year. Dale said he definitely planned on taking it. She said she thought he'd enjoy it. He agreed. Then Mrs. Heath said something else that surprised him.

"Oh, the second test indicated that you have high potential in a field like physics. Have you ever considered taking that? Or maybe majoring in it in college?"

Dale said no. He wasn't even sure what physics was.

"Well, come to think of it, I'm not exactly sure what it is either." She smiled. He liked her self-deprecating sense of humor.

Dale said Mr. Smedley had told him he should think about studying business. Mr. Smedley seemed to think he didn't have the right kind of "background" for anything else.

"Well, there's nothing wrong with studying business," Mrs. Heath said. "Economics, for example, is a demanding field. But according to this test you have the intellectual capacity to study anything you prefer."

Dale had thought there was something wrong with Mr. Smedley's evaluation. He should have said something last fall.

"You know," he said, "I'm taking business machines and bookkeeping this year. Do you think that was a mistake?"

Mrs. Heath hesitated. "Well, frankly, Audie, I do. You should have taken more intellectually challenging courses."

Dale agreed. He said he would in the future.

Mrs. Heath said good, and smiled. Dale said he had better get going. He thanked her for the cake. Mrs. Heath thanked him for helping her. She said to visit whenever he liked. She then asked Thea to see him to the door.

Dale walked out of the kitchen with Thea into the living room. The Heath house was small but extremely clean, neat, and well ordered. The air smelled faintly of vanilla and pine trees.

Dale opened the door and prepared to leave. He turned to Thea. She smiled her quiet smile and thanked him for helping her mother.

"Glad to do it," he said. Thea reminded him a little of Juliette, except her eyes were blue.

"I heard you're dating Wendy," said Thea, her small hand holding the knob of the door.

The question embarrassed Dale. He looked out the screen door to their yard. It needed to be raked. Gold and brown leaves covered the walkway.

"Yeah, I guess I am."

Thea smiled. "Wendy's a nice girl."

Dale nodded.

"Well, goodbye, Audie," Thea said softly.

"So long, Thea. I'll see you in school."

Dale opened the screen door and heard the front door shut quietly behind him. He jumped off the porch and kicked at the leaves as he walked to his car. He felt a melancholy shadow pass over him. There was something a little sad about the Heath household even considering how clean and neat it was and how nice both the mother and daughter were. Dale smiled at himself. It was just his feminine traits talking. He jumped in his car, revved the engine, and drove fast down the street.

The chartered Greyhound bus seemed to float over the highway. Dale looked out the large passenger window at a fallow field. Behind it a full Hunter's moon shone. The sky was so clear and the moon so large and bright that he could see the faint outlines of its craters.

Inside the bus, Dale heard the murmuring of quiet conversations and a few sniffles. The cheerleaders, and some of the guys, had cried when boarding the bus. Galilee had lost its playoff game, 12-7, to Maverick High at their stadium.

The Gophers had played a tough game. They scored late in the fourth quarter when Terry Harte broke two tackles for a three-yard touchdown. Harte kicked the extra point and Galilee led, 7-6, with five minutes to go. All the Gophers had to do keep the Maverick Mustangs from scoring.

But Maverick wore down the smaller Gophers. They ran twelve straight running plays and drained all the time off the clock. They marched down the field, made a key fourth and inches at Galilee's thirty-five, and scored on a quarterback sneak with only ten seconds remaining. Maverick failed on the two-point conversion. On the ensuing kickoff, they shrewdly squib kicked the ball. Billy Joe caught it at the forty, then lateraled the ball back to Harte, who cut across the field, dodged one tackler, busted through two more tacklers, then swung wide and raced down the right sideline. The Galilee bench and Galilee fans stood on their feet cheering wildly. It looked like Harte might do the impossible. He dashed past the thirty, the twenty, the ten, and at the seven a Maverick player hurled himself in desperation at Harte's ankles and caught the heel of his foot. That was enough to trip Harte. He sailed in the air for four yards before crashing down at the dusty three-yard line. Time had expired. Galilee had lost its first playoff game in five years.

Dale had started on both offense and defense for the fifth game in a row. He'd played okay, he thought. Maverick, a wishbone team like Galilee, only threw five passes, completing two. Dale's man didn't catch a pass and he'd made five tackles. On offense, he carried the ball only seven times. But one of the runs put Galilee in scoring position. Dale was supposed to run through the four hole on a counter. But out of the corner of his eye, he saw the defensive end crashing down, so he cut right and raced around the end for a twenty-eight-yard gain, setting up Harte's touchdown run. That kind of running drove Dorfman crazy. He always told Dale to run the play how it was drawn up. Follow the blockers and run to where the hole was supposed to be. But once Dale got the ball, his instincts took over and he ran to daylight. Sometimes it worked well; other times it didn't. That time it had worked.

Sitting on the luxurious chartered bus, Dale didn't feel heartbroken like the seniors. Galilee had won eight games and lost only three, including the playoff game. They'd won their district, handily beating Agra and Oilville in their last two games. Against Oilville, Dale had one of his better games. He rushed for eighty-four yards on just ten carries and made seven tackles on defense and didn't allow his man to catch a pass. In school on the following Monday, Mrs. Page had told him he'd played a "very good game." Dale, pleased to be complimented by one of his favorite teachers, had no idea that Mrs. Page came to the football games, especially a road game.

Dale looked to the front of the bus where the cheerleaders were. He saw Wendy sitting with Mary Jane. Wendy had cried with the other cheerleaders. He'd seen her board the bus with tears streaming down her cheeks. He'd wondered if he should do something, but he sat ten rows back from her and he'd have felt silly rushing past all the guys to comfort his girlfriend. Fortunately, Mary Jane had hugged her so he'd been relieved of that responsibility.

Harte had cried, too, when he stood up and told the team how proud he was to have played his last high school game with them. But he didn't bawl or anything. Tears welled up in his leonine eyes, his voice broke once, and he had to brush the tears away a couple of times, but Dale thought, under the circumstances, he'd acted manly enough.

Galilee had chartered two buses for the big game. On the other bus, fans that had been willing to pay for the seats got to ride in style. A lot of other people drove their cars all the way from Galilee to Maverick, a town about thirty miles south of Tulsa. Dale had been amazed to see how many people from Galilee were standing in the visitors' bleachers. Most of them were decked out in crimson and cream and some of them wore these goofy Gopher hats, baseball caps with a cartoon gopher painted on the front. Dale had always been a little embarrassed by their school nickname. How formidable can a gopher be? But when he saw the gopher mascot on the sideline – not wearing a whole suit, just the head – that sight filled him with pride.

Chris, sitting next to Dale, leaned over and asked him if he thought next year's team would be as good.

"No," Dale said.

Chris reacted with surprise at Dale's candor. "Why not? We've learned to win."

"Yeah, but we're losing a lot of good players."

Dale thought they were losing three of their big linemen, including MacDonald who'd done quite well his senior year, although they would still have Leroy Lemmon. But they wouldn't have Harte or Charlie Comingdeer. Harte was the school's best player since Robin Comingdeer.

"Maybe we'll do just as well," Chris said. "You gotta have a positive attitude."

"Yeah, but even a positive attitude can't change reality."

"There you go again, talking philosophy."

Dale didn't really know any philosophy. But he planned to read some in college. Maybe major in it. Until then, he just thought about things. Sometimes he said them out loud to Chris.

"Harte was just a fingertip away from scoring," said Dale, remembering the last play. "Why did the Maverick guy reach just far enough to trip him up? Did the Maverick player have just an ounce more positive energy than Harte? Was it luck? Was it fate?"

Chris shrugged. "Maybe it was God's will."

"Why would God care about the Galilee-Maverick playoff game?"

Chris's face had an earnest expression that Dale had seen before, on the faces of Witnesses. "Because God cares about everything and everybody."

"I guess," Dale said, not wanting to debate that point with Chris. He knew Chris was a sincere Nazarene boy. He turned back to the window and looked out at the dark, flat land and the big, gleaming moon. If what Chris said was true, Dale thought, then that idea raised other questions. For example, why did God allow Maverick to win? Galilee had suffered through five losing years. Maverick had won the Class A state championship just last year. Why didn't God favor Galilee in this game? Why didn't He blow a single breath and move the hand of that Maverick player just an inch and then Harte would have scored? Galilee held a team prayer before kickoff; Dale assumed their opponents did the same. Which team did God listen to?

"Boy, we're going to get home really late," said Chris.

Dale turned to his friend, welcoming a change of topic to the mundane.

"Yeah," he said, "we won't get back until tomorrow."

Chris looked puzzled. "No, we'll get home by one at least."

Dale thought of the immense power of Time. Football season was over. The biggest game of his life was over. But in the larger sense of time, every second of every day passed like the previous seconds of every day. He looked out the window. The moon seemed to be floating higher in the sky and in a few more miles, a few more minutes, it would be out of sight. For eons people had stared at that same moon until they had ceased to exist. Dale thought how he was just one link in a long chain of human beings all caught up in some invisible stream of Time. He felt awed about Time. Time ruled the universe. Maybe that's all there really was in life, just Time.

Dale turned and tapped his finger on Chris's wristwatch. "Yeah, one in the morning. The morning of a new day."

Chris nodded. "Oh, yeah. I guess that's how it works."

"Yeah, that's how it works."


It was almost two o'clock in the morning by the time Dale got to his house. He'd taken Wendy home, but it was so late and both were so tired that he'd just kissed her good night. Usually, when Dale was out he got home around midnight and Blackie would still be up, either watching the end of Johnny Carson or reading his college textbooks. But tonight, since it was so late, Dale knew his father would already be in bed.

Dale parked the Chevy on the street curb in front of his house and quietly walked to his dark home. Since he didn't yet have a house key, he supposed he'd have to ring the doorbell and wake Blackie. He didn't want to do that. He knew Blackie hated being roused from his deep sleep. Dale knew Blackie usually didn't lock the garage door. His father did lock the door that led from the garage to the kitchen, but he knew the small window would be unlocked. He thought he could slide the window up, then reach his hand down and unlock the door. He'd tried doing that a year ago but his arm hadn't been long enough to reach the door handle. But since he was two inches taller and had a longer reach, he figured he could now reach the door handle.

Dale lifted the garage door as quietly as he could, but the steel wheels still made a harsh, clanking noise. He raised the door three feet, then slipped under it into the dark garage. He crept toward the door, almost expecting to bump into his motorcycle, except that Blackie had sold it the past summer. Dale reached the door leading to the kitchen, pushed up the small glass window, and shoved his arm through and down. He had to stand on his tiptoes in order to reach the doorknob. His fingers encircled the knob, and unlocked the lock. He pulled his arm back through the window and opened the door.

As he stepped into the kitchen, Dale noticed that the hall light was on, which illuminated the kitchen enough so that he clearly saw the barrel of a .38 revolver aimed at his head. He stopped in his tracks and blinked. Blackie, extending his arms through the kitchen shutters from the living room, took aim and Dale thought he heard the cocking of the hammer before his father said, "Goddamn, boy!"

"It's just me," Dale said, in a voice so calm that it even surprised him.

Blackie lowered the gun and glared at his son. He walked around the wall separating the living room and kitchen. When he got to the kitchen, he shook his head and Dale stared at the revolver clutched in Blackie's right hand.

"What the hell are you doing sneaking into the house? Why didn't you just ring the doorbell?"

Dale shrugged. "I didn't want to wake everyone."

"Well, I almost blew your goddamned head off."

Dale looked again at the gun in Blackie's hand and remembered hearing the click of the gun's hammer being cocked. He realized that Blackie had almost shot him. For the first time, he felt a wave of fear sweep through him. He looked at his father and saw his face twisted in both anger and another, less familiar emotion. Maybe fear, too.

"It's late," Dale said, trying to explain. "I didn't want to wake everyone."

"You thought opening the garage door wouldn't wake me?"

Actually, Dale did think that. Blackie was ordinarily a heavy sleeper.

"I thought you were burglar, boy. You're lucky I didn't shoot when I first saw you take a step into the kitchen."

Dale felt sick to his stomach. He imagined Blackie's finger putting just a little more pressure on the trigger that would have resulted in the gun's firing. Blackie was a good shot. He wouldn't have missed. Dale knew the bullet would have probably killed him. He shook his head and felt a strange sense of relief and excitement at coming so close to death.

Blackie took a deep breath to relax himself. Dale did the same. He saw that Blackie was just dressed in his white boxers. His father always slept in his "skivvies," even in winter. Apparently, Blackie hadn't even bothered pulling on his trousers. He'd just grabbed his gun and waited.

"We lost the game," Dale said. He didn't know what else to say.

"Yeah, I heard on the radio."

Dale didn't know the game had been broadcast on the radio. He started to ask which station when he noticed that Blackie was still scowling at him.

"Don't do that again," Blackie said.

"Okay."

Blackie said he'd get Dale a copy of the house key. Now, they had better get to bed.

Dale nodded and followed his father down the hall. Blackie glanced at him but didn't say good night as he entered his bedroom. Before he closed the door almost shut, Dale thought he heard Jesse softly snoring from her twin bed.

Dale went into his room, closed the door, took off his street clothes, and put on sweatpants and a T-shirt. He got into bed but he didn't feel sleepy. His body felt tired. His muscles already felt sore from the contact from the game. His mind, however, felt wide awake.

The idea that he'd almost been shot still lingered in his mind. He tried to think of something soothing, as he often did to help calm him for sleep. He didn't want to think of the football game because he'd get excited again. So, instead he thought of Amanda. He still thought about her most nights before going to sleep, even though he knew he was being emotionally unfaithful to Wendy. Tonight, he knew he had to think of Amanda or he'd never fall asleep. He remembered sitting on the team bus and looking out the window and seeing her as she walked with the other pep club girls to the second bus after the game. She hadn't cried like Wendy over the team's loss. But her expression had been somber and the idea that she was unhappy both disturbed and intrigued him. Dale hadn't seen her upset before. She always seemed to have a tranquil expression on her pretty face. The idea that Amanda could feel unhappy made him feel an odd, conflicted feeling. He felt sympathy for her but also a feeling akin to excitement. He felt that way because her unhappiness meant that everything wasn't perfect in her life and maybe he could do something for her. Maybe he'd get the chance to be of service; do something to prove his devotion to her and make her appreciate him.

Dale wondered how Amanda and the other kids at school would have reacted if Blackie had killed him. He supposed his friends would mourn his death, but he suspected that most everyone would get used to his absence pretty quickly. He guessed Amanda wouldn't be too affected, except that he thought she was such a kind and religious girl that maybe she'd be more deeply moved than the others. Dale guessed he would get a full page photo in the back of the yearbook to commemorate his short life, just the way the school honored the last Galilee kid who'd died early, a guy who'd been killed in Vietnam when Dale was in seventh grade.

None of these thoughts soothed Dale. He didn't like the idea of getting killed and no one really caring. Especially Amanda. But since he hadn't been killed, Dale decided that maybe God had saved him for some reason. Maybe God had decided that now wasn't time to have his life end. Maybe God wanted him to do something with his life; maybe He wanted him to stay alive so he could prove himself to Amanda. Maybe that's why Dale hadn't drowned those three times; why he hadn't been killed in the motorcycle accident, and why he hadn't been shot by Blackie.

As Dale lay in his bed in the dark of his room, he decided that God really had saved him. Ordinarily, Blackie would have shot an intruder without hesitating. Maybe God had whispered to Blackie to wait just a second more.

Dale decided God had a purpose for his life. He thought it had something to do with Amanda.

He closed his eyes and after offering a short prayer of thanks for not having been killed, he imagined performing heroic deeds. Not just athletic exploits, but noble deeds like saving Amanda from a burning building or a flood or, even more exciting, from a villain. Perhaps the Mad Sickle Man. Dale grew relaxed as he half dreamed of vanquishing the Sickle Man and rescuing Amanda. As he untied her and removed the gag from her lovely mouth, just as he was about to kiss her and dry her tears, he fell asleep.

**Chapter 6: *Parental problems; a near fight; Wendy's mother***

Dale had heard the story before. But he listened anyway.

Jesse said she met Blackie at a social function at the enlisted men's club at the naval air station in Norman. This was in the fall of 1955. Jesse noticed this man standing at the refreshment bar, wearing his blue dress uniform. Blackie came over and asked her to dance, but since she didn't dance she said no and then he asked if she'd like a drink of punch and she said yes and the two of them sat down at a table and talked a while. Three days later, Blackie asked Jesse out for a date. They went to movies and nightclubs and drives in the country and one thing led to another and they got married three months later, before Blackie shipped off on a Pacific cruise.

"Did Daddy call himself Blackie?" June May asked.

"He said, 'My name is Forrest Smith but all my friends call me Blackie' and I said, 'okay, I'll call you Blackie.'"

"Didn't you feel funny calling him that name?"

"No," said Jesse. "It reminded me of a dog we use to have when I was a kid. He was a big, black mutt and he'd run around the fields chasin' jackrabbits. His name warn't Blackie though. It was Midnight."

"What happened to Midnight?"

"He caught distemper and Poppy had to shoot him."

June May thought that was a sad story. "What happened next with you and Daddy?"

Jesse told her that she went to San Diego with him and stayed there until Blackie got back from his sea duty. Then they went to Rhode Island so Blackie could go to some navy school. Then she came back to Oklahoma when Blackie shipped out for another tour. That's when Dale was born, when Blackie was over in Japan. Then they went to California again, then she came back to Oklahoma while he went on another tour, then they went to Hawaii for two years.

"That's where I was born," said June May.

"That's right. At the navy hospital in Honolulu."

"I don't remember Hawaii," said June May.

"Of course not, dummy," Dale butted in. "You were just a baby."

"I'm not a dummy. I just don't remember Hawaii."

Dale shook his head, then got up and went into the kitchen. He opened the fridge and grabbed the milk carton and chugged some down. He heard Jesse yelling at him to use a glass.

"It tastes better right out of the carton," he said.

"I don't care," Jesse said. "Use a glass."

"Yeah," June May cried. "I don't want your germs!"

Dale put the milk away. "You don't even drink milk anymore," he told his sister. He heard the front door open and Blackie walked in. He wasn't in uniform. Dale followed him into living room.

"I'm late," Blackie said.

"Don't I know it," said Jesse.

"Yeah, well. Work.

"Oh, that's right, *work*." Jesse reached for a cigarette, lit it, sucked in smoke then expelled it through her nose.

"So, are you ready to go?" Blackie asked Jesse.

"Don't I look it?" She was wearing new red pedal pushers and a new blue blouse. She stabbed the just-lit cigarette into the ashtray.

"Okay, then let's go." Blackie looked at Dale and June May. "You kids going to be all right by yourselves?"

"Of course," said Dale.

"Yeah," said June May.

Blackie said they'd be back by ten. They were going to dinner, then they'd stop off for a while and play some pool.

"At a beer joint," said June May, disapprovingly.

"No, at a nice bar," said Blackie.

"Same thing."

Blackie looked like he might swat her, but instead he motioned for Jesse and they walked out of the house. June May turned on the television, then sat on the couch.

"Hard to believe they've been married eighteen years," said Dale.

He looked at June May, who was immediately absorbed in *The Newlywed Game*.

Dale started to go to his room when he heard the door being flung open and his mother's cussing.

"That sonofabitch," she said. "Why I ever married that bastard is beyon' me!"

She walked so fast into the living room that her shorter leg had a hard time keeping up. She sat down on the couch next to June May and picked up her cigarette from the ashtray, lit it, and sucked on it like it was oxygen and she were suffocating.

"Where's Daddy?" asked June May.

"Who the hell cares!" Jesse growled out of the side of her mouth.

"Daddy's not leaving, is he?" June May cried. She jumped up from the couch and ran to the front door. "I don't see him."

"He's just gone for a drive," said Dale.

Actually, he didn't know where his dad went during arguments like these. He was often gone as long as two hours. But he always came back.

June May ran to her room and slammed the door shut. Dale looked at his mother.

"What started it this time?" he asked.

"I don't want to talk about it." She noticed the television show. Her mouth turned down in annoyance. "Change the channel."

Dale reached over and turned the dial. He left it on *The Gong Show*.

"I'm going to my room," he said.

Jesse just nodded and puffed.

Dale walked into his room and shut the door. He thought about a topic he ordinarily didn't allow into his mind: his parents' sex life. As far as he could determine, the last time they had been intimate was the weekend of Blackie's return from the navy. That was more than two years ago. Dale wasn't completely certain. But he'd learned to read the clues of when they had been together. The last time, the bedroom door had been shut the whole night and morning. He'd heard some curious noises from their room. But since then, no noise, at least not any friendly noise, and their bedroom door remained conspicuously open in the mornings. Now that he was beginning to penetrate a little into the mystery of sex himself, he wondered if that was the source of his parents' increasing antagonism.

Dale walked over to his records and flipped through them. As he grew older, he was beginning to appreciate irony. He put the Turtles' "Happy Together" on the stereo just to celebrate his parents' eighteenth anniversary.


Dale put a hand in Comingdeer's face. After Comingdeer shot, Dale turned and blocked out. The ball skidded over the back of the hoop and fell into the open hands of Tim Middleton. Dale felt Comingdeer elbow him in the back. Throughout the scrimmage, Comingdeer had been playing dirty. He'd shove, elbow, and once even tried to knee Dale in the groin. Comingdeer was shrewd enough to do these infractions when the action was elsewhere on the court. Dale had tried ignoring him. He knew Comingdeer was an aggressive player. He thought it was best to keep his cool.

Coach Carpenter blew the whistle. The players took a short break. Dale walked over to the water fountain and took a drink. Chris, who was playing on the second team with Dale, told him he was doing a good job against Charlie. Dale wiped the sweat off his forehead and looked over at Comingdeer standing with the first team. So far, he'd held him to just one basket. One thing Dale was pretty good at was playing defense. It was mostly quickness and anticipation, and Dale knew how to hound Comingdeer and keep him from scoring.

One month into basketball season and Dale had yet to play in a varsity game, a fact that didn't bother him at all. He still found basketball an unnerving game. In practice, he felt at ease, but during an actual game he still felt nervous and self-conscious. He played on the junior varsity and sometimes did fairly well. He never scored much. The most points he'd scored in any of the eight J.V. games so far was seven. But he played steady defense, didn't turn the ball over nearly as much as he used to, and felt like a contributor rather than a liability.

The varsity, in spite of not having any player taller than six foot two, was playing competitive basketball. They had a losing record at 7-11, but most of the losses had been close. Dale thought Coach Carpenter was doing an excellent job considering how short his team was. He thought it must have been especially frustrating for Coach Carpenter, at six foot seven, to not have a real center to train in the art of the playing the post.

Coach blew his whistle signaling the resumption of play. Dale joined his scrimmage team, and waited for the starters to take their place on the court. The varsity starters were Harte, Comingdeer, Stephenson, Billy Joe, and Rusty. Tim Middleton, Sonny, Erickson, Chris, and Dale were the second team. Dale, in fact, usually wasn't part of the 10-member scrimmage crew, but Cary Phillips, a gangly senior, was out of practice with the flu.

The starters took the ball and ran their offense. The subs, playing man-to-man, reacted quickly. Comingdeer took the pass from Rusty and drove toward the basket. Dale moved with him and before he could bring the ball up for a layup attempt, Dale slapped at the ball, knocking it free and Sonny grabbed it and started a fast break.

"Foul," growled Comingdeer.

But Coach didn't call it. Dale started to turn and follow the fast break when Comingdeer shoved him. Dale said, "watch it." Comingdeer threw a punch and Dale turned his head just in time. He felt a glancing blow against his jaw. Comingdeer cocked his arm again.

"Try it," Dale said.

"And what will you do, junior?"

"Just try and see."

Comingdeer drew his fist back and Dale prepared to duck the blow when he heard Coach Carpenter's booming voice.

"Comingdeer! What the hell are you doing?"

"He fouled me. He's been playing dirty all game."

Dale threw his hands up in the air. "That's not true. He's the one playing dirty. He just punched me."

Coach Carpenter walked over to them. The rest of the team stood at the other end of the court, watching.

"Get off the court, Charlie," Coach said.

"Smith started it," growled Comingdeer.

"I saw you hit him. Get off the court now."

Comingdeer hesitated. He glared at Dale. He started to walk by, then suddenly reached out and shoved Dale, knocking him to the floor.

"That's it. You're suspended, Comingdeer!"

Comingdeer marched toward Coach Carpenter with his chest pushed out in defiance. Coach took a step forward, and staring down at him told him not to try it. Comingdeer stopped, turned and peered at Dale with dark, angry eyes, then stormed off the court, descended the stairs, and banged open the locker-room door.

Coach Carpenter looked at the now standing Dale and asked if he were okay. Dale said yeah, wishing Coach hadn't called attention to him. Dale resisted touching his jaw; it hurt a little. Coach told Erickson to join the starters and Wally to join the subs. Then he blew his whistle and the scrimmage resumed.

After practice, Dale got the feeling he was being blamed for the whole thing. He thought Harte and Middleton gave him funny looks as the team descended the stairs. Dale especially didn't understand Harte's reaction. He and Comingdeer had gotten into a fight during football season in the locker room. Dale remembered them sitting at the other end of the bench when suddenly they both jumped up and started punching. Most of their blows missed, but Harte landed one right on Comingdeer's left eye. Before any more damage could be done, Dorfman and Blocker broke it up. Comingdeer had a black eye for a week.

Dale never found out what caused the fight. Maybe Comingdeer was jealous of Harte being mentioned more in the Oklahoma City newspaper's article than he had been. But then, it might have been something even more trivial. Like a typical bully, Comingdeer picked on smaller underclassmen, but unlike one, he also antagonized tough guys like Harte.

After showering and dressing, Dale and Chris walked out of the locker room to find Rusty and Erickson waiting. Rusty shook his head.

"Way to go," he said. "Get in a fight with the toughest guy in school."

"I didn't get in a fight," Dale said.

"I didn't see the punch," said Erickson. "Did it land?"

Dale said it didn't land square; just brushed his jaw.

"Why didn't you hit him back?"

"Because then he'd hit me all the harder."

"So, you were scared," said Erickson.

Dale thought about it. He hadn't been afraid. Nervous, excited, but not really afraid. When he said, try it, he'd looked right into Comingdeer's eyes, expecting to be hit hard. And he hadn't been afraid. He didn't know why.

"Not really," Dale said.

"Yeah, right," scoffed Erickson.

"Shut up, Rich," said Chris. "You wouldn't have done anything either."

Erickson decided to change the subject. "So, how long is Comingdeer suspended for?"

"I heard Stephenson say he heard Coach Carpenter tell Dorfman it was for a week," said Chris.

"Great," said Rusty, giving Dale an annoyed glance. "He'll miss our last two regular season games."

Dale stared at Rusty. He seemed to be blaming him for the whole thing. Rusty knew Comingdeer was a bully. Last year, Comingdeer shoved Rusty around in scrimmages.

Erickson said he had to go. Rusty did too. Their meeting broke up and they walked to their cars. Chris, who was getting a lift from Dale, said he shouldn't let any of what was said bother him.

"Maybe I should have hit back," Dale said. "Now everyone will think I was chicken."

"I don't. I saw you stand your ground. You didn't look chicken to me."

Dale grinned wryly. "I don't think anyone else thinks that."

"Who cares what guys like Erickson think. You know, I know, and I bet Comingdeer knows."

Dale thought about that. Yeah, maybe. He knew he could never win a fight against Comingdeer. But he thought it was important for Comingdeer to know he wasn't afraid of him.

After Dale dropped Chris off, he thought about the incident. He decided not to tell Blackie. He knew what his father's reaction would be.


"Why didn't you hit Comingdeer back?" asked Dorfman.

Dale knew Dorfman would say that when he saw him in bookkeeping class. He shrugged.

"You shouldn't let yourself be pushed around. Not even by a bigger kid like Charlie."

Dale said he didn't let himself be pushed around. He said he stood his ground.

Dorfman had a dubious look on his big, broad face. The bell rang and he walked away from Dale's desk in back to the front of the classroom. Dale saw some of the girls in the front glance back at him. Wendy had an especially troubled look on her face. He felt annoyed. Did she think that he should have fought Comingdeer, too? It amazed him how quickly people found out about certain things. And he knew most school gossip was only about half right. People were probably saying that Comingdeer had beaten him up.

Dale hardly listened in class. Dorfman spent most of the class flirting with girls in the front row. Dale wondered if Amanda had heard about the incident. He looked at her sitting at her desk in the front row, wearing her pep club uniform, a typically placid expression on her lovely face. One of the things he admired about Amanda was she didn't seem to gossip. He'd never overheard her talking mean about anyone.

When class was over, Wendy said bye to Mary Jane, Amanda, and the other girls and walked out the classroom with Dale. Wendy wore her cheerleading outfit. Galilee had a basketball game that night at Agra. Dale noticed she looked upset. Surely, she wasn't this upset about what happened with Comingdeer.

They walked out of the school without saying anything. It wasn't until they were at Dale's car in the parking lot that Wendy looked at him. She had tears in her eyes.

"What is it?" he asked.

Wendy looked around to make sure no one was near. "My mother," she said.

Dale was surprised. He actually thought she was going to complain about him not fighting Comingdeer.

"What about her?"

"She told me I had to come home right after the game tonight."

Dale noticed Wendy wringing her hands. She was fidgeting, too, the way she did when nervous.

"All right," said Dale.

"Don't you understand?"

A few tears squeezed out of her green eyes and trickled down her cheeks. She quickly wiped them with away with her fingers.

"Yeah. Your mother wants you home early."

"She thinks we're seeing too much of each other. We're going out too much, staying out too late."

"Well …" Dale wasn't sure what else to say. Maybe that was true.

"She also *saw* us last Saturday," Wendy said quietly.

Dale felt an emotion stronger than embarrassment; he felt ashamed. He hadn't felt such a feeling for a while. He'd forgotten how the feeling turned him inside out and left him feeling all raw and exposed.

Last Saturday night, Dale brought Wendy home later than usual. *Gone with the Wind* was a long movie and they had to drive to Oklahoma City to see it. Wendy invited him into the dark, quiet house and they went to the same small room they had gone to before and immediately started making out. The smooching progressed to other things. Eventually, Dale took Wendy's bra off and both had their shirts pulled up and he was lying on Wendy and sort of grinding himself into her. He still had his jeans on but Wendy's skirt was up above her hips. Dale remembered he was about to head to third base when he stopped. He thought he heard some faint noise in the next room. Also, he knew he had better stop before it went too far. He'd kept on expecting Wendy to stop him, but she seemed to encourage his every advance. That noise he'd heard must have been Wendy's mother. He doubted she saw much in the dark, but she probably heard plenty to know what was going on. Wendy was rather expressive.

"Wow," Dale said. That was about all he could think to say. He let out a deep breath.

"But I don't want to," said Wendy. "I want to see you as often and long as I can."

She suddenly hugged Dale, her arms clasping around his neck. She pressed herself against his chest and sobbed.

"Come on," Dale said. "It's not that bad."

He patted her on the back, then thinking that wasn't very comforting, stroked her blond hair.

"Don't you care?" Wendy asked, her voice muffled because her face was pressed into his shoulder.

"Of course I do. But maybe we should cool it for a little while."

Wendy jerked back and stared at him with an alarmed expression.

"I mean still go out," he quickly added. "Just not stay out so late. And not do certain things in your house."

Wendy seemed somewhat reassured. "Okay," she said. "Momma doesn't know exactly when the game ends anyway. As long as I get home around the same time as Wally, she won't expect anything. Maybe I can talk him into staying out a little longer. Then we can have some time together."

Dale said that sounded like a good plan.

He walked Wendy to her Volkswagen Beetle and said he'd see her after the game tonight. Wendy, the rims of her eyes red, smiled and said okay, and he watched her drive away.

Dale got in his car and started it up. He sat there listening to the engine rattle. Maybe

Wendy's mother was right. When they started making out, they lost track of time. And lately, they seemed to have gotten increasingly close to home plate. Dale still didn't exactly know what he was doing. He still felt incredibly ignorant of the subtleties of lovemaking. But he discovered that it was really easy to lose control even if he was sort of playing it by ear. He counted on Wendy to enforce the rules and she seemed to get as easily carried away as he did.

More troubling, he feared that she was taking all this too seriously. Dale knew Wendy was an emotional girl. Sometimes the intensity of her feelings scared him. He enjoyed making out with her, but he never felt himself fully involved in it. He was worried that Wendy was fully involved in it, and who knows where that could lead.

He drove out of the parking lot, his mind consumed with these concerns, when he almost ran the stop sign. He saw a dark Lincoln Townhouse out of the corner of his eye entering the intersection and he jerked his Chevy to a stop. He looked over to see Amanda's mother staring at him with a disapproving look on her face. In the passenger seat sat Amanda, who looked straight ahead in her typically serene sort of way as Mrs. Meeks proceeded to drive the car safely through the intersection.

Dale took a deep breath. That's all he needed. To crash into Amanda's mother's car. He smiled at the absurdity of it all and drove home.


### Chapter 7: *Mr. Smedley; needing a tall guy; Gopherette banquet*

Dale sat at his desk reading *A Streetcar Named Desire*. It wasn't for class. He'd seen the book in the library and had remembered the author from another play his junior English class had read, *The Glass Menagerie*. He'd liked that play pretty well; the girl in it had been crippled sort of like Jesse.

Dale was just getting to the good part where Stanley attacks Blanche when Mrs. Page interrupted him.

"Audie," she said, "you're supposed to see Mr. Smedley."

She handed him a note. Dale put the paperback book down and Mrs. Page noticed it.

"I see you're reading another Tennessee Williams play."

Dale detected a disapproving note in Mrs. Page's voice that surprised him. "Yeah."

"Hmmm," Mrs. Page said.

Dale glanced at her face. She had sharp, intelligent light blue eyes that seemed to see everything in her classroom. Her perceptive eyes along with her long, sharp nose made Dale think of a hawk or a falcon. She was pretty in spite of that avian quality. She had a sensual mouth and an attractive oval shaped face. She dressed impeccably in tasteful dresses, nylons, and two-inch pumps, and she styled her auburn hair in rather elaborate hairdos.

"I considered that play for class," she said, "but I thought it was a little risqué for high school."

She looked at Dale with her quick, alert eyes. "How do you find the play?"

Dale said he found it in the library.

Mrs. Page ignored his faux pas and said modern playwrights were neurotic. O'Neill, Williams, and especially Albee enjoyed wallowing in depravity. She preferred the work of Thornton Wilder, Moss Hart, William Saroyan, Maxwell Anderson. The classicists of American drama. She said Dale might do better starting with those playwrights. "Modernists have such bleak world views," she added.

Dale nodded. He didn't have any idea of what she was talking about but he knew it was important so he listened intently.

"Have you read any C. S. Lewis?" she asked.

"Did he write plays?"

Mrs. Page considered the question. "I don't think so. But he should have. Anyway, I think you'd enjoy his work. Perhaps you should start with *The Chronicles of Narnia*. Don't be put off by its classification as a children's book. It's really an allegory."

Dale said he wouldn't be put off. Mrs. Page smiled and said she'd bring him a copy if he liked. He said okay. Mrs. Page said she was gratified to see him taking such an interest in literature. Then she turned and walked back to her desk, her skirt swishing as she walked.

Rusty leaned over and whispered to Dale, "What was she talking about?"

"Books."

"Books?"

Rusty used to read a lot of books, but that was before he dedicated himself to basketball and girls. Rusty seemed to go out with a different girl every couple of weeks. Lately, he'd been dating Mary Jane. Dale always suspected Rusty liked her best, but Rusty was fickle. He was a busy bee. So many flowers to buzz to, so little time.

Before the bell rang signaling the end of fifth hour, Dale went to Mr. Smedley's office. He knocked, heard "come in," and when he did he didn't see Mr. Smedley, just piles of files arranged in six tall columns like skyscrapers on his desk.

"You may sit down," said a voice behind the skyscrapers.

Dale removed a couple of files from the dusty chair and sat down. He looked at the disarray of Mr. Smedley's office. Cabinet drawers yawned open; papers and empty files were tossed everywhere; even a soiled paper plate and a glass of what had contained milk, now only the crusted remains, stood on a cafeteria tray on the corner of Mr. Smedley's desk.

A pair of hands appeared between two towers of files and carefully scooted them apart. Dale saw Mr. Smedley peering at him through the gap.

"How are you…" Mr. Smedley searched for the name.

"Audie Smith."

"Ah, yes, Mr. A. Smith."

Mr. Smedley stood up and only his head cleared the six imposing towers of files. Dale guessed every student in school was represented in those stacks. He observed that the counselor's square glasses were speckled with dust and bits of stuff. He mentioned that to Mr. Smedley in case he hadn't noticed.

"Oh, thank you, A. Smith," Mr. Smedley said. "I'm sometimes a little absent minded. I get so wrapped up in my work that I tend to forget little grooming requirements."

Mr. Smedley removed his glasses and cleaned them with the end of his not-so-clean tie. Dale thought his unshielded gray eyes looked small and vulnerable. Mr. Smedley blinked them several times as if he were just waking up.

Mr. Smedley donned his glasses and looked at first one stack, then another. Dale waited. He was glad he didn't wear glasses. He wore contact lenses. He'd got them in the fall in time for football. He didn't want to be a four-eyes while playing football. The contacts worked well. They were the soft lens kind and he'd gotten so used to them he didn't even feel them on his eyes anymore.

"Ah, here we go, A. Smith," he said, as he slipped a folder from the middle of one of the tall towers. Dale uneasily watched the stack tremble.

Mr. Smedley flipped through the file, then looked at Dale. "There seems to be a mistake."

Dale waited. He couldn't think of a mistake he'd made involving Mr. Smedley.

"It appears, Au-Au-Au-"

"Audie."

"Yes, exactly. That's the problem." Mr. Smedley dropped the file on his desk and sat down. Dale shifted to his left in order to see Mr. Smedley through the stacks. "You see, your folder became confused with another A. Smith. I'm afraid I thought you were *that* A.

Smith and he were you."

"You mean Andy Smith?"

Dale didn't see how anyone could confuse him with the red headed, paler-than-a-fish-belly Andy.

"Yes, exactly. At any rate, Audie, I've made the correction."

Dale considered the implications of this mistake. "Is that why you recommended I take business machines and bookkeeping?"

"Are you taking those two courses?"

Dale said yes, of course.

"Ah, well, you probably shouldn't be. You probably should be taking courses that we in the profession call college-prep courses. You are planning on going to college?"

"I think so," Dale said. He wanted to, but Blackie hadn't told him anything specific.

"Well, I'd encourage you to do so. According to your test scores you're definitely college material."

Dale wondered what college Mr. Smedley had attended.

"Well, Audie, if there is anything else I can do for you, please let me know." Mr. Smedley stood up and peered at Dale from above the stacks. "I just wanted to clear up this little mistake."

Dale nodded, got up, and started to leave when Mr. Smedley asked him to wait. The counselor came over and handed him a paperback book. Dale looked at it. *The Collected Poems of Rod McKuen.*

"I heard you're quite a reader," Mr. Smedley said.

"You sure it was me?"

Mr. Smedley laughed an odd, high-pitched wail. "Of course. At any rate, I thought you might enjoy this book of poems. I remember fondly the hours of enjoyment I had reading them. I was, however, a little older than you when I first encountered their intoxicating rhythms and rhymes. A freshman in college, I believe."

Dale said thanks. He'd return the book after he read it. Mr. Smedley handed him a tardy slip for his next class and said good-bye and Dale left his office. Walking down the deserted halls – sixth hour had already started – he looked at the cover of the book. The author stood staring into space from a wind-swept craggy cliff. He had a beard, wore a turtleneck sweater and chinos, and had a soulful look in his eyes. Dale thought he'd seen him on TV once. The name sounded familiar. He flipped open the book and read one of the poems. He shut the book. He didn't like it.

Dale wondered if he should have asked Mr. Smedley if he could take other courses rather than business machines and bookkeeping for spring semester. He guessed he couldn't. Actually, he didn't mind business machines much. Students worked at their own pace and Dale was almost finished with all the assignments for the year. He always read after zipping through a ten-key assignment. Maybe that's why he'd earned a reputation among the teachers as a reader.

Bookkeeping was another matter. He disliked the class. The work was boring. Dorfman showed off before the girls too much. Dale didn't understand why a middle-aged man liked teasing and flirting with high school girls. He didn't know why the girls responded so eagerly to Coach's attentions. Also, Dorfman had given Dale his only B for fall semester. Five As and one B. Dale had calculated his grade at 89, but Dale knew his coach wouldn't give him the extra point to get an A. That was just Dorfman being Dorfman. But bookkeeping had at least one compensation. Dale got to gaze at Roxanne, Mary Jane, Gretchen, and, of course, Amanda. He didn't count Wendy among the subjects of his gaze, since he saw her all the time.

As for Wendy's mother, that situation seemed to have calmed down. Dale didn't keep Wendy out as long, he didn't come in for make-out sessions, and so far he'd been allowed to see her on weekends. Wendy still seemed too lovey-dovey for his taste. But the new arrangement had reached a sort of satisfactory routine.

Dale opened the door to the art room and saw his classmates busy with an assignment. He handed Miss Roach the tardy slip and went to take his seat next to Rusty when he saw someone sitting in his usual seat. It was Sadie.

He'd heard she was back in school. Dale hadn't seen her yet and he wondered how she was going to make up missing almost two months of spring semester. He grabbed a free chair and scooted in next to Rusty on the other side. Rusty grinned at him and asked if he were late for a reason or just late. Dale noticed Sadie glancing at them with an odd flush on her face.

"Had to talk to Smedley," Dale said.

"Smudgely? What did our great guidance counselor have to say?" Before Dale could answer, Rusty added, "Hey, have you ever gotten a load of his ties? I think he uses them for a bib."

Dale noticed Sadie looking at them again. Her expression was so melancholy that he felt he had to say hello.

"Hi, Sadie."

"Hi, Audie."

Rusty turned to her and smiled. "Yep, she's back. In time for spring semester. Well, a little late. But we're glad she's back. She'll certainly enliven this dull class. Say Sadie –"

Sadie suddenly got up and walked out of the classroom, her head held low. Miss Roach started to ask what was the matter but Sadie walked out so fast she didn't have a chance. Miss Roach looked over at Dale and Rusty.

Rusty shrugged. "Hey, she sat next to me."

Dale tried to look as non-involved as he could, like an innocent bystander, but when he looked down at the other end of the room where K. C. and Bigelow sat, he saw Butch staring at him and Rusty.

"What's Bigelow's problem?" Rusty asked lowly.

"Bigelow," said Dale.

"Hey, that's pretty good. Bigelow's problem is Bigelow."

Dale started working on his assignment, a watercolor. Dale didn't like watercolor. He always put too much water on the brush and ended up soaking the paper. Rusty was even worse. Give them a good old pen-and-ink assignment any day.

Sadie didn't come back to class. Dale guessed she just left. June May was still friends with Sadie's younger sister, Sheba. June May had Sheba over occasionally and Dale had thought about asking her how Sadie was doing. But he never did. He thought it would just embarrass both of them.

The bell rang and Dale fussed around with his watercolor mostly to make sure Bigelow left before he did. He wasn't in the mood to go through any huffing and puffing with him. Rusty, in a hurry as usual, said he'd see Dale in the locker room.

A few minutes later, he left the art room, walked down the hall, and exited the building on his way toward the back entrance to the gym. As he started to open the gym door, he looked to his right and saw Sadie at the far end of the building, leaning against the brick wall talking to someone. The kid stood with his back to Dale, but judging from his long, greasy hair and black leather jacket it looked like Dean Hogue, one of the pseudo-hoods in school. He was a skinny, pimply senior who smoked cigarettes in the alley during lunch and liked listening to heavy metal music. Dale didn't really know him and right now Hogue and Sadie seemed involved in a rather intense conversation. Hogue, noticing Sadie looking Dale's way, turned around and Dale confirmed his suspicion. Hogue scowled but Dale looked past him to see a sad, weary look on Sadie's face. Then Dale opened the gym door and walked inside.

The six feet eleven Agra center pivoted and hurled a perfect hook shot over the outstretched hands of Billy Joe. The ball skimmed through the basket, hardly ruffling the net. Dale, sitting on the back row of the bench, looked at Coach Carpenter sitting in front of him. He wore a thoughtful expression on his Superman-lookalike face. Dale wondered if he were imagining how nice it would be to coach that tall Agra center.

Erickson, the tallest Galilee player at six foot two, had first guarded the Agra guy whose name was Skinner. But Erickson couldn't jump high. The Agra center couldn't jump high either but at his height he could almost stand under the basket and get rebounds. Coach then had Billy Joe, at six foot one, guard Skinner. Billy Joe did better, but Skinner still almost scored and rebounded at will. Thanks to Skinner, Agra led by ten, 54-44, with seven minutes to play.

It didn't look good for Galilee. If they lost this game, the first game in district tournament, then the season was over. During the regular season, Galilee had won eight and lost twelve, which wasn't too bad considering how short the team was. Rusty, who was still growing, was five eleven and played shooting guard. He'd led the team in scoring, averaging almost seventeen points a game. But Galilee, no matter how well they shot and defended, couldn't beat a team with a good, tall player.

The funny thing, Dale thought, was that this Skinner guy wasn't that good. Dale had seen him play in the Sundance Invitational Tournament and he hadn't done well at all against the big man on the Sundance team. Skinner had one of those uncannily appropriate names. He was the skinniest kid Dale had ever seen. At six eleven, he probably only weighed 150 pounds. He looked like one of those emaciated Africans Dale saw on TV, except that he had really white skin and blond hair. In the game against Sundance, Skinner had been shoved all over the court by the Sundance center that was five inches shorter but outweighed the cadaverous Skinner by fifty pounds. Skinner had scored only three points in the loss. Dale remembered feeling sorry for him. He imagined that Skinner had been required as a little kid to play basketball because he was so tall. But he was so skinny and weak that he wasn't very good unless he came up against a short team like Galilee. Dale had always thought a guy could never be tall enough, but that wasn't so in the case of Skinner. He imagined it must be difficult to be so tall and have people expect so much out of you, only to disappoint them because you're really not all that athletic.

But against Galilee, Skinner looked like he was all-state caliber. He tipped in another basket, hardly jumping, and now Agra led by twelve. Coach Carpenter called time out and took out the three senior starters, Harte, Comingdeer, and Stephenson. He substituted Erickson, Sonny and the senior Middleton, keeping the two junior starters, Billy Joe and Rusty, in the game.

Dale watched as the three seniors took a seat on the bench. They looked depressed. Comingdeer turned and noticed Dale looking at him but he didn't scowl or make any threats. He'd been suspended for one week for knocking Dale down. After the suspension, he had to apologize. Before practice, they met in the gym. Comingdeer hemmed and hawed a bit, but finally he told Dale he was sorry. Dale said okay but added that he thought Comingdeer pushed guys around too much. Instead of getting mad, like he thought he would, Comingdeer considered the criticism and said he knew he sometimes overdid it. He said he had a lot of pressure on him and things weren't going so well at home. Dale said he understood. After a pause, Dale asked him about his famous cousin, Robin Comingdeer. Had Charlie seen him lately? Comingdeer's dark eyes flashed. Robin was in prison. Dale couldn't believe it and wondered how the heroic Robin Comingdeer could do anything criminal – forgetting of course, that his heroism was confined to the football field. Charlie shrugged and said he got caught up in bad company. He'd helped rob a gas station in the City and had been convicted for armed robbery and assault.

Dale said he was sorry to hear that. Comingdeer said yeah, and then he held out his hand and they shook hands. While walking away, Dale realized that he and Charlie had at least one thing in common: they both had cousins in prison.

Now, Comingdeer sat on the bench with the other two senior starters watching their team lose the last game of the season. Dale felt sorry for them. It was a bitter end to a fairly good season.

Agra called time-out and substituted for Skinner, who finished with twenty points and ten rebounds. But it didn't matter. Agra's subs continued to increase the lead. With four minutes left, Coach took out Rusty and Billy Joe, subbing Wally and Chris. With one minutes left, and Galilee trailing by fourteen, Coach turned and looked at the two remaining varsity players, a senior named Cary Phillips and Dale. Phillips, gangly, uncoordinated, and further handicapped by a bad foot, hardly ever played. He, like Dale, suited up with the varsity only because they were upperclassmen. Coach nodded at Phillips and he jumped off the bench and peeled off his warm-up jacket. Then Coach looked at Dale. Dale felt his face flush. He felt like his eyes were popping out of his head from the anxiety. He shook his head. He didn't want to go in. Coach Carpenter looked puzzled at first; most players wanted to play. Then he grinned. He knew Dale was shy and he didn't want to force him to play. He turned around and sent in Phillips in for Erickson.

Dale sighed in relief. He'd been reprieved from making a fool of himself. Going onto the court with a minute left in the last game of the season branded him as a charity case. He had too much pride for that. If he'd been crummy in other sports, maybe he wouldn't have refused to go in. But he knew what it was like to be good at sports and he didn't want to be seen as one of the pathetic benchwarmers who gets in for a few seconds. He'd rather not play at all.

The game ended, Galilee lost by fifteen, and the players shook hands. The Galilee players showered and dressed in the visitors' locker room and boarded the bus. Rusty, sitting next to Dale, asked him why Coach didn't put him in.

"He would have, but I didn't want to go in."

Rusty gave him a puzzled look, not comprehending how anyone wouldn't want a chance to play with the varsity. Then Rusty shrugged and slumped in his seat. He hadn't played up to his expectations. He'd only scored twelve points.

"What we need is a tall guy," Rusty said. "Then we'd be good."

"Where do we get one?" asked Dale.

"Yeah, why are all you Galilee guys so short?" asked Erickson.

After two years of living in Galilee, Dale realized that Erickson still didn't think of himself as one of them. He didn't like that and he didn't like Erickson calling them short, although they were.

"Are all the guys in Nebraska so tall?"

"Taller than you guys. At my last school, we had two guys in *junior high* who were six four."

"Six four would be good," Rusty said, imagining a center that tall.

"You're just a Yankee," said Dale, who had heard his grandpa say that to a salesman who talked with Erickson's nasal accent.

"No, I'm not. Yankees live in New England."

Dale knew that was technically right. Dale had gone to most of second grade in Rhode Island when Blackie went to some navy school. He'd hated it. Everything was different there. He had to ride a bus. The milk carton tops were flat instead of angled. The kids all talked with a strange accent. They cussed, too, even some of the grade school kids. They, including the teachers, thought Dale had the odd accent. He'd had to take speech lessons. He got out of regular class and went to see a nice lady who helped him with his speech. Dale had liked the lady. She was friendly and let him draw some of the time. When Dale returned to Oklahoma with his family, he no longer had much of a southwestern accent. Now it was the kids in Oklahoma who said he talked funny. Dale remembered Mary Jane telling him that in third grade.

"All northerners are Yankees," Dale said, mostly to annoy Erickson.

"No, they're not," Erickson said, but before he could continue Rusty interrupted.

"Hey, that's what we need."

"A Yankee?" Dale asked.

Rusty ignored his jest. "To find a big guy. Maybe we can get someone to transfer. Do you guys know anyone six four or so?"

No one did.

"We gotta find one," said Rusty with unusual determination, "or we don't stand a chance next year."


For a change, it was Wendy who stopped the make-out session. She removed Dale's hand from her thigh, but allowed his arm to remain around her shoulders.

"We got to be careful," she said.

Dale knew that. He was the one who usually signaled the end. After about an hour, he couldn't take it anymore unless it proceeded to the next level. Since they couldn't, he'd stop kissing and fondling her and lean back in the seat and sigh. Wendy would straighten herself up and make some cheerful small talk.

"After all, look what happened to Sadie," Wendy said, straightening and smoothing her gown.

Dale thought about seeing Sadie with Hogue. He hadn't known Sadie knew that guy. He wondered why he even cared. Maybe it was because he and Sadie had the same last name. Maybe he felt a certain odd connection to her because for years he'd sat behind her.

"Yeah, what *did* happen to Sadie?" he asked, wanting to see how Wendy would react.

She looked at him with a bemused look on her face. "You *know*."

"Not really. Everybody thinks they know what happened to Sadie, but they really don't."

Wendy didn't answer right away. She was thinking that through. "Well, one boy knows what happened."

"You're making assumptions," said Dale. He'd just learned that concept in English class and had been looking for a way to use it.

"It's obvious, Audie. Why did Sadie have to leave for six months? Why did she have to go to her grandmother's in Fort Worth?"

"I'm just saying we don't know for sure."

"No, not for sure as in having evidence," Wendy admitted. "But it's almost certain." Wendy looked at Dale. "Everyone's wondering who the boy was."

"I'm not."

"You don't want to know? Well, I'm curious. We have three candidates, after all."

Wendy named Rusty, Bigelow, and a third guy, Dale hadn't known about, a guy who'd graduated last year, Jerry Dewberry.

"Jerry Dewberry?" Dale asked.

"Yes. Sadie dated all three of them last spring and summer."

Dale wondered how someone as skilled at gathering gossip as Wendy had overlooked Hogue. He also wondered how someone handled dating three different people at the same time. Well, he guessed he should ask Rusty.

Dale saw a cop car gliding down the road about three blocks away. He started the car. It was hard to go parking in Galilee. The cops liked to catch kids making out. It was even worse at Galilee Park. Billy Joe once told him that a cop appeared out of nowhere and shined his flashlight in his car and caught Merry with her blouse and bra off. Dale enjoyed imagining that. Merry had the biggest breasts of all the junior girls. He hadn't known she was so naughty though.

Dale pulled out of a spot concealed by a bush and a rare tall tree, and drove down the road. He'd found a couple of good parking spots not too far from Wendy's house, too.

"I hope Wally's not home yet," Wendy said.

Dale asked Wendy why Thea Heath asked Wally to the Gopherette banquet. When Dale

192

saw them together earlier that night, he first noticed how odd they looked as a couple. Wally stood almost a foot taller than Thea.

"They're in chemistry together," she said, as if that explained it. Then Wendy talked about the other couples: Mary Jane and Rusty, Roxanne and Harte, Gretchen and K. C., Billy Joe and Peggy, Quentin and Carrie, Merry and Bigelow, Wally and Thea, and Carmen and Chris. She evaluated the dresses the girls wore, why the girl asked whom she did, and other stuff that Dale didn't care much about. He thought about Amanda and her date, Bobby Henshaw. Amanda had asked him last year too. He asked Wendy as nonchalantly as he could if Amanda and Bobby Henshaw were going out.

"I don't think so," said Wendy.

"But that's the second time they've gone to the banquet."

"Is that so?"

Dale didn't want to say too much in case he made her suspicious, so all he said was "yeah, I think so."

"Well," Wendy said decisively, "they're not going out. At least not on a steady basis."

"How do you know?" Dale asked, pretending to be skeptical, as if challenging Wendy's expert knowledge about such matters.

"Because Amanda's mother won't let her date anybody steady."

Dale thought about that time when he almost ran into Mrs. Meeks's car. That incident as well as her rule made him smile.

"What are you smiling about?" Wendy said, smiling too.

"Nothing."

"C'mon. Tell me."

Dale tried to think of a plausible reason. "I was just thinking how funny Wally and Thea looked together." He glanced at Wendy to make sure she found him credible. "You know, the difference in height."

"Oh," Wendy said, disappointed.

## Chapter 8: *A stormy track meet; Wendy surprises Dale*

Dale didn't like the new track uniforms. They weren't made of cloth but some ultra-light material. The shirts even had tiny holes in them. When he complained, Dorfman told him that even half an ounce of lighter material could make the difference between winning a race and finishing second. Dale supposed that was true. But he still didn't like the way the uniforms felt.

He took off his sweats and stood in the paper-thin uniform waiting for his heat of the 100 to begin. Dale remembered the beginning of track season almost two months ago. The blustery weather, the raw-looking Oklahoma sky, that familiar anxiety before running the series of 440s to get into track shape. Most of all, he remembered sprinting down the track one sunny day later that week and feeling that he'd broken into a newer, more satisfying sphere of speed and strength.

Dale finished warming up and got in his blocks and waited for the gun. He timed the start well, leapt forward, and quickly accelerated to full speed. He raced down the track, not seeing anyone ahead of him and only seeing one other runner at his right in his peripheral vision. This was his favorite part of the race. When he ran without strain, his arms pumping, his legs easily carrying him down the track, his spikes hardly touching the cinder while they made a faint *tsk tsk* sound – sort of how a brush makes on a snare drum. At that moment, he felt joyously free.

He leaned into the tape at the finishing line knowing that he'd won his heat. Hardly winded, he gradually decelerated, then walked back in his lane until the official recorded his time: 10.2. His best ever.

Dorfman had him unofficially timed at 10.15. He nodded at his stopwatch as if it were solely responsible for the time. "You'll qualify," Dorfman said. Rusty tossed Dale his sweats and he put them on even though it was a warm, humid day. Dale, now seventeen, was still bashful about showing his body. He thought the shorts were too short and as for the shirt, it hardly covered his chest.

Dale and Rusty waited to see how Chris would do. Dale felt a fraternal sense of pride for Chris. Last year, Chris had tried hurdles, then switched to mostly middle distance events and didn't do too well. Then, at a dual meet at the start of the track season, Dale said Chris should try running the 220. Dale was the only Galilee runner scheduled for it, and he had a hunch that Chris could do well as a sprinter. Chris now stood about five foot eleven and had a lean, fairly muscular build. Dale thought he looked more like a sprinter than an 880 man. But Chris, diffident by nature, wasn't sure he should enter the 220 unless Dorfman gave him permission. Dale said he should because there wasn't any pressure in a dual meet; they were like tune-ups for the bigger meets, the invitationals, where schools came from all over from the region. Dual meets were sort of fun. If you flopped, so what? Finally, Dale convinced Chris to enter and he finished just a few yards behind him for third place. Dorfman had come over to the two of them after the race and told Chris he was a sprinter. Dorfman didn't even ask why Chris entered the 220 or whose idea it was or anything. Dorfman acted like he just forgot to tell Chris. Dale didn't care. Chris did so well in the 100 and 220 that Dorfman put him on the 440 relay team, too, replacing Stephenson, who really wasn't fast enough to be on the team. The relay team of Chris, Rusty, Harte, and Dale took off and had won at least third place in every track meet so far.

Dale and Rusty watched as Chris leaned into the finish line, tying for second in his heat. Dale glanced at Dorfman's stopwatch and read 10.4. "DeVille won't make the finals," Dorfman said, "but not bad for a former middle man."

Dale, Rusty, and Chris walked back to the Galilee camp and sat down on the old gym mats. In a track meet as large as the Wheaton Invitational, several events were taking place at the same time. They watched Sonny pole vault. Across the infield, Leroy Lemmon and Doug MacDonald heaved the shot. Billy Joe was getting loose, waiting for his middle-distance events. Harte was getting ready to make his first try at the broad jump. Stephenson had already made his first attempt at the high jump. The Galilee track team had won several duals and placed high in a couple of invitationals. They had a good team. The kind of athletes they had, somewhat small but fast and well trained, was ideally suited for a sport like track. Dorfman, Dale had to admit, was a good coach. He got them in shape, knew enough technique in every event to help them with strategy, and knew how to adjust their training in practice so they wouldn't peak too soon.

In fact, it looked like Galilee was peaking at the right time. Their guys were qualifying in most of the events in Class A and that was against competition from all over the central, west and north of the state. Just about the only schools not here were from the Tulsa region and from the southeast, the "Little Dixie" part of the state.

Dale liked seeing where all the guys came from. At a big invitational like this, he'd see uniforms with school names he'd never heard of, places like Ada, Cushing, Elk City, Hominy, Fairview, Tomahawk Top, Squaw River, Black Mesa, and dozens more. He liked all the different colors and lettering of the uniforms. He liked the variety of nicknames: from the commonplace like Braves, Buffaloes, and Stallions to the unusual like Horned Toads, Hoot Owls, and Bushwhackers. An invitational was like an athletic circus: lots of high school athletes, coaches, and other people milling around, something going on in every area of the track, and a crowds of people in the stands creating a buzz with their quiet talking and occasional cheers.

The only thing he didn't like much about track meets, especially these big invitationals, was how long it took to conclude them. To help pass the time, Dale had taken to reading while waiting for his events. At that moment, he was reading Somerset Maugham's *Of Human Bondage*. K. C. noticed the book.

"Hey, Smith, what's that book called?"

Dale hesitated. "It's called *Of Human Bondage*."

"When you get finished, let me see it."

"It's not that kind of book," Dale said, not moving his eyes from the page.

"Yeah, right."

"I think Audie was reading this morning when he came to pick me up," said Chris.

Dale looked up from his book.

Rusty asked Chris to elaborate.

"Well, he must have had his eyes on something else because he ran right into the ditch in front of our house."

Chris, Rusty, and K. C. laughed.

"And he just sat in his car," said Chris, "like nothing had happened."

"I was half asleep," said Dale.

He had been. He'd driven Chris home dozens of times but coming to pick him up he'd forgotten about the ditch outside the front of his yard. He'd curved in farther than he should and wham! the next thing he knew, the Chevy's right front was tilted down at a twenty-degree angle. Chris was right. He had just sat in the car staring straight ahead like nothing had happened.

Chris's dad had to tow him out with his truck. Dale thought Mr. DeVille was quite agreeable. Chris always talked about how strict he was, but every time Dale interacted with him he seemed like a mild-mannered fellow.

"My father told me he hoped Audie had a better sense of direction on the track field than in the car," said Chris.

The guys laughed again. Dale smiled at their teasing. One thing he liked about the track team was that most of the guys were friendly and relaxed. Bigelow was on the team, but he did field events so he wasn't around much when the runners were relaxing. Comingdeer, the other overly aggressive guy, hadn't come out for track, which helped ease the tension. On the other hand, he was a good middle-distance man and he would have helped in that area. Some seniors didn't come out for track. They only ran as sophomores and juniors because Dorfman made them in order to play football. Even though Comingdeer would have helped the team, Dale didn't miss him.

Wendy had told Dale to come over at eight o'clock. The baby would be asleep by then.

Saturday night, a week after the Wheaton track meet, and Dale was looking forward to seeing Wendy. He parked his car outside Wendy's brother's house a little after eight. He felt uneasy sneaking into Denny Wainwright's house. He'd met him briefly four years ago when he stayed the night with Wally. Now, Dale was slipping into his house at night in order to make out with his younger sister.

Before Dale could knock, Wendy opened the door and let him in. She immediately hugged him. They kissed and Dale walked over to the couch while Wendy brought them Cokes. He looked around the house. It sort of reminded him of Wendy's parents house except it wasn't as junky and didn't have that comfortable lived-in feeling yet. The house smelled clean and fresh. He wondered if Wendy had done some cleaning.

They dimmed the lights, watched television, and drank their Cokes. Nothing good was on. Wendy went to check on her one-year-old nephew. Dale didn't hear him squawking so he thought he must be sound asleep. Then he heard Wendy softly call him. He got up and turned to walk down the hallway when he saw her standing at the end of the hall naked from the waist up.

Dale stared. He felt his heart flip over and his breath evaporate. Wendy smiled and sauntered over to him. Her breasts were impressively large. Her areolas and nipples were a little pale for his taste, but he liked the way her breasts jiggled as she walked.

"Wow," Dale said.

She threw her arms around his neck and hugged him. He felt her bare chest through the thin cloth of his T-shirt. Dale had never actually seen Wendy topless before. It had always been dark or at least semi-dark when their make-out sessions got that far. He'd seen the outlines of her breasts under the moonlight in the car when he'd pushed her bra and shirt up, but he'd never seen them so clearly.

They went to the couch and Dale, unencumbered with her top half, began to work on the lower half after a few minutes of kissing and fondling. He felt greatly motivated. He thought it was sort of funny how visual stimulation energized him. Wendy reclined on the couch and he tugged at her slacks. He'd already unbuttoned them and he figured the rest would be easy. But the slacks were tight and they didn't want to slide off her ample hips and thighs. He remembered Erickson disparaging Wendy to the other guys for being "too hippy" and now Dale, who especially liked girls with curvy hips, began to experience the practical difficulty of de-pantsing a girl of such proportions.

Wendy helped him by pushing from the top. Finally, he got the tight pants to her ankles and decided that was enough. He turned his attention to her pink panties. He peeled them down to her knees, gasping when he saw her smooth white thighs and the tuft of blond pubic hair in the V above them. When he looked at Wendy's face, he saw her eyes were wide with alarm. Dale wondered if maybe he was doing something wrong but he couldn't think what that could be so soon. Then he heard a car turning into the driveway and saw headlights flash across the wall above the couch.

"Oh, my God!" cried Wendy. "They're home early!"

Wendy struggled to get up from the couch. Dale slipped and fell on her and she wailed for him to get off. He tumbled to the floor and Wendy stood up and tugged her panties up over her jiggling bottom. She reached down and fumbled for her slacks. He tried to help.

"Stop it!" she cried. "You're bunching them up!"

Wendy bunny-hopped down the hall. Dale followed and watched how her plump buttocks quivered and quaked underneath her panties. He fell against the wall, almost delirious from the combination of arousal and panic.

He heard a key jostling in the door and he scampered over to the couch. He tried to look nonchalant. He crossed his legs, but that proved too painful. He uncrossed them, leaned back, then righted himself and leaned his elbows on his knees and pretended to be watching the almost silent television.

The door opened. He glanced over to see Denny Wainwright and his wife staring at him. Dale nodded. Denny didn't seem pleased to see him. Denny closed the door and glanced around the room. His wife, Shari, a pretty brunette, looked alarmed. Dale supposed she had never seen him before.

"Where's Wendy?" Denny asked.

Dale was surprised by how deep his voice was for a rather short man.

"She's back there," he said, standing up and pointing to where he thought the bedrooms were. Then he thought he better not show too much familiarity with that part of the house and awkwardly jerked his hand like it had suddenly been set afire and brought it down to his side. "With the baby," he added.

Shari immediately left for the baby's bedroom. Dale heard two female voices murmuring from down the hall as Denny continued to stare at him from the front door.

"Aren't you Audie?" he asked, his eyes narrowing as he tried to remember.

Dale said yep, that's who he was all right.

Before Denny could interrogate him further, Wendy and Shari appeared. Shari said the baby was fine. He was sleeping. Dale glanced at Wendy's flushed face. She smiled nervously, unconvincingly, as if she'd been ordered to by a firing squad.

"I don't remember you saying your boyfriend was coming over," said Shari.

"I thought I mentioned he was," Wendy said, a new wave of scarlet rising from her neck to her face.

Dale took a step forward. "I – I just stopped by for a few minutes," he said, not quiet stammering. "I've never seen a baby before."

All three of them looked at him closely.

"I mean, obviously, I've seen a baby before, but never one that young." He paused wondering if he'd made any sense at all. "I guess I better get going."

"Would you like to stay longer?" asked Shari. "If the baby wakes up you could see him then."

"I better not. I got to get home. I have a baseball game tomorrow."

"Tomorrow's Sunday," said Denny.

Dale had forgotten. He nodded. "Yeah, it's a special game. A make-up game. For a rainout."

"I'll show you out, Audie," Wendy said.

Dale walked over to the door, and as he did Denny circled in the other direction toward the couch. Dale noticed that he and Denny were about the same size.

Dale said bye and Denny and his wife said good night and he followed Wendy out the door. They both stood under the porch light without saying anything.

"Guess I'll see you in school Monday," Dale said.

He started to leave when Wendy touched his arm and kissed him quickly on the lips. "Good night," she said.

He nodded and dashed off to his car. He got in and started it as Wendy disappeared inside her brother's house. Dale drove back to his home, feeling more frustrated than he'd ever felt before. He felt like a famished man who gets a glimpse of a smorgasbord and is then is arbitrarily denied its sustenance. Then, to further add to his frustration, he thought about Wendy's nudity. She was the first non-relative female he'd ever seen naked. He'd seen Tammy without clothes when he was eleven and she was thirteen. He'd gone looking for her and found her standing naked before her mirror in her room. Dale's eyes were riveted first to Tammy's plump bottom, then to the reflection in the mirror of her apple-sized breasts. Dale had no idea what she was doing, but in spite of his girl-hating convictions then, he was interested in finding out. She screamed and told him to scram. He'd also seen one of Wanda's daughters breast-feeding. And then he'd seen Wanda once, coming out of the shower, a sight he wished to forget.

He'd seen hundreds of pictures of nude women by now. Dale felt almost blasé about it. But one thing was for certain: seeing a naked girl in the flesh, so to speak, was a lot more exciting. He wondered when he would get another chance.

**Chapter 9: *Winning a game; getting in a fight; and Mr. Smedley***

Dale waited. The Quanah Parker pitcher wound up and hurled a pitch that missed the outside corner of the plate. Three balls, one strike. He stepped out of the box and thought about the next pitch. The pitcher had struck him out in his last at-bat with an inside fastball. Dale figured the pitcher would try to do that again.

He got back in the box and saw Chris getting a lead off second. With two out, a hit would score Chris and win the game and give Galilee a winning record for the season.

The Quanah Parker pitcher threw the ball just where Dale guessed he would. Dale smoothly swung the bat and felt that kinetic pleasure of his bat making solid contact with the ball. He heard the crack of the bat, and while sprinting down the first base line, he saw the ball sail over shortstop and bound between the centerfielder and leftfielder. He knew he had a sure double and as he rounded first and headed to second he saw Chris crossing home plate with the winning run. Dale stopped at second and saw his teammates jump out of the dugout, waving their arms in jubilation.

Game over. Galilee 5, Quanah Parker 4. Dale trotted over to his team's bench. He felt pretty good. He'd never gotten the game winning hit in his team's last at-bats. Not even in little league.

Chris, Rusty, and his other teammates congratulated him. Even Comingdeer said "good hit" in his gruff voice. Then the Galilee players went over and shook hands with the Indian guys from Quanah Parker. They had a good team. In fact, they were going to the state playoffs and had played some second teamers for today's game. But Dale didn't care. Galilee finished the season with a 9-7 record, the first winning baseball season in six years. What made the accomplishment even greater was that half the team ran track. Because of that, the baseball team didn't have regular hours to practice. All of that meant a lot to Dale. He hadn't been on a winning baseball team since little league. He went over to his pals and threw one arm over Rusty's shoulder and another over Chris's. All three of them let out a victory whoop. They felt like they'd won the World Series.

The Quanah Parker guys thought they were crazy.

Dale boarded the bus and sat down with Chris. Coach Blocker arrived and told them he was proud of them. They'd done a good job considering the lack of practice and not having a pitching machine. Blocker said this year might be the start of a new and promising chapter in Galilee baseball history. After his talk, the players cheered themselves and chanted Goph-ers! Goph-ers! Goph-ers! then collapsed into chatter and teasing.

On the ride back to the locker room, Dale felt optimistic about next year. Maybe they'd win their district and make the state playoffs. Finally, they weren't losers.


The next day in art class, Dale molded the clay into a grotesque mask. Most of the kids were fashioning the clay into bowls and cups and pots, but he thought that stuff was mundane. He'd made two faces so far, all of them looking like weird Mardi Gras masks. This one was the best yet. The face itself was long, the eyes had a scary sort of squint to them, the nose hooked, and the mouth was thrown open as if it were howling in pain.

Miss Roach came over and looked at Dale's creations. She asked what he was making.

"Faces," he said.

"I can see that, but why?"

"I like faces. Especially grotesque ones."

He almost added, faces like hers, but he didn't. Actually, Miss Roach didn't have a grotesque face. She had a prosaic face. All her features except her nostrils were small and undistinguished. Small eyes, small nose, small mouth. From a distance, her nose looked like it consisted of nothing but nostrils. Just two holes in the middle of her face.

"Do you think those, er, masks, will hold up in the kiln?"

After molding their creations, they were to paint them with some sort of finishing, then bake them in the kiln. Dale was looking forward to seeing how his masks would look in red, blue, and black glaze.

"Sure. Why not?"

Miss Roach didn't respond but she hovered over him for a few more minutes. Dale knew she thought he was a weird kid. He had a taste for the surreal and grotesque. He didn't like painting flowers or birdies or making watercolors of quaint pastoral scenes. He liked weird, dramatic things. He'd seen one of Salvador Dali's paintings in a book, the one with the melting clocks, and he aspired to that kind of art. The first time he'd freaked out Miss Roach was when he drew a cemetery with a reddish sky and a purple field sprouting green stalks with pinkish gray brains on top. He'd also written a poem that went like this:

See the field of brains
Some think it a curious crop;
All they need is one drop
of blood and they will grow,
Sustained by our remains.

When Miss Roach had seen the drawing and read the poem, her small eyes narrowed and her small mouth thinned so much it almost disappeared in her face. Dale thought his next work would be a portrait of Miss Roach. Just a head, with curly black hair, no eyes, no mouth, just two dots for nostrils. She said, "Isn't that rather morbid?" and Dale said no, he thought brains were very interesting. Miss Roach nodded, unconvinced, and left to coo over the pretty pastoral scenes the girls were drawing, although Carmen drew a cool picture of a stallion rearing up on his hind legs. She didn't draw the horse's genitalia, though; she just sort of smudged that part.

Now, Dale finished shaping the third mask. He glanced at Rusty, who had been goofing off the whole time. Rusty didn't want to mold any bowls or pots either, but Dale knew he wouldn't make a mask since he had thought of the idea first. Instead, Rusty leaned back in his chair and flicked a piece of clay in the direction of Sadie, sitting over in the other corner with K. C. and Bigelow. The little chunk of clay flew across the room and landed in Sadie's snowy hair. She scowled at Rusty and reached up and carefully removed it from her locks.

"Hey, why are you doing that?" Dale asked.

"I was aiming for Bigelow."

Dale wondered. Rusty was usually a better shot than that. Rusty pinched off another piece of clay and flung it across the room. This piece hit Sadie in the chest. She looked more sad than mad. Her brown eyes reminded Dale of a scolded puppy.

Rusty flicked another chunk. This one bounced off Butch Bigelow's head. Dale tried not to laugh. Rusty said, "Bingo!"

Dale bent his head down closer to his masks, trying to stifle a chuckle. Bigelow didn't keep his hair in a burr or crewcut anymore; but his hair was still comparatively short and springy. Dale thought the clump of clay bounced off his round head really good.

"Uh-oh," said Rusty.

Dale glanced up and saw Bigelow stalking toward them. His boarish face was set in a scowl. He circled the interconnected Formica tables clockwise and approached Dale, who sat at the end of one table.

"I don't mind you clowns throwing something at me, but you shouldn't have hit Sadie."

Dale knew that was a lie. Bigelow did mind being hit with little clumps of clay. Bigelow minded it when he and Rusty just looked at him the wrong way. And as for Sadie, since when was he her protector?

Dale waited for Rusty to insult Bigelow but he didn't. Dale noticed Butch eyeing his masks. Bigelow reached down to the one Dale had already nicknamed "sinner in hell" and opened his hand like a claw. Dale jumped up from his seat and shoved Bigelow's hand out of the way. A moment passed. Bigelow glared and Dale thought how piggish Butch's eyes looked stuck so far back under his heavy brow. Then he felt Bigelow grab him around the shoulders. Dale squirmed free and threw his arms around Butch's beefy waist. Bigelow turned, Dale pushed, and they knocked apart the tables, scattered three chairs, then fell hard to the floor. He heard Carmen scream.

Dale had never wrestled Bigelow. He'd heard the weight and conditioning guys sometimes wrestled after lifting weights. But he was surprised how well he was doing. Bigelow tried throwing the bulk of his body against Dale, but he was too quick and he slipped out of Butch's grasp. Bigelow tried to throw an arm around Dale's neck, but he fended that off and shoved a hand toward Butch's face. Bigelow grunted and tried to bite a finger, but Dale pushed his hand under Butch's chin. If he had wanted, he could have choked Bigelow but he wasn't a dirty fighter. The two of them rolled over once, then twice, knocking over more chairs. Although Butch was bigger, Dale was quicker, more agile, and almost as strong, and soon it became apparent that they were engaged in a stalemate.

Dale heard his classmates shouting. He heard Rusty say, "get him, Dale!" and K. C. saying, "break it up, Butch!" And he definitely heard Miss Roach shrieking above the din. She kept saying, "stop it, boys, stop it!" Finally, K. C. and Rusty broke them apart. They stood up, panting. Dale noticed that Bigelow had a busted lip. He didn't remember hitting him, but maybe he'd accidentally head-butted him. Dale sensed he'd been scratched on the left side of his face. That area burned and throbbed. But he didn't reach up and touch it. He didn't want Bigelow to think he'd inflicted any pain.

Bigelow glared at him, his big nostrils flaring. He gritted his teeth, and Dale knew he wanted to curse or threaten him but he was out of breath. Dale was out of breath, too. Wrestling was exhausting.

Miss Roach told them to straighten up the room. She told them to sit down. She told them to stop fighting. Dale thought she was issuing contradictory commands, but he didn't say so. Bigelow gave Dale one last glare, then walked back with K. C. to the other side of the room.

Dale and Rusty helped to pick up the chairs, aligned the desks together, and clean up squashed pieces of clay and loose papers. Dale remembered his masks. He anxiously looked for them on the floor but didn't see them. He turned to his table, which hadn't been overturned, and saw all three were unmolested.

He sat down and examined them. They looked as grotesque as ever.

"Hey, man," Rusty said, "what got into you?"

"He was going to crush my masks."

"So?"

"Couldn't let him do that."

"Who do you think you are, man, Picasso?"

Dale didn't think Picasso worked in clay but he didn't argue. "I wasn't about to let Bigelow put his paws on my masks." He noticed Carmen looking at him.

"The side of your face is bleeding," she said.

Dale reached up and felt blood next to his ear and around his jaw. He thought he'd probably have to have a tetanus booster. He was certain Bigelow had filthy nails.

Dale got up and asked Miss Roach if he could go to the restroom and wash the blood off. Miss Roach looked ill; her face was pale and her hand trembled as she wrote something in her notebook.

"Of course," she said.

Dale left the room, ignoring Sadie's and K. C.'s questioning eyes as he passed them. A restroom was just down the hall. Dale threw open the door and entered. He saw Bigelow at the sink, pressing a damp paper towel against his busted lip. Dale waited a few feet behind him. He prepared himself just in case Bigelow tried something. Butch glared at him in the mirror but said nothing until he finished with his lip. Then, still gazing in the mirror at Dale's reflection, he said almost matter-of-factly, "Someday we'll finish it," and strutted out of the restroom.

Dale washed the blood off the left side of his face. Some blood had spilled on the collar of his baseball undershirt that he sometimes wore as a regular shirt. But the blood didn't show much because the collar was red, too. He winced when he dabbed at the scratch. It was a pretty good gouge. He'd once been scratched on the face by June May and this scratch was deeper than that, and June May had long fingernails even as a ten year old.

Now that the fight was over, Dale felt sort of giddy. When they were wrestling, everything around him seemed to blur. He hadn't felt any pain, any fatigue, any fear. He just felt angry and full of adrenaline.

Dale thought about Bigelow's threat. He rarely saw Bigelow during the summer. He thought Butch would probably forget their fight by next fall. Dale already felt his anger long gone. If Bigelow hadn't tried to harm something he cared about, he wouldn't have fought him.

He dried his face, tossed the paper towel in the wastepaper basket, and walked straight to the gym, not bothering to go back to art class.

The following Monday, Miss Roach told Dale that Mr. Smedley wanted to see him. He couldn't detect any disapproval in her voice or face. She looked as bemused as usual. Rusty whispered, "now you're in trouble." As Dale left the class, he thought he probably was in trouble. Bigelow hadn't been in class. Maybe the principal had suspended him already. What puzzled Dale, however, was why he was reporting to Smedley. The academic counselor had nothing to do with punishing students.

Dale knocked on Mr. Smedley's door, heard him say come in, and he entered his office expecting to see the usual disarray. Instead, he saw an immaculate office. No towers of files, no dirty dishes, no pulled out drawers, no litter. The office looked spotlessly clean. Everything seemed in its proper place. It even smelled like lemons and sunshine.

Mr. Smedley, however, still remained as disheveled as ever. His suit seemed thrown on him. His yellow tie had greasy blotches on the tail end. His glasses were almost opaque with dust and smudges. He sat at his neat and tidy desk, holding one piece of paper.

"Sit down, Audie," he said.

Dale thought, he *would* remember me now. He sat down on the wooden chair and tried to look contrite.

"I wanted to notify you in person that you've been –" Mr. Smedley sneezed. Dale saw him resist the impulse to use his tie for a tissue. Instead, Mr. Smedley opened his lower drawer and produced a tissue and loudly blew his nose. "Excuse me. Allergies."

Dale wondered if he were allergic to cleanliness.

Mr. Smedley cleared his throat. Dale in his mind finished the sentence for him. Suspended. Or worse, expelled. Or even worse, arrested.

"I wanted to notify you in person that you've been selected to represent Galilee High School at Boys State." Mr. Smedley stifled another sneeze and looked at Dale.

"You mean, I'm not in trouble?"

"Not unless you consider the honor of your selection as trouble."

Dale wasn't sure how to consider the selection. He asked what Boys State was. Mr. Smedley looked like he wanted to rescind the offer but he explained anyway. High schools across the state selected distinguished students to attend Boys State and Girls State. The boys and girls spent a week at a state college with other selectees and learned how government and politics function. The highlight of the week was a reenactment of a political campaign in which boys ran for office – the highest office, of course, being governor of Boys State.

Dale thought he understood. A bunch of boys got together and pretended to be politicians. Oh yeah, that sounded fun.

"Why me?"

He wasn't interested in politics. He never ran for class office. Rusty, who was junior class president, or K. C., who was vice president, seemed like more appropriate choices.

"If I tell you, will you keep it confidential?"

Dale nodded. He was beginning to feel like a politician already.

"You were the compromise candidate. Some on our selection committee wanted Isaac Gould because of his impeccable academic record. Others objected because of Isaac's lack of extracurricular activities, especially in the area of athletic involvement. A couple of other boys were considered but were deemed to be lacking in seriousness. Well, to make a long story short, we settled on you. You make good grades, although not excellent like Isaac; you play sports. You appear to be the epitome of the well-rounded young man."

"Yeah, but I've never held any class office."

Mr. Smedley nodded. "Yes, that was considered. But sometimes the people elected to class offices are elected more for their popularity than their leadership skills. That's what Boys State and Girls State is designed for. To develop leadership skills in the attendees."

Dale remained doubtful. He knew the reason Rusty or Erickson hadn't been selected was because teachers thought they goofed off in class too much. K. C. didn't make very good grades. Dale still thought one of them should have been picked, but he was relieved that he wasn't getting in trouble.

"So, do you accept?"

Dale said okay.

Mr. Smedley explained he'd be receiving materials and additional instructions in the mail soon. Both Boys State and Girls State took place at the end of July.

Dale got up to leave when Mr. Smedley asked him if he were curious who was selected to Girls State?

Dale hadn't thought about that. "Who?"

"Wendy Wainwright," Mr. Smedley said, smiling. "How about that? High school sweethearts attending their respective political conventions."

Dale didn't like hearing him and Wendy referred to as sweethearts. Although, he guessed they were. It bothered him, though, that they both were going. He wondered if being Wendy's boyfriend had something to do with his selection. Wendy was the ideal choice for girls state. She was smart, gregarious, socially adept, liked people, and held the usual class position for a girl: secretary. Dale on the other hand was solitary, socially inept, and never held or wanted to hold class office. He allowed that he was smart, though. Not brilliant like Isaac but smarter than most of his classmates when he tried.

"Anything else?" Mr. Smedley asked.

Dale shook his head, said thanks, and left his office. He walked back to the art class and sat next to Rusty.

"What happened?"

"Smudgely said I was suspended," Dale said somberly.

"You're kidding! For that little tussle?"

"Yeah, I'm kidding."

The bell rang and the students filed out of class. Rusty asked again what was going on and Dale was about to tell him when Wendy came bounding up to them.

"Oh, Audie, I just heard! Imagine, we're both going!"

Rusty said just where in the heck they were both going to.

"I'm going to Girls State," she said, smiling broadly, "and Audie's going to Boys State."

Dale saw Rusty eyeing him with a skeptical expression. Dale shrugged.

"Isn't that *wonderful*?" Wendy said, almost gushing.

"Yeah, that's *wonderful*," Rusty said, mocking her.

Wendy giggled and said she had to go to the cheerleading tryouts and for Audie to call her tonight so they could talk all about Boys State and Girls State. Still smiling like a Hollywood starlet at a premiere, she waved goodbye and said, "isn't this great!" before disappearing around the corner.

"That's funny," Rusty said, in an almost philosophical tone of voice. "I'm running for student government president and you're running for yearbook editor, but they pick you for Boys State. What do they think? That Boys State is a convention for student journalists?"

"I didn't even know there was a Boys State, did you?"

"Yeah, I knew."

"Do you care that you didn't get it?"

Rusty shrugged. "Not really. Heck, I don't even want to be stuco president. You're the one that talked me into running."

That was true. Dale had talked Rusty into running for the office. He had decided to run for yearbook editor. It was an elected position, which Dale thought rather odd. The school newspaper editor wasn't an elected office. He'd rather be that, but Mrs. Snow advised the newspaper and Dale knew she controlled the paper more than advised it. He didn't really like her much. She was a tall, big-bodied, raven-haired woman of forty whose mouth smiled a lot but not her eyes. He didn't like the idea of being editor when Mrs. Snow made all the decisions. So, he decided to do something bold for him. Run for something.

Dale had also talked Chris into running for parliamentarian. Parliamentarians were supposed to keep order at stuco meetings. The idea of Chris, rather diffident and easygoing, keeping order amused Dale. He was sure Chris would win.

Dale said he was glad Rusty didn't mind his selection.

"No, I don't mind," Rusty said. "Go and have fun. It sounds sort of boring actually."

Dale said he thought so, too.

"I would have missed too much work if I'd been selected."

Dale agreed.

Rusty asked if he was ready to go to track practice. The regional track meet was Saturday. Dale said sure and they walked to the locker room. He glanced at Rusty, wondering what he was thinking since he was uncharacteristically quiet. But he knew. Rusty was wondering why they hadn't selected him. He minded after all.

## Chapter 10: *A mawkish junior-senior banquet; meeting Henshaw*

Dale thought there were too many banquets. He'd already been to the Gopherette banquet in February; in March, he'd gone to the all-sports banquet; and now in May, here he was attending the junior-senior banquet.

Banquets were boring but he had to go to them. He had buy Wendy a corsage. He had to buy tickets. He had to wear a suit. He had to sit and eat fancy food he didn't care for and pretend to be polite and well-mannered and sophisticated. About the only interesting thing about banquets was seeing who went with whom, but even that was getting predictable. For the all-sports banquet, most of the guys asked out the girls who had invited them to the Gopherette. The only notable exception was Amanda. Billy Joe had asked her to the all sports and she had accepted. Since Dale liked Billy Joe – he was the best athlete among the juniors – he didn't mind; and yet he did. Dale didn't know which was worse: a guy he liked asking out Amanda or a guy he didn't like, especially a guy like Bigelow.

Now, at the junior-senior banquet, Dale sat with Wendy and Rusty and Mary Jane at a table and listened to the seniors congratulate themselves on being seniors. Actually, it was the juniors who were supposed to praise the seniors and wish them well as they graduated from high school and got booted out into the real world or college. But a lot of the seniors were singing their own praises as well.

The theme of the banquet was "The Way We Were," taken from the movie that Dale disliked. He'd seen it with Wendy a few months back and hadn't understood the politics the characters were always talking about and didn't like having to look at Barbra Streisand for two hours. He couldn't figure out how Barbra Streisand became a movie star. She looked like Marty Feldman, this weird-looking British comic that Dale had seen on TV. But Barbra Streisand wasn't funny, just funny looking. Even worse, in the movie Robert Redford supposedly found her irresistible – not for her odd looks, but because she had such spunk, spirit, and soul. The movie made Dale wanna talk to Earl.

Now, Amy Mears was reminiscing and once again someone played the sappy song from the movie. Dale heard some sniffling. How bad could it get, he wondered? Dale only knew a few seniors well: the guys he played sports with. In fact, he was glad some of them were leaving. Guys like Comingdeer, for instance. He knew even fewer of the senior girls.

He didn't think many of them were very pretty or nice. Well, Valerie Long, who'd been crowned all-school queen, was very pretty.

So, instead of listening to more maudlin reminiscences, Dale thought about some recent events. Galilee finished second to Ellison in the regional track meet. The team got a big trophy to put in the trophy case. Several Galilee runners qualified for the state meet. Dale qualified in the 100 and 220. He'd won over a dozen medals in track that spring. In the student government elections, Rusty won president; K. C., vice president; Wendy, secretary; Chris, parliamentarian; and Dale, yearbook editor. He'd ran against Carmen, which sort of annoyed him because she'd said she wasn't going to run. Dale heard that some of the girls, including Amanda, had urged Carmen to run. He had to admit that Carmen would probably have been a better selection; she drew really well and had a more advanced understanding of art than Dale. But Dale had won probably because Rusty and Erickson were so funny in the campaign skit they did for him.

Dale was glad he'd won. He was looking forward to editing the yearbook. He'd always enjoyed getting it at the end of the school year although he didn't get one in seventh grade because Jesse didn't want to spend ten dollars. He felt excited when the yearbooks came out, usually the week before classes ended. His excitement was more than just looking at pictures of himself and his friends like most kids. He felt keenly interested in the book itself; its symbolic quality, the way it served as a historical and cultural record for one year. He liked the idea of determining, to some degree, how that symbolism would look. He was interested in art and writing and photography and all the things that went into making a yearbook. He knew he didn't understand all those things very well yet, but he felt art provided a kind of truth that he used to think the Jehovah's Witnesses provided. It didn't explain the mysteries of life so much as explore them. Dale liked exploring for truth more than pretending that he already knew the truth.

Now some of the girls were actually bawling. Dale glanced at Wendy. She was crying, too. Well, Wendy was friends with some of the senior girls. She cheerleaded with three of them. And Wendy was emotional to begin with. But Dale felt embarrassed seeing her cry at this silly banquet. She put her hand in his and squeezed hard. Dale winced. She had sort of a strong grip for a girl.

That mawkish music came on again. Dale wondered where the record player was located. Maybe he could find it and accidentally trip and smash it.

Finally, it ended. The room brightened and Dale saw Wendy wipe away a few lingering tears. She excused herself and went over and hugged some of her senior friends. Dale looked at Rusty, who shared his low opinion of the whole proceedings. Mary Jane had been crying, too. Cheerleaders were an emotional bunch. Mary Jane had joined Wendy in saying good bye to the noble seniors.

"Girls," Rusty said dismissively.

Dale nodded. "Banquets."

They tried to ignore the sentimentalism sweeping the room.

"Are you and Mary Jane going steady?" Dale asked. This was the second banquet they'd been to.

"Not really. Her mother doesn't want her to go steady while in high school."

Mrs. Morgan sounded like Amanda's mother. Well, both families were Nazarenes. "You don't want to go steady, anyway, do you?"

Rusty grinned. "Not really." Then he grew serious. "But I don't like it when Mary Jane dates other guys."

"What other guys?"

"Guys from First Church, mostly."

"But you go to First Church."

Rusty had kept going to the impressive Nazarene church even when Mr. Benedict buzzed off to California.

"Yeah, that's another reason I don't like it. I know who the guys are."

Dale thought about all the girls Rusty dated in addition to Mary Jane. Sadie, Peggy, Gretchen, Merry, Roxanne, and a couple of sophomore girls, too. Rather ironic he'd be jealous of Mary Jane dating some guys from her church.

Dale started to say so when he saw the crowd of girls part in front of the master of ceremonies table. Standing in the middle, as if the other girls had parted just to reveal her to him, was Amanda. She had tears on her cheeks, too. Dale felt a pang. He thought maybe he'd been too harsh in dismissing these sensitive creatures' feelings.

Amanda hugged one senior girl, then another, brushed the tears from her lovely face, and returned to her table. Dale discreetly watched. She smiled at Kevin Stephenson, her date. Dale felt himself disliking Kevin, although he'd always thought he was a nice guy. Unpretentious, a hard worker, a good student. Now, he felt a surge of enmity for him, which Dale knew was unfair. Kevin, like Amanda, was a Nazarene kid, too.

Dale saw Wendy and Mary Jane walk over to Amanda and Kevin.

"They're going to gab forever," said Rusty.

Dale nodded. He'd changed his mind. Rusty's jealousy wasn't ironic at all.


The Northwest Oklahoma City post of the American Legion had invited Dale, as the Galilee Boys State representative, to lunch on Tuesday. Dale drove his Chevy to American Legion #84, got out, and went into the big, old building. He met one of the veterans, an old guy with reddish hair and a bulbous nose, who shook his hand, congratulated him on his selection, and escorted him to a long table with a white tablecloth over it. Already sitting there were the three representatives from Cimarron City. The old guy introduced Dale to them. Only the last guy caught his attention: Bobby Henshaw.

Dale took a seat next to him. Henshaw smiled at Dale, then turned back to the Cimarron City guy on his right who'd asked him a question. Dale had seen Henshaw twice before, both times at the Gopherette banquet as Amanda's date, but he'd never seen him up close. To Dale's disappointment, he was a handsome fellow but in a regular-guy kind of way, not like some pretty boy you'd see in a television commercial. He had brown, wavy hair, intelligent-looking gray-blue eyes, a perfectly shaped Roman nose, a wide mouth, and a strong chin. He didn't smile much, which Dale approved of, since he too wasn't a smiler – at least not in the big-grin-show-your-teeth kind of way. In fact, Henshaw seemed unpretentious and earnest. He didn't talk much to the other two guys. They were more like the usual student government types, sure of themselves and not hesitant to express their opinions. They ignored Dale. After all, they were from Cimarron City High School, one of the largest and best schools in the state. He was from podunk Galilee. Dale hardly deserved to sit at same table with them.

Henshaw, however, didn't have that preemptory attitude. He grew tired of his pals' discussion, something to do with President Nixon, and turned to Dale.

"Politics," he said with a shy smile, nodding his head at his two loquacious friends.

Dale shrugged.

"Are you interested in politics; I mean, national politics?"

"Not really."

Henshaw smiled a little. "That's unusual. I mean, coming from someone going to Boys State. It's all about politics there."

Dale said he thought politics tended to be mostly talk. People talking about things they really couldn't do a whole lot about. Instead of doing something, they talked about doing something.

"So, you're more of a man of action rather than a man of talk," said Henshaw.

Dale didn't know if he was making fun of him or not. He already felt foolish defining politics. He didn't know anything about politics except what little he'd heard from Blackie or his grandpa, and Dale didn't think their opinions would be relevant at Boys State.

"No, not really. I guess I'm more interested in what goes on inside us rather than what goes on outside us," he said, not sure where he got that idea from.

Henshaw looked at him thoughtfully, as if he were really considering Dale's point.

"That's interesting. Maybe that's what politics should be more concerned about. What's going on inside us."

Dale said maybe. Actually, he was more interested in finding out how well Henshaw knew Amanda. He tried to think of a way to make inquiries discreet enough to avoid suspicion.

"I saw you at the Galilee pep club banquet."

Henshaw's face brightened. "Yeah, I remember you, too. You were sitting with Wendy."

"You know Wendy?"

"A little. I see her at church sometimes."

Dale had forgot that Wendy went to First Church occasionally. Her parents were southern Baptist though.

I guess you see other Galilee girls at the First Church, too," Dale said.

"Yes."

Dale waited.

Henshaw picked up on the clue. He did have political skills.

"Mary Jane, Gretchen, Amanda, and a few others all attend First Church regularly."

Dale noticed how nonchalantly Henshaw recited the names. He'd put Amanda last, too. That worried Dale.

"Nice girls," he said.

Henshaw nodded. "Oh, yes." He looked at Dale. "Why don't you attend First Church? A lot of your friends do."

Dale just told the truth. "I'm antisocial."

Henshaw laughed. "You'll make a great politician."

"Like I said, I'm not interested in politics, really."

"That's probably the best kind of politician, one that isn't interested in politics."

Dale liked the paradoxical nature of that statement. Before they could engage in any more discussion, their meals arrived. They ate mostly in silence. The main course was a breaded chicken with hot butter sauce inside. Dale shoved the fork in too hard and the butter squirted out. He glanced around to see if anyone had witnessed the chicken's impaling, but everyone was too busy chowing down to notice.

Dale wanted to get more information out of Henshaw but after their meal they had to listen to an old veteran welcome the guests and talk. He introduced the four Boys State representatives and they all had to stand one at a time and be applauded. Afterwards, Dale looked around at the mostly old men. Many of them, he imagined, had fought in World War II. A couple of even older guys looked so ancient that he wondered if they'd fought in the first world war.

Dale didn't pay too much attention to the talking. He was ruminating about Henshaw and Amanda. The two times he'd seen them together, they didn't appear lovey-dovey. In fact, they seemed friendly and nothing more. He wondered if Henshaw had kissed her. He glanced at Henshaw. He wanted to dislike him, but so far he hadn't found any compelling reason except for Amanda.

After the talk, the three Cimarron City guys rose and said they had to go. Dale stood up, and noted to his chagrin that Henshaw stood at least six feet tall. He wasn't really well built, but he wasn't skinny. His suit looked pretty good on him and it made him look like a real adult.

Henshaw shook Dale's hand, a firm, confident shake, and said he'd see him at Boys State. Dale said okay. Then the three Cimarron City boys left. Dale plopped down in his chair. He realized to his dismay that he liked Bobby Henshaw.

**Chapter 11:** *A peek of cheek; somnolent Sonny; Blackie's politics*

The girls wanted to go for a swim before lunch. Wendy and Mary Jane got up and walked over to a tall elm tree. Dale and Rusty, curious to know what they had packed in the large, wicker picnic basket, flipped the top open and peered inside.

"Man, look at all the stuff," said Rusty.

Dale saw half a dozen sandwiches wrapped in brown butcher paper, and plastic baggies containing carrots, pickles, olives, and radishes. Lying on top were one bag of corn chips and one bag of potato chips. What especially caught Dale's eye was a plastic container of brownies. He smelled the enticing aroma indicating that they had been freshly baked that morning.

"Not a bad birthday already," said Rusty.

He had turned seventeen that day and Mary Jane had organized a birthday picnic. The four of them drove to Turner Falls, a state park known for its cold spring water, streams, and the falls. Since it was a weekday in early June, the park wasn't crowded. They'd left at nine in the morning for the two-hour trip.

"I think I'll get a root beer," said Rusty. "Want one?"

Dale said no. Rusty walked back toward the park's entrance to the Coke machine. Dale walked over to the tree where Wendy and Mary Jane stood. The two girls had worn regular clothes over their bathing suits. As Dale approached, Wendy and Mary Jane were taking off their shirts and cutoff shorts. Wendy pulled her shirt over her head. Mary Jane, with her back to Dale, tugged down her tight-fitting cutoffs and in the process also pulled her bikini bottom down. Dale stared in astonishment as Mary Jane exposed most of her buttocks. She chirped in embarrassment, quickly yanked the bottom up, and glanced around to see if anyone had noticed. When she saw Dale staring at her, she blushed. Dale pretended he hadn't seen anything. But it was no use. She knew he'd seen her.

"What's wrong?" Wendy asked. She gathered up her clothes and walked toward Dale.

"Uh, n-n-nothing," Dale stammered.

"You have a funny look on your face," Wendy said.

Dale saw Mary Jane looking at him. She'd recovered from her embarrassment and now had a small smile on her face, no doubt from seeing how stunned he still looked.

"So, are we ready?" asked Dale, now sufficiently recovered to speak.

The girls said yes, and they walked back to the blanket and the picnic basket and tossed their clothes down. Rusty returned drinking a root beer. Mary Jane took a sip and smiled at him. Then she and Wendy tiptoed to the river bank. Rusty gazed appreciatively at Mary Jane in her bikini.

"She has a nice figure, doesn't she?"

Dale nodded.

The girls waded into the cold water and screamed. Rusty and Dale took off their shirts, and, wearing cutoffs instead of swim trunks, jogged toward the lagoon.

"Dare ya," Rusty said, meaning he was going to jump right into the cold river water. Would Dale?

Dale never backed down from a Rusty challenge. He dived alongside Rusty into the water. Its sheer cold shocked the breath out of him. He splashed to the surface alongside Rusty. They both gasped.

"Man, that's cold!" shouted Rusty.

The girls were standing mid-thigh in the water. Rusty waded over to them. Mary Jane shrieked and flailed her arms at his advance. Rusty grabbed her by her small waist and tossed her into the water. When she surfaced, she let out a wail.

"It's too cold!" she cried.

She stumbled toward the bank. Rusty followed. Dale waded over to Wendy. She reached down and threw a handful of water at him and giggled. Dale suddenly ran at her. She screamed, turned, and tried to get away. Dale playfully shoved her into the water. She surfaced with a delighted shriek and hugged Dale. Her slick body felt warm even with the chilled water streaming off it.

"The water *is* too cold," said Wendy. "Let's go back."

Dale agreed and they climbed out of the stream and joined Rusty and Mary Jane on the blanket. Dale looked at the brilliant blue sky. The day would heat up quickly. By early afternoon, the temperature would be in the nineties and the cold water would feel refreshingly cool.

Mary Jane and Wendy sang happy birthday to Rusty, then they ate lunch. Rusty wolfed down his two sandwiches, half of Mary Jane's, and handfuls of chips. He guzzled two cans of root beer. Dale ate almost as much. The girls, however, ate in a dainty fashion that Dale found a little suspicious. Girls never seemed to eat heartily in public.

They lolled around for an hour or so, then went back in the cold stream and splashed and frolicked and had loads of fun. The four returned to their blankets and the girls lay on their backs basking in the sun.

Dale asked Rusty how he liked his job. He was roofing again, but this time for Mr. Erickson, Rich's dad. Rusty said it was hard work but good money. He said he was saving for a better car. Dale wished he had Rusty's handyman talent. After last summer's disappointments with food service and roofing, he'd decided to run a paper route and mow lawns like he had in previous summers. He didn't make much money, but he didn't need much. Just enough to pay for gas and take Wendy to movies or to the Sooner Shack. Wendy got a job as a salesgirl at a downtown department store. She got a ten percent discount to buy clothes. Unfortunately, she bought so many clothes that she spent half her paycheck. Dale didn't understand the female fascination for clothes. June May was the same. Her closet was stuffed with all kinds of clothes and yet every few months she demanded a new dress, a new outfit, new shoes. Dale preferred his old jeans and worn T-shirts. The older the clothes, the better they felt.

Dale and Rusty walked over to the concession stand and bought Cokes for the four of them. Then they walked back to the girls. As they approached, they heard them gossiping. Wendy asked Mary Jane if Roxanne was still seeing Terry Harte or if she'd had gotten back with Sonny. Mary Jane said Roxanne was still seeing Terry, but that would be over in a few months because he was going off to college. She doubted Roxanne would start seeing Sonny again.

Wendy asked why. Mary Jane said Sonny had changed. Before she could say more, she noticed the boys. She and Wendy accepted the cans of diet Coke and graciously said "thank you" as if they'd been given something fancy, like champagne.

While drinking their Cokes, Dale thought about what he'd heard. Harte had gotten a football scholarship to Wichita State. He'd made second team all-state in football and was also named to the state track team. Dale guessed Harte was the best athlete Galilee had ever produced, even better than Robin Comingdeer.

After more idle chitchat, the girls stretched out to sunbathe, this time on their stomachs. Dale and Rusty talked a little, trying not to stare at them. Dale was amazed that Mary Jane wore such a skimpy bikini. It had just a thin strip covering her hips and the top just had strings for shoulder straps. He thought about how certain parts of the body had special status. A few hours ago when he'd seen Mary Jane's bare bottom, it gave him a thrill. Now, she lay a few feet from him, wearing just a few pieces of cloth and it all seemed proper. Well, it probably wouldn't seem proper to Mary Jane's mother, who probably didn't know her daughter had worn such a tiny suit. As for Wendy, her suit, although not a bikini, was a two piece and revealed a lot more of her than the one-piece she used to wear. Dale thought it was interesting that people accepted this bathing suit convention.

The girls asked them if they would like to rub lotion on their backs. The boys said okay. Dale smeared lotion over Wendy's freckled back and rubbed it in while she sighed. Rusty did the same to Mary Jane. In the middle of their labors, Rusty winked at Dale as if to say "hard work, ain't it?"

Dale breathed in the scent of cocoa butter, grass, water, and brownies; he looked around at the beautiful day with the cloudless blue sky and sparkling water and rich, green grass; he gazed down at Wendy and over at Mary Jane. The day, the time, the place, seemed Edenic. It was one of those times he would always remember.

Dale and Rusty didn't see each other much during the week, but on weekends they often played baseball at the Seventh Day's Adventist field not far from Dale's home. Dale enjoyed playing in those sandlot games. When Vern, Wally, and Rusty's brothers and their friends all came, they had enough guys to have a pretty good game. Playing under the hot sun reminded him of all the games they'd played when they were kids and how the dream of being a major leaguer seemed tangible.

As usual, Dale didn't see much of Chris during the summer. Mr. DeVille kept Chris busy working at his uncle's lumberyard and during the evenings Chris was required to keep company with his family. Dale had called him a couple of times to join him in a pickup baseball game, but Chris always had "family responsibilities." Dale almost began to think that having strict parents was worse than having parents like Blackie and Jesse. At least Dale didn't have to do all kinds of chores, spend time with them, and perform other filial rituals. About the only thing he did with his parents was go to the drive-in, and that wasn't often anymore because Jesse disliked the current violent and "dirty" movies.

One day in mid-June, Dale drove down a street in the north end of town, not too far from the place Vern stabled his horse, and saw Sonny Schoendienst leaning against an old, green Chevy van. Dale slowed down and noticed that Sonny had a curious expression on his face. His eyes were closed and his mouth hung open. Dale wondered if he was sick and stopped his car beside the van.

"Hey, Sonny," he yelled through the open passenger window. "What's wrong?"

Sonny opened his eyes and looked in Dale's general direction.

"Smith. Is that you?"

Dale said it was and repeated if anything was wrong.

"Naw. Just ran out of gas."

Dale said get in. He had a gas can in the trunk. He'd take Sonny to get some gas.

Sonny ambled over, opened the car door, and slid in. He slumped against the seat and closed his eyes again.

"Are you okay?" Dale asked.

"I'm fine, man," Sonny said, still keeping his eyes closed. An odd smile appeared on his face.

Dale drove to the nearest gas station eight blocks away. On the way, he asked Sonny a few general questions like people do to make chitchat, but Sonny only gave monosyllable replies. They lapsed into silence. Dale remembered Sonny's mother, an English teacher at the high school who advised the yearbook, talking to him after he had won the race for editor. She said she had "concerns" about Dale being yearbook editor. She said she didn't know if he could edit the yearbook and play sports. Mrs. Schoendienst said they'd never had an editor who was also an athlete as long as she'd been advising the yearbook. She also didn't want Dale to let Rusty or Rich to be part of the yearbook staff. She knew they'd be bad influences on him. The yearbook was too great a responsibility to miss deadlines and make mistakes.

Mrs. Schoendienst had a reputation as a mean teacher. Dale had her as a freshman and thought she was strict but fair. She didn't buddy around with the kids. She had a sharp tongue and could make cutting remarks about students who goofed off too much or caused trouble. But he thought she was one of the better teachers in the school. She took her job seriously and sincerely tried to educate the class of fourteen year olds, which wasn't easy.

Dale had told her that he thought he'd have enough time to edit the yearbook. First, he planned on organizing the yearbook this summer. Second, he decided not to play basketball, so he'd be free during the busiest time. Thirdly, he said he really wanted to do a good job. He didn't run for editor just for the heck of it. And fourth, he'd already decided not to ask Rusty or Erickson to be on the staff. He knew they might entice him to goof off, and besides, they played basketball and wouldn't have time to be on the staff anyway.

Mrs. Schoendienst gave Dale a slightly surprised look. She had a long, sharp face with heavy-lidded eyes. She said he had helped alleviate her concerns and she was looking forward to advising him that fall.

Now, driving to the gas station with her youngest son, Dale wondered what she thought of Sonny. He wasn't much of a student. He never got in trouble, but he seemed to be friends with some of the pseudo-hoods that hung around in the alley during lunch. He did well at sports, but he never evinced any "leadership" qualities that coaches always talked about, especially from the quarterback. Sonny did fine at quarterback or point guard or pole vaulting, but he never showed much passion or determination. He'd never been shy like Dale; he told jokes and goofed around and went to parties and dated girls earlier than most of the guys. He just seemed indifferent to the more serious concerns in life. Dale wondered if having two teachers for parents had anything to do with that. He'd never heard Sonny say anything bad about his parents; in fact, he never talked about them. Both his mother and father were active in First Church and community activities. They both demonstrated a certain kind of civic motivation that Sonny entirely lacked. Dale imagined that must be a source of conflict in their home.

Dale stopped at the gas station and glanced at Sonny. His clothes – holey jeans and a shabby black Rolling Stones T-shirt – had a funny scent on them. His eyes were still closed. Dale didn't think he was asleep; he didn't breathe like he was and his body didn't have that slumbering slump to it. He just seemed oblivious.

Dale got out and filled the gasoline container, stuck it in his car trunk, then drove back to Sonny's van. Sonny remained unresponsive. Dale tried to think of Sonny's real first name. It was George. Since first grade, everyone had called him Sonny. Even his parents called him that.

Sonny, along with Rusty and K. C., had always been one of the most popular boys in Dale's class. In junior high, Dale had heard girls whispering about how cute Sonny was. He looked a little like David Cassidy, then a teen heartthrob for millions of silly girls like June May. These past few years, Sonny's hair had gotten even longer and his clothes even shabbier. During two-a-days last year, Dorfman had told Sonny to get his hair cut to at least his collar or he'd be off the team. Dale had wondered if Sonny would comply. When he did, Dale felt relieved. The team needed him at quarterback and Dale, although he never hung out with Sonny, nevertheless liked him. For all of Sonny's lackadaisical qualities, he was essentially a nice guy. Dale had never seen him taunt or harass anybody, not even mistake-prone sophomores.

Dale parked next to Sonny's van, a '67 Chevy with grayish spots in the green paint where rust had been scrubbed away. He told Sonny they were back.

Sonny opened his eyes. Dale noticed his blue eyes looked sort of watery. Little red threads networked around the whites of his eyes. Sonny smiled without showing his teeth and said, "thanks, man." They got out and Dale opened the trunk and watched as Sonny took the gas can and poured its contents into his van's tank. Sonny returned the container, dug a hand into the pocket of his worn jeans, and asked Dale how much he owed him.

"Forget it," Dale said. "You can buy me a Coke sometime."

Sonny nodded his head. "Okay, man, that's cool."

As Dale drove off, he looked in the rear view mirror at Sonny climbing into his van. He thought about the funny smell, his bloodshot eyes, and oblivious attitude. Maybe the rumors were right. Sonny was doing drugs.

A few days before Dale had to leave for Boys State, he found his father sitting in his chair watching television. Blackie was on vacation and spent most of his day fishing or going to the shooting range. He and Jesse had gone fishing yesterday. Dale hoped spending time together doing something they both liked would improve the situation at home. But they came back after only an hour arguing. Dale didn't find out what they were fighting about. It hardly mattered anymore.

Dale asked where Mom was.

"Out with Wanda," Blackie said.

Jesse spent quite a bit of time with Wanda. She also went over to Grandma's a lot. Otherwise, she sat in the house smoking like a chimney and watching inane television shows. She and Blackie couldn't even have a normal conversation anymore.

"What are you watching?" Dale asked.

"Nothing. The same goddamned stuff is on all the channels."

"What is it?"

"Congressional hearing."

"About what?"

"You're going to that Boys State thing and you don't know?"

Dale admitted to himself that was sort of funny. But he wasn't going to Boys State because he liked politics; he was going because he was the compromise candidate.

Blackie got up to turn off the TV. "Just a fishing expedition. Nixon's not done anything the rest didn't do."

Dale didn't understand what fishing had to do with a congressional hearing. He asked Blackie what Nixon had done.

Blackie ignored the question. "The Kennedys were worse. In fact, old man Kennedy could teach Nixon a thing or two about dirty tricks."

Dale had no idea what his father was talking about. Blackie never explained his cynical statements. Dale wondered how the guys at Boys State would react if he parroted his father. He'd probably be kicked out.

"I thought you didn't like Nixon."

"I don't. He's a sonofabitch."

"Then why do you care about these hearings?"

"I don't."

Blackie slapped the on/off button and the screen washed black.

## Chapter 12: *Misadventures at Boys State; a tryst at Girls State*

Dale had never driven so far alone. He left Galilee Friday morning in late July and drove 200 miles to Northeastern Oklahoma State University in Tahlequah. At first, the trip was fun. He avoided driving through Oklahoma City and Tulsa so he didn't encounter any heavy traffic. But when he turned off the interstate at Muskogee and headed north, he encountered small roads twisting alongside rivers, narrow bridges, and steep climbs and descents. Dale had no idea that this part of Oklahoma was so hilly and had so many lakes and rivers. He'd expected the same kind of dry, flat land as back home. But in the northeast part of the state, he had to adjust to much more difficult driving conditions. The worst part of the trip was when he crossed a narrow bridge and a semi truck roared by him in the other lane. He tightly gripped the steering wheel and kept the car as far to the right as he could. Even so, the truck came within inches of his car and rattled the bridge. Dale let out a sigh of relief only when he made it off the old bridge.

He arrived at Northeastern in the late afternoon and reported to registration where they checked off his name, gave him his room key, a Boys State T-shirt, an ID badge, study materials for the bar exam and an Oklahoma government manual. Dale gathered up the stuff, thinking Boys State didn't seem much different than school.

He checked into his room and claimed the bed closest to the window. A few minutes later his roommate arrived. He was a tall, thin kid with neat, sandy hair and round spectacles. He introduced himself as Farley Watkins. They shook hands and Dale, after giving his name, told Farley he thought there was something familiar about the name Watkins. Farley said he was the grandson of Congressman Watkins. One of the cities in Boys State was named after his grandfather.

Farley asked Dale what city office he wanted.

"None."

"I don't think that's allowed. You have to run for something."

"What if I don't want to run for anything?"

Farley looked at Dale as if he were an inferior species of humanity. "That's what Boys State is all about," he said emphatically, "running for office."

Dale asked Farley what office he wanted.

"Oh, mayor. Then after I win that, I'll run for governor."

Dale said why limit yourself to governor? He wanted to say dictator but he didn't want to antagonize his roommate too soon. He'd never had a roommate before.

"Boys Nation is where I'll run for president."

"There's a Boys Nation?"

"Yes. It's composed of those superior boys who earn the right to attend. The governor and lieutenant governor automatically qualify."

"Then you'll be a cinch to go to Boys Nation," Dale said.

Farley looked pleased.

"Is there a Boys World?"

"No," said Farley, adjusting his round specs.

"There should be. Maybe when you become president of Boys Nation you can propose that."

Farley nodded. "That's not a bad idea. Sort of a Boys United Nations." Farley looked more carefully at Dale. "Where are you from?"

Dale said Galilee. Farley obviously had never heard of it. He said he was from Kerrville. A suburb of Tulsa.

Dale had never heard of it either. Their conversation running out of steam, Farley said he was going to canvass the dorm. Dale said it's never too early to start campaigning. Farley smiled a thin smile and excused himself.

Dale flipped through the bar exam stuff and thought it looked boring. He then read about the man his "city" was named after, Charles "Duster" Cook. He was nicknamed Duster because he'd been an oil wildcatter in his younger years before going into politics and he'd always come up with "dusters" or dry holes. Dale noticed that Duster Cook was still alive. He'd been born in 1895, the same year as Dale's grandpa. That made Cook more interesting.

Farley returned in time for dinner and they walked over to the cafeteria in the student union. They sat together, but Farley devoted his attention to the other guys at the table who shared his enthusiasm and ambition. After dinner, Dale took a walk around campus while Farley continued to make contacts. Then Dale went back to his room and read *Anthem*, a novel by someone named Ayn Rand. He'd seen Carmen reading it in school last spring and she said he ought to read it sometime. So far, Dale thought it was okay. He was halfway through and thought the "we" narrator was gimmicky but he was curious to see how the book ended.

Farley returned just before lights out and told Dale of his success at making contacts. Dale told him about collective identity. Then they hit the sack and both fell easily asleep.

Boys State activities began in earnest the next day. First, the boys of Cook City gathered together and marched over to a large building for orientation. Afterwards, they took the pre-law exam. Then lunch. Then the different cities had their meetings. Then they took the bar examination. Then dinner. Then all the boys gathered for the general assembly, where they listened to various adults drone on about parliamentary procedure, caucus protocols, tomorrow's schedule, and other bureaucratic information.

Dale walked back to his room alone. Farley was meeting with more Farleys, all of them plotting strategy. So far, Dale didn't like Boys State. He doubted he would like it any better the following days. It looked like the whole event was a tightly orchestrated series of city meetings, instruction classes, county meetings, caucuses, elections, and finally after the last big election, a day of pretending to run Boys State like real politicians.

For a kid with an interest in politics, like Farley, attending Boys State must be a blast. But for Dale, it was tedious and exasperating.

Sitting in his room, finishing *Anthem*, Dale heard a knock. He answered the door and his city's counselor, a guy in his early twenties named Lawrence, told him he had a phone call. Dale didn't think Jesse or Blackie would call unless it was an emergency. He followed Lawrence to the desk on the first floor and took the phone. It was Wendy.

She sounded upset. At first, Dale thought maybe her father had gotten in an accident driving back home after taking her to Girls State at East Central State College in Ada. He asked what was wrong. She said she missed him. He said they'd only been apart for three days. Wendy said she knew but she really, really missed him and just wanted to hear his voice. He said they weren't supposed to use the phone unless it was an emergency. Wendy said she knew, but she just had to speak to him. She said she'd already mailed one letter and she'd write another tomorrow. She asked if he'd written her a letter. He said he was just finishing it and would mail it tomorrow. He said they had to get off the phone now. Wendy's voice got that teary, throaty sound like it did when she was trying not to cry. She said okay, she loved him, and asked if he loved her and Dale said, "sure, I do," and then they said good-bye.

Dale noticed Lawrence looking at him disapprovingly as he hung up the phone.

"The phone's only supposed to be used in emergencies," Lawrence said.

Dale nodded. He went back to his room to start Wendy's letter.

Reveille sounded at six-thirty the next morning and Dale wished he could sleep in. Boys State was worse than school. It was like school but instead of only six hours a day, it lasted all day and most of the evening, and instead of friends to help pass the time, Dale only had Farleys. He'd yet to meet a normal guy.

Another source of irritation was the food – or lack of it. If he got to breakfast, lunch, or dinner a little late all that was left were scraps. At breakfast, Dale had been so hungry that he even ate eggs. He had always refused to eat eggs, one of his peculiar eating habits that bewildered his grandparents. The boy won't eat eggs? They couldn't believe it. Well, Dale was eating them now. His father had warned him more than once at the dinner table when he refused a hunk of spam or one of Jesse's unappetizing, overcooked vegetables that one day he'd be so hungry that he wouldn't turn up his nose at a piece of stale bread. Well, that day had arrived.

Also, boys weren't supposed to have seconds. But Dale noticed some guys were getting seconds and thirds. Those guys seemed to be the city leaders. The privileges of office, he supposed.

After lunch, Dale attended a county caucus where they would   nominate boys for county offices. Dale, sitting in the middle of the room, barely listened as boys made their nominations and gave speeches in behalf of the nominee. Then, to his utter surprise, he heard a voice from the past. The voice nominated Audie Smith for county judge.

Dale turned around and saw Clifford standing in the back of the room giving reasons why Dale would make an excellent judge. Dale stared at his former friend. He wondered if Clifford was paying him back with a brilliant prank. But no, Clifford was, as always, completely serious. He stood erect, spoke in his slightly countrified voice, and paused once to adjust his Clark Kent glasses. Dale didn't listen to what he said. What could Clifford say, anyway? That Dale hadn't teased him as mercilessly as Rusty, therefore he had demonstrated ideal judicial temperament?

Incredibly, another boy seconded the nomination and now Dale was officially on the ballot for county judge. When the meeting ended, Dale pushed through the boys to Clifford, who stood next to the back door.

Dale asked how he was doing. Clifford said fine.

"Look, Cliff, I want to apologize for the stuff that happened at the football game last fall. I had nothing to do with it."

Clifford, his eyes as intense as ever behind the spectacles, nodded. "I didn't think you did."

Dale said it was sort of funny that they both were at Boys State. Clifford didn't respond; he obviously didn't find it amusing that *he* was at Boys State.

Dale asked him what city he was in. Clifford said Rogers. Dale said that was supposed to be a good city. An awkward pause followed.

"Now some of the Lyons guys call me Mouthpiece," Clifford said.

"Because of the sign?"

Clifford nodded. "One of these days, Rusty is going to get his."

"Well, what's a nickname? Besides, you must be doing pretty well at Lyons. They picked you for Boys State."

Clifford said the teachers and administrators picked him for Boys State.

"Same here," said Dale. "Actually, I was a compromise candidate."

Clifford eyes narrowed, an indication of confusion, but before Dale could elaborate, a tall, gangly guy told Clifford he was wanted. Clifford nodded and turned to Dale.

"I gotta go."

"Hey, Cliff," Dale said, as Clifford walked away, "if I don't see you again, good luck here in Boys State."

Clifford nodded and followed the gangly guy out of the room. Dale shook his head at the odd coincidence of he and Clifford both being at Boys State. He didn't know if Clifford would make a good politician. Clifford was smart enough, but he seemed so tightly wound up that in a crisis he might explode.

Wendy called again Tuesday night. She asked if he'd gotten her letter. Dale said he did. She asked if he'd mailed hers yet. He said he had. He didn't tell her it wasn't as mushy as hers. It had embarrassed him, reading her letter. He'd hid it in the Ayn Rand book to prevent anyone from finding it. Wendy told him how much she missed him. Dale said he missed her, too. Then she reminded him that he was picking her up Saturday on his way back to Galilee. He said he remembered. He said he couldn't wait to see her. More mushy stuff from Wendy. Then, with Lawrence staring at him, Dale said he had to go. Wendy said good-bye in a tremulous voice.

He handed the phone to Lawrence, avoiding his censorious look. Before Lawrence could issue his reprimand, Dale said, "I know, I know."

For an hour during the afternoon, the boys got free time. It was supposed to be used for recreation. The Boy Staters had created a basketball league and a baseball league. Dale had been interested in the baseball team, but when he went to the first practice he could tell the team would be based more on who you knew than how well you played the game. He sat on the bench the entire practice and didn't go back the next day. He was also interested in the *Boy Stater*, the official newspaper of Boys State. But the same kind of cronyism prevailed there, too. Besides, the newspaper was really just a record of all the activities, elections, and important people at Boys State and that didn't interest Dale much. He didn't go back to the newspaper after the first meeting, either.

So, Dale actually had free time. He explored the campus while all the other guys played basketball, baseball, volleyball, tennis, Frisbee, golf, and other sports befitting future leaders of tomorrow. Dale rather liked the solitude. He visited the library a couple of times. Classes were not in session, so the library was open only for Boy Staters, and only a couple of people were present in the building.

One of the advantages of not going to any of the activities during free time was being able to use the shower without waiting in a crowded bathroom. Dale walked to the bathroom carrying a towel, a shaving kit, and a change of clothes. No one else was present. He liked the privacy. He showered, got out and dried himself, and wrapped a towel around his waist and went to the sink to shave. At the sink, he looked in the mirror and saw a reflection of Lawrence in the mirror. The image startled Dale and he turned and saw the counselor walking in from the shower room. Dale thought that was odd. He obviously hadn't been showering. He wore his usual street clothes. Dale watched him in the mirror as he walked down toward the toilet stalls and looked under them.

"You haven't seen a shaving kit?" he asked Dale.

Dale said no. He squeezed the top of the shaving cream bottle and felt the cool foam spread over his hand. He rubbed it on his face. He'd started shaving just a few months ago, more out of hope than need. He had such a light beard that he needed to shave only once a week. He took his razor and glided it down his cheek to his jaw. He hardly felt a tug.

Dale noticed Lawrence watching him. Dale had never really looked closely at the counselor. Now, he saw a young man of average height, green eyes, neat blond hair, an ordinary sort of doughy face, and a lumpy body. Lawrence wasn't fat; but he didn't have a muscular or lean build. Just sort of lumpy, as if his torso were a big stocking stuffed with potatoes.

"One of the boys said he thought he left his shaving kit somewhere in here," said Lawrence. He had a pleasant voice. Not deep but with fine clarity.

Dale shrugged. He was shaving around his chin and didn't want to speak. He felt self-conscious shaving while wearing only a towel with Lawrence present. He flicked the foam off the razor and watched as Lawrence walked past him and leaned against the doorway.

"You have a good build," Lawrence said matter-of-factly. "Do you wrestle?"

Dale shook his head. "We don't have wrestling at my school."

"Too bad. I bet you'd be good at it."

Dale thought he probably would be, but the idea of grappling with some guy in front of hundreds of spectators while wearing silly-looking tights bothered him. He wasn't sure he could do it.

"You especially have well-defined pectorals," Lawrence observed in the same overly casual voice.

Dale glanced at him. He thought Lawrence was getting a little weird. Was he some kind of coach? Why else would he be interested in pectorals if he weren't a coach, unless …

"Do you know what pectorals are?"

Dale said yes. Actually, he knew most of the names for the muscles. In ninth-grade gym Coach Carpenter made each guy take a major muscle and write a report. Dale had been assigned gluteus maximus. The other guys laughed. He actually found the report edifying. The gluteus maximus is the single largest muscle on the human body. Only humans really have such a muscle. It's the muscle that helps people stand upright and walk. It's an important muscle. Dale wondered if that was when he became especially interested in the female gluteus maximus. A lot of guys liked breasts best, but he was partial to the posterior. His mind flashed back to seeing Wendy's bare bottom and Mary Jane's partially exposed buttocks. Dale, his mind not fully on the task, pulled the razor too fast over his somewhat stubbly chin. He felt a sting. He looked in the mirror and saw a welt of blood appear.

"Hey, careful there," said Lawrence.

Dale felt annoyed with the counselor. Why was he still here? He almost blamed him for cutting himself. Dale turned and started to tell him to look elsewhere for the missing shaving kit when another guy walked into the bathroom. The guy gave both of them a curious look then proceeded to the urinal. Lawrence said he had to go. He paused, looked at Dale and started to say something, then stopped. Dale, out of the corner of his eye, saw him leave. Then he washed the traces of foam off his face and pressed a finger against the welling blood. He'd cut himself pretty good.

The other guy, who hadn't flushed the urinal, walked by. "Hey, you cut yourself," he said.

Dale nodded. Yet another perceptive junior politician, he thought.

Dale stood in line waiting for dinner on Thursday night. He'd lost the election for county judge. He didn't care. He hadn't even campaigned. He thought the whole Boy State enterprise a little absurd. While it was true that enacting these mock campaigns helped him understand the political process, everything had to be done in such a short time frame that it emphasized the superficial. The elections at Boys State were based even more on appearance and image than they were in high school.

Dale thought maybe he was being too critical. Bobby Henshaw had won governor of Boys State, after all.

While contemplating his deep thoughts, a tall, stooped, wizened man wearing blue slacks, a white shirt, and a red jacket with a star-and-stripes tie accosted him.

"So you're the young man who's getting all the phone calls," the old codger said. "Come here. I want to speak to you."

Dale didn't want to leave his place in line, but the old man was adamant. He stepped out and the old guy told him how he should respect the rules here at Boys State. Phone calls were only for emergencies. He told Dale to tell his disturbed girlfriend to stop calling. Otherwise, he and the supervisors at Boys State would have to take further action.

At first, Dale endured the old man's verbal attack. After all, he thought he looked like Uncle Sam and that alone earned him some respect. But as the old guy kept railing at him, he grew annoyed. It wasn't his fault Wendy kept calling. He'd told her not to. Dale blurted out that Wendy was worried about her father. He had a heart condition but still had to drive his rig all over the country to support his family. So, his girlfriend wasn't disturbed; she was just worried.

Uncle Sam ignored those valid points and continued to chastise him. Dale had enough. He turned and walked away, leaving the old man spluttering. He went back to the place in line where he'd been, but the guys standing there acted like he was trying to cut in. One of the boys was in Cook City, too. They said, you can't cut in, man. Dale was in no mood to argue. He shoved two of them aside and took his place. They stared at him but didn't do anything. He knew they wouldn't. They were like all the other guys he'd met. All talk and no action.

One tall fellow, two places ahead, asked Dale if he knew who that old man was? Dale shook his head no. He didn't care.

"That's Mr. Cook," said the tall guy, someone Dale recognized belonging to his city but he didn't know his name.

"You mean Duster?"

The tall guy nodded and smiled an unsympathetic smile. "You sure made an impression with Mr. Cook; just not a favorable one."

Dale shrugged. So what? What would the officials at Boys State do? Take away his voting privileges? Impeach him? Dale looked down the hallway and saw Duster Cook creeping away. He now felt sorry about getting angry with the old man, but he didn't like him yelling at him about something that wasn't his fault. He'd gotten angry mostly because he already felt embarrassed by Wendy calling so much, and the old man made it worse by yelling at him in front of all the guys. Still, he regretted his anger. Duster seemed like he'd been a pretty good guy back in his day.

The next day, Dale spied Clifford marching with his city members to the general assembly. The Rogers guys marched with military efficiency. Dale noted Clifford's erect bearing, his stiff-legged walk, and the expression of grim determination plastered on his face. Dale looked past Clifford and the Rogers guys and spotted Bobby Henshaw walking with a group of his guys, all of them tall and impressive looking. Dale hadn't had an opportunity to talk to Henshaw. He stayed in a city in a residence hall on the other side of campus. Dale, because of his lateness, never saw him at any of the meals either. Now, as governor of Boys State, Henshaw seemed to exist in a higher realm than Dale, one that floated above the mundane clutter where the rest of them dwelled.

Dale walked into the auditorium and took a seat near the back. Tonight's general assembly was supposed to be the highlight of the week. The featured speaker was the actual governor of the state. Dale tried to listen as various dignitaries and officials took their turn droning at the microphone. His mind was elsewhere. He hadn't enjoyed the Boy State experience, but it wasn't something for a guy like him. The entire week he hadn't met anybody he liked. He had drifted through the endless meetings and events and puzzled over why so many of the boys took it so seriously.

Dale became more alert when Bobby Henshaw spoke. He thought Henshaw looked impressive standing at the podium, even wearing his Boys State T-shirt and not a jacket and tie. Henshaw's short speech was pretty conventional stuff until he said he hoped that real politics could aspire to something greater than the necessary duties of everyday life. He hoped it could address, to some degree, the inner concerns of its citizens. Dale smiled to himself when he heard that. He remembered their conversation at the American Legion lunch. He hadn't realized his off-the-cuff remarks had made any impression on Henshaw. For some odd reason, Henshaw seemed to like him. Bobby had appointed Dale to the Boys State Supreme Court. Dale hadn't asked him; he just saw his name listed on the bulletin board for governor appointees to various offices. He sort of appreciated the act, except that earlier today he had to attend the Supreme Court session and pretend he was a judge all afternoon. They even listened to pretend lawyers argue pretend cases before them.

Henshaw concluded his speech and sat down. Then the real governor stood at the podium. He was a tall man with abundant silver hair swept back off his broad forehead. The governor smiled, showing his large teeth, then said that before launching into his speech, he wanted to convey an important message to one of the boys here. The governor said he'd been given a letter that afternoon from a delightful young lady when he visited Girls State. The young woman had made such a favorable impression on him that he'd agreed to personally deliver the letter to her boyfriend here at Boys State. He said he was especially heartened to know that such wonderful young people involved in such important political training at Boys State and Girls State could still maintain such devotion to each other. He said he was delighted to bring this letter from Wendy Wainwright to Audie Smith. The governor held up the letter. He then handed it to one of the counselors – Lawrence – and instructed him to give it to the lucky boy.

Dale shrank in his seat. As soon as the governor had mentioned the delightful young lady at Girls State, he'd felt a foreboding. His heart somersaulted and his stomach churned as he waited for the inevitable. He'd put his hand over his brow to shield his face when the governor said his name. A few guys knew him by name. He saw them glance at him in a

217

puzzled way. Then as Lawrence walked down the aisle, asking where Audie Smith was located, Dale knew he had no choice. He thought about bolting from the auditorium but that would have been even more humiliating. So, he shyly raised his hand and accepted the letter from the counselor. Dale tried not to look too directly at Lawrence. Dale had managed to avoid him for the most part since that strange encounter in the shower room. But now, Lawrence stared at him with an almost hostile expression, as if he blamed Dale for turning him into a messenger boy.

Dale accepted the letter and quickly glanced around. The guys sitting with him gazed at him with more appreciative expressions than had Lawrence. The looks on their faces seemed to say, "this Smith guy must be some Romeo if a girl is that desperate to get a letter to him."

After the general assembly ended, Dale rushed out of the auditorium and swiftly walked to his room. Once there, he opened the letter. Maybe it was something important, like Wendy had decided to convert to Catholicism and become a nun. But no. Dale quickly read the letter, penned in Wendy's own enthusiastic, loopy script. It was just more mush.

Dale collapsed on his bed. He was getting worried. Wendy seemed to have become more than infatuated; she seemed to have developed some inexplicable passion for him. What bothered him was that he didn't think he could reciprocate. He liked her. He liked making out with her. He appreciated all her fine qualities. She was cute, she had a generous, good-natured personality, if given to gossiping too much. She was smart. She liked people; they liked her. But Dale didn't feel the same kind of intensity for her that she felt for him and that troubled him.

Farley entered the room. He considered Dale with a more thoughtful expression than usual. Dale had hardly seen him since that first night, usually just for a few minutes before lights out when Farley regaled him with his efforts to forge a new political alliance. That is, until yesterday, when he lost the race for governor to Bobby Henshaw. Dale didn't tell him that he knew Henshaw. Instead, he tried to console Farley by telling him that even FDR lost elections before winning four straight presidential terms. Dale said Farley reminded him of FDR. They both had an impressive patrician bearing. Dale could tell that Farley felt better after that comparison. Farley had then taken off his round specs, not quite like FDR's but close, and polished them. He squinted his eyes as he said thanks.

Now, Farley stood appraising Dale in a manner that suggested he had hidden depths that Farley hadn't divined before.

"Your girlfriend has a lot of nerve to ask the governor to deliver a letter for her."

Dale agreed.

"I mean, the governor isn't a mailman."

Dale nodded.

Farley glanced enviously at the letter Dale held in his hands. "Boy, I wish I could inspire that kind of devotion. I might win more elections then."

Dale left Boys State as early as possible Saturday morning. He didn't eat breakfast. He turned in his key, ID badge, and Oklahoma government manual. He got to keep the T-shirt.

The drive to Ada would take two hours. In the letter, Wendy said she'd received permission to stay in her dorm room after the eight a.m. checkout deadline. Dale reckoned he'd make it to the southeastern campus by nine if everything went well.

Unfortunately, everything didn't go well. While driving sixty, he heard a pop outside the car. He slowed the car down so he could hear better when blam! the left front tire blew. The Chevy swerved to the left. Dale tugged on the steering wheel and then the car lurched to the right. He gripped the wheel tightly and slowed. The car stabilized and he coasted to a stop on the side of the road.

He got out and looked at what remained of the tire. The road had shredded it. He looked around. He was in the country. He looked down the road both north and south. No car in sight. He shrugged. He could fix the tire, although he'd never changed a tire by himself. He got the spare from the trunk and changed the tire in the manner Blackie had taught him a couple of years ago outside First Church. For a moment, he remembered how lovely Amanda had looked.

The tire now changed, Dale resumed the trip. He was now half a hour behind schedule. He pushed the Chevy almost to seventy and drove to Ada without incident, only stopping once for gas and to scrub the grime from off his hands.

Dale drove to the college campus, found Wendy's dorm, and parked in the almost empty parking lot. He walked inside the first floor, didn't see anyone at the desk, then climbed the stairs to the fifth floor. He'd knocked only once when Wendy opened the door and without saying a word threw her arms around his neck and hugged him.

Maybe it was the intensity of her hug or the way her voice sounded so soft and pleading in his ear when she whispered how much she loved him, but as Dale held her he also felt a strong emotion engulf him and when he said he loved her too, he almost believed it.

Dale kicked the door shut, still holding onto Wendy. He kissed her and they moved toward her bed. They fell onto the neatly made bed and wrapped themselves around each other. Dale felt his tenderness turn into a kind of passion he'd never felt before. The kisses and caresses led to the next stage and instead of stopping, they continued. They moved under the bedspread, and he removed their clothes and awkwardly consummated their passion.

Afterwards, Dale looked around Wendy's room as she laid her head on his nearly hairless chest. He saw to his consternation three photographs of him tacked on her bulletin board. One, his class portrait. Another, a candid from the school yearbook showing him drawing in Miss Roach's class. And third, another photo from the yearbook of Dale posing for his track letterman picture. He ran toward the camera, the muscles in his arms and legs bulging in an impressive way. But he didn't like the fact he was only dressed in his paper-thin track shorts and jersey. Dale felt embarrassed that Wendy would have these photos in full view. But Wendy had none of his bashfulness. He'd not put one photo of her on his bulletin board. Not even her class portrait or her cheerleading photo.

Wendy lifted her head and smiled broadly at Dale. "Guess what? I won secretary of state."

Dale nodded. He wasn't surprised.

# BOOK 4: *Senior Year*

### Chapter 1: *A wound and a worry*

Dale caught the flat pass, faked out one tackler, cut back against the grain eluding two other Maverick players, then burst into open ground for five yards before a vicious collision knocked his helmet off. Dale, sprawled on the ground, didn't know at first he'd been de-helmeted. But when one of the Maverick tacklers "accidentally" shoved his knee in his face, he figured it out.

He got to his feet and felt a warm liquid trickling down the right side of his head. Thinking it was sweat, he reached up and wiped it away. He looked at his hand and saw bright crimson smears on his fingers. He felt some pain at his temple but nothing serious.

The referee handed him his helmet and told him he had an injury.

K. C. trotted over and told Dale he was replacing him. Dale asked why, and K. C., buckling his helmet, said because you're bleeding, dummy.

Dale looked over at the sideline and saw Coach Dorfman motioning for him. He jogged over, carrying his helmet. Dorfman grabbed his head and examined the wound.

"It's still bleeding," he said. Dale didn't like Dorfman's rough fingers on his face. "Let's clean it and put on a butterfly."

Coach Blocker came over with a clean cloth, a bottle of alcohol, a cotton swab, and a butterfly bandage. He wiped away the blood with the cloth, then dabbed the cut with the alcohol-soaked cotton swab. Dale winced at the sting.

"This is more than a cut. More like a gash. You might need stitches." Blocker looked into Dale's eyes. "How you feeling?"

"I feel fine."

Blocker told him to hold the cotton ball against the wound. Blocker opened the butterfly bandage. Dale removed the cotton ball and Blocker applied the butterfly.

Dorfman reappeared. "How you doing? Feel any pain?"

"I feel fine," Dale said emphatically.

The coaches looked at each other. Blocker said Dale might need stitches. The two coaches actually looked concerned. Dorfman told him to go take a seat on the bench. Dale said he was ready to go back in. Dorfman said take a seat. He'd go back in when they thought he was ready.

Dale walked over to the bench. Ten yards away, where the cheerleaders stood, he saw Mary Jane, Roxanne, and Carmen comforting Wendy. He briefly saw Wendy's face. Tears streamed down her cheeks. Her mouth opened wide as she sobbed. He heard her wails from where he sat. He felt a surge of anxiety swell inside him. Did her father have a heart attack? But if so, then Wendy wouldn't be on the sidelines at the stadium. So, he wondered, what was making Wendy bawl so loudly?

He considered going over to her. She was only ten yards away. But that didn't seem right. He was at a football scrimmage. Dale thought it was sort of like being in the army. You didn't leave your post even if your girlfriend was weeping her eyes out. He nervously glanced over to the cheerleaders. Wendy seemed to have calmed down. She wiped her eyes and looked in his direction. When she saw him she smiled, but her eyes still looked teary and worried.

Dale didn't know what the heck was going on. He walked over to Dorfman and told him he was ready to go back in. Dorfman said no. The scrimmage was almost over. No need to take any chances.

Dale wondered what was wrong with Dorfman. Ordinarily, he'd want him to go back in the game, injured or not. A chance to prove his toughness. Were the coaches showing so much consideration because they thought he was valuable or because he'd bled? He guessed blood made a more dramatic injury than a pinched nerve. It was funny just the same how they were fussing over him now when they hardly cared last year.

He walked a few feet down the sidelines and watched as Matt Jones gained three yards on a counter. Maverick played just as tough this year as last. All scrimmage they'd pounded the smaller Gophers. They hit with a savage intensity. Dale thought they hit harder than Sundance even. Galilee had held their own against them in the scrimmage just the same. Maverick scored twice on six possessions; Galilee had scored once on five possessions. The score came when Dale took a pitch from Sonny and instead of running wide right, he cut against the grain as soon as he saw a hole. The Maverick defenders, aggressive in pursuit, didn't react in time. Dale broke one tackle, sidestepped another, faked out a third tackler, then cut back left and sprinted past the Mustang secondary to score on a fifty-yard run.

He thought it was his best run ever. Too bad it was only a scrimmage game.

When Galilee failed to get a first down, the referee blew his whistle signaling the end of the scrimmage. Dale joined his teammates as they formed a line and shook the hands of the Maverick players. Several of the Maverick guys said "good game" to Dale as if they really meant it. He felt himself swell with pride. He had ambitious hopes for his senior year. He still was undersized, but now standing almost five foot seven and weighing 158 pounds he didn't feel like a shrimp among the whales – more like a little fish. More importantly, he thought he had the speed and strength pound for pound to be a good player.

The team trotted over to the end zone and the coaches led them in a post-game prayer. Then Dorfman gave a short speech, saying they'd played pretty well against a tough opponent. But he reminded them that all their games were tough this year. Dale frowned. Galilee had been placed in a new district and the decision by the high school football administrators seemed absurd. Instead of playing similar-sized rural schools, they had several games against schools in the City. They even had Ralph Ellison High in their district. Ellison, a black school from the City, always had good teams. Galilee's chances of winning their district were poor.

Dorfman, to Dale's disappointment, had changed the offense. Dorfman said they didn't have a fullback so he put in a new offense, the veer, that only had two halfbacks. The obvious problem with the new offense was that not having a fullback to help block weakened the running game. That meant they would be throwing the ball more and the team would depend even more on Sonny.

Coach concluded his comments and K. C. and Bigelow led the team in chanting Go-phers! Go-phers! Then Dale joined Chris as they walked over to the picnic tables in the practice field for watermelon.

"You played good," Chris said.

"Thanks."

"That was a nifty run," Chris said, referring to Dale's touchdown. "I didn't even have time to make a block."

"Sorry about that," Dale said, grinning at Chris's frowning face.

"Don't be. Do it whenever you can." They walked over to the watermelon lines. "How's your cut?"

Dale had forgotten. He reached up and touched the butterfly bandage. It seemed to be holding well. "It's fine."

"Good deal. We don't want you injured again."

No kidding, thought Dale. He'd missed the first two games each of the last two years. He wasn't about to let that happen this year.

Dale looked over at the pep club senior girls serving slices of juicy red watermelon. He noticed Amanda serving guys in the middle line. Dale told Chris they were getting in that line.

"Why? The first line's shorter."

Dale didn't answer. He slipped over to the middle and Chris followed. Dale, already growing nervous, wiped the sweat off his face. Sweat soaked his crimson jersey. It had been a hot and humid day. He hoped he didn't stink too bad.

A few minutes later, Dale stepped up and accepted his slice of melon from Amanda. She smiled at him and Dale took in her entire face, especially her blue eyes and full lips. He also stared for a moment at that spot, the groove, above her upper lip that was more defined than most people's. He wondered how it would feel to kiss it.

"You played a good game, Audie," she said, her voice sounding musical to his ears.

"Thanks," he said, almost dropping the slice of melon. He smiled a little in embarrassment, then reluctantly stepped away. He watched as she served Chris. Dale noticed she spoke to Chris in a more familiar way. Of course, she and Chris went to First Church. They'd known each other for years, even before Amanda moved to Galilee.

Dale and Chris walked over to the benches next to several tall green trash cans. The players weren't supposed to spit the seeds on the turf.

"Amanda's nice," said Chris.

Dale remembered the beginning of last school year. "You think all the girls are nice."

Chris bit off a chunk of melon and slurped it down. "True, but some are nicer than others."

Something in Chris's tone of voice nettled Dale. Chris had once told him that he and Amanda had gone out casually a couple of times after church. Chris had wanted to ask her out on a real date, but he didn't have the nerve. Now, Dale wondered what he'd do if Chris got the nerve. Dale decided he was worrying about nothing. Chris dated occasionally, but his parents forbade him from going steady. However, Chris, who bought an old, hulking, white '65 Plymouth over the summer, which he'd nicknamed "the bomb," had already confided in Dale that he was going to have some fun during his senior year.

After eating their fill of the watermelon, the football team boarded the bus and drove back to the high school. Dale showered and dressed quickly. He and Wendy were going out. They were going to see *The Towering Inferno* and he had to hurry so they would have time to drive to the City. He was about to walk out with Chris when Dorfman told him to take care of his cut. He said he might want to see a doctor. Then he asked how he felt. Dale said okay. Just a little headache. Dorfman gave him a couple of aspirin and Dale swallowed them without water.

Outside the gym, Dale said so long to Chris and walked over to his car, got inside, and waited for Wendy. A couple of minutes later, he heard the passenger door open and Wendy climbed in. Immediately, he sensed something was wrong.

"I'm late," she announced, her normally sunny face scrunched in worry.

Dale didn't understand. "I've only been here for a few minutes."

"I don't mean that," Wendy said. She looked at him, her green eyes tearing up. "I mean I'm *late*."

Dale, now understanding, felt like he'd been slammed by the whole Maverick football team. He slumped back in his seat, stunned and hollow inside.

"Are you sure?"

"Of course," she said. She began to cry.

Dale swallowed hard and thought back to that time in the dorm room at Girls State. They hadn't done anything like that since. He felt exasperated. How could this happen from just one time? What were the odds? Admittedly, he didn't know much about how all this stuff worked, but still?

Wendy draped herself over him and sobbed against his shoulder. He stroked her hair but said nothing. After a few minutes, she stopped crying and Dale glanced around to see if anyone was watching. He always parked at the far end of the lot and no one seemed to be around.

Wendy lifted herself off him and peered at the side of his face. She gingerly touched the bandage.

"Are you alright?"

Dale said yeah. It wasn't bad.

"It looked bad. Blood streaming down the side of your face." She started to cry again.

"Good grief," Dale said, putting his arm around her. "It was just a cut. I don't know why it bled so much. It doesn't hurt or anything."

Wendy murmured against his shoulder, what are we going to do?

Dale didn't know. He couldn't imagine many things worse than this. He guessed Wendy would have to go to her aunt's or grandmother's and wait it out. He felt a cold dagger cutting inside him when he thought of Wendy's parents. What would they do? What would they think of him? Wendy's father might shoot him or run him over with his rig. Dale thought he deserved it. He berated himself for being so stupid, for not having enough self-control. Too bad someone hadn't walked in on them. It would have been humiliating but not as humiliating as this. But no one did. They lay in her bed for half an hour before leaving. Dale remembered how uncharacteristically shy Wendy had been. She wouldn't let him watch her dress.

He asked Wendy if she still wanted to go to the movie. She sniffled, then said yes. She didn't want to go home yet.

They drove to the City mostly in silence. They sat in the theatre and held hands while watching the movie. Dale couldn't quite get involved in it. The story seemed too soap operaish for his taste. He liked the death scenes, though. Some of the characters perished in inventively gruesome ways. By the time of the rescue scene, he'd almost forgotten their big problem.

The movie ended and they drove back to Galilee mostly in silence. Dale parked on the curb outside Wendy's house and looked at her. She looked tired and worn out. She'd done a lot of crying. He felt desperately sorry for her. He didn't know what to say.

"Do you want to talk?" Dale asked.

Wendy shook her head no. "I'm tired. We can talk tomorrow."

Dale said okay. He got out, opened the car door for her, and walked her to the porch. They kissed without passion. He could taste the tears in her mouth.

They said good night. She went inside as Dale walked to his car. He waited until she turned off the porch light, then he drove home.

A half moon shone high in the clear night sky. Stars shimmered. Dale prayed to be forgiven. He prayed for Wendy to be all right. He wasn't sure what all right meant, but he wanted her to be safe and happy again. If God would punish him instead, he would gladly accept it.

When Dale arrived home, he noticed all the lights were off. His parents and June May were in bed. Dale never wore a watch but he guessed it was a half an hour past midnight.

He unlocked the front door, quietly entered the still house and went to his room. As he fell upon his bed, he considered a possible solution: he could marry Wendy. That seemed like a drastic choice. They were only seventeen. He decided that was not a logical option and lay in his bed for what seemed like hours trying to think of some solution before he finally fell asleep, exhausted.

The next morning, Wendy called. Dale, just waking up, heard the phone ring and jumped out of bed and told his sister he would answer. He knew it was Wendy. He dreaded hearing her wounded voice.

"Hello," he said.

"Hi," she said. Her voice sounded subdued but not despairing.

Dale ached all over. His head, especially where it was cut, throbbed. "How are you?"

A dramatic pause.

"I'm fine. I mean, *really* fine. I got my period this morning."

Dale tightened his hold on the neck of the receiver and pulled it away from his ear. He stared at it. He heard Wendy's distant voice saying, "Audie, Audie."

"I thought you were – " he hated saying the word – "late."

"Yes, I was."

"Then what happened?"

"I guess I just skipped one period."

"Skipped?" Dale thought that was such a simple word for such a complicated situation.

"Yes. It's never happened to me before but I know Mary Jane had it happen. Maybe Gretchen. I dunno. I guess I should ask."

"Don't ask," said Dale. "Don't tell anyone about this."

"Oh, I'm not! I was just thinking of other girls who've had irregularities."

Dale shook his head in bewilderment. Late. Periods. Irregularities. What kind of words were these? He felt overwhelmed by the mysterious complexity of the female.

"It's good news, isn't it?" Wendy asked.

Dale said it certainly was.

"I guess we have to be extra careful from now on."

Dale said those were his thoughts exactly. Extra careful.

Wendy asked where they were going tonight. He wasn't sure. She said he could come over and watch some TV and eat popcorn. Dale said that sounded okay. Wendy said to come by around seven. He said he would. Then she said good-bye, her voice still not full of cheeriness as usual, but certainly not full of woe.

Dale hung up the phone. He saw June May looking at him from down the hall. He fought an urge to warn his sister of the malign motives of men. He walked inside his room and wondered if God had answered his prayer or simply had played a joke on him.

## Chapter 2: *'Surfing' and a close vote for all-school queen*

Dale wished he could surf for real. He thought he'd be good at it. He leaned back in his seat as Rusty's new car, a '67 orange Chevy Malibu SS, roared down the highway. The Beach Boys' *Endless Summer* blared from the tape deck. Dale looked out at the wheat fields flashing by and imagined he and Rusty were driving along the white sands of a California beach.

Dale closed his eyes and felt the hot air flow over him from the open window. It felt like Southern California. Today was a perfect Indian summer day. Late September and almost ninety degrees. He listened to the throaty growl of Rusty's car as it maintained an even sixty miles per hour.

Dale was glad Rusty was in a good mood again. He'd been dismayed hearing over the summer that Coach Carpenter had resigned to go to Cimarron City and coach the junior varsity. But Rusty and Erickson had met the new basketball coach a few days ago and they thought he seemed like a good guy.

"Listen to that engine," Rusty shouted through the noise of both the motor and the wind. "It's a 396 cubic with a dual carb."

Dale nodded. He didn't know much about engines or cars. He had to admit that the Malibu was a lot louder than Rusty's old Rambler.

Rusty slowed the engine to a purr, then turned down a dirt road that ran alongside Lake Overholser. They coasted to a stop. They listened to the end of "Little Deuce Coupe" at full blast. Then Rusty turned the volume down.

"I thought you didn't like the Beach Boys," Dale said.

"Never said that, my man. Although I admit, I never knew they were so *cool*."

Dale smiled. The Beach Boys became cool again this past summer. For some curious reason, he supposed another wave of '60s nostalgia, their double album became the number-one record of the late summer. He thought it was about time the Beach Boys enjoyed a renaissance. He felt a swelling of pride that he'd been a fan through all those lean years when they were dismissed as hopelessly passé. The first records he'd bought were Beach Boys and Beatles records back when everyone else was listening to The Three Dog Night.

A year ago, Dale discovered a specialty record store in the City named *Woody's* that sold all kinds of old records. The store was located in an older part of the City that he'd never been to before. As soon as he walked into the store and smelled the intoxicating smell of vinyl and saw rows and rows of 45s and albums, he knew he'd discovered his musical Shangri-la. All kinds of old records were stuffed in the place. Not only Beach Boys and Beatles records, but Jan and Dean; the Four Seasons; girl groups like the Shirelles and the Angels; great Motown groups; and bands from the British Invasion: the Animals, the

Hollies, the Kinks, the Troggs, the Zombies. He bought a handful of 45s then and had returned every month for more. Now, with the surprising success of *Endless Summer*, Dale felt his taste in music had been vindicated.

"Are you sure this is going to work?" Rusty asked.

"Sure, why not?"

Rusty put the car in park and they got out. Rusty opened the trunk. Dale pulled out a trash can lid. It was kind of stinky. He'd earlier removed the handle from the top and it looked smooth enough to work.

Rusty tied the rope to the back of the car and Dale threaded the other end through a hole he'd bored at the edge of the lid. Rusty tied a second rope higher on the car. That would be the one Dale would hold onto. Dale tossed the lid on the dirt road and looked at his pal.

"I think it'll work."

"We'll see." Rusty surveyed the red dirt road. "I think this is the flattest, smoothest road I've seen. That should help."

Rusty got back in his car. Dale squatted on the lid, grabbed hold of the second rope, and nodded. Rusty slowly advanced the car. Dale struggled to keep his balance. He almost fell but recovered and nodded for Rusty to pick up speed. Rusty eased the car to ten. Dale held the rope and rode the lid. The car's speed increased to twenty. He squinted his eyes and tried not to breathe in all the smoky red dust. The car moved on to twenty-five. He saw the weeds on the side of the road flash dizzily by. Dust coated his face. His hands burned from holding the rope. The lid hit a little bump and he lost his balance and tumbled onto the dirt road, rolling into the weeds. Rusty stopped the car. He threw it in park and raced over. Dale lay sprawled out in a thicket of dry, brown grass and sticky weeds.

"Wipe out!" Rusty said.

Dale nodded. He grabbed Rusty's outstretched hand and pulled himself up. He shook the dust off his jeans and shirt.

"It's more like water skiing than surfing," Dale said.

"You mean dirt skiing."

"Yeah." Dale spit dirt out of his mouth and rubbed it out of his nostrils. "You wanna try?"

"Are you crazy?" Rusty said. "You're the Beach Boy."

Dale was a little late. He'd had to wash up at home after his surfing fiasco and then had trouble tying his tie. He rushed through the back door of the high school auditorium and saw them all waiting for him. Mrs. Heath, the faculty organizer of the ceremony, waved an admonishing finger at him. He shrugged and joined Wendy to make the fifth couple. Dale, who'd heard "Wendy" on Rusty's eight track on their way back from the lake, smiled an uncharacteristically full smile. Whenever he heard that song, he thought of Wendy and how she could be a surfer girl. Wendy, dressed in a green gown that matched her eyes, smiled back although she wrung her hands out of nervousness.

"What are you smiling about?" she asked.

"Oh, nothing."

He looked at the other four couples. Rusty and Roxanne; K. C. and Amanda; Billy Joe and Gretchen; Chris and Mary Jane. He and Wendy were the only two dating that were paired together. Dale didn't like that. He could tell from Rusty's grimace that he didn't like it either. Rusty had wanted to be paired with Mary Jane but she didn't want to. She thought that would brand them as a steady couple and that was against her principles. Dale wondered why K. C. and Gretchen weren't matched together. They were dating and neither had objected to being paired together. It didn't matter anyway; Dale thought the whole affair silly. He admitted to himself he was pleasantly surprised when he'd been elected as one of the "favorites." That's what the school called the five couples who made up the all-school court. One boy and one girl would soon be crowned all-school king and all-school queen. Dale remembered when he was in junior high thinking how mature the senior couples had looked when they walked down the aisle arm in arm and mounted the stage. Now, he felt silly dressed in his suit, knowing he had to walk down that aisle soon with Wendy and partake in a superficial ritual that he sort of objected to.

Dale thought all the girls looked nervous. Even Amanda. She bit her luscious lower lip and kept looking at the walls as if she might see something unusual materialize there. Dressed in a tasteful light blue gown, not gaudy or frilly like Gretchen's and Roxanne's, she really did look regal. Her long, light brown hair almost looked blond. Maybe the summer sun had bleached it a little; Dale doubted she'd ever dye her hair. Dale noticed she wore some makeup too; not much, a few splashes of color to enhance her natural comeliness. Dale thought she looked lovely.

All the girls looked lovely, he thought. Dale felt proud of them. He thought the five of them were the prettiest court of girls he'd ever seen. Roxanne, dressed in a sort of silly frilly pink gown, still looked ravishing. The guys he knew expected her to be crowned queen. But since all the kids in both the junior high and senior high voted, he wasn't certain. He'd heard some of the girls talk about the different advantages Roxanne, Wendy, Mary Jane, Amanda, and even Gretchen had. Did they have siblings in junior high? Did they date the right guy? Were they nice to the different groups of kids or were they snobby? Dale thought such talk was a waste of breath. Why speculate? But he supposed for most people that was half the fun, especially if they weren't one of the candidates.

The guys, on the other hand, were determinedly trying to look bored. Maybe they were bored. This kind of thing was really for the girls. Just another occasion to dress up and buy a corsage and make a spectacle of yourself in public. Generally speaking, not something guys cared about.

Dale had been surprised that he and Chris had been voted to the esteemed group of ten. Sonny had always been one of the "favorites" in junior high. Dale supposed his general slovenliness and rumored drug use had eliminated him. Chris, one of the real nice guys in school, had, in a sense, taken his place. Chris was one of those guys who are overlooked in junior high; not the best athlete, not the most talented, not the smartest, not the cutest, his more substantial qualities are recognized as his peers mature. Everybody Dale knew liked Chris for his kindness, self-deprecating good humor, and high character. Dale was glad he'd made the ten.

As for himself, he was surprised he'd been picked. Even though he thought the ritual somewhat ridiculous, he did feel a warm glow come over him when he saw his name listed with the others. School officials had posted the names of the ten favorites on the big bulletin board in the lobby and that day he'd been congratulated by his friends and a lot of kids he didn't really know well. Even Vern, known for his contempt for school traditions, congratulated him. So did some teachers. Dale felt especially pleased when the two teachers he respected, Mrs. Page and Mrs. Heath, said how well deserved the honor was.

He didn't let any of that go to his head. In fact, he thought the congratulations business was sort of strange. What had they really done to be congratulated for?

Dale had thought Erickson might be one of the favorites. A lot of girls thought he was cute, and he was bright and played sports. But he was beginning to get a reputation as a troublemaker. He smarted off in class and taunted kids he didn't like, usually the awkward and uncool kids. He'd been kicked off the baseball team. Dale guessed all those things worked against him. The other guy that might have been picked was Bigelow. If Dale's inclusion meant Bigelow's exclusion, then he accepted all the attendant silliness.

The music began. Mrs. Heath organized the couples. They got into line. Dale and Wendy were third. Wendy put her hand on his arm. He felt her trembling from nervousness. He glanced at her, saw her face looking more pale than usual, then looked down at her feet and noticed she was wearing pumps with only two-inch heels. That was considerate of her. Now, Dale stood a couple of inches taller than she did.

When their turn came, they entered the dark auditorium and as they walked down the aisle, a spotlight appeared from above and lit their way. Dale felt Wendy's hand in the crook of his arm. He glanced at her and saw her smiling proudly at all the assembled kids. Dale noticed a few faces. He saw Vern looking at him with a sardonic smile on his face. He saw Carmen, too. She smiled sincerely, looking genuinely happy for them. Dale tried to keep his gaze forward; seeing the faces of people he knew made him even more nervous. He thought about his feet. He feared he might trip and take them both down. He could imagine the whole auditorium of kids and teachers screaming with laughter.

As they walked to the stage, he heard the announcer listing all their accomplishments. Their activities, the academic awards and honors, the sports, the clubs, all that stuff. Hearing it spoken aloud, and amplified, made it sound more impressive than it really was.

Dale helped Wendy climb the stairs to the stage. They took their place to the right of Rusty and Roxanne. Dale tried not to blink as the spotlight hit his eyes. Then the light swerved back to the aisle where the next couple, K. C. and Amanda, appeared. Dale watched Amanda as she walked toward the stage. She smiled modestly, obviously not carried away with the ceremony. Dale liked that. He heard the announcer list her honors and activities. Honor society, drama society, vice president of the pep club, choir, Oklahoma City youth orchestra, Future Teachers of America, Future Homemakers of America. Dale found Amanda's musical talent especially impressive. She sang in the school choir and with a smaller ensemble, the "Choraleers." She also played flute in the City's youth orchestra. Dale tried not to watch her too closely as she took her graceful steps up to the stage.

After the last couple, Chris and Mary Jane, arrived, the ten of them stood on the stage as the announcer, whose silky voice Dale finally identified as belonging to Mr. Werhmeier, paused before announcing the 1974-75 king and queen. Dale glanced over to Rusty and Roxanne. He expected both of them to win. Maybe that's why Mrs. Heath had them paired.

In junior high, Rusty had been voted one of the four class favorites all three years; K. C. had won once, and Sonny twice. Roxanne had won all three years; Wendy twice, and Mary Jane once. That was junior high, of course, but Dale thought those awards were as good predictors as anything else.

Mr. Werhmeier intoned the names of the winners: Rusty Grimes and Amanda Meeks.

Dale felt Wendy squeeze his hand. He heard some girls in the audience shriek, either out of delight or surprise. Then the entire audience burst out in applause. Dale looked at Amanda. Her face, illuminated by the soft light of the spotlight, looked radiant. She smiled her modest but becoming smile, then accepted Rusty's escort as he led her to the middle of the stage where the king and queen "thrones" were located. Dale thought the thrones looked more like wicker chairs painted red and white and adorned with flowers and ribbons, but they served their purpose.

Dale glanced at Wendy. She smiled, but he saw the disappointment in her eyes. Her hand still clung tightly to his. Dale had expected Roxanne or Wendy would be queen. In fact, he was sort of hoping Wendy would win. He knew she'd like that and perhaps being crowned queen with Rusty as king would make Dale and Wendy less of a couple.

He felt a perplexing brew of emotions well up inside him. On one hand, he liked that Amanda had won. He'd voted for her. He, of course, didn't tell anyone that. Even if Roxanne was technically prettier, Dale thought Amanda was the epitome of high school royalty. Not only was she comely but she was kind, talented, well mannered, smart, unpretentious – he couldn't list all her virtues. But on the other hand, he didn't want her to be queen. That would confirm her elite status. It would place her at an even higher plane of existence, one he could never hope to equal.

Dale tried not to show his displeasure as Rusty and Amanda exchanged crowns and bracelets and then Rusty put his arms around her waist and kissed her. It wasn't a long kiss or one with much ardor; it wasn't a kiss of lovers or even dating partners, but it wasn't a short kiss or one completely devoid of emotion. To Dale, it seemed entirely inappropriate.

He watched with envy as Rusty pressed his mouth to hers. He impatiently noted the few seconds that passed before Rusty removed his face from Amanda's. When Amanda's face reappeared, Dale felt a pang deep inside him as he saw that her eyes were still closed. Then her eyes fluttered open and she smiled and the audience clapped and cheered again. Dale forced his hands together, too, and tried to manage a smile. But inside he felt almost sick with envy and jealousy. He kept thinking about Amanda's soft lips and how it must have felt to have kissed them. He took his eyes briefly off Amanda and looked at Rusty. He grinned in his usual insouciant way. Dale imagined he rather liked kissing Amanda; Rusty had kissed a lot more girls than he had and never before had he begrudged his best friend that advantage. But now he did.

The ceremony over, the ceiling lights came on and the audience members noisily filed out of the auditorium happy for school to be out half an hour early. Dale remained with the favorites on stage for yearbook and newspaper photos. Mr. Werhmeier, who in addition to his musical expertise was an excellent photographer, took some of the photos while his son, Mark, a sophomore, assisted him. Dale had selected Mark for the yearbook staff although he didn't like him much. Unlike his father, he was sort of arrogant; but he was already a good photographer at age fifteen.

Mr. Werhmeier took photos of each couple, then a group portrait. Dale had also asked him to take a few photos of them outside for the yearbook. So all of them trooped outside, walking a short way to a nice spot that looked like a little park with grass, a tree, and a bench. Dale thought this little pastoral place would provide an excellent backdrop. On the way, the four couples who hadn't won congratulated Rusty and Amanda. When Dale gave his congratulations, he shook Rusty's hand so hard that Rusty winced and he hardly looked Amanda in the eye because he didn't want her to see his jealousy.

After the photographers left, the ten favorites awkwardly looked at each other. Now that it was all over, they felt a little silly standing around in gowns and suits. K. C. said why didn't they all meet at West Oaks in thirty minutes. That would give them all a chance to change. They all nodded. That was the usual procedure for the favored ten. Dale asked Wendy if she wanted a ride home and she said she'd dressed over at Roxanne's and she'd ride with her back there and then meet him at West Oaks. Dale said okay. He watched the girls leave, then Billy Joe and K. C. left, leaving Dale, Rusty, and Chris together.

"Boy, I'm glad that's over," said Chris.

Rusty and Dale agreed.

"Pretty silly stuff," Dale said.

"It's for the girls," said Rusty.

"Yeah," Dale said. He loosened his tie. He hated wearing ties.

A pause appeared in the conversation. Chris, his hands jammed in his pockets, peered down the sidewalk where the girls had walked. "Mary Jane's pretty nice."

Dale looked at Rusty. He didn't smile.

"I mean, I didn't used to think she was that pretty," he added. "She has sort of a bump on the bridge of her nose. But I think it's kinda cute now."

Dale, still resenting that Rusty kissed Amanda, decided to needle him. "Yeah, she's cute. She reminds me of Cher, but better looking."

Chris nodded. "Same kind of hair and figure."

Dale glanced at Rusty. Rusty tried to hold his face in a neutral expression, but it kept slipping into annoyance. Dale thought one more comment would do it. "But prettier face."

Rusty said he'd see them at West Oaks and stormed off.

Chris turned to Dale. "What's wrong with him? I thought he and Mary Jane weren't seeing each other anymore."

"I think they're still dating."

"Oh. Well, they're not going steady or anything."

Dale said he thought that was right.

"Maybe we shouldn't have said anything."

"Maybe not."

"Just keeping my options open."

Dale went over and slapped his friend on the back. "I understand. What we need to do is find you a girl. Just not some other guy's girl."

Chris nodded. He said he better go get changed. He'd see Dale at West Oaks. Dale said so long and after Chris left, he decided to stop by the yearbook office. He walked in the high school's back entrance, and headed for the small office located at the corner at the end of the hallway. He noticed the door was opened a crack; he paused and heard two girls on the staff talking.

"A lot of the girls didn't vote for Roxanne."

Dale recognized Linda Blaine's voice. She was a tall girl with short, curly blond hair and a friendly face. She was the business manager.

"A lot of the boys did, though."

That voice belonged to Carrie Bacon, the copy editor. She had fluffy brown hair, stylish glasses, and full cheeks. Dale thought she was kinda cute.

"I heard the vote was *awfully* close between the girls," said Linda.

"Where did you hear that from?" asked Carrie.

"From Mrs. Heath and you're not supposed to tell anyone."

"Why did she tell you then?"

"Because I helped with organizing the whole affair."

"Oh." A pause. "How close?"

"Very close. In fact, very, very close."

"Now, what are you getting at?"

"You promise not to tell absolutely anyone?"

Carrie said she promised.

"Well, it was actually a tie."

"A tie? Really? Between who?"

"Between Amanda and Wendy."

"Wow! Well, how was Amanda picked then?"

"Mr. Smedley tossed a coin. Well, he tossed two. The first quarter rolled under a file cabinet. The second toss came up tails for Amanda."

"Wow."

"And Roxanne was only two votes behind Amanda and Wendy."

"Were you surprised Amanda got so many votes?"

"Yes and no."

"Amanda's pretty," said Carrie.

"She's also nice to everyone," said Linda. "And not in a fake way."

"And she has a popular brother in ninth grade."

"Yes. Another plus."

"Still, I'm a little surprised."

"Well, it was a close vote. Very, very close."

"Yeah, as close as it can get. I wonder if it's better to lose by a little or a lot?" Carrie said. "I mean, losing by a lot seems more embarrassing but losing by a little must be more excruciating."

"None of them know if they lost by a little or a lot. And let's keep it that way."

"Of course."

Dale wanted to wait until they stopped talking before he entered but he knew that would be probably be forever in the case of the two loquacious girls, so he finally pushed open the door and walked in.

"Oh, hi Audie," said Linda.

"Hi Audie," said Carrie.

229

"Hi girls."

He noticed them looking at him in a curious way. "What's up?"

"Not much," said Linda.

"Yeah, not much," said Carrie.

Dale sat down in a chair in front of a long table used for laying out pages. He flipped through a couple of contact sheets. There weren't many photo assignments so early in the school year but Dale had asked the two photographers Mark and another sophomore, a girl named Natasha, to shoot some candids of students.

From the corner of his eye, Dale caught Linda and Carrie looking at him in a sympathetic way. He glanced at them.

"How's Wendy?" Linda asked.

Dale shrugged. "Fine."

"She's not upset, is she?" asked Carrie.

He said he didn't think so.

"That's good," said Linda.

"I was hoping Wendy would win," said Carrie. "But I thought they all were worthy," she quickly added.

"I know," said Linda. "What a difficult decision."

"We wanted you to win, too, Audie," said Carrie.

Dale shook his head. "Believe me, I don't care about that."

"But it would have been so nice if you and Wendy both won," said Carrie.

That was exactly what Dale wouldn't have wanted. Then they would have forever been branded as *the* high school couple.

Dale got up without answering. "You haven't seen Don around lately?" Don was Don Fargo, the sports editor. Dale didn't really need him. He just wanted to change the subject.

"No, not this afternoon," said Linda.

Dale said okay. He was leaving. He told the girls to make sure they locked up. They said okay. Then they both said "bye" in their sweet, feminine voices.

Dale walked out the building, back to his car. On his way, he thought about what he'd heard. He realized that if he hadn't voted for Amanda, then Wendy would have won by one vote. Dale felt a little guilty for not voting for his own girlfriend. He would never tell Wendy, of course. He decided he was glad Amanda won. He liked the way she didn't seem to take the win too seriously. She had behaved graciously. She was happy but in a modest way that was really becoming. She was sensitive to other people's feelings. She knew Roxanne and Wendy and Mary Jane and even Gretchen were disappointed. All four of them had attended Galilee since first grade.

Dale got in his car and paused before starting it. He realized that if he ever told Amanda of his feelings for her, she wouldn't laugh at him. She was too kind and considerate for that. Even though Amanda was now all-school queen, he thought there might still be hope for him.

**Chapter 3:** *Race dating; homecoming; Blackie with woman*

Mrs. Heath handed the class the results of the racial attitudes survey. Dale took his copy from Wally and handed the rest to Chris sitting at his left. While the results were being passed out, Mrs. Heath reminded the students of her sociology class that their responses had been given in anonymity and would remain that way.

Dale looked at the survey with surprise. He'd expected his classmates to be less critical of other races. Sixty percent said they wouldn't hire a black person if they owned a business. Half said they wouldn't hire a non-white. The same percentages said they didn't think blacks were trustworthy. Fifty percent said it was best for blacks and whites to live separately. Forty percent said they wouldn't rent to a person of another race. Seventy percent said they wouldn't date a person of another race. Eighty percent said they wouldn't marry a person of another race. The percentages opposed to blacks were even higher than for the other races. There were twenty juniors and seniors in the class, so Dale figured between twelve and sixteen students seemed to have reservations about interacting with blacks. Dale thought his classmates' attitudes were especially odd since they'd just seen *Brian's Song* at last year's homecoming.

Mrs. Heath said the students didn't have to discuss the survey if they didn't want. But frankly, she was a little disturbed by the results. She hoped that some discussion might help her understand their attitudes.

She asked the class in general about segregation. Why did they think so many people in class thought segregation a necessary if not a good policy? Dale's classmates weren't eager to answer. Mrs. Heath, however, wasn't afraid to let silence prompt answers from them.

Finally Bigelow spoke up. "People like being with their own kind."

Dale had to admit that Bigelow wasn't afraid of what other people thought of him. Not that Bigelow's attitude would surprise anyone, but few kids would come out and say it.

Mrs. Heath admitted that was generally true. But why? And was it right?

The class remained silent for a minute. Then Bonita Potts, sitting in the front with the other girls, including Amanda, said she thought people would get along better if they knew each other. Maybe it was a good thing for people of different races to live around one another.

Dale looked at Bonita. She was the smartest girl in his class. She always made straight As. She had long, reddish brown hair, wore glasses, and had sort of a square-shaped face. She wasn't considered pretty. She was nice and polite, like most of the girls, but she also expressed her opinions more forthrightly. Back in junior high, Dale had heard she liked him. In eighth grade, she'd even asked him to the pep club picnic. He and Rusty, who'd been asked by Wendy, acted terrible. They ignored Bonita and Wendy and threw food at each other. Dale supposed that Bonita, mature even as an eighth grader, had stopped liking him after that. He didn't care, really; he respected her intelligence but didn't find her especially attractive. She was the right height for him, though; she stood about five foot three, but she was on the skinny side.

Mrs. Heath said Bonita had an interesting point. She asked why some people wouldn't hire a person of a different race than themselves. A couple of people gave vague answers and the class discussion seemed to have hit an impasse.

"Okay," Mrs. Heath said, "let me ask a question that interests all of you. About dating. Why do people not want to date someone of a different race? "

Instead of being provoked, the students seemed even more reticent about answering that question. Mrs. Heath waited.

"Audie," she said, surprising Dale by asking him directly, "would you date a girl of a different race?"

Dale fought his feelings of embarrassment. He liked Mrs. Heath and didn't want to disappoint her. Also, he saw Amanda, Bonita, Mary Jane, and the other girls looking at him from the front of the room.

Dale thought about the question. He'd answered yes on the survey. But answering the question in public was a different matter. Then he visualized Marilyn McCoo, one of the singers of the Fifth Dimension. He remembered a few years ago seeing her sing on television. He thought she was beautiful. She was black. He'd definitely date her if that were possible.

"Yes," Dale said. "I would."

He caught Bigelow staring at him. Billy Joe, Sonny, and even Wally seemed to be looking at him askance.

"Why would you do that?" Mrs. Heath asked.

"Well, I guess it depends on who she was. But if I liked her, liked her as a person, then it wouldn't matter to me if she were white or black. Or any other race."

Dale added that last part even though he wasn't exactly sure how many other races there were.

Mrs. Heath nodded and tried not to smile. When Dale looked toward the front and saw Amanda still looking at him, a slight smile on her face, he felt justly rewarded.

"People ought to stick with their own kind," said Bigelow. "That goes for race and religion. People just get along better with people like themselves. There's a social –" Bigelow tried to think of the word to intellectually justify his view. "It's more socially responsible."

Mrs. Heath asked what he meant.

"If people get along better, there's less fighting and arguing. That makes for more social responsibility."

"Do you mean social stability?" Mrs. Heath asked.

"Yeah, that's what I meant."

Mrs. Heath nodded and started to ask another question from the survey when the bell rang. The students quickly gathered their books and papers and left as she reminded them of their reading assignment. Dale walked with Chris and Wally to their lockers.

"Would you really do that?" asked Wally.

"Do what?" replied Dale.

"You know. Date a colored girl."

"Yeah." Dale was certain now. It didn't even have to be Marilyn McCoo if he liked her. "Wouldn't you?"

Wally shook his head. "If you want my honest opinion, I don't think so." Wally looked at Chris. "How about you?"

"Yeah," Chris said, "but I wouldn't have any luck with them either."

The boys laughed, opened their lockers, and got their books for their next class.


Dale and Wendy stopped by the homecoming party for an appearance. Dale saw Chris talking to Carrie Bacon. Dale walked by and winked at Chris and he winked back. Dale had told Chris about Carrie. She laughed easily and was a good listener. Chris obviously was making a play.

"Sorry, I got in your way on the kickoff return," Chris said, as Wendy and Carrie chatted.

"That's okay," Dale said.

After Dale tackled an opponent in the end zone for a safety, he almost broke the ensuing kickoff for a touchdown. Chris tried to make a block but instead slowed Dale down enough that two Agra players tackled him at the Armadillo's thirty yard line. Three plays later, Dale scored on a twenty yard touchdown run and the Gophers went on to defeat the Armadillos, 20-6.

Now Chris looked over at Carrie. Dale beat him to the punch.

"Yeah, I know, she's a nice girl."

Chris smiled and wagged his eyebrows as if to say, "I hope not *too* nice." Dale playfully shoved him. Even nice Nazarene boys could lust.

On their way out of the school, Dale noticed Sadie standing alone, staring out of the large windows that looked out at the courtyard. He stopped and glanced at Wendy. She whispered that Sadie had been missing a lot of school. Dale wondered if she were with anyone at the homecoming party. Sadie seemed almost frozen in place as she stared at the dark courtyard. Dale felt sorry for her. He thought about going over and speaking to her, but since Wendy seemed anxious to leave, he didn't.

They walked outside. The October air was warm, even at nine at night. Dale asked Wendy what she wanted to do. She said some of the gang was going to Pizza Hut. Dale said let's go for a while. When they got there, they crowded into a booth with Rusty, Erickson, Roxanne, and Becky Brown. Dale and Wendy congratulated Roxanne on being voted football queen. She smiled and Dale noticed once again her sly violet eyes and full lips. He envied Billy Joe and Bigelow. Dale glanced around to see if Amanda was present. He didn't see her. He'd heard that she was with Billy Joe. Before he left, Dale asked Rusty where Mary Jane was. Rusty twisted his face into a big "who cares" look and turned his attention to Becky. As Dale and Wendy prepared to leave, Dale told Rusty, "good luck" and his buddy grinned.

Having made their social calls, Dale now drove to the best parking place he knew: a shaded nook he'd found in the north of town when he'd delivered papers last summer. If Dale angled the car just right when he parked, the bushes and two birch trees effectively camouflaged the car. It helped that Dale's Chevy had recently been repainted a dark blue.

After kissing for awhile, Dale helped removed Wendy's cheerleader blouse and unhooked her bra. Dale fondled her breasts and nuzzled her neck as Wendy murmured indistinct words as if she were learning a new language. Then he removed another article of clothing. They almost went as far as they had at Girls State, but they prudently stopped. Dale thought he needed a new baseball definition for the kind of activity they engaged in. He wasn't getting all the way home, but it was more than a triple. Maybe he was rounding third and had to retreat back to the bag.

A week ago they'd gone to the drive-in movie a week after learning she was all right. Wendy's parents were out of town for some truckers' convention, and after Wendy checked in with her sister-in-law, she snuck out with Dale. Playing at the drive-in was a dusk-to-dawn quadruple feature of all the *Planet of the Apes* movies. He'd seen the first ape movie seven years ago at the same drive-in. He'd been ten years old and really liked *Planet of the Apes*. He still remembered his shock and awe at the end when he learned that the United States and civilization itself had been destroyed by a nuclear war and the world had been left to the apes.

That night at the drive-in he and Wendy watched the first film without fooling around much. But the second one wasn't as good and they began their usual make-out routine. The drizzly, moonless night intoxicated them and they moved beyond their usual boundaries. That was also the first time Dale had touched her in her most intimate place. After he took her home, he drove to his house smelling the scent of her on his fingers. It was a potent, musky smell that reached deep into his brain beyond the ordinary categories of good smell, bad smell. It seemed somehow an important moment, a totemic moment. Dale thought it was a lot more appealing than olives.

Now, while cuddling, Wendy chatted about all her usual concerns. She didn't seem at all dispirited as she had when she didn't win all-school queen. She said she was glad Roxanne won. Roxanne was the perfect homecoming football queen. Dale thought so too, but he didn't say so aloud. She judiciously critiqued each of the candidates' gowns. Wendy then again complimented Dale on his play. He admitted to himself that it was his best game so far that season. He'd only rushed for sixty-nine yards but he'd made the decisive plays in the game. Take that, Bigelow!

Dale listened to Wendy talk for another half an hour. Now both physically and emotionally satisfied, he drove her home, gave her a good night kiss, and watched her go inside. Then he drove back to his house. As he did, he felt rather dissatisfied. He'd done well in the football game; he had a pretty cheerleader for a girlfriend who loved him. And yet, he felt something missing. He wanted to feel something deeper, more profound; he wanted to feel something transcendent.

A few weeks ago in senior English, something like that had happened. He'd been sitting in class reading Herman Melville's *Moby-Dick*. For the last year, Dale had been taking his studies more seriously and not just to make better grades. Rather, he'd discovered that he really wanted to understand ideas, especially aesthetic and philosophical ideas.

He'd been reading serious books out of school for over a year. He even read them at track meets. But he never felt like he fully understood what he was reading. Then that day while reading *Moby-Dick*, it was almost as if the book "opened up" for him. Dale felt his mind enter into the book on a deeper level. It was almost as if his mind had briefly connected with old Herman's mind. It excited Dale. He thought he understood the rather difficult book. For one thing, he realized that parts of *Moby-Dick* were funny. Not so much in an overt way, but in a subtle, sly way. Also, he began to more fully appreciate the book as an allegory.

Later, during class discussion, Dale felt frustrated with his classmates and his teacher, a young woman named Miss Cartland. He thought they were just skimming the surface of Melville. They didn't really understand him. Even Isaac Gould, boy genius, hadn't seemed to have penetrated Melville's sinewy prose and found the soul.

Later, when the class studied the transcendentalists, Dale felt an affinity for them. He didn't think his classmates genuinely appreciated the ideas of Thoreau or Emerson. He didn't think Miss Cartland did either. She seemed like a conventional teacher who taught in a predictable, boring way. Read this. Answer the obvious questions with the obvious answers. Dale knew there was more lurking under the words. He knew it the same way he knew there was more lurking under the conventional, ordinariness of life. He wanted to discover that larger meaning. He wanted to seize it and penetrate into its mystery before the mundane absorbed him.

Dale had been so busy of late, that he hadn't bought Wendy her birthday gift. He wasn't supposed to get her anything expensive or fancy, not that he had the money for that anyway. But he'd already ordered a small bouquet of flowers because he knew she liked flowers a lot. But he also wanted to get her another present, a small one with a personal touch. He decided to buy her the 45 recording of "Wendy."

The problem was that none of the record stores in Galilee had it. The stores carried *Endless Summer* and the album had "Wendy" on it, but Dale wanted to give her just the 45. That seemed more special to give her just one record with her name on it.

So, he decided to drive into the City to Woody's and buy it there. After dinner, he told Jesse he was going out, but didn't say where because he knew she wouldn't like him driving to the City in the evening. He drove out of Galilee, down Highway 66. He'd knew the route to the store by memory, but as he drove into the City, he had a hard time finding all the landmarks because he'd never driven there in the dark. He missed one turn. Then he turned the wrong way. Finally, he got to the store just before closing. He dashed inside the store, flipped through the Beach Boys 45s until he found it. He paid for it and felt satisfied that he'd accomplished his mission. He knew Wendy wasn't a big Beach Boys fan like he was. But he was sure she'd like this record, especially since listening to it would have special meaning.

Dale walked back to his car parked on the street curb. Located about twenty blocks away from downtown, the record store stood across the street from a restaurant, a bookstore, and a coffee shop. Dale glanced across the street, his interest initially attracted by the bookstore, when he saw something out of the corner of his eye. He turned and looked at the coffee shop and saw his father opening the door for a woman Dale had never seen before. At first, he thought Blackie was just being polite, but as he watched it was obvious that Blackie knew the woman and, in fact, was with her.

Dale watched as they walked to the counter together. Then the woman, who didn't look young or old, maybe in her mid-thirties, walked away and sat down in a booth. Then Blackie joined her. He sat down across from her and talked to her in a way that meant he knew her and she wasn't a recent acquaintance or a casual friend. Blackie, wearing his thin black leather jacket that Dale didn't like because it made him look like an older guy trying to be young, listened as the woman talked. She had fluffy blond hair, and a face that from a distance looked full of color from the heavy makeup she wore. She was dressed in a scarlet blouse under a gaudy, sequined blue jacket and a short red skirt. She reminded Dale of one of those female country and western singers that his grandma watched on TV; like one of the women who sang on the Porter Wagoner show.

Dale knew the OSU extension center was a few blocks away. He knew Blackie went to night classes four times a week. In fact, he knew Blackie had a sociology class in family structure tonight. What Dale didn't know until now was the real reason why Blackie sometimes got home late. Blackie had explained his lateness to Jesse by saying he'd been studying at the library. But now Dale knew Jesse's suspicions were right.

Dale took one last look at them. They didn't seem to be in love or anything. They weren't holding hands or leaning forward while gazing at each other. They were just talking. At least, she was talking in an animated way; Blackie seemed to be listening mostly. That was sort of odd, too, thought Dale. Blackie had never seemed like much of listener.

Dale got in his car and drove away, still thinking about his father. On the one hand, he didn't blame him. Jesse was difficult. He doubted they slept together anymore; that is, had sex. They slept in separate beds in the same room. He imagined his father was sort of lonely. Blackie worked hard. He worked his ranger shift, then took college classes four nights a week. But on the other hand, Dale didn't like it. Right now, Jesse sat at home smoking another pack of cigarettes and watching some stupid TV show. He didn't necessarily think Blackie should be doing the same thing, but he didn't think he should be with another woman drinking coffee. If for no other reason, he knew Blackie's deception would cause trouble. And if it caused trouble between him and Jesse, then that would bring trouble for Dale and June May.

Dale realized that was the problem with doing bad things: it never only affected one person.

**Chapter 4:** *Questions about two Smiths; Lyons game; Jesse suspicious*

Dale sat at his desk in the yearbook office and flipped through the prints. The photos looked pretty good. The first section he wanted to complete was the classes section. All the class pictures had been organized and stacked, and he and Carmen were working on the layouts. All he needed was to select the candids to fill in the pages.

Dale enjoyed editing the yearbook more than he had expected. He discovered a knack for organizing things. He had to schedule photo shoots with people or organizations, assign photographers, get the film developed, make contact sheets, select prints to be made, sketch a rough layout, and finally put all the elements – the photos, the copy, the headlines – together to make a page. He enjoyed all aspects of the job. He'd even learned how to shoot pictures, develop film, and make prints.

He'd bought a fairly inexpensive camera through the mail. Mr. Werhmeier had told him that was the best way to get a good camera at a cheap price. Dale read a book explaining picture composition, exposure readings, and all the other technical concerns of taking photos. But what he liked even better was working in the darkroom. He liked developing the film, learning how to thread it into the stainless-steel reel in the dark. He liked mixing the chemicals, turning on the big clock, and developing the film. He especially liked making the prints. The first time he took an exposed piece of photo-sensitive paper and put it in the developer tray and watched the image gradually appear was magical. Soon, even the smells of the darkroom didn't bother him. He actually began to like the chemical stink on his fingers.

Dale looked at the senior class portraits, photographed in color rather than the usual black and white. The seniors went to the Lake Overholser near Amanda's house and had their photos taken by a professional photographer friend of Mr. Werhmeier's. Dale thought it was an excellent setting. The trees in Amanda's neighborhood were the most colorful and attractive in Galilee. Taken in Mid-October, some of the leaves had already turned gold, orange, even red.

He looked at Wendy's photo. Dressed in a white and green dress, she sat on a bench and beamed a smile at the camera. He liked how the sunlight made her yellow blond hair gleam. The green in her dress highlighted her green eyes.

He looked at the photos of some of the other girls. Roxanne stood in front of a large rose bush that provided an interesting backdrop to her strawberry blond hair. She smiled her characteristically soft smile, not too broad, that emphasized her full, lipstick red lips.

Mary Jane stood beside a tree and held a basket of flowers. Her long, brown hair hung to her shoulders and her limpid brown eyes looked invitingly at the camera. She smiled warmly, showing her straight, white teeth.

Amanda reclined in the grass, her light blue dress covering her legs to her knees. She held a flower, a daisy, and smiled at the camera. Dale thought it was a perfect smile. Not too broad to stretch her lips too wide and reduce the fullness of her lower lip. She tilted her heart-shaped face toward the camera. That angle, along with her wide-open blue eyes, gave her an endearingly innocent quality. Dale felt himself pleasantly ache inside when he stared at her picture.

He glanced at some of the his pals' pictures. Rusty posed with one foot on a bench while resting his elbow on his knee. He stared someplace off to the side of the camera, not smiling. Dale thought the photo didn't capture Rusty's restlessness. His reddish blond hair flowed over his shirt collar, the longest it had ever been.

Chris stood straight against a tree and stared into the camera, smiling shyly, and his golden hair was so short it showed all of his ears

Dale then looked at his own portrait. He sat on the grass, leaning against a tree. He wished he hadn't complied with the request to sit. His blue and gray checked suit looked too sporty for his taste. But Blackie, who took him to buy a new suit at the beginning of the school year, insisted he not buy the simple dark blue suit that he wanted. Blackie said such a suit was old fashioned and not in style. He said Dale should get a suit with a more youthful style and cut. Dale went along with Blackie, but now, looking at his photo, he wished he hadn't. Most of all the other guys had similarly showy and colorful suits, but he liked classic understatement.

In the photo, Dale smiled his usual semi-smile, the corners of his mouth upturned but not showing teeth. He noticed how dark his hair looked in the photo, its length somewhere in between Rusty's long hair and Chris's short. He also thought his eyes looked surprisingly dark as they stared at the camera. Part of the reason he noticed this was because most of his classmates had light-colored hair, blond, red, or light brown. Most of his classmates also had blue, green, or gray eyes. Not many had dark brown eyes. Dale guessed that was because a lot of people in town came from English, Welsh, Scotch, and German backgrounds. Some French and Scandinavian as well. But that realization made him wonder about his own background. He knew his mother's family was Irish; well, Scots-Irish, though Dale didn't really know how that was different than plain old Irish. His Walsh relatives looked like his classmates. So he figured he must take after his father's family, but Smith was just a common English name.

He'd once asked Blackie about his background and he'd just grunted and said "white." Another time he said, "we're American." Both responses hadn't been very revealing. Dale suspected there was something different in their background that Blackie didn't want to talk about.

Dale tossed the photos back on the desk and resolved to ask Blackie to be more specific.

His thoughts on that matter were interrupted by footsteps outside the yearbook office. He'd left the door cracked open and since the office was in the corner near a curve in the building, sound seemed swirl around the walls and rush into the office. He got up to shut the door when he heard the voices of Amanda and Gretchen. He listened more closely.

"Are you sure?" Amanda said. "Is she really leaving?"

"She's already dropped out," said Gretchen. "She hasn't been in class for a week."

"That's a shame."

"The real shame was what she did. And then what happened to her."

"Yes, what she did was wrong. But I still feel sorry for her."

"So do I," said Gretchen, "but she got herself in trouble. It's her own fault. I bet she doesn't even know who the father is."

"We weren't friends, but maybe we should have done more. Done something to help her."

"What, for instance? She didn't like us. She thought we were stuck up. Besides, after it happened, there was nothing we could do to help her."

"I suppose."

"A girl that behaves like that is going to get in trouble eventually."

"I know."

"Amanda, you're too soft hearted. You almost seem to think she didn't do anything so bad."

"No, what she did was wrong. It was foolish. It was … bad. I just feel some sympathy for her."

"Me, too. But she should have been smarter. You're supposed to wait until marriage for that sort of thing. If you don't, you end up disgracing yourself."

"But to drop out of school."

"Probably the best thing for her. People know. She can't hide it. She can't escape from it."

Suddenly they stopped talking. Dale wondered if they'd noticed the yearbook office door not completely closed. But when he heard the footsteps of girls' shoes, he knew they'd been interrupted. He walked back to his desk and sat down just as Linda and Carrie pushed open the door and walked in.

"Did you hear the news?" asked Linda.

Dale pretended that he didn't know. Linda and Carrie filled him in. Both of them felt sorry for Sadie. They didn't go into any detail as to why she was dropping out. He guessed everyone in school knew the reason; well, at least the girls. While Linda and Carrie talked, he thought about Sadie. He'd known her since second grade. He sat behind her throughout grade school. He didn't talk to her much, but he never talked much to girls. Now, he wished he had spoken to her more. He wished he'd spoken to her that night at the homecoming party when he saw her standing alone and staring out the window.

"Well, Audie," Carrie asked, "what do you think?"

She wanted his reaction to their discussion that Dale hadn't been following. He stood up. "I think it's time for me to go."

He walked past the two girls and out the door as they gaped at each other.

Dale had a bad feeling about the Lyons game. Coach Dorfman had decided to experiment with a two-platoon system. Dale guessed Dorfman felt so confident about winning that he didn't think not playing his best players on both offense and defense would hurt. After all, Lyons had won only one game all season. Galilee had beaten them by fairly large margins in the previous two games of the Dorfman era. And now Dorfman had decided to utilize a two-platoon system.

But from the start nothing went right for the Gophers. Steady rain hampered the offense. The Lions scored two quick touchdowns against a Gopher defense missing five of the usual starters. In the second half, Galilee rallied but in the end lost 21-14 when Dale fumbled a wet, slick football while racing down the sideline for a possible tying score.

After Lyons recovered the ball at its thirty-five, Dale watched forlornly as the Lions players celebrated, their mud-caked bodies leaping in the air. Dale recognized one of them as Clifford.

He and his teammates trudged over and shook the hands of the Lyons players. When Dale got to Clifford, he saw mud splattered on his face and glasses. They shook hands and Clifford, without his mouthpiece in, said, "revenge is sweet."

Dale nodded and joined his team as they trotted off the field to their bus. The Gophers hadn't been allowed to use the visitors' locker room to suit up for the game. Lyons officials said the room had been flooded. So, Galilee had to endure an uncomfortable ride over and now would take an even more uncomfortable journey back home.

Dale slumped in his seat next to Chris. Someone threw him a towel and he tried wiping off some of the mud. It caked his hands and coated his uniform. He wanted to blame some force for this debacle of a game. Dale felt like he had been a football Cassandra and had foreseen the Gophers' terrible fate, but had been helpless to change it. He hated that lonely, isolated, powerless feeling.

Dorfman didn't have much to say. He boarded the bus and said, "at least you guys didn't give up." Then he looked at them with a pitying expression on his big face. Dale blamed him in part. If Dorfman hadn't fooled around with the defense, they wouldn't have lost.

Silence spread over the bus like a heavy, wet blanket. Then Cookie started the bus and Dale welcomed the noisy rattle of the engine. As the bus drove away, it exited through the visitors' parking lot and Dale, looking forlornly out the window, saw Rusty, Erickson, and Wally standing beside Rusty's Malibu. The three of them stood there like they were frozen in place. As the bus passed, Dale saw the shattered side windows and back window of Rusty's car. Rusty shouted, "shit!" and then sounds of the engine's rumble and tires crunching gravel filled the bus.

Dale quietly asked Chris if he saw that? Chris nodded. Dale wondered if Clifford's revenge included more than just the football victory.


The next morning when he awoke, Dale still felt sorer than usual. He always felt sore all day Saturday after a game. He rarely bruised, but all the pounding he took made him feel like he'd been knocked down by a truck. He got up, dressed, and walked stiffly to the kitchen. He expected to see Blackie sitting at the table, drinking coffee and reading the sports section. He usually read about the Galilee road games because he didn't go to them.

Dale drank some orange juice out of the carton and walked into the living room. Jesse sat on the couch reading a book. She used to be a big reader, although she only read children's books and the Bible. Now, as Dale walked over to her, he saw she was reading an astrology book. He remembered she used to believe in astrology. When she became a Witness, she gave up astrology because it was pagan.

He remembered when he was little Jesse telling him his horoscope and explaining his personality based on his astrological sign. He was an Aries, a ram. Jesse said that was why he was so solitary and independent. Then Dale, who was only six at the time, asked Jesse about her sign. She was Scorpio, the scorpion. He looked at the picture of her sign and felt sorry for her. A scorpion didn't sound like a good sign. It stung people and was poisonous. He asked about his dad and sister. Jesse said Blackie was Leo, the lion. Dale envied his father his sign. He thought the lion was the best sign of the twelve. Jesse then said June May was Virgo. Dale asked, Virgo what? Jesse changed the subject.

Dale glanced at the wall clock and noted with surprise that it was almost eleven. He'd slept much later than usual.

"Where'd Dad go?"

Jesse looked up from her paperback and said she didn't know.

"You don't know?"

Jesse shook her head.

"He didn't have to go to work, did he?"

Sometimes in the past Blackie traded with another ranger for different days off, but he stopped doing that when he made sergeant.

Jesse resumed reading her book and said, "I don't know where the hell he is."

Dale shrugged. He wasn't in the mood to listen to Jesse rant about Blackie. They never got along now. Their marriage was like a strange weather pattern that only had gathering dark clouds, thunder, lightning, and a storm. Then, after a brief lull, another round of the same. Never any sunshine.

Dale started to walk out of the room when Jesse asked him if *he* knew where Blackie was.

"What do you mean?" asked Dale.

"You know what I mean, mister."

"No, I don't."

"Your daddy never tells you nothin'?"

"He never tells me anything about his personal business, if that's what you mean." As soon as Dale said it, he knew he'd made a mistake.

"Personal business? What does that mean?"

"Nothing. Just an expression."

"Do you know if your daddy has *personal* business?"

"It's just an expression. I meant stuff like hunting, fishing, and playing cards and –" Dale suddenly realized that Jesse liked doing those things, too, and in fact used to do them with Blackie. "I mean, he doesn't tell me anything."

"Uh-huh," Jesse said, putting aside the astrology book.

Dale thought he'd try changing the subject. "So, where's Junie?"

"She's baking a cake."

Dale wondered for a moment if his mother was losing her marbles again. He looked at her. Her eyes didn't have that peculiar shine to them. Maybe she was making a joke. Although that would be a first.

"Baking a cake, huh? Well, she must be doing it in the bathroom because she's not in the kitchen."

"I reckon she's missing, too, then."

"Did June May and Dad go somewhere together?"

"Now, why would they do that?"

His mother had a point. "So where is she?"

"She walked to the store," said Jesse. There was a 7-11 a couple of blocks away. "To get some baking powder for her cake."

So, June May really was baking a cake. Dale thought that rather strange, too. She had inherited Jesse's baking prowess, which meant she probably would be better off buying a Jiffy cake mix.

"She's making one from scratch?"

"I s'ppose so."

"Who is she making the cake for?" Dale knew she wouldn't make a cake, especially one from scratch, for one of them.

"For some boy. For his birthday. Marvin, I think his name is."

"Marvin?" Dale had never heard of a Marvin. Except Lee Marvin, but Jesse didn't mean him. "Do you mean Martin? Martin Dewberry?"

"That's the one."

Dale knew him. He played basketball and ran track. Dale recalled last spring seeing him run the 880 with his shaggy-dog hair flopping. Dale didn't like him much. He never had. It wasn't just his hair; Rusty had long hair that flopped when he ran, too. What Dale especially didn't like about Dewberry was that he pretended to be smart when he wasn't. He often misspoke. For example, he'd say "irregardless," when he should say "regardless." And Dale remembered Dewberry talking snidely about Thea once. She'd asked him to the Gopherette banquet, and Dewberry had turned her down. Dale had overheard him say dismissively that Thea wasn't good-looking enough for him. Dale didn't like June May getting involved with "Marty."

"Great. I thought she wasn't allowed to date any boys until she was sixteen."

"She'll be sixteen soon."

"Not until next September."

"Well, that's not so far off."

Dale didn't like the idea that his little sister was more socially advanced than he was. When he was fifteen, he couldn't even work up the nerve to say hello to the opposite sex.

"I don't think she should bake a cake for a boy until she's sixteen," said Dale. "Or better yet, not until she can bake one that's edible."

Jesse didn't get the joke. After putting away her book, she'd lit a cigarette. Now, she exhaled a plume of smoke in Dale's general direction. He waved the acrid stuff away.

"All right," he said, "I'm going."

"Where to? To find your daddy?"

"No, to my room to watch football."

Jesse nodded, sucked in more smoke, and kept it inside for so long that Dale wondered if she'd developed some other way of expelling it. Finally, it streamed out of her nostrils.

Dale walked out of the living room and as he did he heard a car pull up in the driveway. He went to the door, opened it, and saw Blackie getting out of his Olds along with June May. She cradled a brown paper sack.

"About time you got up," Blackie said.

"Yeah, I've been up since eight," said June May.

"That's cause you still watch cartoons," said Dale.

"I do not!" She opened the door and as she brushed by she stuck her tongue out at him.

"Naw, you're too *mature* to watch cartoons."

"I never got to sleep late when I was a boy," said Blackie, entering the house.

"I know. You had to get up at four to milk the cows."

"No, I had to get up to shovel cow shit."

Dale shook his head in disgust at his father's scatological humor. "Mom said she didn't know where you went."

"I told her when I was walking out the door."

"She said she didn't know."

Dale gave his father a longer look than usual, and Blackie stared back.

"Well, she's got an active imagination," Blackie said, glancing over to June May at the kitchen counter.

"I told her that you probably just went out for a cup of coffee or something."

Blackie continued to stare. Dale noticed his dark eyes narrowing. The look reminded him in an unpleasant way of Comingdeer.

"Why would I do that? We have coffee here. Of course, you don't drink coffee, do you, boy?"

He didn't like the way Blackie said boy. "No, I don't drink coffee." He didn't like the bitter taste. "But you like coffee. You drink a lot of coffee."

Blackie closed the door. "Why are you trying to get under my skin?"

Dale thought he could tell Blackie that he'd seen him that night with that woman at the coffee shop. He wondered what would happen if he did tell him. But he chickened out. Besides, it wouldn't do any good to confront him. If Jesse overheard, she'd throw a fit and they'd get into it and maybe Blackie would throttle her again. Dale wondered if he could stop Blackie now. He was still three inches shorter and maybe twenty pounds lighter than his father. And he didn't have Blackie's ferocity, although Dale increasingly thought it was mostly bluster.

"I'm not," Dale said, turning away from his father. "I'm just teasing."

Blackie called after Dale as he walked away. "Better remember that I don't like being teased."

Dale closed the door to his room, walked over and flipped on the TV, sat down and watched the Sooners play Kansas. He loved the Sooners. They'd achieved back-to-back undefeated seasons. They ran the wishbone to perfection. They played the game the way it was supposed to be played.

## Chapter 5: *Sinning in speech class; Ellison game; Blackie walks*

Dale had forgotten to read the assignment. Ordinarily, it might not have mattered much. But this time he'd forgot to read his speech class assignment. From the Bible.

He sat at his desk in the back and listened as Mrs. Page went from student to student asking if they'd read the first chapter from *Ecclesiastes*. So far, each student had said yes.

Dale hated to disappoint Mrs. Page. She and Mrs. Heath were the two best teachers he'd ever had. Mrs. Page might chastise him in front of the whole class. She was very good at that. She didn't yell, she just fixed the malefactor with her sharp, intelligent eyes and gave him a disapproving look that made the student wither.

The fact that the assignment was from the Bible compounded the transgression. If Dale had forgotten to read a chapter from the textbook or even from *Our Town* or another one of Mrs. Page's favorite plays, then his oversight might have been tolerated. But the Bible? He felt he'd not made a mistake so much as sinned.

Mary Jane said yes. Amanda said yes. Becky said yes. Mrs. Page continued to work her way to Dale.

He could lie. Mrs. Page hadn't asked for any evidence. She hadn't required a report or anything. As far as he could tell, he could say yes and get away with it.

Mrs. Page finally came to Dale. "Audie Smith," she said, her eyes focused on her grade book.

Dale wavered. Lying would be easy. He'd told a few lies before. He'd sort of lied to his mother just last week about Blackie's personal business. He could lie again.

"No," he said.

Mrs. Page looked up. Her acute, almost predatory eyes peered at him. Dale felt the attention of his classmates upon him, even though they all sat looking straight ahead at Mrs. Page.

"I'm disappointed that you didn't read the assignment, Audie," she said. "But I commend you on being honest about it."

Dale felt his face burning. Her compliment embarrassed him more than her criticism. He didn't know why he'd told the truth. It just popped out of him. Maybe he just didn't want to tell a lie to someone he respected.

Mrs. Page worked her way down the other row of desks. All the kids said yes. Then she came to Matt Jones, who sat in the back across from Dale. He said no.

Mrs. Page paused, looked at Matt who sat in his usual dignified way that Dale called his "Buddha" look, then she smiled slightly, and proceeded to call the last few names.

Dale glanced over to Matt. A slight grin crossed his lips and Dale matched his subtle expression. Dale liked Matt. Unlike most of the high school kids he knew, Matt had an understated manner about him. Dale didn't think it had anything to do with his being half-Japanese. Matt was just naturally calm and perceptive. He'd met Matt's mother once. She was a petite woman with a shy demeanor. She reminded Dale a little of the Japanese geisha doll that Blackie had given Jesse years ago when he came back from Japan. The doll sat in their bedroom and as a kid Dale had examined it and found its delicate features and tiny hands and feet interesting. The doll wore a red kimono and her black hair was rolled up and held in place with wooden sticks.

Dale didn't usually have any interest in dolls, except to behead and dismember them. Once he'd captured June May's Barbie doll and tied her to a homemade stake and burned her. June May had cried hysterically as if the doll were a real person. But the geisha doll enticed Dale in some curious way. Jesse always told him to keep his hands off it. It wasn't for play, just for looking.

Mrs. Page began discussing *Ecclesiastes*. Dale remembered why he'd forgotten to read the assignment. He'd been busy reading *Invisible Man*. Not the book about the invisible guy, but the one about the colored guy. He'd seen the novel in the library and remembered that Ralph Ellison had been born in Oklahoma. Since Galilee's football team was going to play Ralph Ellison High on Friday, he was curious about Ellison's only novel. So far, he liked the book. Dale knew he didn't quite understand some important ideas, and the book was a little hard to read, but he liked the idea that the narrator was metaphorically invisible. Dale understood that feeling, even though he wasn't colored.

Ralph Ellison High used to be called something else. Dale tried to remember. Something like Jiggstown. Then again, maybe that was the disparaging nickname some guys called it. Anyway, the school changed its name a couple of years ago to honor Ralph Ellison. The school's nickname was the Scribes. He didn't know what that meant so he'd looked it up. It meant writers, but more in the old sense, like monks used to be. He thought it was an interesting name, except that it didn't seem very athletic.

The class bell rang and instead of rushing out of the room like he usually did, Dale sat at his desk and flipped through *Invisible Man*. He thought the book's narrator called himself different kinds of names and he wondered why the school didn't use one of them for its nickname. So, he checked. Ectoplasm. Spook. Phantom. No, he guessed those names wouldn't do.

Dale sensed someone standing before his desk and when he looked up he saw Amanda. Seeing her stunned him. He forced his heart to start beating again and looked at her face. He noticed she had a puzzled but interested expression as if Dale were an exotic animal that she'd once seen and now she was trying to recall where. She reached into her purse and pulled out a small, white New Testament. She offered it to him.

"I thought maybe you didn't read the Bible assignment because you didn't have one."

She smiled a little and Dale felt entranced by her full lips and that enticing groove between her upper lip and nose. He broke off his gaze and looked at the Bible. He started to reach for it, then stopped.

"No, I have a Bible. I just forgot."

"Oh," Amanda said.

"Besides, that's only the New Testament." He nodded at the Bible that Amanda still extended in her hand.

"Oh, yes, you're right," she said, smiling now out of embarrassment. "I guess this wouldn't help with *Ecclesiastes*."

Dale smiled his small, shy smile. "No, it wouldn't."

She put the Bible back in her purse and Dale stood up. He noticed with some satisfaction that he was a couple of inches taller than she. Still, he wished he were taller. They walked slowly out of the classroom. He surprised himself by not feeling as intensely shy as he used to feel. He looked at Amanda and thought she was the one who seemed shy. She swung her purse by its strap and wouldn't quite look him in the eye. They exited the classroom and Dale noticed Mary Jane stood down the hall waiting for Amanda.

"Well, I better go," she said.

Dale nodded, trying to hide his disappointment. Amanda paused and bit her lower lip. He'd observed she did that when she was nervous.

"I just wanted to say your honesty was refreshing even if your behavior wasn't."

She smiled again, then turned and walked over to Mary Jane. The two girls left together and Dale watched them, glad that Amanda had a fuller figure than the lithe Mary Jane. Then he thought of Amanda's words. He wasn't sure if she had been complimenting or criticizing him. He guessed a little of both. He felt a warm glow spreading in his face. He walked over to the yearbook office that was down the hall from Mrs. Page's classroom. He noticed the door stood slightly ajar. He pushed it open and saw Linda sitting at her desk looking through invoices. She glanced up and smiled.

"What happened to you?" she asked.

Dale asked what she meant.

"You're smiling. I mean, actually smiling."

Dale hadn't been aware of that. Linda often made fun of his stoical demeanor. She was just the opposite, frank and open with her feelings, just like Wendy.

"Now you're not," said Linda.

Thinking of Wendy had sobered him. He sat down and looked at Linda, who stared at him, no doubt wondering the cause for his sudden shift in mood. Before she could ask another question, the other staff members arrived. The yearbook staff met during sixth hour and with the arrival of Carrie and Carmen, the three girls forgot about Dale and immediately became engaged in their usual deep conversation about feminine concerns.

The Gophers played the black school from the City, Ellison, tough but in the end the Scribes had too much talent and won, 20-12. Dale had scored one rushing touchdown and intercepted a pass. He'd also hurt his right hand when a big lineman stepped on it. He and his teammates had played perhaps their best game of the season but Ellison simply had too much speed and size for the smaller and slower Gophers.

On the way back to the high school, the players didn't sulk in silence. The season was over and as they thought about their last game, they realized they had played pretty well. Ellison ordinarily would have beaten them by twenty points; but Galilee had outhustled and outhit them and stayed in the game. Heck, Dale thought, they almost won.

"I guess you were right," Chris said.

"About what?"

"About not being as good as last year."

Dale had almost forgotten about that prediction. Well, it made sense. They didn't have a stud like Terry Harte. Still, he thought 6-4 wasn't too bad. It wasn't as impressive as last year's 8-2 regular season record, but it was a lot better than what it used to be.

"Remember winning only one game in ninth grade?" asked Dale.

Chris nodded, then smiled. "Yeah, we were really crummy."

"We're not crummy anymore."

But somehow that wasn't enough, thought Dale. Once you get good, you expect to get better. This season was disappointing no matter how he looked at it.

After showering and getting dressed, Dale, Chris, and Matt walked out of the locker room and stood outside feeling that odd feeling of a season ending. For Dale and Chris, they'd never again leave the locker room after playing a football game. Dale felt a nostalgic melancholy come over him. His hand still hurt, too. He hadn't even bothered asking Dorfman to look at it. No blood, no worry.

Matt, who seemed unusually dejected, said see ya later, and Chris and Dale nodded. Chris said some of the seniors were going over to West Oaks. The restaurant was staying open late as a special occasion for the last game of the season. Chris was taking Carrie and Dale waited for Chris to tell him Carrie was a nice girl, but he didn't. Maybe he was hoping for the opposite. If so, Dale figured Chris was bound to be disappointed.

Chris spotted Carrie in the parking lot and said he'd see Dale at West Oaks. Wendy was talking to her fellow cheerleaders at the courtyard. He walked over. When she saw him, she said goodbye to Mary Jane, Roxanne, Carmen, and Becky. She met him at the sidewalk and they turned and walked to his car.

Rusty walked by. He said "Sm-m-m-ith," in one of his goofier voices and smiled. He was in a good mood. Football season was over. Basketball season would soon start. Dale turned and watched him greet Becky. He understood why Rusty liked her. She was tall and slender with long, auburn hair and a pretty face. Dale thought she looked a little like Mary Jane but with a more conventionally pretty face. Dale knew Matt Jones had been dating Becky. He wondered how Matt was taking the new competition.

"I thought Becky was dating Matt," he said.

"She was. But not anymore." Wendy put her hand on Dale's arm as they walked to his car. "I'm glad we don't have those kinds of problems."

"What kinds of problems?"

"The problems of wanting to date other people."

Dale opened the car door for her. He didn't say anything as he closed it a little too hard.

Dale knew something was wrong as soon as he saw Blackie's Olds missing from the driveway. He parked on the curb and went inside the dark house. He saw light coming from under the door of his sister's bedroom. As he walked by, she came out. Dale knew by the red rims of her eyes that she'd been crying.

"Daddy and Momma had a big fight," June May said, "and he left."

Dale told her not to worry. He'd be back soon.

"No," June May said, her lower lip trembling, "he said he was moving out."

Dale looked down the hall to his parent's bedroom. The door was closed and no light shone underneath the door.

"Is she asleep?"

June May nodded. "After Daddy left, she went in there and didn't come out."

Dale told June May to go back to bed. Everything would be all right. They'd had fights before.

"I think this one's different," she said as she closed the door.

He flipped on the hall light and walked to Jesse's bedroom door and slowly opened it. The weak light illuminated his mother's curled up body asleep on one of the twin beds. The room smelled funny. He sniffed and realized that it smelled of alcohol. Maybe she'd sleep late and he wouldn't have to wake up to more fighting. That is, if his father came home tomorrow.

Dale closed Jesse's door and went to his room. He felt more weary than sleepy. He sat down in the chair with the light off. He felt lonely. If Wendy wasn't already in bed, he would have gone back over there. He wouldn't have told her about his parents, though. He never talked about his home. Wendy had asked him a few times about his family but when he didn't say much, he guessed she got the message. She never asked again. He wondered how much she knew about his family. Wendy seemed to know a lot about a lot of people, but her interest and knowledge only seemed to include kids at school. He'd never heard her talk much about the parents of any of her friends. So he doubted she knew much about his home life and he hoped none of his other friends knew or cared about his family problems. The whole ugly situation was too humiliating for him to ever talk about.

Dale didn't even bother getting ready for bed. He just took off his cowboy boots, then flopped on his bed and fell quickly asleep just like a drunken man would.

The next morning, Blackie called and told Dale, who'd answered, that he wanted to see him. Dale walked to the end of the block as instructed and Blackie came by and picked him up. Blackie drove north and he and Dale sat in silence for a few minutes.

"Where are you staying?" Dale asked.

"In a motel until I find an apartment."

"So, you're really moving out? I mean, for good?"

Blackie didn't look at Dale. He stared at the road. They were heading out of town and the two-lane road didn't have much traffic on it.

"I'm not sure," Blackie said.

"Then why get an apartment?"

"Maybe I won't." He glanced from the road to Dale. "I saw your game last night."

Dale waited to be criticized.

"Your team played pretty well against those colored boys."

Dale felt surprised by both the qualified praise and Blackie using the word colored.

"Yeah, but we still lost."

"Yeah, well, you gave them a good game." Blackie glanced over. "How's your hand?"

Dale tried flexing his left hand. It hurt when he tried. "I don't know. I think I hurt it pretty good."

"Do you need to see a doctor?"

Dale looked at Blackie. He drove calmly, as if the two of them were going for a nice Saturday morning drive just for a chance to have a father and son chat. Dale knew why he was being nice to him. He really was going to move out for good.

"I don't know."

"Well, if you do, I'll take you to Tinker."

"I think I'll just try soaking it first. It feels better today than it did last night."

Blackie nodded. He turned the car around and drove back to the house. They didn't say anything for a few miles. Then Blackie said he wanted Dale to do him a favor.

"What?"

"I want you to pack some of my clothes. Not all of them, just what's hanging in the closet and what's in the dresser. Also, get all my textbooks. Then meet me at the end of the block tomorrow at noon. Can you do that?"

Dale said he could.

"Good. I only had time to pack my uniforms and get my gun last night."

Dale asked why he just didn't come in and get his own stuff. After all, it was still his house.

"I don't want to get into another argument with your mother."

"What's one more argument?"

"Because the next one might be the last."

Dale looked to see if his father was joking. But his face wore a grim expression.

"Okay. I'll get your stuff."

Blackie said good. He turned onto their street. He stopped the car and Dale started to get out.

"Dale," Blackie said.

He paused.

"We'll still see each other. You can come over when I get my place. You and June May."

Dale thought his father looked different. His face didn't look so dark and contemptuous as it usually did. His eyes even looked sort of sad.

"Sure," Dale said.

He got out of the car. He didn't bother watching Blackie drive off as he walked inside the house.

Dale felt strange. He'd played basketball every year since seventh grade, but not this year. Standing on the side of the court watching the varsity scrimmage, he felt a twinge of regret. He wasn't any good at basketball; because of the yearbook he didn't have any time for it. And yet, watching Rusty, Chris, Billy Joe, Erickson, Wally, and the other guys run up and down the court, he felt utterly left out.

He was in the gym to make sure the sophomore photographer, Mark Werhmeier, knew what he was doing when he took the basketball team and returning lettermen photographs. Dale didn't question Mark's skill. The kid knew photography inside and out. But Dale still worried about him. First, he might not show up. Second, he might want to take some odd kind of photograph, an "arty" one rather than just a plain old team photo. Dale wanted to use more unusual photos in the yearbook, but he thought team photos should be strictly journalistic.

The new basketball coach, Herbert Rayze, blew his whistle and told the team to go downstairs and change into their white home uniforms for the yearbook photo. Dale nodded at Rusty and Chris as they trotted by. Already, he felt a little distance between him and them. He ruefully thought the law of propinquity was already enforcing itself.

Coach Rayze came over and told Dale and Mark that the team would be ready in a few minutes. Then he walked out on the court, picked up a basketball, and shot a few jump shots. He missed four of five.

Dale was glad about one thing concerning his decision not to go out for basketball: he wouldn't have to play for a new coach. He missed Coach Carpenter, although he wouldn't have had much contact with him even if Coach had stayed at Galilee since Dale hadn't taken gym and wasn't playing basketball. But he felt the absence of Coach Carpenter just the same. He thought he was the best coach he'd ever had.

He'd heard from Matt Jones and Sam Mears that Coach Rayze was an easy teacher. He taught social studies and driver's ed. But most coaches were easy if not indifferent teachers. So far, Chris and Rusty seemed to like him. They said he wasn't the yelling kind of coach. He was low-key and friendly. He'd installed a new offense; a run and gun, one more suited to the short Gophers. The guys were excited about that. They expected to score a lot of points off fast breaks.

As Coach Rayze missed another jump shot, Dale thought he looked almost like a high school kid himself. He didn't know his exact age. He guessed around twenty-four. He'd coached the Cimarron City junior high team for two years after graduating from Galilee Nazarene College. His Cimarron City team did pretty well, so Dale guessed that was why he'd been offered the high school job at Galilee when Coach Carpenter went to Cimarron City to be assistant head coach of the varsity.

Rayze was of average height and slender. He had a nondescript face, except that Dale had noticed he had rather long, sandy-colored eyelashes. When he'd come over to talk to him and Mark, he'd closed his eyes for a moment and Dale noticed them. His eyelashes looked almost as long as a girl's and he obviously didn't put any stuff on them. Dale watched as he jogged down the court. He wore his dirty-blond hair long. It hung over his ears and over the back collar of his dress shirt. As he jogged down the court, Dale saw it flopping just like Rusty's did.

The basketball team returned wearing their game uniforms and Dale watched as Mark organized them for the photo. Mark took the stepladder he'd borrowed from Cookie and placed it at the top of the key, then climbed it to get a better angle for the team photo. Dale again felt the pang of not belonging.

After the team photo, Mark took pictures of the returning lettermen. Dale told him he wanted action shots, or at least the pretense of action shots. Get shots of them shooting or dribbling or defending, something more than just the standard mug shots.

While watching the shoot, Dale saw Dorfman walk into the gym. The coach waved without much enthusiasm in the direction of Rayze. He stopped beside Dale and watched the photographs being taken.

"You're so busy with this yearbook stuff you can't even work out," he said.

Dale glanced at Dorfman and saw him staring at him. Dorfman had wanted him to work out with the weight and conditioning guys since he wasn't playing basketball. He hadn't had time so far.

"I'll have more time after making this deadline. Then I'll join in."

"You better. The longer you wait the more out of shape you get."

Dale nodded.

"It'll just be that much tougher for you when track starts," Dorfman warned.

"I'll be in shape for the start of baseball," Dale said, deliberating not mentioning track just to annoy the coach.

"What baseball?"

Dale looked at him. "Our baseball. The high school team."

"We're not fielding a team this year. Or probably ever."

Dale stared at Coach. For a moment, he thought Dorfman was teasing him. But Dale had never seen a shred of evidence that he possessed a sense of humor. Realizing that Dorfman was completely in earnest, he felt like he'd been punched in the belly.

"The school board just decided a few weeks ago. We don't have the money or the coaching staff to field both a boys and girls track team and a baseball team."

"What girls track team?" Dale asked.

There had never been a girls track team. He knew the school had started a girls basketball team this season, but he didn't know the girls would also get to run track.

"The school has to offer girls sports," said Dorfman, although Dale could tell by the tone of his voice that he had as much disdain for that decision as Dale did. "Something has to go. It's baseball."

Dale felt the sting of injustice. "Why baseball?" he said more loudly than he intended.

"I just told you why. Galilee has to have sports for girls now. It's some kind of federal regulation. Cimarron City has had girls teams for a couple of years now. Next year, we're adding volleyball in the fall."

Dale thought this all sounded crazy. Cutting baseball in order to have girls' sports?

"Well, why not eliminate track?"

Dorfman looked at him as if he'd suggested Dorfman would look more attractive in a skirt and high heels.

"You've been sniffing chemicals in the darkroom if you think that, Smith."

Dale had been wrong. Coach did have a sense of humor. A warped sense of humor.

"Of course, you don't care about baseball," Dale muttered.

"No, I don't. And you shouldn't either anymore since it doesn't exist." Dorfman laid a big paw on Dale's shoulder. "Get over it, son. You'll be better off concentrating on track anyway. We're going to have an excellent team this year. But you had better stay in shape."

Dale nodded and heard Dorfman lumber down the stairs to his office in the locker room. Dale didn't even pay attention to the rest of the shoot. He gritted his teeth and wallowed in the mire of indignation. He'd been betrayed by Dorfman, by the school board, by the federal government, by everybody. He thought it was absolutely un-American not to have a baseball team. He could tolerate not having a wrestling team, but not baseball.

Mark sauntered over to him and said the photo shoot was a wrap. That was one of the things Dale didn't like about Mark. The way he used photographer slang in such a smug way. As Dale walked out of the gym with him, he glanced back at the basketball team. Now, he wished he'd gone out.

Wendy didn't share Dale's outrage over the elimination of the baseball team. She thought it was only right that girls got to play sports too.

"Why do girls need to play sports anyway?" asked Dale.

They were sitting in Wendy's yellow Volkswagen Beetle. She'd offered to drive Dale home since he didn't have his car. Jesse had wanted the Chevy. Now that Blackie had moved out, Dale had to share his car with his mother. He didn't tell Wendy the real reason why he didn't have his car. He just said the Olds was being repaired and his parents needed his car.

"Shouldn't girls be treated equally with the boys?" Wendy asked.

As a general proposition, Dale agreed. But he wasn't so sure when it came to something important like sports.

"Equal in what sense?"

"Equal in the sense that girls get to play, too. It isn't fair we haven't had sports of our own all these years."

"You want to play basketball? Run track?"

"I would if I wasn't cheerleading."

Dale wasn't surprised. He'd seen Wendy beat Wally in tennis. Of course, Wally was the slowest non-fat kid he'd ever seen. Still, he acknowledged that Wendy probably would be pretty good at sports. For a girl.

"But baseball. They're cutting baseball."

It was as if the school board had proposed removing flags from school or forcing all upperclassmen to eat at the school cafeteria. Dale felt appalled that Wendy didn't share his indignation.

"It's necessary to give girls sports equality," Wendy said.

Dale glared at her. She sounded like a politician. She'd learned too much at Girls State.

"If this is about real equality, then let's have the girls compete with the boys on the same teams."

"That's silly."

"Why? It would be equal, really equal. We all compete on the same team. Then we could keep baseball."

"Or have softball."

Dale almost said softball was for sissies but he didn't want to let Wendy evade the issue. "What about that? What about having true sports equality?"

"That wouldn't be fair," said Wendy.

"Why not?"

"It just wouldn't."

That was an example of a girl's definition of equality that exasperated Dale. Girls were all for equality but only when it worked to their advantage. Did Wendy register for the draft? No. Did Wendy pay for anything? No. She worked during the summer and made more money than Dale. But he still paid for their cheap dates. She blew her money on clothes and makeup and other feminine expenditures. All the banquets and royalty stuff was for the girls' benefit. Dale and the other guys didn't care about that nonsense. Girls had their own clubs like Future Homemakers of America and they still could join the boys' clubs like Key Club and Future Farmers of America, although only a couple had ever dared. All this equality stuff seemed like a ploy to allow girls to have even more than they had now. Dale ordinarily wouldn't have cared. He didn't like politics. But sports? Baseball? He cared about that.

"You haven't answered the question, Wendy," he said, using a prosecutorial voice that he'd heard while sitting on the Boys State supreme court during oral arguments; that is, when he'd paid attention. "Why wouldn't it be fair? In fact, isn't requiring boys and girls to compete equally for a spot on a sports team the exact definition of equality?"

Wendy stared at him, her green eyes tearing a little as they did when she got annoyed. "I suppose you have a point," she admitted, "but it still wouldn't be fair."

"And why not?"

"You know why not."

"Why?" Dale wanted her to say it.

"Because…" Wendy tried to think of an intellectually valid reason.

"Because the girls wouldn't get to play," Dale finished for her. "Isn't that the reason?"

Dale remembered with satisfaction back in grade school when the boys played the girls in kickball. The boys creamed them. In junior high, the boys easily beat the girls in softball, too.

"All right, yes, it is. And that wouldn't be fair."

"But it's fair to cut baseball. It's fair to take something away from the guys in order to be fair to the girls. In order to be *equal*."

"I don't know why you're getting so angry, Audie. You're really being something of a bully."

Dale thought she was getting a little angry, too, which surprised him.

"Why can't you see my point?" he said, knowing he said the words with such vehemence that it proved Wendy's point about him being a bully.

"I see your point; I just don't agree with it!"

Dale glared at her. She reminded him of Dorfman, of Blackie, of Mrs. Snow, of all the people that seemed unreasonable, selfish, and unfair. He yanked on the door handle and got out.

"Audie," he heard Wendy call, "where you going? Don't you want a ride home?"

Dale stormed through the parking lot. He liked hearing the gravel crunch underneath the heel of his boots. He heard the puttering sound of the Bug as it pulled up beside him.

"Don't be mad," Wendy called. "Get in. I'll give you a ride home."

The idea of getting a ride from a girl filled him with disgust. He'd walked home plenty of times before. He angrily thought about his silly mother wanting his car to drive to Hardees for coffee in the morning and then not using it for the rest of the day. Didn't matter if he needed the car. Didn't matter if the car sat parked in the driveway all day just because she didn't want to be "stuck" at home. What about him? It was his car. He despised the injustice of everything. And now baseball being cut because some girls wanted to play sports? Everything was going crazy.

"Come on, Audie," Wendy pleaded.

The Bug puttered beside Dale as he walked through the parking lot. He ignored Wendy's pleas. He didn't even look at her.

"All right, then," Wendy yelled. "Have it your way!"

She stepped on the gas and the little car zipped past Dale, throwing up puffs of dust that drifted in his face. He waved it away. He'd had worse things flung in his face.

The walk home didn't calm Dale. Every step he took he railed against the injustice of the universe. Wendy didn't understand how important baseball was to him. But she should have known. If she really cared for him she would have understood. She just said mushy things for the sake of feeling romantic. She didn't really know him at all. If she did, she'd understand that baseball was one of the most important things in his life. He'd been looking forward to playing his senior year. His last year. He'd probably wouldn't get to play organized baseball ever again. He didn't think he'd get to play baseball in college because he probably would have to work to pay for his tuition. Blackie hadn't said anything about helping him out. Blackie was too busy going to college himself to think about him. Dale tasted the bitterness of having a dream destroyed. He had imagined playing the best baseball of his life that spring. Now, he wouldn't get a chance to live out his dream.

He saw his Chevy parked in the driveway, just parked there, not doing a thing. He slammed open the house front door, hearing the knob crack the plaster of the wall. He marched into the house. He planned on telling his mother that the Chevy was his and he'd drive it to school if he wanted. He stormed into the living room and didn't see her. He went to her bedroom. Not there. He threw open June May's door. She screamed. She stood in her panties and bra before her mirror as she prepared to step into her new dress. Blackie had bought it for her as a way to expiate his guilt.

"Get out!" she yelled.

Dale quickly shut the door. His embarrassment cooled his anger. He heard June May wailing behind the door that he should *always* knock. She was going to buy a lock for her door. She was going –

Dale walked back into the living room. He couldn't figure out where Jesse was. The bathroom door wasn't closed. That left only the garage. He turned to check there when he saw her climbing the small, leafless tree in the backyard.

What the heck, he thought. He slid open the patio glass door and watched as his mother raised her shorter leg and tried putting it in the crook of the tree's trunk. Her hands clutched two branches above the crook. She tried hoisting herself up. But she couldn't make it. She looked like a short, pudgy cowgirl trying to climb on a tall horse.

"What are you doing?" asked Dale.

Jesse turned and smiled at him.

He went out and looked into her face. Her eyes didn't have that eerie glow to them, the look that told him she was about to change over into a lunatic. But she smiled at him in a peculiar way. He thought maybe she was just being eccentric rather than crazy.

"I used to climb trees when I was a little girl," she said. "I could climb them as good as the boys."

"Well, you shouldn't be climbing this one."

Dale looked at the pathetic tree. Blackie had planted it five years ago and the stunted thing had grown only to ten feet. It was the only tree in the backyard. Dale hadn't liked it. As a kid, it got in the way of him playing baseball and football. Now, he just felt sorry for it. It didn't keep its leaves for very long and it looked spindly and sad standing alone in the backyard.

"Let's go back inside," Dale said.

Jesse nodded and they walked back inside. She immediately resumed her usual behavior. She sat down on the couch and pulled a cigarette out of its pack. She lit it, breathed in its fumes, and looked at Dale with a strange equanimity.

"Have you spoken to your daddy recently?"

Dale said yeah. Blackie had called him a few days ago asking how his hand felt. Dale told him it was okay. It had been sore for a couple of weeks. Dale asked him how college was going. Blackie said fine. Just a typically friendly, wide-ranging conversation between father and son.

"Is he livin' by hisself?" Jesse asked.

Dale said he didn't know.

Jesse impressively blew out smoke from her nostrils. The smoke looped and curled in the air like skywriting. She looked almost thoughtful sitting there, smoking, staring into the air.

"A man shouldn't desert his family," she said.

"He hasn't deserted us."

Blackie sent them a check every couple of weeks. He paid all the bills. In fact, Blackie seemed even more conscientious than he had before in fulfilling his paternal responsibilities, at least in a monetary way.

"A man is s'pposed to provide and protect."

Dale didn't disagree. He'd been taught that. Jesse, in spite of growing up a tomboy and still liking to fish, hunt, and play pool, had always imparted traditional notions to Dale and June May. Jesse had never worked outside the home. While watching the news, he'd heard her once utter a rare comment about politics: she thought the women libbers were crazy.

Jesse grew silent and smoked the cigarette down to the end. Dale watched her for signs of mental instability. She looked fine. But her tree-climbing episode disturbed him. Would a sane woman do that?

"What are you looking at?" she asked, finally taking notice of him.

"Just seeing if you're all right."

Jesse opened her arms wide as if inviting his scrutiny. Then she resumed her contemplative posture. "I reckon that's a question you should ask your daddy."

Dale didn't know how to respond. He couldn't tell if she were being uncharacteristically astute or simply saying something to deflect his attention from her mental state. He decided she was fine for the time being. He said he was going to his room and Jesse nodded and when Dale closed his door he realized he'd forgotten to tell his mother he wanted his car back. Oh well, he thought, he'd let her have it for a while. He could walk.


## Chapter 7: *Musical Amanda; Blackie's presents; Dale's decision*

Dale picked up Wendy to take her to a Christmas concert in the City. Before he knocked on her door, she opened it, said good-bye to her mother, and grabbed Dale's arm as they walked to his car. Once in the car, Wendy told him about all the colleges she had applied to. Only state schools, she added, smiling at him.

Dale had thought about breaking up with Wendy after their argument of a month ago. But he hadn't. She'd called and apologized to him. She hadn't meant to make him mad. She knew he loved baseball. Maybe he was right to be angry about baseball being cancelled just to give girls a chance to run track. She apologized so completely and so sincerely that Dale didn't have the heart to break up with her. In fact, he felt churlish not begging her pardon. Wendy wasn't to blame for baseball being cut. None of the girls were at school. Maybe there were even a few girls in school who loved playing basketball or running track as much as he loved baseball, although he doubted it.

So they were back together, and they spent the next month going on their usual dates. But tonight's date was different. Rather than go to a movie or to West Oaks to eat or simply go over to Wendy's and watch TV, Dale was taking her to a fancy concert in the City. Well, it wasn't that fancy. It was only the Oklahoma City Youth Orchestra's annual Christmas concert held at the Oklahoma City fine arts center. Dale liked Christmas music and two Galilee students were playing in the orchestra, Isaac Gould and Amanda.

They arrived at the music hall and Dale and Wendy found their seats near the front in the middle section as the auditorium slowly filled. The musicians took the stage and tuned their instruments. Dale spotted Amanda right away. She was dressed in a red satin gown and wore her hair up. He'd never seen her without her hair loose and he found her new look compelling if not a little disturbing. It made her look more like a young woman than a girl, and Dale wasn't sure if he completely liked that because he still felt pretty immature himself.

"Look, there's Isaac," said Wendy, pointing to their classmate. Isaac served as concertmaster, the top violinist in the orchestra. "And there's Amanda."

Dale pretended not to be very interested. "Yeah," he said without any enthusiasm. Inside, however, he felt his heart thumping almost as if it were one of the percussive instruments in the orchestra.

Wendy held Dale's hand tightly as the orchestra played a series of light classical pieces associated with the holidays. Then the more religious Christmas songs like *O Holy Night*. Then they played some traditional carols. Throughout the concert, Dale watched Amanda. He followed her every move: watched how she pursed her lips and blew into her flute. Watched her delicate fingers tumble over the keys. Watched her smile slightly when her part wasn't in play.

251

Afterwards, Wendy wanted to congratulate them. Dale hesitated. He didn't really want Amanda to see him with Wendy although she obviously knew he was going steady with her. Wendy insisted so they moved forward to the stage, threading their way through exiting audience members. They stood close to the stage and waved at Isaac. He adjusted his glasses, smiled slightly, and waved his violin bow to acknowledge their praise. Then they moved down and Wendy called out to Amanda. Amanda saw them, smiled, and walked closer to the front of the stage.

"How nice of you two to come," she said.

Wendy said she played so well. And Amanda had such an attractive gown, too.

"Thank you," Amanda said graciously.

Dale stood silent, looking. He gazed at her as if trying to absorb every detail. He noticed she wore tiny earrings. A thin necklace encircled her slender neck and a small silver pendant of an angel hung at the hollow of her throat. Her blue eyes seemed to sparkle in the subdued light of the music hall. She wore lipstick, a creamy pink, and subtle splashes of other makeup.

Amanda sensed Dale staring and her eyes flickered over to him and looked him straight in the eyes before darting back to Wendy.

Wendy noticed Mary Jane standing in the front of the center section and said she wanted to say hi. She dashed off and left Dale still gazing at Amanda.

Amanda, a little flustered by his gaze, smiled and asked him how he liked the concert.

"Fine," he said.

He continued to stare at her. He'd never looked so long at a girl before. He didn't care if she thought him rude. He wanted to memorize every detail of her.

Amanda looked away and smiled uneasily. She reached a hand up to her face, then her hair, as if checking for some embarrassment.

"Is something wrong with me?" she asked, laughing out of nervousness.

"No," Dale said. "You're perfect."

He had spoken quietly, almost reverently. Amanda wasn't sure she heard correctly. She leaned forward a little, her mouth open just enough for Dale to see the white tips of her teeth.

"Pardon?" she said.

Dale didn't dare repeat his words. He just looked at her with the same longing as she stood on the stage, bent over a little, the soft light illuminating her while everyone else on stage seemed obscured in darkness and insignificance.

Before any more words could be exchanged, Wendy and Mary Jane appeared. Dale stepped aside as the three girls conversed. He didn't join in. He snuck glances at Amanda while the three of them talked and he noticed she glanced his way a few times.

The brief conversation over, the four exchanged good-byes. Dale and Wendy walked back to his car. As he opened the door for her, Wendy said Isaac played very well. "And Amanda played very well, too," she added.

Dale said she certainly did.

Christmas eve and Dale sat in his father's chair and read *A Christmas Carol*. Sitting on the couch watching television were June May and Jesse. They were watching *The Grinch Who Stole Christmas*. Dale wasn't interested. He liked it, especially the grotesque Grinch, but he'd seen it many times before. They showed it every year.

They heard a rapping at the door. Dale looked over to June May and Jesse but they kept watching television. Dale got up but before he left the living room, he heard the door open. He stopped and waited. Blackie came in, carrying three wrapped Christmas presents. They even had bows on them.

"You can open them now," Blackie said.

He put them on the coffee table instead of under the four-foot artificial tree that June

May had fished out of the hallway closet and put up. Dale didn't like the tree. It had silver fake tree limbs that were stuck in the holes in the cylinder-like trunk. The limbs had silver bristles that were supposed to resemble the leaves of an evergreen tree. June May had tied small red and green ornaments to the brushy fake limbs. The tree stood in the corner on an end table and looked absurdly out of place.

"We used to open presents on Christmas Day," said Jesse.

"Why wait until then?" Blackie said. He motioned for them to open them. "Go on, June May, Dale."

June May reached over and picked up the package with her name scrawled on a card. She quickly unwrapped it. She opened the box and pulled out a red and white sweater with sewn-on reindeers frolicking over the chest.

"Oh." June May forced a smile on her face. "Thank you, Daddy."

Dale knew she considered the gift a kid's kind of sweater. She would have preferred a cashmere sweater with a plunging neckline.

"You're welcome," said Blackie.

Dale opened his gift. He tore open the wrapping and pulled the box apart and lifted up a new baseball glove.

"Thanks, Dad."

"It's a Joe Morgan model. Especially made for infielders. I thought your old glove was looking a little ragged."

Dale hadn't told Blackie about the high school eliminating baseball as a varsity sport. The glove was nice, though. Joe Morgan, a short but dynamic second baseman for the Cincinnati Reds, was one of his favorite players.

Blackie looked at Jesse. "Ain't you going to open yours?"

Jesse didn't exactly scowl at Blackie, but her expression clearly said she hadn't completely forgiven him. Blackie had called a few days ago wanting to come back home. Dale had been surprised. He thought his father was gone for good. He was even more surprised when Jesse said he could return.

Jesse unwrapped the small box, revealing a purple jewelry case. She opened it and removed a silver cigarette lighter.

"It's real silver," said Blackie.

Jesse considered the gift. She held it in her palm and rubbed the smooth surface with her small fingers.

"Why don't you try it?" Blackie said.

Jesse reached for a half-smoked cigarette from the ashtray, put it to her mouth, flipped open the lid, and flicked the small wheel of the lighter with her thumbnail. Immediately, a small flame burst into view. She nodded, lowered her cigarette to the flame, and puffed.

She flipped the lid down, extinguishing the flame. She took a couple more puffs, then said, with the cigarette dangling out of the corner of her mouth, "it lights real good."

June May frowned. "Daddy, we didn't get you nothing."

Blackie took possession of his favorite chair. He sat down and tugged off his dress shoes. "That's all right, honey. I don't need any presents."

Dale saw Jesse start to say something – something critical, no doubt – but instead she blew smoke out of her nostrils.

"But you oughta get something," June May said.

"Well, I did get a present of sorts." Blackie waited until all of them turned his way. "I got a promotion."

"To lieutenant?" Dale asked.

"That's right," said Blackie. "And when the chief retires in a few years, he said he's going to recommend me as his successor. Of course, that means the city council will have to appoint me."

"You're going to be chief of the rangers?" Dale asked.

"Yeah, eventually."

In spite of his lingering resentment for his father, Dale was impressed. He didn't know much about his dad's job because Blackie hardly ever talked about it. But chief of anything sounded pretty important.

"That's good," said Dale.

"Yeah, Daddy, that sounds really good," said June May.

Jesse took the cigarette out of her mouth. "Whattaya get?"

Blackie waved his hand, dismissing such a trivial question. "That's not so important. It's the satisfaction of getting ahead. Of being recognized for doing a good job."

"Uh-huh," said Jesse.

Dale was used to Blackie's vagueness about his job. He never talked about how much money he made or what benefits he got or anything like that. He didn't like being asked about it either.

"Well, maybe we should celebrate," Blackie said.

Jesse crushed the smoked cigarette in the ashtray. She reached for another, then after putting it in her mouth, tried her lighter again. She looked at it favorably when it instantaneously produced a flame on the first flick.

"Whattaya have in mind?" she asked.

"I ran into Dewey and Pearl and I suggested their coming over for some poker and beer."

"Oh, Daddy, it's Christmas Eve," said June May.

"What were you planning for Christmas Eve?"

"Nothing," June May said with a pout.

"You can still watch TV. We'll play in the kitchen."

June May frowned.

"You can make us some popcorn. Maybe we'll let you sit in for a few hands."

"Really?" June May said, brightening.

"She's too young for cards and beer," said Jesse.

"I didn't say anything about beer for her." Blackie looked at his son. "You're old enough, Audie Dale, to join us."

The idea of joining the four of them as they played poker and drank beer did not appeal to him. "No thanks."

"Suit yourself," said Blackie. He turned to Jesse. "What do you say?"

"I don't mind," she said, the fresh cigarette in her mouth.

Blackie stood up and rubbed his hands. He said he'd go call Dewey and tell him to come over around eight. He walked into the kitchen to the wall phone. June May scampered off the couch and followed him.

Dale wondered why Blackie was trying so hard. When Jesse told him that Blackie was returning home, he thought maybe it had to do with Christmas. He'd heard that people, even those like his father, got lonely during the holidays. He'd read that more people commit suicide then. Now, Dale had another theory. Maybe Blackie's return and his unusual cheeriness had to do with his promotion and the promise for yet another. Maybe Blackie thought it would look better for the prospective chief of the rangers to be living with his family.

Dale told Jesse he'd be in his room. She nodded, still looking with approval at her new lighter. Dale walked down the hall to his room holding the Dickens story in his hand. He sat down in the old chair and thought about finishing the story. He wasn't in the mood. He flipped the booklet on the floor and stared at the blank television screen.

A day before New Year's, it snowed. Every now and then it snowed in Galilee during the winter, but usually just a dry, almost dusty coating that blew away or melted in a day or two. This time the snow fell steadily all night and part of the morning. When Dale awoke, he looked out the window and stared in wonder at the thick layer of snow covering everything. The last time he'd seen so much snow was the winter when he was in second grade in Rhode Island.

Dale got dressed and drove to the high school. He'd convinced Mrs. Schoendienst to give him a key so he could get into the high school over the holidays and work on the yearbook. He opened the back door exit of the building, not too far from the yearbook office. Before going to the office, he first walked through the halls of the deserted, gloomy building. He listened to his footsteps echo. He liked the feeling of being the only one in the school. He felt like an explorer or maybe an archeologist visiting the ruins of some great past civilization. He liked the idea that he alone was in a place that was usually full of people. It made him feel that he knew something about the school that no one else knew. He knew how quiet it could be.

He had brought his camera and after working several hours in the yearbook office, he went outside and took photos of the school shrouded in snow. Thick, wet clumps of snow clung to the boughs in the trees. It blanketed the benches and the brick landmarks. It made the school look unfamiliar and almost mysterious. He took photos until his roll of film ran out.

Dale took the last picture of the courtyard outside the entrance to the school. The snow contrasted dramatically with the red brick and the red benches. He knew the red would show as black in a black-and-white photo. As he snapped the last picture, he realized that this coming semester would be his last in this building. And he knew he didn't want it to be like the others had been. He wanted it to be better. He'd already started taking his studies more seriously. He studied and had made straight A's for two semesters in a row, but more importantly he tried to learn at a deeper level than just learning to make a good grade. Whether the subject was literature or history or psychology, he wanted to do more than learn; he wanted to understand. He liked feeling his mind develop, but he wanted to develop in additional ways. He wanted to assert himself intellectually, physically, and emotionally. He wasn't sure what all that entailed, but he knew he only had one more semester to find out.

"Why are you doing this to me?" Wendy asked, tears streaming down her cheeks. "What have I done?"

Dale said she'd done nothing. He just didn't want to go steady anymore.

"But why? I thought you loved me."

Wendy started crying so hard that Dale thought people walking through the parking lot would hear.

He waited until her wails subsided to sobs. "You know I care about you," he said, careful not to use *that* word, "but it's time for us to take a break for a while."

"But I don't want to," she said, her voice muffled from burying her face into her hands.

"I'm sorry," Dale said.

Wendy removed her hands and stared at Dale with her tear-stained face. Her pale skin looked blotchy and red. The rims of her eyes were red, too. "Do you want to see other girls? Is that it?"

"I don't know."

He looked out the side window of his car. Snow still covered the parking lot. He'd asked her to meet him here after school. He thought they would have a little privacy.

"You *do*," Wendy said. She wiped her nose with her fingers. Dale searched his pockets for a handkerchief or a Kleenex. He didn't have any with him. "That's what this is all about," she said and burst into another round of sobs.

Dale sighed. He couldn't believe how hard and long she could cry. He reached over and opened the glove compartment. He grabbed several napkins and gave them to her. Still sobbing, Wendy took them and pressed a couple against her face. The napkins immediately became soaked with her tears.

He stared out the window again. He saw some kids walking past his car, kids he didn't know well. He heard Wendy's crying ebb for a moment, then heard her blow her nose. She started weeping loudly again.

"What have I done?" she wailed.

Dale felt sick inside. He knew this would be difficult, but he didn't know it would be this painful for both of them.

"You haven't done anything wrong. It's just time to take a break."

"You keep saying that," Wendy said, now her voice less woeful and more accusatory, "but I don't know what that means."

Dale noticed that the front window and Wendy's side window were fogged up. He was glad. The fog would hide Wendy from people's prying eyes.

He sighed and leaned back against the seat. He felt cold. He tightened his letter jacket around him and stared out the frosted window. He listened to Wendy's crying grow quieter, then she made loud, stuttering sounds before lapsing into sobs.

Dale looked at her. He felt nauseous. He felt sweat on his forehead even though he still felt cold.

"I wish you wouldn't cry so," he said softly.

"I can't help it!" she cried, looking at him and gasping for breath. "It hurts so much."

Dale reached for her and she collapsed into his arms. He slipped an arm around her and hugged her and her weeping grew quieter. He didn't know what to say. Everything he thought sounded banal. He did want to date other girls; well, just one girl. He thought it was time to try. This was his last semester in high school and he'd hate himself if he didn't at least try. But he knew he couldn't tell Wendy any of this.

He held her until she stopped crying and instead just made whimpering sounds. She took more napkins and blew her nose again. She laid her head against his chest and asked him how long the break would last.

"I don't know."

She didn't start weeping again. Dale figured she had cried herself out. She raised her head from off his shoulder and looked at the opaque windshield.

"I don't feel well," she said quietly.

"Do you want me to walk you to your car?"

She shook her head no. She kept her face forward and even in profile he could see her eyes were incredibly puffy. She reached for Dale's nearest hand and squeezed it. Without looking at him, she opened the door and slipped outside. She shut the door too softly; it didn't close all the way.

Dale turned around in the seat to watch her walk away. But the back window had fogged, too. He heard the soft tread of Wendy's shoes on the gravel for a few seconds and then silence.

## Chapter 8: *Test scores; basketball homecoming; Jesse*

Seniors were whispering in the halls. Seniors were whispering in class. Some were visibly upset. Most of them had received their college entrance exam results, the ACT, and the senior hallway and classrooms were abuzz.

Dale got his a couple of days ago. He'd done pretty well. He'd scored twenty-eight overall. He'd done best on the social studies and science sections, scoring thirty on both. His worst section, unsurprisingly, was math. He'd only scored twenty-two. He did quite well on the arithmetic questions; it was the algebra and geometry questions he didn't know. He'd never taken geometry and only guessed at the questions about angles and circles and pi.

Vern did well. He scored thirty overall. Erickson also scored thirty. Wally scored twenty-three, but his mediocre English score brought down his other impressive scores. Isaac, of course, scored highest of all with a perfect score of thirty-six.

Bonita scored highest among the girls. She got a twenty-nine, one point higher than Dale, which sort of annoyed him. Carrie did well; she got a twenty-four. Carmen got a twenty-two. Wally said Wendy scored a twenty-four. He could hardly say her score without an edge of resentment in his voice. He hated it when Wendy outperformed him, even if it was by a point.

But the real surprise concerning the exams was that many of the college-bound seniors had done much worse than expected, including some students who made good grades. Chris scored only nineteen. K. C. got a sixteen. Mary Jane scored a seventeen. Gretchen's score was the lowest Dale had heard about, an anemic twelve.

A few seniors who were expected to go to college, including Rusty, hadn't taken the December exam. But Amanda had and Dale hadn't heard her test score yet. She wasn't in his first-hour senior English class; she, along with Mary Jane, Wendy, Rusty, and Chris, took Mrs. Snow's newspaper class instead.

The class bell sounded and Dale walked to the locker he shared with Rusty and Chris. His two friends were already there, grabbing their books for their second-hour history class that Dale also had. When Rusty saw Dale, he pointed to all the glum-faced seniors milling around.

"It's only a test, man," he said, showing his typical indifference to standardized tests, even though he always scored high. "You'd think they got a prison sentence or something."

Rusty clapped Chris on the shoulder and gave him a friendly shove. Chris looked at Dale with a sorrowful countenance. "Only a nineteen," he whispered.

Dale said not to worry about it. Maybe Chris could retake the test. He'd heard a few seniors were going to.

"I don't think so. It's high enough to get into GNC." Chris referred to Galilee Nazarene College. "I guess I have to get used to being just average. Average in sports, average in grades, average in tests, and average with girls."

Ninteen was actually a little higher than average, Dale thought, but he didn't interrupt his friend's doleful recitation. He realized it might be more difficult to be average than below average. Maybe the average students were so close to being good that they more keenly felt the gap. A lot students in Dale's class didn't even take the ACT. Most of the boys, including Sonny, Leroy, Billy Joe, and Quentin, didn't bother. They weren't going to college. Many of the girls, including Roxanne, Merry, and Peggy, didn't take the exam either.

"What did Bigelow get?" Dale asked Chris.

"I don't know," he said quietly. "He hasn't said. So it must be low."

Dale tried not to smile.

Down the hallway he heard some commotion and turned and saw a couple of sophomores invading senior territory, but the two boys quickly turned around and left. But what caught Dale's eye next was more interesting: Mary Jane and Amanda hugging. It looked like the two girls were comforting each other. He strained to see more clearly. He stood on his tiptoes to look over the heads of the taller boys. He saw the two girls hug, then separate but still holding each other's arms. They quietly talked before separating completely. When Amanda turned so Dale could see her face fully, he saw she'd been crying a little. She wiped away a few tears from her cheeks with a fingertip and he felt a pang of sympathy mingled with a jolt of desire. He leaned against his locker as if suddenly stricken ill and Chris asked him what was wrong.

"Nothing," Dale said. He watched as Amanda walked away with Mary Jane and Gretchen. He stood up straight and nudged Chris. "What's wrong with them?"

Chris looked down the hall at the retreating three girls. "Oh. They got scores even lower than me. Well, except Amanda. She got a twenty."

Dale recognized the tone in Chris's voice. It was the same slight note of resentment that he'd heard in Wally's.

Dale saw Wendy staring at him from down the hall. Ever since he'd broken up with her, she continued to gaze at him from a distance. She always had a wounded look on her face. If Dale had made a mask of woe with one of his clay faces, it would have looked a lot like Wendy.

Wendy turned away and shuffled off to her class. Dale felt sorry for her. He knew she was suffering. He wished she wouldn't look at him like that though. He knew she couldn't hide her emotions like he could. Already the girls in school were clucking sympathetically over Wendy and giving him accusatory glances.

Dale shut the locker and he and Chris walked to history. Twenty wasn't so bad, he thought. Why would that upset Amanda? Maybe she was more upset for Mary Jane and Gretchen. That's how she was, thought Dale. More concerned about her friends than herself. Amanda made good grades. She had one of the highest grade point averages in the class, maybe the fourth ranked. At least that was what Mr. Smedley had told him, although Dale wasn't sure he could rely upon Mr. Smedley's accuracy. Dale's class rank, because he'd made C's in driver's ed and algebra, was ninth. When he made his C in algebra, he had been so ignorant that he hadn't even known freshman year counted. He now wished he'd taken his studies more seriously sooner. He could be ranked in the top tier along with Isaac, Bonita, Wendy, Amanda, Mary Jane, and Carrie.

Dale sat down at his desk in history. Since the teacher, Mr. Braddock, was quite accomplished at being boring, Dale's thoughts quickly turned to Amanda. He wanted to comfort her. He wanted to tell her that twenty wasn't so bad. What was the ACT anyway? An arbitrary examination that measured only how well you did on an isolated set of questions. He nodded. That sounded pretty good. He wasn't sure if he believed it. After all, he got a twenty-eight. But he imagined telling her that to comfort her. He imagined something even more appealing: he imagined kissing away her tears.

Mr. Braddock, a fairly tall, flaxen-haired, young teacher that the girls thought looked a little like Robert Redford, asked Dale what the root cause of World War I was?

He hadn't been listening. "Turnips?"

Rusty burst out laughing. Chris shook his head and smiled. Mr. Braddock, however, was not amused.

Dale stood at the water fountain near the entrance to the gym watching the basketball homecoming ceremony. All five candidates, Mary Jane, Wendy, Gretchen, Carmen, and Becky Brown smiled as the spotlight hovered over them. Rusty and Billy Joe, the captains, stood awaiting the winner.

He thought Wendy, in spite of her smile, didn't look happy. Her eyes looked heavy-lidded like she was weary of the whole thing and wanted to go home and sleep. Chris, her escort, looked a little uncomfortable standing next to her. Dale wasn't sure why. Chris liked Wendy.

Dale glanced down at the front of the home bleachers where the pep club girls sat. He saw Amanda sitting on the front bleacher on the end. Dale thought that an advantageous position for what he had in mind. He moved closer in her direction and felt with his finger that his camera's power was on and that the flash was working.

Mr. Werhmeier's voice, resonant with amplification, said the 1975 Galilee High School Basketball Queen was ... Mary Jane Morgan.

The spotlight immediately targeted her and she smiled as the audience applauded. The pep band played a few bars of the school song as Wally relinquished Mary Jane to Billy Joe and Rusty. Billy Joe slipped the bracelet on Mary Jane's wrist, then quickly kissed her. He didn't kiss Mary Jane nearly as long as had kissed Roxanne during football homecoming; but then, Mary Jane's sometime-boyfriend, Rusty, stood by. Rusty then crowned her and to

Dale's surprise, gave her just a medium-length smooch. Dale had expected him to kiss her in an exaggerated, romantic way if for no other reason than to add a little comedy to the affair.

Dale felt happy for Mary Jane but disappointed for Wendy. He glanced at Wendy and saw her applauding like everyone else, a big smile on her face. She looked pleased now. He realized that maybe he'd been too critical of Wendy in the past. She really was a generous kind of girl. Mary Jane smiled and waved at the crowd as the photographers snapped her picture. Dale thought she must feel better now after being crowned homecoming queen after the disappointment with her test scores.

Dale noticed that Rusty had grown a couple of inches since last basketball season. He looked like he was as tall as Billy Joe, which meant he was six one. Erickson, at six feet two, was the tallest player on the team. Rusty had been right about the team needing a big man to play center. The basketball team had won its first game of the season a month ago and since then had proceeded to lose ten straight games. Coach Rayze's new offense wasn't working. He'd forgotten that a fast break team needed speed or at least quickness. Rusty, Chris, and Billy Joe had speed but Erickson and Wally were slow. The only junior who ran well was Matt Jones and he was only five nine. So, the Galilee team wasn't fast enough to compensate for their lack of height.

Another problem with the team was the coach. Rayze just didn't seem to exert any leadership on the team. Dale had seen Rusty arguing with him more than once. The team looked disorganized and, after the losses began to mount, dispirited.

Dale was now glad he hadn't gone out for basketball. He remembered from the not-so-long-ago past how unpleasant losing was. If he'd gone out, he'd just be sitting on the bench watching his teammates lose game after game by making stupid fouls, turning the ball over, and not blocking out on rebounds. Last week at the Sundance Invitational, Galilee had the misfortune to draw Sundance Prep for its first game and had lost 89-43, a mark of genuine shame when a team gets beat by twice its own score. Rusty, however, had a good game. He scored twenty-one points before fouling out with two minutes left. Dale, who'd been there to help with the photographs, thought Rusty played well but without discipline. Not only did he commit senseless fouls out of frustration, but also he took too many quick shots. He didn't give his teammates time to position themselves for the rebound in case he missed. Dale was certain that Coach Carpenter wouldn't have tolerated that. Coach Carpenter always emphasized the fundamentals.

Dale thought Galilee had a good chance of winning their second game tonight. They led the Humble Horned Toads, 25-22, at half. Galilee had beaten Humble in their gym to start off the season. Dale thought the Gophers should win easily. Humble also didn't have any really tall guys. But like the previous games, Galilee had played sloppy basketball and only led by three.

The lights in the gym still hadn't been turned all the way up. Dale thought he had an excellent opportunity to get a good picture of Amanda. He crept closer to her, kneeled in the aisle between the two sections of bleachers, found her image in his viewfinder, and pushed the button. The flash exploded and a wave of light bathed Amanda with its silvery glow. Alarmed, she turned toward the source of the light. When she saw Dale with the camera still positioned over his face, her frightened look faded and she smiled. He immediately took another picture. After the second surge of light, she shielded her eyes and frowned at him.

"Oh, Audie," she scolded, "you're hurting my eyes."

Dale moved closer. "Sorry about that. I forget how bright the flash is." He fiddled with his camera as she rubbed her eyes.

"Well, it's very bright," she said, now smiling.

Dale looked at her. Even though he'd rehearsed his lines for days, now he didn't know how to broach the subject.

"So, how are you?" Amanda asked.

Dale said fine.

After a pause, Amanda said she'd heard he'd scored high on the ACT.

"I did all right."

"A lot better than me," Amanda said, with a rueful smile.

"Those tests don't mean much. They're just an arbitrary measurement of a …" Dale couldn't remember how it went. He gritted his teeth in frustration. He'd thought that phrase sounded just right. "Well, they don't mean much."

"I suppose we tend to exaggerate their importance."

Dale nodded. "Besides, we all know how bright you are."

Amanda looked surprised and pleased. "Oh?"

"Yeah. Tests are so … arbitrary." Dang, he thought, he wished he could remember that phrase. "And besides, you have so much talent. You sing really well and you play your flute like, like a real musician."

Amanda overlooked his inarticulateness. "Oh, thank you. Do you really think so?"

"Yeah, I do. I don't know much about music myself. I mean, I'm trying to learn."

"You're learning an instrument?"

"No," Dale said, again fiddling with his camera. "I'm just listening to classical music. I'm even going to a few concerts."

"Really? Where?"

"I'm going to the Oklahoma City Philharmonic next Saturday night."

"Oh, yes. I've been to a few of the concerts."

"I have two tickets." Dale looked at her. Her blue eyes looked back at him without any guile. "I thought we could go together, if you're not doing anything."

Amanda's lips puckered in surprise. Dale immediately became entranced at how plump and pink they looked.

"Well," she said, "I don't know. Saturday?"

"Yeah," he said, looking more intently into her eyes now. "Saturday. I could come by at six thirty. The concert starts at seven thirty."

"Well, I don't know. Let me think. What am I doing Saturday night?"

"Going to the concert with me," he said, surprised by his boldness.

"Well…"

Dale could tell she was leaning toward saying yes. He didn't know why she was fussing so much. Maybe he hadn't been romantic enough. Maybe she was worried about hurting Wendy's feelings. Maybe she had another date. With who? He'd heard she'd gone on a date with some guy from her church but it wasn't Henshaw.

"If you don't say yes," he said, aiming his camera at her, "I'll take your picture again."

Amanda held up a hand to shield her face and laughed. "All right, Audie, you win."

Dale lowered the camera and looked straight into her eyes. "Okay. I'll stop by at six-thirty Saturday." He started to leave, but turned back. "I mean, next Saturday, not tomorrow."

Amanda laughed and said she assumed it was next week. Dale waved and said so long, feeling momentarily foolish. As he walked away, his foolish feeling gave way to a sense of accomplishment. He'd actually done it! As he walked out of the front doors of the gym on his way to the yearbook office, he felt so happy he thought he might burst. He let out a yee-haw! and didn't even feel embarrassed when an older couple gawked at him as if he were crazy.

At first, Dale thought he was dreaming. He woke up in darkness and listened. He heard the voice again, high and thin, coming from outside his room. His eyes grew accustomed to the dark and he got up. Wearing sweats, as he always did in winter, he walked out of his room. The voice came from the living room. He didn't feel afraid. He knew it wasn't a burglar or an intruder. In fact, he already knew who the voice belonged to, although he couldn't understand why Jesse was making that odd noise. It wasn't like singing, more like a loud humming. Dale walked down the hall and before he entered the living room he saw her appear briefly in his view, then disappear as she danced out of his field of vision. Dale rubbed his eyes. He still felt sleepy and he didn't quite believe what he'd seen.

He entered the living room and saw Jesse, clothed only in shadows, dancing in a small circle as if she were performing a burlesque version of a rain dance. As she danced she made that odd humming sound, as if incapable of speaking or singing – as if that noise was the only way she could communicate her agitated feelings. Dale glanced at the floor and saw her recently shed underwear and pajamas. He looked back at her and watched in amazement as she continued her odd ritualistic dance, throwing her arms up in the air, circling, and making that strange *hmmm hmmm hmmm* sound.

No light came from outside. A moonless night, the sky looked black and formless through the glass patio doors. The darkness concealed details of Jesse's nudity, but knowing that his mother was in that state, and worse, insane again, filled him with a strange mixture of fear and revulsion. He didn't dare come closer. He didn't go over and try to calm her because then he might have to touch her. Instead, he walked down the hall to his parents' room and peered inside and saw Blackie deeply asleep in his bed. Lying on his back, he snored. Blackie, like June May, had always been a deep sleeper. Dale knew he had to shake him awake and he didn't want to do that either, but he had no choice.

He pushed Blackie's shoulder. He snored louder. Dale shoved him hard and Blackie snorted and awoke.

"What the hell," he said, drowsily.

"It's Mom."

Blackie immediately became fully awake. He got out of bed, wearing only his skivvies. He pulled on his pants and threw on a T-shirt.

"Where is she?"

"Can't you hear her? She's in the living room."

Dale wondered if he should warn Blackie about her being naked. Just thinking that word embarrassed him so he didn't. He followed Blackie as he walked down the hallway. Blackie stopped when he saw Jesse dancing in circles. He looked at Dale and said, "my God."

Blackie stooped and gathered Jesse's clothes. He started to go to her, when he stopped.

"You better go back to your room, Audie Dale."

Dale said all right and passed by June May's room. Unsurprisingly, she was still sleeping; at least, no light or sound came from behind her door. Before he got to his room, he heard Jesse shout, "stop! Go away! Leave me alone!" Then Dale heard what sounded like slapping. He turned and walked quickly back to the living room. He saw Jesse slapping Blackie with her open hand as he struggled to get a pajama top on her. Blackie must have sensed Dale had returned. Without turning to him, he said, "get a towel or a blanket, something to cover her with."

Dale went to the bathroom and grabbed a large bath towel. He thought that should easily cover Jesse. He returned and handed the towel to his father as he struggled to hold the squirming Jesse. She kept saying, "no, no, no."

Blackie threw the towel over Jesse. She clawed at it, throwing it off once, then twice, before Blackie hugged the towel to her.

"I want to be free," Jesse chanted, "free as a bird."

She tried to do her dance again which Dale realized was her imitation of flight. She tugged at the towel. "Birds don't wear clothes. Birds are free!"

"She's batty again," said Blackie.

Dale nodded, and almost smiled at the absurdity of the image in his mind: a bird metamorphosing into a bat. Blackie told Dale to go and get his belt from his room. Dale fetched it. Blackie, holding Jesse in the towel with one hand, looped the belt around her arms and fastened it. She stopped squirming and looked in surprise at her binding. She suddenly began crying. Dale felt sick. Jesse had never been much of a weeper. Seeing tears streaming down her face in the shadows scared him more than her deranged antics.

Blackie steered Jesse to the couch and sat her down. "Watch her," he told Dale. "I don't think she'll do anything now. I'm going to call the cops."

"Why the cops?"

"We're going to have to commit her."

"What do you mean?"

"I mean send her to Norman. To do that, you have to get a court order. She'll have to go through the legal process."

He started to leave and Dale held out a hand to stop him. "What about taking her to that hospital? The sanitarium you took her to last time?"

"I can't. The city doesn't offer enough in health insurance anymore. Not for mental problems."

Dale wondered if that were true. "Well, why can't you pay for it?"

"You know how much that kind of care costs?" Blackie hissed. Dale shook his head. Of course, he didn't know. "No, she's going to have to go to Norman this time."

Blackie left to call. Dale sat close enough to Jesse on the couch to grab her if she tried anything. He prayed she wouldn't try anything.

"I want to be free," Jesse muttered.

In the shadows he thought he could see that peculiar shine to her eyes. He'd felt a foreboding for weeks. One day she seemed on the verge of going crazy; the next day she seemed fine. He'd hoped Blackie's return would have helped her. But it seemed to have only delayed the inevitable.

"Purt-ty bird," Jesse said, chanting, "pur-ty bird."

Dale had heard her say those very words but in a different, sane voice when he was a kid and they were over at his grandma's looking at her new bird. Grandma had kept a parakeet in a cage for years. Dale remembered feeling sorry for the poor caged bird. It had blue and red plumage and twittered in its cage, and Jesse kept trying to get it to talk by saying "purty bird, purty bird."

Blackie, now fully dressed, came back from making the call and said he'd sit with her until the cops arrived. When Blackie got near Jesse, she suddenly became agitated.

"You goddamn bastard!" she screamed. She struggled against her bindings and almost fell off the couch. Blackie grabbed her and held her still. "You sonofabitch! You bastard!"

Dale waited in the room and tried not to listen to all the vile things Jesse said. She called Blackie every foul name she could think of. She mocked him. She said he should go back to his whore. She said she was a purty bird. She spat at him.

Throughout the abuse, Blackie held her still and kept her from falling. His face was grim and merciless. Dale wondered if he wanted to squeeze her with his big hands until she stopped squirming and cussing him.

He told Dale to go pack some things for Jesse. A toothbrush, a comb, some clothes, her eyeglasses, all the stuff she'd need. Dale left, and put all the stuff in a big, brown paper bag and came back in the living room.

Jesse calmed down and they waited. The cops finally arrived and Dale let them in. Two cops, one tall and older, the other short and younger. Blackie seemed to know the older one. He talked to him outside the living room while Dale watched Jesse. She seemed tired now, almost on the verge of falling asleep. When the cops entered, Jesse suddenly became animated again. She swore at them. She struggled against her binding. Dale thought the cops didn't seem disturbed by what they saw. They didn't take her insults personally. They consulted with each other and decided to leave the belt on her until they got her to the police station. Then a matron would help Jesse get into her clothes or at least a robe.

Blackie pulled Jesse off the couch and told Dale he'd go along with cops to the police station. He'd take a taxi back home. Dale should go back to sleep.

Dale nodded and tried to ignore Jesse's cries. She didn't want to go with the cops. She must have known it was the first step to Norman. She squirmed and screamed, cursed and spit. Blackie almost had to carry her out the door.

Dale watched from the front door as Blackie put her in the backseat of the squad car and climbed in. The car then backed out of the driveway, its headlights momentarily blinding him as their beam swept over him. Then the patrol car disappeared down the street.

He closed the door and locked it. He walked back to his bedroom when he saw June May looking at him from a crack in her bedroom door.

"Mom's sick again," she said.

Dale noticed how large and afraid her eyes looked.

"Yeah. Go back to sleep."

June May shut her door and Dale heard her crying. He realized that all this was harder on her than him. He was older. He'd been through it more times so maybe he was getting a little used to it. And she was a daughter, not a son. That must have made it a little harder for June May, too.

Dale didn't know how to comfort his sister. So, he let her cry by herself. He walked to his room and sat in the dark and tried to think of something good. He thought of Amanda.

## Chapter 9: *Dating Amanda; stuco meeting; Blackie's mishap*

The first two dates with Amanda had gone well. On their first date, she had worn a light blue dress, a necklace, and short-heeled pumps. Her face had a little makeup on it. She enjoyed the concert. Dale made sure they had good seats and afterwards he asked her questions about the music and her own playing. They stopped off for a snack at West Oaks and talked. She told him about her family. Her father worked as a vice president at an Oklahoma City bank in the northwest part of the City. Her mother was a professor of education at Galilee Nazarene College. That was main reason why they moved to Galilee for her freshman year. Her mother wouldn't have to spend as much time traveling to campus as she had when they lived in the City. Amanda had an older sister, Elizabeth, who attended GNC; she was a senior majoring in business. "A very practical girl," Amanda said. Her younger brother, Kenny, was in ninth grade at Galilee. She said her brother loved sports and knew who Dale was from watching all the high school games. She said she was very fond of her family.

When Amanda asked Dale about his family, he told her as little as possible without looking like he was hiding something. He told her Blackie was a lieutenant lakes and parks ranger. He didn't mention that he was going to college on the GI bill or that he'd been a career man in the navy. He told her Jesse was a homemaker. He didn't tell her that she was currently in the loony bin in Norman. He told her June May was a freshman and a cheerleader.

"Then Kenny and June May must know each other," Amanda said. "I don't think I've heard him mention her, but then he doesn't talk about his friends."

Dale said boys were generally like that. Amanda laughed and he listened to her dulcet voice and admired the dimples in her cheeks.

He took her home on time. He didn't want to make a bad impression with her folks. He walked her to her door. The porch light shone so brightly that it discouraged any ideas he had of kissing her good night. He wasn't planning on it anyway. Amanda seemed too ladylike for him to presume such a bold move on the first date. She thanked him for the concert, he thanked her for accepting, and he said he'd see her in class Monday. Then he stepped off her porch, and before turning for his car, he watched her go inside her home. He had thought about asking her for another date at her door, but he didn't want to be pushy. Better to call her in a few days and ask.

Which he did and she accepted. On their second date a week later, he took her to a musical play also in the City. He thought he couldn't go wrong with more music. She had worn a creamy-white dress this time, with the same kind of shoes as before, and earrings instead of a necklace. Her face had a few more touches of makeup on it this time; mascara and blush, Dale thought. It made her pretty face look even more colorful. The play, *The Fantastics*, bored him but Amanda seemed to enjoy it. Dale actually thought musicals were rather silly. He didn't even like the movie versions much. Once again, they stopped off for a soft drink at West Oaks and this time Dale asked her about college. She was going to GNC, of course. Even if her mother hadn't taught there, she'd still want to go. Her mother and father had graduated from GNC and all three of the kids planned to graduate from there.

Amanda asked what college Dale would attend. He said he wasn't sure. Maybe OU or Central State. He'd stay in state, though. Then he said something he hadn't really considered before. He said he might go to Galilee Nazarene.

Amanda was surprised. Really? she said. That would be wonderful. She thought Dale would like going to GNC. It was fairly small and everyone knew each other and the professors took a personal interest in the students. He nodded. Yeah, he said, he was definitely thinking of going.

He got her home on time again and walked her to the door. He looked resentfully at the glare of the porch light as if it were a competitor. Amanda offered her hand to him. Dale took it, not actually shaking it, but held it for a few seconds and felt how warm and soft it was. That was the first time he'd ever really touched her, and just holding her hand took away his breath and made him feel all abuzz inside. Amanda slipped her fingers out of his hand and said good night. Dale responded in kind and backed up and watched her enter her house. When he turned and walked away, he almost tripped over a garden hoe. He regained his balance and hoped she hadn't seen his near fall from inside her home.

The third date was an important date. They were feeling more comfortable with each other and Dale intended to kiss her when he brought her home; that is, if everything went all right.

When he arrived at her door to pick her up, Amanda asked him to please come inside to meet her mother and father. Amanda's mother looked exactly like he remembered her looking, a tastefully dressed, carefully coifed middle-aged woman, pretty – but not beautiful like Amanda. Mrs. Meeks' nose was a little long and her lips were thinner. But a nice-looking woman all the same, mostly due to the same kind of bright blue eyes that Amanda had. He hoped Mrs. Meeks wouldn't recognize him from the time he almost rammed into her car with his. She apparently didn't because her smile of welcome was genuine.

Amanda's father looked about as tall as Blackie, around five ten. He wore a gray sweater over a white shirt and had black slacks on. He had short, brown hair, a blunt nose, a strong jaw, and hazel eyes that peered at Dale as if he'd already judged him unworthy to date his daughter. Dale shook hands with Mr. Meeks and noted his strong grip. Mrs. Meeks asked where the two of them were going.

"A movie," Dale said. He noticed that Mrs. Meeks raised a brow. Mr. Meeks's rather critical expression didn't change at all.

"Which one?" asked Mrs. Meeks.

Dale said *The Return of the Pink Panther*.

Mrs. Meeks nodded, but her eyes looked doubtful. Mr. Meeks said he remembered seeing a movie called *The Pink Panther* several years ago.

"Yeah, I think this is a sequel to that movie," Dale said.

"I remember that film as rather funny."

Dale said he'd seen it on TV and Mr. Meeks was right. It was funny.

Mr. Meeks seemed satisfied. He looked at his wife and she seemed satisfied, too, so they told Amanda and Dale to have fun. On their way to Dale's car, Amanda said her parents were just concerned about what they were seeing. He said he understood.

They drove to the City to see the movie at a new multiplex. When they got there, ten minutes before the film was to start, the ticket girl told Dale it had sold out. He asked Amanda if she wanted to see anything else. She didn't know. She didn't go to movies very often. He looked at the choices. Of the three other films, he'd heard that *Godfather II* was really good. The first one had won an Academy Award. Since *Godfather II* had been showing for several months, there were plenty of tickets left. He bought two tickets and they walked inside the movie theatre and found two seats near the middle.

Dale asked if Amanda wanted anything from the concession. She said a Diet Coke. He left and brought back the Diet Coke for her and a 7-Up for himself. When the lights went down, he moved a little closer to Amanda. He felt the heat from her body and smelled her light perfume. They sat through the coming attractions and finally the movie started. Dale rested his arm on the armrest and noticed that Amanda kept her hands folded in her lap. She wore a pink dress this time, and unlike the other two, the neck was scooped a little and showed all her soft throat and maybe two inches of the top of her chest. He noticed she was a little small on top, but he didn't mind too much. She had an attractive figure otherwise.

They watched the movie and Amanda seemed to like it until Robert DeNiro shot the neighborhood gangster guy. Dale saw her flinch. She didn't seem to like the other action scenes either. He felt her tense when someone was murdered. He was glad there weren't a lot of swear words in the movie, but when one was uttered he felt embarrassed.

When the movie was over, they left the theatre and walked to the car in silence. Inside the car, Dale looked at Amanda. She didn't seem upset; just lost in thought.

"You didn't like the movie, did you?" he asked.

"No," she said, "it was interesting."

"It's gotten really good reviews," Dale said, hoping that would help his cause.

"No, it was interesting. I've just never seen a movie like that. Was it R-rated?"

Dale said he thought so.

"I'm not supposed to see R-rated movies," she said, smiling a little.

"Sorry about that. I didn't even think about it."

"Oh, that's all right. It was awfully violent, though."

"Yeah, but the violence wasn't gratuitous." That was a word he'd learned from reading a movie review.

"I suppose that's true," said Amanda, smiling. "That is, if you tell me what gratuitous means."

Dale said it meant without justification. Bad movies had guys killing guys just for the heck of it. That was gratuitous. "Or," he added, "when they have nude scenes just to have nude scenes." He realized he'd made another mistake in an effort to impress her. Amanda gave him a slightly disapproving look. "That's what I've read, of course."

"Audie, do you go to a lot of R-rated movies?"

Dale had never kept track. "I've gone to a few," he said, reluctantly. "But only to the good ones."

Amanda smiled and Dale thought maybe the danger was over so he started the car and asked her if she'd like to stop for a snack somewhere. She said okay. He didn't want to go to West Oaks for the third time but that was the only good but casual place in Galilee. He drove for several blocks and before getting on the highway to Galilee he saw a nice-looking restaurant called *Mulligans* on a corner across from a Big Boy. He parked and they went in. The place was sort of busy and noisy, but it looked like a nice place with plants and Celtic decorations and comfortable furnishings. They sat in the booth and Dale ordered another Diet Coke for Amanda and a 7-Up for himself and some nachos for both of them.

They talked more about the movie. Amanda said the film, in spite of all its violence, had a moral to it. The bad men were punished.

"Yeah, and the worst guy of all, Michael Corleone, is punished most," said Dale.

"But he didn't die in the end."

"No, but his fate was worse than death."

"Oh? What was that?"

"Isolation. Complete loneliness. Sitting on the bench all alone."

Amanda nodded. "Maybe that is worse than death."

They drank their soft drinks and munched on the nachos and talked about school. She asked him about the yearbook and he asked her about chorus. Then Amanda noticed a man carrying a pitcher of beer.

"Does this restaurant serve beer?" she asked.

Dale looked around and saw some people drinking beer. Others were smoking cigarettes. He felt like he'd committed another mistake.

"I guess so." He wondered if he should apologize. Instead, he took a different tactic. "Would you like some?"

Amanda opened her mouth in surprise. Dale quickly added that he was kidding.

"Oh," she said, smiling with relief. "You have a mischievous side."

"That I do," Dale admitted. "Really, I didn't know they served beer here."

Amanda said that was all right. They talked for a few more minutes, then he asked if she was ready to go and she said yes. It was getting late. Dale was supposed to bring her home before midnight and it was a quarter til.

They drove back to Galilee and Dale noticed that Amanda sat closer than she previously had. Her thigh almost touched his. As the car hurled itself into the night, he glanced at her. She returned his look with a smile.

Dale parked at the curb and walked Amanda to her front door, frowning at the bright porch light. Before stepping onto the porch, Amanda paused and said she wanted to go in the back way. Would he mind walking her there? He said not at all. They went around the house and Amanda stopped at a side door that didn't have a light above it.

Dale saw his chance. After she put the key in the lock, he moved toward her and waited for her to turn to him. When she did, he put his left arm around her waist and gently pulled her toward him. He didn't feel as nervous as he thought he would. Instead, he concentrated on her face and lowered his enough to find her mouth. He kissed her for a few seconds, savoring the softness of her lips. Inside he felt like electricity had zapped him. His senses soaked in everything about her. How pliable her waist felt; how her body seemed to radiate warmth; how her perfume mingled with her own scent to insinuate itself in his mind. The kiss only took a few seconds but it would remain seared in his memory for the rest of his life.

She pulled away and softly said good night. Dale waited until she opened the door to say good night, his voice sounding surprisingly husky in his own ears. She slipped inside and he walked back to his car.

A crescent moon hung in the sky. He stared at it and then looked at the stars and tried to memorize all the details of that night. He drove away, still thinking of how she looked, how she smelled, how she felt.

Dale sat in the chair at the end of the table reading *Time* magazine and trying to ignore Wendy's doleful glances. She sat at the other end of the table taking minutes as secretary of the student council. In between them sat Mr. Smedley, Rusty, K. C., and Chris. The four of them were discussing ways to raise funds for volleyball equipment. Dale had no interest in the discussion. He didn't understand why, as yearbook editor, he had to attend these tedious stuco meetings. What made it worse of late was being in the same room with Wendy. Since he didn't have any classes with her, he usually could avoid her except in the halls. When he encountered her there, they would exchange hellos and he would ask her how she was and she'd say fine, but she looked so depressed that he knew she was lying for his benefit.

Dale glanced over and saw Wendy looking at him again. She stared without seeing him, as if she were really looking at an image directly behind him, or maybe her memory of him when they were going steady. He thought she didn't look well. Her face looked paler than usual. Her mouth slumped in a frown. A sad look ringed her eyes. He thought she looked seriously depressed. He turned away, feeling a little angry with her. He didn't know why she was taking their breakup so hard. She was hurting herself. Her attitude made him feel guilty, but he resented feeling responsible for her state of mind. She was behaving so tragically that she reminded him of Natalie Wood in a movie he'd seen on TV a few years ago, *Splendor in the Grass*. In that film, Natalie got so distraught over Warren Beatty breaking up with her that she went bonkers. She jumped in a reservoir and tried to drown herself. Her parents had to institutionalize her. By the end of the movie, she'd recovered and Natalie and Warren had some bittersweet meeting where she realized her mad passion had faded. Dale didn't think Wendy would go as far as Natalie, but he wished he didn't have to see her suffer.

"Wendy, my dear," Mr. Smedley said in a condescending voice, "you aren't recording the minutes."

Wendy murmured she was sorry and began writing again as Mr. Smedley resumed his droning. Dale looked from Wendy to Rusty. He, too, was unhappy, but for an entirely different reason. He despised Mr. Smedley. Rusty detested the inactivity of the stuco meetings; he hated the endless discussion of minutia; he loathed being responsible for organizing the various student council activities. Usually, Rusty deferred almost all his executive duties to K. C., who carried them out with cheerful efficiency. For all intents and purposes, K. C. really ran the student government. Rusty, however, had to serve as titular head during these weekly lunch-hour meetings in the library, and each week he grew increasingly restless and exasperated.

"We've discussed this before," Rusty said irritably. "We discuss the same stuff week after week."

"We have discussed these issues before," Mr. Smedley said, removing his spectacles for a pointless cleaning, since when he donned them again they looked just as smeary as before, "but we haven't resolved them yet. Therefore, we must consider them again."

Rusty threw up his hands and sighed loudly. K. C. said, how about having a car wash? He, Mr. Smedley, and Chris discussed the pros and cons as Rusty stewed, Dale read, and Wendy scribbled with as much energy as if she were composing a suicide note. After ten minutes of unproductive talk, Mr. Smedley concluded the meeting. Wendy handed him the two sheets of notebook paper.

"Wendy," he said, looking at the pages, "these minutes are nearly illegible."

"Sorry, Mr. Smedley," Wendy quietly said.

She got up and shuffled out of the room. Mr. Smedley and K. C. soon followed, resuming the discussion that had been officially tabled. Rusty and Chris stayed behind with Dale.

"Glad that's over," said Rusty. "Smudgely is the most boring man on the face of the earth."

Dale tossed *Time* aside and looked at Rusty. "He's imperturbable. That's why you dislike him."

"What's that mean?" asked Chris.

"It means he can't be perturbed," said Rusty.

"Thanks," said Chris, "that was really helpful."

"It means Mr. Smedley doesn't respond to teasing or taunting or insults," said Dale. "He just remains calm and even-keeled."

"That's because he doesn't have a brain."

"He's just very methodical about being disorganized."

"I don't know what you guys are talking about," said Chris. "But I know one thing. Wendy isn't unperturbable. What is wrong with her?"

Dale knew. She was unhappy. But he didn't say anything. Both Rusty and Chris looked at him. Dale wondered how much they knew. He hadn't told them anything about breaking up with Wendy. He hadn't told them he was dating Amanda, either. Dale shrugged. His two pals did the same and they left the library just as the fifth-hour bell sounded and the halls swarmed with kids.

With Jesse in the hospital, June May took over cooking duties. She performed her task with a sullen inefficiency that concerned Dale but not Blackie. Dale knew his father could eat anything. He often boasted of the dreadful slop he'd eaten in the navy and the weird food he'd sampled while in the world's ports. He'd eaten fish heads, worms, walrus, monkey, and even dog. When he mentioned the dog he'd sampled on port call in Bangkok, June May said, "yuck."

Dale and Blackie sat at the kitchen table while June May prepared to fry chicken. She poured the grease in the skillet, then checked on the tater tots and canned biscuits in the oven. Blackie told them how Jesse was doing. He'd driven to Norman to see her yesterday and said she was improving. The doctors were allowing her to smoke again. The first few weeks she'd been denied tobacco. Now, she smoked like a fiend.

Dale asked how long Jesse would be in the hospital. Blackie said it depended on how well she responded to treatment. They were using electroshock therapy on her and she was beginning to think a little more clearly. He thought another four weeks and she'd be able to come home.

June May, listening to Blackie, hadn't been paying attention to her cooking. Suddenly, the grease in the pan caught fire. She shrieked, grabbed a potholder, and picked up the skillet by its handle and ran to the sink. Blackie jumped up, told her to stop, and rushed to her just as June May threw the pan in the sink. Blackie reached for it. June May turned on water. Flames shot out of the skillet and roasted Blackie's outstretched right hand.

"Goddamn it!" he yelled.

He waved his burned hand and Dale, now on his feet, saw melted skin hanging off his fingers. Blackie, grimacing, shoved the stunned June May out of the way, grabbed a handful of sugar with his left hand, and threw it on the burning skillet. The flames faltered. Blackie tossed two more handfuls of sugar, finally snuffing the fire.

June May burst into tears and ran out of the kitchen. Blackie held the wrist of his burned hand with his left hand. He cursed under his breath and glared at Dale.

Dale thought the burn looked bad. The flesh on his father's hand glistened and looked darkly pink like partially cooked meat. The skin hung in shreds at the fingertips and the wrist.

"I'll call an ambulance," said Dale.

"No ambulance," said Blackie. "You drive." He gritted his teeth and breathed so hard and short that he almost snorted.

Dale grabbed the keys to the Chevy and yelled outside June May's door that he was taking Dad to the emergency room. They rushed out of the house and got into the car. Dale drove fast, but not recklessly, to the Galilee hospital's emergency room. He followed his father inside and watched as a doctor and nurse immediately took him into a treatment room. Dale went to a waiting room and wondered how bad Blackie's burn was. It looked bad. It smelled bad. Dale now knew a little of what Blackie had meant when he had talked about the stench of burning human flesh. Recalling the stink made him feel sick to his stomach.

Dale thought his father had behaved with admirable stoicism. He knew the pain must have been excruciating. Broken bones and pinched nerves were nothing compared to severe burns. Dale felt chagrined that his father was tougher than he was.

Dale remembered when he'd nearly cut off his fingers when he was five. He'd been playing in the yard while Blackie and Jesse landscaped. This was back in Texas the summer before he started first grade. Dale saw a knife sticking in the earth and picked it up and stabbed the ground, imagining he was an Indian engaged in a knife fight. Blackie told him to put the knife down. Dale ignored him. Blackie stood up and stalked over, his face angry, and Dale decided to stab his enemy one more time. He thrust the knife with all his might into the ground in defiance of his father, and felt his hand slip down the handle. The knife was double-edged and the force of his blow had resulted in him nearly severing his two smaller fingers on his right hand.

Dale felt a sting, held his hand up, and saw blood gushing from his dangling two fingers. He remembered feeling surprised that it didn't hurt. But a moment later, the pain roared through him, and that along with the flowing blood scared him and he started bawling as Blackie picked him up and carried him to the bathroom. Blackie washed his hand, but the blood kept flowing. Blackie wrapped his hand in a towel and then he rushed him to the car. Jesse got June May, only two then, and they all raced to the navy base and the emergency room. Dale didn't remember the rest very well. He remembered the doctor and the nurse and the pain and trying not to cry now that strangers were around. Then he went to sleep and woke up the next morning in a hospital bed with his right hand bandaged. Blackie and Jesse visited him that afternoon and Blackie told him he was lucky that the surgeon had saved his two fingers.

Now, Dale flexed his right hand. Those two fingers wouldn't bend in the middle. He could only make a fist by pressing his two good fingers against the two bad ones and folding all of them together. He remembered the painful exercises he had to do after he got his stitches out. Blackie put Dale's hand in his and squeezed, forcing his fingers to fold. It hurt like heck.

Half an hour later, he saw Blackie walking toward him along with a nurse. A thick, white bandage covered Blackie's right hand. He nodded to the nurse, then met his son in the waiting room.

"Let's go," Blackie said.

"How's your hand?"

"Mostly second-degree burns. Got to be careful about infection."

Blackie and Dale walked to the Chevy and got in. Dale started it and looked at his father.

"I'll tell you one goddamned thing. June May ain't cooking anymore."

Dale nodded but didn't smile. Blackie wasn't joking.

As he had the previous two weeks, Dale called Amanda on Monday night. When she said hello, he thought he detected something in her voice. Not coolness but maybe a touch of wariness.

Dale asked how she was. She said fine. He told her that the Oklahoma City planetarium had a special program Saturday night. She murmured a vague response. He could tell from her voice she wasn't very interested. He'd tried to think of somewhere appealing to take her that didn't cost a lot of money. The concert and the musical hadn't been expensive exactly, but they cost more than a movie. Dale didn't want to take her to another movie so soon. She might think he really did see a lot of R-rated films.

"We could go somewhere else if you aren't interested in the planetarium," he said, hoping that she might suggest coming over and watching TV like Wendy often did.

"To tell you the truth, Audie, I won't be able to do anything with you next Saturday."

Dale tried to hide his disappointment. "Okay," he said as casually as he could.

After a pause, Amanda said she already made a date for Saturday.

Dale felt all the air go out of him. He felt as flat as a deflated football.

"You did?"

"Yes, I'm sorry, Audie."

Dale wanted to ask who was taking her out, but he didn't want her to think he was jealous. "Gee, Amanda," he said, trying to make his voice sound as normal as possible, "I thought we had a good time these past three dates."

"We did. But that's part of the problem, Audie. Three dates in a row is getting close to, you know, making it a steady thing."

"What's wrong with that?"

"My parents don't want me to go steady with anyone while I'm in high school."

"You're almost eighteen."

"Yes, I know."

"That means you're going to be an adult soon. Shouldn't you make your own decisions?"

"I am making my own decision. I agree with my parents."

Dale didn't know how much he should say. He didn't know if he should tell her how much she meant to him, how much she'd always meant to him from that first time he'd seen her in the school auditorium. If her voice didn't sound so detached, maybe he would have. But at that moment he didn't want her to know how desperately he felt about her.

"We can still go out on occasion," Amanda said. "I've enjoyed our dates. Even the last one."

Dale enjoyed that one the most. But the idea of sharing her with other boys filled him with an anger born of frustration and jealousy.

"But you'll still go out with other guys."

"Well, yes, if I want to."

"I don't know if I could do that," Dale said, hearing a certain intensity of feeling creep into his voice.

"Do what?"

"Go out with you knowing you're seeing other guys."

Amanda didn't respond right away. When she did her voice sounded different, too. He thought he heard a touch of melancholy in it. "I'd just be going out for fun. I mean, it wouldn't mean anything serious. That's the point, Audie. That's why I'm not supposed to go steady with anyone."

"How can you really get to know anyone then?"

Amanda sighed. "I don't know."

Dale tried to think of some additional argument to make her change her mind. But his emotions were in such turmoil that he couldn't think clearly.

"There's another problem," she said.

"What?"

"Well, you're not a Nazarene."

"Does that matter?"

"Yes."

"To who? You or your parents?"

"Both. I mean, it matters to me and my parents."

"Okay. I'll start going to First Church."

"You shouldn't do that."

"I thought you said it mattered to you."

"Yes, but you shouldn't go to church simply so I'll date you. You should go because you want to go. Because you believe in it."

Dale knew how important church was to her. He didn't quite understand it, but he respected her feelings. Maybe if he could get her to understand how strong his feelings were for her without sounding silly, she might relent.

"Amanda, I just want to see you. To get to know you better." He paused. He didn't want his feelings to show too strongly in his voice.

"I, I sort of feel that way, too. But I can't. I can't go steady. If we did and I started feeling … well, I can't. It would cause too many problems."

Dale tried to speak, but he was afraid to. Afraid his voice would betray him and sound as torn up as he felt inside. He heard her soft breathing from the other side of the phone. The air between them was heavy and tense and impenetrable.

"I have to go," Amanda said, almost in a whisper. "Good-bye, Audie."

Dale couldn't speak. He heard her line go dead and he held the receiver until the static ended and the beeping started. Then he slammed the phone down.

He'd been standing during the conversation, pacing out of nervousness and frustration. Now he tossed himself into the old chair and stared into space. He felt as if fate, as if God, had been toying with him. He'd been given a taste of ambrosia only to be denied complete satisfaction. Dale felt that perverse pride rise inside him. If he couldn't have it all, he didn't want any.

### Chapter 10: *Basketball scandal; someone missing at the pep club banquet*

It was easy for Dale to avoid Amanda. He only had two classes with her. She sat in the front, he in the back. He just waited until she left the classroom with her friends, then he slunk out.

That was exactly what he did after his speech class eight days after speaking with her on the phone. He watched her walking away with Mary Jane and Gretchen then he went into the yearbook office to work on the next-to-last deadline. His yearbook duties had kept him extremely busy these past few months – arduous activity that he welcomed. It helped him forget about his problems with Wendy, Amanda, and his mother. He usually worked several hours a day scheduling and supervising photos, working in the darkroom, writing copy, doing layouts, and supervising his small staff of five. He even worked on the yearbook on weekends now. He was rather glad he didn't have a girlfriend to interfere.

While sitting at his desk finishing a layout, Dale saw Don Fargo, the sports editor, walk in. Don had an unusual face for a high school kid. He looked almost old. He had long hair like most of the boys, straight light brown hair that hung almost in his eyes. But what gave him an elderly appearance was his long, hooked nose, thin lips, and mottled skin. Dale remembered him having had a serious acne problem a few years back. It had apparently scarred his skin to such a degree that from a distance it looked a little like wrinkled skin. In keeping with his older-than-his-years quality, Don was also a rather quiet, responsible, mature kind of guy. When he applied to be on the yearbook staff, Dale worried that Don might be sort of boring. However, Don had turned out to have a good sense of humor. He often teased Linda and Carrie. Dale liked him and was glad he was on the staff. He was the only male other than Dale in a room with three talkative girls.

"Hey, Don," Dale said.

Don nodded and sat down in a chair opposite Dale's desk. He put his big feet, shod with Timberline boots, on the edge of Dale's desk.

"Did you hear about the basketball team?"

Dale shook his head. He'd been too busy to go to the away games and he hadn't talked much to Rusty or Chris. The only time he saw them was at their locker or at the stuco meetings. Even then, the two of them seemed a little removed from him. Not playing basketball seemed to have cost him some common ground with his two best buddies.

"They tore up the Lyons' locker room last night," Don said.

"Oh, yeah? How bad?"

"Pretty bad. They busted several lockers, broke some benches, shattered a mirror, cracked a sink."

"All because they lost?"

Dale had heard that Galilee lost to Lyons, 53-52. Rusty could have won the game with a last second shot but he'd missed. Dale could imagine how Rusty and the rest of the guys felt losing to Lyons. They were a team Galilee was supposed to beat. They'd beaten the Lions a few weeks ago at home when Rusty sank a last-second shot. But no déjà vu on the road.

"They got cheated on a lot of calls," said Don. "Still, they shouldn't have busted up the place."

"No, they shouldn't."

Dale didn't think Clifford played basketball anymore, at least he hadn't seen him on the team when Lyons visited Galilee. But Clifford might have been at the game. Dale bet Rusty was still sore about his car windows being smashed at the football game at Lyons. It had cost him several hundred dollars to replace them.

"Where was Coach Rayze during all this?"

Don shrugged. "I heard he'd left the locker room already." Don took his feet off the desk and scooted closer. "That's not the only thing that happened, though."

Dale looked up from sizing a photograph for the layout. "Oh yeah. What else happened?"

"On the way back, some of the guys gave the finger and mooned motorists from the back of the bus."

"Which guys?"

"Sounded like most of them made obscene gestures. Erickson was the only one who mooned anybody."

Dale shook his head in disgust. He wasn't surprised that Erickson would stoop so low. He hoped Rusty and Chris weren't involved in the misbehavior. Knowing Rusty's impressionable ways, he probably was. But Dale doubted Chris would have done anything so rude.

"Who were they doing these things to?"

"Some people from Lyons. A couple of cars full of Lyons people followed the bus out of town. The problem was, an older couple happened to be on the road at the same time. They reported the antics to the cops."

"This all happened last night?"

"Yeah. The cops stopped the bus, too."

"Really? What happened?"

"Just a warning. But the cops called Principal Zook last night and Coach Rayze and players are in trouble."

"What's going to happen to them?"

"We might forfeit Friday's game. Cancel the rest of the season."

Dale thought that sounded harsh. There were two weeks left in the regular season. "Will they get to play in the district tournament?"

Don shrugged. "I don't know. Maybe. The school officials are meeting with Rayze and Dorfman this afternoon to decide."

Dale was impressed with Don's access to information. He sounded more like a gossip columnist than a yearbook sports editor.

"You were at last night's game?"

Don said he was. But he didn't hear about everything until this morning before school. His mother was principal Zook's secretary.

Dale had forgotten that. He rarely saw the principal and never went into his office. Before Dale could ask any more questions, Linda, Carrie, and Carmen walked in, interrupting them. The three girls were laughing and took seats around the worktable.

"Sorry we're late, Mr. Editor," said Linda.

Dale said in a gruff voice, don't let it happen again. The three girls stopped laughing and looked at him.

"Just joking," he said, and Linda and Carrie giggled.

They started talking about the pep club banquet: who the guest speaker was, the theme of the banquet, where it was going to be held, and other boring stuff that Dale successfully tuned out. When he did glance at them a few minutes later, he noticed Carmen studying him. When she saw him notice, she turned away and started talking to Linda again.

Dale imagined he must have done something to offend Carmen but he wasn't sure what. For the last few weeks, she'd been cool to him during the yearbook meetings. She talked to everyone else, but she seemed to avoid him, which wasn't easy to do in the rather small office. She helped him with the layouts but she never initiated conversation. She didn't smile at him, either, which was odd because ordinarily she smiled easily.

Dale knew Carmen was Wendy's best friend. Maybe that was it. Carmen disliked him for hurting Wendy's feelings. Linda and Carrie had been a little aloof too for a few days but they'd returned to their old ways of teasing him about being so serious and obsessed with making deadlines.

Dale pretended to ignore them when they talked about who they were going to ask to the banquet. Linda said she was going to ask her fiancée. He thought she meant Phil Greene, the older brother of a former friend, Eugene, who'd moved to the City after sixth grade. Dale thought Phil went to GNC. Dale waited to hear who Carrie and Carmen were thinking about asking. But the girls sensed he or Don might be eavesdropping, so they lowered their voices. Dale wondered if Carrie or Carmen would ask Chris. He'd briefly dated both of them. Poor Chris, thought Dale. All the girls liked him, but only as a "friend."

Dale had hoped that Amanda might ask him. He pretended that if she did he would turn her down. He was still angry and frustrated with her. His pride was hurt. He especially didn't like the timing of Amanda's change of heart. He'd only got to kiss her once. He hadn't even held her hand except briefly when he kissed her and when they shook hands good night on the second date. He felt cheated and a little angry with Amanda. He tried not to think about her before he fell asleep at night, and the only reason he fell asleep rather easily was because he was so exhausted with all the yearbook stuff.

But Amanda hadn't asked him so he didn't have to struggle with his pride. Dale expected her to ask Henshaw, but instead she'd asked Eugene Greene, who went to First Church. Eugene, like Henshaw, attended Cimarron City High School. Dale had been good friends with Eugene back in grade school. Dale's only better friend was, of course, Rusty. Now, with Amanda asking Eugene to the Gopherette banquet, Dale reckoned that Amanda had never asked or been asked by the same boy more than two times. That must have been one of her rules, too.

Sixth hour ended and Linda, Carrie, and Don left. Dale was so engrossed in working on the clubs section that he hadn't noticed Carmen hanging around until she sharpened her pencil. He looked up and saw her giving him that strange look again.

"Can I ask you a question?" she said.

"Shoot."

"If Wendy asked you to the banquet, would you go?"

Dale put down the grease pencil and examined Carmen's face. She had a pretty face in spite of her cat's eye glasses with her warm, brown eyes and beauty mark near her lower left lip. She was one of the few kids in his class that had a similar dark complexion as Dale's. He remembered in biology class when the teacher, an old hag named Mrs. Huxtable, pointed that out. The class had been looking at the page that showed all the skin tones and colors of the human race and Mrs. Huxtable mentioned the one named "olive" and as a human example pointed to him. He remembered feeling overwhelmed with embarrassment. Not only had he been singled out in class but he'd been identified as having "olive" skin. He felt the eyes of the whole class looking at him and probably thinking what he was thinking: why is that skin color called olive? Aren't olives green? Dale didn't have green skin; just sort of dusky. Mrs. Huxtable must have noticed his humiliation because she quickly identified

Carmen as the other example of that *attractive* skin color. Dale remembered Carmen shyly smiling.

"I think it would be best for both of us if I didn't," Dale said. He returned to his work.

Carmen nodded but she didn't leave. Dale looked up again. Her expression was still odd but she didn't have that critical look in her eye. "Has anybody asked you to the banquet yet?"

Dale felt annoyed. "Yeah."

Bonita Potts had asked him. She'd called Sunday night and said even though she was friends with Wendy she would like to ask him. He said he wasn't sure he wanted to go to the banquet. Bonita said she had to have a date. She was president of pep club. It was getting too late to find another boy. She said they could go just as friends. Please?

Dale gave in. Another banquet. Another wasted evening. Another fancy schmancy meal at a refined restaurant or hotel dining room. What fun.

"Oh," said Carmen. "May I ask who asked you?"

"Bonita."

Carmen's face darkened. Dale wondered why. He thought they were friends. He sometimes thought Carmen didn't like having another girl in class with a Spanish first name. Bonita, however, didn't have that attractive olive skin like Carmen; she had typically pale, freckled skin. Dale wondered why her parents called her Bonita. Rusty, who'd taken Spanish with Mr. Benedict, informed him once that Bonita meant "pretty" in Spanish. He wondered what plain was in Spanish.

"You're going with her?"

"Yeah, I guess."

Dale thought Carmen was acting strange. He knew she was doing this on Wendy's behalf but he didn't want to talk about this too much. He added one more sentence, hoping that would suffice. "I'd rather not go at all, but I said I would."

Carmen nodded and Dale waited. Then she said she was leaving unless he needed anything from her.

"No. Go ahead and go."

Carmen said bye and Dale said so long and she disappeared out the door. He shook his head. He only had one thought: *girls*.

Dale came home later that afternoon and found Blackie sitting in his chair, drinking a beer. He noticed that his father didn't have the bandage on anymore. He walked over and looked when Blackie held up his scarred hand. The skin covering the back of his hand looked like plastic.

"How does it feel?" Dale asked.

"It's sore," Blackie said. "But now I can write with my right hand again."

Blackie had learned to write a little with his left hand. Just enough to sign his name. Dale thought he had surprisingly good handwriting for a man. He remembered how neat his script looked when Jesse showed him  his dad's letters. Blackie used to write fairly regularly when he was on ships or later on shore.

Dale rooted around in the refrigerator for his dinner. He found some ham and tossed it on white bread for a sandwich. He ate chips with it and drank a 7-Up. He decided he needed a vegetable, too, so he grabbed some carrots and munched on them like he was a reluctant rabbit. Blackie came into the kitchen as Dale was finishing.

"Have you decided which colleges you're applying to?"

Dale drained the can of soda. He burped. "I've applied to Central State and OU." He glanced at Blackie. "I was also thinking about applying to Galilee Nazarene."

"That religious school? You don't want to go there."

"Why not?"

"For one thing, it costs too much. It's a private school."

Dale nodded. He wasn't sure how much tuition was, but he guessed it would be a lot more than the state schools.

"If I'm paying for tuition you got to go to a state school," Blackie said.

"All right."

"Why would you want to go to a damn church school anyway? You're not even Nazarene."

"I might start going to the Nazarene church. Maybe I'll become one."

Blackie shook his head. "Haven't you got your fill with religion, boy? It's for suckers."

"You got to believe in something."

"Well, maybe you do when you're young."

Dale noticed Blackie looking at his hand. He wondered if Blackie thought it an alien part of him, the way Dale did about his leg when he got his cast off.

"Where's June May?" Dale asked.

"She's in her room talking on the phone."

Dale thought she was always talking on the phone. He hoped she didn't blab about stuff at home. He didn't think she did. June May seemed as ashamed of their problems as Dale did; but she was girl and he feared she'd get talking and then everything would come out.

Blackie opened the refrigerator and got another beer. He saw Dale looking at him. He unscrewed the top and took a drink. "You can have one, too."

"No, thanks."

"You're going to turn eighteen in a few weeks. Then you can drink legally."

"I don't like drinking."

"How do you know if you haven't tried it?"

"I've tried it a little. Remember? You let me take sips before. But I didn't like it."

Dale didn't mention it, but so had Wanda and some of his older cousins. Once, when he was thirteen, he drank quite a bit and got sick. Everybody in his family seemed to want him to drink and smoke.

"You don't drink beer. You don't drink coffee. You don't smoke. Damn boy, you should be a Mormon, not a Nazarene."

Blackie laughed at his joke. Dale said, "ha ha."

"You don't have any bad habits?" Blackie asked.

Dale shrugged.

"You like girls, though? You *do* like girls."

"Yeah, I like girls." Dale saw his father looking at him a little skeptically. "I like girls a lot."

"You know how not to get them in trouble, don't you?"

Dale wondered why Blackie was having this conversation with him now? Was it because Jesse was in the hospital?

"Yeah, I guess."

"You gotta use a rubber. You know what that is, don't you?"

Dale nodded. He'd heard the older boys talk about them way back in junior high. "You can't buy any in town though."

Blackie took a swig of his beer. "Well, if you ever need one, let me know. I'll get some for you."

Dale thought how he could have used that advice a year ago. He shrugged his shoulders in response. He didn't want to know how his father got hold of rubbers.

Blackie saw that Dale was no longer interested in pursuing their conversation. He went back into the living room and sat in his chair. He drank his beer in silence.

Dale sat at the dining room table and thought how different he was than his father. He was different than his relatives, too. His uncles, aunts, cousins. None of them seemed interested in books or learning or culture. He knew Blackie was smart; he made almost all A's in his college coursework. But he didn't learn for the love of it. He learned because it would help him with his job. Dale didn't care about the pragmatic benefits of getting an education so much. He wanted to learn because he wanted to know.

Dale wished he hadn't consented to go to the pep club banquet. Since Bonita was president, he had to sit at the head table with her and the guest speaker, a former Gopherette president from ten years ago who, along with her husband, owned a dry cleaning business. Also sitting at the head table but on the other end were Amanda, the vice-president, and her date, Eugene Greene. They all had been introduced to one another before the banquet began. When Dale said hello to Amanda he didn't say it very nicely, and he thought she looked a little hurt. Seeing a brief look of discomfort pass over her face made Dale feel mean. But before he could make up for it with a compliment – Amanda dressed in an azure blue gown looked lovely as always – Eugene gave him a hearty hello and stuck his hand out. Dale shook it, noting Eugene's strong grip.

Dale hadn't seen Eugene since sixth grade, but he looked about the same except that he'd grown up, of course. Dale guessed he was around five eleven and he still had his unusual build: long legs but a comparatively short torso. Rusty used to make fun of Eugene's physique by pulling up his own pants over his belly and making his upper body appear short.

Eugene still had the same friendly face with big brown eyes and a mop of brown hair. He had a large mouth and now he smiled at Dale, showing his straight, white teeth. Eugene asked how him how he was doing. Dale said fine. They chatted for a while. Eugene said he played basketball at Cimarron City and mentioned that he and Rusty were going to play on the same summer league basketball team starting in June. Eugene said Dale ought to join them. Dale said he was the worst basketball player in town and Eugene laughed and said it was good seeing him again. Dale said the same and they returned to their respective ends of the table. When he sat down, he looked over at Eugene and Amanda. They were obviously friendly, but he didn't see any evidence of romance. He didn't hold her hand and she didn't make goo-goo eyes at him. Dale felt a little better. Just talking briefly with Eugene reminded him of why he liked him as a boy. He was friendly, optimistic, and good natured. He thought Amanda could do a lot worse for a date.

Sitting at the head table, Dale could see just about everybody in the audience. What he didn't like, of course, is that they could see him. As he discreetly looked over the audience, he detected a certain pall in the air. He hadn't really spoken to Rusty or Chris since he'd heard about the basketball team scandal four days ago. Just the usual banter at the locker. But Friday's game had indeed been forfeited, which made their record 3-13. The school officials had allowed the team to finish the regular season and play in the district tournament. But since all four teams left on the schedule had beaten Galilee by wide margins during their first meeting, Dale doubted they would win any more games. If so, the basketball team would finish the season with the worst record in school history. At least, that's what Don had told him.

Dale figured the poor season and the lingering scandal was the reason why this banquet seemed so low on energy. He spotted Erickson sitting in the back with Roxanne. They didn't look too happy. Dale had heard from Linda and Carrie that Roxanne was on the verge of breaking up with Rich. Roxanne thought his behavior appalling. Erickson had been kicked off the team. He might be suspended from school, too. Dale was surprised he'd shown up. But then Erickson probably enjoyed attending the banquet with the taint of scandal lurking around him. Dale thought he was sort of odd in that way.

Sitting at the same table with Rich and Roxanne were Rusty and Becky Brown. They didn't look too happy, either. Dale noticed Rusty glancing over to a table a few feet away where Mary Jane sat with Billy Joe. Sitting with them were Chris and Carrie. So, she'd asked Chris after all. The two of them seemed to be having a fine time. He saw Chris smiling. Dale had heard that Chris hadn't engaged in any of the improper behavior at Lyons. But Dale wondered why he hadn't tried to prevent it.

Dale saw some of the other senior couples: K. C. and Gretchen, Sonny and Merry, Bigelow and Peggy, Wally and Carmen. As Bonita rose and went to the microphone to welcome the guests, Dale noticed something odd. He hadn't seen Wendy among the crowd. He scanned the audience again, trying not to look too obvious. He didn't see her. How was that possible, he thought? Wendy, as a cheerleader, was one of the most important people in pep club. Surely she would come. He looked again. No sign of her.

Since Dale sat at the head table, he had to pretend with even more conviction that he found the festivities interesting. He tried to listen to Bonita as she gave her opening remarks. He tried to respond to her persistent efforts to have a polite discussion during the fancy meal. He tried to listen to the guest speaker, the dry cleaning woman. But his mind kept drifting back to Wendy's absence. Was she sick? Or did she deliberately not come just to make him feel guilty? He'd seen her yesterday at school, moping through the hallway on the way to class. She hadn't looked sick; just depressed. He couldn't quite believe she would miss the Gopherette banquet during her senior year.

Even when K. C. was named Gopherette Beau, Dale didn't pay much attention. K. C., smiling broadly, accepted the crown from Bonita and kissed her in a friendly way. After all, Gretchen was in the audience.

The banquet ended and Dale said hello to his friends and classmates as they shuffled out of the room while he waited for Bonita. Dale noticed that some of them, Mary Jane and Carmen in particular, looked at him oddly. When they smiled, their eyes peered at him in a critical way like they were examining his face for signs of callousness.

Finally, Bonita was ready to go. They walked to Dale's car while Bonita chattered about the banquet, how well it had gone, how sumptuous the food had been, how delightful the decorations. He hardly listened.

While driving back to Galilee, Bonita stopped in mid-chatter and asked Dale what she'd done wrong. Why was he ignoring her? He'd hardly said a word all evening.

"Sorry, Bonita," he said, glancing at her and seeing her long, thin mouth pressed even thinner in disapproval. She wasn't bad looking, but he couldn't imagine kissing a girl with such thin lips.

"You know, Audie, if you were a little friendlier, you might have won Gopherette beau. K. C. only won by a few votes."

Dale looked at her and wondered how such an intelligent girl would think winning Gopherette beau would matter to him. K. C. was the kind of guy who should win. He was a nice guy. Friendly, happy-go-lucky, enthusiastic. He'd always been one of the popular guys in their class. Dale thought Bonita was just trying to get back at him for his indifference to her.

"Say, Bonita, I hope you don't mind if we don't go anywhere else. I'll just drop you off if that's okay."

Dale glanced at her and saw her gaping at him as if he'd suggested a quickie at a motel.

"If you dislike me so, Audie, then why on earth did you accept my invitation?"

"I don't dislike you."

He saw the exit to Galilee and took it. Bonita lived on the south side of town, not too far from Amanda.

"Then why are you behaving so …"

Dale waited for her to come up with just the right word. He could think of several: callous, mean, boorish, churlish, aloof, bumptious. So when she finally said, "rudely," Dale felt disappointed.

"I don't mean to," he said, turning down her street. "It's just that I have something important to do."

Bonita shook her head in exasperation. "I've always thought you were a little different, a little offbeat. In fact, that's part of your appeal. But I never thought you were so bizarre and selfish."

Dale pulled in front of her house. It was a nice house, a two-story brick with a double garage. Dale couldn't remember what her father did, but it was something quite remunerative in the City. Dale put the car in park. He turned to her.

"I'm really sorry, Bonita. I didn't mean to ruin your evening. I do like you. I like how smart you are and how you're nice even when expressing your opinion. But you said yourself that we were going to the banquet as friends. So, I'm asking you as a friend to excuse my rudeness. I have a reason for it. I just need to go."

Bonita looked at him as if she were considering slapping his face. But then her face relaxed and she nodded and Dale hopped out of the car, ran around to open her door, and rather too quickly walked her to the porch.

Dale paused and looked at her. She'd made herself up quite splendidly, he thought. Her hair was up, she wore tastefully applied makeup, and the light blue eye shadow emphasized her attractive light blue eyes. Her gown, a rich red color, rather daringly bared her small, freckled shoulders. She looked at him with a puzzled expression. But she was no longer angry.

"I hope whatever you're doing goes well," she said. "Oh, and thanks for being my date."

"You're welcome, Bonita." He started to go, then paused, and leaned over and kissed her on the cheek. "Good night, and thanks."

Dale dashed off the porch and scrambled into his car. He glanced back and saw Bonita shaking her head as she went inside her home. He drove away, wishing he could drive faster but knowing he had to be careful in a residential area. He headed north. He now felt his anger returning. He had to tell Wendy to her face that she'd behaved childishly and had not only ruined her senior Gopherette banquet by missing it, but had ruined Bonita's fun as well.

Five minutes later, Dale turned down Wendy's street and parked his car in front of her house. The lights were on. It wasn't late: maybe nine-thirty. He bounded up her porch and banged on the door. Wendy answered. She looked startled to see him.

"Audie!"

"Why didn't you ask somebody to the banquet?" he asked, trying to keep his anger in check.

Wendy's expression changed from surprise to a rather sly expression. "I didn't want to," she said.

"You didn't want to go to your own senior pep club banquet?"

Wendy said nothing. She just looked at him with a rather defiant look.

"Are you just trying to make yourself miserable? There a lot of nice guys you could have asked."

Wendy looked at him with her big, green eyes. They were tearing up. She looked down, and the tears fell from her eyes and trickled down her face.

"I didn't want to go with any of them. I only wanted to go with you."

Dale felt his anger disappear. He looked at her standing at her door, quietly crying, and he felt both shame for himself and sympathy for her.

"I'm sorry, Wendy." He said those words softly. Just saying her name, which Dale usually didn't do, made her turn her face to him.

"Are you, Audie?"

"Yeah, I am. Sorry for what I've done to you."

He looked into her eyes and felt a not-entirely-welcome, warm feeling surge inside him. She must have seen it in his eyes. She moved toward him and Dale embraced her and he heard her say she missed him so. Then they kissed and Dale tasted tears in her mouth. When they parted, he saw Wendy smiling like herself. Her eyes sparkled from the tears and her happiness.

"Mama, I'm going out for a little while," she called back into the house. Her mother said where, with who? "Just out. With Audie."

278

Dale heard the same old cheerfulness in her voice. They walked to the car and he opened the door for her. Dale got in, feeling a little funny wearing his suit with Wendy dressed in jeans and a sweater. She hugged herself when she got in.

Dale asked if she was cold and she nodded, even though for a mid-February night, the weather was rather warm and humid. He took off his suit jacket and gave it to her. Then he turned on the heater. It sputtered. It didn't work very well.

"Where do you want to go?" he asked.

Wendy gave him a suggestive look. "You know."

Dale realized that he'd missed Wendy's warmth these past few weeks. He guessed she missed being close in that way, too. Still, it sort of surprised him that she'd admitted it so candidly, not even disguising her intentions by saying first they should go to West Oaks or the Sooner Shack.

He drove the two miles to their spot and parked the car under the canopy of trees and bushes. As they kissed, it began to rain. As their passion increased, so did the rain. He removed her sweater and heard muted thunder. He removed her bra and fondled her breasts. A streak of lightning flashed across the fields, not far away. Wendy helped him take off his dress shirt. He was surprised by her eagerness. He pressed himself against her, feeling his bare chest rub against the softness of her naked torso. He unbuttoned her jeans and tugged them down to her thighs. For a moment, he remembered that night over at her older brother's and how much difficulty he had with her pants then.

As it rained, Dale reacquainted himself with her fleshy, pale body. He felt more ardor for her than he had in the past. He had missed touching and caressing her. He heard low rumbling in the sky and occasionally Wendy's impassioned face became illuminated when the lightning flashed not too far away. They were going almost as far as they had back in her dorm room at Girls State.

But he stopped at third base. They cuddled for a few minutes and Wendy said she was cold. Dale started the car and turned on the heat. The windows were completely fogged. Wendy wore his suit coat until she felt warm.

"How was the banquet?" she asked.

Dale shook his head, but smiled, too.

**Chapter 11:** *Talkin' to Earl at track; Sonny; Jesse comes home*

Dale was out of shape. He bent over, hands on his knees, and threw up. Chris and Rusty passed him on the track. Rusty said in a sing-song voice that Dale shouldn't have had that hamburger, fries, and shake at Braum's. Dale stood up, and feeling a little woozy, yelled thanks, he'd remember that next time.

Dale jogged toward the finish line. Dorfman watched him straggle in.

"I warned you," he said. "You've got a lot of catching up to do."

Dorfman told them to line up again. He said on your mark, get set, go! The fifteen runners took off around the track again. Dale felt better now that he'd earped. He faded only near the 330 mark, the part of the quarter where most guys "hit the wall," even when in good condition. He still finished ahead of most of the underclassmen.

"Again," Dorfman barked. "Line up."

The guys groaned. They reluctantly lined up. When Dorfman said go! they lurched forward. Dale started off strong again and trailed only Billy Joe, Rusty, and Chris, all three who were in fair track shape from basketball. Then, rounding the last curve, he hit that proverbial wall and coasted to a stop. Panting, sweating, feeling his muscles burn, what he feared the most happened. A tidal wave of nausea surged in his belly and rushed upward.

He bent over at the waist and tried to vomit. But nothing came out but flecks of foam. He caught his breath, then threw up nothing again. Then a third time. Still nothing. His guts churned and he felt dizzy. He breathed in deeply and jogged back to the starting line.

Dorfman stared at him with contempt. "Completely out of shape," he growled. "Sitting on your duff all winter doing the *yearbook*."

Dorfman said the last word with such vehemence that Dale wondered what Coach had against yearbooks.

"Okay, take a five-minute break."

The guys groaned. That meant another round of 440s. They'd already run two rounds.

Dale wandered out to the infield of the track, his arms slung around his neck. He'd never felt so rotten in all his life. Dorfman had warned him. He should have gotten more conditioning in. Of course, he didn't have to go out for track at all. Some seniors didn't. Comingdeer and a couple of other guys didn't last year. But Dale didn't want to be like that. He'd teased Dorfman a few times during the winter about not coming out. Coach had given him a baleful look, no doubt thinking it was possible. Dale had considered it. He felt like paying Dorfman back for cutting baseball. But he knew in the end he would run track. He was good at it and the idea of not coming out just to spite the coach didn't seem right to him. Dale still aspired to behave nobly. Quitting track his senior year wasn't noble.

Rusty and Chris came over. They watched Dale as he trudged in irregular circles.

"You were really talking to Earl back there," Rusty said.

"Then you got the dry heaves," said Chris.

"I don't know which is worse," said Rusty thoughtfully, "throwing up on a full belly or dry heaving."

Dale stopped trudging and glared at them. Rusty and Chris laughed.

They heard Dorfman blow the whistle. The three of them trotted over to the starting line, resigned to their fate.

Dale posed with Wendy for the Mr. and Miss Spirit photograph. Wendy sat on the bench wearing her white cheerleader jacket, smiling. He stood behind her, wearing his crimson letterman's jacket, not smiling. Dale, in fact, felt annoyed that he'd been picked as Mr. Spirit. He knew he'd only been selected because he'd made up with Wendy. He had never been a rah-rah kind of guy and even though the title was more an indication of popularity than an award for demonstrating school spirit, he still felt like a bit of a fraud. Wendy, on the other hand, certainly deserved the award. He couldn't think of any girl who oozed more school spirit than she did.

Mark Werhmeier said cheese and snapped the photo. "Hey, man," he said to Dale, "you weren't smiling."

Dale told him to go and develop the film. He walked Wendy back inside the school. She had a fourth-hour class. She said she'd see him later. He watched her walk briskly back to her accounting class. She seemed pleased to finally have won something, even if it was sort of the fourth-place award.

He didn't have a fourth-hour class, so he walked out of the main entrance of the school to go to the gym. Rusty was often there shooting basketballs or practicing his pacing for the high hurdles. Dale looked at the sunny sky. He smelled the air. It had that refreshing rawness that he liked this time of year. He was about to open the gym door when he saw Sonny across the street standing in the alley talking to Dean Hogue. Dale wondered what Sonny was doing hanging out with Hogue. He saw Sonny give Dean a curt wave and then turned to walk back to the school. Dale waited as Sonny crossed the street. He then went out to meet him.

"Hey, Sonny."

Sonny nodded.

Dale didn't know how to approach the topic. He saw Sonny looking at him, wondering what he wanted. Sonny hadn't gone out for basketball and had been mostly a no-show at the weight and conditioning class. He hadn't shown up for any track practices either. Dale was concerned that Sonny was giving up sports and if that happened, he knew he'd fall in with the wrong crowd for good.

"You shouldn't be hanging out with guys like Hogue," Dale said, deciding on the candid approach.

Sonny smirked. "Oh, yeah? What's it to you?"

"Ordinarily nothing. But we need you in track."

Sonny looked at Dale in his sort of sleepy way.

"We're going to have a good team, but with you pole vaulting and hurdling, we'd have even a better team."

Sonny shrugged. "I dunno."

"Well, it's up to you. But wouldn't it be better to do something good the last months of your senior year like helping your buddies win, rather than hanging out with a bunch of losers?"

Dale expected Sonny to argue his definition of losers. But instead Sonny stood there looking at him in his somnolent way.

"Well, I just wanted to let you know we could use you."

Sonny nodded but didn't say anything as Dale walked into the gym.


Dale thought everybody was talking about Jesse as if she weren't there. Grandma and Wanda, in particular, were making personal comments even though Jesse sat right next to them on the plaid cloth couch.

"I think she's had too many of those shock treatments," said Wanda. "They scramble a body's brains."

Dale looked at his mother. She didn't seem to be offended by her sister's comments – which he thought sort of proved Wanda's point. Jesse sat on the couch with a blank expression on her no-longer-pudgy face. She'd lost weight in the hospital.

"She looks peak-ed to me," said Grandma.

Dale looked over to Yancy and Grandpa sitting on the other couch, the tattered green one. They both looked at Jesse with neutral expressions as if they were judging her sanity and weren't quite sure which way they were going to rule.

"Mama just needs some good home cooking," June May said.

Dale was tempted, but he didn't say anything. He just looked at her and June May stuck her tongue out at him.

"I don't know how Blackie could put her in there," said Wanda.

She meant the state hospital at Norman. Dale thought about telling her Blackie's reasons, but he wasn't sure he agreed with them.

"Forrest knowed what was best," said Grandpa.

"I ain't so sure," said Wanda. "That place ain't even clean."

Dale had visited Jesse a couple of times during the weekends when family members could visit patients in the large, sunny room the attendants called the "family room." He had thought the room looked clean. It smelled pretty good, too. Not like the hallways that he'd walked through to get there.

"Where'd he take her instead?" Grandpa asked.

He grabbed his Folger's can and spat into it. Yancy had brought Grandpa a new package of Red Man tobacco and Grandpa had already gnawed off a plug.

"I just think a real husband wouldn't take his wife of twenty year to an old state institution," Wanda said.

Dale wondered what qualified Wanda as an expert on real husbands. She'd had five now, three different, but none were real in the sense she meant it.

"Well, Dale," said Yancy, "you're turning eighteen pretty soon. How do you think you'll like being a man legal and all?"

Dale knew his uncle was trying to change the subject so he played along. "Fine, I guess. I can't wait to go out and get drunk."

They all stared at him, even Jesse.

"I'm joking," he said.

Grandpa and Yancy laughed. The women didn't think he was funny.

"I bet you're glad there ain't a draft," said Yancy. "They might nab you and send you overseas."

Dale shrugged. "I'd go if I had to."

He had to register for the selective service just the same in case the government revived the draft. He and a couple of other seniors registered in Mr. Smedley's office last week. Mr. Smedley had given them the Peace Corps applications at first.

Then Dale added, "But I'd rather go to college."

Grandpa said Dale would be the first in the Walsh family to go to college. "Ain't that sumthin'?" he said, smiling and showing some tobacco juice between his teeth.

Wanda said Blackie was going to college so that didn't mean much of nothin'. Dale stared at her, wondering why she was so critical of Blackie. Dale guessed she never really liked him but she'd never bad-mouthed his father so openly before.

"Forrest is a good man," Grandpa said. "Just doin' what he has to."

"If he's so all-fired good, then why did he stick Jesse in Norman?" Wanda asked. "He had the money to put her in a decent private hospital."

Dale wondered how she knew that. It annoyed him to hear her make that accusation although he had wondered the same thing.

Then Grandpa and Wanda started bickering over the point, and soon Grandma joined in. Dale looked at Yancy, who looked like he didn't have the patience for another family feud. Yancy got up and said he had to go to work.

"Always workin'," said Grandpa.

He got up and shook Yancy's hand. Yancy walked over to Jesse and put a hand on her shoulder.

"You take care, now," he said.

Jesse looked at him, her eyes a little glazed, but she half-smiled. Yancy then shook hands with Dale and waved at June May, Grandma, and Wanda and left. Grandpa followed him out to his car.

"I don't know why they stick up for Blackie," said Wanda. She caught Dale staring at her and she frowned at him but didn't say anything.

Dale didn't like agreeing with Wanda on principle, but he wondered if she knew more than he did about Jesse's hospitalization. Still, he didn't like her yakking about his dad. She had no room to talk about Blackie or anybody else. He didn't even think she was a good mother. He also held it against her that she'd been on welfare when she wasn't married, which was about half the time.

"I'm ready to go," said Jesse.

Grandpa, who'd just come back in, said she ought to stay a little longer. Grandma asked her if she wanted some lemonade. Or maybe a bite to eat. She'd eaten so little of her Sunday dinner. Wanda said she needed her rest.

Jesse stood up. Grandpa, Grandma, and Wanda hugged her as Dale waited for her. He noticed that Grandma took off her glasses and dabbed her eyes with the end of her apron. Dale opened the door for Jesse and she and June May walked out to the car.

"Now, take care of her, Dale," said Grandpa.

Then he heard Wanda's brassy voice say she'd be visitin' soon. They had some talkin' to do.

Dale didn't look back at his aunt, but he knew that sounded like trouble.

Dale brought the last pages of the yearbook to Mrs. Schoendienst to sign. He carried the mailing package, unsealed, to her classroom. She had a free period for fourth hour and usually sat at her desk preparing for her next class. He knocked on her half-open door, heard her say come in, and presented her with the completed work.

"I'm impressed," Mrs. Schoendienst said. "You're three days ahead of the deadline."

Dale said he wanted to finish before deadline. He had a track meet Friday and the all-sports banquet Saturday.

Mrs. Schoendienst took out a few envelopes containing layouts, photos, and copy and glanced at the work. She said it looked fine. She'd review all the pages today and if they all were correct and proper, she would mail the package tomorrow.

Dale nodded and started to leave when Mrs. Schoendienst asked him to stay for a minute.

"I wanted to say, Audie, that I had reservations about you as editor. I wasn't sure if you were mature enough to handle the responsibilities. And then there was the issue of time. As I told you before, we've never had an athlete edit the yearbook before." She paused and looked at Dale with her heavy-lidded eyes. "But I must say that my qualms were unjustified. You've done an excellent job. Not only did you meet all the deadlines, which is nearly unprecedented, but you showed some creativity as well."

Dale wasn't so sure he'd done a good job. He really didn't know much about the technical aspects of editing a yearbook. He already knew he'd made mistakes in the more subtle areas of design. Some of his photographs weren't very good. But he had worked hard and met all the deadlines.

"Thanks, Mrs. Schoendienst. I had a lot of fun doing it. I learned a lot, too."

"You ought to consider majoring in journalism in college."

Dale said he was considering that. She nodded and turned back to her class prep and he left her classroom.

He walked back to the yearbook office and looked at the disorder: left over layout sheets, contact sheets, grease pencils, pica poles, tape, and wadded-up copy pages littered the room. Dale sat down and took the room in. He thought he liked this room even more than the gym or the football field or the track, other places he spent a lot of time. He thought this was his favorite place of all. And now the monumental project of the yearbook was completed. He felt nostalgic already.

Mrs. Page wasn't expected to be in class for fifth hour speech. Her eldest daughter, Portia, had been rushed to the hospital the day before to give birth. Apparently, there were some complications with the delivery and Mrs. Page had spent a lot of time at the hospital in Oklahoma City. Dale, sitting at his desk at the back of the room, remembered seeing pictures of Portia in an old yearbook. In spite of her old-fashioned puffy hairdo, a style popular back in the mid '60s, he thought she was attractive in a refined, ladylike way. She had light brown hair and light-colored eyes, and in every photo she had an endearing smile on her face. She'd been crowned all-school queen and had graduated with high honors. All three of Mrs. Page's daughters had been excellent students and popular girls. Laurie, the youngest, had been all-school queen and head cheerleader during his sophomore year. Whenever he thought of Laurie, he still felt the sweet pang of adolescent lust.

The substitute teacher, an older woman with glasses, began class with roll. She had almost gotten to Dale when the principal, Mr. Zook, came on the intercom. Dale could tell by his heavy voice that something serious had happened. He listened as Mr. Zook told the students of the junior and senior high that he had the sad duty to inform them that Mrs. Page's daughter, Portia, a 1970 graduate of Galilee High, had died in childbirth just before noon today.

Dale heard several students gasp. Some of the girls began crying. The principal said there would be a memorial service for students tomorrow after school. Today's fifth hour and sixth hour classes would be cancelled. Before dismissing classes, he asked the students to join him as he offered a prayer.

Dale bowed his head with the rest of his classmates. He hardly heard the prayer. He kept thinking of the young woman he'd seen in the 1969-70 yearbook. He remembered all the photographs of her: pictures of her smiling as head cheerleader; the photo of her as an academic honors student. Candid photos of her cheerleading, working on the homecoming float, laughing with her friends. And now she was dead. Dale felt sick inside. It didn't seem fair for someone so young and vivacious to die, especially in childbirth. He didn't even know such deaths happened anymore. He didn't know Portia, but he'd seen her from afar a few times. She'd been a senior when he was in seventh grade, but junior high kids, especially seventh graders, kept pretty much to themselves on the other side of the large building. However, being in such general proximity back then, and having seen all her photographs in the old yearbook, and knowing her mother and younger sisters, made Dale feel her death more keenly than he could have imagined.

During the principal's prayer, Dale heard crying and even some sobbing. When the prayer ended and the substitute teacher dismissed class, he looked at the front of the class where the girls sat and saw Amanda and Mary Jane hugging. He saw Amanda's tearful face and felt his own eyes burn. He wished he could comfort her. He wished he could dry her tears. He turned away, knowing that his feelings for her were as powerful as they had ever been.

He walked out of the classroom and went to the yearbook office. He wasn't sure what to do. He wondered if they'd have track practice. Hearing soft footsteps outside, he got up and went to the office door where he saw Wendy.

"Oh, Audie, isn't it awful?"

Dale took a step toward her and she fell into his arms. He hugged her and looked down the hall and saw Amanda and Mary Jane leaning against each other for emotional comfort as they walked. He heard crying echoing in the hall. He saw Mrs. Heath brushing away tears as she consoled students.

"Yeah," Dale said, "it's awful."

The last time anything this bad had happened was in fifth grade. Two grade school teachers, Mr. and Mrs. Thisbee, husband and wife, were killed in a car crash. Dale hadn't been in either of their homerooms but he had seen them every day in the halls. He thought they seemed like nice people. They both were young. The kids liked them, especially Mrs. Thisbee. Dale hadn't felt any anguish about their deaths. But the teachers and a lot of the students were distraught for days. Rusty had Mrs. Thisbee for homeroom in fourth grade. Dale thought he seemed pretty shook up but he didn't bawl or anything. He just grew uncharacteristically quiet for a few days.

Wendy wiped her tears away and said she was going with Carmen and some of the other girls to the Page's house. They were going to help in any way they could. Prepare some meals. Help answer phones. Just be with all the people that knew and loved Portia and the Page family.

Dale said sure, that was fine. Wendy asked what he was going to do. He said he didn't know. He guessed he'd go to the gym and see if they were having track practice. Wendy asked him to call her that night and he said he would. He watched as Wendy walked down the hall, found Carmen, hugged her, and the two of them walked toward the building's front entrance.

Dale left by the back exit and walked around the building to the gym's back door. He walked in and saw Dorfman sitting in the bleachers talking to Coach Blocker. Dale asked if they were having track practice.

Dorfman said yes, at the regular time. He then added that Dale could be excused if he wanted, considering the circumstances.

284

Dale walked down to the locker room but no one was there. He came back up and walked down to the other end of the gym and stopped. He had two hours to kill. He didn't know what to do. It struck him as almost funny. He'd been busy all these months with football, track, the yearbook, his classes, and pretending to co-direct the all-school play. Mrs. Page had done the real directing. He didn't mind. He and Carrie, who like him was too shy to actually act in a play, enjoyed "conferring" with Mrs. Page on how to direct all their friends in *Our Town*. Rusty and Roxanne had played the leads. Dale had been surprised by how well Rusty performed in a serious role. Amanda played Mrs. Webb and in the last act had to wear makeup to make her look old and haggard. The make-up didn't work. Dale thought no makeup could ugly up Amanda.

He realized he didn't want to think too much about Mrs. Page right then. He was afraid he might start bawling like the girls. Instead, he thought how for months he'd not had five minutes of free time, let alone two hours. He thought about all the things he'd done to keep himself busy. Even with the yearbook, he'd kept reading important books. Then he realized he didn't even have his latest book with him, Chekhov's collected plays, which Mrs. Page had recommended he read. Dale sat down on a bleacher and realized he'd forgotten how to do nothing for two hours.

Girls were on the bus. Dale didn't approve. It was five thirty on a Saturday morning and as he boarded the bus, he saw seven girls sitting in the front. Most were sophomores. Still half-asleep, at first he didn't know why the girls were present. Then he remembered. They were members of Galilee's girls track team.

Dale walked to the very back seat and sat down by the window. A few minutes later, Rusty and Chris showed up. Rusty sat next to Dale and Chris took the opposite seat with Leroy. Billy Joe, Sonny, K. C., and Bigelow filled in the other back rows. The junior boys took the middle seats and the sophomore boys sat in the seats behind the girls. The bus filled, Dorfman told Cookie to head north to the Wheaton Invitational.

Everyone except Dorfman and Cookie slept while the bus lumbered one hundred miles north. Dale awoke an hour out of Wheaton and looked out the window at the waving wheat fields. He looked beyond them at the sky. Clear and serenely blue, with a morning freshness. But Dale knew that didn't mean anything. A storm could brew in a matter of minutes and come swooping onto the plains. It had happened last year.

Once they arrived at the Wheaton track, the coaches and runners got off the bus to do their usual routines. Dale remembered his book, *Tess of the D'Urbervilles* that he'd left on the bus. He turned around and headed back and while bounding up the steps he encountered Sheba Smith coming down.

"Oops," said Sheba, holding a pair of spikes she'd apparently forgotten. She smiled and tried to step aside.

Dale thought about squeezing by but thought it best not to brush up against her. He jumped down and waited impatiently for her to exit.

"Thanks," she said, smiling and looking at him with her interesting blue-green eyes.

Dale grimly nodded and watched her as she trotted over to the other girls. He heard her giggle as they walked away. He grabbed the paperback and jogged back to the track.

This was the first meet that the girls had rode with the boys. The only other meets the girls had gone to were the smaller ones and they'd rode in cars. Dale wasn't sure why they were coming to the Wheaton Invitational. None had a chance of winning anything.

Dale read when he wasn't warming up or running his events. His senior English class had read *The Return of the Native* and he'd liked it so much he'd decided to read another Hardy novel. About halfway through *Tess*, he thought it was pretty good.

The other guys teased him about reading at track meets. He'd read *1984, Brave New World, Oliver Twist*, and *Cyrano de Bergerac* at previous track meets. It helped pass the time, plus he enjoyed reading. He just ignored guys like Bigelow who couldn't believe he was reading for fun. "What are you, some kind of weirdo?" Butch had asked when he saw him reading *Brave New World*. Dale had replied that Bigelow was an epsilon minus. Butch didn't get the joke.

So far, the Galilee track team was enjoying a successful season. They'd won every dual meet they ran in and placed in the top three at five invitationals. The team had gone on a two-day trip to western Oklahoma in early May and had placed second in the first meet on Friday, and after staying the night, had won the Panhandle meet on Saturday. Dale loved running in the Panhandle meet. There hadn't been any fast black guys at that meet. He'd won four gold medals in the 100, 220, 440 relay, and the medley relay.

The Wheaton Invitational didn't have a medley relay event this year, so Dale wasn't sure what his fourth event would be. At the other meets that didn't have a medley relay, he'd broad jumped. He supposed he would do that again, even though he didn't have long-enough legs to broad jump well. He'd only got fifth place the last time.

Dale sat around with the other guys when Dorfman showed up to make sure everyone knew the time for their events. He didn't want anybody screwing up. Marty Dewberry had missed one of his events at the Panhandle Invitational, the 880. It hadn't mattered; Galilee had won anyway. But Coach wasn't taking any chances this time.

Dale asked Dorfman if he could broad jump since there wasn't a medley relay. Dorfman said no. Dale waited for a reason, but Dorfman walked away without giving one. He thought he was lucky. Maybe he'd only have three events.

He and Chris walked over to where they were staging the 100-yard dash. Just as Dale feared, the events were running late because of adding girls' events. He and Chris decided to wait. The last heat of the girls' race was about to be run. Dale looked down at the starting line and saw Sheba Smith. He remembered her as a kid back when she and June May played together after school. He recalled thinking she was sort of cute as a little kid. He really hadn't seen much of her since. She was a year ahead of June May and the two of them had sort of drifted apart. Now, Dale noticed she was still sort of cute and when she took off her sweats he had ample evidence that she wasn't a child any more. The girls wore the same kind of thin running shorts as the boys; instead of sleeveless jerseys they wore T-shirts with sleeves. As Sheba warmed up, he stared at her shapely legs, especially her thighs. When she turned around to walk back to her blocks, he said "wow" at seeing her curvaceous buttocks jiggling under the thin material of her shorts. Maybe having girls at track meets wasn't such a bad idea after all.

Chris, who'd been looking the other way, asked him what he meant.

"Wow, it's taking a long time to run this event," Dale said.

For some reason, he didn't want to direct Chris's attention to Sheba's plush bottom. He'd find out anyway if he watched her run. As Sheba kneeled down at her blocks, Dale noticed she was rather flat-chested. Well, he thought, you can't have everything.

Sheba looked quite a bit like Sadie; the same snowy hair and fairly plain face, except when she smiled the dimples in her cheeks made her cute. But unlike her older sister, she had blue-green eyes that Dale found especially interesting.

The starter's gun popped and the girls ran down the track. Dale watched as Sheba started well but slowly fell behind. Still, she wasn't bad for a sophomore.

Ten minutes later, Dale won his heat in a time of ten flat, tying his best time for the year. Chris recorded a 10.3, which didn't qualify.

Back to the camp Dale and Chris went. Dale resumed reading *Tess* and occasionally glanced up as the guys goofed around. Some of the girls had moved from their little camp to the boys' camp. One of them was Sheba. He glanced at her from time to time. She had put her sweats back on.

The day methodically wore on. Dale qualified for the 220. The 440-relay team qualified, too. Other qualifiers included Rusty in the 110 high hurdles, the 330 intermediate hurdles, and the broad jump; Sonny in the pole vault; Billy Joe in the 440, 880 and long jump;

Bigelow and Mears in the discus; Leroy in the shot; Matt Jones in the 330 intermediate hurdles; and Marty Dewberry in the mile and high jump. The team was in good shape for the finals. Everything seemed in place except for the mile relay team.

Dorfman had been shuffling players on the mile relay team all season. The concluding event, Dorfman still hadn't found the best four. Billy Joe always ran on it. Matt, Chris, Rusty, and the sophomore, Jason Jordan, who also ran on the 440 relay, had tried it. Since Dale almost always had four events, including two other relays, he'd never been on it and he was glad. He hated running quarters. He'd told Dorfman and anyone else who'd listen that he didn't have long-enough legs to run the quarter. Of course, Matt's legs were pretty short, too, but he gutted it out. That was one of Dorfman's favorite phrases: gut it out. Well, Dale didn't mind gutting it out; he minded vomiting his guts out. He painfully remembered running all those 440s to get into shape.

After lunch, Billy Joe asked who was on the mile relay team. Dale, sitting Indian-style on the old gym mats, noticed that Dorfman didn't answer right away. He looked up and saw Dorfman staring at him. Dale didn't know if he was staring because he still couldn't get used to a guy reading at a track meet or if Dorfman was considering the length of his legs. When Dorfman strode off to watch Sonny pole vault, Dale felt an uneasy foreboding.

Late in the afternoon, Dale and Chris walked over to the start of the 100 finals. Chris nodded in the direction of the three Ellison sprinters who'd made the finals. Dale wasn't surprised. Ellison was the only black school at the meet. He knew Ellison had fast sprinters.

While warming up, Dale noticed one of the Ellison guys looked familiar. Dale thought about it and recognized him as the guy that looked sort of like Bill Cosby. He smiled to himself as he kneeled at his blocks.

The official told them to take their marks. Get set. Then Dale heard the crack of the starter's pistol. He got a good jump. He leapt out of his blocks nearly in full stride and raced down the track. He listened to the song of his spikes on the cinder. He kept his head straight and didn't look to either side, although he knew he was neck and neck with all three of the Ellison guys. The tape suddenly jumped at him and he ducked his shoulders and broke through the finish line. His momentum carried him another twenty yards as he gradually slowed down. He glanced back at the officials. They were gathered by the field box comparing times and talking over who'd won and placed. Dale knew it was a close race but he figured he'd gotten beat by inches by at least two of the Ellison sprinters.

He strolled back to the finish line as the officials continued conferring. He looked over at the Cosby guy, who met his glance and frowned.

Finally, the officials pointed to the shortest Ellison guy as the winner. The tallest Ellison sprinter finished second. And Dale edged out the Cosby guy for third. Dale walked over to Dorfman, who told him he'd run a 9.9. Wow, Dale thought, he'd broken ten seconds. He thought it was interesting how 9.9 sounded so much faster than ten flat.

Dale noticed the Cosby look-alike walking by with his two teammates. Dale grabbed his sweats and jogged over to the three Ellison guys. He told them they all ran a good race. The two Ellison guys that had finished first and second didn't respond. They were sort of arrogant guys or at least didn't like talking to competition. But the Cosby guy said thanks. Dale looked at him and waited. Finally it came.

"Man, I remember you," said the Cosby guy. "You stole that football from me."

The Ellison guy was referring to Dale's interception of a pass in the Ellison-Galilee football game. Dale outfought the Cosby guy for the football.

"Man, I thought I had that ball all the way. Just like I thought I had you beat in that hunnad."

Dale couldn't help but smile. The guy really did look like a younger version of Bill Cosby.

"What you laffin' at, man?"

Dale told him.

"Yeah, I get that all the time." But he laughed, too.

Dale asked him his name.

"Maurice Morris," he said. He pronounced his first name, "Mo-reese."

"Almost like Mercury Morris," said Dale, referring to a Miami Dolphins halfback.

"You like him, too?"

Dale teasingly said he liked Csonka better.

"Being a white boy, I guess you would." But Maurice laughed, too.

Dale said he was glad he didn't have to run against the three of them at all the track meets.

"Yeah, wez usually go south for our meets."

Dale didn't say so, but he was glad. There were a lot more black guys running in meets in the south of the state. Galilee usually went to meets in the north or west where the slower white guys ran.

Dale noticed the other two Ellison guys staring at them. He said he'd see Maurice at the 220 finals.

"Not me, just those two. Ah didn't qualify."

Maurice waved goodbye and ran to join his two teammates.

Dale walked back to the Galilee camp. He liked ol' Maurice. He had a good sense of humor. He put on his sweats when Bigelow walked by, cradling his discus.

"I saw you talking to them."

"Who?"

"The colored guys."

"I was just talking to Maurice."

"So you know one of their names already."

"Just found out. What's it to you, Bigelow?"

"Nothing, Smith. You run like one of them, anyway."

"That's a compliment."

"You sort of look like one, too."

Dale stared at Bigelow. Dale tanned easily and now in mid-May his skin had been burnished bronze by the sun. But that was a long way from being black. He didn't know why Bigelow was provoking him. Maybe he wanted to finish their fight.

"No, I don't," said Dale. "But I'll tell you one thing, Bigelow. I'd rather look like them than you."

Bigelow feinted throwing his discus at Dale's groin. Dale flinched and Butch snorted. Then he strolled off to the discus area.

Chris came up to Dale and asked what he and Bigelow were discussing. Dale gave him a rough version of the conversation.

Chris shook his head in disgust. "Just ignore the jerk."

"Sure. But I want you to do me a favor."

"Okay. What?"

"I want you to ask Amanda out to the junior-senior banquet."

Chris opened his eyes wide in surprise. "What's that got to do with Bigelow?"

"I don't want him to ask her."

Dale felt Chris scrutinizing him. He didn't want to go into details but he knew he might have to. A month ago, Bigelow had taken Amanda to the all-sports banquet. When Dale saw them sitting together he almost felt steam coming out of his ears like a character in those goofy cartoons. He couldn't believe Amanda accepted Bigelow's invitation. Dale's worst fear had been realized. He sat with Wendy at their table and tried not to stare at Amanda and Bigelow together. Dale knew Butch went to First Church. He knew Amanda had known him for years. He knew she was probably too polite to turn him down. But he couldn't believe she knew the real Bigelow. If she did, Dale was positive that she'd never go anywhere with him.

But Bigelow had a few points in his favor. He said what was on his mind, which Dale preferred over phoniness. He wasn't afraid of anything. Dale had seen him take on guys thirty pounds heavier than him in football and not back down. Dale guessed even some girls, if they liked pigs, thought him cute. Bigelow still had a porcine look to him with his bristly blond hair and his pug nose.

The banquet had been an ordeal to sit through. Almost as painful as watching Bigelow grinning at Amanda, Dale had to watch him win the award for best football player. On one hand, he admitted that Bigelow had played well at linebacker. But he only started on defense. Dale played both ways. He hadn't expected to win the award. He felt he'd had a disappointing senior season, which led to a disappointing team record. But he thought he was just as deserving as Bigelow. Actually, Dale had expected Leroy to win. He deserved it. He anchored the line. He'd also been named the district's best defensive player. But the coaches obviously didn't agree. Just another example of Dorfman being unfair, thought Dale.

The other awards given out at the banquet were acceptable. Rusty won best basketball player. Billy Joe won best all-around athlete. Since he starred in all three sports, that was an obvious choice.

After the banquet, Wendy had tried to cheer Dale up, thinking he was annoyed at not having won the football award. He couldn't tell her that what really bothered him was knowing that Amanda was with Bigelow at that very moment.

"Why do you care if Bigelow asks Amanda?" inquired Chris.

"Because I don't like Bigelow," Dale said. "And I like Amanda." He didn't quite look Chris directly in his eyes. "As a friend."

Dale didn't think Chris completely believed him. He knew Dale had dated Amanda for a while.

"I don't know," Chris said.

"Why not?"

"I don't think she'll go with me."

Dale almost said if she'd went with Bigelow to the all-sports she'll go with you. Instead, he said Chris didn't have enough confidence.

Chris shrugged.

"See?" Dale said, playfully shoving his friend. "Look, you've known Amanda for years, right?"

"Yeah. As long as I can remember."

"Well, then you're friends. She'll go with you."

Chris looked uneasy. "Look, Audie, that's the problem. I don't know if I want her to go with me just as a friend."

Dale hadn't anticipated that. "I didn't know you were really interested in her."

"I've always liked her. But she's like all the other pretty girls. She only likes me as a friend."

Dale wasn't sure what to say. He felt awkward knowing his second best friend liked his favorite girl, who really wasn't his girl. Things were certainly complicated.

"Take her as a friend," Dale said. "Just accept that for the time being. After all, you don't want her going with Bigelow. She doesn't know the real Bigelow. You don't want her to find out, do you?"

Chris nodded thoughtfully. "Yeah, I see what you mean. Amanda's so nice she tends to think everyone else is as nice as she is."

"Then you'll do it?"

Chris said he would.

"Then call her tonight." The junior-senior was two weeks away.

"It'll be too late tonight when we get home."

"Then ask her first thing at church Sunday."

"Okay, okay. But I don't know why you care so much."

Dale tried to think of a plausible answer. "Because you're my buddy. And Bigelow is my enemy."

That made sense to Chris.

They walked over to see Rusty run the finals of the 110 high hurdles. Rusty had to race against two Ellison guys. He beat one of them for second place.

Dale ran the 220 and predictably the two Ellison guys beat him. But he came in third and got another medal.

The 440-relay team finished second. Ellison's relay team won first. It looked like Ellison would easily win the invitational in class A. But the race for second was close between Quanah Parker and Galilee. The second-place team won a bigger trophy and Dale thought it would look pretty good in their fairly empty trophy case.

The day stretched into early evening and there were only a few more events before the meet's finale, the mile relay. Dorfman strolled over to Dale and the rest of the guys and looked at them with a rather mysterious air. Dale knew he was deciding who would be on the relay team. No one liked running the mile relay. Even Billy Joe didn't like running it, although he ran both the open quarter and anchored the mile relay. For the past six weeks, he'd listened to the candidates for the remaining three spots worry and fret about being picked. Dale wondered if Dorfman wasn't changing the relay team just to keep them on edge. If so, he thought that was psychological torture. If a guy only had three events, then he went through the whole meet wondering if he'd be picked for the mile relay. It ruined the entire day. Now, Dale had experienced the anxiety, worrying throughout the Wheaton meet if he'd be on the mile relay team. Finally, the moment of truth had arrived.

Dorfman first named, as usual, Billy Joe. Then Matt, who tried to disguise a frown. Then he picked Jordan. Only a sophomore, Jordan was already a strapping kid, almost six-feet tall and swift. He probably would make a better quarter man than a pure sprinter as he got older. Then Dorfman coolly looked over the other candidates. Dale felt a sinking feeling. He'd guessed once Coach hadn't let him broad jump that he'd be picked.

"And you, Smith. Okay, men, get ready. The mile relay will get us second if you place above Quanah Parker."

Dale flopped on his back and stared at the darkening sky. He didn't have long-enough legs to run the quarter. It was a race for tall guys, he thought, conveniently forgetting Matt.

When he sat up he saw Rusty and Chris grinning at him. For weeks, they both had been tormented with the possibility of being on the mile relay team. Rusty, who often was named, probably would have been picked but he'd tweaked an ankle during the 330 intermediate finals. Both Rusty and Chris thought it was funny that Dale was now getting a taste of torture.

"You'll love it," said Rusty. "Just remember to take l-l-l-l-long strides."

Dale wanted to punch him. "Why don't you volunteer to run in my place?"

"I'd like to, man, but I got this ache in my little finger." Rusty held up his pinky and grimaced.

Dale jumped up and grabbed Rusty's little finger and gave it a twist.

"Hey, man, that hurts." Rusty pulled his finger out of Dale's hand. "Save your aggression for the race."

Chris slapped Dale on the back and said it wasn't so bad. Sure, a guy ran out of breath after three hundred yards of sprinting, but who needed air?

Dale saw Dorfman waving at them to get ready. Dale joined the three other relay guys and walked over to the starting line. They watched as two heats were run, then got ready for their race. Dorfman wanted Jordan to lead off; Coach often wanted the inexperienced guys to lead off a relay. That way they only had to pass and not receive the baton. Dorfman put Matt second, then Billy Joe third, with Dale running anchor. Dale shook his head and muttered to himself. Running anchor meant that everyone would be counting on him if they were in contention. He thought Dorfman should have left Billy Joe as anchor.

The race started and Jordan did okay. He passed the baton to Matt with Galilee in sixth place out of eight teams. Matt chugged around the track and lost one spot. He passed off to Billy Joe, who started out fast. Dale got in the third lane. He had to stay in that lane until he passed the marker, then he could cut into the first lane. He jogged in place, keeping loose as he watched Billy Joe race around the track. Billy Joe passed one man, then on the last curve passed two more. Three teams were still ahead – one of them, in first, Quanah Parker. Dale felt his stomach flipping and flopping. His mouth was already dry from nervousness. He felt that familiar fear of not wanting to fail. He gritted his teeth and watched as Billy Joe, his equine face gasping for air, raced toward him.

Dale timed his takeoff, reached back, and grabbed the baton. He sprinted around the first curve, then cut in. He passed one guy on the straightway. He felt his legs flying underneath him. He pumped his arms and tried not to think about anything. In some ways what he disliked most about running longer distance was that his mind always seemed to be thinking about how far he'd run, how far he had to go, how tired he was beginning to feel, how close the other runners were getting. If he could stop himself from thinking as he ran, then the longer race wouldn't be so bad.

To Dale's surprise, he passed the runner from Agra and closed the gap with the Quanah Parker guy at the 300-yard mark. He felt his muscles burning and his lungs straining for air. But he forced more speed out of his legs and began to pass the Quanah Parker runner. Dale glanced at his opponent's face. He looked in agony: his dusky face contorted in pain as his long black hair fluttered behind him.

Dale suddenly hit the wall. He felt his legs turn to jelly. He felt like he was melting as he ran down the straightaway. He struggled to keep his small lead but the Quanah Parker kid slowly moved in front of him. Dale felt the futility of running as hard as he could while falling behind.

He still held to the second spot as he crossed the finish line. He stumbled a few more yards down the track, dropped the baton, and threw his hands on top of his head. He was so out of breath that he could hardly breathe in without his sides aching terribly. His lungs felt as if they had exploded inside him. Sweat poured down his face and stung his eyes. The muscles of his legs and arms burned as if on fire. He wandered off the track and onto the infield. His stomach felt like it was a trampoline and some vile, viscous stuff was jumping up and down on it.

Dale hated the mile relay.

Dorfman told the team to assemble over by the short bleachers. The girls team had already left for the bus. Dale walked in a daze over to the bleachers and collapsed on the first row. He slowly caught his breath and lowered his head into his hands. He felt really, really sick.

Dorfman told them they'd done a good job overall. He critiqued a few performances. Winning third was an accomplishment at Wheaton. Most of the better teams in their class were competing here.

Dale half-listened to Coach and half-listened to his rampaging belly. Dorfman asked some of the guys how they thought they'd done as a team. He wanted them to show their spirit. It was especially important to show grit when you're tired. He wanted them to show him the guts he knew they had.

Dale, leaning over, his hands on his knees, his head hanging low, noticed that Coach had new white track shoes with a crimson trim. Then he heard Dorfman ask him what he thought. Did this team have the guts to win?

Dale knew he was about to talk to Earl. He thought about what an inviting target Dorfman's shoes made. He was tempted. He resented Dorfman for a lot of things. But he couldn't do it.

Dorfman repeated his question. Instead of speaking, Dale got up and took five steps away from Dorfman's shoes and replied in a totally different way. He loudly vomited.

He wiped his mouth with the back of his hand and returned to the bleachers and resumed his seat. Dorfman asked Chris if he thought this team could win. Chris said yes.

After the pep talk, Dale joined Rusty and Chris as they walked back to the bus.

"Why didn't you do it?" Rusty asked Dale.

"Do what?"

"You know. Talk to Earl right on Dorf's shoes."

"I was thinking about it."

"Thinking about it? That's your problem, Dale. You're always thinking rather than doing."

Rusty was joking but Dale thought maybe he was right. Rusty probably would have puked on Coach's shoes. Dale hoped Rusty had a chance at the next track meet.


The track team got back to Galilee at eleven that night. He met Wendy at the high school and they drove to Sooner Shack for a Coke, then went to their favorite spot to park. After an hour and a half, Dale took Wendy home. When he arrived at his own home at one, he observed that Blackie's Olds wasn't parked in the driveway. His patrol car wasn't there either.

Dale went inside. He knew everyone was asleep so he'd have to wait until the morning to find out where Blackie's cars were. Exhausted from all the day's activity, he quickly fell asleep in his bed.

The next morning he awoke to the chirping of birds along with the chirping of three female voices. He lay in bed for a few moments and identified the voices of Jesse, June May, and Wanda. What was Wanda doing here on a Sunday morning? Dale quickly got ready and walked into the living room and saw Jesse and Wanda looking at him with expressions that seemed to say he was intruding.

"Momma's divorcing Daddy," June May blurted out.

"What?" Dale looked at Jesse. She stuck a cigarette in her mouth and lit it with the lighter that Blackie had given her for Christmas. "Is that so?"

Jesse took a puff and nodded.

"Why? He just moved back a few months ago."

Jesse took the cigarette out of her mouth and gave him a reproachful look. "Reason number one, he put me in Norman."

"He had to, Mom."

"No, he didn't," said Wanda. "He coulda put her in a private hospital like he did before."

Dale wished Wanda would butt out. "That's not what Dad told me. He said he didn't have the money for a private hospital."

"Pshaw," said Wanda.

Dale didn't know what that meant.

"He has plenty of money socked away somewhere," said Jesse, waving her cigarette for emphasis. "He just don't want to spend it on me." She paused to take another drag. "Anyways, that's not the only reason."

He waited. Jesse puffed. Dale looked at his aunt.

"He was tom-cattin' behind her back," Wanda said.

"How do you know?" Dale asked, but he knew already.

"I *saw* him," Wanda said, with evident satisfaction.

For a moment, Dale wondered if Wanda was the woman he saw having coffee with Blackie that night. She looked like her. Both had puffed-up blond hair and wore too much makeup. But the woman Dale saw was at least ten years younger. He felt relieved that it couldn't have been Wanda.

"What do you have to say about that, mister?" Jesse asked in an accusatory voice.

"About what?"

"What you just heard. You knew about your daddy gallivantin' around with ... whores.'"

Dale doubted that woman he saw was so professional. "No, I don't. Why would I know about Dad's business? I'm busy with my own –" Dale almost said "affairs" but caught himself in time. "— stuff. School stuff. And track."

"Yeah, I bet," said Jesse.

"Oh, that's right. After I go to all my classes, edit the yearbook, help direct the all-school play, go to a track meet all day and half the night, and see my girlfriend, I manage to find a couple hours to assist Dad with his illicit paramours."

Jesse didn't quite follow Dale's recitation. In particular, she didn't understand the words *illicit paramours*. Neither did Wanda or June May. Nevertheless, Dale had made a valid point.

"Maybe so," said Jesse. "But I'm divorcin' him anyway."

Dale looked at Wanda. He knew it was her fault. She had put Jesse up to it. After all, Wanda had plenty of experience.

Wanda noticed the truculent look in Dale's eyes and gathered her big, junky purse and got up to leave.

"I gotta get goin'. Clyde's awaitin'."

Dale guessed Clyde was her new husband. "Why don't you just give them numbers?" Dale said, as Wanda flounced out of the room.

"Least I marry mine," called back Wanda. Dale had to give her credit for at least getting the numerical reference.

Jesse hadn't. "What on earth are you gabbin' about?"

Dale threw up his hands. "Are you really going to do this?"

"Yeah, Momma," June May chimed in. "You ain't really going to divorce Daddy?"

"Yes, I am. I have my particulars."

Dale looked at his mother. He recognized that self-satisfied, self-righteous smirk on her face. He'd seen it before when she was a Witness. He knew he couldn't reason with her.

"It doesn't make sense. But go ahead. It will just make things worse."

"Thank you, Mr. Audie Dale Smith, for givin' your mother your permission to divorce your no-account sonofabitch daddy!"

Dale was in no mood to argue. He still felt a little sick from yesterday's strenuous activities. Especially the throwing-up part. He said he was going out and Jesse said, "pshaw." He grabbed his car keys and walked out the house into the bright sunshine of a late spring day.

He drove his car north, past the pasture where Vern's horse roamed and toward the fertile fields teeming with vegetation. He parked by the side of the road and stared at the vast blue sky and big, puffy clouds. Why did he care if Jesse divorced Blackie? He never saw his father much anyway. He and Blackie were so busy that they hardly were in the house at the same time except to sleep. Dale decided what really bothered him was the shame of it all. Aside from Rusty, he didn't know any kids in school whose parents were divorced. Well, maybe no one would find out. He sure as heck wasn't going to tell anyone.

He started the Chevy and drove back home, thinking he'd have to talk Blackie into buying Jesse a car. She wouldn't get his.

**Chapter 13: *Mrs. Page returns; regional track meet; Wendy's plans***

Dale sat in his desk in speech class and watched as Mrs. Page took roll. She didn't look quite the same. Even from where Dale sat, he saw blueish smudges under her eyes. When she glanced up to check on a student's presence, her normally alert eyes had a heavy, sorrowful look to them.

Mrs. Page had been on bereavement leave for the past two weeks. Portia and her baby had been buried ten days ago. Most people thought Mrs. Page wouldn't return to school for the rest of the semester, but Wendy told Dale that Mrs. Page had wanted to resume teaching. Wendy thought that made sense. Being busy was better than thinking too much about the death of her eldest daughter and her first grandchild.

The class was very quiet. Dale sat almost motionless at his desk as if the slightest movement might disturb Mrs. Page. He sensed the rest of the students' uneasiness. It was strange having a teacher present who was emotionally suffering.

Mrs. Page stood up and told them to turn in their textbooks to page 147. They would pick up where the class left off yesterday. Dale flipped to page 147. They had been reading the play *A Doll's House* by some Norwegian guy named Ibsen. He thought the play was sort of interesting. He liked the names. There weren't many Scandinavians in Galilee.

Mrs. Page began reading from the play. Her voice lacked the vibrancy that it usually had. Once she had to pause because she lost her place. Another time she read the same line twice. When she came to the part where Nora leaves Torvald, Mrs. Page paused again. Dale looked up and saw tears dripping from Mrs. Page's eyes and dropping on the text. She suddenly slammed the book shut and rushed from the room.

The class sat in stunned silence. Everyone was disturbed and felt sorry for Mrs. Page. She'd come back to school too soon. Dale had heard Mrs. Page had almost become hysterical at the funeral. She had wept bitterly and openly, and the idea of Mrs. Page behaving with so little self-control amazed him. She'd always shown admirable self-possession in class. Her voice was always under command and her no-nonsense attitude always conveyed complete control. The sight of seeing her emotionally unravel frightened him and the rest of the students.

Dale felt like he was not quite in his body. He felt that self-conscious glow he felt when something really awful was happening and he couldn't do anything about it. It reminded him of how he felt when he was a little kid and Blackie and Jesse got into fights.

He heard the clatter of high heels in the hall, but instead of Mrs. Page returning, Mrs. Heath appeared. She looked upset, too, but her voice was steady and she asked where they were in the play. No one said anything. Dale thought he heard some of the girls in the front sniffling. He surprised himself by answering. Page 147, he said. Mrs. Heath thanked him and started to read.


Dale reclined on the gym mat, shielding his eyes from the sun. He'd finished his three final events but suspected he'd be named to the mile relay. As usual, Dorfman hadn't named the four legs. Billy Joe would certainly be one of them. Probably Rusty. As for the other two spots, it would be between Dale, Chris, Matt, and the sophomore, Jordan.

Dale had decided to be a fatalist when it came to the mile relay. If he was named, so be it. He wasn't going to sit around all day and worry about it. Worse than the race itself was the anxiety of worrying about running it.

The other four candidates, however, weren't so fatalistic. Dale had listened to their speculation all day. Even Matt, whom he regarded as the most philosophical, had worried if he'd be named.

Dale had decided if Dorfman was not naming the team until near the end of the track meet just to keep them on edge, then the best strategy was to not care. In the last four meets, he'd been named both times when the meet didn't have the medley relay. He'd also thrown-up both times after finishing the anchor leg of the mile relay.

Dale had done well so far in the regional track meet. So had Galilee. With just a few events to go, Galilee was tied for first with Quanah Parker. He had expected Ellison to be in the regional, but they had been placed in a different one. He thought that was a break for Galilee.

He'd won the 100 and the 220. The 440-relay team of Dale, Chris, Matt, and Jordan had won first place. He'd accounted for 12 points and broken school records in the 100, with a 9.8 time, and in the 220, with a 22.3 time. The 440-relay team had also broken the school record that the four of them had just established at the Wheaton Invitational. He thought he'd more than done his part and he hoped Dorfman wouldn't make him run the mile relay. But he knew Dorfman wasn't especially impressed with any of his efforts, so he'd decided to maintain his fatalistic approach.

Chris came over and sat down next to Dale.

"Who do you think will be on the mile relay team?" he asked.

Dale, lying on his back, shrugged his shoulders.

"Think I will be? I hope not. I haven't been on it since the Panhandle Invitational. I don't think I can run it anymore."

"Don't sweat it," Dale said.

He almost smiled at the phrase because it was a hot day at Agra. They had a good track, though. A new, modern asphalt track with big white stripes and large numerals for the lanes.

"Yeah, that's funny. Don't sweat it."

Dale thought Chris sounded genuinely worried. He thought back to the 220. It was run with the corner the way Dale preferred rather than on the straightaway. The important thing was to get a good lane. With his fatalistic attitude in place, he'd waited as the official shook the red gourd-like container and offered it to each runner. Dale enjoyed this ritual, especially if he got the lane he wanted. He reached in and pulled out a small black disk with the numeral three printed on it. A good lane. He felt lucky. He watched Chris pull out number two. Dale nodded at Chris. That was a good lane, too.

He'd been lucky all season. He usually got the inner lanes in the 220. Dale used to question the whole concept of luck. Back when he'd sort of been a Witness, he'd been taught there wasn't such a thing as luck. He didn't believe that now. He didn't know how to define it or how to directly influence it, but he definitely thought good luck and bad luck existed. He had begun to think that a person could influence luck a little with a determined, positive attitude. Not the "olive" philosophy. He still thought the olive as totem was ridiculous. But he thought resolve was important. He believed if he tried his best and didn't fret over stuff he couldn't change, then he could tap into a certain positive force inside himself.

Dale remembered crouching in his blocks at the start of the 220 finals, gazing down the shimmering black track. He saw the heat rising in waves above the steamy asphalt. The heat was good. It helped make the track fast. The starter's gun banged and Dale lunged forward and felt fast and strong as he raced to catch the guys in front of him. He swept around the first part of curve and passed two runners. That was a good omen. He passed two more guys at the end of the curve. That left one guy still in front of him for the straightaway. Dale felt his legs carry him easily past him. He ran without any strain. He ran feeling faster than the wind. It was a good feeling.

As he approached the finish line, he turned his head to his left and saw Chris a few feet behind him. Dale was pleasantly surprised. He ducked his shoulders and broke the tape, finishing first. Chris, finishing third, pumped his left fist and threw his right arm around Dale's shoulders as the two of them coasted to a stop.

Chris had also run his best 220 of the year and at the right time, at regional. When they walked back to their camp, Dale congratulated his buddy.

"Thanks," Chris had said. "I just followed you."

Now, lying on the mat, Dale thought that had been one of the best races he'd ever run. Everything had gone perfectly. Having Chris do so well, too, made it even more memorable.

"If Coach picks you," Dale said, still thinking of their 220 performance, "you'll do fine."

"You think so?"

"Yeah."

Dale stretched out on the mat. He felt sort of tired. He'd sprinted 860 yards already. That was nearly half a mile of running flat out. Surely, Dorfman wouldn't pick him for the mile relay. He told himself to stop thinking about it. If Dorfman did, he did.

On cue, Dorfman appeared. He said Sonny won third in the pole vault but the Quanah Parker guy had won second.

Dorfman took two large strides and stood before Dale. Dale looked up and squinted. The sunlight made a halo around Dorfman's bald spot. His broad face was obscured in shadows.

"How you feeling?" Coach asked.

Dale said he felt a little tired.

"Think you can run anchor on the mile relay?"

Dale wondered why Dorfman was asking. He never asked. He told. Dale considered saying no. If he did, he wouldn't get sick. He'd won first in two events and helped win first in another. After all, he'd done his part. He felt himself getting a little angry that Dorfman was putting him in this position.

"I guess," he said without any enthusiasm.

"Good."

Dorfman moved out of his vision and the sun nearly blinded Dale. He got up and walked over to where Dorfman and the rest of the team stood. He looked at the stands with all the people in them. It surprised him that so many people were here for a track meet. He noticed dozens of Galilee students present. Several cars full of them had driven the fifty miles. Dale saw in particular six senior girls sitting together: Wendy, Carmen, Roxanne, Mary Jane, Gretchen, and Amanda. Seeing them made him want to do well. He forgot about feeling tired and steeled himself for the task ahead.

Dorfman said if they wanted to win the regional, then they had to beat Quanah Parker in the mile relay. He thought they could do it. He named the team: Jordan, Grimes, Barton, and Smith.

Dale glanced at Rusty. He didn't look pleased. He'd finished first in the 110 high hurdles, third in the 330 intermediate, and second in the long jump. He was tired, too.

The four of them walked over to the starting line and watched the first heat of the mile relay. Agra, the team that won, had run a good but not great time. Dorfman was sure they could beat it. Quanah Parker was in the second heat with Galilee. Dorfman told them all they had to do was beat them. If Galilee did, they'd win the meet.

Dale watched Jordan run his leg. For a sophomore, he did fair, fading in the end to seventh. He handed off to Rusty. Dale watched as Rusty stretched out his long legs and made up some ground. Dale saw him limping a little at the end, but he put Galilee in fifth place as he handed off to Billy Joe. Barton raced around the first curve. Billy Joe had already run the open quarter and had finished second. He'd also finished first in the 880 and won third in the long jump. As Dale got on the track in his lane and watched Billy Joe grimace, it was obvious he was exhausted.

Dale decided not to worry. He'd just do his best. Instead of the usual anxiety that almost made him sick, he felt just a little nervous. The last time he'd felt this calm in a pressure situation was last year in the baseball game against Quanah Parker when he'd spanked the game-winning hit.

Dale turned and watched Billy Joe almost pass the guy from Oilville on the curve for third, but instead he hit the wall and faded. Dale got ready. He reached back for the baton, took it, and exploded forward.

Dale saw three runners ahead of him. He decided not to think about them. He decided not to think of anything. He slowed down a little; he had to pace himself. He couldn't sprint flat out the whole 440. As he rounded the first curve, he lengthened his stride. He loped down the backstretch and to his surprise he passed the guy from Oilville.

He picked up his speed and gritted his teeth as he rounded the last curve. His eyes settled into a stare. He didn't focus on anything in particular. He tried not to think about how his lungs squeezed themselves for air or how his legs and arms seemed to be burning in their very bones or how his stomach churned. Most of all, he tried not to think of that wall that he was about to collide into in about ten yards.

Dale leaned into the curve. He kept expecting to hit the wall. He didn't. He raced around the curve and passed the guy from Humble. Instead of disintegrating, he felt surprisingly strong. He heard himself breathing hard, felt the pain, but his body didn't want to shut down. His legs kept pumping, his arms kept churning, and as he approached the straightaway to the finish line he saw the Quanah Parker runner five yards ahead of him.

Dale vaguely heard the cheers of the crowd. Their collective voices sounded like a dull roar, as if he were listening on a phone with a bad connection. He thought he distinguished the voices of Rusty and Chris and Billy Joe and Dorfman yelling at him to go, go, go!

Suddenly, Dale felt his muscles tighten and his breath grow short. He'd not busted through the wall; it had just been moved twenty yards further down the track. He gritted his teeth and willed himself forward. He felt as if the asphalt were sucking at his feet. He felt the sun beating him down. He felt like collapsing and never getting up.

He blinked his eyes and saw the Quanah Parker runner slowing. He, too, had hit the end of his endurance. Dale lurched forward. He felt as if he were somehow picking himself up and throwing his exhausted body a few more yards ahead. Five yards from the finish line, he caught up with the Quanah Parker runner. He heard the guy gasping for air. Dale fought a brief feeling of pity. He called up a reserve of ruthless resolve and propelled himself ahead.

As soon as Dale crossed the finish line, he dropped the baton. He wanted to fall to the ground. He felt his teammates pounding his shoulders and back and shouting congratulations. He saw Dorfman running toward him. His coach wrapped a hairy arm around Dale's neck and hugged him. Dale could barely make out what Dorfman was yelling in his ear. Something about being a stud. High praise coming from Dorfman. He nodded at his coach and teammates, mumbled thanks, and walked down the track in a daze.

Even some of the coaches from opposing teams congratulated Dale. He said thanks, wondering if they were patting him on the back because they had short legs, too.

Dale knew Galilee had won the regional track meet. He knew it, but all he could think of was how miserable he felt. His jersey felt clammy with soaked-up sweat. His sides ached when he breathed. Inside he felt as if the marrow of his bones were burning. His belly churned. He wanted to find a place to throw up.

He moved farther down the track. There were too many people gathered around to talk to Earl. Dale thought he should try and find a restroom. He veered off toward the entrance to the stands. He paused, letting several people pass. Dale thought he saw Mary Jane and Gretchen walk by. He wiped the sweat from off his face. Some of it got in his eyes. It stung. He closed his eyes and staggered forward, only to bump into someone. Then he heard *her* voice.

"Oh, Audie!"

Dale opened his eyes and saw Amanda with her arms pressed against her chest. He'd run right into her.

"Are you okay?" he asked.

He reached a hand out and touched her arm above the elbow. He no longer felt the fatigue and pain. It was replaced by a more pleasant sensation. The recent memory of how sleek, soft, and warm her body felt when they had collided.

"Yes," she said. "Are you?"

He wondered if he looked as bad as he felt. "Yeah."

His eyes cleared completely and he looked at her face. She looked back at him with concern. Dale thought the blue color of her eyes seemed more brilliant than today's luminous sky. Her lovely lips puckered slightly in concern. He hadn't been this close to her since the night he kissed her. He felt a delirious rush of desire flood through him. All his senses took her presence in.

Dale sensed her responding to him. Her face softened. Her eyes seemed dewy. He wanted to reach out and touch her again.

"Amanda," Mary Jane called, "come on."

Mary Jane's voice broke the spell. Amanda smiled shyly. She slowly moved away. "You ran really fast, Audie."

"Thanks."

Dale stepped aside and watched Amanda and Mary Jane join the other girls. He noticed with surprise that Amanda wore rather short cutoff jeans. The fringe came to mid-thigh. He remembered again the wonderful brief feeling of his raised knee brushing against her thigh.

Chris appeared at Dale's side.

"Hey, where are you going? The guys are waiting for you at the trophy presentation."

"I thought I was going to throw up."

"Did you?"

"Naw," said Dale. "The feeling went away."

After making out for an hour, Wendy got fully dressed and became loquacious. After talking for a few minutes about her friends she excitedly said she'd almost forgot the wonderful news: She'd won a scholarship to Oklahoma State.

"Isn't that great?" she asked.

Dale, feeling a little unsatisfied, said yeah, it was great.

"It's not a full scholarship," Wendy continued, "but it pays for all my tuition. An advisor also told me that I could be a resident assistant and get my room and board free. What do you think about that, Audie?"

Dale thought it was terrific.

"That means I'll have to go to campus a week early. Resident assistants have to spend a week in orientation before the rest of the students arrive."

Dale nodded.

"Wouldn't it be great if you went to OSU, too? Have you heard from them yet? I thought you said you applied a couple of months ago."

"I said I was thinking about applying."

"Thinking about it? But you have to apply, Audie."

Wendy, now fully dressed, scooted over and leaned her head against Dale's shoulder.

"Do you think you'll live in a dormitory, too?"

"I don't know."

"I think freshmen have to. Unless they commute. But you wouldn't want to commute all the way from Galilee. That'd take, oh, I don't know, a couple of hours?"

"Yeah, about that long."

"Then you definitely have to stay in a dorm."

Dale didn't say anything. He was pondering how he'd pay for college. Blackie had said he'd pay for tuition at one of the state universities. Both OU and OSU cost more than the regional colleges like Central State. That left Dale with figuring out how to pay for room and board – that is, if he stayed on campus. At any rate, he'd have to get a better job this summer than delivering papers or mowing lawns.

"Audie, you're not saying anything."

"Just thinking."

Wendy leaned up and looked at his face. "About what?"

"I'm not sure I want to go to OSU."

"Why not?"

"It's too big. I don't think I'd like going to a school with twenty thousand students."

"You'd get used to it."

"I don't think so. We go to a small high school. We know everyone in school."

"That's what makes college so exciting. Think of all the people you'll meet."

"Too many people. Too big of a place."

Dale remembered visiting the Stillwater campus with the glee club and going there with the lettermen's club to watch a couple of college football games. He'd felt overwhelmed by the big campus.

"Audie you have to go. If you don't, then I won't."

"Don't be silly."

"I'm not being silly," Wendy said. "I have it all planned. We both go to OSU. That way we'll get to see each other all the time."

"Yeah." He wasn't so sure about that either, but he didn't say so.

Wendy leaned back against his arm. "If you didn't go to OSU, then where would you go?"

"I was thinking maybe Central State."

"Why Central State?"

"Then I could commute." Dale thought he better stay at home until June May graduated from high school. But he didn't want to tell Wendy this.

"I guess so," she said. "How far is it to Edmond from Galilee."

Dale said about forty miles if he took the direct route that was only a two-lane road. If he drove into the City and took the highway north the drive was about sixty miles. But it was all highway.

"How far is Edmond from Stillwater?" Wendy asked.

"I don't know. Not that far."

Wendy pressed her head against his chest. "Too far."

## Chapter 14: *Home; Jr.-Sr. banquet; senior week; graduation*

Jesse got her divorce. The papers came in the mail Saturday and she sat down at the dining table and tried to read them.

"I can't make heads nor tails out of this gobbledygook," she said. She gave them to Dale. "Just show me where the important part is."

Dale scanned over the legalize and found the important part – the money. "Here," he said, and gave the papers back to Jesse.

She understood that part. "I reckon it's the way my lawyer said it would be."

He knew his mother got four hundred dollars alimony every month and one hundred for Dale and one hundred for June May for "child support." Dale, now eighteen, was legally an adult, but he qualified for child support if he went to college. Blackie had also agreed to give Jesse the house and pay for a used car. Jesse had wanted a new car, but Blackie adamantly refused to buy her a new car when he drove a two-year-old car.

Jesse seemed satisfied. She walked over to the coffee table, lit a cigarette, and sat down on the couch for a celebratory smoke. She pointed her cigarette at Dale as if admonishing him.

"Just because your daddy gives a hundred for your support don't mean you ain't getting a job."

"I'll get a job after graduation."

Dale thought his mother had been acting a little bossy since Blackie moved out. He didn't like that. He had considered staying with Blackie, but his father didn't seem so keen on the idea. Dale hadn't asked him directly, but he'd hinted. Blackie didn't encourage him. Dale thought that not living with his dad was probably just as well. Blackie had moved to an apartment in the City. If Dale went to Central State as he planned, the commute would be shorter if he lived with Jesse and June May.

June May strolled into the room. She had adjusted to not having Blackie around pretty well. Dale thought she'd figured out that she'd get more presents and clothes from Blackie. All she had to do was make him feel a little guilty that she didn't have a father around and he'd buy her whatever she wanted. Dale wasn't so sure about her plan. Blackie, as Jesse had often attested to, was a bit of a tightwad. In fact, Dale was surprised he'd agreed to the divorce terms so quickly. He thought his father might contest some of the stipulations, especially the monetary ones. But the divorce had gone smoothly and now it was official.

June May saw the divorce papers lying on the coffee table.

"What'd you get?" she asked. Jesse told her.

"I need more than a hundred for my child support," June May declared. "A good, new dress costs almost that much."

"You'll have to make due, li'l lady."

June May frowned and sat down on the couch next to her mother. She looked at Dale and her expression changed to a mischievous one.

"You taking Wendy to the banquet tonight?"

Dale said yes.

"When are you gonna marry her?"

Dale saw Jesse staring at him. Maybe she was worried that Dale might *have* to marry her.

"Never," Dale said.

"I bet Wendy doesn't think that. I heard one of your friends, a senior girl, is getting married in a few weeks." June May looked at Jesse. "And she's just eighteen."

"Eighteen is too young nowadays," said Jesse.

Dale guessed June May was talking about Linda. It was true. Linda was getting married June 21. He'd been invited. Carrie and Carmen were going to be bridesmaids.

"I bet Wendy's getting ideas," said June May.

Dale stared at June May until she stopped smiling. He glanced at Jesse. She puffed on her cigarette and looked at him with the same critical gaze he'd seen her give Blackie.

"He don't even have a full-time job yet," she said. "He can't get married."

Dale said she was right about that. He left his mother and sister and walked to his room. He wasn't sure he liked the idea of Blackie being gone.


The junior-senior banquet wasn't any better as a senior than as a junior. Dale thought it was mostly a lot of sentimental reminiscences. He and Wendy sat at the same table as Quentin and Roxanne. Wendy had told him that Quentin and Roxanne were now going steady. That information surprised him. Quentin was a nice guy but he'd never been considered one of the popular kids like Roxanne. Usually, the popular went with the popular. Dale admired Quentin for changing the rules.

Across the room, Dale saw Chris and Amanda sitting with Rusty and Mary Jane. The four of them had gone to the banquet together, which sort of annoyed Dale. He'd thought Chris and Amanda would double date with him and Wendy. After all, he'd been the one to convince Chris to ask Amanda. The two couples seemed to be having a good time. Dale noticed that Rusty was in high spirits. He'd asked Mary Jane to the all-sports banquet too. Dale guessed they were going steady or as close to it as Mary Jane would permit.

K. C., as president of the senior class, sat at the head table along with his date, Gretchen. Wendy had told Dale that the two of them might get engaged this summer. Bonita, as class vice president, sat with her date, Wally. When Dale said hello to Bonita earlier, she replied with sufficient friendliness that convinced him she didn't hold any grudges.

Some of the other couples present were Sonny and Merry, Billy Joe and Peggy, Erickson and Becky, Leroy and Carrie, and Bigelow and Carmen. It bothered Dale that Carmen had accepted Bigelow's invitation. He wished Butch would have asked a girl Dale didn't like, like Peggy. Actually, Dale thought, the two of them were suited to one another if for no other reason than they both were porcine. But maybe that old saying, opposites attract, was right, because Bigelow didn't seem to like Peggy anymore or vice versa.

During the banquet, a number of popular songs were played to help establish the proper nostalgic mood. Dale didn't like any of them. He thought rock and pop music was in a serious decline. He preferred music from the '60s but he liked some of the early '70s romantic songs. He remembered listening to "Without You," "Precious and Few," and "Nights in White Satin," and feeling a romantic melancholy descend on him. Invariably, he daydreamed of Amanda. Of course, he'd never confessed his weakness for such music to Rusty or any of the guys. But he didn't hear that kind of music much anymore. Instead, the current music lacked passion or romantic intensity. It all seemed fluffy and predictable. And the newest stuff, called disco, he despised.

Just as he was finishing his musical evaluation, he heard a song he sort of liked. Well, it was one of those songs he both liked and disliked. It was called "Mandy" and had been a big hit during the winter.

Dale glanced over to Amanda. She sat in her seat with her usual perfect composure. When Chris spoke to her, she smiled her typically serene smile.

Dale listened to the song and responded emotionally to the melody but he didn't like the lyrics much. They were sort of vague and he didn't like the part where the singer says Mandy held him while he was shaking. That sounded like the guy was bawling or something. Dale didn't like the idea that Mandy – which, of course, reminded him of Amanda – would comfort some sappy guy.

The banquet finally came to its lachrymose end and Dale endured witnessing the sniffles and eye dabbing and all the other mush. He shook hands with Matt and Sam Mears, two of the junior guys he liked. He impatiently waited for Wendy to stop hugging and talking with everyone and when she returned he escorted her to the car so swiftly that she asked, "what's the hurry, Audie?"

Driving back to Galilee, Dale listened as Wendy talked about the wonderful evening. What an exciting time, she said. She felt sad that high school was almost over but she felt excited about the future, too. Dale, not in such a good mood, mentioned that he was a little puzzled why Chris hadn't wanted to double date with them. When he glanced at Wendy, he noticed she had a funny look on her face.

"What is it?" Dale asked.

Wendy gave him an evasive look, with her eyes darting away from his.

"Come on, give."

"All right." She looked at him with a small smile on her lips. "I think I know why Chris didn't want to double date with us."

Dale, growing annoyed, looked at her.

"Well, you see, Audie, Chris sort of asked me out back when we weren't seeing each other."

Dale hadn't known that. He looked at Wendy and she had that same small smile that he now thought looked a little smug.

"He asked you out?"

Wendy nodded. Then she realized that Dale might misinterpret. "Oh, I didn't accept. He just asked once and I said no."

Dale didn't know if that information bothered him or not. Chris was his friend. He'd broken off with Wendy. Chris had every right to ask her for a date. Indeed, Dale would prefer a guy he liked, a friend like Chris, to date Wendy rather than some jerk like Bigelow.

"So, I guess Chris felt awkward going on a double date with us. Plus –" Dale heard Wendy's tone shift now to a more confidential note "— there's the whole Amanda question."

Dale felt himself tighten inside when Wendy said her name. He didn't know how much Wendy knew about him and Amanda. He'd never talked about it. Knowing Wendy's expertise in gathering gossip, he imagined she knew more than he wanted her to know. Of course, a lot depended on Amanda, and he had the impression she was unusually discreet for a girl.

Dale tried to think of something in response. He didn't know what to say. So, he remained silent and stared at the road.

"How many dates did you have with her?" Wendy asked in a deceptively casual voice.

Dale said a few.

"A few? Two, three?"

He said he forgot.

"I heard three." Wendy's voice sounded irritatingly breezy like she was discussing something utterly trivial. "That's about the limit for Amanda, all right."

Dale glanced at Wendy, trying to keep his face from showing his irritation.

"Is that so?"

"Amanda doesn't date a boy more than three times in a row. Usually, not more than twice. It's some sort of rule, I think. Her parents trying to protect her, I guess."

He said nothing.

"Three times? I guess that meant she liked you. At least a little."

"Why are we talking about this? All that happened a long time ago."

"Well, you brought it up."

"I did not."

"You most certainly did."

"I asked about Chris."

"Well, it's the same thing. I mean, it's connected."

"It's not connected."

Dale felt himself growing angry. All his frustration he felt at the banquet had come back. He didn't think he'd feel much worse if Bigelow had asked Amanda after all.

"Don't get mad."

"I'm not mad."

"You sound mad."

Dale breathed out, trying to prevent his anger from building. He looked at the speedometer and saw he'd been speeding. He quickly slowed down. Cops would be out on a Saturday night.

Wendy grabbed hold of his right arm with both her hands. "I'm sorry if I made you angry. You're right. It was a long time ago."

Dale nodded and Wendy scooted closer to him. He noticed again that she'd worn a rather low-cut gown. He didn't like the yellow color much, but he'd glanced several times at her freckled cleavage during the banquet. Of all the girls at the banquet, Wendy had the most impressive bosom except for the bovine Merry.

Wendy laid her head against his shoulder and Dale relaxed some. As he drove, he thought how difficult it was for two people to like each other in the same way; with the same intensity, with the same expectations. He knew he ought to be grateful that Wendy cared about him. He should like her as much as she liked him. But he didn't. He wanted to, but he couldn't find the same emotional intensity for her that she had for him. Instead, he felt that way for Amanda, a girl above him in social status and with a perfect family. Still, he knew Amanda liked him, too. He'd felt it more than once. At the regional track meet, he'd felt it. The only things preventing her from accepting that feeling were the stupid rules of her parents and the fact that he wasn't a Nazarene.

"What are you thinking about?" Wendy asked, snuggling up against him.

"Nothing," Dale said.

Senior week began with a trip to Red Rock Canyon, the same state park and recreation area where the football team began two-a-days. Most of the seniors went and wore bathing suits underneath their regular clothes. Isaac and Vern didn't go because their religious convictions forbade public swimming. A few other seniors didn't go because they didn't want to. But most of Dale's class crammed into the school bus and rode the fifty miles to the park. Dale sat with Wendy in the back across the aisle from Rusty and Mary Jane. When they got to the park, they stripped to their swimsuits and frolicked in the water. They ate their lunches and played Frisbee. They swam some more. They went on boat rides. The weather was perfect. Sunny, not quite hot. It was an idyllic day.

Dale reclined on Wendy's blanket as she and Roxanne, Mary Jane, Gretchen, and Amanda prepared to jump into the water from the fifteen-foot rocky cliff. The girls held hands and hesitated. They were standing on the lowest cliff but more than one of them seemed reluctant to take the plunge. Rusty, sitting on Mary Jane's blanket not far away, said he bet at least one of them would chicken out.

Dale nodded and watched. Only Wendy and Mary Jane wore two-piece bathing suits, neither a real bikini. The other three girls wore modest one-pieces. Amanda's suit reminded him of an animal skin suit with its brown and gold striped pattern. Compared to a bikini, it didn't show that much skin, but it revealed more of Amanda than Dale had ever seen before.

Finally, the five girls jumped holding hands. They screamed and splashed into the water. Roxanne, on one end, held her nose with her free hand. They climbed out of the water and Dale discreetly watched Amanda walk to her blanket. Drops of water glistened in the sunlight as they clung to her sleek, fair skin. She dried off and pulled on a baby blue T-shirt. She wrung her long light brown hair, the color slightly darkened by the water. She sat down next to Carmen and laughed, pointing to the spot on the lower level of the cliffs that she'd jumped from.

Wendy dropped down next to Dale and shook her head, spraying him with water. He said hey, and she laughed her husky, throaty laugh.

Aside from Dale and Wendy, Rusty and Mary Jane, K. C. and Gretchen, and Roxanne and Quentin, who sat together as couples, the rest of the seniors divided into boy and girl groups. Dale saw Wally and Chris walking up to the taller cliffs. Both wore the long, baggy trunks that most of the boys wore. Wally jumped feet first and made a big splash. Chris dived in and hardly disturbed the water. Dale didn't know Chris could dive so well.

The afternoon came to an end and the group ambled back to the bus. As before, Dale sat next to Wendy with the other couples also sitting in the back. He occasionally glanced forward to where Amanda sat with Carmen. Chris and Wally, sitting in front of them, turned around and chatted with them most of the way back to Galilee.

Dale leaned back in his seat and felt the warm air stream through the window. He smelled the suntan lotion and the musty smell of wet bathing suits. This would be his last ride on a school bus. It was a good last ride.

The yearbook arrived the next day. Dale had devised a different kind of system to pass them out. Rather than mere numbers assigned by grade and alphabetized by name, he decided to employ the *Brave New World* model. Seniors were alphas, juniors betas, sophomores deltas, and so forth down to the lowly seventh-grade omegas, which of course weren't in the novel because there were only five classes of test tube humans.

Only a few kids and teachers understood the meaning of the designations. One of them was Thea, who smiled at Dale when he handed her the yearbook. She said she protested the designations based on class seniority. Dale said he had to do it that way or else most of the kids would be epsilon minuses. Thea laughed and said the cover looked interesting. She was being kind. He'd designed it himself and it hadn't turned out as well as he'd hoped. Instead of the usual cartoonish gopher, he'd tried to draw a fiercer gopher like the kind on the football helmets. Unfortunately, it looked less like a gopher than a big rat. Dale had already heard a couple of kids whispering, "what's with the rat?"

The other problem was that by having an original drawing, the yearbook didn't have the usual embossed cover. Instead, he had to use a silk screen cover and it didn't look or feel as good as the traditional embossed ones. He'd heard some people complain about that, too.

Otherwise, the yearbook looked pretty good and Dale was generally satisfied. Some of the seniors decided to go to the park and sign them. Dale drove with Wendy and about twenty of them wrote sentiments and signed their names. Amanda and Dale exchanged books and wrote a sentence and signed their names. He wrote, *To Amanda, truly an alpha plus female. Best wishes, Audie Dale.* When she saw what he wrote she smiled, but he could tell she was a little puzzled. She wrote a more conventional message: *To Audie, a good friend and an excellent yearbook editor, love Amanda.* Dale didn't take the love part seriously. All the girls wrote that if they were friendly with the guy.

That night some of the seniors who'd gone to the park met for a weenie roast at Lake Overholser, not far from Amanda's home. Dale went with Wendy and sat around the campfire with Rusty, Mary Jane, K. C., Gretchen, Roxanne, Quentin, Chris, Amanda, Carmen, Wally, Peggy, and Carrie. Billy Joe, Sonny, Erickson, Leroy, and Bigelow didn't show. Dale didn't know why. Of those five, only Billy Joe had gone to Red Rocks. Already it seemed that some seniors were going in their own direction.

The school held the senior assembly Thursday. It was an event where the seniors performed skits, some mocking the underclassmen and teachers but mostly spoofing television or media personalities. Dale had been talked into being a television anchorman because he didn't have much of an accent. He went along with it and even wore a tie and jacket. Rusty convincingly imitated Clint Eastwood and even wore Western garb. K. C. and Mary Jane portrayed Sonny and Cher. Erickson played Kung Fu and Chris played his master. Chris showed some impressive creativity with his costume. Not only did he wear a robe, but he found a way to make himself look bald and cut a ping-pong ball in half and used each half to cover each eye, giving him an eerie blind look. He also said "grass-hoppa" in a passable Chinese way.

But the best moment had been when Rusty, Erickson, and Chris did an absurd song and dance called "the Stomp." The three of them had dressed in ridiculous, incongruous clothing. Erickson played the bongos while Chris strummed a ukulele and Rusty did a bizarre "stomping" dance while grunting like an ape. Dale thought the performance was hilarious. It reminded him of the time when Rusty imitated the monkey part of *Gitarzan* at Lake Thunderbird.

Dale attended the awards assembly Friday. Aside from getting his letters, he didn't win anything. He thought he might win the senior English award, but like most academic awards it went to Isaac Gould. For all of Isaac's brilliance, Dale thought he'd shown more perception about the readings in class than Gould. Isaac tended to be literal-minded. Dale didn't think he fully understood the more subtle aspects of *The Odyssey, Macbeth, Moby Dick* or the other classic works they'd read. But Dale didn't think their teacher, Miss Cartland, was especially astute either.

Dale had been nominated, along with Wendy and Amanda, for the West Oaks's Moral Leadership Award. He had no idea why he'd been one of the finalists. He supposed maybe for an athlete he was considered well behaved. He also suspected Mrs. Heath, who was one of the committee members, had something to do with his being nominated. Amanda won. Dale thought that was appropriate. The award came with a five hundred dollar scholarship, which he could have used. But he knew Amanda was the best choice.

Most of the college-bound seniors had already decided which schools they were going to. Isaac had received a full music scholarship to Tulsa University. Wendy was going to OSU. Bonita had won a partial scholarship to attend Southern Methodist in Dallas. Amanda, Mary Jane, K. C., Gretchen, Bigelow, and Chris were all going to GNC. Wally, Carmen, and Carrie said they were probably going to Central State. Don Fargo was going to OU. Rusty told Dale he was thinking about going to Oscar Rose Junior College in Oklahoma City and play basketball there. He hadn't gotten an athletic scholarship, but the team's coach liked him and thought he might earn one for next season. As for the rest of the seniors, none, including Roxanne, Merry, Peggy, Sonny, Billy Joe, and Leroy, were going to college. Oddly enough, both Vern and Erickson, who'd scored high on the ACT, weren't going to college either. Both were going to work as carpenters.

Baccalaureate was Sunday afternoon, and Dale felt as bored as he had during the Witnesses' meetings years ago. He tried to listen because he knew the minister was doing his best to inspire and edify. But his mind was elsewhere. He thought about getting a decent-paying summer job. He thought about which college he was going to. He'd applied to OU and Central State. OU, like OSU, offered a five hundred dollar scholarship for attending Boys State, but Dale still didn't like the idea of going to a big state university. He knew he'd feel overwhelmed by the vast campus and lost in the huge crowd of students.

He then thought about the state track meet that had been held in Norman at the spectacular Oklahoma University track. Dale had done pretty well. He'd won three medals. He'd won third in both the 100 and 220. He'd been lucky. The tall Ellison guy had false-started twice in the 220. The shorter Ellison guy had pulled a muscle in the 440 relay final and couldn't run in the 100 final.

Galilee finished third in the 440 relay. Ellison won. Then, with Dale running the anchor of the mile relay, they almost won a medal, but he couldn't close the gap at the end.

Dale spoke to Maurice after the 440 relay and still thought he was funny. He asked him if he was going to college and Maurice had said yeah, with a note of pride in his voice. Maurice said he was the first Morris to go to college. Dale didn't tell him he was the first of the Walsh family, too. Instead, he asked where. Maurice said South Central in Ada. Dale grinned. The same college where Girls State had been held last year.

Dale and Maurice wished each other luck, shook hands, and left to join their pals. He looked for Maurice after the 100 and 220 finals but he didn't see him. Dale thought how odd it was to get to know someone a little and then never see him again.

Then Dale thought about his parents. He had only seen Blackie a couple of times since he'd moved out. Jesse surprised Dale at how well she was handling being on her own. She'd bought a car with Blackie's money, a '72 red Cougar. When Dale saw it parked in the driveway a week ago, he'd been jealous. It was a lot cooler car than his old-fashioned '67 Chevy.

Then Dale thought about Wendy. He knew she was planning for them to stay together; maybe she had ideas they would eventually get married. Dale wasn't sure how to extricate himself. Wendy had always been too serious about them as a couple. He'd gotten back with her mostly because he couldn't bear seeing her miserable during school. He liked all the other stuff, too. It was good having a girlfriend, especially after a game or for the weekend. Dale liked Wendy's warmth. He liked her for a lot of things. But he didn't want to marry her.

The baccalaureate ended and that left only one other event: graduation on Monday evening.

The seniors meet in the auditorium at six in the evening wearing their caps and gowns. The boys wore red, the girls white, and they marched into the auditorium from different auditorium doors and sat in separate sections. When the speaker was introduced, Dale almost laughed. It was the governor, the same fellow who'd spoken at Boys State. Dale wondered if he'd remember him and Wendy. Well, he might remember Wendy. Dale knew it was a big deal having the governor speak at the Galilee graduation. After all, they were a small school. He wondered who'd arranged it. Later, he heard that the governor had an aide that had went to school at Galilee twenty years ago.

The governor gave the usual polished speech. Dale especially noticed his slicked back silver hair and expensive suit. He was an impressive guy. He laughed easily and told a few jokes and seemed completely sincere in wishing the graduates of 1975 the best of luck in their future endeavors.

Then the seniors' names were called and they walked up to the stage and received their diplomas and shook hands with the principal and the governor. Most of them seemed a little nervous to be in the august presence of the governor. When Dale's turn came, he was tempted to say "remember me, gov'? The Romeo of Boys State?" But he didn't. Instead he nodded at the governor's bright smile and shook his hand firmly and took his diploma.

After the ceremony, the audience applauded, the seniors flipped their tassels and threw their caps in the air to celebrate their liberation. They then gathered in the auditorium's lobby and congratulated each other. A lot of parents were present taking pictures of their kids. Blackie and Jesse weren't there. Since neither had graduated from high school, neither thought the occasion that significant. Jesse, of course, rarely went out in public. Blackie might have come if Dale had reminded him. But he didn't. His father took college classes during the summer and his abnormal psychology class met on Mondays.

Dale felt self-conscious that among his friends he was the only one not to have parents present. Rusty's stepfather and mother had come for the ceremony. Chris's parents, too. He saw Wendy's parents, including her truck-driving father. Mr. Wainwright had made certain he'd be home for his daughter's graduation. Wendy had wanted Dale to go with her and her family out to eat to celebrate their graduation, but he'd made an excuse. Something about how he had to see his dad who hadn't made his graduation because of an emergency at work.

As Dale lingered in the lobby, he spotted Amanda and her family. He saw Amanda's mother give her a hug. Amanda blinked back tears. Dale wondered what it would feel like to have a close-knit family that cared about each other.

Dale hung around long enough to tell his best friends congratulations. He shook hands with Dorfman and Blocker. He also found Mrs. Heath and told her he'd enjoyed her class. She hugged him, which embarrassed him a little. He looked around for Mrs. Page, his other favorite teacher, but he didn't see her. He hadn't expected her to come. She'd missed the last month of classes. She still hadn't come to grips with losing Portia.

As the minutes passed and the parents took photos of their children and friends, Dale felt increasingly left out. He slipped out of the auditorium and stood on the steps and looked at the approaching twilight. He thought how strange it was to experience an important passage in life. It didn't seem as significant as he'd imagined. In fact, he felt it was a little anticlimactic. He knew he'd miss the school and seeing his friends every day. He'd gone to school with most of them for over ten years. He knew people always said they'd keep in touch but he was becoming enough of a realist to know that usually didn't happen. That made him sad. He wished people did stay in touch. Especially friends that he'd known almost his entire life.

He heard the door open behind him and he felt a little annoyed at the intrusion. He turned and saw Amanda looking at him. She smiled and Dale tried not to show his surprise and pleasure.

"I thought you might be leaving," she said.

"Yeah, I was thinking about it."

"Well, I wanted to say good-bye before you left."

Dale knew he'd miss looking at her face. It wasn't only her attractive features; it was also the kindness in her eyes. Right now, her eyes looked a little moist, no doubt from all the emotional good-byes she'd already bestowed on her friends.

"Yeah, well, thanks," Dale said.

Amanda smiled softly again and paused. She looked at Dale with an even more considerate expression.

"Oh, and Audie. I wanted to say how sorry I am about your parents' divorce."

Dale felt that old feeling of mortification sweep over him. The emotion left him glowing inside like a hot wire, and he fought to keep the heat away from his face. The embarrassment passed then a jolt of anger replaced it. He fought that emotion, too. He didn't want to get angry with Amanda the last time he saw her.

"What do you mean?" he asked stiffly, knowing even as he said it he sounded foolish.

"My mother read it in *The Daily Oklahoman*," Amanda said, now feeling embarrassed herself. Her fair skin flushed.

"Oh, yeah." Dale didn't know newspapers printed such personal stuff. "Well, thanks."

Amanda seemed about to say more when the door next to hers flung open and K. C., Bigelow, and Gretchen appeared in the doorway.

"Well, here you are, Amanda," Gretchen said. "Your parents want you."

Amanda glanced at Dale, smiled sort of sadly, and slipped inside with Gretchen. Dale nodded at K. C. He'd already shaken his hand and congratulated him as a new graduate. He hadn't done that with Bigelow and wasn't going to. Butch gave him a mocking grin and joined K. C. as they went inside. The door closed shut behind them, leaving Dale outside, alone.

# BOOK 5: *The Existential Man*

### Chapter 1: *Seeing Sheba; summer job search; a scary movie*

Dale emerged from his room ready for a break. He'd been reading *For Whom the Bell Tolls* for three hours. He felt like going into the backyard and tossing the ball against the garage's brick wall. But first he stopped at the refrigerator and grabbed a can of 7-Up. He popped open the can and drank almost half of it with his first guzzle. He was about to finish it when Jesse came into the kitchen.

"When you gonna get a job?" she asked.

Dale drained the last of the soda pop. He suppressed a burp. "School's only been out for a week."

"A week's long enough to find a job."

Jesse stood with a hand on the kitchen table to help keep her balance. Her left foot fell flat against the floor. Her right foot stood on tiptoe.

"I'm looking," he said.

"Doesn't look like you're looking right now."

"I read the Sunday classifieds this morning."

"Well, mister, maybe you should go out and look in person."

"I'll look first thing tomorrow."

"You better because you ain't gonna laze around here all summer." Jesse walked out of the kitchen but continued talking. "Money's tight around here now that your daddy's left. You're gonna have to make do on your own."

Dale started to tell her that he'd never "lazed around" during the summer. He'd always worked, since he was twelve, even if it was only delivering papers. But he couldn't even make such valid points to Jesse without provoking an argument. The problem with getting a good summer job was that there weren't many in Galilee. A guy could get a job at a fast food restaurant or maybe get a job helping builders or carpenters, but he already knew he was unsuited for that kind of work. Some college guys worked in the oilfields during the summer, but the nearest active oilfield was two hours away. Maybe he could find a job in sales like Wendy had, but since those jobs paid mostly in commissions, he knew he didn't have the sales savvy to make the job worthwhile. He had to find a job, though; he needed to save some money this summer for college. He needed money for meals and gas and other expenses like clothes. He knew Jesse wouldn't help out.

Dale walked over to the patio door and started to open it when he heard the lilting voices of his sister and another girl. He looked through the glass and saw June May and, judging from the white-blonde hair, Sheba Smith. He wasn't certain, because she'd cut her hair fairly short. Just to make sure, he asked Jesse.

"Who's that with June May?"

"Her friend, Sheba." Jesse held a book in her lap. When she raised it, Dale noticed the title: *An Astrological Guide to Life*. "She used to come aroun' here a lot a few years ago."

Dale remembered. He remembered her even better from the Wheaton track meet. He watched as Sheba and June May got up and moved their towels farther into the sunny part of the yard. Like June May, Sheba wore a two-piece bathing suit, and although not a skimpy bikini, it was more revealing than most bathing suits Galilee girls wore. He didn't like the lime green color much, but otherwise the suit showed Sheba to near perfection. As she bent over to spread the towel, he noticed again how her hips curved spectacularly from her narrow waist. She stood straight, her back to him, and Dale felt something kick inside him when he saw the dimples above her swimsuit bottom. Sheba then dropped to her hands and knees and raised her well-proportioned rump in the air, before stretching herself out on the towel.

Dale turned away from the window and took a deep breath. He saw Jesse peering at him.

"Somethin' wrong with you?" she asked.

Dale shook his head. "Nothing's wrong with me," he said, a little too emphatically. He wanted to spy on Sheba some more, but Jesse might think that odd, so he walked back to his room and tried to read more of *For Whom the Bell Tolls*.

The next day, Dale looked for a job. He drove to downtown Galilee and looked at the storefront windows for any "help wanted" signs. There weren't any. He even went inside the bakery and the five-and-ten cent store to ask. Both ladies said they didn't need any help. He checked again at the *Galilee Gazette*, the weekly newspaper. But the managing editor said they didn't need any help for the summer. He told Dale to return in the fall. They might use him as a sports stringer. Dale said okay, not entirely sure what a stringer was but thinking he'd like to work at the newspaper anyway.

Dale drove down the expressway to the other commercial area on the eastern part of town. He didn't even bother with Whataburger or Pizza Hut or the other fast food places. He stopped by the car wash and asked. No openings. He considered the used car lot, but he doubted they'd hire an eighteen year old to sell cars. Maybe wash and clean them, though. He stopped by and the manager said they had all the help they needed. He considered inquiring at Reinhardt's trucking, but he didn't have any mechanical skills.

He was about to give up when he turned north on a smaller street and noticed a help wanted sign in the window of the small business. The place, called Otto's Arts and Industrial, intrigued him.

He parked his car in the gravel lot and walked inside the building. It looked like an office supply store in some ways. He saw lots of paper, pens, ink, notebooks, ledgers, and graphic supplies. There was also a section for business signs and posters. One thing that interested him was a large black felt board with grooves in it. He'd seen such boards encased in glass covers at school and at hospitals or business offices. White plastic letters were stuck in the grooves to form words, usually names of the people working in the building. For some odd reason that Dale couldn't explain, the black felt boards fascinated him. He looked at the price tag at a smaller one. Almost twenty bucks. He thought that was a lot. He entertained the idea of buying such a board sometime when he had an extra twenty bucks, even though he didn't know what he'd use it for. He didn't have a business. But the idea of putting the board in his room and sticking letters on it to form words appealed to him in some murky kind of way.

A middle-aged woman approached him. She asked if he wanted to buy anything.

"No ma'am," Dale said. "I'd like to apply for a job."

The woman, average height and build, with a plain face, short, curly brown hair and tinted ladies' glasses, scrutinized him. She said they did have an open position. She asked him why he was interested in their business.

Dale said he needed a summer job. He also found their business with its signs and graphic arts stuff interesting.

The woman asked him his experience and qualifications. Dale told her the truth. He told he didn't have much of either. He briefly mentioned his past summer job experiences, not dwelling on how brief some of them were.

The woman told Dale to follow her. She took him into a small, neat room where a middle-aged man, completely bald and bespectacled, sat at a desk going over accounts. The woman told him that this young man was interested in a job. The man, who looked oddly like the woman in that he, too, had rather nondescript features, peered at him through his round, old-fashioned glasses and asked Dale his name. He told him, using his middle name. Then the man introduced himself as Mr. Otto and the woman as Mrs. Otto. Dale said hello. Neither smiled. Dale began to wonder if they were capable of any emotion. So far, their plain faces had kept nearly blank expressions. The only emotional change he'd seen so far was an occasional blinking of the eyes behind their eye glasses.

Mr. Otto asked Dale a series of questions: how old was he? Where did he go to school? Was he a hard worker? Was he dependable and reliable? Dale answered the questions and emphasized that he was a hard worker and dependable. He mentioned that he'd not missed one day of class last year and as yearbook editor had made every deadline. Neither Mr. nor Mrs. Otto looked especially impressed, but then he had a hard time reading their impassive faces.

Mr. Otto gave Dale an application to fill out. Then he left the room with his wife. Dale quickly completed the application. While waiting for the Ottos to return, he looked around the office. The plain, white walls were nearly bare. A couple of samples of the business's work were displayed on the wall behind the desk. Two neat stacks of documents stood on the desk along with an open ledger. Otherwise, the office was immaculately clean and relentlessly tidy. Even the black-and-white checkered tile floor didn't have a smudge of dust on it.

As he waited, he grew a little uneasy. He thought the Ottos were odd. The office he sat in seemed *too* clean and organized. Just when he was thinking about getting up and saying he'd changed his mind, the Ottos returned. Mr. Otto took the application and looked it over. While he did, Dale noticed that Mr. Otto's head looked as smooth and white as a light bulb. It even had that kind of shape to it. He looked like a light bulb with glasses, Dale thought.

Mr. Otto said he needed someone right away. They had an important job to complete. The previous worker had let them down. He'd injured himself in a car accident and the Ottos had to let him go. What Mr. Otto wanted to know for certain was whether Dale would be dependable? Would he be able to work right away?

Dale said yes to both questions. Still, he wasn't sure he wanted to take the job. He wasn't sure what the job was. So he asked.

Mr. Otto said the job involved a lot of different things, mostly working on making signs for businesses in town and the City. Dale thought that sounded interesting. Mr. Otto said the current job involved making aisle display signs for a local supermarket. That interested Dale, although he wasn't sure what an aisle display sign was. But he liked signs. He liked the lettering, the colors, and the artistic aspect to an otherwise pragmatic object.

Then Mr. Otto told Dale what the job paid. It paid a little more than the minimum wage, which didn't sound bad. He'd never had a job that paid much money; the roofing job had paid almost a buck over the minimum but he hadn't lasted long enough to benefit from that.

Mr. Otto asked if he wanted the job. Dale hesitated. He had doubts about the job itself; he still didn't know exactly what his position was. And the Ottos were odd. But he needed a job, the sooner the better. It paid okay. He doubted he'd find anything better anytime soon. He said yes.

Mr. Otto said fine and reached over his desk and gave Dale a short, efficient handshake. Dale thought his hand felt a little cold. Then Mr. Otto asked him if he could come in tomorrow morning at eight o'clock sharp. Dale said yes.

Mrs. Otto showed him to the front door. When Dale opened the door to leave, he said good-bye but she said nothing. She just looked blankly at him as if he wasn't there. Dale shrugged, closed the door, and walked to his Chevy. As he backed his car out of the parking lot, he realized that the Ottos hadn't had one customer while he'd been there.

Dale couldn't believe the length of the line. It snaked through the mall for thirty yards. He didn't know why so many people were coming to see this movie. Since *Jaws* had just started that day, he knew all the people weren't coming based on word of mouth. He knew the book had been a bestseller. He'd borrowed the paperback version from Carmen a couple of months ago. It was an okay book. Nothing literary, but sort of fun to read.

"Man, look at all these people," said Rusty. He turned and scanned the long line that extended so far back that he couldn't see the people at the end. "Who'd thought people liked sharks so much?"

"Is the movie about sharks?" asked Mary Jane.

"Why do you think it's called *Jaws*?"

"Jaws could refer to all sort of things."

"Like what? Bunny *wabbits*?" Rusty laughed and Mary Jane gave him a girlish slap on his arm.

"How are all of us going to fit in the theatre?" asked Wendy.

"We won't," said Rusty. "Those people –" he pointed in the direction of the end of the line "—won't get in."

"I don't like sharks," said Mary Jane. "Why are we going to see this movie?"

"Is the movie scary?" asked Wendy.

"Ask Dale," said Rusty. "It was his idea to see it."

The girls looked at him. Their faces were tight with concern.

"If it's like the book, then it won't be too scary."

Mary Jane and Wendy seemed to relax a little.

"In the book, only six or seven people get eaten."

"Eaten?" Mary Jane cried.

"Will they show that in the movie?" asked Wendy.

"I hope so," said Rusty. "What's the point otherwise?"

"Maybe we should see another movie," said Mary Jane.

"C'mon," said Rusty. "It'll be fun. When the scary parts come on I'll cover your eyes with my hand."

He grabbed Mary Jane's small waist and tried to pull her against him, but she squirmed away and gave him a scolding look.

"Is this movie R-rated?" asked Mary Jane.

"No," said Dale. "It's PG."

Mary Jane didn't look completely reassured.

"Oh, it'll be all right," Wendy said to her. "It'll be like a roller coaster. Scary but fun."

"I don't like roller coasters either," Mary Jane said.

Rusty leaned over to Dale. "They make her talk to Earl," he said lowly, grinning.

Mary Jane overheard but wasn't familiar with the phrase. She blinked her big brown eyes at them. "What are you talking about?" she asked, with a touch of asperity in her voice.

Ordinarily, Mary Jane was an agreeable girl. She smiled and laughed easily. Dale wondered why she was out of sorts. He looked at Rusty. He frowned and shook his head.

As they moved closer to the ticket window, Rusty stood next to Dale. He glanced back at Wendy and Mary Jane, who were quietly chatting. Exchanging gossip, no doubt.

"What's wrong with Mary Jane?" Dale whispered to Rusty.

"Beats me. She's been snapping at me since I picked her up this evening."

Dale asked Rusty when the summer basketball league started.

"Next week. You ought to come see the game in August. We're playing at the high school."

Dale said he would.

"Sometimes area college coaches come see the games. Maybe I'll get lucky and have a good game then."

Dale asked him if he'd heard anything more about college scholarships. Coach Rayze had sent film of Rusty's best games to a few schools like El Reno junior college and Southwestern State. He also sent film to Galilee Nazarene, which actually had a good team for its division.

"Naw. Coaches don't care about a guy who plays on a lousy high school team."

Rusty had averaged over twenty points a game during his senior year. He'd been voted the district's most valuable player. He was almost six foot two. He'd received some inquiries from a few small state colleges, but no definite offers yet. Dale thought the reason the scouts had doubts about him was because of his sometimes erratic play. Rusty had talent, but he hadn't learned how to be disciplined. Dale blamed Coach Rayze for a lot of that. If Rusty had a better coach for his senior year, like Carpenter, Rusty would have been compelled to learn how to play with more discipline and self-control.

Dale asked Rusty about work. Rusty was working with Erickson and his dad as a carpenter again. He said the work was fine. It paid pretty well but it got a little routine.

Dale said he understood. He told Rusty about his job, which he'd been working at for four days. He went into the basement of the Otto's building and made some kind of bread sign. He took a twelve-by-six-inch plank of plastic and put it through some kind of machine that softened the plastic in a horizontal line about two inches up. Then Dale bent the plastic at that point, making something of a stand. Then he pasted the label on the stand and stacked it. Then he did another. And another. He did the same thing for eight hours.

"Man, that sounds really boring," said Rusty. Dale nodded.

Rusty turned around and said something to Mary Jane. Dale turned in the opposite direction and looked at the line ahead of them. They were getting closer to the ticket window. Then he noticed three girls standing in line about ten people ahead of him. One of them was Sheba Smith. He guessed that the other two girls had been blocking his view of her before. He wasn't sure if he liked her shorter hair. It wasn't as short as Maria's in *For Whom the Bell Tolls,* but it was short enough that it didn't touch her ears at all, although some hair extended down the front of her ears like fake sideburns.

Dale watched as the three girls – he didn't remember the names of the other two – got their tickets and strolled into the theatre. Sheba wore a pink T-shirt, cutoffs, and sandals. She looked like she was going to the beach instead of a movie.

Finally, they got to ticket window, and Dale bought his two tickets and Rusty bought his and the four of them walked into the cool, dark theatre. Rusty found four seats near the middle front and they scooted over to them, Rusty leading the way and Dale bringing up the rear. Dale usually preferred sitting in the back but he didn't even bother suggesting that because he knew the girls didn't like sitting there. But sitting where they were didn't bother him because he noticed Sheba and her two friends seated in the row in front of them, just a few seats to his right.

The coming attractions came on and Dale watched while sneaking glances at Sheba. She seemed to be watching the trailers with avid interest. She turned every now and then and whispered to her friend, then giggled. He knew she was going to be a junior in high school in the fall. He guessed that made her sixteen.

The movie came on and Wendy's hand tightened in his as soon as she heard the anxiety producing music. Dale hoped she wouldn't overreact to the movie. They hadn't been to many scary movies; Wendy preferred romances or musicals or comedies.

As they watched the movie, he couldn't accuse Wendy of overreacting to the scary scenes, because it seemed everyone in the theatre jumped and screamed when the shark attacked the boats or devoured one of the swimmers. Dale didn't think any of those scenes were particularly scary. He'd seen lots worse, but having five hundred people stuffed in the theatre did encourage him to react like the others. He felt silly when he jumped at the scene where the shark leaps out of the sea and almost snaps Roy Scheider's arm off. When he glanced at Sheba, he smiled to himself when he saw her try to stifle a scream by putting her hand over her mouth.

The movie ended and the house lights came on and Dale heard the sighs of relief and murmurs of enjoyment. He got up and stretched his legs and pretended to be looking at the people in the audience while he really watched Sheba. She smiled and talked to her friends and seemed to have enjoyed the movie a great deal. As she inched down the aisle, she turned toward Dale. She saw him, recognized him, and smiled but didn't say hello.

Dale nodded. Wendy noticed.

"Isn't that Sadie's little sister?" she asked.

Dale said he thought so.

"She looks a lot like Sadie. She won one of the cheerleading spots for next year."

He remembered Wendy telling him about the cheerleading try-outs that spring, but he didn't remember her mentioning Sheba.

The four of them left the theatre and decided to get a snack at one of the places in the mall. Wendy and Mary Jane had Diet Cokes; Dale got a root beer float; Rusty ordered chili fries and a large mug of root beer. Dale teased Rusty about his enormous appetite. For such a lanky guy, Rusty sure could eat a lot of food.

"Hey, I'm still a growing boy," he said, while dangling a fry smeared with chili above his open mouth. He dropped it in and slurped it down. Dale and Wendy chuckled but Mary Jane didn't look amused.

Rusty's eighteenth birthday was next week. Dale remembered last year's trip to Turner's Falls and the good time the four of them had there. Then he remembered the incident with Mary Jane's bikini bottom and almost blushed at the memory. He glanced at Mary Jane. She sucked on the straw of her drink and gazed into the distance. He thought she looked a little bored.

They finished their drinks and the four of them walked into the parking lot, said good night, and separated. Dale walked Wendy to his car. As they drove to the exit, they saw Rusty's Malibu zoom onto the highway while honking at them. Dale didn't honk back; he thought it might scare the people walking in front of his Chevy. But he did ask Wendy what was wrong with Mary Jane.

"I think she's about to break up with Rusty."

Dale turned onto the highway and drove toward the rural road that would take them back to Galilee. "Why?"

"She thinks he's too immature."

"It took her a long time to find that out," Dale said, half-jokingly.

"Well, it's different now we're out of high school."

"Rusty doesn't seem to be aware of this impending breakup," said Dale. In fact, he thought Rusty seemed more buoyant than he had been in several weeks. Dale thought he'd finally accepted his fate of not getting a basketball scholarship.

"Well, I think he's going to be very much aware of that after tonight," said Wendy.

Dale wondered how Rusty would take it. He was a happy-go-lucky guy, but he knew Rusty liked Mary Jane more than any of the other girls he'd dated.

"It's sad when couples can't stay together," said Wendy, leaning against him as he drove the car down the dark highway toward their hometown.

Dale agreed.

## Chapter 2: *Linda's wedding; Blackie's apartment; seeing Terry Harte*

If Linda hadn't been the yearbook business manager, Dale wouldn't have gone to her wedding. Nothing against Linda. He liked her. But he didn't like social functions and attending a wedding sounded awfully boring to him.

Dale sat with Wendy in one of the back pews of the charming chapel at Galilee Nazarene College. Linda and her betrothed, Phil Greene, Eugene's older brother, were exchanging vows. Dale thought Linda, not naturally pretty, looked quite lovely in her understated white wedding dress. Her face glowed and her smile looked radiant. Standing not too far away in the wedding party were Carmen and Carrie as the two bridesmaids. They smiled as Linda repeated the vows. He glanced around the chapel. Not many of his former classmates were in attendance. Linda always seemed to have more friends outside of school than most girls. However, he noticed Amanda and Mary Jane sitting near the front. From his angle, he could barely see the profile of Amanda's face. When she turned to whisper to Mary Jane, he got a better view and Dale felt a wistful melancholy fall over him.

He tried not to look at her. He focused on the wedding. The couple finished their vows and Phil kissed Linda. Dale glanced over at Amanda but her face was turned from his view. Then he looked at Wendy. She smiled and wiped away a tear.

At the reception, Dale congratulated Linda and Phil. He shook hands with both couple's parents and grandparents and the minister. He and Eugene exchanged a friendly handshake and chatted for a few minutes. He hardly knew any of the guests except for Carrie and Carmen. He scanned the room and didn't see Amanda or Mary Jane. He ate a piece of the wedding cake and drank a cup of punch while Wendy chatted with Carrie and Carmen.

Finally, Dale got Wendy to leave and they drove back to her house. Wendy talked about how wonderful the wedding was and how lovely Linda looked. Personally, he didn't understand all the fuss about weddings. His parents hadn't had a wedding. Blackie and Jesse had gotten married at the justice of the peace in Oklahoma City. Of course, their marriage didn't turn out so hot, so maybe a wedding did help dedicate people to their matrimonial duties.

"I suppose eighteen is awfully young to marry," Wendy said, still musing on the wedding.

"Yes, it is," said Dale.

"But if two people love one another, then why wait?"

He didn't say anything. He turned down her street.

"I mean, if you find the right one, then you should go ahead and get married or at least make plans."

"How do you know when you find the right one unless you look around a little."

"Oh, you know when you find the right one."

"But you got to look around some." He stopped the car outside her house.

"Not if you *know*."

"Yeah, but how do you *know*?"

"You feel it."

"How do you feel it unless you have a means of comparison?"

Wendy turned to him. Her lips were pressed into a frown. "Why are you arguing so much?"

"I'm not arguing. I'm just disagreeing."

"You don't believe that people can know when it's right for them? If a person knows she – or he – loves someone, then why should they go on looking?"

"Yeah, but how do they know there isn't someone else they might love better out there?"

"They know because they *feel* it," said Wendy emphatically. "It's called love."

"I know what it's called."

"I don't think you do."

"Of course I do. Don't be silly."

"I'm not silly! And I'm not going to sit here and argue with you, Audie. If you don't believe in love then I don't know what to tell you, except –" Wendy shut her mouth and tears came into her eyes. She let out a cry of frustration, something like "ooohhh," and threw open her door and ran as fast as she could in her long dress and high heels to her front door.

"Wendy," called Dale. "Come back here."

Wendy opened her front door and slammed it shut. He waited for a few seconds, then reached over and closed the passenger door and drove away.

Dale didn't call her that night to apologize. He half-wished that Wendy wouldn't call and it would be over between the two of them. But she called the next night and apologized. She sounded so unhappy that he said he was sorry, too, and they made up. He went over and picked her up, even though they usually didn't go out on Sunday nights. They went for a Coke and afterwards went parking for an hour. But during their make-out session, Dale felt distant from it all and he even got a little irritated with Wendy because she clung to him so tightly and moaned in his ear and he began to feel what he was doing was more a duty than a pleasure.

As Dale drove her home, Wendy gossiped like she always did, but her voice didn't have the same enthusiasm. She told him that Mrs. Page wasn't doing much better; she was depressed and was still taking medication, three months after Portia's death. She said Carmen was dating Billy Joe. She said Roxanne and Quentin were still dating and it looked like they were serious about each other. Then she said Terry Harte had moved back to Galilee for the summer and was planning on going to OSU in the fall to run track. He'd given up football. But he thought he could make the OSU track team.

Dale had heard, maybe from Dorfman, that Harte had been injured in a freshman game at Wichita State. He'd missed half of the season. Dale wasn't completely surprised he'd dropped football. For all of Harte's talent, he wasn't especially big or fast for the college game.

Dale didn't say much while Wendy chattered. He walked her to her door. He still felt a bit irritated and when he kissed Wendy goodnight he didn't do it with much feeling, but Wendy hugged him and pressed her mouth hard against his and then said good night in a sort of wounded way.

He drove home feeling annoyed that as he grew more distant, Wendy grew more desperate. He thought she should show more pride. He wished she'd accept his dissatisfaction and end it herself. But the more he drew away, the more she clung to him.


Blackie asked Dale how he liked his job.

"I hate it," Dale said. He did, too. Boring, repetitive work.

"That's the working life," said Blackie. "Better get used to it."

Dale told Blackie how for a month he'd done nothing but make plastic bread signs. He worked down in the basement of the building and did the same menial task over and over again.

"Sounds like my work when I first joined the navy. Except we sometimes worked sixteen-hour days chipping paint. Try that before complaining."

Dale knew it was no use trying to tell Blackie about his crummy job. Sometimes he didn't see anyone but the Ottos, who came down to check on him from time to time. If he wasn't working as diligently as they thought he should, they threatened to dock his pay. The only other employees besides him were a middle-aged lady who helped with sales at the front desk and a lean, bearded fellow in his twenties who worked in the garage painting signs and doing the graphic work and print jobs. He wished he had that guy's job.

Dale got up and walked around the apartment's living room. Blackie didn't have much furniture in it. Just a couch, a chair, a table, and an old black-and-white television. The yellowish carpet looked old and smelled musty. The beige walls were bare.

"Ain't much," said Blackie. "But it's temporary."

Blackie grabbed a black boot with one hand and with the other hand rubbed a rag smeared with polish onto the leather. He sat in the ratty old chair in his slacks and a T-shirt.

"I had to get something quick. Your mother didn't give me much time when she kicked me out."

Dale knew that was right. He asked if Blackie was going to try and find a place in Galilee.

"Are you kidding? Why in the hell would I do that?"

Dale thought to make it easier to see him and June May, but he didn't say so. "You like living in the City?" he said instead.

"Sure. It's a more central location. And I don't run into as many religious nuts here."

"People in Galilee aren't religious nuts."     Dale thought of Mrs. Page and Mrs. Heath. They were educated and nice. He bet a lot of people in Galilee were.

"To me they're nuts. Anyone who's religious is a bit of a nut."

"That's quite a broad generalization," said Dale.

He'd learned that concept recently by reading a book on English usage. He was trying to get a head start on college. He had learned he could take exams for college credit. If he scored high enough, he got credit just like a real class. One batch of them was called CLEP, short for college level examination placement.

"Is that so?" said Blackie, pausing in his polish job.

Dale had always noticed how Blackie's boots and shoes gleamed. He guessed his father learned how to polish footwear to perfection in the service.

"Religious people tend to be irrational; they feel more than they think," said Blackie. "It's easy for them to become nutty."

"A lot of people are irrational. Including people who aren't religious."

Blackie regarded Dale with some satisfaction. "Maybe you'll do fine in college. You seem to like to think and argue."

Dale did. He didn't like working at a boring job, though. He'd much rather read and contemplate. He wished there were a job like that. *Wanted: Intellectual apprentice.* Sometimes he daydreamed while making those stupid bread signs and he wouldn't quite bend them straight or he'd paste the label on crooked. The Ottos, of course, docked his pay.

Blackie asked how June May was.

"Fine," Dale said. She didn't have a job and Jesse hadn't made her get one yet. Of course, she was only fifteen. But he had worked a paper route at twelve. "She mostly sunbathes and goes to the pool and talks on the phone with her friends."

"Well, I want you to watch out for her now that I'm not around."

Dale thought that was a rather odd request, since Blackie hadn't been around much even when he was living with them.

"And watch out for your mother, too," Blackie added.

Dale wondered if his father felt guilty about the divorce. Of course, Jesse had divorced him but Blackie knew Jesse did so because of his adultery. That is, if Blackie actually committed adultery. Dale wasn't certain. He'd only seen that one woman and he couldn't tell if they were lovers or not. He wasn't even sure what that meant except for those sappy scenes in romantic movies.

"Sure," Dale said. He hesitated. He decided to ask the question as simply as he could. "Dad, why did you marry Mom?"

Blackie had started to spit on his rag when he stopped in mid-motion. He looked at his son as if he'd asked a particularly impertinent question.

"Your mother was a good-looking woman when she was young."

"That's it?"

"No, there were other reasons."

"Such as?"

Blackie rubbed the rag vigorously for a few seconds, then paused and looked at the big, blunt toe of his boot. "Your mother wouldn't sleep with me until I married her."

Dale thought that reason was rather similar to the first. He wondered if that was all there was to it or if there were things his father didn't want to tell. He started to ask another question when Blackie got up.

"That's enough questions. You're almost as nosy as a woman."

Blackie walked into the kitchen. Dale didn't like it when his father impugned his manhood by suggesting he was feminine in some way. He didn't know why curiosity was exclusively feminine anyway. He wondered what Blackie would say if he told him about that test he took for Mrs. Heath. The one that said he had both high masculine and feminine traits. Actually, he knew. Blackie would say that proved what he'd always known: that Dale was a weird, mixed-up kid.

Blackie came back with a beer and Dale said he had to go. Blackie nodded, popped the beer open, and sat down in the chair.

"I'll let you know when I move to my next palace."

"All right. I'll see you."

Blackie waved him away and Dale left his apartment and walked down the stairs to the ground floor. He passed a couple of heavily made-up women wearing short shorts and halter tops and they smiled at him. Dale glanced back at them and observed the exaggerated swing of their hips. He wondered what kind of place Blackie was staying in.

Driving back to Galilee, Dale thought about what his father had told him. Maybe that was all there was to it. Blackie found Jesse attractive and wanted to have sex with her but she wouldn't until he married her. Dale wondered if that sort of thing was common back in the '50s.

Then again, maybe things weren't that much different now – at least in Galilee. Wendy hadn't asked him to marry her before having sex. But Dale knew what she expected. That was one reason why he hadn't tried to have sexual intercourse with her again. Not only did he not want to get her into trouble, he also didn't want to promise something through his actions that he couldn't deliver. However, he knew Wendy already expected something from him and he was determined not to give it to her.

Wendy called the Thursday before Independence Day and said she couldn't go see the movie with him Friday. She said Mary Jane had to see her. It was important or otherwise Wendy wouldn't break their date. She said Mary Jane wanted to talk to her about whether she should break up with Rusty. Dale had thought Mary Jane had already done that, but he just said okay. He'd see Wendy Saturday.

That Friday night, Dale sat in his room reading English romantic poetry in a thick textbook in preparation for one of his CLEP exams when the phone rang. June May knocked on Dale's door and said it was for him. When he took the phone, he expected Wendy, but instead he heard Rusty's voice.

Rusty wanted him to come out. Dale wasn't sure he wanted to; he felt a little tired from a week of the incredible monotony of pasting labels on bottles. That was his latest project at work. But Rusty was insistent and Dale felt bored, so he said okay.

Rusty came by fifteen minutes later and honked. Dale dashed out and got in his Chevy Malibu. Rusty took off. When he turned south, Rusty reached down and turned down the volume on his eight track. Dale recognized an Eagles song, "Already Gone."

"We're on a mission," Rusty said.

Dale moved his head closer to the open window and felt the warm air flow over his face. "Oh, yeah? What kind of mission?"

"We'll call it Operation MJM."

Dale leaned back in his seat and gave Rusty a skeptical look. "What about her?"

Rusty face grew sly. "She said she was going out with Wendy. They needed to talk."

Dale nodded. He said that's what Wendy told him.

"Well, I don't believe her."

Dale asked why.

"I think she's on a date with Gene Greene."

"Are you sure?"

Rusty shrugged. "Not exactly. But K. C. said Eugene told him he had a date with Mary Jane tonight."

Dale thought about the implications of what K. C. had said. If true, then Wendy wasn't with Mary Jane because Mary Jane was with Eugene. That must mean that Wendy was covering for Mary Jane. But he didn't understand why Wendy wouldn't tell him that was the case, unless she thought he'd blab to Rusty.

"Hey, drive down Wendy's street," Dale said.

Rusty turned and drove three blocks south, then turned on Wendy's street. His car crept down the road and Dale noticed that Wendy's Volkswagen Beetle wasn't parked in the driveway.

"Maybe K. C. was wrong," Dale said. "Maybe Wendy and Mary Jane are together at Mary Jane's."

Rusty said there was one way to find out. He drove south, across town to Mary Jane's house. Her Subaru was parked in the driveway but Wendy's Bug wasn't.

"This is getting interesting," said Rusty.

"Well, they could be out in Wendy's car."

"Let's find out."

Dale asked if he planned on driving all over town just to find Wendy and Mary Jane.

"You bet. It's our mission."

Dale said okay. He was beginning to find the mission interesting. It reminded him of when they were kids and they'd pretend they were secret agents or detectives. One summer they cased out the Baptist church, certain the minister and his staff were running a counterfeiting ring. Dale couldn't remember where they got such an absurd idea. Probably from some dumb TV show, like *The Wild, Wild West*. Since both Dale and Rusty had vivid imaginations, at one point they actually believed the fantastic story. Dale remembered some guy chasing them off the church property after a particularly unsuccessful day of sleuthing.

As they drove around the more obvious spots in Galilee, Dale wondered why Wendy would be talking to Mary Jane about Rusty if she'd already broken up with him.

"Did you and Mary Jane break up?"

Rusty shrugged. "She won't go steady. But we're still going to date."

"Then why does Mary Jane need to talk to Wendy about that?"

Rusty considered the question. "Well, you know girls." He stroked his chin as he drove out of the West Oaks parking lot. No sign of them there. "Yeah, you're right. It doesn't make much sense."

They drove to the Sooner Shack and the Pizza Hut mostly in silence, since both of them were wondering what was really going on. Dale said Wendy had told him that Mary Jane wanted to talk to her about breaking up with Rusty.

317

"Yeah, I knew it," Rusty said. "She's out with Eugene. She's just using Wendy as an excuse."

"Why would she do that?"

"Who knows how their minds work."

Dale didn't buy it. There was something they were missing. Also, they'd been to all the usual teenage haunts. No Wendy and no Mary Jane.

"If they are together, then they must be at a place that both of them would like to go to," said Dale.

Rusty thought about that. He nodded. "I know. Mary Jane likes going to that new place, the *Java Joint*. We ought to check there."

Dale had never been there. It was a coffee shop and deli. It kept late hours for the college students. He remembered some people in Galilee objecting to the name. Wasn't joint a slang term for a marijuana cigarette? The owner said in the *Galilee Gazette* that the name had nothing to do with illegal drugs; it was just a slang term for a business.

Rusty drove down 39th Expressway and turned on Wesley Street and they saw that the *Java Joint* was still open. Dale pointed to Wendy's car parked in the lot. Rusty nodded grimly. He pulled his car into an open space next to the yellow Volkswagen Beetle and they got out.

They walked inside. The joint was fairly busy but not noisy. People were mostly talking quietly as they drank their coffee and ate. Dale scanned the room and saw Wendy sitting in a booth in the back. The two couples sitting in the booth in front of her blocked his view of Mary Jane. Dale took two steps forward and that improved his perspective so he could see that the person sitting with Wendy wasn't Mary Jane, but Terry Harte.

Rusty came up behind him. "Man, that sure isn't Mary Jane."

A waitress appeared and asked if they would prefer a table or a booth. Dale said neither. Then he told Rusty, "let's go." As they were about to turn and walk out, Wendy noticed them. Her mouth dropped open and her eyes widened in surprise and alarm.

Dale and Rusty walked to the car, got in, and were driving out of the parking lot when they saw Wendy at the coffee shop's front glass doors. Rusty asked Dale if he wanted to stop and he said no.

Dale didn't understand it. What was Wendy doing with Terry Harte? He remembered her mentioning he was back in town. He remembered that they used to date, but that was a long time ago. He didn't even think they dated for long. Wendy spoke of him as if he were only a friend. She had a lot of friends, including male friends. When Dale first saw them together, he'd been angry. It incensed him that she'd lied to him. But as Rusty drove through town, his anger faded. Instead, he felt puzzled. He couldn't imagine Wendy doing this. Was she secretly dating Harte?

Rusty finally broke the silence. "Man, I never would have suspected Wendy of doing such a thing."

"Doing what?"

Rusty shrugged. "Going out with another guy behind your back."

Dale admitted that it did look like that.

"I bet Mary Jane's doing the same thing," Rusty said. He looked at Dale. Now Rusty was angry. "I bet they planned it. They covered for each other."

"I guess so."

"Yeah, that's what they did." Rusty's hands tightly gripped the steering wheel. "Man, what liars."

Dale knew that wasn't like Wendy. He'd never heard her tell a lie except white lies out of politeness.

Rusty asked if Dale wanted to go along with him to see if he could find Mary Jane. Rusty wanted to confront her – if he could find her. Dale said no; he'd just go home.

Rusty dropped him off and Dale said he'd see him later. Rusty nodded and zoomed his car down the street.

Dale went inside. June May was spending the night with a friend; not Sheba, but a friend in her own class. Jesse had gone to bed already. He unplugged the phone in case Wendy tried calling. He didn't want her to bother his mother. He went to his room and turned on the light and picked up the poetry. Now he didn't find the poems of Keats, Byron, and Shelley especially interesting. He couldn't concentrate. He kept mulling over Wendy's betrayal. It didn't bother him too much. In fact, it gave him a reason to break up with her. Still, his pride was hurt. She'd always seemed so smitten over him. Now, he wondered how much of that was pretending.

Ten minutes passed and Dale heard the distinctive hum of Wendy's Volkswagen Bug outside. He looked through the curtain and saw her sitting in her idling car. She looked upset. He could tell she had been crying. Her face had that scrunched-up look.

Dale walked outside and approached her. She rolled the window down and looked at him with a contrite expression. She wiped tears from her cheeks and smiled tremulously.

"I'm sorry I lied to you, Audie," she said. "But it wasn't a date."

Dale didn't say anything.

"Won't you get in? Let's go somewhere and talk. Let me please explain."

"No."

"Please, please, Audie," she said, crying. "It's not what you think. I would never do that to you."

Her crying grew louder and Dale worried that one of the neighbors might hear her. It was a warm night. Windows were open. And Wendy could weep loudly.

"Okay," he said. "I'll get in."

He walked over to the other side and got in. Wendy blew her nose with a Kleenex and wiped her eyes with her fingers. "I don't know if I can see well enough to drive."

Dale got out and walked over to her side and told her to scoot over. She climbed into the passenger seat with some awkwardness because of the stick shift. He got in and put the car in gear and it lurched forward. He'd only driven a manual a few times. He concentrated on shifting as Wendy told him that it wasn't a date. She had just went out with Terry so he could talk to her about all his problems. Terry had problems just like everybody else. People always thought he had it made, but he didn't. People, especially his father, expected a lot from him. But he'd let them all down. He'd flopped at college football. Now, he was going to concentrate on track at OSU. He just wanted to talk to Wendy because they'd been friends and he knew she was going there, too. He just wanted to know what she thought about all of that. Did she think OSU was a good place for him? Or should he go to a smaller college? He might have a better chance of doing well at track at one of the state's regional colleges. He just wanted to talk, she said. That's all. It wasn't a date.

Dale managed to drive Wendy's Bug back to her house without grinding any gears. She only lived five blocks away. He parked her car in the driveway behind Wally's pickup truck.

"Why are we here?" Wendy asked. "I thought we were going to go someplace and talk?"

"We can talk here."

"Okay." Wendy wiped her eyes again. She smiled. "You believe me, don't you? It's the truth. Oh, Audie, I'd never do anything to hurt you. I'm so sorry that I lied. I just didn't want you to think the wrong thing. I mean, Terry needed someone to talk to so badly. He has to leave tomorrow to go to Little Rock for his grandparents' anniversary. Their fiftieth. He had to go. That's why he had to talk to me tonight."

Dale didn't say anything. He thought about yelling at her, calling her a liar, starting a fight. That would be an easier way to end it all. But he thought that would be wrong. It wouldn't be honest.

"You do believe me, don't you?" she asked.

Dale said he did.

"You do? Then you're not mad at me? I'm so sorry I lied to you. I don't know why I did it. I guess I was just afraid you'd be mad if I told you the truth."

"Why would I be mad?"

"I don't know. I wasn't thinking."

Dale wondered if he would be jealous of Terry Harte. He didn't think so. Actually, he liked Harte. He admired his athletic ability and Harte had never been a bully or stuck up.

"Audie, what are you thinking?"

"I believe you, Wendy."

"You do? I'm so glad."

She reached for him but Dale stopped her before she could embrace him. Wendy stared at him.

"I thought you said you believed me. You're not mad? You've forgiven me for lying to you?"

Dale had thought he could break up with her because she'd lied to him. But if he used that for an excuse she might feel guilty for a long time. He didn't want to do that to her.

"I do forgive you if there's anything to forgive," he said. "I understand why you lied. It wasn't a big lie, really."

"Oh, I'm so glad you understand."

"But I do think we should end it."

"End what?"

"Not because you lied, because that doesn't really matter. But because things are getting too serious."

"What do you mean? End *us*? Break up?"

"That's what I mean."

"Oh, Audie, I knew you were mad." Wendy began to cry.

"I'm not mad. It's just time to end it. Before we get too involved."

"But we are *involved*." Wendy started sobbing. "I'm sorry, Audie. I'm so sorry."

"Stop saying that. You have nothing to be sorry about. I'm the one who should be sorry. I let this go on too long."

"What do you mean? I thought you loved me again."

"I care about you, Wendy. But I don't love you. Not in the way you expect."

Wendy stopped crying. "You don't?"

"Not in the way you want. Not in the way you deserve."

"But I love you," she said, starting to cry again.

"I'm sorry." Dale opened the door.

"Audie, please don't leave." Wendy reached for him.

Dale took her hands and held them and looked into her eyes. The rims were red. Her cheeks were salty from the tears. He pressed her hands together and held them as gently as he could.

"It's over. I'm sorry, Wendy."

She took her hands away from Dale's and covered her face. She sobbed.

Dale got out of her car. He started walking. He was glad he'd driven her back home to tell her this. He didn't want her driving after he'd broken up with her.

He heard a loud and prolonged beep. He turned and saw Wendy weeping in her car, her hands pressed against the horn of the steering wheel. She mashed it again and the car horn wailed long and loud like a bawling calf.

Dale turned and walked away faster. The horn still blared and he started running. Finally, the horn went silent but still he ran. He sprinted all the way home.

**Chapter 3:** *Quitting the Ottos; Harte gives Dale a tip; a fickle girl*

Dale had to pee. Standing before his workbench in the basement of the Otto's business, he tried to hold it in until he got off work. He concentrated on the pasting the label on the bottle of vinegar. He'd already pasted 224 labels today. The urge, however, wouldn't go away.

There was a restroom in the basement but he wasn't allowed to use it. He'd asked Mr. Otto if the door could be unlocked so he could use the restroom. Mr. Otto had replied that the facilities didn't work. Dale knew that wasn't true because one day the bearded guy unlocked the door, went inside, and a minute later he heard a toilet flush and water running from a faucet.

So, if he had to use the restroom, he had to clock out then walked up the stairs to the first floor and then walked down to the other end of the building next to the business office to use that toilet. The first time he'd done so, he had to endure the disapproving gaze of Mrs. Otto at the front desk and the critical stare of Mr. Otto in the business office. When Dale came out of the restroom, Mr. Otto had asked him if he'd "clocked out." Dale had forgot and Mr. Otto wrote down the estimated time he'd spent walking upstairs to relieve himself and said, three and one half minutes would be deducted from his pay. Dale said okay, but he wanted to tell Mr. Otto he ought to get a stopwatch so he'd get a more precise time next time.

Dale now wiggled his right leg to help fight the urge. He looked at the clock on the wall above the machine that he used to clock in and out. 4:09. He had twenty-one minutes to go. He didn't think he could wait that long.

Standing there in urinary misery, Dale thought how much he hated his job. The basement was dank and gloomy. A small, smudgy window on the north side allowed in a few weak rays of sunlight, otherwise he had to make due with the blueish fluorescent light above his worktable. He worked alone, which he didn't especially mind, except that the work was so excruciatingly boring. He came in at eight sharp, worked four hours, ate his home-brought lunch for thirty minutes outside – the only pleasant part of the day – and returned to work for four more hours. The Ottos didn't permit any breaks. They paid him to work, they said. Mrs. Otto had even scolded him for washing his hands before lunch "on their time."

Dale reminded himself he only had one more week to endure. He planned on quitting a week before classes started at CSU. He'd thought about asking the Ottos if he could work part-time, but he couldn't imagine continuing this drudgery. So, he'd made up his mind to quit next week and hope he could find a part-time campus job.

Dale now shook both his legs as if doing an Elvis impersonation. He knew he couldn't wait and he dreaded walking up to the first-floor bathroom and feeling the Ottos' rebuking eyes on him.

His present predicament reminded him of the time in second grade in Rhode Island when he'd wet his pants in class. It happened during his first week at school. Dale was afraid of the teacher, even though she was a small woman. That day the biggest boy in class, almost as tall as the teacher, had smarted off to her and she'd slapped him hard on his face. As class neared its end, Dale had a fierce urge to urinate but he didn't want to ask the mean teacher. He, as a new kid from the South, was extremely shy. The idea of walking up to the teacher in front of the class and asking permission to go to the restroom seemed impossible to him. The teacher might scold him in front of his classmates or even slap him. All these objections were exaggerated in his mind, of course, because being a new kid from a different part of the country had intensified his natural shyness. So, he sat at his desk wiggling his leg, trying to ignore the demands of his bladder, counting the seven minutes until class ended so he could race to the boys' restroom and relieve himself of the awful pressure.

Then it happened. He couldn't hold it in any longer. The urine oozed out and Dale gave up and let the dam break. The resulting flow felt mighty good. For a moment, he forgot the shame of peeing in his pants and enjoyed the warm feeling of relief spreading through him. Then he felt his jeans getting soaked in the crotch. Worse, the urine began dripping down his pants leg and pooling on the tile floor.

Dale, mortified, glanced around him. No one seemed to have noticed. The other kids were busy, like he was, working on an art project. He desperately tried to think of some way to save himself from this great shame. He'd already completed three crayon drawings on thick construction paper. He hesitated. He hated sacrificing his drawings. He took them and as casually as he could, dropped them to the floor and scooted them with his shoe to cover the puddle on the floor.

Dale looked down and saw most of the urine soaking into the construction paper. He looked at the clock. He had a minute to go. He waited and counted the seconds. The bell rang. The kids gathered their stuff and raced out of the classroom. He waited until all the kids had left except one, a little red-haired girl he found cute in spite of his official disapproval of the opposite sex. The little girl kept the teacher busy and he stood up, wrapped his sweater around his waist so that it disguised the wet area on his jeans. He grabbed a couple more sheets of construction paper and used them to mop up and then sneaked the soaked papers to the trash can and tossed them in.

He slipped out of the classroom, left the dingy building, and stood apart from the rest of the kids waiting for the bus. He rode in the front, away from the tough boys in the back, and made sure he sat close to the window, opening it up just enough to let in some fresh, cold air. When his stop came up, he hopped off, amazed he'd gotten away with it all.

Now, eleven years later, he felt like he was in a similar position. Of course, he could have walked to the upstairs restroom but he didn't want to. He hated how the Ottos stared at him. So, glancing at the stairs just to make sure no one was coming, he walked over to the sink and unzipped.

The sink was high enough that Dale was reminded again of some of the practical benefits of being taller. He stood on his tiptoes to get Gilbert over the sink's rim. He aimed, fired, and felt sweet relief. He was about finished when he heard the familiar clacking of Mrs. Otto's heels on the stairs.

He forced the rest of the urine out and hurriedly reached up and turned on the tap. Water swirled in the sink and washed the lingering fluid down the drain. He was about to zip up when he heard Mrs. Otto asking why he was washing his hands now?

Dale turned his head just enough to catch a glimpse of her frowning face. Her thin lips looked like a gash on her white face. Her glasses obscured her small eyes, but he could see just enough to know the expression in them was not kind.

"I had to. I got stuff on them."

Dale remained with his back to her. He dipped his hands in the stream of water, then turned off the tap. He grabbed a large handful of paper towels and dried his hands and mopped the sink.

Mrs. Otto asked if he'd clocked out.

"Sorry. I forgot."

He couldn't turn and face her until he tucked away Gilbert and he didn't want to reach down and zip up with Mrs. Otto watching.

Mrs. Otto launched into a tirade of how employees had to clock out for any personal business. The Ottos weren't obliged to pay for employees' hygienic needs. She said he had been warned several times before.

Dale tried to think of a way to get Mrs. Otto to leave so he could tuck and zip. His mind remained blank.

Mrs. Otto asked him to turn and face her while she spoke. He had to think of something quick. He wadded up the paper towels into a baseball-sized ball and tossed it over his shoulder like he was attempting a basket with his back to the goal.

As soon as the paper towel ball left his hand, he reached down and popped his pecker back in and zipped. It took a deft touch to accomplish both tasks in the few seconds he had, but Dale pulled it off. He turned around just in time to see the paper ball bounce off Mrs. Otto's head.

Mrs. Otto screeched her outrage. She said how dare he throw wastepaper at her. She would promptly inform Mr. Otto of his misdeed.

Dale watched her stumble up the stairs, her thick ankles wobbling above her narrow shoes. He walked over and clocked out. He carried the time card with him as he walked up the stairs and down the hall to Mr. Otto's office.

He arrived just in time to hear Mrs. Otto's finishing remarks, something about how Dale had assaulted her with soiled paper goods.

Mr. Otto, seeing him in the doorway, asked if what he'd heard was accurate.

"I wasn't trying to hit her," said Dale. That was true. He just wanted to distract her.

Mr. Otto asked why he threw used paper towels in the direction of Mrs. Otto in the first place.

"Good question."

They waited.

"Here's my time card," Dale said, handing it to them. "I've clocked out for today. And for good. You can mail my last check to me."

The Ottos' expression remained almost as blank and unresponsive as it had from the first day he'd seen them. Except their thin mouths slightly parted and their eyes blinked once or twice.

Dale said "so long" and walked out of the building to his car, got in, and started it. He saw the bearded guy in his overalls emerge from the garage holding a large paintbrush smeared with yellow paint. As Dale backed his Chevy out of the parking lot, he waved. The bearded guy stopped and stared. Then he slowly raised the hand holding the paintbrush and waved it as Dale drove away.


The high school gym was stifling. The heat from a sweltering day had penetrated the old building and Dale wiped the perspiration from his face even though he was just a spectator. Down on the court, Rusty and the other guys for the Greater Northwest team were drenched in sweat. Two large steel fans blew mostly hot air from the east end of the gym. The noise from their engines made it hard to hear the referee's whistle on the court.

Dale watched Rusty take and miss a twenty-foot jump shot. Dale thought that was an example of his undisciplined play. Rusty had an open shot but he didn't have any teammates under the basket. When the ball careened off the goal, the Oklahoma City Northeast center easily snatched the rebound.

Dale looked around and saw K.C. and Bigelow sitting farther down on the front bleachers. Dale didn't recognize anyone else. He guessed the other twenty people were friends of the players, most of them from Cimarron City or other schools in the City.

He decided the heat was worse in the bleachers, so he climbed down and stood on the west end near the entrance to the gym. Only a couple of minutes were left in the game. The Greater Northwest team trailed by five, 67-62. The team was composed of players from high schools in northwest Oklahoma City and Galilee. Rusty was the only guy from Galilee. Erickson had tried out but hadn't made the team. Dale guessed he was too slow. The only other guy Dale recognized was Eugene Greene. He started at point guard and Rusty played shooting guard. Both of them had done pretty well but the Northeast team had a big center, a black guy who was going to play at Oral Roberts, and he'd dominated the game.

Dale wasn't much interested in the game. He'd come only because he'd told Rusty he would. He would have rather been playing baseball, or even Wiffle ball like he and Rusty and his brothers used to do on summer evenings.

The gym door opened and Dale turned and saw Terry Harte and Kevin Stephenson walk in. They nodded at him and he nodded back. They walked over and sat down on the front bleacher and watched the game. Dale glanced at Harte. He wore cutoffs and a T-shirt. He looked tan and fit. But what attracted Dale's attention was Harte's right knee. Even from where he stood, he saw the scar. It snaked around the outside of his knee for about five ugly inches.

During a time-out, Harte, who'd glanced at Dale a couple of times, walked over. Dale noticed he walked fine. No limp or anything.

"How ya doin', Smith?" Harte asked.

"Fine, Harte. How about you?"

"Doin' good." Harte paused and rubbed his face. Dale observed the blond stubble over his chin. Then Harte turned his rather leonine greenish-gold eyes to him. "I just wanted to say me and Wendy are just friends, you know."

"I never thought otherwise."

"Oh. Okay." Harte looked like he wanted to say something else. "You know, I didn't want you to think the wrong thing."

"I didn't. Wendy and I didn't break up over that. There were other reasons."

Harte nodded. "Oh, okay, good. Well, I don't mean good. I mean I'm glad I wasn't the cause of it or anything."

Dale nodded. He felt a little awkward talking to Harte, although Terry really had nothing to do with his breakup with Wendy. Well, maybe he'd been the catalyst. If Dale hadn't seen them together, he wouldn't have broken it off that night. But the end was imminent.

It had been over a month since he'd broken up with Wendy. She'd called a few times. Just to say hello. They'd talked for a few minutes. Wendy told him about her job and how she was looking forward to going to OSU in a few weeks. Dale didn't say much but he tried to sound friendly. He liked her and didn't want her to be unhappy. He didn't tell Wendy about Sheba. Dale had asked her out after busting up with Wendy. They'd been on seven dates. Nothing special. He took her to the movies or for a Coke and a bite to eat. Wendy hadn't told him if she was seeing anyone. He didn't want to know. That was her business now.

"I hear you're going to CSU for college," said Harte.

Dale said yeah. He asked Harte if he was going to run track at OSU like he'd heard. Harte said he was going to give it a try. He wasn't sure if he had the pure speed to do well, but he'd just about perfected his technique. Harte asked Dale if he were going to play any sports at CSU. Dale said no, he wouldn't have time. He'd have to get a part-time job.

"Oh, yeah?" said Harte. "I know of an opening for a good part-time job."

"Really?"

Harte told Dale about an opening for the weekend shift at the Cimarron City Campus Police force. Harte knew about it because he'd worked there for the summer. The guy who had a weekend shift had graduated from college in August and was leaving the state. Harte told Dale if he was interested he ought to go apply.

Dale said he was interested. Harte told him to go see Chief Dewberry at the Cimarron City campus police headquarters. It was located in the Cimarron City school administration building.

"I will," said Dale. "Thanks for giving me the tip."

Harte said no sweat. He left to join Stephenson on the bleachers.

The game ended and the Greater Northwest team lost. The players shook hands and Rusty came over. He mopped his sweaty face with a towel and glanced over at Harte and Stephenson, who were talking with some of the guys from Oklahoma City Northeast.

"What did Harte have to say?" asked Rusty. "Did he apologize for busting you and Wendy up?"

Dale hadn't told Rusty the details of his breaking up with Wendy. He guessed most people who'd heard probably thought it was Wendy who broke up with him. Dale didn't mind. He thought not contradicting that version was the chivalrous thing to do.

"He just told me about a job opening."

"Oh, yeah, man, you're unemployed."

Dale had told Rusty about the unusual circumstances concerning his resignation at Otto's Arts and Industrial a week ago. Rusty had said Dale should have told the Ottos about whizzing in their sink. Dale had replied, "yeah, good idea. I bet they would have given me a bonus."

"They were jerks," said Rusty, referring to the Ottos.

Dale thought so, too, even more so when he reflected on all their petty rules and badgering ways. He didn't understand why he'd stuck it out so long. He guessed he was afraid he wouldn't find another job.

Eugene Greene came over and shook hands with Dale. They hadn't seen each other since Phil's wedding. Dale said he'd played a good game. Eugene shrugged and said he wished he could shoot like Rusty. Rusty made a face. He'd only made seven of seventeen shots. He'd had an off night.

Dale told them that standing here together reminded him of sixth grade. That was the last time the three of them had been together. Eugene and Rusty laughed. Yeah, sixth grade. That seemed like a long time ago. Rusty asked if they remembered the school cafeteria banning straws because the boys used them to shoot spit wads. The three of them laughed, although Dale didn't remember Eugene being one of the perpetrators. Rusty said a few years ago he'd gone into their sixth-grade home room and noticed that the spit wad he'd shot at the clock was still there. A blob of paper, now hardened with time, stuck between the six and the seven.

The three of them shared a few more golden memories from grade school, then Eugene excused himself. He told Dale so long and then he walked down the stairs to the locker room.

"Looks like you and Eugene are getting along fine," Dale said.

Rusty shrugged. "Yeah. Why should I hold Mary Jane's perfidy against him? They're not seeing each other anymore anyway."

"Perfidy." Dale liked that word. "That's a pretty strong word to use."

"Maybe a little extreme."

"Just a little."

Rusty grinned and asked Dale if he wanted to hang around until he got ready. They could go out and do something. Dale said okay, but he knew they wouldn't do anything more than drive around town for a couple of hours. They'd run into a few other people driving around and they'd talk about nothing in particular. But he hadn't done any aimless driving all summer.

Rusty left for the locker room and Dale took off his boots and walked on the court to shoot some baskets. He hit three in a row and thought how he might have been a decent player if he had practiced more.

K. C. and Bigelow walked by on their way out of the gym. K. C. waved and smiled his big, Teddy Roosevelt smile. Bigelow stared at Dale with his piggy eyes but didn't say anything.

Dale aimed the ball for another shot as K. C. and Bigelow resumed their conversation. Just before he released the ball, he heard in the rumble of their words, "Gretchen" and "Amanda."

Dale's shot completely missed the goal and backboard. It was an air ball.

He parked his car on the side of the street, underneath a tree that offered a little concealment and turned to Sheba and kissed her. Dale put his arms around her waist and pulled her close to him. He enjoyed how silky and soft her skin felt, and as his right hand crept lower to her hip the skin and flesh felt even more sleek and substantial. He kissed her lips, then the cheeks of her face, then nuzzled her neck. He heard her make throaty sounds of pleasure. His left hand caressed the small of her back. His fingers found the elastic of her panties and he slipped two fingers farther down and felt the V-like area at the top of her natal cleft. He pushed his hand even farther down and spread his fingers across the soft, cushiony expanse of her right buttock.

"*Dale*," Sheba said, reaching behind her and grabbing his hand and bringing it back in front.

Dale kissed her again and this time opened her lips and probed her mouth with his tongue. With his left hand he reached under her blouse. He slid his hand up and cupped her right breast over her bra. Sheba pulled his hand away.

"You're being bad tonight."

Dale looked at his hands as if they belonged to someone else. "I can't control them," he said. "They're really not mine."

He opened his hands wide and slowly reached for her. Sheba shrank and giggled. Dale moved his hands closer, as he tried to create a maniacal expression on his face: blank stare and slack mouth. His hands crept a few inches closer when he suddenly pushed them at her chest only to be blocked by her elbows. Then his hands reached around her hips, but she squirmed out of his grasp. Then he rested his hands on her bare thighs and caressed them. Sheba permitted that for a few moments, then reached down and put them around her waist.

They kissed for a few minutes, then he tried again to advance to the forbidden territories. Sheba broke away from his embrace and removed his hands from her.

"Dale, we have to stop if you can't behave."

He sighed in frustration and leaned back against the seat. He hadn't asked her to call him Dale. He supposed she'd heard June May call him that. With Sheba, he felt like a different kind of guy – a Dale – rather than an Audie. He behaved more aggressively with her than he had with any other girl. Well, he'd made out only with Wendy. She'd always been so responsive that he didn't have to get aggressive. Sheba was different. She allowed kissing and necking and caressing as long as his hands didn't stray too far up or down. Dale liked touching her. Her flesh was both firm and soft. She felt a little different than Wendy. Not as full-bodied and pillowy. She smelled different, too. Wendy smelled of domestic scents: milky and yeasty. Sheba had an outdoor smell: grassy and woodsy.

"How did you like the movie?" he asked.

"It was okay."

They'd seen *The Sunshine Boys*, a movie about some old vaudevillians. He would have preferred seeing another movie, but the all the other ones at the cineplex were R-rated and Sheba couldn't yet go to them since she was only sixteen.

Sheba's eyes looked almost dark in the shadows. Dale thought she looked a lot like Sadie right then. He hadn't asked her about her older sister. Sheba hadn't volunteered any information either. The two of them didn't really talk that much. She was going to be a junior in high school and he was going to be a freshman in college. They didn't have a lot in common. Dale knew her mother worked as a waitress at West Oaks. She worked inside where the waitresses got better tips. Her parents were divorced. That fact made him feel some sympathy for her in addition to his lust. Sheba didn't talk about her parents any more than he talked about his. He'd heard a few things anyway, maybe from June May. Sheba's parents had been divorced when she was a little kid. She didn't see her father much. The only other thing he knew about her family was Sheba's mother was the estranged daughter of some Nazarene big shot. She'd married a non-Nazarene; in fact, sort of a teenage hood back in the day when there were hoods. It was a sad story, he supposed.

"School's almost about to start," said Sheba.

Dale said yes, it was.

"You remember what we agreed on?"

Dale nodded. On their third straight date, Sheba told him that she'd go with him for the summer if he wanted, but not during school. She was going to be a junior in high school and she wanted to fully experience that. He said he understood. Dating someone out of school was sort of awkward. Besides – and Dale didn't tell her this – he was interested in seeing college girls.

"I've enjoyed this summer," Sheba said.

"Me, too," Dale said, thinking even though she didn't really have a pretty face, he liked looking at it.

He started to reach for her when the beams of a car's headlights swept over Sheba's startled face. Dale turned and looked out his open window and saw Wendy's Bug stopped in the street. Carmen sat in the passenger's seat and she smiled at him. Wendy's face came into view and she smiled, too. She was about to speak when the pleasant expression on her face suddenly changed. She looked shocked and offended. Her eyes grew wide and her mouth fell open then curled down in dismay. She threw her car into first and it lurched forward and then sped down the street.

Dale looked at Sheba. Wendy must not have seen her at first.

"I thought she broke up with you," Sheba said.

He shrugged.

"Then why did she look so angry and unhappy?"

"Beats me," Dale said. "Maybe she's fickle."

## Chapter 4: *Seeing Wally at CSU; getting a job; Jesse a Witness again*

Dale felt anonymous. He sat in the large lecture hall listening to the biology professor. He took notes and tried to pay close attention, but sometimes he looked around at the other two hundred students and wondered if they were as bored as he was.

The biology class ended and he exited with the mass of students and walked to the student union building. He had an hour to kill before the sociology class. As he approached the entrance, he saw Wally Wainwright sitting on a bench. He knew Wally was going to Central State, but he hadn't seen him on campus during the first two weeks.

"Hey, Wally," Dale said, walking over to him.

Wally didn't seem too pleased to see him. He gave him a rather indifferent greeting.

Dale noticed Wally had a bio-chemistry book open on his lap. The two facing pages featured illustrations of chemical processes that puzzled him.

"I'm glad I don't have to take that course," he said.

"I'm pre-med," said Wally.

Dale nodded. He'd heard that. He asked Wally how he liked going to CSU so far.

"It's okay."

Dale thought the campus was strangely impersonal. He'd expected college to be like in the movies. Lots of happy kids attending classes, then going to school events and activities and feeling a joyous loyalty to their alma mater. CSU didn't have much school spirit or camaraderie. Most of the students were commuters like Dale. They drove to the campus from surrounding areas and attended classes, then left to go either back home or to their jobs.

Dale asked Wally if he were commuting.

"No, I'm living in Hayes dorm."

Dale didn't know where that dorm was. He didn't know where anything was except for his classrooms, the student union, and the library. CSU wasn't an especially large campus but he'd been bewildered the first few days. He'd been late to three of his classes because he couldn't find them, even though he had a campus map with him.

"How many hours are you taking?"

Wally said eighteen. Dale said he was taking nineteen. Six regular classes, algebra, biology, Western Civ I, Intro to Philosophy, sociology, English composition, and a one-hour P.E. class, swimming.

"Why are you taking swimming?" Wally asked. "You know how to swim already."

Dale said not very well. He asked Wally if he'd taken any CLEP exams. Wally said no. Dale had. He'd studied most of the summer in preparation for them. He'd received twelve credits for passing humanities, American literature, British literature, and American history. He didn't mention that to Wally, however.

Dale asked Wally if he'd seen any other Galilee grads on campus. Wally said Carmen and Carrie roomed together. He saw them sometimes. He hadn't seen anybody else though. Not until now.

Wally seemed a little aloof to Dale. He didn't look at him or speak with much enthusiasm. He guessed Wally's reserve might have to do with Wendy. Even though the two of them didn't get along that well, they were twins.

"Say, Wally, is there something wrong? You don't seem too happy to see me."

Wally frowned. "You made Wendy really unhappy."

Dale thought that was it. "I didn't mean to. I just thought she was getting too serious. You know what I mean, don't you?"

Wally nodded. "Yeah, I know. I thought she was getting a little goofy, too. She's only eighteen."

"How is she doing, anyway?"

Wally looked directly at Dale for the first time. "She's doing better. She's having a good time at OSU."

Dale said he was glad. He said he better get going.

"Hey, Audie," Wally said. "If you want sometime, stop by my dorm room. It's room 409. I'm there a lot. You can meet my roommate. He's not a dork or anything."

Dale said he would. He waved bye to Wally and went into the student union and walked past all the other nameless students to the far end corner and sat down in a lounge chair. He pulled out his sociology textbook and began reading the chapter on Riesman's *The Lonely Crowd*.

Dale heard the buzzer. He left his book on his chair and walked down to the first floor, opened the door to the principal's office, and saw a woman in her twenties standing at the back entrance. She waved. He nodded and opened the door. She showed him her ID. She was a teacher here at Cimarron City High.

Dale followed her out of the office and walked with her to her classroom. She was dressed casually in slacks and a sweater. She wore her brown hair in a ponytail. Her face wasn't pretty but open and friendly. If he hadn't known better, he would have guessed she was a student and not a teacher.

Dale asked what she taught. She said English. He said that had been his favorite subject in high school. The woman said, "really? Most boys don't seem to like it much."

The walked the empty halls. The clatter of their footsteps echoed. The teacher said the deserted school seemed spooky to her. She asked if he got lonely working by himself in an empty school.

"No," said Dale. "I sort of like it."

The teacher looked surprised. She used her key to open the classroom door. She said she wouldn't be long. She just needed to get some papers. He said okay.

She went inside and Dale strolled down the hall, thinking how lucky he was to have gotten this job. He'd gone to see Chief Dewberry just as Terry Harte had suggested. The chief knew who Dale was. He said he'd seen him play football at the Galilee games. Chief Dewberry's two daughters went to Cimarron City High, but he'd graduated from Galilee twenty years ago. He also had a couple of nephews going to Galilee, so he attended quite a few of the school's games.

The chief had asked Dale a few questions and had him fill out an application. Chief Dewberry was a man of medium height, with broad shoulders, and a barrel chest. He had a long, broad nose, a small mouth and a heavy jaw. His wore his black hair in a short military cut. The chief reminded Dale of a bull with his huge shoulders and big, broad head.

Chief Dewberry had told him that the position he had open was part-time. If he was hired, he would work from six in the morning to two in the afternoon on weekends and holidays. He wondered if a college kid would be willing to get up that early on weekends?

Dale had said he would be willing. He was used to getting up early. He got up early to drive to Edmond every day to attend college.

The chief seemed to like him. They talked a little about Galilee's games last year. Dale mentioned that the referee had missed offensive pass interference in the loss to Ellison. Chief Dewberry agreed. He'd seen that game. The referee really blew the call.

The interview over, the chief had shaken his hand and said he'd call if he got the job. The next day, he called and said Dale could start work that weekend if he wanted. He said he wanted. Chief Dewberry said, "outstanding" and told him to report to the administration building by 5:45 in the morning to pick up the school's keys. He also said he'd forgot to tell him what he got paid. When the Chief told him, he could hardly believe it. He got paid two dollars an hour more than he did with the Ottos.

Now, two weeks later, the teacher came out of her classroom and locked it. Dale escorted her back to the office. She asked him if he worked full time at this job. He told her no, only weekends and holidays. He went to college full time during the week. She smiled and said she was glad to hear it. She couldn't imagine a young man working every day at such a solitary job.

Dale let her out and then did his rounds. It was a solitary job, but he liked it. He walked down the empty halls, checked the auditorium, the backstage area, the dressing rooms, then the gym, the band room, the cafeteria, and the chained front doors. Then he went back to the administrative office and radioed headquarters saying everything was fine.

Most of the time the school was completely empty of people. Occasionally, he let in a teacher to get something. After doing his rounds, he retreated to the second floor. He'd figured that position was best. He could sit in his chair and read and still hear if the office door opened. Sometimes a supervisor stopped by for a surprise visit but since Dale would hear him come in, he'd meet him on the first floor, pretending he'd been doing more rounds. Campus policemen weren't supposed to read, watch TV, or listen to the radio. They were supposed to patrol the whole time. That might have made sense when school was in session but on weekends it didn't make a lot of sense. Sitting in his chair on the second floor he could hear throughout the whole school. If someone tried to break in, he'd hear it. He didn't carry a gun but he did have a nightstick. He thought it was very unlikely anyone would try to break into the school in broad daylight. He felt perfectly justified sitting in his chair reading his book while keeping an ear out for any suspicious sounds and doing his rounds every thirty minutes.

Dale leaned back in his chair with the small, collapsible desk and thought how lucky he was. Essentially, he got paid to read. It was a perfect job for him. People like the teacher might wonder how he could bear the solitude but he liked walking through the silent, empty building even though the lack of people and noise gave it an eerie feeling.

Since he usually did his course work while on campus, he used the time at Cimarron City to read what he wanted. He'd found out that CSU allowed students to take tests for certain courses and if they passed they got credit without going to class. He thought he'd try and test out of several literature and history courses once he'd read the material. Right now, he was reading post-war American novels. One of the required novels, *Invisible Man*, he'd read last year. He thought he'd skim through it and refresh his memory. He read the first paragraph again and felt like it applied to him even more than it did last year. Whether on campus with thousands of other students or patrolling the empty halls of Cimarron City, Dale felt a little like a ghost himself.

After work, Dale drove home and noticed that Jesse's red Cougar wasn't parked in the driveway. He guessed she was over at his grandparents and he walked inside the house and discovered that June May wasn't home either. He changed out of his uniform and turned on the television to watch the end of the Cowboys' game.

An hour later, Jesse and June May came home and walked into the living room. Both of them were wearing nice dresses. Jesse carried a Bible and a *Watch Tower*.

Dale wasn't completely surprised. He'd noticed that Jesse had reduced her smoking from two packs a day to one. Witnesses weren't allowed to smoke cigarettes. If Jesse couldn't quit after a certain amount of time, she'd be disfellowshipped.

"So, did you have a good time?" Dale asked.

"It was boring," said June May. She turned to Jesse. "I don't know why I have to go the meetings if Dale doesn't."

"You're a child, that's why."

"I'm not a child," June May protested.

"You *are* a child and you're goin' to the meetin's with me." Jesse looked at Dale. "You should go, too."

He shook his head. "I'm too busy even if I wanted to go, which I don't."

"Too busy to worship Jehovah? That's mighty close to sacrilege, mister."

Dale stood up and walked over to the TV and turned it off. He would watch the game in his room in peace.

"Brother Trumbo and Mrs. DuBois asked about you," said Jesse.

"And Juliette," added June May.

He hadn't thought about them in a long time. He wondered if Juliette still wore her hair short. He remembered how delicate the back of her bare neck looked.

"How are they?"

"They're happy doin' the work of the Lord," said Jesse.

Dale shook his head. He was amazed how quickly Jesse had grown devout. Just last week she was cursing and smoking.

"Yeah, besides that, how are they?" He looked at June May.

She shrugged her shoulders. "I dunno. They looked the same to me."

June May had been only eleven when they last went to meetings and she wasn't especially perceptive now, so he knew she wouldn't be able to give more details. He wondered if Trumbo still drove his motorcycle. He remembered it as an impressive bike.

"Well, next time you see them say hello."

"We'll see them Tuesday," said Jesse.

"Momma, I can't go Tuesday," said June May.

"You shore can go."

"But I don't wanna."

"So," Dale interjected, "you're going to start going to all the meetings again?"

Jesse nodded. She sat down on the couch, her legs not quite touching the floor, her hose bagging a little at the ankle.

"Are you sure you want to do that?"

A brief look of offense appeared on her face. She reached for a cigarette, then abruptly stopped as if she were about to touch a snake.

"Yes, I do. I've missed servin' Jehovah."

"Why don't you just go to a regular church?"

"Yeah, Mommy. Why don't we go to the First Church? All my friends go there."

"We now go to the one true church," said Jesse. "Other churches are part of Christendom."

Dale didn't think his mother becoming a Witness again was a good idea. But he didn't think he should tell Jesse that. She was stubborn. She'd just want to go even more if he objected.

"All right," he said. "I'm going to my room to watch the game."

He left Jesse and June May still arguing over June May's obligation to Jehovah. Dale shut the door to his room and turned on the TV. The Cowboys were still winning.

He slumped down in the chair and considered the pros and cons of Jesse's return to the Jehovah's Witnesses. On one hand, going to meetings would give her something to do. All she did before was drive to Hardee's for coffee, have lunch with Wanda, visit her folks, and sit on the couch smoking cigarette after cigarette while watching inane television shows. Going to the Jehovah's Witnesses couldn't be worse than that.

Or could it?

## Chapter 5: *Carmen and chemistry; Cleoma and Christmas*

Dale asked Carmen how she liked the movie. They'd just seen *One Flew Over the Cuckoo's Nest*. He hadn't asked her if she could see R-rated movies. He just assumed she could since she wasn't a Nazarene.

"I don't know," she said. "I wasn't sure if I believed it."

They sat in his car at the West Oaks drive-in. Dale thought about taking her to a nicer place in the City after the movie. But he hadn't been to West Oaks in a long time.

"Didn't believe what?"

"That those kind of things happen in a hospital."

Dale knew they gave patients electroshock therapy. Jesse had been given it in the private hospital and in Norman. He didn't tell that to Carmen. Instead he said the movie was set in the '60s. Maybe such stuff – including lobotomies – happened back then.

"Maybe," said Carmen. She smiled and took a sip of her Diet Coke. "I don't know anything about it, of course. The movie just seemed a little melodramatic."

Dale agreed. The other thing he didn't quite like about the movie was that it wanted us to like the Jack Nicholson character, but he hadn't liked him much. He didn't like Nurse Ratchet either, of course. In fact, she was too obvious a villain. But he did like the big Indian character.

Carmen said she liked him too even though he didn't speak at all.

"Maybe I'll read the book and see if it's better," said Dale.

"Was the movie was based on a book?" asked Carmen.

Dale said yeah. He was planning on reading it so he could take the advanced placement exam on contemporary American fiction.

"Why are you in such a hurry to get through college?" asked Carmen.

Dale had told her about the advanced placement exams. He was going to take two exams over Christmas break. He planned on taking four more in the summer.

Why was he in a hurry to get through college? He didn't like living at home. He didn't like worrying about Jesse. He felt restless. Sometimes he couldn't wait until he finished college and left Galilee. Other times, he thought he'd like to stay in Galilee for the rest of his life. Anyway, if he could shave off a year from college, why not? But instead of telling Carmen all these reasons, he just added, "It saves money. You just have to pay for the exam instead of the course."

Carmen said that was a good reason.

Dale told her she ought to take some advanced placement exams, too. She read a lot. He bet she could pass some of the literature ones.

"I don't read the right kind of books. Besides, I'm not in any hurry to graduate."

Dale asked Carmen if she was ready to go. She said yes. He started his car and drove out of the West Oaks' parking lot. Instead of heading east back to Carmen's house, he turned on a road leading west.

"I thought we could go for a drive, if you don't mind."

Carmen said fine. It was a nice night for December.

Dale drove past the park where Galilee's football stadium was located. Darkness shrouded it. The last time he'd seen it was last year's football game against Ellison. He remembered how the stadium lights blazed as the team bus rolled away from the field. Now, the stadium stood dark and quiet. He thought it was strange how time passed and removed you from things that once had seemed so important.

Carmen didn't say much as Dale drove to Lake Overholser. He guessed she knew where he was headed and so far she hadn't objected. He glanced at her. She stared out her window at the trees lost in the shadows. He thought she had a nicely shaped face. She'd got contact lenses and no longer wore glasses. He liked her small mole below her lower lip. She was little but she had a shapely figure. She was nice and polite. She liked to read. She was quiet, maybe a little too quiet for him since he was that way, too. Dale looked at the road and wondered why he was thinking about Carmen's many good qualities. He guessed maybe he was trying to convince himself of something.

This was only their third date. He'd kissed her on their first date but just a brief smack. On the second date, they kissed as long as they dared, since they were standing on her porch. Dale decided it was time to take it a step farther, but he hadn't planned on driving to the lake really. It just came to him after they left West Oaks.

Carmen wasn't complaining. He guessed she liked him. She'd never made cow eyes at him like Wendy but she was more reserved. He remembered feeling a certain spark between them in high school, although they never seemed able to continue a conversation for very long. He had liked her, too, but not in an intensely romantic way. The truth was that Dale missed making out with a girl. He'd been doing it for a long time with Wendy, then a shorter time with Sheba, but he hadn't made out with any girl for the last three months.

He'd dated a couple of girls before Carmen. Both of them were in his classes at CSU. He'd gone on two dates with the first girl, Blanche. She had short bright red hair and really pale skin. She had a boyish figure, which Dale didn't find appealing, but he was sort of fascinated by how white her skin was. After going to an art exhibition on their second date, and stopping off for a snack, he went too far while they sat in his car. She got offended. Blanche had allowed him to kiss her after their first date, so he expected more on their second. A couple of days later, he called for another date and she refused to go out with him. She told him that she didn't really think he *liked* her. He was just *interested* in her. Dale pretended not to know what she meant. After she hung up, he felt annoyed but knew she was right. He didn't like her much. He thought she was pretentious. She spoke with a snooty voice. She was an art history major. He didn't even find her very attractive except for her alabaster white skin. Her refusal had wounded his pride, however, and he didn't like thinking about her.

The second girl he had dated had the unusual name of Greer. On their first date she asked him if he knew who she'd been named after. Dale said sure. Greer Garson. She'd been impressed. So, he and Greer had one thing in common: they both liked old movies. She didn't look anything like the old movie star, however. Rather, she looked a little like Jean Arthur, not the Jean Arthur of the Frank Capra movies, but the Jean Arthur in *Shane*. She had short, curly blond hair, blue eyes, a cute face, and a pleasant personality. Greer also had a nice rear. She didn't have, unfortunately, Jean Arthur's delightfully musical voice. Instead, Greer sort of had a flat voice. Another problem was that she was rather tall. Dale guessed she was over five foot seven. He'd grown to almost five eight. They were essentially the same height. On their first date, Greer wore low-heeled shoes and everything went fine. They saw a classic Capra movie, *Mr. Deeds Goes to Town*, at the new repertory movie theatre in the City. Afterwards, they went to a fashionable bar and grill called *Gatz's*, had a drink, and talked about other Capra films they had seen. Greer, as she sipped a glass of wine, said she liked *It Happened One Night* the best. Dale, who drank hot apple cider, said his favorite was *It's a Wonderful Life*. But he added he loved every Capra movie he'd ever seen. Back on campus, he walked her to her dorm and kissed her good night and didn't feel too awkward, even though they were about the same height.

The second date went fine, too. They went to a play on campus, *Who's Afraid of Virginia Woolf?* They both found it stimulating. Before walking Greer to her dorm, Dale kissed her several times in his car. He found himself starting to like Greer.

Then, on their third date, Greer wore high heels. They went to another movie, this time a new one called *Shampoo*. It was rather risqué but afterwards, Greer didn't complain about it like most Galilee girls would have. Dale felt mixed feelings about that. On one hand, he was encouraged by her broad-mindedness; on the other hand, he felt irked that she was more sophisticated than he was. After a snack, he took her home in the City and as he walked her to her door he once again noticed she was taller than he was. The kiss didn't go well. He raised himself on his toes as she bent her knees and they missed. Then they compensated and Dale landed an awkward smooch on her. They said good night and he left feeling annoyed. He felt awkward trying to kiss a girl taller than he was. He even wondered if she wore high heels on purpose to embarrass him, although he knew that didn't make any sense. Still, he felt she'd been rather inconsiderate. He didn't ask her out again, even though he did like her. When he saw her on campus, she smiled but not with any warmth.

He didn't have any classes with Carmen, but he saw her a few times on campus. Twice he and Wally went over to Carmen's dorm room and talked with her and Carrie. Then, following his two dating disappointments, he called Carmen and asked her out. She hesitated at first, then said yes.

Now, two dates later, Dale drove to the lake and found a fairly secluded spot and parked. He glanced at Carmen and she gave him a rather shy look. He leaned over and put his arms around her waist and kissed her. She responded pretty well so he kissed her more deeply and soon they were making out although he felt a lingering awkwardness to it all.

Carmen put her arms around his neck and he drew her closer. He put his hand on her thigh and even though she was wearing pants he could feel the soft firmness of her thigh through the fabric. He continued kissing and caressing her. Dale still felt a little odd. He couldn't explain it to himself. He felt self-conscious but he tried to ignore the feeling and move forward. He stroked her thigh and hip and liked how his hand curved over that part of her. Then he eased a hand underneath her sweater and stroked the soft flesh of her belly before moving to her breast. He pushed the bra up and cupped her breast and squeezed her nipple. Carmen jerked when he did that, and he wondered if he'd squeezed too hard. Then he noticed that she wasn't responding to the nuzzling of her neck and Dale stopped and looked at her.

"Is there anything wrong?"

Carmen's head hung down so he couldn't see her eyes. "I don't know," she said quietly.

Dale removed his hand from her breast. "What is it?"

"I don't know," she said, almost in a murmur. "It doesn't feel right."

Dale leaned back in the seat. He'd felt that too, although he'd diligently tried to ignore it by concentrating on how soft and warm she felt. But in the back of his mind he'd thought they were going through the motions like they were following an instruction book.

"Yeah, I know what you mean."

"You do?" Carmen reached under her sweater and discreetly pulled down her bra.

Dale looked at her and nodded. "Yeah. Something's missing."

Carmen smiled wanly. "Maybe it's too soon."

"Yeah, maybe."

"You don't mind?"

Dale pretended that he didn't. "No, of course not. I think you're right. It's just too soon."

They sat silently for a few seconds.

He said maybe they should vacate the spot before a cop or ranger checked on them. Dale especially didn't want a ranger to find them. If the ranger asked for I.D., he might guess that he was Blackie's son even though there were a lot of different Smiths around.

Dale started the car and headed back to town.

After a minute of silence, Carmen said she almost didn't go out with him the first time he asked.

"Oh, yeah," Dale said, grinning a little. "Why not?"

"I was sort of mad at you."

He glanced over and saw that she wasn't smiling. He almost didn't want to ask because he thought she might blame him for making Wendy unhappy.

"What did I do?"

"Well, you first made me a little annoyed last year when we working on the yearbook."

"Why?"

"Well, that was it. *We* weren't working on the yearbook. You did almost everything yourself."

Dale thought was true. He did almost all the editorial work. He'd gotten so wrapped up in it that he hadn't even thought how Carmen might want to do more than he allowed her to do.

"Yeah, I guess you're right." He looked at her and shrugged. "Gee, I'm sorry Carmen. I didn't do it on purpose. I just got carried away with it all."

"That's okay. I know you worked hard. You just didn't think about how other people might have helped."

Dale shook his head. "If I'd had you help more, the yearbook would have probably been better."

"Probably."

Dale looked to see if she was joking. When he narrowed his eyes at her, she smiled. Her reaction puzzled him. If she cared so much, she should have said something to him last year.

"It's all right, Audie," she said. "It was a good yearbook. What it lacked in technical skill you made up with creativity."

He nodded but he still felt irked.

"So," Dale asked, deciding he was ready to hear more criticism, "what else made you a little mad at me?"

He glanced at her when she didn't answer right away.

"Well, Wendy."

Dale frowned. "I don't get it."

"Well, rumor has it she broke up with you, but I know the truth. You broke up with her. And you broke her heart."

He didn't like that phrase. It was trite. The stuff of sappy songs. But Dale realized that words were often inadequate to describe powerful emotions. He was feeling something of a powerful emotion right then. He hated thinking he'd hurt Wendy that deeply. He suddenly felt hollow inside, as if he'd turned into a shell of himself.

"Don't feel so sad about it," Carmen said. "She's over it."

Dale glanced at her. In the gloom, her soft brown eyes looked a little sad too.

"Really?"

"For the most part."

They didn't say anything else for the rest of the drive. Dale wondered how often Carmen spoke to Wendy. He wondered if she would tell Wendy about their dates. He doubted it.

When he arrived at her modest house, he walked her to her door. She smiled and thanked him for the date.

"We're still friends aren't we?" Carmen asked.

"Sure," Dale said.

She stood waiting and he noticed how small she was. He remembered back in seventh grade when they were about the same height. Now, he seemed to tower over her. He forgot his irritation and leaned over and kissed her quickly on the lips, like a friend.

"Good night," he said.

"Good night," she replied. She opened her door and went inside.

He walked back to his car and wondered why things hadn't worked out between them. Maybe it was just a lack of chemistry. Maybe it was the ghost of Wendy. Whatever it was, Dale felt a little sad knowing they would never go out together again.


Blackie's new apartment was as sparsely furnished as his first, but at least the place looked clean and maintained. Dale sat in one of the two chairs; there was no couch. The white walls were bare but not dingy. The maroon shag carpet felt thick and freshly vacuumed. The apartment had a temporary feel to it like it was more of a crash pad than a residence. Blackie, however, had been living here for the past five months.

Dale heard his father rooting around in the kitchen. He heard Blackie say something but he couldn't make out the words. Dale was about to get up and go ask what he'd said when the front door opened and a large-bodied woman appeared in the doorway.

Her name was Cleoma. Dale had met her before. She was the manager of The French Quarter, the apartment complex that catered exclusively to singles. She stood in the doorway and smiled at him.

"Hi, sugah," she said, her large lips looking even larger with all the red lipstick smeared on them. "Awful nice to see ya again."

Dale said hello and Cleoma swished in, the material of her tight scarlet slacks making that odd sound as she gyrated her hips. The ample flesh of her body seemed to move in all directions as she walked. As she swung her hips, her large buttocks and thighs jiggled; when she seesawed her shoulders, her low-slung breasts bobbled. Even her belly shimmied with her locomotion.

"Where's yo' daddy, hon'?"

Dale pointed to the kitchen.

Cleoma rambled into that room and he heard her airy, mincing, Cajun-accented voice rolling in from the kitchen. She asked Blackie what in the world he was doin' in this room of all rooms? Dale couldn't make out Blackie's response. His dad's voice was swallowed in Cleoma's trilling laughter.

She came out with Blackie. "Yo' daddy is soooo funnah."

Dale said he'd always thought so.

Blackie gave him a sharp look but didn't say anything. Cleoma launched into the reason why she was here visiting father and son. As she spoke, Dale was reminded of all the reasons why he didn't like her. He didn't like the way she looked, moved, or spoke. He had to admit Cleoma was attractive in a kind of vulgar, grossly sensual way. She had dark medium-length hair, strikingly blue eyes, a pug nose, and a wide, full-lipped mouth. Her figure, no doubt voluptuous in her youth, was beginning to expand and ooze out like the shell of an elaborate dessert unable to contain its own sticky sweetness. She wore low-cut blouses which showed too much of her pendulous breasts and tight skirts and slacks that revealed too much of her thickening thighs and protruding buttocks. She didn't walk, she pranced, swayed, and sashayed; all her movements and gestures were exaggerated and mannered. And worse was the way she talked. She cooed and lisped, calling everyone honey and baby and sweetie and other annoying endearments. When she spoke her mouth hung open, the full lips loose and moist, her tongue rolling in her mouth as she savored each syllable before releasing it in a sibilant drawl. Her thin, breathy voice seemed incongruous coming from so fleshy a woman. But what Dale liked least about Cleoma was a grotesque combination of vulgarity and pretentiousness. She was an ignoramus firmly convinced she had taste and discernment.

Blackie seemed to like her, though.

Dale caught the last part of Cleoma's speech. She wanted the boys to come over to her place and join the party.

"What party?" Blackie asked.

"Why, the Christmas party," Cleoma said incredulously, as if she was astonished that Blackie would forget.

Blackie said he'd forgot.

Cleoma scolded him. "Now, sugah, how in the world could you forget one of my parties? We have the finest liquor, the most tasty of treats, and the best damn music. Wine, women, and song. Well, you gotta make do with old broads like me fo' women. But what mo' could you ask?"

Dale thought he was hearing some of that best damn music blaring from the first floor of the complex.

Blackie said he'd come over in a little while.

"Can I count on that, baby?"

Blackie said yes.

"All righty, then," she said. "Oh, and by all means, bring yo' son. He's old nuff to have some fun, too."

Dale said he had to leave soon.

"Oh, is that right, sugah? Well, maybe you can come to my next shindig. It'll even be grander than this fete." (Cleoma pronounced it "feet," which confused Dale even more than if she'd pronounced it properly as "fate.")

Cleoma strolled toward the door. "Ta ta, honeys. And Blackie I hope to see ya in a li'l while."

Dale and Blackie watched her sashay out the door, using one hand to close it behind her in an impressively rhythmic way.

Dale looked at his father, who had the puzzled, slightly wary expression on his face of a sleepwalker who has just woken up.

"Does she always just barge in here?" Dale asked.

"I'm usually not home."

Dale thought that didn't really answer the question, although he knew it was true that between work and taking night classes Blackie wasn't home much.

"Well, I got to go," Dale said.

Blackie didn't try to convince him to stay. Dale imagined he really wanted to go to Cleoma's big "feet."

He walked out of his dad's apartment on the second floor and descended the stairs. He heard awful music; it sounded like that disco stuff, blaring from the large, corner apartment that Cleoma claimed as manager. Dale thought they were getting a head start. It was only five in the afternoon on Christmas Eve.

He drove back in heavy traffic to Galilee. He knew he should have left earlier. It took him more than thirty minutes to get home. When he pulled up on the curb outside his house, he noticed a white Ford parked behind Jesse's Cougar. He went inside and found his mother sitting on the couch with Greta Hodd. The large woman held open a Bible for both of them to consult.

"Hello, Dale," said Greta.

He said hello back. He thought Greta looked just the same, except that he detected some gray in her piled-up blond hair. Her one wandering eye fixed on him and she smiled that incongruous smile where neither her good eye nor her bad eye seemed to match her grin.

"Dale," said Jesse, "you remember Greta, don't ya?"

He said he did.

"Your mother told me that you're going to college now."

He said yes, he was. He almost expected Greta to remind him that college was pointless since the End would probably come before he graduated. But she didn't. She was polite.

Greta asked if he'd like to join them in their Bible study.

"No, thanks," said Dale. He was going to his room.

Greta said it was good to see him again. He nodded and left the living room. As he walked down the hall, he noticed the door to June May's room was open, meaning she was out. He remembered she was going with her new best friend, a sophomore girl named Jamie, to the First Church Christmas Eve service. Dale had seen Jamie a few times. She was a big girl; around five foot nine, with long legs and short dark hair. He didn't think she was especially attractive although June May said she was one of the more popular girls in school. Jamie and June May made a rather odd twosome because of a difference of seven inches in their height.

Dale shut the door to his room and debated whether to watch TV, put on a record, or read. He didn't feel like doing any of those things, especially reading. He had to work tomorrow and he'd be reading all day. Sometimes, it seemed all he did was read and study. He'd done all right the fall semester of his freshman year. He'd made five As and one B in algebra. He'd been lucky to get that B. He'd had to force himself to study and finish his homework assignments. The professor, or rather teaching assistant, had been generous to him as well. Dale had gotten a seventy-eight on the final but the teacher had liked his diligence and bumped his final grade to a B. Dale was glad that as a probable journalism major, that was the last math course he'd have to take.

The only other difficult class had been swimming. His midterm report showed he had a C in the class. He wasn't about to get a C in a P. E. course, so he dropped it. Dale thought the teacher, a middle-aged, portly woman who seemed to float in the pool as easily as a bar of soap, didn't like him. He didn't know why. He didn't goof off. Of course, he didn't swim well, but that was why he wanted to take the course: to learn how to swim better. He wasn't the worst swimmer in the class, however. Two African guys were even worse than he was. All three of them seemed to sink into the water like rocks when they performed their swimming exercises. The two African guys, both from Nigeria, were, like Dale, broad-shouldered and muscular. He wondered if the reason for their difficulty in swimming had anything to do with their lack of body fat.

Even with the good news about his grades, Dale felt a little depressed. Part of it was sitting in his room on Christmas Eve. Jesse, once again a Witness, didn't celebrate Christmas. June May didn't even bother putting up the artificial tree as she had the past few Christmases. He got up and looked out the window. None of the neighbors had put lights on their houses either. Darkness loomed over his entire block. The few trees were bare and spindly standing in yards with dormant, brown grass.

He threw himself on his bed and rested his head underneath his folded arms. He thought about some of the people he knew and wondered what they were doing on Christmas Eve. He imagined they were spending it with their families. Rusty, Chris, Carmen, Wendy, Amanda. Dale hadn't thought about Amanda too often of late. Being busy helped him put her out of his mind. But sometimes patrolling the large, quiet, almost solemn Cimarron City high school, he thought about her. He imagined her enjoying her freshman year at Galilee Nazarene along with Mary Jane, Gretchen, Chris, K. C., and Bigelow. Dale had bumped into Chris a couple of times, once at the town library and once at his uncle's lumberyard. Chris had been glad to see him and they had talked for a while. Chris told him about how things were going. Mostly, he was busy with classes and work just like Dale. Dale asked him as casually as he could about the other Galilee grads going to GNC. Chris gave him the usual general information. Dale asked if Bigelow was going steady with anyone. He'd heard that he was. Chris said not anyone he knew. That helped ease Dale's mind. He'd been worried ever since he saw K. C. and Bigelow at the gym that Amanda was going with Butch.

Dale imagined Amanda at that very moment getting ready to attend the Christmas Eve service. He knew she and her family, like all the other devout Nazarenes, went to the Christmas Eve service and worshipped as a family. He imagined her wearing a modest but becoming dress and singing a Christmas hymn in her lovely voice.

How odd it was, thought Dale, to be living in the same town with all the people he'd known for almost all his life and yet to be so separate from them. He felt suddenly more lonesome than he had in a long time. If he drank, he'd get drunk. But instead he picked up his book, Camus' *The Stranger*, and opened where he left off and read without joy.

### Chapter 6: *Facing Flack; Mr. Average splits; Ms. Sweet's Class*

Dale had to get permission from the department chairman to take the special creative writing class for the spring. The Thursday before classes were to begin, he drove to campus and walked up to the fifth floor of Warbler Hall where the English department was located. He approached the desk of the department secretary, an older woman with a skinny neck, a long nose, and large pink-tinted eyeglasses.

"Yes?" she asked.

"I'm here to see Dr. Flake."

The woman peered critically at him through her lenses. "You mean Dr. *Flack*."

Dale looked at his crumpled notebook paper. In his haste to write down the name, he'd obscured the C. "Oh, yeah, sorry. Dr. Flack."

The woman checked her appointment book and confirmed Dale's name, then sent him down the hall to the office on the corner. He knocked on the half-open door and heard a refined male voice say enter.

Dale pushed open the door and saw a tall, broad-chested man in his forties standing before his large bookcase. Dr. Flack wore a dark tweed jacket, a white turtleneck, and a peace medallion around his neck. He had a big-featured, handsome face and long black hair swept off his forehead in front and hung three inches over his shirt collar in back.

"Yes?" Dr. Flack said with obvious disinterest. Instead of turning to look at Dale, he continued to survey the books on his shelves.

Dale told him who he was and that he wanted to take the special creative writing course.

Dr. Flack swiftly turned and appraised Dale. He said the class was only open to sophomore-level students and above. Dale said he qualified, which he did. With his eighteen credits from testing and his eighteen classroom hours, he was now officially a sophomore.

Dr. Flack asked him if he'd brought a writing sample. Dale gave him a fourteen-page single-spaced story he'd written last year in high school. Dr. Flack held it at arm's length and scowled at it.

"I can't possibly read all of this," he said.

He glanced resentfully at Dale and proceeded to skim the first few paragraphs. He returned it without comment.

"Have you read any of Alexandra's novels?"

Dale said he wasn't sure who Alexandra was, so he didn't know if he'd read any of her novels.

"Alexandra Sweet. The teacher of the class. You haven't read any of her work?"

Dale said no.

"You want to take a creative writing class from Alexandra Sweet and you haven't bothered to read any of her novels? Very peculiar."

Dale didn't think it was so peculiar. The class schedule didn't list the name of the professor. Also, it was a writing class, not a literature class. But he remained silent and tried looking as oblivious as Dr. Flack apparently assumed he was.

"I'll have you know that Alexandra's latest opus has been optioned for a television movie-of-the-week."

Dale now tried to look impressed. "Which network?"

Dr. Flack tried to ascertain whether or not Dale was being sardonic. He managed to keep that "I'm impressed" look on his face until Dr. Flack was satisfied he'd asked a sincere question.

"I don't know which network," he said crossly. "One of the big ones."

Dale thought all three were big.

Dr. Flack turned from Dale and rummaged through the shelves of his library. He found what he was looking for, snatched a thin paperback from the shelf, and shoved it at Dale.

"This is the novel in question."

Dale took the book. Pictured on the cover was a drawing of a sullen-looking Indian girl. The book's title, *Hannah Horse*, was printed near the top. The author's name, Alexandra Sweet, was printed in even larger type above that.

Dale had never heard of her.

"I'd advise you to read that novel before class begins," Dr. Flack said in his rather huffy, patrician voice.

Dale said okay and dropped his hand with the book in it by his side. Dr. Flack held out his hand and snapped his fingers.

"I don't mean read that exact book," he said. "I mean buy your own copy and read it."

"Oh, sorry."

Dale gave *Hannah Horse* back to Dr. Flack. He gave Dale a half-pitying, half-contemptuous, look the way an imperious teacher might look at an especially slow pupil and carefully placed the novel back in its place in the bookshelf.

"So, am I in the class?"

Dr. Flack resumed his survey of his books. "I suppose. Tell Mrs. Byrd I said to give you a permission slip for the registrar."

Dale thanked Dr. Flack, left his office, got the permission slip from Mrs. Byrd and walked out of Warbler Hall with a sense of satisfaction. The creative writing class would be the first one he'd ever taken. Galilee High didn't offer such a class. He was especially looking forward to taking the class with the renowned Alexandra Sweet. At least, Dale guessed she was renowned. Dr. Flack seemed to have a high opinion of her.

Before leaving campus, Dale decided to stop by the administration building to check on his advanced placement exam results. The secretary of the testing office gave him an envelope and outside the office he opened it and saw that he'd passed all three exams for nine credits. He'd scored an eighty-eight, ninety, and a ninety-three but on his transcript the courses would be listed as "pass."

On his way out, Dale passed the financial aid office and decided to go in. He didn't have to wait long before he spoke to an adviser. He really wasn't sure what financial aid was. The adviser, a woman with long brown hair and granny style glasses, explained the process to him. He listened and realized he might qualify for something called grants. The woman said students whose parents had low income could qualify for federal and state grants. The student received funds for all college expenses. Dale knew Blackie made too much money to qualify but since he lived with Jesse, and she only got alimony and child support, he wondered if she had low enough income. He asked the woman, even though he felt a little embarrassed to discuss his personal situation. The woman said if he was a dependent on Jesse's tax forms (he knew he was because he did his mother's taxes), and if she only received alimony and child support for income, then he would almost certainly qualify for state and federal grants. If he did qualify, he could use those funds to attend any college or university of his choice.

Dale asked the adviser if he could use grant money to attend a private school. She said yes. Students usually received as much grant-in-aid as was necessary to pay for tuition at private as well as public institutions. She gave him some forms to fill out and told him to submit them with tax records as soon as he could. He thanked her and left. On his drive back home, he realized if he received the grants he could go to GNC if he wanted. Blackie wouldn't have to pay the higher tuition. That idea interested him. He decided he would check out the possibilities.

On Friday, Dale went to his favorite used bookstore in the City, a few blocks away from *Woody's*, the record store. Dale had discovered *Pioneer Rare and Used Books* the week after he'd quit the Ottos. He'd bought a few books then and had returned every week or so to buy one or two books. He'd bought several Dickens, a few Hardys, and some George Eliots. More recently, he'd bought novels by American authors: Twain, Melville, Hemingway, and Fitzgerald. He'd bought the cheaper paperbacks but promised himself that one day he'd buy the sturdy hardbacks.

His greatest find, however, occurred a few weeks after discovering the bookstore. Dale found a large, cardboard box full of study guides called CliffsNotes. He pawed through the slender black and yellow pamphlets and saw that they covered all kinds of books and subjects. He felt as excited as he had when he'd first seen all those *Playboys* and *Penthouses* at Wally's. He flipped through a couple of pamphlets and realized that these study guides could be really helpful. Now, after he read an especially difficult novel or poem, he could find out what it meant by reading the guides.

The CliffsNotes were cheap. Most were marked in pencil as costing ten cents. At that price, he could buy dozens of them. He sifted through them all, decided to buy twenty, and couldn't wait to organize his reading by the CliffsNotes.

Now, in early January, Dale walked into the bookstore and breathed in with relish the musty, pulpy aroma. He gazed at the rows and rows of bookshelves. He liked the quiet. The sunlight slanted in from the large, glass window and cast a golden glow on the beige tile floor. He walked toward the contemporary American fiction section and followed the alphabetized rows until he came to Ss. He scanned several titles until he found one remaining copy of *Hannah Horse*.

He took it, along with five CliffsNotes, to the checkout desk. The same woman that Dale had seen his first day waited on him. She was an older woman who let her reading glasses hang on a chain from around her neck. Her small, acute gray eyes peered at the book and the CliffsNotes as she calculated the price in her head. She said one dollar even in her raspy voice. Dale remembered just a few weeks ago when he'd asked her if she had a copy of *Doctor Faustus* by Goethe, except that he mispronounced the name as "Go-thee." The woman stared at him as if he'd spoken an obscenity, then croaked, "you mean Gur-ta." It took Dale a moment to realize she was referring to the play's author.

He paid for the novel and the CliffsNotes and drove home. He was looking forward to reading the novel tomorrow at work instead of the depressing existential novels he'd been lately perusing.

That night, Dale and Rusty went to see *The Man Who Would Be King*. Dale hadn't seen much of Rusty since summer. Both of them had been busy with classes and work. Rusty had called around six, just an hour before the movie was to start. Dale had been alone at home; Jesse and a recalcitrant June May had gone to the Friday night meeting at the

Kingdom Hall. When Rusty suggested seeing a movie, Dale said let's go, and they drove to the discount theatre where it was playing.

After the movie, they drove to Sooner Shack for a snack. Rusty still had the appetite of a horse and ordered a foot-long hot dog, extra-large fries, a jumbo Coke, and a chocolate shake. Dale just had a plain hamburger, fries, and a shake.

"That was a good movie," Rusty said, while chewing on a big hunk of his foot-long.

Dale agreed. Compared to a lot of the recent movies he'd seen, it was enjoyably old fashioned.

Both liked the camaraderie of Sean Connery and Michael Caine. As they used to do when they were younger, they quickly projected themselves on the characters. Rusty identified with Michael Caine because of his sardonic sense of humor. Dale, although six inches too short, took the role of Sean Connery. He especially liked the noble way Connery died.

Dale asked how Rusty was doing at Oscar Rose.

"Oh, man, the coach is a jerk," he said.

He waved his hot dog for emphasis. A few chunks of chili spilled onto his lap. He picked them up and popped them into his already-full mouth.

"How so?"

"He wants me to play point guard, but I told him I'm a shooter, not a playmaker." Rusty grew reflective. "Actually, I'm not getting to play that much."

Dale knew that had to be tough on Rusty. He'd always played. Even as an eighth grader, he played on the freshman team. He'd suited up for the varsity as a sophomore.

"I'm thinking about transferring," Rusty said. He took another savage bite of his foot-long, reducing it to three inches.

"Where to?"

"Beats me. Someplace I can play. I hate sitting on the bench."

They talked some more about the movie. Rusty really seemed to like it, so Dale mentioned that it was based on a Rudyard Kipling story. He'd read a few stories and poems by Kipling. Dale preferred the stories. He said Rusty might like the stories, too. Rusty didn't seem too interested so he didn't tell him that a good, old action movie, *Gunga Din*, was based on a Kipling poem.

Instead, Dale asked Rusty if he was still dating Mary Jane.

"Nope. She's too wrapped up in all that GNC social stuff."

Dale said too bad. Rusty shrugged. He said he'd met some pretty girls at Oscar Rose. But nothing steady so far.

They left Sooner Shack and drove around town for a while listening to Rusty's eight track. Dale heard a tape he liked. He asked Rusty what it was. Rusty said it was *Born to Run* by some guy called Bruce Springsteen. Dale said it sounded like rock 'n' roll used to sound. Rusty said it was a lot better than the disco rot they played all the time on the radio.

While driving, Rusty didn't say much. Dale thought he seemed unusually subdued. Usually, he talked about all sorts of things, offering his opinions from sports to music to girls with confident ease. Tonight he seemed preoccupied.

A little past midnight, Rusty dropped Dale off at his house. Before he got out, Dale asked how his brothers were doing. Rusty said fine. The second brother, Gavin, now a junior in high school, had decided to play football this year instead of basketball. The younger brother, Sandy, a freshman, might turn out to be the best athlete of the three of them. He'd starred on the freshman football team as a halfback and was doing really well on the basketball team, too.

Dale remembered how he and Rusty had always teamed up against his brothers in everything from Wiffle ball to backyard tackle football. Even when Gavin and Sandy recruited two or three other neighborhood kids to their team, he and Rusty creamed them. It hadn't been fair but that was the rule: Dale and Rusty were always on the same team.

"Oh, yeah," Rusty said, almost as an afterthought, "my folks are getting divorced."

The last time Dale had seen Rusty's parents had been last summer when he went over for a visit and they all had watermelon in the backyard. He hadn't felt or noticed any tension then.

"That's too bad," Dale said.

"Yeah. I had a feeling Mr. Average wouldn't last."

Dale couldn't even think of Mr. Average's first name. He guessed it didn't matter now.

"He was an okay guy, I guess," mused Rusty. "We didn't talk much or anything. Actually, it won't be that much different not having him around."

Dale knew the feeling. He wondered if Rusty knew about his folks splitting up. He guessed his pal did, but neither of them had mentioned it. He and Rusty rarely talked about their family lives. Dale sometimes thought they should have talked more; maybe they would have been even closer friends. They were mostly friends who goofed off together. They weren't talking friends. But most guys were that way. Dale didn't have much interest in talking about personal stuff anyway. But he did have an interest in talking about ideas. About books, movies, music, art, and other intellectual stuff. But Rusty had always shown impatience with that kind of talk, too.

"Sorry about your folks splitting up," said Dale.

Rusty shrugged. "Maybe my mom will have better luck next time," he said, forcing a smile. "Well, see ya later."

Dale said so long and he got out and walked to his house as Rusty zoomed away. Dale walked through the dark house. Both Jesse and June May were asleep. He got to his room and thought about going to bed. He had to get up early tomorrow to go to work. But he wasn't sleepy. Instead he thought about Rusty. It sounded that he, like Dale, wasn't having a very good time after high school.

Alexandra Sweet didn't look at all the way Dale imagined her. She waddled into the room, a corpulent, middle-aged woman with strange white hair that reminded him of the powdered wigs people wore back in revolutionary times. She nodded at the class, settled her substantial bulk on the wooden chair behind the desk, and welcomed the students to her class.

The conversational buzz in the classroom abruptly ended. Dale glanced around and saw several people gazing at Alexandra Sweet with rapt attention. He strained to hear as she spoke softly about this class. Sitting in the back, he thought about asking her to speak up, but in a class of thirty-five students, he felt shy and instead leaned forward in his desk, hoping the extra few inches would help him hear better.

Alexandra introduced herself as *Ms.* Sweet. She pronounced Ms. with a buzzing bee-like sound: Mzzzz. At first, Dale didn't understand. Then he recalled that was the title working women were supposed to use now instead of Miss or Mrs., although none of his female teachers in high school had ever used Ms.

Ms. Sweet then talked about her recent work. She talked about her early work. She talked about her novel that had been bought by television producers to be made into a movie-of-the-week. She talked about her favorite books. She even talked about her hobbies and non-work interests. She talked about all kinds of things related to Alexandra Sweet.

Dale sneaked glances at his classmates from time to time. No one seemed disturbed that the class so far consisted of Alexandra Sweet talking about Alexandra Sweet. In fact, most of them seemed fascinated. Maybe if he could hear better, he'd be fascinated, too. He scooted his desk forward a few inches. The action produced a squeal, which prompted a pause in Ms. Sweet's talk and stares from her devotees. Dale felt an embarrassed glow creep into his face. After an awkward moment, the offended faces of his classmates returned their gaze to the once-more chattering Ms. Sweet.

Dale occupied himself by studying his teacher's bloated person. Her face interested him. It was fat like the rest of her, with only a few touches of makeup. Her button eyes, pug nose, wide mouth, and chubby cheeks and jowls reminded him of a bulldog. Her face also reminded him of someone famous, but he couldn't quite make the connection.

Ms. Sweet was dressed in a black pants suit with a black sweater underneath the black jacket. She wore some jewelry – a turquoise necklace and ring. As she sat in her chair, her rotund body settled onto itself like a deflated tire.

Dale felt disappointed. He'd imagined her as tall, lissome, and young. That was partly because her heroine, Hannah Horse, had been described that way. Of course, Hannah was a Navajo and it was obvious that Alexandra's tribe, if it existed and looked like her, would consist of very fat, pale people.

So, Alexandra Sweet wasn't an Indian. She wasn't young. She wasn't pretty. She wasn't tall and slender. Well, Dale supposed that was fiction for you.

After an hour, Ms. Sweet informed the class it was now time for a break. Immediately, five people rushed to her desk and engaged her in conversation. A couple of them carried her novels, including *Hannah Horse*. The rest of the class exited the room to use the restroom, get a drink of water, and gather in the hall and discuss the finer points of literature.

Dale walked out of the room and got a drink of water from the water fountain. He lingered in the hall for a few minutes listening to a group of older students talk with reverence about Alexandra Sweet's work.

The break ended and class resumed and Ms. Sweet talked some about the books that had influenced her as a writer. She talked about some of the fictional techniques she'd employed. Then she asked the class to write down some information about themselves: name, class standing, major, along with naming two of their favorite books and authors. She also wanted to know why they were taking her class.

Dale thought the assignment boring. He put down his real name, class, and major, but for favorite books he wrote *The Joy of Sex* and *The Cannibal Who Ate Himself*, a title he made up. For his favorite author, he wrote Goethe, making sure he spelled it correctly instead of the way the book lady had pronounced it, and Norman Rockwell. Dale was pretty sure Norman Rockwell hadn't written any books, at least not novels, so he hoped listing him would puzzle Alexandra Sweet.

As for why Dale wanted to take her class, he wrote, "to worship her genius." Looking that over, he decided it sounded a little too sarcastic, so he crossed it out and wrote, "to learn from a master." He wasn't sure if he should refer to a woman as a master. So, he crossed that out and wrote, "to learn from a mistress."

After class, another throng of awed students groveled before Alexandra Sweet as Dale exited the classroom and walked to his car for the journey back home. He felt weary. He'd arranged all his classes for Monday, Wednesday, and Friday. Since the creative writing class met for two and a half hours on Monday evenings, he had to stay on campus from eight in the morning to nine at night.

Driving back home, he didn't think the class was worth the effort. Not only had he been disappointed in Alexandra Sweet's appearance, which was silly because he knew a writer wasn't her character, but he'd been disappointed in the novel, *Hannah Horse*.

He'd read it Saturday at work and afterwards he wondered if he'd misunderstood it. Was it intended to be as simple and obvious as it appeared? The book was about a seventeen-year-old Navajo girl who gets in trouble and is sent to a reformatory school. There, she stabs the young doctor while he's treating a boy wounded from a fight in the detention cell. The attack gets the good doctor's attention and he takes an interest in Hannah. After months of trying to get her to trust him and trying to save her from all the awful degradations she suffers, including a rape, the doctor finally gets her released into his care. He takes her to Santa Fe and just as she's about to develop into a well-adjusted, proud Indian girl, a bus hits her.

She dies. The doctor is sad. The book ends.

After finishing the novel, Dale thought maybe the movie would be better. There wasn't much to the book. Hannah is a poor Navajo girl. White people are mean to her. She's abused by "the system." And just when a nice doctor falls in love with her, she's run over by one of the white man's technological monstrosities: a bus.

Dale supposed that was an example of irony. He would have liked it better if Hannah had been run over by a rampaging mare. At least that would have been ironic *and* funny.

As he drove home, he began to suspect that the English department chairman, Dr. Flack, had peculiar taste. Dale wondered what other silly books he kept stacked in his bookshelves. Who knows? Maybe *The Cannibal Who Ate Himself.*

## Chapter 7: *June May gossiping; Ms. Sweet's B; Seductress Sal*

Jesse was getting fat again. She'd lost weight in her last stay in the hospital and her constant smoking had kept her weight off. But since she'd given up tobacco in order to become a Witness again, she'd started gaining weight.

Dale watched her as she ate potato chips from out of the bag. She stuffed them in her mouth, her pudgy cheeks bulging as she chewed. She reached for another handful as she kept her eyes focused on her *Watch Tower* magazine. She was preparing for the Sunday meeting. She looked at Dale and asked him to start coming to the Kingdom Hall again.

"No, thanks," he said.

He reached over and snagged a few chips and popped them into his mouth. They both were sitting at the kitchen table reading. Dale had a copy of George Bernard Shaw's *Man and Superman* open. He was preparing for his next round of advanced placement exams. One exam was for the course on Ibsen, Shaw, and Wilde.

"I don't want you to suffer through the Great Tribulation," Jesse said.

Dale tried to remember what the Great Tribulation was. He recalled it involved the antichrist gaining control of the world and terrorizing all the peoples of the earth, making them put the mark of the beast on their foreheads and so on. Heavy stuff.

"When's that going to happen, Mom?"

"Anytime, Dale. It could happen in a wink of Jehovah's eye."

Dale paused in his reading. He'd just come to the "Don Juan in Hell" section of the play. He needed to concentrate on that part because it offered the most precise account of the Shavian philosophy. He looked at Jesse and saw she was gazing at him in a strange manner like he was dematerializing right before her eyes.

"Mom, I don't believe in that stuff anymore."

As he said those words, he wondered if that was true. He wasn't sure what he believed anymore. The books he read seemed to offer all sorts of philosophies. He found Shaw interesting. He liked his wit and iconoclastic sense of humor. But some of his philosophical musings seemed silly to him, almost as silly as the Great Tribulation stuff.

"The End Times are upon us," Jesse proclaimed. "Wars and rumors of wars. Natural disasters. Plagues. The rise of the antichrist. The Great Beast and the Whore of Babylon. These are signs that should not be ignored."

"Yeah, okay, I won't ignore the signs," Dale said in a half-hearted attempt at humoring Jesse.

"You won't feel so smart, mister, when Armageddon happens."

Dale closed his book and looked carefully at his mother. Her eyes didn't have that weird shine to them. She behaved fairly rationally. But her obsession with the end of the world troubled him. He feared that her religious zealousness would lead her to lunacy. He wasn't sure what he could do about it. He couldn't forbid her to go to the Kingdom Hall. Besides, she'd gone nuts when she wasn't a Witness. He felt that sickening feeling of being powerless and not being able to do anything for her.

"I know thinkin' of the End Time is scary," Jesse said, misinterpreting Dale's somber expression. "But that's because it will be scary. That's why you need to come to the Kingdom Hall and become a Witness a-gin. You might even be one of the 144,000 saints."

"I'd rather not be a saint," said Dale. "They don't seem to have much fun."

As soon as he said it, he realized he wasn't having much fun anyway. All he did was go to class, study, work, and read. He'd played intramural sports. But that hadn't been that much fun either. He hadn't known his teammates well and he didn't like them much anyway. He'd been on a few more dates with CSU girls. But no sparks. He knew why. Only one girl inspired those feelings in him.

"You shouldn't joke about such things," Jesse said quietly. "Satan is real and prowls amongst us like a wolf amongst sheep."

Satan. The Great Beast. The Whore of Babylon. Mythical figures, all of them, thought Dale. Still, myth exerted a potent force on people's imaginations, including his. He'd been raised with these ideas. Jesse had read the Bible to him when he was a little kid. He had grade school teachers who read the Bible before class. He didn't *think* these things were true, but he still felt their emotional power.

Dale was about to change the subject, when June May traipsed in. She smiled at them and suddenly broke into a cheerleading routine. She went through all the jerky movements, ending with her arms in the air and one leg raised and bent at the knee.

"Go, Gophers!" she shouted.

Jesse frowned at June May. "Vanity," she said, "all is vanity."

Dale recognized that reference from *Ecclesiastes* and for once agreed with his mother. "So, you got selected."

June May hopped twice and smiled. "Yes! I'm a varsity cheerleader. And I'm the only junior. Poor Jamie didn't make it."

"She's too tall," Dale said.

"No, she's not. She's helpful at supporting the smaller girls for our jumps."

He didn't really care. He started to return to Shavian world when he overheard June May talk about the other cheerleaders on the squad. He heard her mention Sheba's name.

"Sheba didn't get head cheerleader," June May told her mother. "I could tell she felt bad about that."

Jesse said it was all worldly foolishness. June May ought to prepare herself for The End and stop jumping around in a short skirt. It's indecent, she added.

June May ignored her mother's rebuke and chattered on. Dale pretended to be reading but he listened as June May gossiped about Sheba getting dumped by her boyfriend, Jason Jordan. "She's not having a very good spring," June May concluded.

Jesse scolded June May for being a gossip. "The devil takes delight with waggin' tongues."

Dale wondered if Jesse was quoting the Bible or just making it up. He decided the latter.

June May turned to a more receptive audience: Dale. "Guess what?" she asked. He tried not to show too much interest. "Matt Jones asked me to the all-sports banquet."

"But you're only a sophomore. He's a senior."

"I know. But there's no rule against it."

Dale thought Matt was dating Becky Brown. He'd heard they'd been crowned all-school king and queen. He didn't keep up much with Galilee High social news. June May told him a few things from time to time even though he never asked her. Dale guessed he didn't mind Matt taking his sister to the all-sports banquet. He'd always liked Matt. He was a lot better date than the floppy-haired Martin Dewberry that June May had dated before – even if "Marty" was Chief Dewberry's nephew.

"Why is the all-sports banquet so late this year?" he asked. Last year it was held in mid-April. It was already the first week of May.

"I dunno," said June May. "I think they're adding a track award."

Dale nodded. It figured. After he graduated, they would add an award he probably would have won.

June May turned to Dale and asked him if he was seeing their dad anytime soon.

"Yeah, probably Friday."

"Good. Tell Daddy I need a new dress for the all-sports."

"You got plenty of dresses already, little lady," said Jesse.

"They're *old*!" cried June May.

"And another thing, you're goin' to the Kingdom Hall with me. No more makin' excuses. Your very soul is at stake."

"I'm not going anymore!" exclaimed June May. "I'll be a varsity cheerleader next year and I'll have to go to all the games anyway. I won't be able to go to the *meetings*."

Jesse warned her about turning her back on Jehovah. Dale got up from the table and left them to squabble. He knew June May would win in the end. She was sixteen and could do pretty much as she pleased.


Dale only had ten minutes with Alexandra Sweet. She didn't have any more time to spare. So many students, so little time. She had to attend to the television movie-of-the-week details. Already, some network executive wanted to make changes in her story.

He sat in the vinyl chair that reminded him of the chairs in his high school cafeteria. The professor sat in her large leather chair before her massive desk and glanced over his final project, a rather lengthy short story about the mysterious circumstances of his uncle Otis's death. Dale thought he'd done pretty good. He especially liked the scene where Otis is cut in half by the train. He described the gory scene in grisly detail, and as he scrutinized his teacher's face he could tell she'd arrived at that point in the story.

Ms. Sweet's brow furrowed and she raised a short, pudgy finger to her pursed, pink lips. She blinked her light blue eyes twice and then turned the page.

Dale remembered his first meeting with Alexandra Sweet. He'd sat in this exact chair two months ago and listened to her as she critiqued the three short assignments the students had done to that point. She said he wrote with "impressive energy" but his language tended to be wordy. She said his grammar was faulty. He nodded about her last criticism. He'd always found grammar boring during the rare times they covered it in school.

Ms. Sweet then handed his assignments back to him. Dale noticed she'd given him a B. He didn't think that was fair. After all, how well could she determine his writing ability with three short assignments? She'd asked them to write a short descriptive scene, a short scene consisting only of dialogue, and a character sketch. He thought the assignments were just separate pieces and didn't show much unless the parts were put together as a whole. But he didn't tell his teacher this.

As he had gotten up to leave, she'd said she wanted to ask him a question. She said she'd never heard of *The Cannibal Who Ate Himself* or of one of Dale's favorite authors.

"You mean Goethe?" Dale had replied, trying his best to pronounce the name. He felt his tongue tangle over the Germanic vowels.

"No," replied Ms. Sweet, without amusement. "Norman Rockwell. Well, I've obviously heard of Norman Rockwell, the famous painter, just not Norman Rockwell the author."

Dale admitted that Norman Rockwell was an obscure author. He'd been overshadowed during his lifetime by that other Norman Rockwell. He said his best book was in fact *The Cannibal Who Ate Himself.*

Alexandra Sweet asked what his book was about.

Dale said it was a book about cannibals. The cannibals start killing and eating each other until there is only one cannibal left. He's so depressed, he ends it all by eating himself.

She said that didn't sound very realistic.

Dale said it was sort of a surreal story. It was also … he tried to think of the term… an allegory.

Ms. Sweet said it sounded like an unusual kind of book. Dale agreed, then noticed something about the great author. The first time he'd seen her she'd reminded him of someone famous. Now, he remembered. She looked like Orson Welles. Dale had just seen *Citizen Kane* in his Classic Cinema class. He'd been really impressed with the movie. It looked different than any old movie he'd ever seen before. Anyway, that's who Alexandra Sweet reminded him of. But not the Orson Welles of *Citizen Kane*. Rather the Orson Welles of those wine commercials on TV. She had a similar bulldog face but without the beard.

Dale told her. He said: You sort of look like Orson Welles. Ms. Sweet didn't seem too pleased with the comparison. She looked at him as if he'd compared her to an elephant, which, considering Orson Welles now probably weighed 300 pounds, Dale sort of had.

She'd returned his work to him and said nothing more as Dale slunk out of her office.

Now two months later, he waited for her comments on his latest opus.

"You need to use one point of view," Ms. Sweet said.

He didn't quite understand.

"Instead of shifting the point of view between several characters, keep it on one character. Like this Rufus."

He'd almost forgot the name Rufus. He was modeled after Billy Dee, Dale's cousin who was in prison; Roscoe had been modeled after Otis, Dale's cousin who'd had been bisected by the train.

Dale asked why?

"It's easier for the reader to follow," Alexandra said.

She spoke with a rather distant, nasal voice as if something was plugging her up. Ordinarily, he would have guessed she had a stuffed-up nose; but she always sounded that way.

Dale wondered why it was important to make things easier for a reader to follow. A lot of books he'd read recently didn't do that. But he nodded and took his story from Ms. Sweet and instead of quickly exiting he impertinently flipped to the back page and read the grade: B.

"I got a B?"

Alexandra Sweet raised one eyebrow, which again reminded him of the famous Orson.

"It's not a bad story," she said. "But the confused point of view renders it less effective in a literary sense."

Dale quickly flipped through the twenty-one double-spaced pages. She'd hardly commented on any of the writing. He mentioned that to her and asked, didn't that mean she didn't think there was anything really wrong?

"Well, I didn't have the luxury to read word for word the entire story."

"You didn't read the entire story?"

"Not word for word." Ms. Sweet pursed her lips and stared at Dale. "It is a rather long story."

Dale said he didn't understand how she could give him a B grade if she hadn't read the entire story. You know, word for word.

She conceded he had a point. She said she'd consider raising his grade if he felt that strongly about it.

He said he did feel that strongly about it. He didn't tell her but he was pretty sure he was going to make all A's in his other classes, even in astronomy. It would be embarrassing to make his only B in a class that he should do his best in.

"Very well, I'll raise your grade to an A. Is that acceptable?"

Dale said yeah. He realized he sounded sort of arrogant, so he smiled a little and said thanks. Then he lied and said he'd enjoyed her class.

Alexandra Sweet wished him well with his literary endeavors. Dale liked that phrase. Maybe she wasn't a bad writer after all. He said so long and left her office.

On his way out of the building, he wondered if he should have told her during the previous meeting that she looked like Orson Welles. He had thought she might be impressed with his powers of observation. Weren't writers supposed to be astute observers? Well, Dale bet any keen eye would make the connection between her and Orson Welles except for the obvious masculine and feminine differences. Maybe he should have said she looked like Orson Welles's sister. But he didn't know if Orson had a sister. Anyway, he could have compared her to someone less appealing than Orson Welles, like Charles Laughton for example.

He wondered if she would have liked that better.

Cleoma's apartment was stuffed with junk. Displayed on the walls were colorful lithographs and glass-encased posters of rock stars like Jimi Hendrix and Janis Joplin and movie stars like James Dean and Mae West. Strewn on several coffee tables and end tables were ashtrays, cigarette lighters, coasters, mementos, and knickknacks, along with and all kinds of household things from scissors to letter openers to empty makeup containers. More ceramic and plastic knickknacks decorated the many shelves jutting from the walls. A large black leather sectional couch dominated the living room. It took up a quarter of the large room. Three chairs – two black leather, the other a more typical cloth chair – were arranged at odd angles around the couch. A large color television was mounted on a massive wood platform, and stuck in the three shelves were the individual components of an expensive stereo. The two large speakers stood like sentinels on each side of the room. On one speaker, a lava lamp glowed a reddish hue as the doughy stuff inside oozed and blobbed in endless arrangements. Hanging with strings from the ceiling were pieces of colored metal that clanged when the movement of people's bodies created enough of a breeze to induce them to collide. A long black and red beaded curtain separated the living room from the kitchen and a small dining room.

Dale imagined this was the kind of room that a hippie would feel at home in. He hadn't imagined Cleoma as a flower child at an earlier point in her life, but the style of her living room certainly suggested she had been one.

Dale sat cross-legged on the thick, red shag carpet flipping through Cleoma's album collection. He had to admit she had some good albums. He especially envied her the Yardbirds and Zombies albums. He'd never seen a copy of these particular albums, not even in *Woody's*. About half the albums were from the '60s, the other half were '70s stuff that he didn't care for, K. C. and the Sunshine Band, The Captain and Tennille, and rot like that.

Sal, Cleoma's daughter, strolled over and plunked herself next to him.

"Oh, so you like that old stuff," she said, pointing to the Yardbirds and Zombies.

Dale said yeah, he liked it. Music from the '60s was much better than today's stuff.

"What about Peter Frampton? He's so hot."

"Not to me."

Sal laughed and slapped his shoulder. "Of course, not to you. Not unless you're queer."

"I don't like his music either."

"He's groovy."

Dale guessed she was about his age but she used old slang like that. She reached over and looked at the *Frampton Live* album. He slyly examined her face. Sal was sort of cute. She had curly, black hair that hung in ringlets to her shoulders. Her eyes were dark blue, so dark that they almost looked black at a distance. But up close and in the light, they were deep, dark blue. Her face had a nice shape to it and her features, although small, fit together well. Her eyes were narrow in shape and gave her a sly look. Her nose was not as short and round as her mother's but still sort of a pug nose. A few freckles peppered the bridge of her nose and spilled over to her plump cheeks. She had a small mouth but her lower lip had a nice fullness to it.

Dale had met Sal a week ago. She said she was visiting her mother for a few weeks. That's about all he knew about her. She didn't talk about herself much. She preferred to joke and drink and smoke and listen to records. She teased him about not smoking or drinking.

Cleoma and Blackie entered the room. Cleoma carried a tray of mixed drinks and beer and set them on the long coffee table in front of the ebony couch.

"Baby doll," Cleoma asked Sal, "would ya like a mai tai?"

Sal said no, she'd just take a beer. She reached over, grabbed a bottle, and took a swig.

"How 'bout you, Dale dahlin'?" asked Cleoma.

Dale didn't even know what a mai tai was. He looked at Blackie, who had settled down in the leather chair with what looked like a glass of scotch.

Dale shook his head. Cleoma smiled, her big lips stretching so wide they showed her gums. She settled her lush body on the couch and daintily sipped the mai tai as if she were at teatime.

Sal shook her head at Dale. "Damn, I can't believe you don't even drink beer."

"I don't like the way it tastes."

"Taste is really not the point," said Sal, grinning.

She didn't have perfect teeth. They were white but not completely straight. That didn't really detract from her looks, though.

"You develop a taste for liquor the more you drink it," said Blackie. "I didn't like it much at first either."

Dale glanced at his father and resisted an urge to say he'd certainly acquired a taste for it now. That was his second scotch. Blackie was on vacation, but Dale still didn't like seeing him get drunk.

"You sho' you don't want somethin' to drink, sugah?" Cleoma said. "If yo' don't want a beer, why don't you get yo'self a nice soft drink? We got root beer in the fridge."

"Root beer," snickered Sal.

"All right, I'll take a beer," said Dale. He reached over and grabbed a bottle of Coors and took a swig. He frowned at the bitter taste.

The three of them laughed.

"Why, Dale, baby, don't force yo'self," Cleoma said between chuckles. "It's not some damn med-cine."

He took another drink. He didn't like it any better with the second swallow but he didn't make a face. "I've drunk beer before," he said. That was true. Most recently, he'd shared a bottle over at Rusty's that they got from Rusty's uncle Tim. He just disliked bitter things.

Dale resumed looking at the albums with Sal while Cleoma talked about getting out of the apartment-managing business and doing something more "luc-a-tive." Dale, only partly paying attention, guessed she meant lucrative, but he wasn't sure because of her exaggerated accent.

Sal finished her beer and placed the bottle on the coffee table and stretched her arms.

"I'm bored," she said.

Dale had only been around Sal twice before, but he'd heard her make that claim during both of his visits.

"Put on some music, baby doll," said Cleoma.

Sal took the Peter Frampton record and put it on the turntable. The speakers hissed, then the music swept out of the giant speakers and filled the room. Sal laid down on the shag carpet, stretched her legs, and folded her arms underneath her head. Dale looked at her. She wore cutoff jeans and a faded red T-shirt. He didn't think she was wearing a bra. Her breasts sort of flattened out and he saw the outline of her nipples underneath the rather thin fabric. Her bare arms and legs were deeply tanned.

They listened to the album and didn't talk. Dale still didn't like the music. Like a lot of rock music today, he didn't like the voice or the attitude. He thought it was shallow and lacked joy or passion. He liked music that celebrated or mourned life's experiences. This kind of music just seemed blasé.

The album ended and Sal once again announced she was bored. She suddenly sat up and asked Dale if he wanted to go for a swim. Before he could answer, she asked Cleoma if the pool had water in it.

"Of course, sweet 'ums. Blackie baby filled it last week."

Dale glanced at Blackie baby. He seemed so lost in a pleasant alcoholic haze that he didn't mind being referred to as baby.

Sal asked if Dale had brought a swimsuit. He said yeah, it was over at Blackie's place. She said, what are you waitin' for? Go put it on. She'd meet him at the pool.

Dale walked over to Blackie's. It was hot enough to go swimming. Only mid-May, the high had reached ninety. He thought a swim in the early evening would feel pretty good.

He walked into Blackie's apartment and went over to the chair where he'd left his trunks. He stripped and had his trunks in hand when he heard a quick knock on the door and Sal popped in.

"What the heck," Dale said. He quickly covered himself with his trunks.

"Oops, sorry," said Sal. "I knocked."

"You didn't." He felt embarrassed and angry.

"I did. Besides, why didn't you change in the bedroom?"

Dale didn't feel he was in the position to explain. The trunks were here on the chair and it would only take a few seconds to change. Besides, he didn't think anybody would just walk in.

Sal smiled at his frustration. He grew angrier.

"It's not like I saw something I haven't seen before."

"Turn around," ordered Dale.

She saluted and turned around. Dale quickly stepped into his trunks. He glared at her when she turned back.

"It's not funny."

He didn't know why he felt so incensed. He guessed it was because he'd never been in such a completely natural state with a girl. Not even with Wendy.

"Don't get angry," Sal said. "You have a good body."

That did not mollify him. "You should have said something before you barged in."

"Man, you're so uptight. Relax. Have fun. Look, if it makes you feel better you can see me."

Sal lifted her top and Dale gaped at the two pale breasts that looked like two large scoops of vanilla ice cream against a light chocolate background.

"Seen enough? I bet not."

She pulled her top down and then pulled her bikini bottom down to her thighs. He gazed in astonishment at the dark tuft of narrow pubic hair between the V of her lower abdomen.

"Now we're even," she said. She opened the door. "See, it's no big deal."

But to Dale it was a very big deal. He recovered sufficiently to follow her out the door and down the stairs to the pool. An older couple lounged on beach chairs. Sal walked to the edge of the pool and paused. Dale came up behind her and focusing on the bikini bottom that barely covered her pert rump, he reached down with his palms out and cupped her buttocks and pushed her into the pool.

Sal shrieked as she tumbled into the water. Dale jumped in headfirst and swam over to her. She tried to dunk him but she wasn't strong enough and he turned the tables on her and dunked her. She surfaced, spluttering. She smiled and he liked the way her eyes narrowed. She suddenly submerged and he saw her watery form swimming toward him. She reached out a hand and grabbed at his loins. Dale, still semi-aroused from Sal's flashing, felt a bolt of fire flash through him as he grew completely erect. Sal surfaced again, a mischievous smile on her face and she turned her back to him and swam away. He lunged after her and grabbed her underwater. He ran his hands down her waist and grabbed hold of her hips and pulled. She fell face first into the water and tried to swim away. He pulled her bikini bottom partially down before she got away. She swam a few feet from him, turned, and wagged her finger at him as she treaded water.

They continued their watery foreplay for several minutes, not even noticing the two people that left. Finally, Dale swam underwater so quickly that she didn't have time or didn't want to evade him and he rose swiftly to the surface and threw himself on her. They embraced for the first time and he marveled at how soft and sleek Sal's body felt.

Another middle-aged couple arrived at the pool. Dale and Sal remained attached while treading water and moved to the deep end. He watched the water splash around her face, some of it sloshing in her mouth when she smiled. She asked him if he wanted to go back to his dad's apartment.

Dale nodded and swam over to the pool's edge. He easily lifted himself out of the pool and then turned and helped Sal out. She patted herself with her towel and wrung the water out of her dark hair. They walked upstairs to Blackie's apartment. Dale knocked to make sure he wasn't there. Sal said not to worry. Blackie would be at Cleoma's for some time.

They went inside and Dale suddenly felt shy. The air conditioning hadn't been turned on so the room felt pleasantly hot after swimming in the cool water. He wondered what he should do. He'd never been in such a situation, alone with a girl he hardly knew who seemed to want what he wanted.

He was about to say something silly like would she like a drink when Sal walked away. As she walked, she reached back and unclasped her top, then pulled her suit bottom down to her ankles and kicked it free. Dale gazed at her completely nude body, trying to ignore the strange feeling he felt somewhere in the corner of his mind. After all, he hardly knew Sal. But seeing her naked as she walked without any self-consciousness to the couch overwhelmed any lingering doubts. He stared at her pale buttocks. They were shaped like peach halves. He liked how the rest of her tanned body contrasted with her white bottom and the narrow pale strip across her back. She turned and reclined on the couch and smiled at him.

"Are you coming over?" she asked, grinning. She seemed amused by his awkwardness.

Dale nodded and walked over as best he could considering his tumescent condition. She helped him pull off his trunks. Then he fell on her and caressed her. She turned her face away from him. He kissed her neck and nuzzled her breasts. He sucked on one of her long nipples. Then she helped him enter her. He was so excited that it didn't take long for him to ejaculate. He collapsed and she tolerated him lying on her for a few moments then she slipped from under him and sat upright on the couch.

"God, I wish I had a cigarette," she said.

Dale sat up too, and breathed in heavily.

"Did you enjoy that?" she asked.

"Yeah," Dale muttered. "It was fun."

"Fun?" Sal said, smiling. "I suppose."

Dale suddenly felt self-conscious being naked with Sal. He looked at her and envied her self-possession. She seemed completely comfortable being nude. He reached for the towel at his feet and draped it across his waist.

"You're shy. I like that."

Dale looked at her. Her breasts were sort of small but round and firm. The areolas were so small that the nipples seemed to stand alone. He preferred breasts with large areolas but he wasn't complaining. He looked down and noticed she had a large, "outy" navel. He looked farther down at her narrow, black pubic hair and spread legs. She had some stubble on the inside of her thighs. Even the outer edges of her pubis had little black dots on it.

"It's not polite to stare," Sal said.

Dale jerked his head back up to her face. She smiled.

"Sorry," he said.

"You haven't had much experience, have you?"

He didn't know what to say.

"I thought so. That's one of the things that makes you so cute."

Dale frowned. He didn't like that word.

"How old are you?" asked Sal.

"Nineteen. How old are you?"

"Twenty-two."

"I thought you were only twenty."

"You flatter me." She looked around the nearly bare apartment. "Goddamn, I wish I had a cigarette."

Dale said Blackie might have a pack in the kitchen. Sal rose from the couch and paused.

"I guess I shouldn't walk around bare-assed," she said.

She reached down for her bikini bottom and tugged it up her hips. He watched as her buttocks jiggled. His arousal, which had been subsiding, revived. He thought about asking for another turn. But he still felt shy and instead watched as Sal next put on her top. Then she walked into the kitchen. He quickly found his shorts and pants and put them on. Sal returned with one of Blackie's lit Camels. She offered him a puff. Dale shook his head no.

"I forgot you don't smoke. Well, it looks like you have at least one vice."

She smiled slyly and sat down on the couch next to him. Dale watched as she smoked. She even smoked in a sexy way, slowly and with a delicate turn of her wrist. Not at all like Jesse, who smoked in an almost ravenous way, as if starved for nicotine. Not anymore, of course. She'd quit smoking. Now she was addicted to Jehovah. Dale didn't want to think about that now. He felt a foreboding but he wasn't sure if it was prompted by his thoughts of Jesse or his questions about Sal.

Dale thought about asking Sal some questions. He didn't know much about her. She was just Cleoma's daughter on a brief visit from New Orleans. He was glad she didn't look too much like Cleoma. She was smaller. Everything about her was smaller. Her body, her face, her features. But Dale could see the family resemblance. That connection began to bother him. He wondered if he'd made a mistake.

Sal stared into space and smoked. She exhaled through her nose. The smoke rings floated in the air like two grayish halos. Dale wondered what she was thinking about. Whatever it was, it wasn't about him.

"I'm bored," she said.

**Chapter 8:** *Jesse talks to Jesus; Dale talks to Sal*

Dale thought the shaking was part of his dream. As he slowly awoke, the dream lingered in his mind. He'd dreamed about Sal, Sheba, and Amanda. All three of them sat with him in his car as it slowly filled with water. He sat in the front seat with Sal, who was naked. Sheba, dressed in her cheerleader's outfit, sat in the back with Amanda, who wore a white church dress. Water rushed in from outside. He felt trapped in the front seat. He looked first at Sal, who smiled slyly and then turned into a fish and slithered out through her window. He turned and saw a weeping Sheba, who slowly sank under the rising water. Then he looked at Amanda, who appeared afraid. He heard her voice say, help me, but her mouth remained closed. Dale tried to reach her, but the seat belt that he never used in life tangled itself on his legs and prevented him. He felt the water pushing at him, shoving him toward the open window where he feared he'd be swept out into a dark whirlpool.

June May shook him fully awake. He opened his eyes and the light from the hall made him blink. He saw June May standing beside the bed. She was crying.

"What is it?" he asked.

"Momma."

Dale got out of bed and put his jeans over his gym shorts. He walked into the lit living room and saw Jesse, wearing the dress she went to meetings in, standing before the portrait of Jesus praying in the garden of Gethsemane before His arrest. Jesse spoke directly to the portrait. Her voice was animated and chattering. She spoke to the painted Jesus as if they were close friends and colleagues. Jesse warned Him of His enemies, of all the traitors and betrayers in their midst.

"Mom," Dale said, "why don't you go to back to bed?"

Jesse turned and looked at him as if she'd been expecting such an enemy to appear. "Judas!" she said in a theatrical voice.

"No, I'm Dale."

"I know who you are. Do you know who I am?"

"You're Jesse and you need to get some sleep."

"No, I am *His* witness," she said, turning and pointing to the painted Jesus. "I bear all insults, all scourges, all false testimony for His sake."

Dale told June May to go back to bed. She left the room and he heard her close the bedroom door. He took a couple of steps toward Jesse.

"Are you here to betray us?" she asked.

"No, I'm here to take you to bed. You need sleep."

"You are a betrayer like Judas. You will deny me three times."

Dale approached her and put his hands on her shoulders. She tossed her shoulders free and slapped at him. He grabbed her shoulders more firmly and asked her if she wanted to go to Norman right now.

"No," she said quietly.

"Then you need to go to your room and go to sleep."

"Sleep? There ain't time for sleep. Soon it will happen."

"Jesus wants you to go and sleep," Dale said, nodding at the portrait.

"He does?" Jesse narrowed her eyes with suspicion. "I did not hear Him say that. You are tryin' to deceive me. You are like the Great Deceiver."

"No, I'm not," Dale said firmly. "You didn't hear Jesus because He told me. He said you needed to sleep. To prepare for that time which is coming."

The last part sounded rather Biblical, like a verse from Revelation thought Dale, although as far as he knew he'd just made it up.

"*He* told you that?"

"Yes." Dale took Jesse's arm.

"Very well," she said. "Only for Jesus' sake."

Dale turned off the living room light and led her down the dark hall to her room. He told her to take off her dress and go to sleep. He said if she didn't, Jesus would be disappointed.

Jesse nodded and Dale closed the door to her room. He listened. He thought he heard sounds of her undressing. Then he heard the bed creak. He heard her muttering to herself, too lowly for him to make out the words. But at least she was in bed.

Dale went to his room but didn't close the door. He wanted to hear if Jesse left her room again. He laid down on his bed and closed his eyes. He didn't feel sleepy. It was the middle of the night and he knew he should go back to sleep. He had to get up in a few hours and go to work. It annoyed him that Jesse would get sick over a weekend. June May would have to watch her until he got back.

He knew Jesse would get sick again. At least she hadn't gone crazy during the school year.

For the summer, Dale had decided to only work as a campus policeman during the weekends and study the rest of the time. He'd scheduled five advanced placement exams. If he passed all of them, he'd get fifteen hours of credit. With those credits and the eighteen he'd already earned through testing, he'd be able to skip a whole year of classes.

Dale thought about the dream he was having before June May woke him. What an odd dream. He remembered how vivid the colors were and how certain things seemed distorted and grotesque. The car in his dream wasn't like his Chevy Impala; it was more like an Olds Cutlass. He thought about Sal being naked in the dream and how he'd seen her naked in real life again just yesterday. He stopped himself from thinking about that. It would get him all worked up and he had to go to sleep. Instead, he thought how in the dream she turned into a fish. He wondered what that meant. He'd read a book about sleeping and dreams in high school just for fun. That's what he used to do instead of doing his homework. Now, all he did was read for school; for the exams.

Finally, he drifted off to a dreamless sleep. The alarm woke him and at first he thought he'd only slept a few minutes but the clock read five-thirty, so he must have slept at least a couple of hours.

He put on his uniform and listened at his mother's door. No sound. Jesse must be asleep, which was a good sign. If she slept she sometimes got better. He listened outside June May's door. She was asleep, too. He didn't want to wake her so he wrote a note telling her to watch Jesse, but if anything happened she couldn't handle to call their grandparents. He then slipped it under her door.

Dale got in his car and instead of taking the expressway to the Cimarron City administration building to pick up the keys, he took the northern rural road, even though it took a few more minutes. He liked looking at the open fields, smelling the dew on the grass, hearing the morning song of the birds. He liked being up this early on a Saturday. Most everyone else was asleep. He felt like he was experiencing the beginning of a new day all by himself.

As he drove, he didn't think of all the stuff that was happening to him. He'd think about that later. Right now, he just enjoyed the tranquility of the summer morning.

Dale listened as Blackie told him what to do, although he already knew. Blackie said he had to go to the county courthouse and fill out an order to commit Jesse. Then the sheriff would come pick her up Monday. Then he would have to go to court for the sanity hearing and make sure the judge committed her.

"I have no legal authority over her," Blackie said. "You'll have to go to the sanity hearing."

Dale said he knew that.

"I'm sorry you have to go through this. But I can't intervene. I don't have any –"

"Legal authority," finished Dale. "Yeah, I know."

Blackie asked Dale if he wanted a beer. He said no. Blackie went into the kitchen and returned with a bottle of Coors. He sipped it in a thoughtful manner.

"How's she behaving?"

"Like she's crazy."

"I know that. But in what kind of specific way?"

"She thinks Jesus is talking to her. She seems to think they're connected in some way, like she's a god, too."

Dale thought about Jesse's behavior when he returned from work earlier that day. He'd heard her banging on the piano before he got inside the house. She played that annoying song, "Myriads and Myriads of Brothers" and sang loudly off-key. June May wasn't home. Dale called over to Jamie's and told June May to come home and watch Jesse while he went over and saw Blackie. June May didn't want to, but he promised he'd be back soon to look after Jesse. His promise annoyed him a little because he was pondering the possibilities with Sal. Their last encounter, their third, occurred in Sal's bedroom Friday evening when Cleoma had been over at Blackie's. Practice had helped. Dale didn't shoot off quite as fast. Still, he'd lasted only five minutes and he could tell that Sal hadn't been satisfied. Well, he'd always been fast at everything. Sal didn't seem to mind though. At least, she didn't say she was bored in the middle of it.

"She's delusional," said Blackie. "Is she paranoid?"

Blackie's prognosis startled Dale, who'd been musing on matters quite different in nature. He shook his head clear and said Jesse thought he was Judas or some kind of betrayer. She thought the "authorities" were going to have her arrested and crucified.

"Yeah, that's paranoid," said Blackie, taking a sip of beer. Dale couldn't tell if he was being droll or not.

Blackie told Dale he might want to write down all of Jesse's insane statements and erratic behavior. It might help his case.

"My case? Why is it my case?"

"Because *you're* going to have to commit her." Blackie asked if Dale had told his grandparents.

"Not yet. I'm going to call Grandpa when I get back."

He hadn't wanted to call any sooner. His grandparents were really old and he didn't want them to worry until they had to.

"Her folks have gone through a lot with Jesse," Blackie said. "She first went off her rocker when she was nineteen."

Dale noticed Blackie looking at him with an uncharacteristic look of concern, as if he had said something insensitive.

"Don't worry," his father said. "There's only a small hereditary factor."

"I'm not worrying." Dale didn't fear losing his mind. If anything, he felt as if he was too much in control of himself. "But how many times has she gone crazy?"

"Seven times while I was married to her."

Dale remembered five times. When he was ten, twelve, then during his freshman year of high school, then his senior year. He also had vague memories of something bad happening when he was six. That meant she had gotten sick twice when he was really little or before he was born.

"I think her folks only had to commit her once," Blackie added.

Dale was about to ask if his grandparents took her to Norman the first time when he heard Cleoma's voice outside the door. She said, "yoo who?" and didn't bother knocking before opening the door.

"Hello, darlins," she said, strutting in. "Are y'all going to drop by and say bye-bye to Salome before she leaves?"

It took a moment before Dale figured out Salome – Cleoma pronounced it "Sal-O-may" – was Sal. But he didn't understand what Cleoma meant when she said Sal was leaving.

"She's leaving?" he asked. "Where to?"

"Oh, baby doll, she's goin' back to New Aw-lens. She's goin' back to Bobby Lee."

Dale looked at Blackie. His face was blank as he took another drink of beer.

"Who's Bobby Lee?" Dale asked.

"Oh, sugah, Bobby Lee's Sal's hubby. Don't you know that?"

Dale felt like he'd been punched in the gut. He shook his head. No one had told him that Sal had a husband. Or a boyfriend for that matter.

"I s'ppose I should say *e-stranged* husband," Cleoma said in a softer, more confidential voice. "She up and left him a few weeks ago. That's why she was here visitin'. I told her she should leave that sonofabitch for good. But he called late last night. They had a real heart to heart. So, she's goin' back to the bastard."

"When's she leaving?" asked Dale.

"Tonight, sugah. On the midnight bus to New Aw-lens."

Dale wondered if Cleoma was making a joke about the midnight bus, but probably not. He felt strange. He had no idea that Sal was married. Why didn't she tell him? Why was she so flirty? Why did she do that stuff with him? He couldn't figure her out.

"I reckon you're sorry to see Salome go, ain't you sugah? You and her were just gettin' to know one another, too."

Dale couldn't tell if Cleoma was insinuating something or not. Did she know what happened? Did Sal tell her? He tried to get some information from Cleoma's face. He couldn't read her painted, smiling visage. Cleoma then asked Blackie if she could have one of those, meaning a beer. Dale said he forgot something in his car and he'd be back in a minute. He walked out the open door and headed down to Cleoma's apartment. He heard music blaring from inside. That execrable *Frampton Live!*

Dale knocked. The music's volume was reduced to a rumble. Sal opened the door and gave him an insolent look. She leaned against the doorway and looked past him.

"I heard you're leaving," he said.

Sal shrugged. "Yeah, tonight."

"I also heard you're going back to Billy Dee."

"Bobby Lee," corrected Sal.

Dale resisted an urge to yell "who cares!" but instead took a deep breath. "Why didn't you tell me you were married?"

Sal held out her left hand. Dale noticed a small, unimpressive wedding ring on her slender ring finger. He'd really not examined the ring before.

"I guess you were too busy lookin' elsewhere to notice this ring," she said in a drawl that reminded him of Cleoma.

That was true. He'd looked almost exclusively at her face and body. He remembered glancing at the ring but not thinking anything about it. He didn't care about jewelry. He didn't know any girls who were married and he never checked girls' fingers because all the girls he knew were unmarried. But he realized he should have checked that finger. After all, he'd had sex with a married woman. He'd committed adultery.

"Wow," Dale said, more to himself than to her.

"Wow?" Sal said, smiling a little. "You're sort of a strange kid, Dale. But you are cute."

He decided to think about the implications of his sin later. It was too big to think it through now. He looked at Sal and saw that same sly smile on her face. Her blue eyes slanted in a way that now sort of annoyed him.

"How long have you been married?"

"Oh, I got hitched a long time ago. When I was sixteen."

"Sixteen?"

Sal looked a little offended. "Yeah, so what? Mama had me when she was sixteen."

"You've been married to the same guy all these years?"

"To Bobby Lee and no one else. I've left him a few times. He's sorta on the boring side."

Dale saw that coming. He shook his head.

"You're not the first, if that's what's botherin' you."

He wasn't surprised. "Why stay married if you're fooling around all the time?"

"I don't fool around all the time," said Sal. "Only when I leave him."

Dale asked why didn't she just get a divorce?

"I dunno. I think about it sometimes. But he's not a bad guy. He calls and tells me how much he loves me. He's a hard worker. He's nice to me. We just got married too young."

"You don't have any kids, do you?" asked Dale, thinking for some reason his sin would even be worse if she had children.

"God, no. I miscarried a few years ago. I don't want to go through that again."

Dale felt strange talking to her. She sounded so much more grown up than he did. She'd married, had a miscarriage, had affairs. She smoked marijuana, too. He smelled the lingering odor at the front door.

"And your real name's Salome?"

"My *full* first name," Sal corrected. "But I don't like it. It's something from the Bible."

Dale sort of remembered coming across that name. He didn't think it was a name of someone good.

"Look, Dale," Sal said, leaning a little closer to him, "I gotta get ready. I wished I had more time. Maybe we could have picked up where we left off."

He felt a flash of embarrassment followed by a wave of frustration. He had been looking forward to another swim.

"You didn't tell your mother about, you know …"

Sal laughed. "Of course not. Why would I tell her?"

Dale wasn't sure he believed her. He started to press her some more when he heard Cleoma's airy voice from the second floor. She'd just told Blackie she'd see him in a few minutes at her place. Dale didn't want Cleoma to see him talking to Sal. He took a step back.

"Maybe we'll see each other again sometime," said Sal.

She smiled her sly smile and Dale felt a confusing swirl of lust, anger, and frustration. He heard the patter of Cleoma's bare feet on the cement walk. He looked down and noticed that Sal wasn't wearing any shoes either. Her toenails were painted blood red. He backed up, nodded at her, and mumbled have a good trip. Then he dashed around the corner of the apartment and listened as Cleoma greeted her baby doll. He heard the door close.

Dale rushed up to Blackie's.

"Where've you been?" Blackie asked.

Dale said he thought he'd left his car unlocked. Blackie shrugged and asked him if he wanted to go over to Cleoma's. They were going to have a little party before taking Salome to the bus station.

Dale said he had to get back home. He'd promised June May he'd be back soon to watch Jesse.

Blackie said okay. He looked a little disturbed. Dale guessed he didn't like thinking about Jesse before he went over to Cleoma's party.

"I got to go, Dad."

"So who's stopping you?" Blackie said a little gruffly.

Dale said he'd see him soon.

"Hey, Son," Blackie said as he started to leave. "Let me know how it all goes."

Dale said he would. Then he said thanks. Blackie hadn't done that much. Dale supposed he couldn't. But at least he understood what he was going through.

Dale got in his car and drove out of The French Quarter apartment complex. He drove on Highway 66 back to Galilee. He felt depressed. Even the pleasant evening didn't lift his spirits. He drove right at the setting sun. The big glowing ball sank toward the shimmering purple horizon. Normally, such a sight would please him. But now he felt nothing but dark depression, some anger, and a lot of frustration. He knew he'd done wrong. Fornication was one thing; adultery was far worse. And even worse, he wanted to do it again. He felt cheated that Sal was leaving. He felt worse than he did when a baseball game ended as he stood standing at the on-deck circle. Just one more at bat. That's all he wanted.

But he wasn't going to get it. Instead, he was driving home to his insane mother to wait out the weekend until he could commit her to the lunatic asylum.

**Chapter 9:** *Talking to Trumbo; seeing the King; visiting Jesse*

Dale couldn't help but smile when he saw Trumbo. They exchanged greetings and shook hands. Dale told him to come in and they went into the living room.

"Well, you're a grown man, Dale."

"Unfortunately."

Trumbo's handsome face looked puzzled.

"I mean, I wished I hadn't stopped growing. I wouldn't mind another four or five inches."

Trumbo smiled. "Wouldn't we all."

Dale guessed that was about how much taller Trumbo was. Dale remembered being almost in awe of him. He'd seemed so imposing and larger-than-life. Now, standing before him in tan slacks and a navy polo shirt, he looked rather ordinary.

Dale asked Trumbo if he wanted anything to drink. He declined. Dale asked him to take a seat. Trumbo settled down in the chair that Blackie used to claim as his own.

"We were sorry to hear about your mother," Trumbo said.

Dale said thanks.

"The brothers and sisters at the Kingdom Hall hope the shadow of Satan is cast from her soul."

Dale had never thought of Jesse's illness in quite that way. "Do you really think that's what is wrong with her?"

Trumbo's large featured face grew solemn. "Yes, Dale, I do. Satan works his nefarious power in all sorts of ways. What many of the world's physicians consider to be the sickness of the mind is really the sickness of the soul."

Dale wondered why he didn't feel offended. After all, Trumbo essentially was saying that Jesse was possessed or at least influenced by the devil. Maybe that was because the Sunday before Jesse was taken away, she had acted like she *was* possessed with the devil. She'd gotten angry with him for preventing her going out. He'd confiscated her car keys. He, Grandpa, and Wanda had kept a watch on her so she wouldn't run outside and do something foolish. Two days before, she'd escaped June May and, in her underwear, had rolled the trash can down the street, spilling garbage all over. Angry about being confined to the house, she ranted at them all, but she seemed most antagonistic toward him. She cursed at him and even threatened him by invoking the avenging angel. Dale wouldn't go to sleep unless either Grandpa or Wanda watched Jesse. He really thought she might set the house on fire or stab him while he lay sleeping. He didn't think that was the devil at work in her. But it was a scary feeling to have your mother change into a hostile stranger before your eyes.

The doctors Dale had spoken to would have scoffed if not condemned as foolish superstition that Jesse was possessed. He didn't know what was wrong with her. One doctor had told him her problem was due to a chemical imbalance. Another doctor said her schizophrenia was basically a genetic weakness. Trauma in her youth had caused the weakness to surface.

"So, Jesse is sick in her soul," Dale said. He almost said, aren't we all? But instead he asked Trumbo what should be done.

"Does she have her Bible with her?"

Dale said no.

"Then you must take her Bible and a copy of the *Watch Tower* and *Awake!* to her."

Dale said he'd consider doing that the next time he saw her.

"Please do so, Dale. It's important. The only way she will be truly healed is if she reads Jehovah's word."

Dale said Jesse had been reading the Bible and the other stuff for months. It didn't seem to do her any good then.

"Then she wasn't reading it the right way. She was reading it with only her mind and not her soul."

That was a distinction Dale still believed in, but he didn't think that was Jesse's problem. He didn't tell Trumbo that. He didn't want to argue. He felt tired. He thought about all the pathetic people at the sanity hearing at the courthouse earlier that morning. Jesse had been one of three people being adjudicated for mental incompetence. One was an old, catatonic fat woman who didn't even respond to her name. The second was a thin, middle-aged man who dressed like a kid. He wore tennis shoes and a baseball cap that was at least two sizes too small for him. Then Jesse. She'd hummed while the lawyer presented her case to the judge. At one point, she stood up and waved her arms around as if conducting an orchestra. Dale had no idea why she'd done that. He didn't even think she'd ever seen a man conduct an orchestra. Dale, dressed in his silly checked blue suit that was now a little too small for him, sat next to Jesse and initially tried to keep her under control. Then he thought, why the heck am I doing that? Let the court see how bonkers she is. But disappointingly, she never acted as bizarre in the courtroom as she had at home. She didn't rant, didn't respond to her "voices," didn't threaten anyone with eternal damnation for keeping the witness of Jehovah from spreading the Good News. She didn't even tell the judge that she was a buddy with Jesus.

Dale had worried the judge might not commit her. But he did. The judge, a heavyset man in his fifties, soberly concurred with the lawyer that she was not *mentis compos*. Jesse had cackled with laughter when she heard that term, like the judge had just said the punch line to a joke.

Rousing himself from his reverie, Dale said he didn't want to be rude, but he had to get busy. He thanked Trumbo for coming over and giving him such useful advice. Trumbo seemed a little surprised to be asked to leave so soon, but he rose from the chair.

Dale escorted Trumbo outside and noticed he had a new motorcycle. It was even bigger, shinier, and no doubt faster than the one Dale remembered him having.

"You like it?" Trumbo asked.

"Yeah," Dale said, looking over the black Harley Davidson. "It's an impressive machine."

"Like a ride?"

Dale hesitated. He really did need to get busy with his studies. He was scheduled to take an exam on *Existentialism in the Post-War World* in two weeks. He had to read hundreds of pages by then.

"You have time for a ride, don't you? Just around the block."

Dale said okay. After Trumbo started the cycle with a simple push of a button, he hopped on the back. The seat was so wide that he felt almost like he was riding a horse. Trumbo eased the cycle forward and slowly turned out of the driveway, then quickly picked up speed until they were flying down the street at close to fifty.

Trumbo slowed to take the corner, then accelerated, then repeated the process until they had circled the block and returned to the driveway. Dale was glad no cops had been around. The speed limit was thirty.

He hopped off and said thanks. Trumbo revved the engine once, then gave Dale an earnest look.

"I don't suppose it'll do any good to ask you to come back to the Kingdom Hall," Trumbo said.

Dale shook his head no.

"You know your soul is at stake."

Dale felt a little sorry for him. Trumbo had to give it one more try, even though he knew Dale would never come back.

"I know."

Trumbo shook his head as if saying to Jehovah that he'd tried and then effortlessly drove his Harley out of the driveway and down the street. Dale meant to watch Trumbo fade into the sunset but June May, driving Jesse's red Cougar, pulled into the driveway.

She got out of the car. She wore a pink uniform. She was working at West Oaks as a carhop for the summer.

"Who was that?" she asked.

Dale guessed she'd seen Trumbo riding away. He shrugged. "Just an old friend."

Their seats weren't very good. From the top section Dale and Sheba saw the small figure of Elvis as he walked out on stage. The audience erupted in delirious screams and cheers and flashbulbs popped from all over the cavernous auditorium. The light flashed like fireworks as the music exploded. Then the familiar voice, amplified to an almost godly volume, swept up to where they sat.

Dale looked at the smiling Sheba. He wasn't sure if she would like going to an Elvis concert. He wasn't sure he wanted to go himself, but Cleoma said the tickets would just go to waste otherwise. She and Blackie couldn't go. Besides, didn't Dale like Elvis?

He liked him fine, except that he thought he was a decade past his prime. He didn't tell Cleoma that, of course. So he took the tickets and thanked her, although he didn't trust her and therefore didn't like accepting favors from her. She also said he could drive her ruby red El Dorado Cadillac convertible to the concert. Dale hadn't wanted to do that either. But she made such a fuss that he gave in and thanked her for that, too. He thought it was strange that he ended up thanking her for things he didn't even want.

Dale gazed down at the stage and now with more light he could see the King himself strolling on stage in his white sequined jumpsuit. The suit wasn't very flattering. It revealed his paunch. This was the Elvis that he didn't like much. He preferred the '50s Elvis with his black leather jacket and sneer.

He watched as dozens of women crowded the front of the stage and tossed their panties and bras at Elvis. Dale imagined if he'd invited Wanda, she'd have been one of the middle-aged floozies tossing her undies. Wanda was crazy for Elvis.

Dale hardly listened to the music. It sort of droned in his ears because they were so far away. The concert, just the same, was interesting because it was such a bizarre spectacle. Thousands of people were jammed into the Myriad, the largest indoor venue in Oklahoma City. Some men came dressed in the different incarnations of Elvis, from his swaggering '50s self to his '60s movie star self to his '70s decadent self. Some women tried to look like his female movie co-stars. Some emulated Ann-Margaret (Dale approved), some imitated Nancy Sinatra (Dale disapproved). It was one weird scene and he wondered if other concerts were as strange and circuslike as this one.

He slipped his hand off the armrest and gently laid it on Sheba's thigh. She wore blue-green dressy shorts and a pink blouse. She noticed his hand and put it back on the armrest. He slowly moved his hand back toward her leg. He wiggled his fingers as if his hand were really an independent creature intent on crawling back to her thigh. Sheba watched his approaching hand out of the corner of her eye. When his hand suddenly leapt on her leg, she squealed just as the audience burst into deafening applause. Dale enjoyed feeling the bare skin of her thigh, marveling at how soft and silky it felt, before she reached down and once again removed the intruder.

The concert was their third date of this summer. He'd called her the day of Jesse's commitment. He'd simply said hi, how'd she like to go to a movie? After the movie, they ate at a Chinese restaurant. His fortune cookie read: *expect big changes in the future.* Her fortune cookie didn't have a fortune in it. Sheba hadn't seemed disappointed. When he took her home, he just kissed her at her door. He wanted to do more, but he sensed that was all she thought proper on their first date of a second summer.

On their second date, Dale took Sheba to a special Bicentennial concert and fireworks display at the new Stars and Stripes Park in the City. Maybe the spectacular pyrotechnics excited Sheba's senses. Whatever the reason, he sensed she would be more receptive to his advances. Afterwards, they made out a little in his car beside her house until her mother came home from work at West Oaks.

Now, after chasing his hand away from her leg for a third time, Sheba allowed Dale to hold her hand for the rest of the concert. Ninety minutes later, the concert came to a close with Elvis performing only two encores. Dale guessed he was tired.

Afterwards, they descended the steep stairs and walked out of the building with three Elvis impersonators: a black leather Elvis, a sequined white uniformed Elvis, and a buckskin cowboy Elvis. None of them looked convincing. Dale and Sheba walked two blocks to the parking lot, found the Cadillac, and drove back to Galilee.

Driving such a big car felt strange to Dale. He liked the warm night air flowing over him, though, and Sheba sat close to him as he drove. He put his hand on her thigh again and this time she didn't remove it.

They stopped off at Braum's for ice cream and sat in the car and ate it while talking. Sheba told him about her junior year in high school and Dale told her about his freshman year in college. He didn't tell her about any of the girls he'd dated. After Carmen, he'd only dated two other girls. The dates hadn't been interesting. He'd taken one girl to the movies twice; the second girl he took to a jazz concert on campus. They were nice-enough girls, he supposed, but he felt no connection to them. For whatever reason, he didn't feel much of a connection to any girl except a Galilee girl.

Dale didn't ask Sheba about the high school boys she dated. He didn't want to know. Instead he asked her if she was thinking about college and she said she was planning on going to Galilee Nazarene. He'd forgotten that her mother's parents were Nazarenes. Sheba said her grandparents had told her if she wanted to go to GNC, they would pay for the tuition.

After the ice cream, Dale drove her home and parked on the side street of her house. He realized that convertibles had one drawback; they didn't provide much cover for making out. He leaned over and put his right arm around Sheba's waist and pulled her to him. They kissed for awhile but when he started caressing her too vigorously, Sheba pulled away.

"That's why I almost didn't go out with you again," she said.

Dale turned his hands up in bewilderment.

"You're a little too aggressive."

Dale leaned back and looked at her. Even in the shadows, he could make out the color of her blue-green eyes.

"Don't you like that?"

Sheba turned her face away. "Yes, in a way," she said quietly. Then she turned back to him. "But we shouldn't let things go too far. Otherwise, I won't go out with you again."

Dale felt himself getting angry. Ever since Sal, he'd felt a little knot of anger inside him. He'd been cross with himself for being seduced by Sal – if that was what happened. He didn't know. He remembered himself as being a pretty eager participant. But he thought they'd done wrong. What confused him, however, was in spite of thinking he'd done wrong, he wanted to continue. In fact, he wanted to practice doing wrong until he got pretty good at it. But he'd been cut off after three tries. He wanted to get Sal out of his mind and he thought the best way was to get intimate with another girl.

Dale stared at Sheba. She looked at him in a nervous way, sensing his ire. He calmed himself and smiled a little.

"Okay," he said. "You're right. We ought to slow things down."

Sheba smiled and leaned closer and Dale put his arm around her.

"I'm glad you're not mad."

"Naw, not me."

They talked for awhile about nothing important, then Sheba said her mother would be home soon. On weeknights, her mother usually got home around eleven.

Dale walked her to her door and kissed her. He held her around her waist, resisting the urge to run his hands farther down than the small of her back. They exchanged good nights. Then he got in the Cadillac and motored all the way back to The French Quarter to drop off Cleoma's Caddy and get his old Chevy. When he got to Cleoma's apartment, he heard loud music and a woman he didn't recognize answered the door.

"Hi, baby," she said. "You wanna come in?"

He guessed she looked around thirty. She had feathered blond hair, a long, curved nose but an attractive, wide mouth and sleepy green eyes. Dale realized the sleepy look was probably a result of drinking too much. She smelled of alcohol and he also smelled on the air the acrid scent of marijuana.

"No, thanks." He handed her the keys to the Caddy. "These are for Cleoma."

The woman took the keys and smiled at him. Dale glanced down at the low-cut blouse that revealed her cleavage.

"Are you sure?" she said, swaying with the door.

Dale wasn't sure but he said nothing and turned and walked away, hearing the woman laugh before she shut the door.

Dale drove west on Highway 66 until he came to the old, abandoned children's hospital that stood in disrepair on the edge of town. A few years ago, he'd read in the *Galilee Gazette* that the town government had been in the process of selling the building and property to some developer from the City, but the deal had collapsed for some reason. So, instead of being razed, the ugly, reddish-brown brick building remained standing. Now, as he turned off the highway and drove on the narrow paved road leading to it, he saw the three-story building looming above the rough, weed-choked grounds like some old, haunted mansion.

He drove until he came to a long, thick chain stretched across the road. Nailed to one post, a sign warned, NOT ACCESSIBLE TO THE PUBLIC. He put the car in park, got out, and looked at the old building. He noticed a few broken windows. He guessed some kids had tossed rocks at the windows. The building, in spite of its size and bulk, looked saggy. Dale imagined if he just blew hard enough in its direction, the whole ugly structure would come tumbling down.

He could hardly believe that Jesse had spent four years in there. Of course, back in the early '40s, the building had been new. Still, Dale guessed it must have been an ordeal for a little girl like Jesse to be stuck in such an awful place with sick and dying kids. He knew that was the reason why his grandparents moved to Galilee: to bring Jesse to this new, children's hospital, supposedly the best in the state. The hospital, along with the orphanage and the Nazarene college, were the primary institutions in the small, fairly new town of Galilee. In the late '60s, the orphanage had been relocated to the City, and the hospital had stopped operating. He'd often glanced at the building while driving west on the highway, but he'd never stopped before to get a closer look. He didn't like looking at the place now. It saddened him to think that his mother had gone through dozens of operations on her leg to save it and her life. He could hardly imagine how horrible it must have been for her. Dale had hated staying just a few days in the Tinker hospital and the one in Corpus Christi. No wonder Jesse went crazy from time to time.

Jesse, who often told Dale and June May stories of her childhood, never talked about her years in the children's hospital. She told stories about everything else: about going to school in Checotah, gathering eggs from the hens, climbing trees, playing kick the can and other simple games, and riding a pony they had for a while until they couldn't afford to keep him anymore.

Dale remembered one strange story Jesse told him, about slaughtering a hog for Christmas. She said after Poppy brained it with a club, slit its throat to drain the blood, scraped off the hide, and then heaved the hog into a boiling cauldron, the stubborn beast revived and bolted from the pot and dashed around the kitchen and squealed for several minutes until Poppy and her older brother Dewey killed it again. Dale, who first heard the story when he was five, had been amazed. Now, he doubted whether the story was completely true. However, since he'd never slaughtered anything, maybe the story was accurate. If so, he reckoned hogs were just as hard to kill as Rasputin.

Looking at the abandoned building depressed him, so he got back in his car and drove back to the highway. But instead of heading into town, he turned west. He thought a drive might lift his spirits. As he drove west toward El Reno, a town that used to be a fort, he glanced south and saw in the distance a hill surrounded by a grove of trees.

Dale had always been interested in that hill. Now, he decided to investigate. When he saw a turnoff, he slowed the car and turned south on a gravel road. As he drove toward the elevation, he guessed the hill really wasn't that high; it just looked tall because the land surrounding it was so flat. But at that moment, the modest hill looked as inviting to him as a real mountain, its verdant hump swelling out of the flat grasslands.

Before he got to the hill, the road curved away, so Dale pulled the car off to the side of the road. He turned off the engine, got out, and walked toward the stand of cottonwoods and the hill that curved above them.

He walked through the trees, smelling the musty, leafy odor, and climbed the incline. Dale was surprised by how steep the angle was. He had to dig his boots into the dry grass to propel himself toward the summit. When he got to the top, he felt a little out of breath and sweaty. He realized he needed to get more exercise. Sometimes he went swimming and played baseball with Rusty, his brothers, and a few friends, but otherwise he hadn't done anything very physical that summer.

At the top, he turned and looked at the spectacular vista before him. Wow, he thought, the hill provided an excellent view of not only the dry, flat land and the vast blue sky, but also the oval-shaped outline of Galilee. To his hometown's east, he saw the hazy, almost mirage-like western edge of Oklahoma City. He could even see the vague outline of the few tall buildings that passed for skyscrapers in the heart of the City.

Dale gazed at the panorama of nature and civilization. He couldn't help but notice that the land and sky overwhelmed the roads and buildings of man. That didn't bother him, though. He'd always felt an affinity with nature. He didn't rhapsodize about it like Wordsworth and some of the other nature poets of the nineteenth century, but he understood their profound appreciation for the beauty of nature. He even shared their idea that God expressed His majesty in the workings of the natural world.

Now, standing on the hill's summit, taking in the magnificence of the rolling flat land and the looming bright blue sky, Dale realized he'd been spending too much time indoors reading depressing books. He'd been reading modernist and existential authors in preparation for another advanced placement exam. Those readings, along with Jesse's illness and his lingering frustration over the Sal "affair," had put him in a prolonged bleak mood.

For the first time in awhile, he thought about God. He'd stopped saying his prayers before going to sleep over a year ago, not long after he saw Amanda on graduation night. He still thought about her from time to time. He tried not to, but he couldn't chase the image of her face completely out of his mind.

Standing on the hill, he didn't pray, but he did engage in a kind of meditation. He tried to open his mind and his soul to the sights and sounds and smells before him. He tried to become One with nature. But he felt that wasn't enough. So he uttered a conventional prayer, too. He asked God to help Jesse get well. He asked God to bless June May, Blackie, his grandparents, his relatives (including Wanda), and his friends, especially those he'd hurt such as Wendy and Carmen. He also asked God to bless Amanda, although Dale thought God had blessed her a lot already.

Then he prayed for forgiveness for his sinful ways, especially for committing adultery, even though at the time he didn't know he was engaging in such a terrible sin. Then, even though he didn't really want to, he asked God to bless Sal and Cleoma. He knew Christians were supposed to love their enemies, which was really a hard thing to do. Dale guessed he was still a Christian. He didn't know what else to be. Besides, there was something inside him that still responded to the best in the Christian message.

When he finished his prayer, he felt tears in his eyes. He felt ashamed of himself for feeling such sappy emotions. He blinked and stared at the hard brown fields spread before him in order to compose himself.

Dale heard someone breathing in a rather labored way from behind him. He turned and saw an old man climbing the hill. He watched as the man, wearing old-fashioned blue jeans and a long-sleeved blue work shirt, even though it was a typically hot day, trudged up the hill. He heard him huffing and puffing and worried that the old guy might not make it. As the elderly man got closer, he noticed his bald head, the short gray hair around his big ears, and the ruddy, wizened face.

For the first time, he realized that he was probably trespassing on somebody's property. He doubted this land belong to the town or county. Judging from the way the old guy was dressed, Dale wondered if he was the caretaker of the land. But he seemed awfully old to be a caretaker.

The old man held up a hand in greeting as he neared the top. Dale lifted a hand, too. The elderly man then paused as he reached the top, breathed in deeply twice, and proceeded toward him.

"Are you all right, mister?" Dale asked.

The old man nodded but he didn't speak right away. Dale suddenly thought he recognized him: his face was as wrinkled as a raisin. He was old man Reinhardt.

"You like my hill?"

Dale said he did. Mr. Reinhardt stood beside him and gazed out over the expanse of earth and sky.

"Yes indeedy," he said. "This is the best view in these parts."

Dale looked at the old man and wondered why such a wealthy man would wear such old beat-up clothes. Dale guessed he liked walking in them. The times he'd seen him at the football games, old man Reinhardt dressed nicely, in slacks and a sweater, usually crimson and cream like the Galilee school colors. Dale knew he wasn't a cheapskate. He'd bought the high school new football and baseball uniforms back when Dale was playing. He'd also spent a lot of money last year buying a new scoreboard for Galilee Stadium. The scoreboard wasn't as fancy as the one at Sundance Prep, but it was plenty nice. Dale had seen it in all its glory last fall when he'd seen the Gophers win their homecoming game against Lyons.

"Yes sir, the view is great," Dale said.

He thought he'd better introduce himself. He gave his full name and held out his hand for Mr. Reinhardt to shake. The old guy had a surprisingly firm and dry handshake.

"I think I remember seeing you," said Mr. Reinhardt. "You were in my granddaughter's class in school."

"Yes sir," Dale said. "I know Gretchen."

The old man nodded and gave him a brief smile. His teeth were a little yellowish, the way Dale's grandpa's was. Dale tried not to stare at his amazingly dried-up face. He wondered how he got so wrinkled and desiccated. He guessed from working in the sun or maybe worrying so much about building his trucking empire. He'd overheard some of his friend's fathers talking about Old Man Reinhardt and how he'd worked long and hard making the trucking company into one of the biggest and best in the southwest. They said Mr. Reinhardt was a tough but fair man. He didn't cheat anyone. He built his business from honest hard work and reliability. The trucking headquarters was on the eastside of Galilee, just off Highway 66, and Dale had visited it once with Rusty. The business covered a huge area. It had its own garage and gas pumps. He'd thought about trying to get a job there at the start of summer, but he was so bad at mechanical things that he didn't try.

"Didn't you play football, young man?"

Dale nodded.

"Yes, I thought so." Mr. Reinhardt fell into a brief reverie. "Too bad last year's team didn't win their playoff game."

Dale had attended the game. The Gophers lost a close contest. Dale imagined Matt Jones and Sam Mears and some of the other seniors had been disappointed. But Galilee still had a pretty good year, going 6-5.

He wondered if he should apologize for invading Mr. Reinhardt's property. But the old guy didn't seem to mind. He hadn't yelled at him, or threatened him, or told him to scram and never come back. In fact, the old guy seemed to be enjoying Dale's company as the two of them surveyed the scene.

"A lot of young folks don't seem to take the time to enjoy nature anymore," Mr. Reinhardt said, still looking at the earth and sky.

Dale said this was the first time he'd been here. He'd seen the hill from the highway and was curious about it. He didn't even think about it being private property.

Mr. Reinhardt smiled his craggy smile again. Dale wondered if it hurt him to stretch his mouth. The old man was even more wrinkled than Dale's grandpa, who'd spent a lot of time in the sun out in the fields. His grandpa's face reminded Dale of a cracked patch of earth with all the fissures and wrinkles except that Grandpa Walsh's skin was fairly pale.

"Well, son," Mr. Reinhardt said, "I know who you are. No use letting a view like this go to waste. You're welcome here anytime."

Dale said thanks. He turned and joined Mr. Reinhardt as they watched the fiery sun slowly move toward the shimmering horizon. He realized it was getting late. Probably past seven. He had to get home and make sure June May didn't burn the house down while making supper.

He said he'd better get going. Mr. Reinhardt nodded. Dale started down the hill, paused, and looked back at the old man. Mr. Reinhardt gave him one short wave. Dale did the same. He trudged down the hill, digging his boot heels into the earth to keep from losing his balance and tumbling down the incline. When he got to the bottom, he looked up and saw that old man Reinhardt had disappeared from view.

He decided he'd call the hill Reinhardt's Summit.

The inside of the building smelled funny. Dale couldn't quite define the odor. A strong antiseptic smell masked fainter, less pleasant smells. The more he smelled the air, the less he liked it. In fact, he felt a little sick, so he stopped breathing through his nose and walked down the hall to the visitors' room where Jesse was supposed to be waiting.

Dale realized he'd taken a wrong turn. After checking in at the front desk and getting a visitor's badge, he'd walked through two white doors into a small lobby that offered a choice of three wings. He'd thought the woman had said to turn left, but as he walked down that hallway it became apparent to him that he was going into the patients' wing.

He turned a corner and saw a middle-aged black man sitting on the floor in his pajamas. Suddenly the man started to bang his completely bald head against the hard plaster wall. Dale debated whether he should stop him or find an attendant. He looked down the hall. He didn't see any hospital staff. The large door at the end of the hall and all the side doors were closed. Dale looked at the man. He stopped banging his head. His dark, uncomprehending eyes stared. The man's head was so large and round and the skin so dark and smooth that it reminded Dale of a bowling ball.

Dale nodded as if to excuse himself and turned around and walked in the other direction. A few seconds later, he heard the echoes of the man again thumping his head against the wall.

He took the right wing this time and proceeded down the hall until he came to the visiting room. He opened the door and tried not to look too closely at the patients or their families. He looked for an open seat and turning to his right saw Grandpa and Grandma and Wanda sitting together.

Dale walked over to them and sat down next to Grandpa. The old man patted him on his shoulder.

"Glad you made it, Son," he said.

Dale looked past Grandpa at Grandma and Wanda. They looked back at him but didn't say anything. They didn't even nod. He sat back in his chair and realized he should have called his grandparents and offered to drive them to Norman. A drive of fifty miles had no doubt tuckered them out.

He looked around the visiting room. It looked clean and well kept. Cushioned wooden chairs lined three of the four bright yellow walls. A large glass window on the east wall allowed in plenty of sunshine. On the long, polished coffee table Dale saw several magazines strewn about: *Field & Stream*, *Good Housekeeping*, *Redbook*, *Time*. He reached over and grabbed the *Time* magazine. It was dated three months ago. He flipped through the magazine and tried to read to pass the time.

A large woman with stringy, Raggedy Ann red hair pattered over to Wanda and asked her if she were her momma. Dale lowered his *Time* magazine and watched, amused by the consternation on Wanda's face.

"I ain't your momma," Wanda said, smiling uneasily and looking around the room, avoiding the red-headed woman's blank, pale eyes.

"You're my momma," the woman said, more insistently.

Dale guessed her age to be around twenty-five or so. Wanda, at least in a chronological sense, could have been her mother.

"No, I *ain't*," Wanda said with exasperation.

She looked over at Dale as if he should do something. He shrugged his shoulders and returned to his magazine.

An attendant, a large man, came over and led the woman back to a woman about the same age but with carefully coifed red tresses. Dale guessed she was the woman's sister.

The door to the other room opened and a black female attendant led Jesse over to Wanda, Dale, and his grandparents. Jesse smiled at them. She wasn't wearing her glasses so she squinted her eyes. She wore light blue pajamas, slippers, and a pink dressing gown. The attendant seated her in a chair across from them. Wanda went over and sat next to Jesse. She asked how she was. Jesse asked who she was.

"You don't know who I am?" Wanda asked.

"Yep, but I wondered if you knew?" Jesse smiled at them as if she'd made an excellent point.

Wanda shook her head, dismayed over such obvious evidence of Jesse's continuing madness. Dale, however, thought his mother had made a valid existential point – not on purpose, of course.

Jesse looked at Dale and smiled her manic smile. She muttered something about her son, her only begotten son. He noticed her shiny eyes. This stage of her madness was definitely better than her depressed, almost catatonic stage. In a strange way, she was sort of funny.

In fact, Dale tried, as he had in the past, to see the humorous absurdity of it all. He glanced around the cheery room, no doubt painted bright colors and designed to let the sunshine stream in not so much for the patients but for the guests. No need to make the guests more uncomfortable than they already were.

In her manic stage, Jesse said funny things and did outlandish deeds in a comical way. If Dale tried to see her madness in an objective light and tried to view all of them – his relatives and the family members of the other lunatics – in an emotionally distant way, he could appreciate, if not the humor, then the absurdity of it all. Didn't the existentialists argue that life itself was absurd? Well, here was evidence that they were right. However, he realized that he really didn't take any comfort in that approach. Although he acknowledged what was happening to Jesse and him and his family was philosophically absurd, there was a big difference between theory and reality. Dale, looking into Jesse's deranged eyes, suddenly realized he didn't like being in a Kafkaesque story. He resented it. Deep inside, he'd always resented Fate for doing this to him. He simply disguised his sense of shame by focusing on the absurdity. But he knew now he wasn't an existentialist or an absurdist. He hated those feelings.

Grandma tried talking to Jesse. She responded with nonsense. Grandma, old and fat and confused, gave up and collapsed in her chair and silently cried.

The visit dragged on. Since Jesse couldn't respond rationally, Wanda started talking about her to Grandma, the same way Dale remembered them doing two Christmases ago. Jesse grew silent and regarded them with large, watchful eyes. Finally, visiting time was over and the attendant came over. Wanda and Grandma hugged Jesse. Dale and Grandpa said good-bye. Jesse looked depressed. She was ready to go back to her room. The attendant led her out the door.

"Well," Wanda said, "that hardly warn't worth the trip."

Dale saw Grandpa glare at Wanda. Then he said something about needing some fresh air and left the room. Wanda asked Grandma what was Poppy's problem, but Grandma just sat in her chair and shook her head.

Dale thought he knew what the problem was. He left the room and walked out the building and found Grandpa strolling across the broad expanse of field across from the parking lot. He went over to him and told him he was sorry he'd forgot to drive them to Norman.

"Ain't mad at you, Dale," Grandpa said. "But I'm sure as tarnation mad at that Wanda. She's s'posed to come by for us but didn't."

Dale walked along with Grandpa for a while. Dale remembered Grandpa always liked to go on walks, especially after having an argument with Grandma. Sometimes he'd stay away for a couple of hours if he was really livid. Dale used to wonder where he walked for all that time. He guessed he went across the street and strolled around the big field that served as little league baseball parks in the summer.

They saw Grandma and Wanda leaving the building and walking to the parking lot. Dale and Grandpa met up with them and they all walked to Grandpa's old Falcon. Dale watched them creakily get inside the car. Grandpa waved. Dale guiltily watched as the little blue car rolled out of the parking lot.

"Grandpa said you forgot to pick them up," Dale said to Wanda.

"Did you offer them a ride, mister?"

"No, I forgot."

"Well, then, you ain't one to talk."

She turned and swished her way to her old, rusty Monte Carlo. Dale watched as she drove away, then he got in his mother's Cougar. It was a sporty kind of car and fun to drive. It had a bigger engine than his Chevy. Just the kind of car a middle-aged woman needed.

As he drove through Norman, he saw from the road the tall lights of the football stadium. He remembered a few years ago when Chris's dad took them to a Sooners' football game. OU had slaughtered Baylor and Dale had enjoyed every minute of it.

The last time he'd been in Norman other than visiting his mother was over a year ago at the state track meet. That had been a strange time. He remembered standing on the impressive college track, admiring how smooth and red it was as he warmed up for his heat of the 100. Then the image of Jesse had popped in his head. Dale realized she was institutionalized just a few miles away. It seemed odd to him that he was running track while his mother might be getting electroshock therapy at that same moment.

Now they were both back in Norman again. Dale hoped it was for the last time.

## Chapter 10: *Catching Chris; seducing Sheba*

Coming out of the Galilee Public Library, Dale heard someone call his name. He turned and looked around. He didn't see anyone calling him in the parking lot. Then out in the road, he heard someone shout, "Audie!" and Dale knew who it was.

He turned toward the voice and saw Chris sitting in an idling Toyota Celica. Chris waved at him and Dale ran over to him in the street.

"What's up?" Chris said.

"Not much. How about you?"

Chris said he was driving home from work. Dale remembered that Chris only lived a few blocks away from the library. Dale asked him how work was going. Chris, who still worked summers in his uncle's lumberyard, said okay. Actually, it was sort of boring. He'd been doing inventory on wood. Chris asked how boring that sounded. Dale said really boring.

"Hey, I heard you might transfer to GNC," Chris said.

"I might. It depends on what kind of financial aid I get." Dale wondered how Chris knew about his possible transfer. He didn't remember telling anyone. "How'd you know?"

"My father works in the admissions office," said Chris. "Remember?"

Dale hadn't remembered. He knew Mr. DeVille worked in some capacity for the GNC administration but he didn't know it was admissions.

Chris reached out the window with his free hand and playfully socked Dale on his arm. He looked pleased that Dale might be joining him at college. "Well, I hope you do transfer. School isn't the same without you and Rusty around."

Dale nodded. He hadn't seen much of Chris since high school. He'd seen him only a couple of times that summer. One time he'd seen him at Roxanne's when she threw Quentin a birthday party. Dale had seen some of the other kids from high school, too. Wendy had been there. They'd talked for a while. Wendy seemed relaxed and friendly, which relieved Dale. Amanda hadn't shown.

"Well, I better go," Chris said. "I'm late for dinner."

Dale said he'd see him around.

"Hey, wait, Audie. We have these college Bible studies on Wednesday nights. Well, it's not much studying. Mostly we play volleyball and have fun then sit down for a brief study. You ought to come. You might like it. You'd get to meet some other GNCers."

GNCers. That's what the kids who went to Galilee Nazarene called themselves. Dale thought it sounded like a corporation or government department or something.

"What time Wednesday?"

"Around seven. Look, I'll come pick you up in my nice, new ride."

Dale said he thought Chris's car was new. It was a big improvement over his old bomb.

"I'll say. Gets a lot better gas mileage."

Dale was amused. Chris had always been practical. He remembered him complaining about his Plymouth's bad gas mileage.

"So, you gonna come?"

Dale thought about the offer. He'd wouldn't mind seeing a few college kids, even if they were GNCers.

"Come on," said Chris. "It'll be fun. Even for an antisocial type like you."

"If you put it that way, okay then."

Chris waved and drove away as Dale walked to the parking lot. He'd liked seeing Chris again. Dale thought he was a good guy. He missed talking "philosophy" to him, even though he suspected that Chris thought Dale a little goofy thinking about all those "big" questions.

Besides, Dale felt like seeing some people. He's spent the summer reading book after book, either at work or at home. It had paid off. He'd received the results of his advanced standing tests. He'd passed four of the five. He passed the objective portion of the contemporary history exam but failed the written part. That irked him. The exam covered material for the class Post-World War II America: Conformity and Conflict. The objective portion had been easy. Dale had always been interested in the '50s and '60s. His favorite music and movies were from the '60s. But the professor apparently hadn't appreciated his interpretation of the communist threat, the "conformity" of the Eisenhower age, or his skepticism in regard to '60s radicalism. Dale thought he'd made a balanced, objective argument about the good and bad aspects of that time. But the professor had scribbled objections all over the essay portion. Dale had a difficult time deciphering his scrawl, but it seemed that the professor thought he hadn't fully appreciated the Red Scare and the revolutionary impulses of sixties radicals.

Dale thought the prof hadn't been fair. But neither had the renowned Alexandra Sweet. She'd given him a B for the creative writing class even though she'd told him she would give him an A. Her mendacity bothered him. She seemed to have a casual attitude about the grade as she had toward the class as a whole. So why lie? Well, the 'B' prevented him from making straight A's in college for the first time. What annoyed him the most was that he'd rather get an A in *Ms.* Sweet's class rather than in astronomy. But he was beginning to understand that certain professors were capricious and not at all impartial judges of scholarship.

Dale thought maybe Galilee Nazarene would be different. He'd heard that the professors there provided students with more personal attention. The profs at CSU didn't seem interested in the students as people at all. The large lecture classes discouraged interaction between professor – or graduate teaching assistant, as the case often was – and student. He felt tired of the impersonal, regimented university life. He'd gone to the small Galilee schools for almost eleven years and he thought he'd like the friendly, traditional atmosphere of Galilee Nazarene. He was certain he'd transfer.

Driving home, Dale thought how his year attending Central State and all the reading he'd done had changed him in ways he didn't fully like. He'd developed his mind, he thought; he'd worked hard and studied diligently. But he often felt uneasy about what he'd read and the implications of the ideas. For example, he'd enjoyed the astronomy class. But when he thought about the vastness of the universe, how long it had existed, and how astronomical time overwhelmed human time, he felt rather diminished. Those ideas, combined with all the depressing post-war literature he'd read, along with reading about one bloody atrocity after another during the twentieth century in his history classes, made him question of meaning of life itself. More than once, he'd dropped a novel, a play, or a history book onto his desk and stared into the space of the empty hallway at work and wondered if human beings deserved to exist.

When he talked to Blackie about some of the ideas he was encountering, Blackie simply confirmed Dale's increasingly bleak view of life. Dale remembered when he told his father how many millions of people had been murdered during the World War II era. Not just killed during the warfare, but murdered. The Russians had decimated millions of their own people. The Nazis slaughtered millions, too, including six or seven million Jews. The Chinese liquidated millions during the "Great Leap Forward." And more recently, perhaps a million Cambodians had been annihilated in the "killing fields" under Pol Pot.

Dale remembered Blackie not reacting with the horror he'd felt when he'd read that bloody history and actually thought about it. Dale had tried to go beyond just the mind-numbing numbers and think of each of those poor persons murdered for arbitrary reasons: because he was a Jew or a Jehovah's Witness or a non-Communist or a school teacher. Blackie, who'd started smoking again after his divorce, simply exhaled a plume of smoke. He told Dale that the allies had killed lots of people, too, and not just soldiers. The allies had killed civilians. Dale said it wasn't the same thing as murdering people in concentration camps. Blackie agreed. But Dale shouldn't be fooled. The world was a hellhole. The good were just a step away from being as evil as the bad. It was a miracle that human civilization survived at all. Dale asked, "miracle?" Blackie said that was a poor choice of words. Dale wasn't sure. Maybe the only reason people didn't destroy themselves was because of some higher power. Blackie scoffed at that. It was just a historical accident. Pretty soon humankind would destroy itself.

Dale had wondered why he even talked to Blackie about such things. He always ended up feeling despondent. He remembered when he was ten and Blackie came home on leave and had told him about "friendly fire." He did so while they were watching a World War II movie, *The Longest Day*, on television. Blackie said a lot of soldiers had been killed by their own side. Americans shot Americans by mistake. War was confusing and hectic. People made mistakes. Sometimes bombs were dropped on the wrong guys. Dale remembered feeling shocked. How could the good guys make mistakes like that? Kill their own guys? He didn't want to believe it then. He preferred the simple orderliness of war movies. But somewhere in his developing mind, he realized that Blackie spoke the truth. After all, his dad had been in two wars, although just on warships.

Reflecting on the disorder and carnage of war depressed Dale. He thought it depressed Blackie, too. After their latest conversation, his dad had gone over to Cleoma's to get drunk and who knows what else.

What made the summer even lousier for Dale, of course, was his mother getting sick again. The last time he'd visited her, she seemed to be getting better. She wasn't manic anymore. She didn't prophesize or make paranoid accusations. Instead, she sat in her chair a rather forlorn figure and smoked. The doctors had let her smoke again. That meant that in a few more weeks she might be getting out of the asylum.

As Dale turned into his driveway, he summed up his thoughts about all the things he'd read and learned and how those ideas didn't illuminate life's mysteries, such as his mother's condition. He'd read all those books during the summer, studied history and philosophy and literature, and had even tried to read some medical stuff on schizophrenia. None of those books had provided the answers he'd been seeking. Dale began to think that maybe people didn't know as much as they thought they did.

The air still felt hot as evening fell. It blew in the window from outside as the Cougar sped down the road. Dale could have rolled up the windows and turned on the air conditioner but he liked how the air felt on his face and skin after a swim. He turned and looked at Sheba. She smiled as the wind ruffled her snowy tresses. She hadn't cut her hair since last summer and now it hung to her shoulders. He liked it better long.

"Like something to drink?" he asked.

Sheba nodded. Dale slowed down and turned on the road leading to Sooner Shack. He didn't want to take her to West Oaks where her mom worked, even though Mrs. Smith worked inside at the restaurant.

Dale pulled into the Sooner Shack parking lot. He asked Sheba if she wanted anything to eat. She thought about it. "Hmmm, just some fries."

Dale got out and ordered a chocolate shake, two orders of fries, and a Diet Coke. While waiting for the food, he turned and looked at Sheba sitting in the car. She had her eyes closed and leaned back against the bucket seat. That was the problem with driving the Cougar instead of the Chevy. She couldn't sit close to him.

They'd dated steady through the summer. Dale had been true to his word about taking things more slowly for several dates. But as summer wore on, he began growing more adventurous. He couldn't help it. He loved the way she felt.

He'd taken her to movies and out to eat. They'd seen *Silent Movie*, the reissue of *Jaws*, and *The Outlaw Josie Wales*. After seeing *Jaws* again, he'd reminded her that he'd seen her sitting in front of him the first time they'd seen it. She remembered and thought it was "cute" that he remembered too. That night, after the movie, had been the first time since her warning that she'd been more receptive to his advances. The next week, while watching *The Outlaw Josie Wales*, Dale wondered if Sheba was allowed to see R-rated movies. She didn't complain after the movie even though it was pretty violent and there had been an attempted rape scene. The actress had her britches pulled off and her bottom briefly exposed before Clint Eastwood stopped the assault.

That night, two weeks ago, when he brought her home after the movie, he parked in the secluded spot on the side road next to her house and they made out. He didn't do more than kiss and fondle her. Dale wanted to go further but he knew it was too soon. Then, last week, he'd taken her to his house and they'd made out on the couch. Things had progressed more than what Sheba thought proper and she'd called the next day to apologize. Dale had apologized too, which was what the call was really about.

Tonight, however, he thought she might be receptive again. When he first picked her up, Sheba seemed a little down. He'd asked her what was wrong. She said she'd spoken to her dad on the phone an hour ago and she always felt a little sad after talking to him. He'd remarried a few years ago to a woman who had two children from a previous marriage and she had heard the kids in the background while talking to her father.

Dale had tried to cheer her up. Since the day had been so hot, over one hundred, he suggested an early evening swim. He'd never been swimming with her, but he still remembered seeing her sunbathing with June May last summer. She said okay and went inside to get her bathing suit. At the pool, he waited for her to come out of the changing room. He hoped she would wear the two-piece suit he'd seen her wearing that time in his backyard. He wasn't disappointed. She came out in that suit and Dale tried not to stare. It wasn't a skimpy bikini but it was fairly revealing. He especially liked looking at her bottom as she walked so he slowed to get behind her. When she noticed he wasn't beside her, she'd stop and stare at him. Dale would pick up the pace, then slow it down again. The suit fetchingly hugged her rear end and the dimples above her buttocks reminded him of accent marks pointing to her best feature.

They swam around but mostly Dale teased her by dunking her and lifting her out of the water by her waist then dropping her back in. She laughed and seemed impressed that he was strong enough to easily pick her up. After his climb on Reinhardt's summit, Dale decided to get in better shape. He started exercising. He could still easily do fifty push-ups. He used to do 100 in gym class in high school when he, Rusty, and Matt Jones won the Presidential Fitness Award. But now he thought fifty was enough to keep his arms and shoulders in shape. Sometimes he ran – not jogged – at night. Thrice a week, he'd walk to the track field, not far from Sheba's house, and run a couple of quarters just to see how it felt. He didn't sprint them flat out but he ran at a good clip. Since the only athletic things he'd done since high school were to play intramural football and softball at CSU, he was surprised how easily he got back into good shape.

Whenever Sheba got out of the pool, Dale would watch her walk. When they were sitting on the beach towel for a break, she asked him why he kept looking at her walk. He grinned and said she had "callipygians." She asked what that meant and he said he'd explain it to her soon.

Now, Dale took the order back to the car and they ate the fries and she drank her Diet Coke. He offered her some of his shake. She refused at first. He knew she was like most girls, worried about her weight. She would only get one dip of ice cream at Braum's while he got three. He offered her the shake again, telling her Sooner Shack made good shakes with real ice cream. She smiled like she was doing something naughty and put the straw in her mouth and sucked some in. Then she used the spoon to scoop up some of the ice cream and ate that. She said it really was good.

They didn't talk much while eating. They never talked much about the past or the future. Sheba wasn't very talkative. Dale didn't think she was dumb. He thought she was smarter than Sadie. But she didn't seem to have a reflective mind. If he told her about some of the books he'd read or introduced some of the ideas he'd been pondering, she would listen but without enthusiasm. She didn't even like critiquing movies or music much.

After they finished eating, Dale drove her back to her house and parked in the familiar spot. He told her about the first time he saw her in her bathing suit. He didn't tell her how he'd almost lost his breath when she got down on all fours but he did tell her how pretty she looked that day.

Sheba seemed flattered and Dale put his arm around her. Sitting in the car in the warm night, he felt better than he had in months. He felt full of energy, full of life. He'd liked driving fast on the way back to town. He'd wanted to push the Cougar to seventy or eighty or even a hundred. Even now, he felt restless and calm at the same time.

Sheba asked if he'd like to come in. Dale hid his surprise and said okay and they went inside. The house was small and reminded him of a cheap motel, the kind the high school track team would stay in during their overnight trips. The furniture looked a little shabby and the tile floor just had a couple of thin rugs covering it. The house smelled clean, though; in fact, a little too clean, in the way hotel rooms smelled.

Dale sat on the couch and Sheba turned on the TV but kept the volume on low. *Dr. Zhivago* was on, a movie that he'd seen at the drive-in. He told her it was pretty good. She came over and sat on the couch and he put his arm around her and they watched some of it. They watched the part where Julie Christie's mother tries to poison herself and Dr. Zhivago helps the older doctor pump her stomach. After pumping her out, the doctor wipes the sweat off her naked back. Dale was surprised they'd show that scene on television.

Sheba said Julie Christie was really pretty. Dale didn't agree too enthusiastically. He said yeah she was, but so was Sheba. He told her he first thought so at the Wheaton track meet his senior year. Sheba said she remembered him looking at her, but she thought he was annoyed with her. He said he was just pretending so she wouldn't know how pretty he really thought she was.

They started kissing and forgot about *Dr. Zhivago*. Dale lowered her on the couch and caressed her as they kissed. Sheba seemed unusually receptive. In the back of his mind, he knew why. She'd felt sad before their date and he'd been nice to her. He'd dunked and tossed her in the water at the pool. He'd told her how pretty she was and how he'd noticed her several times before. Dale meant what he'd said. But he also knew he had an ulterior motive. He'd sensed tonight was the night he could seduce Sheba if he could get her in the right mood.

He liked the way she yielded to him. She opened her mouth and let him kiss her deeply. Dale moved down and nuzzled her neck. He smelled the chlorine still on her skin. He tasted the salt where little drops of sweat had dried. His hands felt how small her waist was, then moved down to the amazing curve of her hips. He kissed the top of her chest. With his free hand, he pulled her blouse up and saw the small, white bra. He kissed her again on her mouth, sucking on her lower lip, then moved back down to her neck and chest. He carefully pushed her bra up. He stared at her small breasts. They were like little molehills but pale and smooth.

"I'm sort of flat-chested," she said apologetically.

He'd felt her breasts a week ago at his house but he hadn't seen them. He gazed at them now. They *were* small. The nipples were small, too; pink and not well defined. Almost like a little girl's.

"They're nice just the same," Dale said. He kissed first one breast, then the other.

"But they're so small."

Dale moved his face close to hers. "You shouldn't worry. You have callipygians."

"What are callipygians?"

"Well, it's a Greek word. It means shapely buttocks."

"What?" Sheba's blue-green eyes grew wide.

"That's right. Calli means shapely or beautiful in Greek. Pyge refers to buttocks. So, callipygians means shapely buttocks."

Sheba opened her mouth in astonishment. The flushing of her skin started in her cheeks, then spread to the rest of her face.

"Was that why you kept looking at my … rear?"

"It's hard to resist."

"Dale, you are bad."

He told her how he came across the word. He actually came across it by accident. He'd been reading about Greek art and myth and he learned there was a famous nude statue called Venus Kallipygos. The statue depicts a woman with beautiful buttocks. There was also a story about two Syracuse girls, poor but shapely, who attracted the attentions of two wealthy suitors because they had such ravishing rears. After they married the rich men, they dedicated a temple to Aphrodite and called the goddess the fair-buttocked.

"You're making that up," Sheba said.

"No, it's true. Not only is there a statue but there's that story. Well, it's more like a poem. And there was a religious cult dedicated to Aphrodite's callipygians."

Sheba considered the historical record. "Hmm," she said. "And you think I have callipygians?"

"Definitely."

"I've always thought I was a little fat back there."

"Not at all. That would be steatopygia. You don't have that."

"Oh."

She closed her eyes as he continued to caress her. He kissed her breasts once more then gently turned her over.

"What are you doing?" she asked, but allowing herself to be turned.

"Just a little back rub."

He rubbed the middle of her back below her blouse. He heard her sigh. He rubbed a little farther down. He gazed at her bottom, clad in turquoise dress shorts. He gently stroked her, slowly moving his hands to the small of her back. Then he tugged on the elastic waist of her shorts and pulled them down enough to see the tip of her cleft.

She murmured something but didn't stop him as he tugged her shorts down farther until they got hung on the fullest part of her callipygians. He gently stroked the small of her back and glided his hands down to the swell of her bottom. He pressed his fingers into the soft flesh and marveled how this part of her was even softer and silkier than her thighs.

He wanted to see all of her bottom, especially the lower curve that hung above the thigh. He pulled harder but the shorts wouldn't come down unless unzipped. Seeing her flesh shake aroused him greatly and he reached around to the side of her shorts to unbutton them and unzip the zipper. Sheba turned her head and tensed her body.

"They're down far enough," she said.

Dale didn't think so. He unbuttoned the button.

"Dale, don't."

He held the zipper between his thumb and first finger. Sheba threw a hand back and tried to stop him.

"Please, don't."

Dale pulled the zipper down and was about to pull the shorts off her when Sheba squirmed so hard that she shoved him off the couch. He grabbed her by her hips. Still face down, she awkwardly struggled with him and cried for him to stop. She turned over and he saw tears in her eyes.

"Please, don't! I'm not like my sister."

Her words and tears stunned Dale. He let go of her. He saw the fear in her eyes. He'd never seen that expression in the eyes of any of the other girls he'd been with. He felt ashamed of himself.

"I'm sorry, Sheba," he said.

He sat down on the thin carpet with his back to the couch so she could adjust her clothes without him looking. He sensed her tugging up her shorts before she sat upright. He waited for a few seconds before he glanced at her. She didn't look at him. She hung her head, her white hair dangling enough in front of her face that he couldn't see her eyes.

"I lost my head. I don't know what's wrong with me lately."

He did know. Ever since he'd had his adulterous "affair" with Sal, he'd felt a knot of anger and frustration in him. It wasn't so much that Sal had deceived him or that she obviously didn't care about him in any meaningful way. It was more that he'd gotten a taste of something that excited him even as he knew it was wrong. He wanted to experience more of that sensation but Sal was gone. He thought he could experience it with Sheba. He liked her better than Sal, which was part of the problem. Since he liked her he didn't want to hurt her. And yet he wanted to have her.

Dale also suspected that if Sadie had been seduced, then maybe Sheba could be seduced. Dale realized how wrong he'd been. He didn't want to be like the guy who'd gotten Sadie in trouble. Even though he had no intention of getting Sheba in trouble, he did want to go as far as he could without going that far. He knew he'd been wrong to think of Sheba in that way; he'd also indirectly been callous to Sadie by thinking of her and her sister as easy prey. Dale shook his head and despised himself. He didn't want to turn into a Bigelow or a Dean Hogue.

Dale got up and sat down on the couch next to her. She still wouldn't look at him.

"I'm really sorry, Sheba," he contritely.

"You must think I'm a prude," she said, giving him a shy glance.

"No, I don't. I think you're a nice girl. A wonderful girl. All of this is my fault. I shouldn't have pushed you too far."

"No, you shouldn't," she said, now giving him an admonishing look.

Dale thought her voice sounded almost childlike as it scolded him. It amused him and he tried not to smile. Sheba seemed offended at first, then seeing his amusement was good natured, she smiled too.

"Boy, I don't know," said Dale. "A lot of stuff has happened this summer. This year. I think it's confused me. But I didn't mean to hurt you."

Sheba nodded. "I know. I feel confused a lot, too."

He pointed at the television set. The Tonight Show was on. "We missed the end of the movie."

Sheba smiled a little. She leaned back against the sofa and Dale put his arm around her. He asked about Sadie. He said he always liked her. He didn't say that he had always felt a little sorry for her even before she got into trouble.

Sheba said Sadie seemed happy living in Fort Worth. She had her baby. She wasn't seeing Dean anymore.

Dale remembered he'd seen Hogue and Sadie together that time outside the gym. So, Dean was the guy after all. Not Rusty or Bigelow. Not that Dale seriously thought either of them was the father.

"Sadie liked you. She said you were nice to her."

"Really?" He thought he could have been a lot nicer to her.

"She said you had a bad temper, though."

"Why did she say that?" Dale tried to remember being angry around Sadie. He couldn't think of one incident.

"She said you started a fight in some class she was in."

"Hey, I didn't start the fight. I –" Dale stopped short. It didn't matter.

They talked a little more about the upcoming school year. They had made a tacit agreement earlier that when school started they'd return to their separate worlds just like they did last year. Sheba reminded Dale that she would be staying at her dad's for a couple of weeks. This was probably the last time they'd see each other this summer. He'd forgotten about that. Then he told her she had been the best thing in his life this summer. Sheba smiled and said she'd had fun, too.

It was almost midnight and Sheba's mother would be home soon. Dale said he would wait outside in his car until her mother got home if Sheba wanted to go to bed. She said that would be nice.

He walked to her front door and kissed her good night. He said he'd see her around. Sheba said good-bye.

As Dale walked away, he heard her shut the door to her house. He got in the Cougar and stared out the window at the dark, moonless night. He didn't feel frustrated anymore. He hadn't gotten what he wanted, really. But he'd learned something. He should care about the whole person, the whole girl, just not the parts, even if those parts were awfully nice.

He liked Sheba. He didn't love her though. It was wrong to try and seduce her. She was only seventeen. Dale wondered why he had these powerful feelings if they couldn't be satisfied. He didn't know why life had to be so complicated.

While puzzling over these questions, he saw Sheba's mother's old Ford pull in the gravel driveway. He ducked a little so she wouldn't notice him sitting there. She didn't look in his direction anyway. She looked tired. After she went in, he started the car and drove slowly away.

## Chapter 11: *Blackie and the ladies; Dale accused of malfeasance*

Dale watched Blackie clean the pool. He used a long-handled net and scooped bits of debris out of the placid blue water. He scooped up dead insects, a few soggy cigarette butts, soaked bits of paper, and a couple of small objects Dale couldn't identify.

"Why are you cleaning the pool?" he asked.

"Just helping out Cleoma," Blackie said. "I get cheaper rent."

Dale wondered why that was a concern to Blackie. Even though he never talked about his finances, Dale imagined he made a good salary as the rangers' second in command. Plus, he got his pension from the navy. Dale knew a chunk of Blackie's income went to Jesse but he knew it wasn't so much that he had to be worried about rent.

"How's your mother doing?" Blackie asked.

Dale said she was doing better. She should be coming home sometime soon.

"That's good."

Blackie wore Bermuda shorts, a colorful Hawaiian style shirt, and tennis shoes with dark socks. Dale wasn't sure he'd seen his father wearing shorts of any kind except for his skivvies. He thought Blackie looked rather ridiculous, although his legs weren't skinny and pale like some older men.

"Ready for school?"

"Yeah," Dale said.

"When do you need the check?"

"I don't."

Blackie paused with his chore and looked severely at Dale. "You're not dropping out, are you?"

"Of course not. I just don't need money for tuition."

"And why is that?"

Dale told him about the state and federal grants he'd received. He'd gotten the letter a couple of days ago. He also got a letter from the GNC financial aid office showing that the grants would pay for his tuition with a little left over for books and expenses.

"That's a helluva deal," said Blackie. "I guess you're glad your mother divorced me after all."

Dale wasn't glad about the divorce. It embarrassed him. It made him feel even more strongly that he really didn't have a family – or at least a good one. But he did appreciate the irony of his parents' divorce providing him with some independence. Now, he didn't have to depend on his father or mother; well, except for a place to stay.

Blackie, finished with the cleaning, emptied the net into a green plastic trash can.

"Your financial aid as good as my GI bill. And you didn't have to give up twenty years of your life."

Dale didn't know how to respond. It was like his dad to compare his hard life to Dale's easy one. Well, Blackie was right. But should he feel guilty about it? He rather resented being reminded all the time how Blackie had it so tough. Wasn't a lot of life just timing or circumstances or chance? At least, that's what Blackie often claimed. Dale had doubts about the primacy of luck or chance in life, but if his father was right then why did he seem to blame him? He'd had nothing to do with Blackie's bad luck to be born in depression-era Alabama.

"I'm thinking about going to GNC," Dale said.

"GNC? What the hell is GNC?"

"Galilee Nazarene College."

"You're going to that religious college?"

Blackie walked over and hung up the scooping device, all the while scowling at Dale.

"I think so."

"Why in the hell do you want to do that?"

"I think I might like it better than Central State."

"Then why don't you go to OU or OSU?"

"They're too big. Both have 20,000 students."

"You need to get used to not being the big fish in the small pond," said Blackie.

"As opposed to being the small fish in the big pond?"

Blackie didn't have a ready answer to that point. He walked over to where Dale stood.

"Well, it's your life. You can damn well do what you want."

"Thanks, but I already know that."

"You better watch your mouth, boy."

Dale threw up his hands. "You're the one arguing. I just told you I didn't need any money for tuition. That should make you happy."

Blackie moved closer and pointed his finger in Dale's face. "Just remember I paid your tuition for a year. So don't get smart with me."

"I know you did and I said thanks." Dale saw that his father was still angry. His face grew darker when riled. "Really," Dale added, "thanks. I know you didn't have to pay my tuition. I do appreciate it."

Blackie's face relaxed a little. He leaned back and looked at Dale with something like paternal concern.

"You worry me, Son. You're nineteen and you don't seem to have any fun."

"I'm having fun."

"Reading all the time. Taking tests. You don't drink or smoke or chase women. You're not living life to the fullest. Let me tell you that you don't stay young forever. Make the best of the time you have. It passes very quickly."

"Carpe diem," said Dale.

"What?"

"The philosophy you're espousing. Seize the day."

Blackie shook his head. "See what I mean."

Dale threw up his hands again. "I like reading. I like thinking. And I like a lot of other things, like sports and having fun and chasing women."

"Chasing women?"

Dale didn't know if he chased exactly. He still felt guilty about his last date with Sheba. Was that chasing? What if the woman didn't want to get caught? Then what should he do? Force her? He doubted Blackie would have acted ruthlessly in a similar situation. Instead, the trick was finding a compliant woman. He knew there were women who were more accommodating, he just didn't like them.

Before Dale could explain this to Blackie he saw Cleoma and that other woman walking toward them. Both of them wore small bikinis and carried beach towels. Sunglasses shielded their eyes from the brilliant sunlight.

"Hi, baby doll," Cleoma called to Blackie. The two women walked through the gate and stood before them. "Y'all having a father and son?"

Dale glanced at Blackie, who crossed his chest with his arms and asked how the ladies were doing this morning.

"Us? Ladies? Get him," laughed Cleoma.

Dale tried not to look at Cleoma spilling all out of her suit. The small pieces of cloth choked her ample dimensions and made her overripe flesh swell like a squeezed balloon.

"Oh, sugah," Cleoma said to Dale, "you remember Ceecee?"

Dale studied the other woman, who looked much better in her bikini. He remembered her. She was the woman he'd given the Cadillac keys to. Ceecee smiled and Dale nodded. She wasn't bad looking. She had impressive breasts. But he didn't like her deep tan. With her ash blond hair and green eyes, it just didn't look natural.

"So, sweetie, is the pool cleared of bugs and all that icky stuff so we can go dog-paddlin'?" Blackie said it was.

"Say, Dale honey, you gonna stay for the day? We're gonna have a real shindig tonight."

Dale wished she'd said "fete" again. He knew how to pronounce the word now and he could have corrected her. He said he had to get back home.

"Oh, that's a cryin' shame," said Cleoma.

Dale shrugged. All three of them looked at him, and he tried not to notice the sly look on Ceecee's face. He couldn't figure her out. He couldn't decide whether she was flirting or mocking him. Probably a little of both.

"Well, I got to go," said Dale.

He told Blackie he'd see him later and said good-bye to Cleoma and Ceecee. He walked out of the pool area still listening to Cleoma's voice floating in the air. She said she hoped one Smith man was ready for some fun. Dale walked faster and realized that Blackie's way of having fun was not his. His way of thinking wasn't either. Dale was going find his own way.


When Dale got home from work Saturday, he spotted Wanda's rusty Monte Carlo parked in the driveway. He parked his Chevy on the curb and walked inside. He found his grandparents, Wanda, June May, and Jesse in the living room. They all looked uneasily at him.

"Surprised?" Wanda said.

"Yeah," Dale said. "When I called last week, the doctor said Mom was making progress but wouldn't be getting out for another week."

He looked at Jesse. She sat on the couch dressed in her regular clothes, black pedal pushers, a red blouse, and girls-sized-sneakers. Her eyes looked normal but tired. She looked older, too. It was almost as if she'd been whisked away from her seat on the couch for three months, then returned to the same spot but looking three *years* older.

"We called the doctor yesterday and told him we wanted Jesse released," said Wanda.

"Yes'm," said Grandma, "she'd been in that place too long anyhows."

"Good. I'm glad Mom's back."

"Are you?" Wanda said.

Dale looked at her. She had an accusatory look on her face with her pursed lips and squinting eyes.

"Of course, I am. As long as Mom is well."

The five of them remained silent. Grandma, Wanda, and Jesse sat on the couch with only Wanda staring at him. June May stood over by the patio glass door and didn't look at him. Grandpa sat in Blackie's E-Z Boy chair and looked like he was fed up with the whole thing.

"So, you all drove out to Norman and brought Mom back?" None of them said anything. "Why didn't you tell me?"

"You were working," said June May.

"I mean why didn't you *tell* me?"

Grandpa stood up with some effort. He looked tired even though Dale guessed Wanda had done all the driving on this trip.

"Son, Wanda thinks you had your mama put away so'n you could take her money. Ah don't believe a word of it, but thar it is."

Dale glared at Wanda. "You don't know what you're talking about."

"Is that so? Well, mister Dale, you shore didn't seem to care how long she stayed in that place."

"It's a dread awful place," said Grandma.

"I talked to the doctor. I trusted his judgment. There's no reason to bring her home if she isn't well."

Dale started to say they would have to take her back if she wasn't well, but he didn't want to scare Jesse. He also didn't like talking about her as if she wasn't there.

"Is that so?" mocked Wanda.

"Yeah, that's so. And as for Mom's money, I spent it on stuff like the mortgage and bills."

"And food," June May piped in.

"Yeah, and food."

"And that's all? You weren't gallivantin' around in her car? You weren't runnin' around spending all her money?"

Dale looked at them in exasperation. Why were his grandparents listening to foolish Wanda? "Yeah, I drove her car some. So did June May. What's the point of having it sitting idle in the driveway?"

"That's what I thought," said Wanda. "And you spent all her money, too."

"No, I didn't."

He looked at his mother. She didn't seem to have much interest in this debate. Dale knew it was just Wanda's meddling.

"Okay, I'll show you."

Dale went into the kitchen and opened the drawer by the light switch and grabbed Jesse's checkbook. He returned to the living room and first showed Grandpa. He pointed to the accounts page. It showed that over the past three months Dale had deposited three checks totaling $1800 and had spent a little over $1300. He flipped a page back to April that showed that Jesse only had a $124 balance before that. He went around to each of them and pointed these figures out. He even showed June May, who looked at him apologetically as if it were none of her doing.

"That means nothing," Wanda said. "It's only writin'. You coulda writ anythang down."

"But I didn't," Dale said. "Those are accurate figures. And if you don't believe me, then let's go to the bank and I'll prove it. I'll show you Jesse has five hundred more dollars in her account than she did when she went into the hospital."

"I don't believe it," said Wanda.

"Let's go and I'll prove it. And let's make a bet to boot. I bet you a hundred bucks that these numbers are right."

"Pshaw," said Wanda.

"If you're so all-fired certain, then why don't you make that bet? Okay, I'll bet you just ten bucks. How about that?"

"I'm not bettin'."

"You're not betting because you know you're wrong. You've been making baseless accusations. You're just a foolish old woman."

"I'm not old and I'm not –"

"Get out of here," Dale said. He moved toward her. "Get out before I throw you out."

"Listen, mister, this ain't your house and you can't order me around like –"

"I said get out of here." He stood over her and stared.

"Well, I never," huffed Wanda.

She got up and Dale took a step back to let her by. His anger quickly dissipated now he saw how small and defenseless she was.

Wanda bustled out of the living room saying, "Well, I never been treated so poorly in all my life," and "this is the thanks I get for carin' about my lil' sister." Dale still heard her muttering resentfully as she closed the door behind her.

"You want us out, too, Dale?" asked Grandpa.

"Of course not. You're welcome to stay as long as you want."

"Ah never believed Wanda," Grandpa said. "Ah knows she's a foolish woman."

Dale looked at Grandma. She sat next to Jesse and didn't say anything. He wasn't sure if she believed him. It didn't matter. Jesse looked as indifferent as ever. She picked up a pack of cigarettes and took out one and lit it. She sucked in the smoke and he thought she seemed to age another month in that act alone.

Dale told his grandparents that he would drive them home whenever they wanted. He was going to go change out of his uniform.

After changing into jeans and a T-shirt, he heard a knock on his door. He opened it and June May stood there. She had an unusually thoughtful expression on her face. Dale asked her what she wanted.

"How did you save all that money in three months when Mom hadn't saved hardly any?"

"Why do you think? Because she spends most of it."

"On what?"

Dale almost said "partly on you" because he knew June May inveigled money out of Jesse every month. He doubted it came to much, but then again June May seemed to have a lot of clothes, cosmetics, records, and other stuff.

"I don't know," he said. "Cigarettes?"


**Chapter 12: *Dale comes to the rescue at Wednesday Night Bible study***

Chris honked the horn of his Celica and Dale jogged out of his house and got in. Chris said hey, so did Dale. Chris put the little car in gear and it rolled down the street. Dale remembered all the rides home he'd given Chris in high school. It seemed a little funny for Chris to be giving him a lift.

"So, you actually transferred to GNC?" asked Chris.

"Yeah, I did."

"Great. You'll like going to GNC. The people there are friendly and the professors give you plenty of personal attention if you need it." Chris turned and grinned at Dale. "And I need it."

They drove to the First Church recreation center and baseball field where the Wednesday night Bible study took place. Dale remembered playing little league at the baseball field. He and Rusty sometimes played their pickup baseball games there when the field was free. It was a nice field. They kept the grass watered and green and the infield groomed. Dale saw a group of men playing softball on the field. Another group consisting of young men and women were gathered around a volleyball net in left field.

"Looks like the men's team is still practicing softball," said Chris. "It's for guys out of college. They'll be finished soon."

Chris parked his car in the parking space at the end. He and Dale got out and walked through the gate of the chain-linked fence toward the throng of young people. Dale immediately identified K. C., Butch Bigelow, Bobby Henshaw, Eugene Greene, Kevin Stephenson, Amy Mears, Valerie Long, Mary Jane, Gretchen, and Amanda. As soon as Dale saw Amanda, he felt his heart leap in his chest. Even after a year, he felt a thrill seeing her.

They joined the group and several people said hello to Dale. Henshaw, K. C. and Eugene even shook his hand. When Dale looked over at the girls standing in their own slightly separate group, Mary Jane, Gretchen and Amanda waved and smiled. He nodded at them, and tried not to look too long at Amanda. He noticed she was dressed like most of the girls that summer: rather modest cream-colored shorts that came to mid-thigh and a blue blouse with a couple of buttons unbuttoned so it showed her throat and the top of her chest. Her hair looked a shade lighter than he remembered it. It was still light brown in color but with some blond strands. Her hair still looked thick and straight but shorter. It hung to her shoulders rather than several inches beyond like he remembered. He supposed she'd gotten it cut for the summer.

Henshaw grabbed a volleyball and called them over to start play. Dale wished they'd thought of another game to play. He didn't like volleyball much. It was another game where height was a definite advantage. Of course, the group of college students wasn't playing competitively; they were just playing for recreation. After all, the girls were playing, too.

Dale counted nineteen of them, including himself. Ten girls and nine boys. Dale didn't recognize three of the boys and five of the girls. He guessed they were GNCers from the City.

Stephenson and Henshaw divided the kids into two teams. Dale joined Chris and they walked over to the north side of the net and stood in the back, not too far away from Amanda and Mary Jane.

Dale glanced back at the infield area of the park. The men's softball team was still playing. He heard a tall man yell there was just one more batter. Dale watched as the batter popped up the first pitch. Then he turned his attention back to his group. He watched Amanda and Mary Jane conversing. He couldn't hear anything; they both smiled and seemed to be just making chitchat.

Then Dale heard the thwacking sound of a bat making good contact with a ball and then he heard shouting. He turned and saw a softball flying toward them. The ball spun high in the deepening blue sky and for a moment he thought how perfect it all looked: the white sphere, the blue sky, the green field. Then he realized the ball was headed right at the girls. He dashed over and reached his hands out and caught the ball in front of Amanda and Mary Jane. He felt the ball sting his bare hands and heard an audible plop! He glanced at Amanda and Mary Jane. They were huddled together in an effort to evade the descending ball. When they saw he'd made the catch, they both smiled at him.

"Nice snag," Chris said.

Dale took a step forward and threw the ball back to the infield. He watched with satisfaction as the ball arced through the sky and sailed into the mitt of the catcher. He still had a pretty good arm.

Dale turned and saw Amanda smiling at him.

"Thanks for making the catch," she said. "I guess we were in the way."

Dale felt so embarrassed by the compliment that all he could do was shrug. He watched as Amanda turned to Mary Jane and said something to her that made her smile and glance in his direction. He felt himself glowing inside. That was the first time since graduation that he'd heard Amanda's voice. He played the dulcet sound again in his mind, especially the way she said, "thanks."

Henshaw yelled at the softball team that it was time to quit practice. The ball had almost hit some of them. The tall guy waved and told his guys practice was over. As the softball team trotted off the field, the college kids took their spots for a game of volleyball.

Dale stood in the back line. Mary Jane and Amanda were in the front line. He looked at Amanda's legs and thought they looked quite attractive. They weren't overly tan like Mary Jane's. They weren't skinny or fat, just sleek and softly firm. He looked at Amanda's rear clad in the dressy kind of shorts that all the girls seemed to be wearing that summer. Her bottom wasn't as callipygous as Sheba's, but it was curvaceous.

The volleyball whizzed by Dale's head. He'd been admiring Amanda so intently that he'd forgotten to follow the action. He heard Bigelow say, "where's your head, Smith?" which he thought was typically obtuse because Bigelow was on the other team and should welcome an opponent's inattention. Dale chased the volleyball down and heaved it back to Stephenson. Play resumed and after a point the players rotated positions.

When Dale got to the front line, he stood across the net from Henshaw. Dale nodded at him, and Bobby smiled back, both of them ready for next volley. Mary Jane served, barely getting the ball over the net and Henshaw jumped up and batted the ball down over the net before Dale could block his shot. Dale told him good play, and wished he was as tall as Henshaw, who looked about six foot one.

On the next play, Bigelow, playing opposite Gretchen, hit the ball too hard at her and she shrieked. K. C., standing behind her, came up to the net and told Butch to cool it. Bigelow said he was sorry, he forgot about hitting the ball too hard. Dale wished he'd been in Gretchen's spot. He'd liked to have blocked the ball right back in Bigelow's face.

The tall guy who'd been playing softball and a much shorter young woman walked over from the baseball diamond and interrupted the game. Dale asked Chris who they were. The tall guy was Thad North, the new First Church minister for young adults. The short woman was his wife, Denise. Denise walked over and told Mary Jane that her mother had called. Mary Jane's older sister, Ann Morgan Stephenson, had gone into labor. Mary Jane was supposed to go to the Galilee general hospital. Mary Jane looked excited. She smiled and turned to Amanda and Gretchen and engaged in animated conversation with them. Mary Jane asked Amanda if she'd be all right. Amanda assured her she would. She'd get a ride with someone. Bigelow came up to them and said he'd give Amanda a ride, not to worry. Mary Jane said good-bye to them all and walked toward her car and drove away.

Dale had seen pictures of Ann Morgan in old yearbooks. She'd graduated in 1971, so she was four years older than Mary Jane. Ann was as pretty as Mary Jane. She was blond with a fuller figure than her younger sister. Dale remembered she'd been voted football queen her senior year and had made the National Honor Society.

Thad North waved the rest of them over to the left field foul line for the Bible study. Dale and Chris walked over, following K.C. and Bigelow, Gretchen and Amanda. Dale noticed that when they sat down, Amanda purposely avoided Bigelow. Instead of sitting next to him, she slipped around the others and sat next to Gretchen.

Dale and Chris sat behind the two girls. Dale tried to listen to Thad North as he began the Bible study but his attention was focused more on Amanda. Most of the college kids had brought their Bibles. Dale hadn't, so he shared with Chris. Thad read part of chapter seven of first Corinthians. Dale guessed the youth minister selected that passage because it discusses avoiding fornication and regulating marriage between Christians. Verse nine stuck in his mind. Paul says if they – the early Christians – can't "have self-control, let them marry; for it is better to marry than to burn." Dale smiled a little to himself, thinking about the Jehovah Witnesses' emphasis on early marriage. He wondered if Trumbo had "burned" before he'd married Babs.

As Dale thought of that, he noticed Amanda reaching up with her hand and brushing her hair, perhaps thinking that some grass or a leaf had gotten stuck in it. She must have sensed him looking because she turned her head and smiled shyly at him before returning to her Bible.

During Thad North's brief discussion of the scripture, Dale wondered if he really wanted to go to Galilee Nazarene. It *was* a religious school. He tried to decide if he wanted to become religious again. He never stopped believing in God, but he had increasingly thought of Him as a force or an intelligence. The students and professors at GNC emphasized their personal relationship with Jesus and God. Dale wondered if he could feel like that.

After the closing prayer, the college kids got up and started to leave. Some of them made plans to get a Coke at West Oaks. Dale lingered to see what Amanda did. She stood talking to K. C., Gretchen, and Bigelow for a minute, then the four of them broke into two couples and walked to the parking lot. Dale and Chris followed not too far behind.

K. C. and Gretchen waved at Bigelow and Amanda as they veered off to the other end of the parking lot. Dale kept an eye on Amanda. He sensed something wasn't quite right. Amanda didn't seem to want to walk too closely to Butch. Dale only paid half attention to Chris as he talked about the highlights of his freshman year at GNC, which were few and far between. He and Chris veered farther left to where Chris's car was parked. Amanda and Bigelow continued walking straight and approached Butch's '74 Cutlass. Dale liked that kind of car. He wished Bigelow didn't have one. But at least he didn't like the olive green color.

He watched as Bigelow opened the door for Amanda and she got in. Bigelow bent down at the window and said something to her. Apparently, it was something she didn't like because she frowned. As Bigelow started to walk over to his side, Amanda opened the door to get out. Bigelow noticed and pushed the door shut. An offended look appeared on Amanda's face. She said something to Butch. She tried opening the door again but he leaned on it and prevented her.

Without telling Chris, Dale left him walking to his car alone and trotted over to Bigelow and Amanda. Bigelow still leaned his bulk against the door. Amanda no longer was pushing on it. She looked unhappy and Dale could see her mouth opening as if to say, "please, Butch."

Dale arrived in time to hear Bigelow say. "I said I'd take you home and I am."

"I've changed my mind," Amanda said. She once again tried to open the door.

Dale wondered why she just didn't scoot over to the other side. Maybe Bigelow's Cutlass had a stick shift and Amanda didn't want to climb over it. Or maybe she was just determined to get out the way she wanted.

"Why don't you let her get out?" Dale said, as he approached Bigelow from behind.

Bigelow turned but leaned his back against the door.

"What business is it of yours?"

"She wants out. Let her out."

"What are you going to do about it?"

"Whatever I have to."

Bigelow smiled his humorless smile. "Is that so?"

"Yep."

Dale heard Amanda saying in a placating voice that everything was all right. She was going to get out and that would be that.

Bigelow stood up straight but he didn't move away from the door enough for Amanda to completely open it. He stared at Dale in the way he had before they'd fought in art class. Dale got ready. He didn't really want to fistfight Bigelow. Butch was four inches taller and had a longer reach.

Suddenly, Bigelow drew back his arm and made a fist. Dale got ready to duck and swing back. He heard Amanda say, "Butch!" in a pleading way. Behind him Dale heard Chris running toward them.

"Hey, you guys," Chris said.

Bigelow kept his arm cocked. He smiled mockingly at Dale.

Amanda opened the door as far as it would go. "Butch! Audie! Please don't!"

Chris arrived and stood next to Dale. Bigelow lowered his arm. He looked around almost casually to see if anyone had seen him threatening Dale. Dale didn't take any chances. He kept his eyes on Butch.

"All right," Bigelow said. He stepped out of the way and allowed Amanda to exit his car. "Don't ride with me. I don't want you to anyway. I always thought you were stuck up."

Amanda got out and joined Chris and Dale as they walked a few steps away. They watched Bigelow get in his car, rev the motor loudly, and abruptly back it out of the parking space. The tires squealed when he peeled out.

Amanda smiled at Dale and Chris. "Thanks, guys, for rescuing me."

She said those words in a half-humorous way but Dale detected a note of sincerity, too. He glanced at Chris. He shrugged and smiled as if to say, "what did I do to get such credit?"

"So," Chris asked, "you need a ride?"

Amanda nodded. "I guess I do."

The three of them walked over to Chris's car. Dale opened the passenger door and said he'd get in the back. Amanda said, "oh, thank you" as Dale slipped in.

Chris started his car and looked in the rearview mirror at Dale. "Shall I drop you off first, Audie?"

Dale said no.

Chris smiled and drove through town and headed south to Amanda's. Chris asked her what was going on back there. Amanda said she didn't really know. They were walking over to his car when Butch started acting strange. After she got in, he leaned near the open window and said he'd like to take her out for a Coke or something. Amanda hadn't liked the way he said that. Especially the something. So she decided she didn't want a ride from him. She tried to get out but Butch wouldn't let her.

"Well, you saw the rest," she said.

Chris nodded. He said he wasn't sure what was getting into Butch of late.

Dale knew: what had always been inside Bigelow. He just wasn't as careful about not letting it show. Dale kept these observations to himself though.

Amanda said she was a little worried about Butch.

Chris and Dale didn't say anything. Amanda then turned around in her seat to look at Dale. She said she'd heard he might be transferring to GNC.

"Yeah," Dale said. "I am."

"So it's definite?" said Chris.

Dale knew he was teasing him. "That's right. It's definite."

"Oh, I'm glad," Amanda said.

She smiled at him. Dale thought her smile was more than just a polite one. He looked into her eyes and she held his gaze for a moment before her eyes flickered away from his. She turned back to Chris and asked him how his family was.

"You know," Chris said humorously. "You just saw them at church Sunday."

"So I did." Amanda laughed nervously, or so Dale thought.

Chris followed the wide streets as they winded into the tree area of town. Chris slowed the car and parked it against the curb outside Amanda's home. Dale hadn't seen it since his last date with Amanda. It looked just as solid and sturdy and white as before.

Amanda thanked Chris for the ride. She started to get out when Dale said he'd walk her to her door.

"Oh, that's not necessary," she said.

Chris said he'd walk her, too. Dale frowned at Chris but he ignored his look. Amanda got out, and held the door open for Dale. Chris put the car in neutral and cranked the parking brake and got out, too. The two young men followed Amanda as she walked to her front door.

"You two really don't have to do this," she said, almost laughing.

"No problem," said Chris.

"Our pleasure," said Dale.

The three of them arrived at her front door. Dale remembered that bright porch light. Its glare still seemed to be reprimanding him.

Amanda turned around and faced Chris and Dale. She smiled and clasped her hands together rather nervously.

"Well, good night," she said.

"Good night," Chris and Dale said almost in unison. They turned to go as Amanda opened her door. She called out to them, "and thanks for the ride."

Dale and Chris waved and watched as she slipped inside her house. They walked back to Chris's idling car. They got in and sat silently for a while as Chris slowly drove down the street.

"Why do I get the impression that you like Amanda?" Chris asked.

Dale turned to him but said nothing.

"Yeah, I like her, too," said Chris. "She's such a –"

"Nice girl," Dale finished for him.

Chris laughed. "Yeah, that's right. She likes me, too." Chris gave Dale a knowing look before his face turned into a frown. "Yeah, she likes me all right; as a friend."

"That's too bad."

"Yeah. What about you?"

"I don't think I like her. I think I love her."

Chris stared at him, amazed. "Since when?"

Dale turned and gazed out his open side window. "Since the first time I saw her."

# BOOK 6: *The Philosopher Kings*

### Chapter 1: *A cold Fish; captain Krupp; amazing Amanda*

"I go by Dale."

The professor, Dr. Petry, peered at him through his small spectacles. "Pardon?"

"I go by Dale. My middle name."

He disliked calling attention to himself on the first day of class, but he knew he had to tell the professor which name he preferred or otherwise he'd be called Audie as he had been in high school.

"Very well," Dr. Petry said, making a note on his class roster sheet.

Dale felt some of his classmates looking at him. He fought his feeling of embarrassment. He thought it was time to be less self-conscious and bashful. It wasn't easy for him to develop poise. He was naturally shy. But he'd read about other people in history who had overcome personality shortcomings and he was determined to do so too.

He glanced to his right and saw an unusual young man named Sylvester Fish staring at him. The first thing Dale noticed about Fish was his pallor. His skin looked like it had never seen the sun. It was so pale that it looked like the color of a mushroom. In contrast to the almost translucent whiteness of his skin, Fish had jet-black hair, worn rather short. But most distinctive of all, Fish's gray, beady eyes were made all the more obscure by his heavy-framed, thick-lensed, tinted eyeglasses. In fact, Dale could hardly see Fish's eyes as he returned the odd fellow's stare.

Dale broke off the staring contest when Dr. Petry explained the purpose of the class. Writing for Christian Publications, he said, was a writing class that emphasized the fundamentals of writing, with special attention to mechanics, along with a commitment to spreading the Christian message to believers and non-believers alike. Therefore, the importance of correct writing should not be underestimated. In his view, correctness was proof of the perfection of God. If a writer could write a piece without error, without any mechanical mistakes of any kind, such writing brought the reader that much closer to God.

Dale wasn't sure he understood what Dr. Petry meant. Of course, a writer should strive for correctness, but the professor seemed to think that mattered most. Dale thought meaning or beauty or some other aesthetic concern should be primary. Since this was the only journalism course offered this semester, he decided he'd try and understand the professor's objectives. Still, he felt a little uneasy as Dr. Petry continued to focus on "mechanics."

The classes at GNC were definitely different than CSU. For one thing, most professors had prayer before starting class. Dr. Petry had led the class in prayer and Dale, with the rest of the students, bowed his head and listened as Dr. Petry asked Jesus to guide them in their attempt to find perfection in prose. Dale had thought that was a rather unusual prayer. In his other classes, including New Testament, the professor didn't make such a direct connection between the spiritual and the academic. Dr. Petry seemed to think the more holy the student, the more "perfect" his prose would be.

Class ended and on his way out, Dale felt someone tapping his shoulder. He turned and saw the impassive face of Sylvester Fish staring at him.

"You're new, aren't you?"

"Yeah."

"I thought so," said Fish, with evident satisfaction. "I know everyone on campus."

Although GNC only had 2,000 students, Dale thought that was quite a boast. "Well, I don't live on campus."

Fish looked peeved. "I didn't mean *living* on campus, I meant *on* campus."

"What's the difference?" Dale felt like teasing this odd fellow.

"Well, the difference is –" Fish broke off once he saw Dale's small smile. "I mean I know everyone here at GNC."

"Everyone?"

"Virtually everyone."

"But you don't know me."

"No, I don't but –"

"Then your statement really isn't accurate."

Fish puffed his flabby cheeks in exasperation. Dale noticed that he was unusually dressed. He wore black slacks, a pressed white shirt, and a black bow tie.

"You seem to be pulling my leg," Fish said without humor.

Dale glanced down at Fish's stubby legs. He noticed that he wore white socks with his black dress shoes.

"I don't see my hands attached to your leg."

"Do you always interpret everything literally?"

"I thought most everyone on campus believed in literalism."

Fish's eyes, or what little Dale could see of them, narrowed. "Where are you from?"

"From here. Galilee."

"Do you attend First Church?"

"You mean literally?"

"Of course. How else?"

"Can't someone attend in the spirit and not the flesh?"

Fish seriously considered that question for a moment. Then realizing that he was being toyed with again, drew his thin lips in until they formed a narrow line across his pale, almost chinless face.

"I believe you've answered my questions more fully than you realize," he said, as he prepared to leave.

"I hope so," said Dale, "or otherwise we might have to have another delightful conversation like this one."

Fish paused to fully register Dale's comment, then understanding that it was not a compliment, he puffed his cheeks again and proceeded to march out of the classroom.

Dale couldn't help but think to himself, "what an odd fish."

Chris asked Dale how the first day of classes went.

"Okay," he replied.

Some of the classes, the philosophy and history, seemed interesting; some, like Writing for Christian Publications, didn't. He did like the fact that none of his classes had more than fifteen students in them. He'd never had a class at CSU with fewer than thirty.

Chris told Dale he'd like him to meet some of the guys on his flag football team. Chris said the team needed a good player like Dale. How would he like to play for the Omega Owls?

"Omega Owls?"

"Yeah, that's our team's name."

Chris rattled off the other seven teams: Alpha Avengers, Beta Bears, Delta Dragons, Gamma Rays, Kappa Crushers, Lambda Lions, and Zeta Gators.

"So, they're all named after Greek letters of the alphabet," said Dale. "That's sort of neat."

"What?"

"Alpha, beta, delta, and so on. Greek letters of the alphabet."

"Hey, I'm a business major."

Dale playfully shoved Chris as they strolled across campus to the P. E. building and adjoining fields.

Chris told Dale that although the football was only flag, most of the teams had good athletes on them. Many of the guys had played high school football. Everyone took the flag football league seriously.

"Great," said Dale. "Gung-ho flag football players."

Chris said last year the Omega Owls won only two games and lost eight. "We finished last in our division."

"Does Omega get a first-round draft pick?"

"Yeah, I wish. No, teams recruit their own players. But once you join a team you have to stay on it for at least a season. We try to be fair. The captains of each team meet and divide up the best new guys. But a guy doesn't have to play for that team if he doesn't want to."

"What if two or more teams want the same new guy?"

"Well, he goes to the team of his choice."

Dale understood. Sort of like a fraternity. GNC didn't have fraternities or sororities. Just separate dorms for the boys and the girls. Some students, like Dale, lived off campus, but they had to be upperclassmen.

They arrived at the athletic field and walked over to a group of twelve guys standing near the north goalpost. Most of them wore gym shorts, red football jerseys, and cleats. Dale heard one of them, a guy almost as short as he was, talking to the rest of the team in an earnest manner. Chris tapped the talker on the shoulder and said, "hey, Krupp, I have a friend with me."

Krupp glanced at them. "Just a sec," he said, then turned back to the team. He spoke about the new offense. One to take advantage of a new passing game he had in mind. It was obvious from last year that a team couldn't count on running the ball in flag football. It was too easy to tackle a runner by pulling the flag. So, Omega would have to throw the ball more than ever.

Dale glanced at Chris. He shrugged.

Krupp then told them that he'd heard one of the new guys was really fast. Supposedly, he ran under ten seconds in the 100. Krupp said they needed to find out who this guy was and get him on their team. He said this new guy had played high school football and knew how to play the game. Krupp said he was looking forward to throwing bombs to this guy.

Chris rolled his eyes. Dale got the idea that maybe Krupp was talking about him.

Krupp said just because a guy was fast didn't mean he could play receiver. It took more than speed. It took skill at running patterns. It took discipline and teamwork to read the quarterback. In flag, the chemistry between quarterback and receiver was really important.

"Hey, Krupp," Chris said, interrupting.

"Hey, Chris, I'm talking right now. I'll get to you in a minute, okay, buddy?"

Chris said wryly to Dale, "he's the captain. And quarterback."

Dale understood how Omega went 2-8 last year.

Krupp, detecting a flippant tone in Chris's remarks, turned to him. "Okay, DeVille, what is it?" he demanded.

Dale noticed that Krupp looked a little like a mouse or a rat or some kind of rodent with his little eyes, big nose, and small mouth. He had longish, thin blond hair. His flimsy moustache looked like white whiskers.

"Peter, this is the guy I told you about. Aud – I mean, Dale Smith." Dale nodded approvingly at Chris for remembering to use Dale.

Peter Krupp frowned at Dale. His moustache turned downwards and his small, green eyes narrowed in disapproval.

"This is the guy?"

Chris said yeah. Dale reached out to shake Krupp's hand.

"He doesn't look that fast to me."

Dale pulled back his hand.

"Well, he is," said Chris. "He was faster than me even before I hurt my knee."

Chris had told Dale that last year he wrenched his knee so badly he couldn't run for three weeks. It healed but he'd lost some speed.

Krupp looked doubtful. "He's not very big."

Dale thought, neither are you. But he didn't say anything. He wanted to see how long Peter Krupp kept talking about him like he wasn't there.

"I didn't say he was big, I said he was fast."

"I bet he's not faster than Hammaker."

Dale noticed a tall, lean guy shift his feet and smile. Dale guessed that was Hammaker.

"Why don't we find out?"

Krupp stared at Chris. "What's that?"

"Let's find out. Let 'em race."

Dale leaned over to Chris and told him he was crazy. Krupp looked at Dale, then looked at Hammaker, and said okay, let's.

"Why did you say that?" Dale said to Chris as he followed him down field. "You're putting me in an awkward position."

"Not if you win."

Dale threw his hands up. The only thing worse would be if they bet money. But since they were Nazarenes and gambling was forbidden, he didn't have to worry about that.

Krupp waved Dale over to the goal line. Hammaker, an eager beaver, already stood there. Dale walked over and nodded. Hammaker had shaggy brown hair and a jovial face. He smiled at Dale as if he thought the whole competition funny.

Krupp said they'd race for forty yards. That was the best distance to judge football speed. Dale thought about declining to race, but the rest of the team had gathered around already and he didn't want to look chicken. He took off his boots and socks. He pressed his toes into the ground. It wasn't too hard. He could get a good grip with his toes for his start. His blue jeans were another matter. He tugged on the thick cloth around his knees and raised them enough to provide some room for his pumping legs.

Chris said he'd start them. Krupp jogged forty yards downfield with a couple of other guys. Chris said take your mark. Dale crouched forward and dug his toes into the grass. He glanced over to Hammaker, more advantageously dressed in gym shorts, red jersey, and cleats. Dale thought he could beat him in a start and that was half the trick in running the forty. He'd always won forty-yard sprints in high school football practice, even as a sophomore.

Chris said get set. Dale leaned forward and tensed his muscles. Then Chris said, go!

Dale got an excellent jump. He sprang forward and pumped his arms and legs and sprinted as smoothly as he used to in track. As he flew down the field, he didn't see any sign of Hammaker in his peripheral vision. His feet hardly seemed to touch the scratchy grass. In a few seconds, he crossed the forty-yard line well ahead of Hammaker.

Dale jogged down the field another ten yards, then stopped, turned and walked back. Krupp ran out to meet him. He held out his hand. Dale thought about not shaking it. He thought Krupp was a jerk. But he clasped the captain's hand and shook it hard, watching in satisfaction when Krupp winced.

"Hey, you are fast," said Krupp, removing his hand and flexing it. "You might be the fastest guy in flag!"

Hammaker came up and shook Dale's hand too. He said, "good race" without any resentment.

Chris introduced Dale to the rest of the team. Krupp told Dale they played flag with eight men: three linemen, two receivers, and three backs, including quarterback. He asked Dale what position he wanted.

"Quarterback."

Krupp's face fell blank for a second before Dale grinned a little.

"Hey, that's funny," Krupp said, feigning a laugh. He asked Dale if he had time to practice a little. Dale said sure.

Dale walked over to Chris and asked him how this Krupp guy became quarterback and captain.

"Well," said Chris, "he just sort of made himself captain, then quarterback."

Dale asked if anybody challenged him.

"No. I guess I should have but I didn't. He's not a bad guy. He just thinks he's better than he is."

Dale knew the type. In high school, Middleton was sort of that way. A guy who played hard, who considered himself a "leader," but who was really a mediocre player. Coaches liked those guys. The rah-rah guys. Dale thought it was better when the leader was also a good player. Better to lead by example than by shooting off one's mouth.

Dale and Chris joined the huddle and Krupp put Dale at halfback. That was okay with him, except he'd heard Peter talk about how Omega was going to pass a lot more.

They ran several plays with Dale staying in the backfield to block, then Krupp told him to split out as a flanker and run a post. On the snap, Dale sprinted down the field and easily outran the guy who played cornerback, but Krupp's pass was ten yards short. Dale jogged back to the huddle and wondered how a guy without a strong arm got to be quarterback.

Krupp told Dale he didn't run the pattern quite right but that was okay since it was his first day. Dale glanced at Chris, who shrugged.

Dale had a feeling it was going to be a long season.

Amanda slung the bowling ball awkwardly. Dale watched it skitter on the wooden floor and plop into the trough for a gutter ball. Everyone at their lane laughed. As Amanda walked back to them, she hid her mouth with her hands, but he could tell by the dimples in her cheeks and the sparkle in her eyes that she was smiling.

"In case we forgot to inform you, Meeks," said Bobby Henshaw with mock gravity, "the objective of the game is to knock down those white objects in the back."

"Oh, thanks for reminding me," Amanda said, now showing her laughing mouth. She sat down next to Dale. "Boy, I stink."

Dale breathed in and detected the subtle sweetness of her perfume and the fresh-washed fragrance of her hair.

"No, you don't stink. In fact, you smell mighty nice."

Amanda turned to him and her face had a brief puzzled look on it before she smiled a softer smile than the broad, abashed smile she'd displayed just seconds before. Dale knew she didn't quite get his sense of humor yet.

Abigail Van Brocklin, Henshaw's date, came over and sat down next to Amanda and the two girls began talking. Dale couldn't quite hear what they were saying. He felt a little shy in the company of Abigail, although she was a nice girl. She had fair skin, black hair, green eyes, and a friendly face. She wasn't especially pretty, a fact that surprised Dale because he'd always imagined that Henshaw would have a beautiful girlfriend. Abigail was more the "cute" variety, especially when she smiled, which was quite often. Then she showed her large, perfect white teeth and her eyes twinkled.

Dale had heard that Abigail was the granddaughter of one of the Nazarene church's most important leaders and the daughter of the school's president. Abigail's grandmother had been influential in the church and college as well. That made Abigail one of the elite on campus. But unlike some of the other campus "leaders," Dale thought she was friendly and accessible. She didn't put on any airs and treated him graciously.

Dale listened to the sound of Amanda's voice. She wasn't quite giggling, but her voice had that high-pitched girlish squeal that preceded laughter. He'd never heard Amanda sound that way. She'd always displayed such a placid, serene demeanor in his observations of her in high school that he never guessed she could be so animated. Now she and Abigail laughed heartily. Dale glanced at them and Amanda turned to him and said Abigail had reminded her of the time they had been at summer camp and she'd been so poor at sports that everyone at camp called her Amazin' Amanda to tease her. You know, because she was really just the opposite of amazing. Amanda laughed and Dale nodded. Since he wasn't laughing, she asked if he got the joke. He said yeah, he got it. Amazin' really meant atrocious. The two girls gave him a puzzled look, thought about the uncommon word, then they both laughed and Amanda said, "exactly."

The two girls resumed talking while Henshaw waited to bowl. Holding the bowling ball in his hands, he turned back to Dale and shrugged. There was some problem setting up the pins. The automatic reset device had jammed and they had to be set manually.

Dale thought how this was the important third date in a row. That was all he'd gotten back in high school. He wondered if this school activity counted as a date. He supposed it did. During the first weekend of the school year the student government sponsored several weekend activities. Tonight, bowling night and an ice cream social back on campus. Tomorrow night, a concert. Dale hadn't asked Amanda to that yet. Three weeks ago, just a few days after his rescue of her from Bigelow at the Wednesday night Bible study, he called her. When he heard her soft, inquiring voice, he jumped right in because he knew if he paused and thought about what he was doing he'd get nervous. He said, "Hi, Amanda, this is Dale." She said, "Dale?" After a pause, she remembered that was the name he was going by now. "Oh, yes, Dale. How are you?" He said fine. Would she like to go out with him Friday? She said, "you don't beat around the bush, do you?" He said, "nope, I generally don't beat bushes. So, how about it?" Dale had been astonished at himself. He wondered if he'd been too direct. But after another momentary pause, Amanda said, "all right."

They went to a summer concert at the Stars and Stripes Park. Dale hoped he didn't see Blackie there. The rangers provided security for the park concerts. Dale didn't see him. Amanda liked the concert. It was a "Mostly Mozart" concert. He liked it too, and afterwards he allowed Amanda to explain all the subtleties of Mozart. Then they went to Braum's for ice cream. She only had one dip of French vanilla. Dale had two dips of chocolate almond rather than his usual three. He didn't want to seem excessive. They talked for awhile more in his car, then he took her home and walked her to her door and even with the porch light on he gave her a quick kiss. She seemed surprised but not displeased and said good night.

The second date almost didn't happen. He'd called her a few days later and asked her out again and she said she had to move into her dorm room on Friday and then go with her family on a trip to their cabin over the Labor Day weekend. Dale said that was too bad. She said, yeah, it was. She said it would take her all day to move in the dorm room and she would be too tired to go out that night. He offered to help her move in. She said, that's nice, but she couldn't impose on him. Dale said it wasn't an imposition. She hemmed and hawed for a moment. He said he'd be delighted to help out. He needed the exercise anyway. She laughed and said okay.

In the late afternoon, Dale met her at her dorm, Hayley Hall, and lugged up all the heavy stuff. If he'd known she lived on the fifth floor he might have not offered. The dorm didn't have an elevator, so he had to cart boxes of classical records, books, a small television, a portable stereo, and armful after armful of clothes on hangers. He couldn't believe all the clothes she had. At one point, he asked her if she were moving in for the school year or for the rest of the century. She smiled tolerantly and helped by carrying the alarm clock radio and popcorn maker.

It was a hot day, almost a hundred, and after finishing his labors, Dale's T-shirt was drenched with sweat. He took the tail of it and mopped his brow. He looked at all the stuff in her room. Amanda organized some of it and thanked him for helping her. It would have taken her hours to move all of it. Dale, a little out of breath, nodded. Amanda said usually her father and brother helped her. But her father had strained his back playing golf and her brother had a summer cold. Dale thought, how convenient, but he really didn't mind helping her. In fact, he was glad to be of service.

Amanda's roommate, Hope Jorgensen, walked in and introduced herself. Dale's hands were a little sweaty but he shook hands with her just the same. Hope looked at her hand for a moment, surprised to feel so much moisture, then smiled. She had fairly short blond hair and a pretty face, but he thought she was too skinny. She wore shorts and he thought her knees were knobby.

Hope and Amanda talked for a few minutes. Dale realized that Hope's father must be the guy on TV that owned the largest car dealership in northwest Oklahoma City, Jorgensen Motors. She looked like her father but prettier, of course.

Amanda said she'd finish organizing her things later. She and Dale walked down to the first floor where he drank like a horse from the lobby water fountain. They then walked outside into the early evening sun. Amanda said, poor dear, your shirt is soaked. Dale didn't mind being poor-deared by her. He said he'd come prepared. He walked over to his Chevy and pulled out a fresh T-shirt. It was a gray shirt with CSU written in block letters over the chest. He pulled off his damp T-shirt, wiped off the lingering traces of sweat, then put on his fresh shirt. He glanced at Amanda and noticed she was pretending not to watch him. He suddenly felt embarrassed thinking that she probably had seen him without his shirt on.

He said, "how about a root beer float?" Amanda nodded. "Sounds yummy," she said and Dale resisted the urge to tease her about using that silly word. He opened the door for her and she got in. He glanced at her bare legs. She wore the same style of dressy shorts she had at the Wednesday Bible study but these were light blue in color, which he liked better. He got in and drove to Sooner Shack. Along the way they talked about the coming school year, then after a pause, Amanda thanked him again for helping her move. She hoped it hadn't been too difficult. He'd gotten rather sweaty. Dale said moving her stuff wasn't hard. It was just a hot day. He said he hadn't meant to change his shirt in her presence. He'd just forgot. She said she didn't mind. She had a brother, after all. Then she said she hadn't realized he had such a … strong build. Dale hid his embarrassment with a joke. He said he'd once been told he had good pectorals. Amanda seemed puzzled. What are pectorals? she asked. Dale, feeling even more abashed, said he was just making a joke. He said he'd tell her the source of it sometime. She nodded, still confused. He wondered if she'd noticed his musculature when he ran track. Guys only wore shorts and small track jerseys. Then he said he still did push-ups to keep in shape. Amanda nodded. She seemed to a little embarrassed now so he asked her about her music classes. She perked up and told him all about them, how she was looking forward to her voice lessons in particular since she didn't think she had the talent to play the flute at the college level.

They talked more about her music plans while having their root beer floats. Then they drove around the lake and stopped at a spot with a good view and watched the sun set. Then Dale asked if she'd like to have something to eat. Amanda said she ought to be getting back home. He said her folks had probably already eaten dinner. Amanda agreed, so he took her to West Oaks and they ate in the restaurant and she had chicken salad and he had his favorite, the chicken-fried-steak sandwich.

They talked some more after eating and then Dale drove her home. She thanked him again as he walked her to her door. She stopped before stepping on the porch and said maybe she should go in the back way since it was so late. He nodded even though it wasn't that late. Only about ten thirty.

They walked through the gate to the side door that led to the garage. Amanda put her key in the door lock, then turned to thank him and Dale put his arms around her waist and pulled her to him and kissed her. Instead of releasing her, he held her for a few more seconds and kissed her more deeply a second time. He heard her sigh, and they stood in the dark without speaking. Then he felt her withdraw from his embrace and he let her go. She said good night in a soft voice. Dale said good night. He walked back to his car remembering the last time he'd kissed her at her garage side door and how that had been their last date of high school. Dale was determined not to let that happen again.

He was so keyed up that he went for a drive. He drove north to the less used rural road that ran between Galilee and the City and raced down the smooth, straight asphalt road until his Chevy hit seventy. He calmed down after that, but he still felt a curious feeling of excitement, anxiety, and anticipation. He felt like his whole future had broken open in front of him like a yawning cavern.

That second date happened a week ago. Now, while Amanda and Abigail chatted, he watched as Henshaw tossed the bowling ball down the lane. The ball collided with the pins with a crack. A strike. Henshaw bowled pretty well, thought Dale.

Abigail went up for her turn as Henshaw took a seat. He nodded at Dale.

"You know, I thought you made an excellent point about Plato in our class this morning."

Dale noticed Amanda looking at him. Amanda asked what excellent point?

"He asked whether *The Republic* is meant as a satire or whether we should read it in a "straight" way?"

"*The Republic*?" asked Amanda.

"Yeah, Plato's *The Republic*. That's our first text for our philosophy class."

"Oh," said Amanda.

"Dr. Prescott thought Dale made a good point, too."

"Well, to really understand a book as complicated as *The Republic* I think you need to have an idea of the context in which it was written," he said, hoping he didn't sound pretentious. He glanced at Amanda. She had a look on her face as if she'd just confirmed something she'd suspected for a long time.

"Yes, the context," said Henshaw. "If the book was written as a satire, then it should be read in that context. If it's a serious book, then it should be read in that context."

"Of course, a book such as *The Republic* might be written as satire and as straight philosophy," said Dale. "The trick is knowing when it's strictly philosophical and when it's satiric."

"Yeah, Dr. Prescott made a similar point," said Henshaw, obviously impressed with the teacher.

Abigail came over to them and asked what they were so engrossed in.

"Don't ask me," said Amanda. "I'm hardly following a word of it."

"Philosophy," said Henshaw.

"Oh, philosophy," said Abigail tolerantly. "Well, it's philosopher Dale's turn to bowl."

He got up and grabbed a bowling ball and stepped onto the lane. He'd been bowling several times before. Blackie once took him and Rusty bowling. Dale had been embarrassed at Blackie for drinking beer even though Rusty's uncle Tim drank beer. Blackie had showed them how to throw a hook and a curve. Dale's father was a good bowler. He'd won a trophy in a navy bowling tournament.

Dale thought he'd be a better bowler if he didn't have two bad fingers on his right hand. But he could control the bowling ball pretty well with his two good fingers and thumb. He took two strides and tossed a fast, accurate ball and watched it crash into the pins for a strike.

Henshaw told him good shot when he returned and they watched as Amanda threw another gutter ball. She didn't laugh this time. Henshaw and Abigail offered encouragement and Dale told her she just needed to relax. Amanda looked glum. She really did stink.

At the end of the bowling tournament, the school paper, *Smoke Signals*, took photos of the high and low scorer. Dale had finished third with a score of 175. He thought he could break 200 if he practiced. Henshaw scored 168. But the winner was some guy Dale had heard of but didn't know personally named Virgil Phelps who rolled 189. He stood for his picture, then Amanda, who had scored only 49, smiled gamely for her photograph. Dale noticed again that she'd changed her hair a little from how he remembered it in high school. She parted her hair in the middle like a lot of girls with long hair, but she arranged the front so it curved out into two wings from her forehead and then fell under the rest of her long, straight locks.

The four of them drove back to campus in Henshaw's Chevy coupe and joined Eugene Greene, Hope, Chris, and Mary Jane at a table in the college cafeteria for ice cream. People could make their own sundaes and Dale teased Chris for making a dreadful concoction of chocolate, strawberry, and pistachio ice cream with bananas, marshmallows, chocolate syrup, pineapples, and ketchup. Dale asked how he could eat that. Chris showed him by shoving a huge spoonful in his mouth.

Dale wasn't so adventurous but he filled his bowl with plenty of ice cream. The girls, predictably, had dainty portions. Dale asked Chris how he did at bowling. He, Eugene, Hope, and Mary Jane had shared a lane at the other end.

"Not so hot," he said. "Only 147. The girls made me nervous."

Dale had been a little nervous, too, but he'd been able to concentrate pretty well because he wanted to show off for Amanda.

After the ice cream social, Dale walked Amanda back to Hayley Hall. In the parking lot, they sat on the hood of his car and talked. Amanda seemed a little down.

"I'm so uncoordinated," she said. "I really made a fool of myself bowling."

"No, you didn't," said Dale. "Besides, it's only bowling. You know, rolling a round ball down a lane to knock down pins."

She nodded but didn't seem amused. "I'd probably be a better flute player if I weren't so clumsy."

"Clumsiness has nothing to do with dexterity. Dexterity is what musicians need. Some of the best musicians are clumsy."

"Really?"

"Yeah." Dale tried to think of a famous contemporary classical musician. All he could come up was Leonard Bernstein. "Leonard Bernstein is notorious for falling down when leaving the stage."

Amanda smiled. "Oh, really?"

"That's the truth," Dale said with mock seriousness. "Broke his leg once. Had to conduct with a cast on."

Amanda laughed. She swayed a little as they sat on the hood of the car. Dale thought she looked especially lovely under the moonlight.

"Besides, you don't need to worry about stuff like that. You're beautiful."

Amanda turned to him with a serious look on her face. "I'm not. But even if I were, I'd like to be something more than beautiful."

"You are. You're beautiful inside, too."

Her eyes widened and glistened. "You really think so?"

"Yes, I do. I've always thought you had a special quality. Something more than skin-deep beauty. A sort of an aura."

"An aura?"

"Yeah, a special glow. It's like that special part of you that's inside you lights up." Dale shrugged. "I'm not saying it right."

Amanda smiled and leaned against him. "No, what you said is very nice."

Dale put his arm around her. They sat silently and watched the stars in the sky for a few minutes. Then Amanda said she should probably go in.

He glanced around the parking lot and seeing no one, leaned over and kissed Amanda. He would have liked to kiss her more, but he knew she'd object since they were in public.

He helped her off the hood of the car and walked her back to the dorm. He asked if she wanted to go to the concert tomorrow night.

"I don't know," she said.

Dale knew she was thinking of her rule of no more than three dates in a row. "I could use help in understanding the music."

"Oh, you could?"

"That's right. Without you, I'd be lost."

Amanda smiled. "All right."

Dale said he'd come by for her at seven. They exchanged good nights and he saw Chris bringing Hope back to the dorm. Dale waited for him around the corner of the building. Chris joined him and asked how his date with Amanda went.

"Fine. We're going out again tomorrow."

Chris looked surprised. "Four in a row? Wow, that's a record."

Dale nodded. And he was determined to extend the record even further.

**Chapter 2: *Smoke Signals; bad break for Butch; Twirp date; suspended***

Dale, Sharon Myrick, Teri Boswell, and the editor, Stan Perkins, were sitting around the newspaper office one afternoon in early October when their temporary adviser, Professor Cooper, came in to check on them. Professor Cooper was Dale's academic adviser and also supervised his English lit independent study. Dale liked him; so did everybody on campus. Out of class, a lot of the kids called him "Coop" because he was so friendly, gracious, and informal. He'd been teaching at Galilee Nazarene for almost forty years. Now, nearing seventy, he still taught a full load, and served as adviser for the Bleacher Bums, which was sort of a comical boys' pep club that attended Galilee basketball games dressed in hobo-like clothes and cheered for the Chiefs. With the newspaper's official adviser, Mrs. Genesee, out sick for the semester, Coop had taken over advising duties.

Professor Cooper shuffled into the room and smiled at them. All of them said, "hi, Coop," except Dale, who still didn't feel comfortable calling his teacher and adviser Coop, even out of class. Professor Cooper had a bad back and couldn't stand up completely erect. He walked bent over a little, but he never complained. He always seemed to be smiling. Dressed in his usual attire, un-pressed dark slacks, a rumpled light blue dress shirt, a well-worn herringbone jacket, and a colorful tie (this one a purple, orange, and white paisley), he had the casual look of a man more focused on what was going on in his mind than how he appeared externally. He had a long, ruddy face with a narrow nose and rather small but perceptive-looking light blue eyes. Although bald on top, he wore his gray hair fairly shaggy on the sides. But most noticeable of all was his lower face, with a well-groomed mustache etched over thin lips and, on his chin, a bristling Van Dyke-style beard. The beard and Professor Cooper's somewhat ironic look in his eyes reminded Dale of those old portraits of a Renaissance courtier.

Professor Cooper asked them how preparation for the new edition was going. They said fine. Stan told Coop of some of the ideas for stories and the professor looked over some copy. He asked Dale how he liked reading *Middlemarch*, one of the books Dale had on his reading list. Dale said he liked it but it was long. Professor Cooper nodded. He'd last read that novel twenty years ago. Now, thanks to Dale, he was reading it again.

Coop said so long, and before walking out of the office reminded Dale that their independent study conference would be next Tuesday. Dale said he'd be finished with George Eliot's novel by then. Professor Cooper said not to rush. Better to read slowly and with appreciation than to rush through just to make a deadline.

After Professor Cooper left, Stan said they were lucky to have him for the substitute adviser. Dale asked why. Stan said when Mrs. Genesee became ill, the administration had considered Dr. Petry to serve as temporary adviser.

"Oh, no," said Teri.

She was a short, chubby girl with black, curly hair and brown eyes. She didn't like Dr. Petry any more than Dale did. It wasn't only that Dr. Petry was boring but he was obsessed with mechanical correctness to the extent that nothing else seemed to matter. He didn't even seemed interested in content, as long as it observed Nazarene propriety.

"And he *wants* to advise the newspaper," said Sharon, the physical opposite of Teri. She was tall and thin with light brown hair and gray eyes.

"He thinks it's his duty," said Stan.

"More like his mission," said Sharon.

"I think he'll try to finagle his way into advising the newspaper or yearbook next year. If Mrs. Genesee is still ill, he just might do it, too," said Stan.

"That can't happen," said Teri. She turned to Dale. "You'll like Mrs. Genesee. She's an excellent teacher and newspaper adviser."

"She edits with a velvet dagger," said Sharon.

Dale liked that image. He asked what she meant exactly.

"She'll rip your copy to shreds but she does it so gently that you don't mind."

Stan concurred. "She knows her stuff. She knows how to edit writing to make it breathe, not to suffocate it like Petry."

When Dale first met Stan and asked to be on the staff, he thought he looked rather strange and humorless. Tall and gaunt, with glasses and a beaky nose, he reminded him of a crane or an ostrich. But as he got to know him, Dale thought he was all right. He still didn't smile much, but when Dale called him Stan the Man he got the reference and a sly quiver crossed his thin lips.

Dale liked both Sharon and Teri. Sharon, from rural Colorado, tended to be reserved. She wrote well and was also an excellent proofreader and editor. She wasn't conventionally pretty but he liked looking at her quick, gray eyes as they darted over copy and quickly made corrections. He didn't even mind when she corrected his copy.

Teri, on the other hand, was more talkative. Dale had liked her candid demeanor right from the start. She also liked joking around, and he often teased her about being from Arkansas. He could do that, he told her, because his grandparents were hillbillies from the Arky Ozarks. She didn't believe him and it became sort of an inside joke between them that Dale was really from New England and just pretended to have hick relatives to enhance his social standing on campus.

Like Dale, Sharon and Teri were also on the yearbook, the *Tomahawk*. Unlike him, both of them had actual positions. Teri served as the activities section editor. Sharon served as assistant editor and everyone assumed she'd be editor-in-chief next year as a senior. Dale, although still interested in the yearbook, thought his best chance at an editorship was with the newspaper. Since he was becoming more interested in topical issues and exploring ideas, he thought a newspaper venue would probably be better than a yearbook.

He'd already written a couple of stories for the newspaper. One was about the adviser of the Philosophy Club, Dr. Philip Prescott. Dale had interviewed him and used that information to enliven the story about the start of a new campus club. Along with Dale, Eugene Greene, Bobby Henshaw, and three other guys that Dale didn't know well were in the group. Dale had talked Chris into going to a few meetings but Chris decided that as a business major he was out of his depth at such intellectual meetings.

His second story was a review of the album *Tales of Mystery and Imagination* by the Alan Parsons Project, sort of an art-pop British group. Sylvester Fish, who was also on newspaper staff, complained about publishing a review of a "secular" record. Stan said it was permissible to review secular records since they were allowed on campus.

The four of them talked a little more about Dr. Petry and his designs on advising the newspaper, then Dale said he had to go to flag football practice. Sharon and Stan said bye and Teri said she'd walk with him to the gym if he didn't mind.

They left the student union and walked across the small, attractive campus. The grounds were neatly maintained and filled with shrubs and flowers and even trees. Dale remembered riding his bike on the campus when he was a kid because he liked the way it looked and smelled and because the cement walkways had so few cracks in them. He, Rusty, K. C., and Wally liked racing their bikes over the smooth walkways during the summer when classes were out of session. The sole campus security guard would chase them off the campus if he saw them, and, of course, that was part of the fun.

As they walked, Teri asked him if he'd been the editor of his high school yearbook. Dale said yes, and asked why she asked.

"Oh, I saw one the other day. I thought it was good. But I did wonder why there was a drawing of a rat on the cover."

"It was supposed to be a mean gopher," said Dale, trying to hide his defensiveness.

"Oh, I see. Well, it did look mean."

Dale saw no point in pursuing this conversation, so he said nothing. They walked in silence for a while when Teri asked him which team Omega was playing Thursday.

"Alpha," he replied.

"Aren't they the best team in the league?"

Henshaw, Eugene, K. C., Bigelow, and Virgil Phelps were on the team. Phelps had been a quarterback at Cimarron City a couple of years ago and was really good. He had a great arm. He could throw an accurate pass from fifty yards away. Dale wondered why he hadn't gone to a school that played real football. He guessed because he was a Nazarene.

"Yeah, they're the best." Alpha was undefeated so far.

"Hmm. Maybe I'll come and watch you guys lose Thursday night," she said, smiling.

Dale paused before entering the gym. "Yeah, we need all the moral support we can get."

Teri waved bye and he went inside the gym to his locker to get dressed for practice.

Omega had played Alpha tough from the start but now in the fourth quarter the Owls trailed by six, 22-16. With five minutes left and Alpha on the march, Dale intercepted a third down pass. The Owls had a chance to tie and perhaps win if they made the two-point conversion.

In the huddle, Chris suggested they run a four receiver set and Krupp agreed. Dale lined up at flanker and ran a short pattern across the middle and caught the ball for a seven-yard gain. He felt someone's hand slap his upper thigh and returning to the huddle he thought it was just an accident. But three plays later, on the same route, Dale caught the pass over the middle and he felt someone's hand punch him on his groin. He staggered but kept his feet and his flag was snatched. He tossed the ball to the ref and rested his hands on his knees, trying to ignore the nausea he felt. The ref asked if he were all right. Dale nodded. He trotted back to the huddle and looked behind him and saw Bigelow snickering. Dale knew it. He hadn't seen him but Bigelow was the only guy on Alpha that would resort to playing dirty.

Two plays later, on third and five, Dale told Krupp to look for him. He could easily beat his man over the middle for the first down. Krupp, realizing that Omega actually had a chance at an upset, nodded.

Dale lined up and looked at Bigelow standing at middle linebacker. Butch smiled his humorless, boarish smile.

On hike Dale ran his short pattern and found an opening across the middle. Krupp threw the ball high. Dale jumped for it and as soon as he caught the ball he felt the back of Bigelow's hand hitting just below his groin, not making direct contact. Dale didn't care. As soon as he was "tackled," he kept the ball and walked over to Bigelow and told him he'd better stop.

"Stop what?" Butch asked, with unconvincing innocence.

"You know what."

"And if I don't?"

Dale hurled the ball at Bigelow's groin. His throw was too high and the ball bounced off his Butch's belly and bounded across the field. Butch, realizing he was unracked, rushed at Dale. Dale waited, crouching a little. Bigelow tried to hit him high. Dale ducked, deftly slid to the side, and grabbed Butch around the thighs and threw him forward, using Bigelow's momentum to lift him into the air. Bigelow, surprised to be airborne, flailed at the air before crashing down on his shoulder. As soon as Butch hit the ground, Dale knew something was wrong. He heard a snap like a small tree branch breaking and Bigelow groaned. All the players gathered around Butch, who writhed on the ground, his right hand clasping his left collarbone.

"I think it's busted," Bigelow muttered through clenched teeth.

K. C. and Phelps helped Bigelow to his feet. Since there wasn't a trainer present, K. C. said they'd have to take him to the hospital. Bigelow breathed hard through his nose, trying not to show any pain. Dale had to give him credit. He was a tough guy.

The referee called for the captains and ruled the game officially over. Alpha won, 22-16, even though there were three minutes left and Omega was on the march at the Alpha twenty-two.

Dale didn't feel guilty exactly, although he knew he was mostly responsible for his team's loss. He'd scored both his team's touchdowns and he and Chris had made several athletic snatches of Krupp's erratic passes. When the Owls walked off the field, Dale told Chris and a couple of other guys that he was sorry about losing his cool and costing them the game. Chris shook his head and said Dale had nothing to feel sorry about. His play had kept them in contention.

Dale didn't mean for Bigelow to get hurt; well, not seriously hurt. He had meant to rack him with the football. But since Bigelow had racked him once and had tried two other times, he felt justified.

He didn't know if the other guys agreed with Chris's view. Since the game ended in such a strange way, the two teams didn't shake hands as they usually did. The players just wandered off the field. Krupp didn't say anything encouraging to Dale but he didn't chastise him either.

"I saw Bigelow playing dirty," Chris said. "You just defended yourself."

"Yeah, but if other people didn't see Bigelow playing dirty, they'll think I started it all."

Chris couldn't think of an answer for that.

Dale had never ridden in Amanda's car. Now he sat in the passenger seat of the white

Mercury Marquis and wondered what was wrong with her.

She hadn't said much since he'd got in. Maybe she was nervous driving and had to concentrate so she couldn't talk. Dale watched her as she stared ahead and drove the automobile down the highway to the City. She was taking him to JR's Chicken Ranch as her "twirp" date. He supposed she'd chosen that place because it had really good fried chicken. When she asked him to be her date, she'd asked what his favorite dish was and that's what he'd said.

The twirp date was the real reason for having Twirp Week on campus. The tradition allowed the girls to ask the boys for a date. The girls even paid for the date. Yesterday, the girls had played the annual powder-puff flag football game at Galilee High School stadium. Since Amanda didn't play, Dale hadn't gone. He didn't care about watching girls play flag football even if it was supposed to be a joke. Chris told him about the halftime ceremony where the twirp king is crowned. Five guys actually dressed up in odd costumes, not quite in drag because that would be too weird for Nazarene decorum, but usually wearing their Bleacher Bums clothes along with wigs or clown noses and other odd touches. To Dale, that sounded a little like the lettermen's club initiation in high school where the inductees wore dresses, wigs, and makeup for an afternoon. Dale had refused to participate in the charade. He'd been too shy. He couldn't imagine making a spectacle to himself even if it meant getting into lettermen's club. Dorfman had let him join anyway.

The conventions of the twirp date annoyed Dale. If the point was for girls to ask out boys, then why call them twirps? Weren't they, in fact, the opposite of twirps? Weren't the real twirps the boys that the girls didn't want to ask out? He supposed the whole pretense was a way of protecting the girl's ego. After all, if a boy didn't go out with a girl, then he was a twirp. If he did, the whole role-reversal aspect of the date was an acknowledged aberration. Afterwards, the boys still asked girls out. They still paid for the dates. Dale decided that Twirp Week was just a way of encouraging social interaction between the sexes. After that first date, the girl probably hoped her twirp date would then ask her out on a real date. Dale thought it was a lot of fuss. When he'd pointed out some of these inconsistencies to Amanda, she'd said it was a tradition. Don't overanalyze it. Just have fun. Well, it didn't seem that either of them were having fun.

"So, what's wrong?" Dale asked.

"Nothing."

Amanda wasn't a very good liar. She bit her lower lip, a certain sign she was upset.

"Come on, what is it? I know there's something bothering you. You haven't said hardly a word since we left campus."

Amanda blinked and then bit her lower lip again. She glanced at Dale, then looked back at the road as if uneasy about talking while driving. Since they were already off the highway and driving in the outskirts of the City, Dale told her to pull over to the side of the road. She slowed the car down, turned onto a residential street, and stopped. Dale looked around and noticed that they weren't too far from Trumbo's house. He wondered how Trumbo would react if he and Amanda just showed up at his house the way he had showed up at Dale's house. He smiled a little.

"What are you smiling at?" Amanda asked. Dale detected a note of asperity in her voice.

"Nothing. Just thinking of a guy I used to know."

A moment of silence. Then Amanda asked how Dale could have been so mean as to have hurt Butch.

Dale could hardly believe what he was hearing. He turned to her and saw her staring at him in an accusatory way.

"Were you at the game?" He hadn't seen her in the stands, but then he didn't like looking at the people looking at him. He tried to ignore them.

"Yes, I was. I was with Gretchen and Mary Jane."

"And you saw what happened?"

"Yes, I did."

"Did you see *all* that happened?"

"I saw you attack Butch. I saw you break his collarbone. He had to go to the emergency room."

Dale shook his head in disbelief. He imagined this was the story going through campus. That he had attacked Butch! He didn't like the way Amanda's voice sounded so concerned for Bigelow. Dale wondered if she liked the thug.

"Why do you care so much about what happened to Butch?"

"I don't like seeing anyone get hurt."

"Yeah, but you sound upset. You sound like you are concerned about poor Bigelow."

"I'm concerned about him as I would be for any human being," she said, a note of strain sounding in her voice.

"Bigelow hardly qualifies."

Dale knew he'd made a mistake. He knew he'd sounded cruel. He felt angry with himself and with Amanda for forcing him into his mistake. He stared at Amanda and saw that her eyes were shiny as her face registered her disapproval for his callous words.

"I didn't mean that," Dale said, not entirely being truthful. "But you seem to care about Butch. Why?"

"I just feel a little sorry for him," she said, rather quietly.

Amanda felt sorry for Butch? Dale couldn't figure out girls. Butch was the last guy she should feel sorry for. He had a good family; he had all kinds of advantages; he never seemed to pay for his nastiness. Yeah, Amanda should feel sorry for Bigelow.

"You really feel sorry for him?"

"A little. I've known him for most of my life. I know he overdoes things, but I know he doesn't mean to. He just gets confused."

"How do you know these things?"

"What do you mean?"

"How do you know how Butch *feels* about these things?"

"I don't know. I mean, he's told me."

Dale stared at her. He wondered how many times she'd been with Bigelow. He knew of only one official date. The time Bigelow took her to the all-sports banquet during senior year. But he should have guessed there were other dates. Maybe the two of them had dated a lot last year. Dale felt a little sick in his stomach. Not as bad as two nights ago when Bigelow racked him, but bad enough.

"How many times did you go out with him?"

Dale could tell by Amanda's reaction that his voice was harsher than he intended. Her face flushed and she jerked her hands off the steering wheel.

"That's none of your business, Dale."

"What did he do to you? Did he kiss you?"

"Dale, I'm not discussing such things."

"How many times did he kiss you? Did he do more than that?"

Amanda's blush deepened and her eyes grew wide with offense. She opened her mouth as if to speak, but no words came out. He saw tears glistening in her eyes.

"Okay, I know. It's none of my business."

Dale threw up his hands and stared out his side window. He hated thinking about Amanda and Bigelow together. If he'd thought about it Thursday night he would have tried to do more than just rack Bigelow.

Dale turned back to Amanda and saw a tear trickle down her cheek. She made no noise. She stared out the windshield as still as a statue, but that one tear shamed him.

"I'm sorry, Amanda," he said, sliding closer to her.

She leaned away from him and he heard her stifle a sob. She raised a hand to her mouth and turned her face to her window.

"Amanda, you're too trusting. Butch is a jerk. You don't really know him. If you heard some of the things –"

Dale wondered if he should tell her what Bigelow had said that one time on the bus after the basketball game in ninth grade. How he'd like to stick something up her. He decided not to tell her even though it would make his case stronger.

"He wouldn't let you out of his car," Dale said, thinking Bigelow's actions rather than his words might be just as persuasive. "What kind of guy would do that?"

"He called and said he was sorry," Amanda said, her voice muffled under her hand.

"Yeah, he's sorry. But what would he do the next time? There's something wrong with him. He's a bully. He likes hurting people."

Amanda turned to him and Dale felt a wave of sorrow and regret wash over him seeing the tear stains on her cheeks. But she wasn't crying any longer.

"Well, what about you? You like hurting people, too."

"I do not."

"You hurt Butch."

"Only to protect myself."

Dale wondered if that was true. He didn't have to throw the football at Bigelow. He realized that he did want to hurt Butch. But he wasn't going to confess that to Amanda. Not now.

"You didn't see everything," he said. "You didn't see Butch playing dirty."

"What do you mean?"

"I mean the unnecessary roughness for one thing."

"I saw the penalty. Butch can get carried away at times."

"Yeah, well, he racked me, too."

"Racked?"

Amanda wasn't familiar with that term. Dale guessed her younger brother had neglected to explain that juvenile male rite of passage.

"Yeah, racked."

"I don't know what that means."

She seemed to understand that it was something bad by the tone of Dale's voice. She asked what it meant. He was reluctant to tell her. He tried to describe it without being too graphic.

"It's when a guy hits another guy."

Amanda waited for more information.

"Hits him in a certain area." Dale nodded his head down toward his lap.

"Dale, I don't know –" Then she seemed to understand. Her mouth opened in surprise and her eyes widened with alarm. "Butch did that?"

"Yeah, three times."

"Were you hurt?"

Dale thought about making a joke but he couldn't tease her with that concerned look on her pretty face.

"Yes, of course."

"Oh, I'm sorry. I didn't know."

"Yeah, I guess no one does except some of the guys on the field."

Amanda looked at him with a conciliatory expression. Dale shrugged, then looked her in the eyes. He liked the way the tears made her blue eyes sparkle. He reached for her and she allowed herself to be held.

Dale had to make one last point. "You're such a good person you don't realize that some people aren't."

"I'm not such a good person."

"Yes, you are. But some people aren't. Like Butch."

Dale told Amanda about the time in football practice when Bigelow smashed Clifford and wouldn't stop. How Butch pounded into him even when Clifford lay sprawled on the ground.

"That's awful," she said, shuddering.

"Yeah, well that's why I think there's something wrong with Butch."

Dale put his arm around Amanda and they sat quietly for a few moments. Dale wondered what she was thinking. Just when he was about to ask, she told him that she had gone out with Butch a couple of times. But it was nothing serious.

"Really? Nothing serious?"

Amanda nodded. "I mean, he wanted to keep on dating, but I didn't."

Dale felt that dissipated anger reforming inside him. He loathed the idea of Bigelow dating Amanda even once. He took a deep breath and willed the anger away.

"Once, he did try and do more than kiss me," she said.

Dale felt his arm tighten but he forced himself to relax. "What happened?" he asked, careful to keep his voice under control.

"We were in his car and he kissed me. Then he started putting his hands on me where I didn't want them to be and I told him no, but he kept on. Then I reached over and honked his horn."

Dale thought that was an unfortunate choice of words. But he asked what happened next.

"He stopped. I held the horn for a long time and it made a lot of noise. He apologized and I went in. That was our last date."

Dale said nothing. He remembered Wendy honking the horn of her car that awful night. But she'd honked it for an entirely different reason.

"Butch called and said he was sorry. He said he couldn't help himself."

"Yeah, well, that's what Genghis Khan used to say, too."

Amanda laughed. Maybe she was getting used to his sense of humor.

She leaned closer to him and Dale kissed her. He kissed her longer and more deeply than ever before. He put his free hand on her hip. He felt the fabric of her slip underneath her dress. As he kissed her again, he breathed in her scent. Subtle floral perfume. Clean skin and hair. She smelled sort of dewy. He liked it. He kissed her cheeks and tasted the salt from her dried tears.

She gently separated from him. "Dale," she said, "we're supposed to go to dinner."

He felt disappointed. This would be a good place and time to make out. He really wanted to do that with Amanda. But he knew he had to exercise patience.

"Right," he said. He took his hand off her hip, the tips of his fingers still sensing its full softness.

Amanda scooted back under the wheel. Dale didn't like her driving him. He said, why didn't she let him drive.

"You want to drive?"

"Yeah. I'd like to see how your car drives."

"Oh, this isn't really my car. It's one of the cars my father gets from the bank to drive."

"What do you mean?"

"The bank repossess cars and my father brings them home for a while."

Dale thought that was odd. "Why does he do that?"

"I don't know."

"Well, I've never driven a repo either, so slide over."

Dale got out and walked over to the driver's side and got in. He started the car and started to put it in gear. He smiled when Amanda scooted closer to him.

"The girl is supposed to take the boy on a date during Twirp Week," she reminded him.

Dale drove the car down the street. "Yeah, but I'm not a twirp."

Sylvester Fish caught up with Dale after their Writing for Christian Publications class. He asked Dale if he'd checked his campus mailbox today.

"Yeah, as a matter of fact."

"Oh, I see."

He listened to Fish's labored breath. He wondered if Fish were out of breath from jogging to catch him or because he was simply excited to think that Dale was in trouble.

"How do you know about it anyway?"

Dale referred to the letter from the dean of student activities. He had been asked to speak to Dean Pierce tomorrow afternoon at four.

"I work in the student mail room," Sylvester said, the thin lips of his long mouth turning up at the corners. Dale guessed that was Fish's smile.

"I bet you enjoy your work, don't you?"

"Yes, as a matter of fact, I do. The hours are convenient and –"

"Forget it, Fish. I was being sardonic."

Dale felt a little sorry for Sylvester. He didn't seem to have much understanding for irony. Dale had detected this intellectual blind spot in him in class as well.

"Yes, I see," said Fish in his typically humorless way.

"I got to go," said Dale. He turned, then paused and looked back at Fish. "Say, I'll let you know what Dean Pierce says."

Fish's eyebrows danced in approval. Then, seeing Dale's sarcastic smile, his face returned to its usual impassive state. Dale waved bye and walked across campus to his next class, one he liked, Political Philosophy from Ancient to Medieval. There Dr. Prescott and the class of five students knew and appreciated irony, paradox, and all sorts of other fun intellectual techniques.

The next day at four o'clock Dale sat in the waiting area of Dr. Pierce's office. The secretary, an elderly woman with white hair and glasses, told him he could go in now.

Dale said thanks and opened the door. He saw Dean Pierce sitting at his desk and K. C., Phelps, and Krupp seated in three chairs across from the dean's large oak desk.

The dean told Dale to have a seat. He took the open chair next to Krupp. He felt uneasy being the last one to join the discussion, if that was what it was. Dale studied Dean Pierce. Even sitting, he could tell he was rather tall and thin, with a long, plain, rather sour-looking face and round spectacles. He had short, neatly trimmed gray-brown hair. Dale thought Dr. Pierce looked like Woodrow Wilson, or at least the photos he'd seen.

"Glad to have you with us, Audie – excuse me, you go by Dale, don't you?"

Dale said yes.

"At any rate, these three fellows and I have been discussing the incident that took place last Thursday at the intramural football game."

Dean Pierce turned to Dale. He thought the dean's eyes looked less severe than the rest of him. They were a sort of mild brown. Dale glanced at the three fellows. They returned his glance but didn't smile.

"I wanted to speak to the two captains of the respective teams first before I spoke to you."

Dale nodded but he didn't know what K. C. was doing here because he wasn't the captain of the Alpha team. Phelps was. But Dale didn't mind. Even though K. C. was Butch's best friend, he knew he was a fair-minded kind of guy.

"I've heard what these three gentlemen have had to say and now I'd like to get your version."

Dale thought that was an interesting choice of words, "his version." In a way, he was glad to learn that Dr. Pierce believed in different versions of things.

Dale told him as simply as he could that Bigelow had been playing dirty all game. He not only hit him when he blocked him, which was against the rules, he also hit him in the groin once and tried twice more. Dale got angry, confronted him, and threw the football at him. Then Butch charged him and he defended himself and sort of threw him down. He'd really just used Bigelow's momentum against him.

401

The dean nodded his head after Dale finished his account. He said that was essentially what the other three young men had told him. Dale glanced at them again, a little surprised that Phelps had told the story that favored Dale. He began to like Phelps.

Dean Pierce removed his glasses and cleaned them with a white handkerchief. Dale thought the dean's eyes definitely looked more kindly in their natural myopic state.

"Now, I'd like to know if you intended to hit Mr. Bigelow in the groin with your throw?"

Dale glanced at the other three guys. They didn't look at him. Dale knew he could lie. There wasn't any way they could prove he meant to hit Bigelow in the groin. But he didn't want to lie about his feelings about Butch.

"Yes, that's what I intended to do," Dale said. It was true. He wanted to hurt Bigelow the way Butch had hurt him.

The dean nodded and put his glasses back on. "I appreciate your honesty, Dale. I think a one-week suspension will suffice."

"From school?" Dale asked.

"Oh, no. From intramural football."

When Dean Pierce rose, the four young men did too. The dean reached over and offered his hand to Dale. He shook it. Then the dean shook the hands of the other three guys and thanked them for coming. The four students left his office and walked outside the administration building.

"I don't think you should have gotten any suspension," said Phelps.

"Me neither," said K. C. "Butch deserved what he got. Well, maybe not a broken collarbone, but he deserved to get a taste of his own medicine."

Dale nodded at them. He noticed that Phelps didn't look as imposing in his regular clothes. He was about six feet tall and 170 pounds. Dale sort of liked his long, mulish face. It reminded him of his grandpa's face except that it wasn't so old and wrinkled.

Phelps and Krupp said they had to go to the league meeting for team captains. Dale and K. C. watched them amble off together.

"Some of the Alpha guys wanted you kicked off intramural football for good," said K. C.

Dale asked who. K. C. mentioned five of them. Dale didn't know any of them well except for Bigelow. Then K. C. listed the six guys who thought Dale was justified. Dale knew K. C., Phelps, Keaton, and Eugene of the six. Dale noticed that K. C. hadn't mentioned Henshaw. He asked how Bobby voted.

"Oh, he abstained at first."

"Abstained?"

"Yeah. He said he didn't see enough of the evidence to vote."

Dale felt a little disappointed in Henshaw. Maybe he hadn't seen enough. But he'd been right on the football field. How could he have overlooked Butch's overly aggressive behavior and dirty play?

"You said he abstained at first. So, he finally voted?"

"Phelps and Greene said Henshaw should vote just to get all the team members votes."

"So, how did he vote?"

"He voted in your favor," said K. C.

Dale wondered what would have happened if Henshaw had voted against him. That would have resulted in a six-six tie. Dale wondered how Dean Pierce would have factored that into his punishment.

"You know, Butch is pretty angry with me," said K. C.

"Yeah, I imagine so." Best buddies were supposed to stick up for one another. Maybe even when one of them was wrong. "Sorry about that."

"Ah, that's okay." K. C. smiled his broad, TR smile. "Butch has got to learn not to overdue things. If he doesn't like me for taking a stand against his dirty play, then tough."

Dale slapped K. C. on the shoulder. K. C. said he had to scoot. Dale said so long and the boys parted.

Dale walked across campus to the parking lot. He thought about Henshaw's reluctance to cast a vote. He wondered about Bobby's motive. He knew Henshaw liked him. Maybe Henshaw had just done the politic thing. Dale was beginning to suspect that even though some influential people on campus liked him, he still wasn't one of them.

## Chapter 3: *Sinning in one's heart; bubblegum; ascending from the cave*

Dale thought Dr. Prescott sounded better than he looked. His voice was deep and resonant. In the seminar room, his baritone voice echoed in a Jovian way. His person, however, was less impressive. Slightly taller than Dale, he had a slender, almost boyish build. His suits never seemed to fit him quite right. The dark one seemed too small; the gray one seemed too large. Dale guessed his age at around thirty, but Dr. Prescott already had a bald spot on the crown of his head. He wore his reddish brown hair short. Little curly tufts formed a circle around his forehead, which reminded Dale of the style of hair found on Greek statues. Dr. Prescott had a homely face, with small, sharp brown eyes, a large, flat nose, and a thick-lipped mouth.

Dr. Prescott sat in his chair at the desk with his five students. Besides Dale, there were Henshaw, Eugene, Stan, and a sophomore, Aaron Short, who Dale still didn't know very well personally, although Short spoke a lot in class.

Dr. Prescott leaned back in his chair and balanced it on its two rear legs. He had a tolerant smile on his face as he listened to Eugene debate Stan about the upcoming presidential election. The class was supposed to be discussing Aristotle's political ethics, but as occasionally happened in class, discussion had veered off into the contemporary.

Stan said Ford, although a moderate, was still a Republican and the Nazarene community should vote for him. Eugene said that Carter, although a Democrat, was an evangelical and all evangelicals ought to vote for him. Aaron Short agreed with Stan. Carter couldn't be trusted. After all, he gave an interview in *Playboy* magazine.

Dr. Prescott asked if anybody had read it. All five of the students remained silent. If they confessed to that, who would believe they didn't look at the photos?

Dr. Prescott leaned forward and brought his chair back down on all fours. "Well, I read it," he announced without any self-consciousness. Dale admired that. "It was an honest outreach to a larger community of voters. After all, aren't Christians supposed to minister to sinners? So, too, shouldn't a Christian politician seek out non-Christian voters?"

Dale thought the professor had made a good point. Eugene, and even Stan, nodded, too.

Short pointed out that Carter had confessed to lusting in his heart.

"Yes," said Dr. Prescott. "What's your point?"

"That Carter is a sinner."

"Aren't we all sinners?" asked Dr. Prescott.

Short remained silent. Dale looked more closely at him. He had rather long light brown hair, worn swept back off his forehead. His features were sleek and symmetrical. His hazel eyes weren't especially large but they had a shiny sincerity to them. Most noticeable of all, was his smiling mouth. Aaron seemed to smile all the time. He had different kinds of smiles: big, broad, hearty smiles; medium, good-natured grins; and small, tolerant smirks that he employed for his classroom adversaries. Right now, Short's rather handsome face smirked a little at Dr. Prescott because he couldn't think of a valid reply to his question.

Eugene pointed out that in the *Playboy* interview Carter seemed to say that lusting in one's heart was the same as actually committing adultery.

Dr. Prescott nodded. "In a spiritual sense, isn't that true?"

Dale jumped in. "You mean if we want to sin but don't actually do it, we've spiritually sinned anyway?"

Dr. Prescott smiled.

"But there is a distinction," said Eugene.

Dale hoped so. Otherwise, he'd done an awfully lot of sinning.

"Is there?" asked Dr. Prescott.

The five young men considered the question. Sometimes they didn't appreciate Dr. Prescott's Socratic method of teaching. It put a lot of weight on their shoulders.

"Surely, a man who actually sins is doing something worse than a man who just imagines it," said Short.

Dr. Prescott smiled.

"Maybe not just imagining it," said Dale. "Nothing so casual. But actually wanting, desiring to sin but not actually doing it. Maybe that is the same as actually doing it. In a spiritual sense, I mean."

"Isn't the spiritual the ultimate reality?" asked Dr. Prescott.

"I still maintain there's a distinction between wanting to do something and actually doing it," said Short.

"But isn't that the point of the parable about the prodigal son?" asked Dale.

He'd just reread that part of the Bible for his New Testament class. The parable had bothered him at first. He'd identified with the good, older brother. But after he carefully reread it, Dale began to see it in a different light.

"What do you mean?" asked Stan. "The prodigal son didn't lust in his heart."

Stan, Eugene, and Short chuckled.

"Yes, but the parable reveals that the older brother only did good because he thought he should. His actions didn't really have any spiritual truth to them. He acted out of convention. Therefore, his actions were spiritually empty."

"Isn't truth, like sin, always truth or always sin?" asked Eugene.

"Is it?" asked Dr. Prescott.

"I think so," said Eugene. When Dr. Prescott gave him an inquiring look, Eugene shook his head. "At least, I thought so."

"Isn't this discussion getting off the topic?" asked Stan. "And professor, please don't say, 'Is it?'"

Everyone in the class, except for Henshaw, laughed.

"Robert," Dr. Prescott said, using Henshaw's proper first name, "you've been unusually quiet. What do you say?"

Henshaw smiled. "In spite of your persuasive Socratic method, Dr. Prescott, I'm voting for Ford just the same."

This time, all of them laughed.

Henshaw caught up with Dale outside of class. He said Dale had made some perceptive comments. Dale said thanks. He asked why Henshaw didn't speak more.

"I was thinking," he said.

Even though Dale had been disappointed in Henshaw's reluctance to side with him in the Bigelow incident, he still liked him. Even if he were tall, intelligent, and handsome, he didn't act superior. He had a sincerity, an earnestness, that Dale liked.

"Do you really think the spiritual is the ultimate reality?" Henshaw asked.

"Yeah, I think I do."

Dale also thought people only caught glimpses of it in their daily lives. As in Plato's cave, people were shrouded in darkness and when they ascended from the gloom they couldn't bear the brilliance of the Truth for long.

"Then how does someone reconcile the spiritual with the mundane?" Henshaw asked. "Or, to make it more applicable to class, how does one bring truth to politics?"

"That's a good question." Dale wasn't especially interested in day-to-day politics. For instance, he didn't really care if Carter or Ford won. He guessed he'd vote for Carter just because his grandpa was a Democrat. "You ought to ask Dr. Prescott that."

"Oh, I will." Henshaw snapped out of his reverie. He slapped Dale on the shoulder. "Gotta go. See you around."

Dale said so long and watched Henshaw take his long strides through campus. He was only a sophomore but already everyone thought of him as the one of the student leaders. Across the quad, Dale saw Abigail walking out of the student union. She joined Henshaw. Together they set off to another part of campus, to another kind of world that Dale knew little about.


On the GNC campus, Dale seemed immersed in God. Professors, except Dr. Prescott, prayed before class. Students were required to attend chapel. People openly spoke about their personal relationship with Jesus. Most of the music played on campus was religious contemporary. In the cafeteria, people prayed before every meal. And the magnificent First Church was only three blocks away. Most students attended the First Church on Wednesday night, and twice on Sundays. Some went to the smaller Nazarene church in the City. Those who weren't Nazarene attended their denominational church either in town or in the City. Dale suspected he was one of the few students who didn't go to Sunday school and morning services.

Now, with revival week starting, the religious intensity on campus and in the Nazarene community hit its peak. One of the activities preceding the preaching of the evangelist was the film version of the Hal Lindsey book, *The Late Great Planet Earth*. Dale hadn't read the book, but he recalled some of the Nazarene kids in high school talking about it. So, he decided to go see the film with Chris.

The film made the argument that the Rapture, the Great Tribulation, and Armageddon were close at hand. Dale had heard such notions from when he was sort of a Witness, but the film made a more plausible argument because it focused on Biblical prophesies concerning Israel and the Arab world. According to film, all Biblical prophecies about the End Times were being brought about by the conflict in the Middle East. Soon, very soon, Armageddon would take place. Only true believing Christians would be spared and instantaneously transported to heaven, or "raptured." After a period of intense suffering for those people who convert to Christianity called the Great Tribulation, Jesus would return to earth and lead his celestial army in the battle of Armageddon against Satan and his diabolical forces. Jesus would win, of course, and cast the vanquished devil into the bottomless pit for one thousand years.

While watching the film, Dale couldn't quite believe the message intellectually; but he nevertheless felt a tingling when he imagined all of it happening for real. It was a strange feeling. He wondered what he'd do if Chris, Amanda, and all his other Christian friends suddenly disappeared, with only their clothes left behind. Dale imagined he'd be about the only one left on campus. He was a Christian but he didn't think he was the right kind. He was too doubting and skeptical. Even as he watched the film he felt his skepticism interfering with the message.

After seeing the film, Dale drove home ruminating about the Rapture and how he'd be left behind to face the Great Tribulation. Jesse had warned him about his fate before but he hadn't believed her. Now, after seeing *The Late Great Planet Earth*, he began to have doubts about his doubts.

When he got home, he found Jesse planted on the couch smoking and watching television. The doctor had given her medicine to take to help keep her mentally stable. Dale made sure she took her medicine. He didn't want to have to commit her again.

"Hi, Mom," Dale said.

He noticed she was watching *The Towering Inferno*. He remembered seeing that movie in the theatre with Wendy. He wondered if Wendy was the right kind of Christian.

Jesse nodded at him and continued smoking and watching.

"Hey, do you remember if the Jehovah Witnesses believe in the Rapture?"

Jesse took the cigarette out of her mouth. "The Rapture?"

"Yeah, you know. When Christians are instantaneously transported to heaven before the Great Tribulation."

Jesse took a puff of cigarette. "Can't say I do, Dale."

"Can't *say* you remember, or you *don't* remember?"

Jesse looked at him as if he'd spoken Aramaic. "What in tarnation are you talkin' about?"

Dale shook his head. Maybe his philosophy class was influencing him too much. "Forget it," he said.

Jesse had already forgotten quite a few things. Dale supposed the electroshock therapy had erased some of her memory. He sometimes thought the electroshock therapy was a less violent, less invasive form of a lobotomy. Instead of cutting a chunk out of her brain, the doctors seemed to have short-circuited parts of her brain. It had worked. She was calmer, more docile. But part of her had disappeared. Not only the part that made her crazy, but also some of the part that made her Jesse.

Dale walked down the hall and knocked on June May's door. She said come in. He opened the door and saw June May, chewing gum, wearing her cheerleading uniform and lying on her stomach on her bed.

"Why are you wearing your cheerleader's uniform?"

"I dunno," June May said. She wasn't studying. Instead she was reading *Cosmopolitan*.

Dale hoped Blackie was wrong and schizophrenia wasn't hereditary. June May was starting to look like a prime candidate.

"What do you mean, you don't know?"

June May blew a big bubble at him. Dale waited, hoping it would blow up in her face. She sucked the air out of it and the pink goo collapsed on her lips. She used her tongue to pull it into her mouth. Finally, she spoke. "I just felt like it, *okay*?"

"Why are you reading that magazine?" he asked, although he found the cover interesting. It showed a partially nude woman gazing wantonly at the camera.

"Hey, you're not my father." She started to blow another bubble.

Dale, hardly listening to his sister, was still thinking about the cover. Why was it that magazines for girls had such sexy, half-naked women on their covers? A few weeks ago, he'd picked up an older issue of her *Cosmopolitan* and felt almost as aroused looking at the cover and the ads inside as he did looking at *Playboy*. Well, he'd mostly stopped looking at such magazines since he'd become a Nazarene.

"I don't think you're mature enough to read such a magazine," he said, only partly teasing.

"I'm seventeen. That's old enough to read *Cosmo*."

She blew the bubble. It expanded to an even larger size than the previous one.

Dale couldn't resist. He thrust his arm out like a fencer and poked the bubble with his finger. It burst in her face.

June May wailed.

"Touché," Dale said.

June May clawed at the sticky mess covering her mouth and nose. "Mom!" She cried. "Dale's victimizing me again!"

He closed the door, savoring his sister's wails, and walked to his room. He guessed that wasn't a Christian thing to do, but at least he hadn't victimized her in his heart.

Dale wasn't certain if he really felt moved by the spirit of God or if he just wanted to think he was being moved. He sat in his seat and listened to the music and the evangelist, Roscoe Rose. The evangelist kept saying that Jesus was here waiting to enter his heart. All he had to do was ask. Didn't he want a personal relationship with Jesus? Didn't he want to know the most blessed feeling in the world, in the universe? Didn't he want to dedicate his life to Jesus and know the blessed peace that it would bring?

Dale opened his eyes and glanced at Amanda. She looked almost saintly sitting in her seat, her head bowed, her eyes closed, her lips gently pressed together. At that moment, he thought she displayed that ineffable quality – a spiritual beauty – that he'd always been attracted to.

He closed his eyes and bowed his head and let the spirit of God enter his soul. Or so he thought. Maybe that was his problem, he thought too much. How did he feel? He felt strange. He felt as if his brain was battling with his heart. His head said this was illogical. His heart, or wherever emotions actually resided, felt anxious. He didn't want to go to the altar. He didn't want to get up and walk down in front of everyone, even if everyone had their eyes closed and heads bowed.

The music soothed him *and* provoked him. The sound of the organ annoyed him yet the melody enticed him. Dale thought about the Roscoe Rose's message. It had been simple. He'd delivered it simply. Jesus loves you. He loves *you*. Accept Him and you would have everlasting life. That simple, that beautiful. Open your heart to Jesus and your life will be forever changed. You will be united with the greatest force in the universe. You will be filled with His spirit. You will be saved.

Most of what Roscoe Rose said wasn't intellectually compelling to Dale, but he responded to the part of being united with the greatest force in the universe. He thought about the philosophy he'd been reading. He thought about the Platonic Ideal. He liked the idea that there was a perfect Mind, a perfect Whole, and he thought that was what Jesus and God really were. People called it different names. He didn't care about names. What mattered was the underlying Truth.

Dale felt something happening to him. It wasn't just the music or Roscoe Rose's entreaties. Rather, he felt like he was ascending from the darkness of the cave. He felt like he was drawing closer and closer to the Truth, to the Perfect Ideal, to God Himself.

He rose, feeling lighter than air. He seemed to float toward the altar. He saw other mortals kneeling at the altar and praying to Jesus. He found an open spot and knelt down. He prayed, too. He prayed to Jesus but that was just a name. A name people had to use because they couldn't comprehend the real name of Jesus or God or the Ultimate Truth. That was okay with him. He'd use that name. All he wanted was to be united with God. He wanted to know that which is unknowable. He wanted to penetrate the mystery of life, even if for a moment. That's all mortals could endure: a moment of Truth and then they sunk back down into the darkness of the cave.

Dale felt someone kneeling beside him. Another supplicant. Then he smelled that floral scent. He felt her hand on his. He opened his eyes and glanced over and saw Amanda kneeling beside him. She had her eyes closed and he looked at her perfect lips moving in prayer.

He bowed his head again but his moment of Truth had ended. Dale felt as if he'd already been cast back in the dark depths of the cave. He felt self-conscious and totally aware. He didn't look up when Roscoe Rose moved over to him. But he felt heavily the evangelist's presence. He heard Rose speaking but he didn't listen to the words. Instead, he listened to Amanda's dulcet voice murmuring beside him.

The service ended. Dale heard people leaving the sanctuary. He felt Amanda squeeze his hand. She was almost finished. He held her small, soft hand and felt its warmth. She squeezed his hand again. She'd never done that before. When she'd allowed him to hold her hand in the movie theatre the last time they'd gone, she hadn't offered him any encouragement.

Amanda rose and Dale did, too. She smiled serenely at him. He smiled back. He wasn't sure what kind of smile was on his face. He doubted it was serene. He heard some people crying as they remained at the altar. He guessed they had heavy burdens. He thought maybe he should have prayed for forgiveness. He now said a quick prayer asking to be forgiven for injuring Bigelow and for trying to seduce Sheba. Then he walked with Amanda out of the sanctuary into the cool, fresh air of an autumn evening.

"Wasn't that wonderful?" Amanda asked.

Dale said yes it was.

"Did you feel the spirit of the Lord?"

He said he did.

"Is that the first time you've been saved?"

Dale said yes, it was.

They walked toward the college. Dale saw some of Amanda's friends ahead of them. He slowed down their walk so they wouldn't catch up with them. He didn't want to talk about all this with people he didn't know well.

Amanda didn't seem to notice. She smiled and looked up at the inky heavens. She said she felt light as a feather.

Dale didn't feel quite so light. Amanda seemed content to revel in the spiritual afterglow. He felt like talking. He felt like analyzing what he'd gone through. But he knew that would spoil it for Amanda. He let her exult.

They walked across campus and headed for her dorm. It was Sunday night and she'd have to go in soon. Dale wished he could go up to her room. Just to talk. He'd only been up there one time before, not counting the time he helped her move in. Boys weren't allowed in the girls' dorm rooms except on Halloween to trick-or-treat. A week ago, Dale had been permitted to enter, although he didn't have a trick-or-treat bag with him. He went to Amanda's room and sat in her beanbag chair while she and Hope gave candy to the boys that came by. Dale had examined her room. He thought her side of the room more refined and tasteful than Hope's. Amanda's side was neat and organized and the one poster of a person she had taped to the cinderblock wall was of a classical musician he'd never heard of. She also had a poster of the *Desiderata*, a poem that had been made into a popular recording a few years back. Dale thought the poem interesting. It was intended to be wisdom, he supposed. He liked the alternation between elevated sentiments and mundane realities.

Dale had been pondering so intently that he didn't notice that Amanda's joyous mood had changed. He noticed a pensive look on her face. He asked what was wrong.

"Can't you work the later weekend shift?"

"You mean the two to ten shift?"

"Yes."

"Then I'd be working most of Saturday night."

Amanda remained silent for a moment. "But you could go to Sunday school and morning services if you worked in the afternoon."

"Yeah, but the guy who has the later shift doesn't want to change."

"He doesn't?"

"No. I've already asked him. He's always worked that shift."

Dale knew he wasn't being completely truthful. He'd asked Charles Caron, the guy in question, how he'd liked his shift. Caron had said fine. Dale hadn't explored the matter after that. In fact, he preferred his shift. He had to get up early in the morning but then it was over by two in the afternoon and he had the rest of the day to watch sports, study, and take Amanda out in the evening. Also, the afternoon shift was busier. No, Dale thought his shift was perfect, but he didn't want to tell Amanda that.

"Well, I guess you can't help missing morning service then," Amanda said in a resigned way.

Dale wondered if she were worrying about the state of his spiritual condition.

"That bothers you, doesn't it?"

"Well, yes, it does, Dale. I mean, you're missing Sunday school and the morning service every week."

"Is attending church that important?"

Amanda stopped and looked at him as if he'd said something close to sacrilege.

"Of course. You need a weekly dose of spiritual nourishment."

Dose sounded more like medicine than nourishment, but Dale didn't tell her that. He knew she was sincere.

"Do you have to go to church to get spiritual nourishment?" he asked.

"I would say yes. I mean, that's the point of church. You need to develop a habit or otherwise your spiritual health is at stake."

"Lots of people can't go to church regularly."

"Such as?"

"Doctors. Soldiers. Sailors. People traveling on business. And sometimes police officers because they sometimes are assigned Sunday shifts."

"I suppose," Amanda said, but her voice told Dale she wasn't convinced.

"Look, I have to work."

He hadn't explained his situation to her in detail. She knew his parents were divorced. Dale had suggested that he had to pay for his "room and board" at home, which wasn't exactly so. Jesse hadn't asked him to pay rent yet. But she might. Since he was away from home most of the time, he bought most of his meals. He paid for gas for his car. He bought his own clothes. Jesse got an extra hundred for him but he never asked for any of it.

"I know," Amanda said. "I just wish you didn't have to work on Sunday."

"I can't get out of that."

He saw she seemed genuinely concerned. She bit her lower lip.

They came to her dormitory and Dale took her arm and led her to the parking lot for a little more privacy.

"I have an idea," he said. "It might make you feel better."

"Oh?"

"When I'm at work on Sunday morning, I'll have my own church service."

"What do you mean?"

"I mean, I'll read the Bible and pray. I'll read the same passage as the pastor. And I'll do it at the same time you are at First Church."

Amanda's face brightened. "Really?"

"Sure. That way, even though I won't physically be with you at First Church, I will be in spirit."

"That sounds nice," said Amanda.

Dale usually spent his hours at the Cimarron City high school reading his English novels for his independent study class. But if it made Amanda happy, he'd sacrifice an hour.

"That's a good idea, Dale. I especially like the idea that while I'm listening to the pastor read from the Bible you will be reading it, too. It's like we'll be experiencing the same thing; well, almost."

"No, we *will* be experiencing it together. Just not in the same physical location. In a way, that makes it even more special." Dale thought his plan seemed rather Platonic.

Amanda smiled. "That's true, isn't it?"

Dale walked her to the dormitory front door.

"That's right. Our minds, our souls, will be together. As you read along with the pastor, as you pray, you will know that I am doing the same thing and thinking about you."

The idea seemed to excite Amanda. She smiled as if she'd been told something pleasantly revelatory. She leaned toward Dale, then stopped. They weren't supposed to kiss. This wasn't a date. She'd almost forgot.

Dale wouldn't have minded but he knew she disliked public displays of affection, especially in front of her dormitory. So, he held her hand for a few seconds and said good night. She returned his goodnight and walked inside the dorm. He heard her laugh as she encountered a friend before the large, frosted glass door closed behind her.

He thought he was in trouble. Dr. Petry sat at his desk and perused Dale's latest paper. The professor read while holding a red pen poised above the paper. Dale didn't know why; he turned the paper in three days ago and Dr. Petry must have marked it already.

Dale had heard from Stan that Dr. Petry was twenty-nine. His job at GNC was his first. He'd finished his dissertation the previous summer after laboring four years on it. Dale didn't know if that was good or bad. Four years sounded like a long time to work on anything, but Stan, who had a brother in a doctoral program in theology, said spending four years on a dissertation wasn't unheard of.

Dr. Petry paused in his reading, and took off his tiny eyeglasses. Dale had never noticed before, but Dr. Petry had sort of a handsome face. He was tall, perhaps six foot four, and thin. He probably weighed no more than 160 pounds. But for all his leanness, he had fairly broad shoulders. His face, although long, fit together well. He had short dark hair, a narrow nose, a wide, full-lipped mouth, a strong chin, and large dark eyes that produced a penetrating gaze even when hid by his curious spectacles. His eyeglasses reminded Dale of Ben Franklin's and now as Dr. Petry put them back on, Dale thought they definitely changed his appearance for the worse.

"I believe this is your best paper," Dr. Petry said, handing Dale his work.

Dale could hardly believe it. He'd expected Dr. Petry to be offended by the banality of the paper. He'd deliberately wrote his assignment with clichés and trite phrases and simple, almost elementary sentences. He'd done so as a rebuke to Dr. Petry and his emphasis of mechanical correctness over content. If his teacher wanted perfect but vapid prose, then he would show him. Now, the joke was on him.

He glanced over the first page. Only a couple of red circles with codes written beside them. He'd forgot an apostrophe and he'd split an infinitive. He flipped the page and saw the copy on that page had been unmolested. His grade, a 96. Dr. Petry had deducted two points for each error. All in all, almost an immaculate composition.

But what of the content? What of the meaning? Dale had written nonsense. He'd written banalities. Yes, he'd done so on purpose to test the grammarian. Dale was appalled that Dr. Petry apparently didn't read for meaning at all; he simply saw the words and punctuation as parts of a verbal machine. As long as all the parts of the machine – the syntax, the punctuation, the spelling and grammar – fit together, it didn't matter if it didn't run. It was like checking out the mechanical and structural fitness of a Ferrari but not getting in, starting it up, and racing around the speedway.

"You liked this paper?"

Dr. Petry nodded slightly. He didn't like subjective terms like "like" so much. "It was an impressively correct paper. It was by far your best work."

"So, you think I should continue to write my assignments in this way?"

"Certainly. Continue to write as accurately as possible. You've made excellent progress."

"But Dr. Petry, shouldn't content matter, too? Shouldn't we read as much or more for what a writer says than how he says it?"

Actually, the issue wasn't so much content versus style as much as mere mechanical correctness versus meaning itself. But Dale didn't want to make it sound as if the professor was as oblivious to meaning as he thought he was.

"I'm not especially interested in what a writer *says*," Dr. Petry replied. "I'm more interested *how* he says what he says."

Dale had heard Dr. Petry had received his Ph.D. from a respected secular university in the east. Dale wondered how someone could graduate from a demanding program and not care about what a writer writes. He glanced over to the west wall above the bookcase and saw the framed Doctor of English in rhetoric and composition diploma. He'd vaguely heard of the university.

Perhaps Dr. Petry noticed the look of skepticism on Dale's face after he glanced at his framed diploma, because he added, "In our class, of course, content is important insofar as the proper Christian perspective is conveyed. Your paper did that as well."

Dale nodded. He'd written basically a parody of one of those devotional pieces he'd read in *Bread*, an evangelical magazine for young adults. He'd written that he loved Jesus. He spoke with Him every day. Sometimes he asked Him what clothes he should wear. Sometimes he asked Him what television show he should watch. Dale had written his paper in that kind of elementary prose on purpose to make fun of some of the pieces he'd read in class that *almost* proposed such trivial requests from Jesus. Dale wasn't making fun of Jesus or anyone's personal relationship with Him, but rather the penchant of some students to think of themselves as babies and Jesus as their daddy who dispensed advice on every quotidian and trivial concern. But Dr. Petry hadn't noticed that satiric intent or didn't care. Dale didn't know which.

"Is there anything else I can help you with?"

Dale was tempted to say, yeah, what's a gerund? But he already knew what one was and he feared that Dr. Petry would accept his question in earnest and drone on about the intricacies of grammar and syntax and all the other boring stuff. Instead, Dale said no, thanks, he'd see Dr. Petry in class, and then he left his spartan office.

Walking to the parking lot, Dale told himself that he at least knew how to get good grades in Dr. Petry's class: write correctly; write simplistically; write without adventure or style. Dale knew he had some problems with mechanics. He made mistakes with irregular verbs in particular. His spelling wasn't great. But that sort of thing could be corrected. What about writing with passion and style? What about making an astute point? Another one of Dale's weaknesses was that he tended to be wordy. Well, that was because he wanted to write about complicated issues and themes. It was difficult to write simply about complex ideas. He couldn't do it yet. His prose inevitably became entangled with itself.

He remembered all the red codes on his first two assignments. Dr. Petry had circled one of his sentence fragments in red ink and written "2a frag" in the margin. After class, Dale had told him it was an intentional fragment. Dr. Petry had replied that he didn't think there was any excuse to write a sentence fragment. Ever. Dale almost pointed out that he'd just spoken one, but he didn't.

He had glanced over his other mistakes and saw codes identifying his errors: "6-5 agr," mistake using a relative pronoun as a subject; "3 cs," comma splice; "27a ns," tense, mood, and voice. After his second paper, also bloodied with circles and codes, Dale became convinced that if he asked Dr. Petry to speak an entire sentence, maybe even a paragraph, using just codes, he could do it.

The Gradgrindian Dr. Petry didn't write any actual words on the papers he graded. He didn't comment on the content or the style or anything remotely human. He simply circled mistakes, wrote down codes corresponding to those mistakes, and wrote the numerical score. After receiving 78 and 85 on his first two assignments, Dale knew he was in danger of not getting an A. Now, with his 96, he still had a chance. He'd have to write really boringly in his next five assignments to raise his grade to an A. Dale thought he could do it: just be a machine churning out perfectly correct and perfectly inhuman prose.

For homecoming, Dale took Amanda to *Jacques*, a French restaurant in the City. Even though Amanda was taking a French language course, she didn't feel comfortable ordering in French and like Dale she simply gave the imperious waiter a number. She had number three, *truffles a la fromage*; he had number seven, *mallard l'orange*.

Dale thought the food and the restaurant too fancy, but Amanda seemed to enjoy it. He wondered why girls enjoyed such pretentious and overpriced places. The whole experience sort of reminded Dale of the pep club banquet back in high school. But since he'd never taken Amanda to any of the high school banquets, he didn't mind so much. He'd bought her a corsage, too, an orchid that impressed her. Dale didn't try to pin it on her; instead, Hope, who came down with Amanda to the lobby, did the honors, pinning it quite accurately to the bosom of Amanda's lovely blue satin gown.

The next night, Dale and Chris went to the homecoming game together. They were supposed to meet Amanda and Hope there. They walked into Beaumont gym and Dale was amazed at the huge crowd. He had no idea the Chiefs' basketball games were so well attended. People packed the rather small gym. The pep band blared. The quiet conversations of two thousand people produced a sustained drone. Dale and Chris scanned the student section. Finally, Chris spotted the two girls and they climbed the stairs, wedging their way down a row of bleachers until they came to Amanda and Hope. There was hardly enough room for them to fit, but they squeezed in. Dale didn't mind. His right leg and arm were pressed snugly against Amanda's. She wore a sweater and slacks, a rarity, and he liked feeling her warm leg against his.

GNC was playing one of their rivals, Oklahoma Baptist, and by half the Chiefs led by six. Dale didn't even know who the homecoming queen candidates were except for one: Laurie Page. He'd seen her walking on campus sometimes. She looked even prettier than she did in high school. He remembered gazing at her as she cheered when he was a sophomore. Now, when her name was announced as the 1976-77 homecoming queen, she smiled a dazzling smile.

The Chiefs poured it on in the second half and won easily, 84-70. Dale and Chris escorted the girls down the bleacher steps and were walking out of the gym when they saw Mrs. Page. Dale had last seen her that day in high school when she broke down and ran out of the classroom. The four of them walked over to her. They said hello and Mrs. Page smiled and asked how they all were doing. Dale noticed that she didn't have her old vivacious quality. Her voice was friendly but without music. When she smiled, her eyes, with faint dark circles underneath them, didn't show any happiness. Dale wanted to ask her if she had any good plays to recommend for him to read, but before he could find an opening in the conversation, an older couple appeared. They seemed to be waiting to take Mrs. Page somewhere. The four of them said good-bye and they left the gym and walked into the unseasonably warm mid-November night.

Dale said that Mrs. Page didn't look quite well. And she looked older than she should since the year and a half that he'd last seen her.

The other three seemed uneasy about his observations. He looked at them and wondered what he'd said that was so impolite.

"Did I say something wrong?"

"Not exactly," Amanda said.

She said he probably remembered how hard Portia's death had been on Mrs. Page. Dale nodded. Amanda said on the anniversary of Portia's death last spring, Mrs. Page fell into a deep depression. She became so disturbed that she began questioning her faith. She stopped going to church. She blamed God for allowing Portia to die in childbirth.

Amanda paused. Dale found all this quite interesting. Since he'd been going to CSU then and didn't attend the First Church yet, he hadn't heard any of this. He asked Amanda what happened after that.

"One of the assistant pastors met with her regularly and prayed with her. They read the Bible, especially the parts that describe the sacrifices people have to make. Slowly, she got better. Now, she's back teaching and is attending church."

Dale said he was glad. Mrs. Page was one of his favorite teachers.

Amanda and Chris agreed. Hope, of course, hadn't had her for a teacher. But she said Mrs. Page was a wonderful woman.

Dale almost said "is," but he knew what Hope meant. Mrs. Page was different. He guessed she was only in her late forties, but she had the manner of a much older woman. He missed her vivacity, her energy, that acute look in her blue eyes. All of that was gone.

They walked over to the student union for the ice cream social. They found their seats and Dale and Chris went to the ice cream bar to get sundaes for themselves and to bring the girls just a little vanilla ice cream in a cup. Before going on their errand, Chris had joked with them. "Watching your figures, eh?" Neither Amanda nor Hope looked amused. Dale wondered why Hope would go on a diet. She may have gained a few pounds since school started, but she was still on the scrawny side.

While topping their sundaes, Chris told Dale he had some interesting news. He waited while watching Chris top his ice cream with all the extras. Dale thought it was the ice cream equivalent of mixing one's drinks.

"Bigelow's dropped out of school."

Dale asked him how he knew.

"He's a business major like me. We were in three classes together. He's not been to one class for over a week. Besides, that's what K. C. said."

"Why did he do that?" Dale asked, even though he was sort of glad. That meant there was less opportunity for Butch and him to confront each other.

"I don't know. But it was just a matter of time. He wasn't much of a student."

"So, any idea of what he's going to do?"

"Heal," said Chris. "His collar bone still hadn't completely mended the last time I saw him."

Dale felt a twinge of guilt. He wondered if breaking Bigelow's collar bone would ruin Butch's life. He half hoped so; then Dale quickly recanted. He didn't wish Butch any real harm.

Chris added the final touch to his sundae. A couple of squirts of ketchup.

"Stop worrying. It wasn't any of your doing."

Dale shrugged and they rejoined the girls. He watched as Amanda spooned a tiny dollop of ice cream into her mouth. He asked if she were certain she didn't want a real sundae.

"No, thank you," she said.

Amanda then leaned closer to Dale and whispered she'd gained three pounds since the start of school. He tried to match her concerned expression but he didn't think three pounds mattered that much. Amanda still had an attractive figure.

After finishing their ice cream, Dale and Chris walked the girls back to their dorm. On the way, Chris jokingly asked Dale what book he was now reading.

"He's always reading some important book," Chris told Hope. "He used to read them at track meets if you can believe it."

Hope couldn't quite believe it, but then she didn't like reading books. "They're sort of boring," she said.

Dale said maybe she'd just read the wrong books.

"Well, what are you reading then?"

"*The Catcher in the Rye.*"

Dale was supposed to be reading *Tristram Shandy*, but he found it so confounding that he put it aside and out of curiosity started reading J. D. Salinger. He hadn't planned on reading contemporary American novels until next year.

"I was supposed to read that book in senior English in high school," said Hope. "But my mother wouldn't let me. She had to write the English teacher a note saying I wasn't allowed to read such a dirty book."

"It's not dirty," said Dale.

He noticed Chris and Amanda looking at him in a questioning way.

"Well, it's not. Has anybody here read it?"

No one had. But then apparently they weren't supposed to.

"Isn't it a book about a dirty old man seducing a little girl?" asked Hope.

"No, that's *Lolita*."

Dale realized he probably hadn't helped his cause by knowing the difference between the two books. He also guessed that Hope had been ungenerous with her description of *Lolita*, but since he hadn't actually read it yet he couldn't rebut her.

"Well, *The Catcher in the Rye* is supposed to be bad, too," Hope said.

"It's not," said Dale. "It's a good book." None of them looked convinced. Dale thought he better change the book. "Well, I'm also reading C. S. Lewis's *Mere Christianity*.

"Oh, C. S. Lewis is one of my favorite authors," said Amanda. "I loved *The Chronicles of Narnia*."

Hope liked those books, too. Chris had read them as well, but he said he wasn't crazy about them. He preferred westerns.

Dale felt he'd redeemed himself. He said C. S. Lewis was an excellent writer. He said this with quiet authority although he hadn't finished *Mere Christianity*.

Amanda said he should read *The Screwtape Letters*.

"I will," he said, " as soon as I finish *The Catcher* – I mean, the other C. S. Lewis book."

Dale could tell that the three of them seemed concerned about his interest in controversial books. Well, his major was partly English, and on the GNC campus English majors were considered awfully close to being liberal. He thought maybe they'd make allowances for him.

The conversation now ended, Dale and Chris walked the girls to the front door of Hayley Hall. Chris and Hope said good night and they went their separate ways. Dale waited until Hope went inside before he took Amanda's hand and said good night. No kiss. It wasn't an official date anyway and they were in public. Amanda gave Dale a long look, giving him a brief moment of hope, but then she said good night and went inside.

Dale turned the corner of the dorm and joined up with Chris. They ambled down the walk and passed the other girls' dormitory, Easger Hall. Dale noticed a sedan idling in the parking lot. As they walked by, the door opened and Laurie Page, wearing a royal blue gown, got out, followed by one of the girls in her court. She saw Dale and Chris looking. She smiled and waved, and then she and her friend entered the dormitory. Dale felt pleased that she knew who they were, or at least pretended to. They moved on and he glanced at the car's passenger window and saw Mrs. Page sitting in the seat. She stared straight ahead and he thought she looked tired and lost, as if she'd been on a long, confusing journey and still didn't know where she was.

Dale remembered her suggesting in high school that he read some of the "classic" American playwrights. He'd checked out a book containing the best plays of the '30s and '40s: plays by Hart and Kauffman, Maxwell Anderson, and Thornton Wilder. He liked them. But he thought Tennessee Williams was better.

**Chapter 5:** *Breaking the speed limit at Christmas; seeing Wendy at New Year's*

Dale slapped the paddle forward and the Ping-Pong ball bounced near the end of the green table before flying off into the corner of the rec room.

"Your point," groused Kenny Meeks, Amanda's younger brother.

He trudged over to pick up the ball. Dale, after losing the first two games to Kenny, was getting a feel for the game. He led in the third game, 14 to 10.

Kenny trotted back and tossed the light, hollow ball to Dale. He held the ball in his left hand while wiggling the paddle with his right. He relaxed his wrist. Then he dropped the ball and served with a swift, short stroke that skimmed the ball just over the net and again landed hard near the end of the table. Kenny swung and missed then said, "crud."

"*Kenneth*," cautioned Elizabeth, Amanda's older sister. She sat with Amanda at a small table across the room. They were playing canasta.

"Game," Dale said.

"You want to play another?"

"Maybe later."

Dale was more interested in getting Amanda alone. She and her family were going on a skiing vacation in Colorado the next day and he wouldn't be seeing her for over a week.

"You're my only competition around here," Kenny said. He pointed his paddle at his sisters. "They can't play worth a darn."

"*Kenneth*," warned Elizabeth.

"I only said darn. I could say a lot worse."

Kenny winked at Dale. Dale nodded back with manly understanding. They both played sports. They'd been in locker rooms. They knew plenty of profanity.

"You know, your sister is kinda cute," Kenny said to Dale. Kenny, like June May, was a junior at Galilee High.

Dale nodded. He was glad someone thought so. Actually, Dale supposed she was pretty good looking. But she wanted to be beautiful.

"Why don't you ask her out?" Dale said, teasingly.

"I already have a girlfriend."

"Then you shouldn't be noticing other girls. Your girlfriend won't like it."

Kenny walked closer to Dale and said confidentially that what she didn't know wouldn't hurt her. Dale nodded back. Kenny stood two inches taller than Dale and probably outweighed him by ten pounds and he hadn't stopped growing. He had his father's looks and build. Kenny had sandy hair, hazel eyes, a blunt nose, a somewhat large mouth and a strong jaw. He looked like a young boxer in some B-movie: pugnacious but callow.

They walked over to Amanda and Elizabeth and watched them play a hand. Dale thought Amanda was definitely the better looking of the sisters. Elizabeth was perhaps an inch taller with a chubby figure. She had chestnut brown hair, green eyes, and a feminized version of Kenny's face. She had a different personality than Amanda, more outspoken and bossy. Maybe being the oldest child had something to do with that. She'd graduated from GNC one year ago and was working at her father's bank as a loan officer. Dale wondered if she handled car loans.

"Dale," Elizabeth said, "do you play cards?"

Dale almost said poker, but he caught himself. "Cribbage. A few other games."

"Would you like to join us at canasta?" asked Amanda.

"No thanks." He just wanted them to finish so he could take Amanda on a walk.

Kenny grabbed a miniature football and told Dale to catch. He threw it and Dale caught it with one hand. He took several steps away from the girls and tossed the football back to Kenny. It hit the palm of his hand with a smack and fell to the floor. Dale could tell Kenny played the line.

"Kenneth, don't throw the football in the house."

"It's not a real football," he said.

"Well, don't throw the imaginary football either," Elizabeth said, demonstrating, Dale thought, some unexpected wit.

"Hey, that's funny," Kenny said but he dropped the football on one of the chairs and looked around the rec room. "Well, what can we do now?"

Amanda stood up. "Why don't you play cards with Lizzy?" she suggested, walking over to Dale.

"Ah, she always wins," Kenny said, but he moped over to the table and sat down.

Amanda asked Dale what he wanted to do.

"Why don't we go for a walk?"

Amanda said okay and the two of them walked up the stairs to the main floor, passing the family pet, a white Persian cat named Prudence. Dale waited while Amanda got a jacket. He looked around the room. The Meeks had a splendid home. Everything in the house was handsomely designed, neatly arranged, and fastidiously clean. All the rooms Dale had been in smelled fresh and faintly woodsy. The Meeks' house was like one of those perfect homes featured in women's magazines.

Amanda returned wearing a red wool jacket. Dale liked the color. He thought she looked good in red although she rarely wore clothes that color. She was also wearing blue jeans. He'd never seen her wear any kind of pants before except women's dress slacks. As he followed her to the door, he thought she filled out her jeans quite nicely.

Amanda noticed that Dale didn't have a jacket. "Dale, where's your coat?"

"I didn't bring one."

"But it's chilly outside."

"Not to me."

He wore an undershirt and a flannel shirt with his Levi's and boots. He'd been warm in the basement. He thought the cool air would feel good.

"Just a minute," Amanda said.

She fetched a jacket from the hall closet and handed it to Dale. She said, go on, put it on. Dale did. The sleeves hung a couple of inches past his wrist, which annoyed him. Dale imagined it was Kenny's jacket, although it might have been Mr. Meeks. Both were about the same height.

They walked out the door and headed down the street to the lake a couple of blocks away. Dale hadn't been to Amanda's house during the fall when the leaves fell. He wished he had. Her neighborhood was one of the few that had large, deciduous trees with a variety of leaf colors. He looked at the curbside of the street. Not one leaf. This was also the kind of neighborhood where people raked up and burned every leaf.

"What are you thinking?" Amanda asked.

"About leaves."

"You certainly think some strange things," she said with a smile.

Dale nodded. It was only strange because all the trees were now bare and she didn't know he was thinking about the fall. Amanda put her hand on his arm and they walked together in silence. They came to a small park and walked a hundred yards to the shore of the lake. In the dark, they could see the water shimmering under the moonlight. He unzipped the jacket. He felt warm.

"What are you going to do while I'm gone?" she asked.

"Work. I'll be working three days this week."

Dale worked weekends and holidays but since New Year's Day fell on a Saturday, he'd have to work the Friday before.

"Oh, yes, work," said Amanda.

Dale remembered their last argument. Amanda didn't think it proper for him to work on Christmas Day. After all, it was their Lord and Savior's birthday. He explained that he had to. She thought he should try and trade with someone. He explained that the other men didn't want to work on Christmas. All of them were older and some of them had families. Amanda said, maybe he should get a different job. Dale told her the campus police job was a wonderful job. He essentially got paid to read. She said she didn't know why that was so wonderful. The job sounded lonely and boring to her. He got a little annoyed and she got a little annoyed and when he left her house a week ago he felt something amiss between them.

They were to meet after the Christmas Eve service at First Church so they could exchange presents. Dale sat with Chris and his family. Amanda sat with her family two rows in front. He watched her the entire service and felt even more emotionally full than he usually did when hearing Christmas hymns. When the service ended, Dale took Amanda over to the

*Java Joint* and they talked, but it wasn't until he gave her the gift while sitting in his car that he felt they'd reconnected.

He gave her the new Beverly Sills album. Amanda's face lit up when she unwrapped the Christmas packaging and saw it.

"Oh, you remembered," she said, smiling.

Dale had surprised himself by remembering. He couldn't think of anything appropriate to buy her. He thought about jewelry but he knew she'd think that inappropriate for this stage of their romance. Then he remembered her mentioning Beverly Sills a few times. Amanda liked her. Beverly Sills had a new album coming out for Christmas, so it made sense.

She said thank you and he leaned over and kissed her. She gave him his present. He could tell by how it was shaped that it was a book. He ripped the wrapping off. *The Screwtape Letters*. Dale felt a little disappointed, although he didn't know why. He didn't really think she'd buy him *Lolita*, did he?

He thanked her and they kissed again. She snuggled next to him and Dale told her again how well she sang in the college choir the week before. She seemed pleased to hear him compliment her again. They'd done several things together that month. They'd gone to see the movie, *In Search of Noah's Ark*. They'd attended the college's Christmas dinner, Yuletide. It wasn't anything that special, thought Dale. The college food service prepared fancier Christmas fare and presented it to students in a dining room decorated for the holidays. But Amanda liked going to such things. She liked being involved in all the traditional GNC activities. Dale didn't enjoy such events as much. He wasn't as socially adept as she was. He didn't have any desire to be part of GNC royalty. In fact, he still felt a little detached from the whole GNC social scene even when he and Amanda sat with Henshaw and Abigail at Yuletide.

While sitting with Amanda in his car he thought about attending the collegian choir's Christmas concert the week before. Amanda had sung well and even had a solo. She had a sweet soprano voice and Dale enjoyed watching her sing because she didn't emote too much. But one thing bothered him. After the concert, while waiting for her, he noticed David Hawkins talking to Amanda.

Hawkins was one of those unusual guys who was both an athlete and an arts kind of guy. He played guard on the Chiefs' basketball team and also sang in the choir, acted in plays, and performed in a group that sang Christian contemporary music. He wasn't especially good looking, but Dale imagined girls thought he was cute with his curly brown hair and sensitive blue eyes. In fact, if Hawkins hadn't been a pretty good basketball player, Dale would have thought him a little effeminate. He wasn't that big; maybe five eleven and slender of build. When Dale watched him on the court, he noticed he was a clever, finesse player; a playmaker. And Hawkins was one of those kinds of singers that Dale didn't like watching. He thought he showed too much emotion. Hawkins had sung a solo, too. Maybe that was what he and Amanda were talking about. But Dale thought they were acting a little too friendly.

Dale's displeasure at seeing Hawkins talking to Amanda had put him in a bad mood and that was one reason why he'd argued about his working on Christmas Day. Otherwise, he would have been more patient with her when she complained.

But the lingering tension had disappeared with their exchanging of the gifts. That had been four days ago. Now, Dale stood with Amanda looking at the moonlight on the lake and he felt even closer to her than before and knew he'd miss her while she and her family were away skiing. He wouldn't see her for ten days.

"What are you thinking?" she asked.

"You've asked me that twice."

"Well, you've been quiet. I'm just wondering what you're thinking."

"I was thinking how lovely you looked and sounded at the Christmas concert."

"Were you really?"

He looked at her. She was smiling. She liked compliments, especially when he mentioned something she did as well as how she looked.

"That's exactly what I was thinking."

She moved closer to him and he took her hand. It felt cold. He rubbed it with both his hands.

"Are you cold?" he asked.

"A little."

"Maybe we should walk back to your house."

He held her hand while they walked.

"Is there anything wrong?" she asked.

"What do you mean?"

"Well, you seem awfully quiet. I thought maybe something was on your mind."

Dale realized he had been quiet. The holidays made him a little depressed. He guessed part of it was because he remembered Jesse getting sick twice during that time. Also, for a couple of years she wouldn't celebrate Christmas. At Dale's house, Christmas seemed sad and pathetic. He wondered if he should tell Amanda any of this. She had hinted she'd like to know more about his family. But he decided not to. He didn't think she knew how awful his home life had been, and to some degree, still was. He knew she lived a sheltered, protected life and she'd shrink in disgust at the ugliness of his parents' lives. Dale still felt a little ashamed of them; especially when he saw how pleasant and loving and wonderful a family could be together – a family like the Meeks.

He also felt a little blue at the thought of not seeing Amanda for ten days. She and her family were going skiing in Crested Butte, Colorado with the Jorgensens. Dale didn't think the older Jorgensen boy was going. He was out of college. But he knew Amanda would meet other wealthy young men at the ski resort. That might make her regard him as less appealing.

Dale decided he wasn't going to let her know his shame and doubts. He'd hid such feelings for years. He'd also hid his love for Amanda for years. He still didn't think he was worthy of her. He wanted to make himself better for her. In a year and a half, he'd graduate. Maybe he could find a good job and show her he had potential. But Dale doubted he had the moneymaking skills of her father. That bothered him, too.

He forced himself to perk up. He gripped her hand tighter and increased the pace of their walk.

"Beautiful night, isn't it?" he said.

They looked at the clear, dark sky and the swirl of stars.

"Yes, it is."

He asked her if she was looking forward to the ski trip.

"Oh, yes," she said. "It's loads of fun."

"Well, don't break your leg."

"Why would I do that?"

"Well, you're a little clumsy."

"How dare you!" she said with mock offense.

"You said so yourself."

"Well, to tell the truth, I don't ski that much."

"You don't? What do you do then?"

"I relax. I go to the sauna. I play bridge."

"You play bridge?"

"Oh, yes."

"Are you any good?" Dale didn't really know what bridge was.

"No, but I enjoy playing with the right partner."

"And who is your partner usually?"

"Oh, it varies."

418

Dale glanced at her. She smiled coyly. She was actually teasing him.

They were at her house. Instead of going in the front, Dale led her through the gate and to the side garage door. He leaned toward her and looked into her eyes.

"I don't think I like you changing partners so much."

"Oh, you don't?"

"No."

"Well, to tell the truth, I play with Lizzy. She's an excellent bridge player."

Dale didn't doubt that. Apparently, Lizzy was the clever sister. But Dale didn't care that much about cleverness. He put his arms around Amanda's waist and held her. Then he kissed her.

"It's a little cold standing her," she said. "Let's go into the garage."

She opened the door and Dale followed her in. He shut the door and tried to find the light. She said leave the light off. He felt her hand tugging on his and he followed her over to a shadowy lump. His eyes adjusted to the dark and he saw it was a couch. They sat down. Dale put his arms around her waist. She seemed to be waiting for his kiss. Her open mouth was moist. He kissed her deeply and then he heard her sigh. He smelled the fragrance on her skin and in her hair. He tugged her sweater out of her jeans so he could put his hands on her bare flesh. He hoped his hands were warm enough. When he caressed her waist she didn't complain, so he guessed they were. He kissed her again, this time slightly sucking on her lower lip. He loved her lower lip; the fullness of it. His hands slowly moved lower and he felt the narrowness of her waist curve into the roundness of her hips. He liked how soft and spongy the flesh around her hips felt. It excited him to touch it. He kissed her cheeks, then, lightly, that groove between her nose and upper lip. She seemed surprised by that, but she didn't say anything. Then he nibbled her ear. He sucked just a little on the tender flesh of her neck. He listened to her murmur in his ear.

Dale put his mouth over hers and French kissed her. Then he put his hand under her sweater. He stroked the skin just below her bra then slowly slipped his hand underneath the cup. His hand gently circled her breast, then squeezed it. He heard Amanda moan. The sound of her moan almost made him delirious. His finger carefully rubbed her erect nipple. She moaned louder. Still kissing her, he slipped his other hand down the back of her jeans. His fingers stroked the elastic band of her panties, then inched past and caressed the incredibly soft skin of the top curve of her right buttock. His other hand retreated just enough from her breast to grasp her bra. He lifted it up and felt her breast spring free.

Amanda moved her mouth away from his. "Dale," she said. She moved her elbow in front of her chest. She squirmed against his hand behind her.

"What?" he said lowly.

"We have to stop."

Dale moved his face back enough to look into her eyes. But he left his hands where they were.

"Why?"

"You know why."

He tried to kiss her but she turned her face away.

"I mean it. We have to stop." She wiggled her body, not to entice him, but to free herself. "Your hands."

Dale removed them even though there wasn't a horn to honk.

"Thank you," she said, almost primly.

He threw himself back against the old couch. Even it smelled clean, not musty.

"It's like gradually picking up speed, going ten, twenty, thirty, forty, then wham! Slamming on the brakes."

"Well, I've never gone more than twenty before," Amanda said.

Dale looked at her. He liked the fact that she used his metaphor. Now, he wondered what twenty was for her.

"Really?"

"Yes, really."

She slid her hand under her sweater and adjusted her bra. She lowered her eyes in embarrassment. He remembered how her breast felt. It wasn't large. Smaller than a Nerf basketball. But it felt very nice. Soft and firm and warm. He wondered what kind of areolas she had. He stopped thinking about that. It would only get him excited again.

"I guess you've had all kinds of experience," she said.

"Not so much." He thought, not nearly as much as I would like to have had. Darn Galilee girls.

"Is that true?"

Dale didn't know what she wanted him to say. That he was a virgin like she was? Well, he wasn't, although he wasn't too far removed from that pristine state. Did she want him to tell her how fast he'd gone? What was the speed of going all the way? One hundred maybe? That metaphor was even trickier than the baseball one. Because if one hundred was intercourse, then what was fifty? She said she'd never gone more than twenty. What was that? Several kisses in a row? A hand on her thigh? Maybe more, which he didn't like to think about.

"There's something more important than experience, Amanda."

"Oh? What?"

"Intensity of feeling." Dale leaned toward her and looked into her eyes. "And I've never felt anything more intense than I just did with you."

"Really?" Her voice sounded soft and pleased.

Dale reached for her and was about to tell her something he'd hid from her and everyone else for years when a light flashed on from the room next to the garage.

"Oh, no!" Amanda cried softly.

She sat upright. Dale did the same, but he didn't know why. If her mother or father – he prayed it wouldn't be her father – did enter the garage and found them there in the dark it wouldn't matter much if they were sitting up straight and not touching.

They waited. The light blinked off.

"Oh, my goodness," she sighed.

She slumped back against the couch. Dale suddenly thought the whole experience ridiculous. Absurd. He chuckled.

"What's so funny?"

"You. Me. The whole thing." He leaned back and put his arm around her. "Amanda, you're going to be twenty years old pretty soon. And yet you're acting like a kid."

"My parents are very strict."

"Yeah, I know. And I'm glad."

"You are?"

"Yes. I want them to take care of you. To protect you."

"Even from boys like you?"

"Especially from boys like me."

She giggled. "You know, I almost didn't go out with you. Back in high school, I mean."

"Why?"

"Well, you know there was Wendy. We were friends. And I sort of thought you were, well –"

"What? Bad?"

"Oh, no. Just different than me."

Dale knew that was true. "What made you change your mind?"

"Bobby told me about you."

"Henshaw?"

"Yes. He said you were a good guy. He said you had, ah, perception."

"Perception, huh? That's because I wear contact lenses."

"What?"

"Just a joke."

"Oh. Well, if Bobby thought you were a good guy then I thought I could take a chance."

"So, are you and Bobby good friends?"

"I suppose we are."

"You seem to think a lot of his opinion."

"Yes, I do."

Dale wondered if Bobby was the one she went twenty with. "I remember you asking him to the pep club banquet twice. That sounds like more than friends."

"Yes, I'd say we're good friends. I've known him all my life."

Dale thought not that again. "Did you ever feel strongly about him?"

"You mean romantically?"

"Yeah."

"No, not really. Maybe I had a crush on him."

"Oh yeah?"

"Well, you know how teenage girls are."

"Unfortunately."

"What?"

"Another joke."

"Oh. Well, it was nothing. Just a phase. Anyway, Bobby's very serious with Abigail."

"Do you wish that wasn't the case?"

"Of course not. Dale, are you trying to start an argument?"

He looked at her. Even in the semi-darkness he could tell she was getting upset. "No, I'm not."

"You're not the jealous type, are you?"

Dale thought people get jealous because they're afraid of losing someone they love. He'd never felt that jealous about Wendy. But Amanda? Oh, yes.

"No, not me," he said. "I'm just curious. Still, I guess I should be grateful to Henshaw."

"Why?"

"Because if you hadn't gone out with me back in high school you probably wouldn't have gone out with me now."

"Oh, I don't know."

"Oh?"

"I always thought you were cute."

That word again. Why didn't girls say, handsome? Or heroic? Or super duper?

"And do you want to know something?" Amanda asked in her quiet, soft voice.

Dale felt a jolt of excitement at the confidential tone in her voice. "What?"

"I really wanted to go out with you that time after that track meet."

Dale wondered what track meet. Then he remembered. *That* track meet. The regional. When he bumped into her while on his way to throw up.

"You mean the regional?"

"Yes. You'd run so well. I watched from the stands. Then on the way down we sort of bumped into each other."

"We *did* bump into each other." He still remembered how her thigh felt when he bumped into it with his raised knee.

"Anyway, I felt something then."

"I did, too. Why didn't you let me know?"

"You were back with Wendy. Besides, you weren't –"

"A Nazarene."

"That's right."

Dale felt a knot of frustration form inside him. If only he'd known for sure how she felt, he'd have become one then. Then a whole year wouldn't have been wasted.

"Is that so important?" he asked.

"What?"

"Being a Nazarene?"

"Of course. And anyway, you're one now."

Dale said that's right. He was.

A pause.

"I better go in," Amanda said. "I'm sure my parents are worried about me. They don't know where I am."

"They know you're with me."

"That's what I'm worried about."

"Yeah, all right."

Dale got up and helped Amanda to her feet.

"I'd ask you in again, but my parents go to sleep early."

Dale wondered what time it was. He guessed it wasn't that late. Maybe around eleven.

"That's okay. I know you have to get up early for your trip."

"Yes."

Dale walked over to the door, then turned and put his arms around Amanda's waist. He pulled her against him and felt her arms go over his neck. He kissed her. First, softly, then more forcefully. He felt her hands hug his neck. He pulled her body tightly against his.

She released her arms around his neck and Dale relaxed his grip around her waist.

"Good night," she said.

"Good night." He gave her one last, quick kiss. He opened the door and paused before going out. "Have fun skiing. And remember, only Lizzy as your partner."

Amanda smiled and closed the door.

Dale walked around the house, through the gate, and got into his car. He looked without resentment at the old, intrusive porch light and drove away.


Dale hadn't seen his father since the summer. Blackie looked the same. Maybe a little heavier.

His apartment was just as sparsely furnished and empty looking. Dale sat on the couch and watched Blackie drink his scotch and soda.

"Sure you don't want one?" Blackie said, holding up the short glass with the amber liquid in it.

Dale shook his head no. "Why are you always trying to corrupt me?"

Blackie gave him a surprised if not severe look. "Who says I'm trying to do that? I'm trying to teach you the ways of the world."

"That's what I mean." He was only partly joking with his father.

"I knew that damn religious school would make you a namby pamby."

Dale then told him about breaking Bigelow's collarbone. He made it sound more violent than it actually was. He wanted to see Blackie's reaction.

"You better watch yourself, boy. You might get sued." Blackie got up to fix himself another drink. "Or worse, I might."

Dale hadn't thought about that. He guessed that was the way of the world, too.

"I got in a fight during my first year in the Navy," Blackie said, returning with another drink. "On a voyage to the Orient."

He knew Blackie would have a better story. His father settled into his chair, just an old beat-up ordinary chair. Dale wondered why he didn't buy another E-Z Boy.

"You mean the one where the black boatswain's mate got burned to death?"

"No, this was a different deployment. Maybe it was my second trip. Anyway, I got into a fight over a poker game with an old Asiatic. You know what that is, boy?"

Dale wished he'd stop calling him boy. But he humored his father. "No, what is it?"

"It's an old seaman that's been on so many voyages to the Orient that he becomes buggy.

You know, eccentric, but dangerously so. Maybe he's been cooped up too long in dark, dank below decks that he loses his sense of perspective. Maybe he's rode out too many typhoons. Well, those bastards are dangerous. You learn to stay away from them."

"But you didn't?"

Blackie smiled. "Not on this voyage. Anyway, we're playing poker and he cheated and I called him on it. Next thing I knew he pulled a shank on me and we were rolling around on the floor. I got up, he didn't. His own shank gutted him."

"Did he die?"

"No, it takes more than that to kill those old bastards."

"Did you get in trouble?"

"Damn right I did. I almost lost my stripe. I'd just gotten it, too. But the other guys stood up for me. It was in self-defense. I had to stand captain's mast, though, for a week."

Dale wasn't sure what that meant but he didn't want to ask right then. Blackie's story was better than his.

Blackie finished off his second drink and asked Dale if he wanted to go over to Cleoma's.

"No, thanks. I'll just get going."

"Now, why the hell don't you want to go to Cleoma's?"

"I don't like her."

Blackie looked at Dale as if he had said he didn't like Farrah Fawcet, which he didn't – she was too skinny – or Raquel Welch.

"What has she ever done to you, boy?"

Dale didn't know exactly. He suspected she might have known about Sal trying to seduce him. Maybe she even encouraged it. He just knew he didn't trust her.

"Didn't she give you tickets to see Elvis? Let you drive her big red Cadillac?"

"And for that I will be eternally grateful."

"You have a smart mouth just like your mother."

"I think it's the other way around."

Dale remembered it was Blackie's teasing and quips that prompted Jesse to chuck ashtrays at his head. Of course, Jesse provoked fights too, but she didn't have a smart mouth. She just knew how to needle him.

"Ceecee will be there."

"Ceecee?"

Then he remembered her. The woman with the cleavage. That was tempting. But he didn't think he'd like Ceecee. He didn't trust her any more than he did Cleoma.

Dale got up. "No, I need to get home anyway."

Blackie shrugged with disgust. "Okay, suit yourself."

Blackie got up and asked about Jesse and June May.

"They're okay. June May wants her own car. She made me promise I'd tell you that."

"She doesn't need a car. She's just sixteen."

"Seventeen."

"Well, she's still in school."

"She wants one for summer."

"She can drive your mother's car. Damn well paid enough for that."

"Well, you know how June May is. She wants one for herself."

Blackie knew too well how she was. She always wanted something. She usually got it, too. One thing Blackie had kept doing was buying June May clothes and stuff. Nothing too expensive. He was going to have to buy her a dress for the pep club banquet in a month.

"Tell her I'll look for an old, used car for her this summer. Old. Used. Be sure to emphasize that."

"Absolutely."

"You sure you don't want to go over to Cleoma's?"

Dale shook his head no.

"You don't have any fun, boy."

"I do. We just have different definitions of fun."

Blackie held out his hand. Dale was a little surprised. He shook his father's hand and said so long. Then he left his apartment and got in his Chevy. He didn't start it. Instead, he thought maybe he didn't have any fun. A part of him would like to see Ceecee. See a lot more of her. Dale imagined he could if he tried. But then he thought of Amanda. Thought of her shushing down those slopes in Colorado. Then he thought about her face, especially her big blue eyes, her full lips, and that soft spot between her upper lip and her nose. That interesting groove. He'd have to find out what it was called.

Dale started his car and drove out of the parking lot, back to Galilee where good girls waited to frustrate his desires.

Dale had to talk Rusty into going to Mary Jane's New Year's Eve party. Dale thought that was ironic: he, socially averse, talking the gregarious Rusty into going to a party. But Rusty hadn't seen Mary Jane since the summer. He wasn't sure he wanted to see Mary Jane, even in a social setting. Dale told Rusty to play it cool. Show Mary Jane that it was no big deal seeing her again. Another irony: him giving Rusty advice on how to behave around girls.

Rusty finally agreed to go. Dale ordinarily wouldn't have wanted to go to a New Year's Eve party but Amanda was still skiing in Colorado. She and her family were scheduled to return in three days and in the meantime Dale wanted to keep busy.

He and Rusty had seen a couple of movies already. First, they saw *Rocky*. Rusty liked it a lot; Dale liked it just okay. Rusty said he thought Dale liked old-fashioned movies. He said yeah, but he thought *Rocky* was a movie that pretended to be old fashioned. Also, he couldn't quite identify with Rocky. He was too stupid. Stupid but brave, said his buddy. Dale admitted that was true. But he'd rather Rocky be a little smarter and brave.

The second movie they saw was *Network*. Dale liked it a lot; Rusty not as much. Dale, although he didn't fully understand all the satire, admired the writing. Lots of interesting words like "adamantine" and "ecumenical." Rusty said it was funny but the romance between the old guy and Faye Dunaway was boring. Dale thought it was a little melodramatic but it gave the movie some pathos to help balance the satiric intellectualism. Since *Network* was R-rated, Dale was glad Rusty had agreed to go. He knew Amanda would never have tolerated it.

The following night, Rusty picked up Dale for Mary Jane's New Year's Eve party. Rusty honked. Dale ran out of his house and jumped in Rusty's old, rattling Malibu. Dale asked what was wrong with the car? Rusty shrugged and said the engine was okay. To prove it, he hit the gas and squealed the tires as they zipped down the road.

Rusty had grown a beard over the winter. Dale examined it and thought it looked pretty good. A little more reddish than his hair. He thought the beard made Rusty look like a Viking. He envied Rusty's hirsute ways. Dale had such a sparse beard he couldn't even grow a good mustache.

Before the movies and tonight's party, they hadn't seen each other since late in the summer when they attended – of all things – a Peter Frampton concert. Well, Erickson couldn't go. Rusty had pleaded with Dale to take his place. Afterwards, when Rusty asked how he liked the concert, Dale said he hated it. Rusty couldn't understand why he disliked Frampton so much. Dale didn't tell him that the English rocker's music reminded him of that summer with Sal. He hadn't told Rusty anything about Sal. Instead, he said he just didn't like that "laid back" kind of music.

Dale thought it was sort of odd that he and Rusty never talked about sex. He knew Rusty and Erickson did. He'd overheard both of them boasting to the other about their conquests. Not that they had much to boast about while in high school. However, both of them had apparently had sex with Merry. Dale had been shocked when he overhead them comparing their trysts. Both Rusty and Erickson fornicated with her in their respective cars. Dale thought Rusty's Malibu wasn't very roomy for that sort of thing. But Erickson drove an El Camino and he'd put an old mattress on the flat-bed for his coupling. After Dale got over his astonishment, he felt a little envious. Merry, in spite of her buxom figure, didn't appeal to Dale. However, if he'd known she was one of the few Galilee girls to be so receptive, he might have overlooked her cow-like qualities.

Aside from Merry, Dale didn't know of any Galilee girl that either Rusty or Erickson had made it with. Dale was pretty certain Rusty had never had sex with Mary Jane. He'd complained more than once about how she enforced "strict boundaries." But Dale suspected that Rusty had found a few compliant girls outside Galilee to have sex with. Once, he'd casually remarked to Dale that one girl he knew, a redhead that went to Oscar Rose, didn't have much of a "border patrol."

As Rusty drove to Mary Jane's, Dale asked him how he was doing with college and basketball. Rusty said he'd quit basketball at Oscar Rose but still took classes, although he didn't attend them much. He'd flunked a sociology class because he'd missed twenty-one classes. His work – he still did carpentry for Erickson and his dad – often interfered with going to class.

Dale asked how Erickson was.

"Fat," said Rusty. "He must have gained twenty pounds since high school."

"You're kidding."

"Nope. He sort of has a potbelly. Too much beer."

Dale wondered if Rusty drank beer now. He probably took a drink or two, but Dale guessed Rusty was like him. He'd never developed a taste for the stuff either.

Dale asked Rusty if he'd applied for college financial aid. Rusty said no. He made enough money to pay for his junior college tuition. Dale said that if Rusty was a dependent on his mother's tax returns, he'd probably qualify for grants like Dale had. He told Rusty how the grants paid for his tuition and books at GNC.

"Man, that sounds fine," Rusty said. He told Dale a few years ago his mother had stopped working at the GE plant. Mr. Average made pretty good money so she didn't have to work. But since he'd run off a year ago, things had been a little tight. His mother got her old job back, so things were now better.

Dale said he bet Rusty would qualify for the whole package. Federal and state grants. He said Rusty could transfer to GNC. Play basketball again.

"You know, Eugene Greene plays for the Chiefs."

Eugene didn't play much; he sat on the bench mostly. Dale knew Rusty was better than Eugene.

"Really? Gene Greene plays some?"

Dale said, yeah, some. He played in the Chiefs last game for about five minutes, a lopsided win over Arkansas Wesleyan.

Rusty nodded his head thoughtfully. He said, thanks, man. He'd look into all that stuff.

They arrived at Mary Jane's house and saw several cars already parked on the street and in the driveway. Her parents' handsome two-story Tudor house was located only five blocks north of Amanda's parents' house. Mary Jane's father owned a shoe store in downtown Galilee and still did a thriving business in spite of a cheap chain shoe store that had opened in northwest Oklahoma City last year.

Dale and Rusty sat in his car for a minute looking at the house all lit up inside. They could faintly hear music playing inside, the disco they both despised.

"Man, I don't know if I want to go in now," Rusty said.

"She's got to have something besides that."

"Wanna bet?"

They got out. They ambled up the driveway to the front door. Dale knocked and Rusty pressed the doorbell. Already, they were getting in the mood.

Chris opened the door. He raised his eyebrows as if surprised to see them.

425

"Hey, guys, come on in."

Rusty and Dale came in. They said hey to K. C., Gretchen, Roxanne, Quentin, Carmen, Carrie, Mary Jane, and Wendy. The guys said hey back, and the girls smiled and waved.

Dale noticed that Mary Jane and Wendy, after giving them a brief greeting, stood in the back near the dining room and acted sort of cool to his and Rusty's presence.

Rusty noticed, too. "Ah, who cares about them?"

He proceeded over to Carmen and Carrie and sat between them. They smiled and immediately began chatting. Dale walked over to the stereo where Chris stood.

"Anything else besides this rot?" Dale asked, referring to the Bee Gees record that was playing.

Chris flipped through the LPs on the record stand. "Contemporary Christian. Folk. Mantovani."

"Mantovani?"

Dale had never heard of him. Was he classical? He looked at one of the many Mantovani albums. Not classical. Looked like this Mantovani guy played instrumental versions of hit '60s songs. Dale wondered what was the point of that?

Mary Jane, wearing a pink cashmere sweater and dressy, rather tight-fitting beige slacks, came over and said hi. Dale nodded. She said refreshments were in the kitchen if he wanted any. He said thanks. He and Chris watched Mary Jane walk back to Wendy. Mary Jane sort of wiggled her hips when she walked and Dale noticed she had more to wiggle. She must have gained a few pounds eating at the college cafeteria. Dale thought she looked pretty good. So did Chris. Dale gave Chris a warning look. Chris wisely said nothing.

They walked into the kitchen and saw an enticing spread. Dale ignored the fancy hors d'oeuvres and filled his plate with nuts, cookies, pretzels, potato chips, and a hunk of fudge. Mary Jane's mother was a good cook. He'd been over only a couple of times, but once he'd tasted Mrs. Morgan's cinnamon rolls and they were excellent.

Chris stuffed his plate with even more food and in his typically indiscriminate way by mixing it all together. On their way out, Rusty came in and told them not to hog all the chow. Chris said there was still plenty and Rusty said not for long.

On his way back to the living room, Dale noticed Wendy pretending not to look at him. It wasn't as bad as it had been in high school, but he still felt a little self-conscious. He'd only seen her a few times around town since their breakup. He'd talked to her on the phone a few times. Wendy had been considerate and calm most of the time. Dale had been unencouraging but polite.

Sitting down in an easy chair with his plate of snacks, Dale glanced at Wendy as she walked into the main part of the living room and sat down on a wooden chair. She looked good. She wore a green sweater and blue jeans. Her hair had that same bright yellow color. Her green eyes looked even greener thanks to the sweater. Her face still looked freckled and cute.

She caught him looking at her and she smiled softly. Dale looked down and concentrated on the hunk of fudge that beckoned to be devoured.

They listened to more detestable disco music. They ate. They talked. The time passed pleasantly. Mary Jane finally took off the last disco record and put on some Mantovani. Dale thought it wasn't so bad, at least when he didn't listen closely. Maybe that's what it was for. Music to have on when you didn't really want to listen to music.

Dale looked at his friends from high school. K. C. and Gretchen and Roxanne and Quentin shared the couch. Gretchen's hair looked a little different. Still red, but darker and shorter. Almost all her neck showed. Roxanne looked as pretty as ever. She didn't look like she'd gained any weight; in fact, Dale noted with disapproval that she might have lost a few pounds. What was wrong with all these girls? Roxanne had one of the most curvaceous figures in high school and now she was trying to get thin? Dale guessed it was the times. All the women wanted to look like the emaciated Farrah Fawcet. Oh, how Dale longed for the women of the '50s and '60s.

Rusty, Carrie, and Carmen sat on the loveseat. Carrie and Carmen looked about the same, both cute and sweet, as they smiled and chatted with Rusty. They wore the same kind of sweaters and slacks that Mary Jane, Gretchen and Roxanne wore. Just different colors. Dale wondered if the girls planned that. He'd seen Carmen only once since he'd stopped dating her. She'd been friendly enough. He appreciated that she hadn't held anything against him.

Wendy, Mary Jane, and Chris all sat in chairs adjacent to the couch. They talked with each other and chatted with the two couples on the couch as well. Dale noticed that Rusty and Mary Jane hadn't spoken to each other all evening.

Mary Jane said she'd asked others to come. Bonita said she might stop by but she had to get ready to go back to Dallas the next day. Dale sort of hoped she didn't show. If she were present, that would make three girls with grievances against him. Mary Jane also asked Linda and her husband to come, but they were going to a party with other young married couples. And she'd also asked Butch.

Dale felt their eyes on him. He'd been staring at the carpet, trying to identify the odd color in one of the designs, one of those pastel colors he didn't like, when he heard Butch's name and felt the collective gaze of his friends seize him like a force field. He looked up.

"I heard you broke Butch's collarbone," said Carrie.

Dale detected a slight smile on her face. She hadn't liked him either.

"I didn't break it. He basically broke it himself."

K. C. and Chris laughed.

"I remember Audie getting into a fight with Butch in art class," said Carmen.

Dale couldn't tell if she was teasing him or not. She didn't smile but she didn't frown at him either like Mary Jane and Gretchen seemed to be doing.

"They knocked over desks and chairs and everything. It was quite a brawl. Isn't that so, Rusty?"

Dale didn't remember causing so much damage. Carmen was exaggerating. People always exaggerate after the fact. Dale looked at Rusty. His buddy looked back at him in a strangely wary way as if Dale had turned into Charles Bronson from *Death Wish*. Actually, Rusty had once teased him that he looked like the actor. Not in the face so much as the build. Dale didn't mind the comparison. He'd always liked Bronson, especially in *The Great Escape*, a movie both he and Rusty had liked a lot as kids.

Dale started to protest when K. C. piped in. "Butch's joining the marines."

"You're kidding," Chris said.

"No. He told me yesterday. He's going to enlist after the holiday."

No one said anything for a few moments. Other Galilee kids had enlisted or been drafted. But Bigelow was the first one of their group to join any branch. Dale wondered if Butch was doing a good thing. He thought Bigelow would make a good marine if he learned not to be a bully. Maybe the Corp would kill that inclination in him.

Chris said, good for Butch. K. C. said it was a good move. Quentin said Butch would make a good marine. The girls didn't say anything, but they looked worried. Dale thought that was just the way girls are. The Vietnam War had been officially over for more than a year. Most American ground troops had been pulled out a few years before that. Bigelow wasn't in any immediate danger of going into combat.

After that surprise announcement, the group played some games. First, Mary Jane and Wendy put a kitchen chair against the wall and dared the boys to stand with their legs straight, then bend over at the waist and try to pick up the chair with just using their arms. K. C. tried. Couldn't do it. Then Quentin. Then Chris. They even talked Dale into it. He couldn't do it either. Nor could Rusty. Then Mary Jane, the weakest girl, lifted it several inches.

The girls laughed and Dale thought the oddity had something to do with how men and women have different kinds of hips. He'd learned this interesting anatomical fact in biology. Women have a larger pelvic girdle than men. Their legs also attach on the sides of their hips, whereas men's legs go straight up into the hips. He remembered the professor using her hands to demonstrate this difference. With her hands cupped to the *side* to the imaginary female hips, she twisted her hands, producing a wiggle. The professor said that's why men tend to walk straight and women tend to wiggle. Dale had thought that very useful information to know.

The second party game involved an orange. One person took the orange under his chin and tried to pass it off to the next person without using his hands. Mary Jane and Wendy organized the contestants. It was funnier, they said, when you matched boys and girls of different height. So K. C., the shortest male, was paired with Mary Jane, the tallest girl. Then Dale with Carrie. Then Chris with Wendy. Then Quentin with Roxanne – but that had to be changed because they were a real couple. So, Quentin with Carmen, and Roxanne with Rusty.

The spectators laughed as K. C. tried to pass the orange to Mary Jane, who stood about an inch taller than him. K. C. dropped the orange several times but finally he put in the crook of her neck and then she tried to pass off to Dale. He didn't like this game much either. Even though he was a tad taller than Mary Jane, he felt foolish trying to get the orange from her.

On the positive side, he did get to bump into Mary Jane and even that casual contact was pleasant. Dale and Mary Jane didn't have too much problem with the orange, so he turned and tried relaying it to Carrie. While contorting his neck to land the orange on her neck, he noticed she had a cute face with plump cheeks. He wondered why he'd never dated her in high school. Well, because of Wendy, of course. Dale felt some regret that he hadn't asked her out. Not only did she have a cute face but she had a sweet personality. But she was one of those girls who was content to stay in the background and so was never especially popular.

Dale had a little more trouble handing off the orange to Carrie, in part because he was thinking why he hadn't dated her instead of concentrating on the game, but finally he did so. Carrie turned to Chris and they struggled for a while. Eventually, the orange made it all the way down the line and, as expected, Quentin and Carmen, a foot difference in their height, made the funniest couple.

After a little more talking and a little more food, the New Year arrived. Mary Jane turned on the television and they watched the taped telecast from New York City showing the big apple ascending the skyscraper. The girls counted down. Mary Jane passed out the noisemakers and when the clock turned to zero, everyone blew their noisemakers and cheered. The two couples, K. C. and Gretchen and Roxanne and Quentin, kissed. That left the other seven glancing around awkwardly.

Mary Jane motioned for Chris to come over to her and Wendy. He raised a brow and promptly trotted over and gave Mary Jane a friendly kiss. Dale glanced at Rusty, who narrowed his eyes in disapproval. Rusty then turned to Carmen and gave her a smooch. Dale looked to his right and saw Carrie smiling. He shrugged and leaned over and gave her a peck, the kind of good night kiss he gave Jesse when he was younger but not on the lips, of course. Even though the kiss didn't last long, he thought Carrie's lips felt nice. He looked up in time to see Chris bussing Wendy and Dale surprised himself by feeling a touch of annoyance when Chris's kiss lingered longer on her than his had on Carrie.

They all said Happy New Year to each other and turned and watched all the people on television celebrating, too. Dale thought of Amanda and wondered if she were celebrating in Colorado. Well, she was in mountain time, so she wouldn't celebrate the New Year for another hour. But he imagined that the New Year was being celebrated there at that moment and wondered if she was with anyone. He wondered if some wealthy, handsome playboy type was kissing her. He suddenly felt melancholic.

"What is it, Audie?" asked Carrie.

"What?"

"You have that look on your face that I remember from our yearbook days."

Dale hadn't realized that Carrie was so perceptive. All that time in the yearbook office and he hadn't noticed that.

"Just thinking of something."

"Or someone?"

Dale nodded.

"Me, too," she said.

"Really? Who?"

Carrie briefly told him about her boyfriend, a senior at CSU, majoring in pre-law. She said they planned on getting married in a few years.

Dale said that was great. He was happy for her.

The two couples said they had to go. Everyone exchanged good-byes and promised to keep in touch. Dale waved and felt a surge of regret that he'd never kissed Roxanne. He now wished he'd been voted football captain. He, not Bigelow, should have been the one to kiss her.

Carrie smiled and excused herself and Dale turned back to the television before sensing someone standing next to him. He turned and saw Wendy looking at him. Her eyes had a little of that old searching look to them.

"How are you, Audie? Or should I say Dale?"

"Either one." He didn't want to explain to Wendy that his family had always called him Dale. "I'm fine. How are you?"

Wendy said she was fine, too.

"Where's Wally? I thought he'd be here."

"He's home studying."

"You're kidding?"

"No, all he does is study. He's pre-med. He's determined to get into medical school."

Dale felt surprised that there were guys more studious than he was.

"So, how is Wally?"

Wendy smiled. "Oh, he's fine."

"Doesn't sound like it."

"Why do you say that?"

"Because if he were, he wouldn't be home studying on New Year's Eve."

"Audie, I've forgotten how clever you are."

Dale tried to see if she were teasing him. She didn't seem to be. Her smile looked genuine. Her green eyes had that old sparkle.

"I was never very clever around you," he said.

"Oh, I don't know. You had your moments."

Dale pretended to frown at her and she laughed her throaty laugh. He glanced to his right and noticed Mary Jane observing them. He lost his mock frown.

"How are you, really?" he asked.

"I'm fine," Wendy said. "I'm doing well in school. I'm working part time at the department store. They've offered me a full-time executive position when I graduate."

"Really?"

"Oh, yes. I'm going to be a lady executive."

Dale nodded. He guessed Wendy would like that. He could imagine her as an excellent business woman. Maybe she'd eventually go into politics. The first female governor of Oklahoma or something like that.

"How's Harte?" he asked.

"Terry? Fine, I guess."

Dale thought he'd heard they were going steady. She noticed his puzzled expression.

"We only went out a few times."

"Why only a few times?"

"No chemistry, I guess. We were really just friends, you know, Audie?"

Wendy didn't say it in an accusatory way, but Dale felt a twinge of guilt just the same. "Too bad."

"Oh, I don't know. I always liked Terry but more in a just-friends way. I mean, he was a great athlete but he wasn't especially bright."

"And you like bright guys?"

"Well, I like you, don't I?"

Dale noticed she used present tense. "So, is Harte running track at OSU?"

"Yes, I think so. But it's more difficult for him at the college level."

Dale nodded. He thought it must be difficult to be great at anything in high school and then find out you're not so great later. He guessed quite a few of people eventually discover that.

"How about you?" Wendy asked.

"What about me?"

"I hear you're dating Amanda. Again."

Dale noticed her green eyes now had an accusatory glint to them.

"Yeah, that's right," he said, glancing to his left to see what Mary Jane was doing. She sat in a chair talking to Rusty, who stood before her with a small smile on his whiskered face.

"So, did you always prefer her?"

Dale didn't really want to talk about that. He glanced at her and saw her eyes no longer had a critical look in them. They seemed softer with a shiny coating of tears.

"Wendy, I was always honest when I was with you."

Dale wondered if that was true. He'd never told her he loved her but that one time when he sort of had to in preparation for what they did. He never spoke about Amanda to her ever.

"I guess you were. Maybe that was the problem."

Dale didn't know what to say. What was the problem exactly? Who was to blame? He thought no one. It was just one of those unfortunate things. The turning of Fortuna's wheel.

"Well, I have to go," she said.

Wendy looked at Dale with an expression he'd never seen before. Not indifference, perhaps detachment. But when she said quietly, "good-bye, Audie," her voice didn't seem to match her expression.

Wendy walked over to Mary Jane and told her how wonderful her party was. She chatted with Chris for a minute, then she, Carrie, and Carmen all left together.

Dale went over to Chris and they talked about the bowl games. Chris said Nebraska beat Texas Tech in the Astro Bluebonnet bowl. That annoyed him. Erickson had always liked the Cornhuskers and even rooted for them against the Sooners. Dale, therefore, hated Nebraska.

Rusty was finally ready to go. Dale told Mary Jane she gave a swell party. Then, he, Rusty, and Chris walked out and Chris said he'd see them later.

They got in their cars and Dale thought about Wendy and Amanda and if he'd really been honest with Wendy. He guessed he hadn't. After all, he'd always adored Amanda.

Rusty slapped a tape in the eight track. Springsteen. Finally, some good music.

"Did you see Chris kissing Mary Jane?" Rusty asked, clearly affronted by the spectacle.

"He was just trying to get some practice."

Dale then asked what he and Mary Jane were talking about. Rusty shrugged. Just different stuff. Then he turned and stared at Dale in a pseudo-offended way.

"She said she hated my beard."

**Chapter 6:** *A female in philosophy class; bad news at Heart-Pal*

The philosophy class had a girl in it. Her name, Polly Davis. Dale sat in his usual seat at the right corner of the long, polished, dark wooden table in the seminar room and stealthily glanced at her. She wasn't good looking, which he thought was fortunate. He didn't want a pretty girl distracting him in such an important class. He'd heard she was very smart. She'd been awarded the outstanding freshman award two years ago.

She had a plain face. Small, light blue eyes, a blob of a nose, and a rather big mouth but with thin lips. She wore her dull brown hair short, without any style. She often tucked loose strands behind her ears. Polly also didn't wear any makeup, not even the small touches that most girls on campus wore. Dale guessed it wouldn't have made much difference anyway.

Still, Polly interested him. She clearly had an intelligent look to her unglamorous face. Her eyes, although small, had a mental vitality shining in them that reminded Dale of the pre-tragedy Mrs. Page.

Polly's presence made most of the guys a little uneasy. They had gotten used to the four of them, along with Dr. Prescott, engaging in manly discussions of difficult philosophical issues. The addition of a female, even an acknowledged intelligent one, had changed the class dynamic.

Dale glanced at his three male colleagues: Henshaw, Eugene, and Stan the Man. Aaron Short had declined to join them. All of them, except Henshaw, had more of a diffident manner than in last year's philosophy class. Henshaw, of course, had won the outstanding freshman award last year, so he felt no pressure from Polly. He also possessed such poise that Dale thought nothing much could unbalance him. He sat tall in his chair, almost noble looking like a founding father, minus the wig of course, and stared out the large picture window that displayed the heart of the student quad.

Dr. Prescott was late. He was often late. Finally, almost five minutes after class should have started, he rambled in looking even more disheveled than usual, and plopped his jumbled assortment of textbooks and notebooks on the desk.

"Pardon my dilatory ways," he said. He smiled but Dale detected an undercurrent of concern in his hearty voice. "I became ensnared with bureaucratic red tape and it took longer than I anticipated to hack my way through it."

Dale grinned. He liked the way Dr. Prescott made mental activity seem physically heroic. Dr. Prescott asked the class where they had left off. Henshaw said on the last chapter of *Either/Or*.

They had been studying Soren Kierkegaard's classic text for three weeks. Dale felt lost. He thought his classmates felt the same, even Henshaw and Polly. *Either/Or* was a complicated book because the "author" wasn't Kierkegaard but two of his pseudonyms, "A" and "B" or Judge Williams. To obfuscate the matter even more, the book was edited under another pseudonym, Victor Eremita. Dale found the use of personas fascinating, although he wished Kierkegaard had been a little more creative and given "A" and "B" interesting names. Like, Adolphus Andersson and Bjorn Bjorkastork. Those were the proper names that Dale invented for the pseudonyms, although he wasn't certain if his made-up names sounded Danish, Swedish, or of some other Scandinavian derivation.

Dale especially liked the name Bjorn Bjorkastork, no doubt inspired by the Swedish tennis great, Bjorn Borg. He'd mistakenly used both made-up names in discussion once instead of referring to "A" and "B" and the rest of the class looked at him as if he'd spoken in tongues – a religious affectation of which Nazarenes did not approve.

Dale had even used Bjorn Bjorkastork as his pseudonym for his first analytical paper that he'd turned in last Friday. He felt a little nervous sitting in class waiting for the papers to be returned, which Dr. Prescott said would happen today. He didn't want Dr. Prescott to think he was simply burlesquing *Either/Or* or making fun of him or the class. He just couldn't write an analytical paper on such an intricate book in a straight way. Not only did it freeze him at the typewriter, but worse, it bored him. So, he decided to call upon the sagacity of Bjorn Bjorkastork. At the very least, if the paper stunk, Dale could blame Bjorn.

Last semester's philosophy seminar, Ancient to Medieval Political Philosophy, was easier than the current one, Existentialism: Christian and Non-Christian. Studying Plato, Aristotle, Machiavelli, and other geniuses wasn't easy. But the class had more of a thematic spine to connect the abstract ribs to: the political realm. Since their discussion had to eventually return to the practical necessity of governing, the philosophy had been grounded in reality. But in this seminar, the class sometimes wandered so far into the thicket of theory and abstraction that they foundered. At least, the students did. Dr. Prescott seemed to navigate his way around the bogs and marshes of Kierkegaard with astonishing ease. Just the rest of them were flailing away – or hacking, as the good doctor had recently described his mental exertions.

Dale certainly felt himself to be a hack. He'd almost not taken the class. He'd had his fill of existentialism last year. Reading Camus, Sarte, Beckett, and the others had made him sick. Not physically, just spiritually. He sort of liked Camus. He gave existentialism a sort of heroic sheen that gave Dale a shred of hope. But the other guys were too bleak. In fact, so bleak that he didn't believe them. If life was meaningless, then why bother writing at all. Such a view seemed so extreme that it negated itself. Dale suspected that the atheistic existentialists and the nihilists were putting on an act. They were pretending to both suffer more than the rest of unenlightened humanity and also offer a penetrating assessment of just that condition. He thought they didn't know any more about such things than anybody else; they just pretended to. After all, didn't Socrates say that the first step to enlightenment was admitting one's ignorance? Or, as Dale had put it in a paper last semester, I know that I do not know.

Henshaw had talked him into taking the class. He said he needed to hear Dale's slightly off-key voice in the choir of conformity. Dale wasn't sure that was a compliment. He guessed Henshaw meant his fellow philosophy students were the choir. Bobby was a good friend of Eugene, but Eugene was going to be a minister and his thinking was, perhaps by necessity, becoming more conventional.

Aaron Short, in last semester's seminar, had been conventional in his thinking. In fact, Dale had come to regard Short as a brighter version of Sylvester Fish. But Short had served a purpose in last semester's seminar: sort of the way Euthyphro did for Socrates in *Phaedro*. Short offered his canopy of platitudes and Dr. Prescott shredded it and allowed in the golden light of reason.

Dale had been intrigued by the title of the seminar: Existentialism: Christian and Non-Christian. The inclusion of non-Christian in the title of the class was brazenly bold. Dale still heard some of the religion professors and majors complaining about a class on *this* campus reading and discussing works hostile to Christianity. In fact, that was why Short had refused to take the course. Then there were some people, like Sylvester Fish, who thought philosophy itself was beyond the pale. Dale guessed they'd defend their desire for ignorance by saying they already knew the truth: Jesus was truth, so why look elsewhere? Dale knew what Dr. Prescott would say: There's Truth and then there's truth. There are a lot of those little truths and unless we investigate them, we can never fully understand the Truth.

Another reason he'd decided to take the class was that they were going to read Dostoyevsky. Dale wanted to read the great Russian novelists, Tolstoy and Dostoyevsky in particular. He'd tried reading *Crime and Punishment* last summer but it was too difficult. Dale told himself that it was the wrong time of the season to read Russian literature. He'd wait until winter and maybe that would put him in a more receptive frame of mind. In truth, he thought he wasn't intellectually mature enough to take on Dostoyevsky. In fact, he didn't really understand half of anything he read. But if he gained a glimmer of understanding, he felt encouraged enough to go on.

So, after Kierkegaard, the class would read some Dostoyevsky, then on to Nietzsche. Dale wished Dr. Prescott had picked some writers with easier names. Weren't there any Smiths or Jones out there in the philosophical wilderness? Come to think of it, there was a James: William, brother of the opaque Henry. Dale was looking forward to reading his work. Pragmatism. That was more like it.

Dale realized he'd been so lost in thought that he'd not heard most of the class discussion. It was mostly Dr. Prescott asking questions and Polly, Stan, and Eugene giving halting replies. Dr. Prescott had to carry most of the discussion, something he was loathe to do. But today he didn't seem to have as much patience for Socratic inquiry. In fact, now, as Dale scrutinized his professor, Dr. Prescott appeared distracted and out of sorts. Most unusual.

"From the persistent silence and hesitant replies to my entreaties, I take it that you scholars are ready to end our discussion of *Either/Or*?"

Dale was. He glanced around. All four of his classmates nodded.

"What was the primary problem with it?" Dr. Prescott held up the text like it was an offending intruder.

"It was rather convoluted, wasn't it?" asked Polly. She often answered questions with part of a question.

"I think it's beyond our ken at this point in our development," said Henshaw. That was the first time Bobby had spoken in class today. He smiled but Dale didn't think he was joking.

"Well, the Kierkegaard we'll be reading and discussing next isn't as dense or paradoxical," said Dr. Prescott. The professor often referred to books by the author's name, an eccentricity that Dale had taken up.

Dr. Prescott mentioned the next book on the schedule, *The Sickness Unto Death*. Sounded fun. Actually, Dale had read some of it already, having given up on *Either/Or* a week ago. What had interested him was its dismissal of "the crowd" and how the modern world (for Kierkegaard that was 1850 or so) had become passionless. He also knew that they were about to enter into Kierkegaard's denunciation of Christendom, which for the philosopher mainly meant the institutionalism of the Danish Reformed Church. To Dale, that sounded a little like the Jehovah's Witnesses' condemnation of Christendom. He'd come to realize that the Jehovah Witnesses were initially reformers. They had strived to return to the roots of Christianity before it had become institutionalized and turned into "Christendom."

Dr. Prescott ended class and passed out the papers. He handed one to everyone but Dale. The other four shuffled out of the room while glancing at their papers. Dale felt himself getting tight inside. Dr. Prescott turned and looked at him with a raised eyebrow.

"And now for your paper, Mr. Bjorkastork."

Dale tried not to smile at the ridiculous name. Just having Dr. Prescott say it made the risk of a poor grade worthwhile. He accepted his paper with trepidation. He resisted looking at the third page and the grade in front of Dr. Prescott. He knew that was rude.

"Actually, Dale, I enjoyed the artifice. As for the content, well, it could have been more focused on the work itself. But I thought you made some astute points – or should I say, Bjorn did."

Dale grinned a little. As he prepared to leave the room, he said he hoped next year's philosophy course would cover the American pragmatists.

Dr. Prescott shook his head. "Unfortunately, Dale, there might not be a philosophy seminar at all next year."

He wanted to ask why when the next group of students, led by Sylvester Fish, intruded. They were arriving for the religion class seminar. Dale thought it rather odd that Fish was an English, journalism, *and* religion major. He guessed he wanted to be like his mentor, Dr. Petry.

Dr. Prescott nodded at Dale and trudged out of room. Dale followed and watched as the doctor descended the steps without his usual jauntiness.

Dale turned to the third page. He saw the usual lengthy critique, which continued on the back. He flipped the page and read the critique's conclusion and saw the grade: an A minus. He thought the professor too generous. He'd written in conclusion: "What you somewhat lack in scrupulous analysis of the text, you compensate with imagination. Kierkegaard wouldn't disapprove."

Dale nodded. Good for Bjorn Bjorkastork.


Sharon had been right about Mrs. Genesee: she did edit with a velvet dagger.

Dale's first paper for her Expository Writing class had been returned with many wounds inflicted on it. He'd stalked out of the classroom feeling vexed. But as he examined his mistakes, he saw that she had been right. In fact, her comments were helpful. He knew he had some flaws. First, when he really got going, he forgot about mechanical correctness so he made mistakes in grammar, punctuation, and even spelling. Second, he tended to be wordy. Partly, that was because he wrote as he "heard" language. People tended to use more words than they needed; they often were redundant and vague. That was another reason why he tended to misspell. He "heard" words more than he "saw" them. Often he misspelled homonyms, like "pear" for "pair." He also had been raised in something of a hillbilly household and therefore he rarely heard proper pronunciation of words. He still tended to misspell "carpenter." He spelled it with a "d" because that's how he pronounced it.

Dale knew he had to change his ways or he'd never be selected as the newspaper editor. So, he devised a rigorous regimen to develop his understanding of usage, mechanics, and style: He studied his English handbook. He also tried to "see" words more than "hear" them. His next paper had fewer bloody tracks on it. He'd learned how to write mechanically correct papers that were devoid of content in Dr. Petry's class; now, this semester, he had to learn to write mechanically correct papers that said something. A much more difficult task, but he was making progress with the help of Mrs. Genesee's velvet dagger.

Now, sitting in the Expository Writing class, Dale figured he had a good chance this semester to make all As as he had last semester. In addition to the philosophy seminar, and this writing class, he'd taken a British history course, and three English classes, Milton, the history of the English language, and an independent study in nineteenth century American novels. The Milton class, taught by a lady professor, Dr. Frost, required a lot of study. Most of the class would be devoted to reading Milton's epic, *Paradise Lost*. Professor Cooper, or "Coop" as Dale had finally come to call his professor outside of class, once again tutored him in his independent study class. The novels they'd scheduled were by Cooper, Melville, Hawthorne, Twain, Howells, Crane, Wharton, and the formidable Henry James. Dale had found CliffsNotes for every novel he'd scheduled to read, and as was his principled practice, he never read the study guide until after he'd read – and sometimes struggled through – the novel itself.

Dale had a tendency not to follow class discussion and now Mrs. Genesee asked him to name an influential Christian writer of the twentieth century. Dale said J. D. Lewis when he meant to say C. S. Lewis. Then he made the matter worse by saying he meant J. D. Salinger. He then shook his head and said the right name, C. S. Lewis. Dale realized he had forever connected the two authors together in his mind like literary Siamese twins.

He noticed Fish, Polly, Sharon, and even Teri regarding him in a dubious way. He thought some of them would have looked at him with even a more disturbed expression if they knew Salinger was Jewish, a fact he hadn't known until he read a CliffsNotes after finishing the novel.

Mrs. Genesee, however, simply smiled at his faux pas. Dale liked her. She knew her subject well and taught in a considerate and encouraging way that Dale, so far, thought his female teachers did better than his male ones.

In that respect, Mrs. Genesee reminded Dale of Mrs. Heath. Mrs. Genesee was the wife of the varsity basketball coach and taught writing and journalism courses. She was friendly and approachable and students called by her first name, Jenny, out of class. She had light brown hair, blue eyes, and a pretty oval-shaped face. Dale liked the way she wore her hair, thick and straight, and how it hung like a movie theatre curtain around her shoulders.

After class, Teri walked out of the room with Dale and asked him if he'd said J. D. Salinger on purpose.

"No, just a slip of the initials."

"What? Oh, I get it."

Dale appreciated Teri's quickness. She was also something of a tomboy. She wore jeans most of the time, whereas most girls on campus wore dresses or skirts, or during winter, women's dress slacks. Teri also had something of a temper. In both respects she reminded him a little of Jesse.

"So, how do you like Jenny's style of teaching?"

"She's excellent." He thought she was a superb adviser for *Smoke Signals*, too. "I wished she'd taught Writing for Christian Publications last semester."

"Well, she was supposed to, you know."

"Then why didn't she?"

Teri stopped and gave a quick glance around them. They were standing on the north end of campus and most of the students were already streaming through the quad.

"If I tell, promise not to tell anyone else."

Dale looked at her. She was serious.

"Sure."

"Well, Mrs. Genesee has MS."

Dale wasn't sure what that was. He knew it must be bad because Teri's face looked like it had been slapped.

"You mean a disease?"

Teri nodded. He guessed she really admired Mrs. Genesee because she couldn't quite speak yet.

"Doesn't that stand for Multiple ..." Dale couldn't think of the second word. He'd never known anyone with the illness.

"Sclerosis."

Teri briefly told him how debilitating it was. An autoimmune disease, the myelin sheaths in the brain eroded and produced a number of serious effects, mostly affecting motor control and cogitation.

"Boy, that sounds serious," Dale muttered. Mrs. Genesee didn't even look that old. Maybe thirty.

"Yeah, it is. But it's in the early stage. It sort of attacks, then retreats. At the start of last semester, it attacked. Now, she's a lot better."

"Yeah, she seems fine. I hope it stays in retreat."

"Me, too." Teri looked at him with a different expression on her face. More of the impertinent look she usually had. "Say, are you planning on running for one of the editorships?"

"Yeah," Dale admitted. Sometimes people acted coy about such things, but he saw no reason to.

"Good. Anyone's better than Sylvester."

Before he could say thanks, Teri said she had to go. Dale watched as she walked through the quad, past all the other girls in their nice dress slacks.

The grand non-religious event of the winter at GNC was the Heart-Pal banquet. Dale thought he couldn't escape banquets. Heart-Pal, held near Valentine's day, was similar to his high school's pep club banquet except that the boys asked the girls. And even though the banquet had a Valentine's Day connection, it wasn't necessarily an event for sweethearts; hence, the odd combination, Heart-*Pal*. Sometimes couples went together as friends; even some female friends attended together.

Dale wondered who had asked Amanda last year. He didn't want to ask anyone, so he tried to guess by listening to people reminisce about last year's event. So far, he hadn't divined who had been her beau.

They sat at their charming table near the back of the resplendent hotel dining room where the underclassmen were seated. Henshaw and Abigail sat with them. Dale knew Henshaw hadn't asked Amanda. Abigail had already told him that the Heart-Pal had been their third date. He'd nodded. He understood the importance of the third date. He was certain Abigail abided by the same rule as Amanda; or had, until Henshaw swept her off her feet.

He didn't want to ask Amanda straight out who took her to this marvelous fete. They'd already had a little argument soon after she'd returned from the skiing trip. Dale, anxious to see her, called her the night of her return from Colorado and asked her out. She seemed pleased to hear his voice and said she'd be delighted to go see *The Pink Panther Strikes Again*. Since the movie was rated PG and they had meant to go to the previous Pink Panther film, he thought it was a good choice.

The next day, Dale wondered if he had the Pink Panther curse. As soon as she got in the car, he could tell she was miffed about something. Amanda, like most girls, wouldn't tell him candidly what was bothering her. No, he had to figure it out. He had to read her mind or decipher her facial expressions and body language and then recall all the oversights and insensitivity that he'd committed these last few days. Of course, that's what puzzled him. He hadn't seen her for ten days. What could he have done?

He asked her how her ski trip had been. She gave a laconic account of all her fun. She then asked him how he'd spent his time. Dale said he'd seen a few movies with Rusty, neglecting to mention that one was the R-rated *Network*. Not only did she refuse to see restricted movies, she disapproved when he backslid and saw one.

Then she asked if he'd done anything "special" on New Year's Eve. Dale started to give a brief account of Mary Jane's party when he realized that was why she was acting so huffy.

He said she apparently knew what he did that night. Didn't Mary Jane tell her?

Amanda glanced at him in a wounded way that uncomfortably reminded him of Wendy's rueful looks. Dale hadn't driven very far from Amanda's house, so he turned and parked in the fairly well-lit country club's parking lot.

He said, is that what's wrong?

She said she didn't know what he was talking about.

Is it about Wendy? He didn't know she would be at the party.

Amanda said it wasn't about Wendy. He didn't kiss *her*.

Dale almost laughed. The kiss was just a peck. Like a son gives his mother.

You kiss your mother on the lips?

Amanda had a good point. He never did that, not even as a little boy. Well, it was quick, he said. He hardly felt anything.

Amanda said that's not what Mary Jane said.

Dale wondered why Mary Jane would want to make trouble for him. Maybe she was angry about what he did to Butch. Maybe she blamed him for Rusty coming to her party. But she'd been talking to Rusty just before they'd left. He shook his head. He couldn't figure out girls.

Well, she's wrong, he said. I hardly kissed Carrie. And it was just a friendly little peck. I promise.

Amanda didn't seem mollified.

Look, I'll show you. He leaned over but instead of giving her a peck he kissed her hard. She squirmed and when he took his mouth away from hers, she slapped him. Not too hard, but it still surprised him.

436

What was that for?

He didn't rub his cheek. It stung a little, but he'd been taught in sports to never show an opponent that you'd been hurt.

I don't know, Amanda said. I'm sorry.

Dale looked out his window. He couldn't believe she was jealous, if that was what it was. He looked at her. She sat quietly at the other end of the seat, almost leaning against the door.

Carrie is engaged, he said. It was just a friendly, short kiss. Then he told Amanda he was sorry he kissed her so hard. He was just fooling around.

Amanda looked at him. He saw tears in her eyes. Dale felt a pang in his heart knowing she was about to cry.

He held out an open hand. Come here, he said gently. She didn't budge. He said, a little less gently, come here.

She lowered her face and scooted over. She didn't sit completely next to him so Dale had to move over, too. He put his arm around her. He tried looking into her eyes but she hung her head and there wasn't enough light to see.

At the party, I kept thinking about you, he said. You can ask Carrie. She noticed how pensive I was and I told her it was because you weren't there.

Really?

Yes. I thought about you all evening. I imagined what you were doing. Later, when I left, I thought about you when it was New Year's Eve mountain time.

Amanda looked puzzled. What do you mean?

I mean mountain time. You were in Colorado. Midnight in Oklahoma is only eleven in Colorado.

Amanda covered her mouth with her hand. Dale noticed she'd painted her nails creamy pink. She usually didn't paint her nails.

Oh, my, she said.

What?

I forgot about the time difference. At New Year's Eve I thought about what you were doing, but that meant it was an hour later here.

Dale shrugged. Time zones could be confusing. He was more interested in what she was doing during her New Year's Eve.

So, you thought about me then?

Yes, Amanda said shyly.

Were you alone?

No. She glanced at Dale. My family was around.

Did you kiss anyone?

My father kissed me on the cheek. She looked at Dale resentfully. But I should have kissed someone.

He squeezed her shoulder. No, you shouldn't.

You did.

Quite by accident. K. C. and Gretchen, Quentin and Roxanne were there. They all kissed. The other guys couldn't leave out the other girls. And I didn't kiss Wendy.

That's true. Chris did.

You sure got a complete report.

Amanda smiled. Dale did, too, and he leaned over and kissed her, softly this time.

He promised he would never kiss any other girl on New Year's Eve but her. Then he joked, but I might kiss a boy. Amanda playfully slapped his knee and he asked if she still wanted to see a movie. Amanda said she really wasn't in the mood.

So they decided to go out and eat. Dale got a full meal, she had a salad. He didn't want to scold her about being on a diet, so he said nothing. Afterwards, they drove around the lake but didn't stop to park. He wanted to but he thought Amanda would object. Then he drove her home, parked, and walked her to her door. She asked if he wanted to come in. It wasn't that late yet. Not even ten. He said he wanted to come in, just not that way. Amanda shook her head at him, as if to say, naughty Dale. But when he took her hand, she followed him around the side of the house. When they got to the door, she hesitated. He said he wouldn't go over forty. She remembered the metaphor. Not over thirty, she said. He said okay, although he knew their speed definitions were probably different. Once inside, he decided to observe the speed limit for the most part. He knew she'd object if he pushed her bra up, so he didn't. She allowed him to put his hand over her breast with the bra still on, and she let him touch her bare hip but not dip his hand down the back of her slacks. When he tried, she said *Dale* in the same voice her older sister had used in cautioning Kenny about throwing the imaginary football.

Even though they didn't get to forty, it was still making out. Dale left feeling fairly satisfied. He knew he had to take it slow with Amanda.

Then classes started and Amanda and Dale attended the opening convocation, which wasn't a revival but a week of religious speakers and concerts. The increased religiosity apparently dampened Amanda's ardor, which he found puzzling and frustrating. He didn't think there was anything wrong with what they did. He cared about her deeply; in fact, he adored her but he hadn't confessed it to her yet because he thought it would scare her. He wanted to be intimate with her. But Amanda thought "petting," the term she used, was now improper. The other problem was she was back on campus. Boys weren't allowed in the girls' dorms. She wouldn't go parking with him. When he suggested it after a religious-themed music concert on campus – bad timing on his part – she looked at him as if he'd propositioned her. So, it was back to hand-holding and a good night kiss. No cruising for Dale.

Now, a month later, he and Amanda sat at their table at the Heart-Pal banquet. Dale knew Amanda enjoyed these rituals. He'd bought her an expensive corsage. She was in a good mood. She liked talking with Bobby and Abigail. In fact, she spoke to them so much that he felt rather left out.

They watched the crowning of the Heart-Pal princess. Dale didn't really know the girl, a petite brunette ironically named Tina Valentine. She was cute, but not a beauty, but then the requirements for Nazarene royalty were as much for good character and sociability as beauty.

Dale imagined Amanda eventually being selected either homecoming queen or Heart-Pal princess. She'd surely be one of the candidates by her senior year. He had mixed feelings about that. He'd like to see her honored because she was lovely but he thought these ceremonies were rather silly and he didn't like to have any personal connection to them. Of course, he might not have any personal connection to them then, which was another source of concern.

After the banquet, Dale drove Amanda back to campus. Some of their friends were going to Thad and Denise North's home to wind down the evening. Amanda wanted to go to her dorm and change. Chris had earlier told him that he and his date, Rowena Watson, would be there. When Dale first met Rowena last semester, he said he liked her name. She didn't get it. He told her the Saxon princess in *Ivanhoe* is named Rowena. Rowena still didn't get it. What's Ivanhoe? she had asked.

In spite of that inauspicious meeting, Dale liked Rowena. She sort of looked like a Saxon princess, with her thick, blond hair and blue eyes. She didn't wear her hair loose, though. It puffed around her head and hung above her shoulders like some medieval helmet and hardly swayed when she walked. He also thought her lips were a little thin but maybe it just looked that way because she smiled easily and she had quite large, perfect teeth. Her figure was what some people termed athletic. Her shoulders were a little broad for a girl and her hips were a little narrow, both features he didn't prefer. She was also something of a tomboy, too, because she, like Teri, wore jeans quite a lot. Nevertheless, she was pretty, in a toothy kind of way, and he thought Chris could do a lot worse.

When Dale parked in the Hayley parking lot, near the more private west end, Amanda said she had something to tell him.

Whenever a girl said that, he knew to be on guard. It rarely indicated anything good.

Dale leaned back in his seat. "Okay," he said, "shoot."

She asked him if he'd heard of Lost and Found.

"Did you lose something at the banquet?" He felt a little annoyed she'd waited until now to tell him.

"No, I didn't lose anything. Lost and Found. It's a summer outreach ministry."

He'd never heard of it.

"Well, it's a group of college kids that performs skits, sings, and ministers to young people. Don't you remember it being on campus last summer?"

Dale tried to remember. He wasn't much interested in stuff like that. Also, he wasn't officially a GNCer then. He supposed Amanda had gone to it with her friends. "No, but why?"

"I'm going to try out."

"Oh, yeah? What are you going to do? Sing?"

"Yes."

"Then you're a cinch."

"Well, there's a problem."

Dale detected a concerned note in her voice. Her eyes glanced away from his.

"What's the problem?"

"If I'm accepted, I'll be gone most of the summer."

"How long is most?"

"Two months. All of June and July."

Dale didn't like that. He'd counted on being with Amanda as much as possible during the summer. He counted on getting back up to speed, so to speak.

"Two months?"

"I probably won't make the team, anyway."

He'd heard that note of discouragement in her voice before. She wasn't doing as well as she hoped with her music. She'd already given up the flute. She'd said her voice coach thought she wasn't practicing enough. She couldn't hit the higher notes like she used to.

"Don't be silly." He tried to sound encouraging. "You'll make it. You have a voice of an angel."

"Really?"

"You know I love your voice. It reminds me –" he searched for a metaphor – "of the chimes of heaven."

He didn't know what the heck he was talking about. But he wanted to cheer her up, reassure her. He knew she'd respond better to encouragement than his disappointment.

"The competition is fierce," Amanda said.

"You'll get it," Dale said, waving his hand as if dismissing any different possibility. "Once people hear you sing, they'll feel the same way I do."

Amanda leaned over and hugged him.

"You don't object to me being gone for two whole months? Well, with practice it's more like two and a half."

"Two and a half?"

Amanda leaned away but kept her hands on his shoulders. "Well, we have to practice."

"Aren't you going to practice here? In Galilee?"

"Oh, no, Lost and Found is based in Kansas City."

"You'll be gone for two weeks in Kansas City?"

"Well, more like three weeks considering we have a few days of orientation."

"Amanda, it sounds like you're going to be gone almost the whole summer."

"I know."

Amanda removed her hands from his shoulders and turned and faced the windshield. Dale saw her biting her lower lip. He wished she wouldn't do that.

He felt himself growing annoyed. He fought the feeling. He knew it wasn't the time to get angry.

"We won't get to see each other much this summer," she said. At least she sounded truly sorry.

"I might have to follow you around this summer," he said, jokingly. "Where will the Lost and Found people be most of the time?"

"Oh, all over," she said, without enthusiasm. "It depends on the troupe. One goes west. One goes east. Another south. Another north."

"Sounds like they got all the bases covered."

"There's an international one, too, but it's for graduates."

Dale didn't know what to say. A summer without Amanda sounded dreadful. They'd never really had a summer together. Just part of August.

"I'll just have to keep busy. I'll get another job for the weekdays. I'll take a couple of summer classes."

Amanda peered at him. "You don't mind?"

"Of course I mind. I'll miss you. But I guess this is important to you."

"Yes, it is. I've dreamed about doing it for years."

"I hope you get it, then."

Amanda returned to his arms. "Most sophomores, or juniors-to-be, don't get it."

Dale stroked her hair. He worried she would be an exception.


## Chapter 7: *Nietzsche banned; poems for Bronwyn; spring break dust storm*

They were forbidden to read Nietzsche. Dr. Prescott announced that to his students the last class before spring break. He held one of the texts he'd planned on using and tossed it down on the table where it landed flat and made an explosive sound.

None of the students said a word. Dale glanced at them and they didn't seem particularly concerned. Even Henshaw looked like he'd stumbled upon an embarrassing public scene and had averted his eyes.

"Why?" asked Dale.

Dr. Prescott shrugged, a gesture that Dale had never seen him perform. "Too dangerous."

Dale was disappointed, although he had a feeling Nietzsche would be especially difficult to read. Getting through Dostoyevsky had been mentally exhausting and trying to tackle the mad German seemed like the intellectual equivalent of trying to subdue a wild boar. Dale was certain he'd be gored by Nietzsche's sharp tusks.

Still, being forbidden to do something intellectually risky at an institution of higher education seemed preposterous to him. He had enough of a contrarian impulse to suggest that they read Nietzsche anyway.

Dale glanced at his four colleagues. None of them seemed to welcome his defiance. They looked at him, then turned their eyes away. He understood Eugene and Stan not sharing his convictions. But he felt disappointed in Polly, and especially Henshaw.

"Interesting suggestion, Dale, but Dean Snyder was adamant. No Nietzsche in class." Dr. Prescott raised one of his tufted brows. "However, I certainly can't stop you from perusing Nietzsche on your own out of class."

Judging from the neutral looks on his colleagues, he doubted any of them would engage in such a perilous venture. But Dale promised himself he would. He and the professor shared a fleeting smile.

"What are we going to read instead, Dr. Prescott?" Polly asked.

Dale had found out that Polly was the daughter of the chairman of the physical science department, Dr. Davis. Her father taught physics and chemistry and was reputed to be a brilliant man. GNC science graduates had an impressive record of attending graduate schools and medical schools, which surprised Dale when he learned this from Sharon Myrick.

Dr. Prescott hadn't answered Polly's question yet. He rubbed his homely face, now sprouting short whiskers in the first stage of a beard. Dale thought a beard would help give the professor a more dignified appearance.

"Clive Staples Lewis," Dr. Prescott pronounced.

Initially, the class didn't recognize the author. Then Polly exclaimed, "Oh, C. S. Lewis," and all of them except Dale and Henshaw murmured in approval.

"What texts?" Dale asked, using Dr. Prescott's preferred term for books.

"*The Problem of Pain* and *The Screwtape Letters*."

More murmurs of approbation. Dale nodded, but not exactly in agreement; he'd already read the texts, but no doubt not up to Dr. Prescott's demanding standards. However, this decision bothered him. C. S. Lewis, for all his talent, wasn't really a philosopher. He was an essayist and Christian apologist. Dale glanced at his professor. Dr. Prescott strolled over to the large, picture window and gazed out at the student quad. Dale had the sinking feeling that he had surrendered or at least compromised an important personal principle.

Dale looked at Henshaw. He hadn't said anything so far. He'd not even reacted to the change in the reading. He sat erect in his chair and gazed out the window in the same preoccupied manner as his mentor.

When Dr. Prescott resumed class discussion, not on the biography of Nietzsche, of course, but on Lewis, the class responded more vigorously than it had since the first weeks of the semester. In a way, Dale looked forward to the sunny disposition of Lewis after weathering the gloomy Dane and the saturnine Russian. However, he felt a wave of intellectual nostalgia sweep over him. For all his grappling with the two authors, Kierkegaard in particular because Dostoyevsky wrote fiction and Dale found that a little easier to understand, he thought he would miss the challenge of penetrating into the prose of a complex thinker.

Kierkegaard had stimulated his mind. First, Dale sympathized with old Soren. Kierkegaard had loved one woman all his life, had once been engaged to her, but broke it off because he didn't want to inflict his melancholy personality on her. He'd remained in love with her just the same, and although she later married, she apparently always loved him, too. When she died, many years after Kierkegaard, she requested in her will to be buried next to him.

Second, Dale responded to Kierkegaard's critique on society and Christendom. Kierkegaard denounced the superficiality of "the crowd" and how it tried to stifle the creative individual. Dale also admired the way the philosopher challenged the accepted conventions of the Danish church, and society as a whole. At heart, he was a reformer, just like Martin Luther.

But what Dale found most compelling was Kierkegaard's insistence that doubt was a necessary element in faith. He believed a "leap of faith" was necessary to believe in God, the same way a leap of faith was essential to love another person, such as his love for Regine Olsen.

Dale had been influenced by his reading of Kierkegaard, in part because it mirrored his own thinking of late. He agreed that without doubt one could not truly have faith. He concurred with the philosopher that a faith in God without having first doubted God's existence would be a worthless faith. The doubt gave faith its meaning.

The only student who had wanted to discuss these ideas at any length with him was

Henshaw. They had spoke for hours out of class about Kierkegaard. They even debated his ideas after an intramural basketball game and continued the same discussion for several days. Their last discussion was on the afternoon before the Heart-Pal banquet. They talked so long and intensely that they'd almost been late picking up Amanda and Abigail.

Dale had mentioned some of Kierkegaard's ideas to Amanda. She listened but she really didn't understand why he found this long-dead philosopher so interesting. Frankly, she thought his ideas were a little strange.

Chris, who ordinarily tolerated Dale's forays into the philosophic, had thought this Kierkegaard guy was a kook. A Kookegaard. He told Dale that the idea that doubt was necessary for faith didn't make any sense. It was a contradiction. Dale demurred. It was a paradox. Chris said, same thing.

Class ended and Dale noticed Henshaw striding out of class. Often, he'd linger with Dr. Prescott until the next class drove them out. Dale knew something was afoot. He gathered his stuff and swiftly followed. He caught up with Henshaw outside the building.

"Hey, Henshaw," he called. "What gives?"

Henshaw stopped. He turned and Dale saw he had a rather severe look on his normally placid face.

Dale walked over to him. "I thought you acted strange in class. What's up?"

Henshaw hesitated. Dale could almost see his mind working on the handsome features of his face, the way it did when Dale made a point that he wanted to refute.

"The administration refused to renew Dr. Prescott's contract."

"You mean, they fired him?"

"Essentially."

"Why? He's the best teacher on campus."

"Perhaps that's the reason."

Dale considered the irony of that assertion.

"I got to go," said Henshaw.

"Hey, aren't you going to do anything about it?"

Henshaw stopped in his tracks and walked back to Dale and stood quite close to him. Henshaw stared down at him and even though Dale felt uncomfortable looking up five inches, he stared back. He thought he saw a spark of anger in Bobby's grayish-blue eyes.

"What am I supposed to do about it?"

"You know people. Talk to them. Talk to Dean Snyder."

Henshaw shook his head. His demeanor returned to its usual equanimity.

"No use, Dale. It's a lost cause."

With that fatalistic comment, Henshaw turned and strode away.

Dale entered the all but deserted library and climbed the stairs to the third floor. He walked past the empty desks to the small cubicle where two typewriters – one a manual, the other an electric – were located. He went inside and closed the door.

He paced the small room. He wasn't in the mood to write yet. His thoughts were still on Amanda. She'd left earlier that day with eleven other GNCers to drive to Kansas City to audition for the Lost and Found summer ministry. Dale had met her at her dorm to see her off. She'd been excited and alternated between giddiness about the trip and the upcoming auditions and regret that she wouldn't be seeing him for ten days. After auditioning that weekend, she was going to meet her family and they were driving to the Ozarks to spend spring break together.

Dale feigned good cheer about it all. He told her he wished he could go to Kansas City and encourage her, but he had to work. Amanda understood. She'd be busy all the time anyway.

Dale had carried her suitcase out of the dorm lobby to the van. He heaved it in the back then, seeing there was no privacy in the parking lot, took Amanda by the hand and walked her behind the dormitory. Amanda giggled nervously and asked what he was doing. Saying good-bye, he said. He checked to make sure no one was around, then kissed her. She responded pretty well but he sensed she was nervous about being in public and anxious to board the van. He didn't kiss her again. Instead, he wished her luck, and said he would think about her every day and walked her back to the van.

He watched her board and take her seat. She smiled and waved as the van rolled past. Then, to Dale's intense displeasure, he saw David Hawkins sitting one seat behind Amanda. That was too close as far as Dale was concerned.

Now, sitting before the electric typewriter, Dale felt despondent. He'd wanted to see Amanda over spring break. They hadn't had much personal time since that time just after New Year's.

Dale thought the best way to chase his blues was to write. The *Smoke Signals* literary issue was coming out in three weeks. He'd decided to enter both the prose and poetry contests. He'd already written a short story and some poetry and submitted it. Now, with the deadline just a few hours away, he decided he'd write some more.

Dale inserted a clean sheet of white paper into the electric typewriter and wondered what he'd write. He didn't have time to write another story. He'd have to compose poetry.

He almost wished he'd taken the poetry class that semester. Since the class met at the same time as the philosophy class, Dale had opted for philosophy over poetry. He really didn't know much about poetry. He'd read quite a bit in preparation for all those advanced placement exams. He liked it. He especially admired the poetry of Shakespeare, John Donne, and the English romantics. He thought they composed verse in the proper way, with complex rhythmic patterns and sophisticated word play. He also liked Dickinson and Frost. Even though Dickinson wrote free verse, which Dale didn't regard in as high esteem, he liked her gnomic sensibility.

He'd met the creative writing teacher once. She came by the *Smoke Signals* office to talk to Mrs. Genesee, or Jenny as she called her. The creative writing teacher's name was Bronwyn J. Ayers. Dale remembered seeing her name on the sign attached to her door when he walked through the English department to meet with Coop. Dale thought it was an arresting name, although her using the middle initial bothered him. He wondered was there another Bronwyn Ayers? Unlikely. Then why the initial J? It suggested a proclivity toward pretentiousness, a quality that Dale especially abhorred, although he secretly feared he might have that tendency, too.

That day, two months ago, sitting before the layout table with Teri, Sharon, and Polly, Dale stealthily evaluated at Bronwyn J. Ayers. She looked young, perhaps in her mid-twenties. She wore her auburn hair long and partially braided. Large earrings dangled from her ears. She wore makeup, not a lot, but enough to suggest she was not a prim teacher. She had a fairly pretty face. Her nose had a slightly bulbous end, but she had a wide, full-lipped mouth and large green eyes, which reminded Dale a little of Wendy's. She was on the tall side for a woman, maybe five foot nine, and had a slender but not skinny figure. But her most noticeable feature, as far as he was concerned, was her large breasts.

Dale had never seen a woman so tall and slender with such large breasts before. In high school, the girl with the biggest breasts in his class, the bovine Merry Singleton, was tall but had a full lower figure as well. Her hips were proportional to her bosom. But Bronwyn had a long, slender figure, which seemed to make her ample breasts look even larger than they were. After that first meeting, Dale sort of wished he'd taken her poetry class rather than philosophy.

Aside from that feature, there was something else interesting about Bronwyn. She looked almost like a hippie; well, as close as people came to looking like hippies at GNC. Her clothes had something to do with it: faded jeans, a fairly tight sweater with a large necklace, and knee-high black leather boots. The tall heels gave Bronwyn another three inches of height so she towered over Mrs. Genesee. Dale wondered how Bronwyn got away with dressing like that. He guessed it was because she taught creative writing and even GNC college administrators made some allowances for "artistic" people.

After Bronwyn left, Teri teased Dale about her. She said, you find her interesting, don't you? He said, she's certainly different. Teri said, yeah, she's hip. Well, hip for GNC.

Dale knew that Bronwyn was the faculty judge for poetry. Mrs. Genesee was the prose judge. The third judge was Stan Perkins. Dale began to wonder what kind of style of literature Bronwyn liked. He already had an idea what Stan and Jenny liked. They favored well-wrought prose, concise, and concrete. Dale had no idea what Bronwyn liked. Judging from her appearance, he thought maybe Walt Whitman. She just looked like a free-verse kind of woman.

So, sitting before the electric typewriter, Dale began to compose a free-verse poem. It didn't go so well. He ripped the paper out of the typewriter and started afresh. What he needed, he decided, was a persona. So, he called upon the spirit of Bjorn Bjorkastork and quickly composed a mini-saga. Very mini. Seven stanzas of gloom, heroism, and death. Sort of a modern day *Beowulf*.

Unsurprisingly, it was silly. But Dale decided to keep it and submit it under Bjorkastork's name.

Now, he was having fun. He wrote another poem, a maudlin paean to motherhood and attributed it to Chris.

Just to get even with Mary Jane, Dale wrote the worst poem he could compose, full of juvenile rhyme and baby-talk diction about the travails of being a woman, and typed Mary Jane Morgan at the end.

His next victim would be Krupp. What could he compose that would do justice to the great man? Dale decided to list all his manly virtues in an address to the reader. The last couplet went as follows:

> I am Hercules, I am Adonis;
> I bestride the world like a Colossus.

Not bad, thought Dale. Better than Krupp deserved.

Dale paused in his labors. He now switched to the manual. He felt he needed a whole new persona. One that would capture the essence of his age. Maybe a persona that would express the pain of being an outsider. A poet of protest. Hmmm. Who could that be?

Then it came to him. He typed the name Harry Horse. He x'ed out the Harry and typed Harold. No, too formal. He x'ed Harold and typed just H. After all, Bronwyn was an initials kind of woman. So, that was it: H. Horse.

Dale, imbued with the fury of H. Horse, wrote the first poem: *I Stand Alone*.

> I stand alone
> A man without his people
> A man without his land
> A man that people
> > ignore
> And say that I am not
> > A man.
>
> I watch my brothers
> as they play a game
> > A white game
> Of gaining wealth and
> wasting health
> For their foolish pleasure.

They see not the beauty
of the land.
They see only green …
They feel not unseen things
Only seen.


Dale thought he was getting in the mood. He detected a Platonic note in the poesy of H. Horse. Rather unusual for a Navajo. Dale liked how H. Horse expressed his existential angst in admirably wretched prose poetry.

For his next opus, he first came up with the title, *I am Red.*

Some say a Chinaman is yellow,
I say gold.
Some say a Negro is black
I say he is dun.
Some say that I am red
but what do they know of a
Red man's hope and heart?

My skin is not red, but my blood …
And they who call me so
Are coyotes howling in the wind.
I am swarthy and strong,
A man whose skin is of a different tone
But my heart is red and brave.

Eiiii! I am a red man
in the home of the brave
In the home where my ancestors lay
In their blood red grave …

Dale scrutinized the work. He liked that "Eiii!" And H. Horse seemed to have a penchant for ellipses. However, Dale began to feel some sympathy for H. Horse. He'd meant to write doggerel, and although it was pretty much that, the poem, seen from the perspective of an oppressed American Indian, did contain a few shreds of feeling. More than he intended. Well, he didn't have enough time to slop it up. So, he composed three more poems all in the same kind of wounded, yet prideful, voice.

His literary labors complete, Dale gathered up the sheets of paper, and filled out the submission forms in convincingly different handwriting styles. Chris's jagged handwriting was easy to fake. Mary Jane's graceful, looping style was more difficult. Dale had to concentrate and hold his wrist really limp. For Krupp, he just wrote as illegibly as possible, hoping the judges wouldn't even bother reading it once they saw how Pollacked it was. He provided fake information, of course, for Bjorkastork and H. Horse. For Krupp, Mary Jane, and Chris, he gave as accurate information as he could remember, except for Mary Jane's major, which he listed as "snoop studies."

Then he left the library, walked over to the student union, down the hall to the publication offices, and, giving one last furtive glance, he slipped the poems underneath the newspaper's door.


Dale stood on the porch with Grandpa and watched the towering reddish clouds gathering

445

in the western horizon.

"Does that remind you of anything?" Dale asked.

Grandpa nodded. "Shore do," he said, "shore do."

They went back inside and reported the news about the advancing dust storm to Grandma, Jesse, and June May. Grandpa said it was just like them black dusters he recollected thirty odd years ago.

"Fordy year," Grandma said.

Grandpa hadn't turned up his hearing aid high enough to hear Grandma across the room, so he launched into a brief history lesson of the Dust Bowl era, still getting the chronology wrong.

Dale waited until Grandpa had concluded, then said he had to go. Jesse asked him where. He said he'd already told her he and Rusty were going to a movie.

"In this weather?" she asked.

"It'll be alright. We're driving east."

"What movie you going to?" June May asked.

"Haven't decided."

He said so long to them. Grandpa said he'd better keep a lookout for that black duster. Dale said he would. Actually, the duster looked more red than black.

Dale got in his Chevy and drove to Rusty's. Since it was Saturday night, and he'd spent the whole day working and reading, Dale didn't want to stay home. He thought about Amanda. She might be auditioning that very minute. He hoped she didn't get selected, then he took the ungenerous thought back.

When Dale arrived at Rusty's, he saw the huge reddish cloud getting closer. He smelled dust in the air. Rusty came out and joined Dale as they surveyed the turbulent horizon.

"Looks bad," said Dale.

"Don't worry," Rusty said. "We can outrun it."

Rusty said they'd take his car, and he and Dale jumped in. Rusty roared the Malibu down the road and onto the north rural road that led to the northwest area of the City. Dale glanced out the back window and saw the storm advancing on them. The reddish, swirling cloud nearly blotted out his view through the rear window.

"Guess what?" Rusty said.

Dale thought, we're running out of gas. That had happened once before with Rusty, but that was back in high school when he drove his old Rambler and the fuel gauge didn't work.

"What?"

"I'm transferring to GNC."

Dale said great.

"I talked to Coach Genesee and he said he'd give me a shot to make the team. Well, the JV team."

Dale said he was a sure thing.

"Yeah, man, but I haven't played competitive basketball for a year. I think I need to play summer league again."

Dale said good idea. Get in shape. He told Rusty he ought to take an independent study gym class with him, Chris, Henshaw, and Greene. They were going to lift weights and play basketball on alternate days.

"You're playing basketball?"

"I played intramural this winter. Did okay. Still can't shoot very well because –" Dale held up his right hand and bent his two good fingers, leaving the two bad ones standing crooked.

"Poor baby," Rusty said.

He knew Rusty was skeptical of his two-severed-finger-excuse. Dale just liked to bug him about it. He planned on holding up his right hand with the mangled fingers every time he missed a shot when they played basketball together.

They got to the mall just as the storm swept over them. Rusty parked his Chevy and they sat in the car looking at the reddish dust shower the car.

"Hey, this is cool," said Rusty.

"Oh, yeah," said Dale, mocking his buddy.

They didn't have enough time to ride out the dust storm. When they saw a lull, they jumped out of the car and raced through the nearly empty parking lot toward the theatre. The dust was so bad they had to pull the top of their shirts over their mouth and nose to keep from choking.

They walked up to the ticket window and saw the ticket girl gazing at them as if they were crazy. She said the manager was thinking about closing down.

"Ahh, the storm's passed now," Rusty said.

The girl, a chubby brunette, asked what movie they wanted to see.

"*A Star is Born*," Rusty said.

Dale stared at his buddy. "Why that?"

"'Cause it has Kris in it."

Rusty gave his Kris Kristofferson facial impression. He made his face go blank and his eyes look dim. Then he grinned like Kristofferson. Dale smiled. Rusty, with his beard, did look a little like the movie star.

"Yeah, but it also has her in it."

Dale pointed to the poster showing the unclothed upper torsos of Kristofferson and Barbra Streisand locked in an embrace.

"Well, you can't have everything, man," Rusty said. "Besides, it looks like she might be getting naked."

Dale didn't think that was an inducement. He tried to remember if he'd ever seen a good movie with Barbra Streisand in it. He didn't like musicals. The only non-musical with her in it that he could remember liking okay was *What's Up, Doc?* and she'd just about ruined that movie as well. He thought it was sort of funny but not nearly as good as the real screwball comedies it was modeled after. Certainly no *Bringing Up Baby*, which he'd seen in his film class at CSU. Now, that was a funny movie.

Dale scanned the marquee. Nothing looked much better, so he paid for his and Rusty's tickets. Rusty started to protest but Dale said it was to make up for the gas. They always took Rusty's car when they went anywhere.

They went into the theatre after Rusty bought a big bucket of popcorn and an extra large Coke. Just as Dale feared, the movie made him sick. He didn't like the music, didn't like her, didn't even like Kristofferson, although he'd read the guy was a Rhodes Scholar. He wrote some pretty good songs, too. But Dale didn't think he could act a lick.

After the movie, they walked out into a dust-covered parking lot. Two inches of dust covered the ground and the cars.

"Man, this is weird," Rusty said, kicking at the dust and sending a spray into the air.

It had been a dry winter and spring. Dale remembered a few summers ago a little dust-up. But that had been August.

They got in Rusty's car but it wouldn't start. They got out, Rusty popped the hood, and he cleaned the air filter. Back in the car, it started up fine.

"How'd you like the movie?" Rusty asked.

"It made me want to talk to Earl."

Rusty smiled. He hadn't heard that expression in years.

The day classes resumed after spring break, Dale sat on his customary stool in the *Smoke Signals* office when Bronwyn walked in. He immediately noticed she was carrying the poetry of H. Horse because he recognized the old-fashioned manual typewriter typeface. He watched her as she went over to Delphina Orkins, the business manager, and asked her to call the registrar's office. Dale felt his stomach flatten. He'd not anticipated Bronwyn verifying whether or not the contestants were officially enrolled in college. He felt thwarted. All that work for nothing.

Delphina called the registrar's office. She asked the person on the other end of the line to confirm whether a student by the name of Horse, initial H., attended GNC.

Dale's ears pricked up. Delphina, a tall, skinny girl with short brown hair, didn't have the best articulation. He thought she'd said "Horsth." Well, the jig was up, he thought.

Delphina received the information, nodded, and hung up the phone. "Yesth, Missth Ayersth, he is a student on campusth."

Dale sat stunned on the stool.

Bronwyn nodded with evident satisfaction. She promptly turned on her three-inch heeled, knee-high boots and marched out.

Dale, still bemused, didn't even bother to watch her exit.

Was there really a H. Horse attending GNC? Dale guessed it was possible. GNC did have a few Indian students enrolled. But still: what were the odds?

Four days later, Dale eagerly picked up the literary issue of *Smoke Signals* on his way to his early morning class. He, and any other staffer who'd contributed to the lit issue, were banned from seeing any copy of that section before publication. He had no idea if his poetry or short story had been selected. He hoped so. Ever since he saw last year's issue, he'd imagined seeing his work printed in the special supplement.

He hurriedly flipped through the tabloid newspaper until he came to the pullout literary section. He stared in disbelief. He felt like he'd been kicked by a mule – or a horse. H. Horse had won not only the best poetry entry but also the best overall entry.

Dale couldn't believe it. He stared again at the bold face type below the two poems, *I Stand Alone* and *I am Red* that read **BEST POETRY AWARD** and **BEST OVERALL ENTRY AWARD**.

Dale closed the newspaper. Did Bronwyn really think those were the best poems? Did she and the other two judges really think *I am Red* was the best overall entry? Dale opened the paper again. Apparently so. Not only were those two poems printed on the first page, but a photograph of a bronze sculpture of a plains Indian warrior occupied more than half the page as an illustration to the two winning entries.

Dale laughed at the absurdity of it. He noticed Fish staring at him from clear across the quad. He'd laughed so hard that it had attracted the keen ears of Sylvester forty yards away.

He quickly grabbed another issue of the newspaper and dashed away, lest Fish stroll over and ask him what was the cause for inappropriate laughter at such an early hour.

While walking to the building where his first class The History of the English Language met, Dale flipped through the rest of the supplement. He saw his two poems. But his short story, a first-person account of a young sailor who gets into a brawl with an "Asiatic," didn't make the cut. Instead, Polly's essay on God's design in nature had won best prose award. Dale stopped walking and smiled at the irony of it all. His pseudonym had out-written him.

There was more comedy in the pages. Krupp's poem had been printed, as had Mary Jane's. Dale whooped with laughter. He flipped to the last page. Darn. Chris's poem didn't make it. Nor did Bjorkastork's.

Well, three out of five pseudonyms wasn't bad.

As Dale sat in his chair in the empty classroom, a puzzling question entered his mind. If there was a Horse, who was he? And what would he do when he saw three poems (a third Horse poem had been selected, too) attributed to him?

Just before class started, Teri congratulated Dale on his two poems; He complimented her on her one. Then she said, did you read the winning entries by the Indian guy?

Dale said yeah.

"What did you think of them?"

He shrugged.

"Yeah, not so hot," she said in her typically blunt way.

Before he could ask her to elaborate, Coop ambled in and cut their discussion short. After class, Dale rushed out, leaving Teri to discuss the literary supplement with Polly. On his way across the quad, he saw Krupp walking as usual with his hands jammed in his pants pockets.

"Great poem, Krupp!" Dale yelled, as he passed him.

Krupp looked up, startled. Dale saluted his literary triumph and Krupp smiled in a confused way. Dale waited for him to deny the poem's authorship, but Krupp, momentarily looking like he'd forgotten his destination, recovered and trudged forward like the Colossus he truly was.

Amanda, a music major, didn't have any classes with Dale, but sometimes they met for lunch at the student union. At noon, he tossed open the front door and saw Amanda standing with Mary Jane. He had to stifle a laugh. Mary Jane had a puzzled expression on her face as she and Amanda flipped through the literary supplement.

Amanda complimented Dale on having *two* poems published. He said thanks and looked at Mary Jane.

"Excellent poem, Mary Jane. I didn't know you had a poetic soul."

"It's not my poem," Mary Jane replied, clearly baffled.

Dale looked over her shoulder at the page they were examining. He looked at her poem entitled: *Woman: Born to Suffer*. He read the first stanza:

> If you're born a woman
> You're born to suffer.
> If born female
> It can't get tougher.

Dale pointed to Mary Jane's name. "It says clear as day, Mary Jane Morgan. It must be yours."

"It's not, Dale."

He read the last stanza:

> Woman born of woman
> Is doomed to wail
> Through centuries of pain
> Ages of travail.

Dale thought the words sounded familiar and just not because he'd typed them three weeks ago. Then he realized he must have been influenced by an old '60s song, "Born a Woman." He'd seen the 45 record over at Cleoma's last summer and played it repeatedly just to annoy Sal. The song must have seeped into Dale's memory deeper than he realized. The poem's words weren't exactly like the song's dopey lyrics, but it was the same kind of simplistic lament. In fact, the song was even sillier than the poem. In the end, the singer is glad to be born a woman even though she's mistreated, deceived, and generally abused by the world of men because she gets to come home to her man – and he makes sweet love to her. Dale wished he'd remembered to include those sentiments in the poem.

"I even went over to the *Smoke Signals* office and told them this wasn't my poem. They showed me the application. And you know, the handwriting looked like mine."

"Then it must be yours," said Dale.

"No, it's *not*," Mary Jane said, clearly peeved. "It's a joke or something."

"How can that be?" asked Amanda.

"Well, for one thing, on my application it listed my major as 'snoop studies.' There isn't such a major."

Dale, in order to prevent himself from bursting out laughing, turned and banged his head against the wall.

"Dale, what are you doing!" exclaimed Amanda.

The head banging worked. His laugh impulse immediately disappeared, replaced by a little pain and dizziness.

"Nothing," he said. "Just trying to work out a kink in my neck."

"By banging your head against a wall?"

"It was the only thing handy."

Amanda and Mary Jane stared at him as if he were a madman.

Dale asked if Amanda was ready to go to lunch.

"I suppose." She glanced at Mary Jane and told her she'd see her later in the dorm.

Mary Jane said bye.

"You should start an investigation," Dale told her, pointing an accusing finger at the newspaper. What was he saying? She might do it.

Mary Jane opened her mouth but said nothing. Dale put his hand on the small of Amanda's back and helped her along a little. She asked what he was doing.

"Just in a hurry. I'm hungry."

"Dale, you're acting strange," Amanda said, as they lined up to enter the cafeteria. Dale hated going at this time. Too many people. But Amanda preferred to eat lunch at noon.

After they ate their lunch, Dale walked Amanda halfway to her class, music theory, then told her bye. He'd see her tonight. Then he turned to go to his class, Expository Writing, where he imagined there would be more speculation about the winning author. But to his relief, there was little talk about that. Instead, the students discussed the editorship contests. Sharon and Teri were going for the yearbook; Dale and Sylvester for the newspaper.

Dale waited anxiously for his classes to end so he could find out who H. Horse really was. So far, he'd heard no clues. People either didn't know or didn't care. In fact, most people hardly looked at the literary supplement. Only the small group of writers really cared who had been published. But since H. Horse did exist and apparently was on campus, Dale wondered why he hadn't heard anything yet.

After his last afternoon class, Dale slipped back to the *Smoke Signals* office. Finding no one there, he called the registrar's office and asked to verify the enrollment of a student. He tried to make his voice sound business-like and said he needed the information for the campus newspaper. A minute later, the woman returned to the phone and said there wasn't a Horse, initial H enrolled.

Dale said, are you sure?

The voice replied in a rather offended way, *yes*.

Now he really felt puzzled. He knew Delphina had verified Horse as a student. He'd heard her. Then he recalled the funny way she'd said the name.

Dale found last semester's student register in Stan's desk and flipped through the names until he came to the Hs. Hodge, Hodgkins, Holmes, Hope, Hordern, Horst, Horton …. Dale backed up one name. Horst, Herschel A.

That was H. Horse.

The woman at the registrar's office had misheard Delphina. Dale couldn't blame her. The campus phones weren't known for their clarity and Delphina did have that little lisp. Also, who expected to be asked to look up a name like Horse, H?

Dale tossed the student register into the drawer. Probably no one would find out unless they really investigated. What if Bronwyn decided she wanted to meet this great Indian poet? What if she simply looked in the student directory like he had? Just because Horse wasn't listed didn't mean he wasn't on campus. Some students didn't have their names listed. Yeah, but Bronwyn could call the registrar's office herself.

Well, so what? No one could prove he did this.

Dale smiled to himself. This had turned out to be a pretty good prank – except that he'd pranked himself, too. He thought back to high school and the time he'd invented his footnotes and bibliography for his term paper. The paper was for Mrs. Snow's class and they were supposed to pick an author, research him or her, and write this stupid term paper. Dale thought the assignment boring and pointless. What was the point of a five page term paper? They didn't have time to do any real "research." It was just another meaningless assignment as far as he was concerned. Just another arbitrary exercise that provided very little educational benefit. So, he made up his footnotes and bibliography. That had been sort of fun. He could still remember one of the "sources:" Dr. Waldo Rubenstein, noted scholar on Dickens and nineteenth century literature.

He'd also made up some good names for one of the yearbook pages. Mrs. Schoendienst, who kept a sharp eye for tomfoolery, didn't discover that bit of subterfuge. Well, he had to make up the names. The playbill had been lost for one of the student plays and since he had to print the cast's names and characters' names, he made up the characters' names: Henrietta Gump, Cherubim Lucrece, Hitchcock Sly, Annabelle Geezer, Roscoe Beentween, Oscar Lumph, Mortimer Grip. Dale liked those names. Maybe he'd use some for pseudonyms sometime.

Dale wished he had someone to share the fun with. Rusty would have appreciated the absurdity of all this. Maybe he would tell him about it. But things like this weren't as funny after the fact.

His other concern was finding out who this Herschel Horst was. Dale felt a curious connection to Herschel Horst. After all, Horst had saved Horse. Horst was sort of Horse's doppelganger. Dale wanted to know who he really was.

Dale and Chris were walking out of the English department when Dale saw Bronwyn approaching. He suddenly stopped and pretended to get a drink of water at the fountain. Bronwyn said hello to Chris and told him she was sorry his poem didn't make the literary supplement.

"What?" asked Chris.

Dale continued to pretend to drink from the fountain, careful not to look up and attract Bronwyn's attention, although she might not know who he was. He'd never had a class with her.

"Your poem. It was very sweet. I still recall that one line: 'my mother baked cookies, even though I played hooky.' You definitely show promise, Chris. You ought to take my poetry seminar next fall. Enjoy your evening, bye."

Dale joined Chris who stood looking at the retreating Bronwyn with a confused look on his face.

"What did Professor Ayers want?" Dale asked.

"I think she got me confused with someone else."

"I heard her say your name."

"Yeah, that's what's so odd about it."

"Maybe she confused you with another Chris."

"Yeah, maybe. She said I – he wrote a poem. Something about mother's cookies and hockey."

"Sounds fascinating," Dale said. "I like the incongruity of the images."

"What?"

"Skip it."

Dale wondered if he should tell Chris about the pseudonyms. He thought not. He might want to use them again next year. He definitely wanted to attribute a poem to Chris. He would try and write his buddy a better bad poem.

Dale had just dropped off his last paper for his independent study class with Coop. Now, he was off to see Amanda. He and Chris walked out of Van Brocklin Hall. Dale asked Chris what he planned to do that evening.

"I dunno. Rowena and I might go to the Collegians' concert."

"So, are you and Rowena a steady thing?"

"Not really. We date now and then."

"Making any progress? Got up to twenty yet?"

"Huh?"

Dale forgot he hadn't informed Chris about the speed metaphor yet. "I mean, first base."

"I'm still standing at home plate."

"You're kidding?"

"Well, maybe I've been thrown out at first." Chris shook his head disconsolately. "I just don't have luck with girls."

"Maybe you ought to get a nose job."

"What?"

"Snip off some of that Gallic nose of yours. Make yourself look less like Charles De Gaulle."

"You think?"

"Naw," Dale said, slapping his buddy on the shoulder. "I'm just kidding. Your nose isn't the problem."

"Then what is it?"

Dale said he just needed confidence. And some luck. Chris shrugged. Dale, now thinking about Horst, asked Chris if he knew a guy named that, being careful to emphasize the "st" in the name.

"No, why?"

"So you don't know anyone named Horst majoring in business or in any of your classes?"

"No. Never heard of a guy called that."

Dale said okay. He had to go. Chris said so long. Dale ambled over to Hayley Hall. He told the girl at the desk he was here for Amanda. While waiting for her, he saw the dorm "mother," a tall, raven-haired, middle-aged woman named Pamela Hester, walk by. Mrs. Hester – Dale had heard she'd divorced a philandering husband years ago – said hello. He nodded and Mrs. Hester turned and disappeared behind a door. Dale thought Mrs. Hester was by far the best-looking dorm mother. She had attractive legs. She always wore high heels and fancy hosiery that emphasized her best feature. She was sort of a sexy dorm mother, especially by GNC standards.

Amanda came down and Dale noticed she didn't look happy. He asked what was wrong. Amanda said, "nothing." He asked if she was ready and she nodded. They were going to see *Our Town* in the City. Dale waited until they got inside his car before he asked her again.

Amanda bit her lower lip. "I didn't get selected."

It took a moment before he realized what she was referring to. Then he got it. The Lost and Found troupe.

"I thought you said you made the first two cuts."

"I did. But once you get past that round they don't tell you who's made the final cut until later. I got the letter today."

"And you didn't make it?"

"No."

Dale wondered if Amanda was going to cry. She bit her lower lip again but her chin didn't tremble.

"I'm sorry," he said.

She looked at him. Her blue eyes looked sad but no tears. He reached for her and she slid over and accepted his hug.

"The funny thing is that I don't feel all that terrible," she said.

Dale said she'd make it next year.

"You think so?"

"Definitely. Look how close you came this year. And you said yourself that only a few juniors-to-be make it."

"That's true." Amanda looked at him appreciatively. "You've been so supportive."

Dale shrugged. "I knew it meant a lot to you."

She smiled at him. "I guess I'll be around all summer."

Dale tried not to smile too broadly. "Yeah, I guess so."

## Chapter 9: *A Horse history; a confused encounter; doppelganger Horst*

Dr. Prescott, for the first time in weeks, seemed to be in a good mood. Before class, Henshaw had told Dale that the good doctor had secured a position at Oklahoma University as a lecturer. The GNC administration had graciously allowed Dr. Prescott to teach a lower-division course for the summer.

The last three weeks had gone well in the philosophy class. All five students had participated vigorously in discussion. Dr. Prescott hardly had to employ his Socratic method. All of them had already read several C. S. Lewis books. Even though Dale still didn't think Lewis qualified as a philosopher, he found the discussions edifying.

Dr. Prescott accepted final papers and told everyone he'd enjoyed teaching this class and hoped they kept the philosophy club going. Henshaw said they would. They'd already decided to rename it the Prescott philosophy club. The doctor laughed and said they better not. It might be banned, too.

Dr. Prescott dismissed class a little early and before Henshaw, Polly, and Eugene could command his attention, he asked Dale if he'd read any Nietzsche yet?

Dale had tried to read *Also sprach Zarathustra*, but he gave up after fifty pages.

"Yeah, but I didn't understand it."

Dr. Prescott furrowed his bushy brows. "No one does."

Dale shook the doctor's hand and told him he really enjoyed his class. Dr. Prescott wished him well in his future studies. Before he could say anything more, the rest of the class approached to engage the doctor.

Dale realized he was going to miss Dr. Prescott. He'd been the best teacher he'd ever had. But in spite of Dr. Prescott's admirable example, he'd decided philosophy was not for him. He didn't think he had a rigorous-enough mind for it. He preferred making things up, being creative, and having fun. Dale doubted if philosophers ever had much fun. Too many of them either drank hemlock or went insane.

Dale walked out of the seminar room and bumped into Sylvester Fish. He and Fish exchanged an "excuse me," a courtesy both thought important to extend even to their adversaries. They were about to proceed their separate ways, when Fish asked him to wait a moment.

"What is it?"

Fish stood before Dale with his normally impassive face.

"Simply wanted to congratulate you on being appointed editor of *Smoke Signals*."

Dale said thanks.

Fish waited. Dale told him he ran a good race. Too bad he lost. Maybe next year.

"I'll be a senior next year," Fish informed him.

"Oh. Well, too bad. I guess you won't be editor at all then."

Fish remained stationary. Dale didn't know what he wanted. He wished he'd just go ahead and tell him.

"What is it, Fish?"

"Well, Smith, just wondering if you need an assistant editor."

"Maybe."

Fish's tiny eyes seemed to disappear altogether behind his thick, tinted lenses. He puffed his flabby cheeks in frustration.

"You can apply if you want," Dale said, in a voice that carried no enthusiasm.

"Thank you, Smith. I plan to."

Dale started to tell him that he'd receive no advantage just because he'd applied for editor and lost, but Fish slipped into the classroom before he could complete the sentence.

Dale shrugged and walked over to the *Smoke Signals* office in the student union. Teri and Polly sat on stools facing the desk where Mrs. Genesee stood talking to Bronwyn J. Ayers. They all exchanged hellos.

"So, finally we meet," said Bronwyn in her distinctive, rather husky voice. Dale guessed having an expansive chest helped in producing the pleasing sound. She extended a limp hand and he took it and gently pumped it twice. "Congratulations on being appointed editor," she added.

Dale said thanks and gave Mrs. Genesee a grateful glance. He knew she had been most responsible for getting him the position, along with Coop.

"I also wanted to tell you that I liked the poems you submitted for the literary issue."

"Thanks," he replied.

He really cared more about his short story. He supposed it had been too violent. But Polly's piece was good. Dale had to admit it was well written. He'd congratulated her about it two weeks ago at the start of philosophy class and she had smiled bashfully.

"I hope you'll take a creative writing class next year," Bronwyn said.

Dale said he planned to. Bronwyn said, wonderful. He nodded at her and was about to go over to the layout boards to see how the last issue was coming when she said she had a question for him.

Dale turned and waited. He felt a premonition that Bronwyn's question had to do with *someone* in particular.

"I was wondering, Dale, if you know of a student by the last name of Horse."

He glanced at Teri and Polly. They looked at him with normal expressions. Apparently they didn't suspect him of inventing H. Horse.

"Well, I can say that I do know him," Dale said. "Sort of."

"There!" said Bronwyn. "I knew someone must know this fellow."

Dale sat on a nearby stool and perused the latest proofs. It was customary for the new editor to help edit the newspaper's last issue of the spring semester.

"I was beginning to think this fellow didn't exist," said Bronwyn. "I've been asking every writing student I have."

"Maybe he doesn't take writing or English classes," said Mrs. Genesee, who also said she'd never had him for class.

"That would help explain his curious incorporeality," said Bronwyn with a laugh.

Dale turned around. He liked her laugh. He liked to *see* her laugh.

"Well, I certainly hope this Horse –" Bronwyn stopped short. "Now, what is his first name?"

"I think Delphina said it was Herschel," said Mrs. Genesee.

"Herschel? What a curious name for an American Indian young man." Bronwyn shook her head. "Herschel? Where have I heard that name before?"

"I think he prefers Harry," said Dale. He knew he was skirting the edge but he couldn't help himself.

"Oh? Harry. Well, that's better," said Bronwyn. "Do you know anything else about him?"

"Well, he had a sister."

"Had? Did something happen to her?"

"Yeah. She got hit by a bus."

"That's terrible," said Bronwyn.

The others murmured their sympathy as well.

"What was her name?" asked Mrs. Genesee.

"Hannah."

"Hannah and Herschel," mused Bronwyn. "Interesting names. Do you know their tribal affiliation?"

"Navajo."

"That's interesting. There aren't many Navajos in Oklahoma."

"He's originally from New Mexico. But after Hannah died, he moved here."

"Perhaps that's why he feels so strongly about the plight of the American Indian," said Bronwyn, recalling, no doubt his protest poetry. "You know, I'd like to meet Harry sometime." She looked at Dale.

"Well, he's a very shy guy."

"Ah, yes, I know the type. He communicates through his writing."

"Exactly."

"Well, Dale, if you happen to see him, tell Harry I'd like it very much if he took my poetry seminar next fall."

Dale said he'd tell Harry that. He also told himself that he was crazy. He was making things worse for himself; and yet, he couldn't help it.

Bronwyn said she had to run. She waved, said bye to Jenny, and exited the room with her boots clicking, her long hair swaying, and her impressive bosom kept mostly in check by some grand contraption that Dale tried to imagine.

Mrs. Genesee called Dale's name twice before he responded.

"Oh, sorry, Mrs. Genesee," he said. "I was lost in thought."

A small smile flickered across her lips, before she told him that Polly had volunteered to help with the editing next year if he didn't mind.

"No, that's great," Dale said.

He knew he needed help in that area. That was Mrs. Genesee's only reservation about having him appointed editor. Dale looked at Polly. She looked back with her usual placid expression. He then glanced at Teri, who looked at him with a more dubious gaze. She'd lost to Sharon for editor of the yearbook, but she wanted to work on the newspaper again.

"Do you have someone in mind for business manager?" asked Mrs. Genesee.

"Yeah. I was thinking about Rowena."

Both Chris and Amanda had recommended her. Chris had been Dale's first choice, but he said he was too busy with his studies. Besides, he really wasn't the sales type.

"Good choice," said Mrs. Genesee.

The four of them chatted briefly before Mrs. Genesee and Polly left. Dale noticed Teri still had that skeptical look on her face.

"Do you really know this Horse guy?" she asked.

"Yeah."

"How well?"

"Pretty well."

"How is it that I've never seen him around?"

"He's a recluse."

"A recluse? A Navajo recluse?"

Dale knew he had to change the topic. He asked her if she was interested in being assistant editor. Actually, the paper wasn't large enough to need an assistant editor. But Dale decided to keep the title when it would really be someone doing all the boring stuff he didn't want to do.

"I thought Sylvester was applying."

"Yeah. That's the point."

"Oh. In that case, yeah."

"Good," said Dale.

Before Teri could bring up Harry Horse again, he said he had to go. He told her to lock up when she left. Teri said sure. But he could tell that the mystery of Harry Horse was still on her mind.


Dale walked to the campus telephone in the lobby of the student union. As luck would have it, the ordinarily busy phone was free. He picked up the receiver and glanced at the extension number he'd written on the palm of his hand. He was about to call Herschel Horst.

Dale knew what Herschel Horst looked like. A week ago he'd gone into the *Tomahawk* office and looked in last year's yearbook. He'd flipped through the class photos and found Horst in the sophomore section. He didn't look anything like a Navajo.

He knew a few other things about Horst as well. He lived in Graham Hall, one of men's dorms, hailed from Houston, Texas, and majored in music.

Just yesterday, Dale, as casually as he could, had asked Amanda if she knew of a guy named Herschel Horst. Amanda had looked a little surprised and asked why he wanted to know. He said it was a newspaper thing. Her face relaxed and she said yes, Herschel was a music major. He played the violin. Then she had changed the subject and he decided not to pump any information out of her lest she become suspicious.

Dale called Horst's extension and got his roommate. He pretended to be from the music department and asked where he could find Herschel. The roommate said in a bewildered voice that Herschel was supposed to be in the music building at that very moment. Dale said, oh yeah, I think I see him walking by. He told the roomie thanks and hung up.

Dale rambled across the quad and veered left to the music building. He threw open the front doors and walked inside and paused. He had no idea where Horst would be. He might be stuck inside some soundproof room practicing his violin.

He walked over to the building directory and scanned it when he heard a startling admission.

"I'm Horse," said a young man with his back to Dale.

"I'm sorry," said a young woman facing the young man. "A lot of people are having that problem."

Dale stared at them. The young man had long, brown hair. It hung to his shoulders. He wondered if this guy really was Horse. The young woman, rather attractive with her long red hair, guileless blue eyes underneath her granny glasses, and a soft dimple in her chin, noticed Dale staring at them. She acquired a concerned look on her face, no doubt prompted by Dale's intense gaze. The young man noticed the change in her expression and turned.

He didn't look Indian. His complexion was fair and his features distinctly Caucasian. The young man stared at Dale with a puzzled, slightly offended look.

"Do I know you?" he asked.

"Are you Horse?"

The young man glanced at the redheaded girl and raised a brow, as if to suggest that Dale was an oddball. "Yeah, a little."

That didn't make sense to Dale. "Are you or are you not Horse?"

The young man frowned. "What business is it of yours?" He looked at the young woman again as if to say, "who is this crazy guy and do you know him?"

"I just want to know if your H. Horse?"

"What? H. Horse? What does H have to do with it? I just have a little cold, that's all."

Dale realized he'd misinterpreted. He could tell by the scratchy sound in the guy's voice that he had said *hoarse*.

"Say, do I know you?" The young man coughed. "Don't you play the piccolo?"

"No."

"No, I don't know you or no you don't play the piccolo?"

"No to both. The only thing I play is the field."

Dale looked at the redhead and suggestively raised a brow. He couldn't help it. The whole absurd situation made him goofy.

The young woman cringed toward the young man with a cold. "Stephen, I think we better leave."

"Certainly, Shirley" said Stephen, with a weak cough.

They walked over to the exit. The redhead gave Dale a snooty glance as the door closed behind them.

Dale told himself to remember that H. Horse didn't really exist. He'd made him up. But Herschel Horst definitely existed and he wanted to find him. He scanned the directory again, but it just listed professors and staff. Maybe he should go into the department chairman's office and ask the secretary where Herschel might be.

He walked down the hall when he saw Horst sitting in a chair in the small lounge. He knew it was Horst by the long blond hair. Dale didn't like his hair. It didn't go with his big, broad, blunt face. In fact, the moment Dale had seen Horst's picture in the yearbook, he didn't like him – a reaction that he knew was illogical. He didn't even know the guy.

Dale walked toward Horst. He noticed Herschel seemed to be engaged in a conversation with someone he couldn't yet see. At least, he was opening and closing his mouth and nodding in a supercilious way. As Dale walked closer, his viewpoint broadened and he saw to his consternation Amanda sitting opposite Horst.

They looked up just as Dale stepped down into the sunken lobby. The expression on Amanda's face changed three times: surprise, pleasure, then concern. All three of her faces looked pretty, he thought. Horst, on the other hand, retained the same smug expression.

"Oh, Dale," cried Amanda. "What brings you here?"

He shrugged. "Just checking out piccolos."

"What?"

Dale stared at Horst. There was something familiar about his face, and not because he'd already scrutinized the yearbook version of it.

"Oh, Dale, this is Herschel," said Amanda.

Horst stood up and Dale noticed to his chagrin that he was rather tall. At least six foot.

"Yes, I know. Herschel Horst."

Horst's expression didn't change. Amanda looked surprised.

"You know each other?" she asked.

"No, I don't believe so," said Horst. His voice sounded as arrogant as he looked, with a slight nasal quality.

Dale shook his head. "No, I've just *heard* of Herschel Horst."

Finally, they shook hands. Horst had a firm handshake. No doubt all that violin practice. He seemed pleased that Dale had heard of him before.

"I take it you're a classical music aficionado," he said.

"No," Dale replied. "I like the Beach Boys."

One raised eyebrow indicated Horst's disapproval. When it lowered, Dale remembered who his face reminded him of: Beethoven. That's why he disliked his hair. Beethoven had wild, curly brown hair. This guy looked like Beethoven with Farrah Faucet's hair.

"I hear you're the new newspaper editor," Horst said, but Dale could tell in his flat voice that he wasn't impressed.

"Yes, and that's obviously why I'm here."

Amanda and Horst looked at him expectedly.

"The newspaper would like to do a feature article on you. For next fall, of course."

Horst didn't look pleased so much as impatient as if he'd expected such an invitation for some time and didn't know why it had taken so long.

"I think I could accommodate you," he said.

"Great. Just wanted to let you know. Things get busy in the fall."

He looked at Amanda. She sat looking at the two of them with her usual soft, serene smile.

Dale waited. He became as immobile as Fish. Horst got the point. He told Dale to let him know in the fall when he wanted to do the story. Herschel nodded at Amanda and said, "good luck with your vocal exercises." Horst then exited.

Dale asked Amanda if she were staying. She said she had been taking a break from practicing but now she thought she might go back to her dorm before dinner.

He said he'd walk with her if she liked. She smiled, stood up, and the two of them walked out of the music building.

They didn't say anything for a while, then Dale asked if Herschel was the guy who asked her to Heart-Pal last year.

"How did you know?"

Dale said he had amazing powers of observation.

"You've been acting a little strange of late," Amanda said. "Is there anything wrong?"

Dale considered her question. He had been acting oddly. Maybe it was all the H. Horse stuff. Maybe it was because Dr. Prescott was leaving. Maybe it was because it was near the end of spring semester and soon summer would be here. He was looking forward to that.

"It's just spring fever."

"Oh, is that so?"

Amanda put her hand on Dale's arm, a sign of public affection she rarely indulged in.

"Did you go out with him just that one time?" Dale didn't want to use Horst's name.

"No."

"How many?"

Amanda smiled a little bashfully. "Three."

"Didn't make the cut, eh?"

Amanda nodded. "He's a talented violinist. But he's sort of –"

"Egocentric?"

"You do have amazing powers of observation."

"And don't you forget it," he said, patting her hand with his.

## Chapter 10: *Rusty hears from Benny; a special movie; an idyllic swim*

Rusty told Dale to hand him the screwdriver. Both of them were lying in the floorboard of Dale's Chevy. He couldn't take listening to the radio anymore, so he'd asked Rusty to help him install a car stereo. Since he'd proved to be mechanically incompetent, Rusty was doing most of the work.

"I think that's about it," Rusty said, staring up into the electronic guts of the car. He added a final a twist here, a tweak there, and removed his six-foot-two-inch frame from out of the car.

"Thanks," Dale said. He crawled out of the passenger's side and walked over to the driver's side. "The radio just plays rot all the time."

The oldies station that Dale usually listened to had changed its format from '50s and '60s rock to disco all day and all night. That had been the last straw.

"Let's take her for a spin and see how the stereo sounds," said Rusty.

Dale started up the Chevy and pulled out of Rusty's driveway and drove north. Rusty flipped on the stereo, inserted Dale's cassette tape of the Beach Boys, and they listened to "I Get Around."

"Not bad," said Rusty.

Dale nodded. Sounded good to him, almost as clear as his stereo at home even though he'd bought a fairly cheap car stereo.

"I don't know why you didn't buy an eight track though."

"I like cassettes better."

"Eight tracks have more of a future," Rusty said with a certain authority in his voice that Dale respected. He knew more about such stuff than he did. But Dale still liked cassettes better.

He turned west on the rural road. Going east would take them to the City. Going west took them into the country pretty quickly.

"Guess what?" Rusty asked. Dale waited. "I'm going to California for a week."

"When?"

"I'm supposed to leave in a couple of weeks. I want to get back in time for summer league."

Dale asked where in California.

"San Diego." Rusty looked at Dale and grinned. "Benny invited me."

Dale glanced at Rusty from the corner of his eye while keeping a lookout on the road. He'd almost hit an armadillo the last time he drove this way.

"Who?"

"B-B-B-Benny," said Rusty.

Now Dale got the reference. Mr. Benedict. He remembered how disappointed they had been the summer when "Benny and the Jets" came out because Mr. Benedict had already split and they couldn't tease him with the B-B-B-Benny stuff.

"Mr. Benedict invited you to come out to San Diego?"

"Yep. Got a letter from him a week ago. Said he'd be finished teaching in a week and he thought I'd like to come for a visit. Said he lived just a few blocks from the beach. I could go surfing."

Dale shook his head.

"Hey, sorry, man. I know you're supposed to be the beach boy. But I dig surfing, too."

Dale slowed the car, then eased it off to the side of the road. The tires kicked up clouds of dust. The spring, and now the summer, continued to be dry. He waved away the smoky dust and turned to Rusty.

"What's up, man? Why you stopping here?"

Dale told Rusty about that night in the cabin. How he saw Mr. Benedict standing over Rusty and watching him sleep. He told him what Mr. Benedict said, too.

"That's weird, man," Rusty said, shaking his head with disgust. "It's wiggin' me out."

Dale said maybe Rusty should reconsider visiting Mr. Benedict in California. Surfing or no surfing.

Rusty's animated face grew serious. He didn't talk for several seconds.

"That really happened?"

Dale said yeah.

"What is he? Some kind of pervert or something?"

Dale said he didn't know.

"Why didn't you tell me sooner?"

"He asked me not to. He said nothing ever happened." Dale glanced at Rusty.

Rusty suddenly grew angry. "That's right, nothing ever happened. But if Benny had tried anything –" Rusty slammed his fist down on the dash so hard it made the stereo squawk.

They didn't say anything for a few moments.

"So, that's why he left."

Dale said he guessed so.

"What a –" Dale knew Rusty wanted to curse but since he was going to GNC in the fall, he resisted. "What a weird guy."

Dale agreed. He thought about all the teasing and tormenting they had inflicted on Mr. Benedict. Suddenly, he got an insight into his former teacher. Why he liked to be abused.

"I think he's a masochist," said Dale.

"How so?"

"Well, he obviously enjoys being emotionally abused, even to the point of humiliation."

"Why, man?"

"I guess because he knows his perverted impulses are wrong." Dale turned to Rusty. "I doubt he's ever done anything to anyone."

Rusty was still angry. "Maybe I ought to go out to San Diego and punch his face in."

"That's a long way to go just to smash a guy."

"Yeah, I guess."

They suddenly became aware that the song playing on the car stereo was "California Girls." They couldn't help but laugh.

They laughed for a long time before Dale turned the car around and drove back to Rusty's.


Dale, Amanda, Mary Jane, and a beardless Rusty stood in a long line at the mall waiting to see a movie. Even though the movie was rated PG, Dale had to convince Amanda that it would be okay to see.

"Are you sure this movie isn't naughty in any way?" Amanda asked.

"It'll be fine," Dale said.

The last movie they'd seen together, almost a month ago, had a brief skinny dipping scene and they had seen the actress's bare bottom as she jumped into the pool. Also, a little of her breasts as she treaded water. Dale remembered how tight Amanda's hand grew inside his as they sat in the dark theatre and watched. Afterwards, she complained and he said the nudity had flashed on screen for just a few seconds. Amanda said that didn't matter and they almost had a serious argument over it.

"That's what you said before the last movie," Amanda said, apparently recalling the same scene. "That movie was rated PG, too."

Dale ignored that note of self-righteousness in her voice. He remembered liking the ad he saw in the *Oklahoman* yesterday. The photograph depicted a heroic young man holding some kind of pole as he guarded a princess. An older guy and what looked like a gorilla stood at his side. A gleaming light, like a supernova, bathed all the characters from behind. The ad had an appealing mythic quality.

"I think it will be a really good movie," he said, certain his instincts were correct.

"That's what you said the last time we were here," said Mary Jane. "And that movie was too scary."

Dale and Rusty looked at her. She was talking about *Jaws* but the four of them hadn't seen that together. It was the three of them with Wendy. Mary Jane realized her mistake and her brown eyes grew wide.

"I don't remember the four of us coming to a movie here before," Amanda said.

Mary Jane blinked her eyes. Dale and Rusty looked at each other.

"Man, look how long the line is," Rusty said, nodding behind them at all the people. The line snaked down through the mall, all the way to the hot dog-on-a-stick place.

"The line was long for *Jaws*, too," Mary Jane said.

Dale wondered why she hadn't forgiven him for subjecting her to the horror of that movie.

He looked at Amanda and saw her thinking about what Mary Jane had said. He didn't think Amanda had seen *Jaws* but she knew Mary Jane had. Mary Jane had probably told her all about the carnage the killer white had perpetrated on the hapless residents of Amity.

The thoughtful expression on Amanda's face suddenly changed. She looked at the three of them, her eyes wide with understanding. "Oh," she said quietly.

Dale gave Mary Jane an annoyed look. Great, now Amanda will be thinking about Wendy. He reached over and took Amanda's hand in his and held it. He thought her hand felt a little cold. She looked at him and he could almost read her thoughts in her eyes. She was wondering if he preferred taking Wendy to movies because Wendy didn't complain about naughty stuff. In a way, that was true. Wendy got embarrassed, too, but she had never chastised him afterward.

Dale gently squeezed Amanda's hand, hoping to spread a little warmth from his hand into hers. She looked down at their interlocked hands, then smiled a little sadly.

They finally got to the ticket window and Dale said, "four for *Star Wars*."

As they walked into the theatre, Dale felt optimistic. They found pretty good seats in the middle of the middle section, seats that the girls preferred, and settled down. Dale asked Amanda if she'd like anything. She said a Tab would be nice. Dale and Rusty dashed off to the concession stand and returned with sodas, popcorn, and candy. As Dale sat down next to Amanda, he could tell she'd been talking to Mary Jane. Who knows what Mary Jane had told her? Then he remembered that *Jaws* had been the movie where he'd noticed Sheba. What if Mary Jane had noticed that, too?

While watching the coming attractions, Dale reached over and held Amanda's hand. He rested their hands first on the armrest, then got tired of the armrest cutting into his wrist and moved their hands to Amanda's leg. She was wearing jeans but she still thought it was improper to have his hand on her lower thigh. She began to move their hands back to the armrest, when she changed her mind. She kept their hands on her leg and Dale liked how warm his hand felt with his fingers wrapped around hers and resting on her soft thigh.

Then *Star Wars* began. As soon as Dale saw the prologue flash on screen and scroll up in that odd skewed way, he knew he was right. This would be a good movie.

Afterwards, the two couples refreshed themselves at a mall restaurant and talked about the movie. Dale said it had an old-fashioned quality to it, with more emphasis on story and character than a lot of today's movies. Amanda gave him an inquiring look, as if asking how many movies have you seen without me, but she smiled and agreed that the movie was entertaining. Mary Jane nodded rather enthusiastically. Dale guessed she had been relieved that nobody had been eaten. Rusty said the movie had cool special effects, too.

The two couples said good-bye to each other in the parking lot and Dale drove back to Galilee. He took his favorite route, the north rural road, and unfortunately got stuck behind a slow pickup truck. Just a day away from the summer solstice, dusk was about to fall, and Dale saw the sun sinking into the shimmering purplish horizon as they drove toward it.

Amanda sat next to Dale, lost in thought. He looked down the road and saw a car a mile away in the opposite lane approaching the bridge. He wanted to pass the slow truck before getting to the bridge. He sped up the Chevy, moved his car over to the other lane, and started to pass the truck.

For some stubborn reason, the guy in the truck increased his speed. Dale hit the gas and watched as the speedometer reached fifty, then sixty. Amanda's hand clutched his knee. She asked what he was doing.

Dale watched as the advancing car rushed toward them from perhaps a distance of four hundred yards. He stomped on the gas, pushed the Chevy to seventy, and finally passed the truck. He swerved the Chevy back into the proper lane just as it rumbled over the bridge. Amanda cried, "Dale!" as the car in the opposite lane flew by them.

Dale slowed down to fifty and looked at Amanda. Fright showed in her eyes although her mouth was no longer open.

461

"I knew I'd make it," he said.

Amanda leaned back into the seat and shook her head. Dale thought she was overreacting. He'd been calm the whole time. He never doubted he'd pass the truck in time. If the jerk driver hadn't sped up, he'd have made it easy. He asked Amanda if she was all right. She nodded her head and took a deep breath.

"Please, don't ever do that again."

They got to her house and Dale parked on the curb. Before he turned off the car, Amanda told him that her father had given the couch in the garage to the Salvation Army. He felt the sting of disappointment. He was looking forward to taking Amanda into the garage.

"There's a shady spot on the next street," she said.

Dale stared at her with gratitude and surprise. He drove the car slowly down the street then, with instructions from Amanda, turned right on a cul-de-sac. He pulled over to an inviting clearing between two large trees with conveniently low limbs and parked. It wasn't as good of a spot as the one he used to take Wendy to, but he thought it would do.

"Sorry about scaring you back there," he said.

"For a moment, I thought we might not make it."

They really hadn't come *that* close to dying. He estimated they had at least five seconds to spare.

Dale put his arm around her and kissed her. He kissed her some more and wished it were raining. He liked making out in the rain.

They hadn't had any real private time since New Year's. Dale had been waiting for this for a long time but he was careful not to rush it. He knew Amanda thought "parking" was improper. He contented himself with just kissing her lips and cheeks and neck and feeling the bare skin around her waist. After half an hour of necking, he felt Amanda had had enough, or at least didn't want to go to the next stage, so they stopped and talked for a while.

They talked about their summer jobs. Dale still had his weekend job at the Cimarron City high school and he'd gotten another job working at the GNC physical plant. He'd mow lawns, move furniture, clean the dormitory trash chutes, and other odd jobs. The physical plant boss had agreed to let him off for his two summer classes, Old Testament and Contemporary Christian Beliefs, the former the last required religion course he had to take. Eugene had recommended taking the Old Testament course in summer. Somewhat easier, he said, than the fall course.

Amanda talked about her campus job, too. She was working at the GNC bookstore. Her mother knew the manager of the store and Amanda had an edge over the other people who'd applied. Summer jobs on campus were fairly scarce and the bookstore job was one of the most coveted.

Dale imagined he and Amanda would see each other a lot that summer. He planned to stop by the bookstore from time to time. He'd see her at Wednesday night Bible study. He'd see her at Sunday night church service. He'd go on a date with her on Saturday nights and maybe Friday nights too if her parents let her. Maybe she'd come and watch him play softball for the First Church college-age team on Thursdays. With two jobs, he'd be making plenty of money for his needs. He could take Amanda to concerts and other places that cost more. Yeah, he thought, this was going to be a special summer.

He felt happy. He felt full of life and joy and optimism. Amanda noticed his mood and hugged him and they didn't say anything for a while; they just sat in his car and listened to the sounds of the summer night and stared at the clear sky with its spangled stars.

Amanda said it was getting late and Dale started the car and slowly drove back to her house. He parked on the curb and noticed two odd things: first, a different car was parked in the drive way along with the Meeks' Lincoln Townhouse family car. Dale identified it as a late model Pontiac Firebird. He thought it was interesting that her father always seemed to bring home a sporty repo car.

The second oddity was that the porch light had burned out. It must have burned out while they were parking because he remembered it blazing when he first pulled up outside the Meeks' residence.

Dale walked Amanda to her door. Before he kissed her good night, Amanda asked him if he wanted to come over tomorrow for a swim. Her parents and the Gardners were going to some special event at the country club and would be gone all afternoon and evening. The Gardners, whose backyard extended all the way to the lake, said they could use their dock for swimming.

Dale said that sounded great. Amanda told him to come over around three. He put his arms around her waist and pulled her to him. She threw her arms around his neck and they kissed. He felt surprised by her rather eager response. He continued kissing her and felt her body moving tight against his. Dale moved his hands underneath her blouse and found the bare skin of her lower back. He stroked her there and then slipped one hand lower. His fingertips felt the elastic band of her panties. He pushed his hand farther down and felt the cool flesh of the upper swell of her right buttock. He slowly swept his fingers across the softness and then slipped the tip of his middle finger into the warm natal cleft. He enjoyed the contrast between the cool flesh of the cheek and the warm, humid valley at the top of the V of her rump.

Instead of resisting, Amanda tightened her arms around his shoulders and stroked the back of his neck with her hands. She returned his kisses with unusual fervor. When he removed his mouth from hers and kissed her neck, he heard her moan. He felt almost delirious hearing her voice lose control. He nibbled her ear and pressed his chest hard into her, feeling her breasts flatten against him. He wanted to be part of her. He felt frustrated at not being able to. "Oh, Amanda," he said lowly in her ear, his voice full of desire and frustration.

She gently pulled away and they kissed one more time. He looked into her eyes and saw them glistening. He wanted to tell her something but she smiled and moved away.

"Good night," she whispered. "See you tomorrow."

Dale nodded and watched as she went inside her home and softly closed the door. He walked, with a little difficulty, back to his car. He waited until he saw her upstairs bedroom light come on. He gritted his teeth thinking of how she was getting ready for bed. He felt a wildness nearly possess him. He imagined climbing the side of her castle-like house and breaking through her window and seizing her.

Then he imagined her father shooting him.

He knew he couldn't sleep yet. He drove to Highway 66 and headed west, then turned off a smaller road and drove to Reinhardt's Summit. He parked his car and climbed the hill and looked out at the dark earth and inky sky spread out before him. The city lights of Galilee looked like the flames of candles flickering in the night.

He stared at that sight for quite some time, thinking of Amanda asleep in her bed. Then he walked back to his car, got in, and drove to his own quiet, dark house.

Elizabeth didn't approve. Dale heard her down the hall talking to Amanda. The elder sister's voice sounded almost like an insect's hum as she spoke rapidly and in a high-pitched voice. He couldn't distinguish her words but he could tell by the tone and the insistence that Elizabeth was disturbed by something. Then he heard Amanda tell Lizzy to mind her own business. A few seconds later, Amanda appeared, dressed in cutoffs and a light blue T-shirt. Dale stood up. He wore cut-offs, too, which he normally didn't do. He didn't like wearing shorts of any kind. But it made sense today since they were going swimming in the lake and he didn't want to wear jeans over his swim trunks.

"Ready?" he asked.

Amanda nodded. She seemed a little upset. They walked out of her house and down the street until they came to the Gardner's large, impressive two-story house with the rolling, well-maintained yard. Like a lot of houses in this part of town, the manicured lawn reminded Dale of a golf course. In fact, Galilee's only golf course, at the country club, was only seven blocks away.

"Anything wrong?"

Amanda hadn't said anything since leaving her house. Instead, she had bit her lip and stared at the ground.

"Oh, just Lizzy. She sometimes thinks she's my surrogate mother."

Dale almost said one strict mother is enough, but he didn't. He wanted to enjoy the day. Instead he told Amanda how lovely she looked.

Amanda finally smiled. She especially liked the word "lovely," whether applied to her face or her voice or a clear, bright summer day like today.

They walked around the side of the Gardner's house and he opened the gate and they walked through the long, almost meadow-like backyard. Dale felt a little like an interloper. He'd never been in the Gardner's backyard. He didn't even know them really. He'd seen them at First Church sometimes, usually talking to the minister and other Nazarene dignitaries. Mr. Gardner, like most people who owned homes in this newer, more exclusive part of Galilee, commuted to the City for work.

Dale held Amanda's hand as they walked. He was astonished by how long the backyard was. If Mr. Gardner cut down some of the trees and bushes, he could build an actual football field.

Finally, the yard rolled down in a gentle slope and they walked past a couple of trees and a few shrubs and came upon a small dock with a paddleboat tethered to it.

"Hey, this is nice," Dale said.

It reminded him of some picturesque lake he might see in a nostalgic movie. He gazed at the water, which was the western finger of Lake Overholser.

"Yes, isn't it delightful?" said Amanda. "And the sad part is that all the Gardner kids are grown and out of the house. So no one swims here much."

They walked over to a spot underneath a small tree and Amanda spread the beach towel on the grass and dropped the picnic basket and her sunglasses on it. She asked if Dale wanted to swim right away or wait. He said why wait? They were in the hottest part of the day.

Amanda took a couple of steps away from him and peeled off her T-shirt. Dale pulled off his T-shirt in one swift motion and watched as Amanda then pulled down her cutoffs revealing the bottom half of her two-piece swimsuit. He stared. Amanda wasn't wearing a bikini but the rather revealing two-piece showed more of her than he'd ever seen before. He felt almost out of breath watching her strip down to her suit. He gazed at the plump curves of the lower buttocks that peeked out of her suit bottom. Amanda really was sort of callipygous.

With her back to him, she turned her head and smiled shyly. Now, he knew why the sisters were arguing.

"Ready?" Dale asked in a suggestive voice. He didn't know why he took that tone; they were just going to jump into the lake.

Amanda turned and Dale liked how she looked in front, too. The top was small enough that it showed most of the top half of her breasts. She wasn't large-breasted enough to really produce cleavage, but he didn't mind. He also liked how the bottom hugged her hips in a V, with the suit tapering off about an inch on the sides. Dale focused on her navel. It was the first time he'd ever seen it. He was pleased to see it was an inny; in fact, it was so small and oval and tight that he felt that odd urge to poke his finger in it.

"Nice color," he said, admiring the royal blue shade. "It matches your eyes."

Amanda almost blushed, then turned and ran in her girly gait to the edge of the lake. Dale loped after her and grabbed her by the waist and threatened to throw her in.

"Don't you dare, Dale!"

464

And, of course, he had to after that warning. He scooped her up, surprised by how easily he lifted her, and tossed her into the water. She made a small splash, then surfaced, smiling and rubbing the water off her face.

Dale thrashed in after her and she tried to get away but he grabbed her and they frolicked in the water for several minutes. When they got out to deeper water, he dunked her by pushing her shoulders down. When they wandered closer to shore, he grabbed her by her waist and lifted her up and tossed her into the air. She screamed as she splashed down. When she surfaced, she said, "my, I didn't know you were so strong."

That was music to Dale's ears. He grinned with mock vanity and flexed his arm muscle and Amanda reached over and felt the bulge of his bicep and raised her eyebrows to show she was indeed impressed.

They swam for an hour, then Amanda wanted to take a break. He followed her as she trudged out of the water. The bottom of her swimsuit worked itself up and in as she walked to the shore. Dale nodded in appreciation as the wet suit clung to her half-exposed buttocks and so clearly defined the cleft itself that she almost looked naked. Amanda, realizing her state of semi-nudity, turned around and reprimanded him for looking. She gazed heavenward in embarrassment as she reached behind her and struggled to pull her swimsuit bottom down over her derriere. He couldn't help but grin.

"Dale, you are naughty!" she said, but he could tell that most of her outrage was for show.

He ran out of the water, kicking some of it at Amanda on purpose. "You look fantastic," Dale said, joining her.

"Not from that angle."

"Wanna bet?"

Amanda smiled and a rosy glow appeared in her cheeks before she shyly turned her face away from his gaze. She dropped down on the beach towel and took a small towel and dried her face and hair.

Dale dropped to his knees and watched. "You don't know how beautiful you are, do you?"

She gave him another pseudo-reproving look and tossed the towel at him. "You need to dry off."

"Yeah, I guess you think I am all wet."

She smiled and he wondered if she got his play on words.

Amanda asked if he would like lunch now. He said sure. She suggested they eat while sitting on the dock. Dale said yeah, let's go over and sit on the dock of the bay. He knew she didn't get the reference to Otis Redding's song, but he didn't care. He picked up the picnic basket and walked beside, not behind, Amanda, although he wanted to. But he didn't want to push his luck.

They sat down on the dock and dangled their legs off the edge. Dale looked down and noticed that his wet cutoffs showed his "plumbing." That was the word Mrs. Huxtable, his high school biology teacher, disapprovingly used in regard to kids' wearing tight pants. He'd gotten aroused seeing Amanda in her swimsuit and the wet fabric of his cut-off jeans now clung to the bulge. Dale glanced at Amanda and she blinked her eyes before she abruptly looked down to the picnic basket. He guessed she'd noticed, but she seemed more surprised than offended. She looked into the picnic basket and spoke rather quickly about how she hoped he liked their lunch. She brought out a sandwich wrapped in cellophane, an apple, carrot sticks, celery sticks, a bag of potato chips, a bottle of Tab, and a bottle of 7-Up.

She handed the ham sandwich to Dale, who was now unaroused but still a little embarrassed. He unwrapped the sandwich and peeked inside. Amanda said she remembered. Dale didn't like stuff on his sandwiches; no condiments of any kind. She was right. It was nice and dry. A few months back when they ate at Sooner Shack, his hamburger had mistakenly been

465

prepared with ketchup and mustard on it and he'd gotten angry.

Dale popped open the chips and stuffed a handful in his mouth. He munched and watched as Amanda nibbled the carrot stick. After he swallowed, he asked her if that was all she was going to eat.

"I need to lose weight."

"No, you don't."

"I gained five whole pounds this past year," she said, shaking her head in despair as she snapped off a piece of carrot with her front teeth.

"Girls worry too much about their weight. You look good. Curvaceous."

Amanda gave him a dismissive look. "I have to lose those five pounds by August for my sister's wedding."

"What wedding?"

"Didn't I tell you? Lizzy's getting married in August."

"No, you didn't tell me. Who to?"

"Richard Reinhardt."

Reinhardt? Not that Reinhardt. The guy that went to Galilee High when Dale was a freshman. The guy that collided into him and busted his leg.

"You mean Dick Reinhardt?"

Amanda shrugged. "Lizzy doesn't call him that."

"What does she call him?"

Amanda looked at Dale as if he had said something unusually obtuse. "Richard, of course."

"She always calls him Richard? Not even Richard the Lion-Hearted or something like that?"

Amanda smiled only briefly. She wasn't interested in humor. She was thinking intently on losing weight for the wedding.

Dale guessed he'd have to go to that wedding, too. He already knew he had to attend Roxanne's and Quentin's wedding next month.

"Here, Amanda, have a bite of the sandwich."

She shook her head no.

"C'mon. Just a bite. You got to be hungry after all the swimming."

She said all right and took a bite. Dale kept the sandwich in front of her and she took as second bite.

"That's all," she said with admirable resolution.

She ate another carrot stick, then a stalk of celery, as Dale finished off the sandwich. He offered her *one* potato chip and she frowned at him but took it and ate it without shame.

"Oh, I almost forgot," Amanda said.    She reached into the basket and brought out a bag of chocolate chip cookies with nuts. Dale's favorite. "I baked them myself. Well, Lizzy helped."

Dale said thanks. He grabbed a couple and took a bite of one. It tasted good, but not great like Vern's mother's cookies or Mrs. Heath's baked goods. But he didn't dare voice the comparison. He nodded and said, "excellent."

Amanda smiled and stared out at the water while she finished eating the last carrot stick.

"I guess you don't –" he offered a half-eaten cookie.

"Of course not," she scolded. "I'm trying to lose weight, Dale."

He took another bite, wished he had a glass of milk, and noticed Amanda coveting the cookie. Dale held the remaining chunk of cookie in front of her, then lifted it up and dangled it above her.

"Open wide," he said, amused to be tempting her.

Amanda frowned at him, but complied. She opened her mouth and Dale dropped it in. She almost choked, but recovered and chewed the cookie with satisfaction.

"You got to catch it with your tongue," Dale informed her. "See?"

He tore off a hunk of another cookie and held it above his open mouth, then dropped it.

"You're such an expert," she said.

"Yes, I am a consummate cookie connoisseur. Well, just in the art of eating them."

"You are sort of funny. I never knew that about you until we started dating."

"Well, there's a lot you don't know about me," he said, feigning an air of mystery, although he suddenly realized he'd said the truth. Not wanting to encourage Amanda to inquire, he quickly changed the subject back to Elizabeth's wedding. Amanda took the bait and talked for ten minutes about it. Dale listened mostly out of politeness. He didn't have much interest in all the nuptial details. She finally wound down and he asked if she wanted to go for another swim.

"No, not so soon after eating."

Dale said okay. They both looked out at the water being ruffled by the light breeze.

"I think this is the first time we've been swimming together," she said.

"No, it isn't."

Amanda turned to him. "It's not?"

"The senior field trip. In high school."

"Oh yes. But that was with a whole bunch of other kids."

"Yeah, but I still noticed you."

"You did?"

Dale nodded.

"Well, I noticed you, too. I noticed your broad shoulders and the large muscles in your arms and chest."

"You mean pectorals," he said, briefly thinking of that goofy Lawrence guy.

"Are pectorals chest muscles?"

"Yeah. And one of the things I've always noticed about you is your philtrum."

Amanda stared at him. She didn't know if he was being naughty again. She seemed reluctant to ask. "What's… what's a philtrum?"

Dale grinned and slowly moved his finger toward her face and softly touched the groove between her nose and upper lip.

"That?" she asked.

He felt her upper lip move against his finger. He removed his finger and nodded.

"That's what the spot is called. A lip philtrum. And you have an especially nice one."

"I do?"

"Oh, yeah. It's one of the first things I noticed about you, along with your big blue eyes and your full lips."

"Don't. You're making me blush."

She was blushing. Amanda turned her face away.

"Do you know what philtrum means?" he asked, thinking that was a dumb question since she didn't even know what the word referred to.

"No."

"It's Greek for 'to love, to kiss'."

Amanda looked at him. Her blue eyes were large and bright. "Are you telling the truth?"

"Absolutely."

"I didn't know you knew Greek."

"I just know the best words."

Dale thought he'd tell Amanda about callipygians one day, but not when she was so concerned about her weight.

"Philtrum," Amanda said softly. "It doesn't sound like what it means."

"You know what 'phil' means in Greek, don't you?"

Amanda shook her head no.

"Sure you do. In words like philosophy, philander, bibliophile, Anglophile?"

"Oh, you mean love?"

Dale was glad she defined it first. "Yeah. Philosophy. The love of wisdom. Phil, love; soph, wisdom."

"Hmmm. You are smart."

She said it in a teasing way, but Dale liked hearing her say it anyway.

"And you like my philtrum?" she asked.

"No, I love your philtrum."

They looked at each other in silence for a moment.

"And that spot is especially sensitive." He leaned over and kissed her on that spot.

"Yes, I've noticed before you like doing that."

"You like it, too, don't you?"

"I do now. When you first did it, I didn't know what you were doing."

"No one had ever kissed you there?"

"No." Amanda looked embarrassed.

"Good. That's our special kiss."

He leaned over and kissed her there again. When he finished, he saw Amanda still had her eyes closed.

Her eyes fluttered open. "I'm glad you like kissing me there."

"I like kissing you everywhere," he said lowly.

Amanda's eyes grew large in offense. "Dale! You're being naughty again."

He laughed and after a moment so did she. He told her a little more about the philtrum. He had to look in a medical dictionary to find the darn word. It took hours. He told her that there are five categories of philtrum corresponding to how well defined it is. He thought hers was a four, which was perfect. The five was excessive. Also, the philtrum is usually proportional to the fullness of the lips. That's why she had such lovely full lips. And he told her one of the myths regarding the philtrum. The ancient Hebrews thought just after birth an angel touches a child above the lips, leaving the imprint. That groove that we call the philtrum seals in all the world's knowledge so the baby can't tell anyone and then he forgets it.

"You certainly know some unusual things," Amanda said.

"Those are the most interesting things to know."

He asked Amanda if she were ready for another swim. She said she'd rather go on a paddleboat ride. Dale said okay. He helped her into the boat and they paddled it into the middle of the lagoon-like lake. He said they could paddle this boat all the way to the other end of the lake. Amanda said let's not. So they contented themselves with paddling around in circles before resting and looking at the fresh, clear blue sky, the fluffy clouds, and the pulsing sun. The day was very warm but not hot. Perfect.

But a snake intruded into their paradise. Dale saw it gliding across the water, heading right at them. He paddled the boat to the left and then Amanda saw it.

"Oh, I hate them," she said, hugging his arm as he paddled.

Dale watched as the serpent skimmed the surface of the water and zipped by them.

"Man, that's a cottonmouth," he said.

"What kind?" Amanda asked with a shudder.

"A water moccasin. They're poisonous."

They paddled back to the dock and Dale asked Amanda if she wanted to swim. She shook her head no. She didn't want to get back in the water. Dale said snakes usually didn't bother people. They only acted in self-defense. But she didn't care. She was afraid of snakes. Just seeing them gave her the willies. He said she shouldn't let a snake scare her away. She said, why not? Dale asked if she would ever go swimming here again.

"Not in the water," she said.

Dale didn't point out the contradiction; instead he cursed the darn snake under his breath. He'd wanted to see her get wet and toss her in the air again. Instead, they took the blanket to the grass and lay in the sun. Amanda said she preferred to sunbathe than swim anyway.

She rolled on her stomach and closed her eyes.

Dale asked if she'd like him to rub some suntan lotion on her. She murmured okay. He reached into the picnic basket and grabbed the bottle. He squirted the lotion on her upper back and shoulders and rubbed it in. He noticed she had a few freckles spread across the nape of her neck. He liked that. He squeezed and rubbed her nape, shoulders, and upper back and she moaned and said that felt good.

Encouraged, Dale applied more lotion to the middle of her back. He suggested unhooking her top so the strap wouldn't get in the way. She said okay. He said he'd do it. He unhooked it with his left hand while spreading the lotion with his right. Amanda raised her head a little and asked how he got so good at that.

"At what?"

"Unhooking straps."

"I'm just naturally dexterous."

"And I'm sure you have never practiced," she said, not smiling.

He thought about saying, "and no thanks to you" but he didn't. He thought it was funny how she regarded him as some kind of Casanova.

"How about your legs?"

Amanda didn't answer. He moved down, appraising the generous curve of her bottom as he moved to her thighs. She had nice thighs, too. Dale felt himself grow excited as he squirted lotion on them and began rubbing. He started above her knees, then slowly worked his way up. When his hands caressed the crease between buttock and thigh, Amanda wiggled and said that was high enough.

Dale said okay, but enjoyed seeing the flesh of her thighs and bottom sway. He kneaded her thighs and Amanda said not so hard, so he eased up and he heard her sigh.

"Do you ever put lotion on?" she asked.

"Nope. I never burn."

Amanda said he was lucky. She burned like a piece of toast. Dale thought that was an odd thing to say. Toast was already dark or otherwise it wouldn't be called toast. But he knew what she meant.

Still kneading her thighs, they heard noise coming from the house. Loud music, followed by faint voices. Amanda raised her head up and tightened her body.

"Oh, fudge," she said, uttering her most serious malediction. "I think the Gardner kids are here."

"I thought you said they didn't live here."

"They don't. But they come over sometimes. I guess they're here to host a party. I wish Mrs. Gardner had told me."

"You want to go?"

He didn't want to be around people he didn't know, but he felt frustrated that he and Amanda couldn't bask longer in this paradise.

"Yes, I suppose."

Dale watched her put a hand underneath her chest to support her top as she reached behind her to snap the strap. Dale felt curious to see how she'd manage it, but his gentlemanly ways got the better of his curiosity and he said he'd do it for her. She said thanks. He hooked it without a problem and he helped her to her feet. They put on their outer clothes and gathered their stuff and headed back through the yard. Dale glanced back at the lake and felt a rush of regret.

They heard music blaring from the open windows. Dale frowned. It was a song from the new Fleetwood Mac album, *Rumours*. He heard that music everywhere. It wasn't as bad as disco, but he still didn't like hearing it all the time. Pop slop. That's what he and Rusty called it. The heavy metal stuff that they also didn't like they called rock rot. Dale thought it wasn't easy to find the right balance in music anymore.

They left the backyard undetected. Dale was glad. He didn't want to meet the Gardner kids. He asked Amanda how old they were. She said the twin girls were around twenty-three, Lizzy's age. The son was twenty-seven or so. Amanda guessed the twins were hosting a party while their parents were away. She said that with evident disapproval.

They walked back to Amanda's house and Dale saw another car, a silver Mercedes, parked in the driveway. Amanda said it was Richard's. He wondered how a guy Reinhardt's age could afford such a car. Then he remembered he was the grandson, the heir, to the lucrative trucking business.

As they walked up to the front door, they heard Kenny's voice. He seemed to be arguing with Elizabeth.

Amanda shook her head. "Kenny's home, too."

She frowned and Dale knew why. Even with her parents out, they couldn't be alone. He shrugged as they went inside. It had been a fun day. He could be good for the rest of the evening.

## Chapter 11: *A surprising background; Roxanne's memorable wedding*

"We're German?"

Dale had always thought Blackie's family was just boring English and now he'd found out the Smiths were really part of the bellicose German race. Dale had regarded himself as an Anglophile, in part because he liked English literature and in part because he thought that was his ethnic background. Now, it looked like he'd have to become a Deutschephile.

Blackie took a long drink of his beer and looked at his son as if he were about to impart a secret.

"My father's family is German," said Blackie. "Our name was originally Schmidt. My grandfather anglicized it during World War I."

Dale had never heard this story. "Your grandfather changed his name?"

"Yeah. He hated the damn Krauts for starting the war. Didn't want to have a German name, which made plenty of sense. He was a farmer in Alabama after all."

"Why didn't you tell me this before?"

Blackie shrugged and took another drink. "I wasn't sure about the story myself until recently. Looked up some family records awhile back. Part of an assignment in a course I took."

"German, huh?" Dale thought about that. "Aren't Germans sort of ruddy and blond?"

"Many are," said Blackie. "But some have somewhat darker complexions."

"So, we're that kind of German."

Blackie drained his can of beer. He wiped his mouth with the back of his hand and stared at Dale. "Worse than that. We're part Injun."

"Indian? How did that happen?"

"Hell, how do you suppose? Seems my grandmother, your great grandmother, was a squaw."

"You're kidding?"

"You think I'd kid about a thing like that?"

Dale realized no, Blackie wouldn't. "What kind?"

"Whattaya mean, what kind?"

"What kind of Indian was she?"

Blackie shrugged. "Creek, I think. Maybe Cherokee."

"One of the civilized tribes," said Dale, with a touch of pride.

He actually found the southern plains tribes, like the Kiowa and Comanche, more interesting. He still had a romantic view of the life of Indian warriors.

"What? Oh, yeah, one of those *civilized* tribes."

"It's sort of ironic that we live in Oklahoma," Dale said. "After all, our ancestors were forced to move here."

"Yeah, that's plenty ironic."

"You don't think it's interesting that we're part Creek?"

"No, I don't. But I guess it's better than having nigger blood."

Dale realized that Blackie must have wondered if he'd had Negro blood. Dale never thought his father looked black. He remembered Wanda once saying Blackie looked like a "Chinaman," which was now sort of funny if American Indians really had migrated from Asia during the last Ice Age. He'd been taught that in the American Indian history class he'd taken at CSU. But Dale understood Blackie's unease with his racial background. He'd read some history of the South. He'd also read, with difficulty, a novel by William Faulkner. It dramatized the miscegenation that had happened in southern history. Dale guessed southerners like his father often had doubts about their racial purity. He wondered if that partly explained Blackie's bigotry towards blacks.

"What are you looking at?" Blackie suddenly growled.

Dale guessed he'd been staring at Blackie while ruminating about their impure racial composition. He didn't care about having some Indian blood. In fact, he liked it.

"Nothing. Just thinking how interesting it is that we're part Creek."

"It's not that interesting to me," said Blackie. "Indians were savages."

"Not the five civilized tribes."

"Them, too. Before whites got here, no Indian tribe had a written language. They hadn't even invented the wheel. They were aborigines. Backward people. So don't tell me about *civilized* tribes."

Dale hadn't been taught that in the Indian history class he'd taken at Central State. The professor, a white man, wore a lot of Indian jewelry and had long hair. But the class had been informative and easy. He'd made an A with only moderate effort.

"Well, I think it's interesting we're part Indian."

He'd always thought he might be something other than all white. After all, he looked different than his pale and fair-haired friends. Dale wondered if Comingdeer would have disliked him less if he'd told him he was partly his blood brother. He doubted it. Then he wondered if his unknown ancestral blood had inspired his H. Horse persona. Maybe an authentic Indian sensibility came out in spite of his satiric intent. Maybe they weren't such bad poems after all. He thought about it. Naw.

"Don't go around blabbing this to anyone," said Blackie. "I just mentioned it to you in a moment of weakness."

"Why would anyone care?"

"People still care. Don't be fooled by all the crap you see on television about noble Indians. People just *act* like they don't care if you're not totally white."

"Will Rogers was part Indian," said Dale. "A lot of famous Oklahomans had some Indian blood."

"Not enough to make them look too different. Just don't go around talking about it. A lot of people still don't like mongrels."

Dale didn't know why his father thought that way. If people were prejudiced, they were people like Blackie or even older people. Things were changing. He didn't think many people really cared if you were part something or not.

Just to appease his father, he said he wouldn't tell anyone. But he did want to ask Blackie more about his family. He'd never heard him speak about them at any length. His dad just made cryptic references. So, he asked Blackie about his parents, his three older brothers, and his older sister.

"There's not much to tell."

"Come on," Dale said. He knew his father hated talking about the subject, which puzzled and intrigued him.

471

"I came along in the middle of a depression and I wasn't a welcome addition," Blackie said grimly. "Use your imagination for the rest."

Dale had a good imagination but he needed a few more details. "Didn't you like any of them?"

"I liked my sister. She was the next youngest; seven years older than me. She was kind."

Blackie fell silent and Dale wondered if he was thinking about her. Then Blackie abruptly got up and walked into the kitchen and came back with another beer. He took a swig and asked Dale in a perfunctory way about Jesse and June May. Dale told them they were fine.

"Oh, June May said thanks for the car."

Blackie had bought her a '65 Chevy Nova. The car had a bigger engine than Dale's Chevy. Now both his mother and sister had cars with more powerful engines than his Impala. It was embarrassing. But the Nova leaked oil and had a carburetor problem. June May was already complaining.

Blackie asked Dale how his holiday went. Blackie meant the Fourth of July. He said fine. He didn't tell Blackie that he'd taken Amanda to a fireworks display at the Stars and Stripes Park. He hadn't told Blackie about Amanda at all.

When their conversation hit the usual impasse, Dale said he had to leave. He was going to the Sunday evening service. Blackie got up and walked over to the door with him. He said he didn't know why he wanted to waste his time going to church. Dale shrugged. He didn't want to get into the same old argument. He told Blackie he'd see him soon and his father shook his hand again just like he had the last few times he'd visited. As Dale walked out of Blackie's apartment, he wondered if his father was getting a little sentimental.


Dale sat with Rusty in the back pew of the Baptist church. Dale tugged at his tie. He hated ties. His neck was too muscular for them. He'd had to unbutton the top button to keep from choking himself. He glanced over to Rusty, who looked bored. Then Dale looked over the guests sitting in the pews. A lot of people had showed. He identified his high school teachers, including Mrs. Heath, whom he'd briefly chatted with. Mrs. Page, unsurprisingly, hadn't made it.

The ceremony was already fifteen minutes late. Everyone was waiting for the wedding party to show. So far, not even the Quentin, the groom, or the best man, a guy Dale didn't know, had appeared. Chris, one of the groomsmen, and Amanda, Mary Jane, and Wendy, as bridesmaids, hadn't appeared either.

"When are they going to get the show on the road?" asked Rusty.

Dale nodded. A lot of planning and fussing went into weddings. He didn't see the point. Just run off and get married. He did think it was surprising that of all the boys Roxanne had dated, Quentin was the guy she was going to marry. Dale had always liked Quentin. But he didn't think anyone would have predicted he would marry the prettiest girl in their high school class.

The minister, a bald fellow with glasses, appeared. He told the audience he had an important announcement. Dale noticed he looked nervous. Rusty and Dale glanced at each other. Something interesting was about to happen. Maybe Quentin had been jilted.

The minister asked everyone to please leave the church and walk over to the gymnasium. There was an emergency and everyone needed to leave right away. The guests didn't move. Rusty whispered to Dale that this was a joke. Dale didn't think so. The minister looked genuinely agitated.

The minister urged the guests in a louder voice to please leave now. He almost shouted it. People started to file out, their concerned and puzzled voices filling the church with a low, intense buzz. Dale and Rusty remained seated. No reason for them to rush out. Let the old folks go first.

A couple of minutes later, everyone except the two young men had exited the church. The minister approached them and told them to please leave. Dale noticed the sweat on his shiny, smooth forehead.

"What's going on, man?" Rusty asked.

Dale almost elbowed him for not saying pastor or minister or some other respectful title. But the minister didn't seem to notice. His rather large, almost owlish eyes stared at them behind his spectacles.

"Please leave. Now. Go to the gym."

Dale stood up but Rusty remained seated.

"I'm not going," he said. "We'll just be coming back."

The minister said he had to leave.

"Why?"

"Because there's been a report of a bomb on the premises."

Dale and Rusty looked at each other. They were impressed.

"So, will you two please leave?"

Rusty slowly got up. "Okay, but I bet it's nothing."

Dale thought so, too, but as he and Rusty walked out with the minister they saw a cop with a German shepherd walking in the back way.

"Man, this is for real," Rusty said.

The minister nodded and ushered them into the old gymnasium. Dale and Rusty stopped just inside the door. The guests, maybe one hundred people, were gathered on the other end, some of them milling underneath the basketball goal, most of the others sitting in the bleachers.

"Man, this is weird," Rusty said.

"Surreal," said Dale.

He didn't see Quentin or Chris or any of the girls. He wondered where the wedding party was.

"Maybe in the coach's office," Rusty said.

They walked down toward the office and saw light behind drawn shades and under the closed door. Rusty sneaked over and leaned his ear against the door. His face changed from a sly expression to a concerned one. He walked back to Dale.

"I heard some bawling."

Dale could imagine how upset Roxanne and her family would be. Most weddings didn't have bomb scares.

"Who do you think made the bomb threat?" asked Rusty.

Dale knew that Rusty had dated Roxanne. "You."

Rusty flinched for a minute before grinning. "Yeah, right, man. I last dated Roxanne in eleventh grade."

Dale thought it was their sophomore year, but he couldn't keep track of his pal's paramours.

"What about Erickson?" Dale asked.

Rusty didn't seem to think him a serious candidate. "I don't think so. Rich is planning on getting married himself in a few months."

"Really?"

Rusty nodded. "To some girl from Nebraska."

Dale said that figured. Erickson was too good to marry an Oklahoma girl. He was just a damn Yankee.

Rusty looked surprised at Dale's cussing. Dale told him the phrase was from a Broadway musical so it was okay to say damn in that context.

"I'll have to remember that," Rusty said. After a thoughtful pause, Rusty suggested Tim Middleton.

Dale had heard that Middleton didn't take the breakup very well. But that had happened four years ago. Dale said he doubted Middleton. Rusty listed six or seven other prime suspects. Dale hadn't even known some of those guys had dated Roxanne. He said the

473

perpetrator was probably someone who'd gone steady with her. The candidates were Erickson, Middleton, Terry Harte and Sonny.

Dale and Rusty looked at each other. They both could imagine Sonny doing it. Why? Because he was the most unlikely suspect. Wasn't that the guy who always committed the crime in the movies?

"Yeah," Dale said, "easygoing Sonny."

"Besides, I hear Sonny's gone goofy over the wicked weed."

Now Dale wasn't so sure Sonny was the guy. Dopers usually preferred sitting in their untidy apartments listening to the Grateful Dead while toking it up. At least, that's what he imagined. He didn't think a druggie would show such initiative to phone in a bomb threat.

Rusty said he had a point. Well, they were back to square one in their investigation.

"Maybe we're looking at this in a completely wrong way," Dale said.

Rusty said, how so?

"We're assuming the mad bomber is an estranged lover of Roxanne when –"

"Hey, man, Roxanne's wearing a white wedding dress."

"I'm using lover in the generic sense," said Dale.

That seemed to placate Rusty. He said proceed, Colombo. Dale frowned at Rusty's choice of the short TV detective.

"Well, maybe the real mad bomber is one of Quentin's ex-girlfriends."

They both burst out laughing, and had to stifle their chuckling before incurring the ire of the other guests. A few milling around at the other end of the gym gave them reproving stares.

"Good thinking," said Rusty, "except that Quentin doesn't have any ex-girlfriends."

Dale and Rusty argued over which girls fell under the definition of a Quentin ex. They finally agreed that Quentin didn't have many girlfriends until Roxanne. And he'd not gone steady with any of those girls, including Carrie and Carmen.

Dale said he didn't remember seeing either Carrie or Carmen among the guests.

Rusty nodded solemnly. "Maybe they're in it together."

Dale considered the possibility with equal solemnity. "What would be their motive?"

Rusty shrugged. Both girls had been the ones to break it off.

"Maybe the bomber called the wrong place," said Dale. "Maybe he simply misdialed."

"Yeah, he meant to call the county courthouse or the sheriff's office."

"That's a possible lead."

The two them lapsed into a brief silence.

"Hey, this is a fun wedding," said Rusty.

"Yeah, well, it's certainly different."

"Remember when we used to sneak around here and think the church people were counterfeiters?"

"Yeah, we were really dopey kids."

Then he and Rusty stared at each other.

"Counterfeiters," they said.

"Yeah, maybe the wedding doesn't have anything to do with the bomb threat," said Rusty.

"It's just a coincidence."

But before they could let their imaginations run completely wild, the minister showed up and said everything was okay. The church had been checked out and no bomb. Everyone should please return to the church as promptly as possible.

Dale and Rusty looked at each other and shook their heads in disappointment. They waited until all the other guests had left the gym, then they followed. They both were more serious now that an actual threat no longer existed. After all, someone had called in a bomb threat and caused all this commotion. They walked over to the church and sat in their previous spots in the back pew and considered who was the most likely suspect.

They looked at each other and said, "Erickson."

Dale felt uncomfortable. Amanda to his right, Wendy to his left. He had tried signaling Chris to come into the big, circular booth before Wendy but either he didn't see Dale signaling or he wanted to sit on the end.

Chris sat on the left end, followed by Wendy, Dale, Amanda, Mary Jane, and Rusty. All three girls wore their bridesmaid dresses, pink, frilly things that looked especially incongruous in the modest pizza place, *Salvatore's Italian Pies*. Dale and Rusty, jacketless, let their ties hang loose around their necks. Chris still wore his tux and looked quite dapper.

"Nice wedding," Rusty said.

The three girls gave him harsh looks for his insensitivity.

"Who could do such an awful thing?" asked Mary Jane.

"It ruined poor Roxanne's wedding," said Amanda.

"She was very upset about the whole thing," said Wendy.

Dale knew that was true. He remembered feeling sorry for her as he gently shook her hand in the receiving line. It was obvious she'd been crying. Her eyes were still a little red and puffy. Quentin seemed to be taking a stoical attitude about it all. He nodded at Dale when they shook hands.

As Dale had progressed through the line, shaking the hands of the brides' parents and the grooms' parents, he noticed the grim faces of the fathers and the distraught faces of the mothers. Seeing their disturbed expressions made him feel ashamed of himself for making light of the bomb threat.

Dale shook hands with the best man, a guy he didn't know. Almost as tall and thin as Quentin, the best man fiercely squeezed his hand as if he suspected Dale of being the villain.

When he shook hands with his friends, Dale felt rather silly. He and Chris smirked, and Amanda smiled at him. When he shook Wendy's hand, he saw her looking at him in a studiedly casual way. But her fingers seemed reluctant to let his go.

Now, Wendy sat so close to him that he could feel her thigh touching his leg. When he shifted, she looked at him and smiled a little.

"Too close for comfort?" she asked.

"Not at all."

"Do you remember when we came here for my birthday?"

He remembered. He'd asked Carmen what was the best pizza place in the City. Dale didn't know why he'd asked her. He supposed he'd thought Cubans knew a lot about pizzas. Anyway, she recommended Salvatore's. She'd been right. The pizza was excellent. Dale especially liked the cornmeal dusting on the bottom of the tasty crust.

"Yeah, I remember."

Dale noticed out of the corner of his eye Amanda looking at him. He turned more her way and saw that she wasn't amused by the seating arrangement. He wanted to tell her that it wasn't his doing, but she turned toward Mary Jane and Rusty, who were arguing. Mary Jane reproved Rusty for not being duly sensitive to the dreadful turn of events. Rusty said at least everyone would remember this wedding. How many weddings could you say that about?

"A wedding isn't supposed to be for entertainment," Mary Jane reminded him.

"No kidding," Rusty said. "That occurs afterwards."

He grinned and Dale thought Mary Jane might slap him. Instead, she shook her head and turned to Amanda for moral support. Dale heard them talking and he could tell by the tone in their voices that both of them were displeased with their dates. Amanda wouldn't even look his way. He noticed that she'd inched away from him so they weren't touching. He moved his right leg so it touched hers, but she still didn't look his way.

Finally, the pizza arrived and the six of them began consuming it, with Rusty and Chris quickly devouring their first slice. At the wedding reception, only cake and punch had been served so they all were a little hungry. While eating, Dale heard Mary Jane and Amanda speculating on who had called in the bomb threat. Each named the same suspects that he and Rusty had mentioned earlier. On Dale's left, Wendy and Chris were engaged in a similar conversation. When Chris began eating his second slice, Wendy turned to Dale and asked him who he thought it was.

"Erickson."

"Rich?" Wendy asked. "I know he took the break-up with Roxanne badly, but he wouldn't do such an awful thing, would he?"

Dale didn't bother telling her that Erickson would do most anything. Dale had once found an old slice of pizza in a pizza box that had been lying on the floor of the school bus for who knows how long. Dale bet Erickson five bucks he wouldn't eat the moldy slice of pizza. Erickson did and Dale had to pay up.

"Sure he would."

Wendy said she didn't believe he would. Dale thought it was rather touching of her to have such faith in Erickson. That faith would probably be shaken if he related a few of Rich's comments concerning her. But he didn't say anything. Wendy said something else but Dale didn't quite hear because he felt Amanda's disapproving stare on the side of face. He turned and saw her and Mary Jane speaking quietly to one another.

They drank refills of pop, reminisced about high school, and then Wendy and Chris said they had to go. Chris had given Wendy a ride. They both said bye and Dale noticed Wendy gave him an especially casual good-bye, which he appreciated since Amanda was watching.

For the first time since they'd sat down, Amanda spoke to him.

"Wendy still cares about you."

"I don't think so."

But Dale knew it was true. He knew because if he and Amanda ever broke up, he'd still care for her. Knowing that Wendy shared his intense feelings made him feel both sympathy and resentment towards her.

Amanda returned her attention to Mary Jane and Dale looked at Rusty, who sat glumly at his end of the table. Dale thought both of them would be lucky to get a good night kiss.

Yeah, it had been a nice wedding.

### Chapter 12: *A trip to Lake Thunderbird and a confession*

Another Fleetwood Mac song came on and Dale gave up on the radio. Still looking at the road, he hit the play button on the cassette tape and the melodic harmonies of The Manhattan Transfer wafted through the car.

Dale looked at Amanda. "Like that?"

He rolled up his window so she could hear the song better. She recognized it and smiled.

"Yes, that's "Zindy Lou" from the second album."

That was Dale's favorite song from the album. He told her he bought the cassette to play for her on this trip to Lake Thunderbird.

"You did?"

"Yeah. I knew you liked them. And I knew there wouldn't be anything to listen to on the radio."

Amanda seemed pleased. She moved closer to Dale and he put his hand on her knee. She didn't remove it. She wasn't mad at him anymore. For almost a week she'd been rather cool to him even when he told her that he never thought of Wendy; he only thought of her. If Amanda only knew how much he'd always thought of her from that first time he saw her, she'd never be jealous.

Amanda sang along with the next song, "Chanson d'Amour." Dale listened to her voice as she sang quietly, almost absent-mindedly. When she caught him listening, she stopped.

"Don't stop," he said. "You got a lovely voice. I like hearing it."

Amanda smiled and resumed her quiet sing-along.

He'd been invited to spend a few days as Amanda's guest at the family cabin. Her parents and Kenny were already there, as were Elizabeth and Reinhardt. The Jorgensen family would be at their cabin, too, as the two families had decided to spend a mini-vacation together.

Dale turned off the highway onto a two-lane paved road, drove five miles, then turned onto a gravel road that circled Lake Thunderbird. He remembered this road from the time when he and Rusty spent the night with Mr. Benedict at the cabin. The Meeks cabin was located in the more desirable south section, not far from Little River State Park.

Ten minutes they arrived at the Meeks' cabin. Dale parked and grabbed their stuff and walked with Amanda to the handsome lodging. It sort reminded him of a Swiss chalet he'd seen in an old movie, except that there wasn't any snow, of course.

Amanda's mother opened the door and greeted them and asked about their trip. Amanda hugged her mother, and Dale said hello. He watched them as they talked; noticing how they both had the same bright blue eyes. Amanda's other features, however, favored her father's, but in a distinctly feminine way.

Dale rather liked Mrs. Meeks. She had always been nice and friendly, even though he suspected she still had reservations about him.

Elizabeth, Hope, and a middle-aged woman were the first to return. After the usual chatter, Mrs. Meeks introduced Dale to the middle-aged woman, Nora, Mr. Jorgensen's wife. She was tall and slender, with medium-length straight hair more reddish than blond. She had the same kind of narrow nose with clearly defined nostril wings that Hope had. Her big blue green eyes and pouting lips were especially attractive. Nora said hello to Dale rather coolly. As he listened to the women talk, he got the impression that Nora was naturally aloof. She didn't smile much and spoke less than the rest of the women.

Next to arrive were Kenny, Reinhardt, and a teenage girl that Dale guessed was Faith. She was the youngest Jorgensen child. She looked like her mother except for her undeveloped figure. She wore a one-piece bathing suit that clung unappealingly to her bony thirteen-year old body. He felt sort of sorry for her. She didn't have any curves. She reminded him of Olive Oyl. He wasn't sure if that was the reason why she had such a sullen disposition or if it was just the usual adolescent disagreeableness. Whatever her problem was, she complained bitterly that the boys had been mean to her while swimming. When introduced to Dale, she stared at him as if he'd been in cahoots with Kenny and Reinhardt.

Kenny waved at Dale and Reinhardt came over. Reinhardt didn't look any bigger than he did in high school. An inch taller than Dale, with a leaner build, he had the same kind of dark red hair and sharp, almost vulpine facial features as his sister, Gretchen. His skin wasn't as pale as hers, but Dale guessed that was mostly due to a tan.

Reinhardt didn't seem to have any recollection of Dale. He glanced at him with his light blue eyes, shook his hand, smiled, and asked how he was in that perfunctory way that meant he really didn't want to know.

Ten minutes later Mr. Meeks and Mr. Jorgensen soon arrived. They burst through the door with Mr. Jorgensen talking in a hearty voice. Seeing Mr. Meeks again, Dale was reminded that for all the bluntness of his face, he had an almost sensual mouth and a highly defined philtrum like Amanda. When Rex turned around to make sure the door was shut, Dale noticed a small bald spot at the top of his head, a pale oval in the short, brown hair.

Mr. Meeks looked heavier in the middle than Dale remembered, but his broad shoulders and big chest still gave him a powerful looking physique. He, like Mr. Jorgensen, wore a polo shirt and Bermuda shorts and his exposed limbs were untanned and hairy.

Mr. Jorgensen on the other hand, was taller but less physically imposing than Mr. Meeks. Standing around six one, with a lean build, Dale recognized his smiling face and rather longish blond hair from television. Mr. Jorgensen did his own commercials for his Ford and Mercury dealership, and his gimmick was donning a Viking helmet and saying in a sing-songy Scandinavian accent, "come on-a in folks to Jorgensen's for your Mercuries and Fjords."

The two men ambled over. Mr. Meeks, in his neutral banker's voice that he always seemed to employ for Dale, introduced him to Mr. Jorgensen. Dale shook his hand. Mr. Jorgensen said in a jokingly serious voice that didn't Dale know it was against the law to drive a Chevy around here? Dale confessed to that crime, but said since his mother drove a Cougar that should provide him with some leniency.

Mr. Jorgensen laughed and said he liked people with a good sense of humor. Dale wondered why he and Mr. Meeks were friends, although he'd seen some evidence that Mr. Meeks had a sense of humor – just one so ironic and dry that it was hard to tell when he was joking and when he was serious. Dale wasn't sure if he liked him.

But he liked Mr. Jorgensen. He seemed genuinely friendly and good natured. After meeting Dale, he went over to the women and teased them and even tried to joke with Faith, who continued to sit morosely at the table.

After eating lunch, Mr. Meeks and Mr. Jorgensen took the young people skiing. Dale had never skied before, but on his third attempt he kept his balance and skied for ten minutes before falling when he tried crossing the speedy boat's wake.

Reinhardt was the best skier by far. Dale could easily tell that he'd been skiing hundreds of times before. He could do all kinds of tricks, from skiing backwards to skiing with one ski.

Around seven, they called it a day. While the two fathers took care of the boats, the rest of them rode back to the cabin. An hour later, the men were back in time for dinner, an outdoor barbecue. After Mr. Meeks said grace, they ate their fill of barbecue beef and pork, baked beans, corn on the cob, homemade bread, lemonade, and homemade chocolate chip cookies for desert. Dale was surprised by how good it all was. He asked Mrs. Meeks how she learned to prepare such good barbecue. She said she grew up in Kansas City and just picked it up. Her mother, originally from the east, didn't know anything about it.

Dale asked about her family. She said her father was a minister in the Nazarene church and her mother was a homemaker. Both of them were still alive and well and retired in the Missouri Ozarks. He asked what her family name was. White, she said. She had two brothers, both ministers too, and one sister, a high school English teacher.

Amanda seemed amused that Dale spoke so long to her mother. He said her mother was nice. And a good cook, he added. Amanda said her mother was a much better cook than she was. Dale said, too bad. First skiing, now cooking. Amanda playfully slapped his arm.

It was almost dusk by the time everyone finished eating. The women cleaned up and Dale retreated to the cabin with the men and Kenny. Dale listened to Mr. Meeks, Mr. Jorgensen, and Reinhardt talk business. Mr. Jorgensen worried about gas prices affecting car sales. Mr. Meeks worried about high interest rates. Reinhardt worried about both. His father had taken out a big loan to cover an expansion in their trucking business. Dale pretended to listen and nodded thoughtfully when the three men did, but business matters bored him.

The women and Faith arrived and they cleared the dining table and played bridge. While Dale watched the Meeks, Jorgensens, Elizabeth and Reinhardt play, Amanda and Hope sat on the couch and talked.

Kenny and Faith, both of whom had left the room an hour earlier, came back. Kenny, holding a Ping-Pong paddle in his big right hand, demanded a better opponent than Faith.

He looked at Amanda and Hope. Amanda said, ask Dale. He's good with his hands. Immediately, Amanda covered her mouth with her small hand and blushed. Hope looked over at Dale with a sly look. None of the adults apparently heard; they were too engrossed in their game. Kenny rolled his eyes and Faith asked why Amanda was giggling.

Before more damage could be done, Dale got up and followed Kenny into the garage. Dale lost to Kenny in the first game, then beat him in the second. Then Reinhardt appeared and said he'd rather play Ping-Pong than bridge. They decided to play a "pong" tournament. The two losers would have to jump off the highest point of the Crimson Cliffs. Dale pointed out that with three playing, there would be two losers. An hour later, the deciding game was between Reinhardt and Dale. It came down to game point with Dale leading by one with the serve. He thought he'd try a spin serve. He'd experimented with that against Kenny but he hadn't tried it with Reinhardt yet. He'd been serving hard, low ones. Dale served, turned his wrist, and hit a ball with a lot of backspin. The serve caught Reinhardt off-balanced and he hit the ball too hard and it sailed over the table.

Amanda clapped over Dale's victory. "See, I told you he has good –" she caught herself this time and shut her mouth but her eyes were wide with embarrassment.

Reinhardt said good game. Dale said thanks, but he could tell Richard was annoyed to lose. Then Reinhardt announced that he and Kenny would jump off the Crimson Cliffs tomorrow.

"What?" Amanda said. "Was that the bet?"

Reinhardt said yeah. Amanda asked Dale in a scolding voice if he'd made that bet. Dale said of course not. He didn't even know what the Crimson Cliffs were. Amanda said none of them should be jumping off those cliffs.

Hope agreed. They were too high. She'd heard that one boy had broken his neck when he landed wrong in the water.

Reinhardt shrugged, and Dale and the girls interpreted the gesture as meaning the bet was off. They went back into the living room and Dale noticed that the Jorgensens were losing and that Nora was miffed. She glared at her husband when they lost another trick, but Mr. Jorgensen just shrugged and smiled.

Dale asked Amanda if she wanted to go for a walk. She said okay. As they left, her mother told them not to walk too far from the cabin in the dark.

Amanda asked if he had a conversation with her father the way he'd had one with her mother. He said no. Her father, Mr. Jorgensen, and Reinhardt just talked business. Amanda laughed. She said that's how Daddy was. He liked talking business. He didn't talk much about *personal* things. Sort of like you, she added.

Instead of taking the hint, Dale asked her about her father. All he knew about him was that he was a vice president at a big bank in the City. And he liked driving repossessed cars. And he played golf.

Amanda said he'd grown up in Iowa and came to Oklahoma to work in the oil fields after getting out of the army. He used the GI bill to get an education. He met Amanda's mother at GNC and they married after he graduated. Her father got an MBA from Oklahoma University and worked his way up at the bank.

"Was he a Nazarene?" Dale asked. "I mean, before going to GNC?"

Amanda shook her head. "No. His family wasn't religious. Daddy started college at Central State but after he met mother he transferred to GNC."

Dale thought that sounded a little familiar. He asked how her father met her mother.

"At a revival. Can you believe it? I guess Daddy was going through a difficult time in his life. He'd just got out of the army and was going to college at CSU and felt sort of empty. Daddy went to the altar call, and after he got saved, he saw mother there and something happened between them. They started dating and four years later they were married."

"Four years?"

"Well, they had to wait until Daddy graduated and got a good job."

Dale stopped walking and put his arms around Amanda's waist. He glanced at the dark sky and the almost-full moon.

"Lovely night," he said.

"Yes, lovely night."

They gazed at the stars and moon and the dark heavens for a few seconds.

"So, you think I'm good with my hands."

"Dale," warned Amanda.

But she allowed him to kiss her. He smelled suntan lotion on her skin. He remembered watching her strip off her cutoffs and T-shirt before skiing, revealing her modest one-piece bathing suit. He'd been a little disappointed but not surprised.

They kissed again and Amanda put her arms on his shoulders. Dale pulled her as close as possible against him, then reached down and cupped her buttocks with his hands.

"Dale," she warned again.

"Just demonstrating."

She reached behind her and moved his hands back up to her waist.

"Sometimes I think you have a fixation with my –" she was too modest to complete the thought.

"With what?"

"With my … bottom."

"I wouldn't say a fixation. Just a healthy appreciation."

"It's too big."

"No, it's not. It's perfect."

"I have to lose weight."

Dale swayed her against him. He sighed in frustration. "I don't know what's wrong with girls. They always think they're too fat."

"Don't boys like thin girls?"

"Some. Not me."

"All the girls in the magazines are thin," Amanda said, almost wistfully.

"It's a conspiracy. A conspiracy of thin women to brainwash society into thinking emaciation is a sign of beauty."

Amanda laughed. "A conspiracy of thin women?"

"That's right. And fat men."

"What do the fat men have to do with it?"

"They're the ones who finance the whole plot."

"Oh? And why would they do that?"

"Well, I haven't figured that out yet. But things were different in the '50s and '60s. Buxom women were the standard of beauty. Then something happened."

"You take all of this rather seriously, don't you?"

"You bet. Beauty is something we all should take seriously."

"But what's more important is the beauty that's inside us," Amanda said.

"But you have both, Amanda. You're beautiful inside and out."

They kissed again and he was about to make another move when they heard Kenny running down the path, braying Amanda's name.

"Oh, fudge," Amanda said.

Dale thought of a malediction quite a bit stronger. They separated and walked hand in hand back to the cabin. Kenny almost ran them over. He said Mom was wondering why you're spending so much time outside. Amanda said they were coming. Kenny could now report back to Mother.

Kenny said yes ma'am and turned and raced back to the cabin.

Dale asked Amanda about the Jorgensens. He thought they didn't seem to get along.

"Well," Amanda said in a confidential way that Dale found interesting because her voice got breathy, "I think Nick wanted more kids and Nora didn't."

Besides the two girls, Hope and Faith, the Jorgensens had an older son, Eric. Dale had wondered if Eric and Amanda had any personal interaction since the two families seemed so friendly. He asked and Amanda said she'd never found Eric appealing. He was so tall and skinny that he reminded her of a stork. Dale raised a brow when she said that, thinking, of another "famous" Scandinavian. Amanda said Eric and Elizabeth seemed friendly for awhile, but since Eric seemed to have his father's bridge skills and his mother's temperament, Lizzy cooled on him, too.

"So, they have just three kids?" Dale asked.

Amanda's voice grew sad. "Well, they lost one, too. A blue baby. She was a girl."

Dale thought a blue baby was one that got tangled in its umbilical cord and suffocated before being born. He vaguely remembered one of Wanda's daughters having lost a baby like that.

He didn't have to ask what the baby's name was or would have been. He could guess. He said that was too bad.

Amanda nodded. "Yes, it's very sad."

When they got back to the cabin, only Reinhardt, Kenny, and Mrs. Meeks were sitting in the living room.

"The Jorgensens have already left," Amanda's mother said. "You missed saying good night to them and Hope."

"Sorry," Amanda said.

Dale felt sheepish but not guilty. He and Amanda hadn't had any private time together since they had arrived. Mrs. Meeks asked Dale if he minded sleeping in the living room with Richard and Kenny. He said not at all. She said there was a couch and a couple of sleeping bags. Then she and Amanda said good night and Amanda went down the hall toward the first-floor bedroom she was sharing with her sister while Mrs. Meeks went upstairs to be with her husband.

After washing up, Dale found his sleeping bag and stretched out on it. He still wore his cutoffs. Since Kenny and Reinhardt had claimed the only two pillows, Dale took off his T-shirt to use for a headrest even though he didn't like sleeping shirtless. He felt embarrassed about his nearly hairless chest. And the idea of sleeping only in his skivvies was out of the question. He didn't even do that at home.

Dale had a hard time going to sleep. He heard Reinhardt snoring. Kenny fell asleep easily, too. Dale lay on his back and thought about how dark and quiet it was. He thought about Jesse and June May back home sleeping in their beds. He thought about Blackie and hoped he wasn't sleeping in Cleoma's bed. He suspected he was. He suspected Blackie spent a lot of time over there, which explained why his apartment was so bare. Dale disliked Cleoma. He didn't trust her and thought she was a phony. All that sweet talk. Then he thought about Sal, about how she looked naked, and he forced that image out of his mind. He still felt amazed at how shameless Sal had been. Sometimes Dale wished he could be less bashful and more indifferent to what people thought. But he could never be as uncaring as Sal seemed to be. He thought for someone to act that way, especially a woman, meant that something inside her was paralyzed: the something that made people self-conscious. Dale didn't think being paralyzed there was a good thing. Although it probably made you feel free, it also made you less responsive to other people's feelings. Jesse, when she was sick, was like that. She didn't care what other people thought of her, or how much discomfort or embarrassment she caused them. She seemed to live in the moment, only for herself, only for her most immediate, if crazy, needs.

Dale then thought about Amanda. He imagined her sleeping in her bed. He wondered what she was wearing. The cabin, even with the windows open, was still warm. He imagined she wouldn't be wearing much. Maybe a short nightie like June May wore. He felt himself growing excited. That was the last thing he needed to think about or he'd never get asleep. So, he tried not to think about how Amanda was so close in the next room, or how little she wore. Instead, he thought about baseball. The Reds had acquired Seaver, his favorite pitcher, in May. Now, the Reds had three of his favorite players, Bench, the great Oklahoma catcher, Morgan, and Seaver. He was certain they would overtake the Dodgers and win the division. He imagined himself playing shortstop for them, even though he didn't like their uniforms. He imagined Morgan congratulating him after he'd scored, saying you're pretty good for a little man. Just as Morgan's hand reached out to shake his, Dale fell asleep.

He awoke to find Elizabeth staring down at him. He immediately felt embarrassed at being shirtless. He blinked his eyes and asked what's wrong? Elizabeth said, nothing. Just time to get up. Dale rose and saw that Reinhardt and Kenny were already up. He felt annoyed that he hadn't awoken before them. He wondered how many people had seen him sleeping on the floor without a shirt on.

After washing up, he had breakfast with Reinhardt. Dale asked where Kenny was. Reinhardt said playing Ping-Pong. Dale asked, by himself? Reinhardt shrugged. Dale said, what's he trying to do, make the Chinese Olympic team? Elizabeth laughed, but Reinhardt kept eating his cereal. Elizabeth asked if Dale wanted bacon and eggs. He said no. He would just have cereal. When Dale asked if everyone was up, Elizabeth said her parents and Amanda were still sleeping.

After breakfast, Dale waited in the living room for Amanda. He wondered if she always slept so long. He went over and looked at the books in the bookcase again. Among the religious books he noticed one slim paperback: *The Late, Great Planet Earth*. Dale remembered seeing the film last fall during revival week. He grabbed it and began reading. It was easy to read. He zipped through it, and had almost gotten to Armageddon when Amanda came into the room.

She said good morning and Dale went over to her. He'd never seen her so early in the morning. Her face, freshly washed and without even the small amount of makeup she usually wore, still looked ravishing. But she was frowning a little. He asked what was wrong. She said she didn't feel that great. Dale said she should have some breakfast and she said okay.

While Amanda had breakfast with her parents, he finished *The Late, Great Planet Earth*. He thought the movie was more effective. The book allowed you to think the claims through more. Dale remembered how the movie had sort of excited him. The idea of people simply disappearing into thin air interested him for its sheer drama alone. But he couldn't believe it in the literal way it was presented. He knew he was supposed to. But he'd read too much philosophy and other literature to think in such simplistic terms.

Most of the morning passed with them not doing much of anything. Then the young people left for the park. At eleven in the morning, not many people were present. The girls spread out beach towels and sat down. While the girls sunbathed, the guys decided to head to the cliffs. As they walked, Richard pointed past the swimming area to the reddish cliffs that gradually ascended from ten feet to about fifty feet. Dale thought the cliffs were impressive looking.

They climbed up to the cliffs and all three dived off the twenty-foot ledge. Then they climbed higher and dived from thirty. The water stung a little but Dale liked how he sliced into the dark blue water like a seal.

They started climbing to the top when they encountered a couple of posts with a small chain stretched across the dirt path. A sign said, THIS POINT CLOSED TO PUBLIC. Dale paused, but Reinhardt stepped over the chain and said guys always ignored the sign. Dale looked at Kenny, who shrugged, although his expression didn't look as unconcerned, and they followed Reinhardt. The path became steep and they ascended perhaps twenty feet until they came to the top. The three of them stood on the rocky ledge and looked down.

"Boy, we're up high," said Kenny.

"Not that high," said Reinhardt.

Dale thought otherwise. It almost made him dizzy to look down at the surprisingly dark water below. He looked farther down the beach where the girls sat on the beach towel. Amanda turned his way, and although she was over a hundred yards away, he saw her mouth open in surprise and alarm. She stood up.

"It's too high," Kenny said. He took a step back.

"Don't be chicken," said Richard, with something of a sneer on his face.

Dale now remembered Reinhardt being a bit of a bully back in high school. Nothing like Comingdeer, but Reinhardt was one of the seniors who liked to taunt the younger kids. Dale wondered if he did that because he wasn't a big guy. Sometimes, smaller guys are worse than the big guys because they have more to prove.

Dale said he'd take Kenny's place. Kenny started to protest, but he said since Kenny had beaten him in swimming it was okay for him to replace him. Kenny seemed to think that made some sense and took another step back. Dale looked at Reinhardt. Richard said, who's first?

Dale said let's throw for it. So, they did. Dale threw a rock and Richard threw paper.

Dale looked down at the water. He'd never dived from so high a distance before.

"You going or not?" asked Reinhardt in a provoking voice.

Dale gazed down at the still water. It looked dark and deep and he felt a little afraid. Maybe a big rock lurked not too far below the surface of the water. He decided he needed to have faith that his leap wouldn't take him too deep too fast. He glanced at Kenny, who had a blank look on his face. Dale shrugged and jumped.

Mid-way in his descent, he wondered if he should cover his groin. Some guys who jumped feet first did that. But he thought his cutoffs, with their thick jeans material, and his shorts underneath should provide enough protection. But as the water rushed toward him, he thought otherwise and tried to move his hands down. Unfortunately, he couldn't move his flailing arms. He gave up and simply tried to keep his body straight. His legs remained pressed together, straight as a knife. He hit the water hard, felt surprised by how much it stung, and shot deep into the cool, dark waters.

When he finally stopped descending into the murky depths, he kicked his legs and thrust his arms down, propelling himself toward the surface. He opened his eyes and saw nothing but dark, swirling water. He felt a little explosion of panic inside him since he'd expected to see some indication of light. He calmed himself, and as he swam up, he felt his lungs burning a little, not as bad as his legs and chest, but enough to concern him that he was running low on air. Then he saw the glimmering light above the surface of the water and he thrust himself up, broke through, and gasped for air.

Dale shook the water off his face and looked up, expecting to see Reinhardt plummeting toward the water. But neither Richard nor Kenny stood at the top of the cliffs. Dale treaded water, then saw the two of them appear at the thirty-feet level. They dived, splashing in not far from him, and when they surfaced, they swam over.

Kenny grinned at Dale in an amazed way and asked if he were okay. Dale nodded. His arms, chest, legs, and feet still stung. Reinhardt, not smiling, asked him if he were crazy.

"What do you mean?"

"I didn't think you'd actually do it," Reinhardt said, in a resentful way as if Dale was responsible for putting him in an awkward position.

Then Richard turned and swam away before Dale could remind him that it was his idea to jump from the Crimson Cliffs in the first place.

Dale followed Richard and Kenny to shore. As he neared the beach, he saw Amanda standing with her hands on her hips. Her lips were compressed in disapproval but her eyes looked worried.

When he got to her, she asked him why he'd done it. Dale shrugged. He was curious, he said.

"Curious? That's a silly reason to jump from so high a cliff and risk your life."

"It's not that high," he said. But his stinging skin suggested otherwise.

"It's such a silly thing to do, Dale. You could have been seriously hurt."

Dale wished she'd stop saying it was silly. He had to jump. Otherwise, Reinhardt would have either shamed Kenny into jumping or made him look chicken if he didn't. But Dale didn't tell her that.

Amanda shook her head. She gave him a towel and he dried off his upper body as they walked back to the others. She asked him if the jump hurt.

"Yeah, it did."

"Good," she said. She asked him to never do that again.

"Don't worry. I've tasted the thrill of victory and I don't want to taste the agony of belly flopping from fifty feet."

Dale and Amanda sat down on the beach towel next to Richard and Elizabeth. When Dale rubbed his legs with the towel, he noticed Reinhardt looking at his right leg. Richard asked why his leg looked odd.

Dale guessed he was referring to the bone callous and the two faint circular scars where the pins had been inserted to hold his bones together. He said he'd broken his leg back in high school. As a freshman playing baseball. He collided with some other guy.

Reinhardt took a moment to make the connection. Then his fox-like eyes narrowed and he raised one brow. He said, you were the kid that ran into me?

Dale nodded, although he thought Reinhardt ran into him. After all, it was Richard's tentativeness in centerfield that had prompted him to chase that pop fly.

Reinhardt shook his head. Smith, right? Dale nodded. Reinhardt said he thought that kid's first name was Audie. Dale said, yeah. That's my first name. I now go by my middle name.

Elizabeth asked them what they were talking about. Amanda looked puzzled, too. She hadn't heard the story or had forgotten. Both of them listened with increasing unease as Reinhardt told them of the collision.

"You sure got the worst of it," Reinhardt said.

Dale agreed. That's what happens when a 125 pounder crashes into a 150 pounder. Reinhardt corrected Dale. A 155 pounder.

Dale told them that he'd made it worse for himself when he jumped up on his already-broken leg and put all his weight on it. The girls winced. Amanda said how awful.

Reinhardt said he remembered how Dale's leg looked like a fish tail. The lower half of his lower leg bowed out. He said he remembered how the broken bone pressed against the skin and looked how it was about to pop through.

The girls shuddered. Dale said thanks for the memories.

Reinhardt said it looked like Dale mended okay. He said yeah. It took awhile, but it healed. Amanda said she remembered him using his crutches to get around. She had felt sorry for him. Dale grinned. He was glad she had felt sorry for him.

Kenny interrupted their conversation by yelling at them to come out and swim. Elizabeth and Richard got up and went into the water as Hope came out. Dale asked if Amanda wanted to swim. She said she'd rather sunbathe. Amanda stretched out on the beach towel. Dale pretended to watch the others swimming, but he glanced at her out of the corner of his eye. She wore a different bathing suit than yesterday, but still one modestly cut. However, this one-piece suit was red.

Dale glanced over to Hope and noticed she also wore a different suit than yesterday. Hope's suit was similar to the two-piece she wore yesterday, except for the turquoise color. Dale liked the color. It looked good against her pale skin. She was a little flat-chested, although she actually had a bosom unlike her deprived younger sister. As Hope stretched out prone on the towel, he still thought Hope was on the skinny side, but she had some curvature to her legs and hips.

He felt bored just sitting on the blanket doing nothing. When Amanda turned over and reminded Hope that they should be careful about the sun – they both had burned a little yesterday – he asked if she'd like him to rub some suntan lotion on her. After a pause, Amanda said okay.

Dale reached into her basket and got the bottle. He squirted a big blob on her back. Dale rubbed the lotion over her neck, arms, and back. When he kneaded her shoulders and neck he heard her sigh. Then his hands moved lower. His fingers lingered on her dimples above her suit bottom until he saw her head turn. She didn't say anything, though.

He asked if she'd like some on her legs. Amanda didn't say anything, and Dale took that as a sign of consent. He squirted lotion on her calves and quickly rubbed that in. Then he let the liquid slowly ooze out of the bottle and fall on droplets on her thighs. He liked how fair-skinned she was. She wasn't pale like Hope, just sort of rosy. He slowly worked the lotion into her thighs, starting near the back of her knee, and gradually moving higher. He grew more excited the higher he got. His fingers caressed the firm softness of Amanda's mid-thigh, then slid to her upper thigh. He thought he heard a faint moan escape from Amanda's lips, no louder than a whisper. He pressed his fingers a little harder into her yielding flesh. When his fingertips touched that delightful crease between her upper thigh and buttock, Amanda said, "Dale."

He knew she was warning him but in a way that wouldn't call too much attention to them. After all, Hope was now lying supine just a few feet away. Dale removed his hands from her thigh, admired the curve of her bottom, resisted an urge to playfully slap it, and reclined on an elbow next to Amanda.

"Thanks," she said in a husky voice that Dale had only heard a few times before.

"My pleasure," he said, lowly.

Dale glanced over to Hope, who he could tell was looking at them through her sunglasses. Suddenly, she got up, tossed her sunglasses down, and walked toward the water.

"I think she's feeling a little left out," Amanda said, still lying on her stomach.

Dale asked if Hope had a steady boyfriend.

"Not anymore," Amanda said.

Dale remembered Chris dating her a few times. He asked Amanda what happened with them.

"Nothing."

"I guess that was the problem."

Amanda rolled over and Dale helped her sit up by holding her hand while she curled her legs underneath her hips.

"For a while, she dated Peter."

"Peter?"

"Peter Krupp."

"She dated *Krupp*?"

"Yes. What's wrong with that?"

"Nothing. After all, he's a colossus."

Amanda didn't get the reference. She dismissed Dale's comment with a tilt of her head.

"She and Eugene were dating steady for a while."

"And?"

"She said Eugene thought they were getting too serious. He broke it off."

"Were they getting too serious?"

Amanda shrugged her narrow shoulders. Dale liked the way they bunched up when she did that. "I think so. In fact, I think Hope is ready to get married."

"She's only twenty," Dale said, although he knew Nazarenes sometimes married young. They didn't marry as young as Jehovah's Witnesses, though.

"For some girls that's old enough."

Dale thought twenty was too young, even for a girl. The conversation broke off when Reinhardt and Elizabeth arrived. They sat on their beach towels and dried off. Reinhardt said he was going to check on the status of the boats. He asked Dale if he wanted to come. Dale said no, he'd rather go for a swim. Reinhardt said he'd be back with the car in about an hour. He trudged off.

Dale asked Amanda if she wanted to swim now. She shook her head. He asked if she felt okay. She said she still felt a little "icky."

He jogged down to the swimming area just as Kenny and Faith were leaving. Dale dived into the water and swam out twenty yards. The water felt nice and cool after being bombarded by the sun's rays. But he didn't like to swim just to swim. He preferred some additional activity, such as diving, throwing a Frisbee, or dunking girls.

He treaded water and saw Hope floating on her back. When she skimmed past him, she splashed water on him. Dale said, hey! She smiled and continued floating on her back. He thought about going after her and dunking her. But he didn't think Amanda would like that. Usually, Hope acted cool to him. But here she was flirting with him. Well, he thought, wasn't that like a girl?

When he didn't pursue her, Hope swam back to shore. Dale watched her walk toward Amanda while she squeezed the water out of her medium-length blond hair. As she walked, she swung her hips with more emphasis than he'd seen before. Even though she was skinny, he thought she was sort of attractive.

Dale swam around for a few more minutes, wishing Amanda would come out so he could dunk her. He liked the way her sleek skin felt when it was wet. But she remained seated on the towel and looked at the bright sky through her sunglasses.

Ten minutes later, Reinhardt returned and drove them back to the cabin. Amanda packed a picnic lunch. Mr. Meeks and Mr. Jorgensen were already with the boats so Richard drove them to the dock and like yesterday they divided into two groups and skied. Dale did even better than yesterday. He could even ski over the boat's wake without falling. He thought with practice he could ski as well as Reinhardt. After an hour of skiing, they took a break for lunch. Dale noticed Amanda didn't eat much. He asked her what was wrong? She said cramps.

"Yeah, muscle cramps are bad," he said.

He remembered getting them in football when he sweated away too much salt. They hurt like heck. Usually, it was his calf muscle and it would turn into such a tight knot he couldn't even walk.

"Not those kind of cramps," Amanda said.

Dale looked at her. She sat sort of slumped on the picnic bench wearing her sunglasses. Even without looking into her eyes, he could tell she felt poorly. She seemed to be gritting her teeth. Her lips pressed together tightly.

"Oh, right," Dale said.

While he was looking in the medical dictionary to find the name for the groove between the nose and mouth, Dale read a little about the female reproductive system. He'd taken biology, of course, but most of that stuff hadn't made a deep impression. As he read the information, he'd realized that women were more complicated than men. He thought about being a girl and all the stuff that would happen, and he'd felt a surge of sympathy for the female. He'd wished he'd been kinder to June May, Wendy, and other girls.

After lunch, Amanda said she didn't feel like skiing any more. She'd just watch. She told Dale to go on. After his third turn, he'd gotten so adept with this simple kind of skiing that it started getting a little routine. So, he crisscrossed the boat's wake until he fell. He rather enjoyed tumbling into the water. It was even more fun than falling off Smoky when he used to go over to Vern's and ride his horse. Sometimes, Smoky would gallop to the corral and turn the corner fast, throwing him off. He'd never gotten hurt. Just dusty and a little beat up.

Now, Dale waved off Mr. Meeks and swam to shore and went over and sat down next to Amanda.

"Not feeling any better, huh?"

She shook her head.

"Anything I can do?"

She asked if he could get her a drink of water. Dale took the paper cup she'd used for her Tab and went over to the water fountain and rinsed it out, then filled it up. He returned and gave it to her and watched as she took a couple of pills and drank the water.

She said he ought to go back out and ski. He said he'd had enough. She smiled and took off her sunglasses. He reached over and took her hand. Since they were holding hands underneath the picnic table, Amanda didn't object.

Dale looked out at the boats and watched as Reinhardt showed off. He'd joined the other boat when Dale left. That way he'd get to ski even more.

"You have a scar right there," Amanda said, gently touching the spot close to his left temple.

"I got it in football. During the scrimmage game senior year. When the Maverick guys knocked my helmet off and the buckle cut me."

"Oh, I remember that. You bled a lot."

"I guess so."

He remembered all the fuss. He also remembered Wendy bawling. Of course, his injury was only part of the reason why she'd cried so hard. He felt himself wince at the memory.

Amanda removed her finger. "Does it hurt?"

"No. I was just remembering something painful."

He looked at Amanda and he could tell by how her eyes deepened and her skin flushed that she was remembering the same thing: Wendy's near-hysterical behavior.

"I got this other scar," he said, pointing to his chin. "And it has a funny story to it."

"Oh?" Amanda said, now so interested in the funny story that the memory of Wendy faded just as Dale had hoped.

"Yeah. I got this scar when Roxanne and Mary Jane hit me with a teeter-totter."

"What?" Amanda smiled at the idea of her two friends hitting Dale with a teeter-totter. "How could such a thing happen?"

"We were in fourth grade. Roxanne and Mary Jane were standing by a teeter-totter. I wandered over. I think I was chasing a baseball. Anyway, I saw them and was a little curious about them. I stood too close to the low end of the teeter-totter. Roxanne and Mary Jane both suddenly pushed on the high end and the low end flew up and clocked me right under my chin. It knocked me off my feet and cut my chin pretty good."

Amanda's mouth was open in surprise. "Did they do it on purpose?"

"I don't think so. They might have meant to scare me. Anyway, that's one reason why I was always shy around girls. You never know when they might clobber you with a teeter-totter."

"Oh, right," Amanda said, smiling. "So, did you cry?"

"No, I didn't."

Dale remembered wanting to, but he wasn't about to start bawling around Roxanne and Mary Jane. He also remembered that they didn't seem too concerned about his injury.

"So, you were tough even as a little boy?"

Dale puffed up his chest and nodded. "Oh, yeah, I was the toughest ten year old in school."

He remembered what happened next. He picked himself up off the gravel playground and held his chin. Roxanne and Mary Jane sort of giggled. They didn't understand he was hurt since he hadn't reacted much. Recess ended and he showed his homeroom teacher his chin. She sent him to the school nurse, who put a Band-Aid on it. His head and jaw hurt the rest of the day. Then he went home and told Jesse. She didn't take him to the doctor to get stitches or check his jaw. Jesse didn't like going anywhere much, especially to doctors. So, Dale healed on his own. He remembered going to the movies at the Coronado theater with Rusty that weekend and having a hard time eating his candy and popcorn. His jaw had probably been dislocated a little. Even now, his jaw didn't seem to close quite right. And the accident left a fairly big scar on his chin. Whiskers wouldn't grow in the groove. Dale thought that part of his chin looked funny when he shaved. Like a small path in a field of stubbly grass.

Amanda gave him a playful pat on the arm. "I don't know why boys have to pretend they're so tough."

Dale shrugged. "Human nature. Boys learn to be tough or at least pretend to be pretty early. There's always bigger, older boys ready to bash them."

"Why are boys so mean?"

"I wouldn't criticize boys so much. They just hurt you physically. But girls. They hurt you inside and that takes a lot longer to heal."

Amanda's blue eyes widened as she looked into his dark eyes.

"Has a girl hurt you like that?"

"Not yet."

Dale wanted to kiss her but he heard the boat coming into the launching area. He squeezed her hand instead and walked over to help Mr. Meeks tie up the boat.

After he, Reinhardt, and Mr. Meeks secured the boat, he walked back to the picnic table and saw Amanda talking to her mother. Mrs. Meeks put her hand on Amanda's forehead then her cheek. Dale slowed down, not wanting to intrude.

Back at the cabin, Mrs. Meeks and Mrs. Jorgensen prepared dinner. Amanda went into the bedroom to lie down. Hope went with her. Dale and Kenny went to the garage to play Ping-Pong. Reinhardt and Elizabeth went for a walk.

When Mr. Meeks and Mr. Jorgensen arrived, they all gathered together to say grace before dinner. Mr. Jorgensen said it. Dale, as he sometimes did, sneaked a glance, first at Amanda, who listened to the prayer with her eyes tightly closed and her lips slightly parted, then at Mr. Meeks. There was something about Mr. Meeks that intrigued him. He got the feeling that Amanda's father wasn't exactly what he seemed to be. Dale couldn't quite explain his suspicion. He imagined Mr. Meeks regarded the world and everyone in it with a superior attitude, as if he knew the whole enterprise was absurd but he wasn't going to tell anyone else. Instead, he was going to play along. Such a strategy enabled him to get an advantage over the less perceptive while pretending to be just as conventional.

Dale wanted to see Mr. Meeks in an unguarded moment. He peeked in his direction during the prayer and to his consternation he thought he saw Mr. Meeks peeking right back at him! Dale quickly bowed his head and closed his eyes and then wondered if he'd really seen what he thought he saw. He was about to peek again when Mr. Jorgensen concluded the prayer. Dale glanced obliquely at Mr. Meeks, but his public face was on again: the dignified, calm demeanor of a stalwart family man and shrewd banker.

After dinner, Dale sat on the couch with Amanda while Mr. Meeks, Elizabeth, and the Jorgensens played bridge. He asked Amanda how she felt. She said not too well. On top of everything else, she thought she got too much sun, too.

Dale felt a melancholy feeling descend on him. He usually felt that way as the end of anything – a day, an event – approached. He knew he should leave for Galilee before it got dark. But he didn't want to leave Amanda any earlier than he had to.

"I guess I better be getting home," Dale whispered to Amanda.

She nodded, then asked if he would mind if she came, too.

"You mean, you want me to take you home?"

She said yes. She'd already spoken to her mother and she'd agreed. Also, Hope wanted to come so she could spend the night with Amanda. Did Dale mind?

He didn't mind. Amanda got up and walked over to her mother, who was watching her husband and Elizabeth win yet another game from the Jorgensens. Dale watched them talk, then Amanda went into the bedroom with Hope. A few minutes later, they came out. Dale went over and took Amanda's and Hope's suitcases and put them in the car. When he got back he saw everyone hugging and saying good-bye. He went over and shook hands with Mr. Meeks, Mr. Jorgensen, and Reinhardt. Mr. Jorgensen told Dale to be sure and drive that *Chevy* safely. Dale said in spite of its make, it was a dependable car. Mr. Jorgensen laughed. Dale saw Mr. Meeks regarding him in a thoughtful way, but he didn't say anything like "be sure and take care of my little girl." He didn't have to. Dale knew what he was thinking.

Dale thanked Mrs. Meeks for inviting him and for providing such good food. She smiled, and thanked him for coming and for taking Amanda back with him. Dale waved at the rest of them. Kenny gave him a friendly wave, but Mrs. Jorgensen and Faith hardly waved at all.

He escorted the girls to the car. Amanda sat in front, Hope in the back. Dale looked at the sky. The bright sun looked about an hour and a half from setting. They should make it back to Galilee before nightfall.

The Meeks and Jorgensens waved bye as Dale drove away. They rode in silence for awhile, then Amanda thanked Hope for coming home with her. Hope said she was getting bored with swimming and skiing anyway. She said it especially wouldn't be much fun without Amanda around.

Dale asked Amanda if she wanted to listen to music. She said okay, but not to play it too loudly. Dale first turned on the radio and heard yet another Fleetwood Mac song followed by Barry Manilow. He'd heard enough. He wondered which tape he should put in. He now wished he'd bought a classical tape, maybe Bach, because he knew Amanda would have liked hearing that. Instead, he decided the Carpenters would be a good choice, so he put that in the tape deck and turned the volume down fairly low.

The hum of the tires on the road acted like a lullaby and Dale noticed both Amanda and Hope growing drowsy. Amanda, sitting close to him, leaned her head on his shoulder and in a few seconds he heard her shallow breathing. He glanced at her and saw she was asleep. He noticed she pushed out her lower lip when she slept.

Dale didn't see Hope at all in his rearview mirror. He guessed she'd laid down in the backseat.

As he drove, he listened to the tires beating on the road and smelled the summery air flowing through the vents and his window. The engine made a reassuring thrumming and Dale relaxed and rather enjoyed the protective sense he felt as he drove the two sleeping girls.

He thought about how he'd enjoyed skiing and being with Amanda. But he'd never felt really comfortable staying in the cabin and being around all the people he didn't know well. The more he observed the Meeks and the Jorgensens and Reinhardt, the less he felt he had in common with them. It wasn't only a matter of money and status. Dale knew the two husbands went out into the cruel world and made good livings so their families could be well off and protected from the harsher realities. He respected that. But he couldn't imagine himself enjoying being a businessman; certainly not a banker or a car salesman, even one as successful as Mr. Jorgensen. He had different ambitions and interests.

Hope woke up first. He saw her yawn and rub her eyes from the rearview mirror. She asked if Amanda was sleeping. Dale nodded.

"She's having a bad one," Hope said.

He knew what she was referring to but he was surprised by her frankness.

Amanda woke up just a few miles from Galilee. The sun was nearly setting. Dale asked how she felt. She said she felt better, but he thought she was just saying that so he wouldn't worry.

They drove on Highway 66 until Dale turned off at the Galilee exit. Then he turned south and headed for the Meeks' residence. When they arrived there, he carried their bags into the house. Amanda asked Dale if he'd like to stay for awhile. He asked if she felt up to having him around. She said she'd like him to stay for at least a little bit.

Dale asked if she'd like to see the sunset. Amanda said that would be nice. They walked out into her backyard and sat on the back porch swing that he liked. He held Amanda's hand as they watched the sun finally sink beneath the horizon. He liked the way the Meeks had designed their long backyard so the tall trees stood on each side and gave a frame to the horizon.

The sky slowly deepened and shadows fell upon them as they sat in the swing. Dale gently swung them as Amanda leaned her head against his shoulder. He put his arm around her and they watched night slowly fall upon the earth.

"I'm sorry I don't feel well," Amanda said.

"That's all right."

"Yes, but we can't really do anything."

He wondered if she were talking about making out or just doing something like going out and getting a Coke. He guessed the latter. Dale wondered if she liked doing the former as much as he did.

"That's okay," he said.

"But this is nice, too."

"Yeah, it is nice."

Dale noticed the fireflies flickering through the air. He heard a cricket rubbing its legs and making its dry, rhythmic sound.

He smelled the scent of her hair and felt the warmth and softness of her leaning against him. With his arm around her slight shoulders, he felt protective of her again. He felt that powerful combination of sympathy and physical attraction. Just sitting next to her excited his senses. But knowing she was unwell and vulnerable made him empathize with her.

"You've been so understanding today," she said, her voice soft.

For a moment, he couldn't speak. Dale took a deep breath and told her what he'd wanted to tell her for a long time.

"That's because I love you so much."

Amanda turned her face to him. Dale saw her eyes shining in the shadows.

"Do you?" she asked softly.

"Yes. I've loved you ever since I first saw you."

He told her about that time in the auditorium at the start of their freshman year in high school. He told her about seeing her for the first time when the spotlight illuminated her beautiful face.

"That's a nice story," she said. "I had no idea you felt that way about me."

"You knew I liked you, though, didn't you?"

"Yes. I guessed that much."

"You just didn't know how deeply and desperately in love with you I was. Even as a goofy kid."

Amanda laughed softly. Then she fell silent for a moment. "I'm glad you told me this now. I mean, at a time like this. Not when we're doing the other stuff. It means more, you know?"

Dale wasn't sure. The night when he'd taken her home from the movie or the time while swimming in the Gardner's backyard, he'd felt powerful emotions and he didn't see anything wrong with telling her then. But he knew girls were different. At least, Amanda was different. Passion was less a reason than empathy.

"Yeah, I know," he said, which was true now that he'd thought it out.

"Good," Amanda said, "because I think I love you, too."

He didn't mind that she'd qualified her love. He knew the thought was new to her, not a feeling like his that he'd had for years.

Dale leaned over and kissed her tenderly. He heard her sigh and he hugged her and they looked at the sky now completely dark, the twinkling stars, and the full moon rising above them.

**Chapter 13: *The King and Amanda's callipygians***

"Did you hear the news?" Rusty asked Dale.

Dale had just arrived at the First Church rec center baseball field for softball practice before the Wednesday night Bible study.

"What news?"

"Elvis died."

Rusty nodded solemnly when Dale raised a skeptical eyebrow. After all, Dale had seen him in concert just last year.

"You're kidding."

"Nope. The King is dead."

Rusty threw the softball to Dale who caught it in his mitt. He tossed it back to Rusty. Dale had never been a fanatical Elvis fan. His memories weren't of him when he was a young, rebellious rock and roller, but as a ridiculous movie star. Still, he had a strange fondness for him. Maybe because he'd seen so many of this crummy movies at the drive-in or maybe because he identified with his redneck background. Whatever the reason, Dale felt a little sad.

The softball team practiced for an hour in preparation for their final game tomorrow. They'd had a good season playing other church teams from the City. They'd won nine games and only lost two. With Phelps, Greene, Henshaw, Rusty, Chris, and Dale, they had six good athletes. And they had the league's best pitcher in Phelps. Even though it was a slow-pitch league, Phelps knew how to get hitters out.

During practice, as the college kids started arriving in left field for the Bible study, Phelps hit a long drive that sailed between center and left. Dale chased the ball down and in his haste almost ran over Sheba Smith. He bumped into her, then grabbed her around the waist to keep her from falling. She shrieked more out of fun than fright.

Dale threw the ball back to the infield. He then turned and asked Sheba if she was okay.

"Yeah, I'm okay," she said, smiling. "Are you okay?"

Dale said he was. He hadn't spoken to Sheba since their last date last summer. Feeling ashamed of his behavior, he had sent her flowers and a note of apology to her father's residence in Enid. He'd never heard from her and he thought that was probably for the best. She went back to her high school world, and Dale went back to his college world and began dating Amanda.

Then, a month ago, Sheba showed up at the Wednesday night Bible study with another recent Galilee High graduate, Lila Davis. Dale and Sheba didn't avoid each other, but they never seemed to get close enough to say hello. He noticed Sheba on a few occasions looking in his direction. He, of course, sneaked looks at her, too, especially when she wore tight-fitting cutoffs or shorts. She still had those callipygians.

Now, Dale saw her smiling at him and he thought he should let her know that he didn't feel any resentment. He asked her if she heard about Elvis.

"Yeah, isn't that sad?" she said.

"Yeah and just think. We were two of the millions of people to see him when he was alive."

Sheba laughed. Then she said she appreciated the flowers he'd sent last summer. She meant to write him a thank-you note.

"That's okay," Dale said. "You know I don't read very well, anyway."

She laughed again and playfully slapped him on his arm. Dale remembered how nice she felt when he bumped into her. Her waist was small and the rest of her plump and round; well, the bottom half. For a moment, he enjoyed the pleasant nostalgia of the two summers they'd dated. Then Rusty yelled for him to come in and bat. Dale said he had to go. Sheba smiled and gave him a girly wave of her hand. He turned and sprinted back to the infield and wondered if Sheba had been flirting with him.

After practice, they ambled over to left field and joined the rest of the college kids for the Wednesday night service. Dale saw Amanda standing with Mary Jane, Gretchen, and Hope. He waved with his baseball mitt. She waved back but without much enthusiasm. He wondered what was wrong.

Those who wanted to play volleyball divided into two groups. Dale joined the side with Rusty and Chris. They stood in the back row and joked around. It was almost like high school. Rusty had started coming to Wednesday nights after the summer league basketball league ended.

Eugene Greene walked past them on his way to the other side. As he passed, Rusty said, "hey, Mr. Green Genes."

Eugene had no idea why he called him that. He asked Dale what Grimes meant. Was he talking about that guy on the old Captain Kangaroo show?

Dale told him no. He said Mr. Green Genes – and Genes in the scientific sense – was a song by Frank Zappa on the *Uncle Meat* album.

Eugene shrugged. Zappa and the album meant nothing to him. Dale said it was sort of a notorious record that Rusty and Erickson used to torment Mr. Benedict.

"Mr. Benedict? You mean, Rabbi?"

Dale thought it was funny that Eugene still thought of Mr. Benedict by that moniker.

"Yeah, that Mr. Benedict."

Eugene said he thought Rabbi was teaching in California. Dale said yeah, that's what he'd heard.

Rusty overheard and turned to Eugene and said don't ever go visit Benny in San Diego. Eugene said he had no intention of doing so.

"Glad to hear that, man," Rusty said. "You might never come back if you go."

Eugene gave Dale a "what gives?" look and Dale shrugged.

They were ready to start the volleyball game. The girls had begun to complain a few weeks ago about the games getting too competitive. Volleyball was supposed to be for fun. But ever since Rusty arrived and played with more intensity, the other guys had responded in kind. Dale got the impression that some of the Cimarron City Nazarene guys, Henshaw in particular, didn't like Rusty much. Dale sort of understood. Rusty had a tendency to rub the opposition in the wrong way. He played with a lot of animation and energy and exulted in a comical way when he spiked the ball or briefly got angry if he didn't make a good play. And he was still a new guy.

Initially, Thad North had tried to keep the game casual, but after Rusty had spiked him, he let the game get serious. The last few weeks, Dale had noticed that the teams divided themselves between former Galilee High and Cimarron City High players. Rusty, Dale, Chris, Stephenson, and K. C. on one side; Henshaw, Phelps, Greene, Keaton, and North on the other.

The two teams played the first game more casually with the girls involved. The girls sat out the more intense second game. Usually, thanks to Rusty, the team composed of Galilee High guys won. But tonight, Dale noticed a newcomer in their midst. A former Cimarron City basketball great who'd transferred from OU to GNC just last semester: a seven footer named Gary Lyle.

Rusty spotted him right away. "Say," he said to Dale and Chris, "what's Lyle doing here?"

It was unusual for someone to come to Wednesday night this late in the summer. Dale suspected he'd been recruited.

They played the first game in a friendly, recreational way. Then came the second game, and both sides served the ball harder and aggressively blocked and spiked. Lyle, however, didn't play with much intensity. Still, at seven feet, he scored almost at will and easily blocked any shot that came in his vicinity.

Near the end of the match, Dale found himself paired across the net with Lyle. Dale shook his head and all the guys laughed at the sixteen-inch height disparity. The only guy shorter than Dale playing was K. C., and he was only an inch shorter.

The Cimarron City guys only needed a point to win. Henshaw served. Stephenson volleyed it back. Then Eugene set up Lyle. He hit a looping pass over to him. Dale, determined to do his best, timed the spike. He crouched, waited, then as the ball tumbled toward Lyle, he leapt as high as he could.

For a moment, Dale thought he had a chance. Although comparatively short, he jumped well. He extended his arms for the block, then watched in dismay as Lyle, still standing on his size twenty feet, simply tipped the ball over the top of the net, six inches *below* Dale's fingertips.

Everyone laughed. Even the girls watching from the side laughed. Dale tried to laugh too, but inside he seethed. He had to admit that it was a good play. A sneaky play, but effective.

The comedy of the last play seemed to erase the resentment that had been building up between the two teams. Lyle looked down at Dale and grinning said, "good game." Dale nodded and tried to grin, but for a second he would have liked to knock Lyle's teeth out – if he could have reached them.

Rusty slapped Dale on the back and said the other guys only won because they brought in a "ringer." Dale didn't really care which team won as long as he didn't look silly. But he pretended that he didn't mind and walked over to Amanda and hoped that she wouldn't notice that he was only three inches taller than she was. Dale, from his extensive studies, had determined that the ideal height difference between men and women should be four to eight inches.

But Amanda wasn't concerned about that. Instead she asked how Sheba Smith was.

"Fine, I guess."

"I saw you *bump* into her," Amanda said.

Dale thought that was the problem with being passionate with a girl. She assumed you were passionate with other girls. Well, come to think of it, he *had* been rather passionate with Sheba, but not in the same complete way he felt for Amanda. He doubted he could explain that, though. He thought it best to change the topic.

"Did you hear that Elvis died?"

"Elvis?"

Apparently, Amanda hadn't heard and he could tell she wasn't too disturbed. She never listened much to popular music, especially rock 'n' roll.

"Didn't you used to date her?"

Dale should have known the Elvis gambit wouldn't work. He said, yeah, but a long time ago.

"Wasn't it last summer? Before you started dating me?"

Dale wondered how Amanda got such good information. He imagined an intelligence network of girls throughout Galilee and parts beyond gathering information on who dated who, for how long, how intense, who broke up first, and so on.

He took her by her arm and led her away from the others. Amanda didn't seem to want to go at first, but when he said please, she relented and followed him a few feet away from the group.

"I did date her for awhile, but it was just for fun."

"For fun?"

Dale realized that wasn't the most judicious term to use.

"Last week, I saw you looking at her ..." Amanda couldn't bring herself to say the word.

"Her teeth?"

"Very funny. You know what I mean."

Dale didn't think this was the time to explain the concept of the callipygian. Fortunately, Thad North called everyone to gather for the Bible study. Dale said he'd explain everything later. Amanda still looked miffed but she walked with him back to the others.

Unfortunately, as luck would have it, Sheba sat in front of Dale and Amanda. She wore cutoffs that were a little large in the waist. Sitting Indian-style, Sheba's hips tilted back enough to push open the back of her cutoffs and reveal the bare skin between her panties and blouse. Ordinarily, Dale would have been very grateful for this privilege but with Amanda seeing what he saw, he felt himself in an awkward position. If he peeked, Amanda would know. He tried to concentrate on Thad's religious message but he felt his eyes irresistibly drawn down. When Sheba leaned even farther forward, her white panties slipped down just enough to expose the pink beginning of the natal cleft and he couldn't resist. He looked but just for a moment. Sheba then sat up straighter, the posterior cleavage disappeared, and Dale took a deep breath, closed his eyes, and tried to ignore the heat of Amanda's glare on the side of his face.

After the study ended, he quickly got up and offered to help Amanda to her feet. She not-so-politely refused his assistance. Dale noticed Sheba glancing at them, but fortunately she didn't say anything and walked away with her friend, Lila.

Chris came over and said some of the college kids were going to West Oaks. Dale glanced at Amanda and she looked amendable, so he said they would meet Chris and the rest over there.

Dale and Amanda walked to his car. He remembered when Rusty first started coming to the Wednesday nights, he and Mary Jane accompanied Dale and Amanda to West Oaks or wherever else the college kids met afterwards. But something had happened between Rusty and Mary Jane. They weren't seeing each other anymore. Dale had thought it was one more of their temporary splits, but they hadn't been on a date together for two weeks.

Dale saw Rusty walking to his car with Hope. Dale asked Amanda if she saw that.

"Oh, yes, I *see*," she said, in a tight, disapproving voice as if Rusty's behavior proved her worst suspicions of the male race.

Dale thought Hope was a little too thin even for Rusty's preference for slender girls. But Rusty's grin as Dale waved seemed to suggest otherwise.

At West Oaks, Dale and Amanda sat in the same booth as Chris and a girl named Olivia Szabo. She'd gone to Cimarron City High and now went to GNC. Both Chris and Amanda knew her well, but Dale had only met her a few times on campus. She was a little chubby, but her fluffy blond hair and full bust made her popular with the guys. She had a fairly cute face, thanks to her with blue-green eyes and full cheeks. But Dale thought her lips were a little too thin. Naturally cheerful, she smiled often and he noticed the way her mouth stretched wide and revealed all her front teeth and her gums.

But what interested him more was her big bust. She wore a fairly tight red blouse with a daringly low neckline for a Nazarene girl. Dale could see some cleavage and he avoided peeking as much as he could. Chris, however, wasn't quite so discreet. More than once, Dale caught him staring directly at Olivia's scooped neckline. Amanda saw, too, and that additional confirmation of men's lustful ways didn't improve her mood.

On the way to Dale's car, Amanda said she had to give him credit. At least, he didn't act as disgracefully as Chris had.

"I thought you liked Chris."

"I do," Amanda said. "We've been friends all our lives."

"Well, you should have some sympathy for him."

"Sympathize with his naughty behavior?"

"He's harmless. We're all harmless. We can't help ourselves. We have to look. It's instinct."

Amanda didn't appreciate instinct as much as Dale. When they got in the car and he drove out of the parking lot, she said people were supposed to control their instincts. He agreed.

But you shouldn't expect men to be automatons. Amanda wasn't sure what an automaton was, so he said, robot. She agreed that people shouldn't be robots, but they should control their appetites.

Dale acknowledged they should control their appetites, but not deny them. Amanda said what's the difference? He said controlling your appetites meant not acting on them when it was inappropriate; whereas denying them was not acting on them at all.

Amanda thought about that for a while. Since they were almost to her home, Dale tried to advance his argument.

"You remember how difficult it was for you to lose five pounds?"

Amanda nodded.

"That's because you enjoy eating sweets."

He liked them, too. That was one of the better things they had in common.

"Yes, but what –"

"Let me explain. You denied yourself for a while even though it was very difficult. But now you have a little dessert."

"A little," Amanda said.

"Well, with guys it's like being surrounded by desserts all the time."

"Dale, that's silly. Women aren't like cookies and pies."

"No, they're even more tempting. I just want you to imagine not having any of the food you like the most for not just weeks, but months, years. And then imagine that hunger multiplied by one hundred. That's what it's like."

They were at her house. Since it was a Wednesday night, she had to be in early.

"Really?"

"Yes," said Dale. "And I've been on a diet for an awfully long time."

Amanda didn't say anything, but she looked like she was considering his rather ridiculous analogy. He hopped out of the car and went over and opened her door before she found a flaw in his theory.

Dale walked her to her door. He asked if their date for Saturday was still on.

"Of course," she said.

Dale kissed her. She said good night. He said he'd pick her up Saturday at six sharp. He watched her slip inside her house, then he walked slowly to his car. Since the night he'd confessed his love for her, Amanda had been more receptive to his advances. Dale guessed she'd raised the speed limit to about thirty-five. He still hadn't gotten back to the high of forty that he'd enjoyed that night on the couch in her garage. But he was hopeful that Saturday night would be the night. After all, it was their first anniversary.

So far, the night had gone very well. First, Dale took Amanda to *Jacques*, her favorite fancy restaurant. During dessert, he gave her the present. She carefully unwrapped it and said "he shouldn't have" even before opening the jewelry box. When she did, she gasped, then smiled, and held up the gold necklace with the small sapphire against her bosom.

Dale said he wanted to give her a jewel that matched her beautiful blue eyes. He didn't tell her how surprised he was to learn how much such a tiny stone cost. But he figured he had money to spare. He'd worked two jobs that summer and made more than he needed. She thanked him and reached over and squeezed his hand.

Next, they went to the Oklahoma City Philharmonic's last concert of the summer season. The orchestra played some Mozart that Dale liked, then they played some contemporary stuff that he didn't like and then they finished with *Bolero*, which he really liked.

Now, driving back to Amanda's, he asked her how she liked the concert. She said she loved Mozart. He asked her how she liked the other stuff. He could tell she was reluctant to dismiss the contemporary pieces. After all, she was musically educated, unlike the ignorant Dale. She tried to explain the music's virtues but he guessed she didn't really like that music any more than he did. He asked how she liked *Bolero*. She said, it's a little showy.

Dale agreed. That's why he liked it.

He parked on the curb outside her house. Amanda said she'd almost forgot about his present. She reached into her purse and brought out a gift-wrapped package whose shape indicated it was a book. Dale tried to hide his disappointment. Not another C. S. Lewis tome. He took it, tore off the wrapping, and saw to his surprise and pleasure it was indeed a book: *The Great Gatsby* in hardback.

"Thanks," he said with gratitude. "I can't wait to read it."

Dale had scheduled twentieth century American fiction for his fall semester independent study with Coop. Fitzgerald was one of the authors he planned to read.

He flipped the book's pages. He liked the hearing the soft whirring sound and smelling the paper and ink. He told Amanda thanks again. He was pleasantly surprised she'd given him a "secular" book.

Dale asked if she'd like to wear her necklace. She said okay. She got it out, turned around, and he put it around her slender neck. He fumbled a little with the clasp but finally got it locked.

"Maybe I'm not so good with my hands after all," he said.

Amanda turned around and instead of giving him the scolding look that he'd expected, the look in her eyes seemed encouraging. He told her the jewel matched her eyes, except that her eyes sparkled even more beautifully.

They embraced and Dale felt the warmth of her body underneath the rather thin material of her summer dress. Dale wasn't sure which of her outfits he preferred. When she wore shorts, he liked looking at her legs. When she wore jeans or slacks, he liked the way the tight pants outlined her bottom and thighs. When she wore a dress, he liked the way it highlighted her bosom. Dale found this dress especially appealing. First, it was red, a color Amanda rarely wore. Second, it had a more revealing neckline. It showed all her delicate neck, and most of her soft shoulders and even some of the top of her lightly freckled chest. But best, he liked the way the soft, thin material clung to her body. He even liked touching the material itself. He didn't know what the cloth was, but it felt almost as soft as her skin.

Amanda leaned back and said she had a surprise for Dale.

"What?" he said, tasting the anticipation in his mouth.

She leaned forward and whispered that the garage now had a new piece of furniture: an old love seat. Dale wasn't sure quite what a love seat was, but it sounded promising. He looked at her and she smiled a little suggestively and nodded. He felt a little annoyed. He'd planned to seduce her and now it looked she had beaten him to the punch.

They got out of the car and walked directly to the garage side door. Amanda opened it and they walked into the dark garage. Dale thought he saw the shadow of the love seat. It looked like a smaller version of a couch. He thought that was fine. It just made things cozier.

They walked over to the love seat and sat down. Dale said he ought to thank her parents for their foresight in putting this out for them. Amanda said he should thank her. She'd told her mother several times the past few weeks about how ragged the love seat was getting. Why didn't they just buy another? A few days ago, her mother agreed. Her dad took the old one out to the garage just yesterday.

Dale could hardly believe it. Amanda not only being calculating, but for a naughty purpose.

Amanda said they had to be quiet. Dale said, of course. He thought she was overreacting, though. He knew her parents were already upstairs in bed. Since this was an official date, he'd had to come in before taking Amanda out. Mrs. Meeks, after saying hello to Dale, mentioned that Mr. Meeks was upstairs in bed with a bad back. He strained it playing golf. Dale shook his head in sympathy. He had no idea golf was such a strenuous game.

Dale reached for Amanda and they kissed. He kissed her mouth, found it warm and hot, then kissed her philtrum, her cheeks, back to her lips, then her ear lobes, her neck, and her

496

shoulders. Meanwhile, his talented hands were feeling the soft material of her dress around her small waist before gliding down to caress her hips.

Amanda ran her fingers through his thick hair as his mouth kissed the exposed part of her chest. Dale didn't know what it was, the food, the music, the warm night, or the love seat, but Amanda seemed as eager as he did. He remembered his earlier thought about her beating him to the seduction punch. He'd been wrong. You seduce people who you want to be intimate with but don't love. When you love someone, you don't seduce her. You make love.

Dale thought they had been building up the whole summer to this. All they needed was the right time and the right place. He kissed the flat breast bone and then nuzzled the area where the swell of her breast began. He heard her moan. He loved hearing her moan. He cupped her breast with one hand and squeezed. She moaned louder. He reached up and pulled her dress strap off her shoulder. Amanda surprised him again by pulling down the other strap. The dress sagged and revealed her white bra. Dale carefully lifted the bra up and over her breasts. He wished there were more light in the garage. Moonlight streamed in from the window above them and it gave off just enough light so he could faintly see her nipples. They didn't look very long even now when erect. The areolas looked fairly large and rosy, though, and Dale kissed them, then suckled Amanda's nipples and she gasped.

Her hands tugged on the collar of his polo shirt. Dale quickly reached up and pulled it off in one motion. He then pressed his bare chest against her naked breasts and thought he'd explode. He kissed her passionately and she returned his ardor. His hand reached down her leg and his fingers found the end of her skirt. He lifted it up and stroked her stocking-clad thigh. He hated the barrier of the pantyhose. He knew Amanda had to wear them or else her mother wouldn't have allowed her to go out.

He slid his hand up from her sheathed thigh until he found the waistline. His fingers, then his hand, slipped down into the pantyhose. Her flesh felt incredibly warm and soft. He pulled her body to him, and while kissing her neck, then her breasts, he pushed his hand down farther and felt the fullness of her right buttock. His hand grasped her cheek and he pushed her hips forward as he ground his groin against hers.

He heard her moan. He heard himself panting. Sweat dripped off his forehead and plopped on her chest. He kissed her open mouth. He thrust his body against hers and felt frustrated that the rest of their clothes were in the way. He wanted to touch her in her most intimate place. He removed his hand from behind her and tugged at her pantyhose. He heard her say "don't," but in such as breathy way that he didn't believe her. He almost had the pantyhose down past her hips when she said sharply, "Dale, don't!" like she'd say to a disobedient dog.

He grew angry but when he gazed at her his wrath melted away. The look in her eyes was a mixture of passion and fear. Her eyes glistened. She blinked them. She said she wanted to but they couldn't.

Dale let go of the pantyhose. But he left his hand on the soft flesh of her hip and caressed her. He felt so worked up he wanted to bang his head against the wall. Instead he breathed in deeply and then rested his head on her chest, sticky from his sweat. He felt her hands caress his neck before her fingers fluttered through his hair.

He listened to her heartbeat and gradually calmed down. As his passion subsided, he thought no wonder religious kids get married so young. Otherwise, they might spontaneously combust.

Dale raised his head and looked into Amanda's eyes. They seemed soft and a little teary. He said, "I love you so much, Amanda."

She closed her eyes and tears squirted out of the corners but she didn't make a sound. He kissed her and tasted the different flavors in her mouth and the saltiness of her tears. His lips lingered on hers and then he pulled them upright. He hugged her until they regained their composure.

They de-embraced and leaned back against the love seat. They both sighed.

"I'd say we pushed it past sixty this time," Dale said, in a pseudo-thoughtful voice like he was imitating a pompous professor.

Amanda giggled against his shoulder. He noticed that she felt shy sitting next to him partially clothed. Her arms were folded across her breasts so Dale removed his arm and reached for his shirt so she could slide her bra back down without him looking at her, although, of course, he wanted to look. In fact, he wanted intensely to see her completely naked.

He pulled his shirt over his head while Amanda tugged her dress back into place. Then he put his arm back around her and they leaned back against the love seat.

"What is a love seat, anyway?" he asked.

Amanda said it was a smaller kind of divan. Meant for just two people.

"How appropriate."

He hugged her, then kissed her on the cheek, and Amanda seemed to grow more comfortable.

"Do you think you're off your diet now?"

Dale nodded. It amused him when she used his metaphors. "I guess so. But I'm always hungry around you."

He squeezed her again and she snuggled against him.

"You know that I can't do everything until marriage," Amanda said.

Dale felt a mixed emotional reaction to her statement. On one hand, he appreciated that she didn't automatically include him; she didn't say after *we* are married. On the other hand, it annoyed him that she didn't. Did she have doubts about him? Well, he had doubts about himself, too. Not that he didn't love her. He did. He always would. But he didn't want to talk or plan about marriage. They were only twenty. Marriage was a long way off. He knew Amanda thought this way, too. She was even more practical minded than he was. He knew the only way she would marry him was if he convinced her that he loved her, which he had, and also if he did all the necessary things to prepare for their marriage. At that moment, he thought he would if he could. He'd do anything for her. He might even become like her father.

"I understand," he said.

"Do you really?"

"Of course I do. I know what is important to you. I feel the same way."

"Really?"

Dale nodded. Actually, he wasn't sure if he *felt* the same way. He *thought* the same way; at least he did now. Marriage should be special. People should make it special. He didn't want Amanda not to be a virgin before she got married. She was too special.

"But we can get close, can't we?" he said, deciding it was time to be less serious.

"Dale," she said, a little disappointed.

"I'm joking. I never want to do anything to hurt you or even displease you."

"Oh, is that so?"

"Yes, that's so."

"Then what about Sheba?"

"It was nothing."

"Yes, but I saw you looking at her."

"I was just looking at her callipygians."

"Her calli-what?"

Dale knew he'd made a mistake. Now, he'd have to explain the whole concept and history of callipygians. He tried to evade the issue, but Amanda wouldn't let him. She was curious about that word, especially since it had been applied to Sheba.

So, Dale told her, but focused more on the origin of the word, how it referred to the statue of the Kallipygious Aphrodite and how the two Syracuse girls, the fair-buttocked, built a temple to Aphrodite.

When Dale finished he noticed Amanda staring at him as if he'd confessed to having a closet full of *Playboy* and *Penthouse* magazines.

"What is it?" he asked, puzzled by the shocked look on her face.

"Dale," she said severely, "that's pagan."

For a moment, he thought she was kidding. But her eyes were large with offense.

"Yeah, pagan in the sense that it's Greek."

"It's indecent."

Dale should have known she wouldn't understand. He actually thought the concept was sort of funny. He understood and appreciated the Greek's emphasis on beauty, especially the gluteal kind. After all, that was his favorite area of the female figure. But the idea that statues and temples would be dedicated to callipygians was rather comical. It was like the Greeks were much more philosophical and intellectual Hugh Hefners.

"You're overreacting, Amanda."

"Am I? Paganism is wrong."

"I agree. For us, it's wrong."

"For us? For everyone."

Dale didn't understand why so many Nazarenes, or for that matter Jehovah's Witnesses and other sects, thought everyone should be like they were. There were an awful lot of non-Christians in the world. Even more throughout history. Why insist that everyone think the same way, or worship the same way, or believe the same thing? He thought there was a core of ideas that everyone should believe in: like the intrinsic worth of human beings and that the spiritual was the ultimate reality. Otherwise, ideas should be interpreted in a variety of ways. But he knew he was treading on dangerous ground, so he didn't voice any of these thoughts to Amanda.

"I understand," he said.

Dale remembered that was what Dr. Prescott had said when Aaron Short made a dubious assertion in class. What Dr. Prescott was really saying was that the point wasn't important enough to refute.

Amanda wasn't completely mollified. Now, she returned to Sheba.

"And you think she has these callipygians?"

Dale was impressed that Amanda pronounced the word correctly after just becoming acquainted with it. But she did have a facility with language. As part of her music major, she studied French, German, and Italian.

"You saw her," Dale said, thinking back when Sheba had unintentionally displayed them.

Amanda didn't respond and Dale felt her tense underneath his arm.

"I love you, Amanda. I never loved Sheba." Amanda relaxed a little. "Besides, you have callipygians, too."

Amanda looked at him. "I do?"

"You bet. And I'd build a temple to them, too."

"Dale."

"I'm joking. But you're beautiful all over. Including there." Dale could tell Amanda wasn't sure she liked that. She didn't like the pagan origins. "Marilyn Monroe had callipygians."

"Marilyn Monroe?"

Dale knew she was before their time. But he liked watching her movies, especially *Some Like It Hot*. He knew Amanda hadn't seen nearly as many movies as he had. So, he tried to think of a woman that Amanda admired who had callipygians. Did Beverly Sills? Dale didn't know. Did Maria Callas? He was unsure. Barbra Streisand? Well, sort of.

"Barbra Streisand."

"She does? How do you know? Did you see an R-rated movie with her in it?"

Dale confessed he'd seen *A Star is Born* with Rusty.

"I can't trust you for a second," she said, but she didn't really seem offended. Then she thought about their discussion. "So, do you like my callipygians better than hers?"

Dale assumed she meant Sheba and not Barbra. He reached down and patted Amanda's bottom.

"You know I do."

They kissed and Dale could tell that Amanda was still a little hungry like he was. They kissed for several minutes and he slipped his hands down the back of her pantyhose and caressed her soft flesh while she rubbed his neck and shoulders. He started the making-out process all over again and Amanda went along with it for a while. But when he began nuzzling her breasts, she called a stop to it.

"Let's not get carried away again," she said.

"Oh let's," he replied. But when she resisted, he stopped.

"Lizzy's wedding is next week."

Amanda certainly knew how to throw cold water on him. "Yeah, I know."

"I'm looking forward to it."

"Yeah, I bet you are."

"I hope it goes better than Roxanne's wedding," she said, without a trace of humor.

"Not likely to have two weddings with bomb threats. At least not in the same summer."

"Oh, Dale," Amanda said, but she smiled a little.

"Everything will go fine." He reassured her with a hug.

They kissed a little more and then Amanda said she had better go in. It was late.

Dale said okay. He helped her off the love seat and they walked over to the door. She said, just think, school starts in two weeks.

He asked if she needed help moving into her dorm room.

"Oh, Dale, would you mind? My Daddy's back, you know."

Dale wondered why Mr. Meeks always got a bad back around the start of the school year. Only a coincidence, no doubt.

"No problem. I'll be glad to lug your tons of clothes up to the fifth floor."

"Oh, I'm on the fourth floor this year."

"That'll certainly make the job easier."

They kissed good night. Dale walked out of the garage door and to his car. He got in and waited until he saw the light to Amanda's bedroom come on. Then he slowly drove away.

On his drive home, Dale had an uneasy feeling about Elizabeth's wedding. He didn't really want to go. He knew he'd be out of place. All the finest people in Galilee would be attending. But he had no choice. He'd been invited.


**Chapter 14: *A stormy wedding; Dr. Prescott banished***

Dale stood in the back of the country club's magnificent dining hall talking to Chris. He'd already been through the buffet once, but he'd been shy about filling his plate with all the sumptuous food and now he felt a little hungry. He wondered if he had time for seconds.

Chris asked Dale if he knew where Reinhardt and Elizabeth were spending their honeymoon. Dale said he thought in Acapulco. Chris asked where that was. Dale said someplace in Mexico. On the coast so Dick could get in plenty of skiing when not otherwise engaged.

The bride and groom had departed almost an hour ago after going through the cake ritual. Then Elizabeth, dressed in an elaborate wedding dress with an impractically long train, had tossed her bouquet and Gretchen grabbed it. Dale had glanced at K. C. and he didn't seem embarrassed at all. Rumor had it that he and Gretchen was getting married next summer. Now, with Gretchen's catch, Dale supposed K. C. had to resign himself to that fate.

The reception was winding down. The festivities leading up to the wedding, the wedding itself, and now the reception had gone wonderfully. No problems of any kind. The rehearsal dinner, which Dale had attended as Amanda's date, had been an impressive affair. Held in a splendid dining hall at a fancy hotel in downtown Oklahoma City, he'd been surprised that he actually liked the food. He even got a chance to briefly talk to Old Man Reinhardt. The elderly fellow recognized him immediately, even though he was wearing a suit. He asked Dale if he'd visited his hill lately. Dale said just a month ago. He told the elderly Reinhardt that it had been on a clear day and he felt as though he could see all the way to Canada. Old Man Reinhardt nodded in appreciation.

The wedding went just as planned. Dale sat next to Chris and watched the ceremony. Amanda and Gretchen were two of the four bridesmaids. The only other people Dale knew, besides Reinhardt and Elizabeth, were Ann Stephenson, nee Morgan, as matron of honor and Hank "Hindu" Henderson as best man. Dale hadn't seen Henderson since high school. Although he'd filled out a little, with his lanky, loose-limbed build, he still reminded Dale of a scarecrow – although one incongruously dressed in a tuxedo.

The wedding had been a grand affair. Dale noticed all of Galilee's elite in attendance. Not only the mayor, but other politicians including the U.S. congressman from the fifth district. All the big shots from local businesses were in attendance along with Nazarene church leaders and other dignitaries. He'd been amazed at all the people packing the church. He had no idea that the Reinhardt family was so important, although the trucking company was one of the largest in the Southwest.

Amanda left the church with the rest of the wedding party and rode to the country club in a limo. Dale hadn't spent much time with her. She'd been in the receiving line, then she spent a lot of time overseeing the entertainment. She and two other girls that he vaguely recognized as GNC music majors sang several songs before Elizabeth and Reinhardt departed. Dale had been quite proud of her. She sang in her usual lovely soprano and her face had a becoming glow to it. She wore her hair up, as she usually did for special occasions, and he rather liked that novelty; in fact, he imagined how later that night she would loosen it and let it fall free past her shoulders. The only thing he didn't like was her light green bridesmaid dress.

Even the weather had cooperated with the Reinhardt-Meeks wedding. Thunderstorms had been predicted to start in the early evening, but they were late to materialize.

Dale knew they were coming, however, when he heard the distant rumbling of thunder. He noticed some of the guests were starting to leave. Chris said he better find Olivia. He'd taken her to the reception. Dale asked him how things were going with her. Chris suggestively raised a brow and said he'd find out later tonight.

Dale scanned the room for Amanda. He saw her standing over by the half-eaten wedding cake with Gretchen. He walked over and said they probably had better get going before it started raining. Amanda said okay, but she took so long saying good-bye to everyone that by the time they left the dining hall the storm had almost arrived.

Dale smelled the rain on the wind and felt the electricity in the air. A few fat drops of rain plopped on the sidewalk in front of them. He knew this was just a mild prelude to a much larger storm. He took off his suit jacket and put it around Amanda's shoulders. They walked to the north parking lot, with Amanda walking gingerly in her high heels. She wasn't used to wearing such heels; she always wore shoes with flat heels now, even when going to the evening Sunday service with Dale.

Amanda scolded him for parking in the farthest north lot. He admitted that it wasn't the best decision under the circumstances. When the sky thundered and a streak of lightning flashed before them, Amanda shuddered. They made it to the car just as the rain began to fall lightly, like a spring shower.

Dale turned the ignition, but the motor groaned. Amanda looked at him with alarm. He tried it again. The motor groaned even weaker. He knew it was the battery. No point in trying again. It would just sap the battery even more.

He told Amanda he needed to get a jump. She looked at him like he said they should hitchhike. He said it wouldn't take long. He'd seen Chris's dad walking to his car on their way over to the parking lot.

Dale jumped out of the car and raced over to the east parking lot. He caught Mr. DeVille just as he and his wife were backing out. The rain had picked up its pace. He felt his white shirt sticking to his back as Mr. DeVille rolled down his window. Dale explained the dire situation and Mr. DeVille told him to get in, and they drove over to the north parking lot. By now, most of the parking lot was empty, so Mr. DeVille parked next to Dale's Chevy and the two of them got out, opened the car hoods, made sure the cables were dry, and carefully applied them to the batteries.

They got the Chevy started just before the rain started falling hard. Dale said thanks, helped Mr. DeVille disengaged the cables, thanked him again, and jumped back in his now running car.

Amanda stared out the window at the rain that now fell with fierce intensity. Dale knew she was angry with him. But how did he know his car's battery was weak? He told her not to worry, he'd get her home in a jiffy. She said nothing.

As Dale drove out of the country club grounds, thunder boomed and lightning sizzled across the sky. Wind rocked the car. Rain poured down, making a pounding sound on the car's roof as if they were inside a drum. Amanda cowered. She said maybe they should go back to the country club. He said they were only six or seven blocks away from her home. He turned on the windshield wipers on high but the rain washed over the glass so thickly that he could hardly see. He slowed the car down. The storm had blotted out the rays of the descending sun. It seemed as dark as midnight. The Chevy crept down the road as Dale sat on the edge of his seat and peered through the brief clearing in the windshield when the wipers made their swing.

He wiped the lingering traces of rain from off his forehead and tried to ignore his shirt sticking to his back and arms. He glanced at Amanda. She slumped in the seat, huddled under his jacket. She looked frightened. She jerked when the thunder boomed and winced when the lightning sizzled across the sky.

Then hail started pelting the car, hitting the roof with a loud bong, bong, bong sound. The chunks of ice were the size of golf balls, and Dale thought how that was appropriate since they were not far from the golf course. He slowed the car, then turned it partially off the road and stopped. He couldn't see far enough to even drive five miles an hour down the street.

"It'll be over in a few minutes," Dale told Amanda, trying to sound confident that he knew what he was talking about.

Actually, he was worried that they were stuck in the middle of a terrible storm. He knew they weren't that far from Amanda's house unless he'd taken a wrong turn. He rubbed the fog from his side window and peered out. He didn't recognize this street. In fact, he didn't think they were on a residential street at all. Maybe he'd turned wrong in the darkness and rain and they were back close to the country club's grounds or maybe even close to the lake.

Dale hoped they were close to the lake. He thought he remembered reading that tornadoes didn't hit around water. The funnels tended to jump over lakes and low-lying areas. He hoped so. The storm had all the classic characteristics of a twister.

He reached over and patted Amanda's hand and asked her if she was all right. She nodded but said she felt chilly. The rain had been cold but Amanda had only been exposed to a few sprinkles. He glanced in the backseat but there wasn't anything else to offer her.

The hail suddenly stopped. The storm seemed to have hit a lull. The rain tapered off, the wind died. Dale thought about moving the car. But something didn't feel right to him. He sensed the worst was about to come.

He listened. Then he heard it. A dull roar from somewhere northwest of where they were. He rolled down his window and peered in the direction of the sound. Light rain slapped his face. Then lightning flashed and it illuminated a narrow black funnel swirling toward them from the northwest. Thunder boomed and the wind suddenly revived and rocked the car. Dale looked at Amanda. Her mouth was agape and her eyes were wide in terror. He grabbed her wrist and said they better get out.

"Out? Why?"

"I think a tornado's coming."

He opened his door and pulled on her arm. She slid awkwardly over to him, her dress impeding her slide. She told him to stop, he was hurting her arm. He pulled harder and grabbed her by her shoulders. She asked why they didn't stay in the car.

"We'll be safer outside."

Dale got Amanda out of the car and he looked around for some low-lying ground. Past the car, he saw what looked like a drainage ditch. He pulled Amanda with him as they ran to it. The wind howled and shoved them backward. He grabbed her by the waist and they pushed against the powerful air current. He shoved her into the drainage ditch and told her to lie on her back. She said there was water and mud. He heard an awful roar coming toward them. He jumped on her and pushed against her until she was pressed into the sodden earth.

He heard the shrieking of the storm and felt its fierce winds sweep over them. He stretched his body over Amanda's. She shut her eyes tightly and he held her head close to his. He heard her softly praying.

After a crescendo broke over them, the wind and noise quickly dissipated. Dale lay on top of Amanda and heard their audible breathing. The howling of the wind faded into a whistle, then a murmur. The weak rays of sunlight streamed out of the empty western horizon. Birds began to chirp. The air smelled pure and clean.

He asked Amanda if she was hurt. She quietly said no. He got off her and helped her out of the drainage ditch. Amanda took a few steps, then stopped. She held her arms out and looked down at her wet dress. Then she turned around and he saw that the bottom half of the back was covered in mud.

"It's ruined," she said. She reached her hands up toward her disheveled hair, tried to smooth the wet strands back into place, then felt the back of her head. "And my hair has mud on it." Her arms fell to her sides and she started to cry.

Dale went over, took her hand, and told her it was all right. They walked toward the car. Then he saw it. The force and pressure of the wind had blown out the windows.

"Man," he said. "Look at that."

Amanda stopped crying. She walked with Dale over to his Chevy. Amazingly, it was still running. Dale didn't see any other damage. He thought it was funny how twisters worked. The tornado could have just as easily picked up his Chevy and tossed it five blocks away. Instead, it had just blown out the windows.

"Oh, Dale, I'm sorry," Amanda said. She started to cry again.

Dale hugged her and said it was okay. They both were soaked. He told her to sit on the curb while he cleaned off the seats. He looked around for something to use against the broken glass. He spotted a trash can lid in the middle of the street. He jogged over and grabbed it and used it to shovel the glass into the back seat. He took off his tie and wrapped it around his left hand to help protect it from the jagged edges. Even so, he nicked his fingers a few times. Five minutes later, he'd cleared all the glass he could see from the front seat. He went over to Amanda and said he was ready to take her home.

She looked up at him with her red-rimmed eyes and sorrowful face. He felt guilty that his crummy car had prevented them from leaving before the storm hit. He held his hand down to her and she took it and they walked over and got in his car.

Dale put the car in gear and half expected it to fall apart. But it lurched forward and rolled down the street. Amanda said, "ouch," and He looked over and saw her leaning up and gingerly picking something out of the seat of her muddy dress. She held up a small sliver of glass and glared at it before tossing it down on the floorboard.

"Sorry," Dale said. "You better sit carefully. There might be some more small pieces of glass."

Amanda didn't say anything. Dale wasn't exactly sure where they were. He drove slowly until he found a street sign he recognized, then he knew they were about eight blocks from Amanda's house.

As he drove, he told Amanda about some of the storms he'd been in. He told her about the tornado that hit in the parking lot of the drive-in when he was a little kid. He neglected to tell her how he'd cowered in the back seat, praying and bawling. Then he told her about the storm that swept over the Wheaton track meet his junior year.

Amanda said she'd never been in a storm before.

Dale looked over and saw she had calmed down. "Scary, isn't it?"

Amanda nodded glumly. Then she stared at the soiled three-layered skirt.

"Dale, my dress."

He said he was sorry he'd ruined it. He'd buy her one just like it if she wanted.

Amanda said nothing. She looked like she might cry again, but she didn't. Instead she tried to tuck the loose, wet strands of her hair back into place, then sighed, and gave up.

They arrived at her house and it was completely dark. The storm had knocked out the power in the neighborhood, probably most of town. Dale remembered seeing Amanda's parents and brother leave half an hour before them. They had made it home before the storm hit.

He got out of the car and Amanda didn't wait for him to open her door. They saw the door to her house open and both her parents appeared. Amanda walked quickly toward them, almost stumbling in her high heels. Her mother, father, and Kenny came out and met her. Dale slowly walked over to them, trying to unstick his white dress shirt from his chest. He realized he had no idea where his suit jacket was. Probably stuck in the mud back at the drainage ditch.

He watched as Amanda hugged first her father, then her mother. Mrs. Meeks took her inside. Mr. Meeks and Kenny took a few steps toward him. Dale couldn't tell if they were angry with him or not. They both peered at him with narrow eyes, but their strong jaws didn't jut out in anger.

"We got caught in the storm," Dale said.

Mr. Meeks asked if he needed any help. Dale noticed him looking at the blown windows of his car.

"We weren't in the car when that happened."

Mr. Meeks nodded. Kenny shook his head like he couldn't believe Dale had endangered the life of his sister.

"I guess I better get going," Dale said. "I should check on my mother and sister."

Mr. Meeks said good night. Kenny waved. Dale watched them turn and walk back into the house and shut the door. He paused. He wanted to say good night to Amanda and see if she were okay. He guessed he could call her when he got home. She didn't seem to be in the mood at to say good night to him anyway.

Dale got in his car and slowly drove home, thinking how weird it was to drive a car without a windshield. Most of the lights were out in the southern part of town, but when he crossed 39th Expressway, he felt relieved to see all the shining lights in the northern half.

He was halfway home when his hands began to tremble. He stopped the car and took his hands off the steering wheel. They continued to shake. Even his arms seemed to vibrate. Dale tried to calm himself. He tried relaxing his hands and arms and took deep breaths. A couple of minutes later, the shaking stopped.

He drove home and when he turned on his street, he saw lights on inside his home. He got out. The ground was soaked but it looked like the houses on his block had sustained only mild wind damage.

He walked inside and found his mother and sister sitting on the couch watching television. "What happened to you?" June May asked.

Dale pulled out the wet tail of his dress shirt and let it flop against his wet slacks. "Guess?"

June May looked at Jesse.

"Did you get caught out in that storm?" Jesse asked.

He nodded.

"It warn't so bad here," she said.

"Well, it was bad over there."

"Over where?" asked June May.

Dale didn't bother to answer. He walked in his soggy shoes to his bedroom and closed the door.


Before classes started, Dale had to see Dean Pierce. This time he wasn't in trouble; the dean just had a question about Dale's scholarship. Publication editors were awarded tuition scholarships and Dean Pierce wanted to ask Dale a question about his.

Dale, still working at the physical plant, went over to the administration building during his afternoon break. Sitting in the air-conditioned outer office, he realized he looked like a slob dressed in his sweaty T-shirt and grass-stained blue jeans. He'd just finished mowing a lawn and his shirt sagged a little from the sweat. He mopped his brow with the back of his hand and smiled at the elderly secretary, who looked at him like he was some bum who'd wandered off the street into her cool, clean outer office.

The door to Dean Pierce's office opened and he appeared and told Dale to enter. They shook hands and Dale sat down in the same leather chair he'd occupied almost a year ago when the dean suspended him for one flag football game.

The dean got right to the point. He told him that since his tuition was already paid for by federal and state grants, he could receive the scholarship as a check.

He wasn't sure what the dean meant. Did he mean that he actually got money for editing the newspaper?

"That's right, Dale," Dean Pierce said. "Usually, editors apply their scholarship to tuition. But since you don't need to, you may receive yours in a lump sum disbursement."

Dale liked those words: lump sum disbursement.

"Okay," he said.

Dean Pierce nodded and Dale thought he was looking at him in a curious way. Maybe the dean just noticed his inappropriate attire. He felt a little annoyed. What was he supposed to do? Go home and change into a suit? He didn't even have one, since the only suit that fit him had been ruined in the storm.

"Would you mind if I asked you a personal question?" Dean Pierce asked.

Dale said he didn't mind, although he couldn't imagine what personal information the dean would be interested in.

"Are you by chance Indian?"

Dale's mind lingered for a moment over the words "by chance." Then he looked at the dean's pale, long face and wondered why the dean was interested.

"Well, I'm part Indian. Creek, I think."

The dean nodded and then looked down at some papers on his desk. Dale suddenly felt embarrassed and he didn't know why. Maybe he shouldn't have confessed to his Indian background. But it wasn't much. He thought maybe he looked more Indian now because he'd worked outside in the sun during the summer and he tanned easily. His skin had bronzed, but the deep tan would fade and by winter he'd have his same old "olive" complexion.

"Well, thank you, Dale, for coming by," the dean said with a small smile. He stood up and showed Dale the door. He said he could pick up his check in about three weeks from the bursar's office.

Dale nodded and left the dean's office thinking that they hadn't shaken hands again. Well, that didn't mean anything. Then he remembered what Blackie had told him. He still didn't believe most people were as bigoted as his father.

Still, the encounter with Dean Pierce left him in a bad mood. Dale wondered if the dean had asked him about being an Indian because he received government grants. Did the dean think he was from a poor Indian family? Dale almost laughed. His father made pretty good money and he had his navy retirement pay, too. True, he didn't benefit much from it anymore, but the government grants were really a result of his staying with his divorced mother. But Dean Pierce probably didn't know that.

He knew he was over-reacting. After all, he rather liked the dean. But Dale was sensitive to his background – his hillbilly background. He now felt that the grants were a little like charity. He felt sort of disgusted by his family's problems even if they ironically helped him in some ways.

Dale decided to drop by and see Amanda at the bookstore. Maybe seeing her would lift his spirits. She'd forgiven him for endangering her life. He'd called her last Saturday night after he got home and changed out of his wet clothes. She sounded subdued on the phone. Then she hadn't gone to Sunday night service because she'd caught a cold. Knowing that Amanda was home sick with a cold made him feel even worse. But she called him a couple of days ago and she sounded better. In fact, she thanked him for taking care of her during the storm. She said her father told her that Dale had done the right thing in pulling her out of the car. If they'd stayed inside, the busted windows might have seriously hurt them.

Dale felt better hearing her thank him. But he knew if his car's battery hadn't gone dead, they wouldn't have been in that risky situation to begin with.

He strode across campus to the student union and walked downstairs to the bookstore. He made sure the bookstore manager wasn't around, then he slipped in and surprised Amanda. She and David Hawkins stood behind the desk at the register talking. Dale knew Hawkins worked at the bookstore but he thought at a different time. He didn't like seeing him. He especially didn't like seeing him talking to Amanda.

Amanda smiled at him and Dale motioned her over to the door. She asked David to cover for her and she walked over.

Dale liked the cool air on him. His shirt had almost dried. When Amanda arrived, he took her hand and gave it a friendly squeeze. She leaned closer, but not close enough for him to kiss her.

"Dale," she said disapprovingly, "you're sweaty."

"Yeah, I've been mowing lawns all day."

Amanda's small nose wrinkled. "You sort of smell."

Dale had noticed how sensitive she was to smell before. One of the rare times he'd ever heard her criticize anyone was in high school when he overheard her complain about Mr. Smedley's strong odor; well, she'd been right. Sloppy Mr. "Smudgely" did stink some. But now she was criticizing him. Usually, she didn't mind if he sweated a little. In fact, Dale thought in the right situation his sweat served as an aphrodisiac as long as he was otherwise clean and neat. He'd sweated *on* her that night on the love seat and she hadn't complained.

But this kind of sweating was different, he supposed. Plus, he hadn't put on any deodorant. He never did if he was going to work outside. What was the point? Dale tried to smell himself. His T-shirt did smell a little rank.

"Sorry," he said.

She had an expectant look on her face. She also seemed a little nervous to have him in the bookstore. She wasn't supposed to talk to friends while working.

"I just wanted to make sure about Friday afternoon. You know, helping you move in."

If he'd been in a better mood, he would have teased her about the Herculean effort it took for her to carry up her popcorn maker.

"That will be fine," she said, smiling nervously.

Dale wanted to kiss her, thinking that would make him feel better. But he knew she wouldn't like it. Plus, he was all sweaty and stinky.

He released her hand. "Okay. I'll see you then."

Amanda put the freed hand in her other one and smiled and said okay. She walked back to the register where Hawkins pretended to be organizing Chiefs' knickknacks. Dale didn't like his curly hair. He'd spoken to him a few times, and he'd disappointingly concluded that he was a nice guy, but Hawkins still annoyed him.

Dale turned and stalked out of the bookstore and threw open the double glass doors of the student union. He didn't know why he felt so angry. He strode through the quad and headed for the physical plant when he turned the corner of the business school building too sharply. He almost knocked over Sylvester Fish.

"Pardon," Fish said in a huffy voice.

Dale guessed it was his fault for turning the corner so fast but he didn't say sorry. In fact, he almost wished he had knocked Fish over.

As Dale breezed by, he knew Fish was resentfully gazing at him in disapproval. Fish already had reason to hate him. Sylvester had applied for assistant editor and he'd appointed Teri instead. He remembered Fish's voice when he'd called to inform him of his decision. Fish had not sounded disappointed or frustrated but *disapproving*. Dale's decision wasn't a reflection of Fish's foibles but of Dale's lack of respect for campus proprieties. After all, Sylvester was the connection between the creative world on campus and the religious world. The only problem with that view, thought Dale, was that Fish was about as creative as a rock.

As Dale paused to cross the street, he turned and saw in the nearby parking lot Dr. Prescott toting a box of books to the open hatch of his little blue Datsun. Dale watched. He wondered if he should go over and say good-bye to the professor. But Dr. Prescott seemed lost in thought. His homely face seemed to be concentrated on a conundrum, no doubt the question as to why one of the best teachers on campus had been so unceremoniously fired.

Then Dale saw Dean Snyder strutting down the sidewalk, heading in their direction. Dale couldn't help but compare the dean with Dr. Prescott. The dean: tall, broad-shouldered, dressed in an expensive, dark pin-striped suit, his handsome face distinguished by a rigid crew cut haircut and a cleft chin. Dale had to begrudgingly admit that the dean was an impressive fellow, at least outwardly. Then there was the professor: short, paunchy, homely, dressed in a stained green and gold Baylor T-shirt and baggy slacks. There was no contest as to which fellow looked happy, confident, and successful.

Dale watched as Dean Snyder raised a big hand and waved it at Dr. Prescott. The professor nodded, still clutching the box of his not-so-valuable books, his humiliation complete.

Dale felt his resentment over his favorite teacher's treatment turn into something more profound. He thought it was not just unfair, but a sign of cosmic injustice that Dr. Prescott had been driven off campus.

# BOOK 7: *Through a Glass, Darkly*

**Chapter 1:** *Film flaps; Dean Snyder rules; Amanda's humor*

People were complaining about the movie reviews.

Dale expected some students, faculty, and administrators to protest his decision to include movie reviews in *Smoke Signals*. After all, the college's official policy discouraged students about attending films. No films were shown on campus but many students went to theatres and saw movies, although they confessed to seeing only G or PG-rated films. Because of that, Dale had agreed with Mrs. Genesee's suggestion that he only print reviews of films that had those two ratings. No R-rated movies, even if they were often the more critically acclaimed films.

Dale finished reading the letter to the editor that denounced the two film reviews that appeared in the newspaper's first issue. The writer, Dr. Petry, wrote that "including any information about secular films simply promotes antichristian attitudes and stimulates young people's carnal desires."

Dr. Petry seemed to think that film itself was a devil-inspired invention. The professor said motion pictures "compelled the viewer to vicariously participate in all the sinful experiences of the characters" and didn't allow the viewer "enough time to intellectually distance himself from the violence, illicit sex, and profanity that most contemporary films irresponsibly depict."

Dale thought the letter was interesting mostly because it was so candidly anti-artistic. The two movies that he and a girl named Rosalind Webb had reviewed were two summer releases, *The Spy Who Loved Me* and *For the Love of Benji*. He could sort of understand Petry's objection to the James Bond film. It did contain considerable violence, but of the cartoonish kind, and it had a few sex scenes, although nothing explicit. Dale had written a negative review; he much preferred the old Bonds. But it puzzled him why a G-rated film about a lovable pooch would be included in the grammarian's condemnation except that film as a means of expression was evil in itself.

He tossed the letter on his desk with the five other critical letters. Dr. Petry's letter was by far the best written and reasoned. The other four predictably expressed the writers' offended feelings. He thought it strange how easily offended some people were and how they tended to view everything from a narrow, subjective perspective.

"So, are you gonna print all of the complaining letters to the editor?" asked Teri.

"Just Petry's and one other. We don't have room for the others."

Teri shook her head. She didn't see any reason to print such silly letters.

"People have a right to complain about the change in the paper's content," Dale said, thinking how open minded he sounded.

"Yeah, but complaining about *Benji*?"

He'd never seen the dog's movies. Maybe they were awful. Generally speaking, Dale thought canine actors tended to overact. Lassie was really a ham. Cats, on the other hand, were admirably understated.

"Well, they're really complaining about promoting movies by having reviews in the paper," Dale said.

"Don't they know we're in the twentieth century?"

Dale shrugged. Apparently, some people didn't want to be. In a way, he understood. Such attitudes reminded him of some of the Jehovah's Witnesses he'd known. The larger world was a threatening, confusing place and some people didn't like to be exposed to it. Still, he thought college people should be more intellectually curious and psychologically stalwart. Otherwise, what was the point of becoming educated?

Before he could express these thoughts, the half-dozen staffers walked in for the newspaper class. Dale initially had doubts about his supervision of students who took the one-hour newspaper practicum. He thought they would simply get in the way. But he'd figured how to exploit the students. Mostly, they did simple clerical duties and went around campus verifying information. They could also submit written pieces. Rosalind, the younger sister of Mr. Benedict's Beatrice, and who unfortunately had her sister's canine-like countenance, had done so. Her *Benji* review had been well written, although her opinions predictable. Dale felt a little disappointed in her. She was the youngest daughter of the editor of the *Galilee Gazette*, so she knew how to write journalism. But her taste was utterly conventional.

Dale gave the seven students their assignments and three of them stayed in the office and worked on menial tasks while the other four left to verify information in a couple of feature stories.

He leaned back in his chair. It had rollers and a springy back. He loved this chair. He could zoom around the room on the wheels or rock himself by leaning against the back. In the first staff meeting, he leaned so far back that he'd toppled over. No one laughed except Teri.

Rowena walked in and said she'd sold another two pages of ads. One of the things he wanted to do was expand the newspaper from eight to twelve pages. Now, with three days to go before the ad deadline, Rowena had already sold enough ads to cover another twelve pager.

He told her good job. She smiled. Dale thought she had a becoming smile. He felt confident that she'd do an excellent job of selling ads. If for no other reason, the Galilee businessmen liked buying ads from a cute girl.

With the larger newspaper, he'd added two pages of entertainment and arts. The section featured book, movie, record, and theatre reviews along with advance stories on campus entertainment and arts events. He'd also put in a calendar of off-campus events, such as museum tours, plays, and concerts available to students in the City. Dale had heard a few people complain about that, too. The newspaper was bringing too much of the "real world" to campus, which he thought was a curious objection to make about a newspaper.

Some campus leaders, in particular, the student council vice president for religious life, Aaron Short, had complained to him and Mrs. Genesee that the newspaper was becoming too secular and worldly. In addition to the movie reviews, they didn't like the reviews of secular records. Short, who Dale called Snort because of his tendency to make that sound when he laughed, had argued that the only records the campus paper should review were gospel or contemporary Christian. Dale thought he sounded like a more eloquent Fish.

The three staffers finished their duties and departed, which left Dale, Teri, and Rowena. So far, the three of them along with Polly had done almost all the work. Dale had appointed Rusty as sports editor, even though Mrs. Genesee had some reservations. But Rusty had promised to be reliable and not goof off, so their advisor had relented.

The door opened and Aaron Short walked in. Short, who was in fact on the tall side, moved with a sort of feline grace. In addition to his fairly long, sleek hair, Short also dressed more casually than most of the religious conservatives on campus. He often wore jeans and T-shirts in addition to slacks and dress shirts. In his casual clothes, Short moved in a smooth, fluid way. He smiled easily and broadly. He exuded good-cheer. Dale thought there was a certain silkiness to him that belied his narrow-minded views.

Short, now dressed in jeans and a polo shirt, stood behind the large desk counter that separated the front of the room from the work area. He asked Dale how he was doing. Dale said fine. Short said he was troubled by the review of The Manhattan Transfer's latest record. He wondered if on a religious campus such as theirs, running reviews of rock music was proper.

Dale told him that The Manhattan Transfer was a pop-jazz group, not rock.

Short said, wasn't that was comparing apples and oranges? No, Dale said it was comparing musical genres. Then Short said in his smooth, reasonable-sounding voice that secular music, whether rock or pop-jazz, was demon inspired. Rock music was especially wicked because it deliberately exploited the carnal desires of the young.

Dale patiently listened to Short and then asked if he'd ever listened to any rock music.

Short refused to answer. Dale wondered if that meant he'd listened to some of the taboo music and didn't want to confess or he hadn't and didn't want to confirm the illogic of his position. If he hadn't actually listened to it, then how did he know it was demon inspired?

"That's irrelevant," Short finally said.

Dale said he thought it was particularly relevant.

Short briefly laughed, then snorted, and shook his head as if to say he knew all along his request would be ignored.

"So, I take it that you are refusing to stop running reviews of secular records?"

"That's right," Dale said.

Short smiled without any mirth and glided out of the *Smoke Signals* office.

Dale looked at Teri and Rowena. Rowena shook her head and Teri said Short was simply parroting a youth minister that was scheduled to speak on campus during revival week. The minister, Barry Richardson, had been touring Christian colleges telling students that rock music was demon inspired. But even Richardson didn't think all secular music was wicked.

Dale thought about a song he'd heard and liked that summer. He was certain that Richardson would condemn the Blue Oyster Cult's "(Don't Fear) the Reaper" as demon inspired. Dale had almost run a review of the group's latest album, but he thought the song's message definitely romanticized suicide, which he thought irresponsible. He decided his ambivalent feelings would result in a confused review. Also, he knew a review of a group called Blue Oyster Cult would certainly generate dozens of angry letters.

Now, Dale realized he had two campus "leaders" opposed to him: Fish and Short. But he did enjoy the support of Henshaw, the stuco president, and Abigail, who served as vice president of campus life and organized campus events. He knew he could also depend on the backing of Mrs. Genesee and Professor Cooper, too.

That reminded Dale of Mrs. Genesee's absence in the staff meeting. Dale asked Teri where Mrs. Genesee was.

"She's feeling a little tired," Teri said.

He stroked his chin with concern.

"She's got to be careful not to overtax herself."

Dale said he understood. He hoped she didn't suffer a relapse. Not only for her sake, but also for the paper's.


Dean Snyder said the college could not accept as transfer credit the classic cinema class from Central State University. But all the other credits, including those earned through advanced placement examination, would be accepted.

Dale expected all his credits would be honored. Before he'd transferred to GNC, he'd asked Mr. DeVille to confirm all his CSU credits would be accepted. He hadn't said the classic cinema class wouldn't count.

"Why isn't the film class being accepted?" Dale asked.

"We don't have a course of that nature in our academic curriculum," Dean Snyder said with a smile.

Dale thought Dean Snyder had an impressive bearing. Not only did he have neatly groomed crew cut silver hair and a strong, clefted chin, but his shoulders seemed about to burst out of his expensive pin-striped suit. Dale had heard he'd played football at some Christian university. He'd been pretty good, too.

"But GNC has accepted other courses that don't exactly match the curriculum." Dale mentioned the Ibsen, Shaw, Wilde credits.

"Yes, but that qualifies as a literature course."

"So, the real issue is that the classic cinema course is a film course."

"Yes, that's right."

Dale knew there was no point in arguing with the him. The dean had formidable confidence. But he gave it one more try.

"But isn't film a valid kind of artistic expression?"

Dean Snyder's smile faded a little. Dale knew he was a busy man and only had agreed to see him because he'd argued about the three transfer credits with the registrar.

"No, I wouldn't say that."

"You don't think film is a serious form of art?"

"No."

Dale wondered how many films Dean Snyder had seen. He bet not many. Still, he had to respect his convictions. In some ways, Dale wasn't sure if film was a serious form of art either. He just liked it. It was fun. He even sort of enjoyed watching crummy movies like the Elvis movies. Even movies that were regarded as great, such as *Citizen Kane* or *Stagecoach*, seemed more fun than serious. Dale had doubts whether anything fun could be art. But then, he wasn't sure yet what art was, not in the literary, cinematic, or any other sense.

Dean Snyder, his large smile now fully restored, asked Dale if he had any other concerns. Dale said no. The dean rose to his six feet of height, reached out and shook Dale's hand, and reminded him that the rest of the CSU credits had been accepted and that his other degree requirements had been met. He just had to complete twenty-one more upper-division credits.

Dale thanked him and walked out of his spacious office. He thought the dean was the kind of guy he should like. He'd played football, after all. But Dale didn't like him. If for no other reason, because he'd been unfair to Dr. Prescott.

As for the classic cinema class, it didn't matter. He had to take at least twelve hours in both the fall and spring semesters to receive his grants and scholarship. He'd easily have enough credits to graduate.

Amanda hadn't liked *Annie Hall*. Dale sat with her in a booth at West Oaks and tried to understand her objections. They'd seen the film earlier that evening, something that she only agreed to because it had been rated PG.

"Well, Dale," she said, while sipping on her Diet Coke, "first, I didn't think it was particularly funny."

"Oh, yeah. Why not?"

Dale had liked it. He'd seen a few other Woody Allen movies and he thought this one was by far the best.

"I don't know why exactly. It all just seemed strange to me."

Dale thought about the movies they'd seen together. He couldn't remember Amanda liking the humor in any of them. Well, she did think the robots in *Star Wars* were sort of funny. The Wookie, too. He guessed she liked simpler humor; satire or observational humor didn't appeal to her.

"Isn't he Jewish?" Amanda asked.

She meant Woody Allen. Dale said yeah, he was.

"Well, maybe that's it."

Dale wasn't sure what she meant. "Why does that matter?"

"Oh, I don't know. I get the idea that Jewish people have a dark sense of humor."

"You mean black humor?"

"Yes, I guess that's what I mean."

Dale almost said no wonder considering their history. But instead he said the humor in *Annie Hall* was more of the self-deprecating and satiric kind. Didn't she like that?

Amanda took a drink of her Diet Coke and considered the question. "I don't know what to tell you, Dale. It just wasn't that funny to me."

"Okay," he said.

He felt a little disappointed in her. He liked it when she liked the same things he did. Dale didn't really like the Woody Allen persona that much. He thought he was wimpy and a little whiny. But he did like the movie. He especially liked the way the film combined humor with a touch of pathos.

"Besides, there were some bad words and some bedroom scenes," Amanda said.

"Only a few bad words. And nothing was really shown in the bedroom scenes."

The latter fact had disappointed Dale a little. But if there had been any nudity, Amanda would have insisted they leave.

"Are you sure the movie was rated PG?"

"Of course. You saw the rating appear on the screen."

"Well, if PG movies are going to have such things in them, maybe we shouldn't go to them anymore."

Dale felt himself growing annoyed. He already had to see R-rated movies on his own or with Rusty. Now, Amanda didn't want to see PG movies?

"Sure, we can just see *For the Love of Benjy* or *Herbie Goes to Monte Carlo*. Movies like that."

Amanda looked at him in a puzzled way, not sure if he was teasing or not. Then she smiled. When she did, Dale felt his annoyance fade.

"Sometimes your sense of humor escapes me," she said.

Dale reached over and patted her hand. "Then I guess I better let you know when I'm joking. But you like going to movies, don't you? I mean, when they don't offend you?"

"Oh, sure. I liked *Star Wars*. I like watching musicals when they come on television. I just don't like movies that are violent and full of profanity and naughty scenes."

Dale felt disappointed again. He didn't mind the violence, the profanity, and especially the naughty scenes as long as those things weren't gratuitous or exploitative. Well, he didn't mind seeing the "naughty scenes" even when they were gratuitous.

"You don't like those things in movies, do you, Dale?"

Amanda looked at him with such an innocent look on her face that he didn't want to respond too candidly.

"It's just sometimes those things are necessary to tell a certain kind of story."

"Oh, I don't think so."

He asked her to think back to when they saw the *Godfather, part II*. Didn't that movie have to include some unpleasant things in order to tell the story?

"Well, why do they have to make movies like that in the first place?"

Dale didn't think that was a stupid question. He liked old movies a lot. Most had a more affirmative view of life than today's cynical films. But movies tended to reflect their times. Maybe they were living in an ugly time and movies, like other forms of art, reflected that.

"But aren't you curious to know what is going on in the larger world?" he asked. "And movies sort of show such things."

"I guess I'm not that curious to know about violence and immorality."

He understood what she meant, and in a way he approved of her sentiments. He thought she ought to be protected from the ugly things in life. But on the other hand, it concerned him that she didn't want to open her mind to more than what she could find in the small world of Galilee.

"What are you thinking about?" She had noticed the reflective look in his eyes.

Dale patted her hand again. "Nothing really. Just thinking if it's better to remain in the cave or risk being blinded by the sun."

Amanda smiled. "Sometimes you say rather mysterious things."

Dale asked if she was ready to leave. She said yes. He left enough cash to cover the bill and a decent tip. Even though Sheba's mother hadn't waited on them, he knew most of the waitresses were women like her.

They walked to his Chevy and got in. Dale still hadn't gotten used to the new look of the car windows. The shade of the glass or the cut of it wasn't like the old windshield's. He started the car and the radio came on. He started to turn it off when Amanda told him not to. As he drove out of the parking lot, they listened to the song. He'd heard it a few times already: "You Light Up My Life."

After the song ended, Amanda said she liked that song.

Her approval surprised him. Usually, she didn't like pop songs except songs by Barbra Streisand and a few other similar singers. She definitely didn't like rock or disco.

"Why do you like it?" he asked.

"It has a sincerity I like. It sounds like a devotional song, but I don't suppose it is if it's on this station."

Dale thought she was right. It did have that quality. But some of the lyrics made it seem like a conventional love song. He didn't hate it.

He drove back to campus and parked in the back section of the Hayley parking lot. If there were enough privacy, Amanda would allow him to kiss her. The start of school proved to be a difficult transition for Dale. No more love seat; no more making out even in the secluded cul-de-sac in her neighborhood. The other change he didn't like was all the social activities he had to go to with Amanda. He'd gone to the first weekend's campus party, a luau, and he thought it was boring. Amanda enjoyed herself. She liked seeing all her friends. The next Friday, they'd gone to the ice skating party and that had been okay. He'd been amused seeing her try to skate. She fell a couple of times right on her bottom. The second time she fell pretty hard and after he helped her up she had said she might have bruised herself. When he'd said he'd be glad to offer her first aid, she'd scolded him for being vulgar.

He leaned over and kissed her. She didn't protest. He kissed her again. She let him. But when he put his arms around her waist and pulled her to him, she whispered "not here" in his ear.

"Where then?"

She smiled but removed his hands from around her waist. When he looked grumpy, she asked if doing such things was that important to him.

For a couple of seconds, Dale looked as thoughtful as he could, as if he were considering the most perplexing problem in the universe.

"Naw," he said in an exaggerated way while making a dismissive gesture.

Amanda laughed. He liked the way her voice sounded musical in her throat. He reached over and put his arm around her shoulders and they leaned against the seat and looked out the window. Sitting like that was permissible; she just didn't want anyone to see them necking.

He asked her if she missed testing the speed limit and she smiled a little and said quietly, yes. He didn't press the issue. At least knowing she missed making out made him feel a little less frustrated.

They sat in the car for half an hour talking. Mostly, Amanda talked. She told him about her classes. She was practicing pretty hard training her voice. Dale wondered how she did in her classes. They never talked about her grades. He remembered her making excellent grades in high school. So, he asked. She said she did well in music, but she mostly made Bs in her other courses. She'd made a C in chemistry her freshman year. She asked him if he'd made all As again that summer. He said yes. He'd made straight As last spring as well. She didn't mind that he made better grades than she did. In fact, she liked that he was smart. She'd told him so.

Dale felt better now than he did at West Oaks, so when she said she had better get in, he didn't complain. He walked her to the dorm's front doors and squeezed her hand and said good night and said he'd see her tomorrow night at church.

On his way home, he tried to forgot his disappointment in Amanda for not sharing his taste in movies or his love of literature and for her lack of intellectual curiosity in general. He told himself that wasn't so important. After all, they had other things in common. Unfortunately, one of those things was being denied him since she'd moved back into the dorm.

## Chapter 2: *An Intramural incident; powder puff and smashing the speed limit*

Rusty asked if the Lambda guy was playing dirty. Dale said, sort of. The guy kept chucking him at the line of scrimmage, which was against the rules. He'd warned him twice already, but the guy – Dale didn't know his name – just smiled in a scornful way.

Chris leaned toward them and told Dale and Rusty that the guy was a freshman. He didn't know that Dale broke guys' collarbones if they messed with him. Chris and Rusty laughed and the three of them listened as Krupp called a pass play in the huddle.

They broke huddle and Dale lined up as one of the wide receivers. He'd told Krupp several plays before that he should move to flanker so could stand a yard or two behind the line of scrimmage and thus avoid the illegal contact. But, as usual, Krupp ignored his advice. Krupp, the quarterback, the captain, the colossus, knew better.

Dale looked at the kid standing just a yard away from him. He warned him again: Don't make illegal contact. The kid smirked at him. He reminded him of that crazy guy he had to knock down back in high school football because he wouldn't stop going after him on pass plays. Like that guy, this kid was fairly tall and rangy and Dale knew he could put his shoulder right into the guy's gut and lift him up and throw him down.

Krupp called the signals. The center hiked the ball. Dale faked running a pattern and when the smirky kid tried to jam him, he lowered his shoulder just as he planned.

He let up before he hurt the guy. He could have pile-driven him into the ground. Instead, Dale just fell on top of him. As he lay on the guy, he told him in a deep, threatening voice if the guy kept on cheating, he'd really hurt him.

On the next play, the guy stood five yards away like most defensive backs did. Dale noticed the kid's pale, defiant look. It was an act. He knew the guy was afraid of him now. He felt a little sorry for him. But it was the guy's own fault. He'd told him three times. He didn't know why some guys were jerks. They almost ruined playing flag football.

In the huddle, Dale had told Krupp he'd be wide open if he wanted to throw deep. Krupp grunted. He didn't like being told who to look for. But once he got the ball, he threw it deep. All Dale had to do was fake throwing a block at the kid, then race past him. He'd been so open that even Krupp's wounded duck of a pass got to him in plenty of time for him to grab it and score untouched.

After the game, which Omega won, 20-6, Dale found the kid to shake hands with him. He said good game, but the guy ignored him. Once a jerk, always a jerk, thought Dale.

He joined Rusty and Chris as they walked off the field. With the addition of Rusty to their team, they were actually pretty good. They'd won their first three games. Dale had considered asking Rusty to challenge Krupp for quarterback, but he didn't. Rusty liked playing receiver. And somehow everything was working anyway. Rusty had good speed, big hands, and fine jumping ability. All Krupp had to do was throw the ball high enough and Rusty would grab it. Dale now tended to run shorter routes and if Krupp managed to hit him in stride, he often eluded enough tacklers to gain ten or fifteen yards. He'd even scored a couple of times off short passes when he'd evaded and outran the defenders.

In a couple of weeks, Omega would play Alpha. It looked like those were the best teams in their respective divisions. Dale remembered before the start of the season when Henshaw had asked him to join Alpha. He'd said since Dale ended the career of one of their guys – meaning Bigelow – the least he could do was take his place. Dale thought about it. He'd much rather play with Henshaw, Phelps, Eugene, and K. C. than with Peter Krupp and his cronies. But he felt some loyalty to the Omega team and Chris. So, he reluctantly declined. Anyway, when Rusty joined Omega, Dale got to play with both Rusty and Chris. It reminded him of their freshman year in high school, the last time the three of them played football together.

As Dale walked off the field with his two buddies, Dale remembered being amused watching Rusty interact with the egomaniacal team captain at their first practice. Rusty had regarded Krupp with a pseudo-reverent attitude, the way he used to do with Mr. Benedict when he especially wanted to mock him. After practice, Dale teasingly asked Rusty what he thought of "Peter"? Rusty said simply, "he's full of Krupp."

Now, walking with Chris and Rusty back to the off-campus parking lot, Dale asked Rusty how he'd convinced the junior varsity coach, Titus Meyer, to let him play intramural football. Usually basketball players and the other varsity athletes didn't play intramural sports. Rusty said he didn't convince anybody. He just did it.

Dale shook his head. He told his pal that was not the best way to impress your new coach. Rusty said what he didn't know wouldn't hurt him. Besides, he knew the Owls desperately needed his talent. He clapped both Dale and Chris on the back just for emphasis.

Dale said that was true, but he wondered if Rusty had learned anything from his Oscar Rose debacle.

Amanda had decided to play in the powder puff football game. Rowena had talked her into it. So, Dale decided to attend the silly spectacle with Chris. They sat in the stands of the Galilee High School football stadium and watched the upperclassmen girls play the underclassmen girls. Dale had to admit it was sort of funny. Some of the girls actually took the game seriously. One of them was Rowena Watson. She played halfback and when she raced around end on a handoff, she gritted her big, healthy teeth and outran every girl on the field.

"She's pretty fast," Chris said.

"She's had practice," Dale said. "Being chased by you."

Chris grinned. After failing to get a steady girlfriend (his pursuit of the ample-busted Olivia had proved fruitless), Chris seemed to have succeeded with Rowena on a second try. He'd dated her twice already and had a third one planned after the powder puff game that night.

"So, what was the decisive factor in Rowena accepting your advances this time?" Dale asked.

"She liked the way I factored in depreciation costs in my make-believe business in our finance class."

"How romantic."

Chris shrugged. "You gotta play to your strengths, my friend."

Dale wasn't much interested in the actual playing of the powder-puff game. Instead, he casually evaluated the girls' appearances. Most of them, including Amanda, dressed in baggy sweats and wore too-large football jerseys. However, a few girls, including Rowena and Sheba, wore cutoffs. He tried not to stare too much at Sheba. She was the only good player on the underclassmen team. She played halfback and carried the ball a lot. When she stood in the huddle with her back to the stands, Dale admired how fetchingly her callipygians filled out her cutoffs.

In the fourth quarter, with the uppers leading by three touchdowns, Amanda finally got a chance to play. Dale had been looking at her standing on the sideline more than at the girls playing on the field. He thought she looked cute dressed in baggy sweats and a too-large red jersey with Dale's old high school number "21" printed on it. He realized he'd never seen her dressed in athletic clothes of any kind. She wore her hair in two long braids and he liked that change, too.

She ran onto the field and lined up at end. She was too small to play the line and too slow to play in the backfield, so they'd put her out at end. Dale watched her run around in a confused way on a couple of plays. He didn't think she even knew the basic rules about football, even though the girls practiced a couple of times and had the tutelage of Titus Meyer and Thad North, both of whom had played high school football.

Then, near the end of the game. Amanda somehow got behind the defense and found herself wide open for a pass. The quarterback, Amy Mears, threw an awkward pass toward Amanda. Dale watched as the ball tumbled end-over-end to her. Amanda held out her arms and backtracked. She opened her mouth and leaned back and the nose of the football hit her right in the chest and then the football bounced off onto the field.

Everyone laughed and Amanda hid her face in her hands. When she trotted off the field after the game ended, she discreetly rubbed her chest at the breastbone. Dale thought, not another bruise in a strategic place.

Dale and Chris walked down to the field to tell the girls they'd meet them at their dorm for the twirp date. Teri, who'd also played, and done quite well at linebacker, came up to them and said she was surprised to see two real athletes slumming among the female imposters. Dale said she shouldn't doubt the femininity of herself and her teammates. They weren't imposters; they really were girls.

Teri said, ha ha, and said she'd see them later. Dale and Chris said so long and then told Amanda and Rowena they'd see them at their dorm in a few minutes. The two girls, still in the throes of the happiness that victory brings, laughed and said okay.

While waiting for the girls in front of Hayley, Dale asked Chris where he was taking Rowena – or rather, where she was taking him.

Chris said JR's Chicken Ranch. Dale remembered that's where he and Amanda went last year. Then they saw Rusty and Rose Myrick, Sharon's younger sister who'd played quarterback for the underclassmen team, walking down the sidewalk to the other girls' dorm, Easger. Dale and Chris waved. Chris said he didn't know Rusty was dating Rose. Looked like Rusty and Mary Jane were quits for good. Dale thought Rose was rather pretty. She wasn't as tall as Sharon and had a fuller figure and blond hair.

Amanda's car, containing some of the victorious powder puffs, pulled into the parking lot and Dale and Chris watched as Amanda and Rowena got out and walked to the dorm's front door. The girls said they'd be out after they changed, but Dale grabbed Amanda by her elbow and ushered her to the side of the building. She giggled and asked what he was doing. He asked her if she really wanted to do this silly twirp thing. She said, yes. He said in that case, he didn't want her to change. He wanted to leave right now.

Amanda protested but Dale reminded her that he was her twirp date therefore she should do what he wanted. They walked to the parking lot and he noticed that her car, a Buick LeSabre, was a different repo than the one last month. However, this car looked promising for what he had in mind.

Dale started to get into the driver's side but Amanda reminded him that she was supposed to take him out. He shrugged. Okay, he'd play along. He got in the passenger side and when Amanda got in the driver's seat she asked where to? almost in the same kind of tone that he used when he asked her.

Dale told her to drive back to the football stadium. Amanda looked at him with a wondering expression; he liked how her big blue eyes grew even bigger. She started the Buick and drove it out of the parking lot and toward the stadium.

As she drove, she told him that he was behaving oddly. They were supposed to go out on a date. Dale said they were. He didn't want to go to JR's Chicken Ranch again. She looked at him in a suspicious way, but said nothing, and they drove to the stadium in silence. Once they got there, Dale told her to drive past it. She did as instructed. He told her to drive around the park, then turn onto a small gravel road. She did. Dale could tell that she was growing nervous but also a little excited. He felt an interesting tension in the car. He knew she knew what he had in mind and so far she hadn't objected.

They drove down the gravel road until Dale spied the secluded spot between two trees with low limbs. He'd taken Wendy here a few times when the spot was available. It was a good make-out location. Private, with plenty of cover. The gravel road also provided advanced warning for a snooping cop because Dale could hear the tires of an approaching car grinding the gravel.

He told her to turn into the secluded spot. Amanda did. He said turn off the motor. She complied. He sat at the other end of the car seat and peered at her. To his surprise, she returned his candid look.

He extended his arm and she scooted over. He put his left arm around her shoulders, thinking how odd this position seemed. He'd never been with Amanda with her sitting on his left. Even in her garage they sat on the couch and love seat as if they were sitting in his car. Now, he'd have to execute his moves in reverse. Dale rather enjoyed anticipating that novelty.

Before kissing her, he took one of her braids and looked at the thick, twisted hair. It reminded him of a rope. He noticed that her hair still had its lighter color from the summer sun. Sort of like the color of ripe wheat: a very light golden brown. He took the brushy end of her braid and rubbed it against her small nose. She giggled. He dropped her braid and put his arms around her waist, feeling how light and fluffy the material of her sweats felt. He kissed her very lightly and felt her excitement. For some reason, Amanda seemed especially receptive to him. Maybe it was the warm Indian summer night. Maybe it was the fun she'd had playing powder-puff football and pretending to be athletic. Maybe it was that she, in a sense, had taken him to the lake – an illusion of control. Whatever it was, he sensed she was willing to get back up to speed after a month of poking along.

He continued to kiss her lightly, tenderly, on her lips, then her philtrum, then her cheeks. He felt her growing increasingly excited. He rubbed his hands against the waistband of her sweatpants. He anticipated how easy it would be to slide his hands down them.

Just as she moaned after his last lingering kiss on her neck, he paused and asked her how her chest felt.

"I think I might have bruised it," she said.

Dale said, let me see.

Amanda pulled her jersey down just enough for him to see the top of her breast bone. The light of the nearly full moon gave off enough illumination to see the beginning of a faint purplish bruise. He asked if it hurt.

"A little," she said, quietly.

Dale bowed his head and gently kissed that spot. Amanda threaded her fingers through his hair. He moved his mouth a little lower and started to pull her jersey up. Amanda tugged on his hair.

"You first," she said, smiling in an uncharacteristically suggestive way.

"Me?"

"Yeah. You're my date."

Dale was glad she didn't say twirp date. She knew he hated that word and that concept. He surprised himself by not feeling shy. He leaned back and pulled his baseball undershirt over his head. Amanda reached out and touched his chest, the same spot just above the breastbone where he'd touched her. With her fingertips she traced the sparse hair between his pectoral muscles.

Dale said he didn't have much chest hair.

Amanda said she didn't mind. She spread her hands across his chest and glided them up to his shoulders. She said she'd always liked his muscles. She said she liked how broad his shoulders were and how narrow his waist and hips were.

He felt his face flush out of both embarrassment and pleasure. He told Amanda it was now her turn.

She removed her hands from his shoulders and used them to hide her face. She giggled in a bashful way. Dale said again, this time more insistently, it's your turn. She took her hands away from her face and he saw her looking at him in an almost vampish way. He'd never seen that expression before and he loved it.

"C'mon," he cajoled.

Amanda pulled the jersey over her head but not in one quick motion. It got stuck in her braids and Dale had to help untangle them. She tossed the jersey next to her. He stared at her bra. He'd never seen one like that before. It looked different. Larger and sturdier.

"That too," he said, after debating whether he'd prefer her taking it off or if he'd do the honors.

"*Dale.*"

"C'mon," he said in a low, coaxing voice.

She reached behind her in that way girls do, with their flexible arms bending so easily behind them. She unhooked her bra and it fell to her lap.

Dale gazed appreciatively at her exposed breasts. He felt as if his nerves were aflame. His breathing grew faster. When he examined them critically, he knew they weren't spectacular. Her breasts weren't large. The nipples weren't long or deeply pigmented the way he preferred. But because they were Amanda's breasts, at that moment they looked perfect to him.

"Beautiful," Dale murmured. Amanda, her face still lowered, blushed.

He reached over to her but instead of embracing her he put his hands on the elastic band of her sweatpants. He slipped his fingers under both the waistband of her pants and her panties. He knew they would be easy to pull down. He'd imagined doing so since seeing Amanda wearing them while standing on the sidelines.

"Dale," she said.

"I want to see you. All of you."

He gently slid the sweatpants and the panties down her hips. Amanda didn't look at him or resist. She lifted her bottom so he could pull them under her. He slid them slowly down her thighs, over her knees, and down to her ankles. He watched as she lifted her small feet out of them.

He looked at every part of her as she sat demurely in the nude, bathed by the moonlight. He especially liked how small her waist looked and how curvaceous her hips and thighs were.

"You are lovely," he said.

She raised her face and shyly smiled.

He gently put one hand on her far knee and one hand on her closest hip. He told her to turn around. He wanted to see her from behind.

"Dale," she said, this time with more of a note of complaint in her voice.

"Please, Amanda. You know I especially like the back."

She reluctantly complied. He helped her turn and stretch out across the seat. When she lay flat on her stomach, with her legs stretched over Dale's lap, he reached down and stroked her narrow shoulders. His hands gently followed her backbone from the neck down to the small of her back, and into the cleft of her buttocks. He heard her breathe out, not quite a sigh because she was too nervous, but not an exhalation of protest either.

He looked at her naked back, buttocks, and thighs in the silvery light of the moon. He wished there were more light. He couldn't see as much detail as he'd like. But he did see the small bruise on the upper area of her left cheek. It was about the size and shape of a silver dollar. When he lightly touched it, she squirmed. He asked if she was sore there. She said a little.

He slowly ran his hand over the curve of her right cheek, down to her thigh. He caressed her soft flesh for a few minutes until she wiggled and said she was getting a little cold.

She pulled her legs off him and tried to sit up. Dale put his arms around her waist and helped turn her over. He put his arms around her and hugged her to warm her. He pressed himself against her. He kissed her lips, then moved down to her neck. He liked the way her skin smelled. The scent was more than the usual subtle, floral scent of her perfume. He smelled a slight pungent odor of sweat. He didn't think he'd ever smelled that before. He liked it.

He started to caress her when she said something that stunned him. She said she wanted to see him, too.

"What do you mean?"

"I want to see, too," Amanda said. "You know, it."

It? Gilbert?

"That's getting into dangerous territory."

He was sort of joking, but he was concerned that he might not be able to control himself.

"You saw me," she said.

She reached a hand down to his lap. She didn't pull on his belt or try to unzip his fly. Dale asked her if she was sure. She nodded. He felt a little silly, but that moment of self-consciousness faded as he realized she was sitting next to him naked. He'd gotten the beginning of an erection even before they parked. Now his penis pushed forcefully against his jeans. It wasn't difficult taking Gilbert out. Dale unbelted, unbuttoned, unzipped, pulled his shorts down enough that his engorged member sprung right out. Amanda gasped. He didn't think she could see that well in the dark. The moon had floated farther up in the sky and the moonlight wasn't as strong as a few minutes before. But Amanda seemed impressed.

"It's so big," she said.

Dale doubted that. Probably just average. She reached down and touched it. He felt her small hand tremble and he almost exploded.

"Amanda," he warned.

She curled her slender fingers around and Dale growled in the back of his throat. He felt like he was one of those cartoon thermometers where the mercury rises and rises until it explodes out the top.

"Amanda," he gasped.

His body jerked. He wanted to thrust, but he restrained himself. He didn't want to scare her. He knew she didn't really know how this kind of thing worked. But restraining himself made him nauseous. He breathed in deeply and tried not to groan.

"What happened?" she asked.

When he'd jerked, she had removed her hand. He didn't know exactly where the stuff went. Most of it seemed to have splattered on the leg of his jeans.

"Nothing," he muttered. What a lie, he thought.

"Are you all right?"

"Yeah."

Amanda leaned her head against his sweaty chest. Dale hugged her and tried not to think too much about her naked thigh pressing against his leg. He'd never get unaroused.

"Everything smells sort of funny," she said, sniffing.

Dale almost burst out laughing. She felt his chest heave and she asked what was so funny. He couldn't explain it to her. The smell of sex, even the incomplete variety they'd engaged in, did produce a curious smell. He breathed in. That odd musky odor that didn't smell good or bad. Just potent.

She again asked him what was so funny, and before he could make up an excuse for his mirth, they heard in the distance the crunch of a car's wheels rolling over gravel. He felt

Amanda tense against him. She reached for her jersey and draped it over herself. Dale stuffed the nearly flaccid Gilbert back into his shorts and zipped up.

"Dale?"

He told her not to worry. It was probably a couple trying for this spot. When they saw the back end of the car, they'd leave.

They listened to the crunching sound come closer. Then he heard the wheels turning on the gravel and the beams of the headlights swirled above their heads. Amanda scrunched down in the seat. Dale remained sitting straight. Just as he thought. The intruding car stopped, backed out, and crunched its way back the way it came.

"I told you so," Dale said. "Just someone looking for this spot."

Amanda remained huddled against him. "How embarrassing."

"Why? They didn't see anything. They don't even know who is parked here."

"It's still humiliating."

Dale looked at her. Her attitude had changed. Now, she was thinking about how they'd sinned. She felt ashamed to be naked.

"Don't be embarrassed," he said. "You're with me. You're with someone who loves you very much."

She looked at him. "Really?"

"Yes. More than anything in the world."

She said she loved him, too, but he could tell that she felt like she'd done something wrong. They had really exceeded the speed limit this time.

She shyly reached for her clothes. This time, Dale helped her with them. She didn't protest, but she didn't look at him as he helped her pull up her panties and sweatpants. After she put on that odd bra, he helped her pull the jersey over her head.

She said thank you, and Dale didn't say "my pleasure" because he knew she wasn't in a playful mood.

"I'll drive," he said.

She said okay, and Dale lifted her over him as he slid behind the wheel.

"Hungry?" he asked. He was. After all, they were supposed to go to dinner.

"Famished."

Dale started the car, backed out of the make-out spot, and drove back to town.

"How about West Oaks?" he asked.

"I'm not dressed for it."

He said he meant outside with the carhops. Amanda said that would fine.

A couple of minutes later, Dale parked at West Oaks, asked what Amanda wanted, ordered what he wanted, and when the carhop brought the food and drinks, he paid her. Amanda said she was supposed to pay. Dale joked to himself, you already have, but he didn't say so aloud because he knew Amanda would take it the wrong way. Instead, he asked if she had any money with her?

"No, it's in my purse back in my dorm room."

"It doesn't matter," Dale said. "I don't cotton to the whole twirp concept."

Amanda smiled. "You don't cotton?"

Sometimes Dale lapsed into country talk; usually, around his uncles and cousins. He nodded. "That's right, ma'am. I don't cotton."

She smiled and Dale asked her questions to keep her mind off what had recently transpired. He asked her about her classes, her voice lessons, and how she was getting along with Hope, her roommate for the second straight year. While he was asking these questions, he wondered if Amanda got an allowance from her parents. Probably. Although she had worked the summer at the bookstore.

The food and drinks arrived and they both ate enthusiastically without talking much. Dale had his favorite, a chicken fried steak sandwich, fries, and a chocolate shake. Amanda, instead of her usual Caesar's salad or something light like that, had a flame-broiled cheeseburger stuffed with all the things he didn't like, tater tots and a diet Coke. She even indulged herself by taking a few sips of his shake.

Dale was amused at her hunger. Playing football, even the powder puff variety, worked up an appetite.

After stuffing themselves, he drove her back to the dorm. He kept the conversation going and she answered his questions freely but as the car turned into the parking lot she grew quiet. Instead of parking in a far corner away from a street light as he usually did, this time he parked in a more lit part of the lot. When he turned to her, he glanced down at the seat to see if any evidence of their passion was visible. He didn't see anything. Maybe all of his ejaculate had landed on his jeans. He hoped so.

They talked for awhile about classes and her music. Then, close to her curfew, he kissed Amanda and put his arms around her waist. He told her she looked cute in her braids and playfully pulled one of them. She smiled. But he saw a look of regret already in her eyes.

As he walked her to the front door of the dorm, he asked her who usually drove that car. "Daddy," she said. "Why?"

Dale said no reason. Just wondering. He prayed that Mr. Meeks wouldn't inspect the interior of the car and if he did he wouldn't find anything. He wondered what Mr. Meeks would do if he did discover some evidence. Would Amanda's father track him down and shoot him? Would he demand he marry her? Would he simply clean it up and not say a word but forever feel disappointed in his daughter? Dale knew he was overreacting. He didn't think there was much evidence and it would almost certainly not be detected, especially if it was on the floorboard.

Amanda asked Dale what he was thinking. He said nothing. He asked her how her bruises felt.

She blushed. After all, he'd seen both of them. She said they felt a little sore, that's all. Dale glanced around and not seeing anyone, he quickly kissed Amanda and held her and whispered in her ear that he loved her.

His confession of love seemed to make her feel better. She briefly smiled and opened the dorm door. He thought she looked almost like a little girl going to bed in floppy pajamas as she pattered into the dorm wearing the sweatpants and jersey, her braids swaying. He felt a tingling behind his eyes and in the top of the bridge of his nose, as he did when he felt a strong surge of emotion. He blinked his eyes and fought the emotion. He hoped she didn't feel too badly about what they had done. But he had a feeling she would be visiting the altar tomorrow morning at church to pray for forgiveness.

**Chapter 3:** *TV movie and poetry class; Dale gets pow-wowed*

Dale sat in the chair in his room watching the Dallas Cowboys on Monday night football. He'd been so busy of late that he didn't watch nearly as much sports. He'd only seen a few games of the World Series, which had ended two weeks ago. Seeing so few games hadn't bothered him too much because the despised New York Yankees won. They'd beaten the Dodgers. He'd been wrong about the Reds. They hadn't overtaken LA.

Dale stared with satisfaction at the television screen. The Dallas game was going well. They were creaming the hated Redskins. At halftime, he thought he'd get a snack. He left his room and walked into the kitchen. He opened the fridge when he heard some dialogue coming from the television in the living room. The words sounded familiar. Dale grabbed the bottle of 7-Up, then closed the refrigerator door. He listened. He heard the gruff voice of an actor say, "white man's medicine is sometimes necessary, Hannah."

Dale remembered that inane bit of dialogue from the book. He rushed into the living room and saw his mother and sister watching television. He stared at the screen. A tall man with glasses stood next to an Indian girl on a street in a western city. Dale had forgotten all about the movie version of that silly book. But here it was on television being broadcast to millions of homes. No doubt hundreds of residents of Galilee were tuning in.

"What is this?" Dale asked, even though he knew it was *Hannah Horse*. The odds that another movie would feature a pretty and spunky Indian girl and a solicitous white doctor were extremely low.

Jesse, between puffs of her Pall Malls, said she'd forgot. Dale looked at June May.

"I dunno," she said.

"You're sitting there watching a movie and you don't know what it's called?"

June May shrugged.

Dale grabbed the television guide from the coffee table and flipped to Monday night. At least they'd changed the title. The movie was called *A Girl Named Hannah*. Maybe no one, especially Bronwyn, would make the connection.

"Have any of the characters called her by her full name?"

Jesse and June May looked at him as if he were asking an especially difficult question.

He tried a simpler one. "Has anyone called her Hannah Horse?"

Jesse blew smoke in his general direction. June May, her attention riveted to the screen, which lowered Dale's opinion of her taste to a Death Valley level, frowned at him.

"Shhh, Dale. We're trying to watch the movie."

He thought maybe the screenwriters or producers or director or whoever made such decisions would change the character's name from Horse to something less absurd. Maybe Hannah Hopi. No, that didn't make sense. She was a Navajo. Maybe Hannah Caulder, except he remembered that was almost the name of an old Raquel Welch movie. Maybe Hannah Hosanna, which he rather liked. Or Hannah Puma, which was a more interesting animal name, although not alliterative.

Dale had to watch the awful movie for almost twenty minutes before a racist white woman sneeringly said, "there's nothing worse than a smart Navajo. That Hannah Horse is trouble."

Dang and double dang, thought Dale.

He trudged back to his room and rejoined the Dallas game. At least the Cowboys were routing the Redskins.

The next evening, Dale entered the poetry classroom with trepidation. He feared Bronwyn would soon come in and glare at him, incensed over his making a fool of her. He wasn't sure what he'd say. Maybe that there were two Hannah Horses: the fictional one and the real one. The fact that Alexandra Sweet had written a novel about a Navajo girl by the name of Hannah Horse, then had sold the rights of that book to a television network, which then proceeded to make a movie-of-the-week of said book, and that a real girl by the same name just happened to be the deceased sister of the talented Indian poet on campus by the name of Harry Horse was simply a coincidence. You know, just one of those unusual events that occasionally take place from time to time.

Dale wondered if anybody else who'd seen the TV movie would make the connection to the prize-winning poems of H. Horse? He doubted it. He imagined the few students who had any recollection of last year's literary prizes would be too busy to watch a silly movie-of-the-week. Besides, there could be more than one Horse running around. That is to say, someone could believe that there was a fictional Hannah Horse and a real H. Horse on campus.

Dale took his usual seat in the seminar room. He felt funny sitting in this classroom for a poetry class when last year the same room had been used for Dr. Prescott's philosophy classes. Before classes had started, Henshaw had told him that he was thinking about taking

Dr. Prescott's night class at OU. He wondered if Dale had any interest in taking it, too. He did, but he didn't think he had time to drive all the way to Norman and back twice a week.

His classmates arrived. Two rather plain girls, Charlotte and Emily, that Dale didn't know well. Then Sharon's little sister, Rose, whom he enjoyed sneaking glances at. She had nice lips, fuller than Sharon's, and a pretty good philtrum to boot. Then Polly. Dale nodded at her when she walked in. Polly's poetry wasn't very good. It was well written technically, but didn't have much feeling or musicality.

Then the last student walked in: David Hawkins.

Hawkins took a seat next to Dale. He nodded and Dale returned the unspoken greeting. Hawkins had sat next to him since the first class. Dale didn't know if he did so because they were the only males in class or because David knew he was Amanda's boyfriend.

Sometimes Hawkins came into the gym when Dale, Rusty, Chris, Henshaw, and Eugene were lifting weights and playing basketball for their P. E. independent study. A couple of times he joined them playing basketball to make it an even six – even though Dale knew coaches didn't like varsity players getting involved in pick-up games. Hawkins hadn't showed off. He played in earnest but he didn't hog the ball or act like he was a great player. In fact, he'd played generously, passing to open guys and not stealing the ball when he guarded Dale, even though Dale bet he could have done so easily. Dale found himself liking Hawkins against his will.

He heard the loud clack of Bronwyn's boots down the hall. Dale wondered if she ever wore any other kind of footwear. He tried to steady his nerves. After all, she was probably too busy or had too much taste to watch a ridiculous movie-of-the-week. Well, since she'd liked H. Horse's poems so much that she'd awarded them literary prizes, maybe she didn't really have much taste after all.

Dale lowered his head and peered indirectly at the door when Bronwyn marched in. She said, "good evening, class" in her usual ebullient voice and then took a seat at the head of the table where Dr. Prescott never sat. The Philosopher preferred to stand and roam about the room. Dale guessed he would have preferred to teach outside like Socrates did, roaming the groves of academe with his devoted students.

Dale looked up. She smiled at him. She smiled at all the students. He wondered if this was a sly trick. She'd pretend nothing was wrong until Dale, lulled into a false sense of security, was about to leave, then she'd inform him that she'd already spoken to the dean and he would be expelled for his malicious hoax.

Dale knew he was overreacting. Bronwyn didn't seem to have a calculating bone in her body. If she knew about Hannah Horse, he would have seen it on her face immediately.

Bronwyn said a short prayer, and then she asked who had poems to read. Emily held up her hand. Dale wished he'd not taken this class. He didn't really like poetry that much; at least not the drivel that was written in this class. Most of it was religious in nature. But none of the writers had a T. S. Eliot or G. M. Hopkins or John Donne sensibility. Or, for that matter, a gnomic religious sense like Emily Dickinson. No, it was generally predictable, conventional religiousosity about the wonders of God's natural world or Jesus's ultimate sacrifice or how God and Jesus inspired the greatest expressions of human thought. Dale didn't disagree with the ideas so much; he just thought the ideas were expressed in dreadfully banal language. The two plain girls wrote the worst stuff; Rose, who Dale had some hope for, didn't write much better. She clearly wasn't as clever as her sister. Polly wrote her uninspired but verbally correct verse. And Hawkins, well, he'd only read one of his poems so far and much to Dale's chagrin, it wasn't bad. Not that it was good; it was just much better than Dale had expected from a varsity basketball player. But then, Hawkins did sing and act and do other "artistic" things.

Dale had read one poem in class that expressed his philosophical perspective. It was entitled *The Spark within Man*. It was one of the two poems that had been published in last year's literary supplement. It read as follows:

The spark within Man
May not light a fire;
It may not start a blaze
That will outshine Hades;
It may not rival the sun
In all its luminous glory,
But it continues to shine
No matter how low
One solitary spark
In the eternal dark.


Dale thought it was okay. Bronwyn and the class liked it. Hawkins, in fact, had complimented him rather effusively after class. Dale had told him thanks but he didn't think the poem was that good.

He thought that might be the last poem he'd read in class. He'd asked Bronwyn last week if he could write other things instead of poetry. She reminded him that this, after all, was a poetry class. Dale agreed but said he was working on a play and he'd like to use it to fulfill some of the writing requirements. After all, there wasn't a creative writing class for drama. She looked dubious. Dale said she could pretend it was in blank verse. She'd been amused and gave him permission.

The class crept along. Dale studied Rose's philtrum. It wasn't as good as Amanda's but it was pretty nice. He wondered if Rusty liked Rose's philtrum. He'd have to ask him.

When Hawkins read his poem, Dale caught Rose looking at him in a favorable way. Rusty wouldn't like that. Dale didn't even like it. He also noticed that the two plain girls looked at Hawkins in a way that said, "isn't he dreamy?" Dale wondered if girls took poetry writing classes to find a sensitive man. That alone was enough for him to abandon poetry.

Aside from Rose's lips, the only other attraction in class was Bronwyn's bosom. She'd never worn a low-cut blouse or even one with a scooped neckline, not even at the beginning of class when the weather was hot. She always wore high-necked dress blouses or thin sweaters, and now, thicker turtleneck sweaters. Nevertheless, her prodigious bosom offered an interesting diversion from the turgid verse. Dale was careful not to stare. He sometimes looked in the general direction of her well-concealed breasts with a pensive look on his face, suggesting he had to gaze thoughtfully in the distance in order to fully appreciate a classmate's versifying.

Finally, class ended. Dale busied himself until Bronwyn was free. Apparently, she hadn't seen the movie. But he wanted to make sure. After the two plain girls left the room, he asked Bronwyn if she'd watched TV last night.

"That's an unusual question to ask after a poetry seminar," she said.

Dale said that's exactly why he was asking. He said a documentary about Robert Frost aired on the PBS last night. He wondered if Professor Ayers had seen it.

"No, I'm afraid I didn't watch the Frost documentary. Usually, I don't watch much television. However, I did tune into something last night."

Dale felt his stomach split in two and wrap around his thumping heart like a tourniquet. "What was that?" he managed to croak.

"The Cowboys game."

Dale couldn't believe it. "You were watching the football game?"

"Well," she said with a shy smile, "only because Titus watched it."

"Titus?"

"I'm sorry. Titus Meyer."

Dale nodded. The JV coach. He said he didn't know Titus, er, Coach Meyer was her boyfriend.

"Yes, well, one could say that," she said, smiling in a rather coy way.

Dale understood Coach Meyer's interest in Bronwyn. He'd once seen the coach palm two basketballs, one in each hand.

"Was the documentary illuminating?" she asked.

"What?" Dale was still considering the palming of the basketballs.

"The Frost documentary. The one you said aired on PBS last night?"

"I don't know. I watched the Cowboys game, too."

Bronwyn looked puzzled. Dale said he better go. He started to walk out when she said she had a question for him. He stopped. He already knew what it was.

"I meant to ask you at the start of the semester about your friend, Herschel."

Dale frowned a little at what he was about to say. He couldn't help himself. "You mean, Harry Horse?"

"Of course," Bronwyn said. "I meant Harry. Well, did you ever speak to him? About taking the poetry class?"

Dale nodded. "Yeah, I did. But he said he was too busy with his other classes. They're very demanding."

"Oh, I see. I don't recall what his major is."

"It's veterinarian science."

Bronwyn looked puzzled again. "I don't think GNC offers a major in veterinarian science."

"True. I meant, pre-veterinarian science."

"Like pre-med?"

"Exactly. Except, of course, Harry calls it pre-vet."

"That's interesting," said Bronwyn. "It doesn't surprise me. I can tell from Harry's poetry that he loves animals."

Dale tried to remember if any of H. Horse's poems had animals in them. He recalled one mentioned a coyote. Another alluded to a water buffalo. Not an American buffalo or bison, but an actual water buffalo. The kind that wandered the rice paddies of southeast Asia.

"Yeah," Dale said. "He's a regular animal lover."

"Well, if you see him sometime soon, please mention I'd like to meet him sometime. Perhaps he could stop by my office. Or perhaps he could take next semester's poetry class."

"I will. I'll tell Harry all those things. But, you know, I think he told me he might be transferring. To a school that has a stronger pre-vet program."

Bronwyn nodded in a doubtful way. Dale knew she didn't believe him. But she, as did a few other professors, regarded him as such a strange young man that she wasn't offended by his poetic license.

"Well, at any rate, please forward my interest in his poetry to him. And tell him he should come by for a chat." Bronwyn gave him a somewhat skeptical smile. "Well, I should be off."

She said good night in her husky voice and strode out of the class. Dale listened to her boots click-clacking on the floor for a minute, then he walked out of the room too.

When he got to the first floor, he encountered Hawkins standing in the lobby looking at the painting of C. S. Lewis. He turned when Dale walked by.

"Hey," he said.

Dale stopped, and said what's up?

"Not much."

Dale noticed Hawkins looking at him in an inquiring way. He wondered if David had something to ask him, or tell him. Maybe Hawkins was about to suddenly blurt out his love for Amanda. If so, he thought he might punch him, varsity athlete or not.

When Hawkins didn't say anything, Dale shrugged and said he better get going.

Hawkins said he liked Dale's review of *Annie Hall*.

Dale said thanks. He asked if David liked the movie.

"Yeah. It was both comic and tragic."

Dale didn't think it was tragic, but it did have pathos. Still, he appreciated the fact that Hawkins liked the movie. They seemed to have similar taste. As far as he could tell, they were the only two people on campus who liked it. Well, Teri had liked it, too.

"I guess I better get going," Hawkins said.

Dale said okay. They exchanged nods and walked to different exits of the building. As Dale walked to the north parking lot, he wondered if Hawkins was just being nice to him to get closer to Amanda. That didn't make sense, though. Most guys who coveted another guy's girl didn't hide their intentions. Dale shook his head. He couldn't yet figure out Hawkins.

Dale read the latest letter to the editor complaining about his film review of *Annie Hall*. The writer, a religion major that Dale didn't know, seemed to be disturbed that Dale would review, thus promote, a "Jewish" film. The author's criticism puzzled him. First, how was *Annie Hall* a Jewish film, except that Woody Allen, a Jew, had written and directed it? If the film had been titled *Annie Golda Meier*, then the writer might have a point, although still a silly one. Why should it matter if a Jew or a Christian or a non-believer made a film and it was reviewed in the campus newspaper? Some people on campus seemed to think that the only information or knowledge they should come into contact with had to be theologically pure. Dale felt increasingly exasperated with such close-minded views.

The door opened and Teri walked in. Dale said hi and immediately noticed that she had a knowing look on her face. She walked over and plopped down on a stool, that look still on her features.

"Guess what I saw last night?" she asked.

"The Aurora Borealis?"

"On TV."

Dale didn't bother to look up. He shuffled through a couple more letters to the editor. All negative. Well, people tended to write complaints, not compliments.

"I'm surprised you'd be wasting your time watching television," he said, still flipping through paperwork.

"It wasn't a waste this time."

Dale grew tired of the cat-and-mouse game. He looked at her, noticed she had a sly smile now, and asked what she'd seen.

"A movie called *A Girl Named Hannah*."

"Was it any good?"

"No. But it was about a Navajo girl named Hannah *Horse*."

Dale tried to look surprised. "Really? Well, I think Horse is a common name among the Navajo."

"Yeah, I bet. But didn't you say that Harry Horse's sister was named Hannah? What is the likelihood that a dumb movie-of-the-week would have a character in it with the same name? And didn't you say she got run over by a bus? Well, that happens to the girl in the movie, too."

Dale shook his head with fake sympathy. He suggested that maybe the film was based on the tragic history of Hannah Horse. Maybe the TV people were inspired by her life, sort of like George Bernard Shaw had been inspired by Joan of Arc to write *Saint Joan*?

"I don't think so. The movie was based on a book."

Teri reached behind her and produced a paperback copy of *Hannah Horse* from her back pocket.

"Where did you get that?" Dale asked, as innocently as he could.

"From a used bookstore."

Dale nodded. He wasn't sure how to refute such irrefutable evidence.

"C'mon, Dale. There really isn't a Hannah Horse, is there?"

"It depends on what you mean by 'really isn't.'"

"A real *person*."

"There might be a real person named Hannah Horse running around the mesas and arroyos of Sante Fe or elsewhere for that matter."

"Not the Hannah Horse we thought we knew about. And that means that Harry really doesn't have a sister."

Dale considered her statements. Implicit in them was that Harry Horse actually existed. Well, why wouldn't Teri think that? After all, Bronwyn (Delphina actually) had verified his existence as a student on campus. As long as no one verified the verification, then no one would know that H. Horse was a complete invention.

"Okay," Dale said. "It's true that Harry doesn't have a sister."

"I knew it!" Teri jumped off the stool. She waved the book at Dale and laughed. "You just gave Harry a sister because of this silly book."

Dale admitted he'd read it. He told Teri he'd taken a class with the renowned author, Alexandra Sweet.

"How was the class?" Teri asked.

"It stunk."

"What about this Alexandra Sweet?"

"She was an obese egomaniac. Otherwise, she was quite boring."

Teri walked around the room lost in thought. Dale didn't like seeing that.

"It's strange, though," she said. "You got a real guy named Harry Horse and a character named Hannah Horse. Both are Navajos. How likely is that?"

"Well, how did you think Alexandra Sweet came up with the idea for that book?"

Teri considered his point. "You mean, the novel is based on Harry?"

Dale shrugged. "Let's just say that Harry's life is remarkably similar to Hannah's in the book."

"You mean Alexandra Sweet knew Harry? She used his life for material for her book? She just changed the sex of the character?"

Dale said nothing but tried to match Teri's expression of disapproval that an author would be so exploitative.

"What does Harry think of her book?"

"He hates it," Dale said with conviction.

"I bet he does. Imagine someone taking your life story and using it for her book."

"Well, you know how writers are. Always looking for raw material to exploit."

"But Harry didn't get killed by a bus."

"No, he obviously survived the accident."

Teri began pondering again. Dale wished she'd be like most people and just accept what appeared to be true.

"Did Harry know this doctor guy, you know, the one that gets involved with Hannah?"

"I don't know. I guess."

"But in the book, the doctor and Hannah seem to have a thing for one another."

"Well, remember it is fiction."

Teri nodded. "Yeah, sometimes that's easy to forget. Especially when a character is based on someone from real life."

Dale shuffled through some more papers hoping Teri would get the hint that he was a very busy newspaper editor.

"Tell me, Dale. Harry really exists, doesn't he?"

Dale threw up his hands in exasperation. "You heard Bronwyn verify his enrollment on campus, didn't you?"

"Well, it wasn't Bronwyn exactly –"

"Well, the powers that be said he was enrolled at GNC. You heard that."

Teri considered his point. She nodded and smiled. "Yeah, you're right." Then she looked more critically at Dale. "And you really know this mysterious guy?"

"I'm getting to know him better and better."

Teri was about to ask another impertinent question when Abigail Van Brocklin came into the room after a quick rap on the half-closed door. She asked if she were interrupting anything. Dale said not at all and waved her in.

Abigail stood at the desk counter. Dale got up, ignored Teri's skeptical look, and walked over to her.

"What's up?" he asked.

"Well, I thought you might be interested to know that I asked Dean Pierce if student activities could show a film on campus."

"A film? You mean a real film? I mean, a secular film?" Dale still had a hard time making that distinction.

"Yes. And Dean Pierce agreed."

Dale glanced at Teri. She raised an eyebrow.

"That's progress," he said. "How did you convince him?"

"I said if campus activities showed a secular film from time to time, a good, decent film, of course, then students would be less likely to leave campus to see the indecent films."

Dale was impressed with Abigail's strategic approach. Maybe Henshaw had a reason to get involved with her.

"Great. What films do you have in mind?" He hoped she wouldn't say *In Search of Noah's Ark* or *For the Love of Benjy*.

"Well, we're going to show *Oliver!* on homecoming weekend."

"That's a musical based on *Oliver Twist*, isn't it?" Dale thought Amanda might deign to see that.

"You certainly know your movies, Dale."

He shrugged. He wasn't sure that was a compliment, even coming from Abigail. He said that was a good choice. Abigail agreed. She said most people liked musicals. He suppressed a frown. Then she looked at the clock and asked if that was the real time. Dale said yep. Abigail said she had to run. Teri said she had to go, too. She walked past Dale and gave him a suspicious glance but only said bye. Dale waved to the two girls as they left the office. Then he went back to his desk and wondered how many other people had seen *A Girl Named Hannah*. The only people that knew of his connection to Harry Horse were Jenny, Polly, and Sharon, besides Teri and Bronwyn. Apparently, only Teri had seen the movie. None of the others had said a word to him about the movie-of-the-week. He thought maybe his pseudonym would survive undetected.

Dale sat in the auditorium with Sharon and Polly. Literary types with no theatrical or musical skills tended to sit together at Pow-Wow, the annual GNC talent show. He hadn't attended last year's extravaganza. But since Amanda was in this fall's spectacle, not to mention Rusty, Chris, Eugene, and Teri, Dale decided to attend.

Amanda was part of some comic chorus that sang silly songs between skits. Dale knew where Abigail and Eugene, the organizers of the show, got the idea. From Greek drama. He couldn't wait to tell Amanda that she was part of a Greek chorus. On second thought, maybe he wouldn't tease her. She'd been a little cool to him ever since smashing the speed limit on the twirp date.

Dale had to admit that some of the skits were funny. He'd never suspected that Nazarene kids could have a good sense of humor. Their kind of comedy wasn't his kind; nothing satirical or absurd, really. Most of the humor was good natured, poking fun at certain campus personalities like Henshaw or Short and some teachers and administrators. They made quite a few jokes about religious and denominational matters that he didn't quite get.

Interspersed in the skits were musical interludes. In addition to the Greek chorus, which included Fish, a number of soloists and groups played. One of the groups, a four-member band called "Aaron's Rod," played up beat Christian contemporary rock music. The group had generated some controversy. Some people didn't like the name – especially the rod part. In a stuco meeting, Short complained that the name was suggestive. Dale, jumping at a chance to tease the VP of religious life, asked him suggestive of what? He had enjoyed seeing Short's sleek face turn purple.

The Greek chorus closed the show. Dale watched Amanda, standing in front, sing. He liked the way she sang. She never exaggerated her expression, not even now when doing this silly song. Then he saw her frown for a moment. He looked past her and saw Fish. Dale thought he had more than his usual impassive expression on his odd face. The fact that Fish was in the Greek chorus didn't surprise him. He knew Sylvester sang in the First Church choir. In fact, he was reputed to have a rather impressive bass voice. Dale guessed it was Fish who had been responsible for the guttural sounds emanating from the Greek chorus' performances tonight. The funny thing was that Fish's speaking voice wasn't especially deep.

As far as Dale was concerned, The Stomp was clearly the highlight of Pow-Wow. The Star Trek skit, featuring the seven-foot Lyle as Spock and the ubiquitous Putney as Captain Kirk, was pretty funny too, thanks to Putney's clever parody of William Shatner. But Dale thought nothing could top The Stomp.

After the Pow-Wow ended, Dale told Sharon and Polly he'd see them later, then threaded his way backstage in search of Amanda. On his way to the other side of the stage, he bumped into Rusty, Chris, and Putney.

"What a shocking display of primordial behavior," he told them.

"So, you liked it?" Rusty said, still wearing most of his goofy costume.

"I thought it was great."

Dale saw Putney gazing at him. Dale told him he was excellent, too. In particular, his Nutty Professor was superb. Even better than Jerry Lewis.

"Why, thank you, young man," said Putney, using his Nutty Professor voice.

Dale noticed that he and Putney were similar physically, except that Putney had an animated, agile-featured face like Rusty. When he raised an eyebrow at this observation, Putney did the same. Dale thought he'd found the impossible: someone as funny as Rusty.

Chris asked Dale what he had planned for the rest of the night. Usually, there were two choices: if college kids wanted a quieter atmosphere, they gathered at Java Joint. If they wanted a louder atmosphere, they went to West Oaks. But high school kids hung out there, too. They could also go to the college cafeteria. It usually stayed opened for an hour after campus events.

"Maybe we'll go to West Oaks," he said.

Chris said he'd join them there. Then he asked Rusty and Putney if they wanted to come along.

Rusty said he had other plans. He winked at Putney, who only raised a brow, playing the straight man to perfection. Dale felt a little uneasy about Rusty and Putney teaming up. He felt like a funnier, more accomplished partner was replacing him.

Dale told them so long and walked across stage to Amanda. On the way, he told Eugene, Hawkins, and Phelps he'd been impressed with their band. The three of them nodded in the cool manner expected of rock stars.

Dale saw Amanda talking to that same redheaded girl he'd encountered in the music building last spring. He didn't remember her name. She was cute, with a baby doll face, a soft dimple in her chin, and round granny glasses. As he walked over, he saw Fish lurking in the background. He seemed to be gazing at the two girls in an odd way. When Fish saw Dale approach, he turned around and pretended to be fooling with the zipper of his black robe he'd worn as a member of the Greek chorus.

Dale said hi to Amanda. He noticed the redhead staring at him in a thoughtful way, as if she were trying to place him. Amanda introduced them. She told him that the girl's name was Shirley. She was a music major, too.

"Hello," Dale said. "How's Stephen doing?"

"Stephen?"

Dale thought that was the name of the guy he'd seen her with. "Yeah, Stephen. I guess he's over his sore throat by now."

Shirley looked at Dale more closely. It took her a few seconds to recognize him. He saw her eyes open wide, almost as if in alarm.

"Are you, are you –" she stammered.

"That's right," Dale said. "The piccolo player."

He suggestively raised an eyebrow at her. He couldn't help it.

Shirley's mouth dropped open. She asked Amanda to excuse her. Dale watched as she abruptly turned and walked away.

"Dale, what in heaven's name is going on?"

Amanda must be really annoyed, thought Dale. She hardly ever used any intensifiers.

"Just saying hello."

"Well, yes, but what is this business about being a piccolo player? And why did Shirley leave so suddenly?"

Dale said he'd explain it to her someday. Right now he wanted to congratulate her on her excellent singing.

"Thanks." Amanda didn't smile. She looked annoyed.

"What's wrong?" Dale had hoped she'd be over her guilt about the twirp date. That had been almost a week ago.

"Oh, nothing."

She glanced over her shoulder. Fish and another guy Dale didn't know were standing not far away, talking quietly.

"What is it, Amanda?"

Amanda leaned closer and said that Sylvester had been bothering her all night. During the musical interludes, he leaned down too far and she felt his breath on the back of her neck. He'd been staring at her, too.

"You're kidding? Fish?"

Amanda gave him a severe look. She asked if he thought she was making this up.

Dale glanced over to Fish and the other guy. He had thought Fish too cold-blooded to be interested in girls. Dale could imagine him later in life fertilizing eggs but not actually engaging in any mammalian sexual activity.

"Even now, he's lurking," Amanda said.

"He has a tendency to lurk," said Dale. "But you said he's been bothering you?"

"Practically all night."

She actually seemed angry. Now, Dale felt himself growing angry, too.

"All right. Stay here."

He walked slowly over to Fish. Dale threw his shoulders back and narrowed his eyes. His jaw jutted. He imagined he looked pretty tough. He noticed the other guy, a skinny kid with fashionable spectacles, take his leave of Sylvester.

"Hello, Smith," Fish said. His beady eyes blinked behind his thick lenses.

Dale felt a small drop of sympathy fall in his heart before the memory of Amanda's agitated voice evaporated it.

"Amanda told me you've been bothering her."

Fish's mouth nearly disappeared before reappearing to say Amanda was mistaken.

Dale didn't like hearing him say her name. He stepped closer. Even though Fish was a couple of inches taller than he was, Sylvester shrunk down an inch lower than Dale with that additional step.

"She said you were breathing on her neck."

The image of that put his anger in a higher gear. He now felt his muscles growing taut, in preparation of doing violence to the pathetic Fish.

"If I did, it was entirely by mistake, I assure you, Smith," Fish said weakly, blinking his small gray eyes.

Dale pointed a finger at Fish. "If you ever bother her again, I'll smash your face."

Fish nodded his head emphatically. "Yes, I understand, Smith. It's all been a misunderstanding. No need for violence. No need."

Dale shook his head. He wished all guys he didn't like were as easily scared as Sylvester. "Just remember, Fish. Stay away from her."

Fish lowered his eyes from Dale's stare and nodded. Dale felt another drop of sympathy for Sylvester, but he kept his truculent expression. Fish really was a creep. Amanda had been right to be disgusted. Dale turned around and walked back to her. He took her hand and led her off the stage, down the stairs, and into the empty auditorium. When he glanced at her, she smiled at him with the most warmth he'd seen in a week.

Later, in his car, after they'd visited West Oaks and sat with Chris and Rowena and had a good time, Dale asked her if Fish had ever bothered her before.

"Oh, let's not talk about him." Amanda said. She leaned back against his arm that encircled her shoulders.

"If he ever bothers you again, let me know. I'll thrash him."

"*Dale*," she said in a scolding voice. But she smiled, too. "Would you really do that?"

"You bet I would."

He knew he could easily pummel Fish. He just hoped Amanda didn't attract any tough creeps. He didn't really like fighting. He didn't even like getting into scrapes with jerks like that guy in flag football. But he knew part of the trick of not getting into fights was making it clear that he would if necessary. In fact, ever since he'd sort of broke Bigelow's collarbone, he'd acquired a reputation as a guy with a temper and the muscle to back it up. A lot of people actually thought he'd busted Bigelow's collarbone on purpose. Such a reputation had its advantages on a comparatively pacifist campus like GNC. For example, if there was only one good dessert left at lunch and he and another guy arrived for it at the same time, Dale got it.

He noticed Amanda still smiling at him.

"So, you're not mad at me anymore?" he asked teasingly.

"I was never mad at you," she said. "I was just disappointed in myself."

Dale had felt a little disappointed in himself as well. For not controlling himself. Well, it had all been too exciting. He'd thought about Amanda nude under the moonlight every night that week. He guessed he'd always remember that image until the day he died.

Which might be sooner than he expected if Mr. Meeks had found anything.

"Your father didn't say anything about the condition of the Le Sabre, did he?"

Amanda looked puzzled. "No. Why would he?"

"No reason. Well, maybe driving it on the gravel road." He paused, trying to think of a way to ask the next question. "His attitude hasn't changed toward you, has it?"

"No, it hasn't, but why are you asking? Should his attitude have changed?"

Dale heard the irritated note in her voice. He squeezed her shoulder with his hand. "Of course not."

"Then why are you asking such strange questions?"

"Just a little concerned about the car."

"Well, Daddy didn't say a word about it. In fact, he took it back to the bank and brought back another one."

"What kind?"

Amanda gave him a look that suggested he'd asked another strange question. But she answered anyway.

"Some foreign sports car."

"Do you remember what kind?"

"I don't know. Some kind of Datsun."

"A Datsun 280Z?"

"I don't know. Maybe."

Dale liked those cars. But they didn't have enough room for making out really.

"Why did you feel disappointed in yourself?" Dale knew he was changing the topic to a more thorny issue, but he was curious.

Amanda leaned against his arm and sighed. "You know."

"You regret doing what we did?"

Amanda looked at him. "Don't you?"

"No."

Amanda shook her head. "It's different for men, I guess."

Dale tried to look into her eyes. She wouldn't turn his way. She was still upset about the whole thing. He squeezed her shoulder.

"I don't want to make you do anything you don't want to do," he said. "If you don't want to do that kind of thing, then we won't anymore."

Amanda turned to him and looked into his eyes. "Really? You won't mind?"

"Of course I'll mind. I want to be as close to you as I can. But I don't want you to feel unhappy about it."

"Well, Dale, it's sinful."

Dale nodded. He supposed it was. Amanda felt the sorrow of sinning more keenly than he did.

"Well, then, let's try to arrive at a speed limit that is mutually acceptable."

Amanda smiled a little.

"If what we did last week was going over the speed limit some –"

"A lot," Amanda interjected.

Dale tried to hide his disappointment. "We agree it was speeding. What should the speed limit be now?"

She didn't want to say. She didn't want to define the terms.

"How about sixty?" he asked.

Amanda shook her head, but she smiled slightly.

"You know what sixty is, don't you?"

Amanda tried not to giggle.

"Maybe I should demonstrate." Dale leaned against her, his free hand slowly moving toward her.

She scooted away and giggled. "Dale, stop!"

He returned his wayward hand back to the steering wheel. "Okay, you tell me."

"I don't know," she said shyly.

Dale put his head close to hers. He said she could whisper the rules of the road to him. She almost laughed. He said, come on. Tell me.

"Well," she said quietly, "we have to keep our clothes on."

"All of them?"

"Of course."

"But I can rearrange things a little, can't I?" He spoke lowly. He knew she liked his voice when it got deep.

"Dale."

"Can I push your bra up?"

"*Dale.*"

"I'll leave it on. I'll just slowly slide it up. That's okay, isn't it?"

She didn't say anything. He heard her breathing become more audible.

"I can touch you, can't I? Just slow, gentle caresses on your soft, bare skin."

She exhaled a little. He felt the warmth of her breath on his face.

"I can kiss you, can't I? Not just your lovely face, either. Kiss your downy neck. Maybe a little lower. Soft, tender kisses."

He hadn't touched or kissed her yet. He'd just leaned his face near hers and spoke in a low, husky voice. He felt them both growing excited. He looked in her eyes and saw they were a little teary with emotion.

"See Amanda, it's not just what we do. It's how we feel."

"Oh, Dale," she sighed.

He gently kissed her lips. He felt her tremble. He felt himself breaking up inside. He put his arms around her and squeezed her tight. When he removed his mouth from hers, he heard her sob a little. He kissed her cheek and looked at her. She had her eyes closed. A few tears streamed out of them.

"What's wrong?" he asked.

"I think I'm feeling too much for you."

Dale smiled. "What's wrong with that?"

Amanda turned her face away. He gently took her face in his hands and turned it back to him. He ran the fingers of one hand through her thick hair. He asked again, this time in a somber voice. "What's wrong with that?"

"I don't know."

But he knew. It frightened her. She still had doubts about them. About him. He wasn't exactly what she'd planned on.

"It will be all right, Amanda," he said. He felt that tingling behind his eyes and in the bridge of his nose.

"Will it?"

"Yes, it will."

He kissed her again, and she kissed him back with more fervor than he'd anticipated. He put his hands underneath her sweater and stroked the bare skin of her waist, sliding them down to rest them on the curve of her hip. Their mouths parted and he kissed her neck and heard her moan. He wanted to repeat everything they'd experienced the week before and more, but he knew they couldn't while sitting in his car in the parking lot. In fact, he was surprised that Amanda hadn't called a stop to it already.

He stopped kissing her neck and leaned back. She opened her eyes and looked at him in surprise. Dale had never seen her face look that unguarded and passionate. Her naked face.

"What is it?" she asked in a breathless voice.

Dale had heard a car driving toward them. He nodded toward the sound. Amanda looked startled. She shielded herself with her hands as if she were really naked. He thought maybe she'd drifted back in her mind to last week and had forgot where they were.

The car, a late model Ford, parked beside them. Amanda shrunk in her seat and leaned against Dale as if she expected someone to throw open the door and pull her out. He watched as the car door opened and Eugene and Mary Jane got out. He glanced at them, and saw Mary Jane looking past him, right at Amanda. Dale turned and looked at Amanda and thought he saw what Mary Jane saw: a young woman overwhelmed by her feelings; her eyes a little puffy from weeping. The sight scared him a little. He didn't mean for them to lose their heads and get so carried away.

They watched Eugene walk Mary Jane to the dormitory. Then Dale asked Amanda if she was okay. She didn't answer.

"Are you all right, Amanda?"

She blinked her eyes. She looked at him with a serious, sad look in her eyes.

"I don't know if I should see you anymore."

Dale almost smiled before he knew she was serious.

"You don't mean that."

Amanda nodded. "I do. Maybe I shouldn't."

Dale felt like he'd been decapitated. He didn't feel anything below his neck. His head swirled. His vision blurred. He reached for her but she suddenly scooted away and opened the door.

He jumped out of the car and followed her. She walked with her head down and her arms folded in front of her chest. Dale asked her what was wrong. He asked what he'd done. He said he was sorry. He said she was overreacting. He said he loved her.

She walked toward her dorm without speaking. He saw tears on her cheeks. She wouldn't look at him. When he reached for her, she evaded his touch.

They passed a couple sitting on the bench outside the dorm. Dale ignored their inquiring looks. They walked to the front doors of Hayley Hall. Mary Jane and Eugene stood there, talking.

Dale put his hand on the Amanda's sweatered arm and told her he wanted to talk to her before she went in. She shook her head no. Mary Jane asked her what was wrong. Amanda sdidn't answer. She opened the door and quickly walked in. Before the door swung shut, he saw her running toward the stairs.

He turned to Mary Jane. Her brown eyes stared accusingly at him. Without a word to Dale or Eugene, she opened the door and rushed in after Amanda.

Dale looked over at Eugene. He gazed at him as if he'd come across a pathetic, lost dog, but one he didn't want to take in. Dale turned and walked away.

## Chapter 4: *Dale in print; the bloody Alpha game*

Dale stared out the window in Mrs. Genesee's journalism class as she spoke about libel law. It had been five days since Dale had last seen Amanda and he'd suffered. He couldn't sleep. He hardly ate. He sometimes found himself staring vacantly into space when he should be writing copy or reading his assignments. He tried to keep busy, but increasingly he felt like a zombie walking around campus, dead inside but somehow able to function outwardly so no one knew.

He vaguely heard Mrs. Genesee finish up the discussion on libel, and say that before class ended she'd like to read an essay she'd seen in this morning's *Daily Oklahoman*.

She began reading and the words sounded familiar to Dale. He hadn't seen the City paper today or any other day since Blackie moved out. Jesse didn't read newspapers. He sometimes glanced over the City papers while browsing through the periodical area in the library. But he hadn't been to the library today so he couldn't have perused this essay that Mrs. Genesee was now reading aloud to class.

Then Dale remembered. He'd written it. The *Daily Oklahoman* had held a contest for young people a few months ago. The editors said they wanted teens and young adults from ages fourteen to twenty-one to send in five-hundred word essays and they would publish the best ones. Those selected would receive twenty-five bucks.

He'd seen the contest announcement and rules on a library bulletin board just before classes started. He thought he'd give it a try. He walked up to the third floor and used the very same typewriter he'd used to compose some of the poems for his pseudonyms. This time, of course, he used his real name. He finished in about an hour. He counted the words. About a hundred too many. He had a predisposition to write too much. So, he cut out about ninety words, revised the shorter version, and the next day mailed it to the newspaper. Then he promptly forgot about it.

Dale listened as Mrs. Genesee read it. He remembered the essay as being better than what he was listening to now. He'd written on the topic of the spiritual as being the ultimate reality. He basically said that even though we live in an increasingly matcrialistic and hedonistic world, those concerns are illusions. As such, they ultimately fail to satisfy human beings. The only reality that matters is the spiritual one. Even if the forces of greed and power appear to triumph now, in the end they wouldn't. In the end, spiritual matters transcended all other concerns. He concluded with an allusion to the death of Socrates. Even though Socrates had been defeated politically and ultimately took his life by drinking hemlock rather than accepting banishment from his beloved Athens, he transcended his death and triumphed spiritually over his enemies. He did so by the greatness of his thought and spirit.

Dale knew what inspired him to write that rather pretentious essay: Dr. Prescott's departure from campus. In fact, he'd written the essay the next day after seeing Dean Snyder "salute" Dr. Prescott. Fortunately, since this was twentieth-century America and not fifth-century B.C. Athens, Dr. Prescott hadn't been required to drink poison.

Mrs. Genesse finished and smiled at Dale. He felt embarrassed. He tried to ignore the curious, envious, and critical glances of his classmates. He knew his friends, Teri, Sharon, and Polly, were happy for him. But he knew his adversaries, such as Sylvester, were already disturbed because Dale had used Socrates as an exemplar rather than Jesus.

With the end of class, Mrs. Genesee congratulated Dale on the publication of his essay. He said thanks. He liked Mrs. Genesee. She was an excellent teacher and she didn't provoke controversy. Part of it was that taught journalism and writing, not philosophy. Part of it was her sweet temperament. Dr. Prescott, for all his intelligence, had a thorny personality in some ways. And what else protected Jenny was she believed the tenets and teachings of the Nazarene church. She just didn't insist that everyone believe them in exactly her way.

Teri, Sharon, Polly, and a few others also congratulated him as he walked out of the classroom. He tried to smile. He said thanks. He knew he should have remained behind and talked to them, but he didn't feel like it. On the way out of the door, he saw Fish staring at him. Dale said, "I know, Fish, I know. Jesus would have been a better example."

Fish opened his mouth as wide as he'd ever seen before but didn't make a sound.

Dale walked down the stairs and out the building and strode across campus to the student union and the deserted newspaper office. He went over and looked at what copy and photos they had on the layout pages. Ordinarily, he would have laughed at both photos. The first one showed Rusty, Chris, and Putney doing The Stomp. It was a pretty good picture. It showed the three guys right in the climax of their performance. Rusty looked convincingly simian as he bobbed his shoulders and pushed his mouth out like an ape.

The second photo was funny, too, although maybe not to the humorless girls living in the dorms. Someone – and Dale had a good idea who – had switched one key letter in the two displayed names on the girls' dormitories. The twelve-inch silver letters, about as thick as a horseshoe, were mounted on the brick front of the buildings. One dorm read HAYLEY; the other, EASGER. The clever prankster had removed the Y from Hayley and G from Easger and switched them. The result: HAGLEY and EASYER.

The newspaper photographer, Ansel Van Dyke, got a picture of both dorms before campus maintenance men restored the letters to their proper place. The crime took place sometime in the early morning of Saturday, several hours after Pow-Wow. The funny thing was that no one noticed the switch until Sunday evening. The maintenance guys didn't make the change until Monday morning. So, for more than one full day everyone could walk over and laugh at the new names for the girls dorms. The name change sparked several witticisms, the best being, "were the girls of Easyer really "easier" or was it just more false advertising?"

Several people asked Dale whom he suspected of perpetrating the prank. Some, of course, suspected he'd done it or been in on it. He said he had no idea. However, he knew Rusty worked as a carpenter and had a number of useful tools in the trunk of his car. Also, there were few pranksters with the clever eye of Rusty. Dale had no proof, of course. Apparently, no one did. The pranksters had struck in the dead of night, hours past curfew, and so swiftly that the night watchman hadn't caught sight of them.

Dale couldn't quite smile at the two photographs. Nothing was particularly funny to him of late. He went over and sat down in his mobile chair. Even skating around the office didn't cheer him up. He grabbed a Nerf ball and tossed it into the basket mounted on the side of the wall. Rusty had done the honors for that, too. The walls in the newspaper office were fairly tall and the Nerf basket stood eight feet high, low enough so Dale could easily dunk.

He'd tried calling Amanda the next day after Pow-Wow in her dorm room. She hadn't been in. She usually went home for Saturday afternoons. He thought about calling her at her home, but he decided to wait until early evening and call the dorm again. They were supposed to have a date that night. He called around six. Hope answered the phone and said Amanda wasn't in her room. He called several more times and each time another girl answered and said she wasn't in. Dale didn't believe them. He told Mary Jane, who answered the last time, that he knew she was in. He told her to tell Amanda he called and for her to call him back. Mary Jane just said good-bye in a huffy voice.

He'd tried calling Sunday afternoon after work. He usually picked her up at her dorm for Sunday night service. He got the same treatment when he called Sunday. Dale didn't bother going to church that evening. He knew she'd be surrounded by Mary Jane, Hope, and Gretchen. He doubted if he could even get close enough to apologize to her.

Since Dale didn't have any classes with her, it was easy not to see her Monday. He even went to lunch at the time she usually did, noon, but he didn't see her. He waited in the lunchroom longer than he usually did, too, feeling foolish sitting by himself after Chris and Rusty left.

The same results Tuesday. That night, after his poetry writing class, he walked over to Hayley and went to the desk. As luck would have it, Shirley, the redheaded music major that Dale had teased into believing he was a sex maniac, was on duty. She stared at him like he was there to attack her. He explained that he'd just been joking around. He really wasn't a piccolo player. Could she please notify Amanda that she had a guest?

Shirley told him he better leave or she'd call security.

Dale didn't want to leave. After a little more discussion, Mrs. Hester, the dorm mother, appeared and told him if a young woman didn't want to see him, then there wasn't any way anyone could make her. She said it in a pleasant way. She even smiled. He shrugged and left. He felt like a fool as three girls sitting in the parlor stared at him as he stalked out.

Dale decided it was best not to force a face-to-face meeting. Since Amanda didn't want to speak to him on the phone either, he had decided to write her a letter. He wrote a relatively short letter telling her that, one, he loved her; two, he didn't want to hurt her; three, if his loving her hurt her, then maybe she was right not to see him anymore. All he knew, not seeing her hurt him. But if their being apart made her feel better, then he'd try to bear the pain. Then he added one more sentence: *you light up my life.* He knew it was corny, but he thought it might work.

Along with the letter, he thought about sending her a dozen red roses; he'd that once before, on her birthday last year. He'd sent them to her dorm and she had told him how impressed all the girls were. But this time, he didn't think he should. Instead, he went to the florist and ordered just one red rose. The florist, a small middle-aged lady, said they couldn't deliver just one rose. Dale asked, why? Because the purchase was too small. He asked how much he had to spend to get a delivery. The woman said five bucks. The rose only cost one dollar. So, Dale said he'd pay five bucks but he still only wanted one red rose delivered. The small woman said very well and sent the flower to Amanda.

That had been yesterday. Dale still hadn't heard anything from her. He'd decided not to call her or try to see her. She knew how he felt. It was up to her to respond.

He went over to his desk and sat down and rested his chin in the palm of his hand in a mopey way. He didn't know what he'd do if Amanda broke up with him for good. Maybe he'd transfer to another college. Maybe he'd drop out and join the navy. All he knew was he didn't think he could be on the same campus if he couldn't be with her.

Dale heard a light rapping on the half closed door and looked up. Mary Jane walked in. She looked startled when she saw him sitting at his desk. She said sorry to interrupt. She was supposed to meet Rowena here. He said she could come in and wait if she wanted. Rowena should be here in a few minutes.

Mary Jane frowned a little, but she walked past the desk counter into the work area. Mary Jane was a business major like Rowena. Sometimes they worked together on class projects. Mary Jane occasionally came into the office and used Rowena's nice Selectric typewriter.

Mary Jane sat down in Rowena's chair. She glanced uneasily at Dale. He guessed she didn't like being around him. He didn't think she disliked him. They'd never spoken much in high school but that was because he'd been shy. He'd always liked her. Even when he thought she was on the skinny side, he thought she was pretty. She wasn't stuck up or unkind to anybody. But ever since he started going to GNC, Dale got the feeling that Mary Jane disapproved of him.

Mary Jane noticed him staring at her. She asked how he was.

"Not good," he said.

"I'm sorry to hear that."

"Are you?"

She gave him an offended look. "Well, of course."

When Dale continued to stare at her, she turned away.

"Look, Dale," she said, "if I've been acting a little strange toward you, it's not because I dislike you."

"Then what is it?"

Mary Jane glanced at him, then looked away. "I just don't want you to hurt Amanda the way you hurt Wendy."

Dale thought it was something like that.

"Well, that makes two of us," he said.

Mary Jane glanced at him again but didn't say anything.

"You told Amanda about seeing me talking with Wendy at your New Year's Eve party, didn't you?"

"Yes."

"Why did you do that? You knew my talking to Wendy didn't mean anything."

"Maybe it meant something to Wendy."

"Mary Jane, I don't know what qualifies you to be organizing everyone's life."

She stared at him.

"You don't know what's going on inside me any more than you knew what was going on inside Rusty."

"That's not fair," she said.

"Maybe not. But I care about Amanda more than anything else in the world. I don't want to hurt her. I just want her to know that."

Mary Jane looked at Dale but said nothing. He thought she didn't look as offended or defiant as she had before. Then the door opened and Rowena walked in.

"Oops," she said, noticing their serious expressions.

"It's all right," Mary Jane said.

She got up and walked over to Rowena. They both glanced at Dale. Rowena waved apologetically before they walked out.

Dale wondered why Mary Jane had broken up with Rusty. Rusty never talked much about it. He mentioned a couple of times that they argued over stuff. Where to go, what to do, who they should be around. Dale suspected that Mary Jane didn't like Rusty's wandering eye. He was easily distracted. But Dale didn't have that inclination. The only source of conflict between him and Amanda was how GNCish he was going to be. Amanda grew up a Nazarene, grew up dreaming of going to GNC like her parents; she wanted to be fully involved in the GNC culture. He didn't so much. He only went to the social activities to please Amanda.

Dale didn't know what was going to happen. He just knew he'd rather write a winning letter to Amanda than a winning essay for the *Daily Oklahoman*.

Somehow, the Omega Owls had won their relatively weak division and were now playing for the flag football championship against the formidable Alpha Avengers.

Omega had started the season strong, winning three straight, then hit a rough patch losing three in a row, before recovering to win their last four to finish 7-3. Alpha had easily won their division with a 9-1 record.

Dale thought Omega had a small chance. If Krupp could get the ball to him and Rusty, then they might score enough to match the powerful Alpha offense.

As with last year's championship game, the stands were packed with spectators. He thought it was a little strange that a couple of hundred people wanted to see a flag football game. But he had to admit that the crowd added some excitement to the game's atmosphere. Dale, who'd felt lethargic all day, now felt energized. Even without a lot of sleep or nourishment these past few days, he felt strong and fast, the result of adrenaline shooting through his veins.

Omega kept pace with Alpha during the first half. Rusty caught a touchdown pass in the first quarter and Dale scored on a kickoff return. Alpha, because they converted both their 2-point conversions led at half, 16-14. The two teams traded touchdown in the third quarter (Rusty scoring Omega's score with another TD grab) and going into the final quarter, Omega trailed Alpha, 22-20.

Alpha extended their lead in the fourth when Virgil Phelps threw a beautiful deep touchdown pass but the Avengers didn't convert the 2-point conversion. With five minutes remaining in the game, Omega still had a chance to tie and send the game into overtime. But on a sideline route, Rusty sprained his ankle after catching a pass and trying to make a cut on the slippery grass. He tried playing a few more plays, but it was no use. Dale watched him limp off, gritting his teeth.

Krupp moved Chris from tight end to Rusty's spot at split end. Somehow Krupp's wobbly passes to Dale and Chris found their mark and the Owls moved the ball into Alpha territory. Then, on third and two, Dale suggested they go deep and surprise Alpha. Krupp agreed. Dale lined up like he was going short, but took off down field. Krupp heaved the ball, but as usual, not far enough. Dale stopped his route, raced back, and jumped. Phelps jumped, too, and somehow his elbow hit Dale on the nose. Another Alpha guy collided with both of them and all three collapsed on the ground. Somehow, Dale wound up with the football. Phelps, still on the ground, reached over and pulled out his flag, which was a smart play because technically Dale could have jumped up and ran.

But he wasn't in any condition to jump up and run. He fell hard on his back, whipping his head against the turf. Blood spurted from his nose from Phelps's blow. He lay on the ground, feeling dizzy, blood running down his face.

Phelps bent over him and asked if he were okay. He said he didn't mean to elbow him in the face. Dale said he knew that. Just one of those things.

Phelps and Eugene helped him to his feet. Dale felt groggy. He used his flag to wipe the blood off his face. His nose kept on bleeding, though. He'd always been susceptible to nosebleeds as a kid. Sometimes, his nose bled without being hit at all. Once, while playing little league baseball, his nose started bleeding just before a grounder was hit to him at short. The ball took a bad hop and hit him in the face. When Dale recovered, he grabbed the ball and felt blood smeared all over it. The ump had to call time and replace the ball.

Now, Dale ambled off the field to the water fountain to wash the blood off his face.

Afterwards, he tilted his head up and tried to stop the bleeding. He used his yellow flag and held it against his nose.

By the time the bleeding stopped, the game was over. Omega, for the second straight year, lost the championship to Alpha. The score 28-20.

The Alpha guys were gracious in victory. They shook hands with the Omega guys and even asked Dale and Rusty about their injuries. Dale remembered Henshaw inviting him to join the Alpha team before the season began. If he had, he would have been on a championship team for the first time in his life.

Dale and Chris walked over to see how Rusty was doing. He sat on the bench, looking glum. He said basketball practice began next week. Dale shook his head. He knew Rusty shouldn't have risked injury by playing flag football but he didn't say anything. Without him, the Owls wouldn't have had a chance to make the playoffs.

Chris told Dale he had blood all over his jersey. Dale looked down and saw his jersey streaked with blood. Not yet dry, the red blotches looked moist and ugly but blended in with the red jersey. He hadn't realized he'd bled that much. He had a bad headache, too, from banging his head on the ground.

Dale and Chris said they'd help Rusty to his car. Rusty threw his long arms around their shoulders and leaned on them as they slowly walked to his Chevy. As they entered the parking lot, Dale saw Mary Jane, Gretchen, Hope, and Amanda leaning against Mary Jane's little car. She'd parked her Subaru two spaces away from Rusty's Malibu. For a moment, Dale felt angry. He almost thought they'd come out to see Omega lose. But as he, Rusty, and Chris drew near, he saw that the girls weren't looking at them in a mocking or critical way. Amanda, in particular, looked concerned.

As Dale and Chris deposited Rusty on the hood of his car, he heard the girls say "hi" and "you guys played good." He felt annoyed again. He hated it when girls told him he played good when he lost. He glanced over to the four of them and tried not to look too directly at Amanda. He saw her looking at him in an expectant way. It reminded Dale of the way Wendy used to look at him. Her expression sort of annoyed him, but he told himself he was being perversely proud. After all, he wanted Amanda to look at him in that way.

Mary Jane asked Rusty how his ankle was. He frowned at her and said it was okay. Chris asked Rusty if he needed any assistance driving home. He said no. His ankle was feeling better. Plus, his car was an automatic so he didn't need to use his left foot.

Chris said okay and walked over to the girls and asked if anyone needed an escort back to Hagley or Easyer? The girls didn't laugh. Rusty and Dale tried not to grin. Chris said sorry. Did anyone need an escort back to their dorms? Hope said she did. Gretchen said she'd walk with them until she found K. C. The three of them left and Dale watched them walk away, then glanced at Rusty. Rusty didn't look like he was in much pain now. He bobbed his eyebrows in a comically suggestive way.

Dale looked over to Amanda and Mary Jane. The two girls leaned against the front of the car and didn't look at them. Rusty nodded his head at them, encouraging Dale to make his move. He still felt a little irritated. His pride was hurt. He'd lost the championship game and got bloodied in the process and now he thought Amanda simply felt sorry for him. But he knew it was a chance to get back with her, so he fought that perversely proud feeling and walked over to her. As he did, Mary Jane left her spot and walked over to Rusty.

Amanda didn't look at him until he said hi. Then she asked was he hurt?

"No, just a nose bleed. Nothing serious."

"I saw Virgil hit you on the nose."

"Just an accident. One of the hazards of playing football."

"You bled a lot."

"Well, I have that tendency."

Dale moved closer and leaned against the car, not too close to Amanda.

She looked down at the ground. "I got your letter. And the flower."

Dale waited.

"It was a nice note. It made me feel better."

"I'm glad."

She glanced at him, a small smile on her face. "You light up my life?"

Dale grinned at the corniness of it all. Then he grew serious. "Well, you do."

He reached for her hand. She let him take it. He asked her if she wanted to walk over to his car. She nodded. Dale looked over at Rusty and Mary Jane. They were engaged in some fruitful discussion, too. Mary Jane laughed at something Rusty said. Dale decided not to interrupt. He gently pulled Amanda upright and they walked down the parking lot to his Chevy.

They didn't say anything until Dale started to open the door for Amanda. She turned to him and said she missed him. He said he missed her, too. Then he reached for her and they embraced. She whispered in his ear that she thought the one flower was a very nice touch.

Dale drew back enough to look in her eyes. She looked happy enough, although in an odd, almost reluctant way. He glanced around and then kissed her softly and briefly on the lips. She smiled a little and Dale opened the door for her and she got in. He walked over to his side, got in, started the car, and drove it out of the parking lot.

He asked if she'd like to go to West Oaks for a Coke and she said yes but she couldn't stay out late. Then she said, "oh, goodness."

Dale glanced over and saw her looking at a smudge of blood on her white sweater.

He told her he was sorry. He'd forgot he had blood all over his jersey. Amanda said it was okay. It was old, anyway. He felt badly. He knew she was sort of finicky about her clothes. Dale said he owed her two articles of clothing now.

"What do you mean?" Amanda asked.

"Your sweater and your bridesmaid dress. I ruined that, too."

Amanda heard the dejected note in his voice and she leaned over and hugged his arm.

"You didn't ruin anything."

"Oh, yeah?"

"Oh yeah," she said, mocking his gruff voice. She leaned her head against his shoulder as he drove.

"Dale, I just want to say one thing."

He waited.

"We have to be careful."

"I know."

"I mean not just about *that*. I mean careful about getting too emotionally wrapped up."

"I think it's too late for that, Amanda. At least for me."

"I know," she said, her fingers pressing into the muscle of his arm. "But I don't want to feel that I have to make a decision between you and God."

Dale almost smiled, but he knew she was serious. He said she shouldn't worry. She wouldn't have to.

"Really?"

"That's right. From now on, I'll be good."

Amanda hugged his arm. Dale meant what he said. But he knew that it wouldn't be easy.

**Chapter 5: *Ramakrishna introduced; demon records; prediction at Revival***

Dale stopped by the newspaper office before going to his Chaucer class. He'd decided to take Chaucer and Shakespeare for his last two upper-division English requirements. Next semester, he'd take Shakespeare, a class he was looking forward to. He'd read a few

Shakespeare plays in high school, and more out of class, but he knew he needed tutelage to fully appreciate them.

Dale glanced over the letters to the editor. As usual, more were critical than favorable. Several letters questioned his decision to print photographs of the prank on the girls' dorms and The Stomp. He wondered why so many people lacked a sense of humor. One letter said the dorm prank was insensitive and indecent. He supposed there was some truth to that accusation; that's why it was funny. Another letter, from Short, said the photograph of The Stomp suggested that dancing was permissible on campus when, in fact, all forms of dancing were forbidden. Dale could sort of understand a religious school forbidding the tango and the twist, or for that matter, the Charleston – but The Stomp? It hardly qualified as a dance. It was more like a nervous breakdown.

Some people thought Dale was producing an interesting campus paper. Henshaw and Abigail often defended the paper during stuco meetings whenever Short complained or, more often, said he "heard" other people complaining. Sharon was on his side. So were Jenny and Coop. Professor Cooper often complimented him on the creativity on display in the paper. Dale thought there was really just a handful of reactionaries on campus that thought all expression should be strictly religious and any deviation of that was a sin.

He knew Aaron Short was in the reactionary camp, but Aaron was too smooth to make obvious his allegiance. Rather than complain openly, he tended to express his "concern." Short had started his own small publication, a devotional pamphlet called "His Time." Short had asked Dale if he'd mind putting the pamphlet in *Smoke Signals* as a supplement. Dale said he didn't mind. All Short had to do was come by around five in the morning after they got the press run from the printer and stuff the pamphlets in seven hundred tabloid newspapers. Short had said he needed to reconsider his idea.

Dale left the office and strode through campus to Chester Hall. He arrived just as the Chaucer class was starting. Polly, Teri, Sharon, Hawkins, Fish, Rosalind Webb, and three other girls, the two plain girls he'd had in his poetry class, Charlotte and Emily, and a friend of theirs, also not especially pretty, named Anne, were already sitting at their desks. Dr. Frost, an older female professor with puffed up silver hair, small, twinkling light blue eyes, a small round nose, and a small mouth, placidly sat at her desk at the front of the classroom.

"Glad you've decided to join us," she said.

When she spoke Dale noticed that her two front teeth were considerably larger than the rest of her teeth. They weren't quite buck teeth. They didn't stick out of her mouth or anything, but they, along with her other facial features, gave Dr. Frost a rabbity appearance. Actually, she looked cuter than that. More like a fluffy bunny because she wore frilly, soft dresses and her hair had an almost furry look to it.

Dale, as he often had to do, resisted an impulse to say, "what's up, doc?" Instead, he said, "sorry if I'm late."

He took his usual seat at the desk in the back of the room. Dr. Frost reminded Dale that it was his time to lead the class in a brief devotional and prayer. He'd almost not taken the class because he'd heard that Dr. Frost required an even more elaborate pre-class ritual than the other professors. He could sort of understand such displays of piety in a religion class, but this was an English lit class. Still, he'd wanted to take Chaucer. He didn't think he could understand it on his own. Unfortunately, he didn't think Dr. Frost was that cogent of a reader of Chaucer, especially *The Canterbury Tales*. In fact, she'd completely skipped the Miller's Tale, the tale that he liked best. He knew why. It was indecent. He'd told Coop about that during his independent study session and the old professor had nodded and smiled. He and Dale discussed the tale for a while. Professor Cooper liked that tale as well. In fact, Dale had deduced that Coop had an appreciation for some of the bawdy humor in literature. They'd talked about the ribald comedy in Boccaccio and Rabelais as well as *Tom Jones* when he and Dale discussed that novel last year.

Dale now looked for his piece of paper that had his devotional message written on it. He found it and walked to the front of the class and stood at the small podium. He hated doing this kind of stuff. He glanced at his audience. He noticed Teri sort of smirking at him. He wondered if she knew what he was about to do.

He said he wanted to read a short passage from a book he'd sort of stumbled on. He thought it was interesting. It wasn't the usual kind of devotional message, but he thought in a literature class such as theirs, the passage from Ramakrishna might provide some food for thought. Dale read the following:

> Different people call on God by different names.
> Some as Allah, some as God, and others as Krishna,
> Siva, and Brahman. It is like the water in a lake. Some
> drink it at one place and call it jal; others at another
> place and call it pani; and still others at a third place
> and call it water. The Hindus call it jal, the Christians
> water, and the moslems pani. But it is one and the
> same thing.

As he concluded, still looking at his paper, he felt the heat of several affronted gazes on his face. But when he asked them to bow their heads, he glanced up and saw that all had complied. He said a short, conventional prayer. He didn't want to pray to Allah or Brahman. After all, he was a Christian. But he wanted to let his classmates know that he agreed with Ramakrishna that "as many faiths, so many paths."

When he finished, he walked back to his desk and ignored the stare of Fish. The three girls he didn't know well, Charlotte, Emily, and Anne, gaped at him. Polly and Sharon gave him more discreet, astonished looks. Hawkins sort of grinned. And when he sat down, Teri, sitting beside him in the last row, gave him an inquiring look.

He wondered if she thought he was reading Ramakrishna just to rebel or play a joke. He wasn't. He did come across the passage in a book about literature and religion. Dale found Ramakrishna's ideas interesting. He especially liked his idea about the unity of all religion. He liked the assertion that "truth is one but sages call it by different names." Another idea he liked was that various religions are different ways to reach The Absolute and that the Ultimate Reality could never be expressed in human terms.

But as he read further, he came to one idea he didn't agree with. Ramakrishna believed that sensual desire was part of the dark forces, or "avidyamaya," that struggled with the higher forces, or the "vidyamaya." Evil passions, like greed, lust, and cruelty, entrapped people in the cycle of birth and death. Those evil passions must be fought. With the help of vidyamaya, people could eventually rid themselves of them and also eliminate "maya" or illusion from their lives. They could actually move to a higher plane of consciousness.

Dale agreed that greed, lust, and cruelty were evil passions. But he didn't think sensual desire was. He also didn't know how one could break the cycle of birth and death. After reading several hundred pages, he decided his mind was too western. He didn't feel comfortable with the detachment and the passivity of eastern religions. But he did think they were valid approaches to reach The Absolute and the Ultimate Reality for others.

Dr. Frost thanked Dale for his unusual devotional reading. He could tell she was a little embarrassed in the same way she'd be embarrassed if the class discussed the Miller's Tale. She was a kind, polite woman so he knew she wouldn't chastise him in front of the class.

While they discussed the Wife of Bath's Tale, Dale turned his unexpurgated text to the Miller's Tale. Even in middle English, Dale knew the passage he read would be judged obscene by most in the class. But he reread it anyway.

> Derk was the night as pich or as the cole,
> and at the window out she putte hir hole,

And Absalom, him fil nobet ne wers,
But with his mouth he kiste hir naked ers,
Full savoury, er he were war of this.
Abak he sterte, and thoughte it was amis,
For wel he wiste a womman hath no beerd.
He felt a thing al rough and longe yherd,
And saide, "Fy, allas, what have I do?"

Dale remembered the next line. Alisoun, the young, pretty, and unfaithful wife to old, rich Absalom, says, "tee-hee." Dale almost laughed out loud imagining the naughty wench saying such as silly thing after sticking her bottom out the window to be kissed by her foolish husband.

More scurrilous comedy followed, but Dale preferred the Alisoun scene. His imagination grew bold and he imagined Amanda instead of Alisoun and, of course, had to mentally rewrite the scene so he wouldn't be some old cuckold. He was in the middle of enjoying his R-rated scene when Dr. Frost asked him a question about the Wife of Bath tale: how did this tale contrast with the Clerk's Tale that the class had read last week. Dale said, sorry. He hadn't been listening. Dr. Frost refrained from scolding him and repeated her question and he answered satisfactorily.

After class, Teri walked with him and waited until they were out of the building to ask him a one-word question:

"*Ramakrishna?*"

Dale tried to explain how he'd come across this Hindu saint and how he liked most of his ideas. He thought his classmates should hear some new ideas. After all, hadn't they heard about the mercy of God and the ultimate sacrifice of Jesus many times before? In some ways, he thought it strange they had to hear the same ideas over and over. He didn't necessarily disagree with the ideas, he just found the repetition of them – he said the word – boring.

Teri shook her head. She said he better not advertise such notions.

Dale told her another interesting idea from Ramakrishna. He said when God consciousness falls short, traditions become dogmatic and oppressive and religious teachings lose their transformative power.

"That's what you think?" she asked. "You think the college's traditions have become dogmatic and oppressive?"

"It's not so much the college's traditions. It's more the lack of intellectual and spiritual curiosity on campus. A lot of people aren't willing or capable to see beyond its borders. If they can't see beyond the boundaries of their own time and place, then how can they get in touch with the transformative?"

Teri smiled but she still shook her head. "I think you're taking all of this stuff too seriously."

Dale shrugged. Maybe he was.

Teri said she had to go. He said so long. They parted and he walked back to the student union. On his way, he saw Sylvester Fish talking to Dr. Petry on the other side of the quad. Dale noticed the two of them gazing at him as he walked by.

He realized he could have introduced Ramakrishna to campus at a better time. After all, fall revival was starting tonight.

Dale sat in the back of the auditorium at Van Brocklin Hall with Rusty and Chris and scrutinized Barry Richardson. He was of average height, chubby, with rather short shiny brown hair. A curl hung over his broad forehead. He had a round head with boyish features: button-like eyes, a short, round nose, and a small, smiling mouth. The longer Dale stared at him, the more Barry Richardson began to resemble the Big Boy cartoon character. The forehead curl was the defining touch. If Richardson cut it off or combed his hair differently, then the similarity wouldn't have been nearly as pronounced.

The large auditorium, used for the required chapel during the school week, was about half filled. Not bad attendance, thought Dale, although he thought even more college kids would attend. After all, Richardson was here to denounce rock music. He'd been fulminating about the demon influence in rock music for about thirty minutes so far. He'd played examples, which was the most entertaining part of the talk. Richardson said some of the biggest names in rock were guilty of demon influence in their music and lyrics. He played songs from the Rolling Stones, Led Zeppelin, Alice Cooper, Jefferson Starship, Kiss, Pink Floyd, Steely Dan, and, of course, the Blue Oyster Cult. Richardson even castigated the Eagles for their *Hotel California* album and song. That was a mistake. The Eagles were the most popular secular group on campus. A dozen students got up and left.

Richardson had condemned rock music on two counts: the music itself, with its excessive emphasis on rhythm; and the content of the lyrics, which made subtle and overt references to the occult, pagan mysticism, and demon worship.

Dale understood the part about lyrics, but he didn't quite understand the music part. Richardson said the emphasis on rhythm in rock music resulted in overstimulation and excessive physicality. Such music appealed to the baser instincts. The heavy rhythmic nature of rock music was derived from African demon worship. Enslaved Africans brought their voodoo rituals and drum-oriented music to the New World. Over time that demon-based music gradually insinuated itself into the larger culture. This style of music became popular with the rock 'n' roll revolution in the '50s. Since then, the rhythm part of popular music has become increasingly emphasized, leading to overt demon influence. In contrast to rhythm and its connection to the body, the mind responds to harmony and the spirit responds to melody. With the de-emphasis of harmony and melody in contemporary music, rhythm and its assault on the spiritual began to grow and demonology flourished.

Dale got somewhat lost in all the technical discussion of music. His mind began to wander. He remembered what Eugene had told him yesterday about Barry Richardson. He said he was the son of a famous rock 'n' roller from the '50s. His father had died in a plane crash. Barry had been just a little kid and he now thought his father had died because of the demonic influence of rock music. Dale had tried to think who Barry Richardson's father could be. Off hand, he didn't remember any Richardson in '50s-era rock. So he spent part of the afternoon looking up a connection. One possibility was found in the crash of Buddy Holly's plane. Not only did the rockabilly star die, but so had Richie Valens and the "Big Bopper," whose real name was J. P. Richardson. Could Barry Richardson be the son of the Big Bopper? Was the man now standing before them and denouncing rock music really Barry the "Little Bopper"?

The idea amused Dale. He tried not to smile or else he might be accused of being possessed by a demon.

For a pudgy guy, Richardson was an energetic speaker. He paced back and forth, varied the loudness and pitch of his voice skillfully, gave animated expressions, and performed with theatrical flair. And that, too, was one of the reasons why Dale doubted him. Everything about him seemed exaggerated and thus his message seemed less credible.

Richardson, after exposing the hidden and not-so-hidden demonic references and influences in the albums he had on display, then asked all the people who had these albums to raise their hands. Rusty didn't raise his, although Dale had first heard "(Don't Fear) the Reaper" while riding in his car. Instead, Chris raised his hand. Dale wondered which of the wicked albums he possessed. Chris didn't like hard rock; he liked country. But Dale remembered he had Eagles' records. Maybe he had *The Hotel California* album. Dale had heard the hit single. But he remembered the song seemed more anti-demon than pro-demon. The Eagles didn't exactly endorse staying in the Hotel California.

Dale didn't raise his hand because he didn't have any of those albums. The only current groups or musicians he liked a lot were Bruce Springsteen, The Manhattan Transfer, and The Alan Parsons Project. Richardson hadn't mentioned them.

Then he remembered he did have one album by one of the targeted groups: *Dragonfly* by the Jefferson Starship. Cleoma had given him that album along with a Zombies album for some duplicitous reason. Hmmm. Did that mean Cleoma was a demon? He rather liked to think so. But no, he suspected she was just a conniving woman trying to get him to like her as part of her strategy to hook Blackie.

Richardson then asked all those who had raised their hands, about fifty kids, to come down to the front. Dale glanced at Rusty, who rolled his eyes. But to his Dale's surprise, Chris got up and walked down to the front of the auditorium.

Dale watched Chris gather with the other musical sinners. Richardson then told the rest of the audience that on Friday night, after the final revival service, he would destroy demon-inspired records. He asked everyone to contribute. Don't go out and buy such evil stuff. They should bring the demon records they already had and allow Barry Richardson to smash them to hell where they belonged.

Dale and Rusty thought that sounded fun. They grinned at each other and nodded. At last: something to look forward to.

Then Richardson said a brief prayer, asking God to cleanse the hearts and minds of all present and that they not be tempted to listen to wicked music.

Dale and Rusty decided not to wait for Chris. No telling how long he'd be. As they left, Dale thought Chris and the others had been tricked. Once Richardson got him and the others to raise their hands, they were almost compelled to come down to the front.

Outside, Dale asked Rusty what he thought of Richardson's arguments. Rusty said it was rot. Music was music. Just because he listened to some of that music didn't mean he was influenced by demons. Dale agreed. He thought even though Richardson had made some valid points, he'd exaggerated and taken things out of context.

Dale suspected that Ramakrishna would consider much of rock music as part of the avidyamaya, or dark forces. Dale didn't like a lot of the current music, but it was more on aesthetic grounds rather than for religious reasons. He preferred the '60s rock music because he thought it was better; that era had more musical variety: Brill building, Sun records, Motown, the British Invasion – a whole efflorescence of sound. And that music was more fun. Today's music sounded sort of pretentious or depressing and, in the case of disco, vacuous. But since he didn't know much about music – he'd never even played an instrument – he knew he didn't have any expertise to make a sound judgment.

He and Rusty encountered three members of Aaron's Rod: Eugene, Hawkins and Putney. Rusty asked them what they thought of Richardson's screed. Eugene, who looked troubled, just shook his head. Hawkins said he'd oversimplified the issue. All music was rhythmic. He didn't think more rhythm resulted in depravement. Dale thought he'd made a good point. He told Hawkins he'd like him to write a column for the student newspaper about the issue. David said he'd like to but he was pressed for time. Basketball season was about to start. Dale said he'd help him if he needed it. Hawkins then agreed.

Putney, growing bored with the discussion, began beating imaginary drums. He started slowly, then began banging them like he was possessed with, well, demons. Rusty laughed and joined in. The two of them engaged in a manic drum duet for several minutes while Dale and Hawkins watched with amusement. Eugene, however, walked away. Dale knew what was troubling him. As a minister-to-be, he had to take such issues seriously. The fact he was in a rock band, even if it played Christian contemporary music, made the issue even more difficult for him.

When Rusty and Putney concluded their drum session, Hawkins said he had to go. Dale watched him head in the same direction as Eugene. Putney then suggested they go over to his pad – he lived off campus – and listen to some demon music. Rusty said great idea, man. Dale said he wanted to wait for Chris. Rusty slapped Dale on the shoulder and said he'd see him later. Then he and Putney ambled off and Dale heard Rusty ask Putney if he'd ever listened to "Electric Aunt Jemima." Putney said, what's that, man? And Dale heard Rusty singing it in his weird falsetto, which actually sounded a bit like the voice on the song, as they walked out of hearing range.

Dale walked back to Van Brocklin Hall and saw Chris coming out. He asked Chris why he'd gone down to the front.

"After I raised my hand, I sort of felt I had to," he said.

Dale resented Richardson for that tactic. He thought it was sneaky if not dishonest. He asked Chris what "bad" records he had besides *Hotel California*.

"That's it. But Barry said just about any rock record qualified as demon inspired if it has a heavy enough beat."

"Yeah, I heard. What else did Barry tell you?"

"He want us to help him smash the records, unless he gets a steamroller."

"A steamroller?"

"He said that works best. He can crush a lot more records with a lot less effort."

"I'll bet."

"You know, maybe he's right about all that stuff. But there's one problem."

"What's that?"

"I don't have enough rock albums." Chris looked at Dale and smiled sheepishly. "So, could I borrow some of yours?"

"Borrow? If you borrow them, Chris, they'll be smashed to pieces. What are you going to do? Give me back the shards?"

Chris nodded his head. "Good point."

They started walking towards Chris's dorm when Chris stopped. "You think Rusty would let me borrow some of his?"

Dale shook his head in bemusement.

Daniel Ransom Johnson's dark eyes seemed to be peering straight at Dale. The evangelist's furrowed brow, his jutting jaw, his pointing finger, gave him awesome authority. He gazed at Dale and all of the other sinners. He said, you are damned unless you repent of your sins, ask forgiveness, and surrender your soul to Jesus. If not, your soul will be consigned to the everlasting flames of hell.

Dale had heard such words before, but never delivered with such conviction and theatrical force. Daniel Ransom Johnson spoke with fervor. He pounded the podium. He spread his muscular arms wide. He cupped his large, powerful hands in supplication. His bold-featured, handsome face had such a noble look to it that Dale thought it should be stamped on a coin. His rather longish black hair, worn swept back, eventually fell in thick strands just above his eyes as he preached. He often used one of his large hands to sweep the stray locks off his forehead, while not missing a beat in his rhythmic harangue. His heavy but not oppressive brows narrowed when emphasizing sin, then raised heavenward when describing the splendors of heaven. His dark eyes flashed with intensity. Unusually large, his eyes seemed to penetrate into the collective souls of the faithful gathered in the First Church for the last night of revival. His long, straight nose led to a wide, full-lipped mouth, which might have given him a somewhat effeminate look save for his powerful jaw line, strong chin, and the faint outline of a heavy beard on his clean-shaven face.

Dale had never heard so eloquent and dynamic a speaker. Even Dr. Prescott didn't have the majesty of Daniel Ransom Johnson's deep, expressive voice. It could boom like a bass drum or gradually fade to a warm intimate whisper within a few words.

The evangelist put his whole self into his speaking. Last night, he got so worked up, he tossed off his dark suit jacket, unashamed to show the congregation the sweaty saddlebags underneath his arms. Then he rolled up his sleeves, showing sinewy forearms.

So far tonight, Daniel Ransom Johnson had simply loosened his plain red tie twice. Now,

546

it hung so slackly from his neck that it looked like he was wearing an upside down noose.

Dale leaned back in his seat and considered the appeal of the evangelist. It was simple. He was a tall, handsome, virile man who spoke with an impressively resonant voice and delivered his simple message with intensity and eloquence.

But there was something more. He had charisma. Dale knew the term meant gift of God's grace. The term came from the Greek. *Charis*: grace, beauty, kindness. The more he thought about origin of the word, the more he thought he was partly wrong. The evangelist certainly had grace and a masculine beauty. But Dale doubted the kindness part.

Dale discreetly glanced around. The audience seemed transfixed. Hundreds of people packed the sanctuary of the immense First Church. He doubted this many people attended the church for the Christmas Eve or Easter service. Daniel Ransom Johnson had brought out not only the Nazarenes of the college and town, but he'd attracted hundreds of more people. Dale thought that was what a talented evangelist was supposed to do – and talent was almost an understatement to describe the powers of Daniel Ransom Johnson.

Amanda, sitting to Dale's left, gazed in rapt attention at the evangelist. Past her, he saw Mary Jane and Rusty, Chris and Rowena. In the seats in front, he saw Hope and Hawkins, K. C. and Gretchen, Henshaw and Abigail. Somewhere farther down, he'd seen Eugene, Polly, Sharon, and Teri. Just about everybody Dale knew was present for the climactic Friday night service.

Dale looked more closely at Amanda. She had an almost beatific look on her face. She looked imbued with a spirit that gave her an ethereal beauty. Such a look made him wonder if a feeling of religious ecstasy that was the feeling she most cared about.

It wasn't that look that bothered him; not at all. He felt drawn to it. He'd always seen something of it in her face, even in the most mundane of situations. It was her serenity that he'd been attracted to in the first place. A spiritual beauty that he'd almost forgot about in his concentration on her fleshly beauty. What bothered him, though, was that look seemed to be inspired by the evangelist.

Dale turned his attention back to the evangelist. What struck him about Daniel Ransom Johnson was he seemed to be the opposite of what he ordinarily admired. Instead of being a man of breadth of vision, Johnson was a man of intense narrowness. And yet, Dale saw an advantage in such an approach. Such intensity with its laser-beam-like focus gave his words momentum and power that couldn't be achieved with a more balanced, nuanced, and broad-minded view. Dale disapproved intellectually of such an approach. But he recognized the mesmerizing appeal of that style. It was like admiring an immensely talented actor as he delivered a stunning performance in a play or film, but disliking the simplistic, manipulative story he performed in.

Before Daniel Ransom Johnson said it, Dale felt it. He felt something like a force spread itself throughout the atmosphere of the church. It was as if the air had became filled with rich oxygen. He knew everyone else sensed it, too. Perhaps it was the Holy Spirit descending upon them. Perhaps it was just their imaginations. But whatever the force was, it was powerfully present just as Daniel Ransom Johnson said these words:

"Brothers and sisters, the Time is imminent. I know the Time is always imminent in the sense that God is outside time. But for us believers, there comes a time when prophecy will be fulfilled. That time is before us. Tonight, those of you who become saved will be among those who will be delivered to Jesus into heaven. At the last minute, of the last hour, of the day our Savior rose from the dead and ascended into heaven, so all believers will meet Jesus in the Rapture.

"So, let us prepare for that meeting. Let us dedicate our lives anew to our joining Him in heaven, and the preparations we will make for his second coming.

"Those of you who haven't been saved, or who wish to rededicate yourself to His name, should leave your seats now and come forward. Come down. Come down. Come to me. Let me pray with you so you can be saved and be with Jesus. Come down and join the righteous who will meet our Lord and Savior on that appointed day."

The organist began to play the music for the altar call, but Daniel Ransom Johnson asked her not to play. He said, "please no music. No singing. Just listen to your heart. Let those brothers and sisters who haven't been saved yet or who need to rededicate themselves to Him to come in silence."

Daniel Ransom Johnson began to pray. Dale felt moved by his resonant baritone more than the words. His voice sounded like the deeper notes of an orchestra or the soft rumbling of thunder in the distance.

Scores of people left their seats. Dale watched them before the evangelist asked everyone to keep their heads bowed. Then he felt Amanda stir. He glanced at her and hoped she wouldn't go. She'd already been saved. There was no need for her to go to the altar yet again. She'd been there just last year with him.

But he felt her dress brush his knees on her way to the aisle. He watched her slowly walk to the altar, her ivory-colored, modestly cut dress flowing over her figure in a becoming way.

He felt strangely annoyed. He didn't want her to go. He heard Daniel Ransom Johnson's voice became even more deep and resonant and compelling. The evangelist used his voice as an instrument, and he played it like a virtuoso.

Dale noticed others leaving their seats. He didn't want to go. But he knew he couldn't allow Amanda to be on her own. He feared he'd lose her. He almost bolted out of his seat and walked swiftly down to the altar. He spotted her kneeling on the far right side. He was glad she'd walked farther to the right so she'd be less conspicuous. He walked over and kneeled beside her. She sensed he was there. She didn't glance at him, but she moved her body just slightly enough to tell him. He tried to pray. He glanced over and took in her closed eyes and her perfect lips moving so slightly they looked like they were vibrating. A light glow appeared on her cheeks, matching the faint crimson blush on her throat and neck.

Dale reached his hand over and lightly pressed it on her folded hands like she had done for him the year before. But he knew what he was doing wasn't genuine. He wasn't moved by spiritual concerns. He was motivated by earthly, even sensual concerns. He didn't want her to move so close to God that she left him behind.

Daniel Ransom Johnson finished the prayer. Dale heard the congregation say under their breaths in Jesus Christ's name, amen, but with the hushed force of over one thousand people.

Behind him, he heard people leaving their seats. They made excited, hushed sounds. Their whispers carried an enthusiasm of people who have been thoroughly entertained, emotionally moved, and spiritually satisfied.

Dale waited for Amanda to finish praying. Finally, she did. She said amen, and glanced at him. She smiled softly. Tears welled in her eyes but they did not fall. She slowly rose, and he rose with her, and tried to match her spiritually sated expression. He glanced farther down and saw the magnificent evangelist slowly moving their way, as he briefly paused to touch the head and hands of the supplicants or knelt and whispered a few encouraging words.

Dale wanted Amanda to leave before he arrived. He didn't want her to be in Daniel Ransom Johnson's powerful presence. He tried to prompt her to quicken her pace by taking a couple of swift steps ahead of her, but she moved slowly, patiently from the altar and he almost prayed for God to goose her.

They moved into the sanctuary where many people still gathered. He watched Amanda greet her friends. She hugged Gretchen, who also had visited the altar.

Dale lingered behind as Amanda walked over to her parents and greeted them. She hugged her mother. Then she turned and walked back to him, smiling joyously.

They made their way out of the church, Amanda slowing their progress with small chats with people she knew, including older adults. Dale gave them his customary nod and tried not to look as awkward as he felt.

They finally made it outside. Amanda looked at the dark sky filled with stars and a crescent moon and said isn't God great.

Dale said yes.

Amanda put her hand on his arm as they slowly walked down the sidewalk on their way back to campus. They saw Eugene walking opposite of them and they both said hi to him. Eugene smiled. He looked happy. He'd been saved again, too.

They walked in silence for a while, Dale not wanting to interrupt Amanda's feelings of jubilation. When she looked like she was back to normal, he asked her if she'd heard what the evangelist said about people meeting Jesus in heaven.

"Yes, I remember something about that," she said. "I have to admit that I was almost in a trance. I don't remember every word brother Johnson said."

"Yeah, well, those words were special. I think he predicted the date of the Rapture."

Amanda had a delighted look on her face. "Did he? I didn't hear. Oh, I wish I'd heard."

"I think he said this coming Easter."

Amanda shook her head in amazement. "That's wonderful, Dale. We'll soon be in heaven."

Dale stopped walking. He looked into her eyes.

"Amanda, don't you understand? He did something he's not supposed to do. You're not supposed to predict the Rapture or the Second Coming or anything like that."

"Why not?"

Now that they were standing outside in the brisk autumn night, breathing in the fresh air, and no longer contained in the intense atmosphere of the church, Dale felt his rational mind working at high speed.

"Because the Bible says that no man shall know the time of Jesus' return."

He felt pretty sure that was what the Bible said. He thought he remembered that passage from when he read the New Testament.

"Dale, are you sure? No one else mentioned that after the service."

"Everybody's still caught up in the euphoria. But when they stop and think about it, they'll realize that brother Johnson made a presumptuous statement, to say the least."

"Dale, I think you're sort of making a presumptuous statement."

"Okay, let's go find a religion professor. He'll tell you."

"Don't be silly."

"I'm not the one being silly."

"Oh, do you think I'm being silly?"

"Not you. I mean *Daniel Ransom Johnson*." Dale said the three names with more emphasis than he meant to.

"Now, that's an awful thing to say. Especially after an altar call and being saved again."

Dale knew this wasn't the time to argue with Amanda about all of this. He said okay. Maybe he was wrong. In fact, he did wonder if he'd heard right. How could a responsible minister, or an evangelist, make such a definite statement?

"Dale, you should feel wonderful."

"I do. I feel wonderful if you feel wonderful."

"I do feel wonderful. I'm just wondering if you do."

He patted her hand. "Believe me, I do."

She smiled and they were about to move on when they saw Rusty and Mary Jane walking toward them. Rusty hadn't said much about he and Mary Jane getting back together. He said they still hadn't gone out on an official date. They just did stuff together on campus. But Dale could tell that he was happy about it. He watched them approach. Rusty walked with a slight limp. Mary Jane smiled in the same spiritually satisfied way as Amanda.

"How are you two?" Amanda asked.

They both said fine. Amanda and Mary Jane started talking about the service and the people they saw there. Rusty came over to Dale and asked him if he were going to the record-busting party.

"Yeah, I guess. Are you?"

"Looking forward to it. Maybe next week we'll have some book burning."

They grinned at each other. Dale asked Rusty if he'd heard the evangelist say the Rapture was going to take place this coming Easter.

"Was that what he was talking about? I wasn't sure."

"But you heard him?"

"Yeah, man. I heard."

Dale told Amanda that Rusty had heard the evangelist predict the Rapture.

Mary Jane asked them what they were talking about. Dale told her. She said she didn't remember any such prediction. Dale wondered if Daniel Ransom Johnson had spoken in such a way that only men heard him predict when the Rapture was going to take place.

Rusty asked the girls if they wanted to go to the record-busting party.

"The what?" Mary Jane asked.

Rusty filled her and Amanda in. Both girls hadn't heard about Richardson's anti-demon music event. They didn't know if they wanted to go.

Rusty said it would be fun. Afterwards, they all could go to the college cafeteria for ice cream. Mary Jane and Amanda finally agreed.

They walked over to campus, to the large parking lot outside the college's concert hall. When the four of them arrived, they saw a fairly large crowd had already gathered. Dale estimated a couple of hundred college kids were present.

Dale, Amanda, Rusty, and Mary Jane squeezed their way into the spectators and watched Barry Richardson, standing in front of forty people holding albums, 45s, eight-track tapes, and cassette tapes, welcome them to God's response to demon influence in music. Richardson gave a brief talk, giving the basics about demon influence in rock music. Amanda glanced at Dale and he shrugged. It sounded even sillier now than it did three nights ago.

Richardson, his forehead curl still in place, accepted the Rolling Stones' album, *Goat's Head Soup*, from one of the participants, took the record out of the cover and sleeve, then broke it over his bent knee. Most of the people in the crowd cheered.

Richardson broke a couple more albums, then instructed his confederates to toss their records one by one on the ground. Dale spotted Chris standing near the back of the line, looking embarrassed to be holding only one album. As the college kids threw their music down on the asphalt, Richardson disappeared and a few seconds later, Dale heard the guttural sound of a diesel engine starting.

The crowd of record-tossers parted enough so that he could see Richardson on top of the big, black machine, manipulating it in preparation to getting it rolling.

"Man, look at that," Rusty said. "He's got a steamroller. That's pretty cool."

Amanda leaned closer to Dale. The crowd grew excited at the prospect of mass record destruction. She asked him what the man on the steamroller was going to do.

"He's going to crush the records."

"Oh, Dale, that's terrible."

He was glad she said that. He didn't like what was going on either. Even if the music was bad, he still didn't like seeing it destroyed. It didn't seem right to smash a creation, even an imperfect, if not corrupt, creation.

The more Dale thought about the whole issue, the more he thought Richardson had made a faulty argument. He thought the premise that rhythm was wicked inherently silly. How could something natural be bad? Plus, rhythm didn't necessarily excite bestial or animalistic impulses. Rhythm seemed an element that added energy to music. What was wrong with energy? As with anything, one could overdue it. Bad music was bad because it lacked balance or subtlety or creativity. It was bad because it was predictable. Perhaps a lot of contemporary music overdid rhythm, resulting in an unbalanced song. But he didn't think it was demon inspired.

And even if it were, should they destroy records in response? Dale thought it would be better to create and promote good music instead. Rather than records, he thought of something he knew better: books. Should people burn bad books? Not poorly written or thought-out books like *Hannah Horse*, but books that advocated evil ideals. The only book he could readily think of was *Mein Kampf*. He'd never read it, but he supposed it was an evil book. After all, it laid the "intellectual" foundation for the mass murder of Jews and others. Should they burn every copy of that book? He didn't think so. People shouldn't be afraid of ideas, even evil ideas. He thought they should fight them with good ideas. By destroying evil books or records, people were admitting they were afraid of them.

Richardson put the steamroller in gear. The crowd cheered. He slowly advanced it toward the scattered pile of records.

Amanda tugged on Dale's arm. "I don't like this. Let's go."

Dale said okay. He told Rusty they'd meet him and Mary Jane at the cafeteria.

"Hey, man," Rusty said. "You're missing the best part."

Dale said so long and Rusty shrugged. Mary Jane looked at them with an expression that said she'd rather be going with them, too. The crowd seemed to be getting a little raucous.

As Dale and Amanda walked away, they heard behind them cheers followed by the sickening sound of crunching. The steamroller's engine snorted, then they heard more busting. To Dale's ears, it sounded like breaking ice: sharp, sudden cracks.

The crowd cheered louder.

### Chapter 6: *Short and Fish; homecoming hi-jinx; a censoring paw*

Dale changed records. He took off *I Robot* and put on Jefferson Starship's *Dragonfly*. He didn't like the album much. The first song was okay. But he wanted to see if he could identify any demonic influences. He'd listened to it a couple of times yesterday, and he hadn't been able to detect any demon doings.

He sat in his rolling chair and pushed his feet against the floor and he and the chair flew across the room. He rolled so fast he bumped into the desk counter. He glanced across the room, concerned his accident might have made the record skip. "Ride the Tiger" roared along with missing a beat.

Dale had bought a new stereo and brought it into the newspaper office a week ago. Since he often worked or studied at the newspaper office until late in the evening, he thought he might as well listen to music. He also did it to annoy Short and Fish, who often hung out in the student council offices across the hall.

He heard a rapping on the half-closed door and he said come in. Aaron Short and Sylvester Fish appeared. Short motioned for him to turn down the volume on the stereo. Dale pushed against the floor, and he skated across the room on the chair. He turned the dial down. Then he got up and walked over to where the two young men stood in front of the desk counter.

"Burning the midnight oil, eh, Smith?" asked Short, with his usual broad smile.

Dale said not really. He was just goofing around.

"May I ask what record you're playing?" asked Fish.

Dale reached over and grabbed the album cover and showed it to Sylvester. Fish's beady eyes grew beadier as he examined the rather surreal cover of a creature that looked like part human, part dragonfly, and part space alien. Dale didn't much like the cover art either, but then he hadn't bought the record.

Fish gave Short a disapproving look.

"Smith, some people are concerned about the playing of such music," Short said.

"Some people? Or just you two?"

Fish puffed his cheeks and Short smiled.

"It's just part of a study I'm doing to determine the demon content of records," said Dale. "You know, like movie ratings. I thought I could rate records on the basis of how much demon influence is in them. Instead of a star system, I thought I'd use a pitchfork system. I'd say this album is three forks out of five."

"You shouldn't make fun of such concerns," said Short.

"Yes, Smith. Demons are real and at work in this world," said Fish.

Dale said nothing. He simply looked at the two of them. He didn't even raise an eyebrow.

It took a while for them to get the joke. Fish shook his head in pity while Short snorted.

"Another point before we leave," Short said. "Your editorial concerning revival week was excessively critical. Just because you don't value the work of Barry Richardson –"

"You mean Barry the Little Bopper."

"Excuse me?"

"Isn't Barry Richardson the illegitimate son of the Big Bopper?"

"The Big who?" asked Fish.

"The Big Bopper. You know, of "Chantilly Lace" fame. 'A wiggle in your walk, a giggle in your talk.'"

Fish and Short shook their heads in pity for the wayward Dale.

"I have no idea of what you're talking about, but we are going to leave," said Short.

"Don't go," said Dale. "We could talk more about the Big Bopper. You both might be interested in learning that his music has a very low demon content. Maybe half a pitchfork, tops."

Short and Fish said nothing as they exited the room, not even bothering to close the door. Dale walked across the room and turned up the volume on the stereo. He listened for a minute, then took the album off and then put on something good, *Born to Run*. He wondered when this Springsteen guy was going to release another album.

He heard a rapping on the outside twin window. He pushed open one half of the window and said hey to Rusty. Rusty asked who Dale been talking to. He told him.

"Oh, those two clowns," Rusty said.

The first time he'd met them, Rusty stood listening to them talk for five minutes about the religious organizations and activities available to incoming students. Suddenly, Rusty shrieked in an earsplitting falsetto and walked away. After Fish and Short recovered, they asked Dale why his friend had done that. He told them Rusty had a low tolerance for boredom, which was true. Sometimes while eating lunch in the school cafeteria, just out of sheer tedium, Rusty would stand up and do "the Shriek" and then calmly sit down as if nothing had happened.

"They're not clowns," Dale corrected in a mock serious voice. "They are pillars of society."

"More like pillows of society," Rusty said.

Dale grinned. He thought that was funny. Both Short and Fish had lumpy bodies like slept-on pillows.

Dale asked what was up. Rusty asked him if he was "in" on his latest prank. Dale said sure. Rusty said to meet at Putney's pad tomorrow night at 6:45. Then they'd all go to the homecoming game together. Dale said okay. Rusty said *adios* in his Spanish voice and disappeared into the night.

Dale closed the window and returned to his desk. Both Amanda and Mary Jane were involved in the homecoming festivities and weren't available to sit with at the game. He didn't mind so much. Whenever he watched the Chiefs' games with Amanda, she either bothered him by asking what was going on because she still didn't understand basketball strategy or she talked with Mary Jane or Hope or Gretchen sitting on her other side. She and Dale were still going out after the game, though.

Dale flipped through the latest batch of letters to the editor. He could print a whole newspaper with critical letters. In a way, he liked the idea that the newspaper generated so much feedback from students, faculty, and an occasional administrator. But he wished he received more thoughtful letters. Several writers complained more than ever after the Barry Richardson talk that the newspaper ought to cease printing record reviews. The other controversial topic, of course, was the debate over whether Daniel Ransom Johnson had actually predicted the Rapture. Some people thought he had and admired his prophetic powers. Others thought he had and denounced his presumption in predicting something that could not be predicted. Still others thought the evangelist hadn't predicted anything at all. He'd just spoken metaphorically. Dale had printed as many letters as he could in the last issue on the topic. He'd also asked two religion professors to write their opposing views. He'd received a call from Dean Pierce suggesting that he not seek controversy. Best not to stoke the blazing fire too much or else one might be burned. Dale said he understood.

But he didn't promise he wouldn't stoke any more fires.

The four of them, Rusty, Dale, Chris, and Putney, gave their tickets to the ushers and ignored their gawking faces. The four then proceeded to the door leading to the basketball arena. When they walked in and down the sidelines of the court, most of the crowd of two thousand people cheered their hairy presence.

Putney, who'd brought the bananas, gave one each to Rusty, Chris, and Dale, and they tossed the fruit into the stands. Then the four of them, dressed in realistic looking gorilla suits, waved. A camera's flash momentarily blinded them and they stumbled toward the stairs.

Dale was amazed at how hot he felt encased in the full body suit. Maybe it was the fake fur. Maybe it was the fact that his head was stuck inside a heavy, rubbery ape head. Whatever it was, sweat already dripped from his brow, and parts of his body, in particular his armpits and crotch, were sticky with sweat. If he'd known he'd feel this uncomfortable so soon, he would never have consented to wear the darn suit.

The warmth of the gym didn't help. People packed the stands in tight rows and generated heat. Dale thought the maintenance people also had turned up the heat even though the November night wasn't particularly cool.

They marched up the steps to the top reaches of the bleachers, people laughing and calling after them. Putney scratched under his arms, whether for show or because he too felt itchy under there, Dale didn't know. Rusty loped convincingly like a gorilla. They found a gap in middle of one of the top bleachers and the four of them clambered their way past the knees of seated fans and sat down.

The ape idea had been Rusty's. Wearing jerseys with one large block letter was Dale's. He'd wanted six guys to dress in ape suits and wear a red jersey with one block letter printed on it. In addition to the four of them, they'd asked Henshaw and Phelps. Both declined but said they wouldn't reveal their plans. They couldn't ask Eugene; he was on the varsity now, although he didn't play much. Rusty had mentioned Krupp, but Dale didn't want him, even though he brought an advantage in not needing a suit. Rusty had laughed. So, instead of finding six guys to spell out D-A-R-W-I-N, Dale suggested they just go with the four of them and not use the vowels. Sort of like a baseball box score that shortened players' names by using just consonants, such that Davy Concepcion would be spelled "D.Cncpcn." So, they'd spell the name DRWN.

The other three guys agreed. Even Chris said okay, although he had reservations about advancing the evolutionary theory of Darwin. Dale said they weren't advancing anything. They were just having fun. In fact, maybe they were making as much fun of Darwin as GNCers who didn't believe in evolution.

Now, sitting in the bleachers, Dale was rather glad they only had four guys. This way only the more astute observers would guess what the DRWN letters meant. Of course, no one would guess if they didn't get the seating arrangement correct.

Dale noticed that Chris, the W, was sitting on the far end instead of him, the N. He motioned for Chris to switch. Chris stood up and Dale slid over. When he did he noticed he was sitting next to a cute redheaded girl. The eye holes in the ape head weren't that large, so he had to move his head around a little to get a complete picture of the girl. Attracted by the motion, the girl turned and looked at him and Dale recognized her: Shirley, the music major.

She smiled. She said hello. Dale grunted. The guys had agreed not to speak to anyone. After all, apes don't converse. Dale heard Rusty, the D, grunting on the other end. Dale wondered who he was responding to. Either Hope or Rowena. He'd seen both of their heads when they'd passed them to reach their seats.

"Who are you?" Shirley asked.

Dale grunted twice. She giggled. He looked past her to see if her boyfriend Stephen sat next to her. He only saw another girl, a brunette with a feline face.

Shirley leaned closer. She peered into the eye holes. Her smile faded, replaced by an inquisitive look.

"Do I know you?"

Dale shook his head no. He hadn't lied exactly. Shirley didn't really know him. She'd been harassed by him a few times, but they had never had a real conversation. She probably still thought he played the piccolo.

"Your eyes look familiar," she said.

Darn almond-shaped brown eyes, thought Dale. Not many people on campus had such eyes. He could probably be picked out of police lineup just because of his eyes.

Dale turned away as the game started. He caught Shirley looking his way from time to time, but she left him alone while he watched the contest. The Chiefs played well and at half led Texas Lutheran by eight.

The apes watched the homecoming ceremonies and clapped when the homecoming queen was crowned. Dale didn't really know the girl, a tall brunette by the name of Gay Ludwig. A senior majoring in home economics, she was pretty and waved graciously to the crowd.

As he sat on the bleacher during halftime, Dale felt drenched in sweat. Even his face sweated. He wished he could get a 7-Up, but he couldn't drink it with his simian muzzle. And he couldn't take off his mask or else he'd be identified.

He wished he could speak. Then he'd bet Rusty another ten bucks that he wouldn't go down in the middle of the basketball court and do twenty pushups in his ape suit. Dale had made a similar bet with Rusty during the last home game, and at halftime Rusty, sans ape suit, had simply walked out of the stands, strolled to center court, dropped down and calmly did twenty perfect pushups. Then he got up and walked back into the stands, smiling at all the people gawking at him. Dale had to pay up, but it was worth it.

Shirley and her friend, who'd gone to the concession stand during halftime, returned and Dale scooted over to make room for them. Shirley said thank you. She smiled at the poor, thirsty ape and asked if he'd like a drink of Diet Coke.

Dale nodded. She waited for him to take off his ape head. He shook his head and pointed to his simian muzzle. Shirley giggled and lifted the cup of Diet Coke up to his rubber mouth and Dale pretended to drink by making gulping sounds. She and her friend laughed and Shirley said, "thirsty monkey."

Dale turned to her and nodded his thanks and he noticed she was peering at his eyes again.

"I know I've seen you somewhere," Shirley said. "I know because I remember those cute brown eyes."

She briefly smiled and Dale saw her face go slack with thought. He saw her searching her memory while gazing at his eyes. He knew he should turn away, but the demon in him wouldn't let him.

Her own green eyes grew wide in recognition. She had remembered.

"You!" she said.

Dale shrugged his shoulders. If he had enough room he'd try scratching himself like an ape, but they were all shoulder to shoulder.

"It's him," Shirley told her friend.

Shirley shrank from him, her face screwed up in disgust. Dale thought, how fickle. Just a moment ago, she was just saying how cute his eyes were. He grunted.

"You're a wolf!"

Shirley leaned back against her friend, who shared her repulsed and alarmed expression. Dale guessed she'd told all her friends about the Lothario piccolo player who kept propositioning her.

Dale screeched. He didn't know if gorillas made such noises but it was the best he could do.

Shirley jumped at the noise and spilled some of her Diet Coke on her slacks.

"Look what you've made me do!" she cried.

She stood up and Dale, to keep the pop from soaking into her slacks, pawed at the blotchy stain above her knee. She cried "ugh" at seeing his paw on her leg and stumbled against her friend, causing the brunette to spill her drink on the back of Shirley's slacks. Shirley wailed and turned her head to try and see where the soda pop landed. When she twisted his way, he saw that the Coke had soaked a spot on the seat of her slacks.

She glared at Dale. "It's all your fault," she snapped. "Oh you, oh you ... monkey!"

If he were permitted to speak he would have corrected her. They were gorillas. Instead he threw up his hands and shook his head apologetically as she rushed down the stairs, people pointing and laughing at the blotch on her derriere.

Dale felt sorry for her. Maybe he'd find out her last name and send her a note offering to pay for her dry cleaning.

The Chiefs ran away with the game in the second half. The four gorillas saw Eugene get into the game near the five-minute mark of the fourth quarter. With GNC leading by twenty-one, Dale motioned for them to leave. He wanted to get the suit off and wash the sweat away before he took Amanda out. He knew she wouldn't like the aroma of a sweaty ape suit on him.

They walked down the stairs and waved at the crowd. Several people waved back. Dale thought it was good to know that so many Nazarenes were friendly to their distant cousins. When they got down to the first row, they saw Mary Jane and Amanda sitting with the other organizers of the homecoming festivities. Rusty and Dale leaned over and grunted at them. Amanda and Mary Jane stared back in astonishment. Then, when Dale and Rusty waved, they both smiled and waved back.

During a timeout, Dale noticed some of the basketball players glancing at them while in the team huddle. Even one of the referees looked at them and smiled. Dale thought it was funny how people liked apes.

As the gorillas marched out of the gym, the pep band played "I'm a Believer." Not a bad choice, Dale thought. But he wished they'd picked "Gitarzan."

They left the building and piled into Rusty's Malibu. Some people would recognize his car, but not many since he'd only been on campus for three months. They resisted pulling off their ape heads until the car drove down the street toward Putney's apartment.

Finally, they were safe. Dale tugged off his ape head. His hair was plastered with sweat. His clothes stuck to him underneath his suit. He thought he must have lost five pounds from sweating. He thought that old theatrical saying was right: dying is easy, comedy is hard.

They laughed at the memory of the astonished faces. Dale told them about Shirley and they laughed about that, although he felt sorry for her. Rusty told Dale about Hope sitting next to him and how she hadn't guessed who he was. Dale said Rusty must not have made much of an impression on Hope; he'd dated her several times just a few months ago. Rusty said that's how girls were: they forgot you as soon as you stopped calling.

The next night, Dale took Amanda to see *Oliver!* at the Van Brocklin auditorium. They sat where Amanda preferred in the middle of the middle section and while they waited for the movie to start, he asked her if she'd seen those gorillas at the game. Last night he'd played it cool, waiting to see if she would mention the gorillas grunting at her. She never did.

"Yes, I did," she said. "Very strange fellows."

"How do you know they were guys?"

"I don't know. What girl would do such a thing?"

Dale couldn't think of one. Maybe Carol Burnett if she were a GNC student.

"And you know, a couple of them came over and made noises at me and Mary Jane."

"Oh, yeah? Which ones?"

"The tall one and the short one."

Dale shook his head in annoyance. She would notice their height.

"What's wrong?" she asked.

"Nothing."

He looked around the auditorium. It was about half filled. Not bad attendance for the first secular film to be shown on campus. He glanced at Amanda and when he saw she was relaxed and off-guard, he leaned over and grunted.

She jumped and stared at him. He grinned.

"Dale! Was that you?"

"Yeah, I was the tall ape."

"What? Oh, you're funny." She smiled. "Why did you do such a silly thing?"

"It was Rusty's idea."

"I'm not surprised."

"You don't sound impressed."

"Well, his sense of humor is a little strange. I was having lunch the other day and just as I was about to sip my soup, he stood up and made this awful noise. I almost spilled the soup on my dress."

Dale tried not to smile. He guessed it wasn't funny to stain your clothes. He ought to ask Amanda about Shirley's last name.

"And what was the idea with the shirts with the single letters on them?"

"You mean the D-R-W-N?"

"Well, I thought it was D-R-N-W."

"No. D-R-W-N. Sort of a code."

"A code for what?"

Dale thought about it. "Survival of the fittest."

Amanda considered the phrase. "Dale, that doesn't make any sense."

"You think four guys wearing gorilla suits does?"

Amanda shook her head. "I still don't get it."

"That's the point. You're not supposed to get it. It's an act of absurdity. Just doing something for the fun of it."

"Oh. You thought that was fun?"

"No, I think this is fun. Having this conversation."

Amanda shook her head again. "Sometimes I can't tell if you're serious or not."

Dale decided to stop his teasing. He patted her hand. "I'm just joking."

She smiled at him. He felt a little guilty about teasing her. She tended to take things at face value.

The movie started and they settled back and watched the Dickensian melodrama unfold on the screen, complete with characters dancing and singing. Dale wondered what some Hollywood producer would do next, make a musical version of *A Tale of Two Cities*? Perhaps it would have a scene in it where Sydney Carton sings a ditty before he's guillotined.

Actually, Dale thought the movie was pretty good, except for the singing. He glanced a couple of times at Amanda and she seemed to be having a good time. Then something odd happened. During a saloon scene, while the Nancy character is dancing and singing, a shadow crept into the frame and obscured part of her dress. For a moment, Dale thought something was wrong with the print. But the shadow remained and followed the actress as she swirled and sang and he realized it wasn't a flaw in the print but someone's hand intruding into the light of the projector.

Amanda asked what was happening. Dale knew. He noticed the shadow seemed to reach across a strategic area of the actress's body: her bosom.

He leaned over to Amanda and whispered, "someone's blocking her cleavage."

"What?" Amanda whispered back.

Dale heard murmuring in the audience. He guessed most people didn't know why the shadow had abruptly appeared. When the actress danced toward the edge of the frame, the hand didn't follow quickly enough and he saw the low neckline of the woman's dress. She did show some cleavage. But so what? Was that so shocking it had to be censored? And what a silly way to censor the scene, too. He wondered if they would completely block out the scene where Sikes murders Nancy.

The hand departed after the saloon scene and it didn't reappear. After the movie, Dale told Amanda he wanted to go up to the projectionist booth and see whose hand had blocked the shocking sight of an actress's cleavage.

Amanda remained in her seat as Dale rushed to the back of the auditorium and climbed the stairs to the projectionist booth. He peered through the window and saw Aaron Short standing next to the projector. Short almost frowned before forcing his mouth into a grin. He came over and opened the door.

"Why am I not surprised?" asked Dale.

Short asked if he enjoyed the movie.

"I would have if someone had kept their big paw out of the way."

"Oh, that."

"Yeah, that. Did you really think that was necessary?"

Short said it was a precaution. He didn't want anyone to complain to the administration.

Dale pointed at him. "What do you have against breasts?" he asked in a mock prosecutorial voice.

Short looked startled by the question. "Why, nothing."

"So, you like breasts?"

"Well, yes, I mean, what kind of question is that?"

"Just wondering. It's hard to believe that a man who professes to like breasts would block out an attractive cleavage, that's all."

"Smith," Short said, "you are strange."

Dale grinned. "I'm strange?" He started to leave when he stopped and asked if Abigail knew of his big paw plans.

"Abigail is not in charge of campus decency."

"No, Abigail is VP of student events. You should have at least let her know that you planned to censor the film. What else are you planning on censoring?"

Short didn't speak. He didn't even smile.

"That's what I thought," Dale said. "You better keep your big paw out of the newspaper office or it'll be caught in a weasel trap."

Dale gave Short a severe look but he didn't feel all that angry. Mostly, he'd been teasing Short, although he did think his censoring of the film had been a ludicrous act. College students can't be exposed to a low-cut dress? Next thing Short and his ilk would try to do is forbid male students from looking lower than Bronwyn's neck. Just imagine the consternation on campus if Bronwyn wore a low-cut dress. For a moment, he enjoyed imagining it.

He returned to Amanda who was chatting with Abigail. Dale told them that Aaron Short had been responsible for "the shadow of the valley of breast." The two girls looked at him in a puzzled way, not getting the pun. Abigail, after clearing her head of the odd reference, said she already knew it was Aaron. She'd visited the booth after the scene ended and told him to stop interfering.

Dale asked Abigail what movie she had scheduled next. Considering Short's actions, maybe it should be *Lawrence of Arabia*. At least there weren't any women in it.

Abigail smiled. She said they probably wouldn't show another movie until next semester, but she'd keep Dale's suggestion in mind. She said bye and Dale watched her walk across the auditorium to where Bobby Henshaw stood talking with Eugene Greene. Henshaw saw him, and the two former philosophers exchanged nods.

Dale asked Amanda if she'd like to go out and get a drink, maybe a snack. She said fine. They walked over to the parking lot and got in his Chevy and he drove to the Sooner Shack. He felt like having a shake. Amanda just wanted a Diet Coke. After Dale got the order, they sat in his car and talked about the movie. Amanda liked it. He did too, although he wished it didn't have so many songs in it.

"Well, it is a musical, Dale," she reminded him.

"Yeah, but do they have to sing in the middle of everything?"

After they finished, he drove her back to her dorm. They hadn't done any real smooching since their mini-breakup. Dale hadn't wanted to pressure Amanda. She especially didn't seem in the mood after revival. But that had been two weeks ago. Now as they sat in his car, in the far corner of the parking lot, Dale, with his mind still on the blocked cleavage, put his arm around Amanda and asked her what she thought about Short censoring that scene.

"I thought it was silly," she said.

Dale nodded. "So, seeing cleavage in a movie doesn't bother you?"

Amanda smiled a little. "No."

"It doesn't bother me either," he said, raising an eyebrow.

Amanda shook her head but her smile grew broader.

Dale stroked her shoulder with his hand. "You know, we've been saying good night in a G-rated way for a long time."

"And you want to revise the rating system, I suppose?"

"Well, I know I can't hope for an R yet."

When Amanda turned to him with an exaggerated look of shock on her face, he knew she was back to her easy-going self.

"I'm joking, of course," he said, which wasn't quite true. "But how about a PG good night?"

"We can't. Not in the parking lot."

Dale knew better than to suggest the lake, so he nodded and pretended to forget about the topic. After a few minutes of chatting, he said he needed to stop by the newspaper office. He'd forgot to get some work. How'd she like to go with him? They could walk over there and enjoy the late autumn night. The fresh air would do them good.

Amanda said all right. They got out of the car and walked across campus. They looked at the bright, clear sky and the nearly full moon. Dale took her in the student union by the back entrance. He had a key to the door; all stuco members did. Then they walked into the newspaper office and he pretended to look for his work on his desk, then said he'd forgot he'd already picked it up. He walked over to Amanda, who stood near the desk counter. He reached his arm past her and pushed the door shut.

She gave him a questioning look, although he knew she'd already guessed his intentions.

He flipped off the light switch and the room fell dark. He put his arms around her and kissed her. Unlike their previous good night kisses for the past three weeks, this kiss had passion behind it and she responded in kind.

He hugged her and she whispered in his ear reminding him that it was only going to be a PG good night. Dale knew their definitions of PG were slightly different, but he decided to play out the scene with her definition in mind.

They kissed some more. Dale put his hands around her waist and she put hers around his neck. They leaned against the wall but didn't drop to the floor. He put his hands underneath her sweater but only caressed the delightful curve of her hip. Then he kissed her neck. They kissed some more, this time more deeply, and after they hugged each other, she said she had better go.

Dale didn't complain. He said okay. He opened the door and they walked back to her dorm. He swung her hand in his. She seemed happy.

At her dorm, he held her hand like usual before she went in. She said good night. He did, too. He watched her walk inside her dorm, then he walked back to his car. He thought everything went fine. No powerful emotions were unleashed. He hadn't pushed her farther than she wanted to go. He knew he should be satisfied for her sake.

But he wasn't.


### Chapter 7: *Counseling June May; voodoo music; recommending Coop*

Jesse asked Dale to talk to June May about coming home late. He didn't really want to. He knew what she'd say: *you're not my father*. But June May had come home even later than he did last weekend.

Dale left Jesse puffing away on the couch and knocked on his sister's door. She said "*what?*" in an unencouraging voice. He'd hoped by the time she reached eighteen she would have lost some of her surliness.

He opened the door and saw her lying on her stomach on her bed reading an actual book, *The Scarlet Letter*. She wore a short nightie and Dale tried not to notice her rather voluptuous figure. He knew there were a few things he had to block his mind to, and his sister's figure was one of them.

"Whattaya want?" she asked, not looking at him.

"I remember reading that book."

"Yeah, well, it stinks," she said, tossing it on the bed.

Dale didn't think so. He sort of liked Hawthorne, even if he wasn't very funny.

"Are you reading it for senior English?"

"What else?"

Dale didn't know why June May would take senior English if she didn't like reading. Seniors didn't have to take the class if they didn't want to. Maybe his sister thought it would be easier than other subjects. She disliked math and science.

"Mom said you're coming home too late."

June May gave him *that* look. She rolled over on her back and stared at the ceiling. Dale averted his eyes upward as well.

"Look," he said, "it's your business, I guess. But you don't want to worry Mom, do you?"

June May didn't answer for a while. Dale kept his gaze on the ceiling. He didn't like coming into his sister's boudoir in the first place. He guessed he should have told her to come into the living room, but he didn't want to discuss these matters with Jesse present. She and June May would just get into another argument and interrupt his dispensing of brotherly advice. He glanced at his sister's skimpy attire for just a second. He'd once told her to wear more clothes around the house, but she said she could wear what she wanted in the privacy of her bedroom and he couldn't think of a retort.

"No, I don't want Mom to worry," she finally said.

They both knew Jesse shouldn't be worried. She'd been well for more than a year. The medication she took worked effectively. Dale thought she was nearly chemically and televisually lobotomized, but he guessed that was better than being insane – although not by much. At least it made things easier for him and June May, which made him feel a little guilty when he thought about it at night before going to sleep. He also knew she smoked far too much. But the smoking seemed to calm her, too. All that nicotine and tar and junk impaired her health, but perhaps it was another necessary evil.

"Who you seeing anyway?" Dale asked.

"What's it to you?"

"Just tell me."

"Marty Dewberry."

Dale remembered the guy. He remembered June May had dated him a few years ago. But he was two years older, so that meant he'd been out of high school for a while.

"Does he still have floppy hair?"

"His hair isn't floppy."

"Why? Did it all fall out?"

"Of course not. He has it styled."

"*Styled*?" Dale had always disliked Dewberry for some reason. Now, he was reminded why. Marty was pretentious. "Who does he think he is, John Travolta?"

June May rolled her eyes. She'd never appreciated his sense of humor.

"What does he do?"

"He works at the Unisexy Hair Salon in the City."

Dale shook his head. It was worse than he thought. "Is he a hermaphrodite?" He wondered if he should have used a different personal  pronoun.

"*What?*" June May didn't know what that word meant. "No, he's Irish or something, I think."

Dale shook his head again. And to think June May was going to graduate from high school in a few months.

"So, this guy is a hair stylist at a unisexual salon and you're staying out late with him?"

June May rolled back on her stomach. That position wasn't any more acceptable to Dale. "You got it," she said.

"Well, what's all this leading to?"

"What do you mean?"

Dale didn't want to say anything corny like, are his intentions honorable. He doubted they were. He was curious, though.

"I mean, are you two serious?"

June May narrowed her hazel eyes. "Serious in what way?"

Dale thought, maybe she wasn't stupid. She just didn't read or study vocabulary. There were two kinds of serious, he thought. The first kind usually led to marriage; the second kind sometimes led to a trip to your out-of-town grandmother's or aunt's, or a new possibility, a trip to the doctor. Dale didn't like any of those possibilities.

"I mean are you going to get engaged?"

"*Engaged*? I just turned eighteen."

"Yeah, I know." Dale didn't want to say it, but he supposed he had to. "Well, just don't do anything stupid."

June May smirked. "Look who's talking."

He wondered if she was referring to something specific that she knew about or if she was just smarting off. He guessed the latter. After all, he'd never gotten a girl in trouble.

"June May, you don't need me to spell it out, do you?"

"June."

"What?"

"I'm going by June now."

Dale nodded. "Okay, Junie."

She glared at him.

"I'm joking. June's a good name. About time you just used your first name."

June looked a little mollified.

"Anyway, don't stay out so late and worry Mom. And don't do anything stupid. And you know what I mean."

She smirked at him again. "Yes, father."

Dale shook his head and thought she was right. Blackie ought to be the one warning her. But he hadn't advised them even when he lived at home.

Dale closed her bedroom door. He walked back to his room and thought how June wasn't bad looking. She had an impressive figure and her face, although not beautiful, was cute. She had a lighter complexion than he did. He doubted she'd ever be quizzed about having some Indian "blood."

As he went into his room, he consoled himself by thinking at least this Dewberry guy had a good job. Dale bet hair stylists did all right nowadays. Everybody had long hair. He guessed if guys didn't have straight hair like he did then they might want to have it styled. But Rusty had long hair and it was more wavy than straight and he didn't have it styled. But Dale supposed that was because Rusty liked his "wild man" look.

He decided it was time to forget domestic concerns and prepare for the upcoming exam in Chaucer. He picked up his textbook and reread The Wife of Bath's Tale.

Rusty was in a good mood. He'd been playing more on the junior varsity team. Last game, he scored ten points, a far cry from the big numbers he'd put up in high school, but it was a start.

Rusty sat at Rowena's desk and finished typing his sports story for the last issue of the fall semester. Dale sat at his desk finishing an editorial. Readers like Fish and Short should like it. He thought it was his most conventional editorial ever. Well, the holidays were almost here. Time to stop stoking the fire for a while.

Rusty finished typing and ripped the copy sheet from the Selectric with a flourish. "*Fini!*" he said, putting his fingers to his lips and smacking them like an Italian artist. He tossed the copy sheet on Dale's desk and leaned back in the chair. Like Dale's super chair, Rowena's had a flexible back but it didn't have rollers. Dale noticed his buddy peering over at him. Rusty coveted his chair.

Dale finished typing his copy, too. "All right," he said, standing up and surrendering the chair to his pal. Rusty thanked him with servile deference, then sat down, grabbed hold of the armrests, cocked his long legs against the wall, then sprung them with such force that he propelled the chair and himself across the room until he crashed into the desk counter.

Dale estimated that Rusty might have exceeded his world roller chair speed record. He didn't like that. After all, it was his chair and office. It was like the visiting team setting records on his home field.

He motioned Rusty to return the chair to him. Rusty complied. Dale got in and did the same maneuver as his chum. But he angled the chair a little too much to the right and he and the chair flew toward Rusty at such speed that Rusty didn't have time to get out of the way. Dale collided into him. Both of them, along with the chair, spilled into a heap. He heard Rusty laughing until he got to his feet. Dale looked up and saw Rusty wince.

"Hey, you okay?" Dale asked.

Rusty flexed his right knee. "Me think so," he said in his deep Powhatan voice.

Back in grade school they had made up a song about Pocahontas and Chief Powhatan. Ever since, Rusty occasionally employed both voices, although Dale had originally created the Powhatan voice.

Rusty walked over to the stereo and dropped the needle on the record. The zesty sounds of The Manhattan Transfer's "Zindy Lou" wafted through the newspaper office. Rusty liked this song as much as Dale. They both thought it was funny.

Rusty began groovin' to the beat even though dancing in any form was banned on campus. Dale laughed at his grotesque facial expressions and silly body contortions. He grabbed his camera from off his desk and shot a couple of low angle photos of Rusty in the throes of performance. Then the photo shoot was interrupted by a knock on the nearly closed door. Dale yelled, "entre, Zindy!"

He saw Aaron Short's pale hand first appear on his side of the door, before the grinning visage of the VP for religious life leaned into view. Short asked in a loud voice if they could turn down the music. He and his staff were working on the *His Time* devotional book.

Dale turned down the volume on the song. Rusty stopped contorting but still tapped his foot and nodded his head while gazing at Short.

"What kind of music is that?" Short asked, still smiling but without any mirth behind it.

"Voodoo, man," Rusty said in a deadpan voice while gazing with a vacant, zombie-like stare at Short.

Dale told Short not to worry. The Manhattan Transfer had a very low demon content. Then he walked over and picked up the Nerf basketball. He stared at Short. Aaron's grin faded.

"What did I tell you about putting your weasel paw inside the newspaper office?"

Short's face fell into a confused look of fear and defiance. Dale gave the Nerf ball one short toss in the air and caught it in his open hand. Short looked at it. Then Dale whipped his arm back and flung the ball at Short's face. The Nerf ball hit him right on the nose and bounced back high in the air where Rusty snagged it.

"Smith!" Short squealed, his face scrunched up even though a Nerf beaning would hardly produce any pain. He slammed the door shut.

"I warned him," Dale said in a quiet, resolute mock voice that suggested sometimes a man had to resort to violence to protect his turf.

Rusty walked over to Dale and gave him a high five.

"Good shot, mahn," he said in his Jamaican voice. Then, in his normal voice, he asked Dale what he meant when he referred to Short's "weasel paw."

Rusty hadn't been at the screening of *Oliver!* Dale quickly described the censored scene. An aghast look appeared on Rusty's face. He shook his head in disbelief. He asked, how could any red-blooded man dare cover up the beauty of a woman's cleavage?

"Well, it *was* Short," Dale said, nodding at the closed door.

"'Nuff said," Rusty replied solemnly.

Rusty began to groove again but abruptly stopped. He flexed his right knee. Dale gave him a questioning look.

"Ah, it's nothing. Just a twinge."

Rusty said he better go to JV practice. Dale said he needed to go over to the physical education building and get some sports info from Coach Meyer's secretary. Dale turned off the stereo and locked the office on their way out. He and Rusty walked across campus.

Dale asked how Rusty's classes were going.

"Not so good," he said, shrugging. "I've missed a lot of New Testament. The class is at Revelation and I'm still hanging out with the apostles."

Rusty asked Dale how his classes were going. He said fine. Actually, it had been the easiest semester of his college career. He'd make straight A's again. He only had three real classes, the journalism ethics class, the poetry class, and Chaucer. The other two classes were the independent study in the twentieth century English novel and editing the newspaper. Dale had enough time on hand to help with photography. He took some photos, but most of the time he worked in the darkroom. He liked it. He enjoyed solitary, dark places that stunk of chemicals. He thought he ought to be a mad scientist.

As they approached the P.E. building and gym, Dale asked Rusty if he knew Coach

Meyer was dating Bronwyn.

"Bronwyn?"

"You've seen her. The creative writing teacher. She advises the yearbook. She always wears boots and *sweaters*."

That word rang Rusty's memory bell. "Oh, *Bronwyn*." Rusty nodded appreciatively.

Dale guessed Rusty was more of a leg man. He seemed to prefer long, slender legs like Mary Jane's. But like Dale, he definitely valued a prodigious bosom, too. But it was Chris who seemed obsessed with breasts. All Dale had to do was mention the *color* of Bronwyn's sweater she last wore to class and Chris's eyes grew large and his eyebrows twitched.

"Coach Meyer is dating her, huh?"

Dale said yes. Seriously.

"How else would you date her?" Rusty said with a leer.

They walked into the physical education building and Rusty said so long and Dale went over to the athletic department office and talked to the secretary about getting schedules and press books for the spring sports. That took about twenty minutes. Then on his way out, he saw David Hawkins coming out of the locker room, spruced up after varsity practice. Hawkins said hello. Dale asked him if he was practicing for the Christmas concert. He knew he was because Amanda was, but he asked him anyway just to make small talk. Hawkins said yeah. Between the choir, his classes, and basketball, he hardly had time for anything else. Dale nodded. Hawkins seemed to be lingering for some reason. Then David said he'd been impressed reading part of Dale's play for Bronwyn's poetry class. Dale said thanks. It was in blank verse. Hawkins looked for a moment like he believed him. Dale grinned and said he was joking. David laughed. Then Dale thought he noticed Hawkins looking at him in a kind of funny way, but he decided David was just thinking how goofy he was saying he'd written a play in blank verse.

Hawkins broke off his gaze and said he had to go. Dale said so long. Hawkins waved and walked out of the building. Dale walked into the gym and watched the JV team scrimmaging. Rusty took a shot and missed. Then, on defense, he made a dumb foul and Coach Meyer yelled at him. When Rusty dribbled the ball down court on his team's next possession, Dale noticed he didn't put all his weight on his right leg. Rusty tried cutting to his left, but his right leg buckled a little and he lost control of his dribble and the defender snatched the ball away and raced down court. Rusty fouled the guy hard when he went up for the layup. Coach Meyer blew his whistle and told Grimes to sit out for a while. Rusty, red in the face with anger, walked over to the sideline and threw himself down on the bench and hung his head in frustration.

Dale had a bad feeling things weren't going to get any better for his best buddy.

Teri said Jenny had a relapse. She slumped in Rowena's chair and looked glum. Dale thought he saw tears in her eyes. He asked if Jenny would teach next semester.

"I doubt it," she said. "She doesn't have any energy. She needs to rest and maybe her disease will retreat a little."

"She's not going to advise the newspaper next semester, either," Dale said, sitting at his desk and flipping through the final issue of *Smoke Signals* for the semester.

"I suppose not. But how do you know?"

"I have to go see Dean Pierce this afternoon."

Actually, Dale had anticipated the unfortunate turn of events weeks ago. Jenny had missed two staff meetings in a row.

"God, no," Teri said.

Dale raised an eyebrow at Teri's language. GNCers rarely invoked the name of God unless they were completely sincere. Well, he guessed she was.

"Yeah. It's a meeting about appointing a temporary adviser for the paper. I asked Sharon to come along."

"Why her?"

Dale sometimes thought Teri had reservations about Sharon. Maybe it was because she'd lost the yearbook editorship to her. Or maybe there were other reasons that he didn't know about. Girls seemed to know more about each other than boys ever suspected.

"Just another voice on my side," he said. "You can come, too."

"No, I'd just get angry. But please do one thing."

Dale said okay, what?

"Make sure Dr. Petry doesn't get appointed newspaper adviser."

"Don't worry. I'll do everything I can to prevent that from happening."

They both grew silent pondering about Jenny and the dreadful possibility that Petry would become adviser.

"You know if Petry becomes adviser, he'd try and get you fired."

Dale had already thought of that. Publication advisers had only one vote on the committee but their opinion carried a lot of weight. According to the bylaws, an adviser or administrator could seek the dismissal of an editor if he or she suspected the editor of negligence of duty, unethical actions, or behavior not consistent with Nazarene morality and conduct. All of those stipulations sounded fairly broad to Dale; depending on who was defining those terms, he'd probably broken a couple of the Nazarene conduct rules already.

"Why did God allow Jenny to get sick?" Teri asked.

Dale didn't say anything. He didn't think there was an answer to that question.

"If God loves us, then why does he let people suffer so? Poor Jenny. She has a terrible disease. And she's one of the best teachers on campus. She's smart. She knows her stuff. And she's kind and considerate. Why her?"

Dale thought he might give a philosophical response to that question but he knew Teri didn't care about that. He had doubts about God's unconditional love, too. Christians believed God loved his creations. Nazarenes emphasized their personal relationship with Jesus. Dale understood why. The Old Testament God could be harsh. As it said in several passages, Yahweh could be a jealous God. He had demanded that Abraham sacrifice Isaac; He had allowed the devil to torment Job. He was definitely an Authority Figure; a God of the Law.

Jesus, on the other hand, came to redeem mankind. He sacrificed Himself for human beings. He had to love people or else He wouldn't have suffered and died for them. Jesus, then, was a God of love. Therefore, Dale understood why Christians had such a difficult time resolving the question that Teri had just asked. Would a loving, omnipotent, omniscient God allow such suffering and torment? Dale knew Christian apologists like C. S. Lewis made valiant arguments for a loving God. But Dale increasingly thought those perplexing issues were more easily understood in relation to an Old Testament God. The fact that Jenny had a dreadful disease, or Portia Page had died in childbirth, or Jesse had been damned with schizophrenia, were no worse than Job's suffering.

Dale sometimes thought God wasn't all loving. Maybe what he cared about most was the development of the human species. And in order to grow, people had to suffer. But why did people have to be aware of their suffering? That's what made it so bad. In a way, he thought consciousness was almost as much a curse as a blessing.

He didn't tell Teri any of these thoughts. Because even if his thoughts made any sense, they wouldn't comfort her.

"I got to go," he said.

Teri nodded her head. He walked out of the office and knocked on the yearbook door. Sharon came out and the two of them walked over to the administration building to see Dr. Pierce.

Upon entering his office, Dr. Pierce shook their hands and asked them to sit down. Then, characteristically, he got to the point. He wanted to know their opinion of who should be the temporary adviser of the newspaper. Of course, their opinion had no official standing, but he still wanted to know.

Sharon nodded at Dale to go first; after all, he was the most affected.

Dale said he'd prefer Professor Cooper. He'd served as temporary adviser last year and had done an excellent job. Dale had already taken the initiative to ask him if he'd consent to the job, and he'd said yes. He didn't think there was anyone more capable or prepared to do a better job.

Sharon agreed with Dale.

Dean Pierce nodded. He said he was interested to hear that Dale had taken the "initiative" to talk to Professor Cooper. But Dean Pierce didn't say it in a snide way. In fact, he seemed to appreciate Dale's decisiveness.

But Dean Pierce did say that some of the administrators and some of the faculty thought Dr. Petry might make a better adviser. In addition, Dr. Petry had made it abundantly clear that he'd welcome the role.

Dale glanced at Sharon. She tried to hide a frown.

Dean Pierce wanted to know what the two of them thought about that prospect.

Dale said he didn't like that prospect.

Dean Pierce almost smiled at his candor. He took his glasses off to clean them and Dale once again noticed he had rather mild, if not kind, eyes.

Sharon put it more diplomatically. Dr. Petry didn't have any experience advising student publications. And he didn't have any practical journalism experience.

Dean Pierce, now with his glasses back on, said Professor Cooper didn't have any practical experience either. Sharon conceded the point. But Dale said there was an especially important reason why Dr. Petry shouldn't become adviser.

Dean Pierce asked what that was.

"Dr. Petry's not creative."

Dean Pierce asked why an adviser needed to be creative.

"Well, he needs to have a creative mind. He needs to appreciate the creative act. Otherwise, how can he genuinely advise students on how to be creative? That's what publications are. Creative works."

Dean Pierce considered Dale's argument. He told him that he'd made some cogent points. He'd think them over and let them both know soon who the temporary adviser would be.

Dean Pierce shook their hands again and escorted them out of his office door. Dale and Sharon left the building and on their way back to the student union, she asked him what he'd do if Dean Pierce picked Dr. Petry.

"Then I guess I'd have to get really creative."


## Chapter 8: *Overhearing Cleoma; Christmas and Rex's lesson*

Blackie wanted to celebrate. He'd received his Bachelor of Science degree in criminology/ sociology from Oklahoma State two days ago. He told Dale he'd worked hard for his degree. Holding down a full-time job, especially one as demanding as lieutenant of the rangers, and taking college courses for nearly seven years took a lot of perseverance.

Dale agreed. So far, he'd agreed with his father on everything.

Blackie strolled across the living room of his apartment. He still wore his ranger uniform, but he'd taken off his tie. His shoes, too. Dale thought his father looked sort of funny walking the carpet in his white socks while still wearing his revolver. The holster swayed a little as he walked, but the .38 Smith & Wesson pistol sat snug in the pocket.

As usual, Blackie had beaten him to the punch. Dale was scheduled to graduate next spring, a year early, but Blackie had done the trick this winter. Dale didn't think he was rubbing it in, exactly.

"You've been dealt a lot better hand than I was," he told his son. "But I played my poor hand goddamned well."

Dale said he'd played his cards astutely. Like a real pro.

Blackie stopped pacing and peered at Dale sitting in the big easy chair. Blackie had finally bought a new, comfortable chair, although it wasn't an E-Z Boy.

"Damn right," said Blackie. Then he paused and stared down the hall as if he expected someone to appear. "It's strange, though, how some people have all the breaks and still can't make it."

Dale asked what he meant.

"Found a suicide this morning. At Lake Overholser. The man, about my age, shot himself in the mouth with a .45. Blew off most of the back of his head."

Now, Dale remembered why he liked coming over to Blackie's: to hear his cheerful stories. The last time he came over, just before school started, Blackie had told him the rangers had found two drowning victims or "floaters" in the lake. He described the bloated condition of both bodies. One a man's, the other a woman's. Their swollen skin looked like an overcooked weenie just before bursting open. Later that night, Dale took Amanda out to dinner. She wondered why he didn't have much of an appetite.

"The funny thing was that this guy drove a Caddie," continued Blackie in a pensive voice. "A new one, too. I got to wondering what drove the bastard to blow his head off."

"Did you find out?"

Blackie smiled cynically. "The cops checked it out. The usual. About to go bankrupt. Getting a divorce."

Dale asked if his father knew who the guy was.

"Some big shot from the City. Educated in the east. He drove out to the lake to kill himself. Some suicides like the water. With the holidays, we'll probably get a couple more."

Blackie shook his head as if to clear his mind. He looked over to Dale.

"What's up with you?"

Dale shrugged. Somehow his struggles with Dr. Petry, Short, and Fish didn't sound so dramatic now. At least, Dale had heard from Dean Pierce that Professor Cooper would be the temporary adviser to the newspaper. That alone gave him holiday cheer.

"Going to stay the evening?" Blackie asked, not pressing Dale for news in his life. That's how Blackie was. If you wanted to volunteer information, he'd listen for a while. If you didn't, he didn't beg you.

"I can't," Dale said.

He was going to attend the college choir's Christmas concert so he could see Amanda sing. Dale thought it was odd. His father knew he had a girlfriend, but he didn't know her name.

"Cleoma's throwing a big party," Blackie said.

"Gee, I hate to miss that."

Blackie could detect sarcasm a mile off. He scowled at his son.

"What's Cleoma's last name, anyway?" Dale asked, in part to divert his father's attention from his sass. He didn't really know why he wanted to know. Maybe because he wondered if it was as strange as her first.

"Her maiden or married?"

Dale had a hard time imagining Cleoma as a maid. "Both, I guess."

"Maiden name, Thibodeaux. Married name, Bell. Interesting name. Cleoma Jae Bell."

"Her middle's name is Jay?"

Blackie said yeah, then he spelled it.

Dale wondered why Cleoma still went by her married name of Bell. He knew she'd been divorced for several years now. He preferred her maiden name. Thibodeaux. He guessed it was Cajun. Roxanne's folks were originally from the bayou country of Louisiana. So at least not every girl from there was a swamp thing.

"You ought to come to Cleoma's party," Blackie said.

Dale detected an insinuating note in Blackie's voice. "Why?"

"Sal flew in last night."

Dale wondered why Blackie thought he'd be interested in Sal visiting for the holidays. He wondered if Sal told Cleoma and she told Blackie about Dale's brief adulterous liaison with her. He wouldn't put it past the two women.

"Why do I care?" Dale asked.

Blackie threw his hands up in mock concern. "Well, pardon me all to hell, boy. I just thought you might want to know. Cleoma said you two hit it off a couple of summers ago."

"Yeah, and Sal was married. Which I didn't know at the time. And we didn't hit it off."

"Well, she's not married anymore."

"Hmmm. Why am I not surprised?"

"No, she's no longer Sal Robinson. She's Sal Bell again."

Dale wondered if he'd heard right. He asked Blackie if Sal's married name was Robinson. Blackie nodded. Dale shook his head in amazement.

"Mrs. Robinson?"

Dale chuckled, then grew annoyed. At least Dustin Hoffman got a whole summer. Dale had got just three trysts. Thinking about Sal cutting him off so suddenly angered him.

"What's wrong with you, boy?"

"Damn it, stop calling me boy."

Dale spoke more loudly and angrily than he meant to. He stood up and glared at his father. He didn't know why he felt so angry. Blackie glared back. For a moment, he thought Blackie might escalate things. But instead, his father smiled thinly.

"You've always had a temper. Well, you mostly keep it under control. And if you don't want to go to Cleoma's party, that's fine by me. But you'll miss some fun."

Dale walked across the room to cool down. He glanced at the magazines and newspapers in disarray on the coffee table. He took a deep breath and glanced back at his father. Blackie was an inch or so taller. He outweighed Dale by ten pounds, but it wasn't all muscle. Dale realized he could probably beat his father in a fight. It felt strange knowing he was now stronger than his father. He'd always been a little scared of him. But he wasn't anymore. He then felt a stab of sympathy for Blackie. He walked back and said, yeah, he knew he'd be missing some fun but he had other plans.

Blackie shook his head. He didn't understand his son. Blackie said he had to go out and get some booze for the party. Did Dale want to come? No, Dale did not want to come. Blackie walked into his bedroom, changed into civvies, and came back out wearing his black slacks and a rather garish black-and-gold plaid sports jacket. Dale marveled at his father's bad taste.

"Wait until I get back and we can talk some more," Blackie said on his way out the door. Dale nodded.

His father left and he wandered back to the coffee table and flipped through old *Time* magazines and newspapers. He looked at one newspaper from a two months ago that announced Anwar Sadat visiting Israel. Dale remembered that historic event. It had happened right before revival. He wondered if the event, with its potential Biblical implications, had helped create that strange atmosphere at the revival.

Dale tossed aside the newspaper and went into the bathroom to pee. He unzipped just as he heard the door open and two female voices cooing greetings. One voice, judging from its nasal drawl, had to be Cleoma's. The other sounded like her big busted friend.

He heard them speaking lowly, about Blackie baby not being in. Dale couldn't make out the next few sentences. Then they must have walked into the kitchen because their voices were much clearer. He zipped up just in case but otherwise he didn't move.

"Is Blackie gettin' any closer to makin' it official?"

"Naw, sugah, he's a careful one. You know what they say, once burned, twice careful."

"What's he waitin' for? You ain't gettin' any younger."

"Who the hell knows, honey? I've done hinted till my mouth has turned blue. He's got those two brats and he's payin' all that money to his crazy ex-wife. He's a bit of a tightwad if you wanna know the truth. Don't wanna support a second family."

"Well, there are ways to get what you want, girl."

"Don't ah know it, sugah? Well, he ain't a bad catch, either. He's got his navy pay and he tells me he's gonna be chief of the rangers prettah soon. The old man is retirin' in a few months. When Blackie makes chief, he gets a hefty raise in pay, sweetie. And then you add the moolah he make on the side, and it's not bad. If he just didn't have to fork over so much money to his crazy wife and his spoilt rotten kids, he'd have plenty for all of us."

Their voices faded as they left the kitchen and returned to the living room. Dale strained to hear but he only heard snatches. Nothing especially interesting. Plans for the big party. Then he heard the door open and close and the apartment became silent.

He finished his business, flushed, and walked back into the living room, smelling the lingering fumes of Cleoma's scent. He waved it away. He didn't like the smell of her perfume. It reminded him of overripe fruit; in fact, Cleoma herself seemed like a big, fat overripe tomato just about ready to burst into a sticky, pulpy mess.

What Cleoma said hadn't surprised Dale; it didn't especially insult him. He knew all along she was a phony. What interested him more than her dismissal of him, June May, and Jesse, however, was the phrase, "what he makes on the side." Dale wasn't sure what she meant exactly, but it bothered him. Blackie had told him stories about when he was in the navy and how he "worked the system." Later, when he made chief petty officer, he traded favors to sailors for favors in return. Blackie called them "chits." He said he'd learned to horse-trade chits and play the game. It was a good way to get ahead in the navy. Dale wondered if he was calling in some chits now as a ranger.

Blackie came back carrying a large paper sack full of booze. He carefully took out each bottle and examined it. All kinds of stuff. Vodka, scotch, gin. Dale watched him. He found the bottles interesting. The different colors, the different bottle designs and styles. He even liked the graphics on the labels. He remembered the liquor ads in *Playboy* he'd seen as a teenager. The bottles of booze looked almost as sensual as the women. Too bad he didn't like the stuff in them. If he did, he could easily get drunk while appreciating the aesthetic qualities of the bottles.

Then he remembered that summer with Sal and how one time he had drunk half a bottle of whiskey out of curiosity. The funny thing was that afterwards he didn't feel drunk. His mind seemed almost as clear as usual. He remembered feeling sleepy, though. He guessed he needed a different atmosphere than a quiet apartment along with the booze in order to really get drunk. Afterwards, he worried that Blackie would wonder who drank his whiskey. But Blackie never asked him about it. That was the last time he'd drank any liquor. He really didn't like the stuff.

Dale wondered if he should warn his father about Cleoma's conniving. He decided Blackie already knew about her intentions. Then he thought about asking Blackie about what she meant about his making money on the side. But he decided not to. He didn't want to provoke his father. Blackie was in a good mood. He was looking forward to the party, to drinking and listening to loud music and playing cards. Besides, how serious could his "side work" be? He was only a lakes and parks ranger.

Dale hung around for another hour but he and his father didn't really talk. They never did. Blackie sometimes told him cynical stories and they'd argue a little. It sort of depressed him because they could have spent more meaningful time together. But something prevented them. Maybe because Blackie had never really been much of a father to begin with. Dale suspected he didn't know how.

When Dale left in the late afternoon, his father, as had become his custom, shook his hand. Dale said he'd see him soon. Then he walked to his car and on the way he encountered that woman – the one with the impressive cleavage. He remembered her name when she said, "hi, baby" to him. It was Ceecee.

Dale grinned at her and said, "hi, sugah" in a voice he hoped parodied Cleoma's. Of course, Cleoma's voice already was a parody, but he tried his best. Ceecee stared at him like he'd called her a bad name. Dale walked past her and didn't look back.

After work on Christmas Day, Dale first stopped by his grandparents for a short visit. In addition to Jesse and June, his uncle Yancy and his new girlfriend, an Amazon-sized redhead with a homely face but a pleasant personality, were there. His grandmother said she had a plate set aside for him, but he told her he was going over to his girlfriend's parents' house to have a late Christmas dinner. Grandma said she reckoned he'd get better fed here than there. Dale said no one cooked better than she, but Mrs. Meeks was an excellent cook, too. Shore, said Grandma, for city cookin'.

All his assembled kin seemed interested in hearing about his girl and her family. Dale didn't want to talk about them. He decided to go before they started asking questions he didn't want to answer. Before he walked out the door, June smiled at him and asked when *he* was going to get engaged. Dale felt too embarrassed to think of a clever retort so he just said so long and left.

On his drive over to the Meeks' residence, Dale noticed how different this part of town was from Amanda's. The Meeks lived in the only fancy part of town, with all the trees and the lake, whereas his grandparents lived in the older, crummier part of town. Usually, the difference didn't bother him so much but June's teasing had made him wonder where he and Amanda were headed. They had been dating steady for sixteen months, which was a pretty long time. There seemed to be a momentum to such things, and he got the idea that their romance was still moving ahead or else Amanda wouldn't have insisted he come over and have Christmas dinner with her folks. He liked knowing that she thought they were progressing, but he had mixed feelings about where it seemed to be heading. He didn't doubt what he felt for her, but he knew her feelings were based in part on how well he conformed to her religious and social expectations.

Dale felt like he was conforming now. He'd changed out of his uniform and instead of putting on his old comfortable Levi's and a flannel shirt, he'd put on slacks and a dress shirt. He was even wearing a suit jacket. He refused to wear a tie. He wasn't going to church or anything.

He really didn't want to go over to the Meeks for Christmas dinner. Amanda had talked her folks into having a late holiday dinner so Dale could attend. He felt pressure to behave in an impeccably Nazarene way. He didn't like holidays much. Maybe it was because he associated them with all the unpleasantness with Jesse.

Dale also felt a little annoyed because he'd expected to have more physical contact with Amanda now that she was back home. But the evening of their first date with her back home hadn't turned out well. Before they went out, Reinhardt, who'd been over getting a few odds and ends for his and Lizzy's household, asked Dale to help him move the love seat from the garage to his pickup truck. So, he and Reinhardt hauled the surprisingly heavy love seat out of the garage. Dale felt a touch of poignancy as he shoved the piece of furniture onto the truck's bed. He even patted it good-bye.

Now, with no love seat, they couldn't go into the garage. She didn't like going to the lake. So, she and Dale had parked a few times in the secluded cul-de-sac down her block but they'd never made enough progress to satisfy him. He hadn't pushed her. He thought if he did, she might break up with him again. On one hand, she seemed to take certain things for granted, which suggested she thought of them as a couple with a future. On the other hand, he could easily imagine her getting so upset she'd break up with him if he brought her to that aroused state he had a few months ago in the Hayley parking lot without her explicit consent.

He drove into her neighborhood and admired the beauty of the setting sun and the shimmering glow of the approaching dusk. This area of town, with the large houses, had the best Christmas lights on display. Dale remembered Jesse driving him and June May to this part of town so they could gawk at the elaborate light displays on the houses and in the neat yards. Jesse and June May liked gazing at the blazing lights in the deep dark winter night, but even as a kid he felt like an interloper in this neighborhood.

Dale parked his Chevy on the curb, rang the doorbell, and Amanda invited him in. After everyone exchanged greetings, the women went inside the kitchen to get dinner ready. Kenny and Dale went down to the rec room and played darts and Ping-Pong. Dale let him win. He didn't want to put Kenny in a bad mood on Christmas while he was a guest. Reinhardt came down later and the three of them played Nerf football and talked about the Cowboys' season and how well it had gone. Thirty minutes later, dinner was ready and they all assembled at the large, polished dinner table for the feast. Mr. Meeks said grace and they all politely passed around the food. Dale, sitting next to Amanda, tried to act comfortable. He listened to the conversation as he ate. Mostly Reinhardt, Elizabeth, and Kenny talked. Amanda introduced topics from time to time to help get Dale into the conversation. Mr. Meeks didn't say much. He simply sat at the head of the table and ate the magnificent ham and turkey dinner with all the extra stuff with great dignity.

As they finished their cherries jubilee dessert, Dale complimented Mrs. Meeks for preparing such a delicious meal. She smiled graciously and said Amanda and Lizzy did most of the work. Dale gave Amanda such an exaggerated look of appreciation that she bumped his knee with hers.

When completely finished, the women began fussing about who should clean up. Amanda and Elizabeth wanted to do it all, but Mrs. Meeks refused to sit out. Dale asked Amanda if he could help, although he really didn't want to. His grandmother and female relatives always did all the tidying up afterward. She said he and the other men could help by bringing their plates into the kitchen and cleaning them off. That was all she thought they were capable of doing.

Dale nodded like a dolt and she laughed. He got up and performed the simple task requested of him, then the males retired to the spacious living room and gathered around the fireplace and talked about sports and business. Dale wondered if they'd talk about politics, but they didn't. He knew politics and religion were topics to be generally avoided in social situations, but since they almost certainly shared the same politics and religion, he wondered why they didn't talk about it a little. The more he thought about it, however, he realized he might not share all their convictions if the conversation got far enough along.

Ten minutes later, Mr. Meeks looked at Dale and smiled slightly. He said he wanted to show him something, if he didn't mind.

Dale said he didn't mind. He then followed Mr. Meeks into the parlor, then into a large room with book shelves, a desk with an electric typewriter, an expensive leather chair, a smaller cloth chair, a coffee table, a magazine rack, a large globe, and a tall, impressive-looking walnut cabinet. Mr. Meeks closed the heavy door and gestured at the room and said it was his study. He then walked over to one of the bookcases and removed a book. There was something in his manner that reminded Dale of Dr. Flack that time he'd entered his office and the professor had shown him *Hannah Horse*. He hoped Mr. Meeks wasn't going to show him a similarly silly book.

"I acquired this recently," said Mr. Meeks. He showed Dale a copy of *An American Tragedy* by Theodore Dreiser. "It's a first edition. Signed by the author."

Dale took the book and opened it to the title page and saw Dreiser's forceful signature underneath an inscription he couldn't quite make out.

"Interesting," Dale said.

"Have you read this book?"

Dale said he had. It was good. He didn't know why he liked Dreiser's work. Its pessimism reminded him a little of Hardy. But there was something about the relentless, almost ungainly accumulation of prose that gave his books power. Dale had read *Sister Carrie*, too. He liked both books but he thought *An American Tragedy* a more important book.

"How much do you think a first-edition, signed copy is worth?" asked Mr. Meeks.

Dale gave the book back to Mr. Meeks. He said he didn't know. He didn't know anything about book appraisals. He only bought books for reading, not investing.

Mr. Meeks nodded and returned the novel to its place in the bookcase. Then he asked Dale if he'd like to take a seat. Dale said, okay, since it was obvious that Mr. Meeks wanted him to, and he sat down in the smaller chair opposite the sleek leather one.

Mr. Meeks asked Dale what he had in mind after graduating this spring.

"I'll find a job."

"In what field?"

"I think journalism. A newspaper job."

Mr. Meeks nodded but he didn't look impressed. "Do newspaper jobs pay well?"

"Not really."

Dale thought Mr. Meeks looked like the kind of man who should smoke a pipe. In fact, his two large hands looked rather awkward lying on the armrests doing nothing. Dale then noticed the fingers of his right hand spreading out, then retracting, as if he were caressing the leather. He wore a gray cashmere sweater over his white dress shirt and dark blue tie. His black dress slacks looked freshly pressed and his shoes recently shined. Dale wondered, is this how a successful man relaxes?

"We haven't talked much, have we, Dale?"

"No, Mr. Meeks, we haven't."

"You may call me Rex, if you like."

Dale didn't think he would like, so he just nodded.

"I'd like to tell you a brief story, if I may."

Dale said, sure, go ahead.

Mr. Meeks told him that he grew up on a farm in Iowa. As a boy, he enjoyed drawing. When he got older, he tried his hand at painting. His two influences were his mother and a man who had grown up not far away, an artist named Grant Wood. He asked Dale if knew of Wood.

"Yeah. I've seen a photo of his famous painting, *American Gothic*."

Mr. Meeks looked pleased. He continued. The army drafted him when the Korean war started. He didn't see any action; he was a quartermaster. He asked Dale if he knew what that was.

"Sure. Sort of like a supply clerk."

Mr. Meeks didn't look so pleased with that description, but he continued. While stationed in Korea, he met a young man named Ike Russell who also had an interest in painting. They became friends. After their tour of duty ended, they were scheduled to leave on the same transport plane. Rex, however, became ill and was assigned to the next plane. The one his friend was on crashed and burned and everyone on board was killed. When Rex got back to the States, he decided to look up his friend's family. They lived in Oklahoma. That's why he came to this state. He decided to stay and work in the oilfields. Then he went to college on the GI bill and along the way forgot about painting. He really wasn't very good at it. He met Victoria, became a Nazarene, transferred to Galilee Nazarene College, and majored in business. After graduation, he went into banking. After a while, he regained his interest in painting – not as an artist, but as an aficionado.

Mr. Meeks rose. He asked Dale if he'd like to see a painting by Grant Wood. Dale got up and said yes.

Mr. Meeks walked over to the tall cabinet and opened the double doors wide. Hanging inside wasn't *American Gothic*, of course; Dale knew it hung in a museum somewhere. But this painting impressed him, too. It wasn't done in the satirical-realist style of *American*

*Gothic.* Rather, this painting's style reminded him of the pointillist paintings of Seurat. It showed a boy running through a colorful, splotchy meadow. In the background, past a cornfield, was an orderly, grayish village. Dale wanted to reach out a finger and touch the canvas, but he knew he couldn't. He did lean closer and read the title: *Flight.*

"Like it?"

Dale nodded. "Very impressive."

"One of his earliest," Rex said. "A gift to my mother."

They gazed at it for a little longer and then Mr. Meeks carefully closed the doors to the cabinet as if he were closing the door to a sleeping child's room.

"I developed an eye for observation and detail while studying painting," Mr. Meeks said. "That has helped me enormously in my business dealings. I observe people who come in for loans. I study businessmen, too. In short, Dale, I learned that business can be an art, too. Not like that –" Mr. Meeks pointed an upturned hand to the cabinet – "but an art in a different sense."

Mr. Meeks looked at him. Dale thought he understood. But he didn't agree. He thought there was only one kind of *art*. He still didn't know how to define it, or fully understand it, but he thought Rex's analogy didn't quite hold together.

"Well. Shall we rejoin the others?"

Dale said he was ready. They walked out of the study back to the living room. Dale noticed Amanda looking at him in a curious way. He and Mr. Meeks took seats and listened to the conversation. Christmas music played softly on the stereo. Reinhardt had started a fire in the fireplace. He stabbed at the smoldering log with a poker.

Dale hardly listened to the conversation. Instead, he thought about Mr. Meeks. If he'd been encouraged to ask questions, he would have asked what Rex believed in regard to religion. He suspected he viewed it in the same way he did art. Something to acquire and not really practice.

When the conversation lagged, Amanda glanced at Dale and asked if he'd like to go for a walk. He said sure. They excused themselves, leaving behind the bored-looking Kenny with the two married couples.

Dale held Amanda's hand as they walked to the small park a few blocks away and stood on the bank and looked at the black waters underneath the dark sky. Amanda asked Dale what her father and he had talked about.

"About art."

Amanda looked surprised. "Really? He rarely discusses that

They talked about the Christmas concert she'd performed in last week. Dale praised her singing. She said she didn't think she was so good anymore. Her voice wasn't improving with age. He said that was silly. She wasn't even twenty-one yet. She said she was thinking about getting an education certificate so she could teach high school. He said that made some sense, but she should never give up singing. She said she wouldn't. She'd always sing in the choir and in other ways. Then they fell quiet for a few moments.

"Dale, why don't you ever talk about your family?"

Her question startled him. He didn't answer immediately.

"There isn't much to say," he finally said, thinking he sounded like Blackie.

After a pause, Amanda said she understood how difficult it must be for him.

Dale wondered how much she knew about his family. He wondered how much people in Galilee knew. It depressed him to think that probably more people than he realized knew at least a little about his family's situation.

"You know, you can always talk to me about your problems," she said.

"I don't have any problems."

Amanda tightened her hand on his arm. Dale resisted looking at her face. He didn't know why. He felt ashamed of his family and then he felt ashamed of himself for feeling that way.

"My father doesn't like talking about personal matters, either," Amanda said. "But sometimes I think it helps."

Dale turned to her and saw that her eyes looked soft and sympathetic. He knew she'd try to understand his situation. But he didn't think he should tell her too much.

"My folks just have some problems."

Amanda nodded and Dale saw she wanted him to say more.

"All I know is they're divorced," she said. "I guess that was hard on you and your sister."

Dale shrugged. "Harder on my sister than me."

He could have told her that when his parents were married his home was full of tension and acrimony. Maybe it was better they divorced. At the time, he didn't think so.

Dale felt Amanda's hand stroking his forearm in a sympathetic way. He glanced at her and tried not to show his annoyance. He didn't like people feeling sorry for him.

"Well, if you ever want to talk about any of that," she said, "I'll listen. I'd like to help if I can."

Dale said thanks. They stood gazing at the dark lake and the indigo-colored sky for a few more minutes, then Dale said they should probably get back to her house. He felt melancholic again; he wondered if he had a Kierkegaardian tendency to melancholia.

Amanda said okay and they walked back to her house. Then Amanda said she'd almost forgot. She reached into the pocket of her blue coat and brought out the red ski stocking cap that he'd given her for Christmas. They'd exchanged presents last night after the Christmas Eve church service. Dale had also given her matching leather gloves, which cost more than he thought gloves should cost. Amanda gave him a clock radio. He needed one. His old one had stopped working three weeks ago and he'd been late to his first class a few times.

Amanda pulled the stocking cap on her head and smiled at him. She thanked him again. Dale said when she went skiing, the cap would remind her of him. (She'd told him a similar thing when she gave him the clock radio; how when he woke up every morning he could think of her. He didn't tell her that he already did that.)

"Well, I'm going to have to wait awhile to use my presents," she said, smiling in a secretive way.

"What do you mean?"

"I'm not going skiing over New Year's."

"But your family's going."

"Not Elizabeth. She's staying behind, too."

"Why?"

Amanda leaned close to him, tugging on his arm to bring his ear close to her mouth. "Lizzy's going to have a baby."

"She's pregnant?"

Dale could tell Amanda didn't like that word spoken out loud. He guessed she thought it vulgar like she did a few other words, which were really just medical terms.

"Four months," Amanda said, still whispering.

Dale felt surprised. Elizabeth and Reinhardt hadn't seemed that passionate together. They still didn't. Well, passion wasn't necessary for procreation.

"Isn't that exciting!" Amanda said, almost shouting. She put a gloved hand to her mouth and smiled. "To think I'm going to be an aunt."

"Aunt Amanda," Dale said, grinning. "That sounds fine."

She tugged on his arm. "It makes me sound old."

"You're just a kid."

She looked at him. "So are you, then."

"Not really. I'm going to graduate in five months."

She didn't say anything; she just smiled.

573

## Chapter 9: *A New Year's tryst*

K. C. announced that he and Gretchen were engaged to be married. He stood in the middle of Roxanne and Quentin's living room and made the announcement. Gretchen said they were planning a June wedding. All the guests held glasses of punch and drank to their upcoming marriage.

Dale shook hands with K. C. So did Rusty, Chris, and Quentin. The girls, Amanda, Mary Jane, Hope, and Roxanne, hugged Gretchen.

"Not a bad way to start the New Year," said Chris to K. C.

"Wanna bet?" Rusty said in a loud voice.

He then shoved K. C. a little too hard for it to be playful. K. C. ignored Rusty and maintained his broad smile. He said Rusty could tease all he wanted. He'd been waiting to marry Gretchen since high school.

"What took you so long then?" Dale asked.

K. C. laughed heartily, then said he'd had to prove to Mr. Reinhardt that he was worthy as a son-in-law. "It took me four years to convince him, but a month ago when he gave me the promotion I figured he thought I was."

Dale slapped him on the back. K. C. had started going to college part-time so he could work full-time for Reinhardt trucking. He worked in the accounting office and Dale had heard from Richard Reinhardt that no one gave him any slack just because he was Gretchen's boyfriend. K. C. worked hard and had proved himself.

Dale noticed Rusty walking into the kitchen where the punch and snacks were. He excused himself and followed. He saw Rusty spiking the punch. When he saw Dale, he grinned and stopped pouring the vodka.

"Hey, don't you know the punch has some booze in it already," Dale said.

He'd tasted it right away. Even though he didn't drink, he could detect the slightest amount of alcohol because he disliked it so much. He'd only sipped his punch during the toast.

Rusty shrugged. "So? It can use some more."

Dale had noticed Rusty acting odd tonight. He didn't talk much, for one thing, and when he did he spoke in a ridiculing voice, the way he did to K. C. earlier. And bringing the vodka. Rusty had never been a drinker to Dale's knowledge. He knew he drank beer some. But Dale had never seen him take a drink of hard liquor, although he knew Erickson did.

Dale asked him to step outside with him.

"What, man? You want to take me outside? Hey, buddy, I didn't know you were that kind of *buddy*."

Dale opened the door and shoved Rusty out. Rusty told him to watch it or buddy or no buddy he'd slug him. Dale closed the door and asked what hell was going on. His use of a mild profanity got Rusty's attention.

"I don't know. I guess I'm pissed off."

Dale asked why.

"I flunked out."

"Out of college? How could you do that?"

But Dale already knew. Rusty missed too many classes. He never took it seriously. Rusty always had a quick mind. Dale remembered that the only kid in grade school that read more books or advanced higher in the fifth-grade reading competition than the two of them was Isaac Gould, the boy genius. In high school, Rusty could do pretty well without studying much. But not in college. Especially in the classes that required attendance.

"Man, I bombed my New Testament final. I couldn't remember if Paul went to Ephesus or Corinth or the moon."

"That's only one class."

"I failed the sophomore comp class, too. But I hated that guy."

Rusty meant Dr. Petry.

"I did all my assignments. I passed them all even though he graded in a weird way. But I missed twenty-one classes. He said that alone was enough to flunk."

"How could you miss twenty-one classes?"

"Easy, man." Rusty grinned. "It started at eight. The idea of going to that dude's class that early did not *motivate* me to get up."

Dale had warned him not to take Petry's classes, but Rusty said the other sophomore composition classes had been closed out by the time he registered. Besides, he'd always been a great speller.

"What about basketball?" Dale asked.

"Ah, that wasn't working out either."

"Why? Was it your knee?"

"No, man. My knee is fine."

Dale knew he wouldn't say if it were. He was funny that way. Since Dale had hurt his knee, he'd never mention it. But if Rusty had hurt it in another way, he'd complain and even use it as an excuse, which it would be, of course.

"Then what was it?"

Rusty leaned against the wall and shook his head. "I didn't like the offense. Coach Meyer ran this disciplined, pass-oriented offense. I like to shoot, you know? I like playing free. I felt all penned in. Pass, pick, roll, pass. It's not my style. I started making too many mistakes. He'd get on my case and I'd make more mistakes. He didn't play me much the last game, anyway."

Dale said that was too bad. Too damn bad.

"Hey, man, what's got into you? You don't cuss."

"I've been around my dad recently."

Rusty raised an eyebrow. Then he slumped a little more until he was about eye level with Dale.

"And Mary Jane and me broke up."

"Yeah, I gathered that. You two have hardly said a word to each other all night."

Rusty shrugged. "Not much to say to each other. I guess I'm just not cut out to be a GNCer."

Dale didn't think he was either, but he didn't say so. He guessed Amanda still thought he was. Her father certainly thought he had potential. Dale even planned to take a business course in the spring.

"We better go back inside," he said. "The girls will wonder where we are."

"The girls want me to blow away like a shriveled leaf," Rusty grumbled.

Dale slapped him on the back and opened the door and they went inside. Dale saw Amanda standing at the snack table drinking a cup of punch. Rusty bobbed his eyebrows at him and glided out of the kitchen.

"Amanda, what are you doing?"

Amanda's eyes grew large at the tone of Dale's voice while the upturned cup hid the rest of her face. She finished, put the cup down, and asked him what he meant.

"Did you drink a whole cup of punch?"

"Well, yes, but I was thirsty. The dip is so spicy."

He walked over to her and examined her face. She blinked her eyes at his searching look and then raised a hand to her face.

"What's wrong? Is my lipstick smeared?"

"No, it's fine. Didn't you think the punch tasted strange?"

"Now, that you mention it, yes, I did."

"What did it taste like?"

"I don't know. Sort of bitter, I suppose. Why?"

"Why did you keep drinking it?"

Amanda's mouth opened in alarm. She looked at the empty cup. She looked back at Dale. "Is there something wrong with it?"

"Well, no. I mean, yeah." Dale leaned closer to her and whispered that it had vodka in it.

"Vodka? Is that some kind of liquor?"

Dale nodded.

Amanda put a hand to her mouth. She stared at Dale with her big blue eyes. He almost laughed at how they looked full of fear.

"Don't worry," he said gently. "It's not poison."

She shook her head as if she'd done something irretrievably sinful. "Dale, I've never drank anything like that before."

He put his arm around her shoulders and hugged her. "It won't kill you. But if you drank too much it might make you sick."

The look of fear in her eyes increased. He asked how much she'd drank. She said one cup earlier and one cup, no two cups, just a while ago. He thought that probably wasn't enough to make her sick. He told her she'd be all right. She relaxed some when they heard commotion in the living room. He and Amanda walked into the other room and saw Mary Jane glaring at Rusty. Dale guessed he'd said the wrong thing again.

"Man, I'm splitting," Rusty said, waving his hand at them. "I'm going to find Erickson."

Everyone looked at Quentin and Roxanne. Quentin's jaw tightened and Roxanne's face flushed. Rusty knew he'd made another faux pas, but he waved his hand dismissively and said he was blowing this joint. He threw open the door and stormed out of the little house.

Quentin walked over and shut the door. No one said anything for a moment, then several people began to talk at once, commenting on how rude Rusty had been all night and how he'd upset Mary Jane more than once and listed his other offenses as well.

Dale thought he better tell them. He walked to the middle of the room and said Rusty had spiked the punch.

Quentin said Rusty shouldn't have done that. He'd already put in a little rum.

Mary Jane, Hope, and Gretchen looked almost as disturbed as Amanda had looked in the kitchen. Dale wondered if any of them had tasted the magic elixir before.

Mary Jane shook her head and looked like she wanted to cry. She said, "oooh, Rusty."

K. C. grinned and said he thought he'd have another glass of punch. Gretchen grabbed his arm and said, no you don't.

Everyone was still talking about the spiking when they heard a knock at the door. Everybody expected Rusty. Quentin went over and opened the door. They all gawped, not at Wendy and Carmen, but at Butch Bigelow standing there with the two young women. He was dressed in his marine uniform.

"Hey, man," Quentin said to Butch.

He reached out and shook his hand. He welcomed Wendy and Carmen as well and invited them all in. The girls said hello as did K. C. and Chris. Dale didn't say anything. He was taken aback at seeing Bigelow with Wendy and Carmen. He wondered why they were with Butch.

Everyone chattered for several minutes. Bigelow walked over and shook K. C.'s hand. Quentin told him the news about K. C.'s engagement to Gretchen. Bigelow clapped his old buddy on the back. Then while the girls gathered together and talked, Bigelow walked over to Chris and shook his hand, then looked at Dale.

Dale thought Bigelow looked impressive in his olive green uniform. It fit him well. He looked like he'd lost a little weight around the middle and gained even more muscle in his shoulders and arms. He looked like a real fighting machine. He noticed the chevrons on his shirtsleeve that showed Butch had made lance corporal already. His hair had the classic marine buzz cut. It reminded Dale of the short haircut Butch had sported back in ninth grade football. His head still had a broad, boarish look to it. His features were still porcine.

But when Bigelow grinned at him, Dale thought his smile looked genuine.

Bigelow extended his hand and Dale shook it. He felt everyone looking at the two of them. He was especially aware of Amanda's gaze from across the room.

"How are you, Smith?"

"Fine, Bigelow."

They ended the handshake. Dale was rather glad. Butch had a vise for a hand.

"The last time I saw you was that night playing flag football," Butch said with a grin.

"Yeah, I remember." He couldn't resist. "How's your collarbone."

"It healed a long time ago."

They looked at each other and Dale thought the look in Butch's eyes seemed different. No hostility. He'd always wondered why Bigelow disliked him so much. He didn't like Rusty either. Dale guessed it was just one of those situations where guys take a visceral dislike to one another.

K. C. walked over and slapped both of them on the shoulder. "Hey, you guys aren't going to start another fight, are you?"

K. C. had his big T. R. grin on his face. Dale grinned, too, and Bigelow laughed a short, staccato laugh. Then the three of them walked over to the rest of the gang and everyone asked Bigelow how he liked the marines, what he did, where he'd been stationed, and all the usual questions.

Dale watched with some unease when Amanda talked to Butch. He was still watching when he heard Wendy's voice.

"So, how are you?"

Dale turned and saw her smiling at him. He said fine. He asked how she was. She said she was doing well. An awkward pause settled between them. Dale wanted to see what Amanda and Butch were doing.

"I see you're still dating Amanda," Wendy said.

"Yeah."

"You two must be serious."

Dale noticed that her smile didn't match the look in her eyes. He didn't know what to say.

"I'm sorry," she said. "It's none of my business."

"That's okay. Are you seeing anyone?"

"Oh, I date. But nothing serious so far."

Dale nodded. He thought Wendy looked different than she did when they dated. She didn't have the same girlish quality to her. Her features looked more refined. Then he figured out why. She was wearing makeup. Lipstick, rouge, eye shadow, liner, all that stuff. Dale remembered that she never wore much makeup in high school. She always had a fresh, natural, girl-next-door quality; now, she looked like an adult woman. A polished businesswoman, perhaps.

She smiled more broadly. "What are you looking at?" she asked in her old bubbly voice.

"Oh, I just noticed you're wearing makeup."

Wendy appeared to blush but the makeup hid some of the glow. "Well, you know. Getting older."

"You're twenty-one," Dale said.

"Oh, you remembered."

"Of course. I remember the date even."

Wendy laughed and Dale smiled and he glanced over to Bigelow and noticed that he was now talking to Roxanne and Quentin. He looked around and saw Amanda sitting on the sofa talking to Mary Jane. Dale didn't like seeing the two of them together.

"Is anything wrong?" Wendy asked.

"Naw," Dale said.

He turned back to Wendy and caught her staring at him. She reached a hand out and gently touched his arm and said she had to go. Before Dale could respond, she walked over to Carmen. Dale nodded at Carmen. She smiled, but her eyes had a narrow, rather critical look to them. He guessed she hadn't completely forgiven him for how he had treated her, although during last year's New Year's Eve party she seemed to have. Well, Amanda hadn't been at that one.

Wendy said the three of them had to go. Several people groaned. Roxanne asked them to stay longer. There was punch and snacks in the kitchen. Bigelow held up his hand and said they really had to get going. They were going to another party at a marine buddy's place and they were already late. They just wanted to stop in and say hi.

Everyone gathered around them and wished Bigelow good luck and told Wendy and Carmen to keep in touch. K. C. and Bigelow shook hands again, and then he, Wendy, and Carmen walked out. Quentin and K. C. watched from the door until Bigelow's Cutlass drove away.

Dale walked over to Amanda and as he did, Mary Jane got up and walked into the kitchen. He sat down next to Amanda on the couch. She looked at him without smiling.

"Happy to see your old friends?" she asked.

"Yeah. Especially Bigelow."

Amanda nodded. She didn't get his joke. Dale thought her eyes looked a little glassy. He stared into them.

"What's wrong?" Amanda said in a voice that had a hint of intoxication.

"How do you feel?"

"I feel wonderful," she said, smiling. Then her smile faded. "How was Wendy?"

"Fine." He guessed Amanda was a little tipsy. He wondered how much vodka Rusty had poured into the punch.

"Just fine? You two talked quite awhile to only find that out."

"She told me she was going to join the circus."

Amanda blinked her eyes. "What?"

"Yeah, she said she was tired of ordinary life. She yearned for the smell of greasepaint and sawdust."

Amanda stared at him as if she'd swallowed something that hadn't gone down right.

"Amanda, are you okay?"

She wavered a little. "I don't know."

Dale put his arm around her and looked into her eyes. She looked unwell. Maybe the vodka was bothering her stomach. He asked her if she wanted anything to eat. She shook her head no. He told her she better eat something. She leaned against him and said she wasn't hungry. Dale asked Roxanne if she had any crackers. She said she thought so. He asked if she could get Amanda three or four crackers.

While he waited for Roxanne to return with the crackers, he asked Amanda how her stomach felt. She said it felt funny. They'd eaten before coming over to Quentin and Roxanne's, but Amanda hadn't eaten that much. Just a Caesar's salad.

Roxanne returned with the crackers and Dale told Amanda to eat them. She looked at him as if he'd told her to eat her shoe. He told her the crackers would make her feel better. He took one and held it to her lips and she took a bite. She said they were dry. Dale said that was the point. The crackers would help soak up what alcohol remained on her stomach.

Dale saw Mary Jane return holding a cup of punch. Dale told Amanda to keep eating the crackers. She nodded. Then he went over to Mary Jane.

"You do know that punch has vodka in it?"

Mary Jane took a sip. She had to fight to not wince. "So?"

"You don't drink, do you?"

Mary Jane took a longer drink. This time she winced.

Dale went over to Chris standing next to Hope. He told them they had better look after Mary Jane. They said they would. Dale asked who drove. Hope said she did. Dale suggested she not drink any more of the punch. Hope frowned at him. He told them he and Amanda were leaving. Chris said they'd miss the turning of the new year. Dale said Amanda wasn't feeling well. Chris said, okay buddy. But Dale thought he said it in a funny way, as if he didn't mean it. Dale thought this was a strange New Year's Eve party. No one seemed to be having any fun.

He thanked Roxanne and Quentin for inviting them, but he needed to take Amanda home. She wasn't feeling well. They commiserated and said the usual parting words, then Dale went over to Amanda and saw she'd only eaten two crackers. He said they were going. She protested. But Dale took her hand and helped her up and she said good-bye rather loudly to everyone and gave them an exaggerated wave. Her friends waved back and said bye. Mary Jane came over, still sipping her cup of punch, and hugged Amanda with one arm. Amanda asked if she could have a sip of Mary Jane's punch. Her mouth was dry from the crackers. Dale said no and finally he got her out of the house and into his car.

As they drove away, he rolled down the window to let some fresh air in. The breeze felt bracingly cool. The day had been a little warm for late December but the night had turned chilly.

Dale glanced over to Amanda. She leaned against the seat and closed her eyes. She smiled when he asked her how she felt. She said the air felt good.

Roxanne and Quentin lived on the north side of town. Dale stopped by a 7-11 and got a Diet Coke for Amanda. She sipped it as they drove back toward campus. She reached into her jacket pocket and pulled out her ski stocking cap. She put it on and smiled at him. He guessed she was a little drunk. He asked how she felt. She said, better. She reminded him that Elizabeth and Richard were at her home entertaining the Stephensons.

Dale said, so?

Amanda said they wouldn't have any privacy if he took her home now.

Dale got the point. He glanced at her and wondered if she'd consent to the lake. But then they'd miss New Year's. As they drove through campus, he had an idea. He turned on the road that led behind the student union. He asked Amanda if she'd like to go into the newspaper office. He had his stereo there. They could listen to the New Year's Eve festivities on the radio. That would be lovely, she said a little too loudly.

Dale parked in the lot behind the student union even though it was reserved for staff or faculty. As he got out, he thought he saw someone lurking in the shadows by the building. He waited. Whoever it was, slipped away. Dale helped Amanda out and they went inside the building by the rear entrance. He opened the door to the newspaper office, turned on the overhead lights to find the stereo, tuned it to a station broadcasting the New Year's festivities, then turned on the desk lamp on Rowena's desk. He went over to Amanda, extinguished the overhead lights, and brought her around the long desk counter.

There wasn't a good place to sit in the office. Just chairs and stools. Dale took off his jacket. He wondered if the heat had been kept on even though the day had been unseasonably warm. He asked Amanda if she felt warm. She said yes. He took off her ski stocking cap and her jacket. He put their jackets on the carpeted floor and said they could sit on the floor if she didn't mind. Amanda said fine in an airy voice.

No one was in the student union building on New Year's Eve. Security usually only made a round every four hours. Dale knew the last checkup was about thirty minutes ago if the guy kept his regular schedule. So, the coast was clear for another three hours.

They listened to the radio coverage of the New Year's Eve celebration in New York. Dale put his arm around Amanda and she leaned against him. He asked how she now felt. She said better. Her stomach had settled. She guessed the crackers helped. She asked Dale how he knew to do that. He said he'd read it in a book. Actually, he knew Blackie ate crackers when he drank too much too fast. That is, if he didn't want to get sick. Sometimes he didn't care.

Dale felt Amanda's warmth as she leaned against him. The lamp gave off a golden glow from across the room. It almost looked like candlelight when he squinted. He told Amanda that. She squinted and smiled. You're right, she said, giggling, her voice still sounding a little drunk.

The newspaper office was surprisingly cozy, thought Dale. Even with only one light, sitting on their jackets, and listening to the low murmur of the radio, he thought this was better than the lake. And there was certainly more privacy and room.

Amanda asked him in a soft voice if he liked seeing Wendy again.

"Let's not think about that."

"But you went with her for a long time."

He knew what she wanted to hear. He hadn't told her in a while. He hugged her and whispered in her ear that he loved her only.

"Really?"

"You know it's true," he said lowly.

She said she loved him, too.

He kissed her and even with a few cracker crumbs still in her mouth, it felt wonderful.

"Sorry," she said, when she saw him swallow one crumb that got in his mouth. He said it was okay. He didn't mind sharing her food. She giggled.

He kissed her again and this time he only tasted a faint bitterness of vodka. He put his arms around her waist. She threw her arms around his shoulders. He leaned against her and they slowly fell into a recumbent position. He kissed her open mouth, then sucked a little on her full lower lip. Then he kissed her philtrum and she smiled. Then he kissed her right cheek. He asked her to turn the other cheek. She giggled and he kissed that one too.

When he returned to her lips, the playfulness ended. He kissed her softly, then gradually with more force. His hands went under her sweater and stroked the bare flesh at the small of her back. Her hands rubbed his neck like she was giving him a gentle massage.

They stretched their bodies out on the carpeted floor. He continued to kiss her, now deeply, as she began to moan. His hand stroked her lower back. She had worn jeans without a belt and now his hand easily slipped under her pants. His fingers felt the upper curve of her right buttock. He caressed the soft, cool flesh with his fingertips. Then he glided his hand back to her spine and slipped his middle finger into the warm, humid natal cleft. He liked the contrast of coolness and warmth.

Dale pressed against her and Amanda rolled on her back. He removed his hand from the back of her jeans and put it under her sweater as he kissed her neck. He heard her moan in his ear. He slowly moved his hand up her sleek belly and when he came to her bra he slipped his hand underneath it without pausing. His hand cupped her right breast. He squeezed and she moaned. He gently rubbed her erect nipple between two fingertips. She moaned so loudly that Dale thought he might have hurt her. But her body remained relaxed and so he kissed her lower on her neck. He leaned back and used his other hand to push her sweater up. He lowered his head and kissed her stomach around her navel. Then he softly kissed her flesh as he worked his way up to her breasts. He pushed her bra up. He kissed between her breasts, then nuzzled them with his face. He smelled the slightly milky aroma of her skin there. He squeezed the soft mounds of flesh, one hand on each breast. Then he suckled first one nipple, then the other. She moaned loudly and Dale felt dizzy with the sound of her voice in his ears and his own desire.

He tugged her sweater up and she lifted her arms as he pulled it over her head. Then he turned her on her side and reached around and unhooked her bra on his first try. He felt rather pleased with himself.

He unbuttoned his flannel shirt with his left hand while he caressed her stomach with his right. When he finished unbuttoning, she reached a hand to help him remove his shirt. Then he pulled off his T-shirt. His chest was already a little sweaty. He pressed his chest against her breasts and rubbed. She hummed deep in her throat. He kissed her and she returned his kiss with ardor. He breathed deeply, to slow his building excitement, and reached down and unbuttoned her jeans. He unzipped her. He kneeled so he could use both hands to tug her jeans down. Amanda threw her arms across her face and offered no resistance. Unlike the first time he undressed her, this time he pulled off her pants only. He pulled them down her hips, and watched with pleasure as her thighs came into view. After she slipped off her shoes using just her feet, he tugged the jeans off her legs.

He moved up to her and removed her arms from over her face. Her eyes were closed. He leaned over and gently kissed her eyelids. He heard a faint gasp leave her mouth. Then he kissed her lips softly, then more forcefully, while caressing her breasts.

His lips left her lips, and slowly moved down her neck, to her throat, to her breastbone, kissed first one breast, then the other, then kissed her belly and all the way down to where her panties were. He kneeled again. His fingers felt the sleek material. He noticed she wore modest pink panties that covered most but not all her hips. He stroked the jutting edge of her hipbones. She murmured. Then he took each side of her panties in his fingertips and he slowly pulled them down.

He watched in the low light as the V of her lower abdomen became exposed. He watched the pubic hair appear. Fluffy and light brown. He pulled the panties down her thighs, over her knees, and off her legs.

He said he wanted to see her back. He turned her over. She didn't protest. He caressed the nape of her neck, her back, then slid his hands over her buttocks and squeezed each cheek. He stroked her thighs. He looked at how her hips curved out and how her buttocks rose in two cupped mounds. He caressed them again, feeling the soft, ample flesh. Then he turned her on her back again.

He looked at her face. Her eyes were closed. He put his face close to hers. He waited until she opened her eyes. He looked into them. He told her she was beautiful. She smiled. He told her he loved her. She stopped smiling and he saw her eyes glisten. He kissed her. He slowly slid his hand from her chest to her stomach to her thighs and then to her pubis. He gently moved one finger, then another into her vagina. He'd wanted to touch her in her most intimate place for a long time. She was wet. She moaned, not entirely from pleasure. He looked at her face. She closed her eyes and shook her head once. He stroked her. Even with the wetness, there seemed to be a tightness that he had to overcome. He leaned his chest against hers and continued to work his fingers. She gasped. He watched as she moved her head to and fro. He lowered his face and kept his lips just an inch away from hers. He spoke lowly to her. He said her name. He said Amanda. She moaned. Then she said, Dale. She threw her arms around his shoulders and hugged him. He removed his fingers and thought he felt something a little thicker than wetness.

He held her and she cried softly for a short time. He told her he loved her. She stopped crying and she reached down and tried to unbuckle his belt. He did it instead, then unbuttoned and unzipped. She reached down and helped pull his jeans over his hips. His erect penis sprung out and he enjoyed the relief of not having it confined. With her arms still around his neck, she braced herself against his shoulders and tilted her pelvis. He grabbed her hips and she spread her legs. He felt his phallus touching her inner thigh. He pushed until he felt it touch the small, wet opening and he almost shot off right then. He paused and controlled himself and then he looked at her face. Amanda's lips were open and her eyes tightly closed. He saw tears on her cheeks. She had thrown her arms over her head and she shook her head slightly from side to side. He heard her murmuring. The expression on her face, and the position of her body, looked less like an offering of love and more like a sacrifice. He knew he shouldn't do it.

"Oh, Amanda," he said.

He felt the tingling behind his eyes. He felt overwhelmed by the erotic sensations and his own conflicted sense of desire and responsibility.

"What is it?" she asked, responding to the pain in his voice.

"I love you too much."

She made a quiet, sobbing sound.

He leaned against her and felt his body press against hers but not enter. He loved her too much to take advantage of her. He desperately wanted to be united with her, but he knew he couldn't do it like this.

Dale held Amanda tightly until he felt himself grow slack. He listened to her breathe. He smelled the musky odor around them. He reached down and pulled his jeans up then reached over and grabbed his shirt and spread it over her. She turned away from him. She curled up. Dale reclined and gently moved against her from behind.

"Know what this is called?" he asked, now feeling recovered.

"What?" she asked quietly.

"Spooning."

"Why?"

"Because we're pressed against each other like spoons."

She didn't say anything for a second.

"Why didn't you do it?"

Dale stroked her hair. "Because you would have regretted it."

"Would I?"

"You know you would. And that would have destroyed us."

She said nothing for a moment.

"I'm feeling a little cold."

He reached over and grabbed his jacket and put it over her, too. He still felt hot.

"That better?" he asked.

"Yes."

He listened to her breathe. He stroked her hair.

"My darling Amanda," he said quietly.

"What's going to happen to us, Dale?"

He said nothing. He didn't know what to say. They listened as the announcer said it was 1978. They heard celebrations on the radio.

Dale leaned over and kissed Amanda. He said, Happy New Year. She said the same in a quiet voice.

"You don't want to get married, do you?" he asked.

He didn't even want to use the word. He thought they both were too young. He didn't want to stay in Galilee when he graduated. But he wanted her.

"No." She turned her head to him, but not her body. He still pressed against her from behind. "I mean, not yet."

He hugged her and felt his groin press into her soft, naked bottom. He felt himself growing aroused. He willed himself not to think erotic thoughts. It wasn't the time. Instead, he focused on her breathing and what was going on inside her. He thought he knew. She was wondering if the two of them would make it.

"Don't worry," he said. "Everything will work out."

Amanda didn't answer.


**Chapter 10:** *A scandal; a deserted campus; Shakespeare's identity*

Dale had been gone all week. He walked into the newspaper office and saw Teri and Polly sitting at the two desks. He exchanged hellos with them. Teri started to vacate his chair. He said it was okay. Maybe she ought to get used to sitting at the editor's desk. After all, she might be editor next year. He climbed on a stool by the layout tables and noticed they were looking at him in an odd way.

"How was OU?" Teri asked.

Dale had been at the Scholarship-Leadership Conference at the Oklahoma University campus. He'd applied for the honor last fall. He didn't know why, exactly. Mostly, he wanted to see the OU campus as a quasi-student. The attendees received room and board for a week at the OU campus, were enrolled in a seminar with a distinguished professional, and got a certificate attesting to their general wonderfulness. The committee to select the students had considered scholarship, which meant good grades, evidence of leadership, meaning campus activities, and outstanding character. Dale felt a little doubtful about the last one. How could a committee evaluate outstanding character on an application? Well, he hadn't committed any crimes or alienated too many people, so he had asked Jenny, Coop, and Dean Pierce to write letters of recommendation. All three, including Dean Pierce, had been delighted to do so. All three said he'd make an excellent representative from GNC. He'd been surprised that Dean Pierce seemed to regard him so highly.

"It was okay," said Dale.

Actually, the whole week reminded him a little too much of Boys State except that the educational aspect was more pertinent to his interests. He'd been selected to be part of the mass media and communications seminar. The seminar leader was a middle-aged man who'd served in a number of distinguished capacities in academia, the media, and as director of the Federal Communications Corporation during the Johnson administration. In other words, he was a big shot. Dale rather liked him. He wore his hair fairly long, didn't wear a suit coat or tie, and instead of dress shoes, he wore loafers without socks. Sometimes, he'd slip his feet out of them and cross his legs at the ankles with his big, hairy bare feet showing underneath the seminar table. Dale admired his eccentricity.

"So, what did you do there?" asked Polly. Her small eyes looked at him without any jealousy. She hadn't applied, although Dale thought she should have.

Dale gave them a quick rundown. He stayed in one of the guest dorms. He had a roommate, some guy from the state's Baptist college, who didn't seem especially bright. Dale guessed the organizers had roomed them together because they both went to religious colleges. His roommate was attending the business and technology seminar. He'd drone on about the topics and issues his seminar discussed, ideas that the roommate found fascinating but he thought mundane. The conference attendees ate their meals at a special cafeteria, where the school's athletes dined. Dale had recognized the star quarterback, J. C. Watts, and thought about going over and teasing him about OU blowing the Orange Bowl and losing to Arkansas. But he didn't want to hurt his feelings.

In the evening, they attended a series of special events: lectures by even bigger big shots; a champagne soiree; and, the final evening, a banquet where they all received awards and certificates.

"All that sounds edifying," said Polly.

"Yeah," said Teri. "Sounds more than okay to me."

Dale shrugged. He wasn't the hobnobbing kind. He didn't like talking to people he didn't know. He didn't like pretending he was a junior big shot. In fact, he'd considered splitting early but he found the former FCC guy intriguing.

He asked them if anything interesting had happened while he was gone. They both stared at him with the self-satisfied expression of people who know something amazing and were about to divulge it to a pathetically ignorant newcomer.

"Give," he said. "After all, I'm the editor of the distinguished campus newspaper."

Teri glanced at Polly. Polly nodded, indicating that the honors belonged to Teri since she was assistant editor. Teri turned to Dale with a knowing smile on her lips.

"Dean Pierce and Mrs. Hester ran off together," she said.

Dale thought they were joking. "Nice try."

"No, really," said Teri.

He still didn't believe her. She was pretty good at teasing for a girl, but not good enough to fool him. But when he looked at Polly and saw her serious, earnest expression, he re-evaluated the news.

"You're not kidding."

Both girls shook their heads no. Dale stood up and paced the room. He thought about the plausibility of Dean Pierce, a man of rectitude, and Mrs. Hester, a woman of impeccable reputation as the Hayley dorm mother, skipping off together.

"That's funny," he said.

"Funny?" said Polly. "It's a dreadful scandal."

Dale looked at Polly. He forgot her father was head of the physical science department. Of course, she'd have a different reaction than he did.

"Yeah, Dale," Teri said. "It's a big deal on campus. People are shocked."

Dale thought that made the whole thing even funnier. He didn't tell them that though. He remembered that Dean Pierce was a widower. His wife died three years ago of ovarian cancer. Mrs. Hester had divorced her philandering husband almost twenty years ago.

"Why is it such a scandal?" he asked. "Neither abandoned a family or a spouse."

Polly stared at him as if he were a pornographer selling *Playboy* right in the office. Even Teri gave him a disapproving look.

"It means they were carrying on without anybody knowing for some time," Teri informed him.

Dale thought about that. He imagined Dean Pierce and Mrs. Hester sneaking out somewhere for their trysts. He smiled.

"Good for them."

Polly stood up and prepared to go. She pursed her thin lips and shook her head at Dale. "Sometimes you take this unconventionality of yours to an extreme."

"What do you mean?"

"I mean you don't seem to find anything improper with them –" Polly paused and then lowered her voice "– fornicating while working as employees of the college."

Dale guessed he didn't as long as they loved each other. And apparently they did. But he said that Polly was simply assuming they were fornicating. Maybe they weren't.

"Then why did they run off together?" Teri asked. "If they were in love, why didn't make it official?"

"Yes, if they weren't engaging in prior improprieties, they would not have absconded."

"Maybe they were seized with a moment of passion," Dale said, as he began to pace the room. Polly and Teri watched him with wariness. "Maybe they had tried for months to resist their mutual attraction, and then wham! – " he smacked his fist into the open palm of his other hand, making both girls jump.

Polly had enough. She gathered her books and scurried out while giving Dale a reproving glance. He hoped she wasn't too mad at him. He needed her copyediting expertise, especially with Jenny away.

"You don't really believe that, do you?" Teri asked him.

"I don't know what to believe. After all, I just heard."

He thought about Dean Pierce and Mrs. Hester. He'd suspected that both of them weren't as prim and proper as they pretended. He didn't mean they were hypocrites. He meant that he'd seen a glimmer of warmth in both of them that they apparently repressed publicly. The fact they both had human failings and passions made him like them more, not less.

"Are we going to do a story on it?"

Dale said he didn't think so. It was their business. He asked when everyone found out. Teri said last Monday. Both of them left notes of resignation and apology in their campus mailboxes last Friday. The administration didn't discover them until early Monday.

"So, both didn't show on Monday?"

Teri nodded. Dale asked how Mrs. Hester had managed to avoid her "Mom" duties at Hayley for the entire weekend. Teri said she'd told the assistant dorm mother that she had

584

a family emergency. Dale nodded. That wasn't exactly a lie.

Teri asked him what he was thinking.

"That they must love each other a great deal."

She asked why he thought that.

"Both are middle-aged. Both are leaving behind their jobs, their church, their lives, to run off together. Only people who love each other very much would turn their lives upside down."

Teri said that made sense. But it was also dangerous. They might be making an awful mistake.

Dale nodded. "That's right. That's what's makes it interesting."

"You mean romantic."

"Yeah, that's right."

Dale walked over to the long desk counter that served as a barrier to the public but also provided shelf storage space. He knelt down to see if he could find a back issue of the newspaper that he remembered featured a photo of both Dean Pierce and Mrs. Hester standing with a group of other college representatives at a recent function. He looked through the top shelf, then looked at the lower section. That's when he saw a few drops of blood on the carpet. Puzzled, he looked more closely. Dale reached a finger down and touched the three small stains, brownish red in color, shaped almost like tears. It was dried blood all right. And he knew it wasn't his.

Teri noticed him staring at the carpeted floor. She asked what he was doing.

"Just looking at evidence."

"What?" He heard the amusement in her voice.

Dale stood up. He resisted rubbing the drops with the heel of his boot. He realized he'd made Amanda bleed. It had happened New Year's Eve. He remembered from his reading that one way to verify a girl's virginity was to check to see if her hymen was intact. The breaking of the hymen yielded some small amount of blood. That was where the crude phrase, "busting her cherry" came from. He remembered Bigelow saying the words in a boastful way back in high school in regard to some rather sad, plain girl he'd deflowered. Now, Dale had apparently deflowered Amanda, but not through an act of copulation. Was that possible? Would a young woman of her age still have an intact hymen? Well, he knew she'd never been involved with any man before him. She never did anything athletic. She hadn't even cheerleaded. She'd had gym class, but he imagined she was one of those pretty girls who didn't do much. In a lot of ways, Amanda was rather passive by nature. But didn't she ever rub herself down there? Dale couldn't imagine her not ever doing that. Maybe she just didn't rub vigorously or not too directly. Maybe it took more than rubbing. Once again, the complexity and mystery of the female puzzled him. He felt both emotionally moved and amazed that he'd deflowered Amanda. He felt a surge of sympathy and tenderness for her. Then he felt that annoying tingling behind his eyes. He turned toward the wall. He blinked his eyes and tried to think of something impersonal and physical.

Teri asked him if anything was wrong. Why was he facing the wall?

"Just checking for cracks."

Teri laughed. "Now you're an engineer?"

Dale was over it. He sat down on a stool and wondered about the definitions of things. Virgin. Fornication. Love. Life was more complex than people usually understood. And yet simple, too.

Teri, who been ruminating about Dean Pierce and Mrs. Hester running away, said maybe he was right. Maybe the two of them were passionately in love.

"I hope so," Dale said. He wished them well.

In total darkness, Dale threaded the film into the developing tank reel. He'd gotten pretty good at it. He usually got it right on his first try. He liked how the flexible, chitonous film felt in his hand as he cupped it just enough to slide the edges into the grooves. He wished he could show Amanda how well he did this. She'd really appreciate how good he was with his hands.

Dale thought he shouldn't joke about that sort of thing. He'd not been using his hands much around her of late. With her back on campus, they'd returned to an almost chaste existence of a few goodnight kisses in his car before escorting her to the dorm's front door. He'd suggested visiting the newspaper office once, but she'd acted like she hadn't heard him. He guessed she associated it with sin. Not only had they engaged in some serious sexual activity, but she'd also been under the influence of alcohol. Not that she'd chastised him about that night. She simply didn't talk about it. It was as if it never happened.

Now with the film safely in the tank, he turned on the lights, added the chemicals, agitated the tank, and watched the timer. He liked photography, especially the darkroom work. He liked the magic of developing the film and making prints. He didn't like shooting pictures so much. He had to fool around with people. Most people fussed getting their photos taken. Even Amanda primped a little. He'd taken some photos of her over Christmas break. He was looking forward to seeing how they turned out. This had been his first chance to develop that roll of film along with another roll of newspaper assignments.

Dale poured the chemicals into a reuse jug and rinsed and fixed the film. Then he unspooled it and looked at the negatives. They looked pretty good. Excellent contrast. He studied Amanda's negative image. He taken most of the photos around the park and the lake near her home. He'd taken a couple indoor by the fireplace. Even her negative image looked good to him. The image didn't show much clarity of her features, but it did show how attractive her long, straight hair and her heart-shaped face looked. He couldn't wait to make a contact sheet and see how the positive image looked.

He hung up that roll to dry, then glanced at the second roll. Just campus stuff. A few photos of basketball intramurals, which reminded Dale of how lousy Omega was. Krupp was even more delusional in regard to his basketball abilities. Convinced he was another Pete Maravich, he jacked up shots from all over the court and made about one third of them. He led the team in scoring, but why shouldn't he when he took so many shots?

He then saw three rather strange images that he didn't recognize. He looked more closely. He remembered. Photos of Rusty groovin' to "Zindy Lou." He looked more closely at the most bizarre one. Dale laughed at Rusty's ridiculous, agonized expression. The camera's low angle had exaggerated the distortion of Rusty's grimacing face. His hands looked almost like claws as they slashed at the air. His body had been moving so fast that the camera couldn't quite freeze it. It looked a little blurred. The background, because of the angle and the slight overexposure, looked hazy and almost steamy. Dale couldn't tell that Rusty had been standing in the newspaper office. In fact, he thought not only the background but the entire photo looked otherworldly. It was one weird picture.

Dale liked it. He hung that roll up to dry, too, and walked out of the "inner sanctum" part of the darkroom. That's what he called the room where all the developing and printing went on. He realized he'd lost track of time. He often did that while working in the darkroom. The quiet, isolation, and detailed work seemed to erase time. Sometimes, he imagined the dark room as a time machine. He went in and it was the present. He came out and it was two hundred years into the future. Now, as he left the darkroom in the basement of the science building and walked up to the first floor and into the sterile-smelling, white-tiled hallway, he actually felt a little like a time traveler.

As he walked through the hall, he noticed how strangely quiet it was. Usually, he heard some noise. A professor lecturing or students working in a lab. He thought the lack of people was a little odd, but as he walked outside he forgot about that as his mind turned to his upcoming class assignments and editorial duties.

He crossed the street to the main campus. Still, he saw no one. He didn't know what time it was. He never wore a wristwatch. He ambled up to the student union building and opened the door and didn't see anyone in the lobby. He thought that strange. Instead of going to his office as he planned, he turned and walked to Chester Hall where most of his English classes were held. He threw open the doors, walked down the empty hallway, and peered into the classroom where his Shakespeare class met. No one there. Not one soul.

Dale wondered how long he'd been in the darkroom. Besides developing film, he'd made about ten prints. He guessed he'd been there for an hour and a half. What felt strange was that before he walked over to the darkroom, the campus had been its usual bustling place.

He walked back to the entrance and looked out the window. The day appeared like a typical Oklahoma winter day: a hazy sky, with a mild winter sun, and a breeze rattling the bare limbs of the trees. He listened more closely. He heard nothing but the wind as it picked up speed and gave a low, whistling howl. No sounds of people talking or even moving about.

For a moment, he thought maybe something remarkable had happened. Maybe the Rapture. It made sense he'd be left behind. But would everyone on campus be zapped up into the air to meet Jesus? Even someone like Phelps, who seemed pretty worldly to Dale; or Lyle the seven-foot basketball star who had been rumored to have bad habits involving coeds and pot; or Henshaw, who Dale knew once entertained heretical philosophical views; or even Teri, who had doubted the mercy of God?

He stared out the window at the empty campus and listened to a gust of wind howl like a lost soul before it died down to almost nothing.

Did it really happen?

Dale snapped out of it. There had to be a logical explanation. He was just a little disoriented after an hour or two in the darkroom smelling chemicals and staring into darkness. But why was campus so deserted? He pushed open the door, walked outside, and strode toward Van Brocklin auditorium.

Another factor in his heightened sense in the possibility of supernatural activity was that a strange atmosphere had been developing on campus. Aaron Short's last *His Time* devotional book had been dedicated to the very likely possibility of the Rapture happening on Easter. Short's essay repeated the prediction that it would happen "at the last minute, at the last hour," on the anniversary of our Lord's ascension into heaven as had Daniel Ransom Johnson.

Then, during opening convocation, one of the speakers, a respected Biblical scholar from Dallas, said the Rapture was nearly upon us. He didn't give an exact time, but it made an impression on the congregation. Then Dale had heard from Chris that last Sunday the pastor of the First Church had also mentioned the imminence of the Rapture and the whole End Time scenario.

Dale remembered that the leader of a group of Bible-based Christians who would later become the Jehovah's Witnesses had decided that the End Time would occur at the end of October of 1914. Charles Taze Russell, the founder and leader, had made a study of Biblical prophecy and had calculated that date for the end of "Gentile Times." Jesus's Second Coming would take place then. The fact that World War I later began made Russell seem prescient. As Dale remembered it, his followers gathered together to welcome the return of the Lord on that fateful day only to be disappointed.

Before that, in the nineteenth century, a man named Miller also proclaimed that the Second Coming was nigh. He formed a sect, which became known as the Millerites, and all of them gathered together in a field in October 22nd of 1844 and waited. Jesus didn't return. That event or non-event, was called the Great Disappointment. Dale nodded his head. No kidding.

Dale arrived at Van Brocklin auditorium and walked up the steps to the side door. If he didn't see anyone here, then maybe he had been left behind. He knew that meant he'd have to face the Great Tribulation and the rise of the antichrist and a whole lot of other unpleasantness. Just as he reached for the door, it flew open. He jumped. He half-expected some kind of disembodied creature to fly at him. Instead, a file of students marched past him, down the steps, and out across the quad.

He'd forgot about chapel. That's where all the students and faculty and everyone else but essential campus personnel were. He stood holding the door, watching a long stream of students smile at him as they marched past.

Dale saw Amanda and Mary Jane walking toward him. They both looked at him disapprovingly. They slipped out of line and huddled next to him by the door as the line of students continued to spill out of the building.

"Dale, you missed chapel," Amanda scolded.

"I know, I forgot."

Amanda shook her head and looked at Mary Jane as if to say what a wayward boyfriend she had. Mary Jane nodded. She knew the type.

"I was in the room of darkness," Dale said. He often called it that just for fun. It sounded spookier.

"What?" Apparently, Amanda had forgotten the term.

"The darkroom."

"Well, that's no excuse."

"I know. But it's easy to lose track of time when you're in ..." Dale let his voice fade, before speaking in a low, hushed way like a radio announcer for a scary show, "*the room of darkness.*"

Amanda and Mary Jane were not amused.

"You keep this up and you're going to fail chapel again," Mary Jane told him.

Dale appreciated her concern. He didn't tell her or Amanda but he'd planned that such a fate might befall him. He'd already taken not just the two required religion courses, but *three*. If a student failed chapel more than once, he had to take an additional religion course. Dale remembered failure meant missing more than four chapels. He'd missed five last semester; he'd missed four already this year, but three were excused because he'd been at OU. This absence made two official absences. Anyway, failing chapel didn't affect his GPA. It wasn't for credit.

"So, how was chapel, girls?"

"They gave out T-shirts." Amanda held up one.

"Who gave out T-shirts?"

"The religious life people," said Amanda. "You know, Aaron and his crew."

"Ah, yes, Snort and the gang."

"You shouldn't make fun of Aaron," said Mary Jane.

"Why not? Especially when it's so easy."

"Dale, he works very hard as vice president for religious life," Amanda said.

"Yes, he's one busy weasel."

Amanda shook her head disapprovingly. Before Mary Jane could remind him not to make fun of Aaron again, Dale asked her jokingly if she was dating him.

"None of your business," she said, clearly offended, which puzzled him. Was she insulted that he'd made the joke or because she wanted Snort to ask her out and he hadn't.

"Why are you defending him, then?"

"I'm not defending –" Mary Jane stopped. She told Amanda she was leaving. Amanda asked her to wait for a moment.

"I got to go, too," Amanda said.

"Okay. See you tonight?"

Amanda smiled and said okay. Dale watched them join the thinning stream of students. He turned and nodded like a dutiful doorman as the last few dozen students rushed past.

Dale popped through the door and walked down to the front of the auditorium where Aaron Short and three other students, including Sylvester Fish, were busy tidying up. Dale noticed a few black T-shirts folded on the long table in front of the *His Time* gang. He walked over and picked one up. He read what was printed in white: 3-26-1978-11:59-P.M. Dale wondered why they didn't list the second as well.

Short came over, smiled his usual condescending smile, and asked Dale how he liked the T-shirts.

"I think you should have included the nano second if you're so certain Daniel Ransom Johnson's preposterous prediction will come true."

Short stopped smiling. Fish came over as well.

"You're correct that it refers to brother Johnson's message," said Short. "And it's a message, Smith, that you should behoove."

*Behoove*. Dale rather liked that word. He had to give Short credit; sometimes he used unusual words.

"That's right, Smith," said Fish, his voice genuinely sincere. "You still have time to repent."

"Thanks for your concern, Polonius."

Since Fish was in Dale's Shakespeare class, Dale had started calling him "Polonius" after reading *Hamlet*. Fish, being the literal-minded fellow he was, had thought it was a compliment. Even now, the corners of his thin lips quivered.

Dale turned to Aaron. "But Short, doesn't the Bible say that 'no man knows the time of His return,' meaning Christ's second coming?"

"The T-shirts refer to the time of the Rapture, not Jesus's Second Coming."

"Isn't that the same thing?"

Both Short and Fish looked at each other and smiled. Well, Short smiled; Fish's scar of a mouth just sort of quivered.

"The Rapture precedes the Second Coming," said Short. "It may precede it by quite some time. Some Biblical scholars think as long as seven years."

Dale had to admit he hadn't known that. He shrugged, conceding the point to Short. He then pointed to the T-shirt. "But actually predicting a date? Isn't that silly?"

Short smiled in his patronizing way. "Not at all. The truth has been revealed. Revelation has happened before. It is now happening in our time."

Dale shook his head. Short actually believed it. So did Fish. He almost felt sorry for them.

"What are you going to do when it doesn't happen?" Dale asked.

Short's smile grew larger and more genuine. "What are you going to do when it does?"

"When you're left behind?" Fish added.

Dale knew there was no point in debating the issue. That was the problem. It wasn't an issue to Short and Fish. He turned to go.

"Don't you want a T-shirt?" Short asked, extending one to him.

Dale took it. It wasn't a cheap T-shirt. The material felt substantial. He thought that was sort of funny. People who were raptured left behind their clothes as well as the unbelievers.

"Thanks, Snort," he said.

Aaron didn't smile.

"See you in Shakespeare, Polonius."

Fish nodded, his beady eyes looking brighter than usual behind his glasses.

Dale, the T-shirt oracle in hand, left the building. As he walked across campus, he saw Dean Snyder walking from the opposite direction, also holding a T-shirt. As they passed, Dale held up the hand holding the T-shirt and saluted the administrator. Dean Snyder returned the greeting with a salute of his own. Dale decided that if Short, Fish, and Dean Snyder were going to be raptured, then he wouldn't mind waiting.

The Shakespeare class was focusing on his great tragedies, *Romeo and Juliet*, *Hamlet*, *Macbeth*, *Othello*, *King Lear*, and *The Merchant of Venice*. They were also going to read one comedy, *Much Ado About Nothing*, as well as one of his later plays, *The Tempest*. The class required a lot of work. First, Dale read the play, then he read it again while listening to a recording, then before the exam, he read it a third time. Dr. Frost, the professor, gave mostly detailed objective exams, asking the students to identify lines from the play, define certain words and terms, and briefly describe characters. After his extensive study of the plays, he'd no problem with the exams. He did wonder why the class didn't delve deeper into the themes and ideas explored in the plays. Dr. Frost seemed more interested in the surface of the drama; memorizing soliloquies and dialogue and knowing even minor characters had its place, he thought, but they were skimming over the real meaning. They were overlooking the incredible poetry, philosophy, and insight into not just human nature but life itself contained in the plays.

Sitting in the back of the class, Dale, a little bored with the lecture, flipped through the textbook and read Shakespeare's biography again. He'd read some of his plays in high school; he'd read a few more out of class. But after reading *Hamlet* again, he'd begun to wonder how a man of such modest background could have acquired the political and cultural experience, and the superb education that was so evident in the plays. Dale knew he didn't completely understand what he was reading even when scrutinizing the text three times, but, nevertheless, he felt he was "entering" the text in a more profound way than ever before. He thought he was beginning to understand it on a deeper level – and not just the words and action and speech of the characters, but the psychology, perhaps even the "mind" of the author.

He'd always heard that Shakespeare was a genius, the greatest writer in the English language. He didn't doubt that. But he still wondered how a man with so little if any formal education, no connections to the royal court, and with a background so different than what he wrote about could have made that fantastic leap.

So, when Dr. Frost concluded her initial lecture, Dale asked her. She looked a little startled by his question. After all, the topic under discussion was whether or not Hamlet was indecisive. And if so, was that not a consequence of his loss of faith? But the doctor decided to humor Dale. She asked him to elaborate. He did. She nodded and said "we" (meaning scholars like herself) actually knew very little about Shakespeare's life. However, they made reasonable assumptions that somewhere along the way Shakespeare had made the right aristocratic contacts, traveled abroad, mastered foreign languages, read rare original manuscripts from where he received many of his ideas and characters, studied law, and accomplished all the other impressive achievements that were so brilliantly elucidated in his masterpieces.

Dale said he still didn't understand how a man of such unpromising background could do all that stuff.

Dr. Frost thought about his question for a moment. Then she said with a slight smile on her lupine face that it was a miracle.

Dale felt disappointed. He thought when people couldn't explain phenomena in a convincingly rational way they explained it away as a miracle. He didn't doubt there were miracles, at least in the sense that certain transforming ideas were discovered by human beings who previously hadn't understood them. He appreciated the feelings of awe that those events and occurrences evoked. He also thought there were inexplicable moments of good luck or fate or serendipity or whatever it was that defied logical analysis. But he thought people with curious minds should investigate those inexplicable happenings and not just settle for the "miracle" explanation.

Dr. Frost, confident she had resolved the contradiction, resumed speaking and soon invited questions from the class. Dale thought about pressing her for a better answer to his question; but instead he sat silently and listened to Polly, Sharon, Teri, Fish, and a few others ask perfectly fine conventional questions, which the doctor sagely answered.

After class, Teri asked him if he was going back to the newspaper office, and he said no, he was going to the gym for a short workout. Sometimes when he felt frustrated, he'd go to gym and engage in some intense physical activity and forget his dissatisfaction.

Teri said she'd see him later and Dale left the building and was heading to the gym when David Hawkins caught up with him. He said he was going to the gym, too, and asked if he could walk with him. Dale said sure. While walking, Hawkins said he thought Dale's question about Shakespeare's identity was interesting.

Dale wasn't sure what he meant by "identity." He asked Hawkins to explain.

"Some people aren't convinced that Shakespeare is the real author of the plays and poetry."

"Really?" Dale asked. "Why do they think that?"

"For the same reasons you gave in class. And other things as well, which are more technical in nature."

Dale didn't know that. He'd always been taught the usual Shakespeare biographical stuff: born in Stratford to a glove-maker and his illiterate wife, married the older Anne Hathaway, went to London and became involved in the disreputable theatre, then somehow churned out one masterpiece after another before retiring to Stratford and giving his wife his second best bed in his will.

"How do you know this?"

Hawkins said he'd played Romeo in *Romeo and Juliet* in high school and became almost obsessed with Shakespeare. He'd researched his life quite extensively and discovered there was genuine doubt about Will's identity and the authorship of the plays, as least in certain circles.

"You mean Shakespeare might be a pseudonym?" asked Dale.

"That's one theory."

Dale found all this fascinating. William Shakespeare: sort of an Elizabethan Harry Horse?

Dale said he and David should talk about it more sometime. Hawkins said he'd like that.

They got to the gym and Hawkins said he had to go to the therapy room and soak his knee. Dale said he noticed that he didn't look one hundred percent in the Chiefs' last game. GNC won easily; with Lyle on the squad, the Chiefs had a formidable team and were ranked third in the nation in small college basketball.

Hawkins said his knee wasn't anything serious. Just had to be careful. But he wanted to ask Dale something. Dale said sure, shoot. David wondered if he and Amanda would like to go with him and Hope to the Sooner or Later dinner theatre and see a production of *Man of La Mancha*. He had four tickets for next month's Saturday night performance.

Dale wasn't sure. Hawkins said the tickets were free. A friend of his worked at the dinner theatre and had given him four tickets. David said he bet Amanda would enjoy the musical play.

Dale wished he hadn't brought Amanda into it. But Hawkins was right. She probably would like it. Dale asked if *Man of La Mancha* was the musical version of *Don Quixote*.

"Something like that," Hawkins said. "Anyway, I'd really appreciate it. It's more fun to go with another couple to such an event."

Dale said okay. Hawkins said great. He'd tell Dale more about the arrangements later. David waved and Dale nodded and watched him amble into the part of the gym reserved for varsity athletes.

Dale walked over to the locker room door for non-varsity athletes. He thought Hawkins wasn't such a bad guy. In fact, he rather liked him. He was smart, athletic, and talented. Dale didn't care for David's interest in music and acting, really. But if he had talent for it, then why shouldn't he do that sort of thing? Hawkins, along with Fish, was usually the only guy in Dale's lit classes. Dale guessed he and David had a lot in common. He ought to feel flattered that David wanted to befriend him; after all, he was a starter on the varsity basketball team.

Still, he didn't completely trust Hawkins.

Dale stood in the pizza line with Chris. When he got to the head of the line, he took two slices, one for himself and one for Amanda. Dale noticed that Chris took two as well, although he was alone. Chris and Rowena were no longer a couple. They'd broken up a month before.

Dale and Chris walked back to one of the front tables in the cafeteria and sat down. Amanda and Mary Jane were getting the drinks. Dale noticed that Chris looked depressed. The four of them had just been to the Friday night concert featuring Andrae Crouch and the Disciples, a gospel group. Dale thought it was an excellent concert. The music reminded him a little of some of the Motown music of the early '60s, but with Christian gospel lyrics. He'd hoped the concert would have cheered up his pal.

"Didn't you have fun at the concert?" Dale asked his moping friend.

Chris's melancholy hadn't lessened his appetite. He'd crunched his way through half the first slice already.

Chris shrugged, chewed vigorously, swallowed, and then said he'd felt uncomfortable sitting with Mary Jane.

Dale asked why.

"Because I asked her out three weeks ago and she turned me down."

Dale shook his head. Chris had cut it close. As far as Dale knew, Rusty and Mary Jane had just broken up a week before that.

Chris knew what he was thinking. "Well, she and Rusty were over. I've always thought Mary Jane a nice girl. But it's the same old story. She likes me, but she doesn't like me in *that* way."

Dale said maybe the problem was that Chris was too likable. Sometimes girls were attracted to guys who were not too nice; some of them liked guys who projected a little danger.

"How do you know that?"

"I've seen movies," Dale said, only half joking.

He guessed that some girls liked the idea of domesticating the aggressive male. He thought that was the idea behind some girl's fascination with horses. Carmen had liked drawing horses. He wondered if she'd tamed any stallions yet. He'd ask her the next time he saw her.

"Yeah, I guess that's my problem. I never saw many movies." Chris touched his Gallic nose. "But I think I'd rather get a nose job than change my personality."

The girls returned with the soft drinks. Dale and Chris stood up for them like gentlemen and they slipped by them to their seats. Dale noticed that Mary Jane made sure to sit a few inches farther away from Chris than Amanda did with him. Dale felt sorry for his buddy.

They ate their pizza and Dale listened as Amanda and Mary Jane talked about their usual social concerns. Chris chimed in a few times. Such talk bored Dale. He didn't know half the people the girls were talking about. Just to be contrary, he asked the girls how the new dorm mother was working out.

Amanda and Mary Jane suddenly stopped talking and stared at him. Mrs. Hester's elopement – Dale had heard that she and Dean Pierce got married in Reno, Nevada – was still a taboo topic. Then they both smiled and said that Penelope was an excellent dorm mother. Dale knew they were referring to the fiftyish Mrs. Penelope Peabody, who'd lost her husband in World War II and had never remarried. He thought Mrs. Peabody interesting. Even though she was fairly old, she had extremely long hair. He'd heard the story that on the day she had been informed of her husband being missing in action, she'd vowed never to cut her hair until his return. Her hair, with its gray and blond mixture, supposedly came down to her knees when she unspooled the lengthy tresses. Dale had never seen her with her hair completely undone. In public she kept it coiled in long braids. Her face, although a little wrinkled, was still pretty.

Before Dale could agitate the girls more, Abigail and Henshaw appeared carrying plates of pizza and holding cups of Coke. Amanda asked them to have a seat. Abigail sat next to Amanda and Henshaw next to Mary Jane, across the table from his girlfriend.

Abigail leaned in front of Amanda and said hello to Dale. He nodded. He noticed she had something on her mind. He thought maybe she was going to ask him to recommend a secular film to show before spring break. After all, he was the movie expert on campus. But instead, she asked him if he would serve as master of ceremonies at the Heart-Pal banquet. Dale thought she was kidding. But she nodded her head, while nibbling on a piece of pepperoni, and said she really wanted him to MC the event.

Dale said he didn't think so. She said, please. Then the others, except for Henshaw, chimed in. Dale said he wasn't good at stuff like that. He didn't tell them that he disliked going to those silly banquets. The idea that he'd have to be involved in some way repulsed him. Dale didn't understand why Abigail would want him to be the MC anyway. He asked her, why me?

"You have such an interesting voice," she said.

Dale thought she was teasing. Ever since he'd been required to take speech lessons in Rhode Island, he'd thought he had a funny voice. He suspected that the Yankees had just wanted to erase his Southern accent, which they'd mostly succeeded in doing.

"I don't," he said, annoyed to be even talking about the subject.

Amanda nudged him. "You do," she said.

Dale guessed she thought so. She seemed to like it when he spoke to her in his low, husky voice.

The others, except Henshaw, agreed. Chris and Mary Jane said he had a good announcer's voice.

Abigail pleaded with him with her eyes. Dale had grown fond of her. For the granddaughter of one of the most eminent Nazarenes in history, and the daughter of the college's president, she was unpretentious and good natured. He didn't want to disappoint her.

"Okay," he grumbled. "But I won't do any *performing*."

Amanda laughed. "No one wants you to sing."

"I meant telling jokes," Dale said, wondering if she'd ever heard him really sing. Usually, he just pretended to in church.

"Oh, wonderful," said Abigail. "I know you'll do so well as the MC."

Dale had doubts. He hated doing stuff like that. He looked over at Henshaw. Bobby gave him a slight grin, then turned his attention to Abigail. Dale wondered what had happened to Henshaw. Ever since Dr. Prescott left, he didn't seem quite the same. He and Dale hadn't spoken much during this school year. Part of it was that they didn't have any classes together. Last semester, during their P. E. independent study or after basketball intramurals, they'd engaged in brief discussions, but nothing like their in-depth talks and debates they'd engaged in last school year. Dale was beginning to think that Henshaw had changed into a completely conventional student leader. He didn't seem to question the mores and assumptions of the college or the church. If anything, he seemed as supportive of all the rules and policies as did Short and Fish, but in a more sophisticated and appealing way. After all, Henshaw was a natural leader. Even at age twenty-one, he had a dignified bearing. And Dale knew he had a quick, inquiring mind. He just wondered why Henshaw had decided to pretend otherwise.

Dale thought about raising the issue of the Rapture prediction. The topic had been bubbling under the surface on campus but no one seemed to want to discuss it directly. Short and Fish had sort of turned it into a campaign, but other campus leaders like Henshaw hadn't said much about it. He wouldn't let the topic be discussed in the stuco meetings. Instead, he made sure the student council remained focused on business and educational matters. Dale appreciated that, but he still wondered how Bobby regarded the whole preposterous notion.

Henshaw said he was going for another slice and excused himself. Dale waited a second,

593

then did the same. He caught up to Henshaw before they made it to the pizza line. Bobby turned and acquired that guarded look that Dale had noticed on previous occasions when he'd cornered him.

"Hey, Henshaw." Dale glanced back at the Amanda and the others. They were pleasantly chatting away. "I want to ask you something."

Henshaw waited. The look on his face wasn't entirely friendly. Dale wondered what he'd done to make Henshaw doubt their friendship.

"What do you think about this Rapture stuff?"

Henshaw's handsome face clouded. Dale could see he didn't want to talk about it.

"You mean in general?"

"No. I mean this prediction that has a few people on campus believing it's going to happen."

"It's more than a few."

"That doesn't matter. What do *you* think?"

Dale waited. Henshaw had always been rather non-committal about certain matters. He'd always defended his reluctance to quickly express his opinion on a desire to consider all the information and give it due thought. Dale was beginning to suspect that he just was cautious and canny and wanted to see where the issue or idea was going before he decided to jump out in front and lead in that direction.

"I believe it's possible," Henshaw said.

"Of course it's possible," Dale said. "Anything's theoretically possible. It's possible we're not even standing here talking. But we are. And I want to know what you really think."

Henshaw smiled just a little, but he didn't say anything.

"I see," said Dale, with a small smile of his own. "You're playing Sir Thomas More."

"That's an interesting comparison," Henshaw said, his smile disappearing. Both of them had admired More while studying his *Utopia* in their renaissance and reformation history class last year. "But you remember that More was beheaded. And I have no intention of meeting such a fate, even in a symbolic sense."

## Chapter 11: *A standing O at Heart-Pal; parking after Man of La Mancha*

Dale didn't feel comfortable in his rented tux. He stood in the wings of the stage tugging on the shirtsleeves and pulling on the collar. As usual, the suit coat was a little tight in the shoulders and a tad too long in the sleeves. The ruffled shirt seemed to strangle him. He wished more than ever that he'd told Abigail no to being the MC.

Complicating matters was the fact that Amanda had been named one of the five Heart-Pal sweetheart candidates. Dale had to announce the candidates and the winner, so he couldn't be her escort for the brief ceremony. Since she had to have an escort, Dale had asked Chris to be it. He'd agreed – a little too readily, Dale thought.

Chris didn't get to sit with her. Dale glanced over to him sitting at the far end of the table, almost a forgotten man. Once the ceremony began, Chris would go over and escort Amanda to center stage, then afterward he'd return to his small corner of the table. In a way, Chris was the designated escort. Just as Dale detested the DH in baseball, he despised this absurd arrangement.

Amanda and the other four candidates and their escorts sat at the banquet table on the stage. From the stage wing, Dale looked at Amanda and she waved. She looked lovely. Dressed in an elegant light blue dress with a scooped bosom, rather daring for her, he thought, she was the prettiest of the five sweetheart candidates. He wasn't sure what he'd do in the unlikely event she won; after all, she was the only junior girl among the five. He guessed as soon as he announced her name, he'd walk over to her with the microphone in his hand, cut in front of Chris, and slip the small crown on her head, and then kiss her.

Chris didn't have a date, in part because he'd consented to this charade. Dale told him he could have asked a girl to come along; he'd just have to leave her when the time came to escort Amanda. But Chris didn't even know whom to ask. He'd exhausted his supply of potential girlfriends.

The guests were all seated and it was time to start the proceedings. The trio of musicians, a harpist, a flutist, and a violinist, brought their lilting melody to a close. Dale walked past the dining table with the candidates, escorts, and the two administrators who served as sponsors, and approached the microphone. He hadn't even practiced his master of ceremonies routine. He'd warned Abigail that he'd just wing it. She'd said fine.

He welcomed the guests. He briefly described the history and significance of the Heart-Pal banquet in a concise, accurate manner that would do any newspaperman proud. He refused to use flowery language even at such a mushy occasion as this. As he spoke, he couldn't tell how his voice sounded other than amplified. To him, it sounded a little nasal but he hoped also deep and resonant. He'd always had problems with his sinuses; that's one reason why he had nosebleeds. He was sure his voice reflected his congested sinuses, and for an absurd moment he wondered if Abigail and everyone else had tricked him into doing the MC chores just to laugh at him.

He paused and looked over the audience and noticed that no one was laughing. Now, having concluded his opening remarks, he told the audience that he supposed a polished MC would tell a few jokes at this point. But since he didn't know any jokes and hadn't cared to learn any, he thought they could just pretend that he'd told some really funny ones and laugh anyway.

Dale waited. A few people tittered. He waited some more. More people chortled. Still, he waited and pretty soon everyone in the banquet hall laughed, some even guffawing. Dale thought that was interesting. He knew laughter tended to be infectious. He'd noticed that sometimes people laughed just because someone else was laughing. Amanda was that way.

After the laughter died down, Dale congratulated them on their imaginations. He almost said, now imagine that the banquet is over so they all could go home, but he didn't. Instead, he said they, the audience, had performed so well that they should applaud themselves. And to his amazement, they did.

Dale stood at the podium listening to the applause and he marveled at the power he possessed. He'd made the audience laugh at non-existent jokes and then applaud themselves for engaging in the absurdity of it all! It astounded him that people were so agreeable and willing to comply with the wishes of an authority figure – and he felt pretty authoritative right then. He wondered what other magic he could conjure for the willing audience, but he decided not to press his luck. He really just wanted to get the whole thing over with.

So, he moved on to the ceremony. He announced the candidates and the escorts. His only prank was to introduce Chris as Christian De Gaulle rather than DeVille, which provoked a few chuckles and a frown from Chris. Then he read the candidates' vital information: class standing, majors, hometown, parents' names, and campus activities. He was tempted to add their measurements and perhaps even exaggerate them like they did in *Playboy*, but he didn't. He knew that would be going too far.

He tried not look too closely at Amanda as she walked by with Chris. He half-wished she would win, but if she did he knew it would make things awkward for all of them.

He accepted the envelope containing the name of the winner from Abigail and opened it. He paused dramatically, but not intentionally so. For a moment, he thought the card actually said Amanda Meeks. He found himself about to pronounce her name, when his head cleared and his eyes refocused and he read the actual winner: Amy Mears.

The audience clapped and Dale let out a sigh of relief which, unfortunately, was picked up by the microphone. No one seemed to care. He watched the coronation of Amy, who looked quite comely with her long red tresses while wearing a silver gown. He felt a little pride that a graduate of Galilee High had been named 1978 Heart-Pal Sweetheart.

After the ceremony, Dale got to join Amanda for the splendid roast duck meal. Amanda told him that he was doing just fine, but she said it in such a way that he wondered. He didn't tell her that he'd almost read her name by mistake. He imagined what would have happened if he had. He guessed he'd have to announce a correction and make a fool out of himself. After all, the Heart-Pal committee knew who'd won. He'd probably be accused of trying to rig the election for Amanda. As he chewed on his scrumptious meal, he imagined the lurid scandal his negligence would cause. He found the whole fantasy strangely entertaining.

After dinner, his only duty was to read the engagement announcements. He accepted the list from Abigail and read them in a dignified voice to begin with. But after the thirteenth announcement, he grew bored and injected a little more drama into his voice, almost approaching his deep, hushed *Room of Darkness* voice.

After he read K. C.'s and Gretchen's engagement, which was the last one, he couldn't resist adding one more. He read in a solemn, rather thoughtful voice, with what he hoped was a touch of poignancy, the engagement of Aaron Short to Sylvester Fish.

Quite a few people laughed; more than he expected. However, he noticed some people glaring at him, in particular Aaron Short who sat near the front with his date, Mary Jane.

Dale winked at them. Now he knew why Mary Jane had defended Short and then had been offended by Dale's accusation that they were dating. They were!

He concluded the occasion by complimenting the audience on their patience, their fortitude, and their compliance. He wondered how many people in the audience knew what the heck he was talking about. But they all looked pleased with themselves. He said they had been such an outstanding audience, and this had been such a magnificent banquet and ceremony, that he thought the audience should give themselves a standing ovation.

Dale started clapping. He nodded at them, to encourage them to overcome their natural modesty. And to his astonishment and pleasure, people began to stand and clap. Eventually, almost everyone in the audience stood and clapped except Short, Mary Jane, and Short's friends and associates.

He told them all good night and good luck. The musical trio played exiting music. The banquet hall filled with the buzzing of voices. Dale pulled his stupid bow tie loose. Then Putney, who'd brought Olivia Szabo, came up to the stage and congratulated him on his great MC job. Dale shook his hand and said thanks, but realized if Putney thought he'd done a good job, then he was probably in trouble.

However, no one at the head table denounced him as he walked back to Amanda. Abigail smiled at him, and said he did quite well, even if his imagination seemed to get the better of him. Henshaw waved at him but didn't come forward and shake his hand. Chris frowned at him again and asked why he'd made fun of him. Dale said he wasn't making fun. He'd just got Chris confused with another great Frenchman. Chris forgave him with a grin.

Amanda, however, did not seem pleased. She and Dale, along with Chris, walked out together and didn't speak until they got to the parking lot. Then Chris, who Dale thought had been unusually pensive all evening, said good night, and Dale and Amanda waved.

Dale opened the door for her and when he shut it he couldn't help but think how incongruous the two of them looked dressed in their finery only to be riding in such an old, prosaic car. Dale guessed he should have borrowed Blackie's Oldsmobile. Maybe that would have pleased Amanda.

As he drove back to Galilee, he reckoned he must have attended ten banquets since his sophomore year in high school. But this one had been the best. He got to take Amanda and he got to goof off a little, too.

He glanced over to Amanda. She didn't seem to be in any better mood than she had when he picked her up. He'd even bought her a fancy corsage, too. He asked what was wrong.

"Nothing," she said.

He glanced at her. She'd worn more makeup than usual. He especially liked her red lips. She hardly ever wore red lipstick. It made her lips looks even more voluptuous. They reminded him of ripe, juicy cherries.

"Come on," he said. "You've been mopey all night."

He knew he shouldn't have used that word. He should have used a word she wouldn't quite understand, like saturnine or dyspeptic or bilious. She turned and looked disapprovingly at him.

"You didn't have to act so strangely."

Dale didn't think he'd acted strangely, exactly. Just unorthodox. Well, to Amanda that was the same thing.

"Just trying to provide a little levity to the proceedings."

That was true, but now as he thought about the power he had wielded over the audience he remembered that intoxicating feeling standing on the stage. He felt sort of powerful. He told the audience what to do and they did it. Dale then had an insight. He imagined controlling an audience in a different setting, an even more emotionally charged atmosphere. He could imagine losing his head. Then he understood why Daniel Ransom Johnson might have said what he said, why he'd predicted the date of the Rapture. Maybe the evangelist had simply got carried away. Dale, now having tasted the potent brew of public speaking and swaying an audience, could understand that.

"And I don't know why you had to make fun of Chris and Aaron."

Dale glanced at Amanda. She actually seemed upset. She sat extremely still the way she did when she was disturbed. He even saw her bite her lower lip, which must have scraped a little lipstick into her mouth.

"I was just joking. Chris said he didn't mind."

"Aaron was offended by your tasteless joke."

Dale didn't like the tone of her voice. She sounded more affronted than Mary Jane had when he'd teased her about dating Short.

"Aaron is easily offended," he said, not calling him Snort because he knew that would upset her even more.

"He has important responsibilities so sometimes he comes across as too straight-laced. That's why some people make fun of him."

Dale's mind began working in another direction. He glanced at Amanda. She was too perturbed for it to be just about what he'd done tonight.

"So, what happened with you and Short?"

Amanda turned to him with her eyes wide and her mouth slightly open. Ordinarily, Dale liked that look. He always liked it when she looked caught off guard.

When she didn't answer, he kept his voice calm and professional, the way he would if something embarrassing had happened at the Heart-Pal banquet.

"What happened, Amanda? You can tell me."

She paused, then told him that they had dated during her freshman year. In fact, she'd asked him out for her twirp date.

Dale thought, maybe twirp was an accurate name after all. Then his sense of humor disappeared with the image of Amanda and Short together.

"You asked *him* out?"

Amanda nodded. Dale almost remarked that she had strange taste in men when he realized that comment would include him. Instead, he asked what happened.

"Well, we went out a couple more times after that and then, well, he didn't call."

"And you wanted him to?"

"No, not really. It's just that I had always been the one to, well, to …"

"End things."

Amanda nodded.

Dale could hardly imagine anyone not wanting to continue to date Amanda. Well, Aaron, in spite of his bonhomie, was a sort of peculiar guy. Then he wondered if Amanda really wanted Short to continue to ask her out. He didn't like that idea.

"What else happened?" He said it more forcefully than he meant to, but the tone of his voice prompted her to answer instead of evading his question.

"Well, later we talked. He told me that the reason he didn't call me again was because he knew he'd be too attracted to me. That dating me would distract him in his work. He takes his work for Jesus very seriously, Dale. That's why you shouldn't make fun of him."

Dale felt himself growing angry. Not only with Short, but also with Amanda.

"And you believed him?"

"Of course. I mean, the part about his wanting to concentrate on his service to God. You know, he's going on a mission this summer. To the Philippines."

"Do you still like Short?"

"It's not so much that I like him. It's more that I respect him. And his dedication to his work. He'll make an excellent minister."

Dale didn't know what to say. If Amanda really felt that way about a fool like Short, he didn't know if he could trust her judgment in other matters. Then he wondered if maybe he was wrong about Aaron. He was a pretty smart guy. He made the academic honor societies. He studied Greek. Girls no doubt thought he was cute with his sleek features and big smile. Dale guessed maybe he did have a certain kind of integrity about him. He really seemed to believe in what he did. He sincerely produced the *His Time* devotional book. Then he thought, snap out of it! Short was a narrow-minded, humorless Bible thumper, to borrow a phrase from Blackie. He just hid his fanaticism with his casual clothes and big grin.

Amanda suddenly slid over and put her hand on his arm. He glanced at her and realized he must have a very serious expression on his face. She smiled at him in an apologetic kind of way; he didn't know if she wanted him to forgive her or she had forgiven him.

"Don't worry," she said. "I don't really like him. I mean, I don't *care* about him."

Dale wasn't sure he believed her. He wondered if he had to worry about Hawkins and Short. He still couldn't believe that Amanda and Short had been out together.

"I'm sorry if I criticized your job tonight," she said. "Aside from what you said about Chris and Aaron, I thought you did an excellent job."

"You did?"

"Yes. You were actually pretty funny."

He raised an eyebrow. He'd never been the funny guy; Rusty had always been that. Dale was more like the gag writer that Rusty used for some of his better material.

"But you didn't seem to be enjoying yourself much," he said. They were in Galilee. He turned off the expressway to campus.

"Oh, I just wasn't in the mood."

"Were you bothered that you didn't win Heart-Pal sweetheart?"

Amanda smiled. "Not at all." Then she grew serious. "In fact, I didn't really want to be a candidate."

That admission interested Dale. He'd always thought such rituals silly. Not that he'd want to see them eliminated. He felt the same way about the Academy Awards. Even though the ceremony was ridiculous, he still sort of liked watching.

"Why? You're the prettiest girl on campus."

Amanda shook her head. "I'm not. But that's what bothers me. We shouldn't make such a fuss over unimportant things like, you know, looks."

Dale pulled into the Hayley parking lot and parked in the semi-lit back. He put the car in park and turned off the motor. He leaned back and looked at Amanda.

"Beauty is not unimportant," he said.

"But it's not important either. It fades. What's important is the beauty within."

In theory, Dale thought that was true. But at that moment looking at her bathed in the hazy light of parking lot, he didn't think so.

"Well, maybe because it fades is why it is important. The impermanence makes it precious."

Amanda smiled a little. "I know what you mean. But sometimes I wish I weren't so …" She didn't want to say it.

"Beautiful?"

"I'm not."

"Okay," Dale said. "Not ugly. Let's say you sometimes wish you were not so ugly."

Amanda didn't laugh.

"Amanda, you *are* beautiful. Inside and out. But why does being pretty bother you?"

She leaned against his shoulder and peered out the window at the shadowy parking lot. "Because that's all most people see. And I can't blame them. I'm not good at anything. I'm not smart. I'm not clever or charming or funny. I'm clumsy. I can't do anything that's physical. I don't even cook or sew well like my mother. I'm not talented. I didn't play the flute very well. And I don't think I sing very well either. If all I have is looks, then what will I have when that fades?"

Dale shook his head. "Yeah, you're hopeless."

She smiled a little but didn't laugh.

"Look, first of all, you are not clumsy, you're just not athletic." Dale paused. "Well, maybe you are clumsy." This time she giggled. "But everything else you said is not accurate. You are talented. You have a lovely voice. You're smart, smarter than a lot of people."

"Not as smart as you."

Dale gave her a mock-solemn look. "Few are."

She giggled again.

"But one of the best things about you is that you have a wonderful personality."

"I don't."

"Yeah, you do. Having a wonderful personality is more than telling jokes or being clever or sophisticated or whatever people usually think it is. You're kind and considerate and thoughtful and all those more important things."

"You really think so?"

"I do. In fact, sometimes I think you overdo it."

"Oh? In what way?"

"Well, if you want to know the truth, you tend to attribute virtues to some people who aren't deserving."

"Oh?"

"Yeah, but that's about your only fault."

"I wish."

Dale glanced at her. She still looked a little glum. Most girls would be delighted to have been in the Heart-Pal court as a junior. That meant that Amanda would probably be homecoming queen next year. But Amanda seemed to feel just the opposite. He wondered if she were really as insecure as she sometimes seemed to be. He remembered gazing at her in high school and thinking not only how pretty she was but how serene she seemed. Now, he'd learned that she had a lot of doubts about herself. He wondered if that explained her devotion to religion. Not just an appreciation for the spiritual, which he understood, but a need for ritual, clear boundaries, and a rather simplistic view of life.

Dale then wondered what he'd be doing next year. Maybe working at the town newspaper. He'd spoken to the editor of the *Galilee Gazette* a few days ago. Mr. Webb said they might need some help next fall. Since the paper was only a weekly, it would only be part-time as a sportswriter. Dale felt a little encouraged, but even if he kept his campus cop job he wouldn't be making that much money. But at least he'd be with Amanda for her senior year.

"There's something else that's been bothering me," Amanda said.

"What?"

"Well, the deadline for Lost and Found is soon. I'm not sure if I should apply."

"Of course you should."

"What if I don't get it again?"

"You will."

"If I do, then we won't see each other much during the summer."

Same situation as last year, thought Dale. He told her the same thing, too. He'd just work longer and harder and the time would pass faster. He knew she wanted to be in the Lost and Found troupe. She'd dreamed about it since she was a kid. She ought to try again. If she got it, they'd work it out.

"Okay, I'll apply. But I won't get it."

"You will."

And somehow this time he knew he would be right.


David Hawkins had a pretty cool car, thought Dale, as he and Amanda sat in the back of his Pontiac Firebird. They were driving back to campus after seeing *Man of La Mancha*. Dale had been surprised by how much he enjoyed it. He didn't even mind too much when the singing interrupted the action. They had sat at a table not too far from the stage. He liked watching the comic duels and the exciting near rape-scene of Dulcinea. In the end, Quixote is overwhelmed by the army of mirrors and the deluded knight-errant succumbs. But before he dies, he affirms in song his belief in a romantic ideal.

Dale glanced at Amanda. She'd been rather quiet on the ride back. She hadn't even spoken much to Hope. Well, they were roommates. He guessed they spoke all the time.

Hawkins whistled the "Impossible Dream" as he drove. Dale thought he whistled better than he sang. He watched David reach up and smooth his curly hair while finishing the song. Then he saw him look in his rearview mirror. Dale felt a little annoyed. Hawkins had been doing that quite a lot on the drive back. Dale didn't like him looking at Amanda. David had looked more in his rearview mirror than he had looked at Hope sitting next to him.

"Hey, did you guys like the meal?" Hawkins asked them.

Dale remembered he'd already asked that question once; he guessed Hawkins was trying to give a reason for getting caught looking at Amanda in the rear-view mirror.

The three of them said it was good. Steak, baked potato, green beans, a hard roll, choice of drink, and apple pie. Not bad, thought Dale. He was glad it wasn't some fancy stuff. He wondered how much a ticket to the Sooner or Later dinner theatre cost.

Dale felt like talking about Shakespeare again. He and Hawkins had talked at some length on the way to the dinner theatre. So much, in fact, that the girls had visibly shown their impatience. Neither of them cared much about hearing him and Hawkins speculate about Shakespeare's real identity. David said he leaned toward the Francis Bacon theory. Dale remembered reading some of Bacon's *Novum Organum* when he studied for the humanities CLEP exam. Just based on that one experience, he had doubts about Bacon. His writing style not only was different, but the intelligence displayed in that work didn't seem to match the Shakespearean mind very well. Hawkins said Dale had a good point. He'd check into that Bacon work.

Now as Hawkins drove into the Hayley parking lot, he asked Dale if he was sure he and Amanda didn't want to join them for coffee at the *Java Joint*. Dale said they'd like to but he had to get up early for work the next morning. Hawkins said he understood. Dale and Amanda got out and thanked David again for the tickets. The two couples said bye to each other and then Dale and Amanda watched David and Hope drive away.

Amanda looked at Dale, wondering why he'd said he had to get up early. His job hadn't stopped him before from staying out late on a Saturday night. Dale didn't want to tell her that he needed some excuse to get away from Hawkins. He didn't like the idea of David spending even more time in Amanda's company.

Dale said he'd like to get a Coke. She gave him a look that said then why didn't they join David and Hope, but when he asked if she wanted one she said all right. They walked over to his car and got in and Dale turned north out of the parking lot.

Amanda said, didn't he turn the wrong way? Weren't Sooner Shack and the other places he liked the other way?

He grinned a little.

"Dale, I don't want to go to the lake," Amanda said.

He was surprised by how emphatic she sounded.

"Why?"

"Because I don't. I don't want for us to get caught."

"By the cops?"

"By anyone."

"Don't worry. We're not going to the lake."

Before she could ask where they were going, he asked her how Hope was getting along with Hawkins.

"Oh, she likes him very much."

"Really?"

"Yes. They've been dating steady for several months now."

He wondered if Hawkins could be so sneaky that he'd lead Hope on and befriend him just so he could get to know Amanda better. He didn't know. On one hand, Hawkins seemed like a sincere kind of guy. On the other hand, there was something about him that made Dale suspicious.

"Dale, where are we going?"

He glanced at Amanda. She seemed suspicious herself. He'd already passed the only other fast food joint on the north side.

"Just wait. You'll see."

"I told you I don't want to go to the lake."

"We're not going to the lake."

Amanda looked out her side window. "Then where are we going?"

"To this perfect, secluded little spot that I know about; that is, that I found recently."

Dale wasn't telling the exact truth. It was that perfect spot he used to take Wendy to, the one not too far from the pasture where Vern's horse was stabled. He hadn't been there since that last time with Wendy. But he was certain it would still be as private as before.

Dale glanced at Amanda and saw her staring at him with disapproval. He didn't know what was wrong with her. They hadn't had any real intimacy since New Year's Eve. He grew a little angry.

"I need some physical contact," he told her. He watched her eyes grow large at his blunt declaration but she didn't protest.

Dale drove to the spot and saw with satisfaction that it was as protected by the two large, low-limbed trees and several bushes as he'd remembered it. He slowly turned into the space and parked. He turned and nodded at the back of the car. See, he said, how the trees and bushes hide the car? No one will know we're here.

Amanda still didn't look receptive. She didn't move closer to him. She stared out the window at the night sky and the darker fields spread before it.

Dale asked her how she liked *Man of La Mancha*. She hadn't said much about it.

She said she liked the music but she thought the play had too much violence and vulgarity.

Dale tried thinking what she'd object to. Well, Dulcinea did dress rather revealingly. She wore a low-cut blouse and her skirt often flew to mid-thigh when she cavorted or when she struggled against the rapists. Also, the near-rape scene was pretty realistic. He remembered glancing at Amanda and seeing her blanched face.

"Didn't the violence and vulgarity make a dramatic contrast to the idealism and romance in the play?" Dale asked.

Amanda said she guessed so.

Dale asked her why she didn't scoot over. She glanced at him but didn't move. He reached his hand out and said in a low coaxing voice, come here.

She hesitated, then she slid over and Dale put his arm around her. He asked, didn't she like being alone with him anymore? She nodded. He asked why she was acting like this then? She said she felt uncomfortable sitting in a car. He told her this was a safe, secluded place. She asked how did he know that?

Dale's hand had been caressing the curve of her upper arm, but now he stopped. He didn't like the critical tone of her voice.

"Well, isn't this the kind of place you used to take Wendy to?" she asked again, this time in an even more offended voice.

"As a matter of fact, I used to take Wendy to this exact place," Dale said. "And she never acted the way you're acting."

Amanda stared angrily at him. In the shadows, her eyes flashed.

"So, now I'm just another girl you want to bring here and take advantage of?" She tried to throw off his arm. He squeezed her shoulder tighter with his hand.

"What are you talking about? You're not just another girl."

"I'm not like Wendy, am I? You wish I were, though."

"Sometimes I do."

It was the truth but he knew he shouldn't have said it. She tried to slap him but Dale caught her wrist and squeezed it until she cried out.

"Let go," she said.

But he didn't.

"Please, Dale, let go."

Dale let go of her wrist but he leaned against her, still keeping his arm wrapped tightly around her shoulders. She shrank from him. He leaned closer and tried to look in her eyes, but she turned her head.

"I love *you*, Amanda, but sometimes you drive me crazy. You seem to think that being close to one another is wrong. But it's not. Not when you love someone."

He waited for her to say something, but she didn't. He squeezed her shoulder again and hugged her to him but she still remained silent. He grew a little angry and put his free hand on her face and turned her head to him. She resisted for a moment, then complied. He kissed her, hard. She didn't return his kiss at first. Then she opened her lips and he thrust his tongue in her mouth and he threw both his arms around her and pulled her against him. They began kissing with passion and he put a hand underneath her sweater and squeezed her breast and he heard her moan under his mouth. He kissed her neck and heard her gasp while his hand shoved her bra up and freed her breasts. Then he pulled up her sweater but didn't take it off. He pulled it up high enough so he could kiss and nuzzle her.

She grabbed at his jacket and he threw it off. She tried to unbutton his shirt, but it took too long, so he unbuttoned four buttons then tore the last few when he pulled open his shirt and pressed his chest against her. His hands reached behind her and slid down inside her slacks. He grasped each cheek and he pushed her against the bulge in his pants. He pushed into her, then leaned back and pulled her slacks and panties down past her hips. They kissed, then Dale put his hand between her thighs. He pushed two fingers inside her. She was very wet and not as tight as before. He heard her gasp. She moaned loudly as he worked his fingers with more precision. Then he felt her hand unzip his fly. She began to shudder and moan. Dale tried to hold back, but just feeling her hand on his erection and hearing her voice lose control caused him to explode in his pants. He growled loudly from the sensation and out of angry frustration at climaxing prematurely.

Amanda stopped moaning and pushed his hand away from inside her. She fell against him and began to cry. Dale slumped against her and tried to recover. He felt nauseous as he always did when he didn't ejaculate freely. He held her next to him and heard her weep harder. He didn't know what was wrong. She wasn't crying out of relief or passion; she seemed to be crying out of fear.

He asked her what was wrong. She cried even more loudly. He felt afraid that he'd hurt her. Amanda had never cried this loudly and openly before. Usually, she wept almost silently. Now she sobbed, and Dale felt utterly helpless.

He held and rocked her. Her crying grew quieter. She gasped for breath once, and hiccupped once, then she stopped weeping but still pressed her face against his shoulder.

Dale decided he hadn't hurt her physically. In fact, he was pretty sure she'd climaxed. Could that be what was scaring her?

He held her and said he loved her. He said he was sorry if he'd hurt her or scared her or did anything to her she didn't want.

She didn't speak. She lifted her head from off his shoulder and turned away and reached for her purse. She brought out a hanky and blew her nose and wiped her eyes. She leaned back against the seat and he looked at her swollen eyes and tear-stained cheeks and felt himself crumble inside.

He asked what was wrong. Why didn't she speak to him? When she turned to him, he saw her chin tremble as she bit her lower lip.

"Amanda, what is it?"

She cried again, this time in her usual, almost silent way. He watched the tears ooze out of her eyes and trickle down her face. He wiped away her tears, and took her face between his hands and gently kissed the moisture off her cheeks. He told her he loved her more than anything. Would she please speak to him?

Amanda took a deep breath. She blinked her eyes. She stopped crying. She said she didn't know what was wrong. She felt confused. She felt she wasn't in control of herself and it scared her.

Dale put his arm around her and hugged her.

"Maybe we should get married. Is that what you want?"

"I don't know."

Dale wondered if the Heart-Pal banquet two weeks ago with all the engagement announcements had affected her like it did him. He wanted to have their engagement announced, and yet he didn't. He wanted to be with her, to marry her, but he didn't want to become part of her world.

"What if, after I graduate, we just run away together?"

Amanda stared at him, the rims of her eyes red.

"I mean, elope. Just leave all this behind us. All the frustration and worry. Just leave and be with one another. Love one another."

"What would we do?"

"It doesn't matter. I could find a job. We could go to the west coast. Maybe up to Alaska. We could just live."

"You want me to leave my home? My parents?"

Dale knew what else she'd have to leave. Her town, her church, her friends, her college. Her life. Yes, he wanted that.

"We'd be together, Amanda."

"Oh, Dale."

He knew he was thinking crazy. And yet two older people had done it. Why couldn't they?

He looked into her eyes. "What do you want, Amanda? What do you *really* want?"

"I don't know. I don't know anymore."

He knew what he wanted. Why did she have to be so complicated?

"What about your parents, Dale? Your home?"

"I don't have a home."

Amanda found this interesting. She leaned closer to him. He knew she wanted to hear more.

"Why do you say that?" she asked.

Dale thought about telling her about all the problems with Jesse and Blackie. But why tell her? He could just show her. He wondered how she'd react if he took her to see Jesse perched on the couch puffing like a chimney while watching one inane television show after another. Or better, wait until Jesse went crazy and let Amanda see her babbling nonsense to the cheap portrait of Jesus. Or take her to meet Blackie, especially after he'd had a few drinks. He could tell her some of his charming stories about picking up floaters and scraping up the charred remains of a "nigger" boatswain. Maybe they could double date with his dad and Cleoma. Dale was certain Amanda would hit it off with Cleoma.

"You have such a strange look on your face, Dale. What are you thinking about?"

He knew he had a bitterly amused look on his face. He was thinking that even Amanda didn't have enough understanding and kindness to overlook the grotesquerie of his family.

"Amanda, if we want to be together, we need to leave all of that."

"All of what? Dale, I love my family. I love my church. I love the college. I don't want to leave."

Dale knew that. He blinked his eyes and thought of something impersonal and physical. The best he could do was conjure up the image of Blackie's .38 revolver.

He turned to her and smiled a little. "I know." He hugged her. "I was just talking crazy."

Amanda's expression told him that she agreed. Then her eyes grew large and her mouth opened in alarm.

"Oh, my! Dale, what time is it?"

He said he didn't know. He didn't have a wristwatch.

Amanda became flustered. She yanked her slacks and panties up and pulled her bra and sweater down and made worried sounds in her throat. Dale buttoned his shirt and zipped up. Then he watched her finish straightening up. When she gave him a reprimanding look, he reminded her that she had a wristwatch on.

"Oh, goodness gracious."

She peered at the wristwatch. She said she couldn't see it well enough. He took her wrist and moved it into what little light there was and stared at it.

"Twelve ten," he said.

"Oh, no! I've missed curfew."

For a moment, he thought Amanda might start crying again, but this time out of vexation. Instead she bit her lip and instructed him in an agitated voice that they had to go. Dale started the car and backed out of the spot, then drove fast, but not too fast, down the road and then turned south back to town.

He glanced over to Amanda. She stared out the window, gnawing on her lower lip. He wanted to tell her to stop, but he knew she was worried. She'd never broke curfew before.

He didn't like seeing her worry so much. So what if she were twenty minutes late? He wasn't sure what Mrs. Peabody would do. He doubted anything severe. Just chastise her. Maybe give her a demerit. The girls had some kind of system that charted their misbehavior. He thought that was ridiculous, too.

When they got into town, the streetlights illuminated the inside of the car enough that Dale noticed that Amanda looked a mess. Her clothes looked rumpled, her hair disheveled, her lip-gloss smeared, her eyes red from weeping, her cheeks stained with tears. Then he noticed another disturbing detail: a bruise on the soft inside part of her wrist, the spot where a nurse would take her pulse. A bruise caused by the thumb of his left hand when he'd squeezed her wrist.

He shook his head. He hadn't meant to hurt her. He remembered the time they'd made out passionately in her garage for the second time and how he'd left marks on her neck.

When he saw her next, she wore a turtleneck sweater and scolded him for doing that to her. She actually seemed upset at first, but when he said in an abject voice how sorry he was, she forgave him with a little smile. Since then, he'd been careful not to press too hard on the soft skin of her neck with his mouth or fingers.

He reached over and touched the bruise on her wrist. She looked startled.

"Sorry," he said.

Amanda blinked her eyes and looked down at his finger caressing the bruise. She didn't say anything. Instead, she looked at herself in the mirror and gasped. She hastily tried to make herself more presentable to whoever stood guard in the dormitory. He glanced at her as she fussed. He almost smiled. He'd never seen her become so busy with herself, combing her hair, cleaning her face with a tissue, straightening her clothes.

When they arrived at the dorm, Amanda told him just to drop her off. Dale asked why the rush? She was already late. Why not let him park and walk her to the door?

"Dale!" she cried, pointing to the street curb in front of Hayley. "Just stop and let me get out."

He coasted to a stop beside the curb and she jumped out of the car without letting him kiss her or even say good-bye. He watched her half walk, half run to the front doors in her kind of cute, clumsy way. When she arrived, she turned and gave him a wave at least, but her face looked worried.

Dale watched her disappear inside the dorm. Then he drove west out of town, down the highway past the old, abandoned children's hospital, then turned south on the rural road and drove to Reinhardt's Summit. He parked the car on the side of the road, ascended the hill, and gazed out at the deep night sky, the shining stars, the three-quarter moon, and the slumbering town of Galilee with its flickering lights where Amanda was now safe and secure in her dorm room.

He hoped he hadn't ruined everything.

**Chapter 12:** *Violating locker room etiquette; spring break animals; VPL*

Dale waved at Amanda as she sat in the van. She smiled and waved back. She'd forgiven him two weeks ago, but he'd detected a kind of sadness in her since that night at the secluded spot. Now, leaving for the Lost and Found auditions, she seemed happy again.

They hadn't indulged in any prolonged "physical contact" since that night. Just some kissing and a little petting in his car. Amanda hadn't gotten in much official trouble for missing dorm curfew, but her mother had heard and apparently shamed her. Since then, Amanda had refused to go parking, either at the lake or that secluded spot, and also declined his invitation to visit the newspaper office. Dale was running out of places for trysting.

Even on her twenty-first birthday, after a delightful dinner at Jacques, and after Dale bestowed on her a rather expensive silver charm bracelet, she didn't feel like making out. He attributed part of her reluctance to over celebrating. Her parents had made a big deal of her birthday. They threw a party for her and all her friends had attended. Since her birthday was on Saturday, Dale missed the beginning of her party because of work. But he arrived in time to see her parents present Amanda with a new sky blue Volvo.

Now, a week later, Dale watched the van with Amanda and eleven other GNCers in it roll out of the parking lot. He didn't like Amanda being away so long. Like last year, her parents were going to meet her in Kansas City after she completed her audition, but instead of going to the Ozarks for spring break, the Meeks were going to visit Vicki's relatives in Kansas City before driving to Iowa and visiting Rex's family.

However, Dale didn't feel completely out of luck. Hawkins wasn't on the van. Instead, Hope had, in a sense, taken his place. She was going to audition for the acting troupe where singing wasn't as important.

Hawkins, who'd seen Hope off, came over and stood by Dale as they watched the van disappear down the road on its way to Kansas City. David said since both of them were going to be on their own for spring break, they ought to do something together. Dale said okay, what did he have in mind? David asked if he played racquetball. Dale said yeah. He'd taken a class in it during his spring semester at CSU. Hawkins said they could play at the YMCA gym. The Y had just constructed a "state of the art" racquetball court. They agreed to meet on campus next Tuesday.

Hawkins waved bye and went on his way to the campus gym while Dale turned and walked toward the student union. Since it was the Friday afternoon before spring break, a lot of the students had fled the campus for either home or for recreation areas. Few Nazarenes went to the secular hot spots on the gulf coast of Texas or elsewhere, but some did, like Eugene; they went to minister to the wayward kids partying on the beach. Dale wondered if Eugene was ever tempted to join in on the fun. He doubted it. He guessed Eugene was even less tempted by the drinking, carousing, and casual sex than he was. But he thought it was shrewd of Eugene to minister to college kids on spring break. After all, reality never conformed to fantasy. He bet Eugene made quite a few converts to Jesus among the disillusioned partygoers of Corpus Christi.

Dale threw open the doors to the student union, turned to go down the hall, but cut the corner too sharply and almost knocked Sylvester Fish down.

"Why don't you watch where you're going Fish?" Dale said, although he knew he was at fault.

"Me? Why, Smith, I was just minding my own business –"

Dale laughed scornfully. "You never mind your own business."

Fish drew his lumpy body up as straight as it would go. "I resent that, Smith."

Dale laughed more genuinely. Try as he might, he really couldn't work up any real animus toward Sylvester. He was too ridiculous.

"What are you doing here, anyway?" Dale asked. "Why aren't you on spring break?"

"Need I remind you that I work at the student union?"

Oh, yeah. He'd forgotten that Fish worked in the mailroom and did other menial jobs. Fish spent almost as much time in the student union as he did in the newspaper office. He didn't know that Sylvester stayed on campus through the holidays, though. Well, what else would he do? Go partying at Corpus?

Dale noticed again the top of a small notepad sticking out of Sylvester's shirt pocket. Fish had been carrying that around since the beginning of the school year. Dale guessed he was pretending to be a reporter, jotting down notes and observations for stories he never wrote. After all, he wasn't on either the newspaper or the yearbook this year.

Dale pointed to the notepad. "What have you written there, Polonius? Your recommendations for Laertes?"

Fish shook his head and said nothing.

"You know, Fish," Dale said in a confidential tone, "that Polonius's instructions to Laertes aren't meant to be read as wisdom. They're platitudes." He remembered Fish in class not understanding the irony in that passage in *Hamlet*. "Shakespeare is really satirizing Polonius's hypocrisy and banality. In fact, he's mocking all the Poloniuses of the world."

Fish stiffened. Dale thought maybe Fish finally understood that he'd not been complimenting him all these weeks by referring to him by that moniker.

"May I ask if you are on your way to the newspaper office?" Fish asked with impressive dignity, considering he finally understood why he'd been compared to the fatuous Polonius.

"Yeah, that's where I'm going."

"May I accompany you? I want to submit my work for the literary contest."

Dale studied the impassive face of Fish. Even when insulted, his face didn't change much from its normally solemn state. Well, his eyes grew beadier until they looked almost like dull marbles stuck in his eye sockets behind his thick-lensed glasses.

"Sure. Come on."

He walked to the newspaper office with Fish following a little too closely behind him. When Fish's big foot nicked Dale's heel, Sylvester tubaed a sorry.

Dale opened the door and Fish strolled right in and walked around the desk counter to the editor's desk. Dale had a little difficulty getting the key out of the lock; he tended to turn the key too hard and he'd bent the metal a bit. By the time he freed the key and closed the door halfway, he noticed Fish looking at news copy and a couple of books spread on his desk.

Dale pointed to the open-faced box sitting on the desk counter. "The submission box is over here, Fish."

Sylvester didn't respond with alacrity. Instead, he stood gazing at something on Dale's desk for a few more seconds. Then, with one stubby finger, he pushed his glasses against his face, and trudged over to the desk counter.

Dale watched as Sylvester dropped a rather thick manuscript into the box. He'd always suspected Fish of being prolific. He imagined it was some dreadful quasi-religious essay on the necessity of prayer, fasting, and shunning demon-inspired entertainment.

Fish gave Dale an odd look of satisfaction. "Interesting reading material, Smith," he said, with his long, thin lips forming a thin line with slight upturned corners. Then he nodded and departed the office.

Dale walked over to his desk and examined it. In addition to the news copy, pica pole, and photo-blue correction pen, there were two books: the AP handbook and a book he'd recently bought while visiting the *Pioneer* used bookstore in the City. He'd been intrigued by the subject. He'd been reading it since last weekend. The title: *The Christian Agnostic*.

Dale wondered if Fish even knew what the word "agnostic" meant. He supposed he did; for all his literal-mindedness, Fish wasn't exactly stupid. At least, he understood denotations of words; he just had trouble with the connotations.

So what? Dale thought. Fish saw a book that wasn't approved by Sunday school. He decided to forget about Sylvester and finish his own submissions for the literary supplement. He cleared his desk, moved the typewriter from Rowena's desk to his, and began typing.

He'd already written his poems, as well as five poems by H. Horse. Dale had thought about terminating H. Horse, but he couldn't. Harry Horse existed! True, H. Horse only lived in his imagination, but as far as Dale was concerned that was living. Once he became imbued by the spirit of H. Horse and he put words on paper, the pseudonym ceased to be a just a name and became something real.

This time, however, he'd actually tried to write in earnest about H. Horse's agony over his Indian identity in an uncaring America. Well, not completely in earnest. But he tried to make the poems less overtly silly. One or two of them actually tugged at Dale's heartstrings like the way H. Horse tugged on the wild mane of his prairie pony.

He wished he could submit another mini-epic by Bjorkastork. He didn't think he should since Bronwyn would obviously think it was a made-up name and that might make her more scrupulous than she was last year in checking out the legitimacy of submissions. So, he regretfully retired Bjorkastork as a literary artist. However, he still planned on calling upon the melancholy Dane to write a letter to the editor when the need arose and to contribute to the April Fool's edition that he planned on reviving.

The last time *Smoke Signals* had an April Fool's issue was when Flora Eliot was editor, four years ago. Dale had flipped through that issue in the bound book containing past issues. As with the yearbook, a sly, witty humor was in evidence. The April Fool's edition had featured four pages of news-story parodies and mostly gentle jokes about campus personages. Dale admired Flora's sense of humor; unlike his, it was essentially gentle and good natured.

Besides Bjorkastork, Dale had other surprises planned for the April Fool's issue of the newspaper. He planned on using several other pseudonyms and inventing absurd stories about topical issues on campus and in the "real world."

One of the pseudonyms, in fact, had already made an appearance in the last issue of the paper. Dale had used one of the photographs from his OU Student-Leadership press packet. The photo was of one of the distinguished guests, a renowned man that had led the science seminar and was a physicist from some prestigious college in the east. The man had an interesting face. In fact, it reminded Dale of Einstein's. The seminar leader, probably in his fifties, had a similar lugubrious look in his intelligent eyes, a similar mustache although not as bushy, and a general air of sagacity as he gazed into the camera.

Dale had dubbed him Waldo Rubenstein. He'd first used that pseudonym in high school for a fake literary scholar that he'd listed in his Dickens research paper bibliography. But for the campus newspaper, he'd elevated Waldo Rubenstein from a mere literary critic to a GNC student running for Who's Who. In reality, no one ran for Who's Who; an illustrious panel of college administrators and professors selected them. But Dale thought it was time for some fellow to buck tradition and actually campaign for Who's Who. So, Waldo Rubenstein had come out of the shadows and announced his candidacy on the campus news page in the last issue.

Dale had printed the photograph of the Einstein look-alike, put **WALDO RUBENSTEIN** under the photo in bold cap letters, and listed his qualifications. Underneath that info, Dale printed a brief interview. Waldo's rationale for campaigning for Who's Who was compelling: he wanted the notoriety. The fact that Waldo had an utterly undistinguished if not ridiculous background for such an honor didn't not faze him. He wanted it; he deserved it; he should be accorded the honor. Low grade point, non-existent campus activities, questionable character, and general disagreeableness should not be held against him, he had opined. After all, he planned a career in politics.

Unsurprisingly, the parody had resulted in several letters to the editor. Most castigated Dale for making fun of the august Who's Who tradition. However, one letter in particular drew Dale's interest. The writer apparently thought Waldo Rubenstein was real. The author wondered how such an older man, and one who appeared to be Jewish, could be a student on campus, let alone a candidate for Who's Who.

When Dale read the letter, at first he'd suspected that the author was Fish. But no, it was some other dolt named Lou Staples. Dale printed that "perspicacious" letter along with two reasonable ones.

Now, back at his literary labors, Dale decided to spare Mary Jane from more poetic immortality; he wouldn't write any poems under her name. After all, she'd suffered enough. He'd last heard her speculate on who really wrote *Woman: Born to Suffer* a few months ago. She didn't suspect him. Perhaps she didn't think he had enough insight into the female condition to write even dreadful verse from a woman's perspective.

But he had written poems on behalf of Krupp and Chris. Now, all he had to do was finish his story. He had until Sunday night to finish it.

David Hawkins picked Dale up outside the newspaper office in his splashy Firebird and they drove to the Y. On the way, they heard news on the radio that the Israelis had invaded Lebanon to drive out PLO terrorists. Dale, even though he was the editor of the campus newspaper, didn't follow national or world news much. Often he was too busy to follow it; but another reason was he preferred the cultural and critical side of journalism. *Smoke Signals* under his editorship reflected this emphasis; it seemed less like a conventional newspaper and more like a magazine focused on features, entertainment and art, sports, and cultural issues rather than on "hard news."

"What do you think that means?" asked Hawkins.

Dale didn't know. Sounded like more trouble in the Middle East.

"Could lead to another war."

He guessed David was referring to the Six-Day War of five years ago. Dale hadn't paid much attention to it. The oil embargo hadn't affected him much personally because he just drove to school and the gas prices in Oklahoma had stayed fairly low compared to the coasts. What had made a deeper impression, however, was the PLO murdering the Israeli athletes at the Munich Olympics in 1972. He'd been watching the Olympics and had been shocked and appalled at the killings, even though he only dimly understood the political backdrop.

"It'll probably make everyone on campus even more susceptible to mass hysteria concerning the Rapture," Dale said.

As soon as he said it, he realized he was assuming Hawkins shared his skepticism. Dale glanced over and saw David grinning.

"You don't believe it either," Hawkins said.

"No," Dale said, speaking bluntly for the first time to someone connected to the GNC community. "Of course," he said in his room of darkness voice, "*it could happen.*"

Hawkins had never heard that voice before, but he understood its comic intentions right away. "Yes, it could," he said with mock solemnity, which gave them both enough cover so God wouldn't obliterate them as they drove to the racquetball court.

Dale thought about the recent campus controversy over Daniel Ranson Johnson's Rapture prediction. As the date neared, some students on campus had taken it so seriously that they had stopped going to classes. After all, if they were going to be raptured to heaven in a few weeks, why bother? The administration had sent notices to all students that they were required to attend classes, chapel, church, and other activities just as normal. Dale had been surprised by the administration's good sense; he wrote an editorial commending the decision.

Thinking of the strange atmosphere on campus, Dale told David about another weird time in history, the Munster Rebellion in 1530s Germany. He'd first read about this religious uprising in his renaissance and reformation class that he'd taken last year. Three fanatics – Rothmann, a Lutheran pastor; Matthys, a baker; and Bockelson, a tailor – along with their Anabaptist followers took over the city of Munster, intending to install a theocracy. Franz von Waldeck, the town's expelled bishop, laid siege to the town. On Easter Sunday, Matthys, who had prophesied God's judgment for the wicked on that day, led his thirty men in the surprise attack on von Waldeck's large army. Matthys and his men were slaughtered, of course. The Catholic army desecrated Matthys's corpse; they stuck his severed head on a pole and nailed his genitalia to the city gate.

The Anabaptist fanatics refused to surrender. Bockelson crowned himself king (perhaps he was an ancestor of Krupp), claimed Munster as the new Zion, and then initiated a series of radical "reforms." King Bockelson legalized polygamy, took sixteen wives (one of whom he beheaded in the marketplace for some imagined crime), created a communist-style community of goods, and fomented a revolution lacking in good sense and sane behavior. The fanatics justified all the resulting murder, rape, and injustice by their special status as "saints." Bockelson and others decided that saints were above the law of man – conveniently forgetting that the law of man should be based on the law of God.

After more than a year of such madness, the besiegers finally captured the town of Munster, and Bockelson and his followers were tortured and tried, then executed in the marketplace. Their corpses were displayed in steel cages that hung from the steeple of St. Lambert's church. Dale said, in conclusion, that those cages still hang from the steeple, although the fanatics' bones had been removed centuries ago.

After he finished his history lesson, Hawkins gazed at him in an impressed way. He asked Dale how he remembered all that stuff.

"I just reread it a few days ago."

"Why? Think something like that could happen here?"

"Naw. But people do have a tendency to lose their heads."

"I'm glad I'm not in the sixteenth century."

"No kidding. Beheadings and emasculations. Those guys played rough."

David nodded as he pulled into the Y parking lot.

They changed in the locker room and since it was a Tuesday afternoon, only a couple of older men were present. As Dale stripped, he acquired his locker room stare, which required him to keep his field of vision above the waist of all present. After years of changing in locker rooms, he'd perfected this technique and could even reach down and put on his jock without looking down. As he slipped on his athletic supporter, he noticed in his peripheral vision something odd. Hawkins seemed to be violating locker room etiquette. Dale turned to make sure, but by the time he did Hawkins had slipped on his gym shorts and was busy tying his shoes. Dale thought, maybe he'd misinterpreted.

David had reserved an hour on the court and they squeezed in three games by playing at a fast pace. Hawkins won the first game. Dale appreciated his quickness and agility, both characteristics that Hawkins displayed on the basketball court. However, he also noticed that Hawkins's backhand wasn't very strong, in part because of his sore left knee. Dale, who didn't like losing the first game, decided to exploit David's weakness and hit shot after shot so Hawkins would have to use his backhand. Dale won the second game.

The third and final game remained close. Dale had stopped taking advantage of David's vulnerability; he felt a little sorry for him, although Hawkins was the varsity athlete. At match point, Dale served and hit a fat volley right into Hawkins's forehand zone, but instead of smashing it, David's racket glanced at it and the ball skittered into the corner.

Hawkins said, damn, and then turned to Dale and told him good game. Dale said thanks, they shook hands, and then surrendered the court for two pudgy older men.

On the way back to the locker room, Dale wondered why Hawkins would blow the point. Competitive guys never did that. First of all, it was an insult to your opponent if he figured it out. Hawkins hadn't made it obvious; he had been leaning to his left for a serve to his backhand. But Dale knew he had the quickness to recover and blast a return. It was pretty obvious to him that Hawkins had wanted him to win.

Then in the locker room, Dale caught Hawkins violating etiquette again. It was almost blatant. As Dale stripped to prepare to shower, he glanced over and saw David looking too low. When Dale frowned at him, Hawkins pretended to be looking elsewhere. But Dale had seen his eyes. For a moment, they had gazed at him in a frank, inquiring way.

As they showered, Dale grew a little angry. Hawkins kept his eyes above the waist at all times, as he did when they dressed. On the drive back to campus, Hawkins chattered in an enthusiastic, somewhat nervous way that reminded Dale of how Wendy would gossip and carry on. Hawkins talked about sports. He liked baseball, too. He'd played it at his high school in Tulsa and had been a decent shortstop. He asked what position Dale played. He said second base, mostly. Hawkins said he'd guessed. He had the look of a middle infielder.

Hawkins hadn't played football. He said he'd been too small to play at his 3A high school. He admitted that he probably wasn't tough enough to play anyway. Dale didn't say anything concerning that admission. Hawkins seemed tough enough. He'd seen him hold his position when a bigger player collided with him so he could get an offensive foul called on the other guy.

David then told Dale a little more about Shakespeare. One of the reasons why some people suspected the real author of the plays of using a pseudonym was because of the "Will's" scandalous behavior.

Even though Dale knew the whole point of this tidbit was to provoke him into asking the question, he was curious. So he asked, what "scandalous behavior"?

As the Firebird pulled into the parking lot closest to the student union, Hawkins put the car in gear and looked at Dale.

"Sexual improprieties," he said.

Dale appreciated David's subtlety in some matters, but not this one. He'd mistrusted Hawkins for some reason, but not this reason. It surprised him that he'd misinterpreted David's intentions. He guessed he should have known. After all, he'd experienced the curious behavior of both Lawrence at Boys State and Mr. Benedict at the cabin, although Mr. Benedict had been interested in Rusty and not him. He wasn't completely offended, though. He didn't feel like punching Hawkins in the face. He'd grown to like David. Actually, he now felt a little sorry for him.

"That's interesting," Dale said. "Of course, most people, let alone writers, don't want their sexual improprieties to be made public."

Hawkins looked at him but didn't say anything. He then asked Dale if he'd like to do something else this week. They could play racquetball again, or go to a movie?

Dale said he was going to be very busy this week, even though it was spring break. He wanted to work ahead for the special newspaper issue, which was true. He also said he had to do some things with his parents, which wasn't true.

Hawkins said he understood. He held out his hand and Dale shook it. He got out and David said bye and drove away.

Dale walked back to the newspaper office. He'd been depressed all weekend feeling Amanda's absence. Even rereading *Cyrano d'Bergerac* hadn't helped. His melancholia had served him well, though. He'd finished a pretty good story about a young man who learns that his true love isn't a pure and good woman, but he loves her anyway. In the end, her thug friends mortally wound him. He knew *Man of La Mancha* had influenced him, but his story still seemed to have its own integrity. It was a tragic story, and one that matched Dale's mood as he patrolled the empty halls of the high school.

All weekend, he'd been looking forward to playing racquetball with Hawkins. He'd thought it would lift his spirits. Now, as he walked back to the newspaper office, he didn't feel depressed anymore but he felt strange. Once again, he wondered why things had to be so complicated. He tried to think of something funny to make himself feel less strange. The idea that he'd thought Hawkins was after Amanda seemed a little funny to him now. However, it was possible that Hawkins might still be interested in her. After all, he apparently was getting along just fine with Hope.

Dale thought if he ever saw Hawkins making a play for Amanda, then he would punch his face. Even if he did like him.


The four of them sat in the booth at the Pizza Hut discussing the movie. All of them, with the possible of exception of Chris, had loved it. Rusty and Putney were speaking lines of dialogue from memory. Dale noticed that Rusty took the Tim Matheson lines while Putney took the John Belushi lines. He thought that appropriate; they resembled the actors in stature.

Rusty now mimicked the Matheson speech denouncing the student government investigation of "animal house" misbehavior. They all laughed. Putney said Rusty had captured the actor's attitude really good. He tried to describe it.

"A kind of suave insouciance," Dale interjected before Putney could define it.

The three of them stared at Dale. Even Rusty didn't know what insouciance meant.

"Hey, man," Rusty said, "did you watch the same movie as us dudes?"

The three of them laughed at Dale, who shrugged. Then Putney stuffed three breadsticks into his mouth and wagged his shaggy eyebrows as he vigorously chewed.

"Don't you dare," said Chris, sitting next to Putney and opposite of Dale.

Dale grinned. He knew Putney wouldn't do it.

Rusty, sitting next to Dale on the end, laughed and said they needed a chick sitting with them to get the full comic effect.

Putney stopped chewing and filled his cheeks with the masticated bread.

Chris warned him.

Dale narrowed his eyes thinking the crazy guy might actually do it.

Rusty laughed and waved his hands, signaling Putney to bring it on.

Putney punched his cheeks with his fists and spewed slimy chunks of chewed bread mostly at Rusty. Rusty said, "hey, man!" Only a few chunks hit Dale, who had anticipated the explosion in time to evade most of the fusillade.

Putney burst out laughing, some remaining little blobs of bread falling out of his open, guffawing mouth. Dale thought that was funnier than the prank itself and started laughing. Rusty, wiping the chunks of bread from off his face and hair, and brushing them off his shirt, howled with laughter. Even Chris chuckled, then when he saw specks of bread clinging to Rusty's beard, pointed and honked his laughter.

Chris's face suddenly turned serious as the manager, a short man with expressive eyes and a fuzzy mustache, appeared and asked them what the problem was.

Rusty immediately stopped laughing, and turned mock serious. He said his friend over there had started choking and he'd had to perform the Heimlich maneuver on him.

The manager asked how he'd accomplished that since he was sitting opposite of the afflicted fellow.

"I have really long arms, man," Rusty said, holding his hands high over his head.

The manager said, most amusing, and warned them to settle down or else they'd be asked to leave.

Dale, who'd been watching the manager's Chaplinesque face, thought he recognized him. He asked if he had worked at the Pizza Hut in Northwest Oklahoma City.

The manager looked surprised and said yes, he had. For seven years before coming over to Galilee to get this store in shipshape condition.

Rusty now recognized him and asked the manager, do you remember us? From about five years ago?

The manager said he'd had thousands of customers between then and now.

Rusty asked if he remembered this fat slob of a guy with a flabby face and glasses who'd tried to run off without paying and spoke in this really pompous voice; then Rusty gave a convincing imitation of Mr. Benedict's grandiloquent voice: "I assure you, my good man, that I had no intention of leaving without paying."

The manager's face twitched in recognition. "Yes, I remember that … that –"

"Buffoon," supplied Dale.

The manager nodded. "Whatever happened to that strange man?"

"He's in the California correctional facility at Alcatraz," Rusty said somberly.

"Really?" The manager looked alarmed as if Mr. Benedict might appear at any moment after busting out of the clink. "On what charge?"

"Impersonating a teacher," said Dale.

"I didn't know that was a serious crime."

"It is when you do it for six years," said Rusty.

"Hmmm," said the manager. "Sorry to hear that."

Putney, who preferred physical comedy over verbal, had earlier unrolled a breadstick, flattened it out, and then pressed it over his teeth like he was wearing a mouthpiece. He had been smiling his bread smile during most of the conversation. Putney now broadened his smile as if opening wide for the dentist. Rusty, Dale, and Chris had noticed the bizarre grin but had maintained placid, if not solemn expressions, waiting for the manager to notice.

Finally, the manager noticed. He gawked at the grotesque sight. Rusty, Dale, and Chris burst out laughing again, while Putney continued his weird grin and wiggled his eyebrows.

"Now, young men, I'm not going to warn you again. Please behave. Or else you'll have to leave."

"We're sorry, sir," said Rusty, "but our friend here suffers from imbecility."

The manager gazed warily at Putney, who convincingly managed to make the look in his eyes more vacant. He nodded his head erratically, but too vigorously, because the bread smile suddenly dropped off his teeth and fell to his plate.

"No more warnings," said the manager, who promptly turned and left.

The conversation returned to *Animal House*. They mentioned their favorite scenes and only Chris criticized it for being "too gross." But he said he liked the other parts. Rusty said, what other parts? Then Rusty said not only was it funny, but it had ample nudity in it. They all, even Chris, nodded their approval. Putney said he liked the sorority sisters topless pillow fight the best. Rusty nodded. Chris, recalling the scene, was rendered speechless. Dale said he liked that scene a lot, but he favored the scene where the actress, wearing only a football jersey, is seen from behind.

Rusty asked why he liked that scene best.

"I like callipygians," he said.

All three of them stared at him as if he'd said he liked hieroglyphics. Dale couldn't believe he hadn't told Rusty or Chris about the word.

They demanded to know the meaning of this mysterious word. Rather than simply define it, Dale said he'd give an example. He said, Sheba Smith.

His three friends knew who she was. They'd seen her on campus wearing tight jeans. They'd seen her play powder puff football in tight shorts. Dale observed them searching the lust department of their memories. Rusty's face and Putney's face lit up at the same time.

"Oh, yeah, man," said Rusty. "Is that what you call them?"

Putney nodded. He understood the term as well.

Only Chris didn't get it. "It means flat chested?"

"No," said Dale, "it means shapely buttocks."

"Really?"

Dale briefly explained the Greek origins of the word, the Kallipygous Aphrodite, and the two Syracuse girls who built her a temple because they too shared her posterior beauty.

"The fair buttocked?" asked Rusty. "Are there unfair butts?"

"Fair as in physically attractive," Dale said, although he knew Rusty had understood.

Putney stared at Dale with an appreciative gaze. He slowly lifted his hand and offered it. Dale took it and they shook with great solemnity.

"I'm glad I know this man," said Putney to the other two. "He has interesting things to say."

Then, their conversation deteriorated into a conventional discussion of sports. Dale felt a little sad that their talk had left the lofty heights of Olympus to descend into the lowly sphere of brutes. However, he engaged in the discussion as well, telling them they were crazy if they thought the Yankees would win the AL pennant again. He thought the Red Sox were the team to beat.

Rusty and Chris argued about which team would win the NBA title. Putney talked about the hockey playoffs, although nobody in Oklahoma played or watched hockey. Dale dropped out of the conversation for awhile. He thought about seeing Wendy and Carmen earlier that evening at the new mall multiplex. They were going to see *An Unmarried Woman*. He thought that movie was about a woman who leaves her unfaithful lout of a husband and then becomes an independent woman and refuses to marry a handsome artist she meets because she loves being single. Dale guessed it was a comedy. He bet *Animal House* was a lot funnier.

While standing in line, he'd talked to Wendy. She asked why he was seeing a movie with three guys. He didn't tell her that Amanda didn't go to R-rated movies. After all, *An Unmarried Woman* was rated R. He just said he felt like it. Wendy asked what he was doing during spring break. He said working on the upcoming special newspaper issue. He said he had a lot of typing of copy to do. She asked if he'd like any help typing? Dale remembered she was a good typist and proofreader. He said sure. She said she might stop by sometime. He said he was at the newspaper office most afternoons and evenings. Then the line she and

Carmen were in started moving and Wendy waved good-bye. Carmen didn't.

Now, Dale leaned back and looked out the large window at 39th Expressway. Drizzle fell and he wondered what Amanda was doing at that moment. Maybe her parents were taking her to a classical music in Kansas City. Mrs. Meeks loved classical music just like Amanda. Mr. Meeks, however, didn't seem to appreciate that kind of stuff.

Whatever she was doing, he hoped she was thinking about him, too.

Dale thought he wouldn't have encouraged Wendy to come to the newspaper office and help with the typing and proofreading if he didn't need her assistance. But he wondered if that was true. Even though he had written several of the news-story parodies by hand while at work, he probably could have typed them all himself in plenty of time for the April Fool's issue. After all, that issue wasn't for another week.

He sat at his desk and finished typing a second story. He yanked it out of the typewriter and turned and gave it to Wendy. She stood at the layout table, proofing his copy. He remembered how she had typed a short story he had written in high school. He gave her twenty-one pages of handwritten stuff and she'd typed it all up without any errors by the next day. He'd been impressed by her typing skill and her willingness to do work for him that he didn't like doing himself.

Dale knew he'd had an ulterior motive for accepting Wendy's offer, but he didn't want to admit it to himself. But it was simple: lust. When he'd seen her at the mall multiplex, he'd thought about some of the activity they used to engage in and he remembered how enthusiastic Wendy had been. Actually, in the beginning, she'd been more willing than he had been. That was because he was then still very shy and she had stronger feelings for him than he had for her. But now, after weeks of frustration with Amanda, the idea of having uninhibited physical contact sounded appealing.

He knew, and he thought she knew, that all of this was a bit of a charade. Dale was hungry for some passionate, physical contact and he guessed Wendy was too. He knew what he was going to do was wrong. Unlike some people, Rusty for instance, he always seemed aware of his behavior. He had a hard time hiding his motives from himself. So when he turned and looked at Wendy as she stood with her back to him while proofing his copy, he knew he was about to sin.

Dale frankly appraised Wendy's bottom. She wore tight slacks and he wondered if she did that on purpose. He'd always liked her rear; maybe it was a little broad and not quite as fully rounded as he preferred. She didn't quite have callipygians. But encased in those tight-fitting, sleek slacks, her rump looked quite fetching.

He remembered that funny line in *Annie Hall* about VPL: visible panty line. Yep, Wendy had VPL and now as he stared at that line he noticed it was fairly high up on each cheek. The idea that she'd worn rather skimpy panties underneath her tight slacks aroused him even more. The peculiar focus of his lust surprised him. He wondered if he was becoming like a satyr because of sexual frustration.

He stood up and pinched Wendy on the lower curve of her right buttock. Wendy turned around with a look of pleasure on her face and threw her arms around his shoulders. Dale put his arms around her waist. They kissed. He remembered how her lips and mouth used to taste and the flavor in his mouth now tasted like that.

The switch to the overhead lights was within reach. He reached out and flipped it off. Most of the room fell into darkness. Only the small lamp on Rowena's desk remained on. Dale remembered that same light had been on when he brought Amanda here. He didn't want to think about her now. But when he kissed Wendy a second time, he saw Amanda's face in his mind. He wondered what she was doing at that moment. She was probably staying the night at her aunt's house in Kansas City before driving home with her parents tomorrow. That day a postcard from Iowa had arrived. The postcard had the image of the famous Grant Wood portrait, *American Gothic*, on it. Dale wondered if she had selected that postcard knowing that he and her father had discussed the renowned Iowa-born painter. She had signed it, *love, Amanda.*

As they kissed, Wendy began to moan. She'd always been vocal. Dale remembered being a little embarrassed about that when they were together. Sometimes she even directed him. *Faster, faster.* Or, *higher, higher.* Actually, that had sort of annoyed him at the time. But he knew he'd been clumsy and befuddled and now he didn't blame her. In fact, he envied her uninhibited nature.

In some ways, it was that open, earthy nature of Wendy's that he missed. He loved Amanda, but her reluctance and guilt about being intimate frustrated him.

He stopped kissing Wendy. He heard her swallow. She asked what was wrong.

"I don't know if we should be doing this," he said.

"Don't you want to?"

A part of him did. The satyr. But he didn't want to hurt Amanda. He didn't want to give her cause to end it between them. He thought she would if she found out. Amanda took sinning very seriously.

"I'm still with Amanda," he told her.

Wendy dropped her arms off his shoulders. Dale took his arms from around her waist. She leaned back against his desk and gave him a disappointed look. At least, that's what he thought it was in the gloom.

"I wondered if you were when I saw you at the movie theatre," she said. "I mean, I hadn't heard otherwise, but I don't hear all the news like I used to."

"She's with her folks for spring break."

"Oh."

Dale felt frustrated again. He'd liked the way Wendy felt. He liked the way her large breasts pressed against his chest. Wendy was bigger there than Amanda.

"Frankly, I'm surprised that you two are still together," she said.

Dale wondered if he'd ever heard Wendy say "frankly" before. He didn't think so. She was even talking like a businesswoman.

"Why is that?"

"Because you're so different."

Now Wendy's voice wasn't as evaluatory as before. It sounded more like she used to sound in high school. Sweet and unaffected.

"Yeah, I guess that's true."

"I mean, Amanda's a wonderful girl. I always liked her. But her background is so ..."

"Refined?"

"Well, that too. But I meant religious. I mean, that's good. Some people thought she was a goody-two-shoes, you know. But I respected her."

Dale didn't like talking about Amanda to Wendy. It sounded like they were talking about somebody in both of their pasts.

"Well, if what you're saying is that I'm not good enough for her, then you're right."

"I'm not saying that."

"Well, it's true," Dale said. "And I guess one of these days she might figure that out."

"And you don't want her to?"

"That's right."

Wendy bent down and picked up her purse. He saw her looking for her jacket in the dark of the room. Dale flipped the switch and the overhead lights blazed on. Wendy shielded her eyes and said, "oh, my."

Dale looked at her in the bright light. She'd worn a red sweater. She knew he liked her to wear red. Her tight slacks were gold. Wendy had worn flat shoes, too. He wondered if that was on purpose. She wore quite a bit of makeup like the last time he'd seen her. She wore eyeliner and mascara. He didn't like that. She had blond eyelashes and when she wore black stuff on them they made her look wanton. Her cheeks were rouged, which he liked fine, although Wendy always had appealing, naturally pink cheeks. But she didn't wear any thick lipstick like she had when she'd visited the New Year's party. Instead, she wore the thinner stuff, lip gloss, that Amanda often wore. Dale supposed Wendy had deliberately worn gloss instead of lipstick for the same reason she'd worn the tight slacks and low-heeled shoes. She'd planned to entice him all along. Well, Dale had planned to be enticed. He didn't blame her. He just thought it was sad how people planned things that didn't work out.

"I guess I better go," she said, smiling unconvincingly. She walked over to the coat rack and took her black jacket.

"Would you like me to walk you to your car?"

"That's not necessary. You still have work to do."

She opened the door but before she stepped out, she looked at him. "Seems like lately when we see each other, I'm always leaving before you are."

Dale said, yeah.

She smiled sadly and didn't say good night or good-bye and walked out and closed the door behind her.

Dale paced the room and wondered why he had never felt as passionately for Wendy as he felt for Amanda. If he had, then things would have been simpler. He went over to the window and parted the curtain and watched as Wendy walked to her car, a gold, metal-flaked Datsun 280Z, and got in. Dale knew she made good money at her marketing job. She'd started working full-time last summer and now went to college part-time. She'd bought herself a nice sports car.

He watched her drive away and then, just before he was about to let go of the curtain, he saw a figure creeping down the sidewalk away from the parking lot. Dale watched and thought he knew who it was even before the figure turned and the moonlight revealed the unmistakable profile of Sylvester Fish.


**Chapter 13:** *Not in the mood; the gathering of saints*

Amanda hadn't enjoyed *A Man for All Seasons* that much. Dale knew she would have preferred to stay on campus and attend the religious concert. But since Saturday was the last performance of the play, he had insisted they go.

Now, driving home from the theater in the City, Dale glanced at her and saw that she didn't look happy. He thought he'd ask her about something she cared about, the Lost and Found auditions. She'd already told him last Sunday night after she and her parents arrived home from their spring break trip that her audition went well. But she hadn't given many details. So, now he asked her several questions.

She described the audition hall and told him about the kids who'd come from evangelical colleges all over the country. As she told him about that weekend, her voice grew musical with excitement. When she paused, Dale asked her what songs she'd sung. She'd sang two for the first audition, contemporary Christian songs that he didn't recognize, and when she made that cut, she sang one more. The third song was "You Light Up My Life."

"Really? You sang that?"

Amanda nodded. "All the judges liked my interpretation of it."

Dale said he'd like her to sing it for him. She said she would sometime. He said he wanted to hear it now. She said that was silly. She didn't have any music. He insisted. She had such a lovely voice she didn't need musical accompaniment. Amanda smiled shyly but when he said please, she complied. He listened intently as she sang quietly in her sweet soprano. When she finished, she glanced at him.

"You sound even better than Debbie Boone."

"Oh, I do not."

Dale said she did. He really was impressed. He'd heard her sing several times before, at the Christmas concerts, but that was mostly with a group. He'd also heard her sing at her sister's wedding, but that was in a large dining hall and her voice hadn't projected too well. But this was special because she'd sung just for him.

They were almost back to the campus. Now that Amanda was in a better mood, he asked her why she didn't like *A Man for All Seasons*.

"Oh, I liked it fine," she said. "I suppose I just wasn't in the mood for any heavy drama."

Dale nodded. He turned off the expressway and drove to the Hayley parking lot. When he saw one of the overhead lights out at the east end of the lot, he parked the Chevy there. They really were in the shadows.

"Weren't you interested in Sir Thomas More's decision to remain faithful to his principles even if it cost him his life?"

"Yes, that was all interesting," Amanda said. She paused in thought. "Wasn't he Catholic though?"

Dale wondered if she'd paid attention to play. "Sir Thomas More? Yeah, of course."

He knew that since More had died for his Catholic principles, Amanda wasn't quite as impressed.

"You know, in addition to being a brilliant lawyer and politician, he also wrote the classic book *Utopia*."

Dale remembered reading other stimulating selections from classic books in his renaissance and reformation history class. They read some of Luther's writing, and Erasmus' *In Praise of Folly*. All in translation, of course.

"*Utopia*," Amanda repeated. "I think I've heard of that."

"Did you like it?"

"I said I heard of it, not that I read it."

Dale nodded. Sometimes he wished Amanda read more good books. She read contemporary devotional books and, of course, the Bible. Once, he'd heard Kenny teasing her about a romance book. She'd been embarrassed. Dale had never heard her mention reading any good book. Not even one by a woman author like Jane Austen or Virginia Woolfe. No, on second thought, he remembered she'd once mentioned reading both *Wuthering Heights* and *Jane Eyre*.

"I bet you get selected for Lost and Found," he said.

Amanda tried to hide her pleasure at the possibility. A small smile fluttered across her lips though.

"I've decided that if you get it, I'm going to go to Europe."

"What do you mean?" Amanda looked not only surprised but dismayed.

"I mean for a short trip. I've checked it all out already. You can stay in these cheap places called youth hostels and buy an economy train pass that'll take you all over. It's a good deal."

"How long would you be gone?"

"A couple of months."

Dale was glad she looked concerned. For a moment, he feared she might not care.

"I'll only go if you get picked. That way, even though I'll miss you, I'll be busy and the time will pass faster."

Amanda nodded. She could see the point of that. "Are you going to go by yourself?"

"I'm trying to get Rusty to come along."

"Rusty?"

"Yeah. He's my best pal." Dale noticed Amanda almost bit her lower lip. "I thought you liked Rusty."

"I do. It's just sometimes I think he might be a bad influence on you."

"A bad influence? How?"

"Well, I don't know. I once heard him say a bad word."

"So?" Dale knew he shouldn't have said that.

"So?" Amanda said, hardly believing he didn't take profanity seriously.

"Well, saying a bad word is rather trivial."

Amanda's eyes grew large. "I don't think so. Words reflect what's in our hearts. And, besides, he took the Lord's name in vain. That's even worse."

Dale had never heard Rusty use that swear word before. In fact, Rusty never cussed much unless he was around Erickson.

"He also has stopped going to church."

"How do you know all these things?"

"Mary Jane told me." Then she looked at him with disapproval. "Of course, you don't go to church either."

"I do so."

"Not Sunday morning, the most important service. You won't even go to morning service for Easter. The most important Christian holy day."

Dale didn't want to start talking about religion. The last time they'd discussed religion, she'd been disturbed that he hadn't yet been baptized in the Nazarene church. He'd told her that being baptized in the Baptist church was as baptized as one could get. She didn't find his answer funny.

"You know I have to work," he said. "And I hold my own service while you're in First Church."

Actually, he'd stopped doing that a few months ago. However, he did say a prayer for Amanda when he knew the service was starting.

"Well, that's all fine and good, Dale, but why can't you take off work for Easter? And Christmas, too?"

"I've told you no one will switch with me. Besides, is it that important to simply observe a date?"

"What do you mean, simply observe a date?"

Dale sighed. They'd had this argument before. "What I mean, Amanda, is what really matters is what's in our heart, isn't that true?"

"Well, yes."

"And therefore all the outward demonstrations we make aren't as important as what we feel inside. So, whether or not I'm in church is less important than what I think and feel and believe. Isn't that true?"

Amanda didn't answer right away. He knew he'd spoken a little too forcefully, but sometimes she exasperated him.

"I suppose."

He looked at her. She was trying to understand his point. He knew his unconventionality bothered her. He knew she'd much rather have a boyfriend like Eugene Greene or Bobby Henshaw; that is, in the sense that he would like all the things she liked and be as devoted to the formal observance of religion as she was.

She was sitting too far away. Their legs weren't even touching. Dale asked her to scoot over.

She gave him *that* look, like he was asking for something unreasonable but secretly she didn't think so.

"Come here," he said.

He raised his arm. She scooted over and he put his arm around her shoulders. She'd worn a dress to the play. A becoming deep blue long-sleeved dress that showed a little more of the top of her chest than usual.

"Did you miss me?" she asked.

"You know I did." Dale leaned over but she only offered her cheek. He kissed it and looked into her eyes. "What's wrong?"

"I'm just not in the mood."

"Why not?"

"I don't know. I guess I'm thinking about tomorrow."

"You mean Easter?"

"Of course."

Dale knew religious holidays made her even more devout. During these times, she was less receptive to physical intimacy, something that he couldn't quite understand. He admired her spiritual devotion; he even thought it enhanced her physical beauty. He thought she looked most lovely when praying. But he was increasingly concerned about her spirituality that de-emphasized physical intimacy. He even wondered if they got married if she'd be more focused on being religiously passionate than sexually passionate.

"You know what I heard?" Amanda said in a quieter voice.

"What?"

"Some people are going out to the country tomorrow night and wait for the Rapture."

Dale shook his head. "You mean Short and Fish are getting a bunch of other silly people to go out and wait to be raptured?"

"They might not be silly. It could happen."

Dale didn't think so. But he didn't want to disillusion Amanda or give her reason to think he was an infidel.

"If it happens, then it doesn't matter where they are, does it?"

Amanda said nothing. She knew he was right. Dale knew most Christians even believed the righteous dead would be raptured. If the dead could stay where they were until that time, why shouldn't the living?

"You know people aren't supposed to make predictions about that sort of thing," he said.

"I guess."

Dale turned to her. "You aren't going to join those fanatics, are you?"

She didn't like that word. "No, but you shouldn't call them names."

"People like Short and Fish are Pharisees. They have a legalistic view of religion."

Amanda gave him a puzzled and annoyed look. For all her piety and Bible reading, he sometimes thought she didn't remember certain concepts very well.

"What I mean, Amanda, is that they don't really understand religion or God. They think it's about show. But it's really about what you feel here."

Dale took his hand and placed it on Amanda's chest above her left breast. He saw her eyes grow large. She didn't remove his hand. He could feel her heartbeat through her dress. He saw her lips slightly part. Dale lowered his face and kissed her.

She responded for a moment, then she turned her face away. But she didn't take his hand from off her heart.

"Dale, we shouldn't get started."

"We haven't been together for two weeks."

"We were out last night."

Last night, after yet another religious concert on campus, they'd walked to the coffee shop for a snack and then he'd walked her to the front door of Hayley and didn't even get a good night kiss.

"I mean alone together."

Amanda glanced around. "People can see us."

"No, they can't. We're in the shadows."

He kissed her again and this time he slid his hand down and gently squeezed her breast. For a moment he thought she might give in, but she turned away again and this time she removed his hand.

"I'm really not in the mood," she said.

Dale put the rejected hand under her skirt and on her thigh. Even through the pantyhose he liked the way her thigh felt.

"Dale. You heard what I said."

"You *are* in the mood, Amanda."

"No, I'm not."

"You are. I can tell."

He felt like he was trying to hypnotize her. He caressed her thigh. He kissed her again but this time she kept her lips closed.

He looked at her. She stared at him in an almost defiant way.

"You just don't want to get in the mood."

She took his hand from off her thigh. "I guess I don't."

Dale sat back and stared out the window. Amanda told him maybe if he prayed more he wouldn't feel the need to do this sort of thing so much.

He smiled a little. "Is that what you do?"

Maybe it was the way he said it, in a suggestive voice. Amanda stiffened. Dale turned and said he was sorry. She said she had to go in. He thought about apologizing again, but instead he grew angry.

"Okay," he said. "Go in."

He sat rigid and didn't look at her. He heard her make a soft, annoyed sound, then heard her sliding to her door and opening it. He didn't look at her as she got out. Then he realized he was making a mistake and jumped out of the car and went over to her and apologized. He was just frustrated. Couldn't she understand that?

"Yes," she said, but she didn't say it in a very understanding voice. "But I should go in now. I'm getting up early tomorrow to go home and help with things before church."

"Okay," Dale said, disappointed. He guessed it was only eleven thirty. The play had been fairly long, and they'd stopped off for a snack at a diner in the City. But they still had half an hour to be together. Instead, Amanda was going in before curfew.

He walked her to the door. When he took her hand to say good night, she didn't seem irritated anymore. She smiled at him, but Dale still didn't think things were completely right. She reminded him that she had choir practice and wouldn't be able to sit with him at the Sunday night service. When she had choir practice, she always sat with Mary Jane and Hope for some silly reason. He said he remembered. She said good night and he watched her walk inside her dorm.

He stood there and wondered if praying really would help.

The next day at work, Dale felt depressed. When he walked the lonely halls of the high school, he felt like he was the only man left in the world. He checked the doors and windows, made all his rounds, and even wished that someone would interrupt his solitude. But no teachers or administrators came by. He spent the whole day alone in the school building, trudging down the empty halls, going into the vacant classrooms, and hearing his own footsteps echo in the spacious building.

In between making his rounds, he finished *The Christian Agnostic*. He almost had to force himself to read it, not because it was a bad book, but because of his melancholy mood. Actually, it was an interesting book, and Dale thought maybe he was becoming one. According to the author, a Christian agnostic is someone who believes in the spirit of Christ and seeks to meet "the challenges, hardships and sorrows of life" in that spirit, but does not subscribe to all the conventional dogma. The Christian agnostic is one whose "intellectual integrity makes him say about many things, 'It may be so. I do not know.'"

Dale, although he'd always admired Jesus and felt in awe of His sacrifice, couldn't quite accept the supernatural elements in that story. In many ways, he was drawn more to the Old Testament. He especially liked the "wisdom literature" of Psalms, Song of Solomon, and Ecclesiastes. He also felt intrigued by the book of Job. The story of God allowing Satan to torment Job in order to test Job's faith both fascinated and disturbed him. In the end, Job, who had always been a good man, confesses his worthlessness before God and accepts his punishment. After abasing himself, the Lord restores his health, wealth, and family tenfold. Essentially, the book of Job was a warning to all proud humans that even good men had to succumb to the power and majesty of Yahweh. In that book, God is a demanding, all-powerful, nearly cruel God. Nearly cruel, because the book argues that God is so exacting only for our own good.

Dale wasn't so sure. That's why the book of Job exasperated him. Maybe God *was* cruel. After all, He's God. He can do what He wants.

Dale's favorite Biblical character had always been David. He first heard the story of the great David in grade school. His teacher, a nice elderly woman whose name he now couldn't remember, would read a chapter from the Bible at the start of each class. When he heard the story of David, he became fascinated with him. He admired David's heroism. After all, he slew the giant Goliath, and in a clever way. He admired David's poetic soul. He composed psalms. And he even forgave David for his flawed character. Even as a little boy, Dale understood how a noble man might commit an awful sin because of his love for a woman. David, having spied the beautiful Bathsheba bathing, sent her husband Uriah into the front lines during a battle. As David had planned, Uriah was slain and David claimed Bathsheba as his wife.

Dale liked how the story of David depicted an essentially tragic character. A man of talent and nobility, yet so flawed he'd knowingly commit two terrible sins: adultery and murder. For David, although he hadn't directly killed Uriah, had arranged it. David, in a spiritual sense, had committed adultery and murdered Uriah.

Because he knew a Christian really shouldn't have a Hebrew character as a favorite, for years he'd made a distinction: David was his favorite *Old* Testament personage; Jesus his favorite *New* Testament personage. But really, in his heart, Dale preferred David.

Dale felt better after walking Amanda to her dorm after the Sunday night choir practice. He told her she sang well and she asked how he could tell. He said he could pick her voice out of a choir any day. It was the loveliest one.

His compliments put her in a good mood, too. They held hands on the walk back to the dorm. She even let him give her a quick kiss before they got to the dorm's front door. But she had to go in because she had to study for her music theory exam. He wished her good luck and watched her go inside the dorm with a better feeling than he had the night before.

The church service had lifted his spirits, too. The assistant minister who sometimes conducted the evening Sunday service, had indirectly referred to the prediction of the Rapture. He reminded the congregation that no one knows exactly when Christ will return, even though that miraculous event could be at any time. The important lesson was for Christians to live each moment of their lives as if Christ's return *was* imminent, and to dedicate their lives to His memory, and to act with compassion and charity as He would act.

Dale walked across the campus to the student union building. He still had work to do. The newspaper deadline was Thursday night. In addition to the regular pages, he'd added four spoof pages that only he knew about. He suspected he'd generate a little controversy for including a spoof, so he didn't tell Teri about it, which was a shame because he knew she would have provided interesting parodies. But he wanted to protect her from any possible ramifications if the parodies were poorly received. After all, she was going to run for next year's editor.

He walked inside the student union and turned down the hall to the student newspaper office when he noticed the door to the student council office open. He looked in. Short and Fish were standing in the office looking at a road map.

"Need directions?" Dale asked.

They turned and looked at him. Neither smiled.

"Joking as usual," said Short. "But soon the joke will be on you."

Dale shook his head. "I don't think so. But what I don't get is why you two want to take your apostles to a field somewhere when it doesn't matter where you are when the Rapture happens – or doesn't happen."

"We want to be with our brothers and sisters," Short said. "Something you apparently can't understand."

"I'll tell you what, Short. I'll join your brothers and sisters. I'll be your eyewitness. When you and your associates disappear and leave behind your clothes, I'll be there to verify the miracle."

Short glanced at Fish. They nodded at each other.

"Very well, Smith. Do you know where the old children's hospital is located?"

Dale almost smiled. He said yes.

"We're meeting in the field west of that building," said Short. "We're meeting ten minutes before midnight."

"I'll see you there."

"Don't be late, Smith. Otherwise, you'll miss the blessed event."

Dale gave the two prophets a quick salute and turned and went into his office. This time he completely closed the door.

Throughout the evening, Dale worked on the April Fool's section. He pasted the copy on the layout sheets, blocked out the space for the photos, and saved one large section for a very special parody that he'd write after tonight's event.

At 11:40, according to the clock, he left the office and walked to his car. He drove down the expressway out of town. He estimated the trip to the field west of the abandoned children's hospital would only take ten minutes, tops. He'd get there in plenty of time.

As he approached the hulking shadow of the children's hospital, he noticed several cars parked ahead on the shoulder of the highway. He slowed down and eased his Chevy off the side of the road and parked. He grabbed his camera and flash and walked down the side of the road until he saw the silhouettes of maybe two dozen people standing under the nearly full moon in a field about fifty yards away.

Dale crept along. He didn't really want to disturb the gathered saints. As he stealthily walked, he counted the silhouettes. Twenty-four people. Judging from the shapes of the shadows, twelve women and twelve men.

Dale realized that this was another event where he could have used a wristwatch. Well, the faithful would tell him when the time arrived. He decided to try and get a picture without a flash. He'd have to use a timed exposure. He had fast film in his camera but even so he'd have to expose the film for a couple of minutes. He saw Short's car, a '75 AMC Gremlin, and he decided to use it for a higher angle. He climbed on the hood of the car, careful not to slip. He aimed the camera. The saints were standing in close proximity to one another in the flat field. They were roughly arranged in two semicircles. Dale composed the photo and held his hands as steady as possible and pressed the shutter button. He held the shutter open for one minute. Then he took three more photos at longer staggered intervals. Next he attached the flash. He'd wait until Short, Fish, and their disciples trudged out of the field back toward their cars.

Then it occurred to Dale, what would he do if they really were raptured? Well, after he recovered from the shock of witnessing a supernatural occurrence, he guessed he'd take photographs of the piles of clothes. He thought it was sort of funny that true believers were raptured without clothing. He remembered that the saints weren't actually naked. They were transformed and their earthly bodies were made into some kind of super celestial body. Maybe those bodies didn't have genitalia. He didn't remember reading or hearing exactly what kind of anatomy the saints had. He also thought there weren't any male or female sexes in heaven. If so, heaven didn't sound very fun to him.

He waited, his camera poised, watching the people in the field. He wished they would be raptured, even though that meant he'd be left behind. Then, at least, he'd know that the literalist approach was correct. Dale knew if that happened, then all true Christians would disappear as well. Back on campus, Amanda's clothes would be lying in a pile. She probably was in bed right now. He guessed she'd be wearing a nightgown. She'd whispered that secret information in his ear once, her voice sibilant. That night back in his own bed, he couldn't go to sleep for a long time.

Dale thought it must be time. He'd been standing on Short's car for at least ten minutes. He'd probably gotten here at 11:50. He wondered how long the saints would stand there? Were they thinking that God's watch was slow? Were they thinking that maybe human time and God's time wasn't synchronized? He could believe that. In fact, he thought that was one of the more profound problems in the universe: how mortals and God weren't quite in synch with one another.

Dale looked at the silhouettes. He noticed some of them hanging their heads in disappointment. Others seemed to be shaking theirs. Others held their arms up in supplication. Some were praying. Others stood as stationary and still as plants.

It had to be past time. He wondered when they would give up. Short and his minions might stay out there all night. He considering taking a photo and leaving. But he wanted to record another Great Disappointment. There hadn't been any photographs taken of the Millerites or pre-Witnesses when their predictions of a Second Coming failed to materialize. Maybe Short and Fish should have thought about how embarrassed they would be to have their folly recorded.

Finally, some of the saints gave up. A small group of people slowly walked off the field. A few more followed. Then he heard a voice say something indistinguishable. More people turned to leave. Dale got ready. He wanted to get a good shot. He might not get another chance.

He looked through the viewfinder and found the largest gathered group of people walking toward him. He waited until they crowded the frame and then he pushed the button. The flash shot a wave of instantaneous light at them. Dale heard several saints gasp. One young woman shouted, hallelujah! Maybe she thought they were finally being raptured. Maybe she thought the flash was the spirit of God beaming His power at them. Dale waited for the flash to recharge. Then he shot another. This time he heard disgruntled cries. Getting flashed wasn't fun. It sort of blinded the subject for a couple of seconds.

"Get off my car!"

Dale recognized the voice. Short. He guessed he was in no mood to converse. Dale had wanted to get some quotes for the story.

He climbed down from Short's Gremlin. He waited for the VP for religious life to approach. When he did, Dale aimed the camera and flashed him.

"Damn you!"

Dale was impressed. Short had a temper after all. Dale asked if he could quote him. Short ignored his request. Dale tried to locate Fish. He found him trudging not far behind Short. Good. That shot would have both of them in the picture.

Dale decided to leave them be. He knew they must feel foolish, and he didn't want to rub it in. He guessed guys like Short and Fish would soon find a reason why God did not rapture them or anybody else. They just had to think about it and read some scripture and pray and rationalize it. Maybe they'd be in the mood to talk later.

He walked back toward his car when he glanced at a couple of other figures walking back from the field. One of them looked familiar. In particular, the silhouette's nose looked familiar. Dale slowed and watched as the fairly tall, masculine form stepped into the moonlight and the face became illuminated. It was Chris.

Dale couldn't quite believe it.

He thought about calling his name. But he could tell by the way Chris dejectedly walked that he probably wasn't in the mood to talk to him. Dale couldn't blame him. What would he say, anyway? Dale had made fun of the whole Rapture business. He knew Chris had been depressed since his aunt's death but he hadn't consoled him. The last time he talked to his buddy, a few days after his aunt's funeral, Chris had wondered if he'd been punished for seeing an R-rated movie. Dale told him that no one had been punished. His aunt had been killed in an accident, albeit a strange accident. No one really knew why Chris' aunt – her married name was Karen Anderson – had run across the street in the dark. Maybe she had been chasing her beloved cat since no one could find it in the house or yard. Dale had tried to explain to Chris that the fact he'd seen an R-rated film on the night of his aunt's death was just a coincidence. There wasn't any logical connection. Chris's "sinning" didn't result in his aunt's death. There hadn't been any retribution. Chris still felt guilty.

Now, as Dale stood staring at his friend shuffling out of the field with the other saints, he felt disappointed in both his buddy and himself. He felt disturbed that Chris had joined these silly people. But he felt he'd let down Chris, too. Maybe if he'd been more understanding and just listened to Chris talk about his aunt's death and the other things that had been bothering him, his buddy wouldn't have joined ranks with Short and Fish.

Dale watched Chris cross the drainage ditch and walk to his Toyota. He thought he saw Chris glance his way, but his pal didn't greet him or even show any sign of recognition. Instead, Chris opened the car door and got in.

Dale knew he should have said something to him, something to convince his friend that he didn't think he was a fool. But it was too late. Chris started his Celica and joined the long procession of cars as they slowly drove back to campus, the puffs of exhaust trailing them like a great cloud of disappointment.

**Chapter 14: *April Fool's backlash; whom does Dale love?***

Early Friday morning, five days after the Great Disappointment of 1978, Dale helped the distribution guy stuff the campus newspaper racks with the latest edition of *Smoke Signals*, including the surprise four-page April Fool's section.

An hour later, with newspapers safely tucked in their racks and lying in a neat bundles in the lobbies of buildings and dorms, he decided to wait and see the first reaction.

He lurked by Chester Hall and spotted Dr. Petry ambling toward the building. Dale knew the good doctor was going to his office before teaching his Principles of Grammar class. Dale hid behind a tree and watched as Dr. Petry picked up a newspaper and flipped through it. He knew the teaser on the top front of the paper would get Dr. Petry's attention. He watched as the grammarian turned to the middle section and read. Then, to Dale's amazement and pleasure, Dr. Petry crumpled the newspaper in his long, thin hands and marched into Chester Hall.

Dale couldn't have hoped for a better reaction.

Anxious to peruse the paper more closely himself, he turned and ran to his car. He carried the last two thick bundles of newspapers to the *Smoke Signals* office. He always enjoyed his first thorough examination of the paper. Even though he knew what every page looked like from pasting it up, writing much of the copy and even taking some of the photographs, he still liked how it looked different on newsprint. It looked official. It looked substantial. It looked real.

Dale sat at his desk and scrutinized the front page. Everything looked fine. Even the photographs he'd taken of the saints at the field turned out better than he'd hoped. He'd printed two photos on the front page. The smaller photograph in the middle of the paper showed the rather eerie-looking silhouettes of the saints as they stood motionless in the field awaiting the Rapture. For a manually timed exposure, it didn't turn out too bad. He thought readers would be able to recognize the significance of the photo, even though it was a little murky.

The larger photograph occupied the top corner of the paper under the headline, "The Great Disappointment, 1978." It showed the startled faces of Aaron Short and Sylvester Fish as they trudged out of the field. The flash had worked well. It illuminated a large circle around Short and Fish and showed them in clear detail. The background, however, remained shrouded in darkness. Dale usually didn't like the odd contrast between light and dark in a flash photo. The yearbook staff photographer shot the varsity basketball games with a flash and he'd never liked the effect. A guy driving for a layup looked like he was playing in a cave. Just him and the defender were lit up; everything else was obscured by darkness. However, Dale couldn't have asked for a better effect in this photograph.

Aside from the Great Disappointment lead story that he'd written in an objective, journalistic manner, he didn't think the rest of the regular newspaper would generate much controversy. Polly had written a rather lengthy story on all the religious activities for Easter week. Teri wrote a recap of the cultural festivities of the past week. Even Dale's editorial shouldn't offend too many people. He commended the assistant pastor of the First Church and the college administration for not being swept up in the Rapture hysteria that had gripped a few deluded souls.

Well, he guessed one item in the regular newspaper might incite resentment. Waldo Rubenstein was running for student council. However, Waldo wasn't running for an actual office; he was running for the fictional position of Philosopher King. Dale had been tempted to include Henshaw in that race, but instead, he kept Henshaw in his real race, for a second term as stuco president.

Now, Dale turned to the spoof part. The four-page pullout section, called "Smoke and Mirrors," was like a mini-newspaper tucked away inside the real newspaper. The lead story: The Unrapture. Dale had decided if the Rapture hadn't happened, then the Unrapture had. In the Rapture, believers were whisked away, leaving their clothes behind. In the Unrapture, only the believers' clothes were whisked away, leaving the saints in a state of nature, no doubt perplexed and chilly.

Dale had come across an AP photograph from a thick file of old newspaper stuff from when Flora Eliot was editor. The photograph showed a group of OU students streaking back in 1974 when the desire to run in the nude had seized the impressionable minds of mostly college kids – although he remembered the non-student streaker during the Academy Awards of that year. Ray Stevens, who wrote and sang the immortal "Gitarzan," had a hit with the comic "The Streak," satirizing the goofy trend. While the fad lasted, Galilee hadn't been victimized by any streakers that Dale remembered. The fad hadn't interested him, because most of the streakers were hairy men. If more comely women had joined in the nude parade, he would have heartily approved.

Alas, the OU streaking photograph only showed hairy and not-so-hairy young men. Frat boys, Dale guessed. It didn't show anything below the waist. It was an AP photo, after all. While writing the Unrapture story, he'd remembered seeing the AP photograph and fished it out of the box. He'd thought the photo would serve as a perfect parody photograph for the Unrapture.

He'd concocted the second photograph by getting Rusty to toss a handful of clothes into the air while he snapped the shot. He'd worried that the effect would be unconvincing. Flying clothes? But when he printed the photo, it looked better than he'd hoped. Rusty had done a good job throwing the clothes: a pair of jeans, a T-shirt, socks, sneakers, and a pair of boxer shorts with little hearts all over them. Dale had bought the boxers at a post-Valentine's Day sale a month ago. He did it as a joke, thinking he might use them as a wacky wedding gift for K. C. Now, the boxer shorts with hearts all over them provided a nice comic touch for the photo.

Dale read the Unrapture story. Not bad. Written in objective newspaper prose, it related the strange story of a group of C. S. Lewis club members who had gathered on a small southwestern campus to await the Unrapture. No Great Disappointment for these spiritual pilgrims. The Unrapture happened and the saints' clothes miraculously left their bodies and zoomed to the heavens. Fortunately, a quick-reflexed photographer was present to document the bizarre event. Startled by the Unrapture, the students stampeded *au naturel*.

There were a couple of other brief news parodies of current events. In one, President Carter is proclaimed the antichrist by a renowned seer, Mortimer Grip. In another, Muslims and Jews convert to Christianity but instead of living peacefully, they start a war after differing on their conception of the trinity.

On page two, the editorial page, the editor, Roy Rogers Jones, wrote a blistering editorial denouncing the abominable practice of showing movies on the GNC campus. He especially had harsh words about movies that featured cleavage in them. He condemned a long list of films showing the mammarial cleft, among them *Oliver!, For the Love of Benji, Herbie Goes to Monte Carlo,* and *Annie Hall*. Dale didn't recall any cleavage in *Annie Hall*. All the women seemed rather flat-chested, but Roy Rogers Jones had a tendency to exaggerate.

In keeping with his anti-mammary fulmination, Jones then proposed that any GNC female professor with an ample bosom be required to teach in the classroom facing backward so as to not provide any distraction to male students. If the lady professor also had a curvaceous posterior, she should teach behind a curtain.

The second half of the editorial page featured a guest columnist, the much-lauded Danish philosopher and part-time fisherman, Bjorn Bjorkastork. The melancholy Dane delivered a lugubrious meditation on the philo-religious concept of the "hop, skip, and jump of faith." Bjorkastork said this concept was not only a spiritual idea, but it also served quite well as a technique in hopscotch. In spite of Bjorkastork's astounding foot size of twenty, his concept had enabled him to become Copenhagen's hopscotch champ for three years in a row.

Dale included a picture of Bjorkastork, who vaguely resembled another Danish philosopher from the mid-1800s, except Dale had superimposed a fisherman's hat on the head of Kierkegaard and also gave him a mustache.

On page three, an editor's note apologized for not have an entertainment and arts section. Because of overwhelming demand, "Smoke and Mirrors" had decided to have a full page of religion news and features. The first story, a feature story, chronicled the adventures of two aspiring Christian clowns, Long and Shrimp. The two young men, renowned for their personal piety, had decided to use their natural comic abilities to evangelize among the heathen. They had convinced the organizers of Lost and Found to include a clown troupe. Long and Shrimp (first names Weasel and Polonius) dressed in clown clothes, but since their faces already matched the classic clown countenance, they didn't require such superfluous accoutrements such as red rubber noses. No, Weasel Long and Polonius Shrimp were naturally clownish and they had decided to use their innate gifts to spread the gospel. They also juggled *His Time* devotional books.

The second story featured a guest rant, er, sermon by the awesome evangelist, Hosea Revelations Carter. An editor's note mentioned that HRC, as he was affectionately known, was rumored to be the older, illegitimate half brother of the current president, although Roy Rogers Jones disputed such scurrilous rumors. The editor asserted that the president's mother, Miss Lillian, was an unmarried virgin at the time of Hosea Revelations Carter's conception.

Hosea Revelations Carter's sermon was a powerful one. In it, he proclaimed his personal connection to God, and reminded the readers that only *he* had predicted the Unrapture. Those, such as the C. S. Lewis club members at a small southwestern college, who had heeded his word had experienced the joy and discomfort of being Unraptured. HRC knew the resulting nudity might embarrass some of the more modest brothers and sisters, but he reminded them that God had made us in His image. Since we were born naked, so God must be naked, too. Now, the whole world would witness the bare truth as Unraptured Christians, nude and holy, walked among the clothed unbelievers. HRC demanded that all un-unraptured brothers and sisters repent. For there is a hell. In it, all are doomed to wear leisure suits and listen to disco and other demon-inspired music. Repent! he commanded his brothers and sisters.

Just to emphasize HRC's message, the editor had printed below the sermon a picture of a soul tormented in hell. Actually, it was the most grotesque photo of Rusty groovin' to "Zindy Lou." A couple of months ago, after making a print of the weird image, Dale had decided he had to use this bizarre photo somewhere in the paper. The April Fool's issue provided the perfect opportunity. Rusty, grimacing and frozen in an agonized pose, sort of looked like a poor soul roasting in hell. The murky background sort of suggested smoky surroundings. Now, looking at the photograph, Dale thought it perfectly captured the essence of HRC's message. The photo had two headlines. The smaller headline on top read, "Yes, my friend, there is a hell." The larger headline on the bottom, in all caps read, "REPENT."

Page four featured a fake ad and one sports story with a photo. The story was about two East German refugees that, after successfully seeking asylum in the U.S., had decided to swim for the GNC women's swim team (which didn't exist). The story quoted the swim coach, Mathilda "Roo" Kangaranga, the former Australian Olympic champion, as welcoming the young women and disputing rumors that East German swimmers had been injected with illegal drugs in order to masculinize them.

The photograph showed the torsos of two broad-shouldered, rather brawny young women posing in one-piece bathing suits. Well, actually, the photo showed Rusty and Putney wearing women's swimsuits and smiling with their faces painted with makeup. Putney wore a cute pink bathing cap and smiled demurely. Still, his moustache (he refused to shave it off) and chest hair peeking out of the top of his one-piece sort of spoiled that feminine touch. Rusty, who'd generously shaved off his beard, and combed his long hair neatly down to his shoulders, looked a little more convincingly female. With the red lipstick, rouge, mascara, and eyeliner, he looked like a really ugly Carol Burnett.

Underneath the photo, the cutline read: Former East German swim stars, Heidi "Hans" Evabraunstein and Brunhilda Von Valkyriereich, now frolic for the GNC aquawomen. Dale had thought about naming one of the "girls" after his father's family's German name of Schmidt, but it wasn't funny enough.

As for the fake ad, it informed readers of a new law firm in town: Gilbert, Earl, and Maynard. The trio of ambulance chasers boasted of their success with personal injury lawsuits. If Galileans needed a lawyer to sue on account of personal injuries, very personal in the case of Mr. Gilbert, esq., they should call upon the expertise of these three attorneys. No case was too silly or unjustified. Gilbert, Earl, and Maynard promised results.

Dale felt satisfied with the April Fool's parody. Of course, he hadn't anticipated that some real April fools would have competed with his parody issue. And if he had more time, he could have made the parodies a little subtler. Well, that was journalism.

He glanced at the office clock. Almost nine. His boring business class, Practical Principles of Business Management, met at nine. He'd better hightail it over there.

He locked the office and strode across the quad to the business building. Unsurprisingly, it was one of the newest and largest buildings on campus. He supposed that two-thirds of the student body majored in business, education, or religion.

Dale sat in the back of his exciting business class and read Franz Kafka's *The Trial*. He didn't quite get the book. He'd decided to read it because he'd liked the short story *The Metamorphosis*. But the novel puzzled him. Maybe he wasn't concentrating enough. The professor kept interrupting his concentration by talking about depreciation and adjusted grosses and junk like that.

The only people Dale really knew in the rather large class were Rowena and Mary Jane.

They both sat up front like the diligent students they were. At the beginning of class, he noticed both glancing back at him. They gazed at him with astonished expressions on their faces. He guessed they'd seen the newspaper.

After class, Dale didn't hang around to talk to Rowena or Mary Jane. He hurried across campus to the darkroom in the science building. He'd told Sharon he'd help develop film and make prints for the yearbook's final deadline. He knew how yearbook editors were always under pressure. She'd been two days late with the last deadline. Photography was always the problem. Two yearbook photographers had quit during the school year. Their duties got in the way of their studies or they felt like their work wasn't appreciated or they didn't like being told what to do. Anyway, Dale had picked up the slack. He got paid, too. For him, he was rolling in money. He got his campus cop pay, he'd received his "lump sum disbursement" at the start of spring semester, and he got as much as a hundred bucks a month helping with the photography.

As Dale entered the outer chamber of the room of darkness, the arrogant freshman photographer, Ansel Van Dyke, was leaving. The tall, bearded fellow stared at him. Dale said, hey. Van Dyke asked if he'd taken the two photographs on the front of the newspaper. Dale nodded and said he'd taken all the photographs in the parody issue, too. Van Dyke raised a shaggy, black brow and said, "interesting," then disappeared.

High praise from the kid shutterbug genius. Ansel had taken all the other photographs but Dale had been too busy to really scrutinize them and thus offer his compliments.

He went into the inner sanctum of the room of darkness and followed instructions on developing two rolls of film, then checked the contact sheets and made a dozen of prints. Before he left, he noticed that Ansel Van Dyke had made a print of the "Butte-Kickers" photo that featured Dale, Rusty, Putney, Chris, Teri, and Henshaw. The six of them had dressed up as cowboys (Teri as a saloon girl) and posed for a photo taken at a nearby ranch. It was a joke. The six of them had bought a yearbook ad that would feature the photo. Dale scrutinized the print. They had borrowed cowboy garb from the drama department (the department had staged the musical *Oklahoma* earlier in the school year) and the five guys were decked out in their western duds, cowboy hats, boots, vests, while brandishing rifles. Teri wore a frilly skirt with a petticoat and gartered stockings. The photo looked pretty funny. All of them were in "character" as desperados. Dale remembered that he'd had to persuade Sharon into accepting the photo and ad. At first, she objected to the gang's name. "The Butte-Kickers" (the gang was wanted dead or severely mangled for abusing buttes, plateaus, and other natural geographic resources) sounded rather vulgar. But Dale finally talked her into it.

He'd meant to work only until noon and then go to lunch, but, as usual, he lost track of time. When he dashed over to the cafeteria, it was nearly one. The cafeteria stopped serving lunch at one, so he had to wheedle the old lady that checked the meal tickets to let him enter. He walked inside and only saw a few people finishing up lunch. He didn't know any of them well. He got his tray, piled food on it, got a glass of milk, 7-Up, and orange juice, and sat down at a far table and quickly consumed his lunch.

He decided to visit the newspaper office until it was time for his other class, Shakespeare. He strode through the student union, seeing only a few people because classes were in session, and went to the office. No one was there either, which wasn't unusual for Friday.

Dale thought about the next issue and the literary supplement. He would have nothing to do with the literary supplement. Bronwyn, Coop, and Sharon were already reading all the entries, then would make their selections, and deliver the winning manuscripts to the newspaper office the following week. Dale wouldn't know how much of his stuff made it because he'd "recused" himself from working on the literary supplement. Teri, who hadn't submitted any work, would edit that special section. She said she wouldn't even let him in the office when she was working on it.

So, he planned the other eight pages. He almost lost track of time doing that too, then realized he only had a minute to race to Chester Hall for the Shaky class.

He made it to his seat in the back row just as Dr. Frost began class. He noticed she looked at him in a strange way. Well, she often did that because he was often nearly late. He saw Teri giving him a curious look, too. Maybe she was miffed that she hadn't known about the April Fool's section. He hoped she wasn't mad.

The class was almost finished with *The Merchant of Venice*. As Dr. Frost lectured, Dale almost fell asleep. Because of the newspaper deadline, he'd only gotten four hours of slumber. He noticed Teri giving him strange looks from time to time. Every now and then, Fish, Hawkins, Polly, Sharon, and a few others glanced back in his direction, but they pretended to be looking at the classroom clock.

Dale hadn't spoken much to Hawkins since playing racquetball with him. He felt a little awkward around him and he thought David felt the same. They'd exchanged a few sentences. That was about it. Dale wondered what exactly was going on with Hawkins. As Dale sat at his desk in the back row, he looked ahead two rows at the sharply angled profile of David with his curly brown hair. He wondered if Hawkins was really a homosexual. David had said "sexual improprieties." He'd used the plural. Did he mean to say that he engaged in sexual impropriety with both men and women?

Dale had seen Hawkins and Hope walking on campus and at a couple of social functions. They seemed happy with one another. They didn't seem especially affectionate, but most Nazarene couples frowned on public displays of affection. He'd seen them hold hands. He supposed Hawkins kissed Hope good night. Amanda had told him that Hope and David were serious about one another. Dale didn't really know what to think. Besides, he thought it was Hawkins's business.

Dale tuned in Dr. Frost as she talked about Shylock demanding his "piece of flesh" and then cleverly insisting it be from the heart of Antonio. Then she mentioned the scene where Portia disguises herself as a lawyer and Dale, as he always did when Shakespeare's Portia was mentioned, thought of Mrs. Page and her star-crossed daughter.

Class ended and Dale prepared to dash off; he still had things to do before going home for dinner and then seeing Amanda. Teri followed him out of the classroom and called his name before he rounded the building. He stopped and asked, what's up?

"What's up? Are you crazy?"

"What do you mean?"

Teri held up the parody section of the newspaper.

"Oh, that."

"Yeah, that."

Dale tried to explain why he'd kept Teri in the dark. Why he'd kept everyone in the dark except Rusty and Putney. He told her it was because he was concerned that Teri, Polly, and other staffers might get into a little trouble, but he also admitted he wanted to do all the parodies himself. Four pages wasn't much. He thought if he'd had time he could have filled eight pages, easy.

"Hey, I'm not worrying about that," Teri said.

"Oh, yeah?"

"Yeah. I'm worried that you're going to get into big trouble."

"Come on. It's an April Fool's issue."

"Yeah, but a lot of people don't share your sense of humor."

Dale knew that was true. But he said how much trouble could he get into? He'd made fun of silly things. Some people like Short and Fish and Dr. Petry might be offended, but he doubted many others would be.

Teri shook her head. "For a smart guy, you're pretty naïve."

Dale said he needed to go back to the newspaper office. He asked Teri if she wanted to come along. They could talk more there.

She said okay. After all, he might need a bodyguard. Dale thought that was funny. She was about five foot two.

They walked across campus to the student union. Dale noticed a couple of people he didn't know well staring at him. Otherwise, nothing much happened. The campus tended to empty out by mid-afternoon on Friday.

Dale and Teri passed Fish in the hall on their way to the office. Dale said, "well, if it isn't Polonius Shrimp" and gave him a friendly nod to indicate the parodies were all in good fun. But Fish didn't return the nod. In fact, he glared at Dale, if one could call his beady eyes narrowing to even beadier proportions a glare.

"See what I mean?" said Teri.

"Oh, that's just Fish."

They walked into the newspaper office and already Dale counted eight, nine, ten letters to the editor. He didn't want to read them now. Teri picked them up and stacked them on his desk. He sat down and the phone rang. He answered. A woman, the secretary to Dean Snyder, a rather young, attractive woman with wavy blond hair and a nice figure whom he regarded as sweet-tempered, denounced him over the phone. She said he'd produced a travesty of a newspaper. Dale told her that was the point. It was an April Fool's issue. She said she meant the *whole* paper. Then she hung up.

Dale put the receiver back in its cradle. She had sounded upset. It bothered him that an attractive young woman was upset at him. If it was some old crone he wouldn't have minded as much. She'd also used the word "travesty." He liked that word. He'd used it himself while writing a movie review of the film version of *You Light Up My Life*. Well, the movie had been awful.

Then he heard a knock on the door and Aaron Short threw it open without waiting for Dale to say enter. Dale noticed immediately that Short wasn't smiling.

"I have notified the proper authorities," said Short.

Dale asked if he meant the cops or even higher celestial authorities. Short still didn't smile.

"You've derided everything sacred," Short said with great dignity. "You have created an abomination."

Another word Dale liked. Short snorted once, then turned and left.

"Weasel!" Dale shouted. "Come back. Let's talk!"

Teri shook her head but a smile crossed her face.

Dale looked at her and asked if she thought the April Fool's supplement funny.

"Yeah, I did, but I'm almost as warped as you."

He said he didn't care what Fish and Short thought. Or the other conventional thinkers on campus.

"Well, that's just about everybody, Dale," Teri said.

She had a point. Well, wasn't that the reason for satire? To provoke people? To stimulate debate? To lampoon those pompous fools and self-righteous clowns that too often determined how the rest of us behave?

Then to Dale's utter surprise, Amanda, flanked by Mary Jane and Hope, entered the office. He found that interesting. Amanda hadn't dropped by the newspaper office since her New Year's Eve deflowering. Dale didn't know if she had good memories or bad memories about it. She never talked about it. When he'd alluded to it a week after it happened, she got a far-away look in her big blue eyes and pretended not to hear him.

Now, Amanda looked upset. She stared at him. Her eyes looked teary but out of anger, not sorrow. As Dale got up to go over to her, she pointed to the copy of *Smoke Signals* she held in her hand.

"How could you do this, Dale?"

He thought about answering, easy when there's so much material supplied for him. But he didn't want to be a smart aleck with Amanda. He walked over to the desk counter and asked what she meant. He didn't like how Mary Jane and Hope were staring at him with disturbed, hurt looks on their faces. They regarded him as if he'd just told them that they smelled bad.

Amanda tossed the newspaper on the counter. "You not only made fun of people like Aaron, but you ridiculed something I care about: Lost and Found."

"I didn't ridicule Lost and Found."

"You said they were going to add a clown troupe!"

"That's not ridicule. It's a suggestion."

Dale hoped she'd smile but her frown deepened. He'd never seen her face look so dismayed since the time he saw her find out about her ACT scores.

"Look, I was making fun of Short and Fish. Not Lost and Found."

Amanda then pointed to a photograph on the third page of the regular newspaper. Her lower lip quivered. He felt like he'd been punched in the gut when he saw her lovely lower lip quiver.

"You even made fun of my mother."

"What?"

Dale looked at the photograph in question. It was a shot of several education professors at a tea party for a retiring colleague. Mrs. Meeks, or in this context, Professor Meeks, stood in the background. She'd apparently dropped a piece of cheesecake on her otherwise immaculate pink dress. Her mouth was wide open in an exaggerated manner, like she'd just seen a mouse scurrying across the floor and being an anti-vermin kind of woman she was about to scream.

Dale tried not to laugh. He'd been so busy getting the parody section completed that he hadn't examined every detail of the rest of the paper. In fact, Mrs. Meeks was pretty far in the background of the photo. She wasn't that noticeable. But he knew it was the kind of photo that once a few people discovered her exaggerated expression, they would tell others.

"I didn't take the photograph. I had nothing to do with it."

"You put it in the paper!"

Amanda stopped herself from crying. Now she glared at him like the faithful daughter whose mother has been cruelly abused by a muckraking journalist.

"Believe me, Amanda, I didn't see your mother in the photo."

"How can I believe you, Dale? Everything in this paper is a taunt or a joke or an insult."

"Not everything."

"Making fun of something holy like the Rapture by comparing it to –" Amanda lowered her voice as if she were about to say a naughty word "— *streaking*."

Ordinarily, Dale would be impressed that she'd even heard of streaking, but he was too concerned about her being upset at him. He reached a hand toward her and he felt stunned when she quickly retreated a step as if he were about to strike her. Mary Jane and Hope shrank away, too.

"I don't want to see you tonight," Amanda said, huffily. "Or any other night!"

She turned and walked out with Mary Jane and Hope, both of whom gave him a final rebuking look as they might to an unrepentant roué.

Dale started to dash around the desk counter in pursuit of Amanda when Henshaw and Abigail arrived and stood in the doorway.

"Not you, too," Dale said to Henshaw.

Henshaw looked the way Dale had remembered him looking the day of Dr. Prescott's last philosophy class: sad but resolute.

"You've got yourself in a jam," Henshaw said.

"What's wrong with everybody? It's an April Fool's issue. No one should take it seriously."

Abigail didn't seem to be angry with him. Her mild green eyes regarded him with pity more than anything else.

"You've offended the wrong people," Henshaw said.

Dale almost said, "good," but he didn't know whom Henshaw was referring to aside from Short, Fish, and Dr. Petry. Instead, he shrugged.

"Dale, didn't you consider the implications?" asked Abigail.

"What implications? It's a joke. It's for fun. Come on, didn't you guys think the East German transfer students' story funny?"

He looked around. Teri smiled broadly. Henshaw and Abigail smiled briefly, too.

"Yes, but most of the humor in the "Smoke and Mirrors" is too pointed," said Henshaw. "It hits too close to home." Then the stuco president paused and regarded his semi-friend. "Of course, I know from our classes that you tend to go for the jugular."

"What class did you learn that from? Our anatomy class?"

Dale had no idea what Henshaw was talking about. As he remembered it, Henshaw complimented him more than once on his insight into Plato and Kierkegaard. He wondered if Henshaw was already editing his memory to make his former friend even more iconoclastic than he really was.

Henshaw, seeing that Dale had no intention of expressing remorse, said he and Abigail had to go. They were going out to dinner that evening with Abigail's parents. They would do what they could to explain the true intentions behind the parody section in the newspaper.

Dale said thanks. He wondered if he were really in trouble. He guessed so, if Henshaw and Abigail were thinking about placating her parents. Not only was her father president of the college, but her mother was on several important committees in the Nazarene general assembly.

Henshaw and Abigail left and Dale stared at the door wondering who would come through next. He noticed that none of the staff had showed up. Well, most didn't on Fridays. But sometimes Polly and Rowena dropped by.

Dale asked Teri what Polly thought of the spoof paper.

"She was shocked, Dale." Teri shrugged. "And she spotted several typos."

Well, even in her appalled state, leave it to Polly to identify mistakes. Dale sort of smiled. He imagined Polly, aghast at the spoof, nevertheless reading the whole section closely and spotting a misspelled word, a split infinitive, an improper use of an irregular verb, the whole gamut of mistakes he was prone to do when in a hurry.

Dale put his elbows on the desk counter and lowered his head onto his open hands. Maybe he'd gotten carried away. He didn't mean to offend anybody; well, that wasn't true. He had meant to offend a lot of people he thought silly. But not Amanda. He began to doubt her sense of humor. His jokes sometimes bothered her at first, or she didn't get them (especially when they first started dating), but she'd grown to understand the way his mind worked. He'd have to convince her that he didn't mean to make fun of her mother. He could understand how she'd be upset over that. Her mother was such a proper woman; well dressed, well coifed, and nice, too.

Dale thought he'd let Amanda cool off. He'd wait and call her tonight. Surely by then she'd have thought it over and realized that he hadn't meant anything sacrilegious or unholy. He'd just tried to have some fun. He knew his sense of humor tended to be satirical and a little sharp; he wished he had the gentle wit of Flora Eliot. But he didn't.

He heard the soft creeping of shoes on the hallway carpet and looked up warily. Who would this be? What accuser would enter now and excoriate him?

It was Professor Cooper. He slowly ambled in, his gait stiff because of his bad back. Dale had shown him the regular pages of the paper. Coop had made a few corrections, made one minor suggestion, and then gave his blessing. He hadn't asked about Waldo Rubenstein running for philosopher king. Dale guessed he pretended not to see it, so if any administrator complained he could plead inattention due to age. Dale suspected he was amused by the great Waldo first running for Who's Who and now running for student government. But the parody section? Would Coop be offended like everyone else? Would he think Dale had gone too far and insulted every Nazarene and Christian on campus?

Coop looked at Dale and Teri.

"Happy April Fool's parody," he said, smiling his cavalier smile.


Amanda wouldn't come to the phone Friday or Saturday. Her dorm sisters shielded her and Dale wondered if he'd ever get to speak to her again. He knew if he could just see her, he could explain and she'd forgive him.

He went to work Saturday and patrolled the empty halls of Cimarron City High School. He didn't even feel like reading much.    Saturday night after work, Dale saw Rusty. They were supposed to go see a movie, but they couldn't agree on which one to see. Rusty wanted to see *Animal House* again; Dale didn't feel like seeing it again so soon. He didn't feel like seeing any comedies. He was more in the mood for a depressing movie, something Bjorkastork would like, perhaps Ingmar Bergman if one of his films were playing in the City. Rusty didn't get that. Why see a depressing movie when you're depressed? Why see a depressing movie at all?

So they just drove around town for a while, then ate at Sooner Shack, then went to Braum's for a multi-dip ice cream cone, and then drove around some more. Neither one of them talked about girls. Both knew that their sweethearts were angry and disappointed in them. Both were likely to stay angry and disappointed in them. Best to avoid depressing topics.

Later in the evening, they went over to Putney's pad. He lived at the same apartment complex that Mr. Benedict had lived in five years ago. They sat around and listened to records and talked about "Smoke and Mirrors." Putney loved it. Rusty's enthusiasm was more muted.

Putney suggested they listen to albums with the highest demon content in them. He had hundreds of albums. He even had the *Uncle Meat* album. Putney said after Rusty told him about it, he had to have it. He found it at a record store in the City. Dale asked if the record store was *Woody's*. Putney said, yeah, how did he know? They talked about the record store for awhile and Dale told him about all the '60s albums and 45s he used to buy there. He didn't mention the Beach Boys. Putney didn't seem to have that kind of musical taste. But he told him about some of the great British Invasion groups, like the Kinks, Yardbirds, Animals, Troggs, and Zombies. Putney said he liked British rock. He mentioned some albums of current groups he liked, Queen, Sweet, Jethro Tull, and Uriah Heep.

Putney played the *Uncle Meat* album. Dale hadn't heard it since that time Erickson and Rusty played it at Mr. Benedict's. He liked a few of the songs, especially "Electric Aunt Jemima;" but most of the album was experimental jazz that he didn't care for. The album also had a four-letter taboo word. Dale remembered that was the reason why Mr. Benedict had banned the playing of the record.

Then Rusty and Putney started debating which team would win the NBA playoffs. Dale guessed Putney had given up talking hockey. He thought about Putney's name. Abner Putney. That unusual name sounded familiar. He thought he'd read it somewhere recently. Then he remembered. He'd read that name in a sister publication – that is, a student newspaper from a Nazarene college in Idaho. Abner Putney was the president of that college.

Dale asked Putney if he was a "junior"?

Putney raised a shaggy brow and informed Dale that no man called him that. Dale asked if his father was the president of the Idaho Nazarene college. Putney admitted that he was. He said his father had exacted one promise from Abner junior in exchange for a new Trans Am for high school graduation: please don't attend his college. Putney had agreed and the rest was history.

At midnight, Dale said he had better go. He had to get up at five-thirty in the morning to go to work. The three of them got in Rusty's beat-up car. After Rusty dropped off Dale, he and Putney were going to get into some harmless mischief. At least, Dale hoped it would be harmless.

The next day at work, he felt a little groggy. His shift dragged on, although he did finish *The Trial*. When he got home, he called Amanda at her home. Kenny answered the phone and didn't sound too friendly, but he put Amanda on. As soon as he heard her voice, Dale felt his heart melt. He'd missed hearing her voice and it had only been two days.

Amanda still sounded offended. Dale asked if he could see her. She said she was going to church tonight. She suggested that he should go too; not to see her, but to ask for forgiveness. He told her that he only cared about receiving her forgiveness. She said he should worry about receiving God's forgiveness. He said he didn't think he'd done anything to God to ask His forgiveness for. She begged to differ. He said he didn't want to argue; he just wanted to see her. She said he could come by her dorm before Sunday evening service and they could talk for a little while. He said he'd come by half an hour before church.

Dale noticed the girl at the front desk eyeing him warily. Maybe she thought he would throw off his clothes like an unraptured person or maybe she knew he was the wicked author of the newspaper parody. He studied her and placed her feline face. She was Shirley's friend that he'd seen at the homecoming basketball game.

Dale recognized Amanda's footsteps as she descended the stairs. Since she almost always wore short heeled shoes, he'd learned to identify their soft clicking. He turned and waited. As soon as he saw her face, he felt like confessing or doing anything she wanted. Then, as he looked from her face to the rest of her, he grew concerned.

She came over to him but didn't smile. Dale noticed she'd gotten her hair done. She'd cut it so it now hung only to her shoulders, and she'd made it too wavy. It was the same color, though. Her clothing seemed different too; her attire looked more modest. The skirt of her beige dress draped over her knees. The long-sleeved and high-necked dress covered all her chest and even some of her throat. Her dress approached the no-skin-showing style of Vern's sisters. Dale wondered if she was trying to punish him visually. At the very least, this was a bad sign.

He said hello.

She said hello.

He tried to take her hand, but she clasped her hands together as they walked out of the dorm. They didn't say anything as they crossed the street and headed in the direction of the magnificent First Church.

Dale felt himself growing annoyed. He'd hoped she'd be over her anger and disapproval. She didn't seem angry now, but her attitude, distant and unresponsive, worried him.

They approached a bench on the edge of the main campus and Dale asked her to sit down. He wanted to talk to her.

She sat down in a very demure, proper way. She even tugged on her skirt so it covered her knees. Dale shook his head. He held his palms up in exasperation.

"Amanda, what's wrong? Why are you acting like this?"

"I'm not acting."

"You cut your hair."

She didn't answer. He looked again at her beige dress. He hated beige. He thought she knew this, but maybe not. Beige was for old ladies.

"Look, I'm sorry if I upset you," he said. "But you're overreacting to the newspaper spoof."

"Oh, is that what you call it?"

"Yeah. A spoof. Meaning you're not supposed to take it seriously."

"Dale, I did take it seriously. Many people did. We usually do when our values are attacked."

He didn't like the word "values." He was surprised she'd used it. Why didn't she use good old-fashioned words like morals or principles? Not that it would have made his case any easier.

"Believe me, I didn't see your mother in that photograph. If I had, I would have cropped her out."

Amanda gave Dale a puzzled look. Apparently she didn't know what "cropped" meant.

"I mean, I would have edited her out of the picture."

She still looked at Dale in a distant, rebuking way. He couldn't believe she was acting like this. He thought maybe if he could touch her, she'd snap out of it. He scooted closer. She gave him a warning look.

"What is it, Amanda? Can't I even touch you?"

"Dale, don't you see that's been the problem between us of late?"

"Problem?"

"When you focus on all that … activity, you get frustrated. Perhaps that frustration affects the way you think?"

Dale knew he should be offended. Amanda had just said his feelings for her, his passion, addled his thinking. Well, in a way it did. But it wasn't sexual frustration that had spurred him to write the newspaper parody; it was exposing plain old human folly.

"Don't you like the *activity*?"

Amanda stared at him, offended.

Dale leaned toward her and she leaned away. He couldn't contain his frustration any longer.

"Damn it!"

Amanda stared at him as if she'd been slapped. Her eyes, large with shock, teared. When Dale saw that, he immediately felt sorry. He hadn't meant to yell at her.

"I'm sorry, Amanda. But I'm not the only one who likes being close. Physically close. You like it, too."

He could see she didn't want to admit it. She lowered her head. It was as if she were confessing to an awful sin.

"Yes. But I shouldn't."

"You're wrong, Amanda. You should."

Amanda turned her head away from him.

He drew a little closer but he didn't touch her. He just used his voice.

"If you love me the way I love you, then it's natural and *good* to want to be close. To be intimate, even. It's love, Amanda. There's nothing wrong with that."

She reached up with a couple of fingers and wiped away a tear. When he tried to touch her, she leaned away.

"We're supposed to love God more," she said quietly.

Dale shook his head in anger. Why did she have to bring Him up?

"You do love God, don't you Dale?"

"Of course."

"Do you really?"

Dale wondered if he loved God. He wasn't sure what that meant. To him, God was an omnipotent force. The all-encompassing consciousness. The ultimate reality. The source of all Truth. An enigma.

"I don't know."

Amanda glanced at him. "You don't know if you love God? Love Jesus?"

"I love you, Amanda. That's what matters."

"Not to me. Oh, Dale, don't you see that if we both love Jesus in the same way, then everything will be all right?"

Dale saw that her eyes were clear now. They shined. They were lit up with the love of Jesus. Dale envied her simple faith. She really *believed*.

"Will it, Amanda?"

"Of course. Then all temptation will disappear. All those strong, powerful urges will be under control. Loving Jesus will be the most important, powerful feeling in our lives."

"And you want that?"

"Yes, Dale, I do."

Dale didn't know what to say. He didn't want to hurt Amanda. He realized he'd been doing that. Not intentionally. And yet the idea of being with Amanda but not having her, at least some of her, offended him. He felt anger well up inside him, not for her, but for God. Why did He do this? Bring them together and allow them to fall in love each other and yet prevent them from fulfilling their love. To test them? To instill patience? All he had to do was acquiesce to Amanda and God, practice patience, become a businessman or something practical, and he could have her. In another year, they could marry. Then he'd have her completely. Or would he?

"Dale, tonight at the service, go to the altar and pray for forgiveness. Pray for Jesus to enter your heart. Then we'll be one in Him."

Dale was about to say okay, when he saw Chris walking toward them. He was heading to the evening service. Chris saw them sitting on the bench and started walking over. Dale tried to will him away. He didn't want to see his good friend. He knew he had wounded him, too.

Chris, wearing his dark blue suit, stood before them and after giving Dale a resentful glance, looked at Amanda with a concerned look on his face.

"Are you all right, Amanda?"

Dale didn't like Chris asking her that, especially in that kind of protective voice.

"I'm fine, Chris." She glanced at Dale. "I'm just trying to help Dale understand the mistakes he made."

He knew Amanda would have added sinful if she didn't care about his feelings. But he still felt annoyed. He didn't think he'd made any mistakes – except for a few typos.

Chris shook his head. "Why did you do all of that, Dale?"

"Do all of what?"

"Attack people. Attack God."

"I didn't attack anybody or God. I just exposed folly."

"Folly? You think the Rapture is folly?"

Dale glanced at Amanda. She waited to hear his answer, too.

"Maybe you forgot, Chris. The Rapture didn't happen."

Dale knew he shouldn't have said that. Chris clenched his teeth and stared. He'd never seen Chris so angry with him.

"Dale, you've been my friend for a long time, and I love you like a brother, but I think you've been a bad influence on me."

Dale hoped Amanda wasn't thinking the same thing. "I'm sorry to hear that, Chris."

Dale hung his head and thought about Chris's words. Maybe he had been a bad influence. He talked him into seeing R-rated movies. Worse, maybe he'd caused doubt to creep into Chris's mind. Maybe Chris was like Amanda and he wanted to close his mind off to certain things, certain imponderables. Chris had an accountant's mind. He didn't enjoy contemplating paradox or investigating ambiguity. He liked everything in black and white. Balanced and double checked. Dale didn't blame him. For a lot of people that made sense. He thought closing your mind off to certain things probably helped most people live happy and productive lives. But he didn't think he could. That meant he'd have to become like Rex Meeks or Bobby Henshaw or David Hawkins. Subtle, clever, perceptive people who hid something of their true selves. Maybe such an act was necessary if you wanted to live in a safe, ordered world. Maybe you had to conform to be part of a larger community. To belong. Dale thought he wouldn't mind belonging.

Amanda and Chris had exchanged a few words while Dale thought. He heard Chris say they should be going to First Church. It was getting late. Dale remembered the poster in

Chris's dorm room, the one with the clock and a crucified Jesus displayed in its middle instead of hour and minute hands. The headline read: *It's later than you think.*

"Dale," Amanda said softly as she stood up, "do you want to come with us?"

He rose but when he heard the "us," he felt that old perverse stubborn pride take hold.

Dale looked at Amanda, then at Chris. They both looked back at him in a gentle, forgiving way. All he had to do was go with them, repent his sins, and he'd have his girlfriend, his love, and his good friend back.

"No, Amanda," he said. "I want you to stay with me."

She stared at him. Chris did, too.

Dale knew if he touched her and spoke to her in the way she liked, he might have a chance. He took her hand. He looked into her eyes.

"Stay here with me."

Amanda looked startled. But she didn't take her hand away.

Chris took a step closer. Dale gave him a warning look. He loved Chris like a brother, but he'd slug him if he had to.

"I can't, Dale," she said.

He stroked her hand with his thumb. Even caressing the back of her hand delighted him. Dale knew what Ramakrishna would say: he was full of avidyamaya. Well, to hell with him.

"I knew it," Chris said. "I knew it when I saw him laughing at us at that field. He doesn't believe."

"I do believe," Dale said. "Just not in the silly stuff."

Amanda gently removed her hand from his. Dale had said the wrong thing. His words had broken the spell. Chris, the snake in the grass, had provoked him into saying the wrong thing.

Amanda didn't look offended; she looked sorrowful but resolute.

"Are you *coming*?" she asked.

Dale shook his head. "No."

Amanda's face flushed and her eyes glimmered, but she said nothing. Chris, narrowing his eyes at Dale, said he'd walk with her over to First Church if she'd like. Amanda nodded. Dale watched the two of them walk away.

He sat down on the bench and pulled his tie loose. He didn't like wearing suits or ties or dress shoes. He liked dressing like a rube. Amanda liked dressing properly. He liked her to dress for him. She'd changed her hair. It made her look more grown-up. Less like a girl. But he liked it the way it was before, long and free.

Dale glanced across the long stretch of campus with a view of the front portion of the gleaming First Church. Maybe he should go. Maybe he should show Amanda that he was willing to believe like she did. If he didn't, he knew it was over between them. He wasn't sure if he could bear that.

He vacillated. He made the case one way, then the other. He thought Amanda should do what he wanted. He thought if he waited, she'd return. She loved him. He knew she did. He knew he thrilled her when he let her. He knew she liked the way he touched her, spoke to her in a low, deep voice before he kissed her. He knew she liked making out with him when she allowed herself. He knew she would enjoy completing the act once they got married. When they became one, this other stuff wouldn't matter as much. She'd put it all in perspective. Religion was important, but it wasn't everything. You could overdo that, too. It wasn't as important as love.

Dale didn't know what time it was. He didn't know how long he'd been sitting at the bench debating with himself. She wasn't coming back to him. She was too pure. Too much in love with God. He didn't blame her, exactly. From his reading, he knew some people in history had shared her intense feeling for God. What did Kierkegaard call them? God besotted?

He glanced at his wrist as if he had a wristwatch. Maybe he should wear one. Maybe he should be like her father. Punctilious and regimented and shrewd. Make lots of money. Provide and protect. Disappear into the conventions of business and family and religion. Dale didn't think any of that was bad. It just wasn't for him.

Or was it? He jumped off the bench and jogged toward First Church. Then he ran. He dashed up the stairs. He threw open the glass front doors and quickly walked to one of the entrances, hearing the sublime voices of the choir. He lingered. He lurked. He didn't go in. The choir stopped singing and Dale listened to the pastor read scripture. I Corinthians 13. Verses 9 to 13. Then he commenced his sermon. Dale inched closer to the entrance and looked at the assembled brothers and sisters. He could sense their joy, their rapture. Most of them thought they were going to heaven soon. Dale guessed a few had doubts. Those with rational minds that told them that such simple beliefs were too fantastic. But they were impostors among the believers, like him. They were the wolves in sheep's clothing.

Dale peered down the rows of seats. He saw Amanda sitting in the middle. Always in the middle. He saw her sitting with Mary Jane and Gretchen and K. C. and Chris. He couldn't see if there was an open seat close to her. But he could still walk down there and show her he was there.

He took a breath and tried to calm himself and took a step forward. Then he heard the pleasant, cheerful, confident voice of the pastor as he talked about the imminent return of Jesus. If only the good pastor hadn't said that.

Dale took a step back and looked one more time at Amanda sitting with her friends, her brothers and sisters. He wanted to join her, but he couldn't. He felt that tingling in the back of his eyes and high in his nose and he tried to think of something impersonal and hard. He couldn't do it. He could only see her face. He stepped back and looked at the immaculate white wall that encircled and protected the sanctuary. Even that didn't destroy the feeling. As he wept, he hit his fist against the wall, hoping the sensation would drive that annoying emotion away, and said her name over and over.

A latecomer opened the door farther down and Dale stopped hitting the wall. He walked to the nearest door, threw it open, and burst into the soft, fading sunlight of a spring evening. That annoying emotion was gone. He felt dry inside. To keep it that way, he imagined a baseball in his mind. A perfect, white sphere with that interesting red stitching traversing the ball. He thought how it felt to hold a ball in his hand and throw it. He thought how good it felt to catch it. He loved playing baseball. The grass, the earth, the blue sky. The smell of the spring air. The way the cloth of the uniform felt on his muscles as he ran; the way the spikes pricked the dusty base path and kicked up puffs of dirt.

Thinking about baseball helped. He calmed down. He walked slowly back to campus. He knew it was over with Amanda and he didn't want it to be over. He wanted her but not on her terms. He felt desolate inside. He wondered if this was what God wanted. A merciful God? A God that permitted Portia to die in childbirth? A God that allowed Jesse's mind to collapse into insanity? A God that tormented Mrs. Page and inflicted a horrible disease on Mrs. Genesee? A God that thrust all those terrible burdens on poor, believing women?

Dale wished he didn't believe in God, but he did. He felt His presence in his soul in his moments of joy and in his moments of agony.

But he didn't love God. He loved her.


### April 3, 1978: Part 2

By the time Dale made it to his car from off Reinhardt's Summit, the storm had darkened the whole western section of the sky. He smelled the rain, the electricity in the air, and saw streaks of lightning, followed by deep booms of thunder.

Dale jumped in his car and headed north on the rural road for a mile. By the time he turned east onto the highway, he saw towering thunderheads looming almost overhead. He raced the Chevy down the road and realized he couldn't outrun the storm. He glanced in his rearview mirror and saw dipping clouds, witches' teats, and he knew conditions were ripe for a twister.

He turned onto the road leading to the abandoned children's hospital and drove toward an old building that used to be a storage facility. He remembered how sturdy it looked from the time he'd explored the grounds a few years ago. Since it no longer had a front, Dale drove straight into the building.

As soon as he pulled into the dark, dank place, he heard the sound of the wind increase from a howl to a shriek and saw the sunlight disappear as if a solar eclipse had just taken place.

He shut off the motor and turned around in his seat to watch. Hail pelted the ground. Thunder boomed. Lightning sizzled. The wind howled, then grew muted. Then it roared more fiercely. Then it was over. The fast-moving storm had passed over in five minutes.

Dale started the Chevy and backed up out of the building and noticed that the worst of the storm seemed to be farther north. Thick, turbulent clouds blotted out that whole section of sky. He drove back to Galilee and saw that the traffic lights weren't working. Few people were on the road, however, and he navigated through the town center without incident. As he drove to the college, he saw a couple of cars with significant hail damage. Debris littered sidewalks. A few business had busted windows.

He turned on Luther Street and drove down the road looking at the girls' dorms. Everything looked okay. Some tree limbs lay strewn on campus. But the dorms looked fine, no visible damage.

Dale slowed down at Hayley and wondered about Amanda and the other girls. Since she didn't have any late afternoon classes on Monday, he was sure she had been in the dorm when the storm hit and had gone down into the basement with the others. He felt confident she was safe and secure. Just thinking of her huddled in the basement with her friends made him feel a sharp pain. He wished he could be with her, holding her hand. He knew she was afraid of storms, just like Jesse.

Dale drove north to his home. As he advanced, he noticed more damage. A few smaller trees had been uprooted. Larger trees had limbs severed off. Several houses were battered and damaged.

He grew more concerned the farther he drove north. When he crossed 50th Street, he knew this part of town had been slammed by a tornado. Two blocks later, he turned on his street and saw half the houses down on the other end of his block were in shambles. What few trees the block had were now scattered across the debris-strewn yards or lying in shreds in the street. Amazingly, his house looked okay.

He didn't see either Jesse's Cougar or June's Nova. For a moment, he wondered if the cars had been tossed blocks away. Unlikely, if the house was undamaged. He parked the car and walked up to the house and opened the front door. As he did, he had the strange sensation that he was entering a stage prop. Most of the kitchen and the living room had been sucked away. The glowering northern sky loomed right in front of him, unblocked by those rooms.

The other part of the house, however, looked intact. It was as if a toy house had been pulled apart by powerful hands. The only real debris came from the roof. Some ripped wood and loose tile hung over the severed roof. Otherwise what had been the living room and kitchen was just empty space.

All the living room furniture, including the television, had been blown away. The kitchen appliances, including the electric stove, were gone. The cabinets and dining table, too.

Dale turned and walked down the hall, peering at the roof, wondering if it would hold. It seemed fine. It was as if the house had been built this way: to split almost evenly in two.

For a second, he felt his heart leap in his chest at the thought that Jesse and June had been sucked away with the living room and kitchen. He looked in their bedrooms. No one there. No damage. When he looked in his bedroom, it looked the way he'd left it that morning. Even the book he'd been rereading, *Brave New World*, lay on the chair with the bookmark still stuck between its pages.

Dale retreated from the bedroom area and wondered where Jesse and June could be. The most likely place would be Grandpa and Grandma's. They had a small storm cellar and if Jesse saw the storm coming on television, she might have headed there with June.

Dale drove to his grandparents and as soon as he turned onto their street, he saw both Jesse's and June's cars parked in the yard. He parked on the curb and got out. June's car had sustained some damage, Jesse's less so. Grandpa's Falcon parked in the gravel driveway looked fine. The little house looked mostly undamaged, too. Just a cracked window. The small tree in the front yard had been stripped of most of its leaves and some branches had been torn off. But for the most part, the house and yard hadn't been damaged.

Dale started to knock on the front door when it opened, and Grandpa said, "git on in here, boy."

He entered and saw Grandpa, Grandma, Jesse, and June gathered in the living room. They all stared at him with big eyes.

"Were you out in that there storm?" asked Jesse.

"No, I took cover when I saw it coming."

Grandpa asked if he knew how bad it was. Dale said most of the town hadn't been hit too hard. But the north side probably had been hit by a tornado.

He saw Jesse and June staring at him.

"It took half of our house away."

The four of them gawked at him and started talking all at once. Dale told them what he'd seen. None of them, except for Grandpa, could believe it.

"Why, I've seen a twister carry away a milk cow and leave behin' the pail of milk."

Grandma said he'd seen no such thing.

Grandpa said he shore as hell did see it. Back in Arkansas, before they'd got hitched.

Grandma said he was telling tales.

Dale interrupted them to ask if the power was on. Grandpa said he reckoned it weren't. Dale walked over and flipped the switch. Nothing came on. He looked out the front. The power lines were still up in this neighborhood. He guessed the electricity would be restored pretty soon.

June asked Dale what they should do. Could they go home? She wanted to get her clothes at least. Her record player, too. Her makeup case. And some other stuff. Come to think of it, she could use –"

Dale told her he'd go back later and fetch some clothes and other essentials. She and Jesse better stay here out of the way. They couldn't stay in the house, it was too dangerous.

Grandma asked Dale if he was hungry. He said no. He listened to them fuss and speculate and talk and talk. He went over to the still open front door and looked out the screen door and smelled the fresh, clean air. He thought, what else is going to happen on my birthday?


### Epilogue 1: *A man for all seasons*

Dean Snyder thanked Dale for attending this special meeting of the college publication board. Dale, sitting on a vinyl chair ten feet away from a long, polished oak table where the five members of the board sat, nodded. He thought the fact that the handsome dean had thanked him was typical of his smooth, rather unctuous way. After all, Dale didn't have much choice.

It had been four days since the tornado tore off part of his home. After staying the first night with his grandparents, he'd called Blackie and asked if he could stay with him until he graduated from college – assuming he would graduate. Dale thought it was possible he might be kicked out of GNC. Apparently, the administration had taken his April Fool's special supplement far more seriously than he did.

But first, the publications board had to meet to consider removing him from his editor's position. The five members sat at the handsome oak table, sitting on cushioned chairs. Dale thought it was rather amusing that they seemed to sit in order of how much they either liked or loathed him. Starting on the far left: Professor Edward Cooper, acting adviser to the newspaper; Professor Bronwyn J. Ayers, adviser to the yearbook; Robert Henshaw, stuco president and student representative; Dr. Henry Snyder, dean of academics, who had taken Dr. Pierce's position on the board until they appointed a new dean for student services; and Dr. Thomas Petry, faculty representative.

Well, it was a toss-up who disliked him the most between the dean and the grammarian. Dale guessed it didn't matter much. He was certain both of them would vote to remove him.

As for the other three, Dale guessed they were on his side. But, except for Professor Cooper, he wasn't even sure of that.

Dale shifted in his seat and glanced at the empty yellow vinyl seat to his left. He supposed it was there for witnesses. He'd been told there would be witnesses. He didn't know why. The facts of his case seemed self-evident. In fact, they were in black and white.

"Before we commence this inquiry," said Dr. Snyder, "the board would like to extend its condolences to Dale Smith. We were informed that your home was destroyed in the tornado that hit Galilee four days ago."

The board members nodded their condolences at him and he nodded back, even though Dean Snyder exaggerated a little. The house hadn't been destroyed exactly, although what was left standing would be demolished. Dale, June, and Jesse had salvaged about everything they could, which, considering all their bedrooms had been mostly undamaged, was quite a lot. Since Blackie had so little stuff in his own apartment, Dale had plenty of room for his possessions.

Dean Snyder began the inquiry. The first topic was the notorious April Fool's section of the newspaper, the so-called "Smoke and Mirrors" parody. Dale noticed that Dean Snyder didn't even like pronouncing the parody name.

The five board members took turns asking Dale his thoughts and motives in producing the parody section. He explained that the student newspaper used to publish a special April Fool's issue in the past. He said he wanted to revive that tradition, one that had stopped after Flora Eliot's editorship. When he said Flora's name, he noticed Bronwyn, wearing a red sweater with a rather roomy black jacket over it, looked especially interested.

Dale said he'd brought the parody issue from four years ago to show them if they wished to see it. Coop and Bronwyn asked to look at it. Dale noticed Bronwyn smiling when she flipped through its pages.

Then Dean Snyder and Dr. Petry asked him specific questions about the parody news stories and photos. What seemed to bother them the most was the AP photo of OU frat boys streaking. Didn't he realize how indecent such a photograph was?

"No," Dale said. "It just shows bare chests and arms."

"Yes," Dr. Petry said, "but the viewer knows that these young men are streaking. Therefore, there is a salacious context to it. The viewer knows that these young men are naked even if he or she can't see below their midsection."

Dale wondered how such an intelligent man as Dr. Petry got so narrow minded. Dale responded that what Dr. Petry said was somewhat valid, except that he was attributing salacious desires on the part of the viewer. If someone wanted to think in that way, he could do it without prompting from a photograph. He could just look at other people and think how they are naked underneath their clothes.

Dale didn't mean to look at Bronwyn when he said that, but he thought she was by far the most attractive person on the board. She raised her eyebrows, Coop chuckled, and Dr. Petry scowled, while the dean and Henshaw maintained scrupulously neutral expressions.

"So, you don't see anything unseemly about the photograph?" asked Dean Snyder.

"No. It illustrates the parody news story in a comical way. That's the only reason why it's in the paper. I don't know who would be titillated by the photo, anyway. They're just a bunch of grubby frat boys."

This time Dale looked at Dr. Petry, who stopped scowling and glanced quickly at his colleagues before assuming a more dignified mien.

They asked him about each parody item. Dean Snyder and Dr. Petry were, unsurprisingly, his chief antagonists.

Who is this Bjorn Bjorkastork?

Dale almost laughed when Dean Snyder pronounced the name. He tried to explain the origins of the melancholy Dane. But as soon as he started talking about Kierkegaard and his *Either/Or* text, Dean Snyder became impatient. Henshaw attempted a feeble explanation, but it was clear to Dale that Robert had left behind old Soren and the religious skepticism he'd championed.

Where did you get the idea of the Unrapture? And didn't you realize how offensive that concept would be to the GNC community?

Dale said he thought of it when he saw Short and Fish and the others standing out in an empty field waiting for the real Rapture. He didn't think the Unrapture idea any more offensive than the idea that someone could actually predict the Rapture or the Second Coming or the Apocalypse or any of those things. It was presumptuous of people to predict such things. He was just making that point in an absurd, comic way.

There were two gratuitous slanders concerning our nation's president. Why did Dale refer to President Carter as the antichrist? Why did he mock the president's elderly mother and the concept of the virgin birth?

Dale said he wasn't mocking the president or his mother but the tendency of religious fanatics to misattribute religious concepts to contemporary people and events.

Was the parody story about the evangelist Hosea Revelations Carter meant to be a lampooning of the respected evangelist Daniel Ransom Johnson?

Dale looked at Dr. Petry, who'd asked the question. He said, what did he think?

Dr. Petry said he did indeed think it was a tasteless attack on the esteemed evangelist.

Dale said that was true. But it was Brother Johnson who'd started the whole Rapture hysteria. He'd said the Rapture was going to happen on a specific date and time.

Dr. Petry vigorously disagreed. Some people had simply misinterpreted the evangelist. Dr. Snyder seemed to disagree with Dr. Petry. The two quietly exchanged a few words, then Dean Snyder asked Dale another question.

Regarding the "hell" photo. Did he believe in hell?

"At this moment, I certainly do."

Coop chuckled. Bronwyn smiled. The others remained neutral. Dale was especially impressed with Henshaw's stolidity.

Did he think it funny to satirize two respected students and the admirable Lost and Found organization?

Dale said he didn't know who were the two respected students Dr. Petry referred to.

Long and Shrimp.

Dale suppressed a laugh. If Dr. Petry had said Weasel Long and Polonius Shrimp, he would have burst out laughing. Dale said he wasn't aware of any students on campus with those names.

Dr. Petry said of course not *those* names. But everyone on campus knows to whom Dale was referring.

Dale shrugged. "Do they?"

"Of course," said Dr. Petry.

"Well, who?"

Dr. Petry did not want to say.

Dean Snyder asked about showing disrespect to the Lost and Found organization.

Dale said he meant no disrespect and he apologized if it appeared that he was making fun of that esteemed organization.

Dr. Petry asked him about the strange rant about movies with cleavage in them. What was the point of this Roy James Jones?

Dale was surprised that Dr. Petry had made an error. He respectfully corrected the grammarian. Roy *Rogers* Jones.

Dr. Petry looked peeved. He said he meant Roy Rogers Jones.

Dale almost smiled at how uncomfortable Dr. Petry seemed referring to fictional characters. He didn't even like speaking their names.

Dale tried to explain that the mock editorial was in reaction to Aaron Short's ridiculous censorship of the actress's cleavage in *Oliver!* This time, he didn't look at Bronwyn.

Dean Snyder didn't understand the circumstances of the so-called censorship. Henshaw leaned over and whispered to the dean. Dale guessed he was telling him about Short sticking his paw over part of the lens to block out the offending image. Dean Snyder nodded and asked Dale to respond.

Dale said Short's behavior was ridiculous and he wanted to write a mock editorial to illustrate just how absurd it was. He said when people like Aaron started overreacting to one thing, it was only a short step for them to censor other forms of expression. Dale tried not to stare at the dean or Dr. Petry.

The board seemed to have covered most of its objections about the parody part of the newspaper. Dean Snyder asked Dale if he had anything to say.

"Yeah, did you think the East German swimmers' story funny?"

To his surprise, all the board members, except Dr. Petry, nodded. Dale guessed they watched the Olympics.

He thought, if that was it, then maybe he'd survived. He thought he'd done a pretty good job defending himself. A lot of the questions were silly. Who's Bjorn Bjorkastork? Who does Dean Snyder think he is? A tennis star?

Dean Snyder said they could only make a short inquiry about the other part of the newspaper, the non-parody part, because they were pressed for time. Most of the members of the board wanted Dale to know that the story and photographs about the "Great Disappointment of 1978" were in bad taste. Also, this mysterious character called Waldo Rubenstein that continues to appear in the paper is puzzling to many people. Just who is this Waldo Rubenstein?

"He's a fictional character," said Dale.

"We understand that," said Dean Snyder. "But presumably the photograph is of a real man."

"That's true."

"Well, who is he?"

Dale said he didn't remember his name, then he explained how he got the photo from the OU student-leadership press packet and how the man in the photo is an eminent scientist from a prestigious university in the east. As soon as he finished, he saw all five of the board members staring at him in wonder, even Professor Cooper.

"Do you think that's responsible behavior from a student journalist, not to mention an attendee of the respected Student-Leadership seminar?"

Dale considered the question. He'd never really thought about it in that way. He just thought it was an amusing photo.

"No, I guess not."

Dean Snyder nodded. "And what do you imagine would be the reaction of this eminent scientist if he found out that his image was being used for a fictional character named Waldo Rubenstein?"

"If he has a sense of humor, I think he'd like it."

Dr. Petry let out a frustrated sigh and shook his head. "You really think so?"

"Yeah."

"You don't think it shows disrespect?"

"I don't know him, so how can I show disrespect?"

"Come now, Dale, you know what we mean," said Dean Snyder. "A man of his stature wouldn't want to see his photograph used in some crude satire, would he?"

Dale didn't like his satire being called crude. "Why would he care? If he's so eminent, then he shouldn't care if his photograph is used for a little fun. He has more important things to think about than fussing about some small college paper using his image to satirize silly conventions."

"You think Who's Who and student council are silly conventions?" asked Henshaw.

"In some ways, yes. Those things are perhaps necessary, but some people tend to take them too seriously, don't you think?"

Henshaw didn't answer. Dale thought the Henshaw he knew last year would have agreed with him.

"Very well," said Dean Snyder, "we have to move on. Now we come to the second phase of the investigation in which accusations of poor character have been leveled against you, Dale."

Dale glanced at his two allies, Professor Cooper and Bronwyn. Only Coop looked at him in an apologetic manner.

"Bring in the first witness," said Dean Snyder to a secretary who'd been taking notes in shorthand of the inquiry.

Dale hadn't had a chance to look at her. She'd arrived just before the meeting began and sat somewhat behind him and across the room. Dale turned and glanced at her. She was the same attractive young woman that had called his newspaper a "travesty." Dean Snyder's secretary. He couldn't think of her name. So he decided just to refer to her as Miss Travesty.

Miss Travesty walked over to the closed door, opened it, and Shirley, the music major, walked in. She was about the last person Dale expected. Shirley, wearing an attractive beige suit skirt just like she would at a real trial, swished over to the vinyl seat not too far from Dale. She gave him a reproachful look when she sat down. She saw him looking at her knees when her skirt rose above them. She frowned at him and tugged the skirt down over them.

Dean Snyder asked her to tell the board about Dale's misbehavior.

Shirley, with another reproachful look Dale's way, read from a prepared statement. She said that the young man had accosted her several times. He'd made lewd comments and gave her suggestive looks. He'd upset her. He'd also made her boyfriend suspicious. Stephen thought she might be seeing this fellow, which was, of course, impossible. He'd also followed her to the dorm desk once and harassed her there. She almost had to call campus security.

Dean Snyder asked Shirley if she had knowledge of any other misdeeds Dale had engaged in.

She nodded. He'd been one of the four ruffians who'd dressed up in monkey suits and interrupted the basketball game during homecoming. He'd sat next to her on purpose, teased her, and then ruined her pants when he spilled a soft drink on the front and the back. People in the bleachers had laughed at her when she left to change.

Professor Cooper asked how she knew it was Dale in the ape suit if he was, in fact, wearing an ape suit.

Dale appreciated Coop for not using Shirley's improper monkey term.

Shirley said she'd recognized his eyes.

644

Bronwyn and Professor Cooper found that point interesting. Bronwyn asked if she was so offended by the young man's attentions, why would she remember his eyes so well?

Shirley hesitated. She glanced at Dale. He raised an eyebrow at her. She scowled. She said he had distinctive eyes. Sort of foreign looking.

Dean Snyder asked Dale his version of the events.

Dale said he and Shirley simply had different interpretations of what had transpired between them. He hadn't meant to antagonize her. Mostly, he'd been teasing. He didn't spill Coke on her slacks, but he did cause it to happen. He was sorry about that. He'd pay for a new pair of slacks if she wanted.

Dean Snyder said that was enough. He told Shirley she could leave. Shirley gave Dale one last reproving look and swiveled out of the room. Her skirt was tight. Dale could hear it swishing. He resisted looking at her exiting. No need to give his enemies any ammo.

Dean Snyder asked Miss Travesty to bring in the next witness. Dale didn't bother looking back as he heard the familiar shuffling of feet. When Sylvester Fish took his seat, Dale looked over.

"Et tu, Polonius?"

Fish didn't show any recognition of the allusion, although their Shakespeare class had covered *Julius Caesar* just two months ago. His impassive face looked as inviting as a blank wall, then he turned it to the board members.

Dean Snyder asked Sylvester Fish to tell them the improper behavior he had observed and documented.

Fish pulled out from his shirt front pocket a small notepad and flipped through the pages to the front. He said, charge one, the accused had on several occasions assaulted Sylvester, usually under the pretense of running into him accidentally.

The dean asked Dale if that were true.

"I ran into him a few times, but by accident. If I really wanted to assault Fish, I mean Sylvester, I'd do it in a more effective way than that."

Fish said that Dale had threatened to "punch his face" once.

Dean Snyder asked for Dale's response.

"Yeah, I did. But Sylvester was bothering somebody I care about."

The dean asked if Dale would like to mention the person by name. He said he'd prefer not to. The dean told Sylvester to continue.

Fish said he'd overheard Dale threaten the vice president of religious life on two separate occasions. The accused had also hurled a basketball at the face of the VP for religious life.

Dale said he threw a *Nerf* ball at Short.

Dean Snyder asked him if the ball hit Aaron.

"Yeah, right on the nose."

Bronwyn and Coop chuckled.

The dean asked Sylvester to continue.

Fish said Dale had been involved in a number of a campus pranks. He'd changed the letters on the girls' dorms to insult both residences. He'd dressed up in simian garb and insulted the homecoming audience by tossing bananas at them.

Dale said he didn't change the letters on the girls' dorms. He did dress up as an ape and threw a banana, but people in the crowd weren't insulted. They cheered.

Dean Snyder asked him if he thought it was funny to wear a shirt over the gorilla suit that advocated Darwinism.

Dale was impressed with Dean Snyder's acumen. He assumed the dean read baseball box scores.

"I wasn't advocating anything," he said. "I was just having some fun."

Dean Snyder seemed to have a dim view of that activity. He asked Sylvester to continue.

Sylvester said he'd observed Dale reading several morally questionable books. One that he'd recently seen was a book called *The Christian Agnostic*.

Dean Snyder asked why Dale would read such a book?

"Out of curiosity."

Dale could tell that wasn't an especially compelling reason for Dr. Petry, Fish, or even Dean Snyder.

Then Dr. Petry asked Dale if it were true that he once read a Hindu propaganda message instead of a Christian devotional in one of his classes.

"You mean Ramakrishna?"

Dale could tell that the mere mention of that name disturbed Dr. Petry. He nodded, his distaste as evident as if he'd just bitten into a rotten piece of fruit.

Dale said what he read wasn't Hindu propaganda, although Ramakrishna was a Hindu saint. Ramakrishna respected all religions. He'd even practiced Christianity. That was what the message was about. Tolerance for all religions.

"And you thought that an appropriate devotional message on a Christian college campus?" asked Dean Snyder.

Dale almost said, especially on this Christian college campus, but instead he simply said, "yes."

Dean Snyder didn't seem pleased to hear that. Dale heard Dr. Petry "harrumph."

Then Fish said another example of Dale's lack of Christian commitment was his strange friendship with an older Jewish man. Dale kept putting his picture in the school newspaper.

The board members looked at Fish with puzzled expressions on their faces. Dale glanced at him and grinned. So, Fish was Lou Staples, eh? Dale thought about the pseudonym. Why Lou Staples? He tried changing the names around. He sometimes did that while thinking of pseudonyms. Lou Staples. Staple Lou. Louis. S. L.? S. Louis? Lewis. S. Lewis? That was it. Clive Staples Lewis. C. S. Lewis. Hmmm, thought Dale. Maybe Fish had a little imagination after all.

Dean Snyder told Fish that the board had already covered its objections in regard to the Waldo Rubenstein fictional character.

Now Fish looked puzzled. Dale leaned over and said, "that's right, C. S., Waldo isn't *real*."

Fish puffed his flabby cheeks in frustration.

Dean Snyder then asked Sylvester to tell the board about Dale's sexual improprieties.

Dale started when he heard that term. He glared at Sylvester.

Fish said he knew of two occasions when classes were out of session that the accused took two girls into the newspaper office. The lights then were out for some time.

Bronwyn looked confused. Or maybe impressed. "He took two girls into the office at the same time?"

Fish said negative. He took one girl during Christmas break and another girl during spring break.

Dale shook his head. He knew Fish was a lurker, but not a spy. Then he realized the implications of Fish's charge.

The dean asked Sylvester if he knew who the girls were. They were as guilty as Dale. School policy forbade students from engaging in any kind of sexual activity on campus property.

Fish said he didn't know for certain, but he could assume the identity of at least one young woman. After all, Smith had been dating –

Dale interrupted. "Sylvester doesn't know anything about that. Since it was dark outside and in the office, he obviously couldn't have seen who it was."

Fish said he had seen one girl. She had blond hair. As for the other, it was reasonable to assume it was –

Again, Dale interrupted. "You don't need to assume anything. I'll tell you."

Dean Snyder, the four other board members, and Fish waited.

"There was only one girl. She's my former girlfriend from high school. She's not a student at GNC, so I don't think I have to give her name."

"You admit that you took a young woman into the newspaper office for carnal relations," said the dean.

"Yes."

"But why your ex-girlfriend," said Fish, "and not the one you have, uh, had?"

Dale glared at Fish then realized he had to give a plausible reason.

"Why do you think? Let's just say my ex-girlfriend from high school was more receptive to going to the newspaper office. After all, these trysts took place when my girlfriend was away."

Fish seemed to believe him. After all, it confirmed one of Sylvester's worst suspicions about Dale.

Dale glanced at the five board members. None of them looked at him directly. They seemed embarrassed. It was bad enough that he'd fornicated with a young woman in the newspaper office, but to have betrayed a present one for an ex made the sin even worse.

Dean Snyder thanked Sylvester. Fish said he had more. He said in an excited voice that he had evidence about voodoo music being played in the newspaper office. Dean Snyder said he'd provided enough.

Fish moved his thin mouth into a genuine smile and glanced at Dale in triumph. Dale quietly said, so long Polonius, but even that nickname did not fade the rare Fish smile.

After Sylvester left the room, Dean Snyder asked Dale if he had anything to say. Before he could respond, however, Dr. Petry asked if he could present charges against Dale.

Dean Snyder said he could not. He was on the board conducting the inquiry. Dr. Petry nodded, but Dale could tell he was disappointed.

The dean asked again if Dale had anything to say in his behalf.

"I want to say that I'm the only one responsible for the newspaper parody. No one else even knew about it. Well, except for a couple of my friends who were talked into posing for a photograph. As for the other stuff, well, I'm sorry that I broke campus rules. I guess I am guilty of that."

Dale wasn't sure if he'd really engaged in sexual improprieties or not. It depended on how one defined the term. But he certainly wanted to. So, he guessed he was guilty of committing sexual improprieties in his heart. According to some, perhaps even Dr. Prescott, that was the same as doing it.

The dean asked if Dale minded waiting outside the room for a few minutes while the board members discussed his case. He said, no he didn't mind. The dean thanked him. Dale got up and walked out the door, trying not to take Miss Travesty's glare personally.

Dale paced the halls. Things were going pretty good until they got to the sexual impropriety charges. Well, if he was going to be kicked off the newspaper for something, it might as well be for being a Don Juan.

Of course, he wasn't a Don Juan. At least not a successful one. He wondered what he'd do if he got expelled from GNC. He guessed he'd transfer to another college. He'd still be eligible for another year of financial aid. Maybe he'd go to OU. He still thought it was a big campus with a lot of people, but he wasn't as shy anymore and he wouldn't be so daunted by being with 20,000 other students.

Miss Travesty opened the door and asked him to step in. He could tell by her self-satisfied, tight little smile that he was in trouble.

Dean Snyder told Dale that the board had voted to remove him from his position as editor of the student newspaper. However, it would recommend no further action against him if he agreed to step down.

Dale said okay.

The dean told him he had to surrender his office keys and remove all personal belongings from the office as soon as possible.

Dale said okay.

The dean said the inquiry was over and thanked the board members. Dale started to leave, when Bronwyn motioned for him to stay. She walked over to him. She said she was sorry he'd been removed. Of course, he only had himself to blame.

He agreed. Then he took the opportunity to ask her about Flora Eliot.

Bronwyn said she and Flora were good friends. They still kept in touch. Flora worked for a large metro daily newspaper in Providence, Rhode Island. She said they had good times together at GNC. Bronwyn had been the yearbook editor her senior year while Flora had been the newspaper editor. Bronwyn asked why Dale was interested.

"I've read her stuff. I like it."

Bronwyn nodded. "Yes, she has talent."

Dale saw Coop approach. The professor held out his hand and Dale shook it.

"At least they didn't ask for a pound of flesh," said Professor Cooper.

Dale nodded. "At least not literally."

He apologized to Coop for getting him involved in the controversy.

"Don't apologize, Dale," he said. "I'm an old man. They can't do anything to me."

Coop said he overheard Dale asking about Flora. He said she was one of the best students he'd ever had at GNC. Bright, personable, witty. A real joy.

Dale had almost wanted Bronwyn or Coop to tell him that Flora had a personality disorder or was pretentious or something like that, because she seemed too good to be true. But he knew they wouldn't because he'd read her writing in both the yearbook and the newspaper and thought he had a good sense of her personality and character. She did sound like a real joy. He knew that a writer's writing didn't necessarily reveal the individual's true nature. He suspected that some writers were better people than writers and the obverse. But in Flora's case, he had been certain that her graceful, gently witty writing would be reflective of her personality.

Bronwyn and Coop related a few anecdotes about Flora. Dale listened with interest. He wondered about the vagaries of life, of time. If he'd been born four years earlier, then he would have known Flora himself. He found her appealing even though he didn't know her. But, of course, if Dale had been born four years earlier, he wouldn't really be who he was now. In the complex weave of time, if one strand is removed, then the whole design is changed. So, God had decreed that Dale and Flora not be on the GNC campus at the same time. He had to content himself by knowing her through the work she left behind.

Bronwyn and Coop said they had to be leaving. Coop told Dale not to take this setback too hard. He was one of the best students he'd ever taught at GNC, too.

Bronwyn didn't quite second her colleague's sentiments; Dale knew she thought he was a little strange. But she also encouraged him to forge ahead and learn from his mistakes. He had talent, too. She didn't want him to squander it.

Dale thanked them. They asked if he were leaving, and he said, no, he thought he'd stay behind for a while. He had some thinking to do.

They said good bye and walked out of the meeting room together. Dale listened to their footsteps, Bronwyn's boot click and Coop's softer patter, as they faded down the hall.

Dale thought how mysterious the world was. Fate, Destiny, Karma, Kismet, God, whatever force was at work in the universe truly was inscrutable. For instance, if the tornado hadn't destroyed his home, he probably would have been kicked out of college. He couldn't be sure, but he imagined even the impervious Dean Snyder feeling a little sorry for poor Dale for not having a home. Why kick the kid out of college, too? He's going to graduate in a few weeks, why not let him? He'll be gone then.

Dale guessed Abigail had something to do with his not being further punished. He knew just by looking into her eyes last Friday that she would entreat her father for mercy in Dale's behalf. That was the funny thing about the GNC community: for every Fish, there was an Abigail. For every Dr. Petry, a Coop. For every Dean Snyder, a Jenny. For every Short, an Amanda.

Who knows? Maybe even Henshaw spoke a word in Dale's defense. Even though Dale observed Henshaw turning into a Snyder, he hoped Bobby still had a few shreds of Dr. Prescott in his soul.

Another irony was that the destruction of his home – well, Jesse's home – might prove beneficial to his mother. Blackie had kept up the insurance that fortunately included storm and tornado coverage. Jesse would get the insurance money. It probably wouldn't be as much as the house was worth, but it would provide her with a nest-egg while she moved in with her parents. Dale thought having Jesse stay with Grandpa and Grandma was a good arrangement. They could make sure she took her medicine; she could make sure they took their medicine. Living with her folks also put less pressure on Jesse. Maybe the change of address would keep her sane.

June didn't like it staying with Grandma and Grandpa too much. But she was going to graduate from high school in two months. Dale guessed she could tolerate sleeping in the back room for awhile. Another coincidence: Yancy had built the addition to Grandpa's and Grandma's little house just last summer. Now, it would serve as June's own room. Dale didn't think he had to worry too much about her.

The tornado had damaged only the northern edge of Galilee. Dozens of homes had been destroyed or severely damaged. Fortunately, only five people had been killed: a middle-aged man who Dale didn't know, although he only lived a block away and attended First Church. His funeral was tomorrow. And an elderly couple had been killed when the storm threw their car off the road. They were from the City.

And also Trumbo and his youngest son, Michael. For some inexplicable reason, Trumbo had taken Michael flying that afternoon from Wiley Post airfield. They apparently got a late start, didn't heed the weather advisory, and crashed. The newspaper story didn't say if the tornado directly caused the crash or if the plane crashed due to mechanical failure or pilot error.

Dale first heard about Trumbo and his son while watching the news on television at his grandparents' house the Monday night of the storm. The power had come back on just a few minutes before ten, and Dale had turned on the TV. They heard about the accident five minutes into the broadcast. Jesse didn't even remember who Trumbo was. June asked him if that was the man they knew at the Kingdom Hall. Dale said yeah.

Now, standing in the conference room, looking out the big picture window at the quad, Dale thought about Trumbo. He'd liked him. He didn't understand him. He didn't understand why such an impressive guy would close his mind to the larger world and become a fanatic. Well, Dale was being harsh. Trumbo wasn't a fanatic, just a devout believer. If so, then Trumbo probably wasn't surprised when the twin engine plane nose-dived. He probably thought, about time. The end at last. But maybe not. After all, his son was with him. Maybe Trumbo felt fear and anger and powerlessness until the End overtook him.

Dale heard the scuffling of footsteps in the hall. He turned and saw Teri walk in. She said she'd heard. She was sorry.

He said she shouldn't be. There were only two issues left anyway. Besides, she'd make a good editor.

Teri said she'd seen Robert Henshaw leaving the building. She said he looked disturbed, angry even.

"About what? Did you ask him?"

"He said, he now knew how Richard Rich felt." Teri shook her head. "What does that mean?"

"Not much," Dale said, smiling a little. "It just means Robert doesn't want to be a man for all seasons."

The next night as Dale was gathering his personal things from the newspaper office, Teri came in and looked at him in an inquisitive way. Dale said, what?

"Did you really bring a girl in here and fornicate?"

He frowned. So, already the word had gotten out.

"Well, it didn't get quite that far."

Then he remembered that it almost had.

Teri shook her head and clucked her tongue. "Dale."

He shrugged his shoulders.

"So," Teri asked shyly, "was it with that girl?"

Dale guessed Teri meant Wendy. He didn't think anyone would really suspect Amanda. She had a solid reputation in spite of going steady with him. He shrugged.

"Your ex? From high school?"

Dale nodded. He disliked linking Wendy to a scandal. Quite a few people at GNC knew who she was. But if she heard, and she would, he figured Wendy would just have one more reason to be angry with him. It might even help her to stop caring about him.

"*Dale*," Teri said. She actually sounded a little offended.

He picked up his albums, and a small bag containing a few odds and ends: a couple of books, his Nerf basketball, his bloody Omega football jersey, a towel, a bottle of Aqua Velva. He'd already moved his stereo to his car.

"Good luck with the remaining two issues."

Teri told him he was welcome anytime.

Dale nodded and walked out of the newspaper office for the final time.

**Epilogue 2:** *A literary surprise; a graduation surprise; Blackie; Amanda*

Without the newspaper and without Amanda, campus life was just not the same for Dale. He'd made quite a few people angry; he was actually surprised by how many. After a week, most people didn't glare at him when they saw him walking across campus on his way to class. However, to almost everyone, he'd become *persona non grata*.

Dale's misdeeds had already begun to reach mythical proportions. Not only had he played demon-inspired music in the newspaper office, he'd played voodoo music. Rumor had it that he'd sneaked in other fabrications and sly jokes in past issues of *Smoke Signals*. Dale had actually seen a couple of curious underclassmen skimming through back issues. Some rumors recounted how he had a terrible temper. He'd broken one fellow's collarbone, and had assaulted at least two other guys, including busting the nose of a stuco member by throwing a basketball at him. Not only had he taken Wendy into his office for an illicit tryst, he'd taken other girls although never Amanda. In fact, Amanda, whom Dale only saw from a distance, usually surrounded by two or three of her friends, seemed to have achieved the exalted status of wronged woman. No one suspected her of immorality. Instead, they imagined the satyr-like Dale, frustrated by the chaste Amanda, luring defenseless girls into his lair of an office. When Dale heard these lurid rumors from Teri, he thought at least the last one had a grain of truth to it.

A week after the meeting to remove Dale as editor, the issue of *Smoke Signals* with the literary supplement arrived. Dale, suffering through an understandable bout of depression, had all but forgotten about the supplement. It wasn't until he saw other students in his Practical Principles of Business Management class flipping through the supplement that he remembered.

He got his copy after class and instead of going to the newspaper office like he used to, he walked across the expressway, passed the downtown area and went to the public library.

He didn't look at the literary supplement until he sat down at a table. He flipped to that section and saw that his short story, *The Impossible Dream*, had won best prose entry and best overall entry. Wow. He'd won a total of thirty bucks.

The story was printed on the first page of the literary supplement. Teri had probably chosen the photograph to go along with it, a publicity shot of Sophia Loren as Dulcinea from the movie version of *Man of La Mancha*. She'd tried to disguise it a little by printing it in a special screen process. Dale easily recognized it. He thought it was an excellent decision even if the story made no direct mention of Dulcinea or *Don Quixote* or the musical version of the book. He liked the illustration if for no other reason than it showed Sophia's ample and amazing cleavage. Dale wondered why there weren't more actresses like Sophia Loren starring in movies today.

He read his story. He thought it was okay, although a little derivative. Dale thought how hard it was to achieve true originality. Maybe it couldn't even be done today with the formidable history of literature looming above them from some verbal Mount Olympus. Well, he thought, all you could do is try and maybe you'd make a modest contribution.

Dale turned the page and gaped at the best poetry winning entry. H. Horse had struck again. He read the three selected poems. Now, as he read them in print, they didn't seem completely ludicrous. In fact, he sort of liked the one entitled "Ghosts". It read:

> Black man
> You were a slave
> To the white.
> But what am I?
> No Negro slave
> But a Nomad
> In my own land …
> Black brother
> Let me share your tears
> For though you were a slave
> n a foreign land
> I am a ghost
>    in my own.

Dale felt a little embarrassed with H. Horse's clever exploitation of white liberal guilt. But what the hell? It worked.

Reading the poem again, Dale felt an affinity with the speaker. Not that he thought of himself as a victimized Indian; in spite of his Indian "blood," he knew he wasn't a Creek in any genuine way. But he did share the writer's sense of isolation. He'd lately felt a little like a ghost. The only people he had any contact with were Rusty, Putney, and Teri. Ever since that Sunday night falling out with Amanda, and especially after she heard he'd been kicked out as editor for "sexual improprieties" with Wendy, she'd had nothing to do with him. She refused his phone calls. After a week, he stopped calling and wrote a final letter, including one white rose.

In his letter, Dale wrote the following:

*My Darling Amanda,*

*To really love someone is to care more for her well-being
than for your own. I now know we can't be together.
I've caused you pain and I would continue causing you pain
because I can't accept your world and you refuse to be part of mine.*

*Even though I love you more than you will ever know,*
*even though I began loving you the first time I saw you*
*and will continue loving you until the day I die,*
*the only way I can prove this is to accept your rejection of me.*

*I will never bother you. I will only think of you with tenderness*
*and appreciation. Knowing that you once loved me*
*will sustain me. And even when the day comes when we both perish,*
*our love will not. It existed before we met; it bloomed when*
*we were together; it endures even when we are apart.*
*Not only in my heart, but in some special place in eternity.*

*-- Dale*

It was difficult writing that letter. He had to pause several times to keep his composure. He now smiled sadly at the thought of keeping his composure while composing. Although Dale meant every word he wrote, he also hoped that Amanda would change her mind about him. He had hoped that her love for him would overcome her disapproval for his unconventional thinking and sinful behavior. But she didn't change her mind. He didn't hear from her. Now, Dale realized he wasn't much of writer. If he were, Amanda would have responded.

Chris wouldn't associate with him either. He'd not only been offended by Dale's ridiculing "the saints," of which he'd been a member, but he thought Dale had cruelly used Amanda. After all, he and Amanda had known each other their entire lives. How could Dale humiliate her so? Betraying her with Wendy?

Dale had seen Chris and Amanda together a few times. Last Wednesday night, when he'd come out of the library after losing track of time, he saw them from a distance walking across campus on their way to Wednesday night service.

Dale decided to stop thinking about that. Instead, he returned to the literary supplement. He read H. Horse's other two poems. They weren't as interesting. He wondered if Coop, Bronwyn, Jenny, Teri, Sharon or anyone else suspected him of being the true author of these poems. He didn't think so. He wondered if he should confess. He felt a pang of guilt knowing he'd deceived people he liked. But in a strange way, he liked the idea of the true identity of H. Horse remaining a mystery. Hadn't Fate decreed such a result? Well, Dale wasn't sure if fate decreed anything. Such a concept was too simple. But coincidence and accident had certainly played a role in the publication of the H. Horse persona. Dale had whipped off the poems as a joke. For some reason, Bronwyn liked them. She bestowed on them the coveted literary prize. Then when the ruse should have been exposed, Herschel Horst confused things and the identity of H. Horse survived.

Maybe the fact that H. Horse had written another batch of poems only confirmed Bronwyn's belief in the wounded Navajo lad. Dale liked Bronwyn, but he suspected her of sentimentalism, which to Dale was as serious a literary flaw as cynicism. Eventually, sentimentalism produced cynicism. He could imagine already an anti-H. Horse poet at work somewhere on the GNC campus. He, or she, was busy writing the antidote to Harry Horse's *cri de coeur*. No doubt, those poems would be just as simplistic.

Dale had almost forgotten to see if any of his other pseudonyms had made it. He flipped to the next page and saw "Chris's" poem printed. Instead of writing a ridiculous ode to his mother again, Dale had written in his friend's behalf a love lyric. Entitled, "Love From Afar," the last stanza went as follows:

> We've known each other
> our entire lives; but
> our friendship prevented
> the flowering of love.
> On that night
> when I gazed
> into your eyes
> the bud opened, the flower unfurled
> and our love blossomed
> > like a red, unblemished rose.

Chris's poem made Dale feel a little sad. He'd written it too well. It still wasn't very good but it wasn't preposterous like the poem he'd written last year. Worse, the poem now had a relevance that he hadn't intended or welcomed.

Beside it, another love poem of sorts. But this one wasn't one of Dale's pseudonyms. Rather, it was a poem by D. A. Hawkins. Entitled, "Michelangelo's David", the last stanza read:

> Sinewy arms, muscl'd legs
> of masculine might and beauty
> its art swelled in stone;
> I gaze upon the statue
> knowing that I, the watcher,
> stand apart and alone.

At first, Dale felt a little stunned. Then he thought, that subtle Hawkins. Dale rather wished he'd found a rhyme for pectorals.

Since his trial and punishment, Dale had kept waiting for Hawkins to approach him and whisper, "sexual improprieties, eh?" but, of course, he never did. Hawkins didn't speak to him any longer. Dale supposed he wasn't a pariah to Hawkins as he was to most people on campus; Hawkins just didn't see the point of wooing him anymore. Dale understood. But he still sort of missed talking to David about the identity of Shakespeare and other intellectual speculations. But even art wasn't compelling enough to bring them together after discovering their great natural divide.

He flipped to the last page hoping that one more poem would appear. He found it. Another opus by Peter Krupp. Entitled "Groveling Before God," the last stanza read:

> Like the lowly worm, I crawl;
> I beseech God, then I bawl
> What am I? Just a fallen man:
> My life a farce, my self a sham.

Interesting reversal of attitude for our poet Krupp, Dale thought. His previous published entry acclaimed his greatness by comparing his self to towering Greek heroes. Now, this bathetic poem veers in the opposite direction and wallows in the dusty earth.

Dale closed the literary supplement and glanced at the rest of the newspaper. A big week for news. The Who's Who people were featured. Unsurprisingly, Dale hadn't been selected. He knew he had the grade point and the activities, but apparently he lacked something. Oh, yes. Character.

The student government election results were listed as well. Henshaw won in a landslide for his second stuco presidential term. Abigail won her second term as vice president of campus life. However, in a stunning upset, Weasel Long – er, rather Aaron Short – lost in his bid to a second term as VP of religious life. Eugene Greene defeated him in a close race.

Dale closed the student newspaper and spent two hours reading magazines and newspapers before leaving the public library and venturing back to campus. As he passed by the business building, he spotted Peter Krupp coming out.

Dale accosted Krupp. He hadn't spoken to Peter for over a month. He knew he was risking Krupp's reputation, but he had to convey his admiration for his poetic brilliance.

"Krupp, I have to confess something," Dale said, with a somber tone and expression.

Krupp's pained face seemed to say he had no interest in hearing any Dale Smith confession. The quarterback, the captain, the mad shooter of errant basketballs, nearly cowered.

"What?" he asked warily.

Dale pointed to the newspaper. "I loved your poem."

Krupp's natural vanity returned. His ratty face smiled. He stroked his wispy mustache. "Thanks, Smith."

"I know comparing yourself to a worm was really a leap of imagination for you."

Krupp nodded but his smile faded.

"But I just wanted to say that I've always known about your vermicular tendencies."

Krupp stopped nodding. He had no real idea what Dale was talking about, but he seemed to have an inkling that it wasn't the compliment he'd expected. Dale reached a hand out. Peter reluctantly extended his. Dale shook it and gazed into the bewildered eyes of Krupp.

Then Dale broke off the handshake.

"So long, Krupp," he said, striding away. "And watch out for the birds."

Dale's last day as a campus policeman was, fittingly, uneventful. He patrolled the empty school building, let in one home economics teacher, and finished his last book, *You Can't Go Home Again*. When his shift ended, he returned to headquarters, turned in his keys and badge, and shook hands with Chief Dewberry, who had made a special trip down just to say good-bye.

The chief told Dale he wished he had more employees like him. Dale nodded modestly. The chief said he simply came in, did his job, and left. Too many other officers stayed around and gossiped and jockeyed for position. Too many wanted to be real cops. The chief could use more young men like Dale.

Dale thanked the taurean chief. He told him he liked his job. He didn't tell him why. What other job would have paid him to read and think in the quiet and solitude of an empty school building?

The campus cop job had been a good one. Dale doubted he'd ever find another quite so helpful in his intellectual development. He estimated he'd read nearly two hundred books in the thirty-three months on the job.

After work, Dale drove to his grandparents' house for Sunday dinner. When he got there, he met Wanda leaving. She didn't smile. Dale didn't say hi. Although they didn't like each other, Dale had to give her credit for not pretending otherwise like most people.

Dale went into the bathroom and changed out of his uniform into his civvies. Then he sat down at the kitchen table and ate his fill of fried chicken, mashed potatoes, gravy, biscuits, corn, okra, dumplings, and apple pie. And then washed it all down with lemonade. Grandma told him that was probably the last good meal he'd get for quite a spell. Dale agreed. In fact, he'd already lost a couple of pounds fending for himself at Blackie's. Dale didn't expect he'd find any good country cooking over in Europe, either.

While he ate, his grandfather, who'd stuffed some cornbread into his glass of buttermilk then ate it all with a spoon, asked him what he planned on doing over there in Europe. Dale said travel around, see things, experience things. Grandpa told him he oughta go visit the Walsh's ancestral home in Ireland. Dale said he would. Grandpa said his great great great great grandfather had lived in Ulster. Dale asked if he was an Orangeman. Grandpa said nope, he was as white as a peeled tater.

After dinner, Dale sat in the living room with his grandparents, Jesse, and June. Uncle Yancy came over later, and told them all how he might sell his doughnut business. The work was too dang tiring. Up at the crack of dawn kneading dough and frying doughnuts. Grandpa said Yancy worked too hard. He oughta sell his store and move to the country. Get him some chickens and cows. Yancy said, if he did that he'd still have to get up early and milk the cows. Grandpa slapped his knee and said he reckoned that was so.

Dale thought about the past few weeks while they talked. He'd got all his schoolwork done. He'd made all A's again. He would graduate magna cum laude. He kept busy when not in class, planning his trip to Europe. He bought a map and charted his expected journeys. He didn't really want to go alone. But Rusty backed out. He couldn't miss any work. He had just bought a new car, a sporty burnt orange Camaro.

Dale thought about his trip itinerary. His Eurorail ticket allowed him to go all over Europe. Dale planned on touring the British Isles, then heading over to the continent. He especially wanted to visit Germany and see if he could find the Schmidt ancestral home. He'd done a little genealogical research. He thought Blackie's ancestors, three hundred years ago before emigrating to America, had lived somewhere in Bavaria. Not too far from the Black Forest.

Planning his trip and finishing his college studies had kept him fairly busy. Not too busy, however, not to brood over Amanda. The more he thought about her, the more he realized their romance had been unlikely from the beginning. They were too different, from too different worlds. He now understood that he'd projected his imagination on her; she was a vessel in which he'd poured his romantic ideals and expectations. He supposed all lovers do that with their beloved. He tried to think of her without the illumination of his imagination on her. But he couldn't do it yet. Every time he thought of her, saw her lovely face in his mind's eye, he still felt something break inside him.

At six o'clock, Dale said he better get going to Blackie's. Grandpa asked how Blackie was doing. Dale said fine. He hadn't told any of them about Blackie becoming a father again. June, who rarely saw her father, knew he and Cleoma were a couple. Dale guessed Jesse knew, too. Sooner or later, Jesse would find out about Cleoma having a baby. Dale thought it would be strange having a half-brother twenty-one years younger than he was.

Since Dale wasn't planning on seeing his grandparents or Jesse or June before he left Tuesday, he said good-bye to them all. He shook hands with Grandpa and Yancy. He hugged Jesse and Grandma. He patted June on the shoulder. He wondered why he and his sister had never been close. He knew she didn't like him in some ways. She didn't understand his sense of humor. He teased her too much. Once she'd told him that he had made it difficult for her in high school. Teachers acted like she wasn't as smart as he was. Sometimes they unfavorably compared her to him. She didn't like that. Dale had told her not to worry about it. After all, she'd been more popular. She'd been voted football queen – an honor he'd never received. June hadn't laughed.

As he drove away, he saw Grandpa standing on the porch waving. Even at age eighty-three, his grandfather had a spryness to him. Sometimes he'd burst out singing some old folk tune, his voice still hale and hearty. Dale wondered how a man that had lived such a hard life, who'd survived two world wars, the Great Depression, and the Dust Bowl, could still have such spirit in him.

Dale sat in the Van Brocklin auditorium listening to the commencement speaker, the president of the Nazarene General Assembly, Augustus Van Brocklin. Gus, as he was affectionately called, neared the end of his speech. Dale, sitting near the back with the other S's, had to admit that Abigail's grandfather spoke well. He noticed that he wasn't an especially large man, either. His crimson academic gown almost swallowed him. But he had a deep, compelling voice that flowed out of his large chest and filled the auditorium.

Dale could understand why Augustus was such an influential figure in the church. The man knew how to speak.

Abigail's father, William, the president of the college, sat in one of the chairs on the stage. Two other GNC officials, the new registrar, Mr. DeVille, and Dean Snyder, also sat on the stage. They were prepared to pass out the 287 diplomas at the end of the commencement speech.

Dale had debated whether or not to attend his college graduation. Ordinarily, he wouldn't have. Since he'd jumped a year, and had only attended GNC for two, he didn't really know that many seniors. The only graduating seniors he was friendly with were Sharon Myrick and Virgil Phelps.

Also, he knew he wouldn't feel welcome. But that was the reason why, in the end, he decided to attend. He realized that he didn't want to skip his graduation because he felt ostracized. He was stubborn enough to want to show the campus community that he didn't think he'd done anything to be ashamed about.

Finally, it was time to hand out the symbolic diplomas. Dale would get his real one in a month. He got in line with the other graduates and waited for his name to be read. He sensed some people in the audience staring at him, but he didn't look to make sure. He just tried to keep his mind occupied and not worry about what people in the audience thought of him. He knew he had a few friends in the crowd. Teri, Rusty, and Putney had said they'd come. Dale hadn't seen Rusty or Putney before the commencement started. He wouldn't be surprised if neither came. Both were free spirits and would only come if the spirit moved them.

He stood on the wings of the stage and waited. He heard his full name, Audie Dale Smith, called. He strode forward and took the fake diploma from President Van Brocklin. He was about to shake the president's hand, then the dean's, when Dale heard an isolated series of gasps and shouts that seemed to roll from the back of the auditorium to the front, like some kind of aural wave. Dale, the president, and the dean looked down at the crowd sitting in the pews. That's when Dale saw them: Rusty and Putney, although he couldn't positively identify them because they were wearing gorilla heads. But he recognized Rusty's tall, lanky body and Putney's shorter, stockier body. For a moment, Dale thought they were naked.

They weren't. They were wearing flesh colored body stockings with fake fig leaves pinned to the strategic place on front. The two of them had raced in from the lobby and now dashed down one side of the auditorium. People gawked at them. Some of the women screamed, not in a loud, horrified way but more in a loud, sustained gasp.

Dale tried not to laugh. He glanced at the gaping faces of Dean Snyder, Mr. DeVille, and President Van Brocklin. As Rusty and Putney raced toward the stage, Dale saw that the body stockings didn't quite fit either body snugly. They bagged in the knees, the seat, and under the arms. The bagginess gave both of them a look of little boys dressed in pajamas, the kind that cover even the feet.

There was something written in magic marker on both of their chests. Dale looked more closely. On Rusty's, the letters UN; on Putney's, RAP. He got it. They had been unraptured. That's why they weren't wearing any clothes. As for the gorilla heads, well, Hosea Revelations Carter would have to explain that.

They raced to the front of the stage and grunted. Because of all the murmuring and occasional gasps as more people saw them, the grunts weren't easy to hear. But Dale heard them. So did the dean and the president. The naked apes then scurried away and raced up the other side of the auditorium before dashing out the back door to the lobby.

The gasps, groans, and murmurs died down. Dale smiled a little as he shook the hand of the stunned president. When he shook hands with Dean Snyder, he saw him glaring at him in the manner a cruel prison warden scowls at the recalcitrant prisoner now leaving on parole.

Dale gave his fake diploma a little shake as he strolled across the stage and joined the other new graduates. He heard Mr. DeVille call the next name in a calm voice as if the disturbance had never happened.

Standing in the lobby after the ceremony, Dale saw Teri approach with a smile on her face.

"I guess you didn't have anything to do with that shocking display, did you?"

"Nothing at all."

Dale didn't. Rusty and Putney hadn't clued him in. But he knew that would be one more legend he'd be associated with.

"And I suppose you have no idea who they were?"

"I'd guess just a couple of poor unraptured souls."

Teri hid her smile with a hand. "Oh, so that's it. I guess I should have known that's what UNRAP meant. But I thought maybe they meant they were 'unwrapped,' you know?"

"Unwrapped, unraptured. Not much difference."

Teri waved for Jenny to join them. She slowly walked over and Dale noticed she looked okay; not well, exactly, but not as poorly as she had near the end of the fall semester.

Teri whispered that Jenny was getting better again. She might be well enough to teach next fall. Dale told her good. That meant Jenny would be the newspaper adviser. Teri had won the job in spite of her connection to Dale. He guessed the publications board members had believed him when he said only he had perpetrated the wicked April Fool's parody.

Jenny came over and congratulated Dale. He asked how she felt. She said she was getting better. She didn't mention any of the unpleasantness of the last month. Dale guessed she had more serious matters to worry about than reading or even reflecting about the newspaper spoof.

Then Professor Cooper came over and congratulated Dale. The four of them talked for a while. They asked him what he was going to do. He told them about going to Europe for a couple of months and then try to get a newspaper job. The three of them looked at him as if he'd said a bad word.

"I've learned my lesson," he said. None of them looked convinced. "I think I'd like to be a sportswriter."

Dale had taken over the sports writing duties when Rusty flunked out. Teri, Jenny, and Coop nodded. Apparently, they all thought he'd get in less trouble writing about sports than religion.

They chatted for a few more minutes. When Dale asked Jenny about Flora, she basically confirmed all the wonderful anecdotes he'd already heard. Then the three of them wished Dale a good trip to Europe, said keep in touch, and then Jenny and Coop left. Teri lingered behind. Her manner changed. She looked at Dale as if she had something to tell him. She reached into her purse and pulled out a small, pink envelope and handed it to him.

Dale took it and immediately knew who it was from as soon as he saw the semi-graceful handwriting.

"She gave it to me to give to you. She said she didn't know how to get in touch with you."

Dale guessed he would be difficult to reach by phone. There were about two hundred Smiths in the Oklahoma City telephone book. And she didn't know Blackie's first name because Dale had never told her it was Forrest. He'd been difficult to contact on campus, too. He'd made himself scarce and Amanda also had classes when he had his. Dale understood why she'd need Teri for a courier.

Dale held Amanda's letter in his fingers and wondered why it felt so light. The letter felt wafer thin. It couldn't contain much of anything of consequence and yet he held it as if it were something precious.

Teri said she had to go. She wanted to catch up with Jenny. She told Dale to have fun on his trip. Then she reached out and lightly touched his arm.

"Keep in touch."

Dale said he would and watched as she walked through the milling graduates, their families, and friends.

He decided to leave as well. He felt anxious to read Amanda's note and he wanted to do it in private. On his way out, he passed by Sharon and told her congratulations on graduating. He also said he'd liked the yearbook. She smiled, not with much warmth, and he realized she was still offended by what he'd done. Sharon hadn't liked even the tenuous connection between her position as yearbook editor and the newspaper parody. He understood. Sharon's yearbook, although flawless, was conventional. It didn't have any of the subtle wit of Flora's book.

Dale walked out of Van Brocklin Hall and strode to the parking lot across the street. He got in his car and made sure no one was around. Then he turned on the overhead light and opened the note. It read:

> Dale,
> If you can, please come by my house at noon
> tomorrow. I have something to give you.
> -Amanda

Dale had no idea what she might want to give him. He thought maybe she wanted to return the things he'd bought her. Some girls were like that. It depressed him to think she didn't even want those few mementos to remember him by.

He was tempted to crumple her note. But he didn't. Instead, he lifted it to his nose and sniffed. It smelled just like paper and ink. Nothing more.

Later that night, Dale drove over to Putney's and he, Rusty, and Abner, Jr. celebrated a little. Putney had a bottle of cheap champagne. He popped the cork and the foamy stuff gushed out. He aimed it at Rusty and sprayed him. Rusty laughed and said, hey man. Then Putney poured it in three champagne glasses. Dale held his glass up and looked at the sparkling liquid bubbling in the shapely glass. He'd never drank champagne before.

Putney asked what they should drink to. Rusty said, to Dale. The three of them took a drink. Dale made a face. He didn't think Rusty or Putney liked it much either.

Then Dale said, another toast.

Putney ran over to the kitchenette and grabbed a piece of bread and popped it in his toaster. Dale waited until Putney got back. He glanced at Rusty, who shrugged. Sometimes Putney's physical humor got too literal.

Dale said, "to naked apes."

The three of them drank more of the stuff. Dale felt it tingle his nose. Putney then hurled the empty champagne glass at the kitchen sink. It shattered against the cabinet. Putney shrugged. Then Rusty tossed his glass and it smashed inside the kitchen sink. Dale aimed, fired, and his glass broke into three big shards and dozens of tiny slivers in the sink.

They smelled the toast burning.

They listened to records, one of which was the new album by the English group Sweet. Dale remembered after a track meet in their sophomore year when Rusty played the group's first hit, "Little Willie," over and over at a restaurant just to bug people. He must have played it a dozen times. Several adults got up to leave before finishing their meal.

That restaurant also required customers to give their names so the counterwoman could call them when their order was ready. Dale had told her, "Hitchcock Sly." She either believed him or didn't care. When his order was ready, she said in her amplified voice, "Hitchcock Sly, your order is ready." Dale, Rusty, Chris, and Wally howled with laughter.

Dale remembered another Sweet song, "Fox on the Run." That had been a big hit during the summer when he'd had his adulterous mini-affair with Sal. Dale had liked the song, but now he associated it with her, and that almost ruined the song.

The last time Dale saw Blackie, he had said Sal was coming to visit Cleoma that summer. Dale didn't care. Although he still thought she was sort of attractive, he'd never really liked her. He'd succumbed to her temptation out of lust. Now, after experiencing love, he didn't think he wanted to settle for just lust again.

They didn't drink any more champagne after the second glass. None of them were drinkers; they just naturally acted intoxicated when the spirit moved them. Instead, they drank root beer. Then Putney and Rusty talked about how funny the faces of the old people had looked when they ran in Van Brocklin auditorium in their unraptured state. Dale guessed both of them were safe. Rusty wasn't a student at GNC anymore. Putney still was, although in a tenuous way. Like Rusty, he didn't like attending classes much. But Dale doubted the son of a Nazarene college president would be kicked out.

"Hey, man, do you think anyone recognized us?" Rusty said in his perfect deadpan way.

Dale and Putney looked thoughtful as they considered that difficult question. Then the three of them laughed.

Dale and Rusty reminisced about some of pranks and comical creations they'd perpetrated while in grade school and high school. Putney, normally as manic as Rusty, listened attentively. Dale and Rusty had written and illustrated a "Buddy Boys" adventure "book" back in fifth grade when both of them were devouring Hardy Boys books. The Buddy Boys book, entitled *A Dangerous Dilema* (Dale had misspelled dilemma), was only seven pages. But for ten year olds, that was an epic of writing. They'd taken turns writing chapters. Dale had done most of the drawings. They'd stapled the book together and included a crayon-illustrated cover. They both thought the book superb.

They talked about another book they'd written in tenth grade, entitled *Eloquent Interludes*. It was just silly poems and anecdotes with grotesque drawings. They'd composed the stuff mostly to repulse Mr. Benedict. Just hearing the word "chunk" would almost induce him to vomit.

The topics covered in the *Eloquent Interludes* were appropriately puerile, sophomoric, and crude. Poems referred to "talking to Earl," which produced "chunks" and "blobs." They satirized all the Maynards they encountered in school. They made obscure references to "Gilbert." They also documented their repugnant habit of "flipping spit." Instead of shooting spitballs as they'd done in grade school, they developed a more advanced technique of projecting their saliva. Rusty was especially good at it. He'd drool a drop of saliva on one of his long fingers and flick his wrist. If the spit was especially thick and cohesive, it could fly ten yards with a good snap of the wrist. Dale wasn't as adept and he felt a lingering sense of decorum, so he didn't indulge in the flipping of spit too often. But Rusty became quite skillful. He could hurl a dollop of saliva from such a distance that the victim never knew where it came from. Dale remembered Rusty hitting Clifford on the bus during a class trip and Clifford whirling around, glaring at everyone, unsure who had spittled him.

At the mention of Clifford's name, Rusty asked what became of that dope. Dale said he wasn't a dope, just a strangely intense kind of guy. Putney said the guy probably became a serial killer. Rusty laughed. Then Rusty told Putney about the time they were riding on the bus after a football game at Sequoyah their freshman year. The drive took two hours. Clifford, sitting across the aisle and one seat in front, fell asleep. His mouth dropped open. He began snoring. Rusty tore off bits of paper from a Dairy Queen napkin. He wadded up the paper into little balls and started tossing them at Clifford's gaping mouth. After missing two times – one wad bouncing high in the air from hitting Clifford's thick lensed spectacles – the third wad dropped right into Clifford's mouth. He startled awake, snorted, then coughed, before stiffly turning around and glaring at his teammates. Rusty and Dale pretended to be asleep, trying mightily to stifle their laughter. Clifford kept staring for several seconds, but finally gave up trying to identify the miscreant. He settled back in his seat and soon fell asleep again. Of course, Rusty repeated his prank, and Clifford this time stood up, his fists clenched, but the two of them feigned sleep so convincingly that Clifford accused another guy known for pranks, K. C., and the two of them almost got into a fight. Back in ninth grade, K. C. was almost as big as Clifford, so Dale had been interested to see who would win. But Coach Carpenter shouted at them in his deep, commanding voice to "sit the hell down," and since he used a cuss word, Clifford and K. C. did.

Rusty nodded. Yep, those were good ol' days. Then he asked Dale, what happened to Clifford? Dale said Wendy had told him she'd heard Clifford was attending West Point.

Rusty said, you're kidding?

Dale shrugged. He could believe it. Clifford was smart. He'd gone to Boys State. Dale said Clifford was the best marcher there.

They listened to a few more records, quaffed a few more root beers, and then Rusty and Putney said they wanted to go out and drive around and get into some mischief. Dale said he better not. He had to get back to Blackie's place before it got too late. Putney then solemnly shook hands with Dale, sort of a ritual they'd developed since the time Dale enlightened him about callipygians. They did not exchange any words. Putney performed even better without dialogue.

Rusty slapped Dale on the back and said he'd pick him up tomorrow at two at his dad's place. Then Rusty would drive Dale to the Will Rogers International airport, where Dale would fly to Dallas's old Love Field before riding over to the new airport and then boarding a 747 and flying nonstop to London's Heathrow Airport. All very exciting.

Dale said so long to Rusty and Putney and drove to Blackie's apartment. He opened the door and hoped he wouldn't find Cleoma lounging in the place. He didn't. He'd managed to avoid her while he'd been staying with his father. Actually, Dale had the place pretty much to himself. Blackie, when not working, was either over at Cleoma's or going to graduate school at Oklahoma City University. He was getting his master's in business administration thanks to the GI bill.

Dale sat in Blackie's big chair and watched the sports part of the news on the TV. He guessed he'd root for the Reds again this year. They still had Morgan, Bench, and Seaver. Cincinnati ought to win the NL. Dale still thought the Red Sox would win the AL. Just imagine, he thought. A match-up of teams from the '75 series again.

Blackie walked in. He asked Dale how graduation went. He said fine, but a couple of guys had made monkeys of themselves. Blackie didn't ask for details.

Blackie walked into the kitchen to get a beer. He asked Dale if he wanted one. Dale said no thanks. He didn't like beer any more than champagne.

His dad came back into the sparsely furnished living room and Dale got up and let him sit in his chair. Blackie motioned for him to stay there, but Dale didn't want to. He said he felt like standing anyway. Blackie flopped down in his chair and took a drink of Coors. Dale wondered why he didn't buy a more expensive brand of beer. Well, maybe Cleoma was right. Blackie baby was sort of tight with the moolah.

"So, you're off to Europe tomorrow," Blackie said, in a voice that suggested he didn't find such a trip that interesting.

Dale knew Blackie thought Europe was a dying civilization. They'd been lucky the USA had saved their bacon twice this century. Who knew, America might have to do it again.

Dale said yeah. He'd be leaving in the afternoon. He told Blackie thanks for keeping his car for him.

Blackie shrugged. Dale watched his father take another drink of his beer. Usually, he didn't drink at all on work nights. Certainly not this late.

Blackie noticed him looking. "Just a little celebration before bedtime. After all, you've graduated and I'm getting promoted. To chief."

Dale nodded. Why wasn't he surprised? Of course, Blackie would tell him of his promotion the night of his graduation.

"Congratulations," Dale said, "on your promotion."

Blackie said thanks. He'd take over as chief at the end of the summer. He didn't know why the old man wanted to stick around for the summer. A lot of floaters then. That meant a lot of paperwork.

Dale waited for a lull in the conversation. He couldn't resist a jab. He told Blackie he must have lots to celebrate. Not only his promotion but also becoming a new father.

Blackie didn't quite glare at him, but his look was not amused.

Then Dale imagined the horrifying spectacle of a pregnant Cleoma. He felt a little sorry for his father.

"So, when are you two getting married?" Dale asked, feeling the absurdity of the role reversal.

Blackie grunted. He finished his beer and Dale saw him deliberating about getting another one. But he didn't. He said he and Cleoma were going to fly out to Vegas in June.

Dale thought, how appropriate. He wondered which pop culture theme chapel they'd pick. He imagined them getting hitched in the Antebellum Chapel. Blackie dressed in a confederate uniform, Cleoma decked out in her Scarlett O'Hara duds, complete with a frilly petticoat. He smiled at that image.

Blackie asked in a gruff voice what he was smiling at.

"Love."

Blackie said Dale was one weird kid. He rose from his big, easy chair and said he better hit the sack. He had to get up early for another exciting day of parks and lakes service.

Dale hadn't heard his dad make fun of his job before. He guessed with the acquisition of power came a change in attitude.

Blackie held out his hand. Dale shook it. He told Dale to have a good time on his trip to Europe, but somehow he doubted he'd do that. Then Blackie said it was funny. He had been all around the world. He sailed most all of those proverbial seven seas. He'd even been to Antarctica. But he'd never been to Europe. He'd never drawn a Mediterranean assignment.

Dale asked Blackie about Antarctica. He'd always been curious to hear more about Blackie's two tours there.

"I liked being stationed there," Blackie said. "Cold as hell and it's the most desolate place on earth."

Then Blackie told Dale of one time when he took a snowmobile and drove a few miles out of base camp to look at an immense mountain covered in snow and ice. He stood a mile away and gazed at the mountain, so white it gleamed blue. All around him was snow and ice. Everything whiter than white. Even the sky looked more white than blue on that January summer morning.

Dale asked him why he'd done that.

"I don't know. I guess I was searching for something."

"What?"

"I don't know. But I tell you this. I didn't find anything. Nothing was there. Nothing but ice and snow and sky."

Dale wondered if he'd been with Blackie if he'd have found something. He thought he would have. He didn't share his father's bleak assessment of the Universe. Dale, in spite of everything, believed in an intelligence in the universe. More importantly, he believed that there was a divine spark in all people. That spark – consciousness or soul – enabled people to acquire wisdom. But it came with the price of suffering. That was the paradox.

Blackie said he had to get some shut-eye. He told Dale he'd see him when he got back. Then Dale asked Blackie for a favor. Blackie looked at him a little warily, which amused him since he rarely asked his father for anything.

"Well, what?" Blackie asked.

"Whatever you do, Dad, don't name the kid Damien."

Blackie didn't know what Dale was talking about. He hadn't seen *The Omen*. Blackie shook his head and told him to go to hell, but in a friendly kind of way, at least for Blackie. Dale watched his father trudge to his bedroom.

Dale sat down on the couch, which doubled as his bed. He didn't know if he'd be able to sleep much. He felt excited. Not only about going to Europe, but seeing her tomorrow. He wondered what she wanted. She hadn't spoken to him since that time before Sunday night service. Dale knew she'd closed her mind to him. Not her heart; her mind. He knew it was over. But some part of him, a romantic part of him, hoped seeing him would change her mind.

He stretched out on the couch, kicking off his cowboy boots by just using his feet. He closed his eyes and imagined her changing her mind about him, about everything. He imagined her deciding to go to Europe with him – on the spur of the moment. She'd tell him she still loved him and wanted to run away with him. He'd tell her that he'd always loved her and always would. They'd leave the stifling conventions of Galilee. Be free. They'd first go to Europe and see the sights. Then come back and stay together forever. He imagined them walking along the river Seine. Then in Venice, sharing a kiss under the Bridge of Sighs. He imagined them at a secluded villa in Florence, in a charming, intimate bedroom. He imagined taking her in his arms and kissing her. He imagined --

Just as he got to the really good part, Dale fell asleep.

Dale knew he was cutting it close. He had to be at the airport at three. Rusty was picking him up at Blackie's at two. He doubted Amanda knew he was flying to Europe today. Just one of those coincidences.

He left Blackie's at 11:40. He didn't want to get to her house either early or late. He wanted to time his arrival perfectly. He even carried the watch that Blackie gave him for his birthday and checked it every few miles to make sure he timed the drive. He still refused to wear a watch strapped on his wrist.

Dale turned south off the expressway and drove to Amanda's house. He hadn't been to Amanda's house since her birthday party. Now, in late-Spring, the trees shimmered with greenery, the grass looked thick and verdant, even the houses seemed to sparkle under the warm sun. But none of it made Dale feel better. He felt like a melancholy interloper, someone that didn't belong here and knew it.

He turned on Amanda's street and felt his stomach tighten. He drove slowly toward her home and came to a stop at curbside. Before he could turn off the ignition, he saw her walk out of her home, wearing blue slacks, a pink blouse, and sandals. Her shorter hair still had that fluffiness to it that Dale didn't like. He noticed she was holding a small gift-wrapped box.

She gave him a weak wave. Dale shut off the car and got out. Before he could walk over to meet her, she ran toward him in her awkward way, her arms sort of swaying in front of her, and said hi.

Dale said hi.

He stood at the front of his car, near the left headlight. She stood five feet away, close to the right headlight.

Dale didn't feel shy, exactly. He didn't feel that inhibiting feeling he used to feel seven years ago when he saw her; when he didn't know her but wanted desperately to. But he felt something close to it: a tentativeness; a reserve; a yearning.

Amanda glanced at him, then looked down at her feet. Dale noticed she'd painted her toenails pink.

"I heard you were leaving on your trip," she said, still not looking at him directly.

"Yeah. To Europe. You know, like I told you before. I'm leaving today."

"Oh, I'm sorry if I've inconvenienced you. What time are you leaving?"

"Not for a few more hours. It's no inconvenience." He almost added, *to see you*. But he didn't. He knew she wouldn't like it.

When she didn't speak, he said, "I heard you got accepted to Lost and Found."

Amanda smiled. "Yes, that's right. I heard a few weeks ago."

Dale nodded. She probably heard just after she broke up with him. He told her congratulations. She said thanks. An awkward pause settled between them. Dale shifted his feet. He wanted to get closer to her.

"So, how are you?" she asked.

He said fine. He asked how she was.

"Oh, you know busy. I'll be leaving for rehearsals next week."

"That soon?"

"Yes."

Dale nodded. "I guess that means we'll both be away for most of the summer."

Amanda didn't say anything. Her smile faded and she looked at her feet again.

"I know you didn't want to talk to me before," Dale said. "I understand why. I said about all I could say in the letter."

He looked at her. She blinked her eyes and stared at her feet but didn't say anything. He thought he could just rush over to her and embrace her. Either she'd scream and fight to get away or Amanda would melt in his arms and everything would be okay again. But for some reason, he couldn't make himself move.

"But I wanted to say again that I'm sorry about causing you pain. Especially about that photograph with your mother in it. If I'd seen her, I wouldn't have run it."

He could tell she didn't want to talk about it. She got very still the way she did when feeling upset. But she didn't bite her lip.

"I know it wasn't on purpose," she said. "It's over with anyway."

Dale thought, yes, it's *all* over with.

Amanda looked at him and tried to smile. "I wanted you to stop by because I have this for you." She raised the small box. Suddenly, she started speaking rapidly, nervously. "It's your birthday present. I was going to give it to you on your birthday, obviously, but everything happened and I, well, I didn't. But I wanted you to have it just the same. I bought it for you. No one else should have it. Besides, I think you might need it."

"Okay, thanks."

Dale took two steps toward her and deliberately reached his hand too far and felt her fingers for just a moment before his hand grasped the package. Just touching her made him feel like he'd touched an electric current; like he'd reached into a socket and momentarily touched the live wire.

"Amanda," he said, his voice low.

She backed away.

"That's why I asked you over. I don't want to keep you. Please open it later."

She glanced at the open front door of her house. Dale looked. He thought he saw someone standing in the doorway. A woman. Her mother? No, Dale thought it was her pregnant sister. Dale had noticed Reinhardt's new Mercedes in the driveway when he first drove up.

"Amanda."

She took another step back.

"Have a nice trip, Dale. Have a nice time."

He almost started to go after her, but instead he watched her as she turned and ran in her clumsy way to the front door. He said, *Amanda*, but too quietly for her to hear. He watched as she became lost in the shadows of her porch before going inside her house. The door sealed her off from him.

He looked at the gift in his hands. He could tell by the size, shape and weight that it was something like jewelry. Dale looked one more time at Amanda's house. Its white façade sparkled in the sun. It looked so solid and formidable. It didn't look like a house at all. He imagined her in there. He wondered if she was crying. He doubted it. She'd probably cried some, but she'd done that weeks ago and had gotten it out of her system. She was already in her serene state of mind, protected by her friends, family, house, and church.

Dale had lost the battle for her to God. Well, in the end, God always wins.

He got in his car and tossed the package on the passenger seat. He started the Chevy and drove away without looking back at her house. Dale knew he'd never see it again.

He drove out of her neighborhood, drove almost to the downtown area, when he pulled to the side of the road and put the car in gear. He ripped the gift wrapping off. He opened the box. He felt the light, crinkly paper and knew for certain the gift was jewelry. He reached in and pulled out a watch. A fairly expensive watch with a leather wristband. He smiled a little at the idea that both she and Blackie had thought of the same gift.

Dale held it in his hand and felt its weight. He gently rubbed his fingers over the smooth, round face. No numbers, just Roman numerals. Then he turned the watch over and read the tiny inscription: *Love, Amanda*